THE RUSSIAN ALPHABET

Printed	Russian name	Approximate sound in English
А а	а	*a* in *father*
Б б	бэ	*b* in *bed*
В в	вэ	*v* in *vet*
Г г	гэ	*g* in *get*
Д д	дэ	*d* in *debt*
Е е	е	*ye* in *yet*
Ё ё	ё	*yo* in *yonder*
Ж ж	жэ	*zh* or *s* in *pleasure*
З з	зэ	*z* in *zero*
И и	и	*ee* in *meet*
Й й	и с краткой	used in dipthongs like *y* in *boy*
К к	ка	*k* in *kite*
Л л	эль	*l* in *pool*
М м	эм	*m* in *mule*
Н н	эн	*n* in *net*
О о	о	*o* in *or*
П п	пэ	*p* in *pet*
Р р	эр	*r* in *carrot*
С с	эс	*s* in *star*
Т т	тэ	*t* in *tap*
У у	у	*oo* in *loose*
Ф ф	эф	*f* in *foot*
Х х	ха	*ch* in *loch*
Ц ц	цэ	*ts* in *bits*
Ч ч	чэ	*ch* in *cheep*
Ш ш	ша	*sh* in *short*
Щ щ	ща	*shch* in *fresh cheese*
ъ	твёрдый знак	1.
ы	ы	*i* in *bill*
ь	мягкий знак	2.
Э э	э	*e* in *met*
Ю ю	ю	*yu* or *u* in *use*
Я я	я	*ya* in *yard*

1. — indicates that the preceding consonant is to be pronounced hard.
2. — indicates that the preceding consonant is to be pronounced soft, palatalized.

а, е, ё, и, о, у, ы, э, ю, and я are vowels.
й is a semivowel.
The other letters (apart from the hard and soft signs) are consonants.

RULES OF SPELLING

After ж, ч, ш, щ, and г, к, or х it is not normal to write ы, ю or я: instead и, y and a are written.

After ц it is not normal to write ю or я: instead y and a are written.

After ж, ц, ч, ш, щ it is not normal to write o unless it is stressed, and e is written instead.

These rules of spelling are of great importance in the conjugation of verbs and in the declension of nouns and adjectives. Declensions and conjugations which differ from the norms given below only because of the rules of spelling are not considered to be irregular.

NOUNS

Gender

Nouns which end in a consonant or in -й in the nominative singular are masculine.

Nouns which end in -a or -я are normally feminine.

Nouns which end in -o, -e, -ё are neuter.

It is assumed that the user of this dictionary will be familiar with these rules and therefore the genders of nouns are only indicated when they are exceptions to these rules: e. g. дядя 'uncle' is masculine, although it ends in -я and this is shown дядя *(m.)*; кофе 'coffee' is also masculine, although it ends in -e and this is indicated in the same way — кофе *(m.)*.

Some nouns belong to two genders, e. g. егоза 'fidget', and this is indicated thus: егоза *(m. & f.)*.

Some nouns which end in -ь are masculine and others are feminine. The gender of such nouns is indicated, except where a masculine noun is followed immediately by the feminine form, as in приятель, -ница 'friend'.

Nouns used only in the plural have the genitive plural given in brackets, e. g. сани (-ей).

Declension

The following declensions of nouns are taken as the norm:
Masculine

Singular

Nom	заво́д	слу́чай	прия́тель
Gen	заво́да	слу́чая	прия́теля
Dat	заво́ду	слу́чаю	прия́телю
Acc	заво́д	слу́чай	прия́теля*
Inst	заво́дом	слу́чаем	прия́телем
Prep	(o) заво́де	слу́чае	прия́теле

(* Masculine nouns denoting animate being have the accusative case like the genitive.)

Plural

Nom	заво́ды	слу́чаи	прия́тели
Gen	заво́дов	слу́чаев	прия́телей
Dat	заво́дам	слу́чаям	прия́телям
Acc	заво́ды	слу́чаи	прия́телей
Inst	заво́дами	слу́чаями	прия́телями
Prep	(o) заво́дах	слу́чаях	прия́телях

Feminine

Singular

Nom	ко́мната	бу́ря	мете́ль	ста́нция
Gen	ко́мнаты	бу́ри	мете́ли	ста́нции
Dat	ко́мнате	бу́ре	мете́ли	ста́нции
Acc	ко́мнату	бу́рю	мете́ль	ста́нцию
Inst	ко́мнатой	бу́рей	мете́лью	ста́нцией
Prep	(o) кoмнате	бу́ре	мете́ли	ста́нции

Plural

Nom	ко́мнаты	бу́ри	мете́ли	ста́нции
Gen	ко́мнат	бурь	мете́лей	ста́нций
Dat	ко́мнатам	бу́рям	мете́лям	ста́нциям
Acc	ко́мнаты	бу́ри	мете́ли	ста́нции
Inst	ко́мнатами	бу́рями	мете́лями	ста́нциями
Prep (o)	ко́мнатах	бу́рях	мете́лях	ста́нциях

(In the plural, feminine nouns denoting animate beings have the accusative like the genitive.)

(Feminine nouns which in the nominative singular end in a consonant +ка insert o before the к in the genitive plural; e. g., ла́вка has the genitive plural ла́вок. This is considered to be normal and is not indicated in the dictionary. Where the insertion of o is not possible because of the rules of speling, the genitive plural is given; e. g. ло́жка *(gen. pl.* -жек).)

Neuter

Singular

Nom	ка́чество	уси́лие	уще́лье	питьё	мо́ре
Gen	ка́чества	уси́лия	уще́лья	питья́	мо́ря
Dat	ка́честву	уси́лию	уще́лью	питью́	мо́рю
Acc	ка́чество	уси́лие	уще́лье	питьё	мо́ре
Inst	ка́чеством	уси́лием	уще́льем	питьём	мо́рем
Prep (o)	ка́честве	уси́лии	уще́лье	питье́	мо́ре

Plural

Nom	ка́чества	уси́лия	уще́лья	питья́	моря́
Gen	ка́честв	уси́лий	уще́лий	питей́	море́й
Dat	ка́чествам	уси́лиям	уще́льям	питья́м	моря́м
Acc	ка́чества	уси́лия	уще́лья	питья́	моря́
Inst	ка́чествами	уси́лиями	уще́льями	питья́ми	моря́ми
Prep (o)	ка́чествах	уси́лиях	уще́льях	питья́х	моря́х

Where a noun does not follow the pattern of the appropriate regular declension table given above, the deviation is indicated in the Russian—English section of this dictionary.

Changes of stress are shown as follows:

Masculine nouns which are stressed on the ending throughout the singular and plural have the genitive singular indicated, e. g. стол(-а́).

Nouns whose stress moves from one syllable in the singular to another in the plural are given with the nominative plural in brackets, e. g. звезда́ *(pl.* звёзды).

Noun which are stressed on the ending in the oblique cases in the plural have stress of both the nominative and genitive plurals indicated, e. g. пло́щадь *(f., pl.* -и, -е́й).

Feminine nouns which have end stress in the singular in all cases except the accusative are shown thus: рука́ (ру́ку).

Alternative stress is indicated, e. g. река́ (ре́ку́).

VERBS

In the Russian—English section Russian verbs are given in the Imperfective infinitive (unless only the Perfective is in common use), with a cross-reference from the Perfective infinitive: e. g., взять *see* брать. In order to save space, however, such cross-references have been omitted when the Perfective is formed simply by adding one of the common prefixes (в-, вы-, до-, из-, ис-, на-, о-, пере-, по-, под-, при-, раз-, рас-, с-, у-) to the Imperfective. It is assumed that the reader will realize that, for example, посидеть is the Perfective of сидеть and will look at the latter.

The following groups of Russian verbs are considered to be 'regular'.

1. Verbs of the First Conjugation with the infinitive in -ать and the present tense (or Perfective future) ending: -аю, -аешь, -ает, -аем, -аете, -ают; and the past tense ending: -ал, -ала, -ало, -али; (е. g. читать).
2. Verbs of the First Conjugation with the infinitive in -еть and the present (or Perfective future) ending: -ею, -еешь, -еет, -еем, -еете, -еют; and the past tense ending; -ел, -ела, -ело, -ели; (е. g. бледнеть).
3. Verbs of the First Conjugation with the infinitive in -овать and the present (or Perfective future) ending: -ую, -уешь, -ует, -уем, -уете, -уют; and the past tense ending -овал, -овала etc.; also verbs with the infinitive in -евать and the present (or Perfective future) ending; -юю, -юешь, -юет, -юем, -юете, -юют and the past tense ending: -евал, -евала, -евало, -евали; (е. g. воевать).
4. Verbs of the First Conjugation with the infinitive in -нуть and the present (or Perfective future) endings -ну, -нешь, -нет, -нем, -нете, -нут; and the past endings -нул, -нула, (е. g. пахнуть).
5. Verbs of the Second Conjugation with the i nfinitive in -ить and the present (or Perfective future) endings -ю, -ишь, -ит, -им, -ите, -ят; and the past tense endings -ил, -ила, -ило, -или; (е. g. говорить).
(Verbs of this group whose stem ends in б, в, м, п, ф, insert л before ю in th first person singular, е. g. я люблю.)

Deviations from these norms, even if they are only changes of stress, are indicated in this dictionary in the Russian—English section, but in order to economize on space, irregularities are shown only with the basic verb. An asterisk* alongside a prefixed verb indicates that the verb has some irregularity and that the reader should look at the basic verb. For example, all verbs formed with a prefix + писать (вписать, выписать, дописать, описать, переписать etc.) are conjugated like писать and the asterisk after these words, вписать*, выписать*, дописать* refers the reader to писать.

Exceptions to the following rules are shown:

Imperative mood

The Imperative is formed from the 3rd person plural of the present or Perfective future tense by removing the last two letters and adding -й(те) to a stem ending in a vowel: чита(ют) -читай(те); and -и(те) to a stem ending in a consonant: смотр(ят) -смотри(те). Давать and verbs formed with -знавать and -ставать have Imperative in -авай(те)
  Second-conjugation verbs with stress on the stem and stem ending in one consonant have Imperative in -ь(те): ставить —ставь(те).
  First-conjugation verbs whose first person ends in one consonant + unstressed -у, also have -ь(те) in the Imperative: резать, режу — режь(те).

Participles

The present participle active is formed by removing -т from the third person plural of the present tense and adding -щий: читаю(т) — читáющий; говоря(т) — говорящий.

The present participle passive is formed by adding -ый to the form of the first person plural, e. g. читáемый, хранúмый. But давáемый, признавáемый.

The past participle active is formed by removing the -л from the past tense and adding -вший: e. g. (про)читáвший, говорúвший. If the past tense does not end in -л e. g. нёс, the past participle active is formed by adding -ший to the past tense: нёсший.

(Reflexive participles add -ся).

The past participle passive is formed as follows:

1. First Conjugation. Remove -ть from the infinitive and add -нный. Past passive participles of verbs in -уть end in -утый, e. g. покúнутый. Other participles ending in -тый are indicated.
2. Second Conjugation. Remove -ить from the infinitive and add -енный if the stress is on the stem of the verb throughout the present (or Perfective future) tense (замéдлить — замéдленный); and -ённый if the stress is on the ending throughout the present tense (or perfective future) e. g. удивúть, удивлю, -úшь, -úт hence удивлённый. It will be noted that if the verb has a consonant change in the first person singular of the present (or Perfective future) tense, the same consonant change occurs in the past participle passive, e. g. встрéтить, я встрéчу; — встрéченный.

Gerunds

The present gerund is formed by removing the last two letters of the third person plural, present tense, and adding -я (or -a if the rule of spelling requires it), e. g. чита(ют) -читáя; говор(ят) — говоря; плач(ут) — плáча. But давáть and its compounds and verbs formed from -знавать and -ставать have the present gerund in -авая: давáя, признавáя, вставáя.

The past gerund is formed by removing the -л of the past tense and adding -в or -вши: (про)читáв, (про)читáвши.

Reflexive gerunds add -сь: одевáясь, одéвшись.

(Perfective verbs of motion which are compounds of идти have a past gerund ending in -я; войтú — войдя; перейтú — перейдя.)

ADJECTIVES

It has not been possible, for reasons of space, to indicate the short, predicative, forms of adjectives.

The synthetic, or predicative, form of the comparative adjective (and adverb) is normally formed by adding -ee to the stem, e. g. нóвый — новée. Irregular comparatives are given.

So that more words could be included, the normal rules for the division of Russian words have not always been observed.

ABBREVIATIONS

a.	adjective	*mil.*	military
acc.	accusative case	*min.*	mineralogy
ad.	adverb	*mus.*	music
agr.	agriculture	*myth.*	mythology
arch.	architecture	*n.*	noun
avia.	aviation	*neg.*	negative
biol.	biology	*neut.*	neuter
bot.	botany	*obs.*	obsolete, old-fashioned
build.	building	*os.*	oneself
c.	conjunction	*p.*	participle
chem.	chemistry	*parl.*	parliament
coll.	colloquial	*pers.*	person
com.	commerce	*pf.*	perfective aspect
comp.	comparative	*philol.*	philology
comps.	compounds	*philos.*	philosophy
cook.	cookery	*phon.*	phonetics
dat.	dative case	*phot.*	photography
dim.	diminutive	*phys.*	physics
eccl.	ecclesiastic	*pl.*	plural
econ.	economics	*pn.*	pronoun
e. g.	for example	*poet.*	poetic
elec.	electricity	*pol.*	politics
f.	feminine	*pp.*	past participle
fig.	figurative	*ppa.*	past participle active
fin.	finance	*ppp.*	past participle passive
fut.	future	*pr.*	preposition
gen.	genitive case	*prep.*	prepositional case
geog.	geography	*print.*	printing
geol.	geology	*refl.*	reflexive
ger.	gerund	*rly.*	railways
gram.	grammar	*sew.*	sewing
hist.	history	*sg.*	singular
imper.	imperative	*smb.*	somebody
impers.	impersonal	*sth.*	something
indecl.	indeclinable	*surg.*	surgery
inst.	instrumental case	*tech.*	technical, technology
int.	interjection	*theat.*	theatre
ipf.	imperfective aspect	*v.*	verb
lit.	literary, in literature	*v. aux.*	auxiliary
m.	masculine	*v. i.*	intransitive verb
mar.	marine	*v. t.*	transitive verb
maths	mathematics	*voc.*	vocative
med.	medicine	*zool.*	zoology

RUSSIAN—ENGLISH

A

a and, but; what; **a то** otherwise; **a и́менно** namely.

абажу́р lampshade.

абба́т abbot; **абба́тство** abbey.

аббревиату́ра abbreviation.

абза́ц indentation, paragraph.

абонеме́нт subscription; **абоне́нт**, **~ка** subscriber.

аборда́ж boarding.

або́рт abortion; miscarriage.

абрико́с apricot; **абрико́сный** apricot; **абрико́совый** (made of) apricot.

абсе́нт absinthe.

абсолюти́зм absolutism; **абсолю́тный** absolute.

абсорби́ровать (ipf. & pf.) absorb.

абстра́ктный abstract.

абсу́рд absurdity; **довести́ до -a** to carry to an absurd extreme; **абсу́рдный** absurd.

аванга́рд advance-guard; van; avantgarde; **аванпо́рт** outer harbour; **аванпо́ст** outpost.

ава́нс advance payment; **ава́нсом** in advance.

авантю́ра adventure, shady venture; **авантюри́ст**, **~ка** adventurer; **авантю́рный** risky; adventure (a.).

авари́йность (f.) accident rate; **авари́йный** repair; emergency; **ава́рия** crash, accident; breakdown.

а́вгуст August; **а́вгустовский** August (a.).

авиа|ба́за air base; **~ли́ния** airline; **~но́сец (-но́сца)** aircraft carrier; **~тра́сса** air-route.

авиацио́нный aviation (a.).

авиа́ция air force.

аво́сь perhaps; in the hope; **на а. on the off-chance**; haphazardly.

аво́ська (gen. pl. -сек) string bag.

авра́л emergency work; all hands on deck.

австрал|и́ец (-и́йца), **~и́йка** (gen. pl. -и́ек) Australian; **австрали́йский** Australian (a.).

австр|и́ец (-и́йца), **~и́йка** (gen. pl. -и́ек) Austrian; **австри́йский** Austrian (a.).

автоба́за motor depot.

автобиогра́фия autobiography.

авто́бус coach, bus.

авто|го́нки (gen. pl. -нок) motor race(s); **~заво́д** motor works, car factory; **~ка́р** trolley; **~магистра́ль** (f.) motorway.

автома́т automatic machine, slot machine; submachine gun; **~иза́ция** automation.

авто|маши́на, **~моби́ль** (m.) car, automobile.

автоно́мия autonomy; **автоно́мный** autonomous.

автопогру́зчик fork-lift truck; mechanical shovel.

а́втор author.

авторефера́т synopsis (of thesis).

авторите́т authority; **авторите́тный** authoritative.

а́вторск|ий author's; **-ое пра́во** copyright; **а́вторство** authorship.

авторучка (gen. pl. -чек) fountain pen.

авто|стра́да motorway, highway; **~цисте́рна** road-tanker.

ага́т agate.

аге́нт agent; **аге́нтство** agency; **агенту́ра** secret service.

агита́тор agitator, propagandist; **агитацио́нный** propaganda (a.); **агита́ция** agitation, propaganda; **агити́ровать** (pf. с-) agitate, persuade; **агитпу́нкт** campaign centre.

аго́ния agony.

агра́рный agrarian.

агрега́т aggregate; unit.

агресси́вный aggressive; **агре́ссия** a gression; **агре́ссор** aggressor.

агрикульту́ра agriculture.

агроно́м agronomist; **агроно́мия** agronomy.

ад (в аду́) hell.

адапта́ция adaptation; **ада́птер** adapter; **адапти́ровать** (ipf. & pf.) adapt.

адвока́т barrister, lawyer; **адвокату́ра** the bar.

адепт adherent.

администрати́вный administrative; **администра́тор** administrator; **администра́ция** administration.

адмира́л admiral; **адмиралте́йство** admiralty.

а́дрес (pl. -á) address; **адреса́т** addressee; **а́дресный** address (a.)

1

~стол address bureau; **адресовáть** *(ipf. & pf.)* address.

áдский infernal.

адъю́нкт graduate of military college;scientific assistant.

адъютáнт adjutant.

азáрт excitement, ardour; **азáртн|ый** reckless; passionate; -ая игрá game of chance.

áзбука alphabet; **áзбучная и́стина** truism.

азербайдж|áнец (-áнца), ~áнка Azerbaijanian; **азербайджáнский** Azerbaijanian *(a.)*.

азиáт, ~ка Asian; **азиáтский** Asian, Asiatic.

азóт nitrogen; **азóтистый** nitrous; **азóтный** nitric.

áист stork.

айвá quince.

áйсберг iceberg.

акадéмик academician; **академи́ческий** academic; **акадéмия** academy.

акáция acacia.

аквалáнг aqualung.

акварéль *(f.)* water-colour; **аквáриум** aquarium, tank; **акведу́к** aqueduct.

акклиматизи́ровать *(ipf. & pf.)* acclimatize.

аккомпанемéнт accompaniment; **аккомпаниáтор** accompanist; **аккомпани́ровать** *(dat.)* accompany.

аккóрд chord.

аккордеóн accordion.

аккóрд|ный -ная рабóта piece-work; contract work.

аккредити́в letter of credit; **аккредитовáть** *(ipf. & pf.)* accredit.

аккурáтность *(f.)* neatness; punctuality, conscientiousness; **аккурáтный** tidy; punctual, conscientious.

акр acre.

акробáт, ~ка acrobat; **акробáтика** acrobatics.

аксиóма axiom.

акт act; statement; speech day.

актёр actor.

акти́в 1. assets; 2. activists, active members.

активизи́ровать *(ipf. & pf.)* to make active; **активи́ст** active worker *(in public affairs)*.

акти́вный active.

áктов|ый: -ый зал assembly hall; -ая бумáга headed, stamped paper.

актри́са actress.

актуáльный topical; urgent.

аку́ла shark.

аку́стика acoustics; **акусти́ческий** acoustic.

акушéрка midwife; **акушéрство** obstetrics.

акцéнт accent; **акценти́ровать** *(ipf. & pf.)* accentuate; accent.

акци́з excise.

акционéр shareholder; **акционéрный** joint-stock.

áкция 1. share; 2. action.

албá|нец (-нца), ~нка Albanian; **албáнский** Albanian *(a.)*.

áлгебра algebra; **алгебрáйческий** algebraic.

алéть *(pf.* за-) redden, glow; be(come) red.

алимéнт|ы (-ов) alimony.

алкогóлик alcoholic; **алкогóль** *(m.)* alcohol; **алкогóльный** alcoholic.

аллегори́ческий allegorical; **аллегóрия** allegory.

алл|éя *(gen. pl.* -éй) avenue.

алмáз (uncut) diamond; **алмáзный** diamond *(a.)*.

алтáр|ь (-я́) altar.

алфави́т alphabet;**алфави́тный** alphabetical.

áлчность *(f.)* greed; **áлчный** (к + *dat.*, до + *gen.*) greedy (for).

áлый scarlet.

альбóм album.

альбуми́н albumen.

альманáх almanac.

альпини́зм mountaineering; **альпини́ст**, ~ка mountaineer.

альт viola; alto.

альтернати́ва alternative.

алюми́ниевый aluminium *(a.)*; **алюми́ний** aluminium.

амбáр barn, storehouse.

амби́ция arrogance; self- esteem.

амбулатóрия dispensary, out-patients' clinic; **амбулатóрный больнóй** out-patient.

амвóн pulpit.

амёба amoeba.

америк|áнец (-áнца), ~áнка American; **америкáнский** American *(a.)*.

ами́нь amen.

аммиáк ammonia; **аммóний** ammonium.

амнисти́ровать *(ipf. & pf.)* amnesty; **амни́стия** amnesty.

амортизáтор shock-absorber.

амортизáция amortization; wear-and-tear.

ампе́р ampere.
ампута́ция amputation; ампути́ровать *(ipf. & pf.)* amputate.
амфи́бия amphibian.
амфитеа́тр amphitheatre; back stalls, circle.
ана́лиз analysis; анализи́ровать *(pf.* про-) analyse; анали́тик analyst.
аналоги́чный (+ *dat.*) analogous (to); анало́гия analogy.
анало́й lectern.
анана́с pineapple; анана́сный pineapple *(a.).*
анархи́зм anarchism; анархи́ст, ~ка anarchist; ана́рхия anarchy.
ана́том anatomist; анато́мия anatomy.
анахрони́зм anachronism.
анга́р hangar.
а́нгел angel.
анги́на tonsillitis, quinsy.
англи́йский English, British.
англика́нский Anglican.
англич|а́нин *(pl.* -а́не, -а́н), ~а́нка Englishman, -woman, Briton.
анекдо́т anecdote.
анеми́я anaemia.
анемо́н anemone.
анестези́ровать *(ipf. & pf.)* anaesthetize; анестези́я anaesthesia.
ани́совый aniseed *(a.).*
анке́та form, questionnaire.
аннекси́ровать *(ipf. & pf.)* annex; анне́ксия annexation.
анноти́ровать *(ipf. & pf.)* annotate.
аннули́ровать *(ipf. & pf)* cancel, annul.
ано́д anode.
анони́мный anonymous.
анонси́ровать *(ipf. & pf.)* announce.
анса́мбль *(m.)* ensemble.
антагони́зм antagonism.
анта́нта entente.
антаркти́ческий antarctic.
анте́нна aerial; antenna.
антиква́р antiquarian; ~ный antiquarian *(a.).*
антило́па antelope.
антипа́тия antipathy.
антирелигио́зный antireligious.
антисемити́зм anti-Semitism.
антисе́пт|ика antiseptics; ~и́ческий antiseptic.
антите́за antithesis.
анти́чный classical.
антоло́гия anthology.
анто́ним antonym.
анто́нов ого́нь *(m.)* gangrene.

антра́кт interval.
антраци́т anthracite.
антрепренёр entrepreneur.
антресо́л|и (-ей) mezzanine; balcony.
антропо́лог anthropologist; антропо́лог anthropologist; антрополо́гия anthropology.
анча́р upas-tree.
анчо́ус anchovy.
аншла́г 'sold out'.
апати́чный apathetic; апа́тия apathy.
апелли́ровать *(ipf. & pf.)* (к + *dat.*) appeal to.
апельси́н orange; апельс|и́нный, ~и́новый orange *(a.).*
аплоди́ровать *(pf.* за-) (+ *dat.*) applaud; аплодисме́нт|ы (-ов) applause.
апло́мб self-assurance.
апоге́й climax.
апологе́т apologist.
апопле́ксия apoplexy.
апо́стол apostle.
апостро́ф apostrophe.
апофео́з apotheosis.
аппара́т apparatus.
аппе́ндикс appendix; аппендици́т appendicitis.
аппети́т appetite; аппети́тный tempting.
аппдика́ция appliqué.
апре́ль *(m.)* April; апре́льский April *(a.).*
апси́да apse.
апте́ка chemist's shop; апте́карь *(m.)* chemist; апте́чка *(gen. pl.* -чек) medicine chest.
ара́б, ~ка Arab; ара́бский, арави́йский Arabian, Arabic.
ара́пник hunting whip.
арби́тр arbitrator; арбитра́ж arbitration.
арбу́з water-melon.
аргуме́нт argument; ~а́ция argumentation; ~и́ровать *(ipf. & pf.)* argue, give reasons for.
аре́на arena.
аре́нда lease; аренда́тор tenant; аре́ндная пла́та rent; арендова́ть *(ipf. & pf.)* have on lease, rent.
аре́ст arrest; арестова́ть *(ipf. & pf., & ipf.* аресто́вывать) arrest.
аристо|кра́т aristocrat; ~кра́тия aristocratic; ~кра́тия aristocracy.
арифме́т|ика arithmetic; ~и́ческий arithmetical.
а́рия aria.
а́рка arch.

аркан lasso.

арктический arctic.

арматура reinforcing steel framework; fittings.

армейский army (a.).

армия army.

арм|янин (pl. -яне, -ян), армянка Armenian; армянский Armenian (a.).

аромат aroma; аромат|ический, ~ичный, ароматный aromatic, scented.

арочный arched, vaulted.

арсенал arsenal, store.

артезианский колодец artesian well.

артель (f.) artel.

артерия artery.

артиллерийский artillery (a.); артиллерия artillery.

артист, ~ка actor, artist; артистический artistic.

артишок artichoke.

артрит arthritis.

арфа harp.

архаизм archaism; арха|ический, ~ичный archaic.

археол|ог archaeologist; ~огический archaeological; ~огия archaeology.

архив archive.

архиепископ archbishop; архиерей bishop.

архипелаг archipelago.

архитект|ор architect; ~ура architecture; ~урный architectural.

аршин arshin (= 0.71 metre).

арьергард rearguard.

асбест asbestos; асбестовый asbestos (a.).

аскет ascetic; аскетизм asceticism.

аспид 1. slate; 2. viper, asp.

аспирант, ~ка postgraduate student; аспирантура postgraduate work/studentship.

ассамблея assembly.

ассигнация currency bill, note.

ассигнование allocation; ассигновать (ipf. & pf.) (на + acc.) assign, allocate (to).

ассимил|ировать (ipf. & pf.) assimilate; ~яция assimilation.

ассистент, ~ка assistant (lecturer).

ассортимент assortment, variety; set.

ассоци|ация association; ~ировать (ipf. & pf.) associate.

астма asthma.

астра aster.

астролог astrologer.

астронавт astronaut.

астрон|ом astronomer; ~омический astronomical; ~омия astronomy.

асфальт asphalt.

атака attack; атаковать (ipf. & pf.) attack.

атаман ataman, chieftain.

атеизм atheism.

ателье (indecl.) studio; fashion house.

атлас atlas.

атлас satin; атласный of satin.

атлет athlete; атлетика athletics; атлетический athletic.

атмосфера atmosphere; атмосф|ерический, ~ферный atmospheric.

атом atom; атомный atomic; атомоход nuclear ship/ice-breaker.

атрибут attribute.

атрофия atrophy.

атташе (m., indecl.) attaché.

аттестат certificate; а. зрелости school-leaving certificate; аттестовать (ipf. & pf.) recommend.

аттракцион side show; star turn.

аудиенция audience.

аудитория lecture room, auditorium.

аукцион auction; продавать с -а auction (v.).

афга|нец (-нца), афганка Afghan; афганский Afghan (a.).

афера shady deal; аферист swindler.

афинский Athenian.

афиша bill, placard.

афоризм aphorism.

африка|нец (-нца), ~нка African; африканский African (a.).

аффект fit of passion аффектация affectation.

ахать (ipf.; pf. ахнуть) gasp; он ахнуть не успел before he could say 'knife'.

ацетилен acetylene; ~овый acetylene (a.).

аэро|вокзал air terminal; ~дром airfield, aerodrome; ~порт airport; ~салон airshow; ~стат balloon.

аэрозоль (m.) aerosol

Б

б = бы.

баба (old) woman; снежная баба snow man; баба-яга witch; бабий woman's; бабье лето Indian summer; бабьи сказки old wives' tales; бабка old woman, grandmother; повивальная бабка midwife.

бабочка (gen. pl. -чек) butterfly.

бабушка (gen. pl. -шек) grandmother.

багаж (-á) baggage, luggage; **багажник** luggage compartment, boot, trunk; **багажный вагон** luggage van; **багажная квитанция** luggage ticket.

ба|гóр (-грá) boat-hook.

багроветь (pf. по-) turn purple; **багрóвый** crimson, purple.

ба|дья (gen. pl. -дéй) tub.

база base.

базáльт basalt.

базáр market, bazaar; **базáрный** market (a.); vulgar.

базировать vote; **-ся** be based; **-ся на фáктах** be founded on facts.

бáзис basis.

байбáк (-á) steppe marmot; lazybones.

байдáрка canoe.

бáйка flannelette; **бáйковый** flannelette (a.).

бак 1. tank; 2. seamen's mess; 3. forecastle.

бакалéйный grocery (a.); **бакалéйщик** grocer; **бакалéя** groceries.

бáкен buoy

бакенбáрда side whisker.

баклáн cormorant.

баклýши: бить б. waste time.

бактериолóгия bacteriology, **бактéрия** bacterium.

бал (pl. -ы) ball

балагáн booth, stall; horse-play.

балагýр jester; life and soul of the party; **балагýрить** joke, be gay.

балалáйка (gen. pl. -áек) balalaika.

балам|ýтить (-ýчу, -ýтишь; pf. вз-) agitate, trouble.

балáнс balance; **балансёр** tight-rope walker; **балансировать** balance; (pf. с-) balance (accounts).

балбéс dolt, simpleton.

балдахин canopy.

балерина ballerina.

балéт ballet; **балéтный** ballet (a.).

бáлка 1. beam, girder; 2. gully.

балкáнский Balkan.

балкóн balcony.

балл mark, point; **проходнóй балл** pass-mark.

баллáда ballad.

баллáст ballast.

баллóн balloon; cylinder.

баллотировать vote, put to the vote; **-ся** be voted; **-ся в члéны stand for membership; **баллотирóвка** ballot, vote.

баловáть (ipf.; pf. из-) spoil (children); (pf. по-) give a treat to; **-ся** be naughty; indulge oneself.

бáловень (-вня) pet, favourite; mischievous child.

балтийский Baltic.

бальзамировать (ipf., pf. на-) embalm.

бамбýк bamboo; **бамбýковый** bamboo (a.).

банáльность (f.) triteness; platitude.

банáн banana; **банáновый** banana (a.).

бáнда gang; band.

бандáж (-á) belt, truss.

бандерóл|ь (f.) (postal) wrapper; **послáть книгу -ью** send by book-post/small-packet rate.

бандит bandit; **бандитизм** banditry.

банк bank.

бáнка jar, can, tin.

банкéт dinner, banquet.

банкир banker.

банкнóт & ~а a bank-note.

банкомёт banker (at cards).

банкрóт bankrupt. **банкрóтиться** (ipf., pf. о-) go bankrupt; **банкрóтство** bankruptcy.

бант bow.

бáня bath-house; public baths.

бар bar, refreshment room.

барабáн drum; **барабáнить** (pf. за-) drum; **барабáнная перепóнка** ear-drum; **барабáнщик** drummer.

барáк barrack, hut.

барáн ram; **барáний** sheep's; mutton (a.); **барáнина** mutton.

барáнка 1. ring-shaped roll; 2. steering-wheel.

барахлó goods and chattels; junk.

барáшек (-шка) lamb; (pl.) fleecy clouds; foam.

барельéф bas-relief.

бáржа barge.

бáрий barium.

бáрин (pl. бáре or бáры, бар) landowner, master.

бá|рка (gen. pl. -рок) wooden barge; **баркáс** (small) boat.

барокáмера pressure chamber.

барóметр barometer.

баррикáда barricade.

барс snow leopard.

бáрский lordly; **бáрство** the gentry; quality; haughtiness.

барсýк (-á) badger.

бáрхат velvet; **бархатистый** velvety; **бáрхатный** of velvet.

ба́рщина corvée.
ба́рыня lady of the manor, mistress.
бары́ш (-á) profit.
ба́рышня *(gen. pl.* -шень) young lady.
барье́р barrier, hurdle.
бас *(pl.* -ы́) bass (singer).
баскетбо́л basketball.
баснсло́вный fabulous, incredible;
   ба́|сня *(gen. pl,* -сен) fable.
басо́вый bass *(a.).*
бассе́йн basin *(of river);* pool.
ба́ста that is enough.
бастова́ть *(pf.* за-) (be on) strike.
батальо́н battalion.
батаре́йка *(gen. pl.* -éек) electric
   battery, torch-battery.
батаре́я *(gen. pl.* -éй) battery;
   radiator.
бати́ст cambric; fine lawn; **бати́сто-**
   вый cambric *(a.).*
батисфе́ра bathysphere.
бато́н long loaf.
батра́к (-á) farm labourer, farm
   hand.
ба́тька, ба́тюшка *(m.)* father; old
   chap *(pl.)* good heavens!
бахва́л braggart.
бахрома́ fringe.
баци́лл|а *(acc. pl.* -ы) bacillus.
ба́шенка turret.
башка́ head.
башки́р ~**ка** Bashkir; **башки́рский**
   Bashkir *(a.).*
башлы́к (-á) hood.
башма́к (-á) shoe; под -о́м henpecked.
ба́|шня *(gen. pl.* -шен) tower.
баю́кать *(pf.* y-) lull.
бая́н bard; accordion.
бде́ние vigil; **бдеть** (бдишь) be awake.
бди́тель|ность *(f.)* vigilance; ~**ный**
   vigilant.
бег *(pl.* бегá) run, race; **бе́гать** run.
бегемо́т hippopotamus.
бегле́ц (-á) fugitive.
бе́глость *(f.)* fluency, dexterity,
   speed; **бе́глый** fluent, cursory,
   rapid; fugitive *(as noun).*
бегов|о́й racing *(a.);* -áя ло́шадь
   racehorse; **бего́м** at the double.
беготня́ running about; **бе́гство**
   flight, rout.
бегу́|н (-á) ~**нья** *(gen. pl.* -ний)
   runner.
беда́ *(pl.* бе́ды) misfortune; бедá в том,
   что . . . the trouble is that . . .
бедне́ть *(pf.* o-) become poor.
бе́дность *(f.)* poverty; **беднота́** the
   poor; **бе́дный** poor; **бедня́га** *m.*

poor fellow; **бедня́к** (-á) pauper;
   poor peasant.
бедо́вый bold; sharp, mischievous.
бедро́ *(pl.* бё|дра, -дер, -драм) thigh,
   hip.
бе́дственный calamitous; distressing; **бе́дствие** disaster; **бе́дств-**
   овать live in poverty.
бежа́ть 1. (бегу́, бежи́шь; *pf.* по-)
   run; 2. *(ipf. & pf.)* escape, flee.
бе́жевый beige.
бе́же|нец (-нца), ~**нка** refugee.
без *(gen.)* without; без че́тверти час
   quarter to one; без вас in your absence.
безава́рийный accident-free, free of
   breakdowns.
безала́берный careless, negligent;
   disorderly.
безалкого́льный non-alcoholic.
безбе́дный well-to-do.
безбиле́тный without a ticket.
безбо́жие atheism; **безбо́ж|ник,** ~**ни-**
   ца atheist; **безбо́жный** godless.
безболе́зненный painless; smooth.
безбоя́зненный fearless.
безбра́чие celibacy; **безбра́чный** celibate.
безбре́жный boundless.
безве́стный obscure.
безве́тренный windless; **безве́трие**
   calm.
безвку́сица bad taste; lack of taste;
   безвку́сный vulgar; insipid; taste-
   less.
безвла́стие anarchy.
безво́дный arid; **безво́дье** lack of
   water.
безвозвра́тный irrevocable; free
   (grant).
безвозме́здный gratuitous, unpaid.
безво́лие weak will; **безво́льный**
   weakwilled.
безвре́дный harmless.
безвре́менный untimely
безвы́ездно without going anywhere.
безвы́ход|ный hopeless; -ное поло-
   же́ние hopeless situation; -но
   сиде́ть до́ма stay at home and never
   go out.
безгла́зый eyeless, one-eyed.
безгра́мотный ungrammatical; illiterate.
безграни́чный boundless.
безда́рный ungifted; fatuous.
безде́йств|ие inaction, inertia;
   ~**овать** idle.
безде́лица trifle.

безделу́|шка (gen. pl. -шек) trinket.
безде́лье idleness; безде́льник idler; безде́льничать idle, loaf.
безде́нежный impecunious.
безде́тный childless.
безде́ятельный inactive.
бе́здна abyss, chasm.
бездо́мный homeless; stray.
бездо́нный bottomless.
бездоро́жье bad, impassable roads.
безду́ш|ие callousness; ~ный heartless.
безды́мный smokeless.
бездыха́нный lifeless.
безжа́лостный merciless, ruthless.
безжи́зненный feeble, lifeless.
беззабо́тный carefree.
беззаве́тный selfless, wholehearted.
беззако́н|ие lawlessness; ~ный lawless.
беззасте́нчивый impudent, shameless.
беззащи́тный defenceless.
беззву́чный silent, noiseless.
безземе́|лье lack of land; ~льный landless.
беззу́бый toothless; impotent.
безле́сный treeless, bare.
безли́чный without individuality, impersonal.
безлю́дный uninhabited, sparsely populated; lonely.
безме́рный boundless, infinite.
безмо́зглый brainless.
безмо́лвие silence; безмо́лвный silent, mute; безмо́лвствовать keep silent.
безмяте́жный serene, tranquil.
безнаде́жный hopeless.
безнадзо́рный uncared-for.
безнака́занный unpunished.
безно́гий legless, one-legged.
безнра́вственный immoral.
безоби́дный inoffensive, harmless.
безо́блачный cloudless, serene.
безобра́зие ugliness; deformity; outrage; безобра́зничать act disgracefully; безобра́зный ugly; outrageous.
безгово́рочный unqualified, without reservation.
безопа́с|ность (f.) security; ~ный safe; foolproof.
безору́жный unarmed.
безостано́вочный non-stop.
безотве́тный meek, mild; unanswered.
безотве́тственный irresponsible.
безотка́зный faultless, reliable.

безотлага́тельный pressing, urgent.
безотлу́чный ever present.
безотра́дный cheerless, dismal.
безотчётный uncontrolled; instinctive.
безоши́бочный unerring, correct.
безрабо́тица unemployment; безрабо́тный unemployed.
безразли́чие indifference; безразли́чный (к + dat.) indifferent (to); нам безразли́чно it is all the same to us.
безрассу́дный rash, reckless.
безрезульта́тный ineffectual, unsuccessful.
безро́дный without kith or kin.
безро́потный uncomplaining.
безрука́вка sleeveless jacket, blouse, pullover.
безру́к|ость (f.) clumsiness; ~ий armless, one-armed; clumsy.
безуда́рный unstressed.
безуде́ржный unrestrained, impetuous.
безукори́зненный irreproachable.
безу́|мец (-мца) madman; безу́мие madness; безу́мный mad; безу́мство madness.
безупре́чный irreproachable, faultless.
безусло́в|ный absolute, indisputable, unconditional; -но, он прав he is certainly right.
безуспе́шный unsuccessful.
безуста́нный tireless.
безуте́шный inconsolable.
безуча́ст|ие indifference; ~ный (к + dat.) indifferent (to).
безыде́йный lacking principles and ideals.
безымя́нный nameless, anonymous; б. па́лец ring-finger.
безыску́сственный unsophisticated.
безысхо́дный endless, irreparable, incurable.
бека́р natural (mus.).
бека́с snipe.
беко́н bacon.
белен|а́ henbane; что ты, -ы́ объе́лся? have you gone mad?
беле́ть (pf. по-) become white; (pf. за-) show white; -ся show white.
белизна́ whiteness; бел|и́ла (-и́л) whiting, ceruse; бели́ть (pf. по-) whiten (ceiling etc.,); (pf. на-) whiten (face etc.,); (pf. вы-, от-) bleach.

бе́личий squirrel *(a.)*; **бе́лка** squirrel.

беллетри́ст writer of fiction; **~ика** fiction, belles-lettres.

белови́к (-а́), **белово́й экземпля́р** fair copy.

белогварде́ец (-е́йца) white guard.

бе|ло́к (-лка́) white *(of eye, egg)*, albumen; protein.

белокро́вие leukaemia.

белоку́рый fair-haired.

белору́с, **~ка** White Russian; Byelorussian; **белору́сский** White Russian *(a.)*.

белору́|чка *(gen. pl.* -чек) *(m. & f.)* fine person *(who never does hard work)*.

бело|швейка *(gen. pl.* -швеек) seamstress.

белу́га white sturgeon.

бе́лый white; **-ый медве́дь** polar bear; **-ый свет** the wide world; **-ые стихи́** blank verse.

бель|ги́ец (-ги́йца), **~ги́йка** *(gen. pl.* -ги́ек) Belgian; **бельги́йский** Belgian *(a.)*.

бельё linen; washing; **ни́жнее б.** underwear.

бельмо́ *(pl.* бе́льма) wall-eye.

бельэта́ж first floor, dress circle.

бемо́ль *(m.)* flat *(mus.)*.

бенефи́с benefit *(performance)*.

бензи́н petrol; **~овый** petrol *(a.)*; **~оме́р** petrol gauge; **~охрани́лище** petrol tank;

бензо|ба́к petrol tank; **~запра́вочная коло́нка** filling station, pump.

бе́рег (на -у́; *pl.* берега́) bank, shore; **береговой** waterside, coastal, shore *(a.)*.

бере|ди́ть (-жу́, -ди́шь; *pf* раз-) irritate; **б. ста́рые ра́ны** re-open old wounds.

бережли́вый thrifty.

бере́жный careful.

берёза birch; **берёзовый** birch *(a.)*.

бере́менеть *(pf.* за-) be(come) pregnant; **бере́менная** pregnant.

береста́ birch bark.

бер|е́чь (-егу́, -ежёшь, -егу́т; -ёг, -егла́, -егло́; *ppp.* бережённый) take care of, keep; spare; **б. своё здоро́вье** take care of one's health; **б. ка́ждую копе́йку** watch every penny; **-ся** (*+gen.)* beware (of); **береги́тесь соба́ки!** beware of the dog!

берло́га den, lair.

берцо́вая кость shin bone.

бес devil, demon.

бесе́д|а conversation, talk; **провести́-у** lead discussion.

бесе́дка summer-house.

бесе́довать *(pf.* по-) talk, chat.

беси́ть (бешу́, бе́сишь; *pf.* вз-) enrage; **-ся** be(come) mad, furious.

бескла́ссовый classless.

бесконе́ч|ность *(f.)* infinity, eternity; **~ный** endless.

бескоры́ст|ие unselfishness, disinterestedness; **~ный** disinterested.

бескро́в|ный bloodless, anaemic; **-ная побе́да** bloodless victory.

бесноваться rage, rave.

бесо́вский devilish.

беспа́мятный forgetful; **беспа́мятство** unconsciousness.

беспарти́йный non-Party.

беспереб́ойный uninterrupted, constant.

беспереса́доч|ный through, non-stop; **-ое сообще́ние** through connection.

бесперспекти́вный without prospects; hopeless.

беспе́чный carefree.

беспла́тный free (of charge).

беспло́дие sterility; **беспло́дный** barren, sterile.

бесповоро́тный irrevocable.

беспод́обный incomparable.

беспозвоно́чный invertebrate.

беспоко́ить *(pf.* по-) worry, perturb; trouble; **-ся** (о + *prep.)* worry (about). **беспоко́йный** уneasy; restless; **беспоко́йство** anxiety; trouble, inconvenience.

бесполе́зный useless.

беспо́мощный helpless, feeble.

беспоро́дный cross-breed, mongrel.

беспоря́|док (-дка) disorder, confusion; **беспоря́дочный** untidy; improper.

беспоса́дочный **перелёт** non-stop flight.

беспо́чвенный groundless.

беспо́шлинный duty-free.

беспоща́дный merciless.

беспра́вие lawlessness; lack of rights; **беспра́вный** without any rights.

беспреде́льный boundless.

беспредме́тный aimless, pointless.

беспрекосло́вный absolute, unquestioning.

беспрепя́тственный unimpeded, unhindered.

беспреры́вный continuous, ceaseless.

беспрецеде́нтный unprecedented.
беспризо́р|ник, ~ница waif, homeless child; **беспризо́рный** homeless, neglected.
бесприме́рный unparalleled.
беспринци́пный unscrupulous.
беспристра́ст|ие impartiality; **~ный** impartial.
беспричи́нный groundless, without motive.
беспробу́дный: б. сон deep sleep.
беспрово́лочный wireless.
беспросве́тный gloomy, hopeless.
беспроце́нтный bearing no interest.
беспу́тный dissolute.
бессвя́зный incoherent.
бессерде́ч|ие callousness; **~ный** heartless.
бесси́л|ие debility, impotence; **~ьный** weak, feeble.
бессла́в|ие ignominy; **~ный** inglorious.
бессле́дный without a trace.
бессло́ве́сный dumb, meek.
бессме́нный continuous, permanent;
бессме́рт|ие immortality; **~ный** immortal.
бессмы́сленный senseless; **бессмы́слица** nonsense.
бессо́вестный unscrupulous.
бессодержа́тельный empty, vapid.
бессозна́тельный unconscious, instinctive.
бессо́нница insomnia; **бессо́нный** sleepless.
бесспо́рный indisputable.
бессро́чный permanent; termless.
бесстра́ст|ие coolness, imperturbability; **~ный** impassive.
бесстра́шный intrepid.
бессты́д|ный shameless; **~ство** impudence; shamelessness.
бессчётный innumerable, countless.
беста́ктный tactless.
бестала́нный 1. mediocre; 2. luckless.
бестеле́сный incorporeal.
бе́стия rogue.
бестолко́вый muddle-headed, stupid; unintelligible.
бестре́петный intrepid.
бесфо́рменный shapeless.
бесхара́ктерный weak-willed, spineless.
бесхи́тростный simple, unsophisticated.
бесхозя́йственный thriftless.
бесхребе́тный spineless.

бесцве́тный colourless, insipid.
бесце́льный aimless, pointless.
бесце́нный priceless.
бесце́нок: купить за б. buy for a song.
бесцеремо́нный unceremonious, offhand.
бесчелове́чный inhuman, brutal.
бесче́стный dishonourable; **бесче́стье** dishonour.
бесчи́нств|о outrage, excess; **~овать** commit outrage.
бесчи́сленный countless, innumerable.
бесчу́вст|венный insensible; callous; **~вие** unconsciousness; callousness.
бесшаба́шный reckless.
бесшу́мный noiseless.
бето́н concrete; **бето́нный** concrete (a.); **бетономеша́лка** concrete-mixer.
бечева́ rope; **бечёвка** string, twine.
бе́шенство rage; hydrophobia; **бе́шеный** rabid; frantic; terrific.
библе́йский biblical.
библиогра́фия bibliography.
библиоте́ка library; **библиоте́ка|рь** (m.) **~рша** librarian; **библиоте́чный** library (a.).
Би́блия Bible.
би́|вень (-вня) tusk.
бидо́н can; churn.
бие́ние beat, throbbing.
биле́т ticket; card; обра́тный б. return ticket; **биле́тный** ticket (a.).
биллио́н a thousand millions.
бино́кль (m.) binoculars.
бинт (-а́) bandage; **бинтова́ть** (pf. за-) bandage.
биогра́фия biography.
био́лог biologist; **биоло́гия** biology.
биофи́зика biophysics; **биохи́мия** biochemistry.
би́ржа exchange; **биржево́й ма́клер** stockbroker.
бирюз|а́ turquoise; **~о́вый** turquoise (a.).
бирю́к (-а́) morose person.
бис encore; петь на б. sing an encore.
би́сер beads; **би́серина** bead.
биси́ровать (ipf. & pf.) repeat, do an encore.
бискви́т sponge-cake.
бита́ bat (sport).
би́тва battle.
битко́м наби́тый crammed full.
би́|то́к (-тка́) meat ball.
бить (бью, бьёшь; imper. бей!; ppp.

битый); *(pf.* по-) to hit, beat; (про-) to strike *(of clock)* ; punch a hole in; (раз-) to smash; биться fight; strike (against); beat *(of heart)* ; *(with* с *inst.)* struggle with *(e. g. a problem)*.

бифштекс steak.

бич (-á) whip, scourge; бичевáть lash; castigate.

благ**ó** 1. pleasing; good; 2. since, seeing that ...

благовéщение Annunciation.

благовидный seemly.

благоволéние goodwill.

благо|вóние fragrance; ~вóнный fragrant.

благовоспитанный well brought-up.

благоговéйный reverent.

благодари́ть *(pf.* по-) thank; благодáрность *(f.)* gratitude; благодáрный grateful.

благодаря́ (+ *dat.)* because of.

благодáтный beneficial; благодáть *(f.)* paradise, bliss.

благодéтель, ~ница benefactor, -tress; благодéтельный beneficent.

благодея́ние good deed.

благодýш|ие placidity; ~ный placid, good-humoured.

благожелáтельный benevolent.

благозвýчный harmonious.

благóй 1. good; 2. кричáть благим мáтом yell blue murder.

благонадёжный reliable.

благонамéренный loyal, well-meaning.

благополýч|ие well-being, prosperity; ~ный happy, satisfactory; safe.

благоприя́т|ный favourable; ~ствовать *(dat.)* favour.

благоразýм|ие good sense, wisdom; ~ный sensible.

благорóдный noble; ~ство nobility.

благосклóнный (к + *dat.)* favourable (to).

благосло|вéние blessing; ~вля́ть *(pf.* -ви́ть) bless.

благосостоя́ние well-being, prosperity.

благотвори́тель|ность *(f.)* charity; ~ный charity *(a.)*, charitable.

благотвóрный beneficial.

благо|устрóенный comfortable, well-organized; with all amenities; ~устрóйство organization of public services.

благоухáние fragrance.

благочéстие piety.

блажéнный 1. blissful; 2. simple, silly; блажéнство bliss; блажь *(f.)* whim.

бланк form; заполня́ть б. fill in a form.

блат pull, influence.

бледнéть *(pf.* по-) grow pale; блéдность *(f.)* pallor; блéдный pale.

блёклый faded; блёкнуть *(past* блёк, -ла; *pf.* по-) fade.

блеск brilliance; lustre.

бле|стéть (-щý, -сти́шь *or* -щешь; *pf.* блеснýть) shine glitter.

блёс|тки (-ток) sparkles, spangles.

блестя́щий brilliant; shiny.

блеф bluff.

блéяние bleating; блéять (блé|ет *or* -ёт; *pf.* за-) bleat.

ближáйший nearest, next; бли́же nearer; бли́жний close, near, neighbouring; neighbour.

близ (+ *gen.)* near; бли́зиться approach; бли́зкий *(compr.* бли́же) near.

близнéц (-á) twin.

близорýкий short-sighted.

бли́зость *(f.)* closeness, proximity.

блик patch of light, highlight.

блин (-á) pancake.

блиндáж (-á) dug-out, shelter.

блистáть shine.

блок 1. bloc; 2. pulley.

блокáда blockade; блоки́ровать *(ipf. & pf.)* blockade.

блокнóт note-book, writing pad.

блонди́н, ~ка fair-haired person.

блохá *(pl.* блóх|и, -áм) flea.

блуд lechery; блудли́вый lascivious; блýдный prodigal.

блуждáть roam, wander.

блýз(к)а blouse.

блюдечко *(pl.* -чки, -чек) saucer; блю́до dish; блю́д|це *(gen. pl.* -дец) saucer.

бл|юсти́ (-юдý, -юдёшь; блюл, -á) *pf.* со-; *ppp.* -юдённый) keep, observe; блюсти́тель *(m.)* guardian.

бля́ха number plate, badge.

боб (-á) bean; остáться на бобáх get nothing for one's trouble.

бо|бёр (-брá) beaver (fur).

бобóвый bean *(a.)*

бобр (á) beaver; бобрóвый beaver *(a.)*

бобы́л|ь (-я́) landless poor peasant; lonely person; old bachelor; жить -ём live a lonely life.

бог *(voc.* бо́же, *pl.* -и, -о́в)   god; бо́же мой my goodness!   ей бо́гу really and truly; сохрани́ бог Gcd forbid!

богате́ть *(pf.* раз-) grow rich; бога́тство wealth; **бога́тый** *(comp.* богаче) (+ *inst.)* rich (in).

богаты́рь (-я́) hero, strong man.

бога́ч (-а́), ~чка *(gen. pl.* -чек) rich person.

бога́че *see* **бога́тый.**

боги́ня goddess.

богома́терь *(f.)* Mother of God.

богомо́|лец (-льца), ~лка pilgrim.

богоро́дица Our Lady.

богосло́в theologian; **богосло́вие** theology.

богослуже́ние divine service.

богоуго́дный charitable; godly.

богоху́льник blasphemer; **богоху́льный** blasphemous; **богоху́льство** blasphemy.

богоявле́ние Epiphany.

бода́ть *(pf.* за-; *also* бодну́ть) butt, gore.

бодри́ть stimulate; -ся keep up one's spirits; **бо́дрость** *(f.)* cheerfulness, courage.

бо́дрствовать keep awake.

бо́дрый cheerful, brisk.

боеви́к (-а́) hit, success; thriller.

боево́й battle *(a.),* fighting *(a.).*

боеголо́вка warhead.

боеспосо́бный efficient, battleworthy.

бое́ц (бойца́) fighter, warrior.

бо́же! good God!; **бо́жеский** God's; divine; acceptable; **боже́ственный** divine; **божество́** deity; **бо́жий** God's; divine; **бо́жья коро́вка** ladybird.

бой *(pl.* бои́, боёв) battle; striking *(of clock);* breakage.

бо́йкий *(comp.* бо́йче) sharp, alert.

бойко́т boycott; **бойкоти́ровать** boycott.

бойни́ца loophole.

бо́йня *(gen. pl.* бо́ен) slaughterhouse; carnage.

бок (на -у́, *pl.* -а́) side.

бока́л glass, goblet.

боково́й side *(a.),* lateral.

бокс boxing; **боксёр** boxer; **бокси́ровать** box.

болва́н block-head.

болва́нка pig *(of iron.)*

болга́|рин *(pl.* -ры, -р), ~рка Bulgarian; **болга́рский** Bulgarian *(a.).*

бо́лее more.

боле́зненный ailing, unhealthy; painful; **боле́знь** *(f.)* illness, disease.

боле́ль|щик, ~щица fan, enthusiast.

бол|е́ть 1. (-е́ю, -е́ешь; *pf.* за-) be(come) ill; 2. (-и́т) *(pf.* за-) ache, be(come) sore; **болеутоля́ющий** painkilling *(a.).*

боло́тистый marshy; **боло́тный** marsh *(a.);* б. газ methane; **боло́то** marsh, bog.

болт (-а́) bolt.

болта́ть 1. *(pf.* по-) chatter; 2. *(pf.* с-) stir, mix; 3. *(pf.* за-) dangle *(e. g.* нога́ми); -ся hang loose, dangle; loiter.

болтли́вый garrulous; **болтовня́** chatter, tittle-tattle.

болту́|н (-на́), ~нья *(gen. pl.* -ний) gossip.

боль *(f.)* pain.

больни́ца hospital; **больни́чный** hospital *(a.);* б. лист medical certificate; sick list.

бо́льно 1. it is painful; painfully; 2. *(coll.)* very, extremely.

больно́й sick; patient *(as noun);* sore, bad; б. вопро́с sore point.

большак (-а́) highroad.

бо́льше more, bigger.

большеви́зм Bolshevism; **большеви́к** (-а́) Bolshevik.

бо́льший bigger; **большинство́** majority.

большо́й *(comp.* бо́льше, бо́льший) big, large.

бо́мба bomb; **бомбардирова́ть** bombard, bomb; **бомбардиро́вка** bombardment; **бомбардиро́вщик** bomber; **бомбёжка** bombing; **бомби́ть** *(pf.* раз-) bomb.

бомбоубе́жище air-raid shelter.

бонда́р|ь (-я *and* -я́) cooper.

бор 1. steel drill; 2. boron; 3. (в бору́, *pl.* -ы́) pine wood.

бо|ре́ц (-рца́) champion, fighter, wrestler.

боржо́м Borzhom mineral water.

борз|о́й: -а́я соба́ка greyhound, borzoi.

бо́рзый swift, fleet-footed.

бормаши́на (dentist's) drill.

борм|ота́ть (-очу́, -о́чешь; *pf.* за-, про-) mumble, mutter.

бо́рный boracic, boric.

бо́ров 1. hog; 2. flue.

борода́ (бо́роду, *pl.* бо́роды, боро́д, -а́м) beard.

бородавка wart.

бородатый bearded.

борозда (*pl.* борозды, -розд, -ам) furrow; fissure.

боро|здить (-зжу, -здишь) (*pf.* вз-) plough, furrow; (*pf.* из-) furrow, wrinkle (*e. g.* brow).

борона (борону, *pl.* бороны, -рон, -ам) harrow; **боронить** (*pf.* вз-) harrow.

бороться (борюсь, борешься; *pf.* по-) struggle, fight, wrestle.

борт (*pl.* -á) 1. side (of ship); 2. breast (of coat), lapel; на борту on board; за бортом overboard.

бортпровод|ник (-никá), ∼ница airline steward, -stewardess.

борщ (-á) borshch (*beetroot soup*).

борьба struggle, fight; wrestling.

босиком barefoot; **босой** barefooted; на босу ногу without stockings.

босоно|жка (*gen. pl.* -жек) sandal; **босяк** (-á) vagabond, urchin.

бот 1. boat. 2. high overshoe.

ботан|ик botanist; ∼ика botany; ∼ический botanical.

ботик 1. yawl; 2. high overshoe, galosh.

ботфорт jackboot, wellington.

бочар cooper.

бочка (*gen. pl.* -чек) barrel.

бочком sideways.

бочо|нок (-нка) cask, keg.

боязливый timorous; **боязнь** (*f.*) fear.

бо|ярин (*pl.* -яре, -яр) boyar; **боярыня** boyar's wife.

боярышник hawthorn; haw.

бояться (боюсь, боишься; *pf.* по-) (+ *gen.*) fear, be afraid (of).

бравый gallant.

брази|лец (-льца), ∼лья́нка Brazilian; **бразильский** Brazilian (*a.*).

брак 1. marriage.

брак 2. spoilage, waste; **браковать** (*pf.* за-) reject as defective.

браконьер poacher.

бракосочетание wedding.

брандспойт fire pump; nozzle.

бранить (*pf.* вы-, по-) scold, reprove; -ся (*pf.* по-) quarrel, abuse each other.

бранный 1. abusive; 2. martial, battle (*a.*).

брань (*f.*) 1. bad language; 2. battle.

браслет bracelet.

брасс breast stroke.

брат (*pl.* брат|ья, -ьев) brother.

братание fraternization; **брататься** (*pf.* по-) fraternize.

бра|тец (-тца) brother; old chap; **братия** fraternity.

братоубийство fratricide.

братский brotherly, fraternal; **братство** fraternity; brotherhood.

брать (беру, берёшь; брал, -á, -о, -и; *pf.* взять, возьм|у, -ёшь; взял, -á, -о, -и *ppp.* взятый) take; -ся undertake; -ся за руки join hands; -ся за работу start work; откуда что берётся who would have thought it?

брачный marriage (*a.*); conjugal.

бревенчатый timbered; **бревно** (*pl.* брё|вна, -вен) log.

бред (в -у) delirium; **бре|дить** (-жу, -дишь) rave, be infatuated.

бредн|и (-ей), fancy, ravings; **бред|овой**, delirious, wild.

брезгать (*pf.* по-) (+ *inst.*) be squeamish (about); **брезгливый** fastidious.

брезент tarpaulin; **брезентовый** tarpaulin, canvas (*a.*).

брезжить, -ся dawn, glimmer.

брелок pendant.

бремя (*neut.*) *gen.*, *dat.*, *prep.* бремени, *inst.* бременем, *pl.* -менá) burden.

бренный frail, transient.

брен|чать (-чу, -чишь; *pf.* за-) chink, jingle.

бре|сти (-ду, -дёшь; брёл, -á; *ppa.* бредший; *pf.* по-) drag oneself along; stroll.

бретелька (*gen. pl.* -лек) shoulder-strap (*of underclothing.*)

бр|ехать (-ешу, -ешешь; *pf.* за-, & брехнуть) bark; (*coll.*) tell a lie.

брешь (*f.*) breach, gap.

бригада brigade, team, crew; **бригадир** brigadier, team-leader; foreman.

бриллиант, **брильянт** diamond.

брита|нец (-нца), ∼нка Briton; **британский** British.

бритва razor; blade; **бритвенный** shaving (*a.*).

брить (брею, бреешь; *ppp.* бритый; *pf.* вы-, по-). shave; -ся shave (oneself); **бритьё** shave, shaving.

бров|ь (*pl.* -и, -ей) brow, eyebrow; не в б., а в глаз right on the mark; он и -ью не повёл he did not turn a hair.

брод ford.

бр|оди́ть 1. (-ожу́, -о́дишь) roam, wander. 2. (-о́дит) ferment *(of wine)*.

бродя́га *(m.)* tramp, vagrant; **бродя́чий** vagrant, itinerant.;

бро|же́ние fermentation, ferment.

бром bromide, bromine.

бронебо́йный armour-piercing; **броневи́к** (-а́) armoured car; **бронево́й** armoured; **бронено́|сец** (-сца) battleship.

бро́нза bronze; **бро́нзовый** bronze *(a.)*

брони́ровать 1. (cover in) armour; 2. *(pf.* за-) reserve *(seats)*.

бро́ня reserved quota, reservation.

броня́ armour.

броса́ть *(pf.* бр|о́сить; -о́шу, -о́сишь) throw; -ся rush, dash.

бро́ский garish, striking.

бро|со́к (-ска́) 1. throw; 2. rush, sprint.

бро́|шка *(gen. pl.* -шек), **брошь** *(f.)* brooch.

брошю́ра booklet, pamphlet.

брус *(pl.* бру́сьи, -ьев) beam, *(pl.)* parallel bars *(sport)*.

брусни́ка cowberry.

бру|со́к (-ска́) bar.

бру́тто gross *(weight)*.

бры́згать *(pf.* за-, по-, *&* бры́знуть) splash, sprinkle.

брыка́ть *(pf.* брыкну́ть) kick.

брюзга́ *(m. & f.)* grumbler; **брюзгли́вый** querulous, grumbling; **брюз|жа́ть** (-жу́, -жи́шь) grumble.

брю́ква swede.

брю́ки (брюк) trousers.

брюне́т, / **~ка** dark-haired man / woman.

брюссе́льск|ий: -ая капу́ста Brussels sprouts.

брю́хо belly, paunch; **брюши́на** peritoneum; **брюшно́й** abdominal; б. тиф typhoid fever.

бря́кать *(pf.* бря́кнуть) *(inst.)* bang down; *(coll.)* blurt out.

бряца́ть clank; б. ору́жием rattle the sabre.

бу́|бен (-бна, *gen. pl.* бу́бен) tambourine; **бубе́н|ец** (-нца́) bell.

бу́|бны (-бён, -бнам) diamonds *(card)*.

бу|го́р (-гра́) hill, mound.

буди́льник alarm clock; **буди́ть** (бужу́, бу́дишь) 1. *(pf.* раз-; *ppp.* разбу́женный) waken; 2. *(pf.* про-;

ppp. пробуждённый) arouse *(feelings)*.

бу́дка box, stall, kiosk.

бу́дн|и (-ей) weekdays, work days; humdrum life; **бу́дничный** everyday, humdrum.

будора́жить *(pf.* вз-) excite, disturb.

бу́дто as if, as though; б. бы allegedly, ostensibly.

бу́дущее the future; **бу́дущий** future *(a.)*; **бу́дущность** *(f.)* future.

буера́к ravine, gully.

буза́ 1. buza *(alcoholic drink)*; 2. row, shindy *(coll.)*.

бузина́ elder (bush).

буй *(pl.* буи́, буёв) buoy.

бу́йвол buffalo.

бу́йный wild, violent.

бу́йст|во violent behaviour; **~овать** get violent.

бук beech.

бу́ка *(m. & f.)* bogeyman, bugbear; unsociable person.

бу́ква letter; **буква́льный** literal; **буква́р|ь** (-я́) primer, ABC book; **букво́ед** pedant.

буке́т bouquet.

букини́ст seller of rare and second-hand books.

бу́ковый beech *(a.)*.

букси́р tugboat; tow-line; взять на б. take in tow; *(coll.)* coach, help; **букси́ровать** tow.

булава́ mace.

була́вка pin; англи́йская б. safety pin.

була́ный dun, light bay.

бу́лка roll; **бу́лочная** baker's; **бу́лочник** baker.

булы́жник cobble(s) *(stones)*.

бульва́р avenue; **бульва́рный** avenue *(a.)*; cheap, vulgar.

бу́лькать *(pf.* бу́лькнуть) gurgle.

бульо́н broth, clear soup.

бум *(coll.)* sensation; boom *(econ.)*.

бума́га paper; **бума́|жка** *(gen. pl.* -жек) piece of paper, note; **бума́жник** 1. wallet; 2. paper manufacturer; **бума́жный** (of) paper.

бумазе́я fustian.

бунт 1. riot; 2. bale, bundle; **бунтова́ть** *(pf.* взбунтова́ться) rebel; **бунтовщи́к** (-а́) insurgent, rebel.

бура́ borax.

бура́в (-а́) gimlet, drill; **бура́вить** *(pf.* про-) bore, drill.

бура́н snowstorm.

бурдю́к (-а́) wineskin.

буревéстник stormy petrel.

бурéние boring, drilling.

буржуá (m., indecl.) bourgeois; буржуазия bourgeoisie; буржуáзный bourgeois (a.); буржуй bourgeois.

бурить (pf. про-) bore, drill.

бýрка felt cloak; felt boot.

бурлáк (-á) barge hauler.

бурлить seethe.

бýрный stormy.

буров|óй boring; -áя сквáжина bore-hole.

бурсáк (-á) seminary student.

бурýн (-á) breaker (wave).

бур|чáть (-чý, -чишь; pf. за-, про-) mumble, rumble.

бýрый brown.

бурьян weeds.

бýря storm.

бýсина bead; бýсы (бус) beads.

бут stone (for building).

бутафóрия properties (in theatre); window dressing.

бутербрóд slice of bread and butter, sandwich.

бутóн bud.

бýтс|ы (-ов) football boots.

бутылка bottle; бутыль (f.) large bottle.

бýфер (pl. -á) buffer, bumper.

буфéт sideboard; buffet, bar; буфéтчик, ~чица barman, barmaid.

бухáнка loaf.

бýхать (pf. бýхнуть) thump, bang; blurt out.

бухгáлтер accountant; бухгалтéрия book-keeping; accounts department; бухгáлтерский account (a.).

бýхнуть[1] (past. бух, -ла; pf. на-, раз)- swell.

бýхнуть[2] (pf.) see бýхать.

бýхта bay.

бушевáть rage, storm.

буян rowdy; буянить make a row, uproar.

бы (particle used to form subjunctive); я написáл бы, éсли бы я знал I should have written, if I had known; где бы ни wherever; как бы ни however; ещё бы! I should think so!

бывáло used (to); он бывáло чáсто éздил тудá he would often go there.

бывáлый experienced.

бывáть (pf. по-) be, happen; visit; как ни в чем не бывáло as if nothing had happened.

бывший former, ex-.

бык (-á) 1. bull, ox; 2. pier, support.

былина bylina (Russian epic).

былинка blade of grass.

было nearly, almost; онá пошлá было, да остановилась she was on the point of going, but stopped.

былóе the past; былóй former; быль (f.) fact, true story.

быстротá speed; быстрый quick.

быт (в-ý) way of life; бытиé being, existence; бытность (f.) existence, stay, time; бытовóй domestic, everyday.

быть (fut. бýд|у, -ешь; past. был, -á, -о; imper. бýдьте ger. бýдучи) be; бýдет! that's enough!

бытьё (way of) life.

бы|чóк (-чкá) young bull; bullhead (fish).

бюджéт budget; бюджéтный budget (a.).

бюллетéнь (m.) bulletin; избирáтельный б. ballot paper.

бюрó (indecl.) bureau, office.

бюрокр|áт bureaucrat; ~атизм red tape; ~атический bureaucratic; ~áтия bureaucracy.

бюст bust; бюстгáльтер brassiere.

В

в (+ acc.) into, within; on; at; в три часá at three o'clock; within three hours; он весь в отцá he is just like his father.
(+ prep.) in, at; в десяти шагáх от дорóги ten yards from the road.

вагóн carriage, coach; вагóн-рестораáн restaurant-car; вагонéтка trolley, truck; вагоновожáтый tramdriver.

вáжничать (pf. за-) put on airs; вáжность (f.) importance; pomposity; вáжный important; grand, pompous.

вáза vase.

вазелин vaseline.

вакáнсия vacancy; вакáнтный vacant.

вáкса (shoe) polish.

вáкуум vacuum.

вакцина vaccine.

вал (-ы) 1. roller (wave); 2. bank, rampart; 3. shaft.

валёжник windfall branches, brush-wood.

вáле|нок (-нка, *gen. pl.* -нок *and* -нков) felt boot.

валéт knave, Jack.

вáлик roller, cylinder.

валить (валю́, вáлишь; *pf.* по-, с-) 1. throw down; pile up; в. вину́ на друго́го put blame on someone else; 2. pour, billow.

вáлкий unsteady.

валово́й gross.

валто́рна French horn.

валу́н (-á) boulder.

вáльдшнеп woodcock.

вальс waltz; вальси́ровать waltz.

валю́та currency; валю́тный ку́рс rate of exchange.

валя́ть 1. (*pf.* по-, вы-) roll; 2. (*pf.* с-) roll (*pastry*); в. дурака́ play the fool; валя́й! go on! go ahead! -ся (*pf.* вы-) roll, lie about.

вампи́р vampire.

вани́ль (*f.*) vanilla; вани́льный vanilla (*a.*).

вáнна bath; вáнная bathroom.

вá|нька-встá|нька (*gen. pl.* -нек, -нек) pop-up doll.

вáрвар barbarian; вáрварский barbaric; вáрварство barbarism, vandalism.

вáрево broth, soup.

вáре|жка (*gen. pl.* -жек) mitten.

варёный boiled; варéнье jam, preserve(s).

вариáнт version; вариáция variation.

вари́ть (варю́, вáришь; *pf.* с-) boil, cook; -ся be boiling, be boiled.

варьи́ровать vary, modify.

варя́г Varangian; варя́жский Varangian (*a.*).

васи́л|ёк (-лькá) cornflower; василько́вый cornflower (blue).

вассáл vassal.

вáт|а wadding; cotton wool; пальто́ на -е padded coat.

ватáга crowd.

ватерли́ния waterline; ватерпáс water level (*instrument*); ватерпо́ло (*indecl.*) water polo.

вáтный padded, quilted.

ватру́|шка (*gen. pl.* -шек) cheese cake.

ватт watt.

вá|фля (*gen. pl.* -фель) wafer.

вáхт|а watch; на -е on watch.

ваш, вáша, вáше, вáши your,

вáяние sculpture; вая́тель (*m.*) sculptor; вая́ть (*pf.* из-) sculpt.

вбегáть (*pf.* вбежáть*) run in.

вбивáть (*pf.* вбить*, вобью́ *etc.*) knock, drive in.

вбирáть (*pf.* вобрáть*, вбсру́ *etc.*) absorb, inhale, take in.

вблизи́ close by.

вброд: перейти́ ре́ку в. wade across/ford river.

ввáливать (*pf.* ввали́ть*) throw in; -ся tumble in; become sunken.

введéние introduction.

ввезти́ *see* ввози́ть.

ввек *не* (*coll.*) never.

вве́рить *see* вверя́ть.

вве́ртывать (*pf.* ввернуть) screw in.

вверх up(wards); в. дном upside down; вверху́ above, overhead.

вверя́ть (*pf.* вве́рить) entrust; в. э́то ему́ entrust him with this.

ввести́ *see* вводи́ть.

ввиду́ in view (of); в. того́, что... in view of the fact that...

вви́нчивать (*pf.* ввин|ти́ть, -чу́, -ти́шь) screw in.

ввод lead-in; вводи́ть* (*pf.* ввести́*) bring in, introduce; вво́дный introductory.

ввоз import(ation); ввози́ть* (*pf* ввезти́*) bring in, import; ввозный import (*a.*).

вво́лю to one's heart's content.

ввысь up(wards).

ввя́зывать (*pf.* ввязáть*) mix in, involve; -ся become engaged in, meddle in; -ся в разгово́р join in the conversation.

вгибáть (*pf.* вогну́ть) curve/bend in.

вглубь deep into; в. страны́ into the heart of the country.

вгля́дываться (*pf.* вгляде́ться*) (в + *acc.*) look closely at.

вгоня́ть (*pf.* вогнáть*, вгоню́ *etc.*) drive in.

вдавáться* (*pf.* вдáться*) jut out (into); в. в подро́бности go into details; в. в крáйности go to extremes.

вдáвливать (*pf.* вдави́ть*) press in.

вдалеке́, вдали́ in the distance: вдаль into the distance.

вдáться *see* вдавáться

вдвигáть (*pf.* вдви́нуть) move into, push in.

вдво́е double, twice; в. бо́льше twice as big/as much); уме́ньшить в.

halve; **вдвоём** two together; **вдвойнé** double; платúть в. pay double.
вдевáть (-евáю; *pf.* вдеть*) pass through; в. нúтку в игóлку thread a needle.
вдéлывать *(pf.* вдéлать) fit in(to); set in.
вдобáвок in addition, moreover.
вдовá *(pl.* вдóвы) widow; **вдо|вéц** (-вцá) widower.
вдóволь in plenty, enough; он наéлся в. he ate his fill.
вдовствó widow(er)hood; **вдóвств- овать** to be a widow(er); **вдóвый** widowed.
вдогóнку in pursuit; брóситься в. за + *inst.* rush after . . .
вдоль *(gen.)* along; в. стены along the wall; в. бéрега, в. по бéрегу along the bank; в. и поперёк far and wide, thoroughly.
вдох breath, inhalation.
вдохновéние inspiration; **вдохновéн- ный** inspired; **вдохно|влять** *(pf.* -вúть) inspire; **-ся** be inspired.
вдрéбезги into smithereens.
вдруг suddenly.
вдувáть *(pf.* вдуть*, вдýнуть) blow into.
вдýмчивый thoughtful; **вдýмы- ваться** *(pf.* вдýматься) **(в +** *acc.)* consider, ponder.
вдунуть *see* **вдувáть.**
вдыхáть *(pf.* вдохнýть) breathe in.
вегетариá|нец (-нца), **~нка** vegeta- rian; **вегетариáнство** vegetarian- ism.
вéдать 1. *(inst.)* manage, handle.
вéдать 2. know.
вéден|ие authority; competence; э́то не в вáшем -ии that is not within your province.
ведéние conducting, keeping.
вéдом|о: с моегó -а with my know- ledge; без моегó -а without my knowledge.
вéдомость *(f.)* list, register, record; платёжная в. pay-roll.
вéдомственный departmental; bureaucratic; **вéдомство** depart- ment.
ведрó *(pl.* вё|дра, -дер) bucket.
вёдро fine weather.
ведýщий leading, chief.
ведь you see, you know.
вéдьма witch.
вéер *(pl.* -á) fan.

вéжливый polite.
вездé everywhere; **вездесýщий** omni- present; **вездехóд** cross-country vehicle.
везтú (вез|ý, -ёшь; вёз, -лá, -лú; *pf.* по-, *ppp.* -везённый) convey, take; емý везёт he is in luck.
век *(pl.* -á) age; century; lifetime. на моём векý in my time.
вéко *(pl.* вéки, век) eyelid.
вековóй age-old.
вéксел|ь *(m.* ; *pl.* -я) promissory note, bill of exchange.
велеречúвый pompous.
ве|лéть (-лю, -лúшь, *ipf. & pf.)* or- der, command.
великáн giant.
велúкий great; **великодержáвный** great-power.
велико|дýшие magnanimity; **~дýш- ный** magnanimous.
велико|лéпие splendour; **~лéпный** magnificent.
великорýс, ~ка Great Russian; **вели- корýсский** Great Russian *(a.).*
величáвый stately, majestic.
величественный majestic, sublime; **велúчество** majesty.
велúчие grandeur, greatness; **вели- чинá** *(pl.* -úны) size; quantity; *(maths)* value, magnitude.
велогóнка cycle race; **велосипéд** bicycle, cycle; **велосипедúст, ~ка** cyclist; **велосипéдный** cycle *(a.).*
вельвéт velveteen.
вельмóжа *(m.)* magnate, noble.
вéна vein.
венгé|рец (-рца), **~рка** Hungarian; **венгéрский** Hungarian *(a.); венгр* Hungarian.
венерúческий venereal.
венéц (-нцá) crown, wreath.
вéник besom.
ве|нóк (-нкá) garland; wreath.
вентилúровать *(pf.* про-) ventilate; **вентилятор** ventilator; **вентил- яция** ventilation.
венчáние wedding; marriage cere- mony; **венчáть** *(ipf. & pf;* also *pf.* у-) crown; *(pf.* об-, по-) marry; **-ся** get married; be crowned.
вéнчик halo; corolla.
вепрь *(m.)* wild boar.
вéра (в + *acc.)* faith, belief (in).
верáнда verandah.
вéрба pussy-willow.
верблюд camel; **верблюжий** camel *(a.).*

вербн|ый pussy-willow *(a.)*; -ое воскресéнье Palm Sunday.

вербовáть *(pf.* за-, на-) recruit; win over; вербóвка recruitment.

верёвка rope, cord; верёвочка *(gen. pl.* -чек) string; верёвочный (of) rope.

верени́ца row, file, string.

вéреск heather; вéресковый heather *(a.)*.

вере|тенó *(pl.* -тёна, -тён) spindle.

вере|щáть (-щý, -щи́шь) chirp; squeal.

верзи́ла *(m. & f.)* lanky person.

вери́га chain *(worn by penitent)*.

вери́тельн|ый; -ые грáмоты credentials.

вéрить *(pf.* по-) believe; (+ *dat.)* я не вéрю свои́м ушáм; I can't believe my ears; (в + *acc.)* believe in; вéриться: мне не вéрится, что . . . I cannot believe that . . .

вермишéль *(f.)* vermicelli.

вернопóдданный loyal subject.

вéрность *(f.)* faithfulness, fidelity.

вернýть *see* возвращáть.

вéрный true, correct; loyal.

вéрование belief; вéровать (в + *acc.)* believe (in).

вероисповéдание religion, denomination.

веро|лóмный perfidious, treacherous; ~лóмство treachery; ~терпи́мость *(f.)* tolerance; ~учéние dogma.

вероя́тие, вероя́тность *(f.)* probability; вероя́тный probable.

вéрсия version.

верстá *(pl.* вёрсты) verst *(= 1·06 km.)*.

вéртел spit.

вертéп den, 'dive'.

вертéть (верчý, вéртишь; *pf.* за-, по-) turn, twist, -ся *(pf.* за-) revolve, spin, twist.

вертикáль *(f.)* vertical line; ~ный vertical.

вертля́вый fidgety.

вертолёт helicopter.

вертý|шка *(gen. pl.* -шек) revolving door; revolving stand.

вéрующий believer.

верфь *(f.)* shipyard.

верх (на -ý, *pl.* -и́) top; summit; *(pl.)* the upper ten; upper crust; high notes; вéрхний upper, top *(a.)*.

верхóвный supreme.

верхов|óй (on) horseback; up-river; ~áя ездá horse-riding.

верхó|вье *(gen. pl.* -вьев) upper reaches.

верхóм astride.

верхýшка *(gen. pl.* -шек) top, apex; leaders.

верши́на summit, crest.

верши́ть *(inst.)* manage, direct.

вер|шóк (-шкá) inch.

вес weight.

весели́ть *(pf.* раз-) cheer, gladden; -ся enjoy oneself, be merry; весёлый merry; весéлье merriment.

весéнний spring *(a.)*.

вéсить (вéшу, вéсишь) weigh; вéский weighty.

веслó *(pl.* вё|слá, -сел) oar.

веснá *(pl.* вё|сны, -сен) spring.

весну́|шка *(gen. pl.* -шек) freckle.

вести́ (ведý, ведёшь, вёл, велá; *pf.* по-, *ppp.* -ведённый) lead, take; вести́ себя́ conduct oneself, behave; вести́сь be led, be (in progress).

вестибю́ль *(m.)* entrance hall.

вéстник herald.

вест|ь 1. *(f.; pl.* -и, -éй) (piece of) news.

весть 2.: бог весть goodness knows.

вес|ы́ (-óв) balance, scales.

весь, вся, всё, все all, whole; всё равнó it's all the same; nevertheless; всегó хорóшего all the best; всё everything; always, all the time, still.

весьмá greatly.

ветви́стый branchy; ветв|ь *(pl.* -и, -éй) branch.

вé|тер (-тра) wind; держáть нос по вéтру trim one's sails to the wind.

ветеринáр veterinary surgeon.

вете|рóк (-ркá) breeze.

вéтка branch, twig.

ветлá *(pl.* вé|тлы, -тел) willow.

вéто *(indecl.)* veto.

вéтошь *(f.)* rags, old clothes.

вéтреница anemone.

вéтреный windy: frivolous; ветряной wind *(a.)*; вéтрян|ый: -ая óспа chicken-pox.

вéтхий decrepit, tumble-down.

ветчинá ham.

вéха landmark

вéче *(gen. pl.* веч) veche *(old Russian popular assembly)*.

вéчер *(pl.* -á) evening; вечери́нка

party; **вечёрний** evening *(a.);* **вечёрня** *(gen. pl.* -рен) vespers.

вёчность *(f.)* eternity; **вёчный** eternal.

вёшалка peg, rack; **вёшать** *(pf.* повёсить*) hang; *(pf.* свёшать) weigh.

вещáние broadcasting.

вещевóй: в. мешóк knapsack.

вещёственный material *(a.);* **вещество** substance.

вёщий prophetic.

вещь *(f.; pl.* -и, -ёй) thing.

вéялка winnowing-machine; **вéяние** winnowing; blowing; trend; **вéять** (вéю, вéешь) 1. *(pf.* по-) blow; 2. *(pf.* про-) winnow.

вживáться *(pf.* вжиться*) (в + *acc.*) get accustomed to.

вжимáть *(pf.* вжать*) press in.

взад back(wards); в. и вперёд back and forth.

взаймность *(f.)* reciprocity; **взаимный** mutual.

взаимовыгодный mutually advantageous; **~дéйствие** interaction, reciprocity; **~понимáние** mutual understanding.

взаймы: брать в. borrow; давáть в. lend.

взамéн *(gen.)* instead (of).

взаперти under lock and key; in seclusion.

взбалмошный extravagant, eccentric.

взбáлтывать *(pf.* взболтáть) shake up.

взбегáть *(pf.* взбежáть*) run up.

взбивáть *(pf.* взбить,* взобью) shake up; beat up, whisk.

взбирáться *(pf.* взобрáться,* взберусь) climb up.

взболтáть *see* взбáлтывать.

взбухáть *(pf.* взбухнуть, *past,* -бух) swell up.

взвáливать *(pf.* взвалить*) hoist up, lay on.

взвéсить *see* взвéшивать.

взвести *see* взводить.

взвéшивать *(pf.* взвéсить*) weigh, weigh up.

взвивáть *(pf.* взвить,* взовью) raise, wind up; -ся be raised; soar; rear *(horse).*

взвизгивать *(pf.* взвизгнуть) scream, yelp.

взвинчивать *(pf.* взви|нтить, -нчý, -нтишь) excite, work up; inflate *(prices).*

взвить *see* взвивáть.

взвод 1. platoon, section; 2. notch; **взводить*** *(pf.* взвести*) raise; в. обвинéние на + *acc.* impute fault to ...

взволнóванный agitated, uneasy.

взгляд look, stare; на мой в. to my mind; на пéрвый в. at first sight; **взглядывать** *(pf.* взглянуть) glance.

взгóрье hill.

взгромоздиться *(pf.* -зжусь, -здишься) clamber up.

вздёргивать *(pf.* вздёрнуть) hitch up, pull up; turn up *(nose).*

вздор nonsense; **вздóрный** nonsensical.

вздох sigh.

вздрáгивать *(pf.* вздрóгнуть) shudder.

вздувáть *(pf.* вздуть*) inflate; -ся swell.

вздумать *(pf.)* take it into one's head. -ся: емý. вздýмалось he took it into his head

вздýтие swelling; **вздýтый** bulbous, swollen.

вздымáть raise.

вздыхáть *(pf.* вздохнуть) (по + *prep.,* or о + *prep.)* sigh (for).

взимáть levy, collect.

взирáть *(coll.):* не -ая на лица without fear or favour.

взлáмывать *(pf.* взломáть) break up/ open.

взлезáть *(pf.* взлезть*) climb up.

взлёт flight, take-off; **взлетáть** *(pf.* взлетéть*) fly up.

взлом breaking and entering; **взломáть** *see* взлáмывать; **взлóмщик** burglar.

взлохмáченный dishevelled.

взмах flap, stroke, wave; **взмáхивать** *(pf.* взмахнуть) flap, wave.

взмóрье coastal waters; coast.

взнос payment, due.

взнуздывать *(pf.* взнуздáть) bridle.

взобрáться *see* взбирáться.

взойти *see* восходить *and* всходить.

взор look, gaze.

взорвáть *see* взрывáть 1.

взрóслый adult.

взрыв explosion, outburst; **взрывáтель** *(m.)* detonating fuse; **взрывáть** 1. *(pf.* взорвáть*) blow up; exasperate; -ся burst, explode; **взрывнóй** explosive, blasting *(a.);* **взрывчат|ый** explosive *(a.);* -ое вещество explosive.

взрыва́ть 2. (pf. взрыть*) dig up, plough up.

въезжа́ть (pf. въе́хать*) go up; в. на́ гору drive/ride up a hill.

взъеро́шенный dishevelled.

взыва́ть (pf. воззва́ть*) (к + dat.) appeal (to); (о + prep.) call, appeal (for).

взыска́ние penalty; exaction; взыска́тельный exacting, severe; взы́скивать (pf. взы|ска́ть, -ыщу́, -ы́щешь) exact, recover.

взя́тие taking, capture; взя́тка bribe; взя́точник bribe-taker; взя́точничество bribery; взять see брать.

виаду́к viaduct.

вибра́ция vibration; вибри́ровать vibrate.

вид sight: appearance, shape, form, view; prospect; kind, species; в ви́де (gen.) in the shape of; на виду́ in the public eye; име́ть в виду́ to bear in mind; теря́ть из виду lose sight of; с виду in appearance; под ви́дом (gen.) in the guise of; ста́вить на вид reproach for.

вида́ть (pf. по-, у-) see; ви́дение sight, vision; виде́ние apparition, vision; ви́деть (ви́жу, ви́дишь; pf. у-; ppp. уви́денный) see; ся see each other; ему́ ви́дится . . . he sees.

ви́димость (f.) visibility; semblance, ви́димый apparent, visible.

видне́ться be visible; ви́дный visible; eminent.

видово́й travel. landscape, view (adj.); aspectual (gram.); (of) form.

видоизмене́ние modification видоизмен|я́ть (pf. -и́ть) modify.

ви́за visa.

византи́йский Byzantine.

визг squeal, screech; визгли́вый shrill; ви|зжа́ть (-зжу́, -зжи́ш; pf. за-) squeal, screech.

визи́т visit; визи́тная ка́рточка visiting card.

виктори́на quiz game.

ви́лка fork; electric plug.

ви́ллис jeep, landrover.

ви́лы (вил) pitchfork.

виля́ть (pf. за-, or вильну́ть) wag; в. хвосто́м wag tail.

вина́ (pl. ви́ны) fault, guilt. |

винегре́т Russian salad; medley.

вини́тельный паде́ж accusative case.

вини́ть (за + acc.) blame (for).

ви́нн|ый (of) wine; -ый ка́мень cream of tartar; -ая я́года fig.

вино́ (pl. ви́на) wine.

винова́тый (в + prep.) guilty (of).

вино́в|ник, ~ница culprit; вино́вный (в + prep.) guilty (of).

виногра́д grapes; виногра́дарство viticulture; виногра́дина grape; виногра́дник vineyard; виногра́дный grape, wine (a.).

виноде́лие wine-making; виноку́ренный заво́д distillery.

винт (-а́) screw; ви́нтик small screw.

винто́вка rifle.

винтов|о́й screw (a.); spiral, -а́я ле́стница spiral staircase.

виолонче́ль (f.) cello.

виртуо́з virtuoso; виртуо́зный masterly.

вируле́нтный virulent.

ви́рус virus; ви́русный virus.

ви́рши (-ей) (syllabic) verses.

ви́селица gallows.

висе́ть (ви́шу, -си́шь; pf. по-) hang.

ви́ски (indecl.) whisky.

виско́за viscose.

ви́смут bismuth.

ви́снуть (past вис, -ла; pf. по-) hang.

ви|со́к (-ска́) temple, forehead.

високо́сный год leap-year.

вист whist.

вися́чий hanging; в. замо́к padlock; в. мост suspension bridge.

витами́н vitamin.

вита́ть soar.

витиева́тый flowery, ornate.

вит|о́й twisted; -а́я ле́стница winding staircase; ви|то́к (-тка́) coil, turn.

витри́на shop window, showcase.

вить (вью, вьёшь; imper. вей, ppp. ви́тый; pf. свить, совью́*) twist, weave; ся curl, wave, twist.

ви́тязь (m.) champion, hero, knight.

ви|хо́р (-хра́) tuft (of hair).

вихрь (m.) whirlwind; vortex.

вице-адмира́л vice-admiral.

вицмунди́р dress uniform.

вишнёвый cherry (a.); ви́шня (gen. pl. -шен) cherry.

вишь (coll. particle = ви́дишь) вишь, он како́й so that's what he's like!

вка́лывать (pf. вколо́ть*) stick in; work hard.

вка́пывать (pf. вкопа́ть) dig in, plant; как вко́панный стои́т stands as if rooted to the spot.

вка́тывать (pf. вкати́ть*) roll in.

вклад (в + *acc.*) contribution (to); deposit *(in bank)*; вкла́дка, вкладно́й лист supplementary sheet, insert; вкла́дчик depositor; вкла́дывать *(pf.* вложи́ть,-ожу́, -о́жишь) put in, insert.
вкле́ивать *(pf.* вкле́ить) glue in, stick in.
включа́ть *(pf.* включи́ть) (в + *acc.*) include (in); включи́тельно inclusive.
вкола́чивать *(pf.* вколоти́ть*) drive, hammer in.
вколо́ть *see* вка́лывать.
вконе́ц completely.
вкопа́ть *see* вка́пывать.
вкорен|я́ться *(pf.* -и́ться) become rooted.
вкось obliquely.
вкра́дчивый ingratiating, insinuating; вкра́дываться *(pf.* вкра́сться*) creep in; insinuate oneself.
вкра́пливать *(pf.* вкрапи́ть) sprinkle; intersperse.
вкра́тце in brief.
вкривь wrongly; perversely.
вкруту́ю: яйцо́ в. hard-boiled egg.
вкус taste; вку́сный nice (to taste); вкусово́й gustatory; flavouring *(a.).*
вкуша́ть *(pf.* вк|уси́ть, -ушу́, -у́сишь) taste, partake of.
вла́га moisture.
владе́|лец (-льца), владе́лица owner; holder; владе́ние ownership, possession; property; владе́ть (+ *inst.*) own, possess, have mastery of.
влады́ка *(m.)* lord, sovereign; влады́чество dominion, sway.
вла́жность *(f.)* moisture, humidity; вла́жный moist, damp.
вла́мываться *(pf.* вломи́ться) (в + *acc.*) break (into).
вла́ствовать (над + *inst.*) hold sway (over).
властели́н, власти́тель *(m.)* ruler, master.
вла́стный imperious, commanding; я не вла́стен это сде́лать I have not the authority to do that; власт|ь *(f.; pl.* -и, -е́й) power, authority.
влачи́ть drag along, eke out.
вле́во to the left, on the left.
влеза́ть *(pf.* влезть*) climb in.
влече́ние inclination, attraction *(towards);* влечь (влеку́, влечёшь, влёк, -ла́; *pf.* по-, *ppp.*

-влечённый) draw, pull; в. за собо́й involve, entail.
влива́ть *(pf.* влить*, волью́) pour in.
влия́ние influence; влия́тельный influential; влия́ть *(pf.* по-) (на + *acc.*) affect, have influence (on).
вложе́ние enclosure *(with letter);* investment.
вложи́ть *see* вкла́дывать.
вломи́ться *see* вла́мываться.
влюблённый in love, enamoured; влюбля́ться *(pf.* влюби́ться) (в + *acc.*) fall in love (with).
вма́зывать *(pf.* вма́зать*) fix/ cement in.
вменя́емый responsible, sane; вменя́ть *(pf.* вмени́ть) impute, impose; в. себе́ э́то в обя́занность make it one's duty.
вме́сте together; в. с тем at the same time.
вмести́лище receptacle.
вмести́мость *(f.)* capacity, tonnage; вмести́тельный capacious, roomy; вмести́ть *see* вмеща́ть.
вме́сто *(gen.)* instead (of).
вмеша́тельство interference, intervention; вме́шивать *(pf.* вмеша́ть) (в + *acc.*) mix (into); implicate (in); -ся (в + *acc.*) interfere, intervene (in).
вмеща́ть *(pf.* вме|сти́ть, -щу́, -сти́шь) contain, accommodate; -ся go in, be accommodated.
вмиг in an instant.
вмя́тина dent.
внаём, внаймы́ on hire/rent; сдава́ть в. let.
внаки́дку: наде́ть пальто́ в. put coat over one's shoulders.
внача́ле at first.
вне *(gen.)* outside (of); вне себя́ beside oneself.
внебра́чный natural, extra-marital.
вневре́менный timeless.
внедре́ние inculcation; внедря́ть *(pf.* внедри́ть) (в + *acc.*) instil (into); -ся strike root.
внеза́пный sudden.
внекла́ссный out-of-school.
внеочередно́й extraordinary.
внесе́ние bringing in; payment; entry; внести́ *see* вноси́ть.
внешко́льный out-of-school.
вне́шн|ий outer, external; -яя поли́тика foreign policy; вне́шность *(f.)* exterior; appearance.

вниз down (wards); **внизу́** below, at the bottom.

вника́ть (pf. вни́кнуть) (в + acc.) go into, try to fathom.

внима́ние attention; **внима́тельный** attentive; **внима́ть** (pf. внять past only) (+ dat.) heed, listen to.

ВНИЧЬЮ: сыгра́ть в. play a draw.

вновь anew, again.

вноси́ть* (pf. внести́*) carry in, bring in, enter.

внук grandson.

вну́тренний inner, internal; **вну́тренность** (f.) interior; (pl.) internal organs.

внутри́ (+ gen.) inside (of); **внутрь** (+ gen.) into.

внуча́та (внуча́т) grandchildren; **вну́|чка** (gen. pl. -чек) grand-daughter.

внуша́ть (pf. внуши́ть) inspire; в. ему́ уваже́ние inspire him with respect; **внуше́ние** suggestion; hypnosis; reprimand; **внуши́тельный** impressive; earnest.

вня́тный distinct; **внять** see **внима́ть**.

вобра́ть see **вбира́ть**.

вовлека́ть (pf. вовле́чь*) (в + acc.) draw in (to); involve (in).

во́время in time.

во́все completely, quite; **во́все** не not at all.

вовсю́ with might and main, to the utmost.

во-вторы́х secondly.

вогна́ть see **вгоня́ть**.

во́гнутый concave.

вода́ (во́ду, pl. во́ды) water.

водворя́ть (pf. -и́ть) put in, install, establish.

водеви́ль (m.) vaudeville, comic sketch.

води́тель (m.) driver.

води́ть (вожу́, во́дишь; pf. поводи́ть повести́*) lead, conduct; **-ся** be found; associate (with); как во́дится as usual.

во́дк|а vodka; дава́ть на -у (give a) tip.

во́дный water (a.).

водо́|боя́знь (f.) hydrophobia, rabies; **~воро́т** whirlpool, vortex; **~ём** reservoir; **~измеще́ние** displacement; **~ла́з** 1. diver; 2. Newfoundland (dog); **~ме́р** water gauge; **~непрони́цаемый** waterproof; **~отво́д** overflow pipe; **~па́д** waterfall; **~пой** watering place; **~прово́д**

water pipe, water mains; **~прово́дчик** plumber; **~разде́л** watershed; **~ро́д** hydrogen; **~ро́дный** hydrogen (a.); **~росль** (f.) water plant, seaweed; **~сто́чная труба́** drainpipe; **~храни́лище** reservoir.

водружа́ть (pf. водру|зи́ть, -жу́, -зишь) erect; raise (flag).

водяни́стый watery; **водя́нка** dropsy; **водяно́й** water (a.).

воева́ть wage war; **воево́да** (m.) commander, voevoda (hist.).

воедино together.

военача́льник military leader; **военко́м** (вое́нный комисса́р) military commissar.

вое́нно-возду́шный air(force); **~морско́й** naval; **~пле́нный** prisoner-of-war; **~полево́й суд** court-martial; **~слу́жащий** serviceman.

вое́нн|ый military, war (a.); -oe положе́ние martial law; **вое́нщина** the military.

вожа́к (-á) leader; **вожа́тый** 1. Young Pioneer leader; 2. tram-driver; 3. guide.

вожделе́ние desire.

вожд|ь (-я́) leader, во́жж|и (-éй) reins.

воз (на -ý, pl. -ы́) cartload.

возбуди́мый excitable; **возбужда́ть** (pf. возбуди́ть, -жу́, -ди́шь ppp. -ждённый) excite, arouse; **возбужда́ющий** exciting; stimulant; **возбужде́ние** excitation, excitement.

возведе́ние raising, erection.

возвеличе́ние glorification; **возвели́чивать** (pf. -ичить) glorify, exalt.

возвести́ see **возводи́ть**.

возвеща́ть (pf. возве|сти́ть, -щу́ -сти́шь) announce, proclaim.

возводи́ть* (pf. возвести́*) erect raise; в. э́то в при́нцип make it a principle.

возвра́т return, repayment; **возвра́тный** return (a.); reflexive (gram.); **возвраща́ть** (pf. возвра|ти́ть, -щу́, -ти́шь & верну́ть) return, give back; **-ся** return, go (come) back; **возвраще́ние** return.

возвыша́ть (pf. возв|ы́сить, -ы́шу, -ы́сишь) raise, elevate; **возвыше́ние** rise; dais; **возвы́шенность** (f.) height; loftiness; **возвы́шенный** high, elevated.

возглавля́ть (*pf.* возгла́вить) head, be at head of.

во́зглас exclamation; **возглаша́ть** (*pf.* возгла|си́ть, -шу́, -си́шь) proclaim.

возго́нка sublimation (*chem.*)

возгора́емый inflammable; **возгора́ться** (*pf.* возгоре́ться*) be inflamed; be consumed (*with passion, etc.*).

воздава́ть* ((*pf.* возда́ть*) render.

воздвига́ть (*pf.* воз|дви́гнуть, *past* -дви́г) erect.

возде́йств|ие influence; **~овать** (на + *acc.*) have influence (on).

возде́лывать (*pf.* возде́лать) till, cultivate.

воздержа́ние abstention, temperance; **возде́рживаться** (*pf.* воздержа́ться*) (от + *gen.*) abstain, refrain (from); **возде́ржный** abstemious.

во́здух air; **воздухопла́вание** aeronautics; **возду́шн|ый** aerial; **-ый шар** balloon; **-ые за́мки** castles in the air.

воззва́ние appeal, manifesto; **воззва́ть** *see* взыва́ть.

воззре́ние view, opinion.

вози́ть (вожу́, во́зишь; *pf.* по-, повезти́*) convey, carry; **-ся** (с + *inst.*) romp; be busy (with).

возлага́ть (*pf.* воз|ложи́ть, -ложу́, -ло́жишь) lay, place; **в. наде́жду** (на + *acc.*) put hopes (on).

во́зле (*gen.*) near.

возлия́ние libation.

возложи́ть *see* возлага́ть.

возлю́бленный beloved.

возме́здие retribution.

возмеща́ть (*pf.* возме|сти́ть, -сти́шь) compensate, reimburse; **в. ему́ расхо́ды** pay his expenses; **возмеще́ние** compensation, reimbursement.

возмо́жность (*f.*) possibility; **возмо́жный** possible.

возмужа́лый mature; manly.

возмути́тельный disgraceful; **возмуща́ть** (*pf.* возму|ти́ть, -щу́, -ти́шь) fill with indignation; stir up; trouble; **-ся** be indignant; **возмуще́ние** indignation.

вознаграждать (*pf.* вознагра|ди́ть, -жу́, -ди́шь) reward; **вознаграждение** reward; fee.

возненави́деть *see* ненави́деть.

вознесе́ние Ascension (Day).

возника́ть (*pf.* воз|ни́кнуть, *past* -ни́к) arise, crop up; **возникнове́ние** origin, rise, coming into existence.

возноси́ть*(*pf.*вознести́*)raise; exalt; **-ся** rise; become conceited.

возня́ fuss; noise.

возобновле́ние renewal, revival; **возобно|вля́ть** (*pf.* -ви́ть) renew; revive.

возомни́ть (*pf.*): **в. о себе́** have a high opinion of oneself.

возража́ть (*pf.* возра|зи́ть, -жу́, -зи́шь) (про́тив + *gen.*) object (to); **возраже́ние** objection.

во́зраст age; **на -е** no longer young; **в -е пяти́ лет** at the age of 5; **возраста́ние** growth, increase; **возраста́ть** (*pf.* возрасти́*) increase; **возрастно́й** age (*a.*).

возрожда́ть (*pf.* возроди́ть*) revive; **-ся** revive; **возрожде́ние** Renaissance; revival.

во́зчик carter, drayman.

возыме́ть (*pf.*) conceive (*a wish etc.*).

во́ин soldier, warrior; **во́инск|ий** military, martial; **-ая пови́нность** national service; **вои́нственный** martial, warlike.

вой howl, wail.

во́йлок thick felt; **во́йлочный** felt.

война́ (*pl.* во́йны) war.

во́йско (*pl.* -á) force, army.

войти́ *see* входи́ть.

вока́льный vocal.

вокза́л station; **вокза́льный** station (*a.*).

вокру́г (*gen.*) round; **верте́ться** *or* **ходи́ть в. да о́коло** beat about the bush.

вол (-á) ox, bullock.

вола́н flounce; shuttlecock.

волды́р|ь (-я́) blister.

волево́й volitional; strong-willed.

волейбо́л volley-ball.

во́лей-нево́лей willy-nilly.

во́лжский Volga (*a.*).

волк (*pl.* -и, -о́в) wolf; **волкода́в** wolfhound.

волна́ (*pl.* во́лн|ы, -ам & -а́м) wave; **волне́ние** agitation; roughness (*of water*); **волни́стый** wavy; **волнова́ть** (*pf.* вз-) agitate, trouble; excite; **-ся** (*pf* за-) be agitated, upset, excited; **волноло́м** breakwater; **волнообра́зный** undulating; **волну́ющий** disturbing; exciting.

во́лок portage.

волокита 1. red tape; 2. lady-killer.
волокнистый fibrous; вол|окно (pl.
-óкна, -óкон) fibre, filament.
вóлос (pl. -ы, -óс, -áм) hair; волосáтый hairy; волоснóй capillary (a.);
воло|сóк (-скá) hair; hair-spring;
filament;. быть на -сóк от (+ gen.)
be within a hair's breadth of.
вóлость (f.) volost (Russian rural
district).
волосянóй hair; horse-hair (a.).
волочить (-очý, -óчишь; pf. по-) drag;
-ся be dragged, trail; за (+inst.)
run after, court.
волхв (-á) medicine-man, wizard.
вóлчий wolf's, lupine; волчица she-
wolf.
вол|чóк (-чкá) spinning-top.
волч|óнок (-óнка ; pl. -áта, -áт) wolf-
cub.
волшéб|ник magician; wizard; ~ница
enchantress; волшéбный magic,
bewitching; волшебствó magic,
enchantment.
волынка 1. bagpipes; 2. delay.
вольгóтно (coll.) in freedom, free.
вóльная letter of enfranchisement;
вóльница freebooters.
вольноду́м|ец (-мца) free-thinker.
вольноопределя́ющийся volunteer.
вольнопрактику́ющий private practitioner;
вольнослу́шатель (m.) external student.
вóльность (f.) liberty; вóльный free,
unrestricted; вóльно stand easy!
вольт volt.
вóля will, freedom.
вон away; over there; пошёл вон! go
away! из рук вон плóхо wretched
(ly); вон онó что! so that's it!
вонзá|ть (pf. вон|зи́ть, -жý, -зи́шь,
ppp. -зённый) thrust, plunge.
вонь (f.) stench; воню́чий stinking;
воню́|чка (gen. pl. -чек) skunk;
воня́ть stink.
вообража́ть (pf. вообра|зи́ть, -жý,
-зи́шь) imagine; воображе́ние imagination; воображи́мый imaginable.
вообще́ in general.
воодуше|вле́ние inspiration ~вля́ть
(pf. -ви́ть) inspire.
вооружа́ть (pf. вооружи́ть) arm;
вооруже́ние armament; arms.
воóчию with one's own eyes.
во-пéрвых in the first place, firstly.
вопи́ть (pf.за-) howl,yell;вопию́щий

scandalous; -ая несправедли́вость
crying injustice.
воплоща́ть (pf. вопло|ти́ть, -щý,
-ти́шь) embody; воплоще́ние incar-
nation.
вопль (m.) wail, cry.
вопреки́ (dat.) in spite of.
вопрóс question; вопроси́тельный
interrogative; вопрóсник questionnaire.
вор (pl. -ы, -óв) thief.
ворвáться see врывáться.
воркова́ть (pf. за-) coo.
воркотня́ grumbling.
воро|бéй (-бья́) sparrow;воробьи́н|ый
sparrow's; -ая ночь short summer
night.
ворова́ть (pf. с-) steal, pilfer; ворóвка
thief; воровствó pilfering.
ворожи́ть (pf. по-) tell fortunes.
вóрон raven.
ворóна crow.
воронёный burnished.
ворóнка funnel; crater.
воронóй black.
вóрот collar; windlass.
вор|óта (-óт) gate(s).
вор|оти́ть (pf., -очý, -óтишь) turn;
сде́ланного не ворóтишь what's
done can't be undone.
воротни́к (-á) collar.
вóрох (pl. -и and -á) pile, heap.
ворочáть move; turn; в. делáми have
control of affairs; в. глазáми roll
one's eyes; -ся turn, toss.
вороши́ть (pf. раз-) stir, turn.
ворс pile (on carpet).
ворчáние grumbling; growling; вор|-
чáть (-чý, -чи́шь; pf. за-, про-)
(на + acc.) grumble, growl (at);
ворчли́вый grumpy, peevish.
восвоя́си (to) home.
восемнáдцатый eighteenth; восемнáдцать eighteen; вóсемь eight;
вóсемьдесят eighty; восемьсóт
eight hundred; вóсемью вóсемь
eight times eight.
воск wax.
восклицáние exclamation; восклицá-
тельный exclamatory; восклицáть
(pf. воскли́кнуть) exclaim.
восковóй wax(en).
воскреса́ть (pf. воскр|éснуть, past
-éс) rise again, revive; воскресéние
revival, resurrection; воскресéнье
Sunday.
воскрешáть (pf. воскре|си́ть, -шý,
-си́шь) revive, resuscitate.

воспаление inflammation; в. лёгких pneumonia; воспалённый inflamed; воспалительный inflammatory; воспалять (pf. -ить) inflame; -ся be(come) inflamed.

воспевать (-еваю; pf. воспеть) sing, glorify.

воспитание upbringing; воспитан|ник, ~ница pupil; воспитанный well-bred; воспитательный educative, educational; воспитывать (pf. воспитать) bring up, educate.

воспламен|ять (pf. -ить) set on fire; -ся catch fire; воспламеняемый combustible, inflammable.

восполнять (pf. восполнить) fill, supply, make good (deficiency).

воспоминание recollection.

воспрещать (pf. воспре|тить, -щу, -тишь) forbid; -ся be forbidden; курить воспрещается no smoking.

восприём|ник, ~ница godfather, -mother.

восприимчивый (к + dat.) susceptible (to); воспринимать (pf. воспр|инять, -иму, -имешь; ppp. -инятый) perceive, grasp; восприятие perception.

воспроизведение reproduction; воспроиз|водить* (pf. -вести*) reproduce.

воспрянуть cheer up; в. духом take heart.

восседать (pf. воссесть*) sit in solemn state.

воссоединение reunification; воссоедин|ять (pf. -ить) reunite.

воссоздавать* (pf. воссоздать*) recreate.

восст|авать (-аю, -аёшь, imper. -авай; pf. восстать*) rise up.

восстанавливать (pf. восстановить; -овлю, -овишь) restore, re-establish.

восстание insurrection.

восстановление restoration, reconstruction.

восток east, orient; востоковед orientalist.

восторг delight, enthusiasm; восторженный enthusiastic, rapturous.

восточный eastern, oriental.

востребован|ие: до -ия poste restante

востро: держать ухо в. be on the alert.

восхваление praising, eulogy; восхвалять praise.

восхитительный delightful, exquisite; восхищать (pf. восхи|тить, -щу, -тишь) enrapture; -ся (+ inst.) admire, be enraptured (by); восхищение admiration, delight.

восход rise, sunrise; восходить* (pf взойти*) go up, ascend; go back to; восхождение ascent; в. на Эверест the ascent of Everest.

восшествие (на престол) accession (to throne).

восьмеро eight.

восьми|гранник octahedron; ~десятый eightieth; ~ног octopus; ~сотый eight-hundredth; ~стишие octave; ~угольный octagonal.

восьм|ой eighth; -ая eighth; quaver; восьмушка octavo; eighth of a pound.

вот here (is); there (is); вот и всё and that's all.

вотировать (ipf. & pf.) vote on.

воткнуть see втыкать.

вотум vote; в. доверия vote of confidence.

вотчина patrimony.

воцар|яться (pf. -иться) ascend throne; set in.

вошь (gen. вши, inst. вошью) louse.

воюющий belligerent.

впадать (pf. впасть*) fall in(to); впадение confluence, mouth; впадина cavity, hollow; socket; впалый sunken.

впервые for the first time.

вперевалку: ходить в. waddle.

вперегонки: бегать в. race.

вперёд forward, ahead; часы идут в. the clock is fast; платить в. pay in advance; впереди (gen.) in front (of), before.

вперемежку alternately.

вперемешку pell-mell.

впер|ять (pf. -ить) fix; в. взор в него fix one's gaze on him.

впечатление impression; впечатлительный impressionable.

впивать (pf. впить, вопью* etc) absorb, imbibe.

впиваться (pf. впиться, вопьюсь* etc.) (в + acc.) stick (into), fasten (on to); fix one's eyes (on).

вписывать (pf. вписать*) insert, inscribe, enter.

впитывать (pf. впитать) absorb, imbibe.

впить see впивать.

впихивать (pf. впихнуть) push in.

вплавь: переправляться в. swim across.

вплетать (pf. вплести*) intertwine, plait.

вплотную close; in earnest; вплоть до (+ gen.) right up (to).

вплывать (pf. вплыть*) sail/swim in.

вполголоса in a low voice.

вползать (pf. вползти́) crawl in.

вполне quite, fully.

впопад to the point.

впопыхах in a hurry.

впору just right; сапоги́ мне в. the boots are just right for me; мне в. уéхать домой I might as well go home.

впоследствии subsequently.

впотьмах in the dark.

вправе: быть в. have the right.

вправля́ть (pf. вправить) set (bone etc.) ; reduce.

вправо to the right.

впредь henceforth.

вприкуску: пить чай в. drink tea through pieces of sugar.

вприпрыжку hopping, skipping.

вприся́дку: пляса́ть в. dance squatting.

впроголодь half-starving.

впрок in store; заготовля́ть в. lay in; всё идёт ему́ в. all is grist to his mill.

впросак: попасть в. put one's foot in it.

впросонках half-asleep.

впрочем however.

впры́гивать (pf. впры́гнуть) jump in(to).

впры́скивание injection; впры́скивать (pf. впры́снуть) inject.

впряга́ть (pf. впр|ячь, -ягу́, -яжёшь, -яг, -ягла́, ppp. -яжённый) harness.

впрямь really.

впуск admittance; впуска́ть (pf. вп|усти́ть, -ущу́, -у́стишь) let in, admit; впускной inlet, entrance (a.).

впусту́ю to no purpose.

впу́тывать (pf. впу́тать) (в + acc.) twist (in), implicate (in); -ся get mixed up in.

впух: в. и впрах utterly.

враг (-а́) enemy.

вражда́ enmity; враждебный hostile; враждова́ть be antagonistic; вра́жеский enemy (a.).

вразброд separately, in disunity.

вразва́лку: ходи́ть в. waddle.

вразрез: идти́ в. с (+ inst.) conflict with.

вразуми́тельный intelligible, persuasive; вразумля́ть (pf. -и́ть) make understand, convince.

враньё lies, nonsense.

врасплох unawares.

врассыпную in all directions.

враста́ть (pf. врасти́*) (в + acc.) grow in (to), take root in.

врастя́жку at full length.

врата́р|ь (-я́) goalkeeper.

врать (вру врёшь; pf. со-) tell lies; talk nonsense.

врач (-а́) doctor; враче́бный medical.

враща́ть turn, rotate; в. колесо́ turn a wheel; в. глаза́ми roll one's eyes; -ся turn, revolve; враще́ние rotation, revolution.

вред (-а́) harm; вреди́тель (m.) pest; wrecker; вре|ди́ть (-жу́, -ди́шь, pf. по-; ppp. -ждённый) (+dat.) injure; вре́дный harmful.

вреза́ть (pf. вре́зать*) cut in; -ся cut into; -ся в па́мять he inscribed on memory.

временно́й temporal; вре́менный temporary, provisional; временщи́к (-а́) favourite.

вре́мя (neut; gen., dat., prep. вре́мени, inst. вре́менем, pl. времена́ времён) time; в то в., как whilst; за после́днее в. recently; времена́ми at times; времяпрепровожде́ние pastime.

вро́вень (с + inst.) level, flush (with).

вро́де like; костю́м в. моего́ a suit like mine.

врождённый innate.

вро́зницу retail.

врозь, врознь separately, apart.

рукопа́шную hand to hand, at close quarters.

врун (-а́), вру́|нья (gen. pl. -ний) liar.

вруча́ть (pf. -и́ть) hand to, deliver, present; вруче́ние presentation; вручну́ю by hand.

врыва́ть (pf. врыть*) dig in(to).

врыва́ться (pf. ворва́ться) *burst in, rush in.

вряд: вряд ли hardly, it is doubtful whether.

вса́д|ник, ~ница (horse)rider.

вса́живать (pf. вс|ади́ть, -ажу́, -а́дишь) stick/thrust in.

всасывать (pf. всосать*) suck in, soak up.

все, всё see весь.

всеведение omniscience; всеведущий omniscient.

всевозможный all kinds of, every possible.

всевышний the Most High.

всегда always; всегдашний constant, usual.

всего in all.

вселение establishment, installation.

вселенная universe.

вселять (pf. -ить) lodge, install (in); -ся install oneself; become established.

всемерный of every kind.

всемирный world-wide.

всемогущество omnipotence; всемогущий omnipotent.

всенародный national, general.

всенощная vespers;

всеобщий general, universal.

всеобъемлющий all-embracing.

всеоружие full possession (e. g. of knowledge, faculties).

всероссийский all-Russian.

всерьёз seriously.

всесилие omnipotence; всесильный omnipotent;

всесоюзный all-Union.

всесторонний all-round, comprehensive.

всё-таки nevertheless.

всеуслышание: во в. for all to hear.

всецело entirely.

всеядный omnivorous.

вскакивать (pf. вскочить* -очу, -очишь) jump up.

вскармливать (pf. вскормить*) rear, nurse.

вскачь at full gallop.

вскидывать (pf. вскинуть) throw up; shoulder.

вскладчину by clubbing together, pooling.

всколых|ивать (pf. -нуть) rock; stir; -ся stir, become agitated.

вскользь casually, in passing.

вскоре soon (after).

вскормить see вскармливать.

вскочить see вскакивать.

вскрикивать (pf. вскрикнуть) scream, shriek.

вскричать* (pf.) shout, exclaim, cry.

вскруж|ить (pf.): это -ило ему голову it turned his head.

вскрывать (pf. вскрыть*) open; reveal; dissect; do postmortem on; -ся come to light; burst (open); вскрытие opening, revelation; post mortem.

всласть to one's heart's content.

вслед (за + inst.) after, following; вследствие (gen.) in consequence of.

вслепую blindly.

вслух aloud.

вслушиваться (pf. вслушаться) (в + acc.) listen attentively (to).

всматриваться (pf. всмотреться*) (в + acc.) look closely (at).

всмятку: яйцо в. soft-boiled egg.

всовывать (pf. всунуть) stick/thrust in.

всосать see всасывать.

вспархивать (pf. вспорхнуть) fly up.

вспахивать (pf. вспахать*) plough, till; вспашка ploughing.

вспенивать (pf. вспенить) froth up, whip up.

всплеск splash; всплёскивать (pf. всплеснуть) splash; в. руками throw up one's hands (in dismay etc.).

всплывать (pf. всплыть*) come to surface; come to light.

всполошить (pf.) startle, alarm.

вспоминать (pf. вспомнить) remember; -ся ему вспоминается he remembers.

вспомогательный auxiliary.

вспомоществование assistance.

вспрыгивать (pf. вспрыгнуть) jump up.

вспрыскивать (pf. вспрыснуть) sprinkle.

вспугивать (pf. вспугнуть) scare off/up.

вспухать (pf. вспухнуть*) swell.

вспучивать (pf. вспучить) (v. t.) swell up, out.

вспылить (pf.) flare up; вспыльчивый quick-tempered.

вспыхивать (pf. вспыхнуть) flare up; вспышка (gen. pl. -шек) flash; outbreak.

вспять back(wards).

вст|авать (-аю, -аёшь, imper. -авай; ger. вставая; pf. встать, встан|у, -ешь) get up; stand up.

вставка insertion; inset; mounting; вставлять (pf. вставить) put, fix in; insert.

вставно́й double *(windows)*; false *(teeth)*.

встарь in olden times.

встрево́женный alarmed.

встрепену́ться *(pf.)* rouse oneself; start.

встрёпка scolding.

встре́ча meeting; **встреча́ть** *(pf.* встре́|тить, -чу, -тишь) meet; -ся be met (with); meet each other; **встре́чный** head (wind); on-coming; пе́рвый в. the first person you meet.

встря́ска shaking up.

встря́хивать *(pf.* встряхну́ть) shake up; -ся shake oneself, rouse oneself.

вступа́ть *(pf.* вступи́ть) (в + *acc.)* enter; join; -ся (за + *acc.)* intercede (on behalf of); **вступи́тельный** entrance *(a.)*, introductory; **вступле́ние** entry, introduction.

всу́е in vain.

всу́нуть *see* всо́вывать.

всухомя́тку: пита́ться в. live on cold food.

всу́чивать *(pf.* всучи́ть) foist, palm off; в. э́то ему́ foist it off on him.

всхли́пывать *(pf.* всхли́пнуть) sob.

всходи́ть* *(pf.* взойти́*, взойду́, взошёл) go/come up, ascend; в. на ле́стницу go up the stairs.

всхо́д|ы (-ов) (corn) shoots.

всхра́пывать *(pf.* всхрапну́ть) snore; *(pf.)* take a nap.

всыпа́ть *(pf.* всы́пать*) pour (in); thrash.

всю́ду everywhere.

вся́кий any; **вся́ческий** all kinds of; **вся́чески** in every way; **вся́кая вся́чина** all sorts of stuff.

вта́йне in secret.

вта́лкивать *(pf.* втолкну́ть) push in.

вта́птывать *(pf.* втопта́ть*) trample down.

вта́скивать *(pf.* втащи́ть*) drag in.

вта́чивать *(pf.* втача́ть) sew in.

втека́ть *(pf.* втечь*) flow in.

втира́ть *(pf.* втере́ть*) rub in; -ся insinuate oneself; -ся ему́ в дове́рие worm oneself into his confidence.

вти́скивать *(pf.* вти́снуть) squeeze/ cram in.

втихомо́лку on the quiet.

втолкну́ть *see* вта́лкивать.

втопта́ть *see* вта́птывать.

втора́ second *(mus.)*.

вторга́ться *(pf.* втор|гну́ться, *past*

-гся, -глась) (в + *acc.)* invade; break in(to); meddle in; **вторже́ние** invasion, intrusion.

вто́рить (+ *dat.)* echo, repeat; take second part *(mus.)*; **вторичный** second, secondary; **вто́рник** Tuesday; **второго́дник,** ~ница pupil who has to remain in same class for one more year; **второ́й** second; **второку́рсник,** ~ница second-year student.

второпя́х in haste.

второ|разря́дный second-rate; ~**степе́нный** secondary, minor.

втра́вливать *(pf.* втрави́ть*) drag/ involve in.

в-тре́тьих thirdly.

втри́дорога at an exorbitant rate; **втро́е** three times; **втро́ем** three together; **втройне́** three times as much.

втул́ка plug.

втуне́ in vain.

втупи́к *see* тупи́к.

втыка́ть *(pf.* воткну́ть) stick in, drive in.

втя́гивать *(pf.* втяну́ть) draw in; -ся (в + *acc.)* get used (to), become absorbed (in); **втяжно́й** suction *(a.)*.

вуа́ль *(f.)* veil.

вуз (вы́сшее уче́бное заведе́ние) higher educational institution.

вулка́н volcano.

вульга́рный vulgar.

вход entrance; **входи́ть*** *(pf.* войти́*) go in, enter; в. в дове́рие (к + *dat.)* win someone's confidence; в. в погово́рку become proverbial; **входно́й** entrance *(a.)*; **вхожде́ние** entry; вхо́ж|ий: быть -им к (+ *dat.)* be received at.

вхолосту́ю free, idling.

вцепля́ться *(pf.* вцепи́ться, -еплю́сь, -е́пишься) (в + *acc.)* take hold (of), cling to).

вчера́ yesterday; **вчера́шний** yesterday's.

вчерне́ in rough.

вче́тверо four times.

вчи́тываться *(pf.* вчита́ться) (в + *acc.)* read carefully.

вшива́ть *(pf.* вшить, вошью*) sew in.

вши́вый lousy.

вширь in breadth; widely.

вшить *see* вшива́ть.

въеда́ться *(pf.* въе́сться*) (в + *acc.)* eat into.

въезд entrance; въезжа́ть (pf. въе́хать*) drive in.

въе́сться see въеда́ться.

въявь in waking hours, in reality.

вы you.

выба́лтывать (pf. вы́болтать) blurt, let out.

выбега́ть (pf. вы́бежать*) run out.

выбива́ть (pf. вы́бить*) knock out; dislodge; -ся get out, come out, be knocked out, dislodged; -ся из сил become exhausted.

выбира́ть (pf. вы́брать*) choose; take out; -ся be chosen etc; get out.

вы́бить see выбива́ть.

вы́боина dent; pothole (in road); вы́бор ·choice; selection; option; всеобщие -ы general election; вы́борный elective; electoral; вы́борочный selective; вы́борщик elector.

выбра́сывать (pf. вы́бросить*) throw out; throw up; -ся throw oneself out; be thrown out.

выбрива́ть (pf. вы́брить*) shave.

выбыва́ть (pf. вы́быть*) leave, quit; выбы́тие departure, removal.

выва́ливать (pf. вы́валить) throw out; -ся tumble out.

выва́ривать (pf. вы́варить) boil; extract by boiling.

выве́дывать (pf. вы́ведать) find out.

вы́везти see вывози́ть.

вы́верить see выверя́ть.

вывёртывать (pf. вы́вернуть) unscrew; wrench.

выверя́ть (pf. вы́верить) adjust, regulate.

вы́весить see выве́шивать.

вы́веска 1. sign; 2. weighing.

вы́вести see выводи́ть.

выве́тривать (pf. вы́ветрить) drive out; air, ventilate; -ся be aired away, vanish; be weathered.

выве́шивать (pf. вы́весить*) hang out; weigh.

выви́нчивать (pf. вы́вин|тить, -нчу, -нтишь) unscrew.

вы́вих dislocation; выви́хивать (pf. вы́вихнуть) dislocate.

вы́вод withdrawal; conclusion; выводи́ть* (pf. вы́вести*) take out; remove; destroy; raise; hatch, grow; conclude, infer; draw; в. из себя́ drive (someone) out of his mind; -ся become extinct, go out of use; be hatched out; вы́во|док (-дка) brood, litter.

вы́воз removal; export; вывози́ть* (pf. вы́везти*) take out; export; вывозно́й export (a.).

выволакивать (pf. вы́волочить) drag out.

вывора́чивать (pf. вы́вернуть) untwist, unscrew.

выга́дывать (pf. вы́гадать) gain, save.

вы́гиб curve; выгиба́ть (pf. вы́гнуть) curve, bend.

вы́глядеть* 1. (ipf.) look, appear; в. пло́хо/но́вым look bad/new; 2. (pf.) spy out, discover.

выгля́дывать (pf. вы́глянуть) look out, peep out.

вы́гнать see выгоня́ть.

вы́гнутый convex; вы́гнуть see выгиба́ть.

выгова́ривать (pf. вы́говорить) pronounce; rebuke; вы́говор pronunciation; reproof.

вы́года advantage, gain; вы́годный advantageous.

вы́гон pasture; вы́гонка distillation; выгоня́ть (pf. вы́гнать*) drive out; distil.

выгора́живать (pf. вы́горо|дить, -жу, -дишь) fence off; (coll.) shield, protect.

выгора́ть (pf. вы́гореть*) burn down; fade.

выгреба́ть (pf. вы́грести*) 1. rake out; 2. row; выгребна́я я́ма cesspool.

выгружа́ть (pf. вы́грузить*) unload; disembark; вы́грузка unloading, disembarkation.

выдава́ть* (pf. вы́дать*) hand out, distribute; в. себя́ за (+ acc.) pass oneself off as; -ся protrude; be conspicuous, distinguished; occur.

выда́вливать (pf. вы́давить) squeeze out; push out.

выда́лбливать (pf. вы́долбить) hollow out; (coll.) learn by heart.

вы́дать see выдава́ть.

вы́дача delivery; issue; payment; выдаю́щийся prominent.

выдвига́ть (pf. вы́двинуть) move out, pull out; put forward; -ся move (in and out); come to the fore; выдвиже́|нец (-нца) promoted worker; выдвижно́й sliding, telescopic.

выдворя́ть (pf. вы́дворить) evict, turn out.

выделе́ние detaching, isolation; secretion; apportionment.

вы́делка manufacture; make; **вы-де́лывать** (*pf.* вы́делать) make.

выделя́ть (*pf.* вы́делить) pick out; detach; apportion; isolate; secrete. **-ся** be distinguished, stand out; exude.

выде́ргивать (*pf.* вы́дернуть) pull out.

вы́держанный self-possessed; steadfast; consistent; ripe, matured, seasoned.

выде́рживать (*pf.* вы́держать*) sustain, endure; pass (*exam.*).

вы́держка (*gen. pl.* -жек) self-control, tenacity; exposure (*photo*); excerpt.

вы́дернуть *see* выде́ргивать.

выдира́ть (*pf.* вы́драть*) tear out.

выдолбить *see* выда́лбливать.

вы́дохнуть *see* выдыха́ть.

вы́дра otter.

выдува́ть (*pf.* вы́дуть*) blow out.

вы́думка device; invention; **выду́-мывать** (*pf.* вы́думать) think up; invent.

выдыха́ть (*pf.* вы́дохнуть*) breathe out; **-ся** lose its smell; be played out, used up.

выеда́ть (*pf.* вы́есть*) eat, corrode.

вы́езд departure; exit; **выезжа́ть** 1. вы́ехать*) leave, drive out; 2. (*pf.* вы́ездить*) break in (*horse*).

вы́емка taking out; excavation; hollow, collection (*mail*).

вы́ехать *see* выезжа́ть.

вы́жать *see* выжима́ть.

вы́ждать *see* выжида́ть.

выжива́ть (*pf.* вы́жить*) survive; force out; в. из ума́ drive mad.

выжига́ть (*pf.* вы́жечь*) burn out; cauterize.

выжида́ть (*pf.* вы́ждать*) wait (for); bide one's time.

выжима́ть (*pf.* вы́жать*) press out, squeeze out.

вы́жить *see* выжива́ть.

вы́звать *see* вызыва́ть.

выздора́вливать (*pf.* вы́здороветь) recover, convalesce; **выздоровле́-ние** recovery.

вы́зов call; challenge.

вызрева́ть (-а́ет; *pf.* вы́зреть) ripen.

вызубривать (*pf.* вы́зубрить) learn by heart.

вызыва́ть (*pf.* вы́звать*) call for;

call forth, arouse; **-ся** volunteer. offer; **вызыва́ющий** provocative.

выи́грывать (*pf.* вы́играть) win; **вы́игрыш** win, prize, gain; **вы́-игрышный** lottery (*a.*), winning (*a.*); advantageous.

выи́скивать (*pf.* вы́и|скать, -щу, -щешь) seek; (*pf.*) find.

вы́йти *see* выходи́ть.

выка́зывать (*pf.* вы́к|азать, -ажу, -ажешь) display.

выка́лывать (*pf.* вы́колоть*) prick out.

выка́пывать (*pf.* вы́копать) dig out

выка́рмливать (*pf.* вы́кормить) bring up, rear.

вы́кат: глаза́ на -е bulging eyes.

выка́тывать 1. (*pf.* вы́катать) mangle.

выка́тывать 2. (*pf.* вы́катить) roll out.

выка́чивать (*pf.* вы́качать) pump out; extort.

выки́дывать (*pf.* вы́кинуть) throw out; have a miscarriage; **вы́кидыш** miscarriage, abortion.

выкипа́ть (*pf.* вы́кипеть*) (*v. i.*) boil down/away.

вы́кладка spreading-out; calculation; (*soldier's*) kit; **выкла́дывать** (*pf.* вы́ложить) lay out.

выклёвывать (*pf.* вы́клевать) peck out.

выклика́ть (*pf.* вы́кликнуть) call out.

выключа́тель (*m.*) switch; **выключа́ть** (*pf.* вы́ключить) switch off.

выкля́нчивать (*pf.* вы́клянчить) to get by pestering.

выко́вывать (*pf.* вы́ковать*) forge, fashion.

выко́выривать (*pf.* вы́ковыр|ять, -нуть) pick out.

выкола́чивать (*pf.* вы́колотить*) knock, beat out.

вы́колоть *see* выка́лывать.

вы́копать *see* выка́пывать.

вы́кормить *see* выка́рмливать.

выкорчёвывать (*pf.* вы́корчевать) root out, extirpate.

выкра́дывать (*pf.* вы́красть*) steal.

выкра́ивать (*pf.* вы́кроить) cut out; make

выкра́шивать (*pf.* вы́красить*) paint.

вы́крик yell; **выкри́кивать** (*pf.* вы́-крикнуть) scream out.

вы́кроить *see* выкра́ивать; **вы́кр|ойка** (*gen. pl.* -оек) pattern.

выкрутас|ы (-ов) flourishes; vagaries.
выкручивать (pf. выкрутить*) unscrew; -ся come unscrewed; extricate oneself.
выкуп redemption, ransom;выкупать
(pf. выкупить) redeem; ransom;
see also купать.
выкуривать (pf. выкурить) smoke;
smoke out; (coll.) distil.
вылазка sally, sortie; ski trek.
вылезать (pf. вылезть*) climb out,
come out.
вылет flight, take-off; вылетать (pf.
вылететь*) fly out.
вылечивать (pf. вылечить) cure.
выливать (pf. вылить*) pour out,
empty; cast; он вылитый отец he
is the image of his father.
выложить see выкладывать.
вылощенный glossy, foppish.
вылупливаться (pf. вылупиться)
hatch out.
вымазывать (pf. вымазать*) smear.
выманивать (pf. выманить) entice,
lure.
вымарывать (pf. вымарать) make
dirty; cross out.
вымачивать (pf. вымочить) soak,
steep.
выменивать (pf. выменять) exchange; в. старое на новое exchange the old for the new.
вымереть see вымирать.
вымеривать (pf. вымерить) measure
out.
вымерший extinct.
вымерять = вымеривать.
выметать (pf. вымести*) sweep out.
вымещать (pf. выме|стить, -щу,
-стишь) vent (anger etc.)
вымирать (pf. вы|мереть, -мрет;
past -мер) die out, become extinct.
вымогательство extortion, blackmail; вымогать extort.
вымокать (pf. вымокнуть*) soak.
вымолвить (pf.) say, utter.
вымочить see вымачивать.
вымпел pennant.
вымывать (pf. вымыть*) wash out,
away.
вымы|сел (-сла) invention; fabrica-
tion; fancy; вымышлять (pf. вы-
мыслить) invent.
вымя (neut.; gen., dat., prep., вымени
no pl.) udder.
вынашивать (pf. выносить*) bear
(child); mature, nurture.
вынести see выносить.

вынимать (pf. вынуть) take out,
extract.
вынос: продавать на в. sell for
consumption off the premises.
выносить* 1. (pf. вынести*) carry
out; endure; give (decision).
выносить 2. (pf.) see вынашивать.
выноска removal; footnote; выносливый hardy, durable.
вынуждать (pf. вынудить, -жу,
-дишь) force, compel; вынужденный forced.
вынуть see вынимать.
вынырнуть (pf.) come to surface;
emerge.
вынюхивать (pf. вынюхать) smell,
sniff out.
выпад lunge, thrust; attack; выпа-
дать (pf. выпасть*) fall out;
occur; в. на долю ему fall to his
lot.
выпаливать (pf. выпалить) fire off;
blurt out.
выпалывать (pf. выполоть*) weed
(out).
выпаривать (pf. выпарить) evaporate; steam.
выпекать (pf. выпечь*) bake.
выпивать (pf. выпить*) drink (off);
выпивший drunk.
выпиливать (pf. выпилить) saw
out.
выпирать (pf. вы|переть, -пру,
-прешь, past -пер, ppp. -пертый)
stick out.
выписка writing out; extract; order,
subscription; выписывать (pf. выписать*) write out; extract; order,
send for, subscribe to.
выпихивать (pf. выпихнуть) push
out.
выплавка smelting; выплавлять (pf.
выплавить) smelt.
выплата payment; выплачивать (pf.
выплатить*) pay off, liquidate
(debt.)
выплёвывать (pf. выплюнуть) spit
out.
выплёскивать (pf. выплеснуть)
splash out.
выплетать (pf. выплести*) weave.
выплывать (pf. выплыть*) swim/sail
out.
выплюнуть see выплёвывать.
выполаскивать (pf. выполоскать*)
rinse out.
выползать (pf. выползти*) crawl
out.

выполнéние implementation, execution, performance; **выполня́ть** (pf. вы́полнить) carry out, fulfil.

вы́полоть see **выпа́лывать.**

вы́правка straightening, correction; carriage, bearing; **выправля́ть** (pf. вы́править) straighten, correct; obtain.

выпра́шивать (pf. вы́просить*) obtain, solicit, beg for.

выпрова́живать (pf. вы́проводить*) send packing.

выпры́гивать (pf. вы́прыгнуть) jump out.

выпряга́ть (pf. вы́прячь*) unharness.

выпрямля́ть (pf вы́прямить) straighten, rectify; **-ся** become straight; stand erect.

вы́пуклый protuberant; convex.

вы́пуск issue, output; discharge; graduates; **выпуска́ть** (pf. вы́пустить*) let out; turn out; publish; **выпускн|óй**: **-áя трубá** exhaust pipe; **-ые экзáмены** final exams.

выпу́тывать (pf. вы́путать) unravel; **-ся** extricate oneself.

выпу́чивать (pf. вы́пучить): глазá в. stare.

выпы́тывать (pf. вы́пытать) elicit, extort.

вы́пялить (pf.): глазá в. stare.

выпя́чивать (pf. выпя|тить, -чу, -тишь) (coll.) stick out.

выраба́тывать (pf. вы́работать) make, produce; work out; **вы́работка** make, production; working-out.

выра́внивать (pf. вы́ровнять) make even, level.

выража́ть (pf. вы́ра|зить, -жу, -зишь) express; **выраже́ние** expression; **вырази́тельный** expressive.

выраста́ть (pf. вы́расти*) grow (up); **выра́щивать** (pf. вы́растить*) grow; bring up; cultivate.

вы́рвать see **вырыва́ть**, 1.

вы́рез cut; low neck; **выреза́ть** (pf. вы́резать*) cut out; engrave; **вы́резка** cutting out; engraving; sirloin; **вырéзывать = выреза́ть.**

вы́ровнять see **выра́внивать.**

вы́ро|док (-дка) degenerate, black sheep; **вырожда́ться** (pf. вы́родиться*) degenerate; **вырожде́ние** degeneration.

вы́ронить (pf.) drop.

выруба́ть (pf. вы́рубить) hew down, cut out.

выру́ливать (pf. вы́рулить) taxi (avia.).

выруча́ть (pf. вы́ручить) rescue, help out; gain, net; **вы́ручка** help; rescue; gain, receipts, earnings.

вырыва́ть 1. (pf. вы́рвать*) pull/tear out; extort; **-ся** escape, break away.

вырыва́ть 2. (pf. вы́рыть*) dig up.

вы́садка disembarkation, landing; transplanting; **выса́живать** (pf. вы́са|дить, -жу, -дишь) put ashore; put off; **-ся** alight; go ashore.

выса́сывать (pf. вы́сосать*) suck out; в. из па́льца invent.

высве́рливать (pf. вы́сверлить) drill, bore.

высвобожда́ть (pf. вы́свобо|дить, -жу, -дишь, ppp. -жденный) free.

высека́ть (pf. вы́сечь*) carve, cut; (see also сечь).

выселе́ние eviction, expulsion; **выселя́ть** (pf. вы́селить) evict, expel.

выси́живать (pf. вы́сидеть*) hatch; sit through;

выси́ться rise, tower.

выска́бливать (pf. вы́скоблить) scrape; erase.

выска́зывать (pf. вы́сказать*) state, say; он speak out.

выска́кивать (pf. вы́скочить) jump out, leap out.

выска́льзывать (pf. вы́скользнуть) slip out.

вы́скоблить see **выска́бливать.**

вы́скочить see **выска́кивать**; **вы́ско|чка** (gen. pl. -чек) upstart.

выскреба́ть (pf. вы́скрести*) scrape, scratch out.

вы́слать see **высыла́ть.**

высле́живать (pf. вы́следить*) track, shadow.

вы́слуга long service **выслу́живать** (pf. вы́служить) serve; qualify for (pension); **-ся** (перед + inst.) curry favour (with).

выслу́шивать (pf. вы́слушать) listen, hear out; sound (-..i.).

высма́тривать (pf. вы́смотреть*) look out for; spy out.

высме́ивать (pf. вы́см|еять, -ею, -еешь) ridicule.

вы́сморкать (pf.): в. нос blow one's nose.

высо́вывать (pf. вы́сунуть) put out, push out; **-ся** thrust oneself out.

высо́кий *(comp.* вы́ше) high, tall, lofty, elevated.

высоко|во́льтный high-voltage; **~ка́чественный** high-quality; **~квалифици́рованный** highly skilled; **~ме́рие** arrogance; **~ме́рный** arrogant, supercilious; **~па́рный** high-flown, bombastic; **~часто́тный** high-frequency.

вы́сосать *see* **выса́сывать**.

высота́ *(pl.* высо́ты) height; **высо́тный** high-altitude; many-storeyed; **высотоме́р** altimeter.

вы́сохнуть *see* **высыха́ть**; **вы́сохший** dried up, wizened.

высоча́йший highest; imperial; **высо́чество** Highness.

вы́спаться *see* **высыпа́ться**.

вы́спренний high-flown, bombastic.

вы́ставка exhibition; **выставля́ть** *(pf.* вы́ставить) put forward; exhibit; represent; take -ся exhibit; show off.

выста́ивать *(pf.* вы́стоять) remain standing; hold out.

выстра́ивать *(pf.* вы́строить) draw up, parade; -ся line up.

вы́стрел shot, report; **вы́стрелить** *see* **стреля́ть**.

выступа́ть *(pf.* вы́ступить) cool.

высту́кивать *(pf.* вы́стукать) tap, tap out.

вы́ступ prominence, protuberance; **выступа́ть** *(pf.* вы́ступить) come forward, come out; perform; в. с ре́чью give a speech; **выступле́ние** performance; statement; appearance; departure.

вы́сунуть *see* **высо́вывать**.

вы́сушивать *(pf.* вы́сушить) dry out.

высчи́тывать *(pf.* вы́считать) calculate.

вы́сший higher, superior; highest.

высыла́ть *(pf.* вы́слать)* send (out); banish; **высы́лка** dispatch; banishment.

высыпа́ть *(pf.* вы́сыпать*) pour out; break out *(in a rash)* ; -ся spill out.

высыпа́ться *(pf.* вы́спаться*) have a good sleep.

высыха́ть *(pf.* вы́сохнуть*) dry up; wither away.

высь *(f.)* height.

выта́лкивать *(pf.* вы́толкать, вы́толкнуть) push out.

выта́пливать *(pf.* вы́топить) melt down; heat.

выта́скивать *(pf.* вы́тащить) take out, pull out.

выта́чивать *(pf.* вы́точить) turn; sharpen.

вытве́рживать *(pf.* вы́твердить*) learn by heart.

вытека́ть *(pf.* вы́течь*) flow out; flow from, result.

вы́тереть *see* **вытира́ть**.

вытесня́ть *(pf.* вы́теснить) force out, eject, displace.

выте́сывать *(pf.* вы́тесать*) hew out.

вы́течь *see* **вытека́ть**.

вытира́ть *(pf.* вы́тереть*) wipe, dry; -ся wipe/dry oneself ;become threadbare.

вытра́|вливать *or* -вля́ть *(pf.* вы́травить) remove *(stain on clothes)*.

вытрезвля́ть *(pf.* вы́трезвить) (make) sober.

вытряса́ть *(pf.* вы́трясти*) shake out; **вытря́хивать** *(pf.* вы́тряхнуть) shake out.

выть (во́ю, во́ешь; *pf.* вз-) howl, wail.

вытя́гивать *(pf.* вы́тянуть) draw out; stretch; endure; -ся stretch (oneself); stand erect; **вытя́|жка** *gen. pl.* -жек) drawing out; escape; extract *(chem.)*.

выу́живать *(pf.* вы́удить*) get, catch, fish out.

выу́чивать *(pf.* вы́учить) learn, teach; в. его́ ру́сскому языку́ teach him Russian; -ся learn.

выха́живать *(pf.* вы́ходить*) nurse; bring up; в. больно́го nurse a patient.

выхва́тывать *(pf.* вы́хватить*) snatch out.

вы́хлоп exhaust.

выхлопа́тывать *(pf.* вы́хлопотать*) obtain, get *(after some trouble)*.

выхлопно́й exhaust *(a.)*.

вы́ход going/coming out; exit; yield; publication; **вы́ход|ец** (-дца) migrant (from), native (of); **выходи́ть*** *(pf.* вы́йти*) go/come out; run out *(of time)* ; look, open (on to); **выходи́ть** *see* **выха́живать**; **вы́ходка** trick; prank; **выходн|о́й** outer *(door)*; free *(day)*; он -о́й it's his day off; -о́е посо́бие redundancy/discharge pay.

вы́холенный well cared-for.

вы́хухоль *(m.)* musquash.

выцара́пывать *(pf.* вы́царапать) scratch out.

выцвета́ть *(pf.* вы́цвести*)* fade.
выце́живать *(pf.* вы́цедить*)* filter.
вычека́нивать *(pf.* вы́чеканить*)* coin.
вычёркивать *(pf.* вы́черкнуть*)* cross out.
вычёрпывать *(pf.* вы́черп|ать, -нуть*)* exhaust; scoop out.
вычёрчивать *(pf.* вы́чертить*)* sketch out.
вы́честь *see* **вычита́ть; вы́чет** deduction.
вычисле́ние calculation; **вычисли́тельная маши́на** computer; **вычисля́ть** *(pf.* вы́числить*)* calculate, compute.
вы́чистить *see* **вычища́ть.**
вычита́ние subtraction; **вычита́ть** *(pf.* вы́|честь, -чту, -чтешь; *past.* -чел, -чла; *ppp.* -чтенный*)* subtract.
вычища́ть *(pf.* вы́чистить*)* clean.
вы́чурный fanciful; affected.
вышвы́ривать *(pf.* вы́швырнуть*)* fling out.
вы́ше higher, beyond; **вышеупомя́нутый** aforementioned.
вышиба́ла *(m.)* chucker-out, bouncer;
вышиба́ть *(pf.* вы́|шибить, -шибу, -шибешь, *past* -шиб; *ppp.* -шибленный*)* kick/knock/push out.
вышива́ние embroidery; needlework;
вышива́ть *(pf.* вы́шить*)* embroider.
вы́шивка embroidery.
вышина́ height.
вы́|шка *(gen. pl.* -шек*)* tower.
вышу́чивать *(pf.* вы́шутить*)* ridicule.
выщи́пывать *(pf.* вы́щип|ать*, -нуть*)* pluck out.
выявля́ть *(pf.* вы́явить*)* expose, reveal.
выясне́ние elucidation; **выясня́ть** *(pf.* вы́яснить*)* elucidate, ascertain; **-ся** turn out, prove.
вьетна́|мец (-мца), **~мка** Vietnamese; **вьетна́мский** Vietnamese *(a.).*
вью́га snowstorm, blizzard.
вьюк pack, load.
вью|но́к (-нка́) bindweed, convolvulus.
вью́чн|ый -ое живо́тное pack animal.
вью́щийся curly *(hair);* climbing *(plant).*
вя́жущий astringent; -ee сре́дство astringent.
вяз elm.
вяза́ние knitting, crocheting; tying.

вяза́нка bundle.
вя́заный knitted, crocheted.
вяза́ть (вяжу́, вя́жешь; *pf.* с-) bind; knit, crochet; be astringent; **-ся** tally, accord; **вя́зка** tying.
вя́зкий viscous; oozy; swampy; tenacious; **вя́знуть** *(past* вяз, -ла; *pf.* за-, у-) stick, get stuck.
вязь *(f.)* ligature.
вя́леный dried.
вя́лый flabby, flaccid; languid, limp, inert; slack.
вя́нуть *(past* вял *ppa* вя́дший; *pf.* за-, у-) fade, droop.

Г

г. Mr.; year.
га́вань *(f.)* harbour.
га́га eider; **гага́чий пух** eiderdown.
гад reptile.
гада́лка fortune-teller; **гада́ние** fortune-telling; guess-work; **гада́тельный** problematic; doubtful; **гада́ть** *(pf.* по-) tell fortunes; guess.
га́дина loathsome creature.
га́|дить (-жу, -дишь; *pf.* на-) foul, dirty; make mischief; **га́дкий** *(comp.* га́же) foul, nasty; bad; **га́дость** *(f.)* muck; foul deed.
гадю́ка adder, viper.
га́ер buffoon.
га́ечный ключ spanner.
газ 1. gauze; 2. gas.
газе́та newspaper; **газе́тный** newspaper *(a.);* **газе́тчик** newspaper boy; journalist.
газиро́ванный aerated.
газовщи́к (-а́) gas-man, gas fitter; **га́зовый** 1. gauze *(a.);* 2. gas *(a.);* **г. заво́д** gasworks; **газоме́р** gas-meter;
газо́н lawn.
газо|прово́д gas-main; **~храни́лище** gas-holder, gasometer.
га́йка *(gen. pl.* га́ек*)* screw-nut.
галантере́йный fancy-goods *(a.);* haberdasher's; urbane; **галантере́я** haberdashery.
гала́нтный gallant.
гал|де́ть (-ди́шь) make a din.
галере́я gallery; **галёрка** gallery, the gods *(theat.).*
галифе́ *(pl.; indecl.)* riding breeches.
га́лка jackdaw.
галлюцина́ция hallucination.

галóп gallop; -ом at a gallop.
гáло|чка *(gen. pl.* -чек) tick, mark.
галóша galosh.
гáлстук tie, necktie.
галýн (-á) gold lace.
галý|шка *(gen. pl.* -шек) dumpling.
гальван|изи́ровать galvanize; ~и́ческий galvanic.
гáлька pebbles, shingle.
гам din, hubbub.
гамáк (-á) hammock.
гамáша gaiter
гáмма 1. scale; gamut; 2. gamma.
гангрéна gangrene; гангренóзный gangrenous.
гантéль *(f)* dumb-bell.
гарáж (-á) garage.
гаранти́ровать *(ipf. & pf.)* guarantee; гарáнтия guarantee.
гардерóб cloakroom; wardrobe; clothes; гардерóб|щик, ~щица cloakroom attendant.
гарди́на curtain.
гармонизи́ровать *(ipf. & pf.)* harmonize *(mus.).*
гармóника accordion, concertina; pleats; губнáя г. mouth-organ; гармони́ровать harmonize, be in keeping; гармони́ст accordion/concertina player;. гармони́ческий harmonious *(mus.);* гармони́чный harmonious, in agreement; гармóния harmony; agreement. гармóшка *(gen. pl.* -шек) accordion, concertina.
гарнизóн garrison.
гарни́р garnish, vegetables.
гарниту́р set, suite; спáльный г. bedroom suite.
гарпýн (-á) harpoon.
гарь *(f.)* burning; cinders; пáхнет гáрью there's a smell of burning.
гаси́ть (гашý, гáсишь; *pf.* за-, по-) extinguish.
гáснуть *(past* гас; *pf.* по-, у-) go out, die out.
гастролёр, ~ша actor/actress on tour; гастроли́ровать be on tour; гастрóль *(f.)* tour.
гастронóм epicure; grocery and provision shop; гастронóмия gastronomy; groceries and provisions.
гауптвáхта guard-room.
гашéтка trigger.
гаши́ш hashish.
гвалт din, row.

гвард|éец (-éйца) guardsman; гвáрдия guard.
гвóздик tack, stud.
гвозди́ка pink, carnation; clove.
гвозд|ь (-я́, *pl.* гвóзди, -éй) nail, tack; г. сезóна hit of the season.
где where; где-либо anywhere; где-нибудь anywhere, somewhere; гдé-то somewhere.
гегемóния hegemony.
гéйзер geyser.
гектáр hectare *(=* 10 000 *sq. metres).*
гéлий helium.
гéмма gem, cameo.
гемоглоби́н haemoglobin.
ген gene.
генеалóгия genealogy.
гéнезис genesis, origin.
генерáл general; г.-майóр major-general; генерáльн|ый general; -ая репети́ция dress rehearsal.
генерáтор generator.
генéтика genetics.
гениáльный brilliant, of genius; гéний genius.
геóграф geographer; географи́ческий geographical; геогрáфия geography; геóлог geologist; геологи́ческий geological; геолóгия geology.
геометри́ческий geometrical; геомéтрия geometry.
георгúн dahlia.
геофи́зика geophysics.
герáнь *(f.)* geranium.
герб coat of arms; гéрбовый heraldic; official *(of stamp).*
гермáнский German.
герметúческий hermetic.
геройзм heroism; герои́ня heroine; герои́ческий heroic; герóй hero.
гéрцог duke; герцоги́ня duchess.
гéтман ataman, leader.
гéтра gaiter.
гиаци́нт hyacinth.
ги́бель *(f.)* destruction, perdition; ги́бельный disastrous.
ги́бкий flexible, lithe; pliable, versatile; ги́бкость *(f.)* flexibility; pliability; versatility.
ги́блый wretched; god-forsaken; ги́бнуть *(past* гиб; *pf.* по-) perish.
гибри́д hybrid.
гигáнт giant; гигáнтский gigantic.
гигиéна hygiene; гигиен|и́ческий, ~и́чный hygienic, sanitary.
гид guide.
гидрáвл|ика hydraulics; ~и́ческий hydraulic.

гидро|плáн hydroplane; ~стáнция hydro-electric power station.

гиéна hyena.

гúкать *(pf.* гúкнуть) whoop.

гúльза cartridge-case; cigarette-wrapper; case, sleeve.

гимн hymn, anthem; государственный г. national anthem.

гимназúст, ~ка secondary-school pupil; гимнáзия secondary school.

гимнáст, ~ка gymnast; гимнастёрка field shirt; гимнáстика gymnastics; гимнастúческий зал gymnasium.

гинекóлог gynaecologist; гинекология gynaecology.

гипéрбола hyperbola.

гипнóз hypnosis, hypnotism; гипнотизёр hypnotist; гипнотизúровать *(pf.* за-) hypnotize.

гипóтеза hypothesis.

гипотенýза hypotenuse.

гипотет|úческий, ~úчный hypothetical.

гиппопотáм hippopotamus.

гипс gypsum; plaster (of Paris); plaster cast; гúпсовый plaster *(a.).*

гиревúк (-á) weightlifter.

гирлянда garland.

гúря weight, dumb-bell.

гитáра guitar.

главá *(pl.* глáвы) head, chief; cupola; chapter; во главé *(* + *gen.)* at the head (of); главáр|ь (-я) leader; глáвенство supremacy, domination.

главнокомáндующий commander-in-chief.

глáвн|ый chief, main; -ым óбразом mainly.

глагóл verb; глагóлица Glagolitic alphabet; глагóльный verbal.

гладúльн|ый ironing; -ая доскá ironing board; глáдить (-áжу, -áдишь; *pf.* вы-) iron; *(pf.* по-) smooth, stroke.

глáдкий *(comp.* глáже) smooth; глáдкость *(f.)* smoothness; гладь *(f.)* smooth, mirror-like surface; satin-stitch.

глáженье ironing; глáженый ironed.

глаз (в -ý, *pl.* глазá, глаз) eye; на г. by eye; at an estimate; смотрéть во все глазá be all eyes; за глазá behind someone's back; с глáзу на глаз tête-à-tête.

глазéт brocade.

глазéть (на + *acc.)* stare (at).

глазúровать *(ipf. & pf.)* glaze; ice, candy.

глазнúца eye socket; глазнóй optic(al); глаз|óк (-зкá) 1. eye *(bot., tech.)* ; peep hole; 2. *(with pl.* глá|зки, -зок) eye; анютины глáзки pansies.

глазý|нья *(gen. pl.* -ний) fried eggs.

глазýрь *(f.)* syrup, icing; glaze.

глáнда tonsil.

глас voice; гласúть say, run, read; глáсность *(f.)* publicity; глáсный 1. vowel. 2. public; глашáтай town-crier; herald.

глéт|чер glacier.

глúна clay; глúнистый clayey; глúняный (of) clay.

глúссер glider.

глист|(-á) worm.

глицерúн glycerine

глицúния wistaria.

глóбус globe.

глодáть (гложý, глóжешь, *pf.* об-) gnaw.

глотáть *(pf.* глотнýть) swallow; глóтк|а gullet; во всю -у at top of one's voice; глотóк (-ткá) mouthful.

глóхнуть *(past* глох; *pf.* о-) become deaf; *(pf.* за-) 1. abate, subside; 2. grow wild.

глуб|инá *(pl.* -úны) depth; глубóк|ий *(comp.* глубóк) deep, profound; -ой óсенью in late autumn; глубокомысленный profound; глубокоуважáемый dear *(at start of letter)* ; глубь *(f.)* deep, depth.

глумúться (над + *inst.)* mock (at); глумлéние jeering, mockery.

глупéть *(pf.* по-) become stupid; глу|пéц (-пцá) stupid person; глýпость *(f.)*stupidity; глýпый stupid.

глухáр|ь (-я) capercaillie.

глухóй deaf; hollow, toneless; godforsaken, overgrown; dead, blank; глухонемóй deaf and dumb; глухотá deafness.

глушúтель *(m.)* silencer; глушúть *(pf.* о-) stun; *(pf.* за-) deaden, stifle, extinguish, jam.

глушь *(f.)* backwoods.

глыба clod, block.

глюкóза glucose.

гля|дéть (-жý, -дишь, глядя; *pf.* по-, глянýть) look, glance; г. в óба be on the alert; тогó и гляди пойдёт дождь it looks like rain.

гля|нец (-нца) polish, gloss.

гля́нуть *see* гляде́ть.

гля́нцеви́тый glossy.

гнать (гоню́, го́нишь; *pf* по-) drive, urge on; pursue; distil; -ся (за + *inst.*) chase.

гнев anger; гне́вный angry.

гнедо́й bay *(horse).*

гнезди́ться nest; nestle, be found (in); гнездо́ *(pl.* гнёзда) nest.

гн|ести́ (-ету́, -етёшь, *no past)* oppress; гнёт weight, oppression.

гни́да nit.

гние́ние decomposition, rotting; гнило́й rotten; гнилокро́вие septicaemia; гниль *(f.)* rot, mould; гнить (гни|ю́, -ёшь; *pf.* по-, с-) rot.

гно́йться fester, suppurate; гной pus; гнойни́к (-á) ulcer, abscess.

гном gnome.

гнуса́вить talk through one's nose; гнуса́вый nasal.

гну́сный vile, villainous.

гнуть (гну, гнёшь; *ppp.* гну́тый; *pf.* со-) bend

гнуша́ться *(pf.* по-) (+*gen.)* shun, abhor.

гобеле́н tapestry.

гобо́й oboe.

гове́ть fast.

го́вор sound of voices; dialect; pronunciation; говори́ть *(pf.* по-) talk, speak; *(pf.* ск|аза́ть, -ажу́, -а́жешь) say, tell; говорли́вый talkative.

говя́дина beef; говя́жий beef *(a.).*

го́голь *(m.)* golden-eye duck; ходи́ть -ем strut, swank.

го́гот cackle; loud laughter; гог|ота́ть (-очу́, -о́чешь, *pf.* за-) cackle, roar with laughter.

год *(pl.* го́ды & года́, *gen.* -о́в & лет) year; годи́на time.

го|ди́ться (-жу́сь, -ди́шься; *pf.* при-) be fit (for).

годи́чный a year's, annual.

го́дный (для + *gen.* на + *acc.)* fit (for).

годова́лый year-old; годово́й annual, yearly; годовщи́на anniversary.

гол goal; забива́ть г. score a goal.

голена́стый long-legged; голени́ще top *(of boot)*; го́лень *(f.)* shin.

голла́н|дец (-дца) Dutchman: ~дка Dutchwoman; голла́ндский Dutch.

голова́ (го́лову, го́|ловы, -ло́в, -лова́м) head; как снег на́ -у like a bolt from the blue.

голова́стик tadpole.

голо́вка head *(of lettuce, pin)*; головн|о́й head *(a.)*; -а́я боль headache.

голов|ня́ *(gen. pl.* -не́й) 1. charred log; 2. brand, smut *(plant disease).*

голово|круже́ние giddiness, dizziness; ~кружи́тельный giddy dizzy ~ло́мка brain-teaser ~ло́мный puzzling; ~но́гое cephalopod; ~ре́з cut-throat; dare-devil.

го́лод hunger; famine; голода́ть starve, go hungry; голо́дный hungry; голодо́вка hunger-strike.

гололе́дица ice-covered ground.

го́лос *(pl.* -á) voice, vote; голо|си́ть (-шу́, -си́шь) wail; голосло́вный unfounded; голосова́ть *(pf.* про-) vote; голосово́й vocal.

голуби́ный pigeon *(a.)*; dove-like; голу́бка female pigeon; dear, darling.

голубо́й pale blue.

голу́бчик dear fellow; my lad; го́луб|ь *(m., pl.* -и, -е́й) pigeon, dove; голубя́|тня *(gen. pl.* -тен) dovecot.

го́лый naked; голытьба́ the poor.

го́мон hubbub.

гоне́ние persecution.

го|не́ц (-нца́) messenger; го́нка haste; race.

гонора́р fee.

гонча́р (-á) potter; гонча́рный potter's

го́нчая hound; го́нщик racer.

гоня́ть drive, chase; -ся (за + *inst)* chase, pursue.

гора́ (го́ру, *pl.* го́р|ы, -а́м) mountain, hill; идти́ в го́ру, на го́ру go uphill; под го́ру, с горы́ downhill; стоя́ть горо́й (за + *inst.)* stand by, defend; у меня́ гора́ с плеч свали́лась a load has been taken off my mind.

гора́зд (на + *acc.)* clever (at).

гора́здо much, far.

горб (-á) hump; горба́тый hunchbacked; го́рбить *(pf.* с-) hunch, arch; -ся stoop; горбоно́сый hooknosed; горбу́н (-á), горбу́|нья *(gen. pl.* -ний) hunchback.

горбу́|шка *(gen. pl.* -шек) crust *(at end of loaf).*

горделивый proud, majestic; гор|ди́ться (-жу́сь, -ди́шься) (+ *inst.)* be proud (of); го́рдость *(f.)* pride; го́рдый proud.

го́ре sorrow, grief; ему́ и го́ря ма́ло he doesn't care a hang.
горева́ть grieve.
горе́лка burner.
горе́лки: игра́ть в г. play catch.
горе́лый burnt.
горемы́ка *(m. & f.)* poor creature.
горе́ние burning, combustion.
го́рестный sorrowful; pitiful.
го|ре́ть (-рю́, -ри́шь; *pf* с-) burn.
го́|рец (-рца), **горя́нка** mountain-dweller.
го́речь *(f.)* bitter taste.
горизо́нт horizon; **∼а́льный** horizontal.
гори́стый mountainous, hilly; **го́рка** 1. hill; 2. cabinet, cupboard.
го́ркнуть *(pf.* про-) go rancid, rank.
горла́нить *(pf.* про-) bawl.
го́рлица turtle-dove.
го́рло throat; **го́рлышко** *(pl.* -шки, -шек) little throat; neck *(of bottle).*
гормо́н hormone.
горн 1. furnace; 2. bugle.
горни́ло hearth; crucible *(fig.).*
горни́ст bugler.
го́рничная housemaid.
горно|заво́дский mining and metallurgical; **∼рабо́чий** miner.
горноста́евый ermine *(с.);* **горноста́й** ermine.
го́рн|ый mountain *(а.),* mountainous; mining *(а.);* -ое де́ло mining.
го́род *(pl.* -а́) town, city.
город|ки́ (-ко́в) gorodki *(kind of skittles).*
городни́чий *(hist.)* town governor;
городово́й *(hist.)* policeman; **горо|до́к** (-дка́) small town; **городско́й** municipal; **горо|жа́нин** *(pl.* -а́не, -а́н), **∼а́нка** town-dweller.
горо́х pea, peas; **горо́ховый** pea *(а.);* **горо́|шек** (-шка) pea(s); души́стый г. sweet pea(s); **горо́шин(к)а** pea.
го́рсто|чка *(gen. pl.* -чек), **горсть** *(f., pl.* -и, -е́й) handful, hollow of hand.
горта́нный guttural; laryngeal; **горта́нь** *(f.)* larynx.
горте́нзия hydrangea.
горча́йший most bitter.
горчи́ца mustard; **горчи́чница** mustard-pot.
гор|шо́к (-шка́) pot.
го́рький *(сотр.* го́рче) bitter
горю́чее fuel.
горя́чий hot; cordial, fervent; горя-

чи́ться *(pf.* раз-)get excited, become angry; **горя́|чка** *(gen. pl.* -чек) fever; haste; **горя́чность** *(f.)* ardour; hastiness.
гос = госуда́рственный state *(а.);* госба́нк State Bank;
го́спиталь *(m.)* hospital.
госпла́н State Planning Committee, Gosplan.
госп|оди́н *(pl.* -ода́, -о́д, -ода́м) gentleman; Mr.; *(pl.)* ladies and gentlemen; **госпо́дский** manorial.
госпо́дств|о supremacy; **∼овать** (над + *inst.)* rule, have sway (over).
госпо́дь (го́спода, *voc.* го́споди!) Lord, God.
госпожа́ lady; Mrs.
госте|прии́мный hospitable; **∼прии́мство** hospitality.
гости́ная drawing-room; **гости́ница** hotel; **го|сти́ть** (-щу́, -сти́шь) stay, be on a visit; **гость** *(m., pl* -и, -е́й) guest, visitor; быть в -я́х у него́ stay with him; **го́с|тья** *(gen. pl.* -тий) *(female)* guest.
госуда́рственный state *(а.)* госуда́рство state.
госуда́р|ь *(m.),* **∼ы́ня** sovereign; *(m.)* sire, sir.
гот Goth; **готи́ческий** Gothic.
готова́|льня *(gen. pl.* -лен) case of drawing instruments.
гото́вить *(pf.* при-) (к + *dat.)* prepare (for); -ся prepare (oneself); **гото́вность** *(f.)* readiness, preparedness; **гото́вый** ready.
грабёж (-а́) robbery, pillage; **граби́тель** *(m.)* robber; **граби́тельский** predatory; exorbitant; **гра́бить** *(pf.* о-) rob; plunder.
гра́б|ли (gen. -бель *or* -блей) rake.
гравёр engraver.
гра́вий gravel.
гравирова́ть *(pf.* вы́-, на-) engrave, etch; **гравиро́вка** engraving; **гравю́ра** print, etching.
град 1. hail; 2. *(obs.)* town; **гра́дом** like hail, thick and fast; **гра́дина** hailstone.
градостро́ительство town-building.
гра́дус degree; **гра́дусник** thermometer.
граждани́н *(pl.* гра́ждане, гра́ждан) citizen; **гражда́нский** civil, civic, civilian *(а.);* **гражда́нство** citizenship.
грамза́пись *(f.)* recording *(on gramophone record).*

грамм gram.

грамма́тика grammar; граммати́ческий grammatical.

граммофо́н gramophone.

гра́мота 1. reading and writing; 2. document, deed.

гра́мотность (f.) literacy; competence; гра́мотный literate; grammatical; competent.

грампласти́нка gramophone record.

грана́т 1. pomegranate; 2. garnet.

грана́та shell, grenade.

грандио́зный grand, grandiose.

гранёный cut, faceted.

грани́т granite; грани́тный granite (a.).

грани́ть cut, facet.

грани́ца boundary, frontier; éхать за -y go abroad; быть за -ей be abroad; грани́чить (с + inst.) border (on).

гра́нка galley-proof.

грань (f.) border, verge; side, facet.

граф count.

графа́ column; гра́фик graph, diagram.

графи́н water-bottle.

графи́ня countess.

графи́т graphite, black lead; графи́т|ный graphite, graphitic.

графи́ть rule, draw lines.

графи́ческий graphic.

гра́фство county.

грацио́зный graceful гра́ция grace.

грач (-á) rook.

гребёнка comb; гре́|бень (-бня) comb; crest.

гре|бе́ц (-бца́) oarsman, rower.

гребе|шо́к (-шка́) comb; crest.

гре́бля rowing; гребно́й rowing (a.).

грёза dream, day-dream; vision; грё́зить (-жу, -зишь) dream; -ся (pf. при-) appear in dream.

грек Greek.

гре́лка hot-water bottle.

гре|ме́ть (-млю, -мишь; pf. за-, про-) thunder, clatter; грему́ч|ий thundering, roaring; -ий газ fire-damp; -ая змея́ rattlesnake.

гре|но́к (-нка́) (piece of) toast.

грести́ (греб|у́, -ёшь; грёб, -ла́; pf. по-) 1. row; 2. rake.

греть (ppp. гре́тый; pf. на-, со-) warm, heat; -ся warm oneself; bask.

грех| (-á) sin; как на г. as bad luck would have it; с грехо́м попола́м just, with difficulty; грехово́дник sinner; грехопаде́ние the Fall.

гре́цкий оре́х walnut.

греча́нка Greek woman; гре́ческий Greek.

гречи́ха buckwheat; гре́чневый buckwheat (a.).

греши́ть (pf. co-) sin; грéш|ник, ~ница sinner; гре́шный sinful.

гриб (-á) mushroom; гри|бо́к (-бка́) mushroom; fungus.

гри́ва mane, crest.

гри́венник 10-copeck piece.

грим make-up; grease-paint.

грима́са grimace; грима́сничать pull faces.

гримирова́ть (pf. за-) make up; -ся make oneself up; гримиро́вка make-up.

грипп influenza.

гриф 1. griffin; griffon; 2. signature stamp.

гри́фель (m.) slate pencil.

гроб (в -у́, pl. -ы́ & -á) coffin; grave; гробни́ца tomb, sepulchre; гробовщи́к (-á) coffin-maker.

гроза́ (pl. гро́зы) (thunder) storm;

гроздь (f.; pl. гро́зди, -éй, or -дья, -дьев) bunch, cluster.

гро|зи́ть (-жу́, -зи́шь; pf. по-) (+ dat.) threaten, menace; гро́зный formidable, menacing, terrible; грозово́й storm (a.).

гром (pl. -ы, -о́в) thunder, bolt.

грома́да bulk, mass; грома́дный huge, colossal.

громи́ть (pf. раз-) raid, sack; rout.

гро́мкий (comp. гро́мче) loud; famous; high-flown; громкоговори́тель (m.) loudspeaker.

громово́й thunder (a.); thunderous; громогла́сный loud; open.

громо|зди́ть (-зжу́, -зди́шь; pf. на-) pile up; -ся pile up; climb up.

громо́здкий bulky, cumbersome.

громоотво́д lightning-conductor.

гро́мче see гро́мкий.

громыха́ть (pf. громыхну́ть) rumble.

грот 1. grotto; 2. mainsail.

гроте́скный grotesque.

гротма́чта mainmast.

гро́хать (pf. гро́хнуть) drop with a bang, crash; -ся fall with a crash.

гро́хот 1. crash, din, roar; 2. riddle, sieve; грохо|та́ть (-очу́, -о́чешь) roll, hunder.

грох|оти́ть (-очу́, -о́тишь; pf. про-) sift; screen.

грош (-á) half-copeck; э́то гроша́ ло́маного не сто́ит it's not worth a brass farthing; **грошо́вый** cheap; petty.

грубе́ть *(pf.* за-, о-) become coarse; **груби́ть** *(pf.* на-) *(+dat.)* be rude (to); **грубия́н,** ~**ка** rude person; **гру́бость** *(f.)* roughness, crudity; **гру́бый** coarse, rude.

гру́да heap, pile.

груди́на breastbone, sternum.

груди́нка brisket, bacon.

грудн|о́й breast *(a.),* pectoral; -ая кле́тка thorax; **груд|ь** *(f.,* в -й, *pl.* -и, -éй) breast; стоя́ть гру́дью за *(+ acc.)* champion, defend.

гружёный laden.

груз load, cargo.

гру|зи́н *(gen. pl.* -зи́н), ~**зи́нка** Georgian; **грузи́нский** Georgian *(a.).*

гр|узи́ть (-ужу́, -у́зишь; *pf.* за-, на-, по-) load, embark; **гру́зный** massive, cumbersome; **грузови́к** (-á) lorry, truck; **грузово́й** cargo, goods *(a.);* **грузоподъёмность** *(f.)* carrying capacity; **грузопото́к** goods traffic; **гру́зчик** loader, stevedore.

грунт soil, ground; priming *(painting);* **грунтова́ть** *(pf.* за-) ground; prime; **грунтово́й** earth, soil *(a.).*

групо́рг group organizer.

гру́ппа group; **группиро́вать** *(pf.* с-) group; -ся group, form group(s).

гру|сти́ть (-щу́, -сти́шь) be sad; (по + *dat.)* yearn (for); **гру́стный** sad; **грусть** *(f.)* sadness, sorrow.

гру́ша pear; **гру́шевый** pear *(a.).*

гры́жа rupture, hernia.

грызня́ fight, squabble; **гры|зть** (-зу́, -зёшь; грыз; *pf.* раз-, *ppp.* -гры́зен-ный) gnaw; -ся squabble; **грызу́н** (-á) rodent.

гряда́ *(pl.* гря́д|ы, -áм) bed *(garden);* ridge, range; bank *(of cloud);* **гря́дка** *(dim.).*

гряду́щий approaching, future.

грязево́й mud *(a.).*

грязни́ть *(pf.* за-, на-) make dirty; tarnish; -ся become dirty; **гря́зный** dirty, sordid; **грязь** *(f.,* prep. в -й) dirt, mud; *(pl.)* mud baths.

гря́нуть *(pf.)* burst out, roar, thunder.

губа́ *(pl.* гу́б|ы, -áм) 1. lip; 2. inlet; **губа́стый** thick-lipped.

губерна́тор governor; **губе́рния** province; **губе́рнский** provincial.

губи́тельный baneful, pernicious; **губи́ть** (гублю́, гу́бишь; *pf.* по-) ruin, destroy.

гу́бка 1. lip; 2. sponge; **губн|о́й** labial; -ая пома́да lipstick; **гу́бчатый** spongy.

гуверна́нтка governess.

гу|де́ть (-жу́, -ди́шь; *pf.* за-) buzz, hoot; **гудо́к** (-дка́) hoot; hooter, buzzer.

гужево́й тра́нспорт carting.

гул rumble; **гу́лкий** resounding, hollow.

гуля́нье walking; fête; **гуля́ть** *(pf.* по-) have a stroll; be free of work; make merry.

гумани́зм humanism; **гуманита́рный** humanitarian; **гума́нность** *(f.)* humaneness; **гума́нный** humane.

гу́мми *(indecl.)* gum.

гумно́ *(pl.* гу́мна, гу́мен, гумён, гу́мнам) threshing-floor.

гурт herd, flock; **гурто́м** wholesale, in a body; **гуртовщи́к** (-á) herdsman.

гурьба́ bevy, flock.

гу́сеница caterpillar; caterpillar track.

гус|ёнок (-ёнка *pl.* -я́та, -я́т) gosling.

гуси́н|ый goose *(a.);* -ая ко́жа gooseflesh.

гу́сл|и (-ей) psaltery.

густе́ть *(pf.* по-) become thick; **густо́й** *(comp.* гуще) thick, dense; **густота́** thickness, density; richness.

гусы́ня female goose; **гус|ь** *(m; pl.* -и, -éй) goose; как с гу́ся вода́ like water off a duck's back; **гусько́м** in single file.

гутали́н shoe polish.

гу́ща sediment; thicket.

гэ́льский: г. язы́к Gaelic.

Д

да 1. yes; 2. but; 3. may; 4. and.

дабы́ in order that.

дава́ть (даю́, даёшь: *imper.* дава́й; *pres. p. p.* дава́емый; *ger.* дава́я; *pf.* дать, дам, дашь, даст, дади́м, дади́те, даду́т) give; grant; let; дава́йте чита́ть let's read; -ся yield; come easy; ру́сский язы́к ему́ даётся легко́ Russian comes easy to him.

да́веча recently.

давить (давлю, давишь *pf.* на-, по-)
press; (*pf.* за-, раз-) crush, run
over; (*pf.* у-) choke, strangle;
-ся (*pf.* у-) hang oneself; (*pf.* по-)
choke; давка crush; давление
pressure.

давний old, ancient; давно long ago;
for a long time; давнопрошедший
remote; pluperfect; давность (*f.*)
age; remoteness; prescription
(*law*); давным-давно long, long
ago.

даже even.

далее further, later; и так д. and so
on; далёкий (*compr.* дальше) distant; далеко far; д. за полночь
long after midnight; он д. не дурак
he is by no means a fool.

даль (*f.*) distance; дальневосточный
Far Eastern, дальнейший further.

дальний distant, remote.

дально|бойный long-range; ~вид-
ный far-seeing; ~зоркий long-
sighted; ~мер range-finder; даль-
ность (*f.*) distance, range.

дальше further, farther.

дама lady; queen (*cards*).

дамба dam, dike.

дамский ladies' (*a.*).

данник tributary (*hist.*).

данный given; данные data.

дантист dentist.

дань (*f.*) tribute, contribution.

дар (*pl.* -ы) gift; дарить (дарю, даришь;
pf. по-) present, bestow.

дармоед sponger, parasite.

дарование gift, talent; даровитый
gifted; даровой free, gratuitous;
даром free, for nothing.

дарственный pertaining to an act or
deed of settlement.

дата date.

дательный dative.

датировать (*ipf. & pf.*) date.

датский Danish; датчанин (*pl.* -ане,
-ан), ~анка Dane.

дать(ся) *see* давать(ся).

дача 1. giving, lending; 2. country
house, *dacha*; дачник summer
resident, resident of *dacha*; дачный
local, suburban; summer (*a.*).

два, две two; каждые два дня
every other day; в два счёта in a
trice.

двадцатилетний twenty-year-old;
двадцатый twentieth; двадцать
twenty.

дважды twice.

двенадцатый twelfth; двенадцать
twelve.

дверной door (*a.*); дверца (*gen. pl.*
-рец) door; дверь (*f.*; на -й, *pl.*
двер|и, -ей) door.

двести two hundred.

дви|гатель (*m.*) motor, engine; дви-
гать (-аю & движу, -жешь;
pf. двинуть) move; further; motivate; он двигает ушами he can
move his ears; пружина движет
механизм a spring works the mechanism; им движет гордость he is
motivated by pride; -ся move, be
moved.

движение movement; (physical) exercise; traffic; движимость (*f.*)
movable property; движимый
moved; движущий motive (*a.*); двинуть *see* двигать.

двое two; двое|брачие, ~женство,
~мужие bigamy; двоеточие colon.

двойка two; pair; двойник (-а) double;
двойной double (*a.*); двойня twins;
двойственный dual; double-faced.

двор (-а) court; yard; peasant house-
hold; дво|рец (-рца) palace; двор-
ник yard-keeper; дворня (*obs.*)
domestic servants; дворня|жка
(*gen. pl.* -жек) mongrel; дворовый
yard (*a.*); manor (*serf*); дворцовый
palace (*a.*).

двор|янин (*pl.* -яне, -ян), ~янка
member of dvoryanstvo (*gentry*);
дворянский noble; of dvoryanstvo; дворянство Russian landed
gentry; nobility.

двоюродн|ый -ый брат cousin;
-ая сестра cousin.

двоякий double, of two kinds.

двубортный double-breasted.

двукопытный cloven-footed.

двукратный twofold, reiterated.

двуличный two-faced.

двуногий twolegged.

двуокись (*f.*) dioxide.

двуручный two-hand(l)ed.

двурушник doubledealer.

двусмысленный ambiguous.

двуспальная кровать double bed.

двустволка double-barrelled gun.

двусторонний two-sided, bilateral.

двухгодичный of two years; biennial.

двухгодовалый two-year-old.

двухдневный two-day.

двухколейный путь double track.

двухколёсный two-wheeled.

двухлетний biennial; two-year-old.

двухме́стный two-seater.
двухме́сячный two-month's.
двухнеде́льный two-week, fortnightly.
двухта́ктный дви́гатель two-stroke engine.
двухэта́жный two-storeyed.
двуязы́чный bilingual.
дебати́ровать debate, discuss; **деба́т|ы** (-ов) debate.
дебе́лый plump, buxom.
дебет debit; **дебетова́ть** *(ipf. & pf.)* debit.
дебр|и (-ей) dense forest; the wilds.
дебю́т debut.
де́ва virgin, maid.
девальва́ция devaluation.
дева́ть (дева́ю; *pf.* деть, де́н|у, -ешь; *imper.* день; *ppp.* де́тый) put; -ся get to; disappear.
де́вер|ь *(m; pl.* -рья́, -ре́й) brother-in-law *(husband's brother).*
деви́з motto.
деви́ца girl, unmarried woman; **деви́чий** girlish, maiden *(a.);* **де́вка** wench; **де́во|чка** *(gen. pl.* -чек) little girl; **де́вственный** virgin *(a.):* **де́вушка** *(gen. pl.* -шек) girl; **дев-чо́нка** girl.
девяно́сто ninety; **девяно́стый** ninetieth; **девя́тка** nine; **девятна́дцатый** nineteenth; **девятна́дцать** nineteen; **девя́тый** ninth; **де́вять** nine; **девятьсо́т** nine hundred.
дегаза́тор decontaminator.
дегенера|ати́вный degenerate *(a.);* **~и́ровать** *(ipf. & pf.)* degenerate.
дё|готь (-гтя) tar.
дегуста́ция tasting.
дед, де́ду|шка *(m., gen. pl.* -шек) grandfather; old man.
дееприча́стие verbal adverb, gerund.
дееспосо́бный able to function.
дежу́рить be on duty, watch; **дежу́рный** (on) duty *(a.);* person on duty, monitor; **дежу́рство** duty; watching.
дезавуи́ровать *(ipf. & pf.)* disavow.
дезерти́р deserter; **~овать** *(ipf. & pf.)* desert.
дезинфе́кция disinfection; **~ици́ровать** *(ipf. & pf.)* disinfect.
дезорганиз|а́ция disorganization; **~ова́ть** *(ipf. & pf.)* disorganize.
дезориенти́ровать *(ipf. & pf.)* confuse.
де́йственный effective, active; **де́йствие** action; act; operation; **действи́тельный** actual, real; valid;

active; effective; **действи́тельность** *(f.)* reality; validity.
де́йствовать *(pf.* по-) act, operate, function; (на + *acc.)* have effect (on); **де́йствующ|ий** acting, in force; -ее лицо́ character *(in play).*
дека́бр|ь (-я́) December; **дека́брьский** December *(a.).*
дека́да ten-day period/event.
дека́н dean *(of faculty).*
деквалифици́роваться *(ipf. & pf.)* be disqualified.
деклам|а́ция recitation, declamation; **~и́ровать** *(pf.* про-) recite, declaim.
деклар|а́ция declaration; **~и́ровать** *(ipf. & pf.)* declare.
декольти́рованный low-necked *(of dress, etc.);* **décolleté.**
декорати́вный decorative; **декора́тор** scene-painter; **декора́ция** scenery *(theat.)*
декре́т decree; **декрети́ровать** *(ipf. & pf.)* decree; **декре́тный отпуск** maternity leave.
де́ланный artificial; simulated; **де́лать** *(pf.* с-) make, do; поезд де́лает 80 км. в час the train does 80 km. an hour: -ся become; что с ним сде́лалось? what has become of him?
делега́т, ~ка delegate; **делега́ция** delegation.
деле́ж (-а́) sharing; partition; **деле́ние** division; point *(on scale).*
де|ле́ц (-льца́) (smart) dealer.
делика́тный delicate, ticklish; considerate, tactful.
дели́мое dividend *(maths);* **дели́мость** *(f.)* divisibility; **дели́тель** *(m.)* divisor; **дели́ть** (делю́, де́лишь; *pf.* по-, раз-) divide, share; -ся впечатле́ниями compare notes.
де́ло *(pl.* -а́) matter, business, affair; deed; говори́ть д. talk sense; **делови́тый** efficient, business-like; **делово́й** business *(a.);* business-like; **делопроизводи́тель** *(m.)* clerk; **де́льный** efficient; sensible.
де́льта delta.
дельфи́н dolphin.
демаго́г demagogue; **демаго́гия** demagogy.
демаркацио́нный demarcation *(a.).*
демилитариз|а́ция demilitarization; **~ова́ть** *(ipf. & pf.)* demilitarize.

демобилиз|ация demobilization; ~
-овать *(ipf. & pf.)* demobilize.

демокр|ат democrat; ~ический democratic; демократия democracy.

démon demon.

демонстр|ант demonstrator; ~ативный demonstrative; ~ация demonstration; ~ировать demonstrate.

демонтировать *(ipf. & pf.)* dismantle.

деморализ|ация demoralization; -овать *(ipf. & pf.)* demoralize.

денатурат methylated spirits.

денежный money *(a.)*, pecuniary.

денница dawn; morning star.

денонсировать *(ipf. & pf.)* denounce.

денщик (-а) batman, servant.

день (дня) day; на днях the other day; in a day or two.

деньги (денег, деньгам) money.

департамент department.

депеша dispatch.

депо *(indecl.)* depot.

депонировать *(ipf. & pf.)* deposit.

депрессия depression.

депутат deputy, delegate; депутация delegation.

дёргать *(pf.* дёрнуть) pull, tug; -ся twitch.

дергач (-а) corncrake, landrail.

деревенеть *(pf.* о-) grow stiff/numb.

деревенский rural; дере|вня *(pl.* -вни, -вень, -вням) village.

дер|ево *(pl.* -евья, -евьев) wood; tree; красное д. mahogany; чёрное д. ebony; деревянный wood(en).

держава power, state.

держатель, ~ница holder, user; держать (держу, держишь; *ppp.* держанный) hold, keep; д. себя behave; -ся hold; -ся в стороне stand aside; -ся за перила hold on to the rail.

дерзать *(pf.* дерзнуть) dare; дерзкий impertinent; daring; дерзновенный daring; дерзость *(f.)* impertinence; daring.

дериват derivative.

дерматин artificial leather.

дёрн turf; дернина sod.

дёрнуть *see* дёргать.

дерюга sackcloth.

десант landing.

десерт dessert.

дескать he, she says, they say *etc.*

десна *(pl.* дёсны) gum.

десница right hand.

деспот despot; ~ический despotic.

десятеро ten.

десяти|борье decathlon; ~летие decade; tenth anniversary ~летка (ten-year) secondary school; ~летний ten-year; ten-year-old.

десятина dessiatina *(2·4 acres)*; десятичный decimal; десятка ten; 10-rouble note; десятник foreman; деся|ток (-тка) ten; десятый tenth; десять ten.

деталь *(f.)* detail; component (part); детальный detailed, minute.

детвора kiddies; детдом children's home.

детектив detective.

детёныш young one, cub; дет|и (-ей, -ям, -ьми, -ях) children; детище child; creation.

детонатор detonator.

детоубийство infanticide; детск|ий children's; -ий сад kindergarten; детская nursery; детство childhood.

деть *see* девать.

дефект defect; дефективный defective; дефектный faulty.

дефицит deficit; дефицитный scarce.

деформировать *(ipf. & pf.)* change the form of.

децентрализовать *(ipf. & pf.)* decentralize.

дешеветь *(pf.* по-) become cheap; дешевизна cheapness, low prices; дешёвка low price; cheap sale; дешёвый (дёшев, -а, дёшево, *comp.* дешевле) cheap.

дешифрировать *(ipf. & pf.)* decipher.

деяние deed.

деятель *(m.)* active worker; политический д. politician; деятельность *(f.)* activity; деятельный active.

джаз jazz.

джем jam.

джемпер jumper, pullover.

джигитовка trick horse-riding.

джунгл|и (-ей) jungle.

джут jute.

диабет diabetes.

диагноз diagnosis.

диагон|аль *(f.)* diagonal; ~альный diagonal *(a.)*.

диаграмма diagram, graph.

диадема diadem.

диалект dialect; диалектика dialectic(s).

диалог dialogue.

диа́метр diameter.
диапазо́н range, compass.
диапозити́в (phot.) slide.
диатри́ба diatribe.
диафра́гма diaphragm.
дива́н settee; divan.
диверса́нт saboteur; диве́рсия diversion; sabotage.
дивертисме́нт variety show.
диви́зия division.
диви́ться (pf. по-) (+dat.) marvel (at); ди́вный wonderful; ди́во wonder, marvel; на д. marvellously.
дие́з sharp (mus.).
дие́та diet.
ди́зель (m.) diesel engine.
дизентери́я dysentery.
дика́р|ь (-я), ~ка savage; shy person; ди́кий wild; shy; unsociable; дикобра́з porcupine; дико́вин(к)а wonder; something strange; ди́кость (f.) wildness; absurdity.
дикт|а́нт, ~о́вка dictation; дикта́тор dictator; дикта́торский dictatorial; диктату́ра dictatorship; диктова́ть (pf. про-) dictate; ди́ктор announcer.
ди́кция enunciation.
диле́мма dilemma.
дилета́нт amateur, dilettante.
дилижа́нс coach.
дина́мика dynamics; динами́т dynamite; динами́ческий dynamic; дина́мо-маши́на dynamo.
династи́ческий dynastic; дина́стия dynasty.
диноза́вр dinosaur
дипло́м diploma.
диплом|а́т diplomat; ~а́тика diplomatics (archive); ~ати́ческий diplomatic; ~а́тия diplomacy.
дипло́мн|ый: -ая рабо́та graduation/ diploma thesis.
директи́ва instructions, directives; дире́ктор (pl. -а́) director, principal.
дире́кция board of management.
дирижа́бль (m.) balloon, airship.
дирижёр conductor; ~и́ровать (inst.) conduct.
диск disc; discus.
ди́скант treble.
дисквалифици́ровать (ipf. & pf.) disqualify.
диско́нт discount.
дискредити́ровать (ipf. & pf.) discredit.

дискримин|а́ция discrimination; ~и́ровать (ipf. & pf.) discriminate against.
диску́ссия discussion, debate; дискути́ровать (ipf. & pf.) discuss, debate.
диспансе́р dispensary, health centre.
диспе́тчер controller; диспе́тчерская control tower.
ди́спут public debate.
диссерта́ция thesis, dissertation.
диссоции́ровать (ipf. & pf.) dissociate.
диста́нция distance.
дистилл|и́ровать (ipf. & pf.) distil; ~я́ция distillation.
дисциплин|а discipline; ~а́рный disciplinary; ~и́ровать (ipf. & pf.) discipline.
дитя́ (neut; gen, dat, prep. дитя́ти, inst. -я́тею pl. де́ти) child.
дифтери́т diphtheria.
дифто́нг diphthong.
диффама́ция libel.
дифференц|иа́л differential; ~иа́ция differentiation; ~и́ровать (ipf. & pf.) differentiate.
дича́ть (pf. о-) grow wild; become unsociable; дичи́ться (+ gen.) be shy (of); shun.
дичь (f.) 1. game; 2. nonsense; 3. wilderness.
длань (f.) palm, hand (poet.).
длина́ length; дли́нный long; дли́тельный prolonged; дли́ться (pf. про-) last.
для (gen.) for (the sake of); для того́, что́бы in order to/that.
дневальный orderly, man on duty.
днева́ть spend the day; дневни́к (-а́) diary; дневно́й day (a.), daily; днём in the daytime, in the afternoon.
дни́ще bottom (of ship, barrel); bilge.
дно (pl. до́н|ья, -ьев) bottom; ground; золото́е д. (coll.) gold-mine.
до (gen.) up to, until, before; мне не до э́того it is not my affair; I haven't time for that; мне не до шу́ток I'm not in the mood for jokes.
доба́вка addition; makeweight; добавле́ние addition; supplement; добавля́ть (pf. доба́вить) add; доба́вочный additional.
добега́ть (pf. добежа́ть*) (до + gen.) run up (to).
добела́ till white.

добива́ть *(pf.* доби́ть*)* finish off; **-ся** (+ *gen.*) achieve, obtain; **-ся** своего́ gain one's end.

добира́ться *(pf.* добра́ться*)* (до + *gen.*) get to, reach; д. до су́ти де́ла get to the root of the matter.

до́блестный valiant; **до́блесть** *(f.)* valour.

добра́сывать *(pf.* добро́сить*)* (до + *gen.*) throw (as far as).

добра́ться *see* добира́ться.

добра́чный pre-marital; maiden *(name)*.

добр|о́ good; э́то не к -у it is a bad sign; д. пожа́ловать (в + *acc.*)! welcome(to)!

добро|во́лец (-во́льца) volunter; **~во́льный** voluntary; **~во́льческий** volunteer *(a.)*; **~де́тель** *(f.)* virtue; **~де́тельный** virtuous; **~ду́шие** good-nature; **~ду́шный** good-natured; **~ка́чественный** of high quality; non-malignant; **~серде́чный** kind-hearted; **~со́вестный** honest, conscientious; **~сосе́дский** neighbourly.

доброта́ goodness, kindness.

добро́тный of high quality, durable.

до́бр|ый good, kind; в -ый час! good luck!; по -ой во́ле of one's own free will; чего́ -ого possibly, perhaps.

добыва́ть *(pf.* добы́ть*)* get, obtain; **добы́ча** extraction, output; booty, loot.

дова́ривать *(pf.* довари́ть*)* cook to a turn, finish cooking.

довезти́ *see* довози́ть.

дове́ренность *(f.)* warrant, power of attorney; **дове́ренный** entrusted; *(as noun)* agent.

дове́рие confidence, faith; **дове́рить** *see* доверя́ть.

до́верху to the top.

дове́рчивый trusting, credulous.

доверша́ть *(pf.* -ши́ть*)* complete, crown; **доверше́ние** completion; в д. всего́ to crown all.

доверя́ть *(pf.* дове́рить*)* entrust; д. ему́ та́йну take him into one's confidence; **-ся** *(dat.)* trust.

дове́|сок (-ска) makeweight.

до́вод reason, argument; **доводи́ть*** *(pf.* довести́*)* (до + *gen.*) lead, bring (to).

довое́нный pre-war.

довози́ть* *(pf.* довезти́*)* (до + *gen.*) take (to, as far as).

дово́льно 1. enough; 2. rather.

дово́льный *(inst.)* pleased, content *(with)*; **дово́льствие** allowance; **дово́льство** contentment *(with)*.

дово́льствовать *(inst.)* supply *(with)*; **-ся** *(inst.)* be content *(with)*.

довы́боры (-ов) by-election.

дог mastiff.

дога́дка conjecture; **дога́дливый** quick-witted; **дога́дываться** *(pf.* догада́ться)* guess, conjecture.

догла́живать *(pf.* догла́дить*)* iron.

до́гма dogma; **догмати́|ческий**, **~йчный** dogmatic.

догна́ть *see* догоня́ть.

догова́ривать *(pf.* договори́ть)* finish speaking; **-ся** 1. (до + *gen.*) talk till one reaches *(e. g.* absurdity, hoarseness*)*; 2. (о + *gen.*) agree (on); высо́кие догова́ривающиеся сто́роны high contracting parties; **догово́р** agreement, contract, treaty; **догово́рный** contractual, treaty *(a.)*.

догола́ stark naked.

догоня́ть *(pf.* догна́ть*)* catch up.

догора́ть *(pf.* догоре́ть*)* burn low.

догреба́ть *(pf.* догрести́*)* (до + *gen.*) row (as far as).

догружа́ть *(pf.* догрузи́ть*)* load full.

додава́ть ***(pf.*** дода́ть*)* give (the remainder).

доде́лывать *(pf.* доде́лать*)* finish.

доду́мываться *(pf.* доду́маться)* (до + *gen.*) hit upon.

доеда́ть *(pf.* дое́сть*)* eat up.

доезжа́ть *(pf.* дое́хать*)* (до + *gen.*) reach, arrive (at).

дожа́ривать *(pf.* дожа́рить)* cook to a turn.

дожда́ться *see* дожида́ться.

дождева́ние sprinkling, irrigation.

дождеви́к (-á) 1. puff-ball; 2. rain-coat; **дождево́й** rain *(a.)*; **дожде-ме́р** rain-gauge; **дожди́ть** *(coll.)* rain; **дождли́вый** rainy; **дождь** (-я́) rain.

дожива́ть *(pf.* дожи́ть*)* live long, live out.

дожида́ться *(pf.* дожда́ться*)* (gen.)* wait for.

до́за dose.

дозволя́ть *(pf.* дозво́лить)* allow.

дозвони́ться *(pf.)* ring till one gets an answer.

дозиро́вка dosage.

дознáние enquiry.

дозóр patrol.

дозревáть *(-евáю; pf.* дозрéть) ripen.

дойгрывать *(pf.* доигрáть) finish (playing).

дойскиваться *(pf.* доискáться*) *(gen.)* find out, seek out.

доисторúческий prehistoric.

дойть *(pf.* по-) milk.

дойтú *see* доходúть.

док dock.

доказáтельный conclusive; **доказáтельство** proof, evidence; **докáзывать** *(pf.* доказáть, -ажý, -áжешь) prove, demonstrate; contend.

докáнчивать *(pf.* докóнчить) finish.

докáпываться *(pf.* докопáться) (до + *gen.)* find out.

дóкер docker.

докúдывать *(pf.* докúнуть) (до + *gen.)* throw (as far as).

доклáд report, lecture; **доклáд|чик, ~чица** speaker; **доклáдывать** *(pf.* дол|ожúть, -ожý, -óжишь) make a report; announce.

доконáть *(pf., coll.)* finish, kill.

докóнчить *see* докáнчивать.

докопáться *see* докáпываться.

дóкрасна redness, red hot.

дóктор *(pl.* -á) doctor; physician.

доктрúн|а doctrine; **~ёрский** doctrinaire.

докумéнт document; **~úровать** *(ipf. & pf.)* document.

докучáть *(dat.)* pester; **докýчливый** importunate.

дол dale.

долбúть *(pf.* вы-) chisel, hollow out; learn by rote; repeat.

долг (в -ý, *pl.* -и) debt; брать в д. borrow; давáть в д. lend.

дóлгий *(compr.* дóлее, дóльше) long; дóлго for a long time.

долговóй debt *(a.)*; promissory.

долго|врéменный lasting, permanent; **~вязый** lanky; **~игрáющая пластúнка** long-playing record; **~лéтие** longevity; **~лéтний** of many years; **~нóсик** weevil; **~срóчный** long-term.

долготá length; longitude.

дóлее longer.

долетáть *(pf.* долетéть*) (до + *gen.)* fly (as far as).

должáть *(pf.* за-) *(coll.)* borrow; get into debt; **дóл|жен, -жнá, -жнó, -жны** owing, obliged; (+ *inf.)*

must; должнó быть probably, it must be; должнúк (-á) debtor; должностнóй official; дóлжность *(f.)* post, position; дóлжный due, proper.

доливáть *(pf.* долúть*) add, pour some more.

долúна valley.

дóллар dollar.

доложúть *see* доклáдывать.

долóй down with; д. войнý! down with war!

дол|отó *(pl.* -óта) chisel.

дóльше longer.

дóл|я *(pl.* -и, -éй) portion, share; fate.

дом *(pl.* -á) house; building; **домáшний** domestic.

дóменн|ый: -ая печь blast-furnace.

дóмик house, cottage.

доминиóн dominion; **домкнúровать:** д. (над + *inst.)* prevail (over), dominate.

домúш|ко *(m., pl.* -шки, -шек) little house.

домкрáт jack.

дó|мна *(gen. pl.* -мен) blast-furnace.

домовúт thrifty; **домовлад|éлец** (-éльца), **~éлица** house-owner; **домовóдство** domestic science.

домовóй brownie.

домóвый house *(a.)*.

домогáтельство solicitation; **домогáться** *(gen.)* try to obtain.

домóй (to) home.

доморóщенный home-grown; halfbaked; **домочáдц|ы** (-ев) household; **домрабóтница** domestic servant.

донéльзя to the utmost.

донесéние report, message; **донестú** *see* доносúть.

дóнизу to the bottom; свéрху д. from top to bottom.

донимáть *(pf.* доня́ть, дой|мý, -мёшь; дóнял, -á; *ppp.* дóнятый) harass, weary.

донóс denunciation; **доносúть*** *(pf.* донестú*) report; (на + *acc.)* inform (against); -ся carry be heard; **донóс|чик, ~чица** informer

донскóй (of the) Don.

донúне hitherto.

доня́ть *see* донимáть.

допекáть *(pf.* допéчь*) bake to the finish; harass.

допивáть *(pf.* допúть*) drink up.

допúсывать *(pf.* дописáть*) finish writing.

доплата extra payment; excess fare; **доплачивать** *(pf.* доплатить*)* pay the remainder.

дополнение addition, supplement; **дополнительный** additional; **дополнять** *(pf.* дополнить*)* supplement.

допотопный antediluvian.

допрашивать *(pf.* допросить*)* question, interrogate; **допрос** interrogation.

допуск admittance; **допускать** *(pf.* допустить*)* admit; **допустимый** permissible, possible; **допущение** assumption; admission; permission.

допытываться *(pf.* допытаться*) (gen.)* (try to) find out.

дорабатывать *(pf.* доработать) elaborate, develop.

дореволюционный pre-revolutionary.

дорога road; **железная д.** railway, railroad; **туда ему и д.** it serves him right!

дороговизна high prices; **дорогой** *(compr.* дороже) dear.

дородный portly.

дорожать *(pf.* вз-, по-) rise in price; **дороже** *see* **дорогой; дорожить** *(inst.)* value; take care of.

дорож|ка *(gen. pl.* -жек) path; track; strip of carpet; **дорож|ный** road *(a.);* travelling *(a.);* -ое строительство road-building.

досада annoyance; **досадный** annoying; **досаждать** *(pf.* доса|дить, -жу, -дишь) *(dat.)* annoy.

доселе hitherto.

досиживать *(pf.* досидеть*):* д. до конца sit out.

доска (доску, *pl.* до|ски, -сок, -скам) board; slab.

досказывать *(pf.* досказать*)* finish telling/saying.

доскональный thorough.

дословный word-for-word, literal.

доспех|и (-ов) armour.

досрочный early, ahead of time.

дост|авать (-аю, -аёшь; *pf.* достать*)* get, obtain; suffice; (до + *gen.)* reach, touch; -**ся** fall to one's lot; это -алось ему it fell to his lot; ему -анется за это he'll catch it for this.

доставка delivery; **доставлять** *(pf.* доставить) deliver, supply.

доста|ток (-тка) easy circumstances, prosperity; **достаточный** sufficient, enough.

достигать *(pf.* достигнуть, достичь;

past -нул *or* достиг, -ла) *(gen.)* reach, achieve; **достижение** achievement; **достижимый** attainable.

достоверный authentic, trustworthy.

достоинство dignity; merit; **достойный** (+ *gen.)* worthy (of).

достопримечательность *(f.)* sight, something worth seeing.

достояние property.

достраивать *(pf.* достроить) finish building.

доступ access; **доступный** accessible, available, approachable.

достучаться* *(pf.)* knock till door is opened.

досуг leisure; **на -е** in one's spare time; **досужий** idle.

досуха dry; **вытирать д.** wipe dry.

досыта to one's heart's content.

досягаемый attainable.

дотация grant, (state) subsidy.

дотла completely; **сгорать д.** burn to ashes.

дотоле till then.

дотрагиваться *(pf.* дотронуться) (до + *gen.)* touch.

дотягивать *(pf.* дотянуть) drag out.

дохлый dead *(of animals);* puny; **дохлятина** carrion; **дохнуть** *(past.* дох; *pf.* из-, по-) die *(of animals);* **дохнуть** *(pf.)* breathe.

доход income, profit.

доходить* *(pf.* дойти*)* (до + *gen.)* reach; be done, cooked.

доходный profitable.

доходчивый intelligible.

доцветать *(pf.* доцвести*)* fade.

доцент reader, assistant professor, lecturer.

дочерний daughter's, filial.

дочиста completely.

дочитывать *(pf.* дочитать) finish reading.

до|чка *(gen. pl.* -чек) daughter; **дочь** *(f; gen., dat., prep.,* дочери, *inst.* дочерью, *pl.* дочер|и, -ей, -ям, -ьми, -ях) daughter.

дошкольный pre-school.

дощатый made of planks, boards; **дощечка** *(gen. pl.* -чек) small plank, board.

доярка milkmaid.

драгоценность *(f.)* jewel; something precious; **драгоценный** precious.

дражайший dearest.

др|азнить (-азню, -азнишь; *pf.* по.) tease.

драка fight.

дракон dragon; драконовский draconian.

драма drama; драматический dramatic; драматург dramatist; драмкру|жок (-жка) drama club.

дранка lath.

драный torn, ragged.

драп thick cloth; драпировать (pf. за-) drape; драпировщик upholsterer.

драть (дер|у, -ёшь; pf со-) tear; (pf. вы-) flog; -ся fight; драчливый pugnacious.

дребез|жать (-жит: pf. за-) jingle, tinkle.

древесина wood; древесный wood (a.); д. уголь charcoal.

древк|о (pl. -и, -ов) pole, shaft.

древний ancient, old; древность (f.) antiquity.

древо (poet.) tree.

дрезина trolley.

дрейф drift; дрейфовать (ipf. & pf.) drift.

др|емать (-емлю, -емлешь; pf. за-) sleep, doze; дремота drowsiness.

дремучий dense.

дренировать (ipf. & pf.) drain.

дрессировать (pf. вы-) train (animals); дрессиров|щик, ~щица trainer.

дробилка crusher; дробить (pf. раз-) crush, splinter; дробный fractional; дробь (f.) fraction; small shot; roll (on drums).

дрова (дров) firewood.

дроги (дрог): похоронные д. hearse.

дрогнуть 1. (past дрог; pf. про-) be chilled.

дро|жать (-жу, жишь; pf. дрогнуть 2., past -нул, & задрожать) shiver, tremble.

дро́жж|и (-ей) yeast.

дро́|жки (-жек) droshky, carriage.

дрожь (f.) trembling.

дрозд (-а) thrush.

дроссель (m.) throttle.

дротик dart, javelin.

друг (pl. дру|зья, -зей, -зьям) friend; друг друга each other; друг с другом with each other.

другой other, different; и тот и д. both.

дружба friendship; дружелюбный amicable; дружеский, дружественный friendly.

дружина detachment, brigade.

дружить be friendly; дружный friendly, unanimous.

дряблый flabby.

др|язги (-язг) squabbles.

дрянной worthless; дрянь (f.) rubbish.

дряхлый decrepit.

дуб (pl. -ы) oak.

дубильн|ая кислота tannic acid; -ое вещество tannin.

дубильня tannery; дубильщик tanner.

дубина cudgel, club; blockhead; дубинка truncheon, club.

дубить (pf. вы-) tan.

дублёр understudy; дублировать duplicate; understudy.

дубовый oak (a.); дубрава oakgrove; leafy grove.

дуга (pl. дуги) arc, bend.

дудк|а pipe; плясать под его -у dance to his tune.

дуло muzzle.

дума 1. thought; 2. duma, council; думать (pf. по-) think.

дуновение puff, whiff; дунуть see дуть.

дупел|ь (m., pl. -я) double snipe.

дупло (pl. ду|пла, -пел) hollow (in tree, tooth).

дур|а, дурак (-а) fool; дурацкий foolish; дурачить (pf. о-) make fool of; -ся play the fool.

дурман narcotic; дурманить (pf. о-) drug.

дурнеть (pf. по-) grow plain/ugly; дурной bad; ugly; мне дурно I feel queer/ill; дурнота faintness, nausea.

дурь (f.) nonsense.

дутый hollow; exaggerated.

дуть (дую, дуешь; pf. по-, & дунуть) blow.

дуться sulk; (на + acc.) be in a huff (with).

дух spirit; breath; испускать дух give up the ghost; захватывает дух it takes one's breath away; присутствие духа presence of mind; о нём ни слуху ни духу nothing has been heard of him; он не в духе he is in low spirits; это не в моём духе it's not to my liking.

дух|и (-ов) perfume.

духовенство clergy.

духовка oven.

духовник (-а) confessor; духовный spiritual, ecclesiastical; духовная will, testament.

духово́й wind (a.); д. инструме́нт wind instrument.
духота́ closeness.
душ shower(-bath).
душа́ (ду́шу, pl. ду́ши) soul; serf; heart, mind; с души́/ на ду́шу per head; у меня́ душа́ в пя́тки ушла́ I was terrified;| он не име́ет ни гроша́ за душо́й he hasn't a penny to his name; она́ в нём души́ не ча́ет she dotes on him.
душевя́я shower-baths.
душевнобольно́й insane; душе́вный mental, emotional; sincere.
душегре́йка |(gen. pl. -еек) woman's sleeveless jacket.
душегу́б murderer.
ду́шенька darling, sweetheart.
душе|поле́зный edifying; ~прика́зчик executor; ~раздира́ющий heartrending.
души́стый fragrant.
души́ть 1. (душу́, ду́шишь; pf. за-) smother, stifle, strangle.
души́ть 2. (душу́, ду́шишь; pf. на-) scent, perfume; -ся use scent.
ду́шный close, stuffy.
ду|шо́к (-шка́) slight smell, whiff.
дуэ́ль (f.) duel.
дуэ́т duet.
ды́бом: во́лосы ста́ли д. his hair stood on end; стать на дыбы́ rear, prance; bristle up, kick up.
дым smoke; дыми́ть (pf. на-) (give off) smoke; fill with smoke; -ся smoke, steam; ды́мка haze; ды́мный smoky; дымов|о́й smoke (a.); -а́я заве́са smoke-screen; дымохо́д flue; ды́мчатый smoke-coloured.
ды́ня melon.
дыра́ (pl. ды́ры) hole; ды́рка small hole; дыроко́л (hole-)puncher; дыря́вый full of holes.
дыха́ние breathing; дыха́тельн|ый respiratory; -ое го́рло wind-pipe.
дыша́ть (-шу́, ды́шишь; pf. по-, ды-хну́ть) breathe.
ды́шло shaft, beam.
дья́вол devil; дья́вольский devilish, awful.
дьяк (-а́) official.
дья́кон deacon.
дю́жий stalwart.
дю́жина dozen.
дюйм inch.
дю́на dune.

дя́дька uncle; tutor; дя́дюшка (m. gen. pl. -шек) uncle; дя́д|я (m., gen. pl. -ей) uncle.
дя́|тел (-тла) woodpecker.

Е

ева́нгелие gospel.
евре́й, евр|е́йка (gen. pl. -е́ек) Jew; евре́йский Jewish, Hebrew.
европ|е́ец (-е́йца), ~е́йка (gen. pl. -е́ек) European; европе́йский European (a.).
еги́петский Egyptian (a.); еги́пт|янин (pl. -я́не, -я́н), ~я́нка Egyptian.
егоза́ (m. & f.) fidget.
еда́ food, meal.
едва́ hardly, just, scarcely; е. не nearly; е. ли hardly, (it is) un-likely; е. ли не almost.
едине́ние unity; едини́ца unit; individual; едини́чный single, iso-lated.
единобо́рство single combat.
единогла́сие unanimity; ~гла́сный unanimous.
единоду́шие unanimity; ~ду́шный unanimous.
единокро́вный consanguineous.
единомы́слие agreement, concord; единомы́шленник person of like mind.
единообра́зие uniformity; ~обра́зный uniform.
единоро́г unicorn.
единоутро́бный брат half brother.
еди́нственный only, sole; еди́нство unity; еди́ный united, common.
е́дкий (compr. е́дче) caustic, pungent.
едо́к (-а́) eater, mouth to feed.
ёж (ежа́) hedgehog; морско́й ёж sea urchin.
ежеви́ка blackberries.
еже|го́дник annual, year-book; ~го́дный annual.
ежедне́вный daily.
ежеме́сячник monthly magazine; ~ме́сячный monthly.
ежемину́тный continual, incessant.
ежене́дельник weekly magazine; ~неде́льный weekly.
ежеча́сный hourly.
ёжик crew-cut.
ёжиться huddle up; hesitate.
ежо́в|ый: держа́ть в -ых рукави́цах rule with rod of iron.

езда́ ride, riding; **е́здить** (е́зжу, е́здишь; *pf.* по-, пое́хать*) ride, drive, go; **ездо́к** (-а́) rider.

ей-бо́гу really and truly.

ёкать *(pf.* ёкнуть): се́рдце ёкнуло my heart missed a beat.

е́ле hardly, only just.

еле́йный unctuous.

ёлка, ель *(f.)* fir, spruce; **ело́вый** fir, spruce *(a.)*.

ёмкий capacious; **ёмкость** *(f.)* capacity.

ено́т racoon.

епа́рхия diocese; **епи́скоп** bishop.

ерала́ш hotchpotch.

е́ресь *(f.)* heresy; **ерети́к** (-ика́), **~и́чка** *(gen. pl.* -и́чек) heretic; **ерети́ческий** heretical.

ёрзать fidget.

ермо́лка skull-cap.

еро́шить *(pf.* взъ-) ruffle, rumple.

ерунда́ nonsense.

ёрш (ерша́) 1. ruff *(fish)*; 2. small brush, wire brush.

е́сли if.

есте́ственный natural; **естество́** nature, substance.

естество|ве́д scientist, naturalist; **~ве́дение, ~зна́ние** (natural) science.

есть 1. (ем, ешь, ест, еди́м, еди́те, едя́т; *imper.* ешь!; *pf.* съ-; *ppp.* съе́денный) eat.

есть 2. there is, are; у меня́ е. I have.

есть! 3. all right! aye-aye!

ефре́йтор lance-corporal.

е́хать (е́ду, е́дешь, *imper.* поезжа́й!; *pf.* по-) go, drive, ride.

ехи́дный malicious, venomous; **ехи́дство** malice, spite.

ещё still, yet; е. раз once more, again; е. бы! I should just think so!

Ж

ж = же

жа́ба 1. toad, 2. quinsy; грудна́я ж. angina pectoris.

жа́бра gill.

жа́воро|нок (-нка) (sky)lark.

жа́дничать be greedy; **жа́дность** *(f.)* greed; **жа́дный** (до + *gen.;* к + *dat.;* на + *acc.)* greedy (for).

жа́жда thirst, craving; **жа́ж|дать** (-ду, -дешь) *(gen.)* thirst, crave (for).

жаке́т jacket.

жале́ть *(pf.* по-) *(acc.)* feel sorry for; *(acc. or gen.)* grudge; *(gen.)* regret.

жа́лить *(pf.* у-) sting.

жа́лкий pitiful, wretched.

жа́ло sting.

жа́лоба complaint; **жа́лобн|ый** plaintive; -ая кни́га complaints book; **жа́лоб|щик, ~щица** plaintiff; complainant.

жа́лованье salary; **жа́ловать** *(pf.* по-) grant; be gracious, kind; (к + *dat.)* visit; добро́ пожа́ловать! welcome!

жа́ловаться *(pf.* по-) (на + *acc.)* complain (against).

жа́лостливый compassionate; **жа́лостный** compassionate; plaintive; **жа́лость** *(f.)* pity.

жаль (it is a) pity; ему́ ж. сестру́ he is sorry for his sister.

жалюзи́ *(indecl.)* Venetian blind.

жанда́рм gendarme.

жанр genre.

жар (в -у́) heat, ardour; fever; **жара́** heat, hot air/weather.

жарго́н slang.

жа́реный fried, grilled, roasted; **жа́рить** *(pf.* за-, из-) fry, grill *etc.*; -ся fry, roast; bask.

жа́ркий *(comp.* жа́рче) hot; **жарко́е** roast (meat).

жа́тва harvest, reaping; **жа́твенный** reaping *(a.)*.

жать 1. (жму, жмёшь; *ppp.* жа́тый) press, squeeze; be too tight.

жать 2. (жну, жнёшь; *pf.* с- сожну́; *ppp.* сжа́тый) reap, crop.

жва́чка chewing; cud; **жва́чный** ruminant.

жгут (-а́) plait.

жгу́чий burning.

ждать (жду, ждёшь, *past.* ждал, -а́) *(acc. or gen.)* wait (for).

же 1. as for, but; 2. *emphatic particle;* где же ... where on earth ...

жева́ть (жу|ю́, -ёшь) chew, ruminate; go on repeating.

жезл (-а́) rod, staff.

жела́ние wish, desire; **жела́нный** desired; **жела́тельный** desirable, advisable; **жела́ть** *(pf.* по-) wish; жела́ем вам успе́ха we wish you success.

желва́к (-а́) tumour.

желе́ *(indecl.)* jelly.

железа́ *(pl.* же́лезы, желёз, -а́м) gland.

железнодоро́ж|ник railwayman; ~ный railway (a.).

желе́зн|ый iron (a.); -ая доро́га railway, railroad.

желе́зо iron; ~бето́н reinforced concrete; ~прока́тный заво́д rolling mill.

жёлоб (pl. -á) gutter; жело|бо́к (-бка́) groove.

желте́ть (pf. по-) turn yellow, look yellow; желтизна́ yellow, yellowness; жел|то́к (-тка́) yolk (of egg); желту́ха jaundice; жёлтый yellow.

желу́|док (-дка) stomach; желу́до|чек (-чка) ventricle; желу́дочный stomach (a.), gastric.

жёлуд|ь (m., pl. -и, -éй) acorn.

жёлчный bilious; bitter; ж. пузы́рь gall-bladder; жёлчь (f.) bile.

жема́ниться mince; жема́нный mincing, finicking; жема́нство mincing manners, affectation.

жéмчуг (pl. -á) pearl(s); жемчу́жина pearl; жемчу́жный pearl (a.).

жена́ (pl. жёны) wife; жена́тый married; жени́тьба marriage; жени́ться (ipf. & pf. женю́сь, же́нишься) marry, get married; ж. на ней marry her.

жени́х (-á) fiancé, eligible bachelor.

женонена́вистник misogynist.

же́нский female, feminine; же́нственный feminine, womanly.

же́нщина woman.

жерд|ь (f.; pl. -и, -éй) perch, pole.

жереб|ёнок (-ёнка, pl. -я́та, -я́т) foal; жере|бе́ц (-бца́) stallion, colt.

жерло́ (pl. жéрла) muzzle; orifice; crater.

жёрнов (pl. -á) millstone.

же́ртв|а sacrifice, victim; приноси́ть в -у sacrifice; же́ртвовать (pf. по-) (+ inst.) sacrifice.

жест gesture; жестикули́ровать gesticulate.

жёстк|ий (comp. жёстче) hard, rigid; -ая вода́ hard water.

жесто́кий cruel; жесто́кость (f.) cruelty.

жесть (f.) tin(-plate); жестя́нка tin, can; жестяно́й of tin.

жето́н counter; medal.

жечь (жгу, жжёшь, жгут; past жёг, жгла; pf. с-, сожгу́, ppp. сожжённый) burn.

живи́тельный bracing, vivifying.

жи́вность (f.) poultry, small game/fry.

живо́й living, alive; ни жив ни мёртв petrified.

живопи́|сец (-сца) painter; живопи́сный picturesque; жи́вопись (f.) painting.

жи́вость (f.) liveliness.

живо́т (-á) belly; life (coll.).

животво́рный life-giving.

животново́дство live-stock farming; живо́тн|ый animal (a.); -ое animal.

животрепе́щущий of vital importance; burning;

живу́чий of great vitality; живьём alive.

жи́дкий (comp. жи́же) liquid (a.); thin, scanty; жи́дкость (f.) liquid, fluid.

жи́жа wash, ooze, swill.

жи́зненный vital, living; ж. у́ровень standard of living.

жизне|описа́ние biography.

жизнера́достный cheerful.

жизнеспосо́бный viable.

жизнь (f.) life.

жиклёр (carburettor) jet.

жи́ла vein; tendon, sinew.

жиле́т, ~ка waistcoat.

жи|ле́ц (-льца́) tenant, lodger.

жи́листый sinewy, stringy.

жили́ца (female) tenant, lodger; жил|и́ще (gen. pl. -и́щ) dwelling, abode; жили́щн|ый dwelling, housing (a.); -ые усло́вия housing conditions.

жи́лка vein; fibre.

жило́й dwelling (a.), habitable; ж. дом dwelling house; жилпло́щадь (f.) living space, floor-space; жильё dwelling, habitation.

жи́молость (f.) honeysuckle.

жир (pl. -ý, pl. -ы́) fat, grease.

жира́ф giraffe.

жире́ть (pf. о-, раз-) grow fat; жи́рный fat, greasy; rich; жирово́й fatty, fat.

жироприка́з banking order.

жите́йский everyday, worldly.

жи́тель, ~ница inhabitant, resident; жи́тельство residence.

житие́ life (of a saint), biography.

жи́тница granary; жи́то corn.

жить (живу́, живёшь; past жил, -á) live; житьё life, existence; жи́ться: ему́ хорошо́ живётся he is well-off, he is doing well.

жму́рить (pf. за-) screw up (eyes); -ся screw up one's eyes.

жму́|рки (-рок) blind man's buff.
жн|е́йка (gen. pl. -е́ек) harvester
(machine) ; жн|е́ц (-еца́), жни́ца
reaper; жни́вьё (pl. жни́|вья
-вьев) stubble.
жо́лоб, жо́лудь = жёлоб, жёлудь
жрать (жру, жрёшь; past. жрал, -а́;
pf. co-) devour, guzzle.
жре́бий lot, destiny; ж. бро́шен the
die is cast.
жрец (-а́) priest.
жужжа́ние buzz, hum; жу|жжа́ть
(-жжу́, -жжи́шь) buzz, hum.
жук (-а́) beetle.
жу́лик rogue, swindler; жу́льни-
чать (pf. c-) cheat.
жура́вл|ь (-я́) crane.
жури́ть (pf. по-) reprove.
журна́л periodical, journal; журна-
ли́ст,~ка journalist; журнали́стика
journalism.
журча́ние babble, murmur; жур|
ча́ть (-чи́т) babble, murmur.
жу́ткий terrible, uncanny; мне жу́тко
I am frightened.
жу́хнуть (past жух; pf. за-) dry,
become dull.
жюри́ (indecl.) judges, judging
committee.

З

за (+ inst.) behind, beyond; at;
for; after; because of; за́ го́родом
out of town; за столо́м at the table;
идти́ за до́ктором go for the
doctor; за рабо́той at work; (+acc.)
behind; for; by; е́хать за́ город
go out of town; ему́ за 50 лет
he is over 50; уже́ за́ полночь it's
already gone midnight; за 100 км.
от 100 km. from . . .; за после́дние
пять лет for the past five years;
за два дня до э́того two days
before that; покупа́ть за 10 р.
buy for 10 roubles; я расписа́лся
за него́ I have signed for him;
за и про́тив pros and cons; взять
за́ руку take by the hand.
заба́ва amusement, sport; забавля́ть
amuse; -ся amuse oneself, make
merry; заба́вный amusing, funny.
забаллоти́ровать (pf.) reject, black-
ball.
забасто́вка strike; забасто́вочный
strike (a.); забасто́вщик striker.

забве́ние oblivion.
забе́г heat, round; забега́ть (pf.
забежа́ть*) run, drop in to see
(with к + dat.); з. вперёд run
ahead, put the cart before the
horse.
забива́ть (pf. заби́ть*) drive in;
obstruct; fill up, choke; score
(goal) ; -ся hide; become obstruct-
ed.
забинто́вывать (pf. -ова́ть) bandage.
забира́ть (pf. забра́ть*) take away,
take possession of; -ся climb up,
get (into).
заби́тый downtrodden; заби́ть* (pf.)
start to beat; (see also забива́ть).
заби́яка (m. & f.) bully; rowdy, squ-
abbler.
заблаговре́менный opportune, in
good time.
заблуди́ться (pf.) (-ужу́сь, -у́дишь-
ся) get lost.
заблужда́ться be mistaken; заблужд-
е́ние errог; ввести́ в з. mislead.
забо́й coal-face; забо́йщик (coal-)
hewer.
заболева́ть 1. (pf. забол|е́ть, -и́т)
begin to ache; 2. (pf. забол|е́ть,
-е́ю) fall ill.
забо́р 1. fence; 2. lot of goods bought
in shop.
забо́та anxiety, care, забо́|титы,
(-о́чу, -о́тишь; pf. o-) worry;
-ся (pf. по-) (о + prep.) worry
(about), look after; забо́тливый
considerate, solicitous.
забра́ло visor.
забра́сывать 1. (pf. заброса́ть) pelt,
shower; 2. (pf. забро́сить*) throw;
abandon.
забра́ть see забира́ть.
забреда́ть (pf. забрести́*) stray,
wander; drop in.
заброс|а́ть, -ить see забра́сывать.
забро́шенный derelict, neglected.
забры́згивать (pf. забры́згать) bespatter, splash.
забулды́га (m.) debauchee.
забыва́ть (pf. забы́ть*, ppp. за-
бы́тый) forget; -ся doze off, lose
consciousness; forget oneself; be
forgotten; забы́вчивый forgetful;
забытьё unconsciousness, oblivion.
зава́л obstruction; constipation; за-
ва́ливать (pf. завали́ть*) heap up,
block up; overload; tumble; -ся
fall; be mislaid.

завал|яться *(pf.)* find no market, not sell.

заваривать *(pf.* заварить*)* make, brew.

заведение establishment.

заведование management; **заведовать** *(inst.)* manage, superintend; **заведующий** manager, head.

заведомый notorious **заведомо** deliberately.

заведующий *see* **заведовать.**

заведывать = **заведовать.**

завезти *see* **завозить.**

заверение assertion, protestation; **заверить** *see* **заверять.**

завернуть *see* **завёртывать.**

завертеть* *(pf.)* begin to twirl; turn someone's head; screw up; **-ся** begin to spin; lose one's head.

завёртывать *(pf.* завернуть*)* tuck/wrap up; turn off *(tap)* ; drop in, call; з. за угол turn a corner.

завершать *(pf.* завершить*)* complete, conclude; **завершение** completion, end.

заверять *(pf.* заверить*)* assure; certify, witness; з. его в дружбе assure him of one's friendship.

завеса curtain, screen; **завесить** *see* **завешивать.**

завести *see* **заводить**

завет precept, behest; Ветхий з. the Old Testament; **заветный** cherished; sacred; secret.

завешивать *(pf.* завесить*)* curtain, cover.

завещание testament, will, **завещать** *(ipf. & pf.)* bequeath.

завзятый confirmed, inveterate.

завивать *(pf.* завить*)* curl, wave; **-ся** wave; have one's hair waved, curled; **завивка** waving, wave.

завидный enviable; ему завидно he is envious; **завид|овать** *(pf.* по-*)* envy; не -ую ему его успехам I don't envy him his success.

завинчивать *(pf.* завинтить*)* screw up.

завис|еть (-ишу, -исишь) *(от + gen.)* depend (on); **зависимость** *(f.)* dependence; **зависимый** dependent.

завистливый envious; **завист|ник, ~ница** envier; **зависть** *(f.)* envy.

завитой curled, frizzled, waved; **зави|ток** (-тка) lock; tendril; flourish; **завить** *see* **завивать.**

завком factory committee.

завладевать (-еваю; *pf.* завладеть) *(inst.)* take possession of, seize.

завлекать *(pf.* завлечь*)* entice, lure.

завод factory, works; stud(-farm); winding *(mechanism)* **заводила** *(m. & f.)* *(coll.)* ringleader; **заводить*** *(pf.* завести*)* bring, lead; acquire; establish; wind up; **-ся** be led, acquired, established, wound up; to be in abundance; **заводной** clockwork; **заводской** factory *(a.).*

заводь *(f.)* back-water.

завоевание conquest, achievement; **завоеватель** *(m.)* conqueror; **завоёвывать** *(pf.* заво|евать; *ppp.* -ёванный) conquer, win.

завозить* *(pf.* завезти*)* leave at a place, deliver.

заволакивать *(pf.* заволочь, -оку, -очёшь; *past* -ок, -окла) cloud, cover.

завораживать *(pf.* заворожить) bewitch.

заворачивать 1. *(pf.* завернуть) wrap up; turn; drop in; 2. *(pf.* заворотить*)* tuck/turn up.

завсегдатай habitué.

завтра tomorrow.

завтрак breakfast; **завтракать** *(pf.* по-) breakfast.

завтрашний tomorrow's.

завхоз manager, in charge of premises.

завывать *(pf.* завыть*)* howl.

завышать *(pf.* зав|ысить, -ышу, -ысишь) overstate, overestimate.

завязать *(pf.* завязнуть) stick, get stuck.

завязка 1. string, lace; 2. plot; **завязывать** *(pf.* завязать) 1. tie up; 2. start.

завязь *(f.)* ovary.

загадать *see* **загадывать.**

загадить *see* **загаживать.**

загадка enigma, riddle; **загадочный** mysterious; **загадывать** *(pf.* загадать) set *(riddles etc.)* ; think of *(a number)* ; make plans, guess.

загаживать *(pf.* загадить) make dirty.

загар sunburn, sun-tan.

загвоздка difficulty.

загиб bend, deviation; **загибать** *(pf.* загнуть*)* bend; *(coll.)* exaggerate.

заглáвие title, heading; **заглáвный** title-, capital *(a)*, *(letter)*.
заглáживать *(pf.* заглáдить*) press, smooth; make up for, expiate.
заглóхший neglected, overgrown.
заглушáть *(pf.* заглушúть) muffle, deaden; jam *(broadcast)*; soothe *(pain)*.
заглядéнье feast for the eyes, beautiful sight.
заглядывать *(pf.* заглянýть) peep in; call on (к + *dat.)*; -ся *(pf.* заглядéться*) (на + *acc.)* stare at in wonderment.
загнáть *see* загонять.
загнивáние decay; suppuration; **загнивáть** *(pf.* загнúть*) rot, decay.
загнýть *see* загибáть.
заговáривать *(pf.* заговорúть) 1. (c + *inst.)* speak to, accost; 2. *(acc.)* charm away, cast spell over; -ся talk nonsense; **зáговор** plot; charm, exorcism; **заговóрщик** conspirator.
заголóвок (-вка) heading, title; headline.
загóн enclosure, pen; driving in; **загонять** *(pf* загнáть*) drive in; tire out, override.
загорáживать *(pf.* загор|одúть, -ожý, -óдишь) enclose; obstruct.
загорáть *(pf* загорéть*) become sunburnt, tanned; -ся catch fire, light up; **загорéлый** sunburnt, tanned.
загородúть *see* загорáживать; **загорóдка** fence, enclosure.
зáгородный country *(a.)*, out-of-town.
заготáвливать *(pf.* заготóвить) lay in, store; **заготóвка** State purchases, procurement.
заграждáть *(pf.* загра|дúть, -жý, -дúшь, *ppp.* заграждённый) obstruct, enclose; **заграждéние** barrage; obstacle.
заграницa foreign countries; **заграничный** foreign *(a.)*.
загребáть *(pf.* загрести*) rake up; accumulate, gather.
загрúвок (-вка) withers; back of neck.
загрóбный beyond the grave.
загромо|ждáть *(pf.* загромоздúть*) block up, encumber; **загромождéние** blocking up, overloading.
загрубéлый coarsened, callous.

загружáть *(pf.* загрузúть*) load, feed *(machine)*; **загрýзка** charge, load, *(amount of)* work.
загрызáть *(pf.* загрызть*) bite, worry to death.
загрязнять *(pf.* -нúть) make dirty, pollute;
загс = отдéл зáписей áктов граждáнского состоя́ния registry office.
зад (в -ý, *pl.* -ы́) back, rear part, posterior.
задавáть* *(pf.* задáть*, *past* зáдал -á, -áло) give, set; -ся be given; give oneself airs; -ся цéлью сдéлать чтó-либо set oneself the task to do something; **задáние** task.
задá|ток (-тка) advance, deposit; *(pl.)* ability, promise.
задáть *see* задавáть.
задáча problem, task; **задáчник** book of problems.
задвигáть *(pf.* задвúнуть) push; bolt, bar; **задвú|жка** *(gen. pl.* -жек) bolt; **задвижнóй** sliding *(a.)*.
задевáть (-вáю: *pf.* задéть*) touch, catch against; affect, hurt; з. за живóе cut to the quick.
задéлывать *(pf.* задéлать) do up, close up.
задёргивать *(pf.* задёрнуть) pull, shut.
задеревенéлый hardened, numbed.
задержáние detention; **задéрживать** *(pf.* задéржать*) delay, hold back; arrest; -ся stay too long; be delayed; **задéр|жка** *(gen. pl.* -жек) delay.
задёрнуть *see* задёргивать.
задéть *see* задевáть.
задúра *(m. & f.)* quarrelsome person.
задирáть *(pf.* задрáть*) lift up; tear, split; bully; з. нос turn up one's nose.
зáдн|ий back, rear *(a.)*; -ий план background; -им умóм крéпок wise after the event.
задóлго (до + *gen.)* long before.
задолжáть *see* должáть; **задóлженность** *(f.)* debts, arrears.
зáдом (в + *dat.)* with one's back (to); з. напéрёд back to front.
задóр fervour; **задóрный** provocative; lively.
задохнýться *see* задыхáться.
задрáть *see* задирáть.
задувáть *(pf.* задýть*) blow (out); extinguish.

заду́мчивый pensive, thoughtful; **заду́мывать** *(pf.* заду́мать) plan, conceive; think of *(a number)*; -ся be(come) lost in thought; (над + *inst.)* meditate (on).

заду́ть *see* задува́ть.

задуше́вный sincere, cordial, heart-to-heart.

задыха́ться *(pf.* задохну́ться*) choke, suffocate; (от + *gen.)* choke *(with rage etc.).*

заеда́ть *(pf.* зае́сть*) eat, worry, wear out; jam, stall.

зае́здить* *(pf.)* wear out; ruin *(horse).*

заезжа́ть *(pf.* зае́хать*) (к + *dat.)* call (on), visit.

зае́зженный hackneyed; worn out.

заём (за́йма) loan.

зае́хать *see* заезжа́ть.

зажа́ть *see* зажима́ть.

заже́чь *see* зажига́ть.

зажива́ть *(pf.* зажи́ть*) heal; *(pf. only)* begin to live; -ся overstay one's welcome.

за́живо alive.

зажига́лка cigarette lighter; **зажига́тельный** used for kindling; incendiary; **зажига́ть** *(pf.* заже́чь*) set fire to, light; -ся catch fire.

зажи́м clamp; suppression; **зажима́ть** *(pf.* зажа́ть*) stop up; squeeze; suppress.

зажи́точный prosperous.

зажи́ть *see* зажива́ть.

здздра́вный тост toast.

ззева́ться (-ев ю .ь: *pf.)* (на + *acc.)* gape (at).

зземле́ние earthing *('lectricity)*; **зземля́ть** *(pf.* -ли́ть) earth.

ззн|ава́ться (-аюсь, -аёшься; *pf.* за з а́ться) give oneself airs.

зазо́р *(tech.)* clearance.

ззре́ние twinge *(of conscience).*

зазу́бренный notched, serrated; **зазу́брива́ть** *(pf.* -и́ть*) notch; learn by heart; зазу́брина notch.

за́йгрывание advances; **за́йгрывать** *(pf.* заигра́ть) 1. spoil by playing; 2. (с + *inst.)* flirt (with); -ся play too long.

за́йка *(m. & f)* stammerer; **заика́ться** 1. stammer, stutter; 2. *(pf.* заикну́ться) mention.

займствование borrowing; **займство-ва́ть** *(ipf. & pf., also* по-) adopt, borrow.

за́йндевелый covered with hoarfrost.

заинтерес|о́вывать *(pf.* -ова́ть) interest; interest materially.

за́йскивать (пе́ред + *inst.)* curry favour (with).

зайти́ *see* заходи́ть.

за́йчик little hare; sunbeam, reflection; зайчи́ха doe hare.

закабаля́ть *(pf.* -и́ть) enslave.

закавка́зский Transcaucasian.

зака́дычный друг bosom friend.

зака́з order; заказн|о́й made to order; -о́е письмо́ registered letter; **зака́з-чик** client, customer; **зака́зывать** *(pf.* заказа́ть*) order.

зака́л temper; cast; **зака́ливать** = **закаля́ть; зака́лка** hardening, toughening.

зака́лывать *(pf.* заколо́ть*) stab; pin up.

закал|я́ть *(pf.* -и́ть) temper, strengthen.

зака́нчивать *(pf.* зако́нчить) finish.

зака́пывать *(pf.* закопа́ть) bury; fill up.

зака́рмливать *(pf.* закорми́ть*) overfeed.

закаспи́йский Transcaspian.

зака́т sunset; **зака́тывать** 1. *(pf.* закати́ть) roll up, wrap in; 2. *(pf.* закати́ть*) roll; -ся roll; set *(of sun).*

заква́ска ferment, leaven; mettle.

заки́дывать 1. *(pf.* закида́ть) shower, pelt; fill up; 2. *(pf.* заки́нуть) throw back.

закипа́ть *(pf.* закипе́ть*) begin to boil; be in full swing.

закиса́ть *(pf.* заки́снуть*) turn sour; go rusty *(fig.)*; за́кись *(f.)* protoxide.

закла́д pawning; pledge; bet; би́ться об з. bet, wager; закла́дка laying; bookmark; закладна́я mortgage; **закла́дывать** *(pf.* зал|ожи́ть, -ожу́, -ожишь) put, lay; install; lay foundation of; pawn; harness; нос заложи́ло my nose is stuffed up.

закле́ивать *(pf.* закле́ить) glue up.

закле́пка rivet; **заклёпывать** *(pf.* закл(па́ть) rivet; clinch.

заклина́ние exorcism, invocation; **заклина́тель** *(m.)* charmer *(of snakes)*; заклина́ть adjure; charm, conjure.

заключ|а́ть *(pf.* -и́ть) conclude, infer; close, finish, contract; contain; imprison; -ся end; consist (in) *(with* в + *prep.)* заключе́ние сопclusion, inference; imprisonment; detention; **заключённый** prisoner; **заключительный** final, closing.

заклятие invocation; oath, pledge; **заклятый** sworn *(e. g. enemy).*

заковывать *(pf.* заковать*) chain, put in irons.

заковыка, -ырка hitch, obstacle.

заколачивать *(pf.* заколотить*) board up; drive in *(nails).*

заколд|овывать *(pf.* -овать) enchant; put spell on; -ованный круг vicious circle.

заколка hair-grip.

заколотить *see* **заколачивать.**

заколоть *see* **закалывать.**

закон law; **законность** *(f.)* legality; **законный** legal, legitimate.

законо|ведение jurisprudence; **∼да-тельный** legislative; **∼дательство** legislation; **∼мерность** *(f.)* conformity with law; **∼мерный** regular, natural; **∼проект** bill, draft law.

законченность *(f.)* finish, gloss; completeness

закончить *see* **заканчивать.**

закопать *see* **закапывать.**

закоптелый sooty, smutty.

закоренелый ingrained, inveterate.

закостенелый numbed, stiff.

закоу|лок (-лка) back street; nook. закоченелый numb.

закра́дываться *(pf.* закрасться*) steal, creep in.

закра́ина edge; flange.

закрепление fastening, fixing; consolidation; **закреп|ля́ть** *(pf.* -ить) fasten, fix; consolidate; seal; з. за собой место secure a place.

закрепо|ща́ть *(pf.* -стить, -щу́, -стишь) enslave.

закрой|щик, ∼щица cutter *(of clothes).*

закром *(pl.* -а́) corn-bin.

закругление rounding; curve.

закругл|я́ть *(pf.*-ить) round (off).

закручивать *(pf.* закрутить*) twist; turn tight *(tap etc.).*

закрыва́ть *(pf.* закрыть*) close, shut; -ся close; **закрытие** closing; **закрытый** shut, closed.

закулисный behind-the-scenes.

закупа́ть *(pf.* закупить*) buy in; lay in a stock of; **закупка** purchase.

закупор|ивать *(pf.* -ить) cork, stop up; **закупорка** corking; thrombosis.

закуп|щик, ∼щица buyer.

закуривать *(pf.* закурить*) light *(cigarette etc.).*

закуска hors d'oeuvre; snack; **закусочная** snack-bar; **закусывать** *(pf.* зак|усить, -ушу́, -у́сишь) bite; have a snack.

закутывать *(pf.* закутать) wrap up.

зал hall, room; **зала** (reception) room.

зала́мывать *(pf.* заломить*): з. цену ask too high a price; з. руки wring one's hands.

залега́ние bedding, seam; **залега́ть** lie, be deposited *(geol.).*

заледенелый covered with ice.

залёживаться *(pf.* залежа́ться*) lie a long time; find no market; become stale; **залежный** fallow; **залежь** *(f.)* deposit, bed; stale goods; fallow.

залеза́ть *(pf.* зале́зть*) climb, creep.

зале|пля́ть *(pf.* -пить*) close, glue up.

залета́ть *(pf.* залете́ть*) fly (in); **залётный** stray.

зале́чивать *(pf.* залечить*) cure, heal.

залив bay, gulf.

залива́ть *(pf.* залить*) flood; spread *(e.g. with asphalt)* pour, spill; -ся be poured *etc.;* overflow with, break into *(tears, laughter);* заливной water-, flood-; jellied.

зали́зывать *(pf.* зализать*) lick (clean); sleek down.

зало́г pawning; deposit, guarantee, security; voice *(gram.);* **заложить** *see* **закла́дывать; зало́ж|ник, ∼ница** hostage.

залп volley, salvo; выпить залпом drink at one gulp.

зама́зка putty; puttying; **зама́зывать** *(pf.* замазать*) paint; besmear; putty.

зама́лчивать *(pf.* замолча́ть*) hush up.

зама́нивать *(pf.* замани́ть*) entice; **зама́нчивый** tempting.

зама́тывать *(pf.* замота́ть) roll up.

зама́хиваться *(pf.* замахну́ться) *(inst.)* brandish; з. на него чем-либо threaten him with something.

зама́чивать *(pf.* замочить*) wet.

зама́|шка *(gen. pl.* -шек) manner, way.

зама́щивать *(pf.* замости́ть*) pave.

замедление slowing down, deceleration; **замедля́ть** *(pf.* заме́длить) slow down.

заме́на substitution; **заменя́ть** *(pf.* зам|ени́ть, -еню́, -е́нишь; *ppp.* -енённый)* substitute, replace.

замере́ть *see* замира́ть.

замерза́н|ие freezing; то́чка -ия freezing-point; **замерза́ть** *(pf.* замёрзнуть*)* freeze, be frozen.

за́мертво as good as dead; in a dead faint.

замести́ *see* замета́ть.

замести́тель *(m.)* deputy; **замести́тельство** substitution; proxy; **замести́ть** *see* замеща́ть.

замета́ть *(pf.* замести́*)* sweep up; cover.

заме́тка note, notice; **заме́тный** appreciable, noticeable, visible; **замеча́ние** remark; reproof; **замеча́тельный** remarkable; **замеча́ть** *(pf.* заме́тить*)* notice, observe, remark.

замеша́тельство confusion, embarrassment.

заме́шивать 1. *(pf.* замеша́ть)* involve; implicate.

заме́шивать 2. *(pf.* замеси́ть*)* mix, knead.

замеща́ть *(pf.* заме|сти́ть, -щу́, -сти́шь)* deputize for, replace; **замеще́ние** substitution, replacement.

замина́ть *(pf.* замя́ть*)* smother, hush up; **-ся** become confused, falter.

зами́нка hitch; hesitation *(in speech).*

замира́н|ие: с -ием се́рдца with sinking heart; **замира́ть** *(pf.* замере́ть*)* stand stock-still; die away.

за́мкнутость *(f.)* reserve, reticence; **за́мкнутый** closed; reserved, exclusive.

за́|мок (-мка) castle; **за|мо́к** (-мка́) lock; под замко́м under lock and key.

замо́лвить *(pf.)* : з. слове́чко за него́ put in a word for him.

замолка́ть *(pf.* замо́лкнуть, *past* -о́лк)* fall silent.

замолча́ть *see* зама́лчивать.

заморá|живать *(pf.* заморо́зить*)* freeze; **за́морозк|и** (-ов) frosts.

замо́рский foreign, overseas *(a.).*

замо́чн|ый lock *(a.);* -ая сква́жина keyhole.

за́муж: выдава́ть з. (за + *acc.*)* give in marriage (to); выходи́ть з. (за + *acc.*)* get married (to); **за́мужем**

(за + *inst.*)* married (to); **заму́жний** married *(a.).*

замур|о́вывать *(pf.* -ова́ть)* immure.

замусо́ленный bespattered, marked.

за́мша suede, chamois; **за́мшевый** suede.

замыва́ть *(pf.* замы́ть*)* wash away.

замыка́ние closing *(of circuit)* ; **замыка́ть** *(pf.* замкну́ть)* lock, close; **-ся** be closed *etc.* ; become reserved, sullen.

замы́|сел (-сла) project, plan; **замыслова́тый** complicated; **замышля́ть** *(pf.* замы́слить)* plan, contemplate.

замя́ть *see* замина́ть.

за́навес curtain *(e. g. in theatre)* ; **занаве́ска** curtain; **занаве́шивать** *(pf.* занаве́сить*)* curtain.

зана́шивать *(pf.* заноси́ть*)* wear too long.

занемога́ть *(pf.* занемо́чь*)* fall ill.

занести́ *see* заноси́ть.

зани|жа́ть *(pf.* зан|и́зить, -и́жу, -и́зишь)* lower, understate.

занима́тельный entertaining; **занима́ть** *(pf.* заня́ть, займ|у́, -ёшь; за́нял, -á, за́няло; *ppp.* за́нятый)* occupy; engage, interest; **-ся** be occupied *etc.* ; *(with inst.)* engage (in), study.

за́ново anew, all over again.

зано́за splinter; quarrelsome person; **зано|зи́ть** *(pf.)* (-жу́, -зи́шь) з. себе́ ру́ку get a splinter in one's hand.

зано́с skidding; snow-drift; **заноси́ть*** *(pf.* занести́*)* bring; note down; cover; *(see also* **зана́шивать).**

зано́счивый arrogant.

заня́тие occupation; seizure; **заня́тный** entertaining, amusing; **заня́той**, **за́нятый** occupied, busy; **заня́ть** *see* занима́ть.

заоблачный beyond the clouds, transcendental.

заодно́ at the same time; in concert, at one.

заостр|я́ть *(pf.* -и́ть)* sharpen; emphasize.

зао́чник external student; **зао́чный** extramural, correspondence *(a.),* *e. g. course)* ; by default.

за́пад west; **запада́ть** *(pf.* запа́сть*)* sink; fall; **за́падный** western.

западня́ *(gen. pl.* -не́й)* snare, trap.

запа́здывать *(pf.* запозда́ть)* be late.

запа́ивать *(pf.* запая́ть)* solder; **запа́йка** soldering.

запак|о́вывать (pf. -ова́ть) pack, wrap up.

запа́л 1. broken wind (of horse); 2. fuse, primer; запа́льная свеча́ sparking plug; запа́льчивый quick-tempered.

запанибра́та: быть з. с + inst. hobnob with.

запа́с stock, supply; запаса́ть (pf. запа|сти́, -су́, -сёшь; запа́с, -ла́; ppp. запасённый) stock, store; -ся (inst.) provide oneself with; запа́сливый thrifty; запасно́й, запа́сный reserve; emergency.

запа́сть see запада́ть.

за́пах smell.

запа́хивать 1. (pf. запаха́ть*) plough.

запа́хивать 2. (pf. запахну́ть) wrap up; -ся (в + acc.) wrap oneself (in).

запа́хнуть (pf.) (inst.) start to smell (of).

запа́шка tillage.

запая́ть see запа́ивать.

запе́в introductory verse/part of song; запева́ла (m.) leader (of choir); запева́ть (-ева́ю; pf. запе́ть*) lead the singing, set the tune.

запека́нка shepherd's pie; baked pudding; brandy; запека́ть (pf. запе́чь*) bake; -ся bake; coagulate; become parched.

запере́ть see запира́ть.

запе́ть see запева́ть.

запечатл|ева́ть (-ева́ю; pf. -е́ть) impress, imprint.

запеча́т|ывать (pf. -ать) seal up.

запе́чь see запека́ть.

запива́ть (pf. запи́ть*) take to drinking; wash down (e. g. medicine with water).

запина́ться (pf. запну́ться) stammer, falter; запи́нк|а: без -и fluently, smoothly.

запира́ть (pf. за|пере́ть,-пру́,-прёшь; за́пер, -ла́, за́перло, ppa. запе́рший; ppp. за́пертый) lock; -ся be locked; lock oneself up.

запи́ска note; записно́й 1. note (a.); 2. (coll) inveterate; запи́сывать (pf. записа́ть*) note; enter; record; -ся register; be noted etc. -ся на приём к врачу́ make an appointment to see a doctor; за́пись (f.) writing down; entry, record, recording.

запи́ть see запива́ть.

запи́хивать (pf. запих|а́ть, -ну́ть) push, shove.

заппа́канный tear-stained; запла́кать* (pf.) start crying.

запла́та patch.

заплёванный bespattered; dirty.

заплёсневелый mouldy.

заплета́ть (pf. заплести́*) braid, plait; -ся: у него́ язы́к заплета́ется he mumbles, stumbles.

заплёчье shoulder-blade.

заплыва́ть (pf. заплы́ть*) swim, sail (in); become fat, bloated.

запну́ться see запина́ться.

запове́дник preserve, reserve; запове́дный forbidden, reserved; за́поведь (f.) commandment, precept.

заподо́зривать (pf. заподо́зрить) (в + prep.) suspect (of).

запозда́лый belated, delayed; запозда́ть see запа́здывать.

заполза́ть (pf. заползти́*) crawl, creep (in).

заполня́ть (pf. запо́лнить) fill in (form, time, gap).

запомина́ть (pf. запо́мнить) memorize.

за́понка cuff-link, stud.

запо́р lock, bolt; constipation; дверь на -е the door is locked.

запоро́|жец (-жца) Dnieper Cossack.

запоте́лый misted (e. g. glass).

запра́вила (m.) boss.

запра́вка seasoning; refuelling; заправля́ть (pf. запра́вить) season; trim; refuel.

запра́вочн|ый: -ая ста́нция filling station.

запра́вский real, true.

запра́шивать (pf. запроси́ть*) enquire.

запре́т interdiction; запре́тный forbidden; запреща́ть (pf. запре|ти́ть, -щу́, -ти́шь) forbid; запреще́ние prohibition.

запрода́жа provisional sale.

запроки́дывать (pf. запроки́нуть) throw back.

запро́с enquiry; overcharge; (pl.) needs; запроси́ть see запра́шивать.

запру́да dam, weir; mill-pond; запру́живать (pf. запруди́ть*) dam, dike.

запряга́ть (pf. запря́чь*) harness; запря́жка harness; team.

запря́тывать (pf. запря́тать*) hide.

запу́гивать (pf. запуга́ть) intimidate.

за́пуск launching (of spaceships etc.); **запуска́ть** (pf. запусти́ть*) start, launch; neglect.

запусте́лый desolate, neglected; **запусте́ние** desolation.

запусти́ть see **запуска́ть**.

запу́тывать (pf. запу́тать) tangle, confuse; -ся (в + acc.) become involved (in); **запу́танный** intricate.

запу́щенность (f.) neglect.

запылённый covered in dust.

запыха́ться (pf., coll.) be out of breath.

запя́стье wrist; bracelet.

запята́я comma.

зараба́тывать (pf. зарабо́тать) earn; **за́работн|ый**: -ая пла́та wage, pay; **за́рабо|ток** (-тка) earnings.

зара́внивать (pf. заровня́ть) level, even up.

заража́ть (pf. зара|зи́ть, -жу́, -зи́шь) infect, contaminate; -ся become infected; (inst.) catch (a disease); **зараже́ние** infection.

зара́з at one stroke.

зара́за infection; contagion; **зарази́тельный** infectious; **зарази́ть** see **заража́ть**; **зара́зный** infectious.

зара́нее beforehand, in good time.

зараста́ть (pf. зарасти́*) be overgrown; heal.

за́рево glow.

заре́з: до -у desperately; **заре́зывать** (pf. заре́зать*) kill, slaughter.

зарека́ться (pf. заре́чься; -еку́сь, -ечёшься; -ёкся, -екла́сь) (coll.) renounce, give up.

зарекомендова́ть (pf.): з. себя́ (inst.) present oneself (as).

заржа́вленный rusty.

зарисо́вка sketching; sketch.

зарни́ца lightning, flash.

заро́дыш embryo; **зарожда́ть** (pf. зароди́ть*) engender; -ся be conceived; arise; **зарожде́ние** conception; origin.

заро́к pledge, vow.

зар|они́ть (-оню́, -о́нишь) drop; arouse (e. g. doubt).

за́росль (f.) undergrowth, thicket; **заро́сший** overgrown.

зарпла́та pay, wages.

зару́ба (pf. заруби́ть*) notch; kill; заруби́ себе́ э́то на носу́/лбу! put that in your pipe and smoke it!

зарубе́жный foreign.

заруби́ть see **заруба́ть**: **зару́бка** notch.

заруб|цо́вываться (pf. -цева́ться) cicatrize.

заруча́ться (pf. заручи́ться) (inst.) enlist (e. g. support); **зару́чка** (coll.) 'pull', protection.

зарыва́ть (pf. зары́ть*) bury.

заря́ (pl. зо́ри, зорь) glow, dawn, sunset; на заре́ at daybreak; от зари́ до зари́ all night long.

заря́д charge; supply; **заря́дка** charging; loading; physical exercises; **заряжа́ть** (pf. заря|ди́ть, -яжу́, -я́дишь) load, charge.

заса́да ambush.

заса́живать (pf. заса|ди́ть, -ажу́, -а́дишь) plant; drive in; put (in jail, to work); -ся (pf. засе́сть*) sit down; settle oneself.

заса́ливать 1. (pf. засоли́ть*, ppp. засо́ленный) salt, pickle.

заса́ливать (pf. заса́лить) make greasy.

заса́сывать (pf. засоса́ть*) suck in, swallow up.

заса́хар|ивать (pf. -ить) ice, candy.

засе́в sowing; seed; sown area; **засева́ть** (-ева́ю; pf. засе́ять*) sow.

заседа́ние meeting; session; **заседа́тель** (m.) assessor; **заседа́ть** sit in conference.

засека́ть (pf. засе́чь*) flog to death; notch.

засел|я́ть (pf. -и́ть) populate, settle.

засе́сть see **заса́живаться**.

засе́чь see **засека́ть**.

заси́живать (pf. засиде́ть*) spot; **заси́женный** му́хами fly-blown; -ся stay too long.

заси́лье dominance.

заска́кивать (pf. заск|очи́ть, -очу́, -о́чишь) jump, spring; (coll.) drop in.

заско́к kink, peculiarity.

заскору́злый hardened, horny.

заслёнка damper, oven door; **заслон|я́ть** (pf. -и́ть) cover, shield, screen.

заслу́га merit; service; **заслу́ж|енный**, **-ённый** honoured; **заслу́живать** (pf. заслужи́ть*) deserve, earn; (with gen.) be worthy of.

заслу́шивать (pf. заслу́шать) listen to, hear; -ся listen with delight.

засма́триваться (pf. засмотре́ться*) (на + acc.) be lost in contemplation.

заснежённый snowed up.

заснуть *see* засыпать.

засов bar, bolt; засовывать *(pf.* засунуть) push in.

засол salting, pickling.

засор|ять *(pf.* -ить) litter; obstruct, choke up.

засосать *see* засасывать.

засохнуть *see* засыхать; засохший dry, withered.

заспанный sleepy.

заспирт|овывать *(pf.* -овать) preserve in alcohol.

застава gate, frontier post.

заст|авать (-аю, -аёшь; *pf.* застать*) find, catch in/at home.

заставка illumination *(in manuscript).*

заставлять *(pf.* заставить) compel, make; cram, block up.

застаиваться *(pf.* застояться*) stand too long; go stale.

застарелый ingrained; neglected.

застать *see* заставать.

застёгивать *(pf.* застегнуть) do up, button, clasp; -ся be buttoned *etc.*; button oneself up; застёжка *(gen. pl.* -жек) fastening, clasp; з. -молния zip-fastener.

застекл|ять *(pf.* -ить) glaze.

засте́нок (-нка) torture-chamber.

застенчивый shy.

застигать *(pf.* застигнуть, застичь, -игну, -игнешь; -иг) catch, (take by) surprise.

застилать *(pf.* застлать*, *ppp.* застеленный) cover; lay, spread.

застой stagnation.

застольн|ый: -ая беседа table talk.

застоится *see* застаиваться.

застраивать *(pf.* застроить) build, develop.

застрах|овывать *(pf.* -овать) insure.

застревать (-еваю; *pf.* застр|ять, -яну, -янешь) stick, get stuck.

застреливать *(pf.* застр|елить, -елю, -елишь) shoot, kill; -ся shoot oneself; застрельщик pioneer, leader.

застроить *see* застраивать; застр|ойка *(gen. pl.* -оек) building, development.

застрять *see* застревать.

застуживать *(pf.* застудить*) cool, chill.

заступ spade; shovel.

заступ|аться *(pf.* -иться*) (за + *acc.*) intercede(for), stand up(for); за-

ступ|ник, ~ница defender, patron; заступничество intercession.

застывать *(pf.* заст|ыть, -ыну, -ынешь) thicken, harden; be stiff with cold.

засунуть *see* засовывать.

засуха drought.

засучивать *(pf.* зас|учить, -учу, -учишь) roll up *(e. g. sleeves).*

засушивать *(pf.* засушить*) dry up.

засчитывать *(pf.* засчитать) take into consideration/account.

засылать *(pf.* заслать*) send a long way *or* to wrong place.

засыпать 1. *(pf.* засыпать*) fill up; cover; strew.

засыпать 2. *(pf.* заснуть) fall asleep.

засыхать *(pf.* засохнуть*) dry up.

затаивать *(pf.* затаить) harbour; hold *(one's breath)*; затаённый secret; repressed.

затапливать *(pf.* затопить*) light *(stove)*, kindle.

затаптывать *(pf.* затоптать*) trample down.

затаскивать 1. *(pf.* затаскать) wear out, overwork; затасканный threadbare; hackneyed; 2. *(pf.* затащить*) carry, drag away.

затачивать *(pf.* заточить*) sharpen.

затвердевать (-еваю; *pf.* затвердеть) become hard.

затвор bolt, lock; seclusion; затворник recluse; затворять *(pf.* затв|орить, -орю, -оришь) close, shut.

затевать (-еваю; *pf.* зат|еять, -ею, -еешь) venture, undertake; затейливый ingenious, intricate.

затекать *(pf.* затечь*) flow, pour; become numb.

затем then, thereupon.

затемнение darkening; black-out; затемн|ять *(pf.* -ить) darken, obscure; black out.

затен|ить *(pf.* -ить) shade.

затереть *see* затирать.

затеривать *(pf.* затерять) mislay; -ся be mislaid; be(come) lost.

затечь *see* затекать.

затея undertaking, venture; затеять *see* затевать.

затирать *(pf.* зат|ереть*) rub over; jam.

затискивать *(pf.* затиснуть) squeeze.

затихать *(pf.* затихнуть, *past* -тих) calm down; затишье calm, lull.

заткнуть *see* затыкать.

затмевáть (-евáю; *pf.* затмúть) cover, darken, eclipse; **затмéние** eclipse.
затó in return; on the other hand.
затовáривание glut *(of goods)*.
затóн back-water, creek.
затоплéние flooding; **затоп|лять** *(pf.* -йть) flood; sink.
затоптáть *see* затáптывать.
затóр obstruction, (traffic) jam.
заточáть *(pf.* заточúть 1) incarcerate; **заточéние** incarceration, seclusion;
заточúть 2 *see* затáчивать.
затó|чка *(gen. pl.* -чек) groove, recess; sharpening.
затрáгивать *(pf.* затрóнуть) affect, touch upon.
затрáта expenditure; **затрáчивать** *(pf.* затрáтить*) spend.
затрéбовать *(pf.)* *(acc.)* require.
затруднéние difficulty, embarrassment; **затруднúтельный** difficult; **затрудн|ять** *(pf.* -úть) hamper, make difficult; **-ся** (+ *inf.)* hesitate (to).
затумáн|ивать *(pf.* -ить) cloud, dim.
затуп|лять *(pf.* -úть*) blunt, dull.
затухáть *(pf.* затýхнуть*) go out slowly; be extinguished/damped.
затуш|ёвывать *(pf.* -евáть) shade; conceal.
зáтхлый mouldy, musty; stuffy.
затыкáть *(pf.* заткнýть) stop up; thrust, stick.
затý|лок (-лка) back of the head; neck *(meat).*
заты́|чка *(gen. pl.* -чек) plug; *(fig.)* stop-gap.
затя́гивать *(pf.* затянýть) tighten; cover, close; drag out, prolong; drag in; **затя́|жка** *(gen. pl.* -жек) inhalation; delay, prolongation; **затяжнóй** protracted.
заýмный abstruse.
заунывный mournful.
заурядный ordinary, commonplace.
заусéница agnail.
заýтреня matins.
заýчивать *(pf.* заучúть*) learn by heart, prepare.
заýшница mumps.
зафрахтóвывать *(pf.* -овáть) charter.
захвáт capture, seizure; **захвáтнический** predatory; **захвáтчик** aggressor; **захвáтывать** *(pf.* захватúть*) take, seize.
ахлёбываться *(pf.* захлебнýться) (от + *gen.)* choke, swallow the

wrong way; be beside oneself (with).
захлёстывать *(pf.* захлестнýть; *ppp.* захлёстнутый) overwhelm, sweep over; lash round.
захлóпывать *(pf.* захлóпнуть) slam; shut in; **-ся** be slammed, slam.
захóд sunset; stopping *(at a place)* **заходúть*** *(pf.* зайтú*) call, drop in; (за + *inst.)* call for; (к + *dat.)* call on.
захолýстный remote; **захолýстье** out-of-the-way place.
захудáлый poor, shabby.
зацветáть *(pf.* зацвестú*) blossom, bloom.
зацепля́ть *(pf.* зац|епúть, -еплю, -éпишь) catch, engage, hook on; **-ся** be caught, catch.
зачар|óвывать *(pf.* -овáть) captivate.
зачастýю often.
зачáтие conception; **зачáточный** rudimentary, embryonic.
зачéм what for, why.
зачёркивать *(pf.* зачеркнýть; *ppp.* зачёркнутый) cross out.
зачéрпывать *(pf.* зачерпнýть) draw, scoop (out).
зачерствéлый stale; *(fig.)* unfeeling.
зачéрчивать *(pf.* зачертúть*) sketch; cover with lines.
зачéсть *see* зачúтывать.
зачёсывать *(pf.* зачесáть*) comb/ brush back.
зачёт: получúть/сдать з. pass an exam; постáрить ему з. pass him.
зачúн beginning; **зачúнщик** instigator.
зачисля́ть *(pf.* зачúслить) enter, include, list.
зачúтывать 1. *(pf.* за|чéсть, -чтý, -чтёшь, *past* -чёл, -члá, *ppp.* -чтённый) reckon; pass, accept; 2. *(pf.* зачитáть) read out; **-ся** *(inst.)* become engrossed (in).
зашвыривать *(pf.* зашвырнýчт) throw away.
зашивáть *(pf.* зашúть*) sew up; mend.
зашнур|óвывать *(pf.* -овáть) lace up.
зашпакл|ёвывать *(pf.* -евáть) putty.
зашпúливать *(pf.* зашпúлить) pin up.
защёлка latch; trigger; **защёлкивать** *(pf.* защёлкнуть) snap to; **-ся** close with a snap.
защемля́ть *(pf.* защемúть) jam, nip.

защи́та defence; защи́тник defender; защи́тный protective; защища́ть *(pf.* защи|ти́ть, -щу́, -ти́шь) defend, protect.

зая́вка (на + *acc.)* claim, demand, application (for); заявле́ние statement; application; заявля́ть *(pf.* заяви́ть*)* declare, announce.

зая́длый inveterate.

за́яц (за́йца) hare; traveller without a ticket; за́я|чий hare's; -чья губа́ hare-lip.

зва́ние rank, title; зва́ный обед dinner party; зва́тельный vocative; звать (зов|у́, -ёшь, *past* звал, -а́; *pf.* по-) call, summon; *(pf.* на-) name; как вас зову́т? what is your name?

звезда́ *(pl.* зве́зды) star; звёздный starry; stellar; звёздо|чка *(gen. pl.* -чек) star; asterisk.

звене́ть (-ню́, -ни́шь; *pf.* за-, про-) ring.

звено́ *(pl.* зве́|нья, -ньев) link; team, unit; звеньево́й unit leader.

звери́|нец (-нца) menagerie; звери́ный of wild animal; bestial, brutal; зверово́дство fur farming; зверо́лов trapper; зве́рский brutal; зве́рство atrocity; зве́рствовать commit atrocities.

зверь *(m.; pl.* -и, -е́й) wild beast; зверьё wild animals.

звон peal, ringing; звони́ть *(pf.* по-) ring; з. в ко́локол ring a bell; з. ему́ по телефо́ну give him a ring; звонкий *(compr.* зво́нче) ringing, clear; зво|но́к (-нка́) bell.

звук sound.

звуко|за́пись *(f.)* recording; ~непроница́емый sound-proof; ~подража́ние onomatopeia.

зву|ча́ть (-чи́т; *pf.* за-, про-) sound; зву́чный sonorous.

звя́кать *(pf.* звя́кнуть) tinkle.

зга: ни зги не ви́дно it is pitch dark.

зда́ние building, edifice.

здесь here; зде́шний local, of this place.

здоро́в|аться (-аюсь; *pf.* по-) (с + *inst.)* greet, say how do you do (to).

здорове́нный strong, hefty.

здоро́во! well done!; здоро́во 1. hello; 2. healthily; здоро́вый healthy; здоро́вье health.

здра́вие = здоро́вье.

здра́вница sanatorium.

здраво|мы́слие common sense; ~мы́слящий sober, sane; ~охране́ние care of public health.

здра́вств овать be well, prosper; да -уст . . .! long live . . .!; здра́вствуй(те) how do you do.

здра́вый sensible; з. смысл common sense.

зев pharynx; gullet.

зева́ка *(m. & f.)* idler; зева́ть (зева́ю; *pf.* зевну́ть) yawn; *(pf.* прозева́ть) let slip; зе|во́к(-вка́) yawn; зево́та yawning.

зелене́ть *(pf.* за-, по-) become green; show green; зеленно́й greengrocery *(a.)* : зеленщи́к (-а́) greengrocer; зелёный green; зе́лень *(f.)* verdure; greenery; greens.

зе́лье potion.

земе́льный land *(a.).*

земле|веде́ние geography; ~владе́|лец (-льца) landowner; ~де́|лец (-льца) farmer, agriculturalist; ~де́лие agriculture; ~де́льческий agricultural *(a.)*; ~ко́п navvy, labourer; ~ме́р surveyor; ~ро́йка *(gen. pl.* -ро́ек) shrew; ~трясе́ние earthquake; ~черпа́лка excavator, steam shovel.

земли́стый earthy.

земля́ (зе́млю, *pl.* зе́мли, земе́ль, зе́млям) earth, land; земля́к (-а́) fellow-countryman; земляни́ка strawberry, -berries; земл|я́нин *(pl.* -я́не, -я́н) earthman; земля́нка dug-out; земляно́й earth *(a.);* з. оре́х groundnut; земля́чество society of people from same area; земля́|чка *(gen. pl.* -чек) fellow-countrywoman.

земново́дный amphibious; земно́й earthly; з. шар globe.

зе́мский zemstvo *(a.);* з. нача́льник land captain *(hist.);* з. собо́р assembly of the land *(hist.);* зе́мство zemstvo, organ of local government *(hist.).*

зени́т zenith; зени́тный anti-aircraft.

зени́ца pupil *(of eye).*

зе́рк|ало *(pl.* -ала́, -а́л, -ала́м) mirror; зерка́льный mirror *(a.);* smooth.

зерни́стый grainy, granular; soft *(caviar);* зерно́ *(pl.* зёрна *(a.)* grain; kernel, core; зерново́й grain *(a.);* зернохрани́лище granary.

зефи́р zephyr; soufflé; sweet.

зигзáг zigzag; **зигзагообрáзный** zigzag *(a.).*

зи́ждиться на be based/founded on.

зимá (зи́му *pl.* зи́мы) winter; **зи́мний** winter *(a.);* **зимовáть** *(pf.* пɛрɛ-, про-) spend the winter; hibernate; **зимóвка** wintering, hibernation; **зимóвье** winter cabin; **зимостóйкий** winter *(a.),* cold-resistant.

зипу́н (-á) homespun coat.

зия́ть gape.

злак cereal.

злáто = зóлото gold.

злить *(pf.* обо-, разо-) anger, irritate; **-ся** be angry, annoyed.

зло *(gen. pl.* зол) evil; harm; **злóба** anger, spite; **злóбный** malicious.

злободнéвный topical, vital.

зло|вéщий ominous; **~вóние** stink; **~вóнный** stinking; **~врéдный** harmful.

злодéй villain; **злодéйский** villainous; **злодéйство, злодея́ние** crime, evil deed.

злой wicked, vicious; (на + *acc.)* angry (with).

зло|кáчественный malignant; **~намéренный** ill-intentioned; **~пáмятный** rancorous; **~полу́чный** ill-fated; **~рáдный** gloating, malicious; **~рáдство** malicious joy; **~слóвие** malicious talk.

злóстный malicious; **злость** *(f.)* malice.

злоумы́шленник malefactor.

злоупотреб|лéние misuse, abuse; **~ля́ть** *(pf.* -и́ть) *(inst.)* abuse, misuse.

злю́ка *(m. & f.)* malicious person.

змееви́дный serpentine; **змей́ный** snake *(a.);* **змей** 1. serpent; 2. (paper) kite; **змея́** *(pl.* змéи) snake.

знак sign, symbol, mark.

знакóмить *(pf.* по-) acquaint; **-ся** (с + *inst.)* make acquaintance (of), meet; **знакóмство** acquaintance; **знакóмый** familiar, known; acquaintance.

знаменáтель *(m.)* denominator; **знаменáтельный** significant.

знáмение sign.

знамени́тость *(f.)* celebrity; **знамени́тый** famous.

знаменовáть signify.

знаменó|сец (-сца) standard-bearer; **знá|мя** *(neut.; gen.; dat.; prep.* -мени,

inst. -менем, *pl.* -мёна) banner, flag.

знáние knowledge.

знáтный notable;

зна|тóк (-токá) expert, connoisseur; **знать** 1. *(f.)* nobility, elite.

знать 2. know; **давáть ему́ знать** let him know; **-ся** с + *inst.* associate with.

знáхарка sorceress; quack; **знáхарь** *(m.)* sorcerer; quack.

значéние significance, importance, meaning; **значи́тельный** significant, important, considerable; **знáчить** mean; **-ся** be mentioned, appear.

зна|чóк (-чкá) mark; badge.

знобúть: мɛня́ -и́т I feel shiverish.

зной intense heat; **знóйный** hot.

зоб (в -у́, *pl.* -ы́) crop, craw; goitre.

зов call.

зóдчество architecture; **зóдчий** architect.

золá ashes.

золóвка sister-in-law *(husband's sister).*

золоти́стый golden; **золо|ти́ть** (-чу́, -ти́шь; *pf.* вы́-, по-) gild; **зóлото** gold; **золотоискáтель** *(m.)* gold-prospector; **золотóй** gold *(a.).*

золоту́ха scrofula; **золоту́шный** scrofulous.

золочёный gilt.

зóлушка Cinderella.

зóна zone.

зонд probe; **зонди́ровать** *(ipf. & pf.)* probe.

зонт, -ик umbrella.

зоóл|ог zoologist; **~оги́ческий** zoological; **~óгия** zoology; **зоопáрк** zoo.

зóркий *(compr.* зóрче) keen-sighted; **зóрька** dawn, glow.

зра|чóк (-чкá) pupil *(of eye).*

зрéлище sight, spectacle.

зрéлост|ь *(f.)* maturity; ripeness; **аттɛстáт -и** school-leaving certificate; **зрéлый** mature, ripe.

зрéн|ие sight; **с тóчки -ия** from the point of view (+ *gen.)* (of).

зреть 1. *(pf.* со-) ripen, mature.

зреть 2. (зрю, зришь; *pf.* у-) behold; **зри́тель** *(m.)* spɛctator; **зри́тельный** visual, optic; **з. зал** auditorium.

зря to no purpose.

зря́чий able to see.

зуб *(pl.* зу́б|ы, -о́в) tooth; име́ть з. про́тив *(gen.)* have a score to settle with; зуба́стый large-toothed; sharp-tongued; зу́б|е́ц (-бца́) tooth, cog; зубно́й dental, tooth *(a.).*

зубо|враче́бный dental, dentist's; ~чи́стка toothpick.

зубр aurochs.

зубрёжка cramming, swotting; зубри́ла *(m. & f.)* crammer; зубри́ть (зубрю́, зу́бришь; *pf.* вы́-) cram.

зубча́тый cogged, indented.

зуд itch; зуд|е́ть (-и́т) itch.

зы́биться ripple; surge, swell; зы́бкий unsteady, unstable; зыбу́чий unstable; quick *(sand)*; зыб *(f.)* ripple; surge.

зы́чный stentorian.

зюйд south, south wind.

зя́бкий sensitive to cold, chilly.

зя́блик finch.

зя́бнуть *(past* зяб, -ла; *pf.* о-) shiver, freeze.

зябь *(f.)* autumn ploughing.

зять *(m; pl.* -тья́, -тьёв) son-in-law *(daughter's husband);* brother-in-law *(sister's husband).*

И

и and, even; и.. и... both... and...

ибери́йский Iberian.

и́бо for.

и́ва willow.

ива́н-да-ма́рья cow-wheat.

ива́новск|ая: во всю -ую with all one's might.

ива́н-ча́й rosebay willow-herb.

и́вовый willow *(a.).*

и́волга oriole.

игла́ *(pl.* и́глы) needle, bodkin; spine, quill; spire.

игнори́ровать *(ipf. & pf.)* ignore, disregard.

и́го yoke.

иго́лка, иго́лочка *(gen. pl.* -чек) needle; с иго́лочки spick and span; иго́льное у́шко eye of a needle.

иго́рный gaming *(a.);* игра́ *(pl.* и́гры) game; play; performance; игра́ть *(pf.* по-, сыгра́ть) play; (в + *acc.)* play *(a game);* (на + *prep.)* play *(an instr ment).*

игри́вый playful; игри́стый sparkling *(e.g. wine).*

игро́к (-а́) player, gambler; игру́шечный toy *(a.);* игру́|шка *(gen. pl.* -шек) toy.

игу́мен abbot; игу́ме|нья *(gen. pl.* -ний) prioress.

идеа́л ideal; ~изи́ровать *(ipf. & pf.)* idealize; ~и́зм idealism; ~и́ст idealist; ~исти́ческий idealistic; идеа́льный ideal.

иде́йный ideological; high-principled.

иденти́чный identical.

идео́л|ог ideologist; ~оги́ческий ideological; ~о́гия ideology.

иде́я idea; concept.

идилли́ческий idyllic; иди́ллия idyll.

идио́м|а idiom; ~ати́ческий idiomatic.

идио́т idiot; идио́т|и́ческий, ~ский idiotic.

и́дол idol; идолопокло́нник idolater.

идти́ (иду́, идёшь; *past* шёл, шла; *ppa.* ше́дший; *pf.* пойти́) go, be going *(on foot);* run, be on *(of film, etc.)* костю́м ему́ идёт the suit suits him; де́ло идет о (+ *prep.)* the matter concerns...;

иезуи́т Jesuit.

иена *(Japanese)* yen.

иера́рхия hierarchy.

иеро́глиф hieroglyph.

иждиве́|нец (-нца) dependant; иждиве́н|ие maintenance; он на её -ии she keeps him.

из *(gen.)* out of, from; изо всех сил with all one's strength.

изба́ *(pl.* и́збы) cottage, hut.

изба́витель *(m.)* deliverer, redeemer; избавле́ние deliverance; избавля́ть *(pf.* изба́вить) (от + *gen.)* save, deliver (from); -ся (от + *gen.)* get rid (of).

избало́в|ывать *(pf.* -овать) spoil *(children).*

избега́ть *(pf.* избежа́ть* *or* избегнуть, *past* -бе́г) (+ *gen.)* avoid, evade; избежа́ние: во и. (+ *gen.)* in order to avoid.

избива́ть *(pf.* изби́ть* изобью́ *etc.)* beat unmercifully; избие́ние slaughter, massacre; assault and battery.

избира́тель *(m.)* elector, voter; избира́тельный electoral; и. о́круг/ уча́сток electoral district, constituency; избира́ть *(pf.* избра́ть*) choose, elect.

изби́тый well-worn; hackneyed; изби́ть *see* избива́ть.

избра́ние election; **избра́нник** the chosen one; **избра́ть** see избира́ть.

избу́|шка (gen. pl. -шек) peasant's cottage.

избы́|ток (-тка) surplus; plenty; **избы́точный** surplus, redundant.

изва́ние sculpture, carving.

изве́дывать (pf. изве́дать) experience, come to know, taste (fig.).

и́зверг monster.

изверга́ть (pf. изве́ргнуть, past. -ве́рг) throw out, disgorge; **-ся** erupt; **изверже́ние** eruption; изве́рженная поро́да igneous rock.

изве́риться (pf.) (в + prep.) lose confidence (in).

изверну́ться, извёртываться see изворачиваться.

извести́ see изводи́ть.

изве́стие news; **извести́ть** see извеща́ть.

известко́вый lime (a.).

изве́стность (f.) fame, reputation; **изве́стный** known; famous; certain.

известня́к (-а́) limestone; **и́звесть** (f.) lime.

извеща́ть (pf. изве|сти́ть, -щу́, -сти́шь) inform, notify; **извеще́ние** notification.

извива́ть (pf. изви́ть, изорью́*) twist, coil; **-ся** twist, meander; **изви́лина** bend; **изви́листый** twisting.

извине́ние apology, excuse; **извиня́ть** (pf. -и́ть) excuse; извини́те! excuse me! I'm sorry!; **-ся** (пе́рсд + inst.) apologize (to).

изви́ть see извива́ть.

извлека́ть (pf. извле́чь*) draw out, extract; **извлече́ние** extract(ion).

извне́ from outside.

изво́д waste (of time, money); **изводи́ть*** (pf. извести́*) use up; destroy; exhaust; exasperate.

изво́з carrier's trade; **изво́зчик** carrier, cabman.

изво́лить wish; deign; изво́л те вы́йти! please leave the room; он изво́лил забы́ть he went and forgot.

изворачиваться (pf. извернуться) dodge, twist; **изворо́тливый** resourceful.

извраща́ть (pf. изгра|ти́ть, -щу́, -ти́шь) pervert; distort; **извраще́ние** perversion; distortion.

изга́живать (pf. изга́дить*) soil, befoul.

изги́б bend; **изгиба́ть** (pf. изогну́ть) bend, curve.

изгла́живать (pf. изгла́дить*) efface.

изгна́ние banishment, exile; **изгна́нник** exile; **изгна́ть** see изгоня́ть.

изголо́вье head of bed.

изголода́ться (pf.) starve; hunger (fig.).

изгоня́ть (pf. изгна́ть) banish.

и́згородь (f.) fence; жива́я и. hedge.

изгот|а́вливать, -овля́ть (pf. -о́вить) manufacture; **изготовле́ние** making, manufacture.

изгрыза́ть (pf. изгры́зть*) nibble, gnaw to shreds.

издава́ть* (pf. изда́ть*) publish, promulgate; utter; exhale.

и́здавна since long ago.

издалека́, и́здали from afar.

изда́ние publication; edition; **изда́тель** (m.) publisher; **изда́тельство** publishing house; **изда́ть** see издава́ть.

издева́тельство mockery; **издева́ться** (-ева́юсь) (над + inst.) sneer, scoff (at).

изде́лие make; article.

издёргивать (pf. издёргать) pull to pieces; overtax, worry.

изде́рживать (pf. издержа́ть*) expend, spend; **-ся** run out of money; **изде́р|жки** (gen. pl. -жек) expenses.

издре́вле from time immemorial.

издыха́ть (pf. из|до́хнуть, past. -до́х) die (of animals).

изжёванный chewed; hackneyed.

изжива́ть (pf. изжи́ть*) get rid of.

изжо́га heartburn.

из-за (gen.) 1. from behind; 2. because of.

излага́ть (pf. изл|ожи́ть, -ожу́, -о́жишь) expound, set forth.

излече́ние recovery; cure, treatment; **изле́чивать** (pf. излечи́ть*) cure; **излечи́мый** curable.

излива́ть (pf. изли́ть, изолью́*) pour out, give vent to.

изли́|шек (-шка) excess, surplus; **изли́шество** excess, overindulgence; **изли́шний** superfluous.

излия́ние effusion.

изложе́ние account, statement; **изложи́ть** see излага́ть.

изло́м fracture, break; **излома́ть** (pf.) break to pieces; ruin (e.g. character).

излуч|а́ть *(pf.* -и́ть) radiate; **излуче́ние** radiation.

излу́чина bend.

излю́бленный favourite, pet.

изма́зывать *(pf.* изма́зать*)* smear; use up *(ointment).*

изма́рывать *(pf.* измара́ть) soil, dirty.

изма́тывать *(pf.* измота́ть) exhaust.

изме́на treason, faithlessness; **изме-не́ние** change, alteration; **изме́н|ник, ~ница** traitor; **изме́ннический** traitorous; **изме́нчивый** changeable; **изменя́ть** *(pf.* изм|ени́ть, -еню́, -е́нишь) 1. change, alter; 2. *(dat.)* be unfaithful to, betray; **-ся** change.

измере́ние measuring, measurement; **измери́мый** measurable; **измери́тель** *(m.)* measuring instrument; index; **измеря́ть** *(pf.* изме́рить) measure.

измождённый emaciated.

измо́р: бра́ть-ом starve out, wear out.

и́зморозь *(f.)* hoar frost, rime.

и́зморось *(f.)* drizzle, sleet.

измота́ть *see* изма́тывать.

изму́ченный exhausted, worn out.

измышле́ние fabrication, figment; **измышля́ть** *(pf.* измы́слить) fabricate, concoct.

изна́нка wrong side; и. жи́зни the seamy side of life.

изнаси́лование rape.

изна́шивание wear and tear; **изна́шивать** *(pf.* износи́ть*)* wear out; **-ся** wear out; be used up.

изне́живать *(pf.* изне́жить) make delicate/effeminate.

изнемога́ть *(pf.* изнемо́чь*)* be(come) exhausted; **изнеможе́ние** exhaustion.

изне́рвничаться *(pf.)* become a nervous wreck.

изно́с wear and tear; **износи́ть** *see* изна́шивать; **изно́шенный** threadbare; worn out.

изнуре́ние exhaustion, inanition; **изнури́тельный** exhausting; **изнур|я́ть** *(pf.* -и́ть) wear out; overwork.

изнутри́ from inside, on the inside.

изныва́ть *(pf.* изны́ть*)* pine away.

изо = из.

изоби́лие abundance, plenty; **изоби́ловать** *(inst.)* abound (in), teem (with); **изоби́льный** abundant, pientiful.

изоблич|а́ть *(pf.* -и́ть) expose; и. в + *prep.* find guilty (of); prove to be.

изобличе́ние exposure.

изобража́ть *(pf.* изобра|зи́ть, -жу́, -зи́шь) depict, portray; и. из себя́ make oneself out to be; **изображе́ние** representation, picture; **изобрази́тельный** figurative; fine *(art).*

изобрета́тель *(m.)* inventor; **изобрета́тельный** inventive, resourceful; **изобрета́ть** *(pf.* изобр|ести́, -сту́, -стёшь; *past.* -ёл, -ела́; *ppp.* -стённый) invent; **изобрете́ние** invention.

изогну́ть *see* изгиба́ть.

изолга́ться *(pf.)* tell a lot of lies.

изоли́ровать *(ipf. & pf.)* isolate; insulate; **изоля́тор** insulator; isolation ward; **изоля́ция** isolation, insulation; quarantine.

изо́рванный ragged.

изоте́рма isotherm; **изото́п** isotope.

изошр|я́ть *(pf.* -и́ть) cultivate, refine; **-ся** become refined excel.

из-под from under; буты́лка из-под молока́ an empty milk-bottle.

изразцо́вый tiled.

изра́ильский Israeli.

и́зредка now and then.

изре́зывать *(pf.* изр зать) cut up.

изрек|а́ть *(pf.* изр|е́чь, -еку́, -ечёшь; -ёк, -екла́; *ppp.* -ечённый) utter; **изрече́ние** saying; pronouncement.

изруба́ть *(pf.* изруби́ть*)* chop up, mince; slaughter.

изрыг|а́ть *(pf.* -ну́ть) disgorge; throw up; belch.

изры́тый pitted.

изря́дный fairly good.

изуве́р (cruel) monster.

изуве́ч|ивать *(pf.* -ить) maim, mutilate.

изуми́тельный amazing; **изумле́ние** astonishment; **изумл|я́ть** *(pf.* -и́ть) surprise; **-ся** *(dat.)* be surprised (at).

изумру́д emerald; **изумру́дный** emerald *(a.).*

изуч|а́ть *(pf.* -и́ть*)* study; **изуче́ние** study.

изъеда́ть *(pf.* изъе́сть*)* eat, corrode.

изъе́здить* *(pf.)* travel all over.

изъе́сть *see* изъеда́ть.

изъяви́тельный indicative; **изъявля́ть** *(pf.* -и́ть) express.

изъя́н defect, flaw.

изъясн|я́ться *(pf.* -и́ться) express oneself.

изъя́тие withdrawal, removal; exception; изыму́, изы́мешь; *ppp.* изъя́тый) withdraw.

изыска́ние finding, procuring; investigation; prospecting; изы́сканный refined; изы́скивать *(pf.* из|ыска́ть, -ыщу́, -ы́щешь) procure, (try to) find; investigate; prospect.

изю́бр Siberian deer.

изю́м raisins; изю́мина raisin; изю́минк|а raisin; zest; с -ой piquant.

изя́щество grace, refinement; изя́щный elegant.

ика́ть *(pf.* икну́ть) hiccup.

ико́на icon; иконобо́|рец (-рца) iconoclast; иконопи́|сец (-сца) icon-painter.

ико́та hiccup.

икра́ roe; caviar.

икс-лучи́ X-rays.

ил silt.

и́ли or; и́ли ... и́ли ... either ... or ...

иллю́зия illusion; иллюзо́рный illusory.

иллюмина́тор porthole; иллюмина́ция illumination; иллюминова́ть *(ipf. & pf.)* illumine.

иллюстра́тор illustrator, designer; иллюстра́ция illustration; иллюстри́ровать *(ipf. & pf.)* illustrate.

имби́р|ь (-я́) ginger; имби́рный ginger *(a.).*

име́ние estate.

имени́н|ник, ~ница one whose name-day it is; имен|и́ны (-и́н) name-day.

имени́тельный nominative.

и́менно namely; вот и. exactly.

именно́й nominal; autographed.

именова́ть *(pf.* на-) name.

име́ть have; и. де́ло (с + *inst.)* have dealings (with); и. ме́сто take place; -ся be.

имита́ция imitation; имити́ровать imitate.

иммигра́нт, ~ка immigrant.

иммунизи́ровать *(ipf. & pf.)* immunize; иммуните́т immunity.

импера́тор emperor; императри́ца empress.

империал|и́зм imperialism; ~и́ст imperialist; ~исти́ческий imperialist(ic).

импе́рия empire; импе́рский imperial.

импоза́нтный imposing; импони́ровать *(dat.)* impress.

и́мпорт import; импортёр importer; импорти́ровать *(ipf. & pf.)* import; и́мпортный import *(a.).*

импровиза́ция improvisation; импровизи́ровать *(ipf. & pf.)* improvise.

и́мпульс impulse.

иму́щественный property *(a.);* иму́щество property; иму́щий propertied; wealthy.

и́мя *(neut.; gen., dat., prep.* и́мени *inst.* и́мєнєм, *pl.* имена́) name, noun; и́мя прилага́тельное adjective; заво́д и́мени Ле́нина the Lenin works; во и́мя дру́жбы in the name of friendship.

ина́че differently, otherwise; так или и. in any case.

инвали́д invalid; инвали́дность *(f.)* disablement.

инвента́р|ь (-я́) inventory; stock.

инверти́ровать *(ipf. & pf.)* invert.

инвести́ровать *(ipf. & pf.)* invest.

ингаля́тор inhaler.

инд|е́ец (-е́йца), индиа́нка (American) Indian.

инд|е́йка *(gen. pl.* -е́ек) turkey.

и́ндекс index.

индивидуа́льный individual *(a.);* индиви́дуум individual.

инд|и́ец (-и́йца), индиа́нка Indian; инди́йский Indian *(a.).*

индоевропе́йский Indo-European; индонез|и́ец (-и́йца), ~и́йка *(gen. pl.* -и́йк) Indonesian; индонези́йский Indonesian *(a.).*

индоссаме́нт endorsement.

инду́с, ~ка Hindu; инду́сский Hindu *(a.).*

индустриализ|а́ция industrialization; ~и́ровать *(ipf. & pf.)* industrialize.

индустриа́льный industrial; инду́стрия industry.

индю́к (-а́) turkey (cock); индю́|шка *(gen. pl.* -шек) turkey (hen).

и́ней hoar-frost.

ине́ртный inert; sluggish; ине́рция inertia.

инжене́р engineer; инжене́рн|ый engineer's, engineering *(a.);* -ое де́ло engineering.

инжи́р fig.

инициа́л initial; инициати́ва initiative; инициа́тор initiator.
инквизи́тор inquisitor.
инкорпори́ровать *(ipf. & pf.)* incorporate.
инкрусти́ровать *(ipf. & pf.)* encrust inlay.
инкуба́тор incubator.
инновалю́та foreign currency.
инове́рец (-рца) heterodox.
иногда́ sometimes.
иногоро́дний of another town; инозе́|мец (-мца), ∼мка foreigner; инозе́мный foreign.
ино́й different, other; и. раз sometimes; не кто и., как none other than.
и́нок monk.
инокули́ровать *(ipf. & pf.)* inoculate.
иносказа́тельный allegorical.
иностра́|нец (-нца), ∼нка foreigner; иностра́нный foreign.
иноязы́чный speaking another language.
инсектици́д insecticide.
инспекти́ровать inspect; инспе́ктор *(pl. -á)* inspector; инспе́кция inspection.
инспири́ровать *(ipf. & pf.)* inspire.
инста́нция instance.
инсти́нкт instinct; инстинкти́вный instinctive.
институ́т institute.
инструкти́ровать *(ipf. & pf.)* instruct; инстру́ктор instructor; инстру́кция instructions.
инструме́нт instrument; инструмента́рий set of instruments, tools.
инсули́н insulin.
инсцени́ровать *(ipf. & pf.)* dramatize, stage; feign; инсцениро́вка dramatization, staging; pretence.
интеллектуа́льный intellectual *(a.)*; интеллиге́нт, ∼ка intellectual; интеллиге́нтный cultured, educated; интеллиге́нция intelligentsia.
интенда́нт commissary.
интенси́вный intensive.
интерва́л interval.
интерве́нция intervention.
интервью́ *(indecl.)* interview *(given to press)*; интервьюе́р interviewer; интервьюи́ровать *(ipf. & pf.)* interview.
интере́с (к + *dat.*) interest (in); интере́сный interesting; интересова́ть *(pf. за-)* interest; -ся *(inst.)* be(come) interested in.

интерна́т boarding school.
интернациона́льный international.
интерни́ровать *(ipf. & pf.)* intern.
интерпрет|а́ция interpretation; ∼и́ровать *(ipf. & pf.)* interpret
интерье́р interior.
инти́мный intimate.
интри́га intrigue; интрига́н, ∼ка intriguer, schemer; интригова́ть *(pf. за-)* scheme; intrigue, interest.
интуи́ция intuition.
инфекцио́нный infectious; инфе́кция infection.
инфля́ция inflation *(econ.)*.
информ|а́тор informer; ∼а́ция information; ∼и́ровать *(ipf. & pf., pf. also* про-*)* inform.
инфракра́сный infra-red.
инциде́нт incident.
инъе́кция injection.
ио́н ion.
ио́та: ни на ио́ту not a whit.
ипоте́ка mortgage.
ипохо́ндрик hypochondriac.
ирла́н|дец (-дца) Irishman; ∼дка Irishwoman; ирла́ндский Irish.
ирони́зировать (над) speak ironically (of).
ирони́ческий ironic; иро́ния irony.
иррациона́льный irrational.
иррига́ция irrigation.
иск action, suit.
иска́жа́ть *(pf.* иска|зи́ть, -жу́, -зи́шь)* distort; pervert; искаже́ние distortion; perversion.
иска́ние quest, search; иска́тель, -ница seeker; иска́ть (ищу́, и́щешь; *pf.* по-) seek, look for; и. кни́гу look for a book; и. сове́та seek advice.
исключ|а́ть *(pf.* -и́ть) exclude; except; eliminate; expel; исключе́н|ие exception; elimination; expulsion; за -и́м его́ except for him; исключи́тельный exclusive; exceptional.
исколеси́ть *(pf.* -шу́, -си́шь) travel all over.
иско́мое unknown quantity; иско́мый sought for.
иско́нный age-old.
ископа́емое fossil; ископа́емые minerals.
искорене́ние eradication; искорен|я́ть *(pf.* -и́ть) eradicate.
и́скоса askance.
и́скра spark.
и́скренний sincere; и́скренность *(f.)* sincerity.

искривл|я́ть (pf. -и́ть) bend; distort; -ся become bent, distorted.

искри́стый sparkling; и́скриться sparkle.

искупа́ть 1. (pf. искупи́ть*) expiate, atone for; искупле́ние atonement, redemption.

искупа́ть 2. see купа́ть.

иску́с trial, test; искуси́тель tempter, ~ница temptress; искуси́ть see искуша́ть.

иску́сный skilled, clever.

иску́сственный artificial; иску́сство art; искусствове́д art critic.

искуша́ть (pf. иску|си́ть, -шу́, -си́шь) tempt, seduce; искуше́ние temptation, seduction.

исла́м Islam.

исла́н|дец(-дца), ~дка Icelander; исла́ндский Icelandic.

испа́|нец(-нца), ~нка Spaniard; испа́нский Spanish.

испаре́ние evaporation, exhalation; fumes; испа́рина perspiration; испар|я́ть (pf. -и́ть) evaporate; exhale; -ся evaporate; disappear.

испепел|я́ть (pf. -и́ть) reduce to ashes.

испещр|я́ть (pf. -и́ть) speckle.

испи́сывать (pf. исписа́ть*) use up (paper); write all over; -ся be used up; exhaust one's inspiration.

испито́й haggard.

испове́довать (ipf. & pf.) profess (a faith); confess; take confession of; -ся confess one's sins; unbosom oneself; и́споведь (f.) confession.

и́сподволь little by little, gradually.

исподло́бья distrustfully, sullenly.

испоко́н веко́в from time immemorial.

исполи́н giant; исполи́нский gigantic.

исполко́м executive committee.

исполне́ние fulfilment; execution; исполни́мый feasible; исполни́тель (m.) executor; исполни́тельный executive; исполня́ть (pf. испо́лнить) carry out, fulfil; -ся be fulfilled; ему́ испо́лнилось 10 лет he is ten years old.

испо́льзование use, utilization; испо́льзовать (ipf. & pf.) use.

испо́рченный spoiled, rotten.

исправи́мый rectifiable; исправи́тельный corrective, reformatory; исправле́ние correction; исправл-

я́ть (pf. испра́вить) correct; mend; atone for; -ся be put right; improve.

испра́вник district police officer (hist.).

испра́вность (f.) good repair; punctuality; испра́вный in good repair; punctual, zealous.

испражне́ние defecation; excrement.

испра́шивать (pf. испроси́ть*) ask for and obtain.

испу́г fright.

испуска́ть (pf. испусти́ть*) emit, exhale, utter.

испыта́ние test, trial; испы́танный proved, tried; испыта́тель (m.) tester; investigator; испыта́тельный test, trial (a.); испыту́ющий searching; испы́тывать (pf. испыта́ть) test, try; experience.

иссле́дование investigation, research; иссле́дователь (m.) investigator, researcher; иссле́довать (ipf. & pf.) examine, explore.

иссо́хнуть see иссыха́ть.

и́сстари since olden times.

исступле́ние frenzy; исступлённый frenzied.

иссуша́ть (pf. иссуши́ть*) dry up; consume; иссыха́ть (pf. иссо́хнуть*) dry up; yearn; иссяка́ть (pf. ис|ся́кнуть, past -сяк) run low, run dry.

иста́птывать (pf. истопта́ть*) trample; wear out (shoes).

иста́скивать (pf. истаска́ть*) wear out.

истека́ть (pf. исте́чь*) elapse; и. кро́вью bleed profusely; исте́кший past.

истере́ть see истира́ть.

истерза́ть (pf.) worry to death.

исте́рика hysterics; истер|и́ческий, ~и́чный hysterical.

ис|те́ц (-тца́) plaintiff, petitioner.

истече́ние outflow, haemorrhage; expiry; исте́чь see истека́ть.

и́стина truth; и́стинный true.

истира́ть (pf. истере́ть*) grind, grate.

истлева́ть (-ева́ю; pf. истле́ть) decay; be reduced to ashes.

и́стовый fervent, zealous.

исто́к source.

истолкова́ние interpretation; истолк|о́вывать (pf. -ова́ть) interpret, construe.

исто́ма languor.

истопни́к (-а́) stoker.

истоптáть *see* истáптывать.

исторгáть *(pf.* ис|тóргнуть, *past* -тóрг) throw out.

истóрик historian; истори́ческий historical; historic; истóрия history

источáть exhale.

истóчник source, spring.

истóшный heart-rending.

истощ|áть *(pf.* -и́ть) exhaust, wear out; истощéние exhaustion, emaciation.

истреби́тель *(m.)* destroyer; fighter *(aircraft)* ; истреблéние destruction; истреб|ля́ть *(pf.* -и́ть) destroy.

истрёпывать *(pf.* истрепáть*) fray, wear.

истукáн idol.

и́стый genuine, true.

истязáние torture.

исхóд outcome; исходи́ть* 1. proceed, issue; *(pf.* изойти́) и. крóвью bleed to death; 2. *(pf.)* walk all over; исхóдный initial *(a.).*

исхудáлый emaciated.

исцарáпывать *(pf.* исцарáпать) scratch all over.

исцелéние healing, recovery; исцел|я́ть *(pf.* -и́ть) cure, heal; -ся recover.

исчезáть *(pf.* исчéзнуть, *past* исчéз) disappear, vanish; исчезновéние disappearance.

исчéрпывать *(pf.* исчерпáть) exhaust; исчéрпывающий exhaustive, thorough.

исчéрчивать *(pf.* исчерти́ть*) stripe, cover with lines.

исчислéние calculation; calculus; исчисля́ть *(pf.* исчи́слить) calculate, estimate.

итáк and so.

итальá|нец (-нца), ~нка Italian; италья́нский Italian *(a.).*

итóг total; итогó altogether, total; итóговый total.

итти́ *see* идти́.

иудéйство Judaism.

и́хний their.

ишáк (-á) donkey.

ишь! see!

ищéйка *(gen. pl.* -éек) bloodhound, police dog.

июль *(m.)* July; ию́льский July *(a.).*

ию́нь *(m.)* June; ию́ньский June *(a.).*

йод iodine.

йóт|а: ни на ~у not a whit.

К

к *(dat.)* to, towards; for; by *(a certain time)* ; к томý же moreover.

-ка *(particle)* just.

кабáк (-á) drinking house; *(fig.)* pigsty.

кабалá servitude.

кабáн (-á) wild boar; hog.

каба|чóк (-чкá) 1. vegetable marrow; 2. café, dive.

кáбель *(m.)* cable.

кабестáн capstan.

каби́на booth, cab, cabin, cockpit.

кабинéт study, surgery, consulting-room; cabinet *(of ministers).*

каблогрáмма cablogram.

каблýк (-á) heel.

каботáж coasting(-trade).

кабы́ if.

кавалéр cavalier; escort, *(coll.)* boy-friend; кавалéрия cavalry.

кáверза chicanery, trick; кáверзный tricky.

кавкá|зец (-зца), ~зка Caucasian; кавкáзский Caucasian *(a.).*

кавы́|чки (-чек) inverted commas, quotation marks.

кадéт cadet; Constitutional Democrat.

кади́ло censer.

кáдка tub.

кадр *(film)* sequence, still; *(pl.)* personnel; кáдровый experienced; regular *(soldier).*

кады́к (-á) Adam's apple.

каёмка edge, hem.

каждоднéвный everyday.

кáждый every, each.

кáжущийся apparent.

казáк (-á, *pl.* -áки) Cossack.

казáрма barracks.

казáть (кажý, кáжешь) *(coll.)* show; -ся *(pf.* по-) *(inst.)* seem, appear (as); кáжется apparently; казáлось бы it would seem.

каз|áх, ~áшка *(gen. pl.* -шек) Kazakh; казáхский Kazakh *(a.).*

казáцкий Cossack *(a.).*

казённый fiscal, government *(a.) ;* formal; на к. счёт at public expense.

казинó *(indecl.)* casino.

казнá exchequer, treasury; казначéй treasurer; paymaster.

казни́ть *(ipf. & pf.)* execute; torture.

казнокрáдство embezzlement.

казнь *(f.)* execution, punishment.

ка́зус case.

кайма́ *(gen. pl.* каём) border, edging.

как how, as; как ни ... however ...; как ..., так и ... both ..., and ...; как мо́жно скоре́е as soon as possible; как когда́ it depends.

какаду́ *(m., indecl.)* cockatoo.

кака́о *(indecl.)* cocoa; **кака́овый** со́coa *(a.)*.

ка́к-либо anyhow; **ка́к-нибудь** anyhow, somehow.

как-ника́к after all.

како́в what; к. он собой? what does he look like?; **каково́** how.

как|о́й what; -и́м о́бразом how; -о́й-либо any, some kind of; -о́й-нибудь any, some kind of; -о́й-то some.

ка́к-то somehow, sort of; one day.

ка́ктус cactus.

кал excrement.

каламбу́р pun.

калан|ча́ *(gen. pl.* -че́й) watch-tower; *(fig.)* may-pole, lanky person.

кала́ч (-а́) kalach, *kind of fancy bread;* тёртый к. *(coll.)* old stager.

калго́т|ки (-ок) tights.

кале́ка *(m. & f.)* cripple.

календа́р|ь (-я́) calendar.

кале́н|ие incandescence; доводи́ть до бе́лого -ия rouse to a fury; **кале́ный** red-hot; roasted.

кале́чить *(pf.* ис-) cripple, maim.

кали́бр calibre, gauge.

ка́лий potassium.

кали́льный heat *(a.);* incandescent.

кали́на guelder rose, snow-ball tree.

кали́тка wicket-gate.

кали́ть heat, incandesce.

каллигра́фия calligraphy.

кало́рия calory.

кало́ша galosh.

ка́лька tracing-paper; loan-word; **кальки́ровать** *(pf.* с-) trace; borrow *(a loan-word)*.

калькули́ровать *(pf.* с-) calculate; **калькуля́ция** calculation.

кальс|о́ны (-о́н) drawers, pants.

ка́льций calcium.

ка́мбала plaice, flounder.

камво́льный worsted *(a.)*.

каме́дь *(f.)* gum.

камене́ть *(pf.* о-) harden, petrify; **камени́стый** stony; **каменноуго́льный** coal *(a.);* hard; lifeless.

каменоло́мня *(gen. pl.* -мен) quarry; **ка́менщик** stonemason, bricklayer.

ка́|мень (-мня, *pl* -мни, -мне́й, *& coll.* -ме́нья) stone.

ка́мера cell, chamber, room; camera; inner tube *(tyre);* bladder *(foot ball);* **ка́мерный** chamber *(a.)*.

камерто́н tuning-fork.

ка́ме|шек (-шка) pebble.

ками́н fireplace.

камнело́мка saxifrage.

камо́рка closet.

кампа́ния campaign; sea-voyage.

кам|фара́, ~фора́ camphor.

камы́ш (-а́) rush, reed; **камы́ш|евый, ~о́вый** cane, reed *(a.)*.

кана́ва ditch.

кана́|дец (-дца) **~дка** Canadian; **кана́дский** Canadian *(a.)*.

кана́л canal; channel; **канализа́ция** sewerage system.

кана́лья *(m. & f.)* rascal.

канаре́|йка *(gen. pl.* -е́ек) canary.

кана́т rope, cable; **кана́тный** rope, cable *(a.);* **канатохо́|дец** (-дца) rope-walker.

канва́ canvas; **канво́вый** canvas *(a.)*.

кандал|ы́ (-о́в) shackles.

кандида́т candidate; **~ка** candidate; **кандидату́ра** candidature.

кани́к|улы (-ул) vacation, holidays; **каникуля́рный** vacation, holiday *(a.)*.

каните́литься dawdle, mess about; **кани́тель** *(f.)* gold thread, silver thread; long-drawn-out proceedings.

канифо́ль *(f.)* rosin.

канона́да cannonade; **канонёрка** gun-boat.

канонизи́ровать *(ipf. & pf.)* canonize; **кано́ник** canon; **канони́ческий** canon *(a.)*.

кантова́ть turn over, tip; *(pf.* о-) edge, mount *(photo etc.)*.

кану́н eve.

ка́нуть *(pf.)* fall, slip; как в во́ду к. disappear.

канцел|я́рия office; **канцеля́рский** office *(a.);* **канцеля́рщина** red tape.

ка́|пать (-плю, -плешь *or* -паю, -паешь; *pf.* ка́пнуть) drop, drip.

капе́лла choir; chapel; **капелла́н** chaplain.

ка́пелька drop.

капельме́йстер bandmaster, conductor.

ка́пельница dropper, drip *(med.)*.

капилля́р capillary; капилля́рный capillary *(a.)*.

капита́л capital; капитали́зм capitalism; капитали́ст capitalist; капиталисти́ческий capitalist(ic); капиталовложе́ние investment; капита́льный capital *(a.)*.

капита́н captain.

капитули́ровать *(ipf. & pf.)* capitulate; капитуля́ция capitulation.

капка́н trap.

ка́|пля *(gen. pl.* -пель) drop, drip; ка́пнуть *see* ка́пать.

ка́пор hood.

капо́т house-coat; bonnet, cowling.

капри́з caprice, whim; капри́зничать be naughty, capricious; капри́зный capricious, fickle.

капро́н kapron *(kind of nylon)*; капро́новый kapron *(a.)*.

ка́псула capsule.

капу́ста cabbage; брюссе́льская к. Brussels sprouts; ки́слая к. sauerkraut; капу́стник cabbage field; cabbage worm; party, social evening; капу́стница cabbage white butterfly.

капюшо́н cowl, hood.

ка́ра penalty.

кара́бкаться *(pf.* вс-) clamber.

карава́й round loaf.

карава́н caravan; convoy *(ships)*.

карака́тица cuttlefish; *(coll.)* dumpy person.

кара́кулевый astrakhan *(a.)*; кара́куль *(m.)* astrakhan.

кара́куля scrawl, scribble.

караме́ль *(f.)* caramel.

каранда́ш (-а́) pencil.

каранти́н quarantine.

кара́с|ь (-я́) crucian carp.

кара́тельный punitive; кара́ть *(pf.* по-) punish.

карау́л guard, watch, help!; почётный к. guard of honour; карау́лить guard; lie in wait for; карау́льщик watchman.

кара́чки: на -ах *(coll.)* on all fours.

карбо́ловый carbolic.

карбу́нкул carbuncle.

карбюра́тор carburettor.

карга́ crone, harridan.

кардио́граф cardiograph.

каре́льский Karelian.

каре́та carriage, coach.

ка́рий hazel, brown.

карикату́ра caricature; карикату́рный grotesque.

карка́с frame(work).

ка́ркать *(pf.* ка́ркнуть) croak.

ка́рлик dwarf; ка́рликовый dwarf *(a.)*.

карма́н pocket; э́то мне не по карма́ну I can't afford it; он за сло́вом не ле́зет в к. he is never at a loss for an answer!; карма́нник *(coll.)* pickpocket; карма́нный pocket *(a.)*.

карнава́л carnival.

карни́з cornice, ledge.

карп carp.

ка́рта map; card.

карта́вить burr, lisp.

картёжник gambler.

карте́ль *(f.)* cartel.

карте́чь *(f.)* case-shot.

карти́на picture; *(theat.)* scene; карти́нка small picture; карти́нный picture *(a.)*: picturesque

картогра́фия cartography

карто́н cardboard; карто́нный cardboard *(a.)*; карто́нка cardboard box; hat box.

картоте́ка card index.

карто́фелина potato; карто́фель *(m.)* potatoes; карто́фельный potato *(a.)*.

ка́рто|чка *(gen. pl.* -чек) card, photograph; ка́рточ|ный card *(a.)*; -ая систе́ма rationing system.

карто́шка *(gen. pl.* -шек) potato.

карту́з (-а́) cap; powder bag.

карусе́ль *(f.)* merry-go-round.

ка́рцер punishment room, cell.

карье́р 1. full gallop; 2. sand quarry.

карье́ра career; карьери́ст careerist.

каса́ние contact; каса́тельная tangent; каса́тельно *(gen.)* concerning; каса́тельство (к + *dat.*) connection(with); каса́ться *(pf.* косну́ться) *(gen.)* touch; concern; что каса́ется меня... as for me...

ка́ска helmet.

каспи́йский Caspian.

ка́сса cashbox, till; desk, booking-office, box-office.

кассацио́нный cassation *(a.)*; касса́ция cassation.

кассе́та cassette, film holder.

касси́р, ~ша cashier.

касси́ровать *(ipf. & pf.)* annul; reverse *(legal)*.

ка́ста caste.

кастеля́нша linen manageress.

кастет knuckle-duster.

касто́рка, касто́ровое ма́сло castor oil.

кастрю́ля saucepan.

ката́лиз catalysis.

катало́г catalogue.

ката́ние ride, drive; rolling; к. на конька́х skating; не мытьём, так ката́ньем by hook or by crook.

ката́р catarrh.

катара́кта cataract.

катастро́ф|а catastrophe; ~и́ческий catastrophic.

ката́ть (pf. по-) drive, roll; -ся go for a ride; roll; -ся на конька́х skate.

катафа́лк catafalque; hearse.

категори́ческий categorical; катего́рия category.

ка́тер launch, patrol boat.

кати́ть (качу́, ка́тишь; pf. по-) roll; take, drive; -ся roll.

като́д cathode.

ка|то́к (-тка́) skating rink; roller.

като́л|ик, ~и́чка (gen. pl. -ичек) (Roman) Catholic; ~и́ческий Catholic (a.); ~ици́зм ~и́чество Catholicism.

ка́торга penal servitude, hard labour; каторж|а́нин (pl. -а́не, -а́н), -а́нка convict; ка́торжник convict; ка́торжный penal; (fig.) backbreaking.

кату́|шка (gen. pl. -шек) bobbin, coil, reel.

катю́ша rocket projector.

кау́рый light chestnut.

каучу́к rubber; каучу́ковый rubber (a.).

кафе́ (indecl.) café.

ка́федра chair; rostrum; department, faculty.

ка́фель (m.) glazed tile.

кафете́рий cafeteria.

кафта́н caftan.

кацаве́йка (gen. pl. -éек) woman's short jacket.

кача́лка rocking-chair; rocking-horse; кача́ть (pf. по-, качну́ть) rock, swing; -ся rock, swing; каче́л|и (-ей) swing.

ка́чественный qualitative; ка́чество quality; в -е (gen.) in the capacity (of), as.

ка́чка tossing (at sea).

качну́ть see кача́ть.

ка́ша porridge, gruel; завари́ть ка́шу stir up trouble; с ним ка́ши не сва́ришь you won't get anywhere with him.

ка́|шель (-шля) cough.

каши́ца thin gruel; pulp.

ка́шлять (pf. ка́шлянуть) cough.

кашта́н chestnut; кашта́новый chestnut (a).

каю́та cabin, room; каю́т-компа́ния mess, ward-room.

ка́яться (ка́юсь, ка́ешься; pf. по-) (в + prep.) confess; (pf. рас-) (в + prep.) repent (of).

квадра́нт quadrant.

квадра́т square; квадра́тн|ый square (a.); -ое уравне́ние quadratic equation.

ква́кать (pf. ква́кнуть) croak.

квалифика́ция qualification; -ици́ровать (ipf. & pf.) qualify.

ква́нтовый quantum (a.).

ква́рта quart.

кварта́л quarter, block; кварта́льный of a block; quarterly; (hist.) policeman.

кварте́т quartet.

кварти́ра flat, apartment; billet,quarters; к. и стол board and lodging; квартира́нт, ~ка lodger, tenant; кварти́рн|ый flat, billet (a.); -ая пла́та, квартпла́та rent.

кварц quartz.

квас kvass; ква́сить (-а́шу, -а́сишь; pf. за-) make sour, ferment; квасно́й kvass (a.); к. патриоти́зм jingoism.

квасц|ы́ (-о́в) alum.

ква́шен|ый fermented, leavened; -ая капу́ста sauerkraut.

кве́рху up(wards).

квита́нция receipt, ticket.

кви́ты quits.

кво́рум quorum.

кегельба́н bowling alley; ке́гл|я (gen. pl. -ей) skittle.

кедр cedar; ке́дровый cedar (a.).

ке́д|ы (-ов) light sports boots.

кекс cake.

кельт Celt; ке́льтский Celtic.

ке́|лья (gen. pl. -лий) cell.

кенгуру́ (m., indecl.) kangaroo.

ке́пка cap.

кера́м|ика ceramics; ~и́ческий ceramic.

керога́з primus stove; кероси́н paraffin; kerosene; кероси́нка oil stove; кероси́новый paraffin (a.).

ке́сарево сече́ние Caesarean operation.

ке́та Siberian salmon; ке́товая икра́ red caviar.

кефир *(kind of)* yoghurt.
кибернетика cybernetics.
кибитка hooded cart/sledge; nomad tent.
кивать *(pf.* кивнуть) nod (one's head); **ки|вок** (-гка) nod.
кидать *(pf.* кинуть) throw, fling; **-ся** throw oneself, rush; throw.
кий (кия) cue.
кикимора goblin; fright.
кило *(indecl.)* kilogram.
кило|ватт kilowatt; **~грамм** kilogram; **~метр** kilometre.
киль *(m.)* keel; **кильватер** wake.
килька sprat.
кимвал cymbal.
кинематография cinematography.
кинетика kinetics.
кинжал dagger.
кино *(indecl.)* cinema.
кино|журнал newsreel; **~звезда** *(pl.* -зве́зды) film star; **~съёмка** filming; **~хроника** newsreel.
кинуть *see* кидать.
киоск stall, kiosk.
кипа pile, stack; bale.
кипарис cypress.
кипен|ие boiling; точка -ия boiling point; кипеть (-плю, -пишь; *pf.* вс-) boil.
кипрей rosebay, willow-herb.
кипучий seething; ebullient; **кипятильник** boiler; **кипя|тить** (-чу, -тишь; *pf.* вс-) boil; **-ся** boil, become excited; **кипячёный** boiled.
киргиз, **~ка** Kirghiz; **киргизский** Kirghiz *(a.)*.
кириллица Cyrillic alphabet.
кирка pick-axe.
кирпич (-а) brick; **кирпичный** brick *(a.)*.
кисейный muslin *(a.)*; prim, starched *(fig.)*.
кисёл|ь | (-я) *kind of* jelly.
кисет tobacco-pouch.
кисея muslin.
кислород oxygen; **кислота** acid; **кислотность** *(f.)* acidity; **кислый** sour; **киснуть** *(past.* кис; *pf.* про-) turn sour.
киста cyst.
кисточка *(gen. pl.* -чек) brush, tassel; **кист|ь** *(f; pl.* -и, -ей) brush; cluster; hand.
кит (-а) whale.
кит|ае́ц (-айца), **~ая́нка** Chinese; **китайский** Chinese *(a.)*.

китель *(m.)* tunic.
китобой whaler; **китовый** whale *(a.)*.
кичиться *(inst)* pride oneself (on), boast (about); **кичливый** conceited.
киш|еть (-ит) *(inst.)* swarm, teem (with).
кишечник bowels, intestine; **кишечный** intestinal.
ки|шка *(gen. pl.* -шок) gut, intestine
кишмя swarming.
клавиатура keyboard; **клавиш** key.
клад treasure, hoard;
кладбище cemetery.
клад|езь *(m.)* fount *(e.g. of wisdom)*.
кладка laying *(e.g. of stone)*.
кладовая pantry, store-room; **кладовщик** (-а) storekeeper.
кланяться *(pf.* поклониться) bow.
клапан valve, vent.
кларнет clarinet.
класс class; **классик** classic; **классика** the classics; **классифици|ровать** *(ipf. & pf.)* classify; **классицизм** classicism; **классический** classical; **классный** class, school *(a.)*; first-class; **классовый** (social) class *(a.)*;
класть (клад|у, -ёшь; *past.* клал; *pf.* пол|ожить, -ожу, -ожишь) put, lay.
клёв bite, biting *(of fish)*.
клева́ть (клю|ю, -ёшь; *pf.* клюнуть) peck, bite.
клевер clover.
клевета slander, libel; **клев|етать** (-ещу, -ещешь; *pf.* на-) (на + *acc.*) slander; **клеветник** (-а), **~ница** slanderer; **клеветнический** slanderous.
кле|вок (-вка) peck.
клеврет tool, agent, minion.
клеёнка oilcloth.
клеить *(pf.* при- с-) stick, glue, gum; **-ся** become sticky, stick; разговор не клеился the conversation flagged; клей (на -ю) glue, gum, paste; **клейкий** sticky.
клеймить *(pf.* за-) brand, mark, stamp; **клеймо** *(pl.* клейма) brand, mark, stamp.
клейстер paste.
клёкот screech.
клён maple; **кленовый** maple *(a.)*.
кле|пать (-плю, -плешь *or* -паю; *pf.* за-) rivet; *(pf.* на-) (на + *acc.*) slander; **клёпка** rivet.
клептоман kleptomaniac.

клётка cage; check (on fabric); в -y check(ed); клёто|чка (gen. pl. -чек) small cage; cell; check; клётчатый checked.

клешн|я (gen. pl. -нёй) claw, nipper.

клещ (-á) tick.

клёщ|й (-ёй) pincers, tongs.

клиёнт client; клиентýра clientèle.

клизма enema.

клик cry, shout.

клйка clique.

кл|йкать (-йчу, -йчешь; pf. клйк-нуть) call.

клймат climate; климатический climatic.

кли|н (pl. -нья, -ньєр) wedge.

клйника clinic; клинический clinical.

кли|нóк (-нкá) blade; клинообрáзный wedge-shaped; cuneiform.

клйрос choir (part of church).

клич call; клй|чка (gen. pl. -чек) name; nickname.

клоáка cesspool.

клобýк (-á) cowl, hood.

клок (pl. клóч|ья, -ьєв or клокй) rag, shred.

клок|отáть (-óчєт) bubble, gurgle.

клонйть (клоню, клóнишь; pf. на-) bend, incline; -ся (к + dat.) bow, bend; tend (towards), approach.

клоп (-á) bug, bed-bug.

клóун clown.

кло|чóк (-чкá shred, scrap.

клуб 1. club(house); 2. puff, whirl (smoke).

клу́|бень (-бня) tuber.

клубйться curl, wreathe.

клубнйка garden strawberries; клубнйчное варéнье strawberry jam.

клу|бóк (-бкá) ball, tangle.

клýмба flower-bed.

клык (-á) canine tooth; fang, tusk.

клюв beak.

клюкá crutch.

клю́ква cranberries.

клю́нуть see клевáть.

ключ (-á) key, clue; spring; ключевóй of key importance; spring (a.); ключйца collar-bone, clavicle; клю́чница housekeeper.

клю́|шка (gen. pl. -шєк) club (e.g. hockey).

кля́кса blot.

кляп gag.

кля́сться (кля/нýсь, -нёшься; кля́-лся, -лáсь; pf. по-) swear, vow; кля́тва oath; кля́твенный on

oath; клятвопреступлéние per_jury.

кля́уза cavil; кля́узничать cavil.

кля́ча nag, jade.

кнйга book.

книго|éд bookworm; ~продáвец (-вца) bookseller; ~хранйлище book depository; library.

кнй|жка (gen. pl. -жєк) book(let); кнйжный book (a.); bookish, unpractical.

кнйзу downwards.

кнóпка press-button; drawing-pin; кнóпочное управлéние push-button control.

кнут (-á) whip.

княгйня princess, duchess; кня́жес-кий princely; кня́жнá princess; кня́|зь (pl. -зья, -зéй) prince.

коалициóнный coalition (a.); коалйция coalition.

кóбальт cobalt; кóбальтовый cobalt (a.).

кобéл|ь (-я́) (male) dog.

кобурá holster.

кобы́ла mare.

кóваный forged, wrought.

ковáрный crafty, perfidious; ковáрство perfidy.

ковáть (кую, куёшь; pf. гы-) forge; (pf. под-) shoe (horse); куй желéзо, покá горячó strike while the iron is hot.

ковб|óйка (gen. pl. -óєк) checked shirt.

ко|вёр (-врá) carpet.

ковéркать (pf. ис-) mangle, distort.

кóвка forging, shoeing; кóвкий ductile, malleable.

кóврик mat, rug.

ковчéг ark.

ковш (-á) ladle, scoop.

ковы́л|ь (-я́) feather-grass.

ковыля́ть hobble.

ковыря́ть (pf. по- or коғырнýть) pick.

когдá when; к.-либо some, any time; к.-нибудь some, any time; к.-то once (upon a time), some time.

кó|готь (-гтя, pl. -гти, -гтéй) claw, talon.

код code.

кодейн codeine.

кóдекс code (law).

кодифицйровать (ipf. & pf.) codify.

кóе-где here and there; кóе-как anyhow; with difficulty; кóе-какóй

some; ко́е-кто a few people; ко́е-что something.
ко́ечный больно́й in-patient.
ко́жа skin; из -и лезть *(fig.)* lean over backwards; ко́жаный leather *(a.)*; коже́венный tanning *(a.)*; ко́жица pellicie, film, skin; кожура́ rind, peel; кожу́х (-а́) sheepskin coat; housing, jacket.
коза́ *(pl.* ко́зы) goat, she-goat; ко|зёл (-зла́) billy goat; ко́зий goat's; козл|ёнок (-ёнка, *pl* -я́та) kid; козли́ный goaty.
ко́|злы (-зел) box *(on coach)*; trestle; saw-stool.
ко́зн|и (-ей) intrigues.
козы|рёк (-рька́) peak *(of cap)*; ко́зыр|ь *(pl.* -и, -е́й) trump *(card.)*; козыря́ть *(pf.* козырну́ть) trump; *(inst.)* flaunt; *(+ dat.)* salute.
кой = како́й *or* ко́е.
ко́йка *(gen. pl.* ко́ек) berth, bunk, cot, (hospital) bed.
ко́кать *(pf.* ко́кнуть) crack, break.
коке́тка flirt; coquette; коке́тливый flirtatious; коке́тничать flirt; коке́тство coquetry.
коклю́ш whooping cough.
ко́кон cocoon.
коко́совый coco *(a.)*.
кокс coke; коксу́ющийся у́голь coking coal.
кокте́йль *(m.)* cocktail; (milk) shake.
кол (-а́ *pl.* ко́л|ья, -ьев) stake, post.
ко́лба flask.
колбаса́ sausage.
колго́т|ки (-ок) tights.
колдова́ть conjure колдовство́ sorcery; колду́н (-а́) wizard; колду́н'ья *(gen. pl.* -ий) sorceress.
колеба́ние variation; hesitation; oscillation; кол|еба́ть (-е́блю, -е́блешь; *pf.* по-) shake; -ся oscillate, fluctuate; hesitate.
коле́нка knee.
коленко́р calico.
кол|е́но *(pl.* -е́ни, -е́ней) knee; (-е́нья, -е́ньев) elbow *(tech.)*; joint *(bot.)*; (-е́на; -е́н) bend; коле́нчатый cranked; к. вал crankshaft.
кол|еси́ть (-ешу́, -еси́шь) rove, travel about; колесни́ца chariot; кол|есо́ *(pl.* -ёса) wheel.
коле́|чко *(gen. pl.* -чек) ring(let).
кол|ея́ *(gen. pl.* -е́й) rut; track; входи́ть в -ю́ settle down.

ко́ли if; as.
ко́л|ики (-ик) colic.
колирова́ть *(ipf. & pl.)* graft.
коли́чественный numerical, quantitative; коли́чество number, quantity.
ко́лкий easily split; prickly, biting; ко́лкость *(f.)* causticity; biting remark.
колле́га *(m.)* colleague; колле́гия board; committee.
колле́дж college.
коллекти́в collective (body); коллективизи́ровать *(ipf. & pf.)* collectivize; коллекти́вн|ый collective; -ое хозя́йство collective farm.
коллекционе́р collector; колле́кция collector.
колло́квиум viva voce (examination).
коло́да block; pack *(cards.)*.
коло́|дец (-дца) well.
коло́дка boot-tree, last, *(tech.)* shoe; *(pl.)* stocks.
ко́локол *(pl.* -а) bell; колоко́льный bell *(a.)*; колоко́|льня *(gen. pl* -лен) belfry; колоко́льчик bell; bluebell.
колониа́льный colonial; колониза́ция colonization; колонизова́ть *(ipf. & pf.)* colonize; колони́ст, ~ка colonist; коло́ния colony.
коло́нка column; geyser, fountain; petrol pump; коло́нна column.
колори́т colouring, colour.
ко́л|ос *(pl.* -о́сья, -о́сьев) ear *(corn)*.
колосса́льный huge, colossal.
кол|оти́ть (-очу́, -о́тишь; *pf.* по-) bang, beat.
ко́лотый са́хар lump sugar.
коло́ть 1. (колю́, ко́лешь; *pf.* рас-; *ppp.* раско́лотый) break, split; 2. *(pf.* за-; *ppp.* зако́лотый) kill; stab; *(pf.* кольну́ть) prick, stab; у меня́ ко́лет в боку́ I have stitch in my side
колпа́к (-а́) cap; nightcap; cowl; simpleton; держа́ть под стекля́нным -о́м wrap in cotton wool.
колхо́з kolkhoz, collective farm; колхо́з|ник, ~ница kolkhoz worker; колхо́зный kolkhoz *(a.)*.
колча́н quiver.
колчеда́н pyrites.
колыбе́ль *(f.)* cradle; колыбе́льная пе́сня lullaby.
кол|ыха́ть (-ы́шу, -ы́шешь; *pf.* колыхну́ть) rock, sway; -ся sway, wave, flutter.

ко́лы|шек (-шка) peg.
коль = **ко́ли.**
колье́ (indecl.) necklace.
кольну́ть see **коло́ть.**
кольцева́ть (pf. за-, о-) ring; **кольцево́й** annular, circular, ring (a.); **кольцо́** (pl. ко́льца, коле́ц, ко́льцам) ring; **кольчу́га** chain mail.
колю́ч|ий prickly, spiny; **-ая про́волока** barbed wire; **колю́|чка** (gen. pl. -чек) prickle, thorn.
колю́шка (gen. pl. -шек) stickleback.
коля́ска carriage.
ком (pl. ко́м|ья, -ьев) lump, clod.
кома́нда 1. command, order; 2. party crew; team.
команди́р commander.
команд|ирова́ть (ipf. & pf.) send on business/mission; **~иро́вка** mission, business trip; **~иро́вочные** travelling expenses.
кома́ндный command (a.);
кома́ндование command; **кома́ндовать** command; (inst.) be in command (of); **кома́ндующий** (inst.) commander (of).
кома́р (-а́) gnat, mosquito.
комба́йн combine.
комбина́т group of enterprises; **комбина́ция** combination; slip; **комбинезо́н** overalls, flying-suit; **комбини́ровать** (pf. с-) combine.
коме́дия comedy.
комменда́нт commandant, superintendent; **комендату́ра** commandant's office.
коме́та comet.
ко́мик comic (actor).
комисса́р commissar; **комиссариа́т** commissariat.
комиссионе́р agent, broker.
комиссио́нный commission (a.); к. **магази́н** second-hand shop; комиссия commission, committee.
комите́т committee.
коми́ческий comic; **коми́чный** comical, funny.
ко́мкать (pf. с-) crumple.
коммента́рий commentary; **коммента́тор** commentator; **комменти́ровать** (pf. про-) comment on.
коммерса́нт businessman; **комме́рческий** commercial.
коммивояже́р commercial traveller.
комму́на commune; **коммуна́льный** communal.
коммуни́зм communism.

коммуника́ция communication.
коммуни́ст, **~ка** communist; **коммунисти́ческий** communist (a.).
коммута́тор switchboard.
коммюнике́ (indecl.) communiqué.
ко́мната room; **ко́мнатный** room (a.); indoor.
комо́д chest of drawers, locker.
ко|мо́к (-мка́) lump.
компа́ктный compact.
компа́ния company.
компаньо́н, **~ка** companion, partner.
компа́ртия Communist Party.
ко́мпас compass.
компенс|а́ция compensation; **~и́ровать** (ipf. & pf.) compensate.
компете́нтный competent; authorized; **компете́нция** competence, sphere.
компили́ровать (pf. с-) compile; **компиля́ция** compilation.
ко́мплекс complex; **ко́мплексный** complex, composite.
компле́кт complete set; **компле́ктный** complete; **комплектова́ть** (pf. у-) complete; recruit, staff.
компле́кция build, constitution.
комплиме́нт compliment.
компози́тор composer; **компози́ция** composition.
компоне́нт component.
компо́ст compost.
компости́ровать (pf. про-) punch (a ticket, with date of departure and number of seat).
компо́т stewed fruit.
компре́сс compress.
компромети́ровать (pf. с-) compromise; **компроми́сс** compromise.
комсомо́л Young Communist League, Komsomol; **комсомо́|лец** (-льца), **~лка** Komsomol member; **комсомо́льский** Komsomol (a.).
комфо́рт comfort; **комфорта́бельный** comfortable.
конве́йер conveyor, production line.
конве́кция convection.
конве́нция convention.
конве́рсия conversion.
конве́рт envelope.
конвои́ровать escort; **конво́й** escort.
конву́льсия convulsion.
конгре́сс congress.
конденс|а́тор condenser; **~а́ция** condensation; **~и́ровать** (ipf. & pf.) condense.

кондитер confectioner; **кондитерск|ая** confectioner's shop; **-ие изделия** confectionery.

кондиционирование conditioning; **к. воздуха** air-conditioning.

кондуктор *(pl. -ы or -á)* conductor, guard.

коневодство horse breeding; **конезавод** stud.

ко|нёк (-нька) small horse; hobby; skate.

ко|нец (-нца) end; **в один к.** one way; **к. всему делу венец** all's well that ends well; **в конце концов** ultimately; **сводить концы с концами** make ends meet.

конечно of course.

конечность *(f.)* finiteness; extremity; **конечный** final; ultimate.

конина horseflesh.

конический conic.

конкретный concrete, specific.

конкурент competitor, rival; **конкуренция** competition; **конкурировать** compete; **конкурс** competition.

конница cavalry; **конный** horse *(a.)*, mounted; **конокрад** horse-thief.

коноп|атить (-áчу, -áтишь; *pf.* за-) caulk.

конопля hemp; **конопляный** hemp *(a.)*.

коносамент bill of lading.

консервативный conservative; **консерватор** Conservative, Tory; **консерватория** conservatoire.

консервировать *(ipf. & pf.)* preserve, can, bottle; **консервный нож** tin-opener; **консерв|ы** (-ов) preserves, tinned/canned food.

консилиум consultation *(med.)*.

конский horse *(a.)*.

консолидировать *(ipf. & pf.)* consolidate.

консорциум consortium.

конспект summary, synopsis; **конспективный** concise; **конспектировать** *(pf.* за-) make an abstract of.

конспиративный conspiratorial; secret; **конспиратор** conspirator; **конспирация** conspiracy.

констатировать *(ipf. & pf.)* certify, ascertain.

конституционный constitutional; **конституция** constitution.

конструировать *(ipf. & pf; pf. also* с-) construct, design; form; **конструктор** constructor, designer; **конструкция** construction, design.

консул consul; **консульский** consular; **консульство** consulate.

консультант consultant; tutor; **консультация** consultation; tutorial; **консультировать** *(pf.* про-) advise; (with с + *inst.*) consult; **-ся** (с + *inst.*) consult.

контакт contact.

контейнер container.

контекст context.

контингент contingent; quota.

континент continent; **континентальный** continental.

контокоррент current account.

контора office; **конторка** bureau, desk; **конторский** office *(a.);* **контор|щик, ~щица** clerk.

контрабанда contraband; **контрабандист** smuggler.

контрабас double-bass.

контрагент contractor.

контр-адмирал rear-admiral.

контракт contract; **контрактовать** *(pf.* за-) contract for.

контраст contrast; **контрастировать** contrast.

контратака counter-attack.

контрибуция contribution.

контрнаступление counter-offensive.

контрол|ёр controller, inspector; **контролировать** *(pf* про-) control, check; **контроль** *(m.)* control, check; **контрольный** control *(a.)*.

контр|претензия counter-claim; **~разведка** counter-espionage; security service; **~революция** counter-revolution.

конт|узить *(pf.)* (-ужу, -узишь) contuse, shell-shock; **контузия** contusion, shell-shock; concussion.

контур contour, outline; circuit *(elec.)*.

конура kennel.

конус cone; **конусообразный** conical.

конфедерация confederation.

конферансье *(m. indecl.)* compère, master of ceremonies.

конференция conference.

конфета sweet, candy.

конфиденциальный confidential.

конфискация confiscation; **конфисковать** *(ipf. & pf.)* confiscate.

конфликт conflict.

конфорка ring, burner *(on cooker)*

конфу́з discomfiture; конф|у́зить (-у́ж-у, -у́зишь; *pf.* с-) disconcert; fluster; -ся be disconcerted/shy.

концентрацио́нный concentration *(a.)*; концентра́ция concentration; концентри́ровать *(pf.* с-) concentrate.

концентри́ческий concentric.

конце́пция conception.

конце́рн concern, enterprise.

конце́рт concert; концертме́йстер leader of orchestra.

конце́ссия concession.

концо́вка tail-piece, ending.

конча́ть *(pf.* ко́нчить) finish; -ся end; ко́нчик tip; кончи́на decease.

конъюнкту́ра conjuncture; situation.

кон|ь (-я́, *pl.* ко́ни, коне́й) horse, steed.

конёк|и́ (-о́в) skates; ро́ликовые к. roller skates; конькобе́|жец (-жца) skater; конькобе́жный спорт skating.

конья́к (-а́) cognac.

ко́нюх groom, stable man; коню́|шня *(gen. pl.* -шен) stable.

кооперати́в co-operative (society); кооперати́вный co-operative; коопера́ция co-operation.

коопта́ция co-optation; коопти́ровать *(ipf. & pf.)* co-opt.

координи́ровать *(ipf. & pf.)* co-ordinate.

копа́ть dig; -ся rummage.

коп|е́йка *(gen. pl.* -е́к) copeck.

ко|пёр (-пра́) piledriver.

ко́п|и (-ей) mines.

копи́лка money-box.

копи́рка *(coll.)* carbon-paper; копирова́льный copying *(a.);* копи́ровать *(pf.* с-) copy; imitate.

копи́ть (коплю́, ко́пишь; *pf.* на-) accumulate.

ко́пия copy.

копна́ *(pl.* ко́|пны, -пён, -пна́м) stook; shock *(of hair).*

ко́поть *(f.)* soot.

копоши́ться swarm.

ко|пте́ть (-пчу́, -пти́шь) be smoky, smoke; swot, work hard; ко|пти́ть (-пчу́, -пти́шь; *pf.* за-) smoke, cure; *(pf.* на-) give off smoke, soot; не́бо копти́т he is wasting his time; копчёный smoked.

копы́то hoof.

копь *see* ко́пи.

копь|ё *(pl.* ко́пья, копий) spear, lance.

кора́ bark; rind; crust; cortex.

корабле|круше́ние shipwreck; ~ строе́ние shipbuilding.

кора́бл|ь (-я́) ship; nave.

кора́лл coral.

кор|е́ец (-е́йца) Korean.

коре́йка brisket.

корена́стый thickset.

корени́ться (в + *prep.)* be rooted (in); коренно́й radical, basic; native; molar; shaft *(horse);* ко́|рень (-рня, *pl.* -рни, -рне́й) root; вырыва́ть с ко́рнем uproot, eradicate; коре́н|ья (-ьев) culinary roots.

коре́янка Korean woman.

корзи́н(к)а basket.

коридо́р corridor.

кори́нка currants.

кори́ть reproach, upbraid.

кори́ца cinnamon.

кори́чневый brown.

ко́рка crust, peel, rind.

корм *(pl.* -ы or -а́) forage, feed.

корма́ stern, poop.

корми́|лец (-льца) bread-winner; корми́лица wet-nurse; breadwinner; корми́ть (кормлю́, ко́рмишь; *pf.* на-, по-) feed; -ся feed; *(inst.)* live on, by; кормле́ние feeding; кормово́й 1. fodder *(a.);* 2. stern *(a.),* after-; корму́|шка *(gen. pl.* -шек) trough, feeding rack.

ко́рмчий helmsman, pilot.

корнево́й root *(a.);* корнепло́д|ы (-ов) root crops.

корне́т cornet.

ко́роб *(pl.* -а́) box, chest; коробе́йник pedlar.

коро́бить *(pf.* по-) make warped; warp; -ся warp.

коро́бка box.

коро́ва cow; коро́вий cow's *(a.);* коро́вка little cow; бо́жья к. ladybird.

короле́ва queen; короле́вский royal; короле́вство kingdom; коро́л|ь (-я́) king.

коромы́с|ло *(gen. pl.* -сел) yoke; beam.

коро́на crown; корона́ция coronation; коро́нка crown *(on tooth);* коронова́ть *(ipf. & pf.)* crown.

коро́ста scab.

коросте́л|ь (-я) corncrake, landrail.

корота́ть *(pf.* с-) while away.

коро́тк|ий *(compr.* коро́че) short; на -ой ноге́ с + *inst.* familiar with; ру́ки ко́ротки! just try!

коротко|волновый short-wave; -волосый short-haired.
коротышка *(m. & f.)* little person.
короче *see* короткий.
корпорация association, union.
корпус *(pl. -á)* building; hull; frame; corps; *(pl. -ы)* body *(of a man, animal).*
корректив corrective; корректировать *(pf. про-)* correct; корректный correct, proper.
корректор proof-reader; корректура proof-reading; proof.
корреспондент correspondent; корреспонденция correspondence; report.
коррозия corrosion.
корсет corset; корсетница corsetiere.
кортеж cortege; motorcade.
кортик dirk.
корто|чки (-чек): сидеть на -чках squat.
корунд corundum.
корчевать *(pf. рас-)* root out.
корчить *(pf. с-)* twist, make writhe; pull *(faces)*; к. из себя эксперта pose as an expert; -ся squirm, writhe.
кор|чма *(gen. pl. -чем)* inn, tavern.
коршун kite.
корыстный mercenary; корыстолюбие self-interest; корысть *(f.)* self-interest; profit.
корыто trough; оставаться у разбитого -а be no better off at the finish.
корь *(f.)* measles.
корявый rough; clumsy.
коряга snag *(of wood, log.).*
коса 1. *(косу, pl. косы)* plait, tress; 2. *(acc. косу pl. косы)* scythe; spit *(of land).*
косвенный indirect.
косилка mowing-machine.
косинус cosine.
косить 1. *(-шу, -сишь; pf. по-, с-; ppp. скошенный)* twist; squint; 2. *(кошу, косишь; pf. с-)* mow.
ко|ситься *(-шусь, -сишься; pf. по-)* *(на + acc.)* be(come) twisted; look sideways; look unfavourably (on).
коси|чка *(gen. pl. -чек)* pigtail.
косматый shaggy.
косметика cosmetics; косметический, каби ет beauty parlour.
космический cosmic, space *(a.).*
космо|дром space drome; ~навт cosmonaut, spaceman.

космополит cosmopolitan, man of the world.
космос space.
космы (косм) mane, dishevelled hair.
коснеть *(pf. за-)* stagnate; stiffen; косность *(f.)* stagnation, sluggishness; косноязычный tongue-tied.
коснуться *see* касаться.
косный inert, stagnant.
косо|воротка Russian blouse *with collar fastened at side;* ~глазый cross-eyed ~гор slope, hillside.
косой slanting, oblique; squinting; косолапый in-toed; *(coll.)* clumsy.
костенеть *(pf. за-, о-)* stiffen, grow numb.
кос|тёр (-тра) bonfire.
костистый, костлявый bony; костный correct; *(gen. pl. -чек)* small bone; stone, pip.
костыл|ь (-я) crutch; spike.
кост|ь *(f.; pl. -и, -ей)* bone.
костюм costume; suit; костюмированный fancy-dress *(a.).*
костяк (-á) skeleton; *(fig.)* backbone; костяной bone *(a.).*
косынка neckerchief, scarf.
косьба mowing.
косяк (-á) 1. jamb, door-post; 2. shoal, flock.
кот (-á) tom-cat; покупать кота в мешке buy a pig in a poke.
ко|тёл (-тла) cauldron, boiler; коте|лок (-лка) pot, kettle; bowler-(hat); котельная boiler-room, boiler-house.
кот|ёнок (-ёнка, pl. -ята, -ят) kitten.
котик little cat; seal; sealskin; котиковый seal *(a.).*
котировать *(ipf. & pf.)* quote *(fin.).*
котиться *(кочусь, котишься; pf. о-)* have/give birth to kittens.
котлета cutlet, chop; rissole.
котлован pit, excavation *(for foundations)*; котловина hollow.
котомка knapsack.
который which, who.
коттедж cottage, house.
кофе *(m., indecl.)* coffee; кофеин caffeine; кофейник coffee pot; кофейный coffee *(a.).*
кофта woman's jacket; cardigan; кофточка *(gen. pl. -чек)* blouse, cardigan.
кочан (-á) head *(e.g. of cabbage).*
кочевать roam, be a nomad; кочевник nomad; кочевой nomadic.

кочегáр fireman, stoker.

коченéть *(pf.* за-, о-) become numb.

коче|ргá *(gen. pl.* -рёр) poker.

кóчка *(gen. pl.* -чек) hammock.

коша́чий feline.

коше|лёк (-лькá) purse.

кóшка *(gen. pl.* -шек) cat.

кошмáр nightmare; кошмáрный nightmarish.

кощу́нственный blasphemous; кощу́нство blasphemy.

коэффициéнт coefficient.

краб crab.

крáга legging.

крáденый stolen; крáдучись stealthily.

краевéдческий pertaining to study of local region; краевóй regional.

краеугóльный ка́ ень corner stone.

крáжа theft, larceny; к. со взлóмом burglary.

край (в краю́, *pl.* края́) edge, brink; land, region; крáйн|ий extreme; в -ем слу́чае as a last resort; по -ей мéре at least; крáйность *(f.)* extreme; extremity.

крамóла sedition; крамóльник rebel; крамóльный seditious.

кран crane; крановщи́к (-á) crane-driver.

крап speckles; крáп|пать (-плет) to spot with rain.

крапи́ва nettle; крапи́вник wren; крапи́вная лихорáдка nettle-rash.

крáпинка speck(le); крáпчатый spotted, speckled.

красá beauty; ornament; краса́|вец (-вца) handsome man, boy; краса́вица beautiful girl/woman; beauty.

краси́вый beautiful.

краси́|льня *(gen. pl.* -лен) dye-works; краси́тель *(m.)* dye (-stuff); крáсить (крáшу, крáсишь; *pf.* вы-, о-, по-) colour, paint, dye; adorn; -ся *(pf.* на-) use make-up, dye one's hair; крáска colour, paint, dye.

краснéть *(pf.* по-) go red; show red; -ся show red.

красно|армéец (-армéйца) Red Army man; ~армéйский Red Army *(a.)*; ~бáй gas-bag; ~вáтый reddish; ~речи́вый eloquent; ~рéчие eloquence.

краснотá redness.

красно|флóтец (-флóтца) Red Navy man; ~щёкий rosy-cheeked.

красну́ха German measles.

крáсн|ый red; beautiful, fine; -ый уголóк recreation and reading room; -ая доскá roll of honour; -ое дéрево mahogany.

красовáться stand in splendour/ beauty.

крас|отá *(pl.* -óты) beauty.

крáсочный dye *(a.)*; colourful.

красть (крад|у́, -ёшь; *ppp.* крáденный; *pf.* у-) steal; -ся creep.

крат: во сто к. a hundredfold.

крáтер crater.

крáткий *(comp.* крáтче) short, brief.

кратко|врéменный momentary; short-term; ~срóчный short-term.

крáткость *(f.)* brevity.

крáтный divisible; крáтное multiple.

кратчáйший shortest.

крах crash, failure.

крахмáл starch; крахмáлистый starchy; крахмáлить *(pf.* на-) starch; крахмáльный starched.

крáшеный painted, coloured, dyed.

кревéтка shrimp.

креди́т credit; в к. on credit; креди́тный credit *(a.)*; кредитовáть *(ipf. & pf.)* give to/for; кредитоспосóбный solvent.

крéйсер cruiser; крейси́ровать cruise.

крем cream.

кремáторий crematorium; кремáция cremation.

кре|мéнь (-мня́) flint.

кремлёвский kremlin *(a.)*; кремл|ь (-я́) kremlin, fortress.

кремнёвый flint(y).

кремнезём silica; крéмний silicon.

крéмовый cream.

крен list, bank, turn; tendency; крени́ть *(pf.* на-) turn over; -ся list.

креозóт creosote.

креп crepe.

крепи́ть strengthen; constipate; -ся stand firm; restrain oneself; крéпкий *(comp.* крéпче) firm, strong; креплéние fastening, strengthening; крéпнуть *(past.* креп; *pf.* о-) become strong.

крепостни́к (-á) serf owner; крепостн|óй 1. serf; -óе прáво serfdom.

крепостнóй 2. fortification *(a.)*; крéпость *(f.)* fortress.

крепчáть grow stronger; крéпче *see* крéпкий.

крéсло *(gen. pl.* крéсел) armchair; *(pl.)* the stalls.

крест (-á) cross; поста́вить к. на + acc.
give up as a bad job; put an end to;
крест|йны (-и́н) christening; кре-
сти́ть (крещу́, кре́стишь, ipf. &
pf; pf. also o-) christen; (pf. пере-)
(make sign of) cross; -ся be christ-
ened; cross oneself; крёст|ник,
~ница god-child; крёстный cross
(a.); крёстн|ый, -ая god-parent.
крестóвый похóд crusade; крестонó|-
сец (-сца) crusader.
крестья́нин (pl. -я́не, -я́н) peasant;
крестья́нка peasant woman; кресть-
я́нский peasant (a.); крестья́н-
ство peasantry.
креще́ние christening.
крива́я curve; кривизна́ curvature;
криви́ть (pf. по-, с-) bend, distort;
к. душóй be a hypocrite; -ся become bent etc.; pull a face.
кривля́ться grimace; twist; give
oneself airs.
кривóй crooked, curved.
криво|нóгий bow-legged; ~тóлки
(-ов) false rumours; ~ши́п (tech.)
crank.
кри́зис crisis; кри́зисный crisis (a.).
крик cry, shout.
кри́кет (the game of) cricket.
крикли́вый loud; flashy; кри́кнуть see
крича́ть.
криминáльный criminal.
кри́нка pot.
криста́лл crystal; кристаллизи́ро-
вать (ipf. & pf.) crystallize (v. t.);
криста́льный crystal(line).
крите́рий criterion.
кри́тик critic; кри́тика criticism;
критиковáть criticize; крити́че-
ский critical.
кри|ча́ть (-чу́, -чи́шь; pf. за-, про-,
кри́кнуть) shout; крича́щий loud;
flashy.
кров shelter.
кровáвый bloody, blood (a.).
кровáтка, кровáть (f.) bed.
крóвельный roof (a.).
кровенóсный blood (a.); circula-
tory.
крó|вля (gen. pl. -вель) roofing, roof.
крóвный blood (a.); thorough-bred;
vital.
крово|жáдный blood-thirsty; ~изли-
я́ние haemorrhage; ~обраще́ние
circulation; ~останá́вливающее
styptic; ~пи́йца (m. f.) blood-
sucker; ~подтёк bruise; ~проли́-
тие bloodshed; ~пускáние blood-

letting; ~тече́ние bleeding; ~то-
чи́ть bleed.
кров|ь (f. в -и́) blood; кровяно́й
blood (a.).
крои́ть (ppr. крóенный; pf. вы́-, с-)
cut out (dress).
крокоди́л crocodile.
крóлик rabbit.
крóме (gen.) except, besides, apart
from.
кромéшн|ый; тьма -ая pitch dark-
ness.
крóмка edge.
кромсáть (pf. ис-) shred.
крóна top (of tree); crown
(coin).
крóншнеп curlew.
кропи́ть (pf. o-) sprinkle.
кропотли́вый laborious, painstaking.
кроссвóрд crossword.
крот (-á) mole.
крóткий gentle, meek; крóтость (f.)
meekness.
крохá (крóху, pl. крóх|и, -áм) crumb;
крохобóрство hairsplitting; крó-
хотный, крóшечный tiny; кр|о-
ши́ть (-ошу́, -óшишь; pf. ис-, на-,
рас-) crumble; chop; mince; крó|ш-
ка (gen. pl. -шек) crumb.
круг (в -ý; pl. -и́) circle; кру́глень-
кий chubby, rotund; круглосу́точ-
ный twenty-four-hour; кру́глый
round, circular; кругово́й circular; mutual.
круго|ворóт rotation, succession; ~
зóр horizon, mental outlook.
кругóм round about; (gen.) round.
круго|обрáзный circular; ~свéтный
round-the-world.
кружевнóй lace (a.); кру́ж|ево (pl.
-евá, -ев, -евáм) lace.
кружи́ть (кружу́, кру́жишь; pf. за-)
spin, turn; -ся spin, whirl.
кру́|жка (gen. pl. -жек) mug,
jug.
кру́жный roundabout (a.); кру́|жóк
(-жкá) circle, group.
круп croup, (med.); croupe (horse).
крупá (pl. кру́пы) groats.
кру́|пи́нка, ~пи́ца grain.
кру́пный large, big.
крутизна́ steepness.
крути́ть (кручу́, кру́тишь; pf. за-,
с-) twist, twirl; -ся spin.
крутóй (comp. кру́че) steep; sudden,
stern; кру́тость (f.) slope; stern-
ness; кру́ча steep slope.
кручи́на grief.

крушéние downfall, wreck, ruin; крушить destroy.

крыжóвник gooseberry, -berries.

крыла́тый winged; крылó (pl. кры́л| -ья, -ьев) wing; sail (windmill); wing, mudguard.

крыльцó (pl. кры́|льца, -лéц, -льца́м) porch.

кры́мский Crimean.

кры́нка pot, jug.

кры́са rat; кры́синый яд rat poison; крысолóв rat-catcher.

крыть (крóю, крóешь; ppp. кры́тый; pf. по-) cover; roof; trump; -ся lie, be; be covered (etc.); кры́ша roof; кры́|шка (gen. pl. -шек) lid.

крюк (-á) hook; detour; крючкова́тый hooked.

крючкотвóрство pettifogging.

крю|чóк (-чка́) hook.

крюшóн champagne-cup, cocktail.

кряж ridge; block.

кря́кать (pf. кря́кнуть) quack; кря́ква wild duck.

кря́|хтеть (-хчу́, -хти́шь) groan.

ксилофóн xylophone.

кста́ти to the point, opportunely; by the way.

кто who; ктó-либо, ктó-нибудь anyone, someone; ктó-то someone.

куб (pl. -ы́) cube; boiler.

ку́барем head over heels; куба́р|ь (-я́) top.

куба́ту́ра cubic content; куби́зм cubism; ку́бик cube, block, brick.

куби́|нец (-нца), ~нка Cuban.

куби́ческий cubic.

ку́|бок (-бка) cup; trophy.

кубомéтр cubic metre.

кувши́н jug, pitcher.

кувырка́ться (pf. кувыркну́ться) turn somersaults; кувырко́м topsyturvy.

куда́ where, whither; к. лу́чше far better; к.-либо, к.-нибудь anywhere, somewhere; к.-то somewhere.

куда́хтать cackle, cluck.

куде́с|ник, ~ница sorcerer, -eress.

ку́др|и (-éй) curls; кудря́вый curly; ornate.

кузéн, кузи́на cousin.

кузнéц (-á) blacksmith; кузнéчик grasshopper; кузнéчный forge (a.); ку́зница smithy.

ку́зов (pl. -ы or -á) basket; body (of car).

ку́киш fig (rude sign).

ку́кла (gen. pl. ку́кол) doll, puppet; ку́колка dolly; chrysalis; ку́кольный doll, puppet (a.).

кукуру́за maize.

куку́шка (gen. pl. -шек) cuckoo.

кула́к (-á) fist; kulak, rich peasant; кула́цкий kulak (a.); кула́чество the kulaks; кула́чный бой fisticuffs.

кулебя́ка pie, pasty.

ку|лёк (-лька́) bag.

кули́к (-á) snipe.

кулина́рный culinary.

кули́са wing (theat.); за -ами behind the scenes.

кулуа́р|ы (-ов) lobby (parl.).

куль (-я́) bag.

кульмина́ция culmination.

культ cult.

культиви́ровать cultivate.

культу́ра culture; культу́рный cultural.

кум (pl. кумов|ья́, -ьёв) god-father; кума́ god-mother.

куми́р idol.

кумовствó nepotism; relationship of godparents.

кумы́с kumiss (fermented mare's milk).

куни́ца marten.

купа́|льный bathing (a.); купа́ль|щик, ~щица bather; купа́ние bathing; купа́ть (pf. вы́-, ис-) bath(e); -ся bathe.

купé (indecl.) compartment.

купéль (f.) font.

ку|пéц (-пца́) merchant; купéческий merchant (a.); купéчество the merchants.

купи́ть see покупа́ть.

куплéт couplet.

ку́пля purchase.

ку́пол (pl. -á) cupola, dome.

купорóс vitriol.

ку́пчая deed of purchase.

купчи́ха woman merchant, merchant's wife.

купю́ра 1. cut; 2. note, bond.

курга́н burial mound.

курéние smoking; кури́льница censer; кури́ль|щик, ~щица smoker.

кури́ный hen's, chicken.

кури́ть (курю́, ку́ришь; pf по-, вы́-) smoke; -ся smoke, burn.

ку́рица hen, chicken.

курнóсый snub-nosed.

коровóдство poultry-breeding.

курóк (-рка́) cock, trigger.

куропа́тка partridge.
куро́рт health resort.
курослеп buttercup.
ку́ро|чка *(gen. pl.* -чек) pullet.
курс course; rate of exchange; дер-
жа́ть его в -е дел keep him in-
formed.
курса́нт student.
курси́в italics.
курси́ровать ply.
ку́ртка jacket.
курча́вый curly-haired.
курьёз queer thing; курьёзный
strange.
курье́р messenger; курье́рский express *(a.)*
куря́тина (meat of) fowl; куря́тник
hen-house.
куря́щий smoker.
куса́ть *(pf.* кусну́ть, ук|уси́ть, -ушу́,
-у́сишь) bite; -ся bite.
куса́чки (-чек) nippers, wire-cutters.
ку|со́к (-ска́) lump, piece; кусо́|чек
(-чка) piece.
куст (-а́) bush; куста́рник bushes,
shrubs.
куста́рный domestic, hand-made;
primitive; куста́р|ь (-я́) crafts-
man.
кусти́стый bushy.
ку́тать *(pf.* за-) wrap up; -ся muffle,
wrap up.
кутёж (-а́) debauch, drinking bout.
кутерьма́ chaos, commotion.
кути́ть (кучу́, ку́тишь; *pf.* кутну́ть)
make merry, carouse.
куха́рка cook; ку́|хня *(gen. pl.* -хонь)
kitchen; ку́хонный kitchen *(a.).*
ку́цый dock-tailed; short.
ку́ча heap.
кучево́й cumulus.
ку́чер *(pl.* -а́) coachman.
ку́|чка *(gen. pl.* -чек) heap; group.
ку́шанье food, dish; ку́шать *(pf.* по-,
с-) eat.
куше́тка couch.

Л

лабири́нт labyrinth.
лабора́нт, ~ка laboratory assistant;
лаборато́рия laboratory.
ла́ва lava; drift *(geol.).*
лава́нда lavender.
лави́на avalanche.
лави́ровать tack, manoeuvre.

ла́вка bench; shop; ла́вочник shop-
keeper.
лавр laurel.
ла́герный camp *(a.)* ; ла́гер|ь *(pl.* -и)
camp *(fig.),* party; *(pl.* -я́) camp;
жить в -я́х camp out.
лавса́н *kind of* terylene.
лад (в -у́, *pl.* -ы́) harmony; way;
де́ло идёт на л. things are going
well; на но́вый л. in a new way.
ла́дан incense.
ла́дить (ла́жу, ла́дишь) get on well;
ла́дно all right; ла́дный well-form-
ed.
ладо́нь *(f.)* palm; ладо́ш|а palm;
хло́пать в -и clap hands.
ла|дья́ *(gen. pl.* -де́й) boat; rook,
castle *(chess).*
лаз manhole.
лазаре́т hospital, sick-bay.
лаз|е́йка *(gen. pl.* -е́εк) hole; loophole.
ла́зить (-жу, -зишь) climb.
лазу́рный azure; лазу́рь *(f.)* azure,
blue.
лазу́тчик scout, spy.
лай barking; ла́йка 1. husky. 2. kid
(-skin); ла́йковый kid *(a.).*
ла́йнер liner.
лак varnish, lacquer.
лака́ть *(pf.* вы́-) lap.
лаке́й footman; lackey.
лакирова́ть *(pf.* от-) varnish, lacquer; лакиро́ванная ко́жа patent
leather.
ла́кмус litmus; ла́кмусовая бума́га
litmus paper.
ла́ковый varnished.
ла́комиться *(inst.)* treat oneself (to);
ла́комка *(m. & f.)* gourmand;
ла́комство dainty; ла́комый (до)
dainty; fond (of).
лакон|и́ческий, ~и́чный laconic.
ла́мпа lamp; valve; лампа́да icon-
lamp; ла́мпо|чка *(gen. pl.* -чек)
lamp, bulb.
лангу́ста spiny lobster.
ландша́фт landscape, scenery.
ла́ндыш lily of the valley.
лани́та *(poet.)* cheek.
ланце́т lancet.
лань *(f.)* fallow-deer; doe.
ла́па paw, claw.
ла́|поть (-птя; -пти, -пте́й) bast
shoe.
ла́пчатый web-footed.
лапша́ noodles.
ла|рёк (-рька́) stall; ла́рчик casket;
ларь (-я́) chest, coffer.

ла́ска 1. caress; 2. weasel; аска́ть *(pf.* при-) caress; fondle; -ся (к + *dat.)* caress; fawn (upon); ла́сковый affectionate, tender.
ласт fin, flipper.
ла́сто|чка *(gen. pl.* -чек) swallow.
латв|и́ец (-и́йца), ~и́йка *(gen. pl.* -и́ек) Latvian; латви́йский Latvian.
лате́нтный latent.
лати́нский Latin.
лату́нь *(f.)* brass; лату́нный brass *(a.).*
ла́ты (лат) armour.
латы́нь *(f.)* Latin.
латы́ш (-á), латы́|шка *(gen. pl.* -шек) Latvian; латы́шский Latvian *(a.).*
лауреа́т prizewinner, laureate.
ла́цкан lapel.
лачу́га hovel, shanty.
ла́ять (ла́ю, ла́ешь; *pf.* за-) bark.
лгать (лгу, лжёшь; *past.* лгал, -á; *pf. co-)* tell lies; *(pf.* на-) (на + *acc.)* slander; лгун (-á), лгу́|нья *(gen. pl.* -ний) liar.
лебеди́ный swan *(a.).*
лебёдка winch; female swan.
ле́бед|ь *(m, poet. f.; pl.* -и, -éй) swan.
лев (льва) lion.
леве́ть *(pf.* по-) move to left, politically.
левко́й gillyflower, stock.
левша́ left-hander; ле́вый left; left-wing.
легализова́ть *(ipf. & pf.)* legalize; лега́льный legal.
леге́нда legend; легенда́рный legendary.
лёгкий *(compr.* ле́гче) easy, light; лёгок на поми́не talk of the devil; легко́ it is easy; easily.
легко|атле́т (track and field) athlete; ~ве́рный credulous; ~ве́сный light-weight.
легково́й автомоби́ль car, cab.
лёгкое lung.
легко|мы́сленный thoughtless, frivolous; ~мы́слие flippancy.
лёгкость *(f.)* lightness, easiness.
лёгочный pulmonary.
ле́гче *see* лёгкий.
лёд (льда, на льду) ice.
леденёть *(pf.* за-, о-) freeze; become numb; леде|не́ц (-нца́) candy, fruit-drop; lollipop; ледени́ть *(pf.* о-) chill, freeze; ле́дник (-а) refrigerator; ледни́к (-á) glacier; леднико́вый glacial; ледо́вый ice *(a.);* ледоко́л ice-breaker; ледяно́й icy.

лежа́лый stale, old; ле|жа́ть (-жу́, -жи́шь; *ger.* лёжа) lie; лежа́чий lying; лежебо́ка *(m. & f.)* lazybones.
ле́звие blade.
лез|ть (-зу, -зешь; *past* лез, -ла; *pf.* по-) get(into), climb; intrude; fit; fall out *(hair).*
лейбори́ст member of Labour Party.
ле́йка *(gen. pl.* ле́ек) watering-can.
лейтена́нт lieutenant.
лейтмоти́в leit-motif; burden, tenor.
лека́рственный medicinal; лека́рство medicine.
ле́кар|ь *(pl.* -и *or* -я́) *(coll.)* doctor.
ле́ксика vocabulary.
ле́ктор lector; лекцио́нный lecture *(a.);* ле́кция lecture.
ле|ле́ять (-ле́ю, -ле́ешь) cherish, foster.
ле́мех (ле́меха́) plough share.
лён (льна) flax.
лени́вый lazy.
ленини́зм Leninism; ле́нинский Leninist.
лени́ться (леню́сь, ле́нишься) be lazy; ле́ность *(f.)* laziness.
ле́нта ribbon, tape; ле́нточный tape-, band-.
лент|а́й, ~я́йка *(gen. pl.* -я́ек) lazybones.
лень *(f.)* idleness, indolence; мне л. идти I can't be bothered to go.
лепес|то́к (-тка́) petal.
ле́пет babble, prattle; ле|пета́ть (-печу́, -пе́чешь; *pf.* про-) babble.
лепё|шка *(gen. pl.* -шек) flat cake; lozenge.
лепи́ть (леплю́, ле́пишь; *pf.* вы́-, с-) fashion, model, sculpture; -ся cling; ле́пка modelling; лепно́й plastic; moulded.
ле́пта mite.
лес (в -ý, *pl.* -á) forest, wood; *(pl.)* scaffolding.
леса́ *(pl.* лёсы) fishing-line.
ле́сенка short ladder, flight of stairs.
леси́стый wooded.
ле́ска fishing-line.
лесни́к (-á) woodman, forester; лесни́чество forestry; лесно́й forest *(a.);* лесово́дство forestry.
лесо|насажде́ние afforestation; ~пи́льня *(gen. pl.* ~лен) sawmill; ~ру́б wood-cutter; ~спла́в rafting, floating; ~сте́пь *(f.)* forest-steppe.
ле́стница staircase, ladder; чёрная л. backstairs.

лéстный flattering; **лесть** *(f.)* flattery.

лёт: **на лету** in flight; **хватáть всё на лету** be quick to learn.

летáтельный flying *(a.)*; **летáть** fly; **ле|тéть** (-чý, -тúшь; *pf.* по-) fly.

лéтний summer.

лётный flying *(a.)*.

лéто *(pl.* летá*)* summer; **в летáх** elderly.

лéто|пись *(f.)* chronicle; **~счислéние** (system of) chronology; era.

летýн (-á) rolling stone.

летýчесть *(f.)* volatility; **летýч|ий** flying; volatile; **-ая мышь** bat; **летý|чка** *(gen. pl.* -чек*)* leaflet; short meeting; mobile detachment.

лёт|чик, **~чица** pilot; **л. -испытáтель** test pilot.

лечéбница hospital; **лечéбный** medical; **лечéние** treatment; **лечúть** (лечý, лéчишь) *(от + gen.)* treat (for); **-ся** receive treatment, take a cure.

лечь *see* ложúться.

лéший wood-goblin.

лещ (-á) bream.

лже- false, pseudo; **лжесвидéтельство** false evidence.

лжец (-á) liar; **лжúвый** false; untruthful.

ли whether; *(interrogative particle)*: придёшь ли ты? will you come?

либерáл liberal; **либералúзм** liberalism; **либерáльный** liberal *(a.)*.

лúбо or; **лúбо . . . лúбо . . .** either . . . or . . .

лú|вень (-вня) downpour; heavy shower.

лúвер 1. liver; 2. siphon, pipette.

ливрéя livery.

лúга league.

лигатýра alloy; ligature.

лúдер leader; **лидúровать** be in the lead *(sport)*.

лизáть (лижý, лúжешь; *pf.* лизнýть) lick.

лик countenance; image.

ликвидáция liquidation, abolition; **ликвидúровать** *(ipf. & pf.)* do away with.

ликёр liqueur.

ликовáние rejoicing; **ликовáть** rejoice.

лилéйный lily-white; **лúлия** lily.

лилóвый lilac-coloured.

лимáн estuary.

лимúт limit; **лимитúровать** *(ipf. & pf.)* limit.

лимóн lemon; **лимонáд** lemonade, fruit drink; **лимóнный** lemon, citric.

лúмфа lymph.

лингафóнный кабинéт language laboratory; **лингвúст** linguist; **лингвúстика** linguistics.

лин|éйка *(gen. pl.* -éек*)* line, ruler; carriage; **линéйный** linear; battle *(ship)*.

лúнза lens.

лúния line.

линкóр battleship.

линовáть *(pf.* на-*)* line, rule.

линóлеум linoleum.

линчевáть *(ipf. & pf.)* lynch.

линь| (-я) 1. tench; 2. line.

лúнька moulting; **линючий** fading; **линя́лый** faded; **линя́ть** *(pf.* вы-, по-*)* shed hair, moult; fade.

лúпа lime.

лúпкий sticky; **лúпнуть** *(past* лип, -ла*)* stick.

лúповый lime *(a.)*.

лúра lyre; **лúрик** lyric poet; **лирúческий** lyric; **лирúчный** lyrical.

лисá *(pl.* лúсы), **лисúца** fox; **лúсий** fox *(a.)*.

лист (-á, *pl.* -ы́) sheet; *(pl.* лúст|ья, -ьев) leaf; **листвá** foliage; **лúственница** larch; **лúственный** deciduous; leaf-bearing.

листóвка leaflet; **листовóй** leaf *(a.)*; **лис|тóк** (-ткá) leaf; leaflet.

листопáд fall.

лит|áвры (-áвр) kettledrum.

литéйный завóд foundry; **литéйщик** founder, smelter.

лúтер travel warrant.

литерáтор man of letters; **литератýра** literature; **литератýрный** literary.

литó|вец (-вца), **~вка** Lithuanian; **литóвский** Lithuanian *(a.)*.

литогрáфия lithography.

литóй cast.

литр litre.

литургúя mass, liturgy.

лить (лью, льёшь; *imper* лей; *past* лил, -á; *ppp.* лúтый) pour; cast, mould; **-ся** pour; **литьё** casting, moulding; casts.

лиф bodice.

лифт lift, elevator; **лифтёр** lift operator.

лúфчик underbodice, brassiere.

лихв|а́; с -о́й with interest.
лихои́мство usury, extortion.
лихо́й 1.. dashing, intrepid; 2. evil;
лиха́ беда́ нача́ло the first step is
the hardest.
лихора́дка fever; лихора́дочный
feverish.
лицево́й facial, front.
лице́й lyceum.
лицеме́р hypocrite; лицеме́рие hypocrisy; лицеме́рить dissemble; лице-
ме́рный hypocritical.
лицеприя́тие partiality.
лицо́ (pl. ли́ца) face; person; в л.
by sight; это вам к -у́ it suits you;
на нём -а́ нет he looks awful.
личи́на mask.
личи́нка larva, grub.
лично́й face (a.).
ли́чность (f.) personality; ли́чный
personal, private; л. соста́в personnel.
лиша́|й (-я́) herpes, shingles.
лиша́ть (pf. лиши́ть) deprive of;
л. его́ э́того deprive him of this;
-ся (gen.) lose.
ли́шек (-шка): два́дцать с ли́шком
twenty and a bit, just over
twenty.
лише́ние deprivation, loss; privation;
лиши́ть see лиша́ть.
ли́шн|ий superfluous, unnecessary;
-ий раз once again; де́сять с -им
more than ten.
лишь 1. only; 2. as soon as; лишь бы
if only.
лоб (лба, на лбу) forehead.
лобза́ть (poet.) kiss.
лови́ть (ловлю́, ло́вишь, pf пойма́ть)
catch.
ло́вкий (comp. ло́вче) adroit; ловкость (f.) dexterity.
ло́вля catching, hunting; ры́бная л.
fishing; лову́шка (gen. pl. -шек)
trap.
лог (pl. -а́) ravine.
логари́фм logarithm.
ло́гика logic; логи́ческий, ~ичный
logical.
ло́говище den, lair.
ло́дка boat; ло́дочник boatman; ло́-
дочный boat (a.).
лоды́|жка (gen. pl. -жек) ankle.
лоды́рничать idle, loaf about.
ло́жа 1. box; masonic lodge; 2. gun
stock.
ложби́на hollow.
ло́же couch, bed.

ло́же|чка (gen. pl. (-чек) small spoon;
под -чкой in the pit of the stomach.
ложи́ться (pf. лечь, ля́гу, ля́жешь;
past лёг, легла́; imper. ляг(те) lie
down.
ло́|жка (gen. pl. -жек) spoon.
ло́жный false; ложь (лжи, inst.
ло́жью) lie, falsehood.
лоза́ (pl. ло́зы) rod; vine.
ло́зунг slogan.
локализова́ть (ipf. & pf.) localize.
лока́ут lock-out.
локомоти́в engine, locomotive.
ло́кон curl, lock.
ло́|коть (-ктя, pl. -кти, -кте́й) elbow.
лом (pl. -ы, -ов or -о́в) crowbar;
fragment, scrap; ло́маный broken;
лома́ть (pf. с-) break; л. го́лову
над + inst. rack one's brains over;
-ся break; grimace, put on airs.
ломба́рд pawnshop.
ло́мберный стол card-table.
ломи́ть (ломлю́, ло́мишь) (coll.)
break; charge forward; ло́мит
ко́сти my bones ache; -ся force
one's way; ло́мкий brittle, fragile.
ломово́й dray (a.); carter (as noun).
ломоно́с clematis.
ломо́та rheumatic pain.
ло́|моть (-мтя) hunk, chunk; slice;
ло́мтик slice.
ло́но bosom, lap.
ло́пар|ь (-я) Lapp.
ло́паст|ь (f.; pl. -и, -е́й) blade, fan,
paddle; лопа́та shovel; spade;
лопа́тка shovel, trowel; shoulder-
blade.
ло́паться (pf ло́пнуть) break, burst.
лопоу́хий lop-eared.
лопух (-а́) burdock.
лоси́на elk meat; chamois leather.
лоск gloss, lustre.
лоску́т (-а́, pl. -ы, -о́в, or лоску́тья,
-ьев) rag, shred.
лосни́ться glisten, shine.
лососи́на (flesh of) salmon; лосо́с|ь
(-я) salmon.
лос|ь (-я pl. -и, -е́й) elk.
лот plummet, lead.
лотере́я lottery.
ло|то́к (-тка́) tray; shoot, gutter.
ло́тос lotus.
лото́ч|ник, ~ница hawker.
лоха́нка tub; по́чечная л. pelvis.
лохма́тый dishevelled, shaggy.
лохмо́т|ья (-ьев) rags.
ло́цман pilot.

лошадйный horse (a.); лóшад|ь (f.; pl. -и, -éй, inst. -ьмй) horse.
лощёный glossy, polished.
лощйна dell, hollow.
лощйть (pf. на-) polish, glaze.
лоя́льный loyal.
лу|бóк (-бка́) splint; bast; cheap print; лубóчный cheap.
луг (на -ý, pl. луга́) meadow.
лу́жа puddle.
луж|а́йка (gen. pl. -áек) lawn.
лужёный tinned; (coll.) cast-iron.
лук 1. onions; 2. bow; лука́ (pl. лу́ки) pommel; bend.
лука́вить (pf. с-) be cunning; лука́вство cunning; лука́вый sly, cunning; the devil.
лу́ковица onion; bulb.
лукомóрье curved sea shore.
луна́ moon; луна́тик sleepwalker.
лу́нка hole, socket.
лу́нный lunar, moon (a.).
лу́па magnifying glass.
лупйть (луплю́, лу́пишь; pf. об-) peel, remove bark; (pf. от-) flog.
луч (-á) ray; лучевóй ray (a.), radial; лучеза́рный radiant; лучеиспуска́ние radiation.
лучи́на splinter.
лучи́стый radiant; лучи́ться shine brightly.
лу́чше better; лу́чший better, best.
лущи́ть (pf. об-) pod, shell, crack.
лы́жа ski; лы́ж|ник, ~ница skier; лы́жный спорт skiing; лы́жня ski-track.
лы́к|о (pl. -и) bast.
лысéть go bald; лы́сина bald patch; лы́сый bald.
ль = ли.
львйный lion's; львйца lioness.
льгóта privilege, advantage; льгóтный favourable.
льдй́на ice-floe.
льновóдство cultivation of flax.
льнуть (pl. при-) (к + dat.) cling (to).
льнян|óй flax, linen (a.); -óе ма́сло linseed oil.
льстец (-á) flatterer; льстй́вый flattering, smooth-tongued; льстй́ть (льщу, льстишь; pf. по-) (dat.) flatter.
любéзничать (с + inst.) pay compliments/court (to); любéзность (f.) courtesy, compliment; любéзный amiable, kind.

люб|й́мец (-й́мца), ~й́мица favourite; люби́мый favourite (a.).
люби́тель, ~ница lover, amateur; люби́тельский amateur; люби́ть (люблю́, лю́бишь; pf. по-) love, like.
лю́бо it is pleasant.
любова́ться (pf. по-) (inst. or на + acc.) admire.
любóв|ник lover; ~ница mistress; любóвный amorous, love (a.); лю|бóвь (-бви, inst. -бóвью) (к + dat.) love (for).
любозна́тельный curious.
любóй any.
любопы́тный curious, inquisitive; любопы́тство curiosity.
люд folk; лю́ди (людéй, лю́дям, людьми́, лю́дях) people; лю́дный crowded; людоéд cannibal; людоéдство cannibalism; людскóй human.
люк hatchway.
люкс de-luxe.
лю́|лька (gen. pl. -лек) cradle; pipe.
лю́стра candelabra, chandelier.
лютер|а́нин (pl. -а́не, -а́н), ~а́нка Lutheran.
лю́тик buttercup.
лю́|тня (gen. pl. -тен) lute.
лю́тый ferocious.
ляга́вая собáка pointer, setter.
ляга́ть (pf. лягну́ть) kick.
лягу́|шка (gen. pl. -шек) frog.
ля́|жка (gen. pl. -жек) thigh.
лязг clank; ля́згать (pf. ля́згнуть) clank.
ля́мк|а strap; тяну́ть -y toil.
ля́пать (pf. на-) botch, bungle.
лях (coll.) Pole.

М

мавзолéй mausoleum.
мавр moor.
магази́н shop.
магй́стр master.
магистра́ль (f.) main; highway.
ма́гия magic.
магна́т magnate.
магнети́ческий magnetic.
магнéто (indecl.) magneto.
ма́гний magnesium.
магни́т magnet; магни́тный magnetic.
магнитофóн tape-recorder.

магомет|анин *(pl.* -áне, -áн), ~áнка Mahommedan; **магометáнство** Mahommedanism.

мадéра Madeira wine.

мадь|яр *(gen. pl.* -я́р), ~я́рка Magyar; **мадья́рский** Magyar *(a.).*

мажóрный major *(mus.); ;* buoyant.

мáзать (мáжу, мáжешь; *pf.* вы́-, по-, на-) smear, spread, cover; grease, oil; *(pf.* вы́-, за-, из-) dirty; **мазну́ть** *(pf.)* dab, brush; **мазня́** daub, mess; **ма|зóк** (-зкá) stroke *(of brush)* ; **мазу́т** black oil; **мазь** *(f.)* ointment, liniment; grease.

май May; **мáйка** *(gen. pl.* мáек) vest, shirt.

майóр major.

мáйский May *(a.);* м. жук cockchafer.

мак poppy.

макар|óны (-óн) macaroni.

макáть *(pf.* макну́ть) dip.

макéт model.

мáклер broker.

макну́ть *see* макáть.

мáковка poppy head; dome, top.

мáковый poppy, papaverous.

макрéль *(f.)* mackerel.

максимáльный maximum *(a.);* **мáксимум** maximum; at most.

макулату́ра waste paper.

маку́|шка *(gen. pl.* -шек) top; crown *(of hat).*

мал (too) small; от мáла до велúка young and old.

малáйский Malayan.

малевáть *(pf.* на-) daub, paint.

малéйший smallest; least.

мáленький *(comp.* мéньше, мéньший) little.

малúна raspberry; **малúновка** raspberry brandy; robin redbreast; **мзлúновый** raspberry *(a.).*

мáло little, few, not much, not many; м. тогó moreover; м. ли что! what of it!; ему́ и гóря м. he doesn't care a bit.

мало|вáжный of little importance; ~вéрие disbelief; little faith; ~вероя́тный improbable; ~вóдный shallow; ~ду́шие faintheartedness; ~ду́шный fainthearted; ~крóвие anaemia; ~крóвный anaemic; ~лéтний young; ~лю́дный not crowded.

мало-мáльски *(coll.)* least, slightest; **мало-помáлу** gradually.

мáлость *(f.)* trifle; **мáлый** small, little fellow; **малы́ш** (-á) kiddy.

мáльва hollyhock.

мáльчик boy; **мальчúшеский** puerile; **мальчúшка** *(gen. pl.* -шек) urchin; **мальчугáн** little boy.

малю́тка *(m. & f.)* baby.

маля́р (-á) painter, decorator.

маля́рия malaria.

мáма, мáменька mummy.

мáмонт mammoth.

мангу́ста mongoose.

мандарúн 1. mandarin; 2. tangerine, mandarin orange.

мандáт mandate.

манёвр manoeuvre; **маневрúровать** *(pf.* с-) manoeuvre.

манéж riding school.

манекéн model, tailor's dummy; **манекéн|щик,** ~щица model, mannequin.

манéра manner, style; **манéрный** affected, pretentious.

ман|жéт(к)а cuff.

маникю́р manicure.

манúть (маню́, мáнишь; *pf.* по-) beckon to; lure.

манифéст manifesto; **манифестáция** demonstration.

манú|шка *(gen. pl.* -шек) shirt front.

мáния mania; м. велúчия megalomania.

манкúровать be absent; *(inst.)* neglect.

мáнная кáша semolina.

мановéние wave, nod.

манóметр pressure gauge.

мáнтия cloak, gown.

манья́к maniac.

марáть *(pf.* за-, из-) dirty, sully; *(pf.* вы́-) cross out; *(pf.* на-) daub.

мáрга|нец (-нца) manganese.

маргарúн margarine.

маргарúтка daisy.

мáрево mirage, looming outline.

мариновáть *(pf.* за-) pickle; shelve.

марионéтка puppet.

мáрка stamp; mark, brand; grade.

мáркий easily soiled.

марксúзм Marxism; **марксúст,** ~ка Marxist; **марксúстский** Marxist *(a.).*

мáрлевый gauze *(a);* **мáрля** gauze.

мармелáд fruit sweets.

мáрочный of high grade, reputable.

март March; **мáртовский** March *(a.).*

марш march; **маршировáть** march.

маршру́т route.

ма́ска mask; маскара́д masquerade; маскирова́ть (pf. за-) disguise; camouflage; маскиро́вка disguise, camouflage.

ма́сленица Shrovetide.

маслёнка butter-dish; oil can; масли́на olive; ма́сло butter, oil; маслоб|о́йка (gen. pl. -о́ек) churn; масляни́стый oily; buttery; ма́сляный oil (a.).

масо́н freemason.

ма́сса mass.

масса́ж massage.

масси́в massif; large tract; масси́вный massive.

масси́ровать (ipf. & pf.) massage; rub.

массо́вка mass meeting; excursion; ма́ссовый mass (a.).

ма́стер (pl. -а́) master, foreman; craftsman, expert; мастери́ть (pf. с-) make, contrive; мастери́ца craftswoman, expert; мастерска́я workshop; мастерско́й masterly; мастерство́ handicraft; skill.

масти́ка mastic, resin; floor polish; putty.

масти́стый of good colour (horse).

масти́тый venerable.

маст|ь (f., pl. -и, -е́й) colour, coat (animals) suit (cards).

масшта́б scale.

мат 1. checkmate; 2. floor mat; 3. matt/dull finish.

матема́тик mathematician; матема́тика mathematics.

матереуби́йство matricide.

материа́л material.

материал|и́зм materialism; ~исти́ческий materialist.

материа́льный material (a.).

матери́к (-а́) continent; материко́вый continental.

матери́нский maternal; матери́нство maternity.

матери́ться curse, swear.

мате́рия matter (phil.); pus; material, fabric.

матеро́й, матёрый big, strong; hardened.

ма́тка womb; female.

ма́товый mat, dull, frosted (glass).

матра́с, матра́ц mattress.

матрёшка (gen. pl. -шек) wooden doll containing others, matryoshka.

матро́с sailor, seaman.

ма́ту|шка (gen. pl. -шек) mother; old woman.

матч match.

мать (f.; gen., dat., prep. ма́тери, inst. ма́терью, pl. ма́тер|и, -е́й) mother.

мах sweep, stroke; одни́м ма́хом at one stroke; дава́ть ма́ху miss an opportunity.

маха́ть (машу́, ма́шешь; pf. махну́ть) (inst.) flap, wave; м. руко́й на (+ acc.) give up as a bad job.

махина́ция machinations.

махну́ть see маха́ть.

маховик (-а́), маховое́ колесо́ fly wheel.

махо́рка cheap tobacco.

махро́вый double (bot.); double-dyed.

ма́чеха step-mother.

ма́чта mast.

маши́на machine; car; машина́льный mechanical; механиза́ция mechanization; машини́ст engine-driver; машини́стка typist; маши́нка typewriter, sewing machine; small machine; маши́нный machine, engine (a.); маши́нопись (f.) typing; машинострое́ние mechanical engineering.

мая́к (-а́) lighthouse; beacon.

ма́ятник pendulum.

ма́яться (ма́юсь, ма́ешься) suffer, toil.

ма́ячить loom.

мгла haze, mist; мгли́стый hazy, misty.

мгнове́ние moment, instant; мгнове́нный momentary.

ме́бель (f.) furniture; меблирова́ть (ipf. & pf.) furnish; меблиро́вка furnishing.

мёд (в -у́, pl. -ы́) honey.

меда́ль (f.) medal.

медве́дица she-bear; Больша́я м. the Great Bear; медве́дь (m.) bear; медве́жий bear's; медвежо́|нок (-нка) bear cub.

ме́дик doctor; medical student; медикаме́нт medicine, drug; меди́цина medicine; медици́нский medical.

ме́дленный slow; медли́тельный slow, sluggish; ме́длить linger, be slow.

ме́дный of copper, brass.

медо́вый honey (a.).

мед|осмо́тр medical examination; ~по́мощь (f.) medical service; ~пункт surgery, aid station;

~сестра́ (pl. -сёстры, -сестёр, -сёстрам) nurse.
меду́за jellyfish.
медь (f.) copper.
меж = ме́жду.
меж|а́ (pl. ме́ж|и, -а́м) boundary.
междоме́тие interjection.
междоусо́бица internecine strife.
ме́жду (inst.) between, amongst; м. тем meanwhile; м. про́чим by the way; м. двух огне́й between two fires; чита́ть м. стро́чек read between the lines.
ме́жду|городный inter-city; ~наро́дный international.
межева́ть fix boundaries.
меж|континента́льный intercontinental; ~плане́тный interplanetary.
мезони́н attic; mezzanine.
мел (в -у́) chalk.
меланхо́лия melancholia.
меле́ть (pf. об-) become shallow.
мелиора́ция improvement; land-reclamation.
ме́лкий (comp. ме́льче) small; petty; мелково́дный shallow; ме́лкость (f.) smallness; мелкота́ smallness; small items, small fry.
мелод|и́ческий, ~и́чный melodic, melodious; мело́дия melody, tune.
ме́лочный petty; ме́лоч|ь (f.; pl. -и, -ей) small item, trifle; small change (money).
мел|ь (f.; на -и́) shoal, sandbank.
мелька́ть (pf. мелькну́ть) flash, gleam; ме́льком in passing, cursorily.
ме́льник miller; ме́льница mill.
мельча́йший smallest; мельча́ть (pf. из-) become smaller, shallow; degenerate; ме́льче see ме́лкий; мельчи́ть (pf. из-раз-) make fine/small.
мелюзга́ small fry.
мемора́ндум memorandum.
мемориа́льный memorial.
мемуа́р|ы (-ов) memoirs.
ме́на exchange, barter.
ме́нее less; тем не м. nevertheless.
меново́й exchange (a.).
ме́ньше smaller, less, fewer; меньшеви́к (-а́) Menshevik; ме́ньший lesser, younger; меньшинство́ minority.
меню́ (indecl.) menu.
меня́ть (pf. об-, по-) change, exchange м. кварти́ру на да́чу exchange

a flat for a dacha; -ся change, exchange; -ся ро́лями switch roles.
ме́ра measure; по кра́йней ме́ре at least.
мере́нга meringue.
мере́ть (мрёт; past. мёр, -ла; coll.) die (in large numbers).
мере́щиться (pf. по-) appear; seem.
мерза́|вец (-вца) scoundrel; ме́рзкий vile.
мерзлота́ frozen ground.
мёрзлый frozen; мёрзнуть (past мёрз, -ла; pf. за-) freeze.
ме́рзость (f.) abomination.
мери́ло criterion, standard.
ме́рин gelding.
ме́рить (pf. с-) measure; (pf. по-) try on; ме́рка measure.
ме́ркнуть (past. мерк, -ла; pf. по-) grow dark.
ме́рный measured, regular; меропри́я́тие measure, step.
мёртвенный deathly; мертве́ть (pf. по-) grow numb/stiff; мертве́ц (-а́) dead man; мертвечи́на carrion; мертворождённый still-born, abortive; мёртвый dead.
мерца́ть glimmer, shimmer.
ме́сиво mash; medley; меси́ть (мешу́, ме́сишь; pf. с-) knead.
месте́|чко (gen. pl. -чек) small place.
мести́ (ме|ту́, -тёшь; past. мёл, мела́; ppa. мётший; ppp. метённый) sweep.
месткóм local committee; ме́стность (f.) locality; ме́стный local.
ме́сто (pl. -а́) place, site, seat; име́ть м. take place.
место|жи́тельство residence; ~име́ние pronoun; ~нахожде́ние location, whereabouts; ~пребыва́ние residence; ~рожде́ние deposit, layer.
месть (f.) revenge.
ме́сяц month; moon; ме́сячный monthly.
мета́лл metal; металли́ст metal-worker; металли́ческий metallic; металлоплави́льная печь smelting furnace; металлу́ргия metallurgy.
мета́н methane.
мета́тельный missile (a.); м. снаря́д projectile; мета́ть (мечу́, ме́чешь; pf. метну́ть) fling, throw; -ся rush about; toss (in bed).
метафи́зика metaphysics.
мета́фора metaphor.

метéлица snowstorm; dance 'the snowstorm'; метéль (f.) snowstorm.

метéние sweeping.

метеóр meteor; метеорóлог meteorologist; метеорология meteorology.

метизáция cross-breeding; метúс mongrel; half-caste/-breed.

мéтить (мéчу, мéтишь; pf. по-) mark; (pf. на-) aim; мéтка mark; мéткий well-aimed, neat.

метлá (pl. мётлы, мётел) broom.

метнýть see метáть.

мéтод method; метóдика methods; методический methodical.

метр metre; метрáж metric area; footage (film).

мéтрика 1. metrics; 2. birth certificate; метрический metric.

метрó (indecl.), метрополитéн metro, underground railway.

мех (pl. -á) fur; на мехý fur-lined; (pl. -и) bellows.

механизáция mechanization; механизúровать (ipf. & pf.) mechanize; механúзм mechanism, gear; механик mechanical engineer, mechanic; механика mechanics; механический mechanical; propelling (pencil).

мехóвой fur (a.); меховощúк (-á) furrier.

меч (-á) sword.

мéченый marked.

мечéть (f.) mosque.

мечтá day-dream; мечтáтель, ~ница dreamer; мечтáтельный dreamy, pensive; мечтáть dream.

мешáлка mixer, stirrer; мешáть 1. (pf. по-, с-) mix.

мешáть 2. (pf. по-) (dat.) hinder, prevent.

мешáться (pf. в-) (в + acc.) interfere, meddle (in).

мéшкать linger, loiter.

мешковáтый baggy, clumsy; мешóк (-шкá) bag, sack.

мещанúн (pl. -áне, -áн) petty bourgeois; Philistine; мещáнский narrow-minded, vulgar; мещáнство lower-middle classes, narrow-mindedness.

миг instant, moment; мигáть (pf. мигнýть, -ну, -нёшь) blink; twinkle; мúгом in a flash.

мигрáция migration.

мигрéнь (f.) migraine.

мизансцéна staging (of play).

мизантрóп misanthrope.

мúзерный small; petty; мизúнец (-нца) little finger/toe.

микрóб microbe.

микрóн micron.

микрорайóн micro-district.

микроскóп microscope.

микрофóн microphone.

микстýра medicine; mixture.

мúленький pretty; nice; dear.

милитарúзм militarism.

милиционéр policeman, militiaman; милиция militia.

миллиáрд a thousand millions.

миллиардéр multi-millionaire; миллимéтр millimetre; миллиóн million; миллионéр millionaire.

мúловать (pf. по-) (obs.) pardon.

миловáть caress.

милóвидный pretty.

милосéрдие charity, mercy; милосéрдный charitable.

мúлостивый gracious, kind; мúлостыня alms; мúлость (f.) favour, grace.

мúлый dear, kin :.

мúля mile.

мúмика mime.

мúмо (gen.) past; мимолётный fleeting; мимохóдом in passing; by the way.

мúна 1. mine; mortar shell; 2. countenance.

миндáлина 1. almond; 2. tonsil; миндáль (-я) almonds; almond tree; миндáльный almond (a.).

минерáл mineral; минералóг mineralogist; минералóгия mineralogy; минерáльный mineral (a.).

миниатюра miniature; миниатюрный miniature; tiny.

минимáльный minimum (a.); мúнимум minimum.

министéрский ministerial; министéрство ministry; минúстр minister.

мúнный mine (a.).

миновáть (ipf. & pf.) pass; escape.

минóга lamprey.

миноискáтель (m.) mine-detector; миномёт mortar; минонóсец (-сца) torpedo boat; эскáдренный м. destroyer.

минóр minor key; the blues, dumps; минóрный minor; sad.

минýвший past, last; -ее the past.

мúнус minus.

мину́та minute; **мину́тный** minute *(a.)*, momentary.

мину́ть *(pf.)* pass; ѐй мину́ло 20 лет she is turned twenty.

мир 1. *(pl. -ы́)* world; village community, commune; **2.** peace.

мира́ж mirage, optical illusion.

мири́ть *(pf.* по-, при-) reconcile; **-ся** be reconciled.

ми́рный peace *(a.)*; peaceful.

мирова́я amicable agreement.

мировоззре́ние world-view, philosophy.

мирово́й world *(a.)*; м. судья́ justice of the peace.

миро|зда́ние universe; **~люби́вый** peace-loving.

мирско́й mundane; secular; communal; **мир|я́нин** *(pl.* -я́не, -я́н) layman.

ми́ска basin, tureen.

миссионе́р missionary; **ми́ссия** mission.

ми́стика mysticism.

ми́тинг meeting, rally.

митрополи́т metropolitan.

миф myth; **мифи́ческий** mythical; **мифоло́гия** mythology.

ми́чман midshipman.

мише́нь *(f.)* target.

ми́|шка *(m., gen. pl.* -шек) teddy bear; Bruin.

мишура́ tinsel, trumpery; **мишу́рный** tinsel *(a.)*; tawdry.

младе́|нец(-нца) infant; **младе́нческий** infantile; **младе́нчество** infancy.

мла́дший youngest, junior.

млекопита́ющее mammal.

млеть (от + *gen.*) be thrilled (with).

мле́чный путь Milky Way.

мне́ние opinion.

мни́мый imaginary; sham; **мни́тельный** overanxious about one's health; mistrustful; **мнить** *(obs.)* think.

мно́гие many; **мно́го** much, many; **мно́гое** a lot; many things.

много|бра́чие, -же́нство polygamy.

многогра́нный polyhedral, many-sided.

многокра́тный repeated; frequentative.

многоле́тний of many years' standing.

многолю́дный crowded.

многому́жие polyandry.

многообра́зный varied.

много|речи́вый, -сло́вный loquacious, verbose.

многосло́жный polysyllabic.

много торо́нний multilateral; versatile.

многострада́льный long-suffering.

многото́чие (three) dots.

многоуважа́емый respected; dear *(in letter)*.

многоуго́льник polygon.

многоцве́тный many-coloured; multiflorous.

многочи́сленный numerous.

многоэта́жный many-storied.

многоязы́чный polyglot.

мно́жественный plural; **мно́жество** great number.

мно́жимое multiplicand; **мно́житель** *(m.)* factor, multiplier; **мно́жить** *(pf.* по-, у-) multiply.

мобилиза́ция mobilization; **мобилизова́ть** *(ipf. & pf.)* mobilize.

моги́ла grave; **моги́льщик** gravedigger.

могу́чий mighty; **могу́щественный** powerful; **могу́щество** might, power.

мо́да fashion; **модели́ровать** *(ipf. & pf.)* model; **моде́ль** *(f.)* pattern, model; **моде́льный** model *(a.)*; fashionable.

модернизи́ровать, -ова́ть *(ipf. & pf.)* modernize.

моди́стка milliner.

модифика́ция modification; **модифици́ровать** *(ipf. & pf.)* modify.

мо́дный fashionable; fashion *(a.)*.

мо́жет быть perhaps.

можжеве́льник juniper.

мо́жно it is possible, permitted.

моза́ика mosaic.

мозг (в -у́, *pl.* -и́) brain; **мозгови́тый** brainy; **мозгово́й** cerebral.

мозо́листый callous, horny; **мозо́лить** *(pf.* на-): м. ему́ глаза́ be a nuisance to him; **мозо́ль** *(f.)* corn, hardness.

мой, моя́, моё, мои́ my, mine.

мо́йка washing; sink.

мо́кнуть *(past* мок; *pf.* вы́-, про-) become wet.

мокри́ца wood-louse.

мокро́та phlegm.

мокрота́ dampness, humidity; **мо́крый** moist, wet.

мол 1. pier, jetty; **2.** he, she says *etc.*

молва́ rumour; fame; **мо́лвить** *(ipf. & pf.)* say.

молдав|а́нин (pl. -а́не, -а́н), ~а́нка Moldavian.

моле|бен (-бна) church service; thanksgiving.

моле́кула molecule; молекуля́рный molecular.

моле́ние prayer, supplication; моли́тва prayer; моли́твенник prayerbook; моли́ть (молю́, мо́лишь) implore; -ся (pf. по-) pray.

моллю́ск mollusc, shellfish.

молниено́сный quick as lightning; мо́лния lightning.

молодёжь (f.) young people.

молоде́ть (pf. по-) be rejuvenated.

моло|де́ц (-дца́) fine fellow/girl; молоде́цкий valiant, fine.

молоди́ть (-жу́, -ди́шь) make young, rejuvenate.

молодня́к (-а́) undergrowth, saplings; young animals.

молодожён|ы (-ов) newly-weds.

молодо́й young; мо́лодость (f.) youth; молодцева́тый dashing, spirited; моложа́вый youthful.

моло́чо milk; молокосо́с greenhorn.

мо́лот hammer; молоти́лка threshing machine; мол|оти́ть (-очу́, -о́тишь; pf. с-) thresh; моло|то́к (-тка́) hammer; моло́ть (мелю́, ме́лешь; ppp. мо́лотый; pf. с-) grind; моло́тьба́ threshing.

моло́чная dairy, creamery; моло́чник milkman; milk jug; моло́чница milkwoman; thrush (med.); моло́чный milk(y).

мо́лча silently; молчали́вый taciturn; молча́ние silence; мол|ча́ть (-чу́, -чи́шь; pf. за-) be(come) silent.

моль (f.) moth.

мольба́ entreaty.

мольбе́рт easel.

моме́нт moment; feature; момента́льный instant(aneous).

мона́рх monarch; мона́рхия monarchy.

монасты́р|ь (-я́) monastery; мона́х monk; мона́хиня nun; мона́шеский monastic; мона́шество monkhood; the monks.

монго́л, ~ка Mongol; монго́льский Mongol (a.).

моне́т|а coin; принима́ть за чи́стую -у take at face value; моне́тный двор mint.

моногра́фия monograph.

моноли́тный monolithic.

моноло́г monologue.

монополизи́ровать (ipf. & pf.) monopolize; монопо́лия monopoly; монопо́льный monopolistic.

моното́нный monotonous.

монта́ж assembling, mounting; editing (films.); монта́жная рабо́та installation work; монтёр fitter; монти́ровать (pf. с-) assemble, mount.

монумента́льный monumental.

мопс pug dog.

мор plague.

морализи́ровать moralize; мора́ль (f.) moral, moral philosophy, ethics; мора́льн|ый moral; spiritual; -ое состоя́ние morale.

морато́рий moratorium.

морг mortuary, morgue.

морг|а́ть (pf. мо́рг|ну́ть, -ну́, -нёшь) blink.

мо́рда muzzle, snout.

мо́ре (pl. -я́) sea.

море|пла́вание navigation; ~хо́дный nautical, seafaring; ~хо́дство navigation.

морж (-а́) walrus.

мори́ть (pf. вы́-) exterminate; (pf. за-, у-) exhaust; starve.

морко́вка carrot; морко́вь (f.) carrots.

моровая́ я́зва plague.

моро́|женое ice-cream; моро́жен|щик, ~щица ice-cream vendor; моро́з frost; моро́|зить (-о́жу, -о́зишь; pf. по-) freeze; моро́зный frosty; морозоусто́йчивый frost-resistant.

мороси́ть drizzle.

моро́шка cloudberry, -berries.

морс fruit juice.

морск|о́й sea (a.), maritime, marine; -а́я звезда́ starfish; -а́я боле́знь sea-sickness.

морти́ра mortar (mil.).

мо́рфий morphia, morphine.

морфоло́гия morphology.

морщи́на crease, wrinkle; морщи́нистый wrinkled; мо́рщить (pf. на-, с-) wrinkle, pucker; -ся knit one's brow; be wrinkled.

моря́к (-а́) sailor.

моска́тельный chandler's.

москви́ч (-а́), москви́|чка (gen. pl. -чек) Muscovite.

моски́т mosquito.

моско́вс|ий Moscow (a.).

мост (-а́, на -у́ pl. -ы́) bridge; мо|сти́ть (-щу́, -сти́шь; pf. вы́-, заpave; мост|кѝ (-о́в) plank footway; мостова́я roadway; pavement; мостово́й bridge, (a.)

мот spendthrift.

мота́ть 1. (pf. за-, на-) reel; wind; 2. (pf. про-) squander; 3. (pf. мотну́ть) (inst.) shake; -ся dangle; fuss about.

мотѐль (m.) motel.

моти́в motive; motif; мотиви́ровать (ipf. & pf.) motivate; мотиви́ровка motivation.

мото́вка spendthrift woman; мото́вство extravagance.

мотого́|нки (-нок) motor-races.

мото́к (-тка́) hank, skein.

мотопробе́г cross-country motor-cycle race.

мото́р motor, engine; мото́рный motor (a.); motive.

мотоци́кл motor-cycle.

моты́га hoe.

моты|лёк (-лька́) moth.

мох (мха or мо́ха, на мху́, pl. мхи) moss.

мохна́тый hairy, shaggy.

моцио́н exercise.

моча́ urine.

моча́лка wisp, piece of bast.

мочево́й пузы́рь bladder.

мочи́ть (мочу́, мо́чишь; pf. за-, на-) soak, wet; -ся (pf. по-) urinate.

мо́|чка (gen. pl. -чек) 1. soaking; 2. lobe of ear.

мочь 1. (могу́, мо́жешь; past мог, -ла́; pf. с-) be able, manage; я не могу́ не... I can't help...

мочь 2. (f.) power; что есть мо́чи with might and main.

моше́нник rogue.

мо́шка (gen. pl. -шек) midge; мошкара́ swarm of midges.

мощёный paved.

мо́щ|и (-е́й) relics (of saint).

мо́щность (f.) power; capacity; мо́щный powerful; мощь (f.) power.

мразь (f.) filth.

мрак gloom; мракобе́с obscurantist.

мра́мор marble; мра́морный marble (a.).

мра́чный dark, gloomy.

мсти́тель (m.) avenger; мсти́тельный vindictive; мстить (мщу, мстишь; pf. ото-) avenge; м. ему́ за э́то take vengeance on him for it.

мудрёный odd, tricky, difficult; не мудрено́, что... it's no wonder

that...; у́тро ве́чера мудрене́е let's sleep on it.

мудре́ц (-а́) sage, wise man.

му́дрость (f.) wisdom; му́дрый wise.

муж (pl. -ья́, -е́й) husband; man; му-жа́ть (pf. воз-) reach manhood; -ся take courage; мужеподо́бный mannish.

му́жественный courageous; manly; му́жество courage.

мужи́к (-а́) peasant; man (coll.); мужи́цкий peasant (a.); boorish.

мужско́й masculine; male, men's; мужчи́на (m.) man.

му́за muse.

музе́й museum.

му́зыка music; музыка́льный musical; музыка́нт, ∼ша musician.

му́ка torment.

мука́ flour.

мул mule.

мультипликацио́нный фильм cartoon film.

му́мия mummy.

мунди́р full-dress coat; карто́фель в -е potatoes boiled in jackets.

мундшту́к (-а́) mouth-piece, cigarette-holder.

муниципа́льный municipal.

мурава́ 1. grass; 2. glaze.

мура|ве́й (-вья́) ant; мураве́йник ant-hill.

мура́вленый glazed.

мураве́д ant-eater; муравьи́ная кислота́ formic acid.

мура́шки: от э́того м. по спине́ бе́гают it gives you the shivers.

мурлы́|кать (-ычет) purr.

муска́т nutmeg; muscatel.

му́скул muscle; му́скулистый brawny; му́скульный muscle (a.), muscular.

му́скус musk.

мусли́н muslin.

му́сор refuse, rubbish; му́сорный я́щик dustbin; мусоропрово́д refuse chute; му́сорщик dustman.

мусульм|а́нин (pl. -а́не, -а́н), ∼а́нка Moslem.

мути́ть (мучу́, му́тишь; pf. вз-, за-) stir up; (pf. по-) make dull; меня́ мути́т I feel sick; му́тный muddy, turbid; муть (f.) dregs; haze.

му́фта muff; (tech.) clutch, sleeve.

му́ха fly; мухоло́вка fly-catcher, fly-trap.

муче́ние torment; му́че|ник, ∼ница martyr; му́ченичество martyrdom;

мучи́тель *(m.)* tormentor; **мучи́-тельный** agonizing; **му́чить** *(pf.* за-, из-) torture; -ся worry, be tormented.

мучно́й flour, meal *(a.)*; starchy.

му́|шка *(gen. pl.* -шек) fly; beauty spot, patch; front sight.

муштрова́ть *(pf.* вы-) drill.

мчать (мчу, мчишь) rush, whirl along; -ся rush.

мши́стый mossy.

мще́ние vengeance.

мы we.

мы́лить *(pf.* на-) soap; **мы́лкий** easy-lathering; **мы́ло** soap; **мыло-ва́ренный заво́д** soap-works; **мы́ль-ница** soap-dish; **мы́льн|ый** soap(y); -ая пе́на foam.

мыс cape, promontory.

мы́сленный mental; **мы́слимый** conceivable; **мысли́тель** *(m.)* thinker; **мы́слить** think; **мысль** *(f.)* idea, thought.

мыта́рство ordeal.

мыть (мо́ю, мо́ешь; *ppp.* мы́тый; *pf.* вы-, по-) wash; -ся wash (oneself); **мытьё** washing, wash.

мы|ча́ть (-чу, -чишь) low, moo.

мышело́вка mousetrap.

мы́шечный muscular.

мыши́ный mouse *(a.)*; **мы́|шка** *(gen. pl.* -шек) mouse; armpit; **нести́ под мы́шкой** carry under one's arm.

мышле́ние thinking.

мы́шца muscle.

мыш|ь *(f.; pl.* -и, -е́й) mouse.

мышья́к (-а́) arsenic.

мя́гкий *(comp.* мя́гче) soft; **мяг-косерде́чный** soft-hearted; **мя́г-кость** *(f.)* softness, mildness; **мяг-чи́ть** soften.

мяки́на chaff.

мя́киш crumb *(soft part of bread)*.

мя́кнуть *(past.* мяк, -ла; *pf.* на-, раз-) become soft; **мя́коть** *(f.)* flesh, pulp, soft part.

мя́млить *(pf.* про-) mumble; hesitate.

мяси́стый fleshy, meaty; **мясни́к** (-а́) butcher; **мясно́й** meat *(a.)*; **мя́со** meat, flesh; **мясору́бка** mincing-machine; **slaughter house** *(fig.)*.

мя́та mint.

мяте́ж (-а́) mutiny, revolt; **мяте́жник** insurgent, mutineer; **мяте́жный** rebellious; restless.

мя́тный mint *(a.)*

мять (мну, мнёшь; *ppp.* мя́тый; *pf.* из-, с-, изомну́, сомну́) crumple; *pf.* раз-) knead.

мя́укать miaow.

мяч (-а́), **мя́чик** ball.

Н

на 1. (+ *acc.*) on to; for *(period of time)*; to; till; by; (+ *prep.*) on; at; in; during.

на 2. there! here you are!

набавля́ть *(pf.* наба́вить) add, increase.

набалда́шник knob.

наба́т alarm, tocsin.

набе́г raid; **набега́ть** *(pf.* набежа́ть*)* come (running) together; (на + *acc.*) run (against).

набекре́нь aslant.

на́бело: переписа́ть н. make a fair copy.

на́бережная embankment, quay.

набива́ть *(pf.* наби́ть*)* fill, stuff; pad; print; **наби́вка** packing, stuffing; printing; **набивно́й** printed.

набира́ть *(pf.* набра́ть*)* gather; recruit, take; set up, compose; -ся accumulate, collect; -ся хра́брости pluck up courage; **набрало́сь мно́го наро́ду** a large crowd gathered.

наби́тый packed tight.

наблюда́тель *(m.)* observer; **наблюда́тельный** observant, observation *(a.)*; **наблюда́ть** observe.

наблюде́ние observation.

набо́жный devout, pious.

набо́к on one side, awry.

наболе́вший painful, sore; **н. вопро́с** sore subject.

набо́р admission, recruitment, new candidates; kit, set; type-setting; **набо́рщик** type-setter.

набра́сывать *(pf.* наброса́ть) sketch, jot down; *(pf.* набро́сить*)* cast/throw on; -ся (на + *acc.*) attack, come down on.

набра́ть *see* набира́ть.

набро́|сок (-ска) draft, sketch.

набуха́ть *(pf.* набу́хнуть*)* swell.

наважде́ние temptation, evil possession.

нава́ливать *(pf.* навали́ть*)* heap, pile up; -ся (на + *acc.*) fall on; lean on.

навáр fat.

навевáть (-евáю; *pf.* навéять*) blow; heap up; bring on, induce.

навéдываться (*pf.* навéдаться) (к + *dat.*) call on; enquire of.

навéк, навéки for ever.

навéрно (е) probably; **наверня́ка** for certain.

навёрстывать (*pf.* наверстáть) make up (for) (*e. g. lost time*).

навёртывать (*pf.* навѣрну́ть) screw on; turn on.

навéрх up, upstairs; **наверху́** upstairs, above.

навéс awning, shed.

навеселé in one's cups.

навéсить *see* навéшивать.

навести́ть *see* навещáть.

навéтренный windward.

навéшивать (*pf.* навéсить*) hang up.

навеⱋáть (*pf.* навести́ть, -щу́, -сти́шь) visit.

навѣять *see* навевáть.

нáвзничь backwards, on one's back.

навзры́д: плáкать н. sob violently.

навигáция navigation.

навинчивать (*pf.* нави́нти́ть, -нчу́, -нти́шь) (на + *acc.*) screw (on).

нависáть (*pf.* на\ви́снуть, *past* -ви́с) (over) hang; нави́сшие брóви beetling brows.

навлекáть (*pf.* навлéчь*) bring on, draw on.

наводи́ть* (*pf.* навести́*)(на + *acc.*) direct, aim (at); put on; build; inspire *(fear etc.)*; **навóдка** aiming; building, making.

наводнéние flood; **навод\ня́ть** (*pf.* -ни́ть) inundate.

наводя́щий: н. вопрóс leading question.

навóз manure, muck.

нáволо\ка, -чка (*gen. pl.* -чек) pillow-case.

навостри́ть (*pf.*) : н. у́ши prick up one's ears.

навря́д (ли) hardly, scarcely.

навсегдá for ever.

навстрéчу to meet; идти́ ему́ н. go to meet him; meet him half-way.

навы́ворот inside out.

нáвык habit, practice.

навы́кате bulging, protruding.

навы́тяжку at attention.

навью́чивать (*pf.* навью́чить) load.

навя́зчивый importunate; obsessive.

навя́зывать (*pf.* навязáть*) (на + *acc.*) tie (on); thrust (on); н. ему́ свое мнéние thrust one's opinion on him; **-ся** *(dat.)* foist oneself (on).

наг\áйка *(gen. pl.* -áек) whip.

нагибáть (*pf.* нагну́ть) bend; **-ся** stoop.

нагишóм stark naked.

наглéц (-á) insolent person; **нáглость** *(f.)* impudence.

нáглухо tight(ly).

нáглый impudent.

наглядéться* (*pf.*) (на + *acc.*) see enough (of).

наглядн\ый graphic, obvious, visual; -ый мéтод direct method; -ые посóбия visual aids.

нагнáть *see* нагоня́ть.

нагнетáть (*pf.* нагн\ести́, -ету́, -етёшь) force; supercharge.

нагноéние suppuration.

нагну́ть *see* нагибáть.

наговáривать (*pf.* наговори́ть) record; (на + *acc.*) slander.

нагóй naked; **нáголо** bare.

нáголову: разби́ть н. rout, shatter.

нагоня́й scolding, telling-off; **нагоня́ть** (*pf.* нагнáть*) 1. overtake, make up for; 2. cause, evoke; н. страх на негó put the fear of God into him.

нагорáть (*pf.* нагорéть*) 1. ему́ за э́то нагорéло he got a telling-off for it; 2. be consumed *(fuel)*.

нагóрье upland.

нагота́ nudity.

наготáвливать (*pf.* наготóвить) lay in, prepare *(a large quantity)* ; **наготóве** at the ready.

награ́бить (*pf.*) steal *(a lot of)*; награ́бленное loot.

награ́да reward; decoration; prize; **награднь́е** bonus; **награждáть** (*pf.* награ\ди́ть, -жу́, -ди́шь; -ждённый) award; reward; **награж-дéние** rewarding; decorating, awarding.

нагревáть (-евáю; *pf.* нагрéть*) heat, warm; **-ся** get warm.

нагромождáть (*pf.* нагромо\зди́ть, -зжу́, -зди́шь, *ppp.* -ждённый) pile up; **нагроможде́ние** piling up; conglomeration.

нагру́дник (child's) bib; breastplate.

нагру\жáть (*pf.* нагрузи́ть*) load; **нагру́зка** loading, load.

нагря́нуть (*pf.*) come suddenly.

над(о) *(inst.)* over, above.

надáвливать (*pf.* надави́ть*) **press.**

надба́вка increment; надбавля́ть (pf. надба́вить) add.

надвига́ть (pf. надви́нуть) move, pull, push (on); -ся approach, impend.

надво́дный above the water, surface (a.).

на́двое in two; ба́бушка н. сказа́ла we shall see what we shall see.

надво́рные постро́йки outhouses.

надгорта́нник epiglottis.

надгро́бный grave, tomb (a.).

наддава́ть* (pf. наддать*) add, increase.

надева́ть (-ева́ю; pf. наде́ть*) put on, don.

наде́жда hope; наде́жный reliable.

наде́л allotment.

наде́лать (pf.) (gen.) make (a certain amount of); н. хлопо́т make a fuss.

надел|я́ть (pf. -и́ть) endow, provide (smb. acc.) (with sth. inst.), allot.

наде́ть see надева́ть.

над|е́яться (-е́юсь, -е́ешься; pf. по-) hope; (на + а.с) rely on.

надзе́мный overground; elevated.

надзира́тель, ~ница supervisor; надзира́ть (за + inst.) oversee, supervise; надзо́р supervision, surveillance.

надла́мывать (pf. надломи́ть*) crack, fracture; overtax, break down

надлежа́ть* be proper/fitting/necessary; надлежа́щий appropriate; proper.

надло́м fracture; wretchedness; надломи́ть see надла́мывать; надло́мленный wretched.

надме́нный arrogant, haughty.

на́до 1. = над.

на́до 2. or на́добно it is necessary; так ему́ и н. it serves him right; на́добность (f.) necessity, need.

надоеда́ть (pf. надое́сть*) (dat.) bore, pester; надое́ло чита́ть I'm tired of reading; надое́дливый boring, tiresome.

надо́й yield (of milk.).

надо́лго for a long time.

надо́м|ник, ~ница one who works at home.

надорва́ть see надрыва́ть.

надпи́сывать (pf. надписа́ть*) inscribe, superscribe; на́дпись (f.) inscription.

надпо́чечник adrenal gland.

надре́з cut, incision; надреза́ть (pf. надре́зать*) make an incision.

надруга́тельство outrage, violation; надруга́ться (над + inst.) outrage, violate.

надры́в slight rent, tear; anguish, strain; надрыва́ть (pf. надорва́ть*) tear; overstrain; -ся strain oneself; надры́вный hysterical; heart-rending.

надсмо́тр control, supervision; надсмо́трщик overseer.

надставля́ть (pf. надста́вить) put on a piece, lengthen.

надстра́ивать (pf. надстро́ить) build on to, raise; надстро́йка (gen. pl. -о́ек) superstructure.

надтре́снутый cracked.

надува́ла (m. & f.) swindler; надува́ть (pf. наду́ть*) inflate; swindle; н. гу́бы pout; -ся swell out; надувно́й pneumatic; inflatable.

наду́манный far-fetched.

наду́тый haughty; sulky.

надуше́нный scented.

наеда́ться (pf. нае́ст.ся*) eat one's fill.

наедине́ in private.

нае́зд flying visit; raid; нае́зд|ник, ~ница rider.

наезжа́ть (pf. нае́хать) visit occasionally; (на + асс.) run (into) collide (with).

наём (на́йма) hire, renting; наёмник hireling, mercenary; наёмный hired.

нае́сться see наеда́ться.

нажа́ть see нажима́ть.

наждак(-а́) emery; нажда́чная бума́га emery paper.

нажи́ва gain; profit; нажива́ть (pf. нажи́ть*) acquire, amass; contract (disease) ; -ся make a fortune.

нажи́вка bait.

нажи́м pressure; нажима́ть (pf. нажа́ть, -жму́*) press, put pressure on.

нажи́ть see нажива́ть.

наза́д backwards, ago; тому́ н. ago.

наза́льный nasal.

назва́ние name, title; назва́ть see называ́ть.

назе́мный ground (a.); на́земь to the ground, down.

назида́ние edification; назида́тельный edifying.

назло́ (ему́ etc.) to spite (him etc.).

назнача́ть (pf. назна́чить) appoint, fix, set; prescribe; назначе́ние fixing, appointment, prescription назо́йливый importunate.

назрева́ть (-ева́ю; *pf.* назре́ть) ripen, mature.

называ́ть (*pf.* назва́ть*) call, name; -ся be called.

наибо́лее most; наибо́льший the greatest.

наи́вный naive.

наивы́сший highest.

наи́гранный affected, assumed; наи́грывать (*pf.* наигра́ть) strum, play softly.

наизна́нку inside out.

наизу́сть by heart.

наилу́чший the best; наиме́нее least.

наименова́ние name, designation.

наиме́ньший the least, smallest.

на́искось obliquely.

наи́тие inspiration.

наиху́дший the worst.

найдёныш foundling.

наймит hireling.

найти́ *see* находи́ть.

наказ instruction, order.

наказа́ние punishment; наказу́емый punishable; нака́зывать (*pf.* наказа́ть*) punish.

накал incandescence; нака́ливать (*pf.* накали́ть) make red-hot; -ся become heated.

нака́лывать (*pf.* наколо́ть*) prick, pin down.

накаля́ть = нака́ливать.

накану́не on the eve, the day before.

нака́пливать (*pf.* накопи́ть*) accumulate.

нака́тывать (*pf.* наката́ть) roll, make smooth; (*pf.* накати́ть*) roll, move.

нака́чивать (*pf.* накача́ть) pump.

наки́дка cloak; cushion-cover; extra charge; наки́дывать (*pf.* наки́нуть) throw on; -ся (на + *acc.*) attack.

накипа́ть (*pf.* накипе́ть*) boil up, swell; form scum; на́кипь (*f.*) scum.

накладна́я invoice; накладно́й superimposed; false; накла́дывать (*pf.* нал|ожи́ть, -ожу́, -о́жишь) put in/on; superimpose; imprint.

накле́ивать (*pf.* накле́ить) glue/stick on; накле́йка (*gen. pl.* -е́ек) pasting.

наклёпывать (*pf.* наклепа́ть*) rivet.

накло́н inclination, incline; наклоне́ние inclination; mood (*gram.*); накло́нность (*f.*) inclination; leaning; propensity; накло́нный slop-

ing; наклон|я́ть (*pf.* -и́ть) incline, tilt; -ся bend, stoop.

накова́|льня (*gen. pl.* -лен) anvil.

нако́жный skin (*a.*), cutaneous.

коле́нник knee-cap/-cover.

наколо́ть *see* нака́лывать.

наконе́ц at last.

наконе́чник tip, point.

накопле́ние accumulation; накопля́ть (*pf.* накопи́ть*) accumulate.

накра́пывать fall, drizzle.

накрахма́ленный starched.

накра́шивать (*pf.* накра́сить*) paint; make up.

накрен|я́ть (*pf.* -и́ть) incline to one side.

на́крепко fast; strictly.

на́крест crosswise.

накрыва́ть (*pf.* накры́ть*) cover; catch red-handed; н. на стол lay the table.

накупа́ть (*pf.* накупи́ть*) buy up.

накури́ть* (*pf.*) fill with smoke.

налага́ть (*pf.* нал|ожи́т., -ожу́, -о́жишь) impose; lay on.

нала́живать (*pf.* нала́дить*) adjust, put right.

нале́во to the left, on the left.

налега́ть (*pf.* (нале́ ь*) (на + *acc.*) lie on, lean on; apply oneself (to).

налегке́ light, without luggage; lightly dressed.

нален|ля́ть (*pf.* -и́ть*) stick on.

налёт raid; thin coating; налета́ть (*pf.* налете́ть*) come flying, swoop; налётчик robber.

нале́чь *see* налега́ть.

налива́ть (*pf.* нали́ть*) pour out, fill; -ся ripen; нали́вка nalivka (*liqueur*); наливн|о́й 1. ripe; 2. tanker (*a.*); -о́е су́дно tanker.

нали́м burbot.

налипа́ть (*pf.* нали́пнуть*) stick.

налито́й chubby; кро́вью н. blood-shot.

нали́ть *see* налива́ть.

налицо́ present, at hand; нали́чие presence, availability; нали́чность (*f.*) ready cash; availability; нали́чный on hand, ready.

нало́г tax; налогоплате́льщик tax-payer.

наложе́ние imposition; наложи́ть *see* накла́дывать; нало́женным пла-те́жом cash on delivery.

нало́жница concubine.

нало́й lectern, pulpit.

намагни́чивать *(pf.* намагн|и́тить, -и́чу, -и́тишь) magnetize.
нама́зывать *(pf.* нама́зать*) smear, spread.
нама́тывать *(pf.* намота́ть) wind on.
нама́чивать *(pf.* намочи́ть*) moisten, wet.
наме́дни the other day.
намёк hint, allusion; **намека́ть** *(pf.* намекну́ть) (на + *acc.)* hint (at).
намерева́ться (-ева́юсь) intend; **наме́рен, -а, -ы:** я наме́рен(а) I intend; **наме́рение** intention; **наме́ренный** intentional.
наме́стник viceregent.
намета́ть *(pf.* намести́*) sweep together.
наме́тить *see* намеча́ть.
намётка rough draft; fishing net; tacking thread.
намеча́ть *(pf.* наме́тить*) plan, outline; nominate; mark.
намина́ть *(pf.* намя́ть*) knead; flatten, trample.
намно́го by far, much.
намока́ть *(pf.* намо́кнуть*) get/become wet.
намо́рдник muzzle.
намы́в alluvium.
намы́ливать *(pf.* намы́лить) soap.
намя́ть *see* намина́ть.
нанесе́ние drawing, plotting; infliction; **нанести́** *see* наноси́ть.
нани́зывать *(pf.* наниза́ть*) string, thread.
нанима́тель, ~ница employer; tenant; **нанима́ть** *(pf.* наня́ть, найм|у́, -ёшь; *past* на́нял, -а́; *ppp.* на́нятый) hire; rent.
нано́с alluvium; deposit; drift; **наноси́ть*** *(pf.* нанести́*) carry, drift; mark, plot; inflict; **нано́сный** alluvial; borrowed; superficial.
наня́ть *see* нанима́ть.
наоборо́т on the contrary; back to front, wrong way round.
наобу́м at random
нао́тмашь violently.
наотре́з flatly, point-blank.
напада́ть *(pf.* напа́сть*) (на + *acc.)* attack; come upon; **нападе́ние** attack; forward line *(sport)* ; **напа́д|ки** (-ок) attacks.
напа́ивать 1. *(pf.* напои́ть) give to drink; make drunk; 2. *(pf.* напая́ть) solder on.
напа́сть 1. *(f.)* misfortune; 2. *see* напада́ть.

нап ... une; **напева́ть** (-ева́ю) hum, с ообп; *(pf.* напе́ть*) sing.
напере|бо́й vying with each other; **~вес** atilt; on the slope, **~го́нки:** бежа́ть н. race.
наперёд in advance, ahead;
напере|ко́р in defiance of; counter to (with *dat.); ~*рез интercepting, cutting across; **~чёт** 1. thoroughly; 2. there are few.
наперс|ник, ~ница confidant(e).
наперс|ток (-тка) thimble.
напива́ться *(pf.* напи́ться*) *(gen.)* have a drink (of); get drunk.
напи́льник file.
напира́ть *(pf.* на|пере́ть, -пру́, -прёшь; -пёр, -перла) (на + *acc.)* press (on), emphasize.
напи́|ток (-тка) drink, beverage.
напи́тывать *(pf.* напита́ть) impregnate; -ся become impregnated.
напи́ться *see* напива́ться.
напи́хивать *(pf.* напиха́ть) cram, stuff.
напластова́ние stratification.
наплева́ть* *(pf.):* мне н. *(coll.)* I couldn't care less.
наплы́в influx; excrescence.
напова́л outright.
наподо́бие *(gen.)* like, similar to
напои́ть *see* напа́ивать.
напока́з for show.
наполня́ть *(pf.* напо́лнить) fill; -ся fill, be filled.
наполови́ну half.
напомина́ние mention, reminder; **напомина́ть** *(pf.* напо́мнить) remind, recall.
напо́р pressure; **напо́ристый** energetic, assertive.
напосле́док in the end, after all.
направле́ние direction, trend; order, permit; **напра́вленность** *(f.)* direction, trend; **направля́ть** *(pf.* напра́вить) direct; send; -ся make one's way; be directed.
напра́во on the right, to the right.
напра́слина *(coll.)* nonsense; **напра́сный** vain, useless; wrongful; напра́сно in vain; it is useless.
напра́шиваться *(pf.* напроси́ться*) thrust oneself; suggest itself; н. на комплиме́нты fish for compliments; н. на неприя́тности ask for trouble.
наприме́р for example.
напрока́т for/on hire.
напролёт right through.

напроло́м: идти́ н. stop at nothing.
напропалу́ю recklessly.
напроси́ться see **напра́шиваться.**
напро́тив on the contrary; *(with gen.)* opposite.
напряга́ть *(pf.* напр|я́чь, -ягу́, -яжёшь; -яг,-ягла́; *ppr.*-яжённый)* strain; **-ся** strain oneself; **напряже́ние** tension; **напряжённый** tense, intense, strained.
напрями́к point-blank, straight.
напря́чь see **напряга́ть.**
напу́ганный scared.
напуска́ть *(pf.* напусти́ть*)* let/set on; let loose; fill; н. на себя́ ва́жность try to look important; **-ся** be set on *etc;* *(with* на + *acc)* fall on, fly at; **напускно́й** affected.
напу́тственный parting *(a.);* **напу́тствие** parting words.
напы́щенный pompous.
напя́ливать *(pf.* напя́лить) pull on, don.
наравне́ (с + *inst.)* equal (to).
нараспа́шку unbuttoned; у него́ душа́ н. he wears his heart on his sleeve.
наспе́в in a sing-song voice.
нараста́ть *(pf.* нарасти́*)* grow, increase.
нарасхва́т quickly, like hot cakes.
нара́щивание grafting *(med.);* building up, accumulation.
нарва́ть see **нарыва́ть.**
наре́зывать, нареза́ть *(pf.* наре́зать*)* cut, carve; rifle, thread; **наре́зка** cutting; thread.
нарека́ние censure; **нарека́ть** *(pf.* нар|е́чь, -еку́, -ечёшь; -ёк, -екла́; *ppr.* -е ённый) name; **наречённый** betrothed.
наре́чие 1. dialect; 2. adverb.
нарза́н Narzan mineral water.
нарица́тельный nominal.
нарко́з narcosis; **наркома́н** drug addict; **нарко́тик** narcotic, dope.
наро́д people, nation; **наро́дник** populist; **наро́дность** *(f.)* nationality, national character; **наро́дный** people's, popular.
наро́ст excrescence, growth.
наро́читый deliberate, intentional.
наро́чно on purpose; как н. as luck would have it; **наро́чный** special messenger.
на́рта sledge.
нару́бка notch.

нару́жность *(f.)* exterior; **нару́жный** external; ostensible; **нару́жу** outside.
нару́чник|и (-ов) handcuffs; **нару́чный** wrist *(a.).*
наруш|а́ть *(pf.* нару́шить) break, disturb, violate; **наруше́ние** breach, infringement; **наруши́тель** *(m.)* transgressor.
нарци́сс narcissus, daffodil.
на́ры (нар) plank-bed.
нары́в abscess, boil; **нарыва́ть** *(pf.* нарва́ть*)* gather *(a head);* pick; **-ся** (на + *acc.)* come up against.
наря́д 1. dress; 2. order, warrant; **наряди́ть** see **наряжа́ть; наря́дн|ый** well-dressed.
наряду́ (с + *inst.)* side by side, parallel *(with).*
наряж|а́ть *(pf.* нар|яди́ть, -яжу́, -я́дишь) dress up; appoint; **-ся** dress oneself up; be appointed.
насажда́ть *(pf.* нас|ади́ть, -ажу́, -а́дишь; *ppr.* -а́женный) spread; implant; **насажде́ние** plantation; propagation.
наса́харивать *(pf.*наса́харить) sugar.
насви́стывать whistle.
наседа́ть *(pf.* насе́сть*)* (на + *acc.)* press (on); settle (on); **насе́дка** brood-hen.
насеко́мое insect.
населе́ние population; **насел|я́ть** *(pf.* -и́ть) settle, populate.
насе́ст perch, roost; **насе́сть** see **наседа́ть.**
наси́живать *(pf.* насиде́ть*)* hatch; warm; **наси́женный** long-occupied; **насиде́ться*** *(pf.)* sit, stay for a long time.
наси́лие violence; coercion; **наси́ловать** *(pf.* из-) coerce; rape.
наси́лу with difficulty.
наси́льственн|ый forcible, forced; violent.
наска́кивать *(pf.* наск|очи́ть, -очу́, -о́чишь) (на + *acc.)* collide (with), run (into); fly (at).
наскво́зь through and through.
наско́к sudden attack, swoop.
наско́лько how much; as far as.
наско́ро hastily.
наскочи́ть see **наска́кивать.**
наску́чить *(pf.) (dat.)* bore.
наслажда́ть *(pf.* насла|ди́ть, -жу́, -ди́шь) delight; **-ся** *(inst.)* enjoy; **наслажде́ние** enjoyment.

наследие heritage, legacy; **наслед|ник**, **~ница** heir, successor; **наследный crown** (prince): **наследовать** (pf. y-) inherit; (dat.) succeed; **наследственность** (f.) heredity; **наследственный** hereditary; **наследство** inheritance.

наслоение layer; stratification.

наслушаться (gen.) hear a lot of.

наслышк|а: по -e by hearsay.

насмерть to death, mortally.

насмехаться (над + inst.) sneer (at), mock; **насме|шка** (gen. pl. -шек) mockery, jibe; **насмешливый** derisive; **насмешник** scoffer.

насморк cold (in the head).

насмотреться* (pf.) (gen.) see a lot of; (на + acc.) see as much as one wants of.

насос pump.

наспех in a hurry, carelessly.

наст frozen snow-crust.

наст|авать (-аю, -аёшь; pf. настать*) come; час настал the hour has struck.

наставительный instructive, edifying; **наставлять** (pf. наставить*) piece on; aim; admonish, exhort; **настав|ник**, **~ница** tutor, mentor.

настаивать (pf. настоять*) (на + prep.) insist (on); -ся brew (of tea).

настать see наставать.

настежь wide open.

настенный wall (a.).

настигать (pf. настигнуть, наст|ичь, past -иг) overtake.

настилать (pf. настлать*) lay, spread, cover; **настилка** laying, flooring.

настой infusion; **настойка** nastoika (liqueur); tincture.

настойчивый persistent, pressing.

настолько so, so much.

настольн|ый table (a.); -ая книга handbook, reference book.

настор|аживаться (pf. -ожиться) prick up one's ears; **насторожé** on the alert.

настояние insistence; **настоятель**, **~ница** Father Superior, dean / Mother Superior; **настоятельный** insistent, urgent; **настоять** see настаивать.

настоящий real; present; (neut.) the present.

настраивать (pf. настроить) tune; attune; dispose; **настроение** mood,

frame of mind; **настройка** tuning; **настройщик** tuner.

наступательный offensive; **наступать** (pf. наступить*) come, set in; (ipf.) advance; (на + acc.) tread/stand on; **наступление** coming; offensive.

настурция nasturtium.

насупить (pf.) knit (brows).

насухо dry.

насущный urgent, vital; daily (bread).

насчёт (gen.) as regards, about.

насчитывать (pf. насчитать) count, number; -ся number.

насыпать (pf. насыпать*) pour, spread, fill, heap up; **насыпь** (f.) embankment.

насыщать (pf. нас|ытить, -ыщу, -ытишь) satiate, saturate; **насыщение** satiation, saturation; **насыщенность** (f.) saturation.

наталкивать (pf. натолкнуть) (на + acc.) push/dash (against); direct (towards); -ся (на + acc.) run (against).

натапливать (pf. натопить*) heat; melt.

натаскивать (pf. натащить*) pull on; drag up (a lot of).

нательный worn next to the skin.

натирать (pf. натереть*) rub.

натиск onslaught.

наткнуться see натыкаться.

натолкнуть see наталкивать.

натощак on an empty stomach.

натр natron; **едкий** н. caustic soda.

натравливать (pf. натравить*) (на + acc.) set/hound on.

натрий sodium.

натрое in three.

натуга effort, strain.

натура nature; **натурализовать** (ipf. & pf.) naturalize; **натуральный** natural, **натур|щик ~щица** model.

натыкать (pf. наткнуть) pin in, stick in; -ся (на + acc.) knock, stumble (against); meet.

натюрморт still-life.

натягивать (pf. натянуть) stretch; draw/pull on; **натяжение** tension; **натя|жка** (gen. pl. -жек) stretched interpretation; с -жкой by stretching a point; **натянутый** tight, strained.

наугад, **наудачу** at random.

наука learning, science, knowledge,

наýськивать *(pf.* наýськать) urge on.

наутёк: пустúться н. take to one's heels.

наýтро on the morrow.

наýчный scholarly, scientific.

наýшник ear-flap; ear-phone; informer; **наýшничать** (на + *acc.*) tell tales (about).

нахáл, ~ка impudent person; **нахáльный** impudent; **нахáльство** impudence.

нахвáтывать *(pf.* нахватáть) *(acc. or gen.)* get, pick up; -ся *(gen.)* pick up, gather.

нахлеб|ник, ~ница hanger-on.

нахлобýчивать *(pf.* -ýчить) pull over one's eyes.

нахлынуть *(pf.)* rush, sweep.

нахмýривать *(pf.* нахмýрить) frown.

находúть* *(pf.* найтú*, найдý; нашёл; *ppp.* нáйденный) find; -ся be found; be situated; **нахóдка** find; **нахóдчивый** quick, sharp; **нахождéние** finding.

нацéливать *(pf.* нацéлить) aim.

национализáция nationalization; **национализ|úровать,** *or* **-овáть** *(ipf. & pf.)* nationalize; **националúзм** nationalism; **национáльность** *(f.)* nationality; **национáльный** national.

нáция nation, people.

начáло beginning; basis, principle; **начáльник** head, chief; **начáльный** elementary; initial.

начáльство authorities; command.

начáтк|и (-ов) rudiments; **начáть** *see* начинáть.

начекý on the alert.

нáчерно rough(ly).

начéрпывать *(pf* начéрпать) scoop up.

начертáние tracing, inscription; **начертáть** *(pf.)* trace, inscribe.

начёт deficiency in account.

начёт|чик, ~чица well-read but uncritical person.

начинáние undertaking; **начинáть** *(pf.* на|чáть, -чнý, -чнёшь; нáчал, -á; *ppp.* нáчатый) begin; -ся begin.

начúнка stuffing; **начин|я́ть** *(pf.* -úть) stuff.

начислéние addition, extra charge.

нáчисто clean, fair; openly.

начúтанный well-read.

начищáть *(pf.* начúстить*) clean.

наш, нáша, нáше, нáши our.

нашатýрный спирт liquid ammonia; **нашатýр|ь** (-я́) sal-ammoniac.

нашёптывать *(pf.* нашептáть*) whisper in someone's ear.

нашéствие invasion.

нашивáть *(pf.* нашúть*) sew on **нашúвка** stripe, tab.

нащýпывать *(pf.* нащýпать) grope/ feel for.

наявý in waking hours.

не not.

небезызвéстно it is not unknown, it is no secret.

небéсный heavenly, celestial.

нёбный palatal.

нéбо *(pl.* н(|бесá, -бéс, -бесáм) sky; heaven.

нёбо palate.

небольш|ой small, little; **50 с -úм** a little over 50.

небо|свóд firmament; **~склóн** sky; **~скрёб** skyscraper.

небóсь it is most likely.

небрéжный careless, slipshod.

небывáлый unprecedented; fantastic.

небылúца untruth, cock-and-bull story; **небытиé** nothingness, non-existence.

небьющийся unbreakable.

невáжно poorly, indifferently; **невáжный** unimportant, indifferent.

невдалекé not far off.

невéдение ignorance; **невéдомый** unknown; mysterious; **невéжа** *(m. & f.)* boor; **невéжда** *(m. & f.)* ignoramus; **невéжественный** ignorant; **невéжество** ignorance.

невéрие unbelief, scepticism.

невероя́тный incredible; unlikely.

невесóмый weightless; imponderable.

невéста bride; fiancée; **невéстка** daughter-in-law *(son's wife)*, sister-in-law *(brother's wife)*.

невéсть: н. кудá God knows where.

невзгóда adversity.

невзирá|я (на + *acc.*) regardless of.

невзначáй by chance.

невзрáчный ill-favoured, plain.

невúдаль *(f.)* wonder, prodigy; **невúданный** unprecedented, without parallel; **невúдимый** invisible.

невúнность *(f.)* innocence; **невúнный** innocent; harmless.

невменя́емый irresponsible.

невмóчь: стáло н. it became impossible.

нéвод seine, net.

невозвр|атимый, ~атный irrevocable, irreparable.

невоздержный uncontrolled, intemperate.

невозможный impossible.

невозмутимый imperturbable.

невознаградимый irreparable.

неволей against one's will; неволить (pf. при-) (coll.) compel; невольник slave; невольный forced, involuntary; неволя captivity; necessity.

невообразимый unimaginable, inconceivable.

невооружённый unarmed; naked (eye).

невпопад not to the point.

невралгия neuralgia.

невредимый unharmed.

невроз neurosis.

невтерпёж: сму н. he can't stand it, he's fed up.

невыгода disadvantage.

невыдержанный lacking restraint; uneven; new (e.g. cheese).

невыносимый unbearable, insufferable.

невыполнимый impracticable.

невыразимый inexpressible.

невыход (на работу) absenteeism, non-appearance.

нега bliss; comfort.

негатив negative.

негашёная известь quicklime.

негде (there is) nowhere.

негласный private, secret.

негодный (к + dat.) unfit (for); worthless.

негодование indignation; негодовать (на + acc.; против + gen.) be indignant (at, with).

негодяй good-for-nothing.

негр negro.

неграмотный illiterate; ignorant; rude, crude.

негритянка negress; негритянский negro (a.).

недавний recent; недавно not long ago, lately.

недалёкий near; short; not very intelligent.

недаром not for nothing, not without reason.

недвижимость (f.) immovables, real estate; недвижимый immovable.

неделимый indivisible.

недельный weekly; неделя week.

недобор arrears, shortage.

недоверие distrust; недоверчивый mistru tful.

недовешивать (pf. недо есить*) give short weight.

недовольство dissatisfaction, displeasure.

недогрузка not a full load; undercapacity.

недоделка imperfection, unfinished job.

недодержать* underexpose.

недоедание malnutrition.

недоимка arrears.

недолюбливать have no great liking for.

недомеривать (pf. недомерить) give short measure.

недомогание indisposition; недомогать be unwell.

недомолвка reservation.

недоношенный premature (child).

недооцен|ивать (pf. -ить) underestimate; недооценка underestimation.

недопечённый half-baked.

недопустимый inadmissible, intolerable.

недоразвитый underdeveloped.

недоразумение misunderstanding.

недорогой inexpensive.

недород poor harvest.

недоросль (m.) ignoramus.

недослышать* (pf.) fail to hear.

недосмотр oversight.

недост|авать (-аю, -аёшь; pf. недостать*) (gen.) lack, miss; мне недостаёт денег I am short of money; недоста|ток (-тка) shortage, deficiency; недостаточный insufficient.

недостижимый unattainable.

недостойный unworthy.

недоступный inaccessible.

недосуг lack of time.

недо|считываться (pf. -считаться) (gen.) not count, be missing.

недосягаемый inaccessible.

недо|умевать (-умеваю; pf. -уметь) be perplexed, at a loss; недоумение bewilderment.

недоуч|ка (gen. pl. -чек) (m. & f.) half-educated person.

недочёт deficit; defect.

недра (недр) depths; bosom, womb.

недруг enemy.

недуг ailment.

недурной not bad; handsome.

нежданный unexpected.

нѐжели than.

нѐженка (*m. & f.*) molly-coddled person; нѐжить indulge, pamper; –ся indulge oneself; нѐжность (*f.*) tenderness; (*pl.*) endearments; нѐжный tender, gentle.

незабве́нный unforgettable; незабу́дка forget-me-not.

незави́дный unenviable; mediocre.

незави́симость (*f.*) independence; незави́симый (от + *gen.*) independent (of).

незада́ча ill-luck; незада́чливый unlucky; unpractical.

незадо́лго (до + *gen.*) shortly (before).

незаконнорождённый illegitimate.

незамени́мый irreplaceable.

незапа́мятный immemorial.

не́зачем (there is) no need.

незва́ный uninvited.

нездоро́в|иться: мне -ится I don't feel well; нездоро́вье ill-health.

незнако́|мец (-мца), ~мка stranger; незнако́мый unknown; unfamiliar.

незна́ние ignorance.

незри́мый invisible.

н зы́бл мый firm, immovable.

н избе́жный inevitable.

н изве́данный unknown.

неизглади́мый indelible.

неизлечи́мый incurable.

неизме́нный invariable, unalterable.

неизмери́мый immeasurable, immense.

неизъясни́мый inexplicable.

неиме́ние lack, absence.

неимове́рный incredible.

неиму́щий poor.

неискорени́мый ineradicable.

неисполни́мый impracticable.

неисправи́мый irreparable, incorrigible; неиспра́вный in disrepair, defective.

неиссяка́емый inexhaustible.

нейстовство fury, rage; нейстовый furious, violent.

неистощи́мый inexhaustible.

неистреби́мый ineradicable.

неисчерпа́емый inexhaustible.

неисчисли́мый innumerable.

нейло́н nylon; нейло́новый nylon (*a.*).

нейтрализова́ть (*ipf. & pf.*) neutralize; нейтралите́т neutrality; нейтра́льный neutral.

нейтро́н neutron.

неказ

и́стый plain, not much to look at.

нѐкий some, a certain.

нѐкогда 1. in former times; 2. (there is) no time; мне н. гуля́т.. I haven't time to go for a walk.

нѐкого (there is) nobody; н. посла́ть there is nobody to send.

нѐкоторый certain.

некроло́г obituary.

некста́ти inopportunely; irrelevantly.

нѐкто someone; a certain.

нѐкуда (there is) nowhere; н. идти́ there's nowhere to go.

некуря́щий non-smoker.

нела́дный wrong; нела́д|ы́ (-о́в) discord.

нелёгкая the devil, deuce; нелёгкий difficult.

неле́пость (*f.*) nonsense; неле́пый absurd.

нело́вкий awkward.

нельзя́ (it is) impossible; not permitted.

нелюди́м, ~ка unsociable person; нелюди́мый unsociable; desolate.

нема́ло not a little; not a few.

неме́дленный immediate.

неме́ть (*pf.* о-) become dumb.

нѐ|мец (-мца) German; неме́цкий German (*a.*).

нѐмилость (*f.*) disgrace.

неминуемый inevitable.

нѐмка German woman.

немно́гие not many, few; немно́го a little, some; немно́гое a few things; a little; немно́ж(еч)ко a little.

немо́й dumb; немота́ dumbness.

нѐмочь (*f.*) illness; нѐмощный infirm.

немудрено́ no wonder.

немы́слимый unthinkable.

ненави́деть* (*pf.* воз-) hate; нена́вистник enemy; ненави́стный hated; не́нависть (*f.*) hate.

ненагля́дный beloved.

ненападе́ние non-aggression.

ненаро́ком inadvertently.

ненаруши́мый inviolable.

нена́стный rainy, inclement; нена́стье bad weather.

ненасы́тный insatiable.

необду́манный rash, thoughtless.

необита́емый uninhabited.

необлага́емый not taxable.

необозри́мый boundless, immense.

необосно́ванный groundless, unfounded.

необрати́мый irreversible.

необу́зданный unbridled.

необутый without shoes.
необходимость *(f.)* necessity; **не-обходимый** necessary.
необъяснимый inexplicable.
необъятный immense.
неоднократный repeated.
неодолимый insuperable.
неожиданный unexpected.
неоколониализм neo-colonialism.
неон neon; **неоновый** neon *(a.)*.
неописуемый indescribable.
неоплатный Irredeemable; insolvent.
неопределённый indefinite; infinitive; indeterminate; **неопределимый** indefinable.
неопровержимый irrefutable.
неослабный unremitting.
неоспоримый incontestable.
неосуществимый impracticable.
неосязаемый impalpable, intangible.
неотвратимый inevitable.
неот|вязный, ~вязчивый importunate; constant.
неотделимый inseparable.
неотёсанный uncouth, unpolished.
неоткуда from nowhere.
неотложный urgent.
неотлучный always present.
неотразимый irresistible.
неотступный persistent, relentless.
неотчуждаемый inalienable.
неотъемлемый inalienable.
неохота reluctance.
неоценимый invaluable, inestimable.
непереводимый untranslatable.
непередаваемый inexpressible.
непереходный intransitive.
неплатёжеспособный insolvent.
непобедимый invincible.
неповиновение disobedience, insubordination.
неповторимый inimitable.
непогода bad weather.
непогрешимый infallible.
неподалёку not far off.
неподвижный immovable; motionless.
неподкупный incorruptible.
неподражаемый inimitable.
неподчинение insubordination.
непоколебимый firm, steadfast.
неполадка trouble.
непомерный exorbitant.
неисправимый irreparable.
непорочный chaste, immaculate.
непосвящённый uninitiated.
непоседа *(m. & f.)* fidget; **непоседливый** restless.

непосильный beyond one's strength.
непослушание disobedience.
непосредственный immediate; spontaneous.
непостижимый incomprehensible, inscrutable.
непочатый entire, unbroken, unopened; **н. край ра от**.. an endless amount of work.
неправда untruth.
непревзойдённый unsurpassed.
непредвиденный unforeseen.
непреклонный inflexible; inexorable.
непреложный immutable; indisputable.
непременно without fail; **непременный** indispensable; permanent *(secretary)*.
непреодолимый insuperable.
непререкаемый unquestionable.
непрерывный continuous.
непрестанный incessant.
неприглядный unattractive.
неприкосновенный inviolable, reserved.
неприменимый inapplicable.
непримиримый irreconcilable.
непринуждённый natural, free and easy.
неприступный inaccessible.
неприхотливый unpretentious, undemanding.
неприязненный hostile, unfriendly; **неприязнь** *(f.)* hostility; **неприятель** *(m.)* enemy; **неприятельский** enemy *(a.)*.
непробудный deep, eternal *(sleep)*.
непроглядный pitch-dark.
непроезжий impassable.
непроизвольный involuntary.
непромокаемый waterproof; **н. плащ** raincoat.
непроницаемый impenetrable.
непротивление non-resistance.
непроходимый impassable, impenetrable.
непрочь: я н. это сделать I don't mind doing it.
непрошенный unbidden, uninvited.
непутёвый good-for-nothing *(a.)*.
нерадивый careless, negligent.
неразбериха muddle.
неразделимый indivisible; **нераздельный** inseparable.
неразличимый indiscernible.
неразлучный inseparable.
неразрешимый unsolvable, insoluble.
неразрушимый indestructible.

неразры́вный indissoluble.
нераствори́мый insoluble.
нерасторжи́мый indissoluble.
нерв nerve; нервничать be nervous; нервнобольно́й neurotic; не́рвный nervous, nerve (a.).
нержаве́ющий rust-resisting; stainless (steel).
не́рпа seal.
неруши́мый inviolable.
неря́ха (m. & f.) sloven, slattern; неря́шливый careless; untidy.
несбы́точный unrealizable, impossible.
несваре́ние indigestion.
несгиба́емый inflexible.
несгора́емый fire-proof.
несе́ние carrying, bearing.
несессе́р toilet-case.
несказа́нный unspeakable.
несклáдный incoherent; clumsy.
несклоня́емый indeclinable.
не́сколько several, some; somewhat.
несконча́емый interminable.
неслы́ханный unprecedented; неслы́шный inaudible.
несменя́емый irremovable.
несме́тный innumerable.
несмотря́ (на + acc.) in spite of.
несмыва́емый indelible.
несовершенноле́тие minority (age).
несоверше́нный imperfective; imperfect.
несовмести́мый incompatible.
несогла́сие disagreement; несогла́сованность (f.) lack of co-ordination.
несоизмери́мый incommensurate.
несократи́мый irreducible.
несокруши́мый indestructible.
несомне́нный indubitable; несомне́нно undoubtedly.
несообра́зный incongruous.
несоотве́тствие discrepancy.
несортово́й of low quality.
неспроста́ not without purpose.
несравн|е́нный, -и́мый incomparable.
нестерпи́мый unbearable.
не|сти́ (-су, -сёшь; past. нёс, несла́; pf. по-, ppp. -сённый) bear, carry; sustain; (pf. с-) lay eggs; -сь rush; be carried.
несто́ящий worthless.
несура́зный awkward; absurd.
несча́стный unhappy, unfortunate; н. слу́чай accident; несча́сть|е misfortune; к -ю unfortunately.
несчётный innumerable.

нет 1. no; 2. (gen.) there is not any . . .; there are no . . .; у меня́ нет (не́ было) . . . I have not (had not) . . . .
нетерпе́ние impatience; нетерпи́мый intolerant; intolerable.
нетрудово́й: н. дохо́д unearned income.
не́тто net (weight etc.).
не́ту (coll.) = нет.
неувяда́емый unfading.
неугаси́мый inextinguishable.
неугомо́нный indefatigable.
неуда́ча failure, misfortune; неуда́чливый unlucky; неуда́ч|ник, ~ница failure, unlucky person.
неудержи́мый irrepressible.
неудо́бный uncomfortable; awkward.
неудобо|вари́мый indigestible; ~испо́лнимый impracticable.
неуёмный incessant, indefatigable.
неуже́ли really?
неузнава́емый unrecognizable.
неукло́нный steadfast, unswerving.
неуклю́жий clumsy.
неукроти́мый indomitable.
неулови́мый difficult to catch, elusive, subtle.
неуме́ние inability, ignorance.
неумоли́мый inexorable.
неумо́лчный incessant.
неурожа́й bad harvest.
неуро́чный inopportune, unseasonable.
неуря́дица (coll.) confusion.
неуста́нный tireless.
неуст|о́йка (gen. pl. -о́ек) forfeit (law).
неустраши́мый intrepid.
неусы́пный ever-vigilant.
неуте́шный inconsolable.
неутоли́мый unquenchable.
неутоми́мый indefatigable.
не́уч ignoramus.
неуязви́мый invulnerable.
неф nave.
нефте|добы́ча oil output/production ~наливно́е су́дно oil-tanker; ~очи́стка oil refining; ~перего́нный заво́д refinery; ~про́мысел (-сла) oilfield; ~промы́шленность (f.) oil industry; ~храни́лище oil tank.
нефть (f.) oil; нефтян|о́й oil (a.); -а́я сква́жина oil-well.
нехва́тка (coll.) shortage.
неходово́й unmarketable.
не́хотя unwillingly; inadvertently.

нецензу́рный unprintable, obscene.
неча́янный accidental; unexpected.
не́чего (there is) nothing; н. де́лать there's nothing to do.
не́чет odd number; нечётный odd.
не́что something.
неща́дный merciless.
нея́вка failure to appear; default.
ни not a; ног; ни...ни...neither.. ноr...; ни то ни сё neither this nor that; кто (бы) ни whoever.
ни́ва cornfield.
нивели́ровать (ipf. & pf.) level.
ниве́сть (coll.) nobody knows.
нигде́ nowhere.
нигили́ст nihilist.
нижа́йший most humble.
ни́же lower, shorter.
нижеподписа́вшийся the undersigned; ~упомя́нутый undermentioned.
ни́жний lower; -ее бельё underclothes.
низ (pl. -ы́) bottom; (pl.) the lower classes.
низа́ть (нижу́, ни́жешь; pf. на-) string, thread.
низверга́ть (pf. -ве́ргнуть; past. -ве́рг) throw down, overthrow; низверже́ние overthrow, subversion.
низводи́ть* (pf. низвести́*) (до + gen.) bring down, reduce (to).
низи́на low place.
ни́зкий (compr. ни́же) low; base, mean.
низкопокло́нство servility; ~про́бный of low standard.
низложе́ние deposing.
ни́зменность (f.) lowland; baseness; ни́зменный low-lying; base.
низово́й lower; local; низо́вье lower reaches; ни́зость (f.) baseness; ни́зший lower; lowest.
ника́к in no way; никако́й no, none
ни́келевый nickel (a); ни́кель (m.) nickel.
ни́кнуть (past. ник; pf. по-) droop.
никогда́ never; нико́й no.
никоти́н nicotine.
никто́ nobody, no one; никуда́ nowhere.
никчёмный good-for-nothing.
нима́ло not in the least; ниотку́да from nowhere.
нипочём not for the world; nothing; э́то ему́ н. it means nothing to him.

ниско́лько not at all; none at all.
ниспроверга́ть (pf. -ве́ргнут , past -ве́рг) overthrow, subvert; ниспроверже́ние overthrow.
ни́тка, ни́точка (gen. pl. -чек) thread.
нитрова́ние nitration.
нить (f.) thread; filament.
ниц: па́дать н. prostrate oneself.
ничего́ 1. nothing; 2. it doesn't matter.
ниче́й nobody's; ниче́йный drawn (game).
ничко́м prone, face downwards.
ничто́ nothing; ничто́жество pettiness; nonentity; ничто́жность (f.) insignificance; nonentity; ничто́жный insignificant, worthless.
ничу́ть not a bit.
ничья́ 1. nobody's; 2. draw; сыгра́ть в ничью́ play a draw.
ни́ша niche, recess.
нищета́ destitution, poverty; ни́щий beggar.
но but, and.
нова́тор innovator; нова́торство innovation.
нове́лла short story.
нове́нький brand-new.
новизна́ novelty, newness; нови́нка novelty, something new; нови́чок (-чка́) novice.
новобра́нец (-нца) recruit; ~бра́чный newly-married; ~введе́ние innovation; ~го́дний new year's; ~лу́ние new moon; ~образова́ние new formation; neoplasm, neologism; ~прибы́вший newcomer; ~рождённый newly-born; ~се́лье new home; housewarming; ~стро́йка (gen. pl. -о́ек) new building.
но́вость (f. pl. -и, -е́й) news; novelty; новоя́вленный newly brought to light; но́вшество innovation, novelty; но́вый new; новь (f.) virgin soil.
нога́ (но́гу, pl. но́ги, -а́м) foot, leg; идти́ в но́гу keep in step; положи́ть но́гу на́ ногу cross one's legs; жить на широ́кую но́гу live in grand style; вверх нога́ми upside down; со всех ног as fast as one can.
ноготки́ (-о́в) marigold.
но́готь (но́гтя, pl. -и, -е́й) (finger/toe-) nail; ногтое́да whitlow.
нож (-а́) knife; быть на ножа́х (с + inst.) be at daggers drawn (with);

ножевóй товáр cutlery; нóжик knife.

нó|жка *(gen. pl.* -жек) foot, leg; stalk, stem.

нóж|ницы (-ниц) scissors.

ножнóй foot *(a.).*

нó|жны (-жен) scabbard, sheath.

ноздревáтый porous.

ноздря *(pl.* нóздр|и, -éй) nostril.

нокаутúровать *(ipf. & pf.)* knock out *(sport).*

нол|ь (-я) nil, nought.

нóмер *(pl.* -á) number; size; hotel room; trick; номе|рóк (-ркá) metal disc, label, ticket.

номинáл face value; номинáльный nominal.

норá (нóрý, *pl.* нóры) burrow, hole.

норвé|жец (-жца), ~жка *(gen. pl.* -жек) Norwegian; норвéжский Norwegian *(a.).*

норд north, north wind.

нóрка 1. burrow; 2. mink.

нóрма standard, norm; rate; нормáльный normal.

нормáн|дец (-дца) Norman.

нормúрование rate setting; rationing.

нóров custom, habit; obstinacy; restiveness; норовúть strive.

нос (на носý, *pl.* -ы́) nose; bow *(of ship),* prow; водúть зá нос make a fool of; говорúть в нос talk down one's nose; поéсить нос be crestfallen; экзáмен на носý the exam is very close; нóсик nose; beak; spout.

носú|лки (-лок) stretcher; sedan chair; носúльщик porter; носúтель *(m.)* bearer, carrier; носúть (ношý, нóсишь; *pf.* по-, понестú*) carry, take; wear; -ся rush; fly, wear; -ся (с + *inst.)* make a fuss (over); нóска carrying; wearing; нóский hard-wearing; good at laying *(eggs).*

носовóй nose *(a.),* nasal; н. платóк handkerchief.

но|сóк (-скá) toe *(of shoe)*; sock.

носорóг rhinoceros.

нóта note.

нотáция reprimand; notation.

ночевáть *(pf.* пере-) spend the night; ночёвка spending the night; ночлéг lodging, shelter; ночнúк (-á) night light; ночнóй night *(a.),* nocturnal; ноч|ь *(f.;* в -й, *pl.* -и, -éй) night.

нóша burden.

нóщно: дéнно и н. day and night.

ноя́бр|ь (-я́) November; ноя́брьский November *(a.).*

нрав disposition, temper; *(pl.)* customs, manners; э́то ей не по -у she doesn't like it.

нрáв|иться *(pf.* по-) *(dat.)* please; э́то мне -ится I like it.

нраво|учéние moral admonition; ~учúтельный moralizing.

нрáвственность *(f.)* morality, morals; нрáвственный moral.

ну well! now!

нугá nougat.

нýдный tedious.

нуждá *(pl.* нýжды) need; нуждáться (в + *prep.)* need, require; нýжный necessary; нýжно (it is) necessary.

нул|ь (-я) nil, naught.

нумерáция numeration; нумеровáть *(pf.* за-) number.

нýтрия nutria; coypu.

нутрó inside, interior.

ны́не now, nowadays; ны́нешний present, modern, current; ны́нче *(coll.)* today; now.

ныря́ть *(pf.* нырнýть) dive.

ны́ть (нóю, нóешь) ache; whimper.

нюáнс nuance.

нюх scent; flair; нюхáтельный: н. табáк snuff; нюхать *(pf.* по-) smell, sniff.

ня́нчить nurse; -ся (с + *inst.)* fuss (over).

ня́|нька *(gen. pl.* -нек), ня́ня nurse; у семú ня́нек дитя́ без глáзу too many cooks spoil the broth.

О

о 1. *(+ prep.)* about; with; 2. *(+ acc.)* on, against; удáриться о стол bump against the table.

оáзис oasis.

об = о.

óба, óбе both; смотрéть в óба keep one's eyes skinned.

обагр|я́ть *(pf.* -úть) stain.

обалдéлый stupefied.

обая́ние charm, fascination; обая́тельный fascinating, charming.

обвáл collapse, landslide; обвáливать 1. *(pf.* обваля́ть) (в + *acc.)* roll (in); 2. *(pf.* обвалúть) make fall; heap round; -ся crumble cave in.

обва́ривать *(pf.* обвари́ть*)* pour boiling water on; scald.
обведе́ние enclosing; outlining.
обве́с false weight.
обве́сить *see* **обве́шивать**.
обвести́ *see* **обводи́ть**.
обве́тренный weather-beaten.
обветша́лый decrepit.
обве́шивать *(pf.* обве́шать*)* hang *(window etc.),* cover; *(pf.* обве́сить*)* give wrong weight to, cheat.
обвива́ть *(pf.* обви́ть, обовью́*)* entwine, wind.
обвине́ние accusation; **обвини́тель** *(m.)* accuser; prosecutor; **обвини́тельный** accusatory; о. акт indictment; **обвиня́ть** *(pf.* -и́ть*)* (в + *prep.)* accuse (of).
обвиса́ть *(pf.* об\ви́снуть, *past.* -ви́с*)* droop; become flabby; **обви́слый** flabby.
обви́ть *see* **обвива́ть**.
обводи́ть* *(pf.* обвести́*)* lead round; surround; outline; о. его́ вокру́г па́льца twist him round one's little finger.
обводне́ние irrigation.
обво́дный encircling, surrounding.
обводн\я́ть *(pf.* -и́ть*)* irrigate, supply with water.
обвора́живать *(pf.* обворожи́ть*)* fascinate, bewitch; **обворожи́тельный** fascinating.
обвя́зывать *(pf.* обвяза́ть*)* tie round.
обгла́дывать *(pf.* обглода́ть*)* gnaw round, pick *(e. g. a bone).*
обгоня́ть *(pf.* обогна́ть*)* outrun, overtake.
обгора́ть *(pf.* обгоре́ть*)* be scorched.
обдава́ть* *(pf.* обда́ть*)* splash, pour (over).
обдира́ть *(pf.* ободра́ть*)* fleece, skin; peel.
обду́мывать *(pf.* обду́мать*)* consider.
о́бе both.
обе́д dinner, lunch; **обе́дать** *(pf.* по-*)* have dinner; **обе́денный** dinner *(a.).*
обедне́ние impoverishment.
обе́д\ня *(gen. pl.* -ден*)* mass.
обез\бо́ливать *(pf.* -бо́лить*)* anaesthetize.
обез\во́живать *(pf.* -во́дить, -о́жу, -о́дишь*)* dehydrate.
обез\вре́живать *(pf.* -вре́дить, -е́жу, -е́дишь*)* render harmless.
обез\гла́вливать *(pf.* -гла́вить*)* decapitate.

обез\до́ливать *(pf.* -до́лить*)* deprive of one's share.
обеззар\а́живать *(pf.* -а́зить, -а́жу, -а́зишь*)* disinfect.
обезлю́деть *(pf.)* become depopulated.
обезобр\а́живать *(pf.* -а́зить, -а́жу, -а́зишь*)* disfigure.
обезоп\а́сить *(pf.* -а́шу, -а́сишь*)* make secure.
обез\ору́живать *(pf.* -ору́жить*)* disarm.
обезу́меть *(pf.)* go mad.
обезья́на monkey; **обезья́ний** monkey *(a.);* **обезья́нничать** *(pf.* с-*)* *(coll.)* ape.
обел\я́ть *(pf.* -и́ть*)* rehabilitate, whitewash.
оберега́ть *(pf.* обере́чь*)* defend, guard.
обёртка wrapper; **обёрточный** wrapping, packing *(a.);* **обёртывать** *(pf.* оберну́ть*)* wrap up; turn; -ся turn.
обес\кро́вливать *(pf.* -кро́вить*)* drain of blood, bleed.
обес\кура́живать *(pf.* -кура́жить*)* dishearten.
обеспе́чение guaranteeing, securing; guarantee; maintenance; provision; **обес\пе́чивать** *(pf.* -пе́чить*)* provide *(smb.— acc.)* *(with sth.— inst.);* provide for; secure, ensure; **обеспе́ченный** well-to-do.
обесси́леть *(pf.)* lose strength; **обес\си́ливать** *(pf.* -си́лить*)* enfeeble.
обессме́ртить (-рчу, -ртишь, *pf.)* immortalize.
обесце́нение depreciation; **обес\це́нивать** *(pf.* -це́нить*)* devalue.
обе́т vow, promise; **обетова́нная земля́** the Promised Land.
обеща́ние promise; **обеща́ть** *(ipf. &* *pf.; pf.* по-*)* promise.
обжа́лование appeal; **обжа́ловать** *(pf.)* appeal against.
обж\а́ривать *(pf.* обжа́рить*)* fry, brown off.
обжига́ть *(pf.* обже́чь, обожгу́*)* burn, scorch; -ся burn oneself; *(fig.)* burn one's fingers.
обжо́ра *(m. & f.)* glutton; **обжо́рливый** gluttonous; **обжо́рство** gluttony.
обза\води́ться* *(pf.* -вести́сь*)* *(inst.)* provide oneself *(with),* acquire.

обзо́р survey.

обзыва́ть *(pf.* обозва́ть**) call *(smb.)* names.

обива́ть *(pf.* оби́ть, обобью́**) beat; upholster; **оби́вка** upholstery.

оби́д|а insult, offence; не в -у будь ска́зано no offence meant; **оби́д-ный** offensive, insulting; **оби́д-чивый** touchy; **обижа́ть** *(pf.* об|и́деть, -и́жу, -и́дишь) hurt, offend; **-ся** take offence.

оби́лие abundance; **оби́льный** abundant.

обину́ясь: не о. without hesitation; **обиня́к:** говори́ть без -о́в without beating about the bush.

обира́ть *(pf.* обобра́ть*, оберу́ *etc.)* gather; rob.

обита́емый inhabited; **обита́ть** (в + *prep.)* inhabit.

оби́тель *(f.)* cloister.

оби́ть *see* обива́ть.

обихо́д custom, use; **обихо́дный** everyday.

обка́рмливать *(pf.* обкорми́ть**) overfeed.

обка́тывать *(pf.* обката́ть**) roll, smooth.

обкла́дывать *(pf.* обл|ожи́ть, -ожу́, -о́жишь) edge, face; cover; surround.

обко́м (областно́й комите́т) regional committee.

обкорми́ть *see* обка́рмливать.

обкра́дывать *(pf.* обокра́сть, обкраду́**) rob.

обку́сывать *(pf.* обкуса́ть) eat, gnaw round.

обла́ва raid, ambush.

облага́ть *(pf.* обл|ожи́ть, -ожу́, -о́жишь) assess, tax.

облагора́живать *(pf.* облагоро́дить, -жу, -дишь) ennoble.

облада́ние possession; **облада́ть** *(inst.)* possess.

о́блак|о *(pl.* -а́, -о́в) cloud.

обла́мывать *(pf.* облома́ть & обломи́ть) break off.

областно́й regional; **о́бласт|ь** *(f., pl.* -и, -е́й) region.

обла́тка capsule, wafer.

облаче́ние robing, investing.

о́блачный cloudy, nebulous.

облега́ть *(pf.* обле́чь**) cover; fit closely.

облегча́ть *(pf.* облегчи́ть) facilitate, lighten; ease, relieve; **облегче́ние** making lighter, easier; relief.

обледене́лый ice-covered; **обледене́ть** *(pf.)* become covered with ice.

обле́злый shabby, mangy.

облека́ть *(pf.* обл|е́чь, -еку́, -ечёшь; -ёк, -екла́, *ppp.* -ечённый) clothe, invest.

обле|пля́ть *(pf.* -пи́ть**) stick/paste all over; cover; cling to.

облесе́ние afforestation.

облета́ть *(pf.* облете́ть**) fly(round); fly all over.

обле́чь *see* облега́ть & облека́ть.

облива́ть *(pf.* обли́ть, оболью́**) pour over; **-ся** wash oneself down; spill over; **-ся** слеза́ми melt into tears.

обли́вка glaze.

облига́ция bond.

обли́зывать *(pf.* облиза́ть**) lick all over; **-ся** lick one's lips.

о́блик appearance, aspect.

облипа́ть *(pf.* обли́пнуть**) be(come) covered, stuck all over.

обли́ть *see* облива́ть.

облицо́вка facing, lining; **облицо́вы-вать** *(pf.* -ева́ть) face, cover.

облич|а́ть *(pf.* -и́ть) convict, expose; reveal; **обличе́ние** accusation; exposure; **обличи́тельный** accusatory.

обложе́ние taxation, rating; **обло-жи́ть** *see* обкла́дывать & облага́ть; **обло́|жка** *(gen. pl.* -жек) dust-wrapper, cover.

облока́чиваться *(pf.* облок|оти́ться, -очу́сь, -оти́шься) lean; о. на подоко́нник lean on the window-sill.

облома́ть, -и́ть *see* обла́мывать; обло́|мок (-мка) fragment.

облу́пливать *(pf.* облупи́ть**) peel, shell.

облу|чо́к (-чка́) coachman's seat.

обма́зывать *(pf.* обма́зать**) coat, putty; smear.

обма́кивать *(pf.* обмакну́ть) dip.

обма́н deception; **обма́нный** fraudulent; **обма́нчивый** deceptive; **обма́н|щик, ~щица** deceiver, fraud; **обма́нывать** *(pf.*обману́ть)deceive.

обма́тывать *(pf.* обмота́ть) wind, wrap.

обма́хивать *(pf.* обмахну́ть) fan, wave; brush away.

обме́н exchange; о. мне́ниями exchange of opinions; **обме́нивать** *(pf.* обменя́ть) (на + *acc.)* exchange (for); -ся *(inst.)* exchange; *(pf.* обме́|нить, -е́ню, -е́нишь) change by mistake, take the wrong one.

обме́р measurement; false measure.

обмере́ть *see* обмира́ть.

обмерза́ть *(pf.* обме́рзнуть*)* become frozen/covered in ice.

обме́ривать *(pf.* обме́рить) cheat, by giving false measure.

обмета́ть *(pf.* обмести́*)* sweep/dust off.

обмина́ть *(pf.* обмя́ть*, обомну́)* trample down, flatten.

обмира́ть *(pf.* обме́реть, обомру́*)* be struck dumb; он обме́р от испу́га he was petrified with fear.

обмола́чивать *(pf.* обмолоти́ть*)* thresh.

обмо́лвиться *(pf.)* make a slip; mention; обмо́лвка slip of the tongue.

обмоло́т threshing; обмолоти́ть *see* обмола́чивать.

обморо́женный frost-bitten.

о́бморок faint, swoon.

обмота́ть *see* обма́тывать; обмо́тка winding; *(pl.)* puttees.

обмундирова́ть *(pf.)* fit out, kit out.

обмыва́ть *(pf.* обмы́ть*)* bathe, wash.

обмяка́ть *(pf.* обмя́кнуть, *past* -ил) become soft/flabby.

обмя́ть *see* обмина́ть.

обнаде́живать *(pf.* обнаде́жить) reassure.

обнажа́ть *(pf.* -и́ть) lay bare.

обнаро́довать *(pf.)* promulgate.

обнаруже́ние discovery, revelation; обнару́живать *(pf.* -у́жить) reveal; display; -ся come to light.

обнести́ *see* обноси́ть.

обнима́ть *(pf.* об|ня́ть, -ниму́, -ни́мешь; обня́л, -а́; *ppp.* -ня́тый) embrace, clasp.

обнища́лый impoverished.

обно́в(к)а new acquisition, new dress; обновле́ние renewal, renovation; обновля́ть *(pf.* -и́ть) renew, renovate.

обноси́ть* *(pf.* обнести́*)* enclose; serve *(at table)* ; pass over/leave out when serving;

обно́|сок (-ска) worn out item of clothing.

обню́хивать *(pf.* обню́хать) sniff (at).

обня́ть *see* обнима́ть.

обобра́ть *see* обира́ть.

обобща́ть *(pf.* -и́ть) generalize, summarize; обобще́ние generalization; general conclusion.

обобществле́ние socialization; обобществля́ть *(pf.* -и́ть) socialize, collectivize.

обобщи́ть *see* обобща́ть.

обогаща́ть *pf.* обога|ти́ть, -щу́, -ти́шь) enrich; обогаще́ние enrichment.

обогна́ть *see* обгоня́ть.

обогну́ть *see* огиба́ть.

обоготворя́ть *(pf.* -и́ть) worship.

обогрева́тель *(m.)* heater; de-froster; обо|грева́ть (-грева́ю) *pf.* -гре́ть) heat.

о́бод *(pl.* обо́д|ья, -ьев) rim.

обо́дранный ragged; ободра́ть *see* обдира́ть.

ободре́ние encouragement; ободр|я́ть *(pf.* -и́ть) encourage, reassure.

обожа́ть adore.

обожествля́ть *(pf.* -и́ть) idolize.

обо́з line of carts/sledges; transport train.

обозн|ава́ться (-аю́сь, -аёшься; *pf.* обозна́ться) mistake one person for another.

обознача́ть *(pf.* обозна́чить) designate; -ся appear, show; обозначе́ние designation

обозрева́ть (-ева́ю; *pf.* обозре́ть*) survey; обозре́ние review; обозри́мый visible.

обо́|и (-ев) wallpaper.

обо́йма cartridge clip; iron ring.

обойти́ *see* обходи́ть.

обо́йщик upholsterer.

обокра́сть *see* обкра́дывать.

оболо́|чка *(gen. pl.* -чек) cover, jacket; membran?

обольсти́тельный seductive; обо|льща́ть *(pf.* -льсти́ть*)* seduce; -ся flatter oneself; delude oneself; обольще́ние seduction; delusion.

обомле́ть *(pf.)* be stupefied.

обоня́ние sense of smell; обоня́ть smell.

обора́чивать *(pf.* оберну́ть) turn; -ся turn (round).

оборва́|нец (-нца) ragamuffin; обо́рванный ragged; оборва́ть *see* обрыва́ть.

обо́рка flounce, frill.

оборо́на defence; оборони́тельный defen??ve; оборо́нный defence *(a.)* ; оборон|я́ть *(pf.* -и́ть) defend, protect.

оборо́т turn, revolution; turnover; оборо́тный reverse; seamy *(side)*; working *(capital)*.

обору́дование equipment; outfit; обору́довать *(ipf. & pf.)* equip, fit out; arrange.

обоснова́ние substantiation; basis; об|основывать *(pf.* -основа́ть*)* ground, base; -ся be based; *(coll.)* settle down.

обособля́ть *(pf.* обосо́бить*)* set apart, isolate; -ся keep aloof, stand apart; обосо́бленный detached, solitary.

обостре́ние aggravation, intensification; обостр|я́ть *(pf.* -и́ть*)* sharpen, bring to a head; -ся become sharper/strained/aggravated.

обо́чина side of road; kerb.

обою́дный mutual; обоюдоо́стрый double-edged.

обраба́тывать *(pf.* обрабо́тать*)* process, till, work; обрабо́тка processing, cultivation.

о́браз *(pl.* -ы) shape, form, appearance, image; way, manner; *(pl.* -а́) icon; обра|зе́ц (-зца́) model, pattern; о́бразный figurative; graphic.

образова́ние formation; education; образо́ванный educated; образова́тельный educational; образо́|вывать *(pf.* -ова́ть*)* form, make up; -ся form, appear; turn out alright.

образу́мить *(pf.)* make see sense; -ся see reason.

образцо́вый model *(a.)*; обра́зчик specimen, sample.

обрамля́ть *(pf.* обра́мить*)* frame.

обраста́ть *(pf.* обрасти́*)* become overgrown.

обрати́мый reversible; convertible; обра́тно back(wards); обра́тный return *(a.)*, reverse.

обраща́ть *(pf.* обра|ти́ть, -щу́, -ти́шь*)* turn; pay *(attention)*; -ся (к + *dat.)* turn (to); apply (to); (с + *inst.)* treat, deal (with); use; (в + *acc.)* turn into.

обраще́ние address; appeal; treatment.

обре́з edge; sawn-off gun; де́нег у меня́ в о. I have just enough money.

обреза́ть *(pf.* обре́зать*)* cut off, clip, pare, trim; -ся cut oneself; обре́|зок (-зка) scrap; end; обре́зывать = обреза́ть.

обрека́ть *(pf.* обр|е́чь, -еку́, -ече́шь; -ёк, -екла́; *ppp.* -ечённый*)* doom.

обремени́тельный onerous; обремен|я́ть *(pf.* -и́ть*)* burden.

обрета́ть *(pf.* обр|ести́, -ету́, -ете́шь; -ёл, -ела́; *ppp.* -етённый*)* find.

обречённый doomed; обре́чь *see* обрека́ть.

обрис|о́вывать *(pf.* -ова́ть*)* outline, delineate; -ся appear in outline.

оброк quit-rent.

обр|они́ть *(pf.* -оню́, -о́нишь*)* drop; utter.

обро́сший overgrown.

обруба́ть *(pf.* -и́ть*)* cut/lop off; обру́|бок (-бка) stump.

обрусе́ть *(pf.)* become Russified.

о́бруч *(pl.* -и, -е́й) hoop, ring.

обруча́льный wedding *(a.)*; betrothal *(a.)*; обруч|а́ть *(pf.* -и́ть*)* betroth; -ся (с + *inst.)* become engaged (to); обруче́ние betrothal.

обру́шивать *(pf.* обру́шить*)* bring down; -ся come down; collapse.

обры́в precipice; обрыва́ть 1. *(pf.* оборва́ть*)* tear/break off; cut short; -ся break; lose one's hold, stop suddenly; 2. *(pf.* обры́ть*)* dig round; обры́вистый steep; abrupt; обры́|вок (-вка) scrap; обры́вочный scrappy.

обры́згивать *(pf.* обры́згать, обры́знуть*)* bespatter, sprinkle.

обрю́зглый flabby.

обря́д rite.

обса́живать *(pf.* обс|ади́ть, -ажу́, -а́дишь*)* plant/set round.

обсервато́рия observatory.

обска́кивать *(pf.* обскака́ть*)* gallop round; *(pf.)* out-gallop.

обсле́дование enquiry, inspection, investigation; обсле́довать *(ipf. & pf.)* examine, investigate.

обслу́живание service; maintenance; facilities; обслу́живать *(pf.* обслужи́ть*)* serve; service.

обсо́хнуть *see* обсыха́ть

обставля́ть *(pf.* обста́вить*)* surround furnish; arrange; *(coll.)* cheat.

обстано́вка conditions, situation; furniture, set *(theat.)*.

обстоя́тельный detailed, thorough.

обстоя́тельство circumstance; adverb.

обсто|я́ть*: де́ло -и́т так this is how matters stand.

обстра́гивать *(pf.* обстрога́ть*)* plane.

обстра́иваться *(pf.* обстро́иться*)* be built; build oneself a house.

обстре́л firing; fire; обстре́л|ивать *(pf.* -я́ть*)* fire at; bombard.

обстру́кция obstruction.

обступа́ть *(pf.* обступи́ть*)* surround.

обсужда́ть *(pf.* обс|уди́ть, -ужу́, -у́дишь) discuss; обсужде́ние discussion.

обсчи́тывать *(pf.* обсчита́ть*)* cheat, overcharge; -ся make a mistake in counting.

обсыпа́ть *(pf.* обсы́пать*)* bestrew, sprinkle.

обсыха́ть *(pf.* обсо́хнуть*)* (become) dry.

обтека́емость *(f.)* streamlining; обтека́емый streamlined.

обтере́ть *see* обтира́ть.

обтёсывать *(pf.* обт|еса́ть, -ешу́, -е́шешь) hew; *(fig.)* polish, refine.

обтира́ть *(pf.* обте́ре́ть, оботру́*)* rub, wipe.

обтрёпанный shabby.

обтя́гивать *(pf.* обтяну́ть) cover, fit close; обтя́жк|а: в -у close fitting.

обува́ть *(pf.* обу́ть, -у́ю, -у́ешь; *ppp.* -у́тый) put on shoes/boots; обувно́й boot-, shoe-; о́бувь *(f.)* footwear.

обу́гливать *(pf.* обу́глить) carbonize, char.

обу́за burden.

обу́здывать *(pf.* обузда́ть) curb, bridle.

обурева́ть (-ева́ет) possess *(of passions).*

обусло́вливать *(pf.* обусло́вить) cause, condition; stipulate.

обу́ть *see* обува́ть.

о́бух butt, back *(e. g., of axe).*

обуча́ть *(pf.* обучи́ть*)* teach, train; -ся learn; обуче́ние instruction; education.

обуя́ть *(pf.)* seize *(of emotions).*

обхва́т the grasp of both arms; обхва́тывать *(pf.* обхеати́ть*)* grasp; surround.

обхо́д round; roundabout way; turn; evasion; обходи́тельный pleasant, urbane; обходи́ть* *(pf.* обойти́,* -ойду́; -ошёл; *ppp.* -о́йдённый) go round; -ся (с + *inst.)* treat; (без + *gen.)* do/get by (without); обхо́дный roundabout; обхожде́ние manners; treatment.

обчища́ть *(pf.* обчи́стить*)* clean, brush; *(coll.)* rob.

обша́ривать *(pf.* обша́рить) ransack, go through.

обшива́ть *(pf.* обши́ть, обошью́*)* edge; cover; plank; make clothes for; обши́вка edging; panelling, boarding, plating.

обши́рный vast.

обши́ть *see* обшива́ть.

обшла́г (-а́, *pl.* -а́) cuff.

обща́ться (с + *inst.)* associate *(with).*

обще|досту́пный open to general use; popular; of moderate price; ~жи́тие hostel; ~изве́стный generally known; ~наро́дный public, general.

обще́ние contact.

обще|поле́зный of general utility; ~при́нятый generally accepted; ~сою́зный all-Union.

обще́ственник public figure; обще́ственность *(f.)* society, the public; обще́ственный public, social; о́бщество society; the public; обществове́дение social science.

общеупотреби́тельный in general use.

о́бщий general, common; в о́бщем in general, all in all.

общи́на commune; общи́тельный sociable, amiable; о́бщность *(f.)* community *(of interests etc.).*

объеда́ть *(pf.* объе́сть*)* eat, gnaw round; -ся overeat.

объеде́ние something delicious.

объедине́ние unification; union; organi ation; объедини́тельный unifying; объедини|я́ть *(pf.* -йть) unite, unify; -ся unite.

объе́дк|и (-ов) leftovers, remnants.

объе́зд riding round; detour; объезжа́ть *(pf.* объе́хать*)* travel all over; (вокру́г + *gen.)* drive round/ past; *(pf.* объе́здить*)* break in *(horses).*

объе́кт object; объекти́в lens; объекти́вный objective.

объём volume; объёмистый voluminous, bulky.

объе́сть *see* объеда́ть.

объе́хать *see* объезжа́ть.

объявле́ние announcement, declaration; notice; объяв|ля́ть *(pf.* -йть) declare, announce.

объяде́ние = объеде́ние.

объясне́ние explanation; объясни́тельный explanatory; объясн|я́ть *(pf.* -йть*)* explain.

объя́тие embrace.

обыва́тель *(m.)* the average man, man in the street; Philistine; *(coll.)* resident; обыва́тельский narro w minded, Philistine.

обы́грывать *(pf.* обыгра́ть)*:* о. его́ на пять рубле́й win five roubles from him.

обы́денный commonplace, ordinary; обыдёнщина commonness, the commonplace.

обыкнове́ние habit; обыкнове́нный usual, ordinary.

о́быск search; обы́скивать *(pf.* об|ыска́ть, -ыщу́, -ы́щешь) search.

обы́чай custom; usage; обы́чный usual.

обя́занность *(f.)* duty, obligation; обяза́тельно without fail; обяза́тельный obligatory; обяза́тельство obligation, commitment; обя́зывать *(pf.* об|яза́ть. -яжу́, -я́жешь) bind, oblige, commit; -ся pledge/commit oneself.

ова́льный oval.

ова́ция ovation.

овдове́ть *(pf.)* become a widow widower.

ове́с (овса́) oats.

ове́чий sheep's *(a.).*

овладева́ть (-ва́ю; *pf.* овладе́ть) *(inst.)* seize, take; master.

о́вод *(pl.* -ы & á) gadfly.

о́вощ *(pl.* -и, -е́.) vegetable; овощево́дство vegetable-growing; овощно́й vegetable *(a.).*

овра́г ravine.

овся́нка oatmeal; oatmeal porridge; yellow bunting.

овца́ *(pl.* о́вцы, ове́ц, о́вцам) sheep; овцево́дство sheep-breeding.

овча́рка sheep-dog; Alsatian.

овчи́на sheepskin; овчи́нка вы́делки не сто́ит the game's not worth the candle.

ога́|рок (-рка) candle-end.

огиба́ть *(pf.* обогну́ть*)* bend round; (go) round, skirt.

оглавле́ние (table of) contents.

огла́ска publicity; оглаша́ть *(pf.* огла|си́ть, -шу́, -си́шь) announce, make public; -ся resound; be announced; оглаше́ние publication.

огло́|бля *(gen. pl.* -бель) shaft.

оглуш|а́ть *(pf.* -и́ть) deafen; stun; оглуши́тельный deafening *(a.).*

огля́дк|а: бежа́ть без -и run without looking back; огля́дывать *(pf.* огляде́ть* & огляну́ть) look over; -ся look back, look round.

огнево́й fire *(a.);* огнемёт flame-thrower; о́гненный fiery; огнео-па́сный inflammable; огнестре́льное ору́жие firearm; огнетуши́тель *(m.)* fire-extinguisher; огнеупо́рный fireproof.

огова́ривать *(pf.* оговори́ть) specify, stipulate, slander; -ся make an error; make a reservation; огово́рка reservation, stipulation.

оголте́лый wild; shameless.

огол|я́ть *(pf.* -и́ть) bare, strip.

ого|нёк (-нька́) small light; ого́нь (огня́) fire; light.

огора́живать *(pf.* огор|оди́ть, -ожу́, -оди́шь) fence in, enclose; огоро́д kitchen-garden; огоро́дник market-gardener; огоро́дничество market-gardening.

огорч|а́ть *(pf.* -и́ть) grieve, pain; -ся grieve; огорче́ние grief, chagrin; огорчи́тельный distressing.

ограбле́ние burglary, robbery.

огра́да fence; огражда́ть *(pf.* огради́ть, -жу́, -ди́шь; *ppp.* -ждённый) guard, protect; огражде́ние barrier.

ограниче́ние limitation, restriction; ограни́чивать *(pf.* ограни́чить) limit, restrict; ограни́ченный limited; narrow-minded; ограничи́тельный restrictive.

огро́мный huge, enormous.

огрыза́ться *(pf.* -ну́ться) (на + *acc.)* snap/snarl at; огры́|зок (-зка) bit, end; core *(of apple).*

огу́|зок (-зка) rump, buttock.

огу́льный groundless; sweeping.

огу|ре́ц (-рца́) cucumber.

о́да ode.

ода́л|живать *(pf.* одолжи́ть) lend; oblige *(smb.—acc.)* *(with sth.—inst).*

одарённый gifted; ода́р|ивать *or* -я́ть *(pf.* -и́ть) present, endow *(smb.—acc.)* *(with sth.—inst.).*

одева́ть (-ва́ю; *pf.* оде́ть*) dress; -ся dress (oneself); оде́жда clothes, dress.

одеколо́н eau-de-Cologne.

одел|я́ть *(pf.* -и́ть) present, endow *(smb.—acc.)* *(with sth.—inst.).*

одеревене́лый numb.

оде́рживать *(pf.* одержа́ть*)* gain; одержи́мый possessed.

оде́ть *see* одева́ть.

одея́ло blanket; одея́ние garment, raiment.

оди́н, одна́, одно́, одни́ one; the same alone; only; certain; оди́н на оди́н in private; одни́ ...други́е ... some ... others ...

одина́ковый same, identical.

одинёхонек quite alone.

оди́ннадцатый eleventh; оди́ннадцать eleven.

одино́кий lonely; одино́чество loneliness; одино́|чка *(m. & f., gen. pl.* -чск) lone person; одино́чный individual, solitary.

одио́зный odious.

одич|а́вший, ~а́лый wild.

одна́жды once.

одна́ко however.

одно|бо́кий one-sided.

однобо́ртный single-breasted.

одновреме́нный simultaneous.

огногла́зый one-eyed.

однозву́чный monotonous.

однозна́чащий synonymous.

одноиме́нный of the same name.

одноколе́йный single track.

однокра́тный occurring only once; momentary.

одноку́рс|ник, ~ница student of same course/year.

однолѐтний annual.

одно̀местный single-seater *(a.).*

одноно́гий one-legged.

одно|обра́зие monotony; uniformity; ~обра́зный monotonous.

однородный homogeneous; similar.

однору́|кий one-armed.

односло́жный monosyllabic.

односпа́льная крова́ть single bed.

односторо́нний one-sided.

однофами́лец (-льца), ~лица namesake

одноэта́жный single-storeyed.

одобре́ние approval; одобри́тельный approving; одобря́ть *(pf.* одо́брить) approve.

одолева́ть (-ева́ю; *pf.* одоле́ть) overcome.

одол|жа́ть *(pf.* -жи́ть) lend; oblige *(smb.—acc.) (with sth.—inst.);* одолже́ние favour.

одома́шнивать *(pf.* одома́шнить) domesticate.

одр (-а́) bed, couch.

одува́нчик dandelion.

оду́мываться *(pf.* оду́маться) change one's mind.

одур|а́чивать *(pf.* -а́чить) make a fool of.

одуре́лый mad, crazy.

одурм|а́нивать *(pf.* -а́нить) stupefy, drug; о́дурь *(f.)* stupor; со́нная

о. deadly nightshade; одуря́ть stupefy.

одутлова́тый puffy.

одухотвор|я́ть *(pf.* -и́ть) spiritualize, inspire.

одушевле́ние animation; одушев|ля́ть *(pf.* -и́ть) animate.

оды́шка shortness of breath.

ожере́лье necklace.

ожесточ|а́ть *(pf.* -и́ть) harden, embitter; ожесточе́ние bitterness; ожесточённый bitter, violent.

ожива́ть *(pf.* ожи́ть*)* come to life, revive; оживле́ние reviving, enlivening; animation; ожив|ля́ть *(pf.* -и́ть) revive, enliven; -ся become animated.

ожида́н|ие expectation, waiting; зал -ия waiting-room; ожида́ть *(gen.)* wait for, expect.

ожире́ние obesity, fatness.

ожи́ть *see* ожива́ть.

ожо́г burn, scald.

озабо́чивать *(pf.* озабо́тить*)* worry; озабо́ченный preoccupied.

озагл|а́вливать *(pf.* -а́вить) entitle, head.

озада́чивать *(pf.* -а́чить) perplex, puzzle.

озар|я́ть *(pf.* -и́ть) illumine, light up; -ся light up.

озвере́лый (become) brutal.

оздоровле́ние sanitation; оздоров|ля́ть *(pf.* -и́ть) arrange sanitation of.

озелен|я́ть *(pf.* -и́ть) plant with greenery.

о́земь *(coll.)* to the ground.

озёрный lake *(a.);* о́зеро *(pl.* озёра) lake.

ози́мый winter *(of crops).*

озира́ть view; -ся look back.

озлобле́ние animosity, bitterness; озлобля́ть *(pf.* озло́бить) embitter.

ознакомле́ние acquaintance; ознакомля́ть *(pf.*ознако́мить) acquaint.

ознаменова́ние: в о. + *gen.* to mark the occasion of ...; ознамен|о́вывать *(pf.* -ова́ть) mark, celebrate.

означа́ть mean, signify.

озно́б shivering.

озо́н ozone.

озор|ни́к, (-ника́), ~ни́ца mischievous child, rascal; озорнича́ть be naughty; озорно́й mischievous, naughty; озорство́ mischief.

оказия opportunity; unexpected turn of events.

оказывать (pf. оказать*) render, show; -ся find oneself; turn out, prove (to be).

окаймлять (pf. -ить) edge, border.

окалина scale, slag, cinders.

окаменелый petrified, fossilized.

окантовка framing; frame.

оканчивать (pf. окончить) finish; -ся finish, end.

окапывать (pf. окопать) dig round; -ся dig in.

окачивать (pf. окатить*) pour over, douse.

окаянный accursed, damned.

океан ocean; океанский ocean(ic).

окидывать (pf. окинуть): о. взглядом take in at a glance.

окисление oxidation; окислять (pf. -ить) oxidize; окись (f.) oxide; о. углерода carbon monoxide.

оккультный occult.

оккупант invader; оккупация occupation; оккупировать (ipf. & pf.) occupy.

оклад 1. rate of pay, tax; 2. framework, setting (of icon).

окладистая борода full broad beard.

оклеивать (pf. оклеить) paste over, cover.

оклик call, hail; окликать (pf. окликнуть) call, hail.

окно (pl. окна, окон) window.

око (pl. очи, очей) (coll., poet) eye.

оковы (оков) fetters; оковывать (pf. оковать*) bind; fetter.

околдовывать (pf. -овать) bewitch.

околевать (-евает; pf. околеть) die (of animals).

околесица nonsense.

околица roundabout way; boundary of village; outskirts.

около (gen.) around, by, near, about.

околоток (-тка) (coll.) neighbourhood; district, ward; police station.

окольіш cap-band.

окольный roundabout.

оконечность (f.) extremity, tip.

оконный window (a.).

окончание termination; окончательный final; окончить see оканчивать.

окоп trench; окопать see окапывать.

окорок (pl. -á) ham, gammon.

окостенелый numb, ossified.

окот lambing; окотиться see котиться.

окоченелый stiff with cold.

окошечко (-чки, pl. -чек) small window.

окраина outskirts; outlying districts.

окраска colouring; окрашивать (pf. окрасить*) colour, dye, paint.

окрестность (f.) environs; окрестный neighbouring.

окрик shout, hail; окрикивать (pf окрикнуть) hail, summon with a shout.

окровавливать (pf. окровавить) stain with blood.

окроплять (pf. -ить) besprinkle.

окрошка cold kvass soup; hotchpotch.

округ (pl. -á) district.

округлый rounded; округлять (pf. -ить) round off.

окружать (pf. -ить) encircle, surround; окружение encirclement; environment; окружной district (a.); окружность (f.) circumference.

окручивать (pf. окрутить*) twist round, wind; (pf. coll.) marry.

окрылять (pf. -ить) lend wings to, inspire.

октава octave.

октроировать (ipf. & pf.) grant.

октябрь (-я) October; октябрьский October (a.).

окулист oculist.

окунать (pf. окунуть) dip, plunge; -ся plunge; be engrossed, absorbed.

окунь (m; pl. -и, -ей) perch (fish).

окупать (pf. окупить*) repay, compensate; -ся be paid; pay for itself.

окуривать (pf. окурить*) fumigate; окурок (-рка) cigarette/cigar-end.

окутывать (pf. окутать) wrap up; shroud, cloak.

окучивать (pf. окучить) earth up.

оладья (gen. pl. -дий) pancake, fritter.

оледенелый frozen.

оленеводство reindeer-breeding; олений deer (a.); оленина venison; олень (m.) deer.

олива olive; оливковый olive (a.); olive-green.

олигархия oligarchy.

олимпиáда ·Olympiad, Olympic Games; олимпийский Olympic.

олицетворéние personification, embodiment; олицетвор|я́ть (pf. -и́ть) personify, embody.

óлово tin; оловя́нный tin (a.), pewter (a.).

óлух dolt, clcd.

ольхá alder; ольшáник alder-thicket.

ом ohm.

омáр lobster.

омела mistletoe.

омерзéние loathing; омерзительный abominable.

омертвéлый deadened, numb; омертвля́ть (pf. -и́ть) immobilize.

омлéт omelette.

омола́живать (pf. омолодить) rejuvenate.

омрача́|ть (pf. -и́ть) darken.

óмут pool; в тихом -е чéрти вóдятся still waters run deep.

омыва́ть (pf. омы́ть*) wash.

он, она́, онó, они́ he, she, it, they.

ондáтра musquash.

óный (coll.) that: (off.) the above.

оонóвский U. N.

опадáть (pf. опáсть*) fall off/away; subside (of swelling).

опáздывать (pf. опоздáть) be late; о. на пóезд/к пóезду miss the train.

опáивать (pf. опоить) give too much to drink; poison.

опáл opal.

опáла disgrace.

опáливать (pf. опалить) singe, scorch.

опáловый opal (a.).

опáльный disgraced.

опаса́ться (gen.) fear; опасéние apprehension.

опáсность (f.) danger, jeopardy; опáсный dangerous.

опáсть see опадáть.

опéка guardianship; trusteeship; опекáть be guardian to, take care of; опекýн (-á), ~ша guardian.

óпера opera.

оперативный 1. efficient; 2. operative; оперáтор operator; surgeon; cameraman; операция operation.

опережа́ть (pf. опере|дить, -жу́; -дишь) outstrip, leave behind.

оперéние plumage.

оперéться see опирáться.

оперировать (ipf. & pf.) operate on (med.); operate.

óперный opera(tic).

опер|я́ться (pf. -и́ться) become fully fledged.

опечáтка misprint.

опечáтывать (pf. опечáтать) seal up.

опéшить (pf., coll.) be taken aback.

опи́вк|и (-ов) dregs; опи́|лки (-лок) sawdust; filings.

опирáться (pf. опе рéться, обо|прýсь, -прёшься; опёрся; ger. опершись) (на + acc.) lean (on).

описáние description; описáтельный descriptive.

опи́ска error, misprint; описывать (pf. описáть*) describe; -ся make a slip; óпись (f.) inventory.

óпиум opium.

оплáкивать (pf. оплáкать*) bemoan, mourn.

оплáта payment; оплáчивать (pf. оплатить*) pay (expenses, damages).

оплетáть (pf. оплести́*) braid; entwine; swindle.

оплéуха slap in the face.

оплодотвор|я́ть (pf. -и́ть) fertilize, impregnate.

оплóт bulwark, stronghold.

оплошáть (pf.; coll.) make a mistake; оплóшность (f.) inadvertence; mistake.

оплыва́ть (pf. оплы́ть*) sail/swim round; swell.

оповеща́ть (pf. опове|сти́ть, -щý, -сти́шь) notify; оповещéние notification.

опóек (опóйка) calf-skin.

опоздáние delay; опоздáть see опáздывать.

опознавáтельный identification (a.); опозн|авáть (-аю́, -аёшь; pf. опознáть) identify.

ополáскивать (pf. ополоснýть) rinse.

óполз|ень (-зня) landslide.

ополчáться (pf. -и́ться) take up arms; be up in arms; ополчéние militia.

опóмниться (pf.) come to one's senses.

опóр: во весь о. at full speed.

опóр|а support; bearing; pier; тóчка -ы fulcrum; foothold.

опоражнивать, or опорожн|я́ть (p.-и́ть) empty.

опóрный strong; support (a.).

опостылеть (pf., coll.) become hateful.

опохмел|я́ться (pf. -и́ться) take a hair of the dog that bit you.

опошл|я́ть (pf. опо́шлить) debase, vulgarize.

опоя́сывать (pf. опо|я́сать, -я́шу, -я́шешь) gird; surround.

оппозицио́нный opposition(al); оппози́ция opposition; оппони́ровать (dat.) oppose (in debate).

оппортуни́зм opportunism.

опра́ва setting.

оправда́ние justification; acquittal; оправда́тельный пригово́р verdict of 'not guilty'; опра́вд|ывать (pf. -а́ть) justify; acquit.

оправля́ть (pf. опра́вить) set right; set, mount; -ся recover (from illness, etc.); put one's dress in order.

опра́шивать (pf. опроси́ть*) question.

определе́ние definition; attribute; определённый definite; fixed; определ|я́ть (pf. -и́ть) define, determine; appoint; -ся become formed; find oneself a place.

опресн|я́ть (pf. -и́ть) distil, freshen (water).

опро|верга́ть (pf. -ве́ргнуть) refute, disprove; опроверже́ние refutation, denial.

опроки́дывать (pf. опроки́нуть) overturn; tipple; -ся overturn; capsize.

опроме́тчивый hasty, rash; о́прометью headlong.

опро́с questioning, inquest; опроси́ть see опра́шивать.

опроте́ст|овывать (pf. -ова́ть) protest, appeal against.

опры́скивать (pf. опры́скать, & опры́снуть) spray, sprinkle.

опря́тный neat, tidy.

о́птик optician; о́птика optics.

оптими́зм optimism; оптими́ст optimist; ~и́ческий optimistic.

опти́ческий optical.

опто́вый wholesale (a.); о́птом wholesale (ad.).

опубликова́ние promulgation, publication; опублик|о́вывать (pf. -ова́ть) make public, promulgate.

опуска́ть (pf. опусти́ть*) lower; post (letter); omit; turn down (collar); -ся be lowered, sink; degenerate; у меня́ ру́ки опусти́лись I lost heart; опусте́лый deserted.

опусто|ша́ть (pf. -и́ть) devastate; опустоше́ние devastation; опустоши́тельный devastating.

опу́тывать (pf. опу́тать) entangle, wind.

опуха́ть (pf. опу́хнуть*) swell; о́пухоль (f.) swelling, tumour.

опу́|шка (gen. pl. -шек) border/edge (of forest); edging, trimming.

опуще́ние omission; prolapsus.

опыле́ние pollination; опыл|я́ть (pf. -и́ть) pollinate.

о́пыт experiment, test; experience; о́пытный experienced; experimental.

опьяне́ние intoxication.

опя́ть again; о.-таки (coll.) but again, besides.

ора́ва crowd.

ора́нжевый orange (a.); оранжере́я conservatory.

ора́тор orator; орато́рия oratorio; ора́торствовать harangue.

ора́ть (ору́, орёшь) yell.

орби́та orbit.

о́рган organ, agency.

орга́н organ (mus.).

организа́тор organizer; организа́ция organization; органи́зм organism.

организова́ть (ipf. & pf.; past pf. only), организо́вывать (ipf.) organize.

органи́ческий organic.

о́ргия orgy.

оргработа organizational work.

орда́ horde.

о́рден (pl. -ы) order (e.g. of knights); (pl. -а́) order, decoration.

о́рдер (pl. -а́) voucher, warrant; writ.

ордина́р normal level; ордина́|рец (-рца) orderly; ордина́тор house-surgeon; head of hospital section.

орёл (орла́) eagle; о. и́ли ре́шка heads or tails.

орео́л halo.

оре́х nut; оре́ховый nut (a.); оре́шник nut-tree, hazel.

оригина́л original; eccentric person; оригина́льный original (a.).

ориента́ция orientation; ориенти́роваться (pf. orientate oneself; (на + acc.) be guided(by), take one's bearings (on); ориентиро́вочный reference (a.).

орке́стр orchestra, band; оркестрова́ть (ipf. & pf.) orchestrate.

орли́ный eagle *(a.)*; aquiline.

орна́мент decorative pattern; орнаменти́ровать *(ipf. & pf.)* decorate.

ороси́тельный irrigation *(a.)*; ороша́ть *(pf.* оро|си́ть, -шу́, -си́шь) irrigate; ороше́ние irrigation.

ору́дие instrument, tool; gun; оруди́йный gun *(a.)*.

ору́довать *(inst.)* handle, run; он всем ору́дует he bosses the show.

оруже́йный arms, armour *(a.)*; ору́жие weapon.

орфографи́ческий orthographic(al); орфогра́фия orthography.

оса́ *(pl.* о́сы) wasp.

оса́да siege.

оса́дка settling *(of soil, building)*; draught *(of ship)*.

осади́ть *see* оса жда́ть; оса́дный siege *(a.)*.

оса́|док (-дка) sediment, deposit; *(pl.)* precipitation.

оса жда́ть *(pf.* ос|ади́ть, -ажу́, -а́дишь; *ppp.* -аждённый) 1. besiege; 2. precipitate; -ся fall, fall out.

оса́ живать *(pf.* ос|ади́ть, -ажу́, -а́дишь; *ppp.* -а́женный) check, rein in; *(coll.)* take down a peg or two.

оса́нистый portly, stately; оса́нка bearing, setting.

осва́ивать *(pf.* осво́ить) master, assimilate; -ся feel at ease/comfortable; -ся с + *inst.* make oneself familiar with.

осведомля́ть *(pf.* осве́домить *ppp.* -млённый) inform; -ся enquire.

осве́ж|а́ть *(pf.* -и́ть) refresh; освежи́тельный refreshing.

освети́тельный illuminating; освеща́ть *(pf.* осве|ти́ть, -щу́, -ти́шь) light up, illumine; elucidate; освеще́ние lighting, illumination; elucidation.

освиде́тельствовать *(pf.)* examine.

осви́стывать *(pf.* освиста́ть*) hiss, whistle *(v.t.)*.

освободи́тель *(m.)* liberator; освободи́тельный liberation/emancipation *(a.)*; освобожда́ть *(pf.* освобо|ди́ть, -жу́, -ди́шь; *ppp.* -ждённый) liberate, emancipate; освобожде́ние liberation, emancipation.

освое́ние mastering; assimilation; осво́ить *see* осва́ивать.

освяща́ть *(pf.* освя|ти́ть, -щу́, -ти́шь) consecrate, sanctify.

осево́й axial.

оседа́ть *(pf.* осе́сть*) settle *(of building)*.

осе́длост|ь *(f.)* settled way of life; черта́ -и Jewish pale.

осека́ться *(pf.* осе́чься*) misfire.

осёл (осла́) donkey.

осе|ло́к (-лка́) touchstone; whetstone.

осемене́ние insemination.

осени́ть *see* осеня́ть.

осе́нний autumn(al); о́сень *(f.)* autumn.

осен|я́ть *(pf.* -и́ть) overshadow; dawn on *(of idea)*.

осе́сть *see* оседа́ть.

осет|и́н *(gen. pl.* -и́н), ~и́нка Ossetian.

осётр (-а́) sturgeon; осетри́на (flesh of) sturgeon.

осе́|чка *(gen. pl.* -чек) misfire; осе́чся *see* осека́ться.

оси́ливать *(pf.* оси́лить) overpower.

оси́на aspen tree.

оси́н|ый wasp's; -ое гнездо́ hornets' nest *(fig.)*.

оси́плый hoarse, husky.

осироте́лый orphaned.

оска́ливать *(pf.* оска́лить): о. зу́бы bare one's teeth.

оскверн|я́ть *(pf.* -и́ть) profane, defile.

оско́л|ок (-лка) splinter, fragment.

оско́мина: наби́ть о. set the teeth on edge.

оскорби́тельный abusive, insulting; оскорбле́ние insult, outrage; оскорб|ля́ть *(pf.* -и́ть) insult, outrage; -ся take offence.

оскудева́ть (-ева́ет) grow scarce/poor.

ослабева́ть (-ева́ю *pf.* ослабе́ть) weaken; relax; ослабле́ние weakening; slackening, relaxation; ослабля́ть *(pf.* осла́бить) weaken; loosen; relax.

ослепи́тельный blinding, dazzling; ослепле́ние blinding; dazzled state; blindness; ослеп|ля́ть *(pf.* -и́ть) blind, dazzle.

осли́злый slimy.

осли́ный asinine.

осложне́ние complication; осложн|я́ть *(pf.* -и́ть) complicate.

ослуша́ние disobedience.

ослы́шаться* *(pf.)* mishear; ослы́шка *(gen. pl.* -шек) mistake, mishearing.

осма́тривать *(pf.* осмотре́ть*)* examine, survey; look round; -ся look round.

осме́ивать *(pf.* осмея́ть*)* ridicule.

осме́ливаться *(pf.* осме́литься*)* dare.

осмея́ние ridicule.

осмо́тр inspection, survey; осмотре́ть *see* осма́тривать; осмотри́тельный circumspect; осмо́трщик inspector, checker.

осмы́сленный intelligent, sensible; осмы́сл|ивать, *or* ~я́ть *(pf.* осмы́слить*)* give meaning to, interpret, find the sense of.

осна́стка rigging; оснаща́ть *(pf.* осна|сти́ть, -щу́, -сти́шь) fit out, equip; оснаще́ние equipment.

осно́ва base, basis; principle; stem *(philol.);* основа́ние foundation; base, basis; grounds; основа́тель *(m.)* founder; основа́тельный well-grounded; thorough; solid; основно́й fundamental, basic; основополо́жник founder; осно́вывать *(pf.* осн|ова́ть, -у́ю, -у́ёшь) found; -ся (на + *prep.)* be founded (on).

осо́ба person, personage.

осо́бенно especially; осо́бенность *(f.)* peculiarity, feature; осо́бенный (e)special, particular; peculiar; особня́к (-а́) detached house; особняко́м by oneself/itself; осо́бо apart; especially; осо́бый special, peculiar.

осозн|ава́ть (-аю́, -аёшь; *pf.* осозна́ть) realize.

осо́ка sedge.

о́спа smallpox; ветряная о. chicken-pox.

оспа́ривать *(pf.* оспо́рить) dispute.

оспопрививáние vaccination.

ост east.

ост|ава́ться (-аю́сь, -аёшься; *pf.* оста́ться*)* remain, stay.

оставля́ть *(pf.* оста́вить) leave, abandon; о. за собо́й reserve *(right etc.).*

остально́й remaining; *(neut.)* the rest.

остана́вливать *(pf.* остан|ови́ть, -овлю́, -о́вишь) stop, bring to a halt; -ся stop, halt.

оста́нк|и (-ов) remains, relics.

остано́вка stop.

оста́|ток (-тка) remainder, rest; оста́ться *see* остава́ться.

остекл|я́ть *(pf.* -и́ть) glaze.

остепени́ться *(pf.)* settle down.

остервене́лый frenzied; остервене́ть *(pf.)* become enraged.

остерега́ть *(pf.* остер|е́чь, -егу́ -еже́шь; -ёг, -егла́; *ppp.* -ежён-ный) warn; -ся *(gen.)* beware (of).

ост-и́ндский East-Indian.

о́стов skeleton, frame.

остолбене́лый dumbfounded, stunned.

осторо́жность *(f.)* care, caution; осторо́жный careful, cautious.

остра́стка *(coll.)* warning.

острига́ть *(pf.* остри́чь*)* crop, cut; -ся have one's hair cut.

острие́ point, spike, edge.

остри́ть sharpen; crack jokes.

остри́чь *see* острига́ть.

о́стров *(pl.* -а́) island; островит|я́нин *(pl.* -я́не, -я́н), ~я́нка islander.

остро́г gaol.

острога́ harpoon.

остро|гу́бцы (-гу́бцев) cutting pliers; ~коне́чный pointed; ~ли́ст holly.

остро́та *(pl.* -о́ты) sharpness. witty remark, 'crack'.

остро|уго́льный acute-angled; ~у́мие wit; ingeniousness; ~у́мный witty; ingenious.

о́стрый sharp, acute, keen.

оступа́ться *(pf.* оступи́ться*)* stumble.

остыва́ть *(pf.* ост|ы́ть, -ы́ну, -ы́нешь) cool down, get cold.

осужда́ть *(pf.* ос|уди́ть, -ужу́, -у́дишь; *ppp.* -уждённый) condemn; осужде́ние censure; conviction.

осу́нуться *(pf.)* grow thin, become sunken.

осуша́ть *(pf.* осуши́ть*)* dry, drain; осуше́ние drainage.

осуществи́мый feasible; осуществле́ние realization, implementation; осуществл|я́ть *(pf.* -и́ть) carry out, realize, accomplish; -ся be carried out *etc;* come true.

осчастл|и́вливать *(pf.* -и́вить) make happy.

осыпа́ть *(pf.* осы́пать*)* strew, shower *(smb. sth.-acc., with-inst.);* -ся crumble, fall; о́сыпь *(f.)* scree.

ос|ь *(f.; pl.* -и, -е́й) axis.

осьмино́г octopus.

осяза́емый tangible; осяза́ние touch; осяза́тельный tactile; palpable; осяза́ть feel.

от *(gen.)* from; дрожа́ть от хо́лода shiver with cold; сре́дство от a remedy for.

ота́пливать *(pf.* отопи́ть*)* heat.

ота́ра flock *(of sheep)*.

отбавля́ть *(pf.* отба́вить) *(acc. or gen.)* take away; хоть отбавля́й more than enough.

отбега́ть *(pf.* отбежа́ть*)* run off.

отбе́лка bleaching.

отбива́ть *(pf.* отби́ть, отобью́*)* beat (off); repel; break off; win over; -ся (от + *gen.)* defend oneself (against); fall behind.

отбивна́я котле́та chop.

отбира́ть *(pf.* отобра́ть, отберу́*)* take away; select.

отби́ть *see* отбива́ть.

о́тблеск reflection; sheen.

отбо́й retreat; ringing off *(telephone)*; бить о. beat a retreat; дать о. ring off; от них отбо́ю нет there's no getting rid of them.

отбо́р selection; **отбо́рный** select, choice; **отбо́рочный** eliminating.

отбра́сывать *(pf.* отбро́сить*)* throw off/away; hurl back; reject; **отбро́с|ы** (-ов) garbage, refuse.

отбыва́ть *(pf.* отбы́ть*)* 1. serve *(of time)*; 2. depart; **отбы́тие** departure.

отва́га courage, bravery; **отва́живаться** *(pf.* отва́житься)* dare; **отва́жный** courageous.

отва́л 1. нае́сться до -а eat one's fill; 2. dump.

отва́ливать *(pf.* отвали́ть*)* pull/heave/push off; bestow; -ся fall off.

отва́р broth, decoction; **отва́ривать** *(pf.* отвари́ть*)* boil; unweld; **отварно́й** boiled.

отве́дывать *(pf.* отве́дать) try, taste.

отверга́ть *(pf.* отве́ргнуть, *past* -е́рг) reject, repudiate.

отвердёлый hardened.

отве́рженный outcast.

отве́рстие opening, aperture.

отвёртка screwdriver; **отвёртывать** *(pf.* отверну́ть, *ppp.* отвёрнутый) unscrew, turn back; turn on *(tap)*; -ся become unscrewed; turn back/away.

отве́с plumb; vertical slope.

отве́сить *see* отве́шивать.

отве́сный plumb; sheer.

отве́т answer.

ответв|ля́ться *(pf.* -и́ться) branch off.

отве́тный return, response *(a)*; retaliatory.

отве́тственность *(f.)* responsibility; **отве́тственный** (за + *acc.)* responsible (for); **отве́тчик** defendant; **отвеча́ть** *(pf.* отве|е́тить, -е́чу, -е́тишь) answer; (на + *acc.)* reply to; (за + *acc.)* answer for.

отве́шивать *(pf.* отве́сить*)* weigh out; make *(bows)*.

отви́ливать *(pf.* отвильну́ть) dodge, wriggle out.

отви́нчивать *(pf.* отве|инти́ть, -инчу́, -и́нтишь) screw off, unscrew.

отвиса́ть *(pf.* от|ви́снуть; *past.* -ви́с) hang down; **отви́слый** sagging.

отвлека́ть *(pf.* отвле́чь*)* distract, divert; -ся be distracted, digress; **отвлече́ние** distraction; abstraction; **отвлечённый** abstract.

отво́д removal; objection; rejection *(of candidate)*; allotting; **отводи́ть*** *(pf.* отвести́*)* lead/take/draw aside/off; **отво́дный** drainage *(a.)*.

отвоёвывать *(pf.* отвоева́ть) win (over).

отвози́ть* *(pf.* отвезти́*)* take/drive away.

отвора́чивать *(pf.* отверну́ть: *ppp.* отвёрнутый) turn aside; turn on *(tap)*; unscrew; -ся turn aside/away.

отворо́т lapel, flap.

отворя́ть *(pf.* отво|ри́ть, -орю́, -о́ришь) open; -ся open.

отврати́тельный disgusting; **отвраща́ть** *(pf.* отвра|ти́ть, -шу́, -ти́шь) avert; **отвраще́ние** aversion, repugnance.

отвыка́ть *(pf.* от|вы́кнуть, *past* -вы́к) (от + *gen)* get out of the habit, become unused (to).

отвя́зывать *(pf.* отвяза́ть*)* untie; unfasten; -ся (от + *gen.)* come loose (from); get rid (of); leave alone; отвяжи́сь от меня́! leave me alone!

отга́дка answer (to riddle); **отга́дывать** *(pf.* отгада́ть) guess.

отгиба́ть *(pf.* отогну́ть) unbend; turn back *(sleeve)*.

отглаго́льный verbal.

отгла́живать *(pf.* отгла́дить*)* iron, press.

отгова́ривать *(pf.* отговори́ть) dissuade; -ся excuse oneself; **отгово́рка** excuse, pretext.

отголо́|сок (-ска) echo.

отго́нка distillation *(chem.)*; отгоня́ть *(pf.* отогна́ть, отгоню́*) drive off; distill.

отгора́живать *(pf.* отгор|оди́ть, -ожу́, -о́дишь; *ppp.* -о́женный) fence/partition off.

отграни́чивать *(pf.* отграни́чить) delimit, separate off.

отгреба́ть *(pf.* отгрести́*) 1. rake off; 2. row away.

отгружа́ть *(pf.* отгрузи́ть*) dispatch; unload.

отгрыза́ть *(pf.* отгры́зть*) gnaw off.

отдава́ть* *(pf.* отда́ть*) give back, give up; return; kick *(of gun)*; drop *(anchor)*; pay, show *(respect)*; *(inst.)* taste, smell (of); -ся give oneself up (to); resound.

отда́вливать *(pf.* отдави́ть*) crush, tread on.

отдале́ние removal; distance; отдалённый remote; отдаля́ть *(pf.* -и́ть) remove, postpone; estrange; -ся (от + *gen.)* move away (from), shun.

отда́ча return, recoil; efficiency; output *(tech.)* dropping *(anchor)*.

отде́л section; department.

отде́лать *see* отде́лывать.

отделе́ние separation; department; compartment, section; отдели́ть *see* отделя́ть.

отде́лка finishing touches; decoration; отде́лывать *(pf.* отде́лать) finish, trim; give a dressing down to; -ся (от + *gen.)* get rid (of), shake off; get off/away.

отде́льный separate; отделя́ть *(pf.* отдели́ть*; *ppp.* -ённый) separate, detach; -ся separate, become detached.

отдёргивать *(pf.* отдёрнуть) pull/draw back/aside.

отдира́ть *(pf.* отодра́ть, отдеру́*) tear/rip off.

отдохну́ть *see* отдыха́ть.

отдува́ться *(pf.* отду́ться*) pant, puff; о. за + *acc.* do someone else's work; отду́шина air-hole; *(fig.)* safety-valve.

о́тдых rest; relaxation; отдыха́ть *(pf.* отдохну́ть) rest.

отдыша́ться* *(pf.)* recover one's breath.

отека́ть *(pf.* оте́чь*) swell.

оте́л calving.

оте́ль *(m.)* hotel.

оте́ц (отца́) father; оте́ческий fatherly, paternal; оте́чественный native; of the homeland; оте́чество fatherland, native country.

оте́чь *see* отека́ть.

отжива́ть *(pf.* отжи́ть*) become obsolete.

отжима́ть *(pf.* отжа́ть*) wring out.

о́тзвук echo; repercussion; отзвуча́ть* *(pf.)* stop sounding.

о́тзыв opinion; response; отзы́в recall *(e.g. of ambassador)*; отзыва́ть *(pf.* отозва́ть*, отзову́) take aside; recall; -ся answer, echo; *(inst.)* taste (of); (на + *acc.)* answer; tell upon, influence; отзы́вчивый responsive, sympathetic.

отка́з refusal, repudiation; отка́зывать *(pf.* отказа́ть*) refuse; о. ему́ в про́сьбе refuse him his request; -ся (от + *gen.)* deny, renounce, give up, refuse; он отказа́лся пое́хать he refused to go.

отка́лывать *(pf.* отколо́ть*) chop off; unpin.

отка́пывать *(pf.* откопа́ть) dig up; exhume.

отка́рмливать *(pf.* откорми́ть*) fatten.

отка́т recoil; отка́тка truck haulage *(in mines)*; отка́тывать *(pf.* отка́тить*) roll away/aside; haul, truck; -ся roll away/back; recoil.

отка́чивать *(pf.* откача́ть) pump out; о. его́ give him artificial respира́tion.

отка́шливаться *(pf.* отка́шляться) clear one's throat.

откидно́й collapsible, folding; отки́дывать *(pf.* отки́нуть) throw away/back; -ся lean/settle back.

откла́дывать *(pf.* отл|ожи́ть, -ожу́, -о́жишь) put aside; postpone.

откла́ниваться *(pf.* откла́няться) take one's leave.

откле́ивать *(pf.* откле́ить) unstick; -ся come unstuck.

о́тклик response; comment; откликаться *(pf.* откли́кнуться) (на + *acc.)* respond (to); comment (on).

отклоне́ние deviation; refusal, declining; deflection; отклоня́ть *(pf.* отклони́ть*) deflect; decline; -ся bend; deviate.

отколо́ть *see* отка́лывать

откомандир|овывать *(pf.* -овать) send *(on a mission).*

откормить *see* **откармливать.**

откос slope.

открепля́ть *(pf.* открепить) unfasten; detach.

откре́щиваться *(от + gen.)* have nothing to do with, disown.

открове́ние revelation; **открове́нный** frank, outspoken.

откру́чивать *(pf.* открутить*) untwist; turn off.

открыва́ть *(pf.* открыть*) open; uncover, reveal, unveil; -ся be opened *etc.;* come to light; **откры́тие** opening; discovery; unveiling; **откры́тка** postcard; **откры́тый** open; frank.

отку́да from where, whence; **отку́да-нибудь** from somewhere or other.

о́ткуп *(pl.*-а́) concession, right *(hist.);* отда́ть на о. farm out.

отку́поривать *(pf.* откупорить) uncork.

отку́сывать *(pf.* откусить*) bite off.

отлага́тельство delay; **отлага́ть** *(pf.* отл|ожить, -ожу́, -о́жишь) postpone; deposit *(geol.);* -ся fall away, detach oneself; be deposited.

отла́мывать *(pf.* отлом|а́ть & -ить) break off; -ся break off.

отле́живать *(pf.* отлежа́ть*): о. но́гу sit so that one's foot goes to sleep.

отлёт flying away; start; дом на -е house standing by itself; **отлета́ть** *(pf.* отлете́ть*) fly away/off.

отле́чь* *(pf.):* у меня отлегло́ от се́рдца a load was taken off my mind.

отли́в 1. ebb(tide); 2. change/play of colour; shot *(of colour)* ; **отлива́ть** *(pf.* отли́ть*, отолью́) 1. pour off; found, cast; 2. be shot *(with a colour)* ; **отли́вка** casting, moulding; cast, ingot.

отлипа́ть *(pf.* отли́пнуть*) come unstuck.

отлич|а́ть *(pf.* -и́ть) distinguish; -ся *(от + gen.)* be distinguished, differ; be notable; **отли́чие** difference; merit, distinguished service; honours; **отличи́тельный** distinctive; **отли́чник, ~ница** excellent pupil; **отли́чный** excellent; *(от + gen.)* different (from).

отло́гий sloping.

отложе́ние deposit *(geol.)* ; **отложи́ть** *see* **откла́дывать, отлага́ть.**

отлуч|а́ть *(pf.* -и́ть) excommunicate; -ся absent oneself; **отлуче́ние** excommunication; **отлу́чка** absence.

отлы́нивать *(pf.):* о. от рабо́ты shirk.

отма́лчиваться *(pf.* отмолча́ться*) keep silent/mum.

отма́тывать *(pf.* отмота́ть) wind off.

отма́хивать *(pf.* отмахну́ть) wave away/off; *(pf.* отмаха́ть*) cover *(distance)* ; -ся *(от + gen.)* wave away, brush aside *(e.g. suggestions)* .

отма́чивать *(pf.* отмочи́ть*) soak off.

отмежёвывать *(pf.* отмежева́ть) mark off, draw boundary between; -ся isolate oneself.

о́тмель *(f.)* sandbank.

отме́на abolition; cancellation.

отмённый excellent.

отмен|я́ть *(pf.* отм|ени́ть, -еню́, -е́нишь; *ppp.* -енённый) abolish, annul, repeal.

отмере́ть *see* **отмира́ть.**

отмерза́ть *(pf.* отмёрзнуть*) become frozen.

отме́ривать, отмеря́ть *(pf.* отме́рить) measure off.

отмести́ *see* **отмета́ть.**

отме́стка revenge.

отмета́ть *(pf.* отмести́*) sweep off/ aside.

отме́тка note; mark; *(pl.)* grades; **отмеча́ть** *(pf.* отме́тить*) mark; observe; register.

отмира́ть *(pf.* отме́реть, отомрёт; о́тмер, -ла) die off; disappear.

отмора́живать *(pf.* отморо́зить*) make/allow to become frostbitten.

отмота́ть *see* **отма́тывать.**

отмще́ние *(obs.)* vengeance.

отмыва́ть *(pf.* отмы́ть*) wash off.

отмык|а́ть *(pf.* отомкну́ть) unlock, unbolt; **отмы́|чка** *(gen. pl.* -чк) master/skeleton-key.

отмяк|а́ть *(pf.* отмя́кнуть*) become soft.

отне́киваться *(coll.)* make excuses, refuse.

отним|а́ть *(pf.* от|ня́ть, -ниму́, -ни́мешь; *past.* о́тнял, -а́; *ppp.* о́тнятый) take away, amputate, subtract; -ся be taken away *(etc.)* ; be paralysed.

относительно relatively; *(gen.)* concerning; **относительность** *(f.)* relativity; **относительный** relative; **относить*** *(pf.* отнєсти*) take, carry away; (к + *dat.)* relate (to), attribute (to); **-ся** (к + *dat.)* treat; regard; concern, relate (to), date (from); **отношён|ие** attitude; relation(ship); ratio; по -ию к + *dat.* with regard to.

отныне henceforth.

отнюдь not at all.

отнятие taking away; amputation; **отнять** *see* отнимать.

отображать *(pf.* отобра|зить, -жу, -зишь) reflect, represent; **отображёние** reflection, representation.

отобрать *see* отбирать.

отовсюду from every quarter.

отогнать *see* отгонять.

отогнуть *see* отгибать.

отогревать (-еваю; *pf.* отогреть*) warm.

отодвигать *(pf.* отодвинуть) move aside.

отодрать *see* отдирать.

отож(д)еств|лять *(pf.* -ить) identify declare identical.

отозвать *see* отзывать.

отомкнуть *see* отмыкать.

отопить *see* отапливать; **отоплёние** heating.

оторачивать *(pf.* оторочить) edge, trim.

оторванный (от + *gen.)* alienated (from); **оторвать** *see* отрывать.

оторопеть *(pf.)* be struck dumb; **оторопь** *(f.)* confusion; fright.

оторочить *see* оторачивать.

отослать *see* отсылать.

отоспаться *see* отсыпаться.

отпадать *(pf.* отпасть*) fall away; pass.

отпарывать *(pf.* отпороть*) rip off.

отпевание funeral service.

отпєрєть *see* отпирать.

отпётый inveterate.

отпеча|ток (-тка) imprint; **отпечатывать** *(pf.* отпечатать) print; imprint.

отпивать *(pf.* отпить*) take a sip of.

отпиливать *(pf.* отпилить*) saw off.

отпирательство denial.

отпирать *(pf.* отпереть, ото|пру, -прёшь; отпер, -ла; *ppp.* от-

пертый) unlock; **-ся** (от) denу renounce.

отписка unhelpful answer (to correspondence).

отпить *see* отпивать.

отпихивать *(pf.* отпихнуть) push away/off.

отплата repayment; **отплачивать** *(pf.* отплатить*) pay back; о. ему той же монётой pay him in his own coin.

отплывать *(pf.* отплыть*) sail/swim off; **отплытие** sailing, departure.

отповедь *(f.)* reproof.

отползать *(pf.* отползти*) crawl away.

отпор rebuff.

отправитель *(m.)* sender; **отправка** dispatch, forwarding; **отправлёние** sending; departure; exercise; **отправлять** *(pf.* отправить) send, post; exercise, perform; **-ся** set off; proceed; be sent *etc.*

отправной starting; о. пункт starting point.

отпрашиваться *(pf.* отпроситься*) ask for leave.

отпрыгивать *(pf.* отпрыгнуть) jump/spring back.

отпрыск offspring; offshoot.

отпрягать *(pf.* отпрячь, -ягу, -яжёшь; -яг, -ягла; *ppp.* -яжённый) unharness.

отпрянуть *(pf.)* recoil, start back.

отпугивать *(pf.* отпугнуть) frighten away.

отпуск *(pl.* -á) leave; holiday; **отпускать** *(pf.* отпустить*) let go/off; allocate, give, supply; forgive *(sins)*; crack *(jokes)*; let grow *(beard)*; **отпускной** holiday, leave *(a.)*; **отпущён|ие** remission; absolution *(of sins)*; козёл -ия scapegoat.

отрабатывать *(pf.* отработать) work off *(debt)*; master by practice.

отрава poison; **отравлёние** poisoning; **отравлять** *(pf.* отравить*) poison.

отрада delight, joy; **отрадный** gratifying; cheerful.

отражатель *(m.)* reflector; **отражать** *(pf.* отразить*) reflect; repulse; **-ся** be reflected, repulsed; (на + *acc.)* have an effect (on); **отражёние** reflection; repulse.

отрасль *(f.)* branch, sphere.

отраста́ть *(pf.* отрасти́*)* grow; отра́щивать *(pf.* отра|сти́ть, -щу́, -сти́шь)* grow *(v.t.).*

отре́бье the rabble.

отре́з cut; length; pattern; отреза́ть, отре́зывать *(pf.* отре́зать*)* cut off.

отрезв|ля́ть *(pf.* -и́ть) (make) sober; -ся sober up.

отрезно́й detachable.

отре́|зок (-зка) piece, segment; отре́зывать *see* отреза́ть.

отрека́ться *(pf.* отре́чься, -еку́сь, -ечёшься; -ёкся, -екла́сь) (от + *gen.)* renounce; о. от престо́ла abdicate.

отре́п|ье (-ьев) rags.

отрече́ние renunciation; отре́чься *see* отрека́ться; отреш|а́ться *(pf.* -и́ться) (от + *gen.)* renounce.

отрица́ние denial, negation; отрица́тельный negative; отрица́ть deny.

отро́г (mountain) spur.

о́троду in one's life.

отро́дье spawn, brood.

о́трок *(obs.)* boy; youth; отро́с|ток (-тка) shoot, sprout; appendix *(med.);* о́трочеческий adolescent; о́трочество adolescence.

о́труб farm, holding; отруба́ть *(pf.* отруби́ть*)* chop off; о́труб|и (-е́й) bran.

отры́в breaking/tearing off; alienation; isolation; отрыва́ть *(pf.* ото-рва́ть*)* tear off; interrupt; divert, -ся tear/come off; take off *(of| aircraft);* break away; отры́вистый abrupt, curt; отрывно́й tear off *(a.; e.g. calendar);* отры́|вок (-вка) extract, fragment; отры́вочный fragmentary, scrappy.

отры́гивать *(pf.* отры́гнуть) belch; отры́|жка *(gen. pl.* -жек) belch.

отры́ть *see* отрыва́ть.

отря́д detachment; отряжа́ть *'pf.* отря|ди́ть, -жу́, -ди́шь) assign, tell off.

отряса́ть *(pf.* отрясти́*)* shake off; отря́хивать *(pf.* отряхну́ть) shake down/off.

отса́сывать *(pf.* отсоса́ть*)* suck/ draw off.

отсве́т sheen, reflection; отсве́чивать shine.

отсебя́тина ad-libbing, own words.

отсе́в sifting; eliminating; number of students who do not finish the course.

отсе́ивать *(pf.* отсе́ять*)* eliminate, screen, sift.

отсека́ть *(pf.* отсе́чь*)* cut off.

отсе́ле, отсе́ль from here, hence.

отсече́ние cutting off, severance.

отска́бливать *(pf.* отскобли́ть) scrape off.

отскака́ть* *(pf.)* gallop; отска́кивать *(pf.* отскочи́ть, -очу́, -о́чишь) jump off/aside; rebound, recoil; come off.

отскреба́ть *(pf.* отскрести́*)* scrape off.

отслое́ние exfoliation.

отслу́живать *(pf.* отслужи́ть*)* serve *(a period);* celebrate *(eccl.).*

отсове́товать *(pf.) (dat.)* dissuade, persuade not to.

отсоса́ть *see* отса́сывать.

отсо́хнуть *see* отсыха́ть.

отсро́чивать *(pf.* отсро́чить) postpone; defer; отсро́|чка *(gen. pl.* -чек) postponement, delay.

отст|ава́ть (-аю́, -аёшь; *pf.* отста́ть*)* (от + *gen.)* fall behind, lag behind, be slow *(of clock).*

отста́вка dismissal; resignation; отставля́ть *(pf.* отста́вить) put/set aside; *(coll.)* dismiss; отставно́й retired.

отста́ивать *(pf.* отстоя́ть*)* defend, advocate; -ся settle *(of a liquid);* become settled.

отста́лость *(f.)* backwardness; отста́лый backward; отста́ть *see* отстава́ть.

отстёгивать *(pf.* отстегну́ть, *ppp.* отстёгнутый) unfasten, unbutton, undo.

отсти́рывать *(pf.* отстира́ть) wash off.

отсто́й sediment.

отстра́ивать *(pf.* отстро́ить) build.

отстране́ние pushing aside; dismissal; отстран|я́ть *(pf.* -и́ть) push aside, remove; -ся (от + *gen.)* move away (from); keep aloof (from).

отстре́ливаться *(pf.* fire back, return fire.

отстрига́ть *(pf.* отстри́чь*)* cut off.

о́тступ space *(typ.);* отступа́ть *(pf.* отступи́ть*)* step back, recoil; retreat; deviate; -ся (от + *gen.)* give up, renounce; отступле́ние retreat; deviation, digression; отсту́пник apostate.

отсу́тствие absence; отсу́тствовать be absent.

отсчёт reading *(on instrument)*; отсчи́тывать *(pf.* отсчита́ть) count off.

отсыла́ть *(pf.* отосла́ть*) send off/ back; (к + *dat.)* refer (to); отсы́лка dispatch; reference.

отсыпа́ть *(pf.* отсы́пать*) pour out; measure off.

отсыпа́ться *(pf.* отоспа́ться*) make up lost sleep.

отсыре́лый damp.

отсыха́ть *(pf.* отсо́хнуть*) dry off, wither.

отсю́да from here, hence.

отта́ивать *(pf.* отта́ять*) thaw out.

отта́лкивать *(pf.* оттолкну́ть*) push away; alienate; отта́лкивающий repellent, repulsive.

отта́скивать *(pf.* оттащи́ть*) drag/ pull away/aside.

отта́чивать *(pf.* отточи́ть*) sharpen, whet.

оття́ять *see* отта́ивать.

отте́|нок (-нка) nuance, shade; оттен|я́ть *(pf.* -и́ть) shade, set off.

о́ттепель *(f.)* thaw.

оттесн|я́ть *(pf.* -и́ть) drive back/ away; push aside.

оттира́ть *(pf.* оттере́ть, оторву́*) rub off.

о́ттиск impression; reprint, offprint; отти́скивать *(pf.* отти́снуть) push aside; print.

оттого́ that is why; о. что because.

оттолкну́ть *see* отта́лкивать.

оттома́нка ottoman.

оттопы́риваться *(pf.* оттопы́риться) protrude, bulge.

отторга́ть *(pf.* от|то́ргнуть, *past.* -то́рг) tear away.

отточи́ть *see* отта́чивать.

отту́да from there.

оттуш|ёвывать *(pf.* -ева́ть) shade.

оття́гивать *(pf.* оттяну́ть) draw off; delay.

отума́нивать *(pf.* отума́нить) blur, obscure.

отупе́ние stupefaction.

отутю́ж|ивать *(pf.* -ить) iron.

отуча́ть *(pf.* отучи́ть*) (от + *gen.)* break, wean (from); -ся (от + *gen)* break oneself off; finish learning.

отха́ркивать *(pf.* отха́ркнуть, *&* отха́ркать) expectorate.

отхлёбывать *(pf.* отхлебну́ть) take a mouthful.

отхлы́нуть *(pf.)* rush/flood back.

отхо́д departure; withdrawal; отходи́ть* *(pf.* отойти́* отойду́) (от + *gen.)* move away (from); withdraw; step aside; deviate; отхо́дная prayer for the dying; отхо́д|ы (-ов) waste, scrap.

отхо́жий про́мысел seasonal work.

отхо́жее ме́сто latrine.

отцвета́ть *(pf.* отцвести́*) fade, finish blossoming.

отцепля́ть *(pf.* отц|епи́ть, -еплю́, -е́пишь) uncouple.

отцеуби́йство patricide; отцо́вский paternal; отцо́вство paternity.

отча́иваться *(pf.* отч|а́яться, -а́юсь) (в + *prep.)* despair (of).

отча́ливать *(pf.* отча́лить) push/ cast off.

отча́сти partly, rather.

отча́яние despair; отча́янный desperate; отча́яться *see* отча́иваться.

отчего́ why.

отчека́н|ивать *(pf.* -ить) coin; *(fig.)* say distinctly.

отчёркивать *(pf.* отчеркну́ть) mark off.

отчёрпывать *(pf.* отчерпну́ть) ladle out.

о́тчество patronymic.

отчёт account; отдава́ть себе́ о. (в + *prep.)* be aware (of); отчётливый distinct; отчётность *(f.)* book-keeping; accounts; отчётный report *(a.);* current, accountable.

отчи́зна native country; о́тчий paternal; о́тчим step-father.

отчисл|я́ть *(pf.* -ить) deduct; allot, assign; dismiss.

отчи́тывать *(pf.* отчита́ть) rebuke; -ся give a report.

отчища́ть *(pf.* отчи́стить*) clean off.

отчужда́ть *(pf.* отчу|ди́ть, -жу́, -ди́шь; *ppp.* -ждённый) alienate *(property)*; estrange; отчужде́ние alienation; estrangement.

отшага́ть *(pf.)* walk, trudge.

отша́тываться *(pf.* отшатну́ться) (от + *gen.)* start back/recoil (from); renounce.

отшвы́ривать *(pf.* отшвырну́ть) throw away; kick aside.

отше́льник hermit, recluse.

отши́б: на -е standing apart.

отшиба́ть *(pf.* от|шиби́ть, -шибу́, -шибёшь; -ши́б; *ppp.* -ши́бленный) knock back/off; hurt.

отшпи́ливать *(pf.* отшпи́лить) *(coll.)* unpin.

отшу́чиваться *(pf.* отшути́ться*) dismiss jokingly, laugh off.

отщепе́|нец (-нца) renegade, turncoat.

отщеп|ля́ть *(pf.* -и́ть) chip off.

отщи́пывать *(pf.* отщипну́ть) nip off.

отъеда́ть *(pf.* отъе́сть*) eat/gnaw off.

отъе́зд departure; отъезжа́ть *(pf.* отъе́хать*) depart, drive off.

отъя́вленный inveterate.

оты́грывать *(pf.* отыгра́ть) win back, retrieve.

оты́скивать *(pf.* оты́ска́ть, -ыщу́, -ы́щешь) find; *(ipf.)* look for.

отягоща́ть *(pf.* отяго|ти́ть, -щу́, -ти́шь) burden; отягч|а́ть *(pf.* -и́ть) aggravate; отяжел|я́ть *(pf.* -и́ть) make heavier.

офице́р officer; офице́рский officer *(a.);* официа́льный official; официа́нт, ~ка waiter, waitress.

официо́з semi-official organ.

оформле́ние designing; design, decoration, mounting; official registration; оформля́ть *(pf.* офо́рмить) put into shape, design; make official; -ся take shape; go through necessary formalities.

о́ханье moaning.

оха́пка armful.

о́хать *(pf.* о́хнуть) moan, sigh.

охва́т embrace; scope; outflanking; охва́тывать *(pf.* охвати́ть*) envelop; seize; comprehend; include.

охладева́ть (-ева́ю; *pf.* охладе́ть) (к + *dat.)* grow cool (towards); охлажда́ть *(pf.* охла|ди́ть, -жу́, -ди́шь; *ppp.* -ждённый) cool; oxлажде́ние cooling.

охо́та 1. hunt(ing); 2. wish, inclination; охо́|титься (-чусь, -тишься) (на + *acc.) or* (за + *inst.)* hunt (for); охо́тник hunter; охо́тничий hunter's *(a.);* охо́тно willingly.

о́хра ochre.

охра́на guard; protection; охран|я́ть *(pf.* -и́ть) guard; protect.

оце́нивать *(pf.* оц|ени́ть, -еню́, -е́нишь; *ppp.* -енённый) value, evaluate, appraise; оце́нка estimate, valuation; оце́нщик valuer.

оцепене́лый benumbed.

оцепля́ть *(pf.* оц|епи́ть, -еплю́, -е́пишь) surround, cordon off.

оцинк|о́вывать *(pf.* -ова́ть) coat with zinc, galvanize.

оча́г (-а́) hearth; hotbed, breeding-ground.

очарова́ние charm, fascination; очарова́тельный charming; очар|о́вывать *(pf.* -ова́ть) charm, fascinate

очеви́|дец (дца) eye-witness; очеви́дный obvious.

о́чень very.

очередно́й next in turn; usual, regular; очерёдность *(f.)* sequence, order of priority; о́черед|ь *(f.;* *pl.* -и, -е́й) turn; queue; о. за ва́ми it's your turn.

о́черк essay, sketch.

очерстве́лый callous, hardened.

очерта́ние outline.

очертя́ го́лову headlong.

оче́рчивать *(pf.* очерти́ть*) outline.

о́чи *see* о́ко.

очи́стка cleaning; purification; очи́стк|и (-ов) peelings; очища́ть *(pf.* очи́стить*) clean; clear; refine; purify; peel.

очк|и́ (-о́в) spectacles.

очк|о́ *(pl.* -и́, -о́в) pip; point; очковтира́тельство deceit, eyewash.

очко́вая змея́ cobra.

очну́ться *(pf.)* come to oneself, regain consciousness.

о́чный: -ая ста́вка confrontation.

очуме́лый mad.

оч|ути́ться *(pf.* -у́тишься) find oneself.

ошар|а́шивать *(pf.* -а́шить) dumbfound, flabbergast.

оше́йник collar.

ошелом|ля́ть *(pf.* -и́ть) stun, astound.

ошиба́ться *(pf.* ошиби́ться, оши|бу́сь, -бёшься; ошибся) make a mistake; оши́бка mistake, error; оши́бочный erroneous.

оши́кать *(pf., coll.)* whistle, hiss.

ошпа́ривать *(pf.* ошпа́рить) scald.

ощети́ниваться *(pf.* ощети́ниться) bristle up.

ощи́пывать *(pf.* ощипа́ть*) pluck.

ощу́пывать *(pf.* ощу́пать) feel; о́щупь *(f.)* touch; на о. to the touch; идти́ -ю groping(ly).

ощути́мый appreciable; perceptible, tangible; ощуща́ть *(pf.* ощу|ти́ть, -щу́, -ти́шь) feel, sense; -ся be observed, make itself felt; ощуще́ние sensation, feeling.

П

па́ва peahen.
павиа́н baboon.
павильо́н pavilion; film studio.
павли́н peacock; павли́ний peacock *(a.)*.
па́во|док (-дка) flood; high water.
па́губный baneful, pernicious.
па́даль *(f.)* carrion.
па́дать *(pf.* упа́сть, & пасть, (у)паду́, -ёшь; (у)па́л) fall; п. ду́хом lose heart.
паде́ж (-á) case *(gram.)*; падёж (-á) loss of cattle.
паде́ние fall, collapse; downfall.
па́дкий (на + *acc.,* до + *gen)* having a weakness (for); keen (on).
па́дуб holly.
паду́чая epilepsy.
па́дчерица stepdaughter.
паёк (пайка́) ration.
паж page.
па́зуха bosom.
пай *(pl.* па|и́, -ёв) share; па́йщик shareholder.
пакга́уз warehouse.
паке́т package, parcel, packet.
пакиста́|нец (-нца), ∼нка Pakistani.
па́кля tow; oakum.
пакова́ть *(pf.* за-, у-) pack.
па́костить *(pf.* на-) dirty, soil; *(dat.)* play a dirty trick (on); *(pf.* ис-) spoil; па́костный dirty, mean; па́кость *(f.)* dirty trick; obscenity.
пакт pact; п. о ненападе́нии non-aggression pact.
пала́та chamber, house.
палатализова́ть palatalize.
пала́тка tent; stall.
пала́ч (-á) executioner.
па́левый pale yellow.
палёный singed.
па́л|ец (-льца) finger; toe; смотре́ть сквозь па́льцы turn a blind eye; как свои́ пять па́льцев знать know like the back of one's hand; have at one's finger-tips.
палиса́дник front garden.
палиса́ндр rosewood.
пали́тра palette.
пали́ть 1. *(pf.* вы́-, & пальну́ть) fire *(shots)*; 2. *(pf.* о-, с-) burn, scorch.
па́лица mace, club.
па́лка stick, cane.

пало́м|ник, ∼ница pilgrim; пало́мничество pilgrimage.
па́ло|чка *(gen. pl.* -чек) small stick, cane.
па́лтус halibut, turbot.
па́луба deck.
пальба́ firing.
па́льма palm.
пальто́ *(indecl.)* (over)coat.
памфле́т pamphlet, lampoon.
па́мятка commemorative booklet; memorandum.
па́мятливый having a retentive memory; па́мятник monument, memorial; па́мятный memorable.
па́мят|ь *(f.)* memory; recollection; подари́ть на п. give as a keepsake; без -и unconscious.
панаце́я panacea.
панеги́рик panegyric.
пане́ль *(f.)* footway; panel.
па́ника panic; паникёр, ∼ша alarmist.
панихи́да requiem.
панора́ма panorama.
пансио́н board and lodging; boarding house; *(obs.)* boarding school; пансионе́р boarder; guest.
пантал|о́ны (-о́н) drawers, pants.
панте́ра panther.
пантоми́ма pantomime, dumb show.
па́нцирь, па́нцырь *(m.)* armour, coat of mail.
па́па *(m.)* 1. dad, daddy; 2. pope.
папа́ха Caucasian fur cap.
па́перть *(f.)* porch *(of church)*.
папиро́са cigarette; папиро́сница cigarette-case/box.
па́пка folder, case *(for documents)*.
па́поротник fern.
па́пский papal.
пар (в пару́, *pl.* -ы́) 1. steam; 2. fallow.
па́ра pair; suit.
пара́граф paragraph; paragraph sign.
пара́д parade, review.
пара́дный full-dress; main *(entrance)*.
парадокса́льный paradoxical.
параз|ити́ческий, ∼и́тный parasitic.
парализова́ть *(ipf. & pf.)* paralyse; парали́ч (-á) paralysis.
паралле́ль *(f.)* parallel; паралле́льный parallel *(a.)*.
парано́йя paranoia.
парафрази́ровать *(ipf. & pf)* paraphrase.
парашю́т parachute; парашюти́ст, ∼ка parachutist.

пáреный stewed.

пáр|ень (-ня) lad, fellow.

пари́ (*indecl.*) bet; **держáть п.** lay a bet.

парижáнин (*pl.* -áне, -áн), **~áнка** Parisian.

пари́к (-á) wig; **парикмáхер** hairdresser;

парикмáхерская hairdresser's/barber's shop.

пари́ровать (*ipf. & pf.*) parry, counter.

паритéт parity.

пáрить steam, stew.

пари́ть soar.

парк park.

паркéт parquet.

парлáмент parliament; **парламентáрий** parliamentarian; **парламентáрный** parliamentary; **парлáментский** of parliament; **парламентёр** truce envoy.

парни́к (-á) hotbed, seed-bed.

парни́|шка (*gen. pl.* -шек) lad.

парнóй fresh.

пáрный twin; paired.

паровóз steam engine, locomotive; **паровóй** steam (*a.*).

пароди́ровать (*ipf. & pf.*) parody; **парóдия** parody.

пароксизм paroxysm, fit.

парóль (*m.*) password.

парóм ferry; **парóмщик** ferryman.

парохóд steamer, steamship; **парохóдный** steamship (*a.*).

пáрта (school) desk.

партéр pit, stalls.

парт|éц (-йца) **~йка** (*gen. pl.* -йек) Party member.

партизáн, **~ка** partisan.

парти́йность (*f.*) membership of the Party; Party spirit; **парти́йный** Party (*a.*).

партиту́ра score (*mus.*).

пáртия party; group; game, set; (good) match (*i.e. marriage*).

партнёр, **~ша** partner.

партóрг Party organizer, secretary of local Party organization.

пáрус (*pl.* -á) sail; **паруси́на** canvas, tarpaulin; **паруси́новый** canvas (*a.*); **пáрусник** sailing ship; sailmaker; **пáрусный** sail(ing) (*a.*).

парфюмéрия perfumery.

парчá brocade; **парчёвый** brocade (*a.*).

парши́вый mangy; wretched.

пáсека apiary; **пáсечник** beekeeper.

пáсквиль (*m.*) lampoon, libel.

паску́дный vile, foul.

пáсмурный dull, gloomy.

пасовáть 1. (*pf.* с-) pass (at cards); 2. (пéред + *inst.*) shirk.

пáспорт (*pl.* -á) passport.

пассáж passage; arcade.

пассажи́р, **~ка** passenger.

пассáт trade-wind.

пасси́в liabilities; passive voice; **пасси́вный** passive.

пáста paste.

пáстбище pasture; **пáства** flock (*eccl.*).

пастéль (*f.*) pastel.

пастернáк parsnip.

пасти́ (пасу́, -ёшь; *past* пас, -лá) pasture; -сь graze.

пасту́х (-á) shepherd; herdsman; **пасту́|шка** (*gen. pl.* -шек) shepherdess.

пáстырь (*m.*) pastor.

пасть 1. (*inf.*) see пáдать; 2. (*f.*) mouth, jaws; trap.

пáсха Easter; **пасхáльный** Easter (*a.*).

пáсы|нок (-нка) stepson.

патéнт patent; **патентовáть** (*pf.* за-) patent.

патети́ческий, **-и́чный** pathetic.

патефóн gramophone.

пáтока treacle, syrup.

патриáрх patriarch; **патриархáльный** patriarchal; **патриáршество** patriarchate.

патриóт, **~ка** patriot; **патриоти́зм** patriotism; **патриоти́ческий**, **-и́чный** patriotic.

патрóн 1. patron; 2. cartridge; lampsocket; pattern; **патронтáш** bandolier.

патрули́ровать patrol; **патру́ль** (*m.*) patrol.

пáуза pause.

пау́к (-á) spider; **паути́на** spider's web, cobweb; gossamer.

пáфос inspiration, enthusiasm.

пах (в -у́) groin.

пáхарь (*m.*) ploughman; **пахáть** (пашу́, пáшешь; *pf.* вс-) plough.

пáхнуть (*inst.*) smell (of).

пах|ну́ть (*pf.*, -нёт) puff; -ну́ло хóлодом there was a gust of cold air.

пáхота ploughing, tillage; **пáхотный** arable.

паху́чий fragrant, odorous.

пациéнт, **~ка** patient.

па́че *(obs.)* more, greater; тем п. *(obs.)* the more so.

па́|чка *(gen. pl.* -чек) bundle; packet *(cigarettes)*; parcel *(books)*.

па́чкать *(pf.* вы́-, за-, ис-, на-) dirty, soil, stain.

па́|шня *(gen. pl.* -шен) arable field.

паште́т pâté.

па́юсная икра́ pressed caviare.

пая́льник soldering iron; пая́льщик tinsmith, tinker; пая́ть *(pf.* за-, с-) solder.

пая́ц buffoon.

пе|ве́ц (-вца́), ~ви́ца singer; певу́чий melodious; пе́вчий singing, song *(a.)*; chorister.

пе́гий skewbald.

педаго́г teacher; педагог|и́ческий pedagogical; ~и́чный educationally correct.

педа́ль *(f.)* pedal.

педа́нт, ~ка pedant; педанти́чный pedantic.

педикю́р chiropody.

пейза́ж landscape, scenery.

пека́|рня *(gen. pl.* -рен) bakery; пе́кар|ь *(pl.* -и & -я) baker; пе́кло scorching heat; hell.

пелена́ shroud; пелена́ть *(pf.* за-, с-) swaddle; пелёнка nappie.

пелика́н pelican.

пельме́нь *(m.)* meat dumpling.

пе́мза pumice (stone).

пе́на foam.

пена́л pencil-case.

пе́ние singing.

пе́нистый frothy, foaming; пе́ниться *(pf.* вс-) foam, froth.

пеницилли́н penicillin.

пе́нка skin *(on milk)*.

пенс penny.

пенсионе́р, ~ка pensioner; пе́нсия pen·ion.

пе́нтюх *(coll.)* lout.

пень (пня) stump, stub.

пенька́ hemp.

пе́ня fine; пеня́ть *(pf.* по-) (на + *acc.* or *dat.)* reproach, blame; (за + *acc.)* (for).

пе́|пел (-пла) ashes; пепели́ще smouldering remains; old homestead; пе́пельница ash-tray; пе́пельный ashy, ashen.

пе́рве|нец (-нца) first-born; пе́рвенство superiority, first place; championship; пе́рвенствовать (над + *inst.)* take precedence, have priority (over).

перви́чный primary.

перво|бы́тный primitive; ~исто́чник origin, source; ~кла́ссный first-class; ~ку́рсник, ~ку́рсница first-year student, fresher; ~нача́льный primary; original; ~печа́тный incunabular; ~ро́дство primogeniture; ~со́ртный first-rate; first-class; ~степе́нный paramount.

пе́рвый first; пе́рвое first course.

перга́мент parchment.

переадрес|о́вывать *(pf.* -ова́ть) re-address.

пере|бега́ть *(pf.* -бежа́ть*) run across; cross; desert; перебе́жчик deserter, turncoat.

пере|бива́ть *(pf.* -би́ть*) interrupt; -ся be interrupted; get by, make ends meet.

пере|бира́ть *(pf.* -бра́ть*) sort out; touch with fingers *(e.g. strings)*; turn over *(e.g. in one's mind)*; -ся be sorted out *etc.*; get over/across; move *(house)*.

переби́ть *see* перебива́ть.

перебо́й stoppage, interruption.

пере|боро́ть* (-орю́, -о́решь *pf)* overcome.

перебра́нка squabble, wrangle.

пере|бра́сывать *(pf.* -бро́сить*) throw over/across; transfer; -ся be thrown over, *etc.*; spread; jump over; -ся не́сколькими; слова́ми exchange/bandy a few words; перебро́ска transfer; transport.

перебыва́ть *(pf.)* be in/visit many places.

перева́л crossing; (mountain) pass; пере|ва́ливать *(pf.* -вали́ть*) load, shift across; go beyond; перевали́ло за по́лночь it's gone midnight. -ся (че́рез + *acc.)* fall/tumble over; перева́лка transfer.

пере|ва́ривать *(pf.* -вари́ть*) spoil by overcooking; re-boil/stew; digest bear, stand.

пере|вёртывать *(pf.* -верну́ть, *ppp.* -вёрнутый) turn over; *(pf.* -верте́ть*) overwind.

переве́с preponderance.

пере|ве́шивать *(pf.* -ве́сить*) re-hang; re-weigh; outweigh; -ся (че́рез + *acc.)* lean (over).

пере|вира́ть *(pf.* -вра́ть*) garble; muddle.

перево́д transfer(ence); translation; conversion; пере|води́ть* *(pf.* -вести*) move, lead across; transfer; translate, convert; п. дух take breath; -ся 1. be transferred, etc.; 2. come to an end.

переводн|о́й: -а́я бума́га carbon paper; -а́я карти́нка transfer; переводны́й translated, transfer (a); -ый бланк (form for) postal order.

перево́д|чик, -чица translator, interpreter.

перево́з transportation, ferry; пере|вози́ть* (pf. -везти́*) transport, remove, take across; перево́зка conveyance, transportation; перево́зчик ferryman.

перевоору|жа́ть (pf. -жи́ть) rearm; перевооруже́ние rearmament.

пере|воплоща́ться (pf. воплоти́ться*) re-embody; reshape; перевоплоще́ние reincarnation; transformation.

пере|вора́чивать (pf. -верну́ть, ppp. -вёрнутый) turn over; upset; переворо́т revolution; overturn; coup; cataclysm (geol.); roll (avia).

перевоспита́ние re-education.

перевра́ть see перевира́ть.

пере|выбира́ть (pf. -вы́брать*) re-elect.

перевыполне́ние overfulfilment; пере|выполня́ть (pf. -вы́полнить) overfulfil, exceed.

перевя́зка bandaging, dressing; перевя́зочный пункт dressing station, first-aid station; пере|вя́зывать (pf. -вяза́ть*) tie up; bandage; переви́зь (f.) sling (med.).

перега́р: у него́ па́хнет -ом he smells of spirits.

переги́б bend, twist; extreme; пере|гиба́ть (pf. -гну́ть) bend; п. па́лку go too far; -ся lean, bend over.

перегласо́вка mutation (philol.).

пере|гля́дываться (pf. -гляну́ться) exchange glances.

перегно́й humus.

перегну́ть see перегиба́ть.

переговори́ть (pf.) have a talk; переговор|ы (-ов) talks, negotiations.

перего́н driving (cattle); stage (between stations); перего́нка distillation; пере|гоня́ть (pf. -гна́ть*) outdistance; drive (somewhere else); distil.

перегора́|живать (pf. перегор|оди́ть, -ожу́, -о́дишь) partition off.

пере|гора́ть (pf. -горе́ть*) burn out, fuse.

перегоро́дка partition.

перегре́в overheating; пере|грева́ть (-грева́ю: pf. -гре́ть) overheat.

пере|гружа́ть (pf. -грузи́ть*) overload; overwork; re-load; move; перегру́зка overload; overwork; re-loading.

перегруппир|о́вывать (pf. -ова́ть) re-group.

пере|грыза́ть (pf. -грызть*) gnaw through; bite to death; quarrel.

пе́ред (inst.) in front of; before.

перёд (пе́реда, pl. -а́) front, forepart.

пере|дава́ть* (pf. -да́ть*) pass, give; transmit, deliver, communicate; convey; (coll.) give too much; -ся be given, transmitted etc; be inherited; переда́тчик transmitter; переда́ча transmission; transfer; gears; broadcast.

передвига́ть* (pf. -дви́нуть) move (across); передвиже́ние movement; передви́|жка (gen. pl. -жек) mobile library/theatre etc.; передвижно́й mobile.

переде́л redistribution.

переде́лка alteration; (coll.) mess; пере|де́лывать (pf. -де́лать) remake, alter.

пере|дёргивать (pf. -дёрнуть) cheat; distort; shock; -ся wince.

пере|де́рживать (pf. -держа́ть*) overdo; overcook; over-expose (phot.).

пере́дний fore, front (a.); пере́дник apron, pinafore; пере́дняя anteroom, hall.

передо|веря́ть (pf. -ве́рить) transfer, sub-contract.

передови́к (-а́) person in front rank, leader; передови́ца leading article, editorial; передово́й foremost, advanced.

передра́зн|ивать (pf. -и́ть*) mimic.

переду́м|ывать (pf. -ать) change one's mind.

переды́шка (gen. pl. -шек) respite.

пере|еда́ть (pf. -е́сть*) (gen.) eat too much (of); outeat; corrode.

перее́зд passage, crossing; level-crossing; removal; пере|езжа́ть (pf. -е́хать*) cross; move house (pf.) run over.

пережа́р|ивать (pf. -ить) overroast, overdo.

переж|да́ть see пережида́ть.

пере|жёвывать (pf. -жега́ть*) chew, masticate; repeat over and over again.

пережива́ние experience; **пере|жива́ть** (pf. -жи́ть; ppp. -жи́тый); experience; endure; outlive.

пере|жида́ть (pf. -жда́ть*) wait till something is over.

пережи́|ток (-тка) remnant, survival.

перезаключ|а́ть (pf. -и́ть) renew (e.g. contract).

перезре́лый overripe.

пере|и́грывать (pf. -игра́ть) play again; overdo.

переиз|дава́ть (pf. -да́ть*) republish, reprint.

переимен|о́вывать (pf. -ова́ть) rename.

переина́ч|ивать (pf. -ить) alter.

перейти́ see переходи́ть.

пере|ка́рмливать (pf. -корми́ть*) overfeed.

перека́т sandbank; peal, roll (of thunder).

перекати́-по́ле tumble-weed; (fig.) rolling stone.

пере|ка́шивать (pf. -коси́ть*): у него́ перекоси́ло лицо́ his face was distorted.

переквалифици́ровать (ipf. & pf.) re-train (for new profession).

перекидно́й retractable; **пере|ки́дывать** (pf. -ки́нуть) throw across/over.

пе́рекись (f.) peroxide.

перекла́дина cross-beam; horizontal bar (sport); **перекладны́е** stage-horses; **пере|кла́дывать** (pf. -ложи́ть, -ложу́ -ло́жишь) move across; interlay; set (to music); put in too much (e.g. sugar).

пере|клика́ться (pf. -кли́кнуться) call to each other; **перекли́|чка** (gen. pl. -чек) roll-call.

переключ|а́ть (pf. -и́ть) switch(over).

перекóвка reshoeing (horses).

перекорми́ть see перека́рмливать.

перекоси́ть see перека́шивать; **переко́шенный** distorted, convulsed.

пере|кра́шивать (pf. -кра́сить*) repaint; paint (a lot of); dye.

перекрёстный cross (a.); п. допро́с cross-examination; **перекрёс|ток** (-тка cross-roads;(пере|-

кре́щивать (pf. -крести́ть*) cross (e.g. a line) · (see also крести́ть).

пере|кру́чивать (pf. -крути́ть*) overwind.

пере|крыва́ть (pf. -кры́ть*) re-cover; exceed; перекры́тие flooring, ceiling; overlapping.

переку́пщик second-hand dealer.

пере|лага́ть (pf. -ложи́ть, -ложу́, -ло́жишь) shift (e.g. responsibility): transpose.

пере|ла́мывать (pf. -ломи́ть*) break in two; master, control; (pf. -лома́ть) break a lot of.

пере|леза́ть (pf. -ле́зть*) (че́рез + acc.) climb over.

переле́|сок (-сга) copse.

перелёт flight; transmigration; **пере|лета́ть** (pf. -лте́ть*) fly(over); fly somewhere else; **перелётная пти́ца** bird of passage.

перели́в play (of colours) modulation; **перелива́ние** pouring; transfusion (med.); **пере|лива́ть** (pf. -ли́ть*) pour, transfuse; let overflow; re-cast; modulate, play; **-ся** flow, overflow; modulate, play; **перели́вка** recasting, re-moulding; **перели́вчатый** iridescent; lilting (voice).

пере|ли́стывать (pf. -листа́ть) turn over (pages); look through.

перели́ть see перелива́ть.

переложе́ние arrangement, transposition; **переложи́ть** see перекла́дывать, перелага́ть.

перело́м break, fracture; crisis; turning-point; **переломáть**, **-и́ть** see перела́мывать; **перело́мный моме́нт** turning-point.

пере|ма́нивать (pf. -мани́ть*) entice.

пере|ма́тывать (pf. -мота́ть) (re)-wind.

перемежа́ть(ся) alternate.

переме́на charge; interval, break (school); **переме́н|ивать** (pf. -еню́ -е́нишь) change, alter; **-ся** change, alter; **переме́нный** variable; **переме́нчивый** changeable.

пере|мерза́ть (pf. -мёрзнуть*) be nipped by frost.

перемести́ть see перемеща́ть.

пере|ме́шивать (pf. -меша́ть) (inter)-mix; shuffle; mix up.

пере|меша́ть (pf. -мести́ть, -мещу́, -мести́шь) remove, displace, transfer; **-ся** move, shift; **перемеще́ние** transference, displacement; **пере-**

мещённые лица displaced persons.

пере|мигиваться *(pf.* -мигнуться) wink at each other.

переминаться: ～ с ноги на ногу shuffle from one foot to the other.

перемирие truce, armistice.

пере|мывать *(pf.* -мыть*) wash; rewash.

пере|напрягать *(pf.* -напрячь*) overstrain.

перенаселённый overpopulated.

перенасыщенный oversaturated.

перенесение transfer, removal.

перенимать *(pf.* пер|енять, -еймý, -еймёшь; *past.* перенял, -á, -o; *ppp.* перенятый) adopt, imitate.

перенос carrying over, transfer; пере|носить* *(pf.* -нести*) carry off/across, transfer; endure, bear; -ся be carried away.

переносица bridge of nose.

переносный portable; figurative; переносчик carrier.

перенумеровать *(pf.)* re-number.

перенять *see* перенимать.

переоборудовать *(ipf. & pf.)* re-equip.

пере|обуваться *(pf.* -обуться) change one's footwear.

переодевание changing *(clothes);* disguise; пере|одевать (-одеваю; *pf.* -одеть*) change *(someone's clothes);* переодетый changed; disguised.

пере|оценивать *(pf.* -оценить*) overestimate; re-value; переоценка overestimate; revaluation.

перепалка skirmish; argument.

пере|пархивать *(pf.* -порхнуть) flit.

пере|пекать *(pf.* -печь*) overbake.

перепел *(pl.* -á) quail.

перепеленать *(pf.)* change *(baby).*

перепелятник sparrowhawk; bird catcher.

перепечатка reprint; перепечат|-ывать *(pf.* -ать) reprint.

пере|пивать *(pf.* -пить*) drink to excess; outdrink.

переписка copying; correspondence; переписчик, ～чица copy-typist; copier; пере|писывать *(pf.* -писать*) re-write, copy; make list/census of; -ся correspond; перепись *(f.)* census.

пере|плачивать *(pf.* -платить*) overpay.

переплёт binding; пере|плетать *(pf.* -плести) intertwine, interlace;

bind; -ся interlace; be tangled; переплётчик bookbinder.

пере|плывать *(pf.* -плыть*) swim/sail/row across.

переподготовка re-training, additional training.

пере|ползать *(pf.* -ползти*) crawl/creep over.

пере|полнять *(pf.* -полнить) overfill, overcrowd.

переполох commotion.

перепонка membrane; перепончатый membranous; webbed, webfooted.

переправа crossing, passage; ford; пере|правлять *(pf.* -править) convey across; forward *(letters);* -ся swim/sail/row across; be ferried; be forwarded.

пере|превать (-преваю; *pf.* -преть) rot; *(coll.)* be overdone *(food).*

перепро|давать* *(pf.* -дать*) resell; перепродажа resale.

пере|прыгивать *(pf.* -прыгнуть) *(через + acc.)* jump over.

перепуг: с -y from fright.

перепутывать *(pf.* перепутать) mix up; confuse.

перепутье cross-roads.

пере|рабатывать *(pf.* -работать) 1. process; re-make; 2. work overtime; переработка processing; overtime work.

перераспределение redistribution; перераспредел|ять *(pf.* -ить) redistribute.

пере|растать *(pf.* -расти*) overgrow; outgrow; develop.

перерасход overexpenditure, overdraft.

пере|резывать, -резать *(pf.* -резать*) cut, cut off; *(pf.)* kill.

пере|рождаться *(pf.* -родиться*) regenerate; degenerate; перерождение regeneration, degeneration.

пере|рубать *(pf.* -рубить*) cut/chop in two.

перерыв interruption; interval; пере|рывать 1. *(pf.* -рвать*) tear apart; 2. *(pf.* -рыть*) dig up; turn over, rummage in.

пересадка transplantation; grafting *(med.);* transfer, change of seat; пере|саживать *(pf.* -садить, -сажу, -садишь) put in different place; transplant; -ся *(pf.* -сесть*) change one's seat; change trains *etc.*

пере|сáливать *(pf.* -солúть) put too much salt in; overdo (it).

пере|сдавáть* *(pf.* -сдáть*) sublet; repeat *(exam.)*.

пере|секáть *(pf.* -сечь*) cross, intersect.

переселé|нец (-нца), ~нка migrant, immigrant; пересел|я́ть *(pf.* -и́ть) move; -ся move, migrate.

пересечéние crossing, intersection; пересéчь *see* пересекáть.

пере|сúливать *(pf.* -сúлить) overpower.

пересказ re-telling; exposition; пере|скáзывать *(pf.* -сказáть*) retell.

пере|скáкивать *(pf.* -скочи́ть*) (чéрез ⊥ *acc.)* jump, skip (over).

пересла́ть *see* пересыла́ть.

пересмáтривать *(pf.* -смотрéть*) look over, review; пересмóтр revision, reconsideration.

пересоз|давáть* *(pf.* -дáть*) recreate.

пересоли́ть *see* пересáливать.

пересóхнуть *see* пересыхáть.

переспéлый overripe.

пере|ставáть *(-*стаю́, -стаёшь *pf.* -стáть*) cease, stop.

пере|ставля́ть *(pf.* -стáвить) rearrange, transpose; п. часы́ впе-рёд put the clocks on.

перестанóвка transposition, rearrangement.

перестáть *see* переставáть.

пере|стрáивать *(pf.* -стрóить) rebuild, reorganize; tune; -ся be rebuilt *etc.;* reform; (на + *acc.)* switch over (to).

перестрахóвка reinsurance; *(fig.)* overcautiousness; перестрах|óвы-вать *(pf.* -овáть) reinsure.

пере|стрéливать *(pf.* -стреля́ть) shoot; use up *(cartridges)* ; -ся exchange fire; перестрéлка exchange of fire.

перестрóить *see* перестрáивать; перестрóйка reconstruction; reorganization.

пере|ступáть *(pf.* -ступи́ть*) overstep; п. грани́цы прили́чия overstep bounds of decency.

пересу́д|ы (-ов) *(coll.)* gossip.

пере|су́шивать *(pf.* -суши́ть*) overdry.

пере|счи́тывать *(pf.* -счита́ть, & честь, -чту́, -чтёшь; *past* -чёл, -чла́; *ppp.* -чтённый) count again.

пере|сыла́ть *(pf.* -сла́ть*) send forward; пересы́лка sending, remit-tance, forwarding.

пере|сыха́ть *(pf.* -сóхнуть*) become (too) dry.

пере|тáскивать *(pf.* -тащи́ть*) drag/carry over.

перетасóвка reshuffle.

пере|тира́ть *(pf.* -тере́ть*) wear away; rub.

пере|тряса́ть *(pf.* -трясти́*) shake up.

перéть (пру, прёшь; *past.* пёр) *(coll.)* trudge.

пере|тя́гивать *(pf.* -тяну́ть*) pull, draw across; outweigh; п. на свою́ стóрону win over.

пере|убежда́ть *(pf.* -уб(ди́ть) convince.

переу́|лок (-лка) by-street, alley.

переустрóйство reconstruction.

переутом|ля́ть *(pf.* -и́ть) overtire, overstrain.

переучёт stock-taking; inventory; registration.

пере|у́чивать *(pf.* -учи́ть*) teach again; re-learn.

перефрази́ровать *(ipf. & pf.)* paraphrase.

пере|хва́тывать *(pf.* -хвати́ть*) intercept; *(coll.)* borrow; snatch.

перехитри́ть *(pf.)* outwit.

перехóд passage, transition; пере-ходи́ть* *(pf.* перейти́*, -€йду́; *ppp.* -ейдённый) cross; pass; пере-ходя́щий ку́бок challenge cup; перехóдный transitional; transitive.

пé|рец (-рца) pepper.

пере|чень (-чня) enumeration, list.

пере|чёркивать *(pf.* -черкну́ть) cross out; cancel.

перечéсть *see* пересчи́тывать, перечи́тывать.

пере|числя́ть *(pf.* -чи́слить) enumerate; *(fin.)* transfer.

пере|чи́тывать *(pf.* -чита́ть, & -честь, -чту, -чтёшь; -чёл, -чла́; *ppp.* -чтённый) re-read.

перéчить *(dat.: coll)* contradict.

пéречница pepper-pot.

пере|ша́гивать *(pf.* -шагну́ть) step across; п. (чéрез) порóг cross the threshold.

переше́|ек (-ейка) isthmus, neck of land.

перешёптываться whisper to each other.

пере шива́ть (pf. -ши́ть*) sew; alter (clothes).

перещеголя́ть (pf.) outdo; outswank.

переэкзамено́вка re-examination.

пери́ла (-и́л) (hand)rail, banister.

пери́на feather-bed.

пери́од period; **перио́дика** periodicals; **периоди́ческий** periodical (a.).

пе́ристый feathery; cirrus.

периферия periphery.

перл pearl (obs.); gem; **перламу́тр** mother-of-pearl.

перло́вая крупа́ pearl-barley.

перлюстри́ровать (ipf. & pf.) censor (letters).

пермане́нт permanent wave; **перма́нентный** permanent.

перна́тый feathered.

перо́ (pl. пе́р|ья, -ьев) feather plume; pen; quill.

перочи́нный нож penknife.

перпендикуля́р perpendicular.

перро́н platform.

перс Persian; **перси́дский** Persian (a.).

пе́рс|и (-ей) (obs.) breast.

пе́рсик peach, peach-tree.

перси́|янин (pl. -я́не, -я́н), ~**я́нка** Persian.

персо́на person, personage; **персо-на́ж** character; **персона́л** personnel, staff; **персона́льный** personal.

перспекти́ва perspective, vista; prospects; **перспекти́вный** long-range, long-term.

перст (-а́) (obs.) finger; **пе́рс|тень** (-тня) ring.

перуа́|нец (-нца), ~**нка** Peruvian.

перхоть (f.) dandruff.

перча́тка glove.

пёры|шко (pl. -шки, -шек) little feather.

пёс (пса) dog.

пе́сенка song; **пе́сенник** song-book; singer.

песе́ц (-ца́) polar fox.

пескарь (-я́) gudgeon.

песнь (f.) song; canto; **пе́сня** (gen. pl. -сен) song.

пе|со́к (-ска́) sand; **песо́чный** sandy; sand (a.).

пессими́ст|и́ческий, ~**и́чный** pessimistic.

пест (-а́) pestle; **пе́стик** pestle; pistil.

пе́стовать nurse; foster.

пестре́ть show/appear multi-coloured; be gay; **пестри́ть:** у меня́ пестри́т в глаза́х I am dazzled; **пестрота́** diversity; **пёстрый** variegated, gay; mixed.

песча́ник sandstone; **песча́ный** sandy; **песчи́нка** grit, grain of sand.

пети́ция petition.

петли́|ца buttonhole; tab; **пе́|тля** (gen. pl. -тель) loop, noose; buttonhole; eye; stitch; hinge.

петру́шка parsley.

пету́х (-а́) cock, rooster; **пету|шо́к** (-шка́) cockerel; **идти́ -ко́м** run after, fawning.

петь (пою́, поёшь; pf. по-) sing (v.i.); (pf. про-, с-; ppp. -пе́тый) sing (v.t.).

пехо́та infantry; **пехо́тный** infantry (a.).

печа́лить (pf. о-) sadden; -ся be sad; **печа́ль** (f.) sorrow; **печа́льный** sad.

печа́тать (pf. на-) print; -ся be printed; have work published; **печа́тка** signet; **печа́тник** printer; **печа́тный** printed; **печа́ть** (f.) seal; the press.

пече́ние baking.

печёнка liver.

печёный baked.

пе́чень (f.) liver.

пече́нье biscuit, pastry.

пе́|чка (gen. pl. -чек), **печь** 1. (в печи́, pl. -и, -е́й) stove, oven, kiln.

печь 2. (пеку́, печёшь; past. пёк, пекла́; pf. ис-; ppp. испечённый) bake; -ся bake; -ся (о + prep.) take care of.

пешехо́д pedestrian; **пе́ший** pedestrian; foot (a).

пе́шка pawn (chess).

пешко́м on foot.

пеще́ра cave.

пиани́но (indecl.) (upright) piano; **пиани́ст**, ~**ка** pianist.

пивна́я pub, beer-house; **пивно́й** beer (a.); **пи́во** beer; **пивова́р** brewer; **пивова́ренный заво́д** brewery.

пига́лица lapwing, pee-wit; puny person.

пигме́й pigmy.

пиджа́к (-а́) jacket.

пижа́ма pyjamas.

пижо́н fop.

пик peak, pinnacle; **часы́-п.** rush-hour; **пи́ка** lance.

пика́нтный piquant; crisp.

пике́ (*indecl.*) piqué; dive (*avia.*).

пике́т picket; **пикети́ровать** picket.

пи́ки (пик) spades (*cards*).

пики́ровать (*ipf. & pf.; & pf.*, с-) dive; **-ся** exchange caustic remarks; **пики́ровщик** dive-bomber.

пикни́к (-á) picnic.

пи́ковый of spades (*cards*).

пи́кул|и (-ей) pickles.

пила́ (*pl.* пи́лы) saw.

пила́в pilau, pilaff.

пилёный sawn, filed; п. са́хар lump-sugar.

пили́ть (пилю́, пи́лишь) saw; **пи́лка** saw; file.

пило́т pilot; вы́сший пилота́ж aerial aerobatics.

пилю́ля pill.

пина́ть (*pf.* пнуть) (*coll.*) kick; **пи|но́к** (-нка́) kick.

пио́н peony.

пионе́р pioneer.

пипе́тка pipette.

пир (в -ý, *pl.* -ы́) feast, banquet.

пирами́да pyramid.

пира́т pirate; **пира́тство** piracy.

пирова́ть carouse, feast.

пиро́г (-á) pie, tart; **пиро́жное** pastry, fancy cake; **пиро|жо́к** (-жка́) pasty.

пи́ршество feast; revelry.

писа́ка (*m.*) scribbler; **писа́ние** writing; writ; **пи́сар|ь** (*m.; pl.* -я́) clerk; **писа́тель, ~ница** writer, author; **писа́ть** (пишу́, пи́шешь; *pf.* на-) write.

писк chirp, squeak; **пискли́вый** squeaky; **пи́скнуть** *see* **пища́ть**.

пистоле́т pistol.

пистон (percussion) cap.

писчебума́жный магази́н stationer's; **пи́счий:** -ая бума́га writing paper.

письм|ена́ (-ён, -ена́м) characters.

пи́сьменность (*f.*) literature; **пи́сьменный** written.

письмо́ (*pl.* пи́сьма, пи́сем) letter.

пита́ние feeding, nourishment; **пита́тельный** nutritious; **пита́ть** (*pf.* на-) feed, nourish; entertain, have; **-ся** (*inst.*) feed on.

пито́|мец (-мца) ~мица foster-child; **пито́мник** nursery (*for plants*).

пито́н python.

пить (пью, пьёшь; *imper.* пей!; *pf.* по-) drink (*v.i.*); (*pf.* вы́-; *ppp.*

вы́питый) drink (*v.t.*) ;**питьё** drink; **питьево́й** drinking, drinkable.

пиха́ть (*pf.* пихну́ть) push, shove.

пи́хта fir.

пи́шущ|ий writing (*a.*); -ая маши́нка typewriter.

пи́ща food.

пища́ль (*f.*) arquebus.

пи|ща́ть (-щу́, -щи́шь; *pf.* пи́скнуть) squeak, chirp.

пищеваре́ние digestion; **пищево́д** gullet; oesophagus; **пищево́й** food (*a.*).

пия́вка leech.

плав: на -ý afloat.

пла́вание sailing, voyage; swimming; **пла́вательный** swimming (*a.*); **пла́вать** sail; swim.

пла́|вень (-вня) flux (*chem.*).

плави́льный melting; **плави́льня** foundry; **пла́вить** (*pf.* рас-) melt; **пла́вка** melting, fusing; **плавле́ние** melting.

пла́вленый: п. сыр processed cheese.

плавни́к (-á) fin, flipper.

пла́вный smooth, fluent; liquid (*sound*).

плаву́чий floating.

плагиа́т plagiarism.

плака́т placard, poster.

пла́|кать (пла́|чу, -ешь; *pf.* за-) weep, cry; **-ся** (на + *acc.*) (*coll.*) complain(of), lament (*over*) ; **пла́к-са** (*m. & f.*) cry-baby; **плакси́вый** weepy; **плаку́чий** weeping (*willow*).

пламене́ть flame, blaze; **пла́менный** flaming, ardent.

пла́|мя (*neut.*; *gen., dat., prep.* -мени, *inst.* -менем) flame(s).

план plan.

планёр glider; **планери́зм** gliding.

плане́та planet; **планета́рий** planetarium; **плане́тный** planetary.

плани́ровать 1. (*pf.* за-, рас-, с-) plan; lay out; 2. (*pf.* с-) glide; **планиро́вка** planning; laying out.

пла́нка lath, plank.

планови́к (-á) planner.

пла́н|овый, ~оме́рный systematic, planned.

планта́тор planter.

пласт (-á) layer, stratum.

пла́стика plastic art; rhythmic plastic movements.

пласти́нка plate; record.

пласт|и́ческий, ~и́чный plastic.

пласт|ма́сса plastic; **~ма́ссовый** plastic (*a.*).

пла́стырь (m.) plaster; patch.
пла́та pay, fee.
плата́н platan, plane tree.
платёж (-а́) payment; платёжеспо-
  со́бный solvent; платёжный pay
  (a.); плате́льщик payer.
пла́тина platinum; пла́тиновый
  platinum (a.).
пл|ати́ть (-ачу́, -а́тишь; pf. за-)
  pay; -ся (pf. по-) pay (fig., e.g.
  with one's life); пла́тный requiring
  payment; paid.
плато́ (indecl.) plateau.
пла|то́к (-тка́) kerchief, handkerchief.
платфо́рма platform; truck.
пла́тье (gen. pl. -ьев) dress, gown;
  clothes; платяно́й clothes (a.).
пла́ха (executioner's) block.
плац|да́рм bridge-/beach-head, base;
  ~ка́рта reserved seat, berth.
плач weeping; плаче́вный lamen-
  table.
плашко́ут pontoon, flat boat.
плашмя́ flat, prone.
плащ (-а́) cloak; raincoat.
плебисци́т plebiscite.
плева́ membrane, film.
плева́ть (плюю́, -ёшь; pf. плю́нуть)
  spit; пле|во́к (-вка́) spit; sputum.
плеври́т pleurisy.
плед rug.
племенно́й tribal; pedigree; пле́|мя
  (neut.; gen., dat., prep. -мени,
  inst. -менем; pl. -мена́, -мён)
  tribe: breed; generation.
племя́н|ник nephew; ~ница niece.
плен (в -у́) captivity.
плена́рный plenary.
плени́тельный captivating; плени́ть
  see пленя́ть.
плёнка film; tape; pellicle.
пле́нник prisoner; пле́нный captive; prisoner.
пле́нум plenary session.
плёнчатый filmy.
плен|я́ть (pf. -и́ть) captivate.
пле́сень (f.) mould.
плеск splash, lapping; пл|еска́ть
  (-ещу́, -е́щешь; pf. плесну́ть)
  splash; lap; -ся splash, lap.
пле́сневеть (pf. за-) grow mouldy/
  musty.
пле|сти́ (-ту, -тёшь; past плёл, -а́;
  ppa. плётший; ppp. плетённый;
  pf. с-) weave; -сь trudge along;
  плетёный wattled, wicker; пле|
  те́нь (-тня́) wattle fence.
плеть (f.; pl. -и, -е́й) lash.

пле́чик|о (pl. -и, -ов) shoulder;
  shoulder-strap; (pl.) clothes-hang-
  er; плечи́стый broad-shouldered;
  плечо́ (pl. пле́чи, плеч, -а́м)
  shoulder; э́то ему́ не по -у́ it's
  beyond him/his strength.
плеши́вый balding.
пли́нтус plinth.
плис velveteen.
плита́ (pl. пли́ты) slab, flagstone;
  stove, cooker; пли́тка tile; cooker;
  пли́точный tiled.
плов pilau.
пло|ве́ц (-вца́) swimmer; пловуче́сть
  (f.) buoyancy; пловучий floating.
плод (-а́) fruit; foetus; пло|ди́ть
  (-жу́, -ди́шь; pf. рас-) procreate;
  -ся propagate; плодови́тый fruitful, fertile.
плодово́дство fruit-growing; плодо́-
  вый fruit (a.).
плодо|ро́дие fertility, fecundity; ~
  ро́дный fertile, fecund; ~тво́рный
  fruitful.
пло́мба stopping, filling (in tooth);
  seal.
пломби́р ice-cream.
пломбирова́ть (pf. за-) fill, stop
  (tooth); seal.
пло́ский flat; trivial.
плоско|го́рье plateau; ~гу́бцы (-цев)
  pliers; ~до́нка flat bottomed boat;
  punt.
пло́скость (f. pl. -и, -е́й) flatness; plane.
плот (-а́) raft.
плотва́ roach.
плоти́на dam, weir; dyke.
пло́тник carpenter; пло́тничное де́ло
  carpentry.
пло́тность (f.) density; пло́тный
  dense, compact, thick, close, tight;
  square (meal).
плотоя́дный carnivorous; пло́тский
  carnal; плоть (f.) flesh.
плохо́й (compr. ху́же, ху́дший) bad;
  wrong.
плоша́дка ground, pitch; platform
  (end of carriage); landing (on
  staircase); площадно́й coarse, foul;
  пло́щад|ь (f.; pl. -и, -е́й) square;
  area.
плуг (pl. -и́) plough.
плут (-а́) rogue; плу́тн|и (-ей) swind-
  le, trickery; плутова́тый roguish;
  плутовско́й roguish; picaresque;
  плуто́вство trickery, imposture.
плыть (плыв|у́, -ёшь; past плыл,
  -а́; pf. по-) swim; float, sail.

плюга́вый mean, shabby.
плю́нуть *see* плева́ть.
плюс plus; advantage.
плюш plush.
плющ (-а́) ivy.
плю́щить *(pf.* с-) flatten; laminate.
пляж beach.
пляс, пля́ска dance; пляса́ть (пляшу́, пля́шешь; *pf.* с-) dance.
пневмати́ческий pneumatic.
по along; through; by; according to; on; по телефо́ну by telephone; по среда́м on Wednesdays; по одному́/два/три one/two/three each.
побе́г 1. flight; escape; 2. shoot, sucker *(bot.)*; побегу́шки *(gen. pl.* -шек) errands.
побе́да victory; победи́тель *(m.)* victor, conqueror; побе́д|ный, ~оно́сный victorious, triumphant; побежда́ть *(pf.* побед|и́ь, -ишь; *ppp.* побеждённый) conquer.
побе́лка whitewashing.
побере́жье coast, seaboard.
побла́|жка *(gen. pl.* -жек) indulgence.
поблёклый faded.
поблёскивать gleam.
поблизости near at hand.
побо́|и (-ев) beating; побо́ище slaughter, bloody battle.
побо́льше a little more; somewhat bigger; a little older.
побо́рник advocate, champion; поб|оро́ть *(pf.* -орю́, -о́реш ь) overcome.
побо́чный accessory, side *(a.)*; natural *(child)*.
побуди́тельный stimulating; motive *(a.)*, prompting; побу́дка reveille; побужда́ть *(pf.* побуди́ть; *ppp.* побуждённый) impel, prompt; побужде́ние incentive, inducement, motive.
побыва́ть *(pf.)* spend time, be; побы́ть* *(pf.)* stay, remain.
пова́дка habit.
пова́льный general, indiscriminate; пова́льно without exception.
по́вар *(pl.* -а́) cook, chef; пова́ренный culinary, cookery *(a.)*; пова́риха cook.
по-ва́шему in your opinion.
пове́дать *(pf.)* relate, reveal.
поведе́ние behaviour.
повеле|ва́ть (-ва́ю; *pf.* повеле́ть*, *coll.)* *(inst.)* rule, command; по-

веле́ние command; повели́тельный imperative; imperious.
поверга́ть *(pf.* пове́рг нуть, *past.* -ёрг) throw down, cast; п. в отча́яние plunge into despair.
пове́ренный lawyer, attorney; п. в дела́х chargé d'affaires; пове́рка verification, checking.
повёртывать *(pf.* поверну́ть) turn; -ся turn (round).
по́верх *(gen.)* over; пове́рхностный superficial; пове́рхность *(f.)* surface; пове́рху on/along the surface.
пове́рье popular belief/superstition.
поверя́ть *(pf.* пове́рить, 1. entrust; 2. check, verify.
пове́са *(m.)* rake, scapegrace.
пове́сить *see* ве́шать.
повествова́ние narrative; повествова́тельный narrative; повествова́ть *(о + prep.)* relate, narrate.
пове́стка notice, summons; agenda.
по́вест|ь *(f.: pl.* -и, -е́й) tale, story.
пове́трие infection.
пове́шение hanging.
повиди́мому apparently.
пови́дло jam.
повили́ка convolvulus.
пови́нность *(f.)* duty, obligation; во́инская п. military service; пови́нн|ый guilty; приноси́ть -ую own up, give oneself up.
повинова́ться *(ipf. & pf.) (dat.)* obey повинове́ние obedience.
повиса́ть *(pf.* пови́снуть*) droop; hang; hover.
по́в|од 1. occasion, cause; 2. (на -оду́, *pl.* -о́дья, -о́дьев) rein.
поводи́ть* *(pf.* повести́*) *(inst.)* move; он и бро́рью не повёл; he didn't bat an e elid.
повозка vehicle, carriage.
повора́чивать *(pf.* поверну́ть) turn; -ся turn (round); поворо́т turn; поворо́тливый agile, quick, manoeuvrable; поворо́тный rotatory, turning; п. круг turn-table.
поврежда́ть *(pf.* повреди́ть*; *ppp.* -еждённый) damage; поврежде́ние damage, injury.
повремени́ть *(pf.)* (с + *inst.)* wait a while (with); повреме́нный periodical; by the hour/week *(pay)*.
повсе|дне́вный everyday; -ме́стный general.
повста́|нец (-нца) insurrectionist, rebel.

повсю́ду everywhere.

повторе́ние repetition; revision; повто́рный repeated; повторя́ть (pf. -и́ть) repeat.

повыша́ть (pf. повы́|сить, -шу, -сишь) raise; -ся rise; повыше́ние rise, increase; повы́шенный high, heightened.

повя́зка bandage; повя́зывать (pf. повяза́ть*) tie.

пога́нка toadstool; пога́ный foul, unclean.

по́гань (f.) filth.

погаша́ть (pf. погаси́ть*) liquidate, pay off; cancel; погаше́ние cancellation.

погиба́ть (pf. поги́бнуть*) perish.

погла́живать (pf. погла́дить*) stroke.

поглоща́ть (pf. погл|оти́ть, -ощу́, -о́тишь; ppp. -ощённ|ли) devour; absorb; поглоще́ние absorption.

погля́дывать (на + acc.) keep casting glances (at); (за + inst.) look after.

погово́рка saying, proverb.

пого́да weather.

пого|ди́ть (pf. -жу́, -ди́шь) (coll.) wait; немно́го погодя́ a little later.

пого́дный yearly.

погол́о́вный reckoned per head; general; поголо́вно one and all.

пого́ловье livestock.

пого́н epaulette.

пого́нщик drover; пого́ня chase, pursuit; погоня́ть drive.

пого́ст graveyard.

пограни́чник frontier-guard; пограни́чный frontier (a.).

по́греб (pl. -á) cellar.

погреба́льный funeral (a.); погреба́ть (pf. погрести́*) bury; погребе́ние burial.

погрему́|шка (gen. pl. -шек) (baby's) rattle.

погреш|а́ть (pf. -и́ть) sin, err; погре́шность (f.) error, mistake.

погружа́ть (pf. погрузи́ть*) plunge, immerse; -ся sink, dive; погруже́ние immersion, submergence; sinking, diving.

погру́зка loading; embarkation.

погряза́ть (pf. погря́|знуть, past -з) wallow.

под (+ inst.) under; near; in the environs of; би́тва под Сталингра́дом the battle of Stalingrad;

(+ acc.) towards (of time); to (e.g. music).

подава́ть* (pf. пода́ть*) give; pass, serve; submit; -ся move; yield, give way.

подавле́ние suppression, repression; пода́вленность (f.) depression; подавля́ть (pf. подави́ть*) suppress; depress; overwhelm.

пода́вно all the more.

пода́гра gout.

пода́льше a little farther (off).

пода́|рок (-рка) present, gift.

пода́тливый pliable, pliant; пода́т|ь (f.; pl. -и, -е́й) (obs.) tax, duty.

пода́ть see подава́ть; пода́ча presenting; feed (tech.); serve (sport); n. голосо́в voting; пода́|чка (gen. pl. -чек) sop; tip; подая́ние charity.

под|бавля́ть (pf. -ба́вить) add, mix in.

под|бега́ть (pf. -бежа́ть*) (к + dat.) run up (to).

подбива́ть (pf. под|би́ть, -обью́*) line (clothes); re-sole (footwear); incite; п. сму́ глаз give him a black eye.

подбира́ть (pf. подобра́ть, подберу́*) pick up; tuck up; sort out; -ся (к + dat.) steal up (to).

подби́ть see подбива́ть.

подбодр|я́ть (pf. -и́ть) cheer up, encourage.

подбо́р choice, selection.

подборо́|док (-дка) chin.

подбоче́нившись with arms akimbo.

под|бра́сывать (pf. -бро́сить*) toss up, throw up.

подва́л basement, cellar.

подве́домственный (dat.) under the jurisdiction (of).

подвезти́ see по.(возить.

подверг|а́ть (pf подве́ргнуть, past -е́рг) expose, subject; -ся (dat.) be exposed (to)' undergo; подве́рженный (dat.) subject (to).

подвёртывать (pf подверну́ть) screw up, tighten; tuck up.

подве́сить see подве́шивать; подвесно́й suspended; подве́сок (-ска) pendant.

подве́тренный leeward

подве́шивать (pf подве́сить*) hang up, suspend

по́двиг exploit, feat

подвига́ть (pf. подви́нуть) move

подви́д sub-species

подви́жник ascetic

подвиж|но́й, -ный, mobile; lively; -но́й соста́в rolling-stock; подви́ж-ность (f.) mobility

подвиза́ться work, act

подви́нуть see подвига́ть

подви́нчивать (pf. подв интить, -инчу́, интишь; ppp -инченный) screw up.

подвла́стный (dat.) subject (to).

подво́да cart

под|води́ть* (pf. -вести́*) bring, place; let down; п. ито́г sum up; п. фунда́мент under-pin.

подво́дн|ый underwater; -ый ка́мень reef; -ая ло́дка submarine.

подво́з supply, transport, lift; под|вози́ть* (pf. -везти́*) bring; give a lift to.

подво́х dirty trick.

подвя́зка garter, suspender; под|вя́зывать (pf. -вяза́ть*) tie up.

подгиба́ть (pf. подогну́ть) tuck up.

под|гля́дывать (pf. -гляде́ть*) peep, spy.

под|гова́ривать (pf. -говори́ть) (на + acc. or inf.) incite (to).

подгоня́ть (pf. подогна́ть*, подгоню́) drive on; (к + dat.) adjust (to).

под|гора́ть (pf. -горе́ть*) get burnt.

подго́рье foot of mountain/of hill.

подгот|а́вливать, -овля́ть (pf. -о́вить) (к + dat.) prepare (for) -ся prepare (oneself); подготови́тельный preparatory; подгото́вка preparation.

под|греба́ть (pf. -грести́*) rake up.

под|дава́ть* (pf. -да́ть*) strike, kick; give away (at chess); add; -ся yield; э́то не -даётся описа́нию it defies description.

подда́кивать (pf. подда́кнуть) agree, say 'yes'.

по́дданный subject; по́дданство citizenship.

подда́ть see поддава́ть.

поддёвка (long-waisted) man's coat.

подде́лка falsification, imitation, forgery; под|де́лывать (pf. -де́лать) counterfeit, forge; подде́льный false, fake.

под|де́рживать (pf. -держа́ть*) maintain, support; подде́ржка support.

под|дра́знивать (pf. -дразни́ть*) tease.

поде́лать (pf.) do; ничего́ не поде́лаешь there's nothing one can do; поде́лка odd job; article, item.

подело́м: п. ему́ it serves him right.

подённый daily, by the day; подёнщик day-labourer/-worker.

подёргивать pull, tug; -ся twitch.

подержа́ние: взять на п. borrow; поде́ржанный second-hand.

подёрнуть (pf.) cover.

под|жа́ривать (pf. -жа́рить) fry, grill, roast, toast; поджа́ристый brown(ed).

поджа́рый lean, meagre.

поджа́ть see поджима́ть.

поджига́тель (m.) incendiary; instigator; поджига́ть (pf. под|же́чь, -ожгу́*) set on fire.

поджида́ть (pf. подожда́ть*) await; lie in wait (for).

поджи́|лки (-лок) hamstring, tendon.

поджима́ть (pf. под|жа́ть, -ожму́*) press, push, purse (lips); п. под себя́ но́ги sit cross-legged.

поджо́г arson.

подзаголо́|вок (-вка) heading.

под|заго́ривать (pf. -задо́рить) egg on.

подзащи́тный client (law).

подземе́лье cave, dungeon.

подзо́рная труба́ spy-glass, telescope.

подзыва́ть (pf. подозва́ть, подзову́*) call, summon, beckon.

поди́ 1. go!; 2. I shouldn't wonder, no doubt.

под|ка́лывать (pf. -коло́ть*) pin up.

под|ка́пывать (pf. -копа́ть) undermine.

подкарау́л|ивать (pf. -ить) be on the watch (for).

под|ка́рмливать (pf. -корми́ть*) feed.

под|ка́тывать (pf. -кати́ть*) roll, drive up.

под|ка́шивать (pf. -коси́ть*) cut (down); -ся: у него́ но́ги подкоси́лись his legs gave way.

под|ки́дывать (pf. -ки́нуть) throw up.

подкла́дка lining; под|кла́дывать (pf. -ложи́ть, -ложу́, -ло́жишь) put (under); add.

подко́ва horseshoe; под|ко́вывать (pf. -кова́ть*) shoe (a horse); подко́ванный в + prep. well versed in.

подко́жный hypodermic.

подкомите́т sub-committee.

подкóп undermining; подкопáть see подкáпывать.

подкосúть see подкáшивать.

под|крáдываться (pf. -крáсться*) (к + dat.) creep up (to).

под|крáшивать (pf. -крáсить*) colour, tint.

подкрепле́ние confirmation; reinforcement; подкреп|ля́ть (pf. -йть) confirm, corroborate; refresh; reinforce.

пóдкуп bribery; под|купáть (pf. -купúть*) bribe, suborn; win over; подкупнóй venal.

под|лáживаться (pf. -лáдиться*) (к + dat.) adapt oneself (to), make up (to).

пóдле (gen.) near.

подлежáть* (dat.) be subject (to); не подлежúт сомне́нию it is beyond doubt; подлежáщее subject (gram.).

под|лезáть (pf. -пéзть*) (к + acc.) creep (under).

подле́|сок (-ска) undergrowth.

под|летáть (pf. -лете́ть*) (к + dat.) fly up (to), rush up (to).

подле́ц (-á) scoundrel.

подливáть (pf. под|лúть, -олью́*) pour in, add; подлúвка dressing, gravy, sauce.

подлиза (m. & f.) lickspittle, toady; под|лúзываться (pf. -лизáться*) (к + dat.) suck up (to).

пóдлинник original; пóдлинный authentic, genuine, original, real.

подлúть see подливáть.

подлóг forgery.

подложúть see подклáдывать.

подлóжный false, spurious.

подлокóтник elbow-rest.

пóдлый mean, base.

под|мáзывать (pf. -мáзать*) grease, oil; (coll.) bribe.

подмасте́р|ье (m.; gen. pl. -ьев) apprentice.

под|мáчивать (pf. -мочúть*) wet slightly.

подме́на substitution; под|ме́нивать or -меня́ть (pf. -менúть, -меню́, -ме́нишь) substitute.

подме́тить see подмечáть.

подме́тка sole (of shoe).

под|мечáть (pf. -ме́тить*) notice.

под|ме́шивать (pf. -мешáть) add, mix in; п. сáхару (в + acc.) add sugar (to).

под|мúгивать (pf. -мигну́ть) wink.

подмóга help.

подмоскóвный Moscow (a.), situated near Moscow.

подмóстк|и (-ов) stage; scaffolding.

подмочúть see подмáчивать.

под|мывáть (pf. -мы́ть*) wash; undermine; егó так и подмывáет (+ inf.) he feels a great urge (to).

подмы́|шка (gen. pl. -шек) armpit.

поднадзóрный person under surveillance.

поднебе́сье skies.

подневóльный dependent; forced.

поднимáть (pf. под|нúму, -нúмешь; past пóднял, -á; ppp. пóднятый) raise; -ся rise.

поднов|ля́ть (pf. -úть) renew, renovate.

подногóтн|ая: узнáть всю -ую learn all the ins and outs.

поднóжие foot (of hill); pedestal; поднó|жка (gen. pl. -жек) step, footboard; backheel (sport).

поднóжный корм pasture.

поднóс tray, salver; под|носúть* (pf. -нестú*) bring, take; present; подноше́ние gift; tribute.

подня́тие raising; подня́ть see поднимáть.

подобáть (dat. + inf.) befit, become; подобáющий proper.

подóбие likeness, similarity; подóбн|ый (+ dat) similar (to); и тому́ -ое and so on; подóбно (+ dat.) like.

подобо|стрáстие servility; ~стрáстный servile.

подобрáть see подбирáть; подогнáть see подгоня́ть; подогну́ть see подгибáть.

подо|гревáть (-гревáю; pf. -гре́ть*) warm up.

подо|двигáть (pf. -двúнуть) (к + dat.) move up (to).

пододе́яльник blanket cover, sheet.

подождáть see подждáть; подозвáть see подзывáть.

подозревáть (-евáю) (в + prep.) suspect (of); подозре́ние suspicion; подозрúтельный suspicious, suspect.

подóйник milk-pail.

подойтú see подходúть.

подокóнник window-sill.

подóл hem.

подóлгу long, for hours/days etc.

подóнк|и (-ов) dregs; scum, riffraff.

подопе́чный under wardship, trust (a.).

подоплёка background.

подо́пытный under experiment; п. кро́лик (fig.) guinea-pig.

подорва́ть see подрыва́ть.

подоро́жная order for post-horses; подоро́жник plantain; подоро́жный roadside (a.).

подосла́ть see подсыла́ть.

подоспе́ть (pf.) (coll.) arrive in time.

подостла́ть see подстила́ть.

подотде́л section, subdivision.

подоткну́ть see подтыка́ть.

подотчётный accountable.

подохо́дный нало́г income tax.

подо́шва sole (of foot, shoe); foot (of hill).

под|пада́ть (pf. -па́сть*) fall.

под|па́ливать (pf. -пали́ть*) singe.

под|па́рывать (pf. -поро́ть*) unpick, unstitch.

подпа́сть see подпада́ть.

подпева́ла (m. & f. coll.) yes-man; подпева́ть (-ева́ю;) (dat.) join in (singing).

под|пи́ливать (pf. -пили́ть*) saw down, shorten; подпи́|лок (-лка) file.

подпира́ть (pf. подпере́ть, подопру́|у, -ёшь; past подпёр; ppp. подпёртый) prop up.

подпи́ска subscription; подписно́й subscription (a.); подпи́счик subscriber; под|пи́сывать (pf. -писа́ть*) sign; -ся sign; (на + acc.) subscribe (to); по́дпись (f.) signature.

под|плыва́ть (pf. -плы́ть*) (к + dat.) swim/sail/row up (to).

под|полза́ть (pf. -ползти́*) (к + dat.) creep up (to); (под + acc.) crawl under.

подполко́вник lieutenant-colonel.

подпо́лье cellar; (clandestine) underground; подпо́льный underfloor; underground (a.); подпо́ль|щик, ~щица member of secret underground group.

подпо́р(к)а support, prop.

подпоро́ть see подпа́рывать.

подпору́чик (obs.) second lieutenant.

подпо́чва sub-soil.

подпоя́сывать (pf. подпо|я́сать, -я́шу, -я́шешь) belt, girdle.

под|правля́ть (pf. -пра́вить) adjust, correct.

подпру́га saddle-girth, belly-band.

под|пры́гивать (pf. -пры́гнуть) jump/hop up and down.

под|пуска́ть (pf. -пусти́ть*) (к + dat.) allow to approach.

подража́ние imitation; подража́тель (m.) imitator; подража́тельный imitative; подража́ть (dat.) imitate.

подразделе́ние subdivision; подразделя́ть (pf. -и́ть) sub-divide.

подразумева́ть (-ева́ю) mean; -ся be implied, meant.

под|раста́ть (pf. -расти́*) grow up rise.

под|реза́ть, -ре́зывать (pf. -ре́зать*) cut, clip, trim.

подрис|о́вывать (pf. -ова́ть) touch up.

подро́бность (f.) detail; подро́бный detailed.

подро́с|ток (-тка) juvenile, youth.

под|руба́ть (pf. -руби́ть*) hew; hem.

подру́га (female) friend; по-дру́жески in friendly fashion.

подрум|я́нивать (pf. -я́нить) paint, touch up with rouge.

подру́чный at hand; apprentice (as noun).

подры́в harm, injury; подрыва́ть 1. (pf. подорва́ть*) blow up; 2. (pf. подры́ть*) undermine, sap; подрывно́й blasting (a.); undermining, subversive.

подря́д 1. in succession, running; 2. contract; подря́дчик contractor.

под|са́живать (pf. -сади́ть, -сажу́, -са́дишь) help to a seat; -ся (pf. -се́сть*) (к + dat.) sit near (to).

подса́ливать (pf. -соли́ть*) add salt to, salt.

подсве́чник candlestick.

подсе́кция subsection.

подсе́сть see подса́живаться.

под|си́живать (pf. -сиде́ть*) lie in wait for; (fig.) intrigue against.

под|ска́зывать (pf. -сказа́ть*) (dat.) prompt, whisper (to).

под|ска́кивать 1. (pf. подск|очи́ть, -очу́, -о́чишь) (к + dat.) run up (to); jump; 2. (pf. -скака́ть*) (к + dat.) gallop up (to).

подсла́щивать (pf. подсла|сти́ть, -щу́, -сти́шь) sweeten.

подсле́дственный under investigation.

подслеповáтый weak-sighted.
под|слýшивать (pf. -слýшать) over-
hear, eavesdrop on.
под|смáтривать (pf. -смотрéть*) spy
on.
подсмéиваться (над + inst.)' make
fun (of).
подсмотрéть see подсмáтривать.
подснéжник snowdrop.
подсóбный subsidiary, auxiliary.
под|сóвывать (pf. -сýнуть) (под
+ acc.) shove, push under; (acc.
— sth., dat. — smb.) palm off (on).
подсознáтельный subconscious.
подсолúть see подсáливать.
подсóлнечник sunflower; подсóл-
нечный sunflower (a.).
подсóхнуть see подсыхáть.
подспóрье (coll.) help.
подспýдный hidden, latent.
подстáвка support, rest; под|став-
лять (pf. -стáвить) (под + acc.)
put under; hold up, offer; substitute (maths.); п. емý нóгу trip
him up; подставнóй false.
подстакáнник glass-holder.
подстанóвка substitution.
подстáнция sub-station.
под|стёгивать (pf. -стегнýть; ppp.
-стёгнут й) whip; (fig.) urge on
под|стерегáть (pf. -стеречь*) lie in
wait for.
под|стилáть (pf. подостлáть, под-
стелю*) spread, lay; подстúлка
bedding.
под|страивать (pf. -стрóить) (coll.)
tune up (mus).; concoct, contrive.
это дéло подстрóено it's a put-up
job.
подстрекáтель (m.) instigator; под-
стрекáтельство incitement; подстрекáть (pf. подстрекнýть) excite (e. g. curiosity); (к + dat.)
incite (to).
под|стрéливать (pf. подстрел|úть,
-елю, -елишь) wound (by shooting).
под|стригáть (pf. -стричь*) clip,
trim.
подстрóить see подстрáивать.
подстрóчный line-by-line; foot (a.)
(eg. note).
пóдступ approach; под|ступáть (pf.
-ступúть*) (к + dat.) approach.
подсудúмый defendant, accused;
подсýдный (dat.) under the competence (of).
подсýнуть see подсóвывать.

под|сýшивать (pf. -сушúть*) (v. t.)
dry a little.
подсчёт calculation, counting; под|
считывать (pf. -считáть) count up,
calculate.
подсылáть (pf. подослáть*) send.
под|сыпáть (pf. -сыпать*) add, pour
in.
под|сыхáть (pf. -сóхнуть*) (v. i.)
dry a little.
под|тáлкивать (pf. -толкнýть) push;
urge on.
под|тáскивать (pf. -тащúть*) (к
+ dat.) drag up (to).
подтас|óвывать unfairly shuffle; п.
фáкты juggle with the facts.
под|тáчивать (pf. -точúть) sharpen;
sap, undermine.
подтащúть see подтáскивать.
под|твер|ждáть (pf. -твердúть*; ppp.
-тверждённый) confirm, corroborate; подтверждéние confor-
mation.
подтёк bruise; под|текáть (pf. -течь*)
(под + acc.) flow (under); leak.
подтéкст implication.
подтолкнýть see подтáлкивать; под-
точúть see подтáчивать.
под|трýнивать (pf. -трунúть) (над
+ inst.) chaff, mock.
под|тыкáть (pf. подоткнýть) (coll.)
tuck up/in.
под|тягивать (pf. -тянýть) (к
+ dat.) pull up; bring up; tighten
подтя|жки (-жек) braces, sus-
penders.
подýмывать (pf. подýмать) think.
подý|шка (gen. pl. -шек) cushion,
pillow.
подхалúм, ~ка toady; подхалúмство
grovelling, toadyism.
под|хвáтывать (pf. -хватúть*) catch,
pick up.
под|хлёстывать (pf. -хлестнýть; ppp.
-хлёстнут й) whip up, urge on.
подхóд approach; подходúть *(pf.
подойтú*) (к + dat.) come up (to),
approach; fit; suit; подходящий
suitable.
под|цеплять (pf. подцеп|úть, -еплю,
-епишь) hook/pick up.
подчáс (coll.) sometimes.
под|чёркивать (pf. -черкнýть; ppp.
-ёркнутый) underline; emphasize.
подчинéние subjection; подчин|ять
(pf. -úть) subject, subordinate;
-ся (dat.) submit (to).

под|чищáть *(pf. -чи́стить*)* rub out, erase.

подшéфный under patronage/protection.

подшивáть *(pf.* подши́ть, подошью́*) sew; hem; line; sole.

подши́пник bearing.

подши́ть *see* подшивáть.

под|шу́чивать *(pf. -шути́ть*)* (над + *inst.*) chaff, mock.

подъéзд approach; entrance; **подъезжáть** *(pf.* подъéхать*) (к + *dat.*) drive up (to).

подъём lifting; ascent; rise; **подъём-ник** elevator, hoist; **подъёмный** lifting *(a.).*

подъéхать *see* подъезжáть.

подымáть = поднимáть.

поды́скивать *(pf.* под|ыскáть, -ыщу́, -ы́щешь) seek out.

подытóживать *(pf.* подытóжить) sum up.

подыхáть *(pf.* подóхнуть*) die *(of animals).*

поедáть *see* поéсть*) eat.

поеди́н|ок (-нка) duel.

пóезд *(pl.* -á) train; **поéздка** trip, excursion; **поездно́й** train *(a.).*

поёмный flooded in spring, water *(a.)*

пожáловать *(pf.)* come; добрó п. welcome!

пожáлуй perhaps.

пожáлуйста please.

пожáр fire, conflagration; **пожáрище** site of a fire, ruins; **пожáрник** fireman; **пожáрный** fire *(a.).*

пожáтие press, shake *(of hand);* **пожáть** *see* пожимáть & пожинáть.

пожелáние wish.

пожелтéлый yellowed.

пожéртование donation.

пожив|áть: как вы -áете? how are you getting on?

пожи́зненный life *(a.),* lifelong.

пожило́й elderly.

пожимáть *(pf.* по|жáть, -жму́*) press; **п. плечáми** shrug one's shoulders.

пожинáть *(pf.* по|жáть, -жну́*) reap.

пожирáть *(pf.* пожрáть*) devour.

пожи́тк|и (-ов) belongings, things.

пóза pose.

позавчерá the day before yesterday.

позади́ behind; *(gen.)* behind.

позапрóшлый before last.

позволéние permission; **позволи́тель-ный** permissible; **позволя́ть** *(pf.* позвóлить) permit, allow *(acc. — sth.) (dat. — smb.).*

позво|нóк (-нкá) vertebra; **позво-нóчник** spine; **позвонóчный** vertebrate.

пóздний *(comp.* пóзже) late; **пóздно** late.

поздрави́тельный congratulatory; **поздравлéние** congratulation; **поздравля́ть** *(pf.* поздрáвить) (с + *inst.*) congratulate.

поземéльный налóг land tax.

пóзже later.

пози́ровать pose.

позити́в positive *(phot.);* **позити́в-ный** positive *(a.).*

пози́ция position.

позн|авáть (-аю́, -аёшь; *pf.* познáть) get to know; **познáние** cognition.

позолóта gilding.

позóр shame; **позóрить** *(pf.* о-) disgrace; **-ся** disgrace oneself; **по-зóрный** shameful.

позы́в urge, inclination; **позывнóй** call *(a.).*

по́йлка drinking fountain; feeding-cup.

поимённо by name; **поимённый спи́-сок** list of names.

поймка capture.

поиму́щественный налóг property tax.

по-инóму differently.

пóиск search.

пои́стине indeed.

пои́ть *(pf.* на-) give to drink; water.

по-и́хнему in their way.

пóйло swill.

поймáть *(pf.)* catch.

пойти́ *see* идти́.

покá *(ad.)* for the present; *(c.)* while.

покáз show, demonstration; **покá-зáние** testimony, statement; **покá-зáтель** *(m.)* index; **показáтель-ный** model, demonstration *(a.);* significant; **показнóй** show, ostentatious; **покáзывать** *(pf.* показáть*) show; **-ся** show oneself, come into view.

покáлыв|ать: у меня́ -ает в боку́ I keep getting a stitch in my side.

покáмест *(coll.)* meanwhile.

покáтость *(f.)* slope; **покáтый** slanting, sloping.

покачивать rock; -ся rock; walk unsteadily.

покашливать have a slight cough.

покаяние confession, repentance.

поквитаться *(pf.)* call quits, get even.

покидать *(pf.* покинуть) abandon, leave.

покладая: не п. рук indefatigably.

покладистый complaisant, obliging.

поклон bow; greetings; поклонение worship; поклониться *see* кланяться; поклон|ник, ~ница worshipper, admirer; поклоняться *(dat.)* worship.

покоиться rest, repose.

покой rest, peace; *(coll.)* room, chamber.

покой|ник, ~ница the deceased; покойницкая mortuary; покойный 1. quiet, calm; 2. deceased.

поколение generation.

покончить *(pf.)* (с + *inst.)* finish off; п. с собой commit suicide.

покорение subjugation; покорный obedient, submissive.

покор|ять *(pf.* -ить) subjugate, subdue; -ся *(dat.)* submit (to).

покос haymaking, mowing.

покрапывать drizzle.

покров cover; shroud.

покровитель *(m.)* patron, protector; ~ственный protective; patronizing; ~ство patronage, protection; ~ствовать *(dat.)* be patron to, protect.

покрой cut *(of clothes)*.

покрывало shawl, veil; counterpane; покрывать *(pf.* покрыть*)* cover; -ся be covered; cover oneself; покрытие payment *(of debts)*, defrayment; roofing; покры|шка *(gen. pl.* -шек) cover.

покупатель, ~ница buyer, customer; покупательный purchasing; покупать *(pf.* купить, куплю, купишь) buy, purchase; покупка purchase; покупной bought; purchasing, purchase *(a.)*.

покушаться *(pf.* покуситься, -шусь, -сишься) (на + *acc.)* attempt; encroach (on); покушение attempt; encroachment.

пол 1. (на -у, *pl.* -ы) floor; 2. *(pl.* -ы, n -ов) sex.

пол- half-.

пола *(pl.* полы) skirt.

полагать suppose; -ся 1. be supposed; be due; 2. *(pf.* положиться,

-ожусь, -ожишься) (на + *acc.)* rely (on).

полат|и (-ей) sleeping shelf *(between stove and wall)*.

полвека *(gen.* полувека) half a century; полгода *(gen.* полугода) half a year; полдень *(gen.* полудня or полдня) midday; полдороги half way; остановиться на полдороге stop half way.

поле *(pl.* -я) field; (back)ground; margin; brim *(of hat)*; полевой field *(a.)*; wild.

полезный useful, helpful.

полемизировать argue, enter / into polemics; полемика polemics.

поле|но *(pl.* -нья, -ньев) log.

полесье wooded district.

полёт flight.

ползать crawl, creep; ползком on all fours; пол|зти (-зу, -зёшь, *past* полз) crawl, creep; ползучий creeping.

полива glaze.

поливать *(pf.* полить*)* pour; water; поливка watering.

полигон polygon.

поликлиника polyclinic.

полинезийский Polynesian.

полинялый faded, discoloured.

полировать *(pf.* на-, от-) polish; полировка polishing; полировщик polisher.

полис policy *(e. g. insurance)*.

полисмен, ~ка policeman/policewoman.

полит- political.

поли|техникум polytechnic; ~технический polytechnic *(a.)*.

политик politician; политика politics; политикан intriguer; политический political; политичный politic; политрук political instructor.

политура polish, varnish.

полить *see* поливать.

полицейский police *(a.)*; policeman; полиция police.

полич|ное: поймать с -ым catch redhanded.

полк (-а, в -у) regiment.

полка shelf.

полковник colonel; полково|дец (-дца) military leader, general; полковой regimental.

полмиллиона half a million.

полнеть *(pf.* по-) grow stout, put on weight.

полно! enough!

полно|вéсный having full weight; sound; ~влáстный sovereign (a.); ~вóдье high water; ~крóвный full-blooded; plethoric; ~лýние full moon; ~метрáжный full-length (e. g. film); ~мóчие authority, plenary powers; ~мóчный plenipotentiary; ~прáвный competent, enjoying full rights.

пóлностью completely; полнотá completeness; plenitude; corpulence.

полноцéнный of full value, valuable.

пóлночь (f.; gen. полýночи or пóлночи) midnight.

пóлный full, complete.

половúк (-á) mat.

половúна half; половúнчатый indecisive, half-and-half.

половúца floorboard.

половóдье flood, high water.

половóй 1. floor (a.); 2. sexual.

пóлог canopy, curtain.

полóгий gently sloping.

положéние position, situation; condition, state; regulations, statute.

полóженный fixed, prescribed; полóжим let us assume.

положúтельный positive.

положúть see класть & полагáть.

пóлоз (pl. -óзья, -óзьɛг) runner.

полóльник hoe; полóльный weeding (a.).

полóмка breakage.

поло|мóйка (gen. pl. -мóек) charwoman.

полосá (пóлосу, pl. пóлосы, полóс, -áм) stripe, strip; region, belt; period; полосáтый striped; полóска strip(e); в -у striped.

пол|оскáть (-ощý, -óщɛшь; pf. вы-про-) gargle, rinse; -ся paddle (in water); flap.

пóлость (f. pl. -й, -éй) cavity.

полотé|нце (gen. pl. -нɛц) towel.

полотёр floor-polisher.

полóтнище width (of cloth); section, panel; пол|отнó (pl. -óтна, -óтɛн) linen; canvas; bed (of road); полотнянный linen.

полóть (полю, пóлɛшь; ppp. пóлотый; pf. вы-) weed.

полпрéд (полномóчный представúтель) plenipotentiary.

полпутú (m., indecl.) half-way.

полслóв|а (не -е) half a word; с -а понимáть be quick on the uptake.

полтúна, полтúнник (coll.) fifty copecks.

полторá (m. & gen. полýтора), полторы́ (f., gen. полýтора) one and a half; полторáста (gen. полýтораста) a hundred and fifty.

полу- semi-, half-.

полубáк forecastle, fo'c'sle.

полуботúнки (-нок) low shoes.

полугóдие half year; ~годúчный, полугодовóй half-yearly, semi-annual; полугодовáлый six-months-old.

полугрáмотный semi-literate.

полýда tinning.

полýденный midday; (poet.) southern.

полузащúтник half-back (sport).

полукрýг semicircle; ~крýглый semicircular.

полумёртвый more dead than alive.

полумéсяц half-moon, crescent.

полумéсячный fortnightly.

полунóчничать burn the midnight oil; ~нóчный midnight; (poet) northern.

полуóстров peninsula.

полупроводнúк (-á) semi-conductor.

полуразрýшенный tumbledown.

полуслóво = полслóва.

полутéнь (f.) penumbra.

полуфабрикáт half-finished product; prepared food;

полуфинáльная игрá semi-final;

получасовóй half-hourly.

получáтель (m.) recipient; получáть (pf. пол|учúть, -учý, -ýчишь) receive, obtain; -ся come; be received; turn out; получéние receipt; полý|чка (gen. pl. -чек) (coll.) sum received; pay.

полушáрие hemisphere.

полýшка a quarter-copeck piece.

полцены́: купúть за п. buy at half price, very cheaply.

полчасá (gen. получáса) half an hour.

пóлчище horde.

пóлый 1. hollow; 2. flood (a.).

пóлымя (n., obs.) flame, fire.

полы́нь (f.) wormwood.

полы́|ньá (gen. pl. -нéй) unfrozen patch of water on frozen surface.

пóльз|а use; benefit; в -у (gen.) in favour of; пóльзование use; пóльзоваться (pf. вос-) (inst.) make use of, use; enjoy (e.g. confidence).

по́|лька *(gen. pl.* -лек) Pole *(woman)*; polka; по́льский Polish.
полюбо́вный amicable.
по́люс pole.
поля́к Pole.
поля́на glade, clearing.
поляриза́ция polarization; поля́рник polar explorer; поля́рный polar.
пома́да pomade; губна́я п. lipstick.
пома́зание anointment; пома́занник the Lord's anointed.
пома|зо́к (-зка́) small brush.
пома́рка blot; pencil mark, correction.
пома́хивать *(inst.)* wave, wag.
поме́ньше somewhat smaller/less.
помертве́лый deathly pale.
помести́тельный spacious, capacious; помести́ть *see* помеща́ть.
поме́ст|ье *(gen. pl.* -ий) estate.
по́месь *(f.)* cross-bred, hybrid.
поме́сячный monthly.
помёт 1. dung, droppings; 2. litter, brood.
поме́тить *see* помеча́ть; поме́тка mark.
поме́ха hindrance, obstacle; interference.
помеча́ть *(pf.* поме́тить*)* mark; date.
поме́шанный mad; он поме́шан на футбо́ле he's mad about football; помеша́тельство madness, insanity; craze; помеша́ться *(pf.)* go mad; become obsessed.
помеща́ть *(pf.* поме|сти́ть, -щу́, -сти́шь) place, locate; accommodate; invest, -ся be accommodated; go/fit in; be situated; помеще́ние location; lodging, room, premises.
поме́|щик, ~щица landowner.
помидо́р tomato.
поми́лование pardon, forgiveness; поми́ловать *(pf.)* pardon; поми́луй(те)! for goodness sake!
поми́мо *(gen.)* besides, apart from; without someone's knowledge.
поми́н: лёгок на -е talk of the devil; помина́ть *(pf.* помяну́ть) mention; pray for; не п. ли́хом think kindly (of); помина́й, как зва́ли and that was the last ever heard *(of him, etc.).*
поми́|нки (-нок) funeral feast.
помину́тно every minute.
помира́ть *(pf.* помере́ть*) (coll.)* die.

по́мнить remember.
помно́гу a lot; in plenty.
помно|жа́ть *(pf.* помно́жить) (на) multiply (by).
помога́ть *(pf.* помо́чь*) (dat.)* help.
по-мо́ему in my opin'on.
помо́|и (-ев) slops; помо́йный slop, rubbish *(a.).*
помо́л grinding.
помо́лвить *(pf.)* engage, betroth; помо́лвка engagement, betrothal.
помо́рье littoral, coastal region.
помо́ст rostrum, platform.
помо́ч|и (-ей) leading reins; braces.
помо́чь *see* помога́ть; помо́щ|ник ~ница assistant; по́мощь *(f.)* help, assistance; пе́рвая п., ско́рая п. first aid.
по́мпа 1. pump; 2. pomp.
помрачи́ться *(pf.)* become dimmed.
по́мы|сел (-сла) plan, thought; помышля́ть *(pf.* помы́слить) think; помышле́ние thought.
помяну́ть *see* помина́ть.
помя́тый crumpled; *(coll.)* flabby.
пона́добиться *(pf.)* prove necessary.
понапра́сну *(coll.)* in vain.
понаслы́шке by hearsay.
по-на́шему in our opinion; in our way.
понево́ле willy-nilly.
понеде́льник Monday.
понемн|о́гу, ~о́жку a little at a time.
пони|жа́ть *(pf.* пон|и́зить, -и́жу, -и́зишь) lower, reduce; demote; пони́же́ние fall, lowering; demotion.
понизо́вье lower reaches.
по́низу low, along the ground surface.
поника́ть *(pf.* пони́кнуть*)* droop.
понима́ние understanding; понима́ть *(pf.* поня́ть, пой|му́, -мёшь; по́нял, -а́; *ppp.* по́нятый) understand; realize.
поно|жо́вщина knifing.
пономар|ь (-я́) sexton.
поно́с diarrhoea.
поноси́ть* 1. abuse, revile; 2. *(pf.)* carry/wear for a while.
поноше́ние abuse.
поно́шенный threadbare, worn.
понто́н pontoon.
пону|жда́ть *(pf.* пон|у́дить, -у́жу, -у́дишь; *ppp.* -уждённый) force, compel; понужде́ние compulsion.

понука́ть (coll.) urge/drive on.
пону́ривать (pf. пону́рить) hang (one's head); пону́рый downcast.
по́нчик doughnut.
поню́|шка (gen. pl. -шек) pinch (of snuff).
поня́тие idea, notion; conception; поня́тливый quick (in understanding); поня́тный clear, understandable; поня́той witness; поня́ть see понима́ть.
поо́даль at some distance.
поодино́чке one at a time.
поочерёдный by/in turn.
поощре́ние encouragement; поощр|я́ть (pf. -и́ть) encourage, give incentive to.
поп(-а́) priest.
попада́ние hit; попада́ть (pf. попа́сть*) (в + acc.) hit; (в/на + acc.) get into/onto; мне попа́ло I caught it!; как попа́ло anyhow; -ся be caught; be met.
попад|ья́ (gen. pl. -е́й) priest's wife.
попа́рно in pairs, two by two.
попа́сть see попада́ть.
поперёк (gen.) across.
попереме́нно in turn, alternately.
попере́чина cross-beam, jib; попере́чник diameter; попере́чный diametrical, transverse, cross; ка́ждый встре́чный и п. any Tom, Dick or Harry.
поперхну́ться (pf.) choke.
попече́н|ие care; на -ии ÷ gen. in the care of; попечи́тель, ~ница trustee, guardian.
попира́ть (pf. по|пра́ть, -пру, -прёшь) trample on, flout.
попи́скивать cheep.
попла|во́к (-вка́) float.
попли́н poplin.
попо́вник marguerite.
поп|о́йка (gen. pl. -о́ек) drinking bout.
попола́м in two, in half.
поползнове́ние wish; pretension.
пополне́ние replenishment, reinforcement; пополня́ть (pf. попо́лнить) replenish, fill up, replace (losses).
полу́дни in the afternoon.
попо́на horse-cloth.
попра́вка recovery; repair; amendment; поправле́ние correction; restoration; поправля́ть (pf. попра́вить) repair; correct; set

straight; -ся get well, recover; improve.
попра́ть see попира́ть.
по-пре́жнему as before.
попрёк reproach; попрека́ть (pf. попрекну́ть) reproach.
по́прище field, walk of life.
по́просту simply, without ceremony.
попрош|а́йка (m. & f.; gen. pl. -а́ек) cadger, beggar.
попуга́й parrot.
популяризова́ть (ipf. & pf.) popularize; популя́рный popular.
попусти́тельст|во connivance; ~вовать (dat.) connive (at).
по́пусту in vain, to no purpose.
попу́тный passing; попу́тчик fellow-traveller.
попы́тка attempt.
по́ра pore.
пора́ (acc. по́ру) time; с каки́х пор? since when?; пора́ домо́й it's time to go home.
порабо́ти́тель (m.) oppressor, enslaver; порабоща́ть (pf. порабо́|тить, -щу́, -ти́шь) enslave; enthral; порабоще́ние enslavement, enthralment.
поравня́ться (pf.) (с + inst.) come alongside, come up (with).
поража́ть (pf. порази́ть*) strike, hit, startle; пораже́ние defeat; пораже́нчество defeatism; порази́тельный striking, startling.
пора́ньше a little sooner.
порва́ть see порыва́ть & рвать.
поре́з cut; поре́зать* (pf.) cut; -ся cut oneself.
поре́й leek.
по́ристый porous.
порица́ние blame, censure, reproach; порица́ть blame, censure, reproach.
по́рка flogging.
по́ровну equally.
поро́г threshold; (pl.) rapids.
поро́да 1. race, breed, species; 2. rock; поро́дистый thoroughbred, pedigree (a.).
порожда́ть (pf. породи́ть*) give birth to, engender.
поро́жний (coll.) empty; порожня́к (-а́) empty wagons.
по́рознь separately, apart.
поро́й at times.
поро́к vice; defect.
поросё|нок (-нка; pl., -ся́та, -ся́т) piglet.
по́росль (f.) young shoots/growth.

порóть (порю, пóрешь) **1.** *(pf.* от-, рас-) undo, unpick; **2.** *(pf.* вы-) thrash, whip; **3.** п. ерундý talk nonsense.

пóрох (gun) powder; он -а не выдумает he won't set the world on fire; **порохóвóй** (gun)powder *(a.).*

порóчить *(pf.* о-) cover with shame; discredit.

порóчный vicious, depraved; faulty.

порóша first snow; **порошúть** to snow slightly.

поро|шóк (-шкá) powder.

порт (в -ý, *pl.* -ы, -óв) port, harbour; port-hole.

портáл portal; gantry.

портатúвный portable.

портвéйн port (wine).

пóртик portico.

пóр|тить (-чу, -тишь; *pf.* ис-) spoil, corrupt; -ся deteriorate, go bad.

портнúха dressmaker; **портнóй** tailor.

портóв|ик (-á) docker; **портóвый** port *(a.).*

портрéт portrait.

портсигáр cigarette-case, cigar-case.

португ|áлец (-áльца), ∼áлка Portuguese; -áльский Portuguese *(a.).*

портфéль *(m.)* briefcase; portfolio.

портьéра door-curtain.

порýбка illegal cutting of timber.

поругáние profanation, desecration; **порýганный** profaned; insulted.

порýка, порýки bail, guarantee.

по-рýсски in Russian.

поручáть *(pf.* пор|учúть, -учý, -ýчишь) entrust; **поручéние** assignment, commission, errand.

пóру|чень (-чня) *(usually pl.)* handrail.

порýчик *(obs.)* lieutenant.

поручúтель, ∼ница guarantor; **поручúтельство** guarantee, bail.

поручúть *see* поручáть.

поручúться *see* ручáться.

порфúр porphyry.

порфúра purple.

порхáть *(pf.* порхнýть) flit, flutter.

пóрция portion, helping.

пóрча damage; spoiling.

пóр|шень (-шня) piston.

порыв 1. gust *(of wind)*; **2.** fit *(of passion)*; **порывáть** *(pf.* порвáть*)* (с + *inst.)* break (with); -ся endeavour; **порывúстый** gusty; impetuous.

порядковый ordinal; **поря|döк** (-дка) order; п. дня agenda; order of the day; **порядочный** considerable; respectable, decent.

посáд settlement, suburb.

посадúть *see* садúть & **сажáть**; **посáдка** planting; embarkation, boarding *(train etc.)*; landing *(avia.)*; **посáдочный** planting; landing *(a.).*

посáсывать suck.

посвúстывать whistle.

по-свóему in one's own way.

посвящáть *(pf.* посвя|тúть, -щý, -тúшь) devote; dedicate; consecrate; п. себя нáуке devote oneself to science; **посвящéние** dedication; initiation; ordaining, knighting.

посéв sowing; crops; **посевнóй** sowing *(a.).*

поседéлый grizzled.

поселé|нец (-нца) settler; exile; **поселéние** settlement; **посё|лок** (-лка) settlement; housing estate; **поселя́ть** *(pf.* -úть) settle, lodge; inspire *(e.g. hatred)*; -ся settle, take up residence.

посередúне *(gen.)* in the middle (of).

посетúтель, ∼ница visitor; **посещáемость** *(f.)* attendance; **посеш|áть** *(pf* посе|тúть, щý, тúшь) visit, attend; **посещéние** visit.

посúльный within one's power/ strength; feasible.

поскользнýться *(pf.)* slip.

поскóльку so far as; so long as.

поскорéе somewhat quicker; quick!

поскрёбк|и (-ов) scrapings.

послаблéние leniency, indulgence.

послá|нец (-нца) messenger, envoy; **послáние** message; **послáнник** envoy, minister; **послáть** *see* посылáть.

пóсле afterwards; *(gen.)* after; **послевоéнный** postwar.

послéдний last.

послéдователь, ∼ница follower; **послéдовательный** consecutive; consistent; **послéдствие** consequence; **послéдующий** subsequent; consequent.

после|зáвтра the day after tomorrow; ∼революцнóнный post-revolutionary; ∼родовóй post-natal; ∼слóвие epilogue, afterword.

послóвица saying.

послужнóй списóк service record.

послушáние obedience; послýшник, ~ница novice; послýшный obedient.

посмáтривать (на + acc.) keep looking (at).

посмéиваться (над + inst.) chuckle (at).

посмéнный by shifts/turns.

посмéртный posthumous.

посмéшище laughing-stock; посмеяние ridicule.

посóбие grant, aid; text-book; посóбник, ~ница accomplice; посóбничество complicity.

по|сóл (-слá) ambassador.

посоловéлый bleary.

посóльство embassy.

пóсох staff; crozier; посо|шóк (-шкá) staff; (coll.) one for the road.

поспевáть (-евáю; pf. поспéть) 1. ripen; 2. be in time; п. на пóезд catch the train.

поспéшный prompt; hurried, thoughtless.

посрам|ля́ть (pf. -и́ть) disgrace.

посреди́(не) (gen.) in the middle (of).

посрéдник mediator; посрéдничество mediation.

посрéдственный mediocre; satisfactory.

посрéдств|о: -ом, при -е (gen.) by means of.

пост (-á) 1. fast(ing); 2. (на -ý) post; position, station.

постáвка delivery; поставля́ть (pf. постáвить) 1. supply; постáвить 2. see стáвить; поставщи́|к (-á) supplier.

постамéнт pedestal.

постанóвка erection; production; staging; organization; statement (of question); постановлéние decision, resolution; decree; постанов|ля́ть (pf. -и́ть*) decree, decide; постанóвщик director, producer.

постели́ть see стлать.

постéль (f.) bed.

постепéнный gradual.

постигáть (pf. по|сти́гнуть, past -сти́г) understand; strike, befall; постижéние comprehension; пости-жи́мый comprehensible.

постилáть = стлать.

по|сти́ться (-щýсь, -сти́шься) fast.

пости́чь see постигáть.

пóстный lenten; vegetable (oil); hypocritical; (coll.) lean.

постовóй on point duty.

постóй (coll.) billet.

постóльку in so far as.

посторóнний outside, strange; extraneous; (as noun) stranger, outsider.

постоя́|лец (-льца) (coll.) lodger; постоя́лый двор inn.

постоя́нный constant; постоя́нство constancy.

пострéл (coll.) rogue, little mischief.

постригáться (pf. постри́чься*) take monastic vows.

построéние construction; parade, formation; постр|óйка (gen. pl. -óек) building.

построчный line (a.); by the line.

постскри́птум postscript.

постýкивать tap.

постули́ровать (ipf. & pf.) postulate.

поступáтельный progressive; поступáть (pf. поступи́ть*) act; (с + inst.) treat; (р/на + acc.) join, enter, start; -ся (inst.) forgo, waive; поступлéние joining, entry; accession, receipt; поступóк (-пка) act; пóступь (f.) step, gait.

посты́дный shameful.

посты́лый hateful.

посýда crockery, china; посýдный crockery, china (a.).

посчастли́в|иться (pf.): емý -илось + inf. he had the luck to.

посчитáться (pf.; coll.) (с + inst.) get even (with).

посылáть (pf. послáть*) send; посы́лка sending; parcel; premise; (pl.) errands; посы́льный messenger.

посыпáть (pf. посы́пать*) strew; посы́паться* (pf.) start to fall; pour down.

посяга́тельство encroachment; посяга́ть (pf. посягнýть) (на + acc.) encroach, infringe (on).

пот (в -ý) sweat, perspiration.

потайнóй secret; п. ход secret passage.

потакáть (coll.) (dat.) indulge; п. емý в э́том let him have his own way in this.

потасóвка (coll.) brawl.

потáш (-á) potash.

по-твóему in your (own) way; in your opinion.

потвóрств|о indulgence; connivance; -овать (dat.) connive (at), pander (to).

потёк stain from damp.
потё|мки (-мок) darkness.
поте́ние sweating.
потенциа́л potential; потенциа́льный potential (a.); поте́нция potentiality.
потепле́ние rise in temperature.
потёртый shabby; worn-out.
поте́ря loss; waste.
поте́ть (pf. вс-) sweat; (pf. за-, от-) (coll.) become misty, damp.
поте́ха fun; поте́шный amusing; п. полк regiment of boy soldiers (of Peter I).
потира́ть rub.
потихо́ньку slowly; silently, secretly.
по́тный sweaty.
пото́к flow, stream; production line.
пото|ло́к (-лка́) ceiling.
пото́м then; afterwards.
пото́|мок (-мка) descendant; пото́мственный hereditary; пото́мство posterity.
потому́ that is why; п. что because.
пото́п deluge; потопле́ние sinking.
пото́чный ме́тод line production.
потре́ба (obs.) need.
потреби́тель (m.) consumer, user; потребле́ние consumption; потребл|я́ть (pf. -и́ть) use.
потре́бность (f.) necessity, need, want; потре́бный necessary.
потрёпанный shabby; seedy.
потре́скивать crackle.
потрох|а́ (-о́в) giblets, pluck; потроши́ть (pf. вы-) disembowel; clean.
потряса́ть (pf. потрясти́*) shake; (inst.) brandish; потряса́ющий staggering; потрясе́ние shock; потря́хивать (coll.) (inst.) shake.
пот|у́ги (-у́г) efforts.
потупля́ть (pf. поту́пить) cast down, drop (one s gaze).
потускне́лый dull, tarnished.
потусторо́нний: п. мир the other world.
потуха́ние extinction; потуха́ть (pf. поту́хнуть*) die out, be extinguished.
по́тчевать (pf. по-) regale, treat.
потя́гивать (coll.) sip; draw at (cigarette); -ся stretch oneself.
поутру́ in the morning.
поуча́ть instruct, teach; поуче́ние precept; lecture; поучи́тельный instructive.

поха́бный obscene.
похвала́ praise; похва́льный laudable; praising.
похва́рывать be frequently unwell.
похити́тель (m.) kidnapper, abductor; thief; похища́ть (pf. пох|и́тить, -и́щу, -и́тишь) steal, kidnap, abduct; похище́ние kidnapping, abduction, theft.
похлёбка soup, broth.
похме́лье hangover.
похо́д march, walking tour; campaign; походи́ть* 1. (pf.) walk for a while; 2. (ipf.) (на + acc.) resemble; похо́дка walk, gait; похо́дный marching, route (a.); camp (a.).
похожде́ние adventure.
похо́жий (на + acc.) similar (to); ни на что не похо́же like nothing on earth; unheard of.
похолода́ние fall of temperature; cold snap.
похоро́нный funeral (a.); по́хор|оны (-он) funeral.
похотли́вый lewd, lustful; по́хоть (f.) lust, carnality.
похра́пывать (coll.) snore softly.
поцелу́й kiss.
поча́сно by the hour.
поча́|ток (-тка) ear, cob.
по́чва soil; почвове́дение soil science.
почём what is the price of?, how much is/are?; п. знать? who can say?.
почему́ why; п.-нибудь for some reason or other; п.-то for some reason.
по́черк handwriting.
почерне́лый darkened.
почерпа́ть (pf. почерпну́ть) get, draw, glean.
по́честь (f.) honour.
поче́сть see почита́ть.
почёт honour; respect; почётный honourable; honorary; of honour.
по́чечный nepl ritic, kidney (a.).
почива́ть (pf. по |и́ть, -ию, -йе шь) rest; п. на ла́врах rest on one's laurels; по и́вший the deceased.
почи́н initiative.
почи́нка mending, repairing.
почита́й (coll.) near, nigh on.
почита́тель (m.) admirer, worshipper; почита́ть 1. honour; revere; 2. (pf. по| е́сть, -чту́, - тё ь; - ёл, - ла́) (coll.) consider, think. 3. (pf.) read a while.

почи́ть *see* почива́ть.

по́|чка *(gen. pl.* -че *·)* bud; kidney.

по́чта post, mail; post-office; **почта́мт** post-office.

почта́льон postman; **почта́мт** post-office.

почте́ние respect; **почте́нный** respected, venerable.

почти́ almost.

почти́тельный respectful; **почти́ть*** *(pf.)* honour.

почто́вый postal; п. я́щик letter-box.

пошатну́ть *(pf.)* shake; -ся shake, stagger; **пошатыва́ться** stagger.

поши́б sort; manner.

поши́вка sewing.

по́шлина duty, tax.

по́шлость *(f.)* banality; **по́шлый** commonplace, vulgar, trivial.

поштучный by the piece.

поща́да mercy.

пощёлкивать *(inst.)* click.

пощёчина box on the ear.

пощи́пывать pluck; nibble.

поэ́зия poetry; **поэ́ма** long poem; **поэти́ческий** poetic(al); **поэти́чный** poetic, beautiful.

поэ́тому therefore.

появле́ние appearance, emergence **появля́ться** *(pf.* появи́ться) appear, crop up.

поя́рковый wool, felt *(a.).*

по́яс *(pl.* -а́) belt, girdle; waist; *(pl.* -ы́) zone.

поясне́ние explanation; **поясни́тельный** explanatory; **поясни́ть** *see* поясня́ть.

поясни́ца waist; loins; small of the back; **поясно́й** waist *(a.);* zone *(a.).*

поясн|я́ть *(pf.* -и́ть) explain, elucidate.

пра- great; **прабабу́|шка** *(gen. pl.* -шек) great-grandmother.

пра́вда truth; **правди́вый** truthful.

правдоподо́б|ие verisimilitude, plausibility; **~ный** probable, likely, verisimilar.

пра́ведник pious/righteous man; **пра́ведный** pious, religious; just, righteous.

праве́ть *(pf.* по-) move to the Right politically. **пра́вило** rule; principle; **пра́вильный** right, true, regular.

прави́тель, ~ница ruler; **прави́тельственный** governmental; **прави́тельство** government.

пра́вить 1. *(inst.)* rule, govern; drive; 2. correct; **пра́вка** correcting; adjusting; setting; **правле́ние** government, administration.

пра́внук great-grandson; **пра́вну|чка** *(gen. pl.* -чек) great-granddaughter.

пра́во 1. *(pl.* -а́) right; 2. really, indeed.

право|ве́дение jurisprudence, (science of) law; **~ве́рный** orthodox.

правово́й legal.

право|ме́рный lawful, rightful; **~мо́чный** competent; **~наруше́ние** infringement of law; **~писа́ние** spelling, orthography; **~поря́док** (-дка) law and order; **~сла́вие** orthodoxy; **~сла́вный** orthodox; **~су́дие** justice;

правота́ rightness; innocence.

пра́вый right; right-wing/-flank.

пра́вящий ruling *(a.).*

пра́дед great-grandfather; ancestor.

пра́зднество festival; **пра́здник** holiday; **пра́здничный** festive, gay; **пра́здновать** *(pf.* от-) celebrate.

праздносло́вие idle talk; **праздношата́ющийся** vagabond, idler; **пра́здный** idle, useless.

пра́ктик practical worker; **пра́ктика** practice; **практикова́ть** practise medicine/law; -ся be done; (в + *prep.)* practise; **практи́ческий** practical; **практи́чный** businesslike, efficient, practical.

пра́о|тец (-тца) forefather.

пра́порщик *(obs.)* ensign.

прапра́дед great-great-grandfather; **прароди́тель** *(m.)* ancestor.

прах dust, earth; все де́ло пошло́ -ом everything went to rack and ruin.

пра́чечная laundry; **пра́|чка** *(gen. pl.* -чек) laundress.

пра|ща́ *(gen. pl.* -щей) sling.

пра́щур ancestor.

пребыва́ние stay; **пребыва́ть** stay, be.

превзойти́ *see* превосходи́ть.

превозмога́ть *(pf.* превозмо́чь*) overcome.

превозноси́ть* *(pf.* превознести́*) extol, laud.

превосходи́тельство excellency; **превосходи́ть*** *(pf.* превзойти́*, -ойду́) -оше́л; *ppp.* -ойдённый) excel, exceed, surpass; **превосхо́дный** excellent, superb; **превосхо́дство** superiority.

превратить *see* превращать.

превратность *(f.)* wrongness, falsity; vicissitude; **превратный** wrong; changeful.

превращать *(pf.* превра|тить, -щу, -тишь)* (в + *acc.)* turn, change (into), reduce (to); п. дело в шутку make a joke of it; -ся (в + *acc.)* turn (into); **превращение** transformation.

превышать *(pf.* прев|ысить, -ышу, -ысишь)* exceed; **превышение** exceeding.

преграда barrier, obstacle; **преграждать** *(pf.* прегра|дить, -жу, -дишь; *ppp.* -ждённый)* bar, block up; **преграждение** blocking, hindering.

пред = перед.

предавать* *(pf.* предать*)* give over, hand over; betray; -ся *(dat.)* give oneself up to *(e.g. anger)* ; **предание** tradition; legend; handing over, committing; **преданность** *(f.)* devotion; **преданный** devoted; **предатель** *(m.)* betrayer, **предательский** treacherous; **предательство** treachery, betrayal.

предварительный preliminary; **предвар|ять** *(pf.* -ить)* forestall, anticipate; forewarn.

предвестие omen, portent; **предвестник** herald, harbinger; **предвещать** foretoken, presage.

предвзятый preconceived, biased.

предвидение foresight; **предвидеть*** foresee.

предвкушать *(pf.* предвк|усить, -ушу, -усишь)* look forward to, anticipate; **предвкушение** anticipation.

предводитель *(m.)* leader; **предводительство** leadership.

пред|восхищать *(pf.* -восхитить*)* anticipate.

предгорье foothills.

преддверие threshold.

предел bound, limit; **предельный** maximum, utmost.

предержащ|ий: власти -ие the powers that be.

предзнаменование omen, augury.

предикативный predicative.

предисловие foreword, preface.

предлагать *(pf.* предл|ожить, -ожу, -ожишь)* offer; propose, suggest.

предлог pretext, ground; preposition; **предложение** offer, suggestion; sentence, clause; **предложить** *see* предлагать; **предложный** prepositional.

предместье suburb.

предмет object, subject.

пред|назначать *(pf.* -назначить)* (для + *gen.)* intend, destine, earmark (for).

преднамеренный premeditated.

предначертание outline, plan; **предначертать** *(pf.)* outline, plan; foreordain.

пре|док (-дка) ancestor.

предопределение predetermination, predestination; **предопредел|ять** *(pf.* -ить)* predetermine.

пред|оставлять *(pf.* -оставить)* leave *(to smb.'s discretion)* ; give, grant.

предо|стерегать *(pf.* -стеречь*)* warn; п. его от опасности warn him of danger; **предостережение** warning, caution; **предосторожность** *(f.)* precaution.

предосудительный reprehensible.

пред|отвращать *(pf.* -отвратить*)* avert, prevent; **предотвращение** averting, preventing.

предохранение protection, preservation; **предохранитель** *(m.)* safety device/catch/lock/fuse; **предохранительный** preservative, preventive, safety *(a.)* ; **предохран|ять** *(pf.* -ить)* (от + *gen.)* protect, preserve (from).

предписание direction(s), instruction(s); prescription; **пред|писывать** *(pf.* -писать*)* direct, prescribe.

предплечье forearm.

пред|полагать *(pf.* -положить,-ожу, -ожишь)* suppose, assume; **предположение** supposition, assumption; **предположительный** hypothetical, presumable.

предпоследний last but one, penultimate.

предпосылка prerequisite, precondition; premise.

пред|почитать *(pf.* -почесть*, *ppp.* -почтённый)* prefer; **предпочтение** preference; **предпочтительный** preferable.

предприимчивый enterprising; **предприниматель** *(m.)* owner *(of firm)*, employer; **пред|принимать** *(pf.* -принять*)* undertake; **предприятие** undertaking, enterprise.

предрас|полага́ть *(pf.* -положи́ть, -ожу́, -о́жишь) *(к + dat.)* predispose (to); предрасположе́ние predisposition.

предрассу́|док (-дка) prejudice.

пред|река́ть *(pf.* -ре́чь, -реку́, речёшь; -рёк, -рекла́) *(obs.)* foretell.

пред|реша́ть *(pf.* -реши́ть) prejudge, predetermine.

председа́тель *(m.)* chairman, president; председа́тельство chairmanship, presidency.

предсказа́ние prediction, prophecy; предска́зывать *(pf.* предсказа́ть*)* predict, prophesy.

предсме́ртный death, dying *(a.).*

пред|става́ть (-стаю́, -стаёшь; *pf.* -ста́ть*) appear.

представи́тель *(m.)* representative; представи́тельный representative, imposing; представи́тельство representation; представле́ние presentation; idea, notion; representation; представля́ть *(pf.* -ста́вить) present; produce; represent; -ся occur, seem.

предста́ть *see* представа́ть.

пред|стоя́ть* be coming; be in prospect; мне -стои́т тру́дное де́ло I have a difficult task.

предте́ча *(m. & f.)* forerunner, precursor.

предубежде́ние prejudice.

пред|уведомля́ть *(pf.* -уве́домить) forewarn.

предуга́д|ывать *(pf.* -а́ть) foresee.

предумы́шленный premeditated.

предупреди́тельный courteous, obliging; precautionary; предупре|жда́ть *(pf.* -ди́ть, -жу́, -ди́ь, *ррр.* -ждён й) advise, warn; prevent, anticipate; предупрежде́ние notice, warning; prevention.

преду|сма́тривать *(pf* -смотре́ть*) foresee, envisage; provide for; предусмотри́тельный prudent, provident.

предчу́вствие presentiment; foreboding; предчу́вствовать have a presentiment of.

предше́ственник predecessor; предше́ствовать *(dat.)* precede.

предъяви́тель *(m.)* bearer *(of note/ cheque)* ; предъявля́ть *(pf.* -яви́ть, -явлю́, -я́вишь) show, produce; lay *(claim),* bring.

предыду́щий previous.

прее́мник, ∼ница successor; прее́мственность *(f.)* succession, continuity; прее́мственный successive; прее́мство succession.

пре́жде formerly; преждевре́менный premature.

пре́жний previous, former.

президе́нт president; президе́нтский presidential; президе́нтство presidency; прези́диум presidium.

презира́ть despise; презре́ние contempt; презре́нный contemptible; презри́тельный scornful, disdainful.

преиму́щественный primary, main; preferential; преиму́щество advantage, preference.

преиспо́дняя the nether regions.

прейскура́нт price-list, bill of fare.

преклоне́ние (пе́ред *inst.)* admiration (for).

прекло́нный во́зраст old age.

преклон|я́ть *(pf.* -и́ть) bend, bow; -ся (пе́ред + *inst.)* bend down (before); admire, worship.

прекосло́вить *(dat.)* contradict.

прекра́сный beautiful; excellent.

прекраща́ть *(pf.* прекра|ти́ть, -щу́, -ти́шь) stop, discontinue; -ся stop, cease; прекраще́ние cessation, discontinuance.

преле́стный charming, delightful; пре́лесть *(f.)* charm, fascination.

преломле́ние refraction; прел|омля́ть *(pf.* преломи́ть, -омлю́, -о́мишь) refract.

пре́лый rotten; прель *(f.)* rot, mould.

прельща́ть *(pf.* прель|сти́ть, -щу́, -сти́шь) entice, fascinate; -ся be attracted, tempted.

прелюбодея́ние adultery.

прелю́дия prelude.

премину́ть: не п. *(inf.)* not fail (to).

премирова́ть *(ipf. & pf.)* give award/ bonus to; пре́мия bonus, premium.

прему́дрый most wise.

премье́р prime minister, premier; премье́ра премье́ре.

прене|брега́ть *(pf.* -бре́чь, -брегу́, -брежёшь, -брёг, -брегла́) *(inst.)* neglect, disregard; пренебреже́ние neglect; disdain, пренебрежи́тельный slighting, scornful.

пре́ние rotting.

пре́н|ия (-ий) debate.

преобладáние predominance, prevalence; преобладáть (над + inst.) predominate (over), prevail.

преобра|жáть (pf. -зить, -жý, -зишь) change, transform; -ся change; преображéние transformation; transfiguration.

преобразовáние transformation, reform; преобразовáтель (m.) reformer; преобраз|óвывать (pf. -овáть) change, transform, reorganize.

пре|одолевáть (-одолевáю; pf. -одолéть) overcome, surmount.

препарáт preparation.

препинáн|ие: знáки -ия punctuation marks.

препирáтельство altercation, wrangling.

преподавáние teaching; преподавáтель, ~ница lecturer, instructor; преподавáть* teach.

препод|носить* (pf. -нести*) present give; преподношéние present, gift.

преподóбный reverend; saint (as noun).

препóна obstacle.

препро|вождáть (pf. -водить*) forward, send; препровождéние forwarding; spending (of time).

препя́тствие obstacle, hindrance; препя́тствовать (dat.) hinder.

прервáть see прерывáть.

пререкáние arguing, altercation; пререкáться argue.

прерогатива prerogative.

пре|рывáть (pf. -рвáть*) interrupt, break off; -ся be interrupted, break; прерывистый broken, interrupted.

пре|секáть (pf. -сéчь*) stop; suppress.

преслéдование pursuit, chase; persecution; prosecution; преслéдовать pursue, chase; persecute; strive for.

пресловýтый notorious.

пресмык|áться crawl, creep; grovel; -áющееся reptile.

пресновóдный fresh-water; прéсный fresh; unleavened; insipid (food); feeble (jokes).

пресс press (tech.); прéсса press (newspapers); пресс-конферéнция press-conference.

прессовáть (pf. с-) press, compress; прессовщик (-á) press operator.

преставлéние decease.

престарéлый aged.

престиж prestige.

престóл throne.

пре|ступáть (pf. -ступить*) transgress, violate; п. закóн break the law; преступлéние crime; преступ|ник, ~ница criminal; преступность (f.) criminality; crimes; delinquency; престýпный criminal (a.).

пресыщáться (pf. пресы́|титься, -щусь, -тишься) be satiated; пресыщéние satiety, surfeit; пресыщенный replete, sated, satiated.

претвор|я́ть (pf. -ить) turn, convert; п. в жизнь realize, carry out.

претендéнт, ~ка pretender, claimant; претендовáть (на + acc.) pretend, lay claim (to); претéнзия claim.

пре|терпевáть (-терпевáю; pf. -терпéть*) suffer, endure.

претить: мне претит it sickens me.

преткновéн|ие: кáмень -ия stumbling-block.

преть rot; sweat; stew.

преувеличéние exaggeration; преувели́чивать (pf. -ичить) exaggerate, overstate.

пре|уменьшáть (pf. -умéньшить) underestimate, understate; преуменьшéние underestimation.

пре|успевáть (-успевáю; pf. -успéть) be successful, prosper, thrive.

прéфикс prefix.

преходя́щий transient.

прецедéнт precedent.

при (prep.) attached to, by; in the presence of, in the time of; on, with; при всём том for all that; я здесь ни при чём it's nothing to do with me.

прибáв|ка, ~лéние addition, increase; прибавля́ть (pf. прибáвить) add, increase; прибáвочный additional, surplus.

прибаýтка witty saying.

при|бегáть 1. (pf. -бежáть*) come running; 2. (pf. -бéгнуть) (к + dat.) have recourse(to), resort (to).

прибéжище refuge.

при|берегáть (pf. -берéчь*) save up, reserve.

при|бивáть (pf. -бить*) nail; drive; лóдку прибило к бéрегу the boat was dashed against the shore.

при|бирáть (pf. -брáть*) put in order; put away.

прибить see прибивáть.

приближáть (pf. прибл|изить, -ижу, -изишь) (к + dat.) draw/bring nearer; -ся (к + dat.) approach, draw nearer (to); approximate (to); приближе́ние approach(ing); approximation; приближённый 1. approximate; 2. retainer, close supporter; приблизи́тельный approximate, rough.

приблу́дный stray (animal).

прибо́й surf, breakers.

прибо́р apparatus, device, instrument.

прибра́ть see прибира́ть.

прибре́жный coastal, riverside (a.), littoral.

прибыва́ть (pf. прибы́ть*, past, при́был, -á) arrive; increase, rise. swell; при́быль (f.) profit; increase, rise; прибы́тие arrival.

прива́л halt.

прива́ливать (pf. -вали́ть*) (к + dat.) lean/put against.

при|ва́ривать (pf. -вари́ть*) 1. weld; 2. cook a little more; прива́рка welding; прива́рок (-рка) victuals.

прива́т-доце́нт lecturer.

приведе́ние bringing; adducing.

привере́дливый fastidious; привере́дничать be hard to please.

приве́р|же|нец (-нца) adherent; приве́рженный attached; devoted, loyal.

приве́с (over)weight, increase in weight.

приве́сить see приве́шивать.

приве́т greeting; приве́тливый affable, friendly; приве́тственный salutatory; of welcome; приве́тствие greeting; welcoming address; приве́тствовать greet, welcome; salute.

при|ве́шивать (pf. -ве́сить*) hang up, suspend.

при|вива́ть (pf. -ви́ть*) inoculate, vaccinate; graft; implant, inculcate; -ся take (of vaccine); become established; приви́вка vaccination, inoculation, grafting.

привиде́ние apparition, ghost

привилегиро́ванный privileged; привиле́гия privilege

привинчивать (pf. приви|нти́ть, -нчу́, -нти́шь) (к + dat.) screw on(to).

приви́тие inculcation.

приви́ть see привива́ть.

при́вкус smack, taste.

привлека́тельный attractive; при|влека́ть (pf. -вле́чь*) attract, draw; привлече́ние attraction.

приво́д drive, gear; при|води́ть* (pf. -вести́*) bring; lead; reduce; adduce; -ся be brought etc.; (impers.) (+ dat.) happen; приводно́й driving (a.); homing (a.). (radio).

приво́з bringing, importation; при|вози́ть* (pf. -везти́*) bring; приво́з|ный, ~но́й imported.

приво́лье freedom; spaciousness; приво́льный free.

при|вора́живать (pf. -ворожи́ть) bewitch, charm.

при|вска́кивать (pf. -вскочи́ть*) start, jump up.

при|встава́ть* (pf. -вста́ть*) raise oneself, get up.

привходя́щий attendant (a.).

привыка́ть (pf. привы́кнуть, past. -ык) (к + dat.) become accustomed (to). привы́|чка (gen. pl. -чек) habit, custom; привы́чный usual, habitual.

привя́занность (f.) (к + dat.) attachment, affection (for); привя́зчивый affectionate; importunate, при|вя́зывать (pf. -вяза́ть*) (к + dat.) tie/bind/attach (to); -ся become attached; attach oneself; bother.

при́вязь (f.) leash, tether.

пригвожда́ть (pf. пригво|зди́ть, -зжу́, -зди́шь, ppp. -ждённый) (к + dat.) nail/pin (to).

при|гиба́ть (pf. -гну́ть) bend down (to).

при|гла́живать (pf. -гла́дить*) smooth down.

пригласи́тельный invitation (a.); приглаша́ть (pf. пригла|си́ть, -шу́, -си́шь) invite, ask; приглаше́ние invitation.

при|глуша́ть (pf. -глуши́ть) muffle, deaden; damp down.

при|гля́дываться (pf. -гляде́ться*) (к + dat.) get accustomed (to).

пригна́ть see пригоня́ть.

при|гова́ривать (pf. -говори́ть) (к + dat.) sentence, condemn (to); пригово́р sentence.

пригоди́ться (pf.) prove useful; приго́дный (к + dat.) suitable (for).

приго́жий good-looking.

при|гоня́ть (pf. -гна́ть*) bring/drive home; fit, adjust.

при|гора́ть (pf. -горе́ть*) be burnt (of food).

при́город suburb; при́городный suburban.

пригоршня
157
приклеивать

пригоршн|я *(gen. pl.* -ей) handful.
пригор|юниваться *(pf.* -юниться)
(coll.) become sad.
при|гота́вливать, ∼гото́вля́ть *(pf.*
-гото́вить)prepare; -ся be prepared;
prepare oneself; приготови́тель-
ный preparatory; приготовле́ние
preparation.
при|грева́ть (-грева́ю; *pf.* -гре́ть*)
warm; give shelter to.
при|дава́ть* *(pf.* -да́ть*) add; give;
attach.
придавливать *(pf.* -дави́ть*) press
down.
прида́ное dowry; layette; прида́|ток
(-тка) appendage, adjunct; при-
да́точный additional; прида́ч|а:
в -у in addition.
при|двига́ть *(pf.* -дви́нуть) move
up/near.
придво́рный court *(a.).*
при|де́лывать *(pf.* -де́лать) (к + *dat.)*
attach (to).
придёрживаться *(gen.)* keep to, hold
to; п. пра́вой стороны́ keep to the
right; п. за пери́ла hold on to the
rail.
придира (*m. & f.*) caviller, fault
finder; при|дира́ться *(pf.* -дра́ть-
ся*) (к + *dat.)* find fault (with)
cavil (at); приди́рка captious objection, cavil; приди́рчивый captious
carping.
придоро́жный roadside *(a.).*
при|ду́мывать *(pf.* -ду́мать) think of,
invent.
при́дурь: с -ью a bit crazy.
придыха́ние aspiration, breathing.
прие́зд arrival; при|езжа́ть *(pf.*
-е́хать) arrive, come; прие́зжий
1. on tour; 2. *(as noun)* newcomer.
прие́м 1. reception; admittance; dosage, taking *(of medicine)* dose; 2.
method, way; приёмлемый acceptable; приёмная reception-room;
приёмник wireless receiver; приёмный receiving, reception *(a.) ;*
selection *(a.);* adopted; п. экза́мен
entrance examination; п. оте́ц
foster-father; приёмочный пункт
reception centre; приёмыш adopt-
ed/foster child.
прижа́ть *see* прижима́ть.
при|жива́ться *(pf.* -жи́ться*) settle
in, get acclimatized; take root.
при|жига́ть *(pf.* -же́чь*) cauterize.
при|жима́ть *(pf.* -жа́ть, -жму*)
clasp; press; п. к. стене́ drive into a

corner *(fig.)* ; прижи́мистый tight/
close-fisted.
приз prize.
при|заду́мываться *(pf.* -заду́маться),
hesitate, become thoughtful.
призва́ние calling, vocation; призва́ть
see призыва́ть.
призе́мистый stocky, thick-set.
приземле́ние landing; приземл|я́ться
(pf. -и́ться) land *(avia).*
при́зма prism.
при|знава́ть (-знаю́, -знаёшь; *pf.*
-зна́ть) recognize; admit; -ся (в
+ *prep.)* confess (to).
при́знак sign, symptom.
призна́ние acknowledgement; при́-
знанный acknowledged, recogniz-
ed; призна́тельный grateful, thank-
ful; призна́ть *see* признава́ть.
призово́й prize *(a.).*
призо́р: без -а without care/super-
vision.
при́зрак ghost, spectre; при́зрач-
ный spectral; unreal, illusory.
призре́ние *(obs.)* care, charity.
призы́в call, appeal; при|зыва́ть *(pf.*
-зра́ть*) call, summon; призывни́к
(-á) man called up for service, recruit; призывно́й call-up, military
(a.).
при́иск mine; золоты́е -и gold mine.
прийти́ *see* приходи́ть.
прика́з command, order; *(hist.)* office;
приказа́ние order, bidding; при-
ка́зчик steward, bailiff; *(coll.)* shop-
assistant; henchman; при|ка́-
зывать *(pf.* -каза́ть*) order, command *(smb.* — *dat.) ;* п. ему́
это сде́лать order him to do it.
при|ка́лывать *(pf.* -коло́ть*) pin;
transfix.
при|ка́нчивать *(pf.* -ко́нчить) *(coll.)*
finish off.
при|карма́нивать *(pf.* -а́нить) pocket,
appropriate.
при|каса́ться *(pf.* -косну́ться) (к
+ *dat.)* touch.
при|ка́тывать *(pf.* -кати́ть*) roll up.
при|ки́дывать *(pf.* -ки́нуть) *(coll.)*
estimate; weigh; -ся pretend; -ся
больны́м pretend to be ill.
прикла́д 1. butt *(of rifle)* ; 2. trim-
mings; прикладно́й applied; при|-
кла́дывать *(pf.* -ложи́ть, -ложу́,
-ло́жишь) add; enclose; apply,
affix.
при|кле́ивать *(pf.* -кле́ить) stick,
glue.

приклёпка riveting; **приклёпывать** *(pf.* -клепа́ть*)* rivet.

приключ|а́ть *(pf.* -и́ть) connect; **-ся** happen, occur; **приключе́ние** adventure; **приключе́нческий** рома́н adventure novel.

при|ко́вывать *(pf.* -кова́ть*)* chain, rivet.

при|кола́чивать *(pf.* -колоти́ть*)* nail.

приколо́ть *see* **прика́лывать.**

прикомандир|о́вывать *(pf.* -ова́ть*)* (к + *dat.)* attach (to).

прикоснове́ние touch; concern; **прикоснове́нный** (к + *dat.)* concerned (in); **прикосну́ться** *see* **прикаса́ться.**

прикра́са colouring, embellishment; **при|кра́шивать** *(pf.* -кра́сить*)* colour; embellish.

прикрепле́ние fastening; registration; **прикреп|ля́ть** *(pf.* -и́ть) (к + *dat.)* attach, fasten; register.

при|кри́кивать *(pf.* -кри́кнуть) (на + *acc.)* raise one's voice (to).

при|крыва́ть *(pf.* -кры́ть) cover, screen, shelter; **прикры́тие** cover, escort, shelter.

при|ку́ривать *(pf.* -кури́ть*)* get a light from someone's cigarette.

при|ку́сывать *(pf.* -куси́ть, -кушу́, -ку́сишь) bite; hold *(one's tongue).*

прила|во́к (-вка) counter.

прилага́тельное adjective; **при|ла-га́ть** *(pf.* -ложи́ть, -ложу́, -ло́жишь) enclose; apply; attach.

при|ла́живать *(pf.* -ла́дить*)* (к + *dat.)* fit, adapt (to).

при|лега́ть *(pf.* -ле́чь*)* fit closely; (к + *dat.)* adjoin.

прилежа́ние diligence; **приле́жный** diligent, assiduous.

при|лепля́ть *(pf.* -лепи́ть*)* (к + *dat.)* *(v. t.)* stick (to).

прилёт arrival; **при|лета́ть** *(pf.* -лете́ть*)* come flying; arrive *(by air).*

приле́чь *(pf.)* lie down for a rest.

прили́в flow, flood; rising tide; surge; **при|лива́ть** *(pf.* -ли́ть*)* flow, rush; **прили́вный** tidal.

при|липа́ть *(pf.* -ли́пнуть*)* (+ *dat.)* stick (to); **прили́пчивый** adhesive; infectious.

прили́ть *see* **прилива́ть.**

прили́чие decency, propriety; **прили́чный** decent, proper, respectable.

приложе́ние application, affixing; enclosure; supplement; **приложи́ть** *see* **прикла́дывать** *&* **прилага́ть.**

при́ма first string; first violin; *(mus.)* tonic.

прима́нка bait, lure.

прима́с primate *(of church);* **прима́т** primacy, pre-eminence; primate *(zool.).*

при|ма́чивать *(pf.* -мочи́ть*)* wet, moisten.

примене́ние application, use; **примени́мый** applicable; **примени́тель-но** (к + *dat.)* in conformity (with); **при|меня́ть** *(pf.* -мени́ть, -меню́, -ме́нишь) apply, employ; **-ся** (к + *dat.)* adapt oneself/conform (to).

приме́р example.

при|мерза́ть *(pf.* -мёрзнуть*)* (к + *dat.)* get frozen (to).

приме́рка fitting, trying on; **приме́рный** exemplary, model; **при|меря́ть** *(pf.* -ме́рить) try on, fit.

при́месь *(f.)* admixture.

приме́та sign, token; **приме́тный** perceptible; prominent; **примеча́-ние** note, comment; **примеча́тель-ный** notable, remarkable; **при|меча́ть** *(pf.* -ме́тить*)* notice.

при|ме́шивать *(pf.* -меша́ть) add, admix.

при|мина́ть *(pf.* -мя́ть*)* crush, trample down.

примире́ние (re)conciliation; **примири́тель** *(m.)* conciliator; **примири́тельный** conciliatory; **примир|я́ть** *(pf.* -и́ть) reconcile, conciliate; **-ся** (с + *inst.)* be reconciled (with).

примити́вный primitive.

примкну́ть *see* **примыка́ть.**

примо́рский maritime, seaside; **примо́рье** littoral, coastal area.

примости́ться *(pf.)* find a place.

примочи́ть *see* **прима́чивать**; **примо́чка** *(gen. pl.* -чек) lotion, wash.

примыка́ть *(pf.* примкну́ть) (к + *dat.)* join, side (with); adjoin; fix *(bayonets).*

принадле|жа́ть* belong (to); **принадле́жность** *(f.)* belonging; *pl.* accessories, requisites; п. к па́ртии membership of the party.

прине|во́ливать *(pf.* -во́лить) make, compel.

принижа́ть *(pf.* приниј|зить, -жу, -зишь) humiliate.

при|никáть (pf. -нúкнуть*) (к + dat.) press oneself (to/against).

принимáть (pf. принять, примý, прúмешь, прúнял, -á; ppp. прúнятый) take, accept, receive; п. за + acc. take (for), assume (to be); -ся be taken etc.; start; -ся за рабóту start work.

при|норáвливать (pf. -норовúть) (к + dat.) (coll.) adapt, adjust (to).

при|носúть* (pf. -нестú*) bring.

принудúтельный compulsory; при|нуждáть (pf. -нýдить, -нýжу, -нýдишь; ppp. -нуждённый) compel; принуждéние compulsion, coercion.

прúнцип principle; принципиáльный of principle.

принятие acceptance, taking, reception; прúнятый accepted, adopted; принять see принимáть.

приободр|ять (pf. -úть) hearten.

при|обретáть (pf. -обрестú*) acquire, gain; приобретéние acquisition, gain, purchase.

приобщ|áть (pf. -úть) (к + dat.) accustom (to); join (to); communicate (eccl.).

приодéть* (pf.) dress up, smarten up.

при|останáвливать (pf. -остано-вúть*) hold up, stop, suspend; -ся stop; приостанóвка stoppage, suspension, respite, reprieve.

приот|крывáть (pf. -крыть*) open slightly.

при|падáть (pf. -пáсть*) (к + dat.) fall down, press oneself (to); (coll.) limp; припáд|ок (-дка) fit, attack.

при|пáивать (pf. -паять) (к + dat.) solder (to).

припáрка poultice.

припáс|ы (-ов) stores, supplies.

припéв refrain; припевáючи: жить п. live in clover.

припёк heat (of sun); при|пекáть (pf. -пéчь*) be hot.

припúска addition, postscript; registration; при|пúсывать (pf. -писáть*) add; register; ascribe, attribute.

приплáта additional payment.

приплóд increase; issue.

при|плывáть (pf. -плыть*) come swimming/sailing.

при|плющивать (pf. -плюснуть) flatten.

припля́сывать dance, hop.

при|поднимáть (pf. -поднять*) raise slightly; -ся raise oneself a little; припóднятый elevated.

при|ползáть (pf. -ползтú*) come creeping/crawling.

при|поминáть (pf. -пóмнить) recollect, recall.

припрáва flavouring, seasoning; при|правля́ть (pf. -прáвить) flavour, season, spice.

при|пря́тывать (pf. -пря́тать*) hide; put aside.

при|пýгивать (pf. -пугнýть) scare.

при|пухáть (pf. -пýхнуть*) swell slightly; припýхлость (f.) swelling.

прúрабо|ток (-тка) additional earnings.

при|рáвнивать (pf. -равня́ть) (к + dat) equate (with).

при|растáть (pf. -растú*) (к + dat.) adhere/grow on (to); accrue; прирáщение increase, increment.

при|резáть (pf. -рéзать*) kill, cut throat of; add.

прирóда nature; прирóдный natural; innate.

приро|ждённый innate, born.

прирóст increase.

прирубéжный frontier, border (a.).

прируч|áть (pf. -úть) tame, domesticate.

при|сáживаться (pf. -сéсть*) sit down, take a seat.

при|сáсываться (pf. -сосáться*) adhere (by suction).

присвáивать (pf. присвóить) appropriate, assume; confer, award.

присвúстывать whistle.

присвоéние appropriation; awarding, conferment.

при|седáть (pf. -сéсть*) squat; curtsey; присéст: в одúн п. at one go/sitting.

при|скáкивать (pf. -скакáть*) come galloping.

прискóрбный sorrowful.

прислáть see присылáть.

прислон|я́ть (pf. -úть) lean, rest; п. дóску к стенé lean the board against the wall; -ся lean, rest.

прислýга servant.

при|слýшиваться (pf. -слýшаться) (к + dat.) listen, lend an ear (to).

при|смá⁻ривать (pf. -смотрéть*) (за + inst.) look after, keep an eye on; -ся (к + dat.) look closely (at); присмо́тр care, super-vision.

присовокупля́ть (pf. -йть) add, attach.

присоедине́ние addition, joining; annexation; adherence; присо-един|я́ть (pf. -йть) join, connect; annex; add; -ся (к + dat.) join, go along (with); subscribe to (an opinion) ; adhere (to).

присо́ска sucker.

приспе́шник minion.

приспи́ч|ить (pf., coll.) ему́ -ило . . . he took it into his head to . . .

приспособле́ние adaptation; accli-matization; appliance, device; приспос|обля́ть (pf. -о́бить) (к + dat.) adapt, adjust (to).

прис|пуска́ть (pf. -пусти́ть*) lower slightly.

при́став police officer; bailiff.

при|става́ть (-стаю́, -стаёшь; pf. -ста́ть*) (к + dat.) stick/adhere (to); worry, pester.

приста́вка prefix; при|ставля́ть (pf. -ста́вить) (к + dat.) put/set/lean (against); join; appoint.

при́стальный fixed, intent.

при́стан|ь (f.; gen. pl. -е́й) landing-stage, pier.

приста́ть see пристава́ть.

при|стёгивать (pf. -стегну́ть) fas-ten, button up.

присто́йный decent, proper.

при|стра́ивать (pf. -стро́ить) (к + dat.) build on, add (to); -ся get a place, settle.

пристра́стие (к + dat.) weakness, predilection (for); bias (towards); пристра́стный partial.

при|стре́ливать (pf. -стрели́ть) shoot down, kill; (pf. -стреля́ть) aim, register.

пристро́ить see пристра́ивать; при-стро́йка (gen. pl. -о́ек) extension, annex.

при́ступ assault, storm; attack, fit; при|ступа́ть (pf. -ступи́ть*) (к + dat.) set about, start.

пристяжна́я side-horse, outrunner.

при|сужда́ть (pf. -суди́ть; ppp. -суждённый) (к + dat.) sentence, condemn (to); award; confer; присужде́ние awarding; confer-ment.

прису́тствие presence; (obs.) office; прису́тствовать be present.

прису́щий (dat.) inherent (in); characteristic (of).

при|сыла́ть (pf. -сла́ть*) send.

при|сыпа́ть (pf. -сы́пать*) put/pour in more; присы́пка powder; sprink-ling, powdering.

при|сыха́ть (pf. -со́хнуть*) dry on, adhere.

прися́га oath; прися́гать (pf. при-сягну́ть) swear; п. в ве́рности (dat.) swear allegiance (to); при-ся́жный barrister.

притаи́ться (pf.) hide, lurk.

при|та́птывать (pf. -топта́ть*) tread down.

при|та́скивать (pf. -тащи́ть*) bring, drag.

притво́рный affected, feigned; при-тво́рство pretence, sham; при-тво́р|щик, ~щица pretender, hypo-crite.

притв|оря́ть (pf. -ори́ть, -орю́, -о́ришь) shut, close; -ся 1. close.

притвор|я́ться 2. (pf. -и́ться) (inst.) pretend (to be).

притесне́ние oppression; притесн|-я́ть (pf. -и́ть) oppress.

при|тиха́ть (pf. -ти́хнуть; past. -ти́х) grow quiet.

прито́к tributary; flow, influx.

при́толока lintel.

прито́м besides.

прито́н den, haunt.

при|то́пывать (pf. -то́пнуть) stamp one's foot, tap.

при́торный sickly; mealy-mouthed.

при|тра́гиваться (pf. -тро́нуться) (к + dat.) touch.

притти́ see приходи́ть.

при|тупля́ть (pf. -тупи́ть*) blunt, dull; deaden; -ся become blunt/dull.

при́тча parable: п. во язы́цех talk of the town.

притяга́тельный attractive, mag-netic; притя́гивать (pf. -тяну́ть*) attract; притяжа́тельный posses-sive (gram.) ; притяже́ние attract-ion.

притяза́ние claim, pretension; при-тяза́тельный exacting.

притяну́ть see притя́гивать.

приумноже́ние increase.

приуны́ть (pf.; past only) become sad.

при|уро́чивать (pf. -уро́чить) (к + dat.) time (for).

приусáдебный учáсток kolkhoz farmer's personal plot.

при|учáть (pf. -учúть*) (к + dat.) train/school (to).

прихвáрывать be unwell.

при|хвáтывать (pf. -хватúть*) catch; damage.

прúхвос|тень (-тня) hanger-on.

прихлебáтель (m.) sponger; прихлёбывать sip.

при|хлóпывать (pf. -хлóпнуть) bang, slam.

прихóд arrival; receipts; parish; приходúть* (pf. прийтú, придý*) come, arrive; п. в себя́ come to one's senses; -ся fit; fall (on a certain day); happen; prove necessary; им пришлóсь уéхать they had to go away; -ся по вкýсу to be to someone's liking; прихóдный receipt (a.); прихóдовать (pf. за-) credit, enter; прихóдский parish (a.); приходя́щий non-resident; п. больнóй out-patient; прихож|áнин (pl. -áне, -áн), ~áнка parishioner.

прихóжая entrance-hall, anteroom.

прихорáшивать smarten up.

прихотлúвый capricious, fanciful, intricate; прúхоть (f.) caprice, whim.

прихрáмывать limp, hobble.

прицéл sight (of gun); при|цéливаться (pf. -цéлиться) take aim.

прицéп trailer; прицéпка hitching, hooking; (coll.) objection; при|цепля́ть (pf. -цепúть, -цеплю́, -цéпишь) (к + dat.) hitch/hook (to); -ся stick (to), cling (to); прицепнóй вагóн trailer.

причáл mooring, moorage; line; при|чáливать (pf. -чáлить) moor, make fast.

причáстие participle; sacrament, eucharist; причáстный (к + dat.) concerned (in), privy (to); прича|щáть (pf. -стúть, -щý, -стúшь) give the sacrament.

причём and, moreover.

причёска hair-do, coiffure; при|чёсывать (pf. -чесáть*) do/dress someone's hair; -ся do/comb one's hair.

причúна cause, motive, reason; причúнный causal; причин|я́ть (pf. -úть) cause.

при|числя́ть (pf. -чúслить) add; reckon, attach.

причитáние lamentation; причитáть (над + inst.) lament (over), bewail.

причит|áться be due; емý -áется сто рублéй he is due 100 roubles.

при|чмóкивать (pf. -чмóкнуть) smack one's lips.

причт clergy of a parish.

причýда whim, caprice; причýдливый whimsical; fantastic, queer; причýдник, ~ница crank.

пришварт|óвывать (pf. -овáть) moor, make fast.

пришелéц (-льца) newcomer.

пришепётывать lisp.

пришéствие advent.

при|шибáть (pf. -шибúть, -шибý, -шибёшь; -шúб) (coll.) hurt; kill; пришúбленный crestfallen, dejected.

пришивáть (pf. -шúть*) (к + dat.) sew (to); пришивнóй sewn on; п. воротнúк attached collar.

прúшлый strange, alien; newly arrived.

пришпúливать (pf. -шпúлить) pin.

пришпóривать (pf. -шпóрить) spur on.

прищёлкивать (pf. -щёлкнуть) (inst.) snap, click.

при|щемля́ть (pf. -щемúть) pinch, nip.

при|щýривать (pf. -щýрить) screw up (eyes); -ся screw up one's eyes.

прию́т refuge; (obs.) orphanage, home; прию|тúть (pf., -чý, -тúшь) shelter.

прия́знь (f.) amity.

прия́тель, ~ница friend; прия́тельский amicable.

прия́тный pleasant.

прия́ть = приня́ть.

про (acc.) about, concerning; (coll.) for; говорúть про себя́ say to oneself.

прóба test; sample; standard; hallmark.

пробéг run; про|бегáть (pf. -бежáть*) run (past); cover; skip through.

пробéл blank, gap; flaw.

про|бивáть (pf. -бúть*) make a hole in, pierce, punch; -ся force one's way (through); пробивнóй penetrative.

про|бирáть (pf. -брáть*) (coll.) pierce; scold; -ся make/force one's way.

проби́рка test-tube.

проби́ть *see* пробива́ть.

про́бка cork, stopper; traffic jam; fuse *(elec.);* про́бковый cork *(a.).*

пробле́ма problem; проблемат|и́ческий, ~и́чный problematic(al).

про́блеск flash, gleam, ray; пробле́скивать *(pf.* -блесну́ть) flash, gleam.

про́бный trial *(a.),* hallmarked; п. ка́мень touchstone; про́бовать *(pf.* по-) attempt, try.

прободе́ние perforation *(med.).*

пробо́ина hole, gap; пробо́йник punch.

пробо́р parting *(of hair).*

про́бочник *(coll.)* cork-screw.

пробра́ться *see* пробира́ться.

про|бужда́ть *(pf.* -буди́ть*) awaken, arouse; пробужде́ние awakening.

пробур|а́вливать *(pf.* -а́вить) bore, drill, perforate.

пробы́ть* *(pf.)* stay, be.

прова́л downfall; failure; gap; trap (in stage); про|ва́ливать *(pf.* -вали́ть*) fail *(in exam);* ruin; прова́ливай! be off!; -ся fall through; collapse; fail; disappear.

про|ва́ривать *(pf.* -вари́ть*) boil thoroughly.

проведе́ние construction *(e.g. of road);* installation; execution, conducting.

про|ве́дывать *(pf.* -ре́дать) call on, come to see; *(pf.)* learn.

прове́рка checking; про|веря́ть *(pf.* -ре́рить) check, test.

про|ве́тривать *(pf.* -ве́трить) air.

провиа́нт provisions, victuals.

прови́дность foresight.

провиде́ние Providence.

прови́зия provisions.

прови́зор pharmaceutist.

провини́ться *(pf.)* commit an offence.

провинциа́льный provincial; прови́нция province.

про́вод *(pl.* -а́) wire, lead; conductor; проводи́мость *(f.)* conductívity; про|води́ть* 1. *(pf.* -ре́сти*) take, lead; build, install; conduct, hold; pass *(a law);* spend *(time);* п. руко́й по + *dat.* pass one's hand over; 2. *(pf.) see* провожа́ть; прово́дка conducting, installation, building; wiring; проводни́к (-а́) conductor, guide; про́вод|ы (-ов) seeing off, send-off.

провожа́тый conductor, guide.

провожа́ть *(pf.* проводи́ть*) accompany, see off.

провоз transport, conveyance.

провозгла|ша́ть *(pf.* -си́ть, -шу́, -си́шь) proclaim, enunciate; провозглаше́ние proclamation, declaration.

про|вози́ть* *(pf.* -везти́*) transport, convey.

провока́тор agent provocateur; провока́ция provocation.

про́волока wire; про́воло|чка *(gen. pl.* -чек) wire; проволо́чка *(gen. pl.* -чек) delay; про́волочный wire *(a.).*

прово́рный agile, quick; прово́рство agility, dexterity.

провоци́ровать *(pf.* с-) (на + *acc.)* provoke (to).

про|га́дывать *(pf.* -гада́ть) miscalculate.

прога́лина glade.

про|гиба́ться *(pf.* -гну́ться) cave in, sag.

про|гла́живать *(pf.* -гла́дить*) iron.

про|гла́тывать *(pf.* -глоти́ть, -глочу́, -гло́тишь) swallow, gulp down.

про|гля́дывать *(pf.* -гляде́ть*) look through, skim; overlook; *(pf.* -гляну́ть) be perceptible.

прогна́ть *see* прогоня́ть.

про|гнива́ть *(pf.* -гни́ть*) rot through.

прогно́з prognosis, forecast.

про|гова́ривать *(pf.* -говори́ть) pronounce, utter; talk; -ся let the cat out of the bag.

прого́н 1. well *(of staircase);* 2. baulk; 3. *(obs.)* travelling allowance; про|гоня́ть *(pf.* -гна́ть*) drive away, send away, dismiss.

про|гора́ть *(pf.* -горе́ть*) burn down/through; go bankrupt.

прого́рклый rank, rancid.

програ́мма programme.

про|грева́ть (-грева́ю; *pf.* -гре́ть*) warm thoroughly, heat.

прогре́сс progress; прогресси́вный progressive; прогресси́ровать progress; прогре́ссия progression.

про|грыза́ть *(pf.* -гры́зть*) gnaw through.

прогу́л missing work; truancy; про|гу́ливать *(pf.* -гуля́ть) miss work; play truant; -ся take a stroll; прогу́лка walk; outing; trip; прогу́ль|щик, ~щица shirker, slacker, truant.

продава́ть* (pf. прода́ть*; past про́дал, -á) sell; прода|вéц (-вца́) salesman.

про|да́вливать (pf. -дави́ть*) break through/in.

продавщи́ца saleswoman/-girl; прода́жа sale; прода́жный selling (a.); for sale; venal, corrupt.

про|двига́ть (pf. -дви́нуть) move/ push forward, advance, further; -ся advance, move ahead, progress; продвиже́ние advancement, progress.

про|дева́ть (-дева́ю; pf. -де́ть*) pass/ put through.

проде́лка trick; escapade; про|де́лывать (pf. -де́лать) do, perform, make.

про|дёргивать (pf. -дёрнуть) pass/ run through; criticize.

проде́ть see продева́ть.

про|длева́ть (-длева́ю; pf. -дли́ть) prolong; продле́ние extension.

продово́льственный provision, food (a.); ration (a.); продово́льствие food, provisions.

продолгова́тый oblong.

продолжа́тель (m.) continuer; про| долж́ать (pf. -дóлжить) continue; продолже́ние continuation; продолжи́тельный long, prolonged.

продо́льный longitudinal; lengthwise.

про|дува́ть (pf. -ду́ть*) blow through.

продувно́й sly, crafty.

проду́кт product; (pl.) foodstuffs; продукти́вный productive; продукто́вый grocery, provision (a.); проду́кция output, production.

про|ду́мывать (pf. -ду́мать) think out.

проды́г|являть (pf. -яви́ть) make a hole in.

про|еда́ть (pf. -éсть*) eat; corrode; (coll.) spend on food.

прое́зд passage, thoroughfare; про|е́здить* (pf.) spend some time riding/driving; проездно́й fare (a.); (as noun) travel allowance; про|езжа́ть (pf. -éхать*) ride, drive, pass by; cover (a distance); про́езжий 1. public (road); 2. traveller, passer-by (noun).

прое́кт project, scheme; проекти́ровать (pf. за-) project, plan.

проекцио́нный аппара́т projector; прое́кция projection.

проём opening, aperture.

прое́сть see проеда́ть.

про|жа́ривать (pf. -жа́рить) roast/ fry thoroughly.

про|жёвывать (pf. -жева́ть*) chew well.

прожектёр schemer; прожектёрство hair-brained schemes.

проже́ктор searchlight.

проже́чь see прожига́ть.

про|жива́ть (pf. -жи́ть*, ppp. -жи́тый) live, reside, stay; spend, run through; -ся spend all one's money.

про|жига́ть (pf. -жéчь*) burn through; п. жизнь lead a dissipated life, live it up

прожи́лка vein.

прожи́тие living, livelihood; прожи́точный: п. ми́нимум subsistence minimum; прожи́ть see прожива́ть.

прожо́рливый voracious, gluttonous.

про́за prose; проза́ик prose-writer; проза|и́ческий, ~и́чный prose (a.); prosaic, matter-of-fact.

прозва́ние, про́звище nickname; прозва́ть see прозыва́ть.

прозева́ть (-ева́ю; pf.) miss, let slip.

прозоде́жда working clothes.

прозорли́вый perspicacious; прозра́чный transparent; limpid; про|зрева́ть (-зрева́ю; pf. -зре́ть*) recover one's sight; begin to see clearly; прозре́ние recovery of sight; enlightenment.

про|зыва́ть (pf. -зва́ть*) name, nickname.

прозяба́ние vegetating; прозяба́ть vegetate.

прозя́бнуть* (pf., coll.) be chilled.

прои́грыватель (m.) record-player; про|и́грывать (pf. -игра́ть) lose; play through; -ся lose all one's money (gambling); про́игрыш loss.

произведе́ние work.

производи́тель (m.) producer; производи́тельность (f.) productivity; произ|води́ть* (pf. -вести́*) produce, make; carry out; promote; derive.

произво́дный derivative; произво́дственный industrial, production (a.); произво́дство production.

произво́л tyranny, arbitrary rule; произво́льный arbitrary.

произ|носить* *(pf.* -нести*) pronounce; произношение pronunciation.

произойти *see* происходить.

произ|растать *(pf.* -расти*) grow, sprout.

происк|и (-ов) intrigues.

проис|текать *(pf.* -течь*) (от, из + *gen.)* result, spring (from).

происходить* *(pf.* произ|ойти*, -ойду, ошёл *pp.* происшедший) happen, occur; (от + *gen.)* be descended (from); result (from); происхождение origin; birth; extraction; происшествие incident, event; accident.

пройдоха *(m. & f., coll.)* crafty person, fox.

пройма armhole.

пройти *see* проходить; пройтись *see* прохаживаться.

прок use, benefit.

прокажённый leprous; *(as noun)* leper.

проказа 1. leprosy; 2. mischief, prank; проказ|ник, ~ница mischievous person; проказничать play pranks, be up to mischief.

прокалка tempering.

про|калывать *(pf.* -колоть*) pierce.

про|капывать *(pf.* -копать) dig.

прокат 1. hire; 2. rolling; rolled metal; прокатный 1. let out on hire; 2. rolling *(a.).*

про|катывать *(pf.* -катать) roll, spread flat with roller; *(pf.* -катить*) give a ride, take for drive; roll by; -ся *(pf.* -катиться*) go for a ride.

про|кисать *(pf.* -киснуть*) turn sour.

прокладка laying, construction; padding; washer; про|кладывать *(pf.* -ложить, -ложу, -ложишь) lay, build; interlay.

прокламация leaflet.

проклейка sizing.

про|клинать *(pf.* -клясть*; *past* проклял, -á; *ppp.* проклятый) curse, damn; проклятие damnation, curse; проклятый (ac)cursed.

прокол puncture.

проколоть *see* прокалывать.

прокопать *see* прокапывать.

прокоптелый sooty.

прокорм nourishment, sustenance.

про|крадываться *(pf.* -красться*) steal, creep.

прокурор public prosecutor.

про|кусывать *(pf.* -кусить, -кушу' -кусишь) bite through.

про|кучивать *(pf.* -кутить*) dissipate, squander.

пролагать = прокладывать.

пролаза *(m. & f.; coll.)* crafty person, artful dodger.

про|ламывать *(pf.* -ломать & -ломить*) break through.

пролегать lie, run *(of road).*

проле|жень (-жня) bedsore.

про|лезать *(pf.* -лезть*) get/wriggle/climb through.

пролёт flight *(of stairs);* stairwell; span *(of bridge);* stage *(between stations).*

пролетариат proletariat; пролет|арий, ~арка proletarian; пролетарский proletarian *(a.).*

про|летать *(pf.* -лететь*) fly (past); cover *(a distance, flying);* пролётка cab, droshky.

пролив strait, sound; проливать *(pf.* пролить*, *past* пролил,-á) spill, shed; -ся spill, be shed; проливной дождь downpour; пролитие крови bloodshed.

пролог prologue.

проложить *see* прокладывать.

пролом break, fracture; проломать, -ить *see* проламывать.

про|масливать *(pf.* -маслить) grease, oil.

про|матывать *(pf.* -мотать) squander.

промах blunder, miss, slip; про|махиваться *(pf.* -махнуться) miss; be wide of the mark.

про|мачивать *(pf.* -мочить*) soak, drench.

промедление delay.

промежу|ток (-тка) interval, space; промежуточный intermediate.

про|менивать *(pf.* -менять) (на + *acc.)* exchange (for).

промер measurement, sounding; error *(in measurement).*

про|мерзать *(pf.* -мёрзнуть*) freeze right through.

про|меривать *(pf.* -мерить) measure, survey; *(pf.)* make a mistake in measuring.

промозглый dank.

промоина hollow.

промокательная бумага blotting-paper; промокать *(pf.* -мокнуть*) get wet; let water in; *(pf.* -мокнуть) *(coll.; trans.)* blot.

промота́ть see прома́тывать.

промочи́ть see прома́чивать.

промтова́р|ы (-ов) manufactured goods.

промча́ться* (pf.) rush past.

про|мыва́ть (pf. -мы́ть*) wash thoroughly.

про́мы|сел (-сла) trade, business; (pl.) mines, works, field(s).

промы́шленник industrialist; промы́шленность (f.) industry; промы́шленный industrial; промышля́ть (inst.) deal (in); make a living (by).

прон|за́ть (pf. -зи́ть, -жу́, -зи́шь; ppp. -зённый) pierce, transfix; пронзи́тельный piercing.

прони́зывать (pf. -низа́ть*) pierce, permeate.

про|ника́ть (pf. -ни́кнуть*) penetrate; percolate; -ся (inst.) be imbued (with); проникнове́ние penetration.

понима́ть (pf. проня́ть, пройму́, -мёшь; про́нял, -а́; ppp. про́нятый) pierce; get at, influence.

проница́емый permeable; проница́тельный perspicacious.

проноси́ть* (pf. -нести́*) carry through/past; -ся shoot/sweep/fly past; be carried past.

проны́ра (m. & f.) pushing person; проны́рливый pushing.

про|ню́хивать (pf. -ню́хать) smell/nose out.

проня́ть see пронима́ть.

проо́браз prototype.

пропага́нда propaganda, popularization; пропаганди́ст, ~ка propagandist.

про|пада́ть (pf. -па́сть*) be missing/lost; perish; disappear; be wasted; пропа́жа loss.

про|па́лывать (pf. -поло́ть*) weed.

про́пасть (f.) abyss, precipice; a lot (of).

пропа́щий hopeless, lost.

про|пека́ть (pf. -пе́чь*) bake thoroughly.

пропива́ть (pf. пропи́ть*; past про́пил, -а́) spend on drink; ruin.

про|пи́ливать (pf. -пили́ть) saw through.

пропи́ска visa, registration; прописн|о́й capital (letter); -а́я и́стина truism; про|пи́сывать (pf. -писа́ть*) prescribe, register; про́пи|сь (f.) samples of writing;

писа́ть -сью write out (figures) in words.

пропита́ние subsistence; про|пи́тывать (pf. -пита́ть) impregnate, saturate.

пропи́ть see пропива́ть.

про|пи́хивать (pf. -пихну́ть) shove through.

про|плыва́ть (pf. -плы́ть*) swim/sail/float past.

проповедник preacher; пропове́довать advocate; preach; про́поведь (f.) sermon.

про|пола́скивать (pf. -полоска́ть*) rinse.

про|полза́ть (pf. -ползти́*) crawl, creep.

пропо́лка weeding; прополо́ть see пропа́лывать.

пропорциона́льный proportional, proportionate; пропо́рция proportion.

про́пуск 1. (pl. -и) admission; absence; omission; pass (document); 2. (pl. -а) password; про|пуска́ть (pf. -пусти́ть*) let through/past; omit; miss; пропускно́й blotting (paper); carrying (a.) (capacity).

прора́б work superintendent.

про|раба́тывать (pf.-рабо́тать) study; work up; criticize.

про|раста́ть (pf. -расти́*) germinate, sprout.

прорва́ть see прорыва́ть.

проре́живать (pf. -реди́ть, -режу́, -реди́шь) thin out.

проре́з cut, slot, notch; про|реза́ть (pf. -ре́зать*) cut through; -ся cut, come through.

прорез|и́нивать (pf. -и́нить) rubberize.

про́резь (f.) cut, opening.

проре́ха rent, tear; fault.

прорица́ть prophesy.

проро́к prophet.

прор|они́ть (pf.) (-оню́, -о́нишь) utter.

проро́ческий prophetic; проро́чество prophecy, oracle; проро́чить (pf. на-) predict.

про|руба́ть (pf. -руби́ть*) hack/hew through; про́рубь (f.) icehole.

проры́в break, breach; hitch, breakdown; про|рыва́ть 1. (pf. -рва́ть*) break through; -ся break through; burst open.

про|рыва́ть 2. *(pf.* -ры́ть*) dig/ burrow through/across.
про|са́ливать 1. *(pf.* -са́лить) grease; 2. *(pf.* -соли́ть) salt.
про|са́чиваться *(pf.* -со' и́ться) leak, ooze, percolate.
про|све́рливать *(pf.* -сверли́ть) bore, drill, perforate.
просве́т clear space, gap; gleam o-hope; просвети́тель *(m.)* enlightenf er; просветле́ние enlightenment; clear/lucid interval.
про|све́чивать *(pf.* -сгети́ть*) 1. *(v.t.)* x-ray; 2. *(v.i.)* be translucent, be visible.
про|свеща́ть *(pf.* -сг(ти́ть, -сp(щу́, -ск(ти́шь) enlighten; просвеще́ние enlightenment.
просвира́ communion bread.
про́седь *(f.)* grey hair.
про|се́ивать *(pf.* -се́ять*) sift.
про́сека opening, cutting *(in forest).*
просё|лок (-лка) country track.
просе́ять *see* просе́ивать.
про|си́живать *(pf.* -сиде́ть*) 1. spend time sitting; 2. wear out the seat of.
проси́тель applicant, petitioner; пр|оси́ть (-ошу́, -о́сишь; *pf.* по-) ask, request; -ся ask; *(fig.)* cry out for; -ся с языка́ be on the tip of one's tongue.
про|ска́бливать *(pf.* -скобли́ть) scrape a hole in; scrape through.
про|ска́кивать *(pf.* -ско́чить, -ско́чу, -ско́чишь) rush by; fall through; *(coll.)* creep in *(of mistakes).*
про|ска́льзывать *(pf.* -скользну́ть) creep, steal.
про|славля́ть *(pf.* -сла́вить) glorify, bring fame to.
про|сле́живать *(pf.* -следи́ть*) trace, track; (за + *inst.)* keep track of.
просле|зи́ться *(pf.)* (-жу́сь, -зи́шься) shed a few tears.
просл|о́йка *(gen. pl.* -о́ек) layer, stratum.
про|слу́шивать *(pf.* -слу́шать) hear, listen to; miss, not catch.
про|сма́тривать *(pf.* -смотре́ть*) look through; просмо́тр examination, review, preview.
проснуться *see* про(с іпа́ться.
про́со millet.
про|со́бывать *(pf.* -су́нуть) push through/in.
просо́дия prosody.
просочи́ться *see* проса́чиваться.

проспа́ть *see* просыпа́ть; проспа́ть-ся* *(pf.)* sleep oneself sober; have a good sleep.
проспе́кт boulevard, avenue; prospectus.
про|сро́чивать *(pf.* -сро́чить) exceed the time-limit of; просро́чка *(gen. pl.* -чек) delay, expiration of term.
про|ставля́ть *(pf.* -ста́вить) fill write in.
про|ста́ивать *(pf.* -стоя́ть*) stand idle.
проста́к (-а́) simpleton.
про|стёгивать *(pf.* -стега́ть) quilt.
просте́|нок (-нка) pier *(between windows).*
про|стира́ть *(pf.* -т(ре́ть*) stretch, extend; -ся range, stretch, reach.
про|сти́рывать *(pf.* -стира́ть) wash.
прости́тельный pardonable, excusable.
прости́ть *see* проща́ть.
простова́тый simple(-minded).
простоволо́сый *(coll.)* bare-headed.
просто|ду́шие simple-heartedness, ingenuousness; ~ду́шный simple-hearted, artless.
просто́й 1. *(a.)* simple; 2. *(n.)* time wasted, demurrage.
простоква́ша sour clotted milk.
просто́р space, spaciousness.
проста́ре́чие popular speech, common parlance.
просто́рный spacious.
просто|серде́чие simple-heartedness, frankness; ~серде́чный simple-hearted, artless.
простота́ simplicity.
простоя́ть *see* проста́ивать.
простра́нный extensive, vast; простра́нство space.
простре́л lumbago; про|стре́ливать *(pf.* -стрелить, -стрелю́, -стре́лишь) shoot through; rake with fire.
просту́да chill, cold; про|стужа́ть *(pf.* -студи́ть, -стужу́, -сту́дишь) let catch cold; -ся catch cold.
про|ступа́ть *(pf.* -ступи́ть*) come through.
просту́|пок (-пка) misdemeanour.
про|стыва́ть *(pf.* -сты́ть*) go cold.
простыня́ *(pl.* про́ст|ыни, -ы́нь, -ыня́м) sheet.
просу́нуть *see* просо́вывать.
про|су́шивать *(pf.* -суши́ть*) dry up/out.

просфора́ (pl. про́сфоры, -фо́р, -фо-ра́м) communion bread.
просчёт checking; miscalculation; просчи́тываться (pf. -счита́ться) miscalculate.
про́сып: спать без -у sleep the clock round.
про|сыпа́ть 1. (pf. -сы́пать*) spill; 2. (pf. -спа́ть*) oversleep; -ся (pf. просну́ться) wake up.
про|сыха́ть (pf. -со́хнуть*) dry out.
про́сьба request.
прота́лина thawed patch.
про|та́лкивать (pf. -толкну́ть) push/press (through); -ся force one's way (through).
про|та́пывать (pf. -топта́ть*) wear, tread (path); wear out (shoes).
про|та́скивать (pf. -тащи́ть*) pull through (coll.) force through.
про|та́чивать (pf. -точи́ть*) eat through.
проте|жи́ровать (dat.) pull strings for.
проте́з artificial limb; зубно́й п. denture.
протеи́н pròtein.
про|тека́ть (pf -те́чь*) flow/run through; elapse; proceed.
протекциони́зм protectionism; проте́кция patronage.
протере́ть see протира́ть.
проте́ст protest; протеста́нт, ~ка Protestant; протестова́ть (ipf. £ pf.) (про́тив + gen.) protest (against); (pf. о-) make an appeal/protest against.
проте́чь see протека́ть.
про́тив (gen.) against; opposite; contrary to; as against.
про́ти|вень (-вня) griddle.
проти́виться (pf. вос-) (dat.) oppose, resist; проти́вник enemy opponent; проти́вный opposite, head (wind), contrary, adverse; (coll.) nasty, offensive.
противо|ве́с counterpoise; ~возду́шный anti-aircraft; ~га́з gas-mask.
противоде́йст|вие opposition; ~вовать (dat.) oppose, counteract.
противо|есте́ственный unnatural; perverted; ~зако́нный illegal; ~зача́точный contraceptive (a.).
противо|поло́жность (f.) contrast, opposition; ~поло́жный opposite, contrary; ~поставле́ние opposition, contrasting;~поставля́ть (pf. -поста́вить) (dat.) oppose (to), contrast (with).

противоречи́вый contradictory, conflicting; ~ре́чие contradiction; ~ре́чить (dat.) contradict.
противостоя́ть* (dat.) oppose, resist.
противоя́дие antidote.
про|тира́ть (pf. -тере́ть*) wear through; rub through.
проти́скивать (pf. -ти́скать, -ти́снуть) (coll.) force/squeeze through.
проткну́ть see протыка́ть.
прото́к canal, duct.
протоко́л protocol, minutes, proceedings.
протолкну́ть see прота́лкивать.
протопта́ть see прота́птывать.
протор|я́ть (pf. -и́ть) beat, blaze (trail).
проточи́ть see прота́чивать.
прото́чный flowing, running.
протра́ва mordant (chem.).
протрез вля́ться (pf. -ви́ться) get sober.
протуха́ть (pf. -ту́хнуть*) become rotten, go bad.
про|тыка́ть (pf. -ткну́ть) pierce, skewer.
про|тя́гивать (pf. -тяну́ть*) stretch out; extend; proffer, -ся stretch out; reach; (pf.) last, linger; протяже́ние extent, stretch; period; протяжённый extensive; протяжный drawn-out.
проу́чивать (pf. -учи́ть*) study; (coll.) teach a lesson to.
профа́н ignoramus.
профдвиже́ние trade-union movement.
профессиона́л, ~ка professional; профессиона́льный professional, trade (a.); п. союз trade union; профе́ссия profession.
профе́ссор (pl. -а́) professor; профессу́ра professorship; the professorate.
про́филь (m.) profile; type.
профо́рма (coll.) formality.
профсою́з trade union; профсою́зный trade-union.
проха́живаться (pf. пр|ойти́сь, -ой-ду́сь; -оше́лся) stroll.
про|хва́тывать (pf. -хвати́ть*) pierce, penetrate; criticize.
прохво́ст scoundrel.
прохла́да cool(ness); прохлади́тельный cooling, refreshing; soft (drink); прохла́дный cool; прохла|жда́ться (pf. -ди́ться, -жу́сь,

-ди́шься) refresh oneself; *(ipf.)* loiter, idle.

прохо́д passage, gangway, aisle; duct; проходи́|мец (-мца) rogue; про|ходи́ть* 1. *(pf.* пройти́*, пр|ойду́, -ойдёшь, -ошёл, *ppp.* -о́йдённый) pass; go past; pass through/over; 2. *(pf.)* spend (time) walking; прохо́дной communicating; entrance *(a.);* прохожде́ние passing, going through/past; прохо́жий passer-by.

про|цвета́ть *(pf.* -цвести́*) flourish, prosper.

процеду́ра procedure; treatment *(med.).*

про|це́живать *(pf.* -цеди́ть*) filter, strain.

проце́нт percentage; per cent.

проце́сс process; legal proceedings, trial; проце́ссия procession.

прочёр|кивать *(pf.* -черкну́ть) draw a line on/through.

про|че́рчивать *(pf.* -черти́ть*) draw.

проче́сть *see* чита́ть.

проче́сывать *(pf.* прочеса́ть*) comb; search *(mil.).*

про́чий other.

про|чи́тывать *(pf.* -чита́ть, -че́сть, -чту́, -чтёшь; *past* чёл, -чла; *ppp.* -чтённый) read through.

про́чить intend, destine.

прочища́ть *(pf.* -чи́стить*) clean, clear.

про́чный durable, firm, solid.

прочте́ние reading, perusal.

прочу́вствованный heart-felt, emotional.

прочь away; ру́ки п.! hands off! прошёдш|ий past; -ее вре́мя the past tense.

проше́ние application, petition.

проше́ств|ие: по -ии *(gen.)* after.

прошиба́ть *(pf.* прошиби́ть, -п;ибу́, -бёшь; -ши́б, -ла; *ppp.* -ши́бленный) break through; его́ пот прошиб he broke into a sweat.

про|шива́ть *(pf.* -ши́ть*) sew, stitch.

прошлого́дний last year's; про́шл|ый past, bygone; -ое the past.

прошмы́гивать *(pf.* прошмыгну́ть) *(coll.)* slip, steal (past).

прошнуро́вывать *(pf.* -ова́ть) string through.

проща́й, -те! good-bye; проща́льный farewell, parting *(a.);* проща́ние farewell, parting; проща́ть *(pf.* прости́ть, -щу́, -сти́шь) forgive,

pardon; -ся (с + *inst.)* say goodbye (to).

про́ще *(comp. of* просто́й) simpler; plainer.

проще́ние forgiveness, absolution, pardon.

прощу́пывать *(pf.* прощу́пать) feel.

проявля́тель *(m.)* developer *(phot.);* проявле́ние manifestation; developing *(phot.);* проявля́ть *(pf.* прояви́ть) show, display; develop *(phot.).*

проясня́ться *(pf.* проясни́ться) brighten up, clear.

пруд (в -у́, *pl.* -ы́) pond; пр|уди́ть (-ужу́, -у́дишь; *pf.* за-) dam.

пружи́на spring; пружи́нистый springy; пружи́нный spring *(a.).*

прут *(pl.* -ья, -ьев), пру́тик twig.

пры́галка *(coll.)* skipping rope; пры́гать *(pf.* пры́гнуть) jump, dive; прыг|у́н (-уна́), ~у́нья, *(gen. pl.* -у́ний) jumper; пры|жо́к (-жка́) jump; dive.

пры́скать *(pf.* пры́снуть) sprinkle; п. со сме́ху burst out laughing.

пры́ткий *(comp.* пры́тче) lively, quick; прыть *(f.)* quickness, verve; во всю п. at full speed.

прыщ (-а́), пры́щик spot, pimple.

пряде́ние spinning; пряди́льный spinning *(a.);* пряди́ль|щик, ~щица spinner.

прядь *(f.)* lock *(of hair),* strand.

пря́жа yarn, thread.

пря́|жка *(gen. pl.* -жек) buckle, clasp.

пря́лка distaff; spinning-wheel.

прямизна́ straightness.

пря́мо straight; frankly; *(coll.)* real, really.

прямо|ду́шие straightforwardness; ~ду́шный straightforward.

прямо́й straight; direct; erect; straightforward; real.

прямолине́йный rectilinear; straightforward.

прямота́ uprightness, plain dealing.

прямо|уго́льник rectangle; ~уго́льный rectangular.

пря́ник cake; пря́ность *(f.)* spice; пря́ный spicy; heady *(smell).*

прясть *(пряд|у́, -ёшь, прял, -á; *pf.* с- *ppp.* спрядённый) spin.

пр|я́тать *(pf.* -я́чу, -я́чешь; *pf.* с-) hide; -ся hide (oneself); пря́|тки (-ток) hide-and-seek.

пса|ло́м (-лма́) psalm; **псалты́рь** *(f.)* Psalter.

пса́|рня *(gen. pl.* -рен) kennel.

псевдони́м pseudonym.

психиа́тр psychiatrist; **психиатри́я** psychiatry.

психика psychology; **психи́ческий** psychical, mental; **психо́лог** psychologist; **психоло́гия** psychology; **психопа́т** psychopath.

пте|не́ц (-нца́) nestling, fledgeling.

пти́ца bird; **птицево́дство** poultry farming; **пти́чий** bird *(a.);* poultry *(a.);* **пти́|чка** *(gen. pl.* -чек) little bird; tick *(mark);* **пти́чник** poultry yard.

пу́блика public; audience; **публика́ция** publication; **публикова́ть** *(pf.* о-) publish; **публици́ст** publicist, pamphleteer; **публици́стика** journalism; **публи́чный** public *(a.);* п. дом brothel.

пу́гало scarecrow; **пуга́ть** *(pf.* ис-, на-, пере-; pf. пугну́ть) frighten, scare; **-ся** *(gen.)* be frightened (of); **пуга́ч** (-á) eagle-owl; toy pistol; **пугли́вый** fearful, timid.

пу́говица button.

пуд *(pl.* -ы) pood (16.38 *kilogr.,* 36 *lb. avoirdupois).*

пу́дель *(m.; pl.* -и & -я) poodle.

пу́динг pudding.

пу́дра powder; **пу́дреница** powder-box/case; **пу́дрить** *(pf.* на-) powder.

пуза́тый *(coll.)* pot-bellied; **пу́зо** *(coll.)* paunch, belly.

пузы́|рёк (-рька́) bubble; bleb; phial; **пузы́р|ь** (-я́) bubble; blister; bladder.

пук bunch, bundle; tuft.

пулемёт machine-gun; **пулемётчик** machine-gunner; **пулесто́йкий** bullet-proof.

пульвериза́тор atomizer, spray.

пульс pulse; **пульси́ровать** pulsate.

пульт stand, desk; (control-)panel.

пу́ля bullet.

пункт point; station; item; paragraph; **пункти́р** dotted line. **пунктуа́льный** punctual; **пунктуа́ция** punctuation.

пунцо́вый crimson.

пунш punch.

пуп (-á) navel; **пупови́на**|umbilical cord; **пу|по́к** (-пка́) navel; gizzard.

пурга́ blizzard.

пурит|а́нин *(pl.* -а́не, -а́н), **~а́нка** Puritan; **пурита́нский** Puritan, puritanical.

пу́рпур purple; **пурпу́р|ный, ~овый** purple *(a.).*

пуск start; **пуска́ть** *(pf.* пусти́ть, пущу́, пу́стишь) let, permit; start, set in motion; throw; put forth *(shoots etc.);* пуска́й/пусть идёт! let him go!; -ся set out; embark *(fig.);* **пусково́й** starting *(a.).*

пустельга́ kestrel.

пусте́ть *(pf.* о-) become empty/ deserted.

пусти́ть *see* пуска́ть.

пустова́ть be/stand empty; **пустозво́н** *(coll.)* idle talker; **пусто́й** empty, hollow; uninhabited; idle, shallow; groundless; **пустоме́ля** *(coll). m, & f.* windbag; **пустота́** emptiness, frivolousness, futility; vacuum; **пусто́телый** hollow.

пу́стошь *(f.)* waste land.

пусты́нный deserted, uninhabited; **пусты́ня** desert; **пусты́р|ь** (-я́) waste, vacant land.

пусть *see* пуска́ть.

пустя́к (-á) trifle; **пуст|яко́вый, ~я́чный** trivial.

пу́таница confusion; muddle; **пу́таный** confused; **пу́та|ть** *(pf.* за-, пере-, с-) mix up, tangle, confuse; -ся get mixed up.

путёвка pass; **путеводи́тель** *(m.)* guide; guide-book; **путево́й** travelling, road *(a.);* путём *see* путь.

путеше́ствен|ник, **~ница** traveller; **путеше́ствие** journey, voyage; **путеше́ствовать** travel, voyage.

пути́на fishing season.

пу́тный sensible; worthwhile.

пу́ты (пут) hobble; *(fig.)* chains, fetters.

путь *(m.; gen., dat.; prep.* пути́, *inst.* путём, *pl.* -и) way; path, track; route; journey, voyage; means; путём *(gen.)* by means (of).

пух (в -у́) down; разби́ть в п. и прах rout.

пу́хлый chubby, plump; **пу́хнуть** *(past.* пух, -ла; *pf.* вс-, о-) swell.

пухови́к (-á) feather-bed; **пухо́вка** powder-puff; **пухо́вый** downy.

пучегла́зый goggle-eyed.

пучи́на gulf; abyss; the deep.

пу́чить *(pf.* вс-) *(coll.)* (make to) swell; *(pf.* вы-) *(coll.)* make protrude.

пу|чóк (-чкá) bunch, bundle; pencil *(of rays) ;* bun *(hairstyle).*
пýшечный gun, cannon *(a.).*
пушúнка bit of fluff; пушúстый fluffy.
пý|шка *(gen. pl.* -шек) gun, cannon.
пушнúна furs, pelts; пушнóй fur-bearing; пушóк (-шкá) fluff.
пýща dense forest.
пýще *(coll.)* more, worse.
пчелá *(pl.* пчёлы) bee; пчелúный bee *(a.) ;* пчеловóдство bee-keeping; пчéльник apiary.
пшенúца wheat; пшенúчный wheat-(en).
пшённый millet *(a.);* пшенó millet.
пыл (в -ý) ardour, heat; пылáть *(pf.* вос-) flame, burn.
пылесóс vacuum cleaner; пылúнка speck of dust.
пылúть *(pf.* на-) raise dust; -ся be dusty.
пы́лкий ardent, fervent.
пыл|ь *(f.,* в -ú) dust; пы́льный dusty, dust *(a.) ;* пыльцá pollen.
пырéй couch-grass.
пырнýть *(pf.) (coll.)* jab, stab.
пытáть torture; *(coll.) ;* -ся *(pf.* по-) attempt, try; пы́тка torture; anguish; пытлúвый inquisitive, keen.
пы́хать (пышý, пы́шешь) blaze.
пы|хтéть (-хчý, -хтúшь) pant, puff.
пы́шка doughnut.
пы́шный luxuriant.
пьедестáл pedestal.
пьéса play.
пьянéть *(pf.* о-) become drunk; пьянúть *(pf.* о-) make drunk, intoxicate; пья́ница *(m. & f.)* drunkard; пья́нство drunkenness; пья́ный drunk.
пюпúтр lectern, stand.
пюрé *(indecl.)* purée; картóфельное п. mashed potatoes.
пяд|ь *(f., pl.* -и, -éй) span; *(fig.)* inch; семú пядéй во лбу egg-head; intelligent.
пя́|льцы (-лец) embroidery frame.
пятá *(pl.* пя́т|ы, -áм) heel.
пятáк (-á) *(coll.)* 5-copeck piece.
пятёрка five; five-rouble note; five *(cards) ;* 'excellent' mark; пя́теро five.
пяти|бóрье pentathlon; ~грáнник pentahedron.
пятидеся́тый fiftieth.

пяти|лéтие quinquennium; ~лéтка five-year plan; ~лéтний five-year, five-year-old.
пятисóтый five-hundredth.
пя́тить (пя́чу, пя́тишь; *pf.* по-) (cause to) move backwards; -ся move backwards, back.
пятиугóльник pentagon.
пя́тка heel.
пятнáдцатый fifteenth; пятнáдцать fifteen.
пятнáть *(pf.* за-) spot, stain.
пятнúстый spotted.
пя́тница Friday.
пятнó *(pl.* пя́т|на, -тен) patch, stain; родúмое п. birthmark.
пя|тóк (-ткá) five; пя́тый fifth; пять five; пятьдеся́т fifty; пятьсóт five hundred.

Р

раб (-á), рабá slave, serf; рабовладé|лец (-льца) slave-owner.
рабо|лéпие servility; ~лéпный servile; ~лéпствовать (пред + *inst.)* cringe (to), fawn (on).
рабóта work; job; рабóтать work; (над + *inst.)* work on; рабóтник, ~ница worker.
работо|дáтель *(m.)* employer; ~спосóбный able-bodied; hard-working.
рабóчий worker; worker's, working *(a.).*
рáбский slave *(a.) ;* slavish; рáбство slavery; рабы́ня female slave.
раввúн rabbi.
рáвенство equality; равнéние dressing, alignment; равнúна plain.
равнó equals (+ *dat.) ;* alike; все р. it's all the same.
равно|бéдренный isosceles; ~вéсие balance, equilibrium; ~дéнствие equinox; ~дýшие indifference; ~дýшный indifferent; ~мéрный even, uniform; ~прáвие equality *(of rights) ;* ~прáвный enjoying equal rights; ~сúльный equivalent, equal; ~стóронний equilateral; ~цéнный equivalent, equal.
рáвный equal
равня́ть *(pf.* с-) even, equalize; -ся compete, compare; (+ *dat.)* be equal to.
рад *(dat.)* glad (at/about).
радáр radar.

радéние *(obs.)* zeal.
рáди *(gen.)* for the sake (of).
радиáтор radiator.
рáдий radium.
радикáл radical; радикáльный radical *(a.)*.
рáдио *(indecl.)* radio, wireless; радио|актúвный radioactive; ~аппарáт radio set; ~вещáние broadcasting; ~грáмма wireless- telegram; ~грáфия radiography.
радиó|ла radiogram; ~свя́зь *(f.)* wireless communication; ~стáнция wireless/radio station.
радúровать *(ipf. & pf.)* radio, send wireless message; радúст, ~ка wireless operator; telegraphist.
рáдиус radius.
рáдовать *(pf. об-)* make glad/happy; -ся *(dat.)* be glad, rejoice (at); рáдостный joyful; рáдость *(f.)* gladness, joy.
рáдуга rainbow; рáдужный iridescent; cheerful.
радýшие cordiality; радýшный cordial.
раз 1. *(pl. -ы, gen. pl. раз)* time; one; one time; 2. once, one day; 3. since, as; как раз just exactly; ни рáзу not once; не раз more than once.
раз|бавля́ть *(pf. -бáвить)* dilute.
раз|бáлтывать *(pf. -болтáть) (coll.)* shake up; blab, give away; -ся work loose; *(of person)* get out of hand; be mixed.
разбéг running start; раз|бегáться *(pf. -бежáться*)* scatter; take a run.
раз|бивáть *(pf. -бúть, -обью́*)* break, smash; defeat; divide up; mark out, space out; -ся be broken, divided, *etc.;* hurt oneself; разбúвка laying/ spacing out.
равбинт|óвывать *(pf. -овáть)* unbandage.
разбирáтельство trial, examination; разбирáть *(pf. разобрáть, разберý*)* take to pieces, strip; sort out; analyse, investigate; understand; seize *(of feelings)*; -ся 1. unpack; 2. (в + *prep.)* examine; look into, understand.
разбитнóй *(coll.)* sprightly.
разбúтый beaten; broken; jaded; разбúть *see* разбивáть.
разбóй brigandage, robbery; разбóйник brigand, robber; разбóйничий robber's.

разбóр analysis; trial; critique; разбóрка sorting out; stripping down; разбóрный collapsible; разбóрчивый 1. legible; 2. exacting, fastidious.
разбрáсывать *(pf. -бросáть)* throw about, scatter; -ся dissipate one's energies.
раз|бредáться *(pf. -брестúсь*)* disperse, straggle.
разбрóд disorder.
разбрóсанный scattered; disconnected, incoherent.
раз|брызгивать *(pf. -брызгать*)* splash, spray.
раз|бухáть *(pf. -бýхнуть*)* distend, swell.
разбушевáться *(pf.)* rage.
развáл collapse; disintegration; раз|вáливать *(pf. -валúть*)* pull down; spoil; -ся tumble down, fall to bits; *(coll.)* sprawl; развáлина ruin, wreck.
раз|вáривать *(pf. -варúть*)* boil soft.
рáзве 1. really; 2. (+ *inf.)* perhaps it would be better (to); 3. unless, except.
развевáть *(-ваю; pf. -вéять*)* disperse; blow about; -ся *(ipf. only)* flutter, fly.
развéдать *see* развéдывать.
развéдение breeding; cultivating.
разведённый divorced; *(see also* разводúть).
развéдка intelligence service; reconnaissance; развéдочный exploratory; развéдчик secret service man; intelligence officer; scout; prospector; раз|вéдывать *(pf. -вéдать)* find out; reconnoitre.
раз|вéивать *(pf. -вéять*)* disperse, dispel, scatter.
развéнчивать *(pf. -венчáть)* dethrone; debunk.
разверзáться *(pf.* разв|éрзнуться, *past* -éрзся) *(coll.)* gape, yawn.
раз|вёрстывать *(pf. -верстáть)* allot; assess *(tax)*.
раз|вёртывать *(pf. -вернýть)* unroll, unfold; display, develop; extend; -ся unroll; spread; develop; turn; развёрнутый full-scale; detailed.
развесел|я́ть *(pf. -úть)* cheer up, amuse.
развéсистый spreading, branchy.
развéсить *see* развéшивать; развéска weighing.

разветвле́ние branching; ramification; fork; **развет|вля́ться** *(pf.* -ви́ться) branch; divide.

раз|ве́шивать *(pf.* -ве́сить*) weigh out; spread; hang.

развея́ть *see* **развева́ть** *&* **разве́ивать.**

развива́ть *(pf.* разви́ть, разогью́*) develop; untwist, -ся develop; be untwisted; lose its curls *(hair).*

разви́лина fork, bifurcation.

разви́н|чивать *(pf.* -ти́ть, -чу́, -ти́шь) unscrew; -ся become unscrewed; become unnerved.

разви́тие development; **развито́й** well-developed; intelligent; **разви́ть** *see* **развива́ть.**

раз|влека́ть *(pf.* -вле́чь*) amuse, entertain; -ся have a good time, amuse oneself; **развлече́ние** entertainment; relaxation.

разво́д divorce; **раз|води́ть*** *(pf.* -вести́*) take; take apart; divorce; dilute; light *(fire);* breed -ся be taken etc.; get divorced; grow, multiply, breed; **разводно́й:** р. мост drawbridge; р. ключ adjustable spanner.

раз|вози́ть* *(pf.* -везти́*) convey, transport; deliver.

раз|вора́чивать *(pf.* -гернуть) turn, swing round; (-гороти́ть*) *(coll.)* smash; разворо́т turn.

развра́т depravity; **развра́т|ник, ~ница** libertine; **развра́тный** lewd, debauched; **развра|ща́ть** *(pf.* -ти́ть, -шу́, -ти́шь) corrupt, deprave; -ся become depraved; **развраще́ние** depraving, debauching.

раз|вью́чивать *(pf.* -вьючить) unload.

развя́зка dénouement; outcome; **развя́зный** free-and-easy; **раз|вя́зывать** *(pf.* -вяза́ть*) untie; unleash; -ся come free/undone/untied; (с + *inst.*) have done (with).

разга́дка clue, solution; **раз|га́дывать** *(pf.* -гада́ть) unravel, solve; guess.

разга́р: в -е боя at the height of the battle.

разгиба́ть *(pf.* разогну́ть) straighten, unbend; -ся straighten up.

разглаго́льствовать talk profusely.

раз|гла́живать *(pf.* -гла́дить*) smooth out, iron out.

разгла|ша́ть *(pf.* -си́ть, -шу́, -си́шь) divulge, noise abroad.

раз|гля́дывать *(pf.* -гляде́ть*) examine; discern.

разгне́вать (-еваю; *pf.)* anger.

разгова́ривать talk, converse; **разгово́р** conversation; **разговори́ться** *(pf.)* get talking; warm to one's topic; **разгово́рник** phrase-book; **разгово́рный** colloquial; **разгово́рчивый** talkative.

разго́н dispersal; momentum; distance; **разгоня́ть** *(pf.* разогна́ть, разгоню́*) drive away, dispel; speed up; space *(type).*

разгор|а́живать *(pf.* -оди́ть, -ожу́, -оди́шь) partition off.

раз|гора́ться *(pf.* -горе́ться*) flare up.

разгороди́ть *see* **разгора́живать.**

разграбле́ние plunder, pillage.

разграниче́ние differentiation; demarcation; **разгран|и́чивать** *(pf.* -и́чить) differentiate; delimit.

раз|греба́ть *(pf.* -грести́*) rake; shovel.

разгро́м rout.

раз|гружа́ть *(pf.* -грузи́ть*) unload, discharge; relieve; **разгру́зка** unloading, relief.

раз|грыза́ть *(pf.* -грызть*) crack *(a nut).*

разгу́л revelry; violence, raging.

раз|гу́ливать *(pf.* -гуля́ть) *(coll.)* amuse; dispel; *(ipf.)* stroll about; -ся *(coll.)* go on a spree; break loose, rage; clear up *(of weather);* refuse to go to sleep; **разгу́льный** loose, rakish.

раз|дава́ть* *(pf.* -да́ть*) distribute, give out; -ся be given out; resound; make way; *(coll.)* expand; put on weight.

раз|да́вливать *(pf.* -дави́ть*) crush; run over.

разда́точный distributing; **разда́ча** distribution.

раз|два́ивать *(pf.* -дво́ить) bisect, divide in two.

раз|двига́ть *(pf.* -дви́нуть) move apart; **раздвижно́й** extending; folding.

раздвое́ние bifurcation, split; **раздво́енный** split; cleft; forked.

раздева́|лка, ~льня *(gen. pl.* -лен) cloakroom; **раздев|а́ть** (-а́ю, -а́ешь; *pf.* разде́ть) undress; -ся undress; take off one's coat.

разде́л division, partition.

разде́лать *see* **разде́лывать.**

разделе́ние division; **раздели́ть** *see* **разделя́ть.**

раз|де́лывать *(pf.* -де́лать) dress; cut; р. под оре́х *(coll.)* make smart; **-ся** (с + *inst.)* have done (with); settle accounts (with).
разде́льный separate; раз|деля́ть *(pf.* -дели́ть*)* divide, separate, share.
раздёргивать 1. *(pf.* -дёргать) pull to pieces; 2. *(pf.* -дёрнуть) pull/ draw apart.
разде́ть *see* раздева́ть.
раздира́ть *(pf.* разодра́ть*, разде́ру) tear, lacerate.
раздо|быва́ть *(pf.* -бы́ть*) *(coll.)* get, raise.
раздо́лье expanse; liberty.
раздо́р discord.
раздоса́довать *(pf.) (coll.)* vex.
раздра|жа́ть *(pf.* -жи́ть) annoy; irritate; **-ся** get annoyed; раздраже́ние annoyance; irritation; раздражи́тель *(m.)* irritant; раздражи́тельный irritable.
раздроб|ля́ть *(pf.* -и́ть) break, smash to pieces; divide.
раз|дува́ть *(pf.* -ду́ть) fan, blow; exaggerate; *(impers.)* swell; **-ся** be blown out/up; swell.
раз|ду́мывать *(pf.* -ду́мать) *(coll.)* change one's mind; *(ipf.)* ponder; **-ся** start thinking (about); разду́мье meditation, thoughtful mood.
разду́ть *see* раздува́ть.
разев|а́ть (-а́ю, -а́ешь; *pf.* рази́нуть) *(coll.)* open wide; gape.
разжа́лобить *(pf.)* move to pity.
разжа́ловать *(pf.)* degrade, reduce to the ranks.
разжа́ть *see* разжима́ть.
раз|жёвывать *(pf.* -жева́ть*) masticate.
раз|жива́ться *(pf.* -жи́ться*) get rich.
раз|жига́ть *(pf.* -же́чь*, -ожгу́) kindle; rouse.
раз|жижа́ть *(pf.* -жиди́ть, -жижу́, -жиди́шь) dilute, thin.
раз|жима́ть *(pf.* -жа́ть*, -ожму́) unclasp, undo.
разжи́ться *see* разжива́ться.
рази́нуть *see* разева́ть; рази́ня *(m. & f.)* *(coll.)* gape, gawk.
рази́тельн|ый striking; рази́ть (-жу́, -зи́шь; *pf.* с-) strike, beat; smell.
раз|лага́ть *(pf.* -ложи́ть, -ложу́, -ло́жишь) decompose; resolve; demoralize; **-ся** decompose; become demoralized.

разла́д disorder; discord; раз|ла́живать *(pf.* -ла́дить*) spoil.
раз|ла́мывать *(pf.* -лома́ть) break; pull down; *(pf.* -ломи́ть*) break.
разлёживаться sprawl, lounge.
раз|леза́ться *(pf.* -ле́зться*) come to pieces, fall apart.
раз|лета́ться *(pf.* -лете́ться*) fly away (in different directions).
разле́чься* *(pf.)* stretch oneself out.
разли́в flood; overflow; bottling *(of wine)*; раз|лива́ть *(pf.* -ли́ть*, -олью́) spill, pour out; **-ся** spill; overflow; разливно́й draught *(beer)*.
разлин|о́вывать *(pf.* -ова́ть) rule, make lines.
разли|ча́ть *(pf.* -и́ть) distinguish, discern; **-ся** differ; разли́чие distinction, difference; различи́тельный distinctive; разли́чный different.
разложе́ние decomposition; разложи́ть *see* разлага́ть & раскла́дывать.
разло́м breaking; break, fracture; разлом|а́ть, -и́ть *see* разла́мывать.
разлу́ка separation; разлуч|а́ть *(pf.* -и́ть) separate, part; **-ся** separate, part
разлюби́ть* *(pf.)* cease to love/ like.
раз|ма́зывать *(pf.* -ма́зать*) spread; *(coll.)* spin out.
раз|ма́лывать *(pf.* -моло́ть*) grind.
раз|ма́тывать *(pf.* -мота́ть) unwind.
разма́х swing; sweep; scope; span; раз|ма́хивать *(pf.* -махну́ть) *(inst.)* swing, brandish; **-ся** swing/wave one's arm.
раз|ма́чивать *(pf.* -мочи́ть*) soak, steep.
разма́шистый sprawling, sweeping.
размежева́ние demarcation, delimitation; размеж|ёвывать *(pf.*-ева́ть) delimit.
размельч|а́ть *(pf.* -и́ть) make small, pulverize.
разме́н exchange; раз|ме́нивать *(pf.* -меня́ть) change *(money)*.
разме́р size; dimensions; degree; extent; раз|меря́ть *(pf.* -ме́рить) measure.
размести́ть *see* размеща́ть.
раз|мета́т* 1. *(pf.* -мести́*) sweep.
размётывать *(pf.* размета́ть 2.) disperse, scatter.

раз|ме́шивать (pf. -меша́ть) stir; 2. (pf. -меси́ть*) knead.

разме|ща́ть (pf. -сти́ть, -щу́, -сти́шь) place, put; accommodate; invest; размеще́ние placing; accommodation, investment.

раз|мина́ть (pf. -мя́ть*, -омну́) knead, mash; (coll.) stretch (one's legs).

разми́нка warming/limbering up.

размину́ться (pf.) miss each other; cross (of letters).

размно|жа́ть (pf. -мно́жить) multiply; duplicate; -ся propagate (itself); размноже́ние reproduction.

размозжи́ть* (pf.) smash.

раз|мока́ть (pf. -мо́кнуть*) get soaked.

размо́лвка disagreement, tiff.

раз|мора́живать (pf. -моро́зить*) defrost.

размота́ть see разма́тывать.

размочи́ть see разма́чивать.

раз|мыва́ть (pf. -мы́ть*) erode; wash away.

размыка́ть (pf. разомкну́ть) break, disconnect.

размы́ть see размыва́ть.

размышле́ние reflection, meditation; размышля́ть (о + prep.) reflect/meditate on.

размяг|ча́ть (pf. -чи́ть) make soft; раз|мяка́ть (pf. -мя́кнуть*) grow soft

размя́ть see размина́ть.

раз|на́шивать (pf. -носи́ть*) wear in (make comfortable).

разнести́ see разноси́ть.

разнима́ть (pf. раз|ня́ть, -ниму́, -ни́мешь; ро́знял & разня́л, -а́; ppp. -ня́тый) disunite, disjoint, take to pieces.

ра́зниться differ, be different; ра́зница difference.

разно|бо́й discord, lack of coordination; ~ви́дность (f.) variety; ~гла́сие difference, disagreement; ~мы́слие difference of opinion; ~обра́зие variety, diversity; ~обра́зный various, diverse; ~речи́вый contradictory; ~ро́дный heterogeneous.

разно́с (coll.) delivery, carrying; scolding, rating; раз|носи́ть* 1. (pf. -нести́*) carry, deliver; book, enter; smash; scold; (coll.) scatter; (impers.) swell; 2. (pf.) see раз-

на́шивать; разно́ска (coll.) delivery.

разносторо́нний many-sided; versatile.

ра́зность (f.) difference.

разно́с|чик, ~чица hawker, pedlar.

разно|цве́тный variegated; ~чи́нец (-нца) raznochinets (intellectual of non-noble origin in 19th century); ~чте́ние variant; ~шёрстный of different colour; patchy; scratch (team).

разну́зданный unbridled.

ра́зный different; various.

раз|ню́хивать (pf. -ню́хать) smell out.

разня́ть see разнима́ть.

разоблач|а́ть (pf. -и́ть) disrobe, undress; expose; разоблаче́ние disclosure; exposure.

разобра́ть see разбира́ть.

разобщ|а́ть (pf. -и́ть) separate, disconnect; estrange.

ра́зовый биле́т single ticket.

разогна́ть see разгоня́ть; разогну́ть see разгиба́ть.

разо|грева́ть (-грева́ю; pf. -гре́ть*) warm up.

разо|де́ть* (pf., -де́ну, -де́нешь) dress up.

разодра́ть see раздира́ть; разойти́сь see расходи́ться; разомкну́ть see размыка́ть; разорва́ть see разрыва́ть 1.

разоре́ние destruction; ruin; разори́тельный ruinous; разори́ть see разоря́ть.

разору ж|а́ть (pf. -и́ть) disarm; dismantle; разоруже́ние disarmament.

разор|я́ть (pf. -и́ть) ruin; destroy; -ся ruin oneself.

разосла́ть see рассыла́ть.

разоспа́ться* (pf.) have a long, sound sleep.

разостла́ть see расстила́ть.

разочарова́ние disappointment; разочар|о́вывать (pf. -ова́ть) disappoint; -ся (в + prep.) be disappointed (in).

раз|раба́тывать (pf. -рабо́тать) exploit, work (e.g. mine); cultivate; work out, develop; разрабо́тка exploitation, cultivation; field, pit; working out.

раз|ража́ться (pf. -рази́ться*) break, burst (out); p. сме́хом burst out laughing.

раз|раста́ться (pf. -расти́сь*) grow, spread.
разре|жа́ть (pf. -ди́ть, -жу́, -ди́шь) thin/weed out; rarefy.
разре́з cut, section; раз|реза́ть (pf. -ре́зать*) cut; разрезно́й нож paper-knife; разре́зывать = разреза́ть.
разреш|а́ть (pf. -и́ть) allow; solve; settle; разреше́ние permission, permit; solution; settlement.
разро́зненный odd, separate; разро́зн|ивать (pf. -ить) break up (a set).
раз|руба́ть (pf. -руби́ть*) hew; cut to pieces.
разрумя́н|ивать (pf. -ить) paint, rouge; redden.
разру́ха destruction, ruin; раз|руша́ть (pf. -ру́шить) destroy, demolish, ruin; -ся go to ruin; fall; разруше́ние destruction; разруши́тельный destructive.
разры́в break, rupture; shell burst; разрыва́ть 1. (pf. разорва́ть*) tear asunder; blow up; (c + inst.) break (with); -ся break, tear; explode.
раз|рыва́ть 2. (pf. -ры́ть*) dig up.
разрывно́й exploding, explosive.
разрыда́ться (pf.) burst into tears.
разры́ть see разрыва́ть 2.
разрыхл|я́ть (pf. -и́ть) loosen, hoe.
разря́д 1. discharge; 2. category, sort.
разря́дка discharging, unloading; relieving; spacing; разря|жа́ть (pf. -ди́ть, -жу́, -ди́шь) 1. dress up; 2. discharge; space out; relieve (tension); -ся 1. dress oneself up; 2. run down; subside.
раз|убежда́ть (pf. -убеди́ть*) dissuade; -ся (в + prep.) change one's mind (about).
разува́ть (pf. раз|у́ть, -у́ю, -у́ешь remove shoes of; -ся take off one's shoes.
раз|уверя́ть (pf. -уве́рить) (в + prep.) undeceive, disabuse (about).
разузн|ава́ть (-аю́, -аёшь; pf. -а́ть) find out.
разу|кра́шивать (pf. -кра́сить*) decorate, embellish.
ра́зум reason, intelligence; разуме́ть understand, mean; -ся be understood; разуме́ется it goes without saying; разу́мный reasonable, wise; clever.

разу́ть see разува́ть.
разуха́бистый rollicking, free-and-easy.
раз|у́чивать (pf. -учи́ть*) learn; -ся unlearn, forget.
разъ|еда́ть (pf. -е́сть*) eat away; corrode.
разъедин|я́ть (pf. -и́ть) separate; disconnect.
разъе́зд departure; railway siding; (pl.) journeyings; разъездно́й siding (a.); travelling (a.).
разъез|жа́ть drive about; -ся (pf. разъе́хаться*) depart; (pf. only) pass one another; miss each other.
разъе́сть see разъеда́ть.
разъяр|я́ть (pf. -и́ть) infuriate, madden.
разъясне́ние explanation; interpretation; разъясни́тельный explanatory; разъясн|я́ть (pf. -и́ть) explain, elucidate.
разы́гр|ывать (pf. -а́ть) perform; raffle; (coll.) play a trick on; -ся become frolicsome; warm up; run high.
разы́скивать (pf. разыска́ть, -ыщу́, -ы́щешь) look for; (pf.) find; -ся be looked for; turn up, be found.
рай (в раю́) paradise.
райко́м regional committee; райо́н region; райо́нный regional.
ра́йский heavenly, of paradise.
райсове́т district soviet.
рак crab; crayfish; cancer.
ра́ка shrine.
раке́та 1. rocket; 2. & раке́тка racket.
раки́та broom (bot.).
ра́ковина shell; sink, washbasin; bandstand; ра́ковый crayfish (a.); cancerous.
раку́рс foreshortening.
раку́|шка (gen. pl. -шек) cockleshell; mussel.
ра́ма frame; ра́мка frame; (pl.) limits; framework.
ра́мпа footlights.
ра́на wound.
ранг class, rank.
ра́нее earlier.
ране́ние injury, wound; ра́неный injured, wounded; casualty.
ра́|нец (-нца) haversack, satchel.
ра́нить (ipf. & pf.) injure, wound; р. в но́гу wound in the leg.

ра́нний early; ра́но soon, early; ра́ньше sooner, earlier.

папи́ра foil, rapier.

ра́порт report; рапортова́ть *(ipf. & pf.; pf. also* от-) report.

ра́са race; раси́зм racialism.

рас|ка́иваться *(pf.* -ка́яться, -ка́юсь) (в + *prep.)* repent (of).

раскали́ть *see* раскаля́ть.

рас|ка́лывать *(pf.* -коло́ть*)* cleave, split.

раскал|я́ть *(pf.* -и́ть) make red/ white-hot.

рас|ка́пывать *(pf.* -копа́ть) dig up, unearth, excavate.

рас|ка́рмливать *(pf.* -корми́ть*)* fatten.

раска́т peal, roll; раска́тистый rolling.

рас|ка́тывать *(pf.* -ката́ть) roll out (flat); *(pf.* -кати́ть*)* roll in different direction; make go fast; -ся *(pf.* -ката́ться) be rolled out; *(pf.* -кати́ться*)* roll about; gain momentum.

рас|ка́чивать *(pf.* -кача́ть) rock, swing; -ся swing/rock oneself.

раска́шляться *(pf.)* have fit of coughing.

раска́яние repentance; раска́яться *see* раска́иваться.

расквартирова́ние billeting.

расквита́ться *(pf.)* (с + *inst.)* settle accounts (with).

раски́дистый branchy.

раскидно́й folding.

раски́дывать *(pf.* раски́нуть) spread/ stretch out; pitch *(tent)*.

раскладно́й folding; · раскла́дывать *(pf.* раз|ложи́ть, -ожу́, -о́жишь) lay out, spread; distribute; unpack.

рас|кла́ниваться *(pf.* -кла́няться) (с + *inst.)* exchange greeting (with); take leave (of).

рас|кле́ивать *(pf.* -кле́ить) stick; unstick.

рас|ко́вывать *(pf.* -кова́ть*)* unshoe; unfetter.

раско́л schism, split; расколо́ть *see* раска́лывать; раско́льник dissenter, schismatic.

раскопа́ть *see* раска́пывать; раско́пка excavation.

раскорми́ть *see* раска́рмливать.

раско́сый slanting.

рас|кра́ивать *(pf.* -кро́ить) cut out; *(coll.)* split.

рас|кра́шивать *(pf.* -кра́сить*)* paint, colour.

раскрепо|ща́ть *(pf.* -сти́ть, -щу́, -сти́шь) liberate.

раскрича́ться* *(pf.)* start shouting.

раскрои́ть *see* раскра́ивать.

рас|кру́чивать *(pf.* -крути́ть*)* untwist.

рас|крыва́ть *(pf.* -кры́ть*)* open (wide); expose, reveal; раскры́тие opening, disclosing.

рас|купа́ть *(pf.* -купи́ть*)* buy up.

рас|ку́поривать *(pf.* -ку́порить) uncork, open.

рас|ку́сывать *(pf.* -куси́ть, -кушу́, -ку́сишь) bite; *(pf.)* get to the heart of.

рас|ку́тывать *(pf.* -ку́тать) unwrap.

ра́совый racial.

распа́д collapse, disintegration; рас|пада́ться *(pf.* -па́сться*)* disintegrate, fall to pieces.

распак|о́вывать *(pf.* -ова́ть) unpack.

распал|я́ть *(pf.* -и́ть) make burning hot; incense.

рас|па́рывать *(pf.* -поро́ть*)* rip.

распа́сться *see* распада́ться.

рас|па́хивать 1. *(pf.* -паха́ть*)* plough up; 2. *(pf.* -пахну́ть) throw open. распашо́нка baby's vest.

рас|пева́ть *(pf.* -певаю́; *pf.* -пе́ть*)* sing; -ся warm up.

рас|пека́ть *(pf.* -пе́чь*)* *(coll.)* scold.

рас|печа́тывать *(pf.* -печа́тать) unseal, break open.

рас|пи́ливать *(pf.* -пили́ть*)* saw up.

распина́ть *(pf.* рас|пя́ть, -пну́, -пнёшь; *ppp.* распя́тый) crucify; -ся *(coll.)* take great pains.

расписа́ние time-table; распи́ска painting; receipt; расписно́й painted, decorated; рас|пи́сывать *(pf.* -писа́ть*)* paint; assign; enter *(bills)* ; -ся sign; *(coll.)* register one's marriage; start writing.

рас|пи́хивать *(pf.* -пиха́ть) push, shove apart/into various places.

рас|плавля́ть *(pf.* -пла́вить) fuse, melt.

распла́каться* *(pf.)* burst into tears.

рас|пла́стывать *(pf.* -пласта́ть) split; *(coll.)* spread.

распла́та atonement, payment; рас|пла́чиваться *(pf.* -плати́ться*)* (с + *inst.)* pay off; get even (with).

рас|плёскивать *(pf.* -плеска́ть* & -плесну́ть) splash, spill.
рас|плета́ть *(pf.* -плести́*) untwine, untwist.
рас|плыва́ться *(pf.* -плы́ться*) run *(e.g. of ink, paint)*; **расплы́вчатый** diffuse, dim.
расплю́щивать *(pf.* -плю́щить, -плю́снуть) flatten, crush flat.
распозн|ава́ть (-аю́, -аёшь; *pf.* -а́ть) recognize, discern.
распо|лага́ть *(pf.* -ложи́ть, -ложу́, -ло́жишь) arrange; dispose, win over; *(ipf, only; inst.)* dispose (of); **-ся** settle, make oneself comfortable.
рас|ползаться *(pf.* -ползти́сь*) crawl away; *(coll.)* come to pieces.
расположе́ние arrangement; disposition; situation; mood; **расположенный** (к + *dat.)* disposed (towards); **расположи́ть** *see* **располага́ть.**
распо́рка cross-bar, strut.
распоро́ть *see* **распа́рывать.**
распоряди́тель *(m.)* manager; master of ceremonies; **~ность** *(f.)* good management; **~ный** active capable; administrative.
распоря|до́к (-дка) order; regulations; **распоря|жа́ться** *(pf.* -ди́ться, -жу́сь, -ди́шься) (о + *prep.)* make arrangements (for); *(inst.)* dispose (of); **распоряже́ние** decree, order, instruction; disposal.
распра́ва (с + *inst.)* violence, reprisal (on); **рас|правля́ть** *(pf.* -пра́вить) smooth out; spread *(wings)*, stretch; **-ся** (с + *inst.)* carry out violence (on), deal (with).
распределе́ние distribution; **распредел|я́ть** *(pf.* -и́ть) distribute, allot; assess.
распро|дава́ть* *(pf.* -да́ть*) sell off/out; **распрода́жа** (clearance) sale.
распрос|тира́ть *(pf.* -тере́ть; *past only* -тёр; *ppp.* -тёртый) stretch out, extend.
распростране́ние spreading; dissemination; **распростран|я́ть** *(pf.* -и́ть) spread; **-ся** spread: (на + *acc.)* apply (to), affect; (о + *prep.)* enlarge upon.
ра́спр|я *(gen. pl.* -ей) discord.
рас|пряга́ть *(pf.* -пря́чь*) unharness.
распрям|ля́ть *(pf.* -и́ть) straighten.

распуска́ть *(pf.* -пусти́ть*) let loose; dismiss; loosen; unravel; dissolve; **-ся** open; let oneself slide; dissolve, melt.
распу́тать *see* **распу́тывать.**
распу́тица season of bad roads; slush, mud.
распу́тник, **~ница** profligate; **распу́тный** dissolute; **распу́тство** debauchery.
рас|пу́тывать *(pf.* -пу́тать) untangle; unravel.
распу́тье cross-roads.
рас|пуха́ть *(pf.* -пу́хнуть*) swell.
распу́щенный loose; dissolute; *see also* **распуска́ть.**
распыли́тель *(m.)* atomizer, sprayer; **распыл|я́ть** *(pf.* -и́ть) pulverize, disperse.
распя́тие crucifix, crucifixion; **распя́ть** *see* **распина́ть.**
расса́да seedlings; **расса́дник** breeding-ground; **рас|са́живать** *(pf.* -сади́ть, -сажу́, -са́дишь) transplant; **-ся** *(pf.* -се́сться*) take seats; sprawl; *see also* **рассе́да́ться.**
рассве́т dawn; **рас|света́ть** *(pf.* -свести́, -светёт; -свело́) dawn.
рас|седа́ться *(pf.* -се́сться*) settle and crack.
рас|се́ивать *(pf.* -се́ять*) diffuse, disperse, scatter; **-ся** dissipate, clear away, disperse.
рас|се́кать *(pf.* -се́чь*) cleave, cut.
рассе́лина cleft, fissure.
рассел|я́ть *(pf.* -и́ть) settle *(in a new place)* ; separate.
рассе́сться *see* **рассе́да́ться** & **расса́живаться.**
рассе́янный scattered; absent-minded; **рассе́ять** *see* **рассе́ивать.**
расска́з story; account; **расска́зчик, ~чица** story-teller, narrator; **рас|ска́зывать** *(pf.* -сказа́ть*) tell, narrate.
рас|слабля́ть *(pf.* -сла́бить) weaken.
рас|сла́ивать *(pf.* -слои́ть) divide into layers; differentiate.
рассле́дование investigation; inquest; **рассле́довать** *(ipf. & pf.)* investigate.
расслое́ние exfoliation; stratification; **расслои́ть** *see* **рассла́ивать.**
расслы́шать* *(pf.)* catch, hear.
рас|сма́тривать *(pf.* -смотре́ть*) consider, examine.

рассмея́ться* *(pf.)* burst out laughing.

рассмотре́ние examination; scrutiny; рассмотре́ть *see* рассма́тривать.

рассо́вывать *(pf.* -сова́ть*) (coll.)* shove away/about.

рассо́л brine; pickle.

рассо́рить *(pf.)* set at variance; -ся (с + *inst.)* quarrel (with).

рассортиро́вывать *(pf.* -ова́ть) classify, sort.

расс|пра́шивать *(pf.* -проси́ть*) question; make enquiries; расспро́с question, enquiry.

рассро́чивать *(pf.* -сро́чить) spread out; рассро́чк|а: купи́ть в -у buy on instalment plan.

расстава́ние parting; рас|става́ться (-стаю́сь, -стаёшься; *pf.* -ста́ться*) (с + *inst.)* leave, part (from, with).

рас|ставля́ть *(pf.* -ста́вить) arrange, place; расстано́вка arrangement, order.

расста́ться *see* расстава́ться.

расстёгивать *(pf.* -стегну́ть) undo, unfasten; -ся come undone; undo/unbutton one's coat.

расстила́ть *(pf.* разостла́ть, расст|-елю́, -е́лешь) spread out, lay; -ся spread.

расстоя́ние distance, space.

рас|стра́ивать *(pf.* -стро́ить) disorder, disturb; shatter; upset; -ся fall apart; be shattered; be upset.

расстре́л execution by shooting; рас|стре́ливать *(pf.* -стреля́ть) shoot.

расстри́га *(m.)* unfrocked monk.

расстро́ить *see* расстра́ивать; расстро́йство disorder; upset.

рас|ступа́ться *(pf.* -ступи́ться*) part.

рассуди́тельный sober-minded; reasonable; рассуди́ть* *(pf.)* judge; рассу́|док (-дка) reason, intellect; рассу́дочный rational; рассужда́ть (о + *prep.)* reason (about), discuss; рассужде́ние reasoning, argument.

рассчи́тывать *(pf.* рассчита́ть & расче́сть, разочту́, -чтёшь; расчёл, разочла́; *ppp.* разочтённый) calculate; (на + *acc.)* count (on), depend (on); -ся (с + *inst.)* settle accounts (with).

ссыла́ть *(pf.* разосла́ть*) distripabute, circulate; рассы́лка distribution; рассы́льный errand-boy.

рас|сыпа́ть *(pf.* -сы́пать*) scatter, strew; -ся spill, scatter; crumble; рассыпно́й loose *(e.g. cigarettes, sweets)*; рассы́пчатый friable, crumbly; short.

рас|сыха́ться *(pf.* -со́хнуться*) dry up /out.

раста́лкивать *(pf.* -толка́ть) push apart/away; shake.

раста́пливать *(pf.* -топи́ть*) light, kindle; melt.

раста́скивать *(pf.* -таска́ть) carry away; pilfer; *(pf.* -тащи́ть*) pull apart.

раство́р opening; solution; раство-ри́мый soluble; раствори́тель *(m.)* solvent; растворя́ть 1. *(pf.* -ори́ть) dissolve; 2. *(pf.* -ори́ть, -орю́, -о́ришь) open.

растека́ться *(pf.* -те́чься*) run, spread.

расте́ние plant.

растере́ть *see* растира́ть.

рас|терзывать *(pf.* -терза́ть) tear to pieces.

рас|те́ривать *(pf.* -теря́ть) lose; -ся get lost; lose one's head.

растёртый rubbed; ground.

расте́рянный lost; confused.

расте́чься *see* растека́ться.

рас|ти́ (-ту, -тёшь; рос, -ла́; *pf.* вы́-) grow.

растира́ть *(pf.* растере́ть*, разотру́) grind; make into powder; spread.

расти́тельность *(f.)* vegetation; hair *(on face)*; расти́тельный vegetable; ра|сти́ть (-щу́, -сти́шь; *pf.* вы́-) raise, bring up; grow.

растл|ева́ть (-ева́ю; *pf.* -и́ть) corrupt, seduce.

растолка́ть *see* раста́лкивать.

растолк|о́вывать *(pf.* -ова́ть) explain.

расто́пка lighting, kindling; fire-lighter.

растоп|ы́ривать *(pf.* -ы́рить) *(coll.)* spread wide.

расторга́ть *(pf.* -то́ргнуть, *past* -то́рг) cancel; dissolve; расторже́ние dissolution, annulment.

растро́пный efficient, sharp.

расточ|а́ть *(pf.* -и́ть) dissipate, squander; расточи́тельный extravagant.

рас|травля́ть *(pf.* -трави́ть*) aggravate, irritate.

растра́та spending, waste; embezzlement; растра́т|чик, ~чица em-

bezzler; рас|тра́чивать *(pf.* -тра́-
тить*) spend; waste; embezzle.
растрепа́ть* *(pf.)* tousle; make
tattered; растрёпанный dishevelled; tattered.
растре́скиваться *(pf.* -тре́скаться)
crack, become cracked.
растро́гать *(pf.)* move, touch.
растру́б socket, bell mouth.
растуш|ёвывать *(pf.* -ева́ть) shade.
расту́щий growing.
рас|тя́гивать *(pf.* -тяну́ть) stretch;
strain; drag out; -ся be stretched
etc.; sprawl; растяже́ние tension;
strain; растяжи́мый tensile; ex-
pansible; растя́нутый stretched;
long-winded.
расфас|о́вывать *(pf.* -ова́ть) pack.
расформир|о́вывать *(pf.* -ова́ть)
disband.
расха́живать walk about.
рас|хва́ливать *(pf.* -хвали́ть*)
lavish praise on.
рас|хва́тывать *(pf.* -хвата́ть) *(coll.)*
snatch; buy up.
расхити́тель *(m.)* plunderer; em-
bezzler; рас|хища́ть *(pf.* -хи́тить,
-хи́щу, -хи́тишь) plunder; embezzle; расхище́ние plundering;
embezzlement.
рас|хлёбывать *(pf.* -хлеба́ть) *(coll.)*
disentangle; завари́л ка́шу, тепе́рь
сам и расхлёбывай you've made
your bed, now lie on it.
расхля́банный lax, loose.
расхо́д expense(s), expenditure; рас-
ходи́ться* *(pf.* раз|ойти́сь, -ой-
ду́сь; -оше́лся) disperse; (c + *inst.)*
part (from); расхо́дный of expen-
ses/expenditure; расхо́довать *(pf.*
из-) spend; расхожде́ние diver-
gence.
расхола́живать *(pf.* расхоло|ди́ть,
-жу́, -ди́шь) (make) cool.
расхоте́ть* *(pf.)* not want any
more.
рас|цара́пывать *(pf.* -цара́пать)
cover in scratches.
расцве́т bloom; flourishing, heyday;
рас|цвета́ть *(pf.* -цвести́*) bloom,
flourish; расцве́тка colouring,
colouration.
расцелова́ть *(pf.)* cover with kisses.
рас|це́нивать *(pf.* -цени́ть*) esti-
mate, value; расце́нка valuation;
price.
рас|цепля́ть *(pf.* -цепи́ть, -цеплю́,
-це́пишь) unhook, uncouple.

расчеса́ть *see* расчёсывать; расчёска *(coll.)* comb.
расче́сть *see* рассчи́тывать.
рас|чёсывать *(pf.* -чеса́ть*) comb;
card; scratch; -ся be combed
(etc.); (coll.) comb one's hair;
scratch oneself.
расчёт calculation, estimate; settling *(of bill)*; расчётливый prudent; расчётный calculation *(a.);*
calculated.
расчи́стка clearing.
расчиха́ться *(pf.)* have a fit of
sneezing.
рас|чища́ть *(pf.* -чи́стить*) clear.
расчлен|я́ть *(pf.* -и́ть) dismember.
расчу́вствоваться *(pf.)* be overcome with emotion.
рас|ша́ркиваться *(pf.* -ша́ркаться)
shuffle; bow and scrape.
рас|ша́тывать *(pf.* -шата́ть) shake
loose; scatter.
рас|шиба́ть *(pf.* -шиби́ть, -шибу́,
-шибёшь; -ши́б; *ppp.* -ши́блен-
ный) hurt; smash; -ся hurt oneself.
расшива́ть *(pf.* расши́ть*, разошью́)
embroider; unpick.
расширре́ние expansion; dilation; рас|-
ширя́ть *(pf.* -ши́рить) enlarge,
widen.
расши́ть *see* расшива́ть.
расшифр|о́вывать *(pf.* -ова́ть) de-
cipher.
расшнур|о́вывать *(pf.* -ова́ть) unlace.
расще́лина crevice.
расщепле́ние splitting; fission; рас-
ще|пля́ть *(pf.* -пи́ть) split, splin-
ter.
ратифика́ция ratification; ратифи-
ци́ровать *(ipf. & pf.)* ratify.
ра́тный military, war *(a.);* ра́товать
campaign.
ра́туша town hall.
рать *(f.)* host, horde.
ра́унд round *(sport).*
ра́ут party, reception.
рафина́д lump sugar; рафини́ровать
(ipf. & pf.) refine.
раха́т-луку́м Turkish delight.
рахи́т rickets.
рационализи́ровать *(ipf. & pf.)*
rationalize.
ра́ция portable radio.
рачи́тельный *(obs.)* zealous.
рвану́ть *(pf.)* jerk; -ся dash, rush.
рва́ный torn, lacerated; рвань *(f.)*
rags; scoundrel; riff-raff; рвать

(рву, рвёшь; рвал, -á) tear; pick; pull; его рвёт he is vomiting; -ся break, burst.

рвач (-á) self-seeker.

рвéние zeal.

рвóта vomiting.

рдеть glow.

реабилитúровать *(ipf. & pf.)* rehabilitate.

реагúровать (на *acc.*) react (to).

реактúвный reactive; jet *(a.);* реáктор reactor.

реакционéр reactionary; реакциóнный reactionary *(a.);* реáкция reaction.

реалúзм realism; реализовáть *(ipf. & pf.)* realize; реалистúческий realistic; реáльный real; practical.

ребёнок (-ёнка, *pl.* -я́та, -я́т & дéти) child, infant.

ребóрда flange.

ребрó *(pl.* рёбра, рёбер) rib.

ребя́та *see* ребёнок; ребя́ческий childish; ребя́чество childishness; ребя́читься be childish.

рёв roar.

ревáнш revenge; return match.

ре|вéнь (-ня́) rhubarb.

реверáнс curtsy.

ре|вéть (-вý, -вёшь) roar.

ревизионúзм revisionism; ревизиóнный revisory, auditing; ревúзия revision; ревизовáть *(ipf. & pf., & pf.* об-) inspect; revise; ревизóр inspector.

ревматúзм rheumatism; ревматúческий rheumatic.

ревнúвый jealous; ревновáть be jealous; р. мýжа к нéй be jealous of her on account of one's husband; рéвностный zealous; рéвность *(f.)* jealousy.

револьвéр revolver.

революционéр revolutionary; ~ка revolutionary; революциóнный revolutionary *(a.);* революция revolution.

регáлии (-ий) regalia.

рéгент regent; рéгентство regency.

регúстр register; регистрáтор registrar, recorder; регистратýра registry; регистрáция registration.

регистрúровать *(pf.* за-) register; -ся register (oneself).

реглáмент regulations; регламентúровать *(ipf. &. pf)* regulate.

регрессúровать retrogress.

регулúровать *(pf.* y-) regularize; *(pf.* от-) adjust, regulate; регули-

рóвщик (traffic) controller; регуля́рный regular; регуля́тор regulator.

редактúровать *(pf.* от-) edit; редáктор editor; редакциóнный editorial; редáкция editorial office staff; editing.

редéть *(pf.* по-) (become) thin.

редúска radish.

рéдкий *(comp.* рéже) thin; widely-spaced *(teeth);* flimsy; rare; рéдкостный rare; рéдкость *(f.)* rarity.

редуцúровать *(ipf. & pf.)* reduce.

рé|дька *(gen. pl.* -дек) radish.

реéстр register.

режúм regime, regimen; conditions.

режиссёр producer; режиссúровать produce, stage.

рéзать (рéжу, рéжешь; *pf.* раз-) cut; *(pf.* за-) kill, slaughter.

резвúться gambol, frolic; рéзвый fast, sportive.

резéрв reserve(s); резервúровать *(ipf. & pf.)* reserve; резéрвный reserve *(a.);* резервуáр reservoir.

ре|зéц (-зцá) cutter; chisel; incisor.

резидéнция residence.

резúна (india-)rubber; резúнка elastic; eraser; резúновый rubber *(a.).*

рéзкий *(comp.* рéзче) sharp; short *(temper);* рéзкость *(f.)* sharpness; abruptness; sharp word.

резнóй carved.

резня́ carnage.

резолю́ция resolution.

резонáнс resonance; echo, response.

резонёрствовать argue, reason.

резонúровать resound.

результáт result.

рéзче *(comp. of* рéзкий) sharper; рéзчик engraver.

резь *(f.)* gripe, colic.

резьбá carving, fretwork.

резюмé *(indecl.)* resumé; резюмúровать *(ipf. & pf.)* sum up.

рейд road, roads *(mar.);* raid.

рéйка *(gen. pl.* рéек) lath, pole.

рейс run, trip, voyage.

рейсфéдер drawing pen.

рейт|ýзы (-ýз & -ýзов) (riding) breeches; pants.

рекá (рéкý, *pl.* рéки, рек, рéкáм) river, stream.

реквизúровать *(ipf. & pf.)* requisition, commandeer; рéквизúт properties *(theatre).*

реклáма advertisement; рекламú-ровать *(ipf. & pf.)* advertise;

реклáмный publicity, advertising *(a.).*

рекомендáтельный of recommendation; рекомендáция recommendation, reference; рекомендовáть *(ipf. & pf.: & pf.* по- от-) recommend; advise; -ся be recommended; introduce oneself.

реконструировáть *(ipf. & pf.)* reconstruct; реконструкция reconstruction.

рекóрд record; побить р. break the record; рекóрдный record *(a.);* рекордсмéн, ~ка record-holder.

рéкрут recruit.

ректифицировáть *(ipf. & pf.)* rectify.

рéктор *(pl.* -ы, & -á) rector, chancellor *(of university).*

религиóзный religious;pious; религия religion.

реликвия relic, memento.

рельéф relief; рельéфный in relief, embossed.

рельс rail.

релятивизм relativity.

ремáрка stage-direction.

ре|мéнь (-мня) belt, strap.

ремéсленник artisan, craftsman; ремéсленный handicraft *(a.);* industrial; рем|еслó *(pl.* -ёсла, -ёсел) craft, trade.

ремé|шóк (шкá) strap.

ремóнт repair(s); maintenance; ремонтировáть *(ipf. & pf.: & pf.* от-) repair; recondition; ремóнтная мастерскáя repair shop.

ренклóд greengage.

рéнта rent; income *(from capital);* рентáбельный paying, profitable.

рентгéновский Roentgen, X-ray *(a.).*

реорганизовáть *(ipf. & pf.)* reorganize.

рéпа turnip.

репарáция reparation.

репатриировáть *(ipf. & pf.)* repatriate.

репéйник burdock.

репертуáр repertoire.

репетировáть *(pf.* про-, с-) rehearse; репетиция rehearsal.

рéплика cue; retort; remark.

реполóв linnet.

репортёр reporter.

репрессáлия reprisal.

репрéссия repression.

репродуктор loudspeaker; репродукция reproduction.

репутáция reputation.

ресница eyelash.

республика republic; республикá|нец (-нца) ~нка republican; республикáнский republican *(a.).*

рессóра spring.

реставрáция restoration; реставрировáть *(irf. & rf.)* restore.

ресторан restaurant.

ресурс resource.

ретивый eager, zealous.

ретрансляция relaying *(radio).*

ретроспективный retrospective.

ретушировáть *(ipf. & pf.; also* от-) retouch.

реферáт paper; synopsis.

рефлéкс reflex; рефлéктор reflector.

рефóрма reform; реформáтор reformer; реформировáть *(ipf. & pf.)* reform.

рефрижерáтор refrigerator; refrigerated boat/wagon.

рехнýться *(pf.) (coll.)* go mad.

рецензéнт reviewer; рецензировáть *(pf.* про-) review, criticize; рецéнзия review.

рецéпт recipe; prescription.

рецидив relapse; рецидивист recidivist.

речевóй vocal, speech *(a.);* речистый voluble.

рéчка *(gen. pl.* -чек) river, rivulet; речнóй river *(a.).*

реч|ь *(f.; pl.* -и, -éй) speech; talk.

реш|áть *(pf.* -ить) decide; solve; -ся make up one's mind; (на + *acc.)* decide (on); решéние decision; solution.

решётка grating, grille; lattice; fireguard; реш|етó *(pl.* -ёта) sieve; решётчатый latticed.

решимость *(f.)* determination, resolution; решительный decisive; resolute; решить *see* решáть.

рéшка: орёл или р. heads or tails?

рéять (рéю, рéешь) hover; flutter.

ржавéть *(pf.* за-) rust; ржáвчина rust; ржáвый rusty.

ржáние neigh.

ржáнка plover.

ржанóй rye *(a.).*

ржать (ржёшь) neigh.

рига threshing barn.

риза chasuble; ризница vestry.

римл|янин *(pl.* -яне, -ян), ~янка Roman; римский Roman *(a.).*

ри́нуться *(pf.)* dart, rush.

рис rice.

риск risk; рискну́ть *(pf.)* venture; риско́ванный risky; рискова́ть *(inst., inf.)* risk; р. здоро́гьсм endanger one's health.

рисова́ль|щик, ~щица designer, draughtsman; graphic artist; рисова́ть *(pf.* на-) draw, depict; -ся be depicted; appear; *(coll.)* pose, show off.

ри́совый rice *(a.)*.

рису́|нок (-нка) drawing.

ритм rhythm; ритм|и́ческий, ~и́чный rhythmic(al).

рито́рика rhetoric.

риф reef.

рифлёный corrugated.

ри́фма rhyme; рифмова́ть *(pf.* с-) rhyme.

робе́ть *(pf.* о-) be timid; ро́бкий *(comp.* ро́бче) shy, timid; ро́бость *(f.)* shyness.

ров (рга, го рру) ditch.

рове́с|ник, ~ница person of the same age.

ро́вный even, flat, level; equable; ро́вня *(m. & f.)* equal; ровня́ть *(pf.* с-) make even, level off.

рог *(pl.* -а́) horn; рога́тка turnpike; catapult; рога́тый horned; рога́ч (-а́) stag; stag-beetle.

рогови́ца cornea.

рогово́й horny.

рого́жа bast mat.

рогоно́|сец (-сца) cuckold.

род (на -у́, *pl* -ы́, -о́в) family, kin; generation; birth; kind, sort; gender; р. челогѐчсский mankind; что-то в э́том ро́де something of that kind, something like that; ѐму 30 лет о́т роду he is 30 years old.

роди́льный дом maternity home; роди́мый (of) birth; ро́дина homeland; ро́динка birthmark; роди́тел|и (-ѐй) parents; роди́тельный genitive; роди́тельский parental.

роди́ть (-жу́, -ди́шь; *ipf. & pf.; ppp.* -ждённый) *ipf.* -ила́, -ило, -или; *pf.* -ила́, -ило, -или; *& ipf.* рожда́ть *&* рожа́ть) give birth to; -ся *(ipf.* -и́лся, -и́лась, -и́лось, -и́лись; *pf.* -и́лся, -ила́сь, -ило́сь, -или́сь) be born.

родни́к (-а́) spring, well.

родни|чо́к (-чка́) fontanelle; small spring.

родно́й own, native; dear; *pl.* relatives; родня́ kinsfolk, relative(s).

родови́тый well-born.

родово́й ancestral, tribal; generic; gender *(a.)* : (of) childbirth.

родонача́льник ancestor; forefather; родосло́в|ная genealogy, pedigree; ~ный genealogical.

ро́дствен|ник, ~ница relative; ро́дственный related; родств|о́ relationship; alliance; быть в -ѐ (с + *inst.)* be related.

ро́ды (-ов) childbirth.

ро́жа *(coll.)* ugly mug; erysipelas.

рожа́ть, рожда́ть *(pf.* роди́ть*)* give birth to; рожда́емость *(f.)* birthrate; рожде́н|ие birth; дьнь -ия birthday.

рожде́ственский Christmas *(a.)*; рождество́ Christmas.

ро|жо́к (-жка́) (small) horn; feeding-bottle; gas burner; shoe-horn.

рожо́н: лѐзть на р. do something known to be risky.

рожь *(gen.* ржи, *inst.* ро́жью) rye.

ро́за rose.

ро́звальн|и (-ей) (low, wide) sledge.

ро́зга birch rod.

розе́тка rosette; electric socket.

розни́ться *(coll.)* = ра́зниться.

ро́зница retail; ро́зничная торго́вля retail trade.

ро́знь *(f.)* difference; челове́к челоге́ку р. no two people are alike.

ро́зовый pink.

ро́зыгрыш draw, drawn game.

ро́зыск search, investigation.

ро́иться swarm; рой (в рою́, *pl.* рои́, рое́й) swarm.

рок fate; роково́й fatal.

ро́кот roar, rumble; рок|ота́ть (-о́чет) roar, rumble.

ро́лик roller; ката́ться на -ах go roller-skating; ро́ликовый подши́пник ball-bearing.

рол|ь *(f.; pl.* -и, -е́й) rôle.

ром rum.

рома́н novel; романи́ст novelist; Romanist.

рома́нс song, romance; рома́нский Romanesque; Romance; романти́зм Romanticism; романт|и́ческий, ~и́чный Romantic.

рома́шка *(gen. pl.* -шек) camomile; ox-eye daisy.

ромб rhombus.

роня́ть *(pf.* урони́ть) drop.

ро́пот grumble, murmur; ропта́ть (ропщу́, ро́пщешь) (на + *acc.*) grumble (at).

роса́ dew; роси́нка dew-drop; роси́стый dewy.

роско́шный luxurious; luxuriant; ро́скошь *(f.)* luxury.

ро́слый stalwart.

ро́спись *(f.)* painting.

ро́спуск dissolution, dismissal.

росси́йский Russian.

ро́ссказн|и (-ей) *(coll.)* old wives' tale, cock-and-bull story.

ро́ссыпь *(f.)* deposit, field, mine.

рост growth, increase; height, stature.

ро́стбиф roast beef.

ростов|щи́к, ~щи́ца money-lender, usurer; ростовщи́чество usury.

рос|то́к (-тка́) shoot, sprout.

ро́счерк flourish; stroke *(of pen)*.

рот (рта, во рту) mouth.

ро́та company; ро́тмистр captain *(of cavalry)*; ро́тный компэ́ny *(a.)*; company commander.

ротозе́й gullible person.

ро́ща grove.

рояли́ст royalist.

роя́ль *(m.)* grand piano.

ртуть *(f.)* mercury.

руба́|нок (-нка) plane.

руба́ха, руба́|шка *(gen. pl.* -шек) shirt.

рубе́ж (-á) boundary, border, line; за ~óм abroad.

ру|бе́ц (-бца́) scar, weal; hem; paunch; tripe *(cook.)*.

руби́н ruby; руби́новый ruby *(a.)*; ruby-coloured.

руби́ть (рублю́, ру́бишь) fell, hew; slash; chop, mince; -ся fight with swords.

рубище rags.

ру́бка 1. felling, chopping; 2. deck-cabin; conning-tower.

рублёвый (one-) rouble.

ру́бленый minced.

рубл|ь (-я́) rouble.

ру́брика rubric, heading.

рубцева́|ться cicatrize.

ру́бчатый ribbed; corrugated.

ру́гань *(f.)* abuse, bad language.

руга́тельный abusive; руга́тельство curse, oath; руга́ть *(pf.* вы-) curse, abuse; -ся *(pf.* вы-) curse, use bad language.

руда́ *(pl.* ру́ды) ore; рудни́к (-á) mine, pit; ру́дничный mine *(a.)*; р. газ fire-damp; ру́дный ore *(a.)*.

ру|жéйный gun, rifle *(a.)*; ружьё *(pl.* ру́ж|ья, -ей) gun.

руи́на ruin.

рука́ (ру́ку, *pl.* ру́к|и, -áм) hand; arm; рука́ о́б руку hand in hand; из рук вон пло́хо very bad; руко́й пода́ть very close.

рука́в (-á, *pl.* -á) sleeve; рукави́ца gauntlet, mitten; рука́вчик short sleeve; cuff.

руко|води́тель *(m.)* leader; instructor; manager; ~води́ть (-ожу́, -оди́шь) *(inst.)* lead; direct; -ся *(inst.)* follow, be guided (by); ~во́дство management, guidance; (the) leadership; guide, manual; ~во́дствоваться *(inst.)* follow, be guided (by); ~водя́щий leading.

рукоде́лие needlework; fancy-work.

рукомо́йник washstand.

руко|па́шный бой hand-to-hand fighting; ~пи́сный manuscript; ~пись *(f.)* manuscript; ~плеска́ть *(dat.)* applaud; ~пожа́тие handshake; ~полага́ть *(pf.* -положи́ть) ordain.

рукоя́тка grip, handle, hilt; lever.

рулево́й steering *(a.)*.

руле́т: мясно́й р. beef-roll, meat loaf.

руле́тка tape measure; roulette.

рули́ть taxi *(avia.)*; рул|ь (-я́) rudder, helm, steering wheel.

ру́мпель *(m.)* helm, rudder.

рум|ы́н *(gen. pl.*-ы́н),~ы́нка Roumanian; румы́нский Roumanian *(a.)*.

румя́на rouge; рум|я́нец (-нца) (high) colour, blush, glow; румя́нить *(pf.* за-, на-) make red/ruddy; -ся *(pf.* на-) use rouge on one's face; румя́ный rosy, ruddy.

руно́ *(pl.* ру́на) 1. fleece; 2. shoal.

ру́пор megaphone; mouthpiece.

руса́к (-á) hare.

руса́лка mermaid, water-sprite.

руси́ст specialist in Russian philology; русифици́ровать *(ipf. & pf.)* Russify.

ру́сло channel, bed of river.

русоволо́сый light-haired.

ру́сский Russian.

ру́сый light brown.

рути́на routine; рутинёр, ~ка rigid follower of routine.

ру́хлядь *(f.)* junk, lumber.

ру́хнуть *(pf.)* crash down.

руча́тельство warranty, guarantee; руча́ться *(pf.* пор|учи́ться, -учу́сь

-ýчишься) (за + *acc.*) guarantee, vouch (for).

ру|чéй (-чья) brook, stream.

рý|чка *(gen. pl.* -чек) little hand/arm; handle; pen-holder, fountain pen ручнóй 1. hand, arm *(a.);* manual; 2. tame.

рýшить 1. *(pf.* по-) husk; 2. *(pf.* об-, раз-) knock/pull down; -ся fall down.

ры́ба fish; рыбáк (-á) fisherman; рыбáцкий, ~áчий fishing *(a.),* fisherman's; ры́бий fish *(a.);* cold-blooded *(fig.);* ры́бный fish *(a.).*

рыбо|вóдство fish-breeding; ~лóв fisherman; ~лóвный fishing *(a.);* ~лóвство fishing.

рыв|óк (-кá) jerk.

рыгáть *(pf.* рыгнýть) belch.

рыдáние sobbing, sob; рыдáть sob.

ры́жий red, red-haired.

рыкáть roar.

ры́ло snout; mug.

ры́|нок (-нка) market(-place); рыночный market *(a.).*

рысáк (-á) trotter.

ры́скать (ры́щет) rove, roam.

рысцá jog-trot.

рысь *(f.)* 1. lynx; 2. trot.

ры́твина groove, rut.

рыть (рóю, рóешь; *ppp.* ры́тый; *pf.* вы́-, от-) dig, burrow -ся dig, burrow; rummage; рытьё digging.

рыхлить *(pf.* вз-, раз-) loosen, make light/friable; ры́хлый friable, loose; flabby *(coll.).*

ры́|царский chivalrous, knightly; рыцарство knighthood, chivalry; рыцарь *(m.)* knight.

рычáг (-á) lever; *(fig.)* key factor.

ры|чáть (-чý, -чúшь) growl, snarl.

рья́ный zealous.

рюкзáк (-á) rucksack.

рю́мка wine glass.

ряби́на 1. mountain ash, rowan tree; 2. pit, pock.

ряби́новка ashberry brandy.

ряби́ть *(pf.* за-) ripple *(v. t.);* в глазáх ряби́т I am dazzled.

рябóй pock-marked.

рябь *(f.)* ripple; dazzling.

ря́вкать *(pf.* ря́вкнуть) *(coll.)* bellow, roar.

ряд *(pl.* -ы́) row; line; в рядý in a line/row; в ря́де слýчаев in a number of cases; ря́дом (с + *inst.)* alongside.

ряди́ть (ряжý, ря́дишь; *pf.* на-) dress up; -ся 1. *(pf.* на-) dress up; 2. *(pf.* по-) bargain, haggle.

рядовóй ordinary; private (soldier); pertaining to rows, drills.

ря́дом side by side.

ря́женый mummer.

ря́са cassock.

С

с 1. *(+ acc.)* the size of, about; с мéсяц about a month; 2. *(+ gen.)* from, off; for *(joy, etc.);* 3. *(+ inst.)* with.

сáбля *(gen. pl.* -бель) sabre.

саботáж sabotage; саботáжник saboteur; саботи́ровать *(ipf. & pf.)* sabotage.

сáван shroud.

сáго *(indecl.)* sago.

сад (в -ý, *pl.* -ы́) garden; orchard.

сади́ть (сажý, сáдишь; *pf.* по-) plant; са|ди́ться (-жýсь, -ди́шься; *pf.* сесть, ся́ду, ся́дешь; сел) sit down; shrink.

сáдн|ить: у меня́ в гóрле -ит my throat hurts, is smarting.

садóвник gardener; садовóд horticulturalist; садовóдство horticulture, gardening; садóвый garden *(a.),* cultivated.

са|дóк (-дкá) fish-pond; *(rabbit)* hutch.

сáжа soot.

сажáлка planting machine.

сажáть *(pf.* посади́ть*) seat, give a seat to; put; plant.

сáже|нец (-нца) seedling, sapling.

сáжень *(f., gen. pl.* сáжен & сажéней, -éням) sazhen, (= 2·131 *m.).*

сазáн carp.

сáйка *(gen. pl.* сáек) roll *(of bread).*

саквоя́ж travelling bag, hold-all.

сáкл|я *(gen. pl.* -ей) Caucasian peasant's hut.

салáз|ки (-ок) toboggan, (hand-) sledge.

салáка sprat.

саламáндра salamander.

салáт lettuce; salad; салáтник salad dish.

сáлить *(pf.* за-) grease, make greasy сáлки (-ок): игрáть в с. play tig/touch.

сáло fat; lard; tallow.

салóн salon; saloon.

салфётка serviette, table-napkin.
сáльдо (indecl.) balance (fin.).
сáльный greasy; tallow; obscene.
салют salute; салютовáть (ipf. & pf.;
   & pf. от-) (dat.) salute.
сам, самá, самó, сáми myself, himself (etc.); сам-друг together;
   double.
са|мéц (-мцá) male; сáмка female.
само|бытный original, distinctive.
самовáр samovar.
самовлáстный despotic.
самовнушéние auto-suggestion.
самовозгорáние spontaneous combustion.
самовóльный self-willed; unwarranted.
само|движущийся self-propelled.
самодéльный home-made.
самодержáвие autocracy.
самодержáвный autocratic;~дéржец
   (-жца) autocrat.
самодéятельность (f.) independent/
   spontaneous activity; amateur per-
   formances.
самодовлéющий self-sufficient.
самодовóльный self-satisfied; ~до-
   вóльство complacency.
самодýр obstinate know-all, petty
   tyrant.
самозарядный self-loading.
самозащита self-defence.
самозвáнец (-нца), ~звáнка pretender.
самокáт bicycle; scooter.
самолёт aeroplane, aircraft; с.-снаряд
   missile-plane, flying-bomb; само-
   лётостроéние aircraft construction.
само|любивый proud; ~любие self-
   esteem.
самомнéние conceit, self-importance.
самонадéянный self-sufficient, presumptuous.
самообладáние self-control.
самообслýживание self-service.
самоопределéние self-determination.
самоотвéрженный selfless.
самопишущий (self)-registering; fountain (pen).
самопожéртвование self-sacrifice.
самородок (-дка) native/virgin metal;
   person of natural gifts.
самосвáл dump truck, tip-up lorry.
самосохранéние self-preservation.
самостоятельный independent.
самострéл cross-bow.
самосýд mob law, lynching.

самотёк drift; ~тёком by gravity; of
   own accord; drifting; ~тёчный
   automatic.
само|убийство (act of) suicide; ~у-
   бийца (m. & f.) suicide (pers.).
самоуважéние self-respect.
самоувéренный self-confident.
самоуправлéние self-government.
самоупрáвство arbitrariness.
само|учитель (m.) teach-yourself
   book; ~ýчка (m. & f.) gen. pl.
   -чек) self-educated person.
само|хвáл boaster.
самоходный self-propelled.
самоцвéт semi-precious stone.
самоцéль (f.) end in itself.
самочинный arbitrary.
самочýвствие: у меня отличнос с. I
   feel fine.
самшит box (-tree).
сáмый the very; same; с. нóвый
   newest
сан dignity; order, rank.
санатóрий sanatorium.
сандáл sandal-wood tree; сандáлия
   sandal (footwear).
сáн|и (-éй) sledge, sleigh.
санитáр, ~ка hospital attendant,
   medical orderly; санитáрный sanitary; medical.
санкционировать (ipf. & pf.) sanction; сáнкция approval, sanction;
   sanction, punitive measure.
сáнный sledge (a.).
санóвник dignitary
санóвный stately.
сантимéтр centimetre; tape-measure.
сапёр field engineer, sapper.
сапóг (-á, gen. pl. сапóг) (high) boot;
   сапóжник shoemaker; cobbler;
   сапóжный shoe (a.).
сапфир sapphire; сапфир|ный,~овый
   sapphire (a.).
сарáй barn, shed.
саранчá locust(s).
сарафáн sarafan (Russian dress);
   sun-dress.
сардé|лька (gen. pl. -лек) (small)
   sausage.
сардинка sardine.
сáржа serge.
саркáзм sarcasm; саркастический
   sarcastic.
сарыч (-á) buzzard.
сатанá (m.) satan; сатанинский
   satanic.
сателлит satellite.
сатиновый sateen (a.).

сати́ра satire; сати́рик satirist; сати-ри́ческий satirical.

сафья́н Morocco leather.

са́хар sugar; сахари́н saccharin; са́харистый sugar(y); са́харница sugar-basin; са́харн|ый: -ый песо́к granulated sugar; -ая боле́знь diabetes.

са|чо́к (-чка́) net.

сба́вка reduction; сбавля́ть (pf. сба́вить) take off.

сба́лтывать (pf. сболта́ть) mix/stir together.

сбега́ть (pf. сбежа́ть*) run down/away; -ся come running, flock together; сбега́ть (pf.) (за + inst.) run (for; e. g. a doctor).

сберега́тельный savings (a.); сбере-га́ть (pf. сбере́чь*) save; preserve; сбереже́ние economy; (pl.) savings; сберка́сса savings bank.

сбива́ть (pf. сби́ть*, собью́) bring/knock down; confuse, put out of stride; knock together; beat, churn, whip; -ся с пути́ get lost; сби́в-чивый confused, inconsistent.

сближа́ть (pf. сбли́|зить, -жу, -зишь) draw/bring together; -ся draw together; become close friends; сближе́ние rapprochement; intimate friendship.

сбо́ку from one side, on one side.

сболта́ть see сба́лтывать.

сболтну́ть (pf.) (coll.) blurt out.

сбор collection; gathering; сбо́рище mob; сбо́рка assembling; (pl.) gathers (on dress); сбо́рник collection; сбо́рный combined; collapsible; pre-fabricated (houses); assembly (a.); сбо́рочный assembly (a.); сбо́рщик collector.

сбра́сывать (pf. сбро́сить*) throw down/off; shed; drop (bombs).

сбрива́ть (pf. сбрить*) shave off.

сброд rabble, riff-raff.

сброс drop; fault (geol.) сбро́сить see сбра́сывать.

сбру́я harness.

сбыва́ть (pf. сбыть*) market, sell off; dispose of; -ся come true, be realized; сбыт sale, market; сбы-тово́й market, sale (a.).

сва́дебный wedding (a.); nuptial; сва́дьба wedding.

сва́йный pile (a.), built on piles.

сва́ливать (pf. свали́ть*) knock down/over; pile up, dump; over-throw; -ся fall down, collapse; сва́лка dump; scuffle.

сва́ривать (pf. свари́ть*) weld; сва́рка welding.

сварли́вый quarrelsome, cantankerous.

сварно́й welded; сва́рщик welder.

сват match-maker; father of the son/daughter-in-law; сва́тать (pf. по-, со-) propose someone as wife/husband; -ся к ней or за неё seek her hand in marriage;

сва́тья (gen. pl. -тий) mother of the son/daughter-in-law; сва́ха match-maker.

сва́я (gen. pl. свай) pile.

сведе́ние reduction; contraction, cramp;

сведе́н|ие information, intelligence; knowledge; приня́ть к -ию take into account; take note of; све́-дущий (+ prep.) versed (in), knowledgeable (about).

свежева́ть (pf. о-) dress, skin.

све́жесть (f.) freshness; свеже́ть (pf. по-) become fresh/cooler; све́жий fresh; new; latest.

свезти́ see свози́ть.

свёкла beet; свекло́вица sugar-beet.

свё|кор (-кра) husband's father; свекро́вь (f.) husband's mother.

сверга́ть (pf. све́ргнуть, past сверг) throw down; overthrow; сверже́-ние overthrow.

све́рить see сверя́ть.

сверка́ть (pf. сверкну́ть) sparkle, twinkle.

сверле́ние boring, drilling; сверли́ль-ный boring; drilling (a.); свер-ли́ть (pf. про-) bore, drill, perforate; сверло́ (pl. свёрла) drill, auger; сверло́вщик borer, driller.

сверну́ть see свёртывать & свора́чи-вать.

сверст|ник, ~ница person of the same age.

свё́р|ток (-тка) bundle, roll; свёрты-вать (pf. сверну́ть) roll up; turn: curtail, narrow; -ся curl/roll up; curdle; coagulate, set.

сверх (gen.) over; above, besides; с. того́ moreover.

сверх|звуково́й supersonic; ~при́-быль (f.) excess profit.

све́рху from above; с. до́низу from top to bottom.

сверх|урочный overtime; ~человек superman; ~ъестественный supernatural.

свер|чок (-чка́) cricket; всяк с. знай свой шесток the cobbler should stick to his last.

свершáться (pf. -ться) be done/ fulfilled; свершéние achievement.

сверя́ть (pf. сверить) collate.

свес overhang; свéсить see свéшивать

свет 1. light; 2. world; society; чуть с. at daybreak.

светáть dawn; светило luminary; светильник lamp; светильня (gen. pl. -лен) wick, taper; св|етить (-ечу́, -éтишь; pf. по-) shine; give light, show the way (to); -ся shine; be luminescent.

светлéть (pf. по-) become brighter; (pf. про-) become clearer (of ideas etc.); свéтлый light, bright; светля́к (-á) glow-worm.

светов|ой light (a.); -áя реклáма illuminated sign(s).

свето|маскирóвка black-out; ~преставлéние end of the world; ~тéнь (f.) chiaroscuro; ~тéхника lighting-engineering; ~фóр traffic lights.

свéтский secular, temporal.

свечá (pl. свéчи, свеч or свеч|éй, -áм) candle.

свечéние luminescence, phosphorescence.

свéшивать (pf. свéсить*) lower let down; -ся lean over; overhang.

свивáть (pf. свить*, совью) twist, weave, wind.

свидáн|ие meeting, appointment; до -ия good-bye.

свидéтель (m.) witness; свидéтельств|о evidence; certificate; licence; ~овáть witness.

свинáрка pig-tender; свинáрник pig-sty.

свин|éц (-нцá) lead.

свинúна pork; свúнка little pig; mumps; морскáя с. guinea-pig; свиноводство pig-breeding; свинóй pig, pork (a.); свиномáтка sow; свúнский swinish.

свинцóвый lead(en).

свúнчивать (pf. св|интить, -инчу́, -интишь; ppp. -инченный) screw together; unscrew.

свинья́ (pl. свúн|ьи, -éй, -свúньям) pig; (coll.) swine.

свирéль (f.) reed (-pipe).

свирéпствовать rage; свирéпый ferocious.

свисáть (pf. свúснуть) hang down, dangle, trail.

свист whistle, whistling; св|истáть (-ищу́, -úщешь) whistle (v.t. & i.); сви|стéть (-щу́, -стишь; pf. свúснуть) whistle (v.i.); (pf.) sneak; свисток (-ткá) whistle; свистя́щий whistling; sibilant.

свúта suite.

свúтер sweater.

свú|ток (-тка) roll, scroll.

свить see свивáть.

свихну́ться (pf.) (coll.) go mad; go astray.

свищ (-á) fistula; honeycomb; hollow (in metal); knot-hole (in wood).

свобóда freedom; свобóдный free.

свободо|любúвый freedom-loving; ~мыслие free-thinking.

свод 1. arch, vault; 2. code; compilation.

сводúть* (pf. свести*) take (down); bring together; reduce; remove; у меня́ свелó нóгу I got cramp in my leg -ся (к + dat.) amount, come(to).

свóдка summary; revise (print.); weather report.

свóд|ник, ~ница procurer, pimp; свóдный 1. summary (a.); 2. step (brothers, sisters).

свóдчатый arched, vaulted.

свое|влáстный despotic; ~вóлие self-will.

своеврéменный opportune, timely.

своенрáвный wilful.

своеобрáзие originality, peculiarity; ~обрáзный original, peculiar.

свозúть* 1. (pf. свезти*) bring together; bring/take down.

свозúть 2.* (pf.) take.

свой, своя́, своё, свой one's own; он сам не свой he is not himself.

свóйственник relative; свóйственный (dat.) peculiar (to); свóйство property; свойствó relationship (by marriage); affinity.

свóлочь (f.) riff-raff; scum.

свóра leash; pack (of dogs).

сворáчивать (pf. свернуть) roll up; turn aside.

своя́к (-á) brother-in-law; (husband of wife's sister); своя́ченица sister-in-law (wife's sister).

свыкаться *(pf.* свыкнуться; *past* сгыбся) (с + *inst.)* get used (to).

свысока in haughty manner; свыше 1. from above; 2. *(gen.)* over, beyond.

связанный tied, connected; constrained, halting *(speech)*; связист signaller, worker in communications; связка bunch, sheaf; ligament; copula, link-verb; связный connected, coherent; связывать *(pf.* связать*) bind, tie; connect; -ся be tied *etc.;* communicate; have dealings; связь *(f)* bond; connection(s); communication(s); liaison.

святилище sanctuary; свя|тить (-чу, -тишь; *pf.* о-, -щу, -тишь) sanctify; святк|и (-ок) Christmastide, Yuletide.

святой holy; saint; святотатство sacrilege; святочный Christmas *(a.);* священник priest; священный sacred.

сгиб bend; flexion; сгибать *(pf.* согнуть*) bend, curve; -ся bend, stoop.

сглаживать *(pf.* сгладить*) smooth out/over/down.

сгл|азить *(pf.;* -ажу, -азишь) cast the evil eye over, bewitch.

сгнивать *(pf.* сгнить*) rot.

сговариваться *(pf.* сговориться) (с + *inst.)* come to terms (with); сговор agreement; сговорчивый compliant, tractable.

сгонять *(pf.* согнать*, сгоню) drive away; drive together.

сгорание combustion; сгорать *(pf.* сгореть*) burn/be burnt down; be consumed *(also fig.);* сгоряча in the heat of the moment, rashly.

сгребать *(pf.* сгрести*) rake/shovel together.

сгружать *(pf.* сгрузить*) unload.

сгруппир|овывать *(pf.* -овать) form into group(s).

сгрызать *(pf.* сгрызть*) chew up.

сгус|ток (-тка) clot; сгущать *(pf.* сгу|стить, -щу -стишь) thicken, condense; сгущённое молоко condensed milk; сгущение thickening, clotting; condensation.

сдабривать *(pf.* сдобрить) flavour, spice.

сдавать* *(pf.* сдать*) pass; hand in; deposit; give up; -ся surrender, yield.

сдавливать *(pf.* сдавить*) squeeze.

сдатчик lessor; сдать *see* сдавать; сдача surrender; depositing; change *(money).*

сдваивать *(pf.* сдвоить) double.

сдвиг displacement; improvement, progress; сдвигать *(pf.* сдвинуть) move; push together; -ся move, budge; come together.

сделка agreement, bargain, deal.

сдельный by the job *(a.),* piece-; сдельщина piece-work.

сдёргивать *(pf.* сдёрнуть) pull off.

сдержанность restraint; сдерживать *(pf.* сдержать*) hold back, restrain; *(pf.)* keep *(e.g. one's word).*

сдёрнуть *see* сдёргивать.

сдирать *(pf.* содрать*, сдеру) strip off; fleece.

сдоба fancy bread; сдобный rich; сдобрить *see* сдабривать.

сдружиться *(pf.)* (с + *inst.)* become friends (with).

сдувать *(pf.* сдуть, сдунуть) blow off/away.

сдуру foolishly.

сеанс seance; performance.

себестоимость *(f.)* prime cost, cost price.

себя oneself, myself, yourself *etc;* себялюбие egoism.

сев sowing.

север north; северный north *(a.);* северо-восток north-east; север|янин (-яне, -ян). ~янка northerner.

севооборот rotation/alternation of crops.

севрюга sevruga *(sturgeon).*

сегодня today; сегодняшний today's; present-day.

седалище seat; седальный sciatic.

седеть *(pf.* по-) go grey; седина grey hair.

седлать *(pf.* о-) saddle; седло *(pl.* сёдла, сёдел) saddle.

седоволосый grey-haired; седой grey.

се|док (-дока) horseman, rider; fare *(in cab).*

седьмой seventh.

сезон season; сезонный season(al).

сей, сия, сие, сии this, present.

сейсмография seismography.

сейф safe.

сейчас (right) now; at once; soon.

секáтор secateurs, pruning shears.
секвестровáть *(ipf. & pf.)* sequestrate.
секи́ра axe.
секрéт 1. secret; 2. secretion.
секретáрство secretaryship; секрет|áрь (-аря́), ∼áрша secretary.
секрéтка letter-card.
секрéтничать keep things secret; секрéтный secret.
секрéция secretion.
сéкта sect; сектáнт sectarian.
сéктор sector.
секуляризи́ровать *(ipf. & pf.)* secularize.
секýнда second *(of time)*; секундáнт second *(in duel)*; секýндная стрéлка second hand; секундомéр stop-watch.
сéкция section.
селёдка herring.
селезёнка spleen.
сéле|зень (-зня) drake.
селéн selenium.
селéние village, hamlet.
сели́тра saltpetre.
сели́ть *(pf. по-)* settle; -ся settle, take up residence.
селó *(pl.* сёла) village.
сельдерéй celery.
сельдь *(f.; pl.* -и, -éй) herring.
сельпó *(indecl.)* village stores.
сéльск|ий rural; -ое хозя́йство agriculture; сельскохозя́йственный agricultural; сельсовéт village soviet.
семáнтика semantics.
семафóр semaphore.
сёмга salmon.
семéйный family *(a.)*, domestic; семéйственность *(f.)* nepotism; семéйственный domestic; семéйство family.
семени́ть walk with mincing steps.
семеннóй seed *(a.)*, seminal.
семёрка *(the number)* seven; seven *(at cards)*; сéмеро seven.
семéстр term, semester.
сéме|чко *(pl.* -чки, -чк) seed *(often, sunflower-)*.
семидеся́тый seventieth; семилéтка seven-year school; *(coll.)* seven-year-old child; seven-year plan; семилéтний seven-year, septennial.
семинáр, ∼áрий seminar; семинари́ст seminarist; семинáрия seminary.

семисóтый seven-hundredth; семи угóльник heptagon; семнáдцатый seventeenth; семнáдцать seventeen.
сёмужий salmon *(a.)*.
семь seven; сéмьдесят seventy; семьсóт seven hundred.
семья́ *(pl.* сéм|ьи, -éй, сéмьям) family; семьяни́н, ∼ка person with a family.
сé|мя *(neut.; gen., dat., prep.* -мени, *inst.* -менем, *pl.* -менá, -мя́н, -менáм) seed; semen.
сенáт senate; сенáтор senator.
сéн|и (-éй) passage.
сéно hay; сеновáл hay loft; сенокóс mowing.
сенсациóнный sensational сенсáция sensation.
сентенциóзный sententious; сентéнция maxim.
сентиментáльный sentimental.
сентя́бр|ь (-я́) September; сентя́брьский September *(a.)*.
сень *(f.)* canopy.
сепарáтный separate.
сéра sulphur.
серб, ∼ка Serb; сéрбский Serbian; серб[ск]охорвáтский Serbo-Croat.
сéрвиз service, set; сервировáть *(ipf. & pf.)* serve, lay *(table)*; сервирóвка lay-out.
сердéчный heart *(a.)*, cardiac; cordial, heartfelt.
серди́тый (на + acc.) angry (at); серди́ть (сержý, сéрдишь; *pf.* рас-) anger; -ся be angry.
сердобóльный tender-hearted.
сердоли́к cornelian, sard.
сéр|дце *(pl.* -дцá, -дéц, -дцáм) heart; пó сердцу to one's liking; в сердцáх in a temper.
сердцебиéние palpitation; ∼ви́дный heart-shaped.
сердцеви́на core, pith.
серебри́стый silver(y); серебри́ть *(pf.* по-) silver; -ся become silvery; be silvered; серебрó silver; серéбряный silver *(a.)*.
середи́на middle; золотáя с. golden mean.
серё|жка *(gen. pl.* -жек) ear-ring; catkin.
сéренький grey; dull.
серéть *(pf.* по-) grow/turn grey.
сержáнт sergeant.
сери́йный serial *(a.)*; сéрия series.

се́рна chamois.
се́рный sulphuric, sulphurous.
серова́тый greyish.
серп (-á) sickle.
серпанти́н paper streamer.
сертифика́т (savings) certificate.
се́рум serum.
се́рый grey.
серьга́ *(pl.* сé|рьги, -рёг, -рьга́м) ear-ring.
серьёзный serious.
се́ссия session.
сестра́ *(pl.* сёс|тры, -тёр, сёстрам) sister; **сестри́н** sister's .
сесть *see* сади́ться.
се́тка net, netting; grid; scale.
се́товать *(pf.* по-) (на + *acc.)* complain (of).
сетча́тка retina; **се́тчатый** reticulated, net-like.
сет|ь *(f.;* в -и́, *pl.* -и, -éй) net; network; *(pl.)* meshes.
се́ча battle.
сече́ние section; **сé|чка** *(gen. pl.* -чек)* 1. cleaver; 2. chaff; **сечь** (сєку, сечёшь; сек; *ppp.* сéчен-ный) *(pf.* вы́-) flog; -ся *(pf.* по-) split.
се́ялка seeding-machine; **се́ять** (сéю, сéешь; *pf.* по-) sow.
сжа́литься *(pf.)* (над + *inst.)* take pity (on).
сжа́тие pressing, pressure; compression; **сжа́тый** condensed, concise; **сжать** *see* сжима́ть.
сжива́ть *(pf.* сжить*, *ppp.* сжи́тый): с. со све́та worry to death, hound; -ся (с + *inst.)* get used (to).
сжига́ть *(pf.* сжечь*) burn down; cremate.
сжи́женный liquefied.
сжима́ть *(pf.* сжать*, сожму́) compress; squeeze, clench; -ся shrink, contract; be squeezed *etc.*
сжить *see* сжива́ть.
сза́ди 1. behind, from behind; 2. *(gen.)* behind.
сзыва́ть = созыва́ть.
сиби́рский Siberian *(a.);* **сибиря́к** (-á) **сибиря́|чка** *(gen. pl.* -чек) Siberian.
си́вый grey.
сига́ра cigar; **сигаре́т(к)а** cigarette.
сигна́л signal; **сигнализа́ция** signalling; **сигнализи́ровать** *(ipf. & pf.)* make signal(s); **сигна́льный** signal *(a.).*

сиде́лка (sick-)nurse.
сиде́ние sitting; **сиде́нье** seat; **си|де́ть** (-жу́, -ди́шь, *ger.* си́дя; *pf.* по-) sit; -ся: ему́ не -ди́тся на ме́сте he can't sit still.
сидр cider.
сидя́чий sitting, sedentary.
си́зый dark bluish-grey.
сикомо́р sycamore.
си́ла strength, power, force; в си́лу э́того because of this; on the strength of this; не по си́лам beyond one's power(s).
сила́ч (-á) strong man.
силика́т silicate.
си́литься make efforts, try.
силово́й power *(a.).*
си|ло́к (-лка́) noose, snare.
си́лос silo, silage.
силуэ́т silhouette.
си́льный strong; powerful; fierce; heavy; он силён в матема́тике he's good at mathematics.
си́мвол symbol; **символизи́ровать** *(ipf. & pf.)* symbolize; **символи́зм** symbolism; **символ|и́ческий, ~и́чный** symbolic.
симметр|и́ческий, ~и́чный symmetrical; **симметри́я** symmetry.
симпатизи́ровать *(dat.)* sympathize (with); like; **симпати́ческий** sympathetic; **симпати́чный** likeable, pleasant; **симпа́тия** sympathy, liking.
симпто́м symptom.
симули́ровать feign, simulate; **симуля́нт, ~ка** simulator, malingerer.
симфони́ческий symphonic; **симфо́ния** symphony.
синаго́га synogogue.
синдика́т syndicate.
синева́ blue colour; the blue; **синева́тый** bluish; **синегла́зый** blue-eyed; **сине́ть** *(pf.* по-) turn/go blue; **си́ний** blue.
сини́льная кислота́ prussic acid.
сини́ть *(pf.* под-) blue; **сини́ца** tomtit, blue-tit.
сино́д synod.
сино́лог sinologist.
сино́ним synonym.
си́нтакс|ис syntax; **~и́ческий** syntactic(al).
си́нтез synthesis; **синтези́ровать** *(ipf. & pf.)* synthesize; **синтети́ч:ский** synthetic.
си́нус sine; sinus.

синхронизи́ровать *(ipf. & pf.)* synchronize.
синь *(f.)* blue; синю́ха cyanosis *(med.)*; синя́к (-а́) bruise.
си́плый hoarse, husky; си́пнуть *(pf. o-)* become hoarse.
сире́на siren.
сире́невый lilac *(a.);* сире́нь *(f.)* lilac.
си́речь *(coll.; obs.)* namely, that is.
сир|и́ец (-и́йца), ~и́йка *(gen. pl. -иек)* Syrian; сири́йский Syrian *(a.).*
сиро́п syrup.
сир|ота́ *(m. & f. pl. -о́ты)* orphan; сироти́вый lone(ly); сиро́тский orphan *(a.).*
систе́ма system; системат|и́ческий, ~и́чный systematic.
си́т|ец (-тца) calico, printed cotton, chintz.
си́те|чко *(gen. pl. -чек)* strainer; си́то sieve.
ситуа́ция situation.
си́тцевый calico, cotton *(a.).*
сия́ние radiance; сия́ть shine.
скабрёзный obscene.
сказ tale; сказа́ние story, legend; сказа́ть *see* говори́ть; сказа́тель *(m.)* storyteller; ска́зка fairy-tale; ска́зочный fabulous, fairytale, сказу́емое predicate; сказа́ться *(pf. сказа́ться*)* tell, have an effect.
скака́лка skipping-rope; скака́ть (скачу́, ска́чешь; *pf.* скакну́ть) jump, skip; *(pf. по-)* gallop; скаково́й race-/racing *(a.).*
скала́*(pl.* ска́лы) rock; скали́стый rocky.
ска́лить *(pf. о-):* с. зу́бы grin.
ска́лка rolling-pin.
ска́лывать *(pf.* сколо́ть*)* chop off; pin together.
скаме́е|чка *(gen. pl. -чек)* small bench; скам|е́йка *(gen. pl. -е́ек)* bench; скамья́ *(pl.* ска́|мьи, -ме́й) bench.
сканда́л scandal; сканда́льный scandalous.
скандина́в, ~ка Scandinavian; скандина́вский Scandinavian *(a.).*
ска́пливать *(pf.* скопи́ть*)* store/ save up.
скарб goods and chattels.
ска́редный stingy.
скарлати́на scarlet fever.

скат 1. slope, descent; 2. ray skate *(zool.);* ската́ть, -ить *see* ска́тывать.
ска́терт|ь *(f.; pl. -и, -е́й, & -е́й)* table-cloth.
ска́тывать *(pf.* ската́ть) roll, fold (up); *(pf.* скати́ть*)* roll/send rolling down.
скафа́ндр diving-suit.
скá|чка *(gen. pl. -чек)* galloping; *(pl.)* horse-race(s); ска|чо́к (-чка́) hop, jump.
ска́шивать *(pf.* скоси́ть*)* mow down; bevel; slope.
сква́жина chink, slit; замо́чная с. keyhole.
сквер public garden/square.
скверносло́вие foul language; скве́рный bad, nasty.
сквоз|и́ть 1. show through; 2. -и́т there is a draught; сквозно́й through *(a.);* сквозня́к (-а́) draught; сквозь *(acc.)* through.
скворе́ц (-рца́) starling; скворе́ч|ник, ~ница box/house for starlings.
скеле́т skeleton.
ске́птик sceptic; скептици́зм scepticism; скепти́ческий sceptical.
ски́дка rebate, reduction; ски́дывать *(pf.* скинуть) throw down/ off; knock off; take off.
ски́петр sceptre.
скипида́р turpentine.
скирд (-а́) & скирд|а́ *(pl. -ы, -а́м)* stack, rick.
скиса́ть *(pf.* ски́снуть*)* go sour.
скит (-а́) small monastery, hermitage.
скита́|лец (-льца) wanderer; скита́ться wander.
скиф Scythian.
склад depot, warehouse; constitution; cast of mind; *(pl. -ы́)* syllable; скла́дка fold, pleat, wrinkle; складно́й folding, collapsible; скла́дный well-ordered; well-knit, well-made; скла́дчин|а: в -у clubbing together; скла́дывать *(pf.* сло|жи́ть, -ожу́, -о́жишь) put together; add; fold up; -ся club together; pool resources; take form/shape.
скле́ивать *(pf.* скле́ить) stick together.
склеп crypt, burial vault.
склёпывать *(pf.* склепа́ть*)* rivet.
скло́ка squabble.

склон slope; склоне́ние declination; inclination; declension; скло́нность (f.) disposition; скло́нный (к + dat.) inclined/disposed (to); склоня́ть 1. (pf. склони́ть*) incline; 2. (pf. про-) decline.

скля́нка phial, bottle.

скоба́ (pl. скоб|ы, -а́м) handle; cramp-iron, staple.

ско́бель (m.) spoke-shave.

ско́бка bracket.

ск|обли́ть (-облю́, -о́блишь; pf. по-) plane, scrape.

скобяно́й hardware (a.).

скова́ть see ско́вывать.

сковорода́ (pl. ско́бо|роды, -ро́д, -рода́м) frying-pan; pan.

ско́вывать (pf. скова́ть*) forge; chain, fetter.

скок hop, jump.

скола́чивать (pf. сколоти́ть*) knock together.

сколо́ть see ска́лывать.

сколь = ско́лько.

скольже́ние slip, glide; скольз|и́ть (-жу́, -зи́шь; pf. скользну́ть) slip, slide; ско́льзкий slippery.

ско́лько how much, how many.

скоморо́х buffoon; wandering player/ minstrel.

сконча́ться (pf.) pass away, die.

скопе́ц (-пца́) eunuch; skopets (member of religious sect.)

ско́пище crowd, gathering; скопле́ние accumulation; crowd; скопля́ть (pf. скопи́ть*) accumulate.

ско́пом in a crowd/heap.

скорбе́ть (-блю́,-би́шь) grieve; ско́рбный sorrowful; скорбь (f. pl. -и, -е́й) sorrow.

скор|ее, ~е́й sooner, rather; c. всего́ most probably.

скорл|упа́ (pl. -у́пы) shell (of egg, nut).

скорня́к (-а́) furrier.

ско́ро quickly, soon.

скорогово́рка patter; tongue-twister; ско́ропись (f.) cursive script.

скоро|по́ртящийся perishable; ~по́сти́жный sudden; ~спе́лый premature.

скоростно́й high-speed (a.); ско́рост|ь (pl. -и, -е́й) speed.

скороте́чный transient; galloping (med.).

ско́р|ый quick, fast; forthcoming; на -ую ру́ку hastily.

скоси́ть see ска́шивать.

скот (-а́) cattle; скоти́на beast; ско́тник cowherd; ско́тный cattle (a.).

ското|бо́йня (gen. pl. -бо́ен) slaughter-house; ~во́д cattle-breeder; ~во́дство cattle-raising.

ско́тский bestial.

скра́дывать conceal.

скра́шивать (pf. скра́сить*) brighten; gloss over.

скре|бо́к (-бка́) scraper.

скре́жет gnashing of teeth; скреж|ета́ть (-ещу́, -е́щешь) grind (teeth).

скре́па clamp; counter-signature; скре́пка clip; скрепле́ние fastening; clamp; counter-signature; скрепля́ть (pf. скрепи́ть*) fasten, clamp; coutersign, ratify; скрепя́ се́рдце reluctantly.

скре|сти́ (-ебу́, -ебёшь; -ёб, -ебла́; ppp. -ебённый) scrape; scratch.

скреще́ние crossing; скре́щивать (pf. скре|сти́ть, -щу́, -сти́шь) cross; interbreed; c. мечи́ cross swords.

скрижа́ль (f.) table, tablet.

скрип creak, squeak; crunch (of snow); скрипа́ч (-а́), ~ка (gen. pl. -чск) violinist; скрипе́ть (-плю́, -пи́шь; pf. про-, & скри́пнуть) creak, squeak, crunch; скри́пка violin; скрипу́чий creaking, squeaky.

скро́мничать be too modest; скро́мный modest.

скрупулёзный scrupulous.

скру́чивать (pf. скрути́ть*) roll; twist; tie up.

скрыва́ть (pf. скрыть*) conceal, hide; -ся hide; lie in wait; скры́тничать be furtive/reticent; скры́тный reserved, secretive; скры́тый hidden, secret; latent.

скря́га (m. & f.) skinflint.

скуде́ть (pf. о-) become thin/scanty/ meagre; ску́дный scanty, meagre; скудоу́мие poverty of mind.

ску́ка boredom.

скул|а́ (pl. ску́лы) cheek-bone; скула́стый with prominent cheekbones.

скули́ть whimper, whine.

ску́льптор sculptor; скульпту́ра sculpture.

ску́мбрия mackerel.

скунс skunk.

скупа́ть (pf. скупи́ть*) buy up.

ску|пе́ц (-пца́) miser; скупи́ться *(pf.* по-) (на + *acc.)* be stingy (with); skimp, grudge; скупо́й (на + *acc.)* miserly (with); ску́пость *(f.)* stinginess, miserliness.
ску́п|щик, ~щица buyer.
скуча́ть be bored; (по + *dat./prep.)* long (for), miss.
ску́ченный tight-packed.
ску́чный tedious, boring.
слабе́ть *(pf.* о-) weaken, grow feeble.
слаби́тельное laxative.
слабо|во́лие weak will; ~во́льный weak-willed.
сла́бость *(f.)* weakness.
слабо|у́мие imbecility; weakness in the head; ~у́мный weak-minded.
сла́бый weak.
сла́в|а fame, glory; на -у wonderfully.
слави́ст, ~ка Slavist; слави́стика study of the Slavs, Slavistics.
сла́вить *(pf.* про-) glorify; sing the praises of; -ся *(inst.)* be famous (for); сла́вный glorious; славо-сло́вие glorification.
слав|яни́н *(pl.* -я́не, -я́н), ~я́нка Slav; славянофи́л Slavophile; славя́нский Slavonic, Slavic.
слага́ть *(pf.* сл|ожи́ть, -ожу́, -о́жишь) compose *(verse etc.);* lay down; -ся (из + *gen.)* be composed, made up (of).
слад: с ним -у нет there is no dealing with him.
сла́денький sweetish; sugary; honeyed *(fig.).*
сла́дить *see* сла́живать.
сла́дкий *(comp.* сла́ще) sweet; сла́дкое dessert; сла́достный sweet, delightful.
сладо|стра́стие voluptuousness; ~-стра́стный voluptuous.
сла́дость *(f.)* sweetness.
сла́женный harmonious, well-organized; сла́живать *(pf.* сла́дить*)* arrange.
сла́мывать *(pf.* сломи́ть*)* break (down/off).
сла́|нец (-нца) shale, slate.
сласте́на *(m. & f.)* sweet tooth; сластолю́бие voluptuousness; сласт|ь *(f.; pl.* -и, -е́й) sweetmeat, candy.
слать (шлю, шлёшь; *pf.* по-) send.
слаща́вый too sweet, sugary; сла́ще sweeter.
сле́ва on/from the left.
слега́ *(pl.* слег|и, -а́м) lath.

слегка́ somewhat, slightly.
след *(pl.* -ы́) track, footprint; trace; сле́дом behind, following.
сле|ди́ть (-жу́, -ди́шь) (за + *inst.)* watch, spy on; keep an eye on; look after.
сле́дован|ие movement; по́езд да́льнего -ия long-distance train.
сле́дователь *(m.)* inspector, investigator; сле́довательно consequently; сле́д|овать *(pf.* по-) 1. follow; 2. be bound (for); 3. be fitting, due; с. coре́ту follow advice; (за + *inst.)* follow (after/on); с pac -ует 5 рубле́й you have to pay 5 roubles; по́езд -ует до Москвы́ the train is bound for Moscow; -ует по́мнить you must remember; как -ует properly
сле́дственный of enquiry; сле́дствие 1. consequence; 2. investigation, inquest.
сле́дуемый *(dat.)* due (to).
сле́дующий following.
сле́|живаться *(pf.* слежа́ться*)* become) compressed; deteriorate.
слежка shadowing, following.
слеза́ *(pl.* слёз|ы, -а́м) tear.
слеза́ть *(pf.* слезть*)* come/get down, dismount, alight.
слези́|нка tear; слези́ться water; слезли́вый tearful; сле́зный tearful; lachrymal; слезоточи́вый газ teargas.
слезть *see* слеза́ть.
сле́|пень (-пня) gadfly.
сле|пе́ц (-пца́) blind man/boy; слепи́ть *(pf.* о-) blind, dazzle.
слепля́ть *(pf.* слепи́ть*)* (make) stick together; -ся stick together.
сле́пнуть *(past* слеп; *pf.* о-) become blind; слепо́й blind.
сле́|пок (-пка) copy.
слепота́ blindness.
сле́сарь *(m.; pl.* -и, *or* -я́) fitter; metal-worker; locksmith.
слёт flight; gathering; слета́ть *(pf.* слете́ть*)* fly down; fly away; -ся fly together.
слечь* *(pf.)* take to one's bed.
сли́ва plum; plum-tree.
слива́ть *(pf.* слить*, солью́) pour out/off; pour together; fuse; amalgamate; slur; -ся flow together; merge.
сли́|вки (-вок) cream.
сли́вовый plum *(a.).*
сли́вочный cream *(a.).*

слизистый mucous.

слизня́к (-á) slug; *(fig.)* sluggard.

слизывать *(pf.* слиза́ть*, слизну́ть)* lick off/away.

слизь *(f.)* mucus.

слипа́ться *(pf.* сли́пнуться*)* stick together.

сли́тный unified, together.

сли́|ток (-тка) bar, ingot.

слить *see* слива́ть.

слич|а́ть *(pf.* -и́ть) collate; **сличе́ние** collation.

сли́шком too.

слия́ние confluence; blending; merging.

слобода́ *(pl.* слоб|о́ды, -о́д, -ода́м) large village, settlement.

слова́к Slovak.

слова́рный lexical, vocabulary *(a.)*; **слова́р|ь** (-я́) dictionary, lexicon, vocabulary.

слова́цкий Slovak; **слова́|чка** *(gen. pl.* -чек) Slovak (woman).

слове́|нец (-нца), **~нка** Slovene; **слове́нский** Slovene *(a.)*.

слове́сность *(f.)* literature; **слове́сный** verbal, oral; philological.

слове́чко (-чки, *pl.* -чек) word; **сло́вник** glossary.

сло́вно as if.

сло́во *(pl.* -á) word; **к сло́ву** by the way; **сло́вом** in a word, in short.

сло́во|образова́ние word-formation; **~охо́тливый** loquacious; **~сочета́ние** phrase.

словц|о́: для кра́сного -á for effect; for the sake of a witty remark.

слог 1. *(pl.* -и, -о́в) syllable; 2. style.

слоёный puff *(a.)*; flaky.

сложе́ние composing; addition; build, constitution; **сложи́ть** *see* скла́дывать, слага́ть; **сло́жный** complicated.

сло́йстый flaky; **сло́|й** *(pl.* -и́) layer, stratum; **сло́йка** *(gen. pl.* слоек) puff *(of pastry)*.

слом pulling/knocking down; scrap; **сломи́ть** *(pf.)* break; **сломя́ го́лову** at breakneck speed.

слон (-á), **~и́ха** elephant; **слоно́вая кость** ivory.

слоня́ться loaf about; loiter.

слуга́ *(m. pl.* слу́ги) servant; **слу|жа́нка** servant, maid; **слу́жащий** employee; **слу́жба** service; **служе́бный** service *(a.)*; **служе́ние** service; **сл|ужи́ть** (-ужу́, -у́жит; *pf.*

по-) *(dat.)* serve; *(with inst.)* serve (as).

слух ear, hearing; rumour; по -у by ear; **слухово́й** acoustic; ear *(a.)*.

слу́чай case; event, occasion; chance; несча́стный с. accident; **слу|ча́йность** *(f.)* chance, fortuity; **случа́йный** accidental, fortuitous; incidental; **случ|а́ться** *(pf.* -и́ться) happen, occur.

слу́шатель *(m.)* listener; student; *(pl.)* audience; **слу́шать** *(pf.* по-) listen; **-ся** *(gen.)* obey.

слыть (слыв|у́, -ёшь; *pf.* про-) (+ *inst.* or за + *acc.)* be reputed (to be).

слы́|шать (-шу, -шишь; *pf.* у-) hear; **слы́шимость** *(f.)* audibility; **слы́шный** audible, able to be heard.

слюда́ mica.

слюна́, слюн|и (-е́й) saliva; dribble; **слюня́вый** dribbling, drivelling.

сля́коть *(f.)* mire, slush.

сма́зка greasing, oiling, lubrication.

сма́зливый pretty.

сма́зочный lubricating *(a.)*; **сма́зчик** greaser; **сма́зывать** *(pf.* сма́зать*)* grease, lubricate; slur over *(a question)*.

сма́нивать *(pf.* смани́ть*)* entice.

сма́тывать *(pf.* смота́ть*)* reel, wind.

сма́хивать *(pf.* смахну́ть) flap/ whisk away/off.

сма́чивать *(pf.* смочи́ть*)* moisten.

сме́жный adjacent.

смека́ть *(pf.* смекну́ть) see, realize.

сме́лость *(f.)* boldness, courage; **сме́лый** bold.

сме́на change; shift; **сме́н|щик, ~щица** relief; **сменя́ть** *(pf.* смени́ть, сменю́, сме́нишь) change, replace.

смерка́ться *(pf.* сме́ркнуться) grow dark.

смерте́льный mortal, deadly; **сме́ртность** *(f.)* mortality; **сме́ртный** mortal; **смертоно́сный** death-dealing; **смерт|ь** *(f.; pl.* -и, -е́й) death; ему́ с. как хо́чется кури́ть he is dying for a smoke.

смерч water-spout; sandstorm.

смести́ *see* смета́ть; **смести́ть** *see* смеща́ть.

смесь *(f.)* mixture, medley.

сме́та estimate.

смета́на sour cream.

смета́ть *(pf.* смести́*)* sweep off away.

сметли|вый sharp, keen-witted; **смёт|лый** estimate(d).

сметь *(pf.* по-*)* dare.

смех laugh(ter); **смехотворный** laughable, ridiculous.

смешанный mixed, joint; **смешение** blending, mixing; confusion; **смешивать** *(pf.* смешать*)* mix; lump together; blend; confuse; **-ся** be mixed etc.; be(come) confused.

смешить *(pf.* рас-*)* make laugh; **смешливый** ready to laugh, easily amused; **смешной** funny; ludicrous.

смещать *(pf.* сме|стить, -щу, -стишь*)* displace, remove; **смещение** displacement; removal; *(geol.)* upheaval.

сме|яться (-юсь, -ёшься; *pf.* по-, за-*)* (над + *inst.)* laugh (at).

смирение humility, meekness; **смирительная рубашка** straitjacket; **смирно!** attention!; **смирный** humble, submissive; **смирять** *(pf.* -ить*)* subdue; **-ся** submit, resign oneself.

смоква fig.

смокинг dinner-jacket.

смола resin; pitch, tar; **смолистый** resinous; **смолить** *(pf.* про-*)* resin; pitch, tar.

смолк|ать *(pf.* смолкнуть, *past* смолк*)* fall silent.

смолоду in one's youth; since youth.

смоляной resin, pitch *(a.).*

сморкать *(pf.* вы-*)* blow *(nose)* ; **-ся** *(pf.* вы-, сморкнуться*)* blow one's nose.

смородина currant(s).

смор|чок (-чка) morel *(mushroom)* ; *(fig.)* shrimp, titch.

сморщенный wrinkled.

смотать *see* **сматывать.**

смотр review; **смотреть** (-отрю, -отришь; *pf.*по-*)*watch; (на + *acc.)* look (at); (за + *inst.)* look (after).

смотритель *(m.) (obs.)* supervisor; **смотровой** observation, inspection *(a.).*

смочить *see* **смачивать.**

смрад stench **смрадный** stinking.

смуглый dark-complexioned.

смута discord; Time of Troubles *(hist.)* ; **смутный** vague, dim; troubled *(hist.)* ; **смутьян**, **~ка** troublemaker.

смушковый astrakhan *(a.).*

сму|щать *(pf.* -тить, -щу, -тишь*)* confuse, embarrass; **-ся** be con-

fused, embarrassed; **смущение** confusion, embarrassment.

смывать *(pf.* смыть*)* wash off/away.

смыкать *(pf.* сомкнуть*)* close.

смысл sense, meaning; **смыслить** reason, understand; **смысловой** semantic.

смычка union.

смы|чок (-чка) bow, fiddlestick.

смышлёный intelligent.

смягч|ать *(pf.* -ить*)* soften; alleviate; **смягчение** softening, alleviation, mitigation.

смятение confusion; commotion; **смятый** rumpled; trampled.

снаб|жать *(pf.* снаб|дить, -жу, -дишь*)* supply, provide; с. его продовольствием supply him with food; **снабжение** supply.

снайпер sniper.

снаружи outside; on the outside.

снаряд shell, missile; contrivance, gear; **снаря|жать** *(pf.* -дить, -жу, -дишь*)* equip, fit out; **снаряжение** equipment, outfit.

снаст|ь *(f.; pl.* -и, -ей*)* rigging tackle.

сначала at first; firstly; again.

снашивать *(pf.* сносить*) (coll.)* wear out.

снег (n -у, *pl.* -а*)* snow.

снегирь (-я) bullfinch.

снеговой snow *(a.).*

снего|очиститель *(m.)* snow-plough; **~пад** snowfall; **снегурочка** Snow Maiden.

снедать consume; **снедь** *(f.; coll.)* food.

снежинка snowflake; **снежный** snow(y); **сне|жок** (-жка) light snow; snowball.

снижать *(pf.* сни|зить, -жу, -зишь*)* bring down, lower, reduce; degrade; **-ся** be lowered, etc., fall; **снижение** lowering; reduction.

снизойти *see* **снисходить.**

снизу from below.

снимать *(pf.* снять, сним|у, -ешь; *ppp.* снятый*)* take away/off; photograph; lease, rent; cut *(cards)* ; **сни|мок** (-мка) photograph.

сни|скивать *(pf.* сн|искать, -ищу, -ищешь*)* gain, win *(respect etc.).*

снисходительный condescending; lenient; **снисходить*** *(pf.* сниз|ойти*, -ойду -ошёл*)* (к + *dat.)* be condescending/indulgent (to);**снис-**

хождение condescension; indulgence.

сниться *(pf.* при-) appear in dream; мне снился сон I had a dream.

снобизм snobbery.

снова anew, again.

сновать (сную, снуёшь) dart, rush; warp *(textile).*

сновидение dream.

сноп (-á) sheaf; shaft *(of light).*

сноровка *(coll.)* knack, skill.

снос pulling down, demolishing; wear, wearing out; сносить* *(pf.* снести*) fetch/take down; carry away; demolish; bring together; endure; -ся (с + *inst.)* communicate (with); сносить* *(pf.)* wear out; сноска footnote; сносный tolerable.

снотворный soporific.

сноха *(pl.* снóхи) son's wife, daughter-in-law.

сношение relation(s), dealings, intercourse.

снятие taking down; removal; снятое молоко skimmed milk; снять *see* снимать.

собака dog; собачий canine, dog's; собá|чка *(gen. pl.* -чек) little dog; trigger.

собеседник interlocutor.

собирательный collective; собирать *(pf.* собрать*) collect, gather; -ся gather; (+ *inf.)* be about (to).

соблазн temptation; соблазнитель, ~ница seducer, tempter; соблазнительный seductive; tempting; соблазн|ять *(pf.* -ить) allure, entice; seduce.

соблюдать *(pf.* соблюсти*) keep, observe, соблюдение observance, maintenance.

соболезн|ование condolence; ~овать *(dat.)* condole (with).

соболь *(m.)* sable.

собор cathedral; council, synod; соборный cathedral, council *(a.).*

собрание collection; gathering, meeting.

собрат fellow, brother.

собрать *see* собирать.

собствен|ник, ~ница owner, proprietor; собственно properly; strictly; собственность *(f.)* property; собственный own; true; proper *(noun).*

собутыльник drinking companion.

событие event.

совá *(pl.* сóвы) owl.

совáть (сую, суёшь; *pf.* сунуть) shove, thrust.

соверш|ать *(pf.* -ить) accomplish, perform; perpetrate; -ся happen, be accomplished *etc.;* совершение accomplishment; perpetration.

совершеннолетие majority, full age;

совершенный perfect; complete, absolute; perfective.

совершенство perfection; ~овать *(pf.* у-) perfect, improve.

сóве|ститься (-щусь, -стишься; *pf.* по-) *(gen.; inf.)* have scruples (about); совестливый conscientious; совестно: мне с. I am ashamed; совесть *(f.)* conscience.

совет advice, counsel; council, soviet; совет|ник, ~ница adviser; советовать *(pf.* по-) *(dat.)* advise *(someone);* -ся (с + *inst.)* consult; советский Soviet; совет|чик, ~чица adviser.

совещание conference, meeting; совещательный consultative, deliberative; совещаться consult, deliberate.

совладáть *(pf.)* (с + *inst.)* control, manage; с. с собóй control oneself.

совместимый compatible; совместный combined, concerted, joint; совмещать *(pf.* совме|стить, -щу, -стишь) combine; совмещение combination; matching.

со|вóк (-вка) scoop; dust-pan.

совокупность *(f.)* aggregate; совокупный combined, joint.

сов|падáть *(pf.* -пасть*) coincide; совпадение coincidence.

совра|щáть *(pf.* -тить, -щу, -тишь) pervert, seduce.

современник contemporary; современность *(f.)* the present time(s); modernity; современный contemporary, modern.

совсем entirely, quite.

совхоз sovkhoz, state farm.

согласие agreement, assent, consent; согласно in accord/harmony; *(dat. or* с + *inst.)* in accordance (with); согласный agreeable; concordant; consonant(al); согласование agreement; соглас|óвывать *(pf.* -овáть) co-ordinate, make agree; -ся agree, conform; соглашáтель *(m.)* conciliator; согла|шáть *(pf.* -сить, -шý, -сишь) reconcile; -ся (на + *acc.)* agree(to); (с + *inst.)* agree with; соглаше́ние agreement; trea-ty.

согна́ть see сгоня́ть; согну́ть see сгиба́ть.

согражд|ани́н (pl. -а́не, -а́н) fellow-citizen, fellow-countryman.

согрева́ть (-ева́ю; pf. согре́ть*) warm.

со́да soda.

соде́йствие assistance; соде́йствовать (ipf. & pf по-) (dat.) assist, help, facilitate.

содержа́ние maintenance, upkeep; content(s); substance; содержа́-тельный solid, rich (in content); содержа́ть* keep, maintain; con-tain; содержи́мое contents.

со́довый soda (a.).

содо́м row, uproar.

содра́ть see сдира́ть.

содрога́ние shudder; содрог|а́ться (pf. -ну́ться) shudder.

содру́жество collaboration; com-monwealth.

соедине́ние joining; connection, com-bination; formation; соединённый combined, united; соедини́тельный connecting, connective; соедин|я́ть (pf. -и́ть) connect, join, unite.

сожале́н|ие regret; к -ию unfor-tunately; сожале́ть (о + prep.) regret, be sorry (about).

сожже́ние burning, cremation

сожи́тель, ~ница (obs.) lover; сожи́-тельство living together.

созва́ть see созыва́ть.

созве́здие constellation.

созву́чие accord, harmony; созву́ч-ный consonant/in harmony (with).

создава́ть* (pf. созда́ть*, со́здал, -а́, со́здало) create; -ся be created; arise; созда́ние creation; созда́тель (m.) creator.

созерца́ние contemplation; созер-ца́тельный contemplative; со-зерца́ть contemplate.

созида́ние creation; созида́тельный creative, constructive.

созн|ава́ть (-аю́, аёшь; pf. созна́ть) be conscious of, realize; acknow-ledge; -ся (в + prep.) confess; со-зна́ние consciousness; confession; созна́тельный conscious; delib-erate.

созрева́ние ripening, maturing; со|-зрева́ть (-зрева́ю; pf.-зре́ть) ripen, mature.

созы́в convocation; созыва́ть (pf. -зва́ть*) call together, summon.

соизволя́ть (pf. -во́лить) deign, be pleased.

соизмери́мый commensurable.

соиска́ние competition.

со́йка (gen. pl. со́ек) jay.

сойти́ see сходи́ть.

сок (в -у́) juice.

со́кол falcon.

сокраща́ть (pf. -ти́ть, -щу́, -ти́шь) abbreviate, reduce, shorten; сокраще́ние abbreviation, reducti-on, shortening.

сокрове́нный secret; inmost; сокро́-вище treasure; сокро́вищница trea-sure-house.

сокруш|а́ть (pf. -и́ть) shatter, smash; -ся be distressed, grieve; сокру-ше́ние destruction; grief; сокру-ши́тельный shattering.

сокры́тие concealment; receiving (sto-len goods).

солда́т (gen. pl. солда́т) soldier; сол-да́тский soldier's; солдафо́н mar-tinet.

солева́|рня (gen. pl. -рен) saltworks; соле́ние salting, pickling; salted/pickled goods; солёный salted, pickled.

солидаризи́роваться (ipf. & pf.) (с + inst.) make common cause (with); солида́рный in solidarity; солида́рный solid, strong; reliable.

соли́ст, ~ка soloist.

солитёр tape-worm.

соли́ть (солю́, со́лишь, ppp. со́лен-ный; pf. по-) salt; (pf. за-) pickle.

со́лнечный sun (a.); sunny; со́лнце sun; солнцепёк: на -е in the blaz-ing sun; солнцестоя́ние solstice.

со́ло (indecl.) solo.

соло|ве́й (-вья́) nightingale.

соло́вый light bay.

со́лод malt; соло́довый malt (a.).

солодко́вый ко́рень liquorice.

соло́ма straw; соло́менный straw (a.); с. вдове́ц grass-widower; соло́минка straw.

солони́на corned beef; солёнка salt-cellar; сол|ь (f.; pl. -и, -е́й) salt.

со́льный solo (a.).

соляно́й salt (a.); соля́ная кислота́ hydrochloric acid.

со́мкнутый close(d); сомкну́ть see смыка́ть.

сомнева́ться (-а́юсь; pf. усомни́ть-ся) (в + prep.) doubt, have

doubts(about); **сомнéние** doubt; **сомнúтельный** doubtful.
сомнó|житель *(m.)* factor *(maths.).*
сон (снá) sleep, dream.
сонáта sonata.
сонéт sonnet.
сонлúвый sleepy; **сóнный** sleepy; sleeping *(pills)*; **сóня** sleepyhead; dormouse *(zool.).*
сообра|жáть *(pf.* -зúть, -жý, -зúшь) consider, think; understand; weigh up; **соображéние** consideration; understanding; **сообразúтельный** quick-witted; **сообрáзный** (c+*inst.)* conformable(to), in keeping (with); **сообразовáть** *(ipf. & pf.* (c + *inst.)* make conform (to).
сообщá together.
сообщ|áть *(pf.* -úть) communicate, impart, report; **сообщéние** communication, report.
сóбщество association; **сообщ|нúк, ~ница** accomplice; accessory; **сóбщничество** complicity.
сору|жáть *(pf.* -дúть, -жý, -дúшь) build, erect; **сооружéние** building, structure.
соотвéтственный *(dat.)* corresponding (to); **соотвéтствие** accordance, correspondence; **соотвéтствовать** *(dat.)* correspond (to).
соотвéтчик co-respondent.
соотéчественн|ик, ~ница compatriot.
соот|носúть* *(pf.* -нестú*) correlate, compare; **соотношéние** correlation.
сопéр|ник, ~ница rival; **сопéрничать** compete, vie; **сопéрничество** rivalry.
сопéть (-плю, -пúшь) wheeze.
сóпка hill, mound; volcano.
соплúвый *(coll.)* snivelling, snotty.
соплó *(pl.* сó|пла, -пел) nozzle.
сопоставлéние comparison; **сопо|ставлять** *(pf.* -стáвить) compare; confront.
сопредéльный contiguous.
сопри|касáться *(pf.* -коснýться) (с + *inst.)* adjoin; come in contact (with); **соприкосновéние** contact.
сопричáстный implicated, participating;
сопроводúтельный accompanying; **сопровожда|ть** *(pf.* -водúть, -вожý, -водúшь; *ppp.* -вождённый) accompany, escort; **сопровождéние** accompaniment; escort.

сопротивлéние resistance; **сопротивля́ться** *(dat.)* resist.
сопряжённый (c + *inst.)* attended (by), connected (with).
сопýтствовать *(dat.)* accompany, attend.
cop litter, rubbish.
соразмéрный commensurate, proportionate.
сорáт|ник, ~ница companion (in arms), comrade.
сорва|нéц (-н .á), **сорвиголовá** *(m. & f.)* madcap; tomboy; **сорвáть** *see* **срывáть.**
соревновáние competition, contest.
сорúнка speck of dust/dirt.
сорúть *(pf.* на-) litter; squander.
сóр|ный dirty, littered; -ая травá, & **сорня́к** (-á) weed.
сóрок forty.
сорóка magpie.
сороковóй fortieth; **сорокононó|жка** *(gen. pl.* -жéк) centipede.
соро|чка *(gen. pl.* -чек) chemise; night-shirt/-dress; caul; родúться в -чке be born with a silver spoon in one's mouth.
сорт *(pl.* -á) sort, grade; **сортировáть** *(pf.* рас-) sort, grade; **сортирóвка** sorting, grading; sorting machine; **сортирóв|щик, ~щица** sorter; **сóрт|ный** high-grade/-quality.
co|сáть (-сý, -сёшь) suck.
сосéд *(pl.* -и, -ей), **~ка** neighbour; **сосéдний** neighbouring; **сосéдство** neighbourhood, vicinity.
сосúска sausage.
сóска baby's dummy, soother.
соскáбливать *(pf.* соскоблúть) scrape off.
соск|áкивать *(pf.* -очúть, -очý, -óчишь) jump off/down; come off.
соскáльзывать *(pf.* соскользнýть) slide down/off.
соскоблúть *see* **соскáбливать.**
соскýчиться *(pf.)* (по + *dat.)* miss.
сослагáтельный subjunctive.
сослáть *see* **ссылáть.**
сослóвие estate, class.
сослужú|вец (-вца), **~вица** colleague.
соснá *(pl.* сóсны, сóсен) pine(-tree).
co|сóк (-скá) nipple, teat.
сосредо|тóчение concentration; -тóчивать *(pf.* -тóчить) (на + *prep.)* concentrate (on); -ся concentrate; be concentrated.
состáв composition, structure; staff; train; **составúтель, ~ница** compi-

ler; составле́ние composition, compiling; составля́ть *(pf.* соста́вить) put together, make up; compile; составн|о́й component, constituent, compound *(a.);* -а́я часть component; ingredient.

состоя́ние condition, state; fortune, wealth; состоя́тельный wealthy; solvent.

состоя́ть* 1. be; 2. (из + *gen.)* consist (of); (в + *prep.)* consist (in).

состоя́ться* *(pf.)* take place.

состра́гивать *(pf.* сострога́ть) plane off.

сострада́ние compassion; сострада́тельный sympathetic.

состри́га́ть *(pf.* состри́чь*) cut/shear off.

состяза́ние contest, competition; состяза́ться compete.

сосу́д vessel

сосу́|лька *(gen. pl.* -лек) icicle.

сосу́н (-á) suckling.

сосуществ|ова́ние co-existence; ~ова́ть co-exist.

сосчи́тывать *(pf.* сосчита́ть) calculate, count.

сотворе́ние creation.

со́тня *(gen. pl.* со́тен) hundred.

сотру́д|ник, ~ница collaborator; employee, worker; сотру́дничать collaborate; сотру́дничество collaboration.

сотряса́ть *(pf.* сотрясти́*) shake; сотрясе́ние shaking; concussion.

со́т|ы (-ов) honeycomb.

со́тый hundredth.

со́ус sauce, gravy; со́усник sauce-/gravy-boat.

соуча́стие participation, complicity; соуча́ст|ник, ~ница participator; accomplice.

софа́ *(pl.* со́фы) sofa.

соха́ *(pl.* со́хи, со́хам) wooden plough.

со́хнуть *(past* сох; *pf.* вы́-, за-) (become) dry.

сохране́ние conservation, preservation, reservation; сохра́нность *(f.)* safety; сохра́нный safe; сохран|я́ть *(pf.* -и́ть) keep; preserve; -ся remain; be well preserved.

соц- social, socialist.

социа́л-демокра́т social-democrat; социализа́ция socialization; социализи́ровать *(ipf. & pf.)* socialize.

социал|и́зм socialism; ~и́ст socialist; ~исти́ческий socialist(ic).

социа́льный social.

социо́лог sociologist; социоло́гия sociology.

соцстра́х social insurance.

сочéльник eve of Christmas/Epiphany.

сочета́ние combination; conjunction; сочета́ть combine, bring into accord.

сочине́ние composition; work, writing; сочини́тель, ~ница author; сочин|я́ть *(pf.* -и́ть) write, compose; invent.

сочи́ться exude, ooze; с. кро́вью bleed.

сочлéн co-member; сочленéние joint, articulation.

со́чный juicy, succulent; rich.

сочу́вственный sympathetic; сочу́вствие sympathy; сочу́вствовать *(dat.)* sympathize (with).

сощу́риваться *(pf.* сощу́риться) screw up one's eyes.

сою́з union; alliance; conjunction; сою́зник ally; сою́зный allied, union *(a.).*

спада́ть *(pf.* спасть*) fall down; abate.

спазм, ~а spasm.

спа́ивать 1. *(pf.* спои́ть) make drunk, turn into a drunkard.

спа́ивать 2. *(pf.* спая́ть) solder; unite, weld; спай joint; спа́йка solder, soldering; close cohesion.

спа́лзывать creep off/down; slip/work down.

спа́льный sleeping *(a.);* с. ваго́н sleeping-car; спа́льня *(gen. pl.* -лен) bedroom.

спа́ржа asparagus.

спа́рхивать *(pf.* спорхну́ть) flit, flutter away.

спа́рывать *(pf.* спороть*) rip off.

спаса́тельный rescue *(a.);* с. круг life-belt; спаса́ть *(pf.* спа|сти́, -су, -сёшь; спас, -ла́; *ppp.* спасённый) save; rescue; -ся escape; спасе́ние rescue; salvation.

спаси́бо (за + *acc.)* thank you (for).

спаси́тель *(m.)* rescuer, saviour; спаси́тельный saving *(a.),* salutary; спасти́ *see* спаса́ть.

спасть *see* спада́ть.

спать (сплю, спишь; спал, -á; *pf.* по-) sleep.

спа́янность *(f.)* unity; спа́ять *see* спа́ивать 2.

спека́ться *(pf.* спе́чься*)* coagulate, curdle; become caked.

спекта́кль *(m.)* play, performance.

спектр spectrum.

спекули́ровать *(inst.)* speculate (in); спекуля́нт speculator, profiteer; спекуляти́вный speculative; спе-куля́ция speculation, profiteering.

спе́лый ripe.

сперва́ at first.

спе́реди at/from the front.

спёртый close, stuffy.

спеси́вый arrogant, conceited; спесь *(f.)* arrogance.

спеть *(pf.* по-*)* ripen.

спех: не к -y there's no hurry.

спец expert.

специализа́ция specialization; ~и́ро-ваться *(ipf. & pf.)* specialize.

специали́ст, ~ка specialist.

специа́ль|ность *(f.)* speciality, pro-fession; ~ный special.

спецоде́жда protective clothing, over-alls.

спе́чься *see* спека́ться.

спе́шиваться *(pf.* спе́шиться*)* dis-mount.

спеши́ть *(pf.* по-*)* hasten, hurry; спе́шка hurry, haste; спе́шный urgent.

спива́ться *(pf.* спи́ться*)* become a drunkard.

спи́ливать *(pf.* спили́ть*)* saw off.

спина́ (спи́ну, *pl.* спи́ны) back; спи́нка back *(of chair etc.)*; спин-но́й spinal.

спира́ль *(f.)* spiral; спира́льный spiral *(a.)*.

спири́т(уали́ст), ~ка spiritualist.

спирт alcohol, spirit(s); спиртно́й напи́ток alcoholic drink; спирто́в-ка spirit lamp.

спи́|сок (-ска) list; copy; record; спи́-сывать *(pf.* списа́ть*)* copy; -ся exchange letters.

спи́хивать *(pf.* спихну́ть*)* shove aside/off.

спи́ца knitting needle; spoke.

спич speech.

спи́чечница match-box; спи́|чка *(gen. pl.* -чек*)* match.

сплав 1. float(ing) *(of timber)*; 2. alloy; спла́вка melting; fusion; сплавля́ть *(pf.* спла́вить*)* 1. float; *coll.* get rid of; 2. melt, alloy; сп-ла́вщик 1. wood-floater; 2. melter.

спла́чивать *(pf.* спло|ти́ть, -чу́, -ти́шь)* join, rally, unite.

сплёскивать *(pf.* сплесну́ть*)* splash.

сплета́ть *(pf.* сплести́*)* interweave, pláit; сплете́ние interlacing; plexus.

сплёт|ник, ~ница gossip, tale-bearer; спле́тничать *(pf.* на-*)* tell tales; спле́|тня *(gen. pl.* -тен*)* gossip, scandal.

сплеча́ straight from the shoulder, violently; at random.

сплоти́ть *see* спла́чивать; сплоче́ние rallying; unity.

сплошно́й compact; continuous; solid.

сплошь entirely; everywhere.

сплю́щивать *(pf.* сплю́щить, сплю́-снуть*)* flatten.

сподви́жник associate, fellow-fighter.

спозара́нку *(coll.)* very early.

споко́йн|ый calm, quiet; even-tem-pered; easy; -ой но́чи! good night!; споко́йствие calm; quiet; composure.

спола́скивать *(pf.* сполосну́ть*)* rinse out.

сползá́ть *(pf.* сползти́*)* climb/crawl down; work down.

сполна́ in full.

сполосну́ть *see* спола́скивать.

спор argument, debate, quarrel.

спо́ра spore.

спо́рить *(pf.* по-*)* argue, dispute, quibble.

спо́риться succeed, go well.

спо́рный questionable, moot.

спорт sport; спорти́вный sport(ing), playing *(a.)*; спортсме́н, ~ка sportsman, -woman.

спор|щик, ~щица arguer, wrang-ler.

спо́соб way, mode; спосо́бность *(f.)* ability, aptitude; спосо́бный able, clever; (к + *dat.)* clever (at); (на + *acc.)* capable (of).

спосо́бствовать *(pf.* по-*)* *(dat.)* assist, further.

спотыка́ться *(pf.* споткну́ться*)* (о + *acc.)* stumble (against, over).

спо|хва́тываться *(pf.* -хвати́ться*)* *(coll.)* bethink oneself.

спра́ва on/from the right.

справедли́вость *(f.)* justice; truth; справедли́вый just, fair.

спра́вить *see* справля́ть.

спра́вк|а information, reference; cer-tificate; наводи́ть -и make en-quiries.

справля́ть (pf. спра́вить) (coll.) celebrate.

справля́ться (pf. спра́виться) 1. look up a word (in a dictionary); o + prep.) enquire (about); 2. (c + inst.) manage, cope with.

спра́вочник reference book; спра́вочный enquiry (a.).

спра́шивать (pf. спроси́ть*) ask, enquire; -ся ask permission; be asked.

спринцо́вка syringe.

спров|а́живать (pf. -а́дить, -а́жу, -а́дишь) (coll.) show out, send off.

спрос demand; asking.

спросо́нок half asleep.

спроста́ artlessly, ingenuously.

спрут octopus.

спры́гивать (pf. спры́гнуть) jump off/down.

спры́скивать (pf. спры́снуть) sprinkle.

спряга́ть (pf. про-) conjugate; спряже́ние conjugation.

спу́гивать (pf. спугну́ть) frighten away.

спуд: держа́ть под -ом hide.

спуск lowering; slope; launching; спуска́ть (pf. спусти́ть*) lower; launch; unleash, let out; -ся go down, descend; спусково́й механи́зм trigger mechanism.

спустя́ after, later; c. неде́лю a week later

спу́т|ник, ~ница companion; satellite; sputnik.

спу́тывать (pf. спу́тать) entangle; confuse.

спя́чка hibernation; somnolence.

сравне́ние comparison; сра́внивать 1. (pf. сравни́ть) compare; 2. (pf. сравня́ть) equal, make even; сравни́тельный comparative; сравни́ться (pf.) (c + inst.) compare (with), come up (to).

сража́ть (pf. срази́ть*) strike down; overwhelm; -ся fight; сраже́ние battle.

сра́зу at once.

срам shame; срами́ть (pf. o-) shame.

сраста́ться (pf. срасти́сь*) accrete, knit.

сра́щивать (pf. срасти́ть*) join, splice.

среда́ 1. (сре́ду, pl. сре́д|ы, -а́м) Wednesday; 2. (среду́, pl. сре́ды) surroundings, medium.

среди́ (gen.) among(st); in the middle.

средиземномо́рский Mediterranean.

средне|азиа́тский Central Asian; ~веко́вый mediaeval; ~веко́вье the Middle Ages.

сре́дн|ий middle; average, mean; в-ем on average.

средо|сте́ние partition, wall; mediastinum; ~то́чие focus.

сре́дство means; remedy.

срез cut; section; среза́ть (pf. сре́зать*) cut off; (coll.) fail (in exam); -ся fail.

срисо́вывать (pf. -ова́ть) copy.

сродни́: быть ему́ c. be related to him; сро́дный (dat.) akin (to); сродство́ affinity; сро́ду не never in one's life.

срок date, period, term; сро́чный urgent; at a fixed date.

сруб felling; framework; сруба́ть (pf. сруби́ть*) fell (timber); build (of logs).

срыв breakdown, failure; срыва́ть 1. (pf. сорва́ть*) tear away; vent (anger); spoil, wreck; -ся break away; fall; fail; slip out; 2. (pf. срыть*) level, raze; сры́тие levelling to the ground.

сря́ду running, in a row.

сса́дина scratch.

сса́живать (pf. ссади́ть*) set down (passenger); coll scratch.

ссо́ра quarrel; ссо́рить (pf. по-) set at odds; -ся quarrel.

ссу́да loan, subsidy; ссужа́ть (pf. ссу|ди́ть, -ужу́, -у́дишь) lend, loan.

ссыла́ть (pf. сосла́ть*) deport, exile; -ся (на + acc.) refer (to); call as witness/referee; ссы́лка_ exile; reference.

ссы́льный exile.

ссыпа́ть (pf. ссы́пать*) pour.

ссыха́ться (pf. ссо́хнуться) shrivel, shrink.

стабилиза́тор stabilizer; стабилизова́ть (ipf. & pf.) stabilize; стаби́льный stable, standard.

ста́|вень (-вня) shutter.

ста́вить (pf. по-) put, stand; pose, set; stake; apply; c. э́то ему́ в вину́ accuse him of it; ста́вка rate; headquarters; ста́вленник protégé; henchman.

ста́в|ня (gen. pl. -ней) shutter.

стадио́н stadium.

ста́дия stage.

ста́дность (f.) herd instinct; ста́дный gregarious; ста́д|о (pl. -а́) herd.

стаж length of service; probation; **стажёр**, **~ка** probationer.

стака́н glass, tumbler.

стале|лите́йный заво́д steel mill; **~плави́льная печь** steel furnace.

ста́лкивать *(pf.* столкну́ть*)* push off/away; bring together; **-ся** (с + *inst.)* collide (with), conflict (with).

сталь *(f.)* steel; **стально́й** steel *(a.).*

стаме́ска chisel.

стан 1. figure, stature; 2. camp; 3. mill.

станда́рт standard; **стандартиз(и́р)-ова́ть** *(ipf. & pf.)* standardize; **станда́ртный** standard.

станио́ль *(m.)* tinfoil.

стани́ца Cossack village.

станкостро́ение machine-tool construction.

стан|ови́ться (-овлю́сь, -о́вишься; *pf.* стать, ста́н|у, -ешь) (take one's) stand/position; *(inst.)* become; *(pf. only)* stop; **во что бы то ни ста́ло** at all costs; **становле́ние** formation, growth.

стан|о́к (-нка́) machine(-tool).

станцио́нный station *(a.);* **ста́нция** station.

ста́птывать *(pf.* стопта́ть*)* wear down at heels.

стара́ние diligence; effort; **стара́тель** *(m.)* prospector; **стара́тельный** assiduous, diligent; **стара́ться** *(pf.* по-*)* try.

старе́йшина *(m.)* elder; **старе́ть** *(pf.* по-*)* grow old; *(pf.* у-*)* become obsolete; **ста́рец** (-рца) old man, elder.

стари́к (-а́) old man; **старина́** old times; antique(s); old man; **стари́нный** ancient, antique, old fashioned; **ста́рить** *(pf.* со-*)* make old.

старо|ве́р old believer; **~жи́л** old resident; **~мо́дный** old fashioned; **~обря́дец** (-дца) old believer.

ста́роста *(m.)* village elder; **ста́рость** *(f.)* old age.

старт start; **ста́ртер** starter *(sport, tech.);* **стартова́ть** *(ipf. & pf.)* start.

стару́ха old woman; **ста́рческий** senile; **ста́рше** older; **ста́рший** elder, oldest; senior; **старшина́** *(m.)* foreman; sergeant-major; dean, doyen; **старшинство́** seniority.

ста́рый old, ancient; **старьё** old clothes, junk; **старьёвщик** old-clothes man, rag-and-bone man.

ста́скивать *(pf.* стащи́ть*)* pull off/down.

стати́ст extra *(theat.).*

стати́стик statistician; **стати́ст|ика** statistics; **~и́ческий** statistical.

ста́тный stately.

статс-секрета́р|ь (-я́) Secretary of State.

стату́этка statuette; **ста́туя** statue.

стат|ь 1. *(pl.* -и, -е́й) build, figure; **он ей под с. he is a match for her; с како́й -и? why?; 2. *see* станови́ться; **ста́ться*** *(pf.)* happen.

стат|ья́ *(gen. pl.* -е́й) article; item; point.

стациона́р permanent institution; hospital; **стациона́рный** stationary; hospital/in-(patient).

ста́чечник striker; **ста́чка** *(gen. pl.* -чек) strike.

стащи́ть *see* ста́скивать.

ста́я *(gen. pl.* стай) flock; pack; shoal.

ствол (-а́) stem, trunk; barrel *(of gun).*

ство́рка leaf, fold; **ство́рчатый** folding.

сте́|бель (-бля, *pl.* -бли, -бле́й) stalk, stem.

стёганый quilted, wadded; **стега́ть** 1. *(pf.* вы́-, про-) quilt; 2. *(pf.* стегну́ть) whip.

сте|жо́к (-жка́) stitch.

стез|я́ *(gen. pl.* -е́й) path.

стека́ть *(pf.* стчь*)* flow down; **-ся** flow together; gather.

стекло́ *(pl.* стёкла, стёкол) glass; pane; **стекля́нный** (of) glass; **стеко́льный** glass, **стеко́льщик** glazier.

стели́ть (стел|ю́, -ешь; *pf.* по-) spread.

стелла́ж (-а́) shelves, shelving.

сте́льная коро́ва cow with calf.

стена́ (сте́ну, *pl.* сте́н|ы, -а́м) wall; **стенгазе́та** wall newspaper; **сте́нка** wall, side; **стенно́й** wall *(a.);* **стеноби́тный тара́н** battering-ram.

стено|гра́мма shorthand record; **~графи́ровать** *(ipf. & pf.)* take down in shorthand; **~графи́ст, ~графи́стка** stenographer; **~гра́фия** stenography.

сте́нопись *(f.)* mural painting.

степе́нный sedate, staid; **сте́пен|ь** *(f.; pl.* -и, -е́й) degree; extent.

степно́й steppe *(a.)*; степ|ь *(f.;* в -и́, *pl.* -и, -е́й) steppe.
стервене́ть *(pf.* о-) rage.
стервя́тник vulture.
стерео|ти́п stereotype; ~ти́пный stereotype(d); ~фони́ческий stereophonic.
стере́ть *see* стира́ть.
стер|е́чь (-егу́, -ежёшь; -ёг, -егла́ guard; watch for.
стёр|жень (-жня) pivot.
стерилизова́ть *(ipf. & pf.)* sterilize; стери́льный sterile.
сте́рлядь *(f.)* sterlet.
стёртый rubbed off; worn out.
стесне́ние constraint; uneasiness;
стесни́тельный shy; inconvenient; стесн|я́ть *(pf.* -и́ть) embarrass; hamper; -ся *(pf.* по-) feel shy, be ashamed.
стече́ние confluence; coincidence; стечь *see* стека́ть.
стилево́й (of) style; стилисти́ческий stylistic; стиль *(m.)* style; сти́льный stylish.
сти́мул stimulus; стимули́ровать *(ipf. & pf.)* stimulate.
стипендиа́т grant-aided student; стипе́ндия grant.
стира́лы|ый washing *(a.)*; -ая маши́на washing-machine; стира́ть 1. *(pf.* вы́-) wash, launder; 2. *(pf.* стере́ть*, сотру́; стёр) wipe off; стирка wash(ing).
сти́скивать *(pf.* сти́снуть) squeeze.
стих (-а́) line, verse, *(pl.)* poetry.
стиха́ть *(pf.* сти́хнуть, *past* стих, calm down, subside.
стихи́йный elemental; spontaneous; стихи́я element.
сти́хнуть *see* стиха́ть.
стихо|сложе́ние versification; ~творе́ние poem; ~тво́рный verse *(a.)*.
стлать (стелю́, сте́лешь, *pf.* по-) spread; -ся spread.
сто hundred.
стог *(pl.* -á) stack, rick.
стогра́дусный centigrade.
сто́имость *(f.)* cost, value; сто́ить *(acc. or gen.)* cost; *(gen.)* be worth; не сто́ит it's not worth it; don't mention it.
сто́йка *(gen. pl.* сто́ек) bar, counter; post; stanchion.
сто́йкий *(compr.* сто́йче) steadfast; stable; сто́йкость *(f.)* steadfastness; stability.

сто́йло stall.
стойма́ upright, standing.
сток flow, drainage; drain, sewer.
стокра́т a hundred times.
стол (-á) table; desk.
столб (-á) pole, post; column, pillar; столбене́ть *(pf.* о-) be petrified; стол|бе́ц (-бца́) column; столбня́к (-á) tetanus; stupor; столбова́я доро́га high road.
столе́тие century; centenary.
столи́ца capital, metropolis; столи́чный capital, metropolitan.
столкнове́ние collision, clash; столкну́ть *see* ста́лкивать.
столова́ться board, have meals; столо́вая dining-room; canteen, cafeteria; столо́вый table *(a.)*; столонача́льник chief of department *(hist.)*.
столп (-á) pillar.
столпотворе́ние babel.
столь so; сто́лько so much, so many.
столя́р (-á) joiner; столя́рный joiner's
стон groan; стона́ть (стону́, -ешь & -а́ю; *pf.* по-) groan.
стоп! stop!; стоп-кра́н stopcock; emergency brake.
стопа́ 1. foot; 2. *(pl.* сто́пы) foot *(in poetic metre)*; 3. *(pl.* сто́пы) ream.
сто́пка pile; small cup/glass.
стопо́рить *(pf.* за-) stop.
стопта́ть *see* ста́птывать.
стори́цей a hundredfold.
сто́рож *(pl.* -á, -е́й), ~иха guard, keeper; watcher; сторожево́й guard, watch *(a.)*; сторожи́ть guard, watch over.
сторон|а́ (сто́рону, *pl.* сто́роны, сторо́н, -а́м) side; party; land; aspect; с одно́й -ы on the one hand; шу́тки в -у joking apart.
сторо|ни́ться (-оню́сь, -о́нишься; *pf.* по-) stand aside; *(gen.)* avoid.
сторо́н|ник, ~ница supporter.
сто́чный sewage *(a.)*.
стоя́лый stagnant, stale; стоя́нка stand, stop; park(ing); moorage; ст|оя́ть (-ою́, -ои́шь; *pf.* по-) stand; stay; стоя́чий standing; stagnant.
стра́вливать *(pf.* страви́ть*) set against each other.
страда́ *(pl.* стра́ды) harvest time.
страда́|лец (-льца) sufferer; страда́ние suffering; страда́тельный pas-

sive *(gram.)*; страда́ть *(pf.* по-) suffer.

стра́дн|ый: -ая пора́ busy season.

страж guard; стра́|жа guard(s), watch.

страна́ *(pl.* стра́ны) country, land.

страни́ца page.

стра́н|ник, ~ница wanderer.

стра́нный strange.

стра́нствие wandering; стра́нствовать wander.

страстно́й Holy, Good (Easter); стра́стный passionate; страст|ь 1. *(f.; pl.* -и, -е́й) passion; 2. *(ad.) (coll.)* simply, awfully.

страт|е́г strategist; ~еги́ческий strategic(al); ~е́гия strategy.

стратосфе́ра stratosphere.

стра́ус ostrich.

страх fear.

страхка́сса insurance office; страх|ова́ние ~о́вка, insurance; страхова́ть *(pf.* за-) insure; страхово́й insurance *(a.).*

страши́лище horror, fright; страши́ть frighten; -ся *(gen.)* be afraid (of); стра́шный terrible.

стре́|жень (-жня) deep part of a river.

стрек|оза́ *(pl.* -о́зы) dragon-fly.

стрек|ота́ть (-очу́, -о́чешь) chirp.

стрела́ *(pl.* стре́лы) arrow, shaft; стре́лка point; pointer.

стрелко́вый rifle, infantry *(a.);* стре|ло́к (-лка́) rifleman, shot; gunner.

стре́лочник pointsman, signalman.

стрельба́ shooting; стре́льбище shooting-range.

стре́льчатый with pointed arch.

стреля́ть *(pf.* стрельну́ть, вы́стрелить) shoot; -ся fight a duel; *(pf.* застрели́ться) shoot oneself *(suicide).*

стремгла́в headlong; стреми́тельный swift; impetuous; стреми́ться (к + *dat.)* speed (towards); стремле́ние aspiration, yearning; стремни́на chute, rapid.

стре́|мя *(neut.; gen. dat., prep.,* -мени, *inst.* -менем, *pl.* -мена́) stirrup.

стремя́нка step-ladder.

стреха́ *(pl.* стре́хи) eaves.

стригу́н (-á) yearling.

стриж (-á) swift; sand-martin.

стри́|женый short-haired, shorn; стри́|жка haircut; shearing; стр|ичь (-игу́, -ижёшь; *pf.* о-, об-; *ppp* -и́женный) cut, clip; -ся have one's hair cut.

строга́ть *(pf.* вы́-) plane.

стро́гий *(comp.* стро́же) severe, strict; стро́гость *(f.)* strictness.

строево́й 1. combatant *(a.);* 2. timber *(a.).*

строе́ние building, edifice, structure; строи́тель *(m.)* builder; строи́тельный building, construction *(a.);* строи́тельство building; стро́ить *(pf.* по-, вы́-) build, construct; draw up *(in formation);* -ся build oneself a house; form up.

строй 1. *(pl.* -о́й, -о́ев) structure, system; 2. *(pl.* -о́й, -о́ев) formation.

стр|о́йка *(gen. pl.* -о́ек) building (-site).

стро́йный well-proportioned, shapely, harmonious.

стр|ока́ (-о́ку́, *pl.* -о́ки, -ока́м) line.

стро́нций strontium.

стропи́ло rafter.

стропти́вый refractory.

строфа́ *(pl.* -фы) stanza.

строчи́ть (-очу́, -о́чишь) 1. *(pf.* про-, вы́-) stitch; 2. *(pf.* на-) write; стро́|чка *(gen. pl.* -чек) line.

стру́г plane; boat.

стру́|жка *(gen. pl.* -жек) shaving(s); chips.

струи́ться stream.

структу́ра structure.

струна́ *(pl.* -у́ны, -у́нам) string *(of instrument etc.).*

стру|п *(pl.* -пья, -пьев) scab.

стручо́к (-чка́) pod.

струя́ *(pl.* стру́й) jet, spurt, stream.

стря́пать *(pf.* со-) cook, concoct; стряпня́ concoction.

стря́пчий attorney, lawyer *(obs.).*

стря́хивать *(pf.* стряхну́ть) shake off.

студене́ть *(pf.* за-) become cold; set.

студе́нт, ~ка student; студе́нческий student *(a.);* студе́нчество the students; student days.

студёный very cold, сту́|день (-дня) (savoury) jelly; ст|уди́ть (-ужу́, -у́дишь; *pf.* о-) cool.

студийный studio (a.); студия studio.

стужа hard frost, cold.

стук knock, tap; стукать (pf. стукнуть) knock, give a tap; ему стукнуло 50 he is over 50; -ся (о + acc.) knock (against), bump (into); see also стучать.

стул (pl. стулья, -ьев) chair stool (med.).

ступа mortar.

ступать (pf. ступить, -уплю, -упишь) step; ступенчатый stepped; ступень (f.; pl. -ени, -еней) step; (gen. pl. -еней) stage; ступенька step; ступня (gen. pl. -ней) foot.

стучать (-чу, -чишь; pf. по-, стукнуть) knock; chatter (teeth); с. в дверь knock on the door; -ся knock.

стушёвываться (pf. -еваться) efface oneself.

стыд (-á) shame; стыдить (-жу, дишь; pf. при-) put to shame; -ся (pf. по-) (gen.) be ashamed (of); стыдливый diffident, modest; стыдный shameful; мне стыдно за это I am ashamed about it.

стык joint, junction; стыковка docking (in space).

стынуть & стыть (стыну, -ешь; pf. о-) get cool/cold.

стычка (gen. pl. -чек) skirmish, quarrel.

стюардесса stewardess.

стяг banner.

стягивать (pf. стянуть) draw/pull together, tighten; pull down/-off.

стяжатель money-grubber; possessor (hist); стяжать (ipf. & pf.) get, obtain.

стянуть see стягивать.

суббота Saturday; субботник voluntary day's work on free day.

субсидировать (ipf. & pf.) subsidize; субсидия subsidy.

субтитр sub-title.

субъект subject; (coll.) fellow, chap; субъективный subjective.

сувенир souvenir.

суверенитет sovereignty; суверенный sovereign (a.).

суглинок (-нка) loam.

сугроб snowdrift.

сугубый especial.

суд (-á) court.

судак (-á) zander, pike perch.

сударыня madam; сударь (m.) sir (obs.).

судачить (coll.) gossip, tittle tattle.

судебный judicial, legal; судейство refereeing, umpiring; судимость (f.) convictions.

судить (сужу, судишь) 1. judge, try; referee, umpire; судя по (dat.) judging by; 2. (ipf. & pf.) (pre)destine; нам суждено (+ inf.) it is our destiny, we are destined (to).

судно 1. (pl. судá, -óв) ship vessel; 2. (pl. судна, -ден) bed-pan.

судоверфь (f.) shipyard; судовой ship(s'), naval.

судок (-дкá) cruet-stand; mealcontainer.

судомойка (gen. pl. -óек) kitchenmaid, dishwasher; scullery.

судопроизводство legal proceedings.

судорога convulsion, cramp; судорожный convulsive.

судостроение ship-building; ~строительный ship-building (a.).

судоустройство judicial system.

судоходный navigable; ~ходство navigation.

судьба (pl. судьбы, -деб) fate.

судья (m. pl. судьи, -дей, -дьям) judge; referee, umpire.

суеверие superstition; суеверный superstitious.

суета bustle, fuss; futility; суетиться (-чусь, -тишься) bustle, fuss; суетливый fussy, fidgety; суетный futile, vain.

суждение judgement, opinion.

сужение contraction, narrowing.

суженый betrothed.

суживать (pf. су зить, -жу, -зишь) narrow; -ся contract, taper.

сук (-á, на -ý, pl. сучья, -ьев, & суки) bough, branch.

сука bitch.

сукно (pl. сукна, сукон) cloth; положить под с. shelve, pigeonhole; суконный cloth (a.); (fig.) clumsy.

сулема sublimate (chem.).

сулить (pf. по-) promise.

султан sultan.

сума bag.

сумасброд, mad/wild person; ~бродный mad, wild; ~бродство extravagant/wild behaviour; ~

шéдший mad, insane; ~шéствие madness.

суматóха bustle, turmoil.

сумбýр confusion; сумбýрный muddled.

сýме|рки (-рек) gloaming, twilight.

сумéть (pf.) manage, succeed.

сýмка bag.

сýмма sum, total; суммáрный summary; total; суммúровать sum up, summarize.

сýмо|чка (gen. pl. -чек) small bag, handbag.

сýмрак dusk, twilight; gloom; сýмрачный gloomy.

сýмчатый marsupial.

сундýк (-á) chest, trunk.

сýнуть see совáть.

суп (pl. -ы́) soup.

сýпе|сок (-ска) sandy soil.

сýп|ник, ~ница tureen.

супрýг husband, spouse; супрýга wife; супрýжеский conjugal; супрýжество matrimony.

сургýч (-á) sealing-wax.

сурдúнк|а: под -у on the sly.

сýрик red lead.

сурóвый severe, stern.

су|рóк (-ркá) marmot.

суррогáт substitute.

сурьмá antimony.

сусáльный tinsel (a.); sugary.

сýслик suslik (kind of marmot).

сустáв joint.

сýтки (-ток) twenty-four hours, day.

сýтолока commotion.

сýточный daily, twenty-four-hour.

сутýлиться stoop; сутýлый round-shouldered.

сут ь1. (f.) essence; 2. (there) are.

суфлёр prompter; суфлúровать (dat.) prompt.

сýффикс suffix.

сухáр|ь (-я́) rusk, biscuit.

суховéй dry wind.

суходóл dry valley.

сухожúлие sinew, tendon.

сухóй (comp. сýше) dry.

сухо|пáрый lean, scraggy; ~пýтный land (a.)

сýхость (f.) aridity, dryness.

сухощáвый lean, meagre.

сучúть (сучý, сýчишь; pf. с-) spin, twist.

сý|чка (gen. pl. -чек) bitch.

сучковáтый gnarled, knotty; сý|чóк (- ка) twig.

сýша dry land.

сушéние drying; сушёный dried.

сушúлка drying apparatus; drying-room; сушú|льня (gen. pl. -лен) drying-room; сушúть (сушý, сýшишь; pf. вы́-) (make) dry; -ся (get) dry.

сущéственный essential, vital; существúтельное noun.

существ|ó being, creature; essence; ~овáние existence; ~овáть exist.

сýщий real; сýщность (f.) essence, main point.

сфéра sphere; сферúческий spherical.

сфинкс sphinx.

схвáтка skirmish; (pl.) convulsions; схвáтывать (pf. схватúть*) catch; grab, grasp; -ся grapple, skirmish; (за + acc.) seize.

схéма scheme.

сход gathering.

сходúть* 1. (ipf.; pf. сойтú*, сойдý сошёл) go/come down; alight; come off; pass; 2. (pf.) go; -ся gather, meet.

схóдка gathering, meeting; схóдн|и (-ей) gangway.

схóдный suitable; (с + inst.) similar (to); схóдство similarity; схóжий similar.

сцéживать (pf. сцедúть*) decant.

сцéна stage; scene; сценáрий script; сценúческий stage (a.); сценúчный theatrically effective.

сцеп hook, link; сцéпка coupling; сцеплéние coupling; clutch; сцеплять (pf. сц|епúть, -еплю́, -éпишь) couple; -ся grapple.

счастлú|вец (-вца), ~вица lucky person; счастлúвый happy, fortunate; счáстье happiness; good fortune.

счесть see считáть.

счёт (pl. счет|á, -óв) calculation reckoning; account score; за с. (gen.) at the expense (of); на свой с. at one's own expense; принять на свой с. take as referring to oneself.

счётный account (a.); calculating; счетовóд accountant; счётчик meter; счёт|ы (-ов) abacus.

счислéние numeration; calculus.

считáть (pf. со-, & счесть, со|чтý, -чтёшь; счёл, сочлá; ppp. сочтённый) count, compute; consider; -ся be considered; -ся (pf. по-) (с + inst.) consider, reckon (with).

счищáть (pf. счи́стить*) clean off, brush off.
сшибáть (pf. сши|би́ть, -бу́, -бёшь; сшиб; ppp. сши́бленный) knock down.
сшивáть (pf. сшить*, сошью́) sew together.
съедáть (pf. съесть*) eat; съедо́бный edible.
съёживаться (pf. съёжиться) shrink.
съезд congress; arrival; съéздить (pf.) go (for a short visit); съезжáть (pf. съéхать*) go/come down; move (home); -ся come together, meet.
съём output; съёмка survey; shooting, taking (film); съёмный removable; съёмщик, ~щица surveyor; tenant.
съестнóй edible.
съéхать see съезжáть.
сы́воротка whey; serum.
сыгрáть see игрáть.
сы́змала from childhood; сы́знова afresh, anew.
сын (pl. сыно|вья́, -ве́й; fig. сыны́) son; сынóвний filial; сы|нóк (-нкá) little son.
сы́пать (сы́плю, сы́плешь; imper. с пь) pour, strew; -ся fall, pour, run.
сыпнóй тиф typhus.
сыпу́чий loose, moving, dry.
сыпь (f.) rash.
сыр (pl. -ы́) cheese.
сырéть (pf. от-) become damp.
сы|рéц (-рцá) raw material.
сы́рник cheese pancake.
сыроéжка (gen. pl. -жек) kind of mushroom.
сырóй damp, sodden; raw, uncooked, unprocessed; сы́рость (f.) dampness; сырьё raw material(s).
сыскáть (pf., сыщу́, сы́щешь) find; сыскнóй investigation (a.).
сы́тный nourishing, substantial; сы́тый replete, satisfied.
сыч (-á) barn-owl.
сы́щик detective.
сюдá here, hither.
сюжéт subject, plot.
сюи́та suite.
сюрпри́з surprise.
сюрту́к (-á) frock-coat.
сюсю́кать (coll.) lisp.
сяк: и так и сяк this way and that.
сям: там и сям here and there.

Т

табáк (-á) tobacco; табакéрка snuffbox; табáчный tobacco (a.).
тáбель (m.) table; time-board.
таблéтка tablet.
табли́ца table; plate.
тáбор camp.
табу́н (-á) herd of horses.
табурéт, ~ка stool.
таврó brand, mark.
тавтолóгия tautology.
тадж|и́к, ~и́чка (gen. pl. -и́чек Tadzhik; таджи́кский Tadzhik (a.).
таёжный taiga (a.).
таз (в -ý, pl. -ы́) basin; pan; pelvis.
тáинственный mysterious; тáинство sacrament; тайть hide; bear (malice etc.); -ся be hidden; keep something back.
тайгá taiga (forest area).
тайкóм secretly; (от + gen.) without someone's knowledge; тáйна secret, mystery; тайни́к (-á) hiding place; тайнобрáчный cryptogamic; тáйный secret; privy.
тайфу́н typhoon.
так ео| т. ему́ и нáдо it serves him right; не т. wrongly; т. или инáче one way or the other, somehow; так как since, because.
такелáж rigging.
тáкже also.
такóв such; так|óй such; в -óм слу́чае in that case.
тáкса statutory price; tariff; dacsh hund.
такси́ (indecl.) taxi.
такси́ровать (ipf. & pf.) fix the price of.
такт 1. beat, measure, time; 2. tact.
тáктик tactician; тáктика tactics; такти́ческий tactical.
такти́чный tactful.
талáнт (к + dat.) talent (for); талáнтливый talented, gifted.
талисмáн talisman.
тáлия waist.
талóн check, coupon.
тáлый melting, thawing.
тальк talc, talcum powder.
там there.
тамадá (m.) toastmaster.

таможенный customs *(a.);* **тамо|жня** *(gen. pl.* -жен) customs-house/ -office.

тамошний of that place, local.

тангенс tangent.

та|нец (-нца) **da** ıce.

танин tannin.

танк tank; **танкер** tanker.

тантьéма bonus.

танцевáльный dancing *(a.);* т. вéчер dance; **танцевáть** *(v.t. & i.)* dance; **танцóв|щик, ~щица,** танцóр, **~ка** dancer.

тáпо|чка *(gen. pl.* -чек) slipper; sports shoe, plimsoll.

тáра packing (material); tare.

таракáн cockroach.

тарáн battering-ram; **тарáнить** *(pf.* про-) ram.

тарантáс tarantass *(springless carriage).*

тараторить chatter.

тарáщить *(pf.* вы-): т. глазá на + *acc.* stare/goggle at.

тарéлка plate; cymbal.

тариф tariff.

таскáть drag, pull; *(coll.)* steal; *(coll.)* wear (out); -ся trail along; hang about.

тасовáть *(pf.* с-) shuffle.

тат|áрин *(pl.* -áры, -áр), **~áрка** Tartar; **татáрский** Tartar *(a.).*

татуировать *(ipf. & pf.)* tattoo; **татуировка** tattoo.

тафтá taffeta; **тафтянóй** taffeta *(a.).*

тахтá ottoman.

тачáнка gun-carriage.

тачáть *(pf.* -с) stitch.

тá|чка *(gen. pl.* -чек) wheelbarrow.

тащить (тащý, тáщишь; *pf.* по-) drag; -ся trail along.

тáять (тáю, тáешь; *pf.* рас-) melt *(v.i.).*

твáрь *(f.)* creature(s).

твердéть *(pf.* за-) become hard.

твер|дить (-жý, -дишь) say, repeat; *(pf.* вы-, за-) learn by heart, memorize.

твердолóбый thick-headed; die-hard *(a.).*

твёрдость *(f.)* firmness, hardness, solidity; **твёрдый** *(сотр.* твёрже) firm, hard, solid; **твердыня** stronghold.

твой, твоя, твоё, твои your(s).

творéние creation; creature; work; **тво|рéц** (-рцá) creator; **творитель-**

ный instrumental *(gram.);* **творить** *(pf.* со-) create, do; -ся happen, go on.

творóг curds; cottage cheese; **творóжник** curd pancake.

творческий creative; **творчество** creation; work(s).

теáтр theatre; **театрáл** theatre-goer; **театрáльный** theatrical.

тевтóн Teuton.

тéзис thesis.

тёзка *(m. & f.)* namesake.

текст text.

текстиль *(m.)* textiles; **текстильный** textile *(a.).*

текýчесть *(f.)* fluidity; fluctuation; **текýчий** fluid; unstable; **текýщий** current, present-day.

телевидение television; **телевизиóнный** television *(a.);* **телевизор** television set.

телéга cart, waggon.

телегрáмма telegram.

телегрáф telegraph; **телеграфировать** *(ipf. & pf.)* telegraph, cable; т. соглáсие cable agreement; **телегрáфный** telegraph(ic).

телé|жка *(gen. pl.* -жек) small cart, truck.

телезритель *(m.)* (T.V.-) viewer.

телё|нок (-нка) *(pl.* -ята, -ят) calf.

теле|пáтия telepathy.

телепередáча television transmission.

телескóп telescope.

телéсный corporal.

телефóн telephone; т.-автомáт automatic public telephone; **телефонист, ~ка** telephonist; **телефóнный** telephone *(a.).*

те|лéц (-льцá) Taurus; calf; **телиться** (тéлится; *pf.* о-) calve; **тёлка** heifer.

тéло *(pl.* -á) body.

тело|грéйка *(gen. pl.* -грéек) padded jacket; **~сложéние** build, frame; **~хранитель** *(m.)* bodyguard.

телятина veal; **телячий** veal *(a.),* calf *(a.).*

тéма subject; theme; **темáтика** subjects, themes.

тембр timbre.

темнéть *(pf.* по-, с-) become dark; **темница** dungeon; **тёмно-синий** dark-blue; **темнотá** darkness; **тёмный** dark.

темп rate; tempo.

тéмпера distemper; tempera.

темпера́мент temperament; ~ный temperamental.

температу́ра temperature.

те́мя (neut.; gen., dat., prep. те́мени, inst. те́менем) crown, top of head.

тенденцио́зный tendentious; тенде́нция tendency.

те́ндер tender.

теnево́й shady.

тен|ёта (-ёт) snare.

тени́стый shady.

те́ннис tennis; теннис́ист, ~ка tennis-player; те́ннисный tennis (a.).

те́нор (pl. -ы & -á) tenor.

тень (f.; в -и́, pl. те́н|и, -е́й) shadow, shade.

теодоли́т theodolite.

тео́лог theologian; теоло́гия theology.

теоре́ма theorem.

теор|е́тик theorctician; ~ети́ческий theoretical.

тео́рия theory.

тепе́решний present (a.); тепе́рь now.

тепле́ть (pf. по-) grow warm; те́плиться glimmer; тепли́ца hot house, conservatory; тепли́чное расте́ние hot-house plant.

тепло́ warmth, heat.

тепло|во́з diesel locomotive; ~во́й thermal; heat (a.).

теплоёмкость (f.) уде́льная т. specific heat.

теплота́ warmth, cordiality.

тепло|те́хник heating engineer; ~хо́д motor vessel.

теплу́|шка (gen. pl. -шек) heated goods van; heated shelter.

тёплый warm.

тепля́к (-á) overall shelter (on building site).

терапе́вт therapist; терапи́я therapy.

тереби́ть (coll.) pull; tug.

те́рем tower-room/-chamber.

тере́ть (тру, трёшь; тёр; ppp. тёртый) rub, polish.

терза́ние torment; терза́ть (pf. ис-, рас-) torment, torture; tear to pieces; -ся suffer torments.

тёрка grater.

терм therm; term.

те́рмин term; терминоло́гия terminology.

термо́метр thermometer; те́рмос thermos flask.

термо|ста́т thermostat; ~я́дерный thermo-nuclear.

тёрн sloe; blackthorn; терни́стый prickly.

терпели́вый patient; терпе́ние patience; терпе́ть (терплю́, те́рпишь; pf. по-) bear, endure, suffer; терпи́мость (f.) tolerance; терпи́мый tolerant; tolerable.

те́рпкий (comp. те́рпче) astringent.

терра́са terrace.

территориа́льный territorial; террито́рия territory.

терро́р terror; терроризи́ровать, -ова́ть terrorize; террори́ст terrorist.

тёртый кала́ч old stager.

теря́ть (pf. по-) lose; -ся get lost; lose one's presence of mind.

тёс boards, timber.

теса́ть (тешу́, те́шешь; pf. вы́-) cut, hew.

тесёмка braid, tape.

тесни́на gorge, ravine.

тесни́ть (pf. по) press, squeeze; (pf. c-) squeeze, be too tight; -ся be herded, jostle; теснота́ tightness; те́сный narrow, tight; close; crowded.

тесо́вый board, plank (a.).

те́сто dough, pastry.

тесть (m.) wife's father.

тесьма́ braid.

те́терев (pl. -á, -о́в & -е́й) black grouse.

тетива́ bow-string; stringer.

тётка aunt.

тетра́дка, тетра́дь (f.) exercise book.

тётя (gen. pl. тётей) aunt.

те́хник technician; те́хника technique; equipment; те́хникум technical college; техни́ческий technical; техно́лог technologist; техноло́гия technology.

тече́ние course, flow; течь 1. (течёт, теку́т; тёк, текла́) flow, pour; течь 2. (f.) leak.

те́шить (pf. по-) amuse, entertain; please; -ся (inst.) amuse oneself (with).

тёща wife's mother.

ти́|гель (-гля) crucible.

тигр tiger; тигри́ца tigress.

тик 1. tick; 2. tic; 3. teak.

ти́кать tick.

тимиа́н thyme.

тимпа́н tympanum.

ти́на mud, slime; ти́нистый miry, muddy.

тип type; character; типизи́ровать (ipf & pf.) typify; тип|и́ческий,

~**ЙчНый** typical; **типовóй** standard, model *(a.)*.
типогрáфия printing-works/-press; **типогрáфский** typographical.
тир shooting-range/-gallery.
тирáж (-á) draw *(in lottery)*; edition, circulation; **вы́йти в т.** become superannuated.
тирáн tyrant; **тирáнить** tyrannize; **тиранúческий** tyrannical; **тирáн|ство**, ~**ия** tyranny.
тирé *(indecl.)* dash.
тис yew.
тúскать *(pf.* тúснуть) squeeze, press; **тиск|и** (-óв) vice.
тиснéние stamping; **тиснёный** stamped.
титровáть *(ipf. & pf.)* titrate.
тúтул title; **тúтульный** title *(a.)*.
тиф typhus; **брюшнóй т.** typhoid.
тúхий *(comp.* тúше) quiet, calm; steady; **тихомóлком** without a word; on the quiet; **тихóнько** softly; on the sly; **тишинá** silence; **тишь** *(f.,* в тишú) silence, calm.
ткань *(f.)* cloth, fabric; **ткать** (тку, ткёшь; ткал, ткáлá; *pf.* со-) weave; **ткáцкий** weaving *(a.)*; **ткач** (-á) **ткачúха** weaver.
ткнуть *see* ты́кать.
тлéние decay; smouldering; **тлéнный** perishable; **тлетвóрный** pernicious; putrid; **тлеть** decay, rot; smoulder.
тля aphis.
то 1. *see* тот; 2. а не то then, in that case; otherwise; то ... то ... now ... now ...
-**то** *emphatic particle* just, exactly.
товáр goods, wares.
товáрищ comrade, friend, colleague; **товáрищеский** comradely, friendly; **товáрищество** comradeship; company, association.
товáрка *(coll.)* friend, pal.
товáрность *(f.)* marketability; **товáрный** goods, commodity *(a.)*; **т. знак** trade mark.
товаровéд expert on commodities/goods.
товаро|обмéн barter; ~**оборóт** circulation of commodities.
тогдá then; **тогдáшний** of that time.
тож(д)éственный *(dat.)* identical (with); **тóж(д)ество** identity, sameness.
тóже also, too.
ток 1. current; 2. threshing floor.

токáрный turning, lathe *(a.)*; **тóкар|ь** *(m.; pl.* -и & -я́) turner, lathe operator.
толк 1. sense; use; **знать т.** (в +*prep.*) know all (about); **сбить с -у** confuse; 2. doctrine; trend; 3. *(pl.)* gossip.
толкáть *(pf.* толкнýть) push, shove; **-ся** jostle.
толкáч (-á) pusher, shunter; pushing person, fixer.
тóлк|и (-ов) gossip.
толковáние interpretation; commentary; **толковáть** 1. *(pf.* ис-) interpret; 2. *(pf.* по-) talk; **толкóвый** clear; intelligent; **тóлком** sensibly, seriously.
толкотня́ crush, squash; **толкý|чка** *(gen. pl.* -чек) second-hand market; crush.
толмáч (-á) interpreter, translator.
толóчь (толкý, толчёшь; толóк, толклá; *ppp.* толчёный; *pf.* ис-, рас-) grind, pound; **-ся** hang about; be pounded.
толпá *(pl.* тóлпы) crowd; **толпúться** crowd, throng.
толстéть *(pf.* по-) grow fat.
толстóвство Tolstoyism.
толстокóжий pachydermatous; thick-skinned; **тóлстый** *(comp.* тóлще) fat, thick; **толстя́к** (-á) fat man.
толчёный crushed, ground.
толчея́ crowd, crush; **тол|чóк** (-чкá) bump, push; shock, tremor.
тóлща thickness; the thick; **толщинá** thickness; corpulence.
толь *(m.)* roofing felt.
тóлько only, merely; **как т.** as soon as; **т. бы** if only; **т. что** just (this minute).
том *(pl.* -á) volume.
томáт tomato; **томáтный сок** tomato juice.
тóмик small volume.
томúтельный tiring, wearisome; agonizing; **томúть** *(pf.* ис-) weary; torment; **-ся** languish; be tormented; **томлéние** languor; **тóмный** languid.
тон *(pl.* -ы́ & -á) tone; *(pl.* -á) shade; **тонáльность** *(f.)* key *(mus.)*.
тонизúровать *(ipf. & pf.)* tone up.
тóнкий *(comp.* тóньше) thin, slim; keen; delicate; fine; **тóнкост|ь** *(f.)* thinness; fineness; subtlety; **вдавáться в -и** split hairs.

тóнна ton; тоннáж tonnage.
тоннéль *(m.)* tunnel.
тóнус tone; жизненный т. vitality.
тонýть *(pf.* за-, по-) sink; *(pf.* у-) be drowned; *(pf.* по-) be lost, submerged *(fig.).*
тонфúльм sound film.
тóньше *see* тóнкий.
тóпать *(pf.* тóпнуть) *(inst.)* stamp *(e. g. one's foot)* ; *(coll.)* tramp.
топúть (топлю́, тóпишь) 1. *(pf.* за-, на-) light *(stove)* ; heat; 2. *(pf.* по-) sink; 3. *(pf.* у-) drown; ruin; 4. *(pf.* на-) melt.
тóпка firebox; heating; melting.
тóпкий boggy, swampy.
топлёный baked; boiled; melted; тóпливо fuel.
тóпнуть *see* тóпать.
топогрáфия topography.
тóпол|ь *(m.* ; *pl.* -и & -я́) poplar.
топóр (-á) axe.
топóрный clumsy, rough.
топóрщить bristle.
тóпот tread *(of feet)*, clatter *(of hooves).*
топтáть (топчу́, тóпчешь; *pf.* по-) trample; -ся stamp; -ся на мéсте mark time.
топчáн trestle bed.
топь *(f.)* swamp.
торг (на -ý) bargaining; auction; *(coll.)* market; торгáш (-á) small tradesman, mercenary person; торг|й (-óв) tendering; auction; торговáть trade; -ся bargain, haggle торгó|вец (-вца), ~вка trader; торгóвля trade; торгóвый trade *(a.);* торгпрéд trade representative.
тор|éц (-рцá) end surface *(wood)* ; wooden paving-block; wood pavement.
торжéственный solemn, ceremonial; торжествó ceremony, celebration; triumph; торжествовáть celebrate; *(pf.* вос-) (над + *inst.)* triumph (over).
тормáшк|и: вверх -ами upside-down, head-over-heels.
торможéние braking, inhibition; тóрмоз *(pl.* -á) brake; тормо|зúть (-жу́, зúшь; *pf.* за-) brake.
тормошúть *(coll.)* tug, pull about; pester.
тóрный even, smooth, beaten *(track).*
тор|опúть (-оплю́, -óпишь; *pf.* по-) hurry *(v. t.)* ; precipitate; -ся hurry; тороплúвый hasty.

торпéд|а torpedo; ~úровать *(ipf. & pf.)* torpedo.
тóрс torso.
торт cake.
торф peat; торфянóй peat *(a.).*
торчáть (-чу́, -чúшь) protrude; stand out; *(coll.)* hang about.
тоскá melancholy; yearning; weariness; т. по рóдине home-sickness;
тосклúвый dreary; melancholy; тосковáть be sad; (по + *dat.* or *prep.)* pine for.
тост toast.
тот, та, то, те that; тот и другóй both; тот же the same; к тому́ же moreover.
то-то how?; what did I tell you?
тóтчас immediately.
точúльный кáмень whetstone; точúльщик grinder, sharpener; точúть (точу́, тóчишь) 1. *(pf.* на-) sharpen; 2. *(pf.* вы-) turn; 3. *(pf.* ис-) secrete, shed; 4. eat away, wear away.
тó|чка *(gen. pl.* -чек) 1. point, spot; full stop; 2. sharpening; т. с запятóй semi-colon.
тóчно precisely; тóчность *(f.)* exactness; punctuality; тóчный accurate, precise, punctual.
тóчь-в-тóчь exactly, word-for-word,
тошн|úть: менá -úт I feel sick; тошнотá sickness, nausea; тóшный tiresome; nauseating.
тóщий emaciated, skinny.
травá *(pl.* трáвы) grass; травúнка blade of grass.
тр|авúть (-авлю́, -áвишь) 1. *(pf.* вы-) poison; aggravate; slacken; 2. *(pf.* за-) hunt; hound; 3. *(pf.* по-) trample down, damage; трáвля hunting; persecution.
трáвма trauma.
травоя́дный herbivorous.
травянúстый, травянóй grassy, herbaceous.
трагéдия tragedy; трáгик tragedian;
траг|úческий tragical, tragic; ~úчный terrible, tragic.
традициóнный traditional; традúция tradition.
траектóрия trajectory.
тракт high road, route.
трактáт treatise; treaty.
трактúр inn, tavern; трактúрщик inn-keeper.

трактовáть treat, discuss; interpret; трактóвка treatment, interpretation.

трáктор tractor; трáкторный tractor (a.).

трáлить (pf. про-) trawl; sweep; трáльщик trawler; minesweeper.

трамбовáть (pf. у-) ram, tamp.

трамвáй tram; трамвáйный tram (a.).

трамплúн spring-board; ski-jump; jumping-off place.

транзúт transit; транзúтный transit (a.).

трансатлантúческий transatlantic.

транскр|ибúровать (ipf. & pf.) transcribe; ~úпция transcription.

трансл|úровать transmit; relay; ~я́ция transmission.

трáнспорт transport; транспортёр conveyor; транспортúр protractor; транспортúровать (ipf. & pf.) transport, convey; трáнспортник transport worker; трáнспортный transport (a.).

трансформ|áтор transformer (elec.); ~úровать (ipf. & pf.) transform.

трансфýзия transfusion.

траншéя trench.

трап ladder.

трáпеза meal; трáпезная refectory.

трапéция trapezium; trapeze.

трáсса line, direction, route; plan, sketch; трассúровать (ipf. & pf.) mark out, trace.

трáта expenditure; трáтить (-чу, -тишь; pf. ис-, по-) spend, expend.

трáур mourning; mourning (clothes); трáурный mourning, funeral (a.).

трафарéт stencil; stereotyped pattern; cliché; трафарéтный stencilled; commonplace.

трéбник prayer-book.

трéбование demand, request, claim; (pl.) desires, aspirations; трéбовательный exacting; трéбовать (pf. по-) (gen.) demand; call for; (acc.) summon; -ся be needed.

требухá entrails, offal; rubbish.

тревóга alarm; anxiety; тревóжить (pf. вс-) trouble, worry; (pf. по-) disturb, harass; тревóжный anxious; disturbing; alarm (a.).

трéзвенник teetotaller; трéзвый sober.

трезý|бец (-бца) trident.

трель (f.) trill, warble.

трéнер trainer.

трéние friction.

тренировáть (pf. на-) train; -ся be in training; тренирóвка training; тренирóвочный training (a.).

тре|нóга, -нóжник tripod.

тренóжить (pf. с-) fetter, hobble.

тр|епáть (-еплю, -éплешь; pf. по-, ис-) tousle, shake, hit; make tattered; -ся (pf. по-, ис-) become tattered, etc.; flutter.

трéпет trembling; трепетáть (-ещý, -éщешь; pf. за-) tremble, palpitate; трéпетный trembling, quivering.

трёпка shaking, hiding.

треск crack(le).

трескá cod.

трéскаться (pf. по-, трéснуть) crack, be chapped.

трескóвый жир cod-liver oil.

трескотня́ cracking; chirping; (coll.) chatter; трескýчий very hard (frost); bombastic; трéснутый cracked.

трест trust.

третéйский суд court of arbitration.

трéт|ий third; -ьего дня the day before yesterday.

третúровать treat with contempt, slight.

трет|ь (f.; pl. -и, -éй) a third; третье-сóртный third-rate.

треугóль|ник triangle; ~ный triangular.|

трéфы (треф) clubs.

трёх|годúчный three-year, triennial; ~грáнный three-edged; ~днéвный three-day; ~лéтний three-year, triennial; three-year-old; ~пóлье three-field system; ~стóронний three-sided, trilateral.

тре|щáть (-щý, -щúшь; pf. за-, про- & трéснуть) crackle, crack (sound); chirp; трéщина crack, split; chap; трещóтка rattle; chatterbox.

три three.

трибýн tribune, orator; трибýна platform, rostrum, stand.

трибунáл tribunal.

тригономéтрия trigonometry.

трúдевять: за т. земéль at the other end of the earth.

тридцáтый thirtieth; трúдцать thirty.

трúжды three times.

трикó (indecl.) tricot; tights; трикотáж knitted fabric/clothes.

трилúстник trefoil; shamrock.

трилóгия trilogy.

тримéстр term.

тринадцатый thirteenth; тринадцать thirteen.

триста three hundred.

тритон triton; newt.

триумф triumph; триумфальный triumphal.

трогательный touching, moving; трогать (pf. тронуть) touch; disturb; affect; -ся move, start.

трое three; троекратный thrice-repeated.

троица Trinity.

тройка (gen. pl. троек) three; three horses, coach/sledge and three; тройной treble, triple; тройн|я (gen. pl. -ей) triplets.

тройственный triple.

троллейбус trolley bus.

тромб thrombus, clot.

трон throne.

тронуть see трогать.

тропа path.

тропик tropic.

тропинка path.

тропический tropical.

трос line, rope.

тростник (-а) cane, reed; трость|чка (gen. pl. -чек), трость (f.) cane.

тротуар pavement, sidewalk.

трофей trophy.

троюродный брат, -ая сестра second cousin.

тройкий triple, threefold.

труба (pl. трубы) pipe; chimney, funnel; trumpet; трубач (-а) trumpeter; трубить (pf. за-, про-) blow; trumpet; трубка pipe; трубопровод conduit, pipeline; трубочист chimney-sweep; трубочный pipe (a.).

труд (-а) labour, work; тр|удиться (-ужусь, -удишься) (над + inst.) work (on), toil (over); трудность (f.) difficulty; obstacle; трудный difficult, hard.

трудо|вой working, labour (a.); ~день (-дня) work-day (unit of work); ~ёмкий laborious, labour-consuming; ~любивый industrious; ~любие diligence; ~способный able-bodied, capable of working.

трудящийся worker; тру́же|ник, ~ница toiler.

труп corpse.

труппа company, troupe.

трус coward.

трусик|и (-ов) shorts, trunks.

тру́|сить (-шу, -сишь) 1. shake, scatter; 2. trot; 3. (pf. с-) be cowardly, have cold feet; (перед + inst.) funk; трусливый cowardly; трусость (f.) cowardice.

трус|ы (-ов) shorts, trunks.

трут tinder.

тру́|тень (-тня) drone (bee).

труха rot, dust of dry rotten wood; dust of hay; трухлявый rotten.

трущоба slum.

трюк stunt, trick.

трюм hold (of ship).

трюмо (indecl.) pier glass.

трюфел|ь (m.; pl. -и, -ей) truffle.

тряпка rag; тряпьё rags.

трясина quagmire.

тряска shaking; тряский bumpy; тряс|ти (-су, -сёшь; тряс, -ла; pf. по-; ppp. потрясённый; also pf. тряхнуть) shake; make shiver; трястись shake, shiver, tremble.

туалет dress; toilet; lavatory.

туберкулёз tuberculosis.

тугодум slow-witted person.

тугой (comp. туже) tight, taut; т. на ухо hard of hearing.

тугоплавкий refractory.

туда there, thither.

туже (comp. of. тугой) tighter.

тужить (тужу, тужишь) grieve.

тужурка double-breasted jacket.

туз (-а) ace; big shot; dinghy.

тузе́м|ец (-мца), ~ка native; туземный native (a.).

туловище body, trunk.

тулуп sheepskin coat.

туман mist; haze; туманить (pf. за-) dim, obscure; туманный misty, hazy.

тумба post; stone; pedestal.

тумбо|чка (gen. pl. -чек) night-table, locker.

тундра tundra.

ту|нец (-нца) tunny.

тунея́|дец (-дца), ~дка idler, sponger.

туннель (m.) tunnel.

тупеть (pf. о-) become blunt/dull.

тупик (-а) blind alley; impasse; ставить в т. nonplus.

тупить (туплю, тупишь; pf. за-blunt; тупица (m. & f.) blockhead, dunce.

тупой blunt; obtuse; stupid; тупость (f.) bluntness, dullness; тупоумный stupid, dull.

тур 1. turn (in dance), round (sport); 2. aurochs.

тура́ castle, rook *(chess).*

турба́за tourist centre.

турби́на turbine.

туре́цкий Turkish.

тури́зм tourism; тури́ст, ～ка tourist; тури́ст(и́че)ский tourist *(a.).*

туркме́н, ～ка Turkmen; туркме́нский Turkmen *(a.).*

турне́ *(indecl.)* tour.

турне́пс swede.

турни́к (-а́) horizontal bar.

турнике́т turnstile; tourniquet.

турни́р tournament.

ту́рок (-рка), турча́нка Turk.

ту́склый dim, dull, lacklustre; ту́скнеть *(pf.* по-) grow dim.

тут here; then; тут как тут there he is, they are *etc.*

ту́товник mulberry bush.

ту́|фля *(gen. pl.* -фель) shoe.

ту́хлый bad, rotten.

ту́хнуть *(past* тух) 1. *(pf.* по-) go out, be extinguished; 2. *(pf.* про-) rot.

ту́ча, ту́|чка *(gen. pl.* -чек) cloud.

тучне́ть *(pf.* по-) grow fat; ту́чный fat, fertile; succulent.

туш flourish *(mus.).*

ту́ша carcass; hulk.

тушева́ть *(pf.* за-) shade.

тушёный stewed; туши́ть (тушу́, ту́шишь) 1. *(pf.* по-) stew; 2. *(pf.* за-, по-) extinguish.

тушь *(f.)* Indian ink.

тща́тельный painstaking, thorough.

тщеду́шие feebleness; тщеду́шный feeble, frail; тщесла́вие vanity; тщесла́вный conceited, vain.

тще́тный futile.

ты you; быть на ты с ним be on familiar terms with him.

ты́кать 1. (ты́ч|у, -ешь; *pf.* ткнуть) poke, stick; 2. (ты́ч|у, -ешь, *or* ты́каю) use the familiar 'you' form to; be on familiar terms (with).

ты́ква pumpkin.

тыл (в -у́, *pl.* -ы́) rear.

тын fence, stockade.

ты́сяч|а thousand; ～еле́тие millennium; ～ный thousandth.

тычи́нка stamen.

тьма 1. darkness; 2. vast multitude.

тюбете́йка *(gen. pl.* -е́ек) embroidered skull-cap.

тю́бик tube.

тюк (-а́) bale, package.

тюле́нь *(m.)* seal; *(fig.)* lout.

тюль *(m.)* tulle.

тюльпа́н tulip.

тюрба́н turban.

тюре́мный prison *(a.);* тюре́мщик prison warder, gaoler.

тю́ркский Turkic.

тюрьма́ *(pl.* тю́|рьмы, -рем) prison.

тюфя́к (-а́) mattress; *(fig.)* lifeless person, lump.

тя́вкать *(pf.* тя́вкнуть) yap, yelp.

тя́г(а): дать тя́гу *(coll.)* take to one's heels.

тя́га draught; traction; eagerness, thrust; тяга́ться *(pf.* по-) (с + *inst.)* be in litigation (with); emulate; тяга́ч (-а́) tractor.

тя́гло 1. draught animals; 2. tax, levy *(hist.).*

тя́гостный burdensome, painful; тя́гость *(f.)* тягота́ *(pl.* тя́готы, тя́гот) burden.

тяготе́ние gravity, gravitation; bent, inclination; тяготе́ть (к + *dat.)* gravitate (towards); have an inclination towards); (над + *inst.)* hang (over).

тяго|ти́ть (-щу́, -ти́шь) oppress, be a burden to; -ся *(inst.)* find (something) a burden.

тягу́чий viscous; ductile, malleable.

тягча́йший gravest.

тя́жба lawsuit; *(coll.)* competition.

тяжеле́ть grow heavy; put on weight; grow stout.

тяжело|ве́с heavyweight; ～ве́сный heavyweight *(a., sport).*

тяжёлый heavy; тя́жесть *(f.)* weight, heaviness; gravity; difficulty; тя́жкий heavy; grave; distressing.

тяну́ть (тяну́, тя́нешь; *pf.* по-) draw, pull; drag out; -ся stretch; drag on, last; stretch oneself.

тяну́чка toffee.

тя́пать *(pf.* тя́пнуть) *(coll.)* hit; drink; grab.

У

у *(gen.)* at, near, by; with; у меня́ был слова́рь I had a dictionary.

уа́тт watt.

убавле́ние decrease; убавля́ть *(pf.* уба́вить) diminish; reduce; -ся become smaller, fall.

убаю́кивать *(pf.* убаю́кать) lull.

убега́ть *(pf.* убежа́ть*) run away; escape; *(coll.)* boil over.

убеди́тельный conclusive, convincing; убеди́ть see убежда́ть.

убежа́ть see убега́ть.

убежда́ть *(pf.* убе|ди́ть, -ди́шь; *ppp.* -ждённый) convince, persuade; убежде́ние persuasion; belief, conviction.

убе́жище refuge, shelter.

убел|я́ть *(pf.* -и́ть) whiten.

уберега́ть *(pf.* убере́чь*) preserve, safeguard.

убива́ть *(pf.* уби́ть*) kill; -ся hurt oneself; waste away; уби́йственный killing, devastating; уби́йство murder; уби́йца *(m. & f.)* murderer.

убира́ть *(pf.* убра́ть*) remove; clear away, tidy; decorate; harvest; -ся *(coll.)* tidy up; clear off; get away.

уби́ть see убива́ть.

ублаж|а́ть *(pf.* -и́ть) *(coll.)* humour, indulge.

убо́гий wretched; убо́жество wretchedness.

убо́й slaughter; убо́йный intended for slaughter *(e. g. cattle)* ; destructive.

убо́р attire, dress.

убо́ристый close, small.

убо́рка harvesting; tidying up; убо́рная lavatory; dressing room; убо́рщица cleaner, charwoman.

убра́нство adornment; furnishings.

убра́ть see убира́ть.

убыва́ть *(pf.* убы́ть*, *past* у́был, -а) diminish, subside, wane; у́быль *(f.)* diminution; loss; убы́|ток (-тка) loss; убы́точный unprofitable.

уважа́емый respected; уважа́ть respect; уваже́ние esteem, respect; уважи́тельный valid; respectful.

ува́жить *(pf.)* humour; comply with, grant.

уведомле́ние information; notification; уведомля́ть *(pf.* уве́домить) inform.

увекове́|чивать *(pf.* -чить) immortalize, perpetuate.

увеличе́ние increase; enlargement, magnification; увел|и́чивать *(pf.* -и́чить) increase; enlarge; magnify; -ся increase, rise; ~и́тельное стекло́ magnifying glass.

уве́нчивать *(pf.* увенча́ть) crown.

увере́ние assurance; уве́ренность *(f.)* confidence; уве́ренный confident; assured; уве́рить see уверя́ть.

уве́ртка dodge, subterfuge; увёртливый evasive, shifty; увёртываться *(pf.* уверну́ться) *(от +* gen.) evade.

увертю́ра overture.

уверя́ть *(pf.* уве́рить) *(в + prep.)* assure (of); -ся be convinced.

увесел|е́ние amusement, entertainment; ~и́тельный pleasure *(a.);* ~я́ть *(pf.* -и́ть) entertain, divert.

уве́систый weighty.

уве́чить *(pf.* из-) maim; уве́чье mutilation.

увеши́вать *(pf.* уре́шать) hang; у. сте́ну карти́нами hang a wall with pictures.

увеща́ние exhortation; увеща́ть exhort, admonish.

уви́ливать *(pf.* увильну́ть) *(от +* gen.) evade.

увлажн|я́ть *(pf.* -и́ть) moisten.

увлека́тельный fascinating; увлека́ть *(pf.* увле́чь*) carry away, fascinate; увлече́ние *(inst.)* enthusiasm, passion (for).

уво́д withdrawal *(of troops etc.);* уводи́ть* *(pf.* увести́*) take away, steal.

уво́з abduction, stealing; увози́ть* *(pf.* увезти́*) take away; abduct, steal.

увола́кивать *(pf.* уволо|о́чь, -оку́, -очёшь; -о́к, -окла́) drag away; steal.

увольне́ние discharge, dismissal; увольня́ть *(pf.* уво́лить) dismiss, sack; retire.

увы́ alas.

увяда́ть *(pf.* увя́нуть*) fade; waste away; wither; увя́дший withered.

увя́зка roping; coordination; увя́зывать *(pf.* увяза́ть*) tie/pack up; coordinate.

уга́дывать *(pf.* угада́ть) guess.

уга́р 1. carbon monoxide; poisoning *(by carbon monoxide)* ; 2. waste; уга́рный газ carbon monoxide.

угаса́ть *(pf.* уга́снуть*) go out, become extinct; die down.

угле|во́д carbohydrate; ~добы́ча coal production; ~кислота́ carbonic acid; ~ки́слый carbonic, carbonaceous; ~ро́д carbon.

углова́тый angular, awkward.

угловой corner *(a.)* ; angular.

углубле́ние deepening; depression; **углуб**|**ля́ть** *(pf.* -и́ть) deepen; -ся (в + *acc.)* delve/ plunge into.

угна́ть *see* угоня́ть.

угнета́тель *(m.)* oppressor; **угнета́ть** oppress; depress; **угнете́ние** oppression; depression; **угнетённый** oppressed; depressed.

угова́ривать *(pf.* уговори́ть) persuade; -ся arrange, agree; **угово́р** persuasion; agreement.

уго́д|**а**: в -у ему́ to please him; **уго-ди́ть** *see* угожда́ть; **уго́дливый** obsequious; **уго́дничество** servility; **уго́дный** welcome, desirable; как уго́дно as you like.

уго́|**дье** *(gen. pl.* -дий) land/property in use; advantage.

уго|**жда́ть** *(pf.* -ди́ть, -жу́, -ди́шь) *(dat.,* or на + *acc.)* please; *(pf.)* fall.

у́гол (угла́, в углу́) corner, angle.

уголо́вный criminal *(a.).*

уго|**ло́к** (-лка́) corner, nook.

у́голь (у́гля) coal; **у́гольный** coal *(a.).*

у́гольный corner *(a.).*

у́гольщик coalminer; coal-ship, collier.

угомони́ть *(pf.) (coll.)* calm.

угоня́ть *(pf.* угна́ть*) drive away; steal.

угора́здить *(pf.)* prompt, cause.

угора́ть *(pf.* угоре́ть*) be poisoned by carbon monoxide fumes; **уго-ре́лый** possessed, mad.

у́горь (угря́) blackhead; eel.

уго|**ща́ть** *(pf.* -сти́ть, -щу́, -сти́шь) entertain; treat; **угоще́ние** entertainment; treat; refreshments.

угрева́тый pimply.

угрожа́ть *(dat.)* menace, threaten; **угро́за** threat.

угрызе́ние pang, qualm.

угрю́мый gloomy, morose.

уда́в boa constrictor.

удава́ться *(pf.* уда́ться*) be a success; мне удало́сь... I managed...

уда́вка slip-knot.

удале́ние removal.

уда|**ле́ц** (-льца́) daring person.

удали́ть *see* удаля́ть.

удало́й bold, daring; **у́даль** *(f.),* **удальство́** boldness, daring.

удал|**я́ть** *(pf.* -и́ть) remove; send away; dismiss; -ся go/move away.

уда́р blow, stroke; **ударе́ние** accent, stress; **уда́р**|**ник**, **~ница** shock worker; **уда́рный** shock *(a.),*

urgent; percussion *(a);* **ударя́ть** *(pf.* уда́рить) strike; -ся (о + *acc.)* bump against.

уда́ться *see* удава́ться.

уда́ча good luck; success; **уда́чливый** successful, lucky *(person);* **уда́ч-ный** successful *(e.g.* attempt*),* felicitous.

удва́ивать *(pf.* удво́ить) double; -ся double.

уде́л destiny, lot; appanage.

удели́ть *see* уделя́ть.

уде́льный specific *(phys).*

удел|**я́ть** *(pf.* -и́ть) give, spare.

у́держ: без -у uncontrollably; **удер-жа́ние** retention; deduction; **удер-живать** *(pf.* удержа́ть*) retain; hold back; suppress; -ся hold one's position; (от + *gen.)* refrain (from).

удешев|**ля́ть** *(pf.* -и́ть) reduce in price.

удиви́тельный amazing, surprising; **удивле́ние** surprise, astonishment; **удив**|**ля́ть** *(pf.* -и́ть) surprise; -ся *(dat.)* be surprised (at).

уди́л|**а** (-и́л, -ила́м) bit.

уди́лище fishing-rod; **уди́ль**|**щик**, **~щица** angler.

удира́ть *(pf.* удра́ть*) (coll.)* make off, run away.

уди́ть (ужу́, у́дишь) fish, catch.

удлине́ние lengthening; **удлин**|**я́ть** *(pf.* -и́ть) make longer.

удо́бный comfortable; convenient.

удобо|**вари́мый** digestible; **~испол-ни́мый** feasible, practicable.

удобре́ние fertilization; fertilizer; **удобря́ть** *(pf.* удо́брить) fertilize.

удо́бство comfort; convenience.

удовлетворе́ние satisfaction, gratification; **удовлетвори́тельный** satisfactory; **удовлетвор**|**я́ть** *(pf.* -и́ть) satisfy; supply; *(dat.)* meet *(requirements etc.).*

удово́льствие pleasure.

удо́й milking; yield of milk.

удорож|**а́ть** *(pf.* -и́ть) raise the price of.

удостаивать *(pf.* удосто́ить) favour, honour.

удостовере́ние certificate; attestation; **удосто**|**веря́ть** *(pf.* -ве́рить) certify; -ся в + *prep.* ascertain; be convinced (of).

удочер|**я́ть** *(pf.* -и́ть) adopt *(as daughter).*

у́до|**чка** *(gen. pl.* -чек) fishing-rod.

удра́ть *see* удира́ть.

удруч|а́ть *(pf.* -и́ть) depress.

удуша́ть *(pf.* удуши́ть*) stifle, suffocate;   удушли́вый stifling; уду́шье asthma; asphyxia.

уедине́ние seclusion, solitude; уеди-нённый secluded; lonely; уедин|-я́ть *(pf.* -и́ть) seclude.

уе́зд district, county *(hist.);* уе́зд-ный district *(a.).*

уезжа́ть *(pf.* уе́хать*) go away.

уж(-á) 1. grass snake.

уж 2. = уже́ really.

у́жас horror; terror; ужаса́ть *(pf.* ужасну́ть) horrify; ужа́сный ter-rible, horrible.

у́же *(comp. of* у́зкий) narrower, tighter.

уже́ already; уже́ не no longer.

уже́ние fishing.

ужива́ться *(pf.* ужи́ться*) get on well; become settled; уживчивый easy to get on with.

ужи́мка grimace.

у́жин supper; у́жинать *(pf.* по-) have supper.

ужи́ться *see* ужива́ться.

узаконе́ние legalization; statute; узаконя́ть *(pf.* -о́нить) legalize.

узб|е́к, ~е́чка *(gen. pl.* -е́чек) Uzbek; узбе́кский Uzbek *(a.).*

узда́ *(pl.* у́зды), узде́|чка *(gen. pl.* -чек) bridle; держа́ть в узде́ hold in check.

у́зел (узла́) knot; junction, centre; bundle.

у́зкий *(comp.* у́же) narrow, tight; уз-коло́бый narrow-minded; узлова́-тый knotty; узлов|о́й main; nod-al; -ая ста́нция junction.

узн|ава́ть (-аю́, -аёшь) *pf.* узна́ть) know; find out.

у́зник prisoner.

узо́р pattern; узо́рчатый patterned.

у́зость *(f.)* narrowness, tightness.

узурпа́тор usurper; узурпи́ровать *(ipf. & pf.)* usurp.

у́зы (уз) bonds, ties.

у́йма a huge amount.

уйти́ *see* уходи́ть.

ука́з decree, edict; указа́ние indi-cation; direction; указа́тель *(m.)* index; guide; указа́тельный indi-cating *(a.),* index *(a.);* ука́зка pointer; orders; ука́зывать *(pf.* указа́ть*) show, indicate.

ука́лывать *(pf.* уколо́ть*) prick.

ука́тывать *(pf.* укати́ть*) roll away.

ука́чивать *(pf.* укача́ть) rock to sleep; make sick.

укла́д structure, tenor *(e.g. of life);* укла́дка packing; placing; laying; укла́дывать *(pf.* ул ожи́ть, -ожу́, -о́жишь) lay; pack; put away; -ся 1. *(pf.* уложи́ться) pack (one's things); 2. *(pf.* уле́чься*) lie down.

укло́н gradient, slope; bias; devia-tion; уклоне́ние deviation; digres-sion; укло́нчивый evasive; укло-ня́ться *(pf.* уклони́ться*) (от + gen.)* deviate (from), avoid, shun.

уко́л prick; injection; уколо́ть *see* ука́лывать.

уко́р reproach.

укор|а́чивать *(pf.* -оти́ть, -очу́, -оти́шь) shorten.

укорен|я́ть *(pf.* -и́ть) implant; -ся take root, become implanted.

укори́зна reproach; укори́зненный reproachful.

укороти́ть *see* укора́чивать.

укор|я́ть *(pf.* -и́ть) (в + *prep.)* reproach (with).

уко́с hay harvest.

укра́дкой furtively.

украй|нец (-нца), ~нка Ukrainian; украи́нский Ukrainian *(a.).*

украша́ть *(pf.* укра́сить*) adorn, beautify; decorate; украше́ние decoration, ornament.

укрепле́ние strengthening, consoli-dation; fortification; укреп|ля́ть *(pf.* -и́ть) strengthen, fortify; -ся become stronger.

укро́мный secluded, cosy.

укро́п dill, fennel.

укроти́тель, ~ница tamer; укро-ща́ть *(pf.* укроти́ть, -щу́, -ти́шь) tame; укроще́ние taming; curb-ing.

укрупне́ние enlargement;amalgamat-ion; укрупн|я́ть *(pf.* -и́ть) en-large, amalgamate.

укрыва́тель *(m.)* concealer; у. кра́-деного receiver of stolen goods; укрыва́тельство receiving; har-bouring; укрыва́ть *(pf.* укры́ть*) cover, shelter; receive; harbour; -ся cover oneself; take cover/ shelter; укры́тие cover *(mil.).*

у́ксус vinegar; у́ксусный acetic.

уку́с bite, sting; укуси́ть *see* куса́ть.

уку́тывать *(pf.* уку́тать) wrap up.

ула́вливать *(pf.* влови́ть*) catch.

ула́живать *(pf.* ула́дить*) settle, fix up.

у́лей (у́л я) hive.

улета́ть *(pf.* улете́ть*) fly away; улет|у́чиваться *(pf.* -у́читься) evaporate, vanish.

уле́чься *see* укла́дываться.

ули́ка evidence.

ули́тка snail.

у́лица street.

улич|а́ть *(pf.* -и́ть) expose, convict.

у́личный street *(a.).*

уло́в catch; улови́мый perceptible; улови́ть *see* ула́вливать; уло́вка trap, trick.

уложе́ние code (of law).

уложи́ть *see* укла́дывать.

улучи́ть *(pf.* -и́ть) find; catch.

улучше́ние improvement; улучша́ть *(pf.* улу́чшить) improve, make better; -ся improve, get better.

улыба́ться *(pf.* улыбну́ться) smile; улы́бка smile.

ультима́тум ultimatum.

ультра|звуково́й supersonic; ~коро́ткий ultra-short, of very high frequency; ~фиоле́товый ultra-violet.

ум (ума́) mind, intelligence; без ума́ (от + *gen.)* mad (about); сходи́ть с ума́ go mad; он себе́ на уме́ *(coll.)* he's crafty.

умали́ть *see* умаля́ть.

умалишённый lunatic.

ума́лчивать *(pf.* умолча́ть*) pass over in silence; hush up.

умал|я́ть *(pf.* -и́ть) belittle, detract from.

уме́лый able, skilful; уме́ние ability, skill.

уменьша́ть *(pf.* уме́ньшить) decrease, diminish; уменьше́ние decrease; уменьши́тельный diminishing; diminutive *(gram.).*

уме́ренный moderate, temperate.

умере́ть *see* умира́ть.

уме́рить *see* умеря́ть.

умертви́ть *see* умерщвля́ть.

уме́рший dead, deceased.

умерщвле́ние killing; mortification; умер|щвля́ть *(pf.* -тви́ть, -щвлю́, -тви́шь) kill, destroy; mortify.

умеря́ть *(pf.* уме́рить) moderate, restrain.

умести́ть *see* умеща́ть.

уме́стный appropriate, opportune, to the point.

уме́ть *(pf.* с-) be able, know how (to); *(pf.)* manage.

умеща́ть *(pf.* уме|сти́ть, -щу́, -сти́шь) find room for, put in.

умиле́ние emotion, tenderness; уми́льный sweet; ingratiating; умил|я́ть *(pf.* -и́ть) touch, move; -ся be touched/moved.

умина́ть *(pf.* умя́ть*) knead, press.

умиротвор|я́ть *(pf.* -и́ть) pacify, reconcile.

умира́ть *(pf.* умере́ть, умр|у́, -ёшь; у́мер, -ла́; *pp.* уме́рший) die.

у́мница *(m. & f.)* clever person.

у́мничать philosophize; be over subtle.

умножа́ть *(pf.* умно́жить) increase; multiply; умноже́ние increase; multiplication.

у́мный clever, intelligent.

умо|заключе́ние conclusion, deduction; ~зре́ние speculation; ~зри́тельный speculative.

умоли́ть *see* умоля́ть.

у́молк: без -у incessantly; умолка́ть *(pf.* умо́лкнуть; *past* умо́лк) fall silent.

умолча́ть *see* ума́лчивать.

умоля́ть *(pf.* умоли́ть*) entreat, implore.

умопомеша́тельство (mental) derangement.

умори́тельный laughable, extremely funny, 'killing'.

у́мственный intellectual, mental; у́мствовать philosophize.

умудр|я́ть *(pf.* -и́ть) make wiser; -ся contrive.

умыва́льная washroom; умыва́льник wash-stand; умыва́ть *(pf.* умы́ть*) wash; -ся wash (oneself).

у́мы|сел (-сла) design, intention.

умы́ть *see* умыва́ть.

умы́шленный intentional.

унаво́живать *(pf.* унаво́зить*) manure.

универма́г department store; универса́льный universal.

университе́т university; университе́тский university *(a.).*

унижа́ть *(pf.* уни́|зить ., -жу, -зишь) humiliate; униже́ние humiliation, indignity; уни́женный humiliated; унижённый humble, oppressed; унизи́тельный humiliating.

уни́зывать *(pf.* униза́ть*) cover, stud *(e.g. with jewels).*

уника́льный unique.

унима́ть *(pf.* уня́ть, уйм|у́, -ёшь; уня́л, уняла́; *ppp.* уня́тый) calm, soothe; **-ся** calm down.

унита́з lavatory pan.

унифици́ровать *(ipf. & pf.)* unify.

уничижи́тельный deprecatory, pejorative.

уничто́жать *(pf.* -о́жить) destroy, annihilate; **уничтоже́ние** destruction.

уноси́ть* *(pf.* унести́*) take away, carry off; **-ся** speed away; be carried (away).

у́нтер-офице́р non-commissioned officer.

у́нта high fur boot.

у́нция ounce.

унывать lose heart, be dejected; **уны́лый** mournful, sad; **уны́ние** despondency.

уня́ть *see* унима́ть.

упа́д: до -y till exhaustion.

упа́|док (-дка) decline, decay; **упа́дочный** decadent.

упако́вка packing, wrapping; **упако́в|щик, ~щица** packer; **упак|о́вывать** *(pf.* -ова́ть) pack; **-ся** pack (one's things).

упа́сть *see* па́дать.

упива́ться *(pf.* упи́ться*) *(inst.)* drink one's fill (of), be satiated (with).

упира́ть *(pf.* упере́ть, упр|у́, -ёшь; упёр, уперла́; *ppp.* упёртый) place, rest; у. шест в сте́ну rest the pole against the wall; **-ся** lean, rest.

упи́танный well-fed; fattened.

упла́та payment; **упла́чивать** *(pf.* уплати́ть*) pay, discharge.

уплотн|я́ть *(pf.* -и́ть) condense, thicken; pack.

уплыва́ть *(pf.* уплы́ть*) swim/sail away.

упова́ть(-а́ю, на + *acc.)* put faith (in).

упод|обля́ть *(pf.* -о́бить) liken, compare *(to + dat.).*

упое́ние ecstasy, rapture; **упои́тельный** entrancing.

уполза́ть *(pf.* уползти́*) crawl/ creep away.

уполномо́ченный authorized representative; plenipotentiary; **уполно|мо́чивать** *(pf.* -мо́чить) authorize, empower.

упомина́ть mention; **упомина́ть** *(pf.* упомяну́ть) mention, refer to.

упо́р rest; stop; де́лать у. на + *acc.* lay emphasis on; в у. point-blank.

упо́рный persistent, stubborn; **упо́рство** persistence, stubbornness; **упо́рствовать** persist.

упоря́д|очивать *(pf.* -очить) put in order, regulate.

употреби́тельный generally used, common; **употребле́ние** use; **употребля́ть** *(pf.* -и́ть) use.

упра́ва justice *(coll.);* board, council *(hist.);* **управдо́м** house manager.

управле́ние administration, control, direction, management; government; **управля́ть** *(inst.)* direct, manage; govern *(gram.);* **-ся** *(pf.* упра́виться) (с + *inst.)* deal (with), manage; **управля́ющий** *(inst.)* director, manager (of).

упражне́ние exercise; **упражня́ть** exercise; **-ся** (в + *prep.)* practise.

упраздне́ние abolition; **упраздн|я́ть** *(pf.* -и́ть) abolish.

упра́шивать *(pf.* упроси́ть*) entreat; *(pf.)* win over.

упрёк reproach; **упрека́ть** *(pf.* упрекну́ть) (в + *prep.)* reproach *(with),* upbraid *(with).*

упроси́ть *see* упра́шивать.

упроща́ть *see* упроща́ть.

упро́чение strengthening, consolidation; **упро́ч|ивать** *(pf.* -ить) strengthen, consolidate.

упроща́ть *(pf.* упро|сти́ть, -щу́, -сти́шь) simplify; **упроще́ние** simplification.

упру́гий elastic.

упря́жка team of horses; harness; **упря́жь** *(f.)* harness.

упря́миться *(pf.* за-) be obstinate, persist; **упря́мство** obstinacy; **упря́мый** obstinate, stubborn.

упуска́ть *(pf.* упусти́ть*) let escape/ slip; **упуще́ние** neglect, omission.

упы́р|ь (-я́) vampire.

уравне́ние equalization; equation; **ура́внивать** 1. *(pf.* уровня́ть) smooth, level off; 2. *(pf.* уравня́ть) equalize; **уравни́ловка** wage-leveling; **уравни́тельный** equalizing, levelling.

уравно|ве́шивать *(pf.* -ве́сить*) balance.

урага́н hurricane.

ура́льский Ural *(a.).*

ура́н uranium; **ура́новый** uranium (a.).

урегули́рование regulating; settlement.

уреза́ть, уре́зывать (pf. **уре́зать***) cut off; reduce.

у́рна urn; избира́тельная у. ballot-box.

у́ро|вень (-вня) level.

уро́д freak, monster.

уроди́ть* (pf.) bear (e.g. fruit); -ся bear a crop.

уро́дливый deformed; ugly; **уро́довать** (pf. из-) disfigure; mutilate; **уро́дство** deformity; ugliness.

урожа́й harvest, yield; **урожа́йный** of high yield, of good harvest.

урождённая born, née.

уроже́|нец (-нца), **~нка** native.

уро́к lesson.

уро́н loss(es); **урони́ть** see **роня́ть**.

уро́чище natural break in landscape (e.g. wood in field).

уро́чный fixed, set.

урыва́ть (pf. **урва́ть***) snatch; **уры́вками** in snatches, in fits and starts.

уря́дник (hist.) village policeman; Cossack sergeant.

ус (pl. усы́, усо́в) moustache.

усади́ть see **уса́живать**.

уса́дьба farmstead; country-estate.

уса́живать (pf. ус|ади́ть, -ажу́, -а́дишь) 1. seat; set down; 2. plant; -ся (pf. усе́сться*) take a seat/seats; sit down.

уса́тый with a moustache; whiskered.

усва́ивать (pf. усво́ить) assimilate; master; **усвое́ние** assimilation, mastering.

усе́ивать (pf. усе́ять*) dot, strew.

усе́рдие zeal; **усе́рдный** zealous.

усе́сться see **уса́живаться**.

усечённый truncated.

усе́ять see **усе́ивать**.

усиде́ть* (pf.) remain sitting; **уси́дчивый** assiduous.

у́сик little moustache; tendril; antenna, feeler, horn.

усиле́ние strengthening; aggravation; amplification; **уси́ливать** (pf. уси́лить) strengthen; aggravate; amplify; **уси́лие** effort; **усили́тель** (m.) amplifier, intensifier.

уска́кивать (pf. ускака́ть*) gallop away.

ускольза́ть (pf. ускользну́ть) slip off, steal away.

ускоре́ние acceleration; **ускоря́ть** (pf. уско́рить) hasten, quicken, speed up.

усла́вливаться (pf. усло́виться) agree, arrange.

усла́да delectation; **услажда́ть** (pf. усла|ди́ть, -жу́, -ди́шь; ppp. -ждённый) delight.

усла́ть see **усыла́ть**.

усло́вие condition; **усл|о́вливаться** (pf. -о́виться) agree, arrange; **усло́вленный** agreed, fixed; **усло́вность** (f.) convention; conventionality; **усло́вный** conditional; conventional; relative.

усложне́ние complication; **усложн|я́ть** (pf. -и́ть) complicate.

услу́га good turn, service; **услу́жливый** obliging.

усма́тривать (pf. усмотре́ть*) perceive; (pf. only) за + inst. attend to.

усмеха́ться (pf. усмехну́ться) grin, smirk; **усме́шка** (gen. pl. -шек) grin, smirk.

усмире́ние pacification; suppression; **усмир|я́ть** (pf. -и́ть) pacify, quiet, suppress.

усмотре́ние discretion, judgement; **усмотре́ть** see **усма́тривать**.

уснаща́ть (pf. усна|сти́ть, -щу́, -сти́шь) garnish, adorn.

усну́ть (pf.) go to sleep.

усо́бица intestine strife/war.

усовершенствование improvement.

усомни́ться (pf.) (в + prep.) feel doubt (about).

успева́емость (f.) progress, good results; **успева́ть** (-ва́ю) pf. успе́ть) have time; succeed, make progress.

успе́ние Assumption.

успе́х success; (pl.) progress; **успе́шный** successful.

успок|а́ивать (pf. -о́ить) soothe, calm, quiet; -ся calm down, be assuaged; **успокое́ние** calming, soothing; **успокои́тельный** soothing, reassuring.

уста́ (уст, -а́м) mouth.

уста́в 1. regulations, statutes; 2. large printing (in old manuscripts).

уст|ава́ть (-аю́, -аёшь; pf. уста́ть*) get tired.

уставля́ть (pf. уста́вить) put, set; у. кни́ги на по́лку put the books

on the shelf; у. полку книгами
fill the shelf with books; у. глаза
на + acc.) stare (at); -ся fit in,
have room; (на + acc.) stare
(at).

усталость (f.) tiredness; усталый
tired, weary; усталь|ь: без -и
unceasingly.

устан|авливать (pf. ~овить, -овлю,
-овишь) establish; fix; install,
mount; -ся be established etc; be
settled; установка putting; installation; plant; direction; установление establishment; установщик fitter.

устарелый out of date, obsolete.

устать see уставать.

устилать (pf. устлать*) cover, carpet, pave.

устный verbal, oral.

устой basis, foundation; support;
устойчивый steady, stable.

устоять* (pf.) keep one's balance,
stand one's ground; -ся (pf.)
settle (of wine etc.).

устраивать (pf. устроить) arrange;
establish; be convenient for, suit;
-ся settle, find a place.

устранение elimination, removal;
устран|ять (pf. -ить) eliminate,
remove.

устраш|ать (pf. -ить) frighten;
-ся (gen.) be frightened (of).

устремление aspiration; устрем|лять
(pf. -ить) rush, direct; -ся rush;
be directed.

устрица oyster.

устроить see устраивать; устройство
arrangement; equipment; device,
mechanism.

уступ ledge, projection; уступать
(pf. уст|упить, -уплю, -упишь)
yield, cede; уступка concession;
уступчатый with ledges, stepped;
уступчивый pliant, yielding.

усть|е (gen. pl. -ьев) estuary, mouth.

усуг|ублять (pf. -убить) aggravate,
redouble.

усылать (pf. услать*) send away.

усынов|лять (pf. -ить) adopt.

усыпальница tomb.

усыпать (pf. усыпать*) (be)strew.

усыпительный soporific; усып|лять
(pf. -ить) lull to sleep; hypnotize.

усыхать (pf. усохнуть*) dry up.

утаивать (pf. утаить) hide, keep
secret; утайк|а: без -и frankly,
openly.

утаптывать (pf. утоптать*) trample
down.

утаскивать (pf. утащить*) drag off.

утварь (f.) utensils.

утвердительный affirmative; утвер|-
ждать (pf. -дить, -жу, -дишь;
ppp. -жденный) affirm, maintain;
approve, confirm; утверждение
assertion; approval, confirm-
ation.

утекать (pf. утечь*) flow away;
escape.

уте|нок (-нка, pl. утята, -ят) duck-
ling.

утепл|ять (pf. -ить) warm.

утереть see утирать.

утерпеть* (pf.) restrain oneself;
не утерпел, чтобы не сказать he
couldn't help saying.

утерять (pf.) lose.

утёс cliff, rock; утёсистый rocky,
steep.

утеха delight, pleasure.

уте|чка (gen. pl. -чек) escape, leakage,
loss; утечь see утекать.

утеш|ать (pf. утешить) console;
утешение consolation; утешительный comforting.

утилизировать (ipf. & pf.) utilize;
утилитарный utilitarian; утиль
(m.), ~сырьё scrap.

утирать (pf. утереть*) wipe, dry.

утихать (pf. утихнуть, past утих)
fade; subside, become calm.

утка duck; scare, false report.

уткнуть (pf.) bury, hide.

утконос duck-billed platypus.

утлый frail.

уток (утка) weft, woof.

утолить see утолять.

утолщать (pf. уто|лстить, -лщу,
-лстишь) make thicker; утол-
щение thickening; bulge.

утол|ять (pf. -ить) quench, satisfy;
soothe.

утомительный tiring; утомление
weariness; утом|лять (pf. -ить)
fatigue, tire.

утонч|ать (pf. -ить) make thinner;
refine; утончение making thinner,
refining; утончённый refined,
subtle.

утопать drown, sink; (fig.) wallow,
be submerged.

утопия Utopia.

утоплен|ник, ~ница drowned per-
son.

утоптать see утаптывать.

уточне́ние making more precise; more precise definition; **уточн|я́ть** *(pf.* -и́ть*)* make more precise, specify.

утра́ивать *(pf.* утро́ить*)* treble.

утра́та loss; **утра́чивать** *(pf.* утра́тить**)* lose, forfeit.

у́тренний morning *(a.);* **у́тренник** morning performance; morning frost; **у́треня** matins.

утри́ровать *(ipf & pf.)* exaggerate, overdo.

у́тро (у́тра *but* с утра́, до утра́, *pl.* у́тра, утр, у́тр|ам, по -а́м) morning.

утро́ба womb.

утро́ить *see* утра́ивать.

утряса́ть *(pf.* утрясти́**)* shake down.

утю́г (-а́) iron; **утю́жить** *(pf.* вы́-, от-*)* iron.

уха́ fish-soup.

уха́б (pot-) hole *(in road);* **уха́бистый** bumpy.

ухажёр *(coll.)* boy-friend; **уха́живать** (за + *inst.)* look after, nurse, tend; court.

у́харский daring.

у́хать *(pf.* у́хнуть*)* crash, echo.

ухва́т oven tongs; **ухва́тка** *(coll.)* manner, way; **ухва́тывать** *(pf.* ухвати́ть**)* grasp, seize; **-ся** (за + *acc.)* catch hold of, seize.

ухитр|я́ться *(pf.* -и́ться*)* contrive; **ухищре́ние** contrivance; device; trick.

ухмы|ля́ться *(pf.* -льну́ться*)* smirk.

у́хнуть *see* у́хать.

у́хо *(pl.* у́ши, уше́й) ear; **уховёртка** earwig.

ухо́д 1. departure; 2. (за + *inst.)* care (for); **уходи́ть*** *(pf.* уйти́*, уйду́; ушёл) go away.

ухудша́ть *(pf.* уху́дшить*)* make worse; **-ся** deteriorate; **ухудше́ние** deterioration.

уцеле́ть *(pf.)* remain whole, survive.

уцепля́ть *(pf.* уц|епи́ть, -еплю́, -е́пишь) catch; **-ся** (за + *acc.)* catch hold of, seize.

уча́ствовать (в + *prep.)* take part (in); **уча́стие** participation; share; sympathy.

участи́ть *see* учаща́ть.

участко́вый district *(a.).*

уча́стливый sympathetic.

уча́ст|ник, **~ница** participant.

уча́с|ток (-тка) district; plot; section.

у́часть *(f.)* lot, fate.

учаща́ть *(pf.* уча|сти́ть, -щу́, -сти́шь) make more frequent.

уча́щийся pupil, student; **учёба** studies, training; **уче́бник** textbook; **уче́бный** educational, school *(a.),* training *(a.);* **уче́ние** learning, studies; teaching; doctrine; **уче|ни́к** (-ника́) **~ни́ца** pupil; **учени́ческий** unskilled; **учени́чество** apprenticeship; **учёность** *(f.)* learning, erudition; **учёный** learned, erudite; scholar.

уче́сть *see* учи́тывать; **учёт** calculation; registration; discount. **учётный** discount *(a.);* stocktaking *(a.).*

учетвер|я́ть *(pf.* -и́ть*)* quadruple.

учи́лище school, college.

учин|я́ть *(pf.* -и́ть*)* do, commit.

учи́тел|ь *(pl.* -я́), **~ьница** teacher.

учи́тывать *(pf.* уче́сть, учту́, учтёшь; *past* учёл, учла́; *ppp.* учтённый) take into account; take stock of; discount.

учи́ть (учу́, у́чишь) 1. *(pf.* вы́-*)* learn; 2. *(pf.* на- об-,*)* teach; у. его́ ру́сскому языку́ teach him Russian; **-ся** *(pf.* вы́-. на-, об-*)* *(dat.)* learn.

учреди́тельный constituent; **учре|жда́ть** *(pf.* -ди́ть, -жу́, -ди́шь; *ppp.* -ждённый) establish, found, institute; **учрежде́ние** establishment; institution.

учти́вый civil, courteous.

уша́нка hat with earflaps.

уша́т tub.

уши́б bruise, injury; **ушиба́ть** *(pf.* уши|би́ть, -бу́, -бёшь; уши́б; *ppp.* уши́бленный) bruise, hurt; **-ся** hurt oneself.

у́ши *see* у́хо.

ушива́ть *(pf.* уши́ть**)* take in, make smaller *(clothes).*

ушко́ *(pl.* -и, -о́в) ear; tab; **ушно́й** ear *(a.)* ; aural.

уще́лье gorge, ravine.

ущем|ля́ть *(pf.* -и́ть*)* squeeze; infringe.

уще́рб damage, loss.

ущипну́ть *(pf.)* pinch, tweak.

уэ́льский Welsh.

ую́т comfort, cosiness; **ую́тный** comfortable, cosy.

уязви́мый vulnerable; **уязв|ля́ть** *(pf.* -и́ть*)* hurt, wound.

уясн|я́ть *(pf.* -и́ть*)* clarify.

Ф

фа́брика factory; фабрика́нт manufacturer; фабрика́т manufactured product; фабри́чный factory (a.), factory-made.
фа́була plot, story.
фаго́т bassoon.
фа́за phase.
фаза́н pheasant.
фа́зис phase.
фа́кел torch.
факт fact; факти́ческий real, actual, virtual.
фа́ктор factor.
факто́рия trading station.
факту́ра invoice; technique (mus.); texture (art.).
факультати́вный optional, elective.
факульте́т faculty.
фальсифи|ка́ция falsification; ~цирова́ть falsify.
фальц groove.
фальши́вить (pf. c-) dissemble; sing/play out of tune; фальши́вка false document; фальшивомоне́тчик counterfeiter; фальши́вый false, spurious; artificial; фальшь (f.) falseness.
фами́лия surname.
фамилья́рничать be familiar, take liberties; фамилья́рный familiar, unceremonious.
фанати́зм fanaticism; фана́тик fanatic.
фане́ра plywood.
фант forfeit.
фантазёр dreamer, visionary; фанта́зия fantasy, fancy.
фанта́ст|ика fantasy; ~и́ческий, ~и́чный fabulous; fantastic, unbelievable.
фанфаро́н braggart.
фа́ра headlamp.
фарва́тер channel, fairway.
фарисе́й Pharisee.
фармаце́вт pharmaceutist; ~ика pharmaceutics.
фарс farce.
фа́ртук apron.
фарфо́р china, porcelain; фарфо́ровый china, porcelain (a.).
фарш stuffing; sausage-meat; фарширова́ть (pf. за-) stuff.
фаса́д facade.
фасо́вка packing.

фасо́ль (f.) haricot/kidney beans(s).
фасо́н fashion, style; фасо́нный shaped.
фат fop.
фата́ veil.
фатали́ст fatalist; ~и́ческий, ~и́чный fatalistic.
фата́льный fatal.
фатовство́ foppery.
фаши́зм fascism.
фая́нс pottery, faience; glazed earthenware.
февра́л|ь (-я́) February; февра́льский February (a.).
федера́льный federal; федерати́вный federative; федера́ция federation.
фее́р|ический, ~и́чный fairy-tale (a.).
фейерве́рк firework(s).
фельд|ма́ршал field-marshal; ~фе́бель (m.) sergeant-major; ~шер, ~шери́ца medical assistant; ~ъе́герь (m.) courier, messenger.
фельето́н topical/satirical newspaper article.
феноме́н phenomenon.
феода́л feudal lord; феода́льный feudal.
ферз|ь (-я́) queen (chess).
фе́рма 1 farm; 2 girder.
фермента́ция fermentation.
фе́рмер farmer; фе́рмерство farming; the farmers.
фе́ска fez.
фестива́ль (m.) festival.
фетр felt; фе́тровый felt (a.).
фехтова́ль|щик, ~щица fencer; фехтова́ть fence.
фешене́бельный fashionable.
фе́я fairy.
фиа́лка violet.
фи́бра fibre; фи́бровый fibre (a.); фибро́зный fibrous.
фи́га fig.
фигля́р buffoon.
фигу́ра figure; фигура́льный figurative; фигури́ровать figure, be present; фигури́ст, ~ка figure skater; фигу́рный figure(d).
фи́зик physicist; фи́зика physics.
физио́л|ог physiologist; ~о́гия physiology.
физионо́мия physionomy.
физи́ческий physical.
физкульту́ра physical culture.
фикса́ж fixing agent; фикса́ция fixing; фикси́ровать (pf. за-) fix.

фиктивный fictitious; **фикция** fiction.

филантроп philanthropist; ~**ия** philanthropy.

филателист philatelist.

филе *(indecl.)* fillet; sirloin.

филёнка panel.

филёр police spy.

филиал branch, section.

филигрань *(f.)* filigree.

филин eagle-owl.

филол|ог philologist; ~**огический** philological; ~**огия** philology.

филос|оф philosopher; ~**офия** philosophy; ~**офский** philosophical.

фильм film; **фильмоскоп** viewer *(for looking at film, slides)*.

фильтр filter; ~**овать** *(pf.* про-*)* filter.

фимиам incense.

финал final; **финальный** final *(a.).*

финансировать *(ipf. & pf.)* finance; **финансист** financier; **финансовый** financial.

финик date.

финиш finish; ~**ировать** *(ipf. & pf.)* finish.

финн, финка Finn; **финский** Finnish.

фиолетовый violet(-coloured).

фирма firm.

фисгармония harmonium.

фитил|ь (-я) wick.

фишка *(gen. pl.* -шек*)* chip, counter.

флаг flag; **флажный** flag *(a.).*

флакон bottle.

фламан|дец (-дца), ~**дка** Fleming.

фланг flank, wing.

фланель *(f.)* flannel; **флан|елевый**, ~**ельный** flannel *(a.).*

фля|нец (-нца) flange.

флегм|а, ~**атизм** phlegm, coolness; **флегматичный** phlegmatic.

флейта flute.

флексия inflexion; **флективный** inflected.

флёр crêpe.

флигел|ь *(m.; pl.* -и & -я*)* wing; outbuilding; ф. -адъютант aide-de-camp.

флирт flirtation; **флиртовать** flirt.

флот fleet; **флотский** naval.

флюгер weather-cock.

флюс 1. gumboil, swollen cheek; 2. flux.

фляга, фля|жка *(gen. pl.* -жек*)* flask.

фойе *(indecl.)* foyer.

фок-мачта foremast.

фокус 1. focus; 2. trick; **фокусник** conjurer, juggler.

фолиант volume.

фольга foil.

фольклор folklore.

фон background.

фонарик torch, flash-light; lantern; **фонар|ь** (-я) lantern, lamp.

фонд fund, stock.

фонема phoneme; **фонетика** phonetics; **фонетический** phonetic.

фонтан fountain.

форейтор postilion.

форель *(f.)* trout.

форма form; mould; uniform; **формальность** *(f.)* formality; **формальный** formal.

формат size; **формация** formation.

форменн|ый (pertaining to) form, mould; *(coll.)* absolute, proper; -ая одежда uniform.

формир|ование formation, forming; ~**овать** *(pf.* с-*)* form; mould; ~**оваться** develop; be formed.

формовать *(pf.* с-*)* cast, mould.

формула formula; **формулировать** *(ipf. & pf.; & pf.* с-*)* formulate; **формулировка** formulation; formula.

формуляр (library) card, ticket.

форпост advanced post, outpost.

форсировать *(ipf. & pf.)* force; speed up.

форсить *(coll.)* swagger.

форсунка injector, sprayer.

форт fort.

фортепьяно *(indecl.)* (upright) piano.

форто|чка *(gen. pl.* -чек*)* ventilation pane.

фосфат phospate; **фосфор** phosphorus.

фотоаппарат camera.

фотограф photographer; ~**ировать** *(pf.* с-*)* photograph; ~**ический** photographic.

фотография photography; photograph; photographer's (studio); **фотолюбитель** *(m.)* amateur photographer.

фрагмент fragment.

фраза phrase, sentence; **фразёр** phrase-monger.

фрак dress-coat; tail-coat.

фракционный factional; **фракция** faction, fraction.

франкировать *(ipf. & pf.)* prepay *(postage).*

франкмасон freemason.

франт dandy.
францу́женка Frenchwoman/-girl; **францу́з** Frenchman; **францу́зский** French *(a.)*.
фрахт freight.
фрега́т frigate.
фре́зер cutter, mill.
френч field jacket.
фре́ска fresco.
фриво́льный frivolous.
фриз frieze.
фронт front; **фронтово́й** front-line.
фрукт fruit; **фрукто́вый** fruit *(a.)*.
фта́левый phthalic.
фто́ристый fluoric; ф. ка́лий potassium fluoride.
фуга́|нок (-нка) plane.
фуже́р tall wine glass.
фунда́мент foundation; **~а́льный** solid; basic, main.
фуникулёр funicular railway.
функциони́ровать function; **фу́нкция** function.
фунт pound *(weight, sterling)*.
фура́ж (-а́) fodder, forage.
фура́|жка *(gen. pl.* -жек) peak cap.
фурго́н van.
фуро́р furore.
футбо́л football; **футболи́ст** footballer; **футбо́льный** football *(a.)*.
футля́р case.
фуфа́йка *(gen. pl.* -аек) jersey, sweater.
фы́ркать *(pf.* фы́ркнуть) snort.
фюзеля́ж fuselage.

X

ха́живать go (often).
хала́т dressing-gown; **хала́тный** careless.
халту́ра hack-work; **халту́рщик, ~щица** pot-boiler.
хам boor.
хамелео́н chameleon.
ха́мский boorish, caddish.
хан khan.
хандра́ melancholy, the blues; **хандри́ть** *(pf.* за-) have a fit of the blues.
ханжа́ *(m. & f. gen. pl.* -е́й) bigot, hypocrite; **ха́нжеский** sanctimonious; **ханжество́** bigotry, hypocrisy.
хао́с chaos; mess; **хаот|и́ческий, ~и́чный** chaotic.

хара́ктер character; **~изова́ть** *(ipf. & pf.)* describe; characterize; **~и́стика** characteristic; testimonial; **характе́рный** (для) characteristic (of).
ха́ркать *(pf.* ха́ркнуть) expectorate, spit.
ха́ртия charter.
харче́вня *(gen. pl.* -вен) eating-house; **харч|и́** (-е́й) food, victuals.
ха́та hut.
хвала́ praise; **хвале́бный** laudatory; **хвалёный** much praised; **хвали́ть** (хвалю́, хва́лишь *pf.* по-) praise; **-ся** *(inst.)* boast (about).
хваста́ться *(pf.* по-) *(inst.)* boast (about); **хвастли́вый** boastful; **хвастовство́** bragging; boasting; **хваст|у́н** (-уна́), **~у́нья** *(gen. pl.* -у́ний) braggart, boaster.
хвата́ть 1. *(pf.* хв|ати́ть, -ачу́, -а́тишь, & схвати́ть) grasp, seize; **2.** *(pf.* хвати́ть*)* *(gen.)* be sufficient; э́того ему́ хва́тит that will be enough for him; -ся (за + *acc.)* catch hold of, grasp; **хва́тка** grip; bite.
хво́йный coniferous.
хвора́ть be ailing.
хво́рост brushwood; pastry straws; **хворости́на** switch, long branch.
хвост (-а́) tail; **хвостово́й** tail *(a.)*.
хвоя́ needle(s) *(of pine)*.
хе́рес sherry.
хиба́рка hovel.
хи́жина shack.
хи́лый sickly, feeble.
химер|и́ческий, ~и́чный chimerical, impracticable.
хи́мик chemist; **химика́л|ии** (-ий) chemicals; **химика́т** chemical; **хими́ческий** chemical *(a.)*; **хи́мия** chemistry; **химчи́стка** dry cleaning.
хини́н quinine.
хире́ть *(pf.* за-) grow sickly; fall into decay.
хиру́рг surgeon; **хирурги́ческий** surgical; **хирурги́я** surgery.
хитри́ть *(pf.* с-) be cunning/crafty; **хи́трость** *(f.)* cunning, slyness; ruse; **хи́трый** cunning.
хихи́кать *(pf.* хихи́кнуть) giggle, snigger.
хище́ние plundering; **хи́щник** beast/bird of prey, predator; **хи́щный** predatory.

хладнокро́вие coolness, equanimity; хладнокро́вный cool, composed.

хлам lumber, rubbish.

хлеб 1. (pl. -ы) bread, loaf; 2. (pl. -á) grain, corn.

хлеба́ть (pf. хлсбну́ть) gulp, slurp.

хле́бница bread-basket; bread-plate; хле́бный bread, grain, cereal (a.).

хлебо|заво́д bakery; ~па́шество agriculture; ~пека́рня (gen. pl. -пека́рен) bakery; ~ро́дный grain-producing, fertile; ~со́льство, хлеб-соль (coll.) hospitality.

хлев (pl. -ы & -á) cattle-shed, pigsty.

хлеста́ть (-щу́, -щешь; pf. хлестну́ть) lash; хлёсткий biting, trenchant.

хло́пать (pf. хло́пнуть) bang, slap.

хло́|пец (-пца) (coll.) fellow, lad.

хлопкоро́б cotton grower; хло́|пок (-пка) cotton.

хло|по́к (-пка́) clap.

хлоп|ота́ть (-очу́, -о́чешь; pf. по-) bustle, take trouble; (о + prep.) petition (for); хлопотли́вый fussy; troublesome; хло́п|оты (-о́т, -ота́м) bustle; care, trouble.

хлопу́|шка (gen. pl. -шек) fly-swatter; pop gun; Christmas cracker.

хлопчатобума́жный cotton.

хлопьеви́дный flaky; хло́пья (-ьев) flakes.

хлор chlorine; хло́ристый chloride; хло́рный chloric.

хлороформи́ровать (ipf.& pf.) chloroform.

хлы́нуть (pf.) gush, spout.

хлыст (-á) whip, switch; Khlyst (member of sect).

хлю́пать (pf. хлю́пнуть) squelch.

хля́бать be loose.

хлябь (f.) abyss; trough.

хля́стик strap (on dress).

хмель (m.)hops; intoxication; хмель-но́й intoxicating; drunk.

хму́рить (pf. на-): х. бро́ви frown; -ся frown; хму́рый gloomy, lowering.

хна henna.

хны́|кать (-ы́чу, -ы́чешь) snivel, whimper.

хо́бот trunk; хобо|то́к (-тка́) proboscis.

ход move, motion; course; entrance; пусти́ть в ход set in motion; знать все ходы́ и вы́ходы know all the ins and outs; на ходу́ in motion, on the move.

хода́тай intercessor; ~ство application; intercession; ~ствовать (pf. по-) solicit, petition.

ходи́ть (хожу́, хо́дишь) go, walk; (за + inst.) look after; хо́дкий marketable; fast; ходов|о́й moving, working (parts) ; current, popular; -ые ка́чества performance (of car) ; ходо́к (-á) walker; peasant messenger.

ходу́л|я (gen. pl. -ей) stilt.

ходьба́ walking; ходя́чий walking; current; хожде́ние walking; circulation.

хозрасчёт (basis of) profitability; на -е self-financing.

хоз|я́ин (pl. -я́ева, -я́св) master, proprietor, boss; host; landlord; хоз|я́йка (gen. pl. -я́ек) proprietress, hostess, landlady.

хозя́йничать keep house; hold sway; хозя́йственник business executive; хозя́йственный economic; economical; хозя́йство economy; husbandry; farm; хозя́йствование management.

хокке́й hockey; ice hockey.

хо́леный well cared-for, sleek.

холе́ра cholera.

хо́лка withers.

холм (-á) hill; холми́стый hilly.

хо́лод (pl. -á, -о́в) cold; холоде́ть (pf. по-) get cold; холоди́льник refrigerator; холодн|ый cold; -ое jellied meat/fish.

холо́п bondsman, serf.

холосто́й unmarried; blank, dummy; холостя́к (-á) bachelor.

холст (-á) canvas, linen; sackcloth.

хому́т (-á) (horse's) collar, yoke.

хомя́к (-á) hamster.

хор choir; chorus.

хорва́т, ~ка Croat; хорва́тский Croatian.

хоре́й trochee.

хо|рёк (-рька́) polecat.

хореогра́фия choreography.

хори́ст, ~ка member of chorus/choir.

хорово́д round dance.

хор|о́мы (-о́м) mansion.

хорони́ть|(-оню́, -о́нишь pf. по-) bury.

хоро́шенький pretty, nice; хоро-ше́нько throughly; хороше́ть (pf. по-) grow prettier; хоро́ший (comp. лу́чше, лу́чший) good; beautiful, handsome.

хору́гвь (f.) gonfalon, standard.

хор|ь (-я) polecat.
хоте́ть (хоч|у́, -ешь, -ет, хоти́м; *pf.* за-) want; хо́чешь, не хо́чешь willy-nilly; **-ся:** мне хо́чется... I want to...
хоть 1. if you wish; 2. at least; 3. although; хоть бы if only; хотя́ although.
хохла́тый crested, tufted; хо|хо́л (-хла́) crest, tuft (of hair); *(coll.)* Ukrainian.
хо́хот laughter, guffaw; хох|ота́ть (-очу́, -о́чешь; *pf.* за-) laugh, guffaw.
храбре́ц (-а́) brave man; храбри́ться pretend not to be afraid; summon up courage; хра́брый brave, va!iant.
храм temple.
хране́ние keeping; storage; храни́-лище depository, depot; container; храни́ть keep, guard; -ся be kept.
храп snore; snoring; хра|пе́ть (-плю́, -пи́шь) snore.
храпови́к (-а́) ratchet.
хре|бе́т (-бта́) spinal column; *(fig.)* backbone; mountain range/ridge.
хрен horse-radish.
хрестома́тия anthology, reader.
хризанте́ма chrysanthemum.
хрип, ~е́ние wheeze; хрипе́ть (-плю́, пи́шь) wheeze; хри́плый hoarse; хрипота́ hoarseness
христи|ани́н *(pl.* -а́не, -а́н), ~а́нка Christian; христиа́нский Christian *(a.);* христиа́нство Christ-ianity.
хром chrome, chromium.
хрома́ть be lame, limp.
хроми́ровать *(ipf. & pf.)* coat with chrome; хро́мовый 1. chrome *(a.);* 2. calf-skin.
хромо́й lame.
хромосо́ма chromosome.
хромота́ limp, lameness.
хро́ник chronic invalid.
хро́ника chronicle; newsreel; хро-нике́р reporter.
хроноло́гия chronology; хроно́метр chronometer.
хру́пкий *(comp.* хру́пче) fragile, frail.
хруст crackle, crunch.
хруста́л|ь (-я́) cut-glass, crystal; хруста́льный cut-glass, crystal.
хрус|те́ть (-ти́т; *pf.* хру́стнуть) crunch, crackle.
хрущ (-а́) cockchafer.

хрю́кать *(pf.* хрю́кнуть) grunt.
хряк hog.
хрящ (-а́) cartilage, gristle; gravel *(geol.).*
худе́ть *(pf.* по-) grow thin.
ху́до, *n,* harm, evil; *ad,* badly; нет ху́да без добра́ every cloud has a silver lining.
худоба́ leanness, thinness.
худо́жественный artistic; худо́-жество art; худо́ж|ник, ~ница artist.
худо́й lean, thin; bad; худоща́вый lean; ху́дший worse; worst; ху́же worse.
хулига́н hooligan, rowdy; ~ство hooliganism, rowdyism.
хули́ть censure, criticize.
ху́тор *(pl.* -а́) farm; hamlet.

Ц

ца́пать *(pf.* ца́пнуть) *(coll.)* snatch.
ца́|пля *(gen. pl.* -пель) heron.
цара́пать *(pf.* на-, о-, цара́пнуть) scratch; scribble; **-ся** scratch (oneself); цара́пина scratch.
царе́вич tsarevich, prince *(son of tsar);* царе́вна *(gen. pl.* -вен) princess *(tsar's daughter).*
цари́зм tsarism; цари́ть reign; цари́ца tsarina, empress; ца́рский tsar's, royal.
ца́рство reign, realm; ца́рствование reign; ца́рствовать reign; цар|ь (-я́) tsar.
цвести́ (цвет|у́, -ёшь; цв|ёл, -ела́, *ppa.* цве́тший) blossom, flower.
цвет 1. *(pl.* -ы́) flower, bloom, blos-som; 2. *(pl.* -а́) colour.
цвети́стый flowery, florid; цветни́к (-а́) flower-garden/-bed; цветно́й coloured.
цве|то́к (-тка́) flower, blossom; цве-то́ч|ник, ~ница florist; цвето́чный flower *(a.).*
цеди́лка filter, strainer; цеди́ть (це-жу́, це́дишь; *pf.* про-) strain, filter.
це́дра dried peel.
цейло́нский Singhalese.
целе́бный medicinal; healing *(a.).*
целево́й (for) special purposes; целе-сообра́зный advisable, expedient; целеустремлённый purposeful.
целико́м as a whole, completely

целина́ virgin land
цели́тельный healing (a.).
це́лить (pf. на-) (в + acc.) aim (at).
целко́вый (coll.) rouble.
целлофа́н cellophane.
целова́ть (pf. по-) kiss; -ся kiss
(each other).
целому́дренный chaste; целому́дрие
purity.
це́лость (f.) safety; це́лый whole;
intact, safe.
цель (f.) aim, goal, object, target.
це́льный whole.
цеме́нт cement; ~и́ровать (ipf. & pf.;
& pf. с-) cement; ~ный cement
(a.).
цена́ (це́ну, pl. це́ны) price, cost,
worth.
ценз qualification (e. g. for electoral
right).
це́нзор censor; цензу́ра censorship.
цени́тель, ~ница connoisseur, judge;
цени́ть (ценю́, це́нишь; pf. о-)
estimate, value; appreciate.
це́нность (f.) value; (pl.) valuables;
це́нный valuable.
центиме́тр centimetre; це́нтнер cent-
ner (= 100 kilograms).
центр centre.
централ|иза́ция centralization; ~изо-
ва́ть (ipf. & pf.) centralize.
центра́льный central; центро|бе́жный
centrifugal; ~стреми́тельный centripetal.
цеп (-á) flail.
цепене́ть (pf. о-) become rigid.
це́пкий prehensile, tenacious; це-
пля́ться (за + acc.) catch, clutch
(at), cling (on to).
цепно́й chain (a.); цепо́|чка (gen.
pl. -чек) chain; цеп|ь (f.; на -и́, pl.
-и, -е́й) chain; line.
церемо́ниться (pf. по-) stand on
ceremony; церемо́ния ceremony;
церемо́нный ceremonious.
церко́вник churchman, cleric; church-
-goer;церко́вно-славя́нскийChurch
Slavonic; церко́вный church
(a.), ecclesiastical; це́р|ковь (f.;
gen. -кви, inst. -ковью pl. -кви,
-кве́й, -ква́м) church.
цех workshop; guild.
цивил|иза́ция civilization; ~изо-
ва́ть (ipf. & pf.) civilize.
циге́йка beaver lamb.
цикл cycle.
цикло́н cyclone.
цико́рий chicory.

цили́ндр cylinder; top hat; ~и́ческий
cylindrical; цили́ндровый cylinder
(a.).
цинга́ scurvy.
цини́зм cynicism; ци́ник cynic; ци-
ни́чный cynical.
цинк zinc; ~овый zinc (a.).
цирк circus; ~ово́й circus (a.).
циркули́ровать circulate; ци́ркуль
(m.) (pair of) compasses; цир-
куля́р circular; циркуля́ция circulation.
цирю́льник (obs.) barber.
цисте́рна cistern; water-cart, tanker.
цитаде́ль (f.) stronghold.
цита́та quotation; цити́ровать (pf.
про-) quote.
ци́тра zither.
ци́трус citrus; ~овый citric.
цифербла́т dial, face; ци́фра number,
figure; цифров|о́й: -ы́е да́нные
figures.
цо́кольный эта́ж lowest floor.
цу́гом one behind the other.
цука́т candied fruit.
цыг|а́н (pl. -а́не, & -а́ны, -а́н),
~а́нка gypsy; цыга́нский gypsy
(a.).
цынга́ scurvy.
цыно́вка mat.
цыпл|ёнок (-нка, pl. цыпл|я́та, -я́т)
chicken.
цы́почк|и: на -ах) on tiptoe.

Ч

чаба́н (-á) shepherd.
ча́вкать (pf. ча́вкнуть) champ (v. i.).
чад (в -у́) fumes, smoke; ча|ди́ть
(-жу́, -ди́шь; pf. на-) (give off)
smoke; ча́дный full of smoke/
fumes.
ча́до offspring.
чадра́ yashmak.
чаевы́е tip, gratuity; ча́йнка tea-leaf;
ча|й (pl. -и́, -ёв) tea; дава́ть на ч.
give a tip.
чай (coll.) perhaps, maybe.
ча́йка (gen. pl. ча́ек) gull.
ча́йная tea-rooms; ча́йник tea-pot;
ча́йница tea-caddy; ча́йный tea
(a.).
ча́лить moor, tie up.
чалма́ turban.
ча́лопегий skewbald; ча́лый roan.
чан tub, vat.

ча́рка cup.

чарова́ть bewitch, charm; чароде́й magician; ча́ры (чар) witchcraft; charms.

час (ча́са *but* два часа́, в ча́се & в часу́, *pl* часы́) hour; *(pl.)* watch, clock; кото́рый час? what time is it?; в тре́тьем часу́ after two; стоя́ть на часа́х be on guard.

часо́|вня *(gen. pl.* -вен) chapel.

часово́й clock, watch *(a.)*; hourlong; sentry *(as noun)*; часовщи́к (-á) watch-maker.

часосло́в prayer-book.

части́ца fraction; particle; части́чный partial.

ча́стник private tradesman/craftsman.

ча́стное quotient.

ча́стность *(f.)* detail, particular.

ча́стный private; particular.

ча́сто often.

частоко́л fencing, palisade.

частота́ *(pl.* -о́ты) frequency.

часту́|шка *(gen. pl.* -шек) chastooshka *(folk verse)*.

ча́стый *(comp.* ча́ще) frequent, thick.

част|ь *(f.; pl.* -и, -е́й) part; department; unit *(military, etc.)*.

час|ы́ (-о́в) clock, watch.

ча́хлый feeble, weak; ча́хнуть *(past* чах, *pf.* за-) wither.

чахо́тка consumption; tuberculosis; чахо́точный consumptive.

ча́ша bowl; chalice; ча́|шка *(gen. pl.* -шек) cup.

ча́ща thicket.

ча́ще more often.

ча́яние expectation, hope; ча́ять (ча́ю, ча́ешь) expect, hope; она́ души́ в нём не ча́ет she dotes on him.

чванли́вый boastful; чва́нство conceit, swank.

чей (чья, чьё, чьи) whose.

чек cheque.

чека́ linch-pin.

чека́нить 1. *(pf.* вы́-, от-) coin, mint; 2. *(pf.* от-) ◊ слова́ speak carefully; чека́нка coinage, minting.

чёлка fringe.

чёлн (челна́) dug-out, canoe; челно́к (-á) dug-out, canoe; shuttle.

чело́ *(obs.)* brow; челоби́тная *(obs.)* petition.

...ловéк *(pl.* лю́ди) person; man; -е∼олю́бие philanthropy.

челове́ческий human; humane; челове́чество mankind; челове́чный humane.

че́люсть *(f.)* jaw.

че́лядь *(f.)* servants.

чем 1. *inst. of.* что; 2. than; 3. чем свет at daybreak.

чемода́н suitcase, trunk.

чемпио́н, ∼ка champion; чемпиона́т championship.

че|пе́ц (-пца́) cap.

чепуха́ nonsense.

че́пчик cap.

черви́вый worm-eaten.

червлёный *(obs.)* scarlet.

черво́|нец (-нца) chervonets *(10 rouble note)*; gold coin (= *10 or 5 r.; hist.)*; черво́нный of hearts *(cards)*; pure *(gold)*; *(obs.)* red.

червото́чина worm-hole.

че́рвы (черв) & че́рв|и (-е́й) hearts *(cards)*.

черв|ь (-я́, *pl.* -и, -е́й), червя́к (-á) worm.

черда́к (-á) attic, garret.

че́ред (череда́) turn; де́ло идёт свои́м -о́м the matter is taking its course.

чередова́ть alternate; -ся alternate, take turns.

че́рез *(acc.)* over, across; through; via; in *(e. g.* in 2 days' time).

черёмуха bird-cherry.

чере|но́к (-нка) cutting, graft; handle.

че́реп *(pl.* -á) skull.

черепа́ха tortoise; turtle; черепа́ховый, черепа́ший tortoise *(a.)*.

черепи́ца tile; черепи́чный tiled.

черепно́й cranial, skull *(a.)*.

чере|по́к (-пка́) crock, fragment *(of pottery)*.

чересполо́сица strip-farming.

чересчу́р too.

чере́|шня *(gen. pl.* -шен) cherry; cherries.

черка́ть *(pf.* черкну́ть) *(coll.)* scribble.

черке́с, ∼ка Circassian.

черне́ть *(pf.* по-), -ся grow black; show black.

чернец (-á) *(obs.)* monk.

черни́ка bilberry; bilberries.

черни́|ла (-и́л) ink; черни́льница ink-pot; черни́льный каранда́ш indelible pencil.

черни́ть 1. *(pf.* за-, на-) blacken; 2. *(pf.* о-) slander.

черновик (-á) rough copy; черново́й rough, draft *(a.)*.

черно|зём black earth, chernozem; ~кожий black-skinned; ~лесье deciduous forest; ~морский Black Sea *(a.)*; ~рабочий labourer, unskilled worker; ~слив prunes; ~сливина prune.

чернота blackness.

чёрн|ый black; back *(e.g. stairs)*; на -ый день for a rainy day; держать в -ом теле ill-treat.

чернь *(f.)* the mob.

черп|ак (-ака), ~алка scoop; черпать *(pf.* черпнуть) ladle, spoon.

черстветь 1. *(pf.* за-) become stale; 2. *(pf.* о-) become hardened/callous; чёрствый dry, stale; hard-hearted.

чёрт *(pl.* чёрт|и, -ей) devil.

черта line; feature, trait; boundary.

черт|ёж (-ежа) draft, sketch; чертёжник draughtsman; чертёжный drawing *(a.)*.

чертить (черчу, чертишь; *pf.* на-) draw.

чертовский devilish.

чертог chamber, palace.

чертополох thistle.

чёрто|чка *(gen. pl.* -чек) line, feature; dash.

черчение drawing.

чесать (чешу, чешешь; *pf.* по-) card; comb; scratch; -ся scratch oneself; itch.

чеснок (-а) garlic.

чесотка itch; mange.

чествовать *(v. t.)* feast, honour, celebrate.

честный honest.

often-люби́вый ambitious; ~любие ambition.

честь *(f.)* honour; это делает ему ~ it does him credit; отдать ~ salute.

чесуча tussore silk.

чёт *(coll.)* even number.

чета pair, couple; не ~ ему no match for him.

четверг (-а) Thursday.

четвереньк|и: на -ах on all fours.

четвёрка four.

четверо four; ~ногий four-footed, quadruped.

четвёртый fourth; четверть *(f.)* quarter; school term.

чё|тки (-ток) rosary, beads.

чёткий clear, accurate.

чётный even.

четыре four; четыреста four hundred.

четырёх|местный four-seater *(a.)*; ~сотый four-hundredth; ~сторонний quadrilateral; ~угольник quadrangle, square.

четырнадцатый fourteenth; четырнадцать fourteen.

чех Czech.

чехарда leap-frog.

че|хол (-хла) case, cover.

чечевица lentil.

чё|шка *(gen. pl.* -шек) Czech (woman); чешский Czech *(a.)*.

чеш|уйка *(gen. pl.* -уек) (fish-)scale; чешуя scales.

чибис lapwing, peewit.

чиж (-а) siskin.

чин *(pl.* -ы) grade, rank.

чинар, ~а plane-tree.

чинить (чиню, чинишь) 1. *(pf.* по-) repair; 2. *(pf.* о-) sharpen.

чинить 3. *(pf.* у-) cause; carry out.

чинный sedate; ceremonious.

чиновник official, civil servant.

чирей abscess, boil.

чирикать *(pf.* чирикнуть) chirp.

чиркать *(pf.* чиркнуть): спичкой ч. strike a match.

чис|ленность *(f.)* numbers, strength; численный numerical; числитель *(m.)* numerator; числительное numeral, number; числить count, reckon; -ся больным be on the sick-list.

число *(pl.* чи|сла, -сел) number; date.

чистилище purgatory; чисти́ль|щик, ~щица cleaner; bootblack.

чи|стить (-щу, -стишь; *pf.* вы-, по-) clean; *(pf.* по-, о-) peel; чистка cleaning; purge *(polit.)*; чистовой clean, fair *(copy)*.

чисто|кровный thoroughbred; ~писание calligraphy; ~плотный clean; ~сердечный candid, frank.

чистота cleanness, purity; чистый *(comp.* чище) clean, pure.

чита́|льный зал; ~льня *(gen. pl.* -лен) reading-room; читатель, ~ница reader; читать *(pf.* про-, & про|честь, -чту, -чтёшь; *past* -чёл, -чла; *ppp.* -чтённый) read; читка reading.

чихание sneezing; чихать *(pf.* чихнуть) sneeze.

чище *(comp. of* чистый) cleaner, purer.

член member; limb; article *(gram.)* членить *(pf.* рас-) divide, articulate.

членораздельный articulate; членский membership (a.); членство membership.

чмокать (pf. чмокнуть) smack one's lips; kiss.

чокаться (pf. чокнуться) clink glasses.

чомга grebe.

чопорный prim, stiff.

чорт devil.

чреватый (inst.) fraught, pregnant (with).

чрево maw; womb; ~вещатель (m.) ventriloquist; ~угодие gluttony.

чрез = через.

чрезвычайный extraordinary, emergency, extreme; чрезмерный excessive.

чтение reading; чтец (-а), чтица reader, reciter.

чтить (чту, чтишь) honour, revere.

что what; that; (coll.) why; who; which; что до меня as far as I am concerned; что ни, что бы ни whatever.

чтоб = чтобы that; in order that; я хочу, чтобы он ушёл I want him to go away.

что-либо, что-нибудь something, anything.

что-то something.

чубарый dappled.

чувственный sensual; чувствительный sensitive.

чувство feeling, sense; чувствовать (pf. по-) feel; ч. себя хорошо feel well; -ся be felt.

чугун (-а) cast iron; чугунный cast iron (a.).

чудак (-а) crank, eccentric; чудачество eccentricity.

чудесный wonderful.

чудиться (pf. по-) appear, seem.

чудно wonderful(ly).

чудной queer, strange.

чудный marvellous, wonderful.

чудо (pl. чудеса, -ес, -есам) miracle, wonder.

чудовище monster; чудовищный monstrous.

чудотворец (-рца) miracle-worker.

чужак (-а) stranger; чужбина foreign land.

чуждаться (gen.) avoid.

чуждый alien; stranger (with gen. — to, e. g. intrigue, jealousy).

чужеземец (-земца), ~земка foreigner; чужеземный foreign; чужестранец = чужеземец.

чужой someone else's; foreign, strange.

чулан store-room; larder.

чулок (-лка; gen. pl. -лок) stocking.

чума plague, Black Death.

чумазый dirty.

чурбан block.

чурка chock.

чуткий (comp. чутче) sensitive; keen; чуткость (f.) sensitivity; keenness.

чуточка: ни -и not a bit.

чуть hardly, with difficulty; чуть--чуть slightly; чуть не almost.

чутьё scent; feeling, flair.

чучело stuffed animal/bird; dummy.

чушь (f.) nonsense.

чуять (чую, чуешь, pf. по-) scent, feel.

чьё, чья, чьи see чей.

Ш

шабаш Sabbath.

шабаш that's enough.

шаблон pattern, stencil; mould; cliché; шаблонный pattern etc. (a.); hackneyed, trite.

шаг (-а, but два шага, в -у, pl. -и) pace, step; move; шагать (pf. шагнуть) step; шагом at walking pace; ша|жок (-жка) short step.

шайба puck; (tech.) washer.

шайка (gen. pl. шаек) 1. gang; 2. washtub.

шакал jackal.

шалаш (-а) hut.

шалеть (pf. о-) go crazy.

шалить play pranks; шаловливый playful; шалость (f.) prank; шалу|н (-на), ~нья (gen. pl. -ний) naughty child; playful person.

шалфей (bot.) sage.

шалый crazy.

шаль (f.) shawl.

шальной mad.

шамкать mumble.

шампанское champagne.

шампиньон mushroom.

шампунь (m.) shampoo.

шанс chance; шансы на успех chances of success.

шантаж (-а) blackmail; ~ировать blackmail; ~ист, ~истка blackmailer.

шапка hat; шапочник hatter; шапочн|ый hat (a.); к -ому разбору at the very end.

шар (-а *but* два шара, *pl.* -ы) ball, sphere; воздушный ш. balloon.

шара́хаться *(pf.* шара́хнуться) shy.

шарж cartoon; шаржи́ровать caricature; overact.

ша́рик small ball, bead; corpuscle; globule; ша́риковая ру́чка ball-point pen; шарикоподши́пник ball-bearing.

ша́рить *(pf.* по-) rummage.

ша́ркать *(pf.* ша́ркнуть) shuffle; ш. ного́й scrape one's foot.

шарлата́н charlatan.

шарма́нка barrel-organ.

шарни́р hinge, joint.

шаров|а́ры (-а́р) wide trousers.

шаро|ви́дный, ~обра́зный spherical.

шарф scarf.

шасси́ *(indecl.)* chassis.

шата́ть *(pf.* шатну́ть) *(v.t.)* rock, sway; -ся be(come) loose; stagger; loaf about.

шате́н, ~ка person with dark brown hair.

ша|тёр (-тра́) tent.

ша́ткий unsteady.

шатну́ть *see* шата́ть.

шату́н (-а́) connecting-rod.

ша́фер *(pl.* -а́) best man.

шафра́н saffron.

шах 1. shah; 2. check *(chess).*

шахмати́ст, ~ка chess-player; ша́х-матный chess *(a.);* ша́хматы (-ат) chess.

ша́хта mine, pit; шахтёр miner; шахтёрский miner's.

ша́|шка *(gen. pl.* -шек) 1. sabre; 2. draught; *(pl.)* checkers; draughts.

шашлы́к (-а́) shashlik *(pieces of mutton on spit).*

ша́шн|и (-ей) intrigues, tricks.

шва́бра swab.

швартова́ть *(pf.* при-) moor.

швед, ~ка Swede; шве́дский Swedish.

шве́йный sewing *(a.).*

швейца́р hall porter, doorman.

швейца́|рец (-рца), ~рка Swiss.

швейца́рская porter's lodge.

швейца́рский Swiss *(a.).*

швея́ seamstress.

швыря́ть *(pf.* швырну́ть) fling.

шевели́ть *(pf.* по-, шевельну́ть) move, stir; -ся move, stir (oneself).

шевелю́ра hair-style; head of hair.

шевро́ *(indecl.)* kid *(leather);* шев-ро́вый kid *(a.).*

шеде́вр masterpiece.

ше́йка *(gen. pl.* ше́ек) neck; ше́йный neck, jugular.

ше́лест rustle; шелесте́ть (-и́шь) rustle.

шёлк *(pl.* -а́) silk; шелкови́стый silky; шелкови́ца mulberry; шел-кови́чный червь silkworm; шёл-ковый silk *(a.).*

шелохну́ть *(pf.)* stir, move.

шелуди́вый mangy.

шелуха́ husk(s), pod(s), peelings; шелуши́ть peel, pod; -ся come off.

шельма *(m. & f.)* rogue.

шепеля́вить lisp; шепеля́вый lisping.

шёпот whisper; шепта́ть (шепчу́, ше́пчешь; *pf.* про-, шепну́ть) whisper.

шере́нга rank.

шерохова́тый rough, uneве́н.

шерсти́стый fleecy, woolly; шерсть *(f.)* wool; шерстяно́й wool(len).

шерша́вый rough.

шер|шень (-шня) hornet.

шест (-а́) pole.

ше́ствие procession; ше́ствовать march.

шестёрка six.

шестерня́ *(gen. pl.* -рён) gear.

ше́стеро six,

шести|гра́нник hexahedron; ~-деся́тый sixtieth; ~ме́сячный six-month *(a.);* ~со́тый six-hund-redth; ~уго́льный hexagonal.

шестна́дцатый sixteenth; шестна́д-цать sixteen.

шесто́й sixth.

шес|то́к (-тка́) hearth.

шесть six.

шесть|деся́т sixty; ~со́т six hundred.

шеф chief; patron; chef; ше́фство patronage; ше́фствовать (над) look after.

ше́я *(gen. pl.* шей) neck.

ши́бкий *(comp.* ши́бче) quick, sharp.

ши́ворот *(coll.)* collar.

шик stylishness; шика́рный smart, chic.

ши́кать *(pf.* ши́кнуть) hiss.

ши́ло *(pl.* ши́л|я, -ев) awl.

шимпанзе́ *(m., indecl.)* chimpanzee.

ши́на tyre.

шине́ль *(f.)* greatcoat.

шинкова́ть shred.

ши|но́к (-нка́) tavern;

шип (-а́) 1. pin, tenon; 2. thorn.

ши|пе́ть (-плю́, -пи́шь) hiss, sizzle.
шипо́вник sweet briar.
шипу́чий sparkling; шипу́чка fizzy drink, pop; шипя́щий hissing.
ши́ре see широ́кий.
ширина́ breadth, width; ши́рить (v.t.) widen; -ся become wider.
ши́рма screen.
широ́кий (comp. ши́ре) broad, wide.
широко|веща́ние broadcasting; ~-веща́тельный broadcasting (a.); ~плечий broad-shouldered; ~-экра́нный wide-screen (a.).
широта́ (pl. -о́ты) breadth; latitude.
ширпотре́б consumer goods.
шить (шью, шьёшь; imper. шей; ppp. ши́тый; pf. с-, сошью́) sew; шитьё sewing, embroidery.
ши́фер slate.
шифр cipher; шифрова́ть (pf. за-) put in cipher.
ши́|шка (gen. pl. -шек) cone, bump, lump.
шкала́ scale.
шкап = шкаф.
шкату́лка box, casket.
шкаф (в -у́; pl. -ы́) cupboard.
шквал squall.
шкив pulley.
шко́ла school; шко́ль|ник, ~ница schoolboy, -girl; шко́льный school (a.).
шку́ра hide, skin.
шку́рник self-seeker.
шлагба́ум barrier.
шлак dross, slag.
шланг hose.
шлейф train (of dress).
шлем helmet.
шлёпать (pf. шлёпнуть) slap, smack; splash; -ся fall, splash; шле|по́к (-пка́) slap, smack.
шлифова́льный grinding, polishing (a.); шлифова́ть (pf. от-) grind, polish.
шлюз sluice, lock.
шлю́пка ship's boat.
шля́па hat; шля́пный hat (a.); milliner's.
шля́ться loaf about.
шля́хта Polish gentry.
шмел|ь (-я́) bumble-bee.
шмы́гать (pf. шмыгну́ть) dart.
шнур |(-а́) cord; шнурова́ть (pf. за-) lace up; шну|ро́к (-рка́) lace.
шныря́ть nose about.
шов (шва) seam, stitch; joint.
шовини́зм chauvinism.

шок shock (med.).
шокола́д chocolate; шокола́дные конфе́ты chocolates.
шо́мпол (pl. -ы & -а́) ramrod, cleaning rod.
шо́пот whisper.
шо́рник saddler, harness-maker.
шо́рох rustle.
шо́ры (шор) blinkers.
шоссе́ (indecl.) highway; шосси́ровать (ipf. & pf.) metal (roads).
шотла́н|дец (-дца) Scot; ~дка Scotswoman; tartan; шотла́ндский Scottish.
шофёр driver, chauffeur.
шпа́га rapier, sword.
шпага́т cord, twine.
шпаклева́ть (pf. за-) putty; шпаклёвка puttying; putty.
шпа́ла sleeper.
шпале́ра trellis; (pl.) lines.
шпарга́лка (coll.) crib.
шпат spar (min.).
шпе|нёк (-нька́) peg, pin.
шпиль (m.) spire; capstan.
шпи́|лька (gen. pl. -лек) hairpin; tack.
шпина́т spinach.
шпингале́т (vertical) bolt.
шпио́н spy; шпиона́ж espionage; шпио́нить spy; шпио́нство espionage.
шпиц spire; spitz (dog).
шпо́ра spur.
шприц syringe.
шпрот sprat.
шпу́|лька (gen. pl. -лек) bobbin.
шпунт groove, rabbet.
шрам scar.
шрапне́ль (f.) shrapnel.
шрифт print, type.
штаб staff, headquarters.
шта́бель (m.) stack.
штамп punch, stamp; cliché; штамповать (pf. от-) punch, stamp.
шта́нга bar; weight (sport); штанги́ст weightlifter.
штан|ы́ (-о́в) trousers.
штат state; staff, establishment; штати́в support, tripod, stand; шта́тный regular, established; шта́тский civil, civilian.
штейгер foreman (in mine).
штемпелева́ть (pf. за-) stamp; штемпель (m., pl. -я, -ей) stamp.
штепсель (m., pl. -я. -ей) electric plug.
штиль (m.) calm.
штифт pin, sprig.

што́пать *(pf.* за-) darn; што́пка darning; thread.
што́пор corkscrew; spin *(avia.).*
што́ра blind, curtain.
шторм gale.
штоф damask.
штраф fine, penalty; штрафно́й penalty *(a.);* штрафова́ть *(pf.* о-) fine.
штрейкбре́хер strike-breaker, blackleg.
штрек drift *(mining).*
штрих stroke; trait; штрихова́ть *(pf.* за-) hatch, shade.
штуди́ровать *(pf.* про-) study.
шту́ка piece, thing; *(coll.)* trick; пять штук яйц five eggs.
штукату́р plasterer; штукату́рить *(pf.* о-, от-) plaster; штукату́рка plaster; plastering.
штурва́л steering control; steering wheel.
штурм assault, storm.
шту́рман navigator.
штурмова́ть storm, attack; штурмови́к (-á) low-flying strike aircraft.
шту́чный piece *(a.).*
штык (-á) bayonet.
шу́ба fur-coat.
шу́лер *(pl.* -ы & -á) card-sharper.
шум noise, commotion; шуме́ть (-млю́, -ми́шь; *pf.* за-, про-) make a noise; make a fuss; шуми́ха uproar; шумли́вый boisterous; шу́мный noisy, bustling.
шумо́вка strainer-spoon, skimmer.
шумово́й: ш. орке́стр jazz band; ш. эффе́кт sound effect.
шу|мо́к (-мка́) slight noise; под ш. on the sly.
шу́рин brother-in-law *(wife's brother).*
шурф excavation.
шур|ша́ть (-шу́, -ши́шь; *pf.* за-) rustle.
шу́стрый bright, quick.
шут (-á) fool, jester; шути́ть (шучу́, шу́тишь; *pf.* по-) joke; jest; шу́тк|а joke; в -у in jest; не на -у exceedingly, seriously; шутли́вый witty, jocular; шутни́к (-á) joker, wag; шу́точный humorous; trifling; шутя́ in jest; не ш. seriously.
шушу́каться whisper.
шхе́ры (шхер) sea cliffs, rocky islands, skerries.
шху́на schooner.

Щ

щаве́левый sorrel *(a.);* oxalic.
ща|ди́ть (-жу́, -ди́шь; *pf.* по-) spare.
ще́|бень (-бня) chippings, road metal.
щеб|ета́ть (-ечу́, -е́чешь) chirp, twitter.
ще|го́л (-гла́) goldfinch.
щеголева́тый foppish; щёголь *(m.)* dandy; щегольско́й smart, swell; щеголя́ть *(pf.* щегольну́ть) cut a dash; *(inst.)* flaunt.
ще́дрость *(f.)* generosity; щедр|о́ты (-о́т) *(obs.)* bounty, gifts; ще́дрый generous, liberal.
щека́ *(pl.* щёки, щёк, щека́м) cheek.
щеко́лда latch.
щек|ота́ть (-очу́, -о́чешь; *pf.* по-) tickle; щеко́тка tickling; щекотли́вый ticklish, delicate.
щёлка chink.
щёлкать *(pf.* щёлкнуть) click, crack; ш. па́льцами snap one's fingers; ш. оре́хи crack nuts.
щелкопёр scribbler.
щелку́нчик nutcracker.
щёлок alkaline solution; щелочно́й alkaline; щёлоч|ь *(f.; pl.* -и, -е́й) alkali.
щел|чо́к (-чка́) crack, smack.
щел|ь *(f.; pl.* -и, -е́й) chink, crack, slit.
щеми́ть squeeze, hurt.
ще|но́к (-нка́; *pl.* -нки́ & -ня́та, -ня́т) pup, cub.
щепа́ *(pl.* ще́п|ы, -а́м) (wood) chips, kindling.
щепети́льный punctilious; delicate *(e.g. matter).*
ще́пка wood chip.
щепо́тка, щепо́ть *(f.)* pinch.
щерба́тый pock-marked; chipped.
щети́на bristle; щети́нистый bristling; щети́ниться *(pf.* о-) bristle.
щётка brush; fetlock.
щи (щей) cabbage soup.
щи́колотка ankle.
щипа́ть (щип лю́, -лешь) 1. *(pf.* щипну́ть) nip, pinch; 2. *(pf.* о-, об-) pluck; щи|по́к (-пка́) nip, tweak; щипц|ы́ (-о́в) pincers, tongs; щи́пчик|и (-ов) tweezers.
щит (-á) shield; shell *(of tortoise);* щитови́дный thyroid.
щу́ка pike.

щуп probe; щýпа|льце *(gen. pl.*
-лец) tentacle, antenna; щýпать
(pf. по-) feel, touch.
щýплый puny, small.
щýрить *(pf.* co-): щ. глазá, щýрить-
ся) screw up one's eyes.

Э

эбéновый ebony *(a.).*
эваку|áция evacuation; ~ировать
(ipf. & pf.) evacuate.
эвкалúпт eucalyptus.
эвол|юциони́ровать evolve; ~юциóн-
ный evolutionary; ~юция evolution.
эвфемúзм euphemism.
эгúда aegis.
эгой|зм egoism; ~ст, ~стка egoist;
~стúческий, ~стúчный egoistic(al).
эзóповский Aesopian.
эквáтор equator.
эквивалéнт equivalent.
экзáмен examination; экзаменáтор,
экзаминáтор examiner; экзамена-
циóнный examination *(a.);* экза-
меновáть *(pf.* про-) examine.
экземплáр copy.
экзотúческий exotic.
эквивóк quibble.
ёкий what.
экипáж carriage; crew.
эконóмика economics; экономúст
economist.
эконóмить *(pf.* c-). save; эконо-
мúческий economic; экономúчный
economical.
экономúя economy; экономка housekeeper; экономный thrifty, frugal.
экрáн screen; ~изировать *(ipf. &
pf.)* make a film of.
экскавáтор excavator; экскавáция
excavation.
экскурсáнт tourist, person on excursion; экскýрсия excursion; экс-
курсовóд tour guide.
экспансúвный effusive, expansive;
экспáнсия expansion.
экспатрийровать *(ipf. & pf.)* expatriate.
экспед|ировать *(ipf. & pf.)* dispatch,
expedite; ~úтор forwarding agent;
~úция expedition; dispatch office.
эксперимéнт experiment.
экспéрт expert; экспертúза examination; commission of experts.

эксплуат|áция exploitation; running,
use; ~ировать exploit; work.
экспозúция exposition; exposure,
экспонáт exhibit.
экспонéнт exhibitor; exponent
(maths); index.
экспонúровать *(ipf. & pf.)* exhibit; *(phot.)* expose.
ёкспорт export; ~ёр exporter; ~-
úровать *(ipf. & pf.)* export;
ёкспортный export *(a.).*
экспрéсс express *(train, coach etc.).*
экспрóмт impromptu.
экстáз ecstasy.
экстéрн external student.
экстраги́ровать *(ipf. & pf.)* extract.
ёкстренный extraordinary, special.
эксцентр|úческий eccentric; ~úч-
ный odd, eccentric.
эксцéсс excess.
эластúчный elastic.
элевáтор elevator.
элегáнтный elegant.
элéгия elegy.
элéктр|ик electrician; ~ификáция
electrification; ~ифицúровать *(ipf.
& pf.)* electrify; ~úческий electric-
(al); ~úчество electricity; ~úчка
(gen. pl. -ичек) electric train.
электровóз electric locomotive; элек-
трóд electrode; электрóлиз electrolysis; электромонтёр electrician;
электрóн electron.
электро|провóдность *(f.)* conduc-
tivity; ~стáнция power-station;
~тéхник electrician; ~энéргия
electrical energy/power.
элемéнт element; ~áрный elementary.
элиминúровать *(ipf. & pf.)* eliminate.
эмáлевый enamel *(a.);* эмалиро-
вáть enamel; эмáль *(f.)* enamel.
эмансип|áция emancipation; ~-
ировать *(ipf. & pf.)* emancipate.
эмблéма emblem.
эмбриолóгия embryology.
эмигр|áнт, ~áнтка emigrant; ~áция
emigration; ~úровать *(ipf. & pf.)*
emigrate.
эмоционáльный emotional; эмóция
emotion.
эмпирéй empyrean.
эмпирúзм empiricism.
эмýльсия emulsion.
энергéтик specialist in power/energy;
энергúчный energetic; энéргия
energy; power.

Энный unspecified; Энский a certain.
Энтомология entomology.
Энтузиазм enthusiasm.
Энциклопедия encyclopedia.
Эпигон imitator.
Эпиграмма epigram; эпиграф epigraph.
Эпидемия epidemic.
Эпизод episode.
Эпилеп|сия epilepsy; ~тик epileptic.
Эпилог epilogue.
Эпитафия epitaph.
Эпитет epithet.
Эпический epic.
Эпопея epopee, epic.
Эпос epic.
Эпоха, эра epoch, era.
Эрозия erosion.
Эрудиция erudition.
Эрцгерцог archduke.
Эскадр|а naval squadron; ~илья (gen. pl. -илий) air squadron; ~он cavalry squadron.
Эскалатор escalator.
Эскиз sketch.
Эскимос eskimo.
Эскорт escort; ~ировать (ipf. & pf.) escort.
Эсми|нец (-нца) (naval) destroyer.
Эссенция essence.
Эстакада pier; bridge, flyover.
Эстафета relay-race; baton.
Эстет aesthete; ~ика aesthetics; ~ический aesthetic.
Эсто|нец (-нца), ~нка Estonian; эстонский Estonian (a.).
Эстрада stage; variety; эстрадный концерт variety concert.
Этаж (-á) storey, floor; этажёрка bookshelves.
Этак so.
Этап stage; halting place.
Этика ethics.
Этикет etiquette; этикетка label.
Этил ethyl.
Этимология etymology.
Эт|ический, -ичный ethical.
Этнический ethnic.
Этно|графия ethnography; ~логия ethnology.
Этот, эта, это, эти this.
Этюд study.
Эфемерный ephemeral.
Эфир ether; эфирный etheric; ethereal.
Эффект effect; ~ивный effective; ~ный spectacular; effective.

Эхо echo.
Эшафот scaffold.
Эшелон line, echelon.

Ю

Юбилей anniversary, jubilee; юбилейный anniversary (a.).
Юбка skirt; нижняя ю. petticoat.
Ювелир jeweller; ювелирный jeweller's (a.).
Юг south; юго-восток south-east; юж|áнин, ~анка southerner; южный south(ern).
Юла humming top; fidget.
Юлить fuss; fidget.
Юмор humour; юмористический humorous.
Юнга m., ship's boy.
Юность (f.) (age of) youth; юнош|а (m., gen. pl. -ей) (a) youth; юношество young people; youth юный young, youthful.
Юр: на -ý in an open place.
Юридический juridical, legal.
Юрис|консульт legal adviser; ~пруденция jurisprudence.
Юрист lawyer; law student.
Юркий nimble.
Юродивый foolish; fool in Christ; юродство being a fool.
Юрта nomad's tent.
Юрьев день: вот тебе, бабушка, и ю. д. this is a fine kettle of fish.
Юстиция justice.
Ютиться (ючусь, ютишься) huddle.

Я

Я I.
Ябеда slander; slanderer, gossip.
Яблоко (pl. яблоки, яблок) apple; яблоня apple tree; яблочный apple (a.).
Явка appearance, attendance; secret address; явление appearance, phenomenon; scene (of play); являть (pf. явить, явлю, явишь) show; -ся appear; (inst.) be; явный evident.
Явственный clear; явствовать be clear, obvious.
Явь (f.) reality.

ягнё|нок (-нка, *pl.* ягня́та, ягня́т) lamb.
я́года berry.
я́годица buttock.
ягуа́р jaguar.
яд poison.
я́дерный nucleur.
ядови́тый poisonous, venomous.
ядрёный healthy; succulent.
ядро́ (*pl.* я́дра, я́дер) kernel; nucleus; shot (*sport*); cannon-ball.
я́зва sore, ulcer; pest, plague; язви́тельный caustic, biting; язви́ть make biting remarks.
язы́к (-á) tongue; language.
языко|веде́ние, ~зна́ние linguistics.
язык|ово́й linguistic; ~о́вый lingual.
язы́ческий pagan (*a.*); язы́чество paganism; язы́ч|ник, ~ница pagan.
яи́чник ovary; яи́чница omelette; fried-/scrambled-eggs; яи́чный egg; (*a.*); яйцо́ (*pl.* я́йца, яи́ц) egg; ovum.
я́кобы as if; supposedly.
я́кор|ь (*m.*; *pl.* -и & -я́) anchor.
яку́т, ~ка Yakut; яку́тский Yakut (*a.*).
я́лик skiff.
я́ловый barren, dry (*cow*); calfskin.
я́ма pit; hole; я́мо|чка (*gen. pl.* -чек) dimple.
я́мщик (-á) coachman.

янва́рский January (*a.*); янва́р|ь (-я́) January.
янта́рный amber (*a.*); янта́р|ь (-я́) amber.
япо́|нец (-нца), ~нка Japanese: япо́нский Japanese (*a.*).
яр steep bank, ravine.
яре́мная ве́на jugular vein.
я́ркий (*comp.* я́рче) bright.
ярлы́к (-á) label.
я́рмарка fair.
ярмо́ (*pl.* я́рма) yoke.
ярово́й spring (*a.*; *e. g. crops*).
я́ростный violent; я́рость (*f*). fury.
я́рус circle (*theat.*); layer (*geog.*).
я́рый ardent; violent.
я́сень (*f.*) ash tree.
я́сл|и (-ей) crèche; nursery school; crib.
яснови́|дец (-дца) clairvoyant; я́сность (*f.*) clarity; я́сный clear.
я́ства (яств) viands, victuals.
я́стреб (*pl.* -ы & -á) hawk.
я́хта yacht.
яч|е́йка (*gen. pl.* -еек) cell; foxhole (*mil.*).
ячме́н|ь (-я́) 1. barley; 2. stye (*on eye*).
я́шма jasper.
я́щерица lizard.
я́щик box, drawer; откла́дывать в до́лгий я. shelve, put off.
я́щур foot-and-mouth disease.

ГЕОГРАФИЧЕСКИЕ НАЗВАНИЯ

Абха́зская АССР Abkhazian Autonomous Soviet Socialist Republic.
Австра́лия Australia.
А́встрия Austria.
Аджа́рская АССР Adzhar ASSR.
Адриати́ческое мо́ре the Adriatic Sea.
Азербайджа́нская ССР the Azerbaidzhan SSR.
А́зия Asia.
Азо́вское мо́ре the Sea of Azov.
Алба́ния Albania.
Алеу́тские острова́ the Aleutian Islands.
Алжи́р 1. Algeria; 2. Algiers.
Алма́-Ата́ Alma-Ata.
Алта́й Altai.
А́льпы (Альп) the Alps.
Аля́ска Alaska.
Амазо́нка the Amazon.
Аме́рика America.
Амстерда́м Amsterdam.
Аму́-Дарья́ the Amu-Darya.
Ангара́ the Angara.
А́нглия England; Great Britain.
А́нды (Анд) the Andes.
Анкара́ Ankara.
Антаркти́да, Анта́рктика the Antarctic.
Антве́рпен Antwerp.
Апенни́ны (-ин) the Apennines.
Ара́вия Arabia.
Ара́льское мо́ре the Aral Sea.
Аргенти́на the Argentine.
А́рктика the Arctic.
Армя́нская ССР the Armenian SSR.
Арме́ния Armenia.
Арха́нгельск Archangel.
Асунсьо́н Asuncion.
Атланти́ческий океа́н the Atlantic Ocean.
Афганиста́н Afghanistan.
Афи́ны (Афи́н) Athens.
А́фрика Africa.
А́шхаба́д Ashkhabad.

Байка́л Lake Baikal.
Баку́ Baku.
Балка́нский полуо́стров the Balkan peninsula.
Балти́йское мо́ре the Baltic Sea.
Ба́ренцово мо́ре the Barents Sea.
Баффи́нов зали́в Baffin Bay.
Башки́рская АССР the Bashkir ASSR.

Бейру́т Beirut.
Белгра́д Belgrade.
Бе́лое мо́ре the White Sea.
Белору́сская ССР the White Russian SSR; Белору́ссия White Russia.
Бе́льгия Belgium.
Бе́рингово мо́ре the Bering Sea.
Бе́рингов проли́в the Bering Straits.
Берли́н Berlin.
Берн Berne.
Би́рма Burma.
Бирминге́м Birmingham.
Биска́йский зали́в the Bay of Biscay.
Болга́рия Bulgaria.
Боли́вия Bolivia.
Бомбе́й Bombay.
Бонн Bonn.
Борне́о Borneo.
Босто́н Boston.
Босфо́р the Bosphorus.
Ботни́ческий зали́в the Gulf of Bothnia.
Брази́лия 1. Brazil; 2. Brasilia;
Брета́нь Brittany.
Брюссе́ль (m.); Brussels.
Будапе́шт Budapest.
Буря́тская АССР the Buryat ASSR.
Бухаре́ст Bucharest.
Буэ́нос-А́йрес Buenos Aires.

Варша́ва Warsaw.
Вашингто́н Washington.
Везу́вий Vesuvius.
Великобрита́ния Great Britain.
Веллингто́н Wellington.
Ве́на Vienna.
Ве́нгрия Hungary.
Венесуэ́ла Venezuela.
Вене́ция Venice.
Ве́рхнее о́зеро Lake Superior.
Вест-И́ндия the West Indies.
Ви́льнюс Vilnius.
Ви́сла the Vistula.
Владивосто́к Vladivostok.
Во́лга the Volga.
Вьетна́м Vietnam.

Гаа́га the Hague.
Гава́йи Hawaii.
Га́на Ghana.
Гвиа́на Guyana.
Гвине́я Guinea.

238

Герма́ния Germany.
Гибралта́р Gibraltar.
Гимала́и (-а́ев) the Himalayas.
Гла́зго Glasgow.
Голла́ндия Holland.
Гонко́нг Hong Kong.
Го́рький Gorky (formerly Nizhny Novgorod).
Гренла́ндия Greenland.
Гре́ция Greece.
Гри́нвич Greenwich.
Грузи́нская ССР the Georgian SSR.
Гру́зия Georgia.
Гудзо́нов зали́в Hudson Bay.
Гулль (m.) Hull.

Дагеста́нская АССР the Dagestan ASSR.
Дама́ск Damascus.
Да́ния Denmark.
Данди́ Dundee.
Дарданéллы (-éллы) the Dardanelles.
Де́ли Delhi.
Джака́рта Jakarta.
Днепр the Dnieper.
Днестр the Dniester.
Дон the Don.
Ду́блин Dublin.
Дувр Dover.
Дуна́й the Danube.
Ду́ргам Durham.
Дюнки́рк Dunkirk.

Евро́па Europe.
Евфра́т the Euphrates.
Еги́пет Egypt.
Енисе́й the Yenisei.
Ерева́н Erevan.

Жёлтое мо́ре the Yellow Sea.
Жене́ва Geneva.

За́мбия Zambia.

Иерусали́м Jerusalem.
Изра́иль (m.) Israel.
Инд the Indus.
Инди́йский океа́н the Indian Ocean.
И́ндия India.
Индокита́й Indo-China.
Индоне́зия Indonesia.
Иорда́ния Jordan.
Ира́к Iraq.
Ира́н Iran.
Ирла́ндия Ireland.
Исла́ндия Iceland.
Испа́ния Spain.
Ита́лия Italy.

Йе́мен the Yemen.

Кабарди́но-Балка́рская АССР the Kabardino-Balkarsk ASSR.
Кабу́л Kabul.
Кавка́з the Caucasus.
Каза́хская ССР the Kazakh SSR.
Казбе́к Kazbek.
Кале́ Calais.
Каи́р Cairo.
Канбе́рра Canberra.
Ка́ра-Калпа́кская АССР the Kara-Kalpak ASSR.
Карака́с Caracas.
Кара́чи Karachi.
Каре́льская АССР the Karelian ASSR.
Кари́бское мо́ре the Caribbean (Sea).
Карпа́ты (-а́т) the Carpathians.
Ка́рское мо́ре the Kara Sea.
Каспи́йское мо́ре the Caspian Sea.
Квебе́к Quebec.
Кёльн Cologne.
Ке́мбридж Cambridge.
Ке́ния Kenya.
Ки́ев Kiev.
Кипр Cyprus.
Кирги́зская ССР the Kirghiz SSR.
Кита́й China.
Ки́то Quito.
Кишинёв Kishinev.
Коло́мбо Colombo.
Ко́льский полуо́стров the Kola Peninsula.
Ко́ми АССР the Komi ASSR.
Ко́нго the Congo; the Congo River.
Копенга́ген Copenhagen.
Кордилье́ры (-е́р) the Cordilleras.
Кра́сное мо́ре the Red Sea.
Крит Crete.
Крым the Crimea.
Куве́йт Kuwait.
Кузба́сс the Kuznetsk Basin.

Лаго́с Lagos.
Ла́дожское о́зеро Lake Ladoga.
Ла-Ма́нш the English Channel.
Лао́с Laos.
Латви́йская ССР the Latvian SSR.
Лахо́р Lahore.
Ле́йпциг Leipzig.
Ле́на the Lena.
Лива́н the Lebanon.
Ливерпу́ль (m.) Liverpool.
Ли́вия Libya.
Лидс Leeds.
Лисабо́н Lisbon.

Лито́вская ССР the Lithuanian SSR.
Лихтенште́йн Liechtenstein.
Ло́ндон London.
Лос-А́нжелес Los Angeles.
Лотари́нгия Lorraine.
Лофоте́нские острова́ the Lofoten Islands.
Льеж Liège.
Люксембу́рг Luxembourg.

Магелла́нов проли́в the Straits of Magellan.
Мадагаска́р Madagascar.
Македо́ния Macedonia.
Мала́ви Malawi.
Мала́йзия Malaysia.
Мала́йя Malaya.
Ма́лая А́зия Asia Minor.
Манче́стер Manchester.
Мари́йская АССР the Mari ASSR.
Марсе́ль (m.) Marseilles.
Ме́ксика Mexico.
Ме́льбурн Melbourne.
Мёртвое мо́ре the Dead Sea.
Ме́хико Mexico City.
Миссиси́пи the Mississippi.
Молда́вская ССР the Moldavian SSR.
Мона́ко Monaco.
Монбла́н Mont Blanc.
Монго́лия Mongolia.
Монреа́ль (m.) Montreal.
Мордо́вская АССР the Mordovian ASSR.
Москва́ Moscow.
Му́рманск Murmansk.
Мыс До́брой Наде́жды the Cape of Good Hope.
Мю́нхен Munich.

Найро́би Nairobi.
Нахичева́нская АССР the Nakhichevan ASSR.
Неа́поль (m.) Naples.
Нева́ the Neva.
Не́ман the Niemen.
Ниге́рия Nigeria.
Нидерла́нды (-ов) the Netherlands.
Никози́я Nicosia.
Нил the Nile.
Ни́цца Nice.
Но́вая Зела́ндия New Zealand.
Но́вая Земля́ Novaya Zemlya.
Но́вый Орлеа́н New Orleans.
Норве́гия Norway.
Но́ридж Norwich.

Но́ттингем Nottingham.
Нью-Йо́рк New York.
Ньюка́сл Newcastle.
Ню́рнберг Nuremberg.

Объединённая Ара́бская Респу́блика the United Arab Republic.
Обь (f.) the Ob.
О́гненная Земля́ Tierra del Fuego.
О́ксфорд Oxford.
О́лстер Ulster.
Оне́жское о́зеро Lake Onega.
Оркне́йские острова́ the Orkneys.
О́сло Oslo.
Отта́ва Ottawa.
Охо́тское мо́ре the Sea of Okhotsk.

Па-де-Кале́ the Straits of Dover.
Пакиста́н Pakistan.
Палести́на Palestine.
Пами́р Pamirs.
Пана́ма Panama; Пана́мский кана́л the Panama Canal.
Пенджа́б the Punjab.
Парагва́й Paraguay.
Пари́ж Paris.
Пеки́н Peking.
Пе́ру Peru.
Пире́й Piraeus.
Пирене́и (-е́ев) the Pyrenees.
Пли́мут Plymouth.
По́льша Poland.
Порт-Саи́д Port Said.
По́ртсмут Portsmouth.
Португа́лия Portugal.
Пра́га Prague.
Пхенья́н Pyongyang.

Рейкья́вик Reykjavik.
Рейн the Rhine.
Ри́жский зали́в the Gulf of Riga.
Рим Rome.
Роде́зия Rhodesia.
Ро́дос Rhodes.
Ро́на the Rhone.
Росси́йская Сове́тская Федерати́вная Социалисти́ческая Респу́блика the Russian Soviet Federated Socialist Republic.
Росси́я Russia.
Роттерда́м Rotterdam.
Румы́ния Rumania.
Рур the Ruhr.

Саа́р the Saar.
Саксо́ния Saxony.
Сан-Франци́ско San Francisco.

Саўдовская Арабия Saudi Arabia.
Саутгемптон Southampton.
Сахалин Sakhalin.
Сахара the Sahara.
река Святого Лаврентия the St. Lawrence.
остров Святой Елены St. Helena.
Севастополь *(m.)* Sebastopol.
Северное море the North Sea.
Северный Ледовитый океан the Arctic Ocean.
Северо-Осетинская АССР the North Ossetian ASSR.
Сена the Seine.
Сибирь *(f.)* Siberia.
Сидней Sidney.
Сингапур Singapore.
Синцзян Sinkiang.
Сицилия Sicily.
Скалистые горы the Rocky Mountains.
Соединённое Королевство Великобритании и Северной Ирландии the United Kingdom of Great Britain and N. Ireland.
Соединённые Штаты Америки the United States of America.
Соломоновы острова the Solomon Islands.
Солсбери Salisbury.
Сомали Somaliland.
София Sofia.
Союз Советских Социалистических Республик the Union of Soviet Socialist Republics.
Средиземное море the Mediterranean Sea.
Стамбул Istanbul.
Стокгольм Stockholm.
Страсбург Strasbourg.
Суонси Swansea.
Суэцкий канал the Suez Canal.
Сьерра Леоне Sierra Leone.

Таджикская ССР the Tajik SSR.
Таиланд Thailand.
Тайвань Taiwan.
Танганьика Tanganyika.
Танжер Tangier.
Танзания Tanzania.
Тасмания Tasmania.
Татарская АССР the Tatar ASSR.
Тегеран Teheran.
Тель-Авив Tel-Aviv.
Темза the Thames.
Тибр the Tiber.
Тигр the Tigris.

Тироль *(m.)* the Tyrol.
Тихий океан the Pacific Ocean.
Тувинская АССР the Tuva ASSR.
Тунис 1. Tunis; 2. Tunisia.
Туркменская ССР the Turkmen SSR.
Турция Turkey.

остров Уайт the Isle of Wight.
Уганда Uganda.
Удмуртская АССР the Udmurt ASSR.
Узбекская ССР the Uzbek SSR.
Украинская ССР the Ukrainian SSR.
Урал the Urals.
Уругвай Uruguay.
Уэльс Wales.

Фарерские острова the Faeroes.
острова Фиджи the Fiji Islands.
Филиппинские острова the Philippines.
Финляндия Finland; Финский залив the Gulf of Finland.
Фолклендские острова the Falkland Islands.
Формоза Formosa.
Франция France.

Хайдарабад Hyderabad.
Ханой Hanoi.
Хартум Khartoum.
Хельсинки Helsinki.
Хиросима Hiroshima.
Хорватия Croatia.

Цейлон Ceylon.
Цюрих Zurich.

Чёрное море the Black Sea.
Чехословакия Czechoslovakia.
Чечено-Ингушская АССР the Chechen-Ingush ASSR.
Чили Chile.
Чувашская АССР the Chuvash ASSR.
Чудское озеро Lake Chud.

Шанхай Shanghai.
Швейцария Switzerland.
Швеция Sweden.
Шербур Cherbourg.
Шетландские острова the Shetlands.
Шеффилд Sheffield.
Шотландия Scotland.

Эвере́ст Everest.
Эге́йское мо́ре the Aegean Sea.
Эдинбу́рг Edinburgh.
Эксетер Exeter.
о́стров Эльба Elba.
Эльза́с Alsace.
о́зеро Эри Lake Erie.
Эсто́нская ССР the Estonian SSR.
Эфио́пия Ethiopia.

Югосла́вия Yugoslavia.

Ю́жно-Африка́нская Респу́блика the Republic of South Africa.
Юра́ the Jura Mountains.
Ютла́ндский полуо́стров Jutland.

Ява Java.
Яку́тская АССР the Yakut ASSR.
Ялта Yalta.
Яма́йка Jamaica.
Япо́ния Japan; Япо́нское мо́ре the Sea of Japan.

ENGLISH—RUSSIAN

A

A, a: *from A to Z* от а до зет, от начáла до концá.

a, an *indefinite article: no equivalent in Russian.*

aback, *ad: taken* ~ смущённый, застигнутый врасплóх.

abacus, *n,* счёты.

abaft, *ad,* на кормé, в стóрону кормы́; ¶ *pr,* позади́.

abandon, *v.t,* оставля́ть, покидáть; бросáть; ~ *oneself to* предавáться *(dat.);* ¶ *n,* непринуждённость; ~ed, *p. p. & a,* (за)брóшенный, поки́нутый; распýтный; ~ment *n,* оставлéние.

abase, *v.t,* унижáть; ~ment, *n,* унижéние.

abate, *v.t,* уменьшáть, смягчáть; *v.i,* уменьшáться; ослабевáть; утихáть *(of storm);* успокáиваться *(of anger);* ~ment, *n,* уменьшéние; смягчéние; сниже́ние.

abattoir, *n,* скотобóйня.

abbess, *n,* настоя́тельница монастыря́; **abbey,** *n,* аббáтство; **abbot,** *n,* аббáт.

abbreviate, *v.t,* сокращáть; **abbreviation,** *n,* сокращéние.

abdicate, *v.t,* отказываться (от прáва); отрекáться (от престóла); **abdication,** *n,* отречéние от престóла; откáз.

abdomen, *n,* брюшнáя пóлость; живóт; **abdominal,** *a,* брюшнóй.

abduct, *v.t,* похищáть; ~ion, *n,* похищéние; ~or, *n,* похити́тель.

abed, *ad,* в посте́ли.

aberration, *n,* заблуждéние; отклонéние от нормáльного ти́па; аберрáция.

abet, *v.t,* поощря́ть; содéйствовать *(dat.);* подстрекáть.

abeyance, *n,* врéменное бездéйствие; врéменная отмéна.

abhor, *v.t,* ненави́деть; **abhorrence,** *n,* отвращéние; **abhorrent,** *a,* отврати́тельный.

abide, *v.i,* пребывáть, жить; *v.t,* выноси́ть, терпéть; **abiding,** *a,* постоя́нный.

ability, *n,* спосóбность; умéние.

abject, *a,* жáлкий, ни́зкий; ~ion, *n,* унижéние.

abjuration, *n,* отречéние, откáз; **abjure,** *v.t,* откáзываться/отрекáться от.

ablaze, *a,* в огнé; *(fig.)* сверкáющий; возбуждённый.

able, *a,* спосóбный; умéлый; be ~ мочь, умéть, быть в состоя́нии; ~-bodied, *a,* работоспосóбный; здорóвый; крéпкий; **ably,** *ad,* умéло.

abnegation, *n,* откáз, отречéние.

abnormal, *a,* ненормáльный.

aboard, *ad,* на бортý; на борт.

abode, *n,* жили́ще, местопребывáние; *take up one's* ~ поселя́ться.

abolish, *v.t,* отменя́ть, упраздня́ть; **abolition,** *n,* отмéна, упразднéние.

abominable, *a,* отврати́тельный, проти́вный; **abominate,** *v.t,* ненави́деть; **abomination,** *n,* отвращéние; что-то отврати́тельное.

aboriginal, *a,* тузéмный, кореннóй; ¶ *n,* тузéмец, кореннóй жи́тель.

abort, *v.i,* преждеврéменно разрешáться от брéмени; ~ion, *n,* абóрт; вы́кидыш; ~ive, *a,* преждеврéменный; неудáвшийся.

abound, *v.i,* изоби́ловать; кишéть.

about, *pr,* о, относи́тельно; óколо; по; вокрýг, кругóм; ¶ *ad,* прибли́зительно, óколо; недалекó; вокрýг, кругóм; *be* ~ *to* собирáться *(+ inf).*

above, *pr,* над; бóлее, вы́ше, свы́ше; ¶ *ad,* наверхý, навéрх; вы́ше; *from* ~ свéрху; ~ *all* прéжде всегó.

abrade, *v.t,* стирáть, сдирáть; **abrasion,** *n,* ссáдина; стирáние; шлифóвка; **abrasive,** *n,* абрази́вный/шлифовáльный материáл.

abreast, *ad,* в ряд; на ýровне; *keep* ~ *of* идти́ в нóгу с

abridge, *v.t,* сокращáть; ограни́чивать; ~ment, *n,* сокращéние, ограничéние.

abroad, *ad,* за грани́цей; за грани́цу; вне дóма; повсю́ду; *from* ~ из-за грани́цы; *there is a rumour* ~ хóдит слух.

abrogate, *v.t*, отменя́ть; abrogation, *n*, отме́на.

abrupt, *a*, отры́вистый; внеза́пный; круто́й, обры́вистый; ре́зкий *(manner)*; ~ness, *n*, отры́вистость; крутизна́; ре́зкость; внеза́пность.

abscess, *n*, нары́в, гнойни́к.

abscond, *v.i*, скрыва́ться.

absence, *n*, отсу́тствие; недоста́ток, неиме́ние; absent, *a*, & absentee, *n*, отсу́тствующий; absenteeism, *n*, абсентеи́зм; нея́вка на рабо́ту, прогу́л; absent-minded, *a*, рассе́янный.

absinth, *n*, абсе́нт.

absolute, *a*, по́лный, соверше́нный; чи́стый; неограни́ченный; абсолю́тный; ¶ *n*, абсолю́т; ~ly, *ad*, соверше́нно, абсолю́тно.

absolution, *n*, проще́ние; освобожде́ние; отпуще́ние грехо́в.

absolutism, *n*, абсолюти́зм.

absolve, *v.t*, освобожда́ть; проща́ть; отпуска́ть.

absorb, *v.t*, поглоща́ть, впи́тывать, вса́сывать; увлека́ть; absorbent, & absorbing, *a*, поглоща́ющий; *(fig.)* увлека́тельный; absorption, *n*, поглоще́ние, впи́тывание; погружённость.

abstain, *v.i*, возде́рживаться; abstemious, *a*, возде́ржанный; уме́ренный; трёзвый; abstention, *n*, воздержа́ние; уклоне́ние; abstinence, *n*, воздержа́ние; уме́ренность; abstinent, *a*, возде́ржанный, уме́ренный.

abstract, *a*, абстра́ктный, отвлечённый; ¶ *n*, конспе́кт; резюме́; ¶ *v.t*, извлека́ть; абстраги́ровать; резюми́ровать; ~ed, *a*, рассе́янный, заду́мчивый; ~ion, *n*, извлече́ние; абстра́кция, отвлечённость; рассе́янность.

abstruse, *a*, тру́дный (для понима́ния), глубо́кий.

absurd, *a*, неле́пый, абсу́рдный; ~ity, *n*, неле́пость, абсу́рд.

abundance, *n*, изоби́лие, бога́тство; abundant, *a*, оби́льный, бога́тый.

abuse, *n*, брань; злоупотребле́ние; ¶ *v.t*, брани́ть; злоупотребля́ть *(inst)*; abusive, *a*, бра́нный, оскорби́тельный.

abut, *v.i*, грани́чить, примыка́ть.

abysmal, *a*, бездо́нный; abyss, *n*, бе́здна, про́пасть.

acacia, *n*, ака́ция.

academic, *a*, академи́ческий; ака-

демти́чный; ~ian, *n*, акаде́мик;

academy, *n*, акаде́мия.

accede, *v.i*, соглаша́ться; вступа́ть.

accelerate, *v.t*. *(& i)*, ускоря́ть(ся); acceleration, *n*, ускоре́ние; accelerator, *n*, ускори́тель.

accent, *n*, ударе́ние; акце́нт; accentuate, *v.t*, подчёркивать; де́лать ударе́ние на; accentuation, *n*, ударе́ние; подчёркивание; произноше́ние.

accept, *v.t*, принима́ть; соглаша́ться с, допуска́ть; ~able, *a*, прие́млемый, допусти́мый; ~ance, *n*, приня́тие, приём; одобре́ние; ~ed, *a*, общепри́нятый, распространённый.

access, *n*, до́ступ; подхо́д; при́ступ (боле́зни); ~ary, *n*, помо́щник, соуча́стник; ¶ *a*, дополни́тельный, вспомога́тельный; ~ible, *a*, досту́пный, достижи́мый; пода́тливый; ~ion, *n*, вступле́ние (на престо́л); прирост; согла́сие; припа̂ок; ~ories, принадле́жности; ~ory, *a*, дополни́тельный, по о́чи й.

accidence, *n*, морфоло́гия.

accident, *n*, несча́стный слу́чай, ава́рия; слу́чай, случа́йность; ~al, *a*, случа́йныи; ~ally, *ad*, случа́йно.

acclaim, *v.t*, приве́тствовать; аплоди́ровать *(dat)*; провозглаша́ть; acclamation, *n*, шу́мное одобре́ние; ова́ция.

acclimatization, *n*, акклиматиза́ция; acclimatize, *v. t*, *(& i)*, акклиматизи́ровать(ся).

acclivity, *n*, склон, подъём.

accolade, *n*, обря́д посвяще́ния в ры́цари.

accommodate, *v.t*, предоставля́ть помеще́ние *(dat.)*; помеща́ть; ока́зывать услу́гу *(dat.)*; accommodating, *a*, услу́жливый; вмеща́ющий; accommodation, *n*, помеще́ние; жильё.

accompaniment, *n*, сопровожде́ние; аккомпанеме́нт; accompanist, *n*, аккомпаниа́тор; accompany, *v.t*, сопровожда́ть; аккомпани́ровать *(dat.)*.

accomplice, *n*, соуча́стник.

accomplish, *v.t*, заверша́ть; выполч ня́ть, исполня́ть; ~ed, *a*, соверше́нный; превосхо́дный; зако́н ченный; ~ment, *n*, заверше́ниедостижение; *pl*, образо́ванность; досто́инства.

accord, *n*, согла́сие; соглаше́ние; соотве́тствие; акко́рд; ¶ *v.i*, соотве́тствовать, гармони́ровать; *v.t*, ока́зывать; ~ance, *n*, согла́сие, соотве́тствие; *in* ~*ance with* в соотве́тствии с; ~ing to согла́сно *(dat.)*; ~ingly, *ad*, соотве́тственно.

accordion, *n*, аккордео́н, гармо́ника.

accost, *v.t*, загова́ривать с; пристава́ть к.

account, *n*, счёт; расчёт; отчёт; *settle an* ~ своди́ть счёты; *take into* ~ учи́тывать, принима́ть во внима́ние; *call to* ~ призыва́ть к отве́ту; *on* ~ *of* по причи́не, из-за; *on no* ~ ни в ко́ем слу́чае; *turn to* ~ испо́льзовать; ¶ *v.t*, счита́ть; ~ *for* объясня́ть; отчи́тываться в; ~ancy, *n*, счетово́дство; ~ant, *n*, бухга́лтер; ~ing, *n*, расчёт; учёт; *cost* ~ калькуля́ция сто́имости.

accoutrement, *n*, снаряже́ние.

accredit, *v.t*, аккредитова́ть, уполномо́чивать; ~ed, *p.p. & a*, аккредито́ванный.

accretion, *n*, разраста́ние, сраста́ние, прираще́ние.

accrue, *v.i*, достава́ться, выпада́ть на до́лю; нараста́ть; происходи́ть.

accumulate, *v.t*, нако́пля́ть, *v.t*, скопля́ться; **accumulation**, *n*, накопле́ние, скопле́ние; **accumulative**, *a*, накопля́ющийся; **accumulator**, *n*, собира́тель; аккумуля́тор *(elec.)*.

accuracy, *n*, то́чность, аккура́тность; **accurate**, *a*, то́чный, аккура́тный.

accursed, *a*, прокля́тый.

accusation, *n*, обвине́ние; **accusative**, *n*, вини́тельный паде́ж; **accuse**, *v.t*, обвиня́ть; ~r, *n*, обвини́тель.

accustom, *v.t*, приуча́ть; ~ed, *p.p. & a*, привы́кший; обы́чный; *become* ~ привыка́ть.

ace, *n*, туз *(cards)*; ас; *within an* ~ *of* на волосо́к от.

acerbity, *n*, ре́зкость; те́рпкость.

acetylene, *n*, ацетиле́н.

ache, *n*, боль; ¶ *v.i*, боле́ть; ~ *for* жа́ждать *(gen.)*; *my head* ~s у меня́ боли́т голова́.

achieve, *v.t*, достига́ть *(gen.)*; успе́шно выполня́ть; ~ment, *n*,

достиже́ние; по́двиг; выполне́ние.

acid, *a*, ки́слый; кисло́тный; ¶ *n*, кислота́; **acidify**, *v.t*, окисля́ть; **acidity**, *n*, кисло́тность.

acknowledge, *v.t*, признава́ть; допуска́ть; подтвержда́ть получе́ние (письма́); ~ment, *n*, призна́ние; подтвержде́ние.

acme, *n*, вы́сшая то́чка.

acne, *n*, прыщ.

acolyte, *n*, служи́тель; после́дователь.

acorn, *n*, жёлудь.

acoustic, *a*, акусти́ческий, звуково́й; слухово́й; ~s, *n. pl*, аку́стика.

acquaint, *v.t*, знако́мить; осведомля́ть; ~ *oneself with* знако́миться с; *be* ~ *ed with* быть знако́мым с; ~ance, *n*, знако́мый; знако́мство.

acquiesce, *v.i*, соглаша́ться (мо́лча); **acquiescence**, *n*, согла́сие; поко́рность; **acquiescent**, *a*, поко́рный, пода́тливый.

acquire, *v.t*, приобрета́ть, получа́ть; овладева́ть *(inst.)*; ~ment, *n*, приобрете́ние; овладе́ние; позна́ние; **acquisition**, *a*, приобрете́ние; **acquisitive**, *a*, стяжа́тельный; восприи́мчивый.

acquit, *v.t*, опра́вдывать; освобожда́ть; выполня́ть; ~ *oneself well* хорошо́ справля́ться; **acquittal**, *n*, оправда́ние, освобожде́ние; **acquittance**, *n*, упла́та до́лга; распи́ска об упла́те.

acre, *n*, акр.

acrid, *a*, о́стрый, е́дкий; ре́зкий; ~ity, *n*, е́дкость; ре́зкость.

acrimonious, *a*, е́дкий, язви́тельный; раздражи́тельный; **acrimony**, *n*, е́дкость; жёлчность.

acrobat, *n*, акроба́т; ~ic, *a*, акробати́ческий; ~ics, *n*, акроба́тика.

across, *ad*, поперёк; на ту сто́рону; на той стороне́; крест-на́крест; ¶ *pr*, че́рез; *come* ~ встреча́ться с.

acrostic, *n*, акрости́х.

act, *n*, де́йствие, посту́пок, акт; постановле́ние; акт (пье́сы); ¶ *v.i*, поступа́ть, де́йствовать; *v.t* игра́ть (роль); ~ *on* влия́ть/ де́йствовать на; ~ing, *a*, де́йствующий; исполня́ющий обя́занности; ¶ *n*, игра́; **action**, *n*, посту́пок, де́йствие; суде́бный процесс; бой; ~able, *a*, дающий основание для судебного преследования.

active, *a*, активный, деятельный, энергичный; activity, *n*, деятельность, активность, энергия.

actor, *n*, актёр; actress, *n*, актриса.

actual, *a*, действительный, настоящий, текущий; ~ity, *n*, действительность, реальность; ~ly *ad*, на самом деле, фактически.

actuary, *n*, актуарий.

actuate, *v.t*, приводить в действие; побуждать.

acumen, *n*, проницательность.

acute, *a*, острый; проницательный; ~ness, *n*, острота; проницательность.

adage, *n*, пословица.

adamant, *a*, непреклонный; твёрдый.

Adam's apple адамово яблоко, кадык.

adapt, *v.t*, приспособлять; переделывать; ~able, *a*, легко приспособляемый/приспособляющийся; ~ation, *n*, приспособление, адаптация; переделка; ~er, *n*, адаптер *(tech.)*.

add, *v.t*, прибавлять; добавлять *(say)*; складывать *(maths)*; addendum, *n*, приложение.

adder, *n*, счётная машина; гадюка *(zool.)*.

addict, *n*, наркоман *(drug)*; ~ed, *a*: become ~ to предаваться *(dat.)*, пристраститься *(pf.)* к; ~ion, *n*, наркомания; склонность, пристрастие.

addition, *n*, прибавление, дополнение; сложение *(maths)*; ~al, *a*, добавочный, дополнительный.

addled, *a*, тухлый; путаный; addlepated, *a*, безмозглый, пустоголовый.

address, *n*, адрес; обращение, речь; ¶ *v.t*, адресовать; обращаться к; ~ a meeting выступать с речью на собрании; ~ee, *n*, адресат.

adduce, *v.t*, приводить.

adenoids, *n*, *pl*, аденоиды.

adept, *a*, ловкий, сведущий; ¶ *n*, эксперт.

adequacy, *n*, соразмерность, соответствие, адекватность; adequate, *a*, соразмерный, соответствующий, адекватный.

adhere, *v.i*, прилипать; держаться; adherence, *n*, верность, приверженность; adherent, *a*, вязкий, липкий; ¶ *n*, приверженец; adhesion, *n*, прилипание; верность (принципам, *etc.*); adhesive, *a*, клейкий, липкий.

adipose, *a*, жирный, сальный.

adjacent, *a*, примыкающий, соседний.

adjectival, *a*, в качестве прилагательного; adjective, *n*, имя прилагательное.

adjoin, *v.t*, присоединять; *v.i*, примыкать, прилегать; ~ing, *a*, соседний.

adjourn, *v.t*, откладывать, отсрочивать; объявлять перерыв (в работе); ~ment, *n*, отсрочка; перерыв.

adjudge, *v.t*, осуждать; присуждать *(prize)*.

adjudicate, *v.t*, выносить решение о; осуждать; *v.i*, решать.

adjunct, *n*, дополнение; помощник.

adjure, *v.t*, заклинать, умолять.

adjust, *v.t*, приспособлять; приводить в порядок; регулировать; ~ment, *n*, приспособление; регулирование; выверка.

adjutant, *n*, адъютант.

administer, *v.t*, управлять *(inst.)*; отправлять *(justice)*; давать; наносить *(blow')*; ~ an oath приводить к присяге; administration, *n*, управление; администрация; правительство; administrative, *a*, административный; administrator, *n*, администратор.

admirable, *a*, замечательный; похвальный; восхитительный.

admiral, *n*, адмирал; Admiralty, *n*, адмиралтейство, военно-морское министерство.

admiration, *n*, восхищение; admire, *v.t*, восхищаться/любоваться *(inst.)*; ~r, *n*, поклонник.

admissible, *a*, допустимый, приемлемый; admission, *n*, допущение; принятие; признание; доступ; вход; ticket of ~ входной билет; admit, *v.t*, впускать; допускать, признавать; принимать; admittance, *n*, вход, доступ; admittedly, *ad*, признаюсь; по общему признанию.

admixture, *n*, примесь, смесь.

admonish, *v.t,* убежда́ть; сове́товать *(dat.);* предостерега́ть; де́лать замеча́ние/вы́говор *(dat.).*

admonition, *n,* замеча́ние, вы́говор.

ado, *n,* шум, суета́, хло́поты.

adolescence, *n,* о́трочество, ю́ность; **adolescent,** *a,* ю́ношеский; ю́ный; ¶ *n,* ю́ноша; де́вушка; подро́сток.

adopt, *v.t,* усыновля́ть, удочеря́ть; принима́ть, усва́ивать; займствова́ть; **~ion,** *n,* усыновле́ние; приня́тие, усвое́ние; **~ive,** *a,* приёмный.

adorable, *a,* восхити́тельный; **adoration,** *n,* обожа́ние; поклоне́ние; **adore,** *v.t,* обожа́ть; поклоня́ться *(dat.);* **~r,** *n,* обожа́тель, покло́нник.

adorn, *v.t,* украша́ть; **~ment,** *n,* украше́ние.

adrift, *ad,* по тече́нию; *be ~* дрейфова́ть; *set ~* пуска́ть по тече́нию; *(fig.)* пуска́ть на самотёк; *set oneself ~ from* порыва́ть с; *turn ~* выгоня́ть; увольня́ть.

adroit, *a,* ло́вкий.

adulate, *v.t,* льсти́ть *(dat.),* низкопокло́нничать пе́ред; **adulation,** *n,* лесть, низкопокло́нство; **adulatory,** *a,* льсти́вый

adult, *a. & n,* взро́слый

adulterate, *v.t,* фальсифици́ровать; **adulteration,** *n,* фальсифика́ция, подде́лка.

adulterer, *n,* измени́вший жене́; измени́вшая му́жу; **adultery,** *n,* супру́жеская изме́на; прелюбоде́яние.

adumbrate, *v.t,* опи́сывать в о́бщих черта́х; предвеща́ть; затемня́ть.

advance, *n,* продвиже́ние, наступле́ние *(mil.);* прогре́сс, успе́х; ссу́да, ава́нс *(fin.); in ~* зара́нее, вперёд; ¶ *v.t,* продвига́ть; выдвига́ть *(theory);* плати́ть ава́нсом; повыша́ть; *v.i,* продвига́ться; де́лать успе́хи; **~guard** аванга́рд; **~d,** *a,* передово́й; ста́рший *(pupil);* продви́нутый; **~ment,** *n,* продвиже́ние; прогре́сс; повыше́ние.

advantage, *n,* преиму́щество, вы́года; *take ~ of* воспо́льзоваться *(inst.) (pf.); gain the ~* получа́ть преиму́щество, брать верх; **~ous,** *a,* вы́годный, благоприя́тный.

advent, *n,* прихо́д; вступле́ние, появле́ние; прише́ствие *(eccl.).*

adventitious, *a,* доба́вочный; побо́чный, случа́йный.

adventure, *n,* приключе́ние; риско́ванное предприя́тие; авантю́ра; ¶ *v.t,* рискова́ть *(inst.);* осме́ливаться на; *v.i,* осме́ливаться *(+ inf.);* ¶ *a,* приключе́нческий; **adventurer,** *n,* иска́тель приключе́ний; авантюри́ст; **adventurous,** *a,* сме́лый, предприи́мчивый; риско́ванный.

adverb, *n,* наре́чие; **~ial,** *a,* наре́чный.

adversary, *n,* проти́вник, сопе́рник; **adverse,** *a,* неблагоприя́тный; проти́вный *(wind);* **adversity,** *n,* бе́дствие, несча́стье.

advertise, *v.t,* реклами́ровать; де́лать объявле́ние о; **~ment,** *n,* рекла́ма; объявле́ние; **~r,** *n,* помеща́ющий объявле́ние; **advertising,** *n,* рекла́мное де́ло.

advice, *n,* сове́т; консульта́ция; извеще́ние; **advisable,** *a,* целесообра́зный; жела́тельный; **advise,** *v.t,* сове́товать *(dat.);* уведомля́ть; **advisedly,** *ad,* обду́манно, созна́тельно; **adviser,** *n,* сове́тник, сове́тчик; консульта́нт; **advisory,** *a,* совеща́тельный, консультати́вный.

advocacy, *n,* защи́та; пропага́нда; **advocate,** *n,* защи́тник, сторо́нник, адвока́т; ¶ *v.t,* защища́ть; отста́ивать; пропаганди́ровать.

adze, *n,* тесло́; струг; ¶ *v.t,* теса́ть.

aegis, *n,* эги́да.

aerate, *v.t,* гази́ровать; прове́тривать; **aeration,** *n,* гази́рование; прове́тривание.

aerial, *a,* возду́шный; эфи́рный; нереа́льный; ¶ *n,* анте́нна.

aerodrome, *n,* аэродро́м; **aeronautics,** *n,* авиа́ция, воздухопла́вание; аэронавтика; **aeroplane,** *n-*самолёт, аэропла́н.

aesthete, *n,* эсте́т; **aesthetic,** *a,* эсти́ческий; **~s,** *n,* эсте́тика.

afar, *ad,* далеко́, вдали́; *from ~* и́здали, издалека́.

affable, *a,* приве́тливый, любе́зный.

affair, *n,* де́ло; *love ~* рома́н; *have an ~ with* име́ть рома́н с.

affect, *v.t,* де́йствовать/влия́ть на; волнова́ть, тро́гать; затра́гивать *(interests);* **~** *ignorance* прикидываться незнающим; ~ation, n, притворство; жеманство; искусственность *(of style);* ~ed, *a* притворный; жеманный; искусственный; affection, n, привязанность, любовь; болезнь; ~ate, *a,* нежный.

affiance, n, доверие; обручение; ¶ *v.t,* давать *(dat.)* обещание при обручении; обручать, помолвить *(pf.);* ~d, *p.p. & a,* обрученный.

affidavit, n, письменное показание под присягой.

affiliate, *v.t,* присоединять в качестве филиала; принимать в члены; усыновлять; устанавливать отцовство *(gen.);* affiliation, n, присоединение; принятие в члены; усыновление; установление отцовства.

affinity, n, родство; родственность, сходство.

affirm, *v.t,* утверждать; подтверждать;~ation, n, утверждение; подтверждение; ~ative, *a,* утвердительный.

affix, *v.t,* прикреплять; приклеивать; прикладывать *(seal);* ¶ n, аффикс.

afflict, *v.t,* огорчать; причинять боль *(dat.);* ~ion, n, огорчение; несчастье.

affluence, n, изобилие, богатство; наплыв; приток; affluent, *a,* обильный, богатый; приливающий.

afford, *v.t,* позволять себе; предоставлять *(possibility);* доставлять *(pleasure); I can't ~ it* мне это не по карману.

afforest, *v.t,* засаживать лесом; ~ation, n, лесонасаждение, облесение.

affray, n, драка, скандал.

affront, n, оскорбление; ¶ *v.t,* оскорблять, бросать вызов *(dat.).*

Afghan, *a,* афганский; ¶ n, афган|ец, ~ка; афганский язык.

afield, *ad,* в поле; *far ~* далеко.

afire, *ad,* в огне; *set ~* поджигать.

afloat, *ad,* на воде; в ходу.

afoot, *ad,* пешком; в движении; *be ~* затеваться, готовиться.

aforesaid, *a,* вышесказанный.

aforethought, *a,* преднамеренный, умышленный.

afraid, *a,* испуганный; *be ~* бояться.

afresh, *ad,* снова, заново.

aft, *ad,* на корме.

after, *pr,* за *(behind);* после, по, за *(time);* по *(in the manner of)* ¶ *ad,* позади, сзади; позднее, потом; ¶ *a,* задний; *day ~ day* день за днём; *~ all* в конце концов; несмотря на; *take ~* походить на.

afterbirth, n, послед.

aftermath, n, последствия.

afternoon, n, время после полудня; *in the ~* днём, после полудня, после обеда.

aftertaste, n, остающийся привкус.

afterthought, n, запоздалая мысль; *it was an ~* это пришло мне в голову потом.

afterwards, *ad,* впоследствии, потом.

again, *ad,* ещё раз, опять, снова; *time and ~* то и дело, неоднократно.

against, *pr,* против; напротив; о, об; на; к; рядом с; *lean ~* прислоняться к; *knock ~* ударяться о; *run ~* наскакивать на; *~ a background of* на фоне *(gen.).*

agate, n, агат.

age, n, возраст; век, эпоха; *old ~* старость; *be of ~* быть совершеннолетним; *I haven't seen you for ~s* я целую вечность не видел вас; ¶ *v.t,* старить; *v.i,* стареть; ~d, *a,* пожилой; в возрасте...; *~ ten* десяти лет.

agency, n, агентство, бюро; орган; фактор; действие; деятельность; посредничество; *by the ~ of* через посредство.

agenda, n, повестка дня.

agent, n, агент; исполнитель; фактор; вещество *(chem.).*

agglomerate, *v.t,* собирать, скоплять; agglomeration, n, скопление.

agglutinate, *v.t,* склеивать; agglutination, n, склеивание; агглютинация *(philol.)*

aggrandize, *v.t,* увеличивать; повышать; возвеличивать, aggrandizement, n, увеличение; расширение; повышение.

aggravate, *v.t,* ухудшать, отягощать; обострять; aggravation, n, ухудшение; обострение.

aggregate, n, совокупность; агрегат; ¶ *a,* совокупный, общий; ¶ *v.t,* соединять; *v.i,* собираться.

aggression, n, агре́ссия; **aggressive**, a, агресси́вный; **aggressor**, n, агре́ссор.

aggrieve, v.t, огорча́ть.

aghast, a, поражённый у́жасом; ошеломлённый.

agile, a, прово́рный, живо́й; **agility**, n, прово́рство, жи́вость.

agitate, v.t, волнова́ть, возбужда́ть; меша́ть, взба́лтывать; v.i, агити́ровать (polit., etc.); **agitation**, n, волне́ние; разме́шивание, взба́лтывание; агита́ция; **agitator**, n, меша́лка; агита́тор.

aglow, a, пыла́ющий; раскалённый докрасна́.

agnostic, n, агно́стик; ~**ism**, n, агностици́зм.

ago, ad, тому́ наза́д: a week ~ неде́лю тому́ наза́д; long ~ давно́.

agog, a, в возбужде́нии.

agonize, v.t, му́чить; v.i, быть в аго́нии; му́читься; **agonizing**, a, мучи́тельный; **agony**, n, муче́ние, аго́ния.

agrarian, a, агра́рный.

agree, v.t, соглашо́вывать; v.i, соглаша́ться; уславливаться; соотве́тствовать; быть подходя́щим (food, climate); ~**able**, a, согла́сный; прия́тный; соотве́тствующий; ~**ment**, n, согла́сие; догово́р, соглаше́ние; согласова́ние (gram.).

agricultural, a, сельскохозя́йственный, земледе́льческий; **agriculture**, n, се́льское хозя́йство, земледе́лие; **agriculturist**, n, агроно́м.

aground, ad, на мели́; в затрудне́нии; run ~ сади́ться на мель; выбра́сывать на бе́рег.

ague, n, озно́б, маля́рия.

ahead, ad, вперёд, впереди́; ~ of time ра́ньше вре́мени; get ~ of опережа́ть.

aid, n, посо́бие, по́мощь; помо́щник; ¶ v.t, помога́ть (dat.).

aide-de-camp, n, адъюта́нт.

ail, v.t, беспоко́ить; причиня́ть боль/страда́ние (dat.); v.i, боле́ть; ~**ing**, a, больно́й; ~**ment**, n, боле́знь; неду́г.

aim, n, цель; наме́рение; прице́л; прице́ливание; ¶ v.t, наводи́ть (на цель); v.i, стреми́ться, намерева́ться; ~ at ме́тить/це́лить(ся) в; ~**less**, a, бесце́льный.

air, n, во́здух; атмосфе́ра; вид, нару́жность; мело́дия; ~**s** and graces жема́нство; ¶ a, возду́шный; ¶ v.t, прове́тривать; суши́ть; ~**borne** перевози́мый по во́здуху; находя́щийся в во́здухе; авиаде́сантный; ~ conditioning. кондициони́рование во́здуха; ~**craft** самолёт; ~**field** аэродро́м; ~**less** безвозду́шный; ду́шный; ~**line** авиали́ния; ~**liner** ре́йсовый/пассажи́рский самолёт; ~**mail** авиапо́чта; ~**man** лётчик; ~ pocket возду́шная я́ма; ~**port** аэропо́рт; ~**ship** дирижа́бль; ~ tight воздухонепроница́емый; ~ way возду́шная тра́сса; ~**worthy** го́дный к полёту; ~**y**, a, возду́шный, лёгкий; весёлый; ве́треный.

aisle, n, прохо́д; боково́й неф.

ajar, a, приоткры́тый.

akimbo, ad: with arms ~ подбоче́нясь.

akin, a, бли́зкий, ро́дственный, сродни́.

alabaster, n, алеба́стр, гипс.

alacrity, n, жи́вость, быстрота́; гото́вность, рве́ние.

alarm, n, трево́га; страх; raise ~ поднима́ть трево́гу; ~ burglar ~ сигнализа́ция; ¶ v.t, трево́жить; ~ clock, n, буди́льник; ~ ing, a, трево́жный.

alas, int, увы́.

albatross, n, альбатро́с.

albeit, c, хотя́.

albino, n, альбино́с.

album, n, альбо́м.

albumen, n, бело́к, альбуми́н.

alchemist, n, алхи́мик; **alchemy**, n, алхи́мия.

alcohol, n, алкого́ль, спирт; спиртны́е напи́тки; ~**ic**, a, алкого́льный; ¶ n, алкого́лик.

alcove, n, алько́в, ни́ша; бесе́дка.

alder, n ольха́.

alderman, n, ольдерме́н; член городско́го управле́ния/сове́та гра́фства.

ale, n, эль, пи́во; ~**house**, n, пивна́я.

alert, a, бди́тельный; прово́рный; ¶ n, трево́га; be on the ~ быть настороже́/наготове.

algebra, n, а́лгебра.

Algerian, a, алжи́рский; ¶ n, алжи́р|ец, -ка.

alias, n, вы́мышленное и́мя, про́звище; кли́чка; ¶ ad, ина́че (называ́емый).

alibi, *n,* а́либи.

alien, *a,* иностра́нный; чу́ждый; несво́йственный; ¶ *n,* иностра́н|ец, ~ка; ~**ate,** *v.t,* отчужда́ть; отвраща́ть; ~**ation,** *n,* отчужде́ние; умопомеша́тельство.

alight, *v.i,* сходи́ть, выса́живаться; спе́шиваться; спуска́ться; сади́ться *(of birds);* ¶ *a,* в огне́, зажжённый; освещённый.

align, *v.t,* ста́вить в ряд; выстра́ивать в ли́нию; выра́внивать; ~**ment,** *n,* выра́внивание, вы́верка; равне́ние, ли́ния стро́я.

alike, *a,* похо́жий, подо́бный; схо́жий; ¶ *ad,* то́чно так же; одина́ково.

alimentary, *a,* пищево́й, пита́тельный; ~ *canal* пищевари́тельный кана́л; **alimentation,** *n,* пита́ние, кормле́ние.

alimony, *n,* алиме́нты.

alive, *a,* живо́й, бо́дрый; ~ *with* киша́щий *(inst.).*

alkali, *n,* щёлочь; **alkaline,** *a,* щелочно́й.

all, *a,* весь, всё, вся; вся́кий ~ *the year round* кру́глый год; ~ *the better* тем лу́чше; ~ *the same* всё равно́; ~ *right* хорошо́, ла́дно; ¶ *n,* всё, все; це́лое; *after* ~ ведь; в конце́ концо́в; *at* ~ вообще́, совсе́м; *not at* ~ ниско́лько, ничу́ть; пожа́луйста, не́ за что; *in* ~ всего́; ¶ *ad,* по́лностью; вполне́; целико́м; ~ *over* повсю́ду; ~ *the world* по всему́ све́ту; ~ *around* круго́м.

allay, *v.t,* успока́ивать; ослабля́ть.

allegation, *n,* заявле́ние, утвержде́ние; **allege,** *v.t,* заявля́ть, утвержда́ть; **allegedly,** *ad,* я́кобы.

allegiance, *n,* ве́рность, пре́данность.

allegorical, *a,* аллегори́ческий, иносказа́тельный; **allegory,** *n,* аллего́рия.

allergic, *a,* аллерги́ческий; *be* ~ *to* име́ть аллерги́ю к, не выноси́ть; **allergy,** *n,* аллерги́я.

alleviate, *v.t,* облегча́ть, смягча́ть; **alleviation,** *n,* облегче́ние.

alley, *n,* алле́я; переу́лок; прохо́д.

alliance, *n,* сою́з; **allied,** *a,* сою́зный; бли́зкий, ро́дственный.

alligator, *n,* аллига́тор.

allocate, *v.t,* распределя́ть, назнача́ть; ассигнова́ть; **allocation,** *n,* распределе́ние, назначе́ние; ассигнова́ние.

allot, *v.t,* распределя́ть, раздава́ть; назнача́ть; отводи́ть; ~**ment,** *n,* распределе́ние, разда́ча; до́ля; уча́сток земли́, наде́л.

allow, *v.t,* позволя́ть, разреша́ть; допуска́ть, выдава́ть; ~ *for* учи́тывать, принима́ть во внима́ние; ~**ance,** *n,* позволе́ние, разреше́ние; допуще́ние; ски́дка; вы́дача; содержа́ние, паёк; посо́бие; де́ньги на расхо́ды; *make* ~*('s) for* принима́ть во внима́ние; де́лать ски́дку на; *family* ~ посо́бие многосеме́йным; *travelling* ~ де́ньги на доро́жные расхо́ды.

alloy, *n,* сплав; при́месь; ¶ *v.t,* сплавля́ть (metals); подме́шивать.

all-round, *a,* всесторо́нний.

allude, *v.i:* ~ *to* упомина́ть; намека́ть/ссыла́ться на.

allure, *v.t,* завлека́ть, зама́нивать; пленя́ть; ~**ment,** *n,* обольще́ние; прима́нка; **alluring,** *a,* соблазни́тельный, зама́нчивый.

allusion, *n,* намёк; ссы́лка; **allusive,** *a,* содержа́щий намёк; иносказа́тельный.

alluvial, *a,* аллювиа́льный, нано́сный; **alluvion, alluvium,** *n,* аллю́вий, нано́сные образова́ния.

ally, *n,* сою́зник; ¶ *v.t,* соединя́ть; ~ *oneself* соединя́ться, вступа́ть в сою́з.

almanac, *n,* альмана́х.

almighty, *a,* всемогу́щий.

almond, almond tree, *n,* минда́ль.

almost, *ad,* почти́, чуть не.

alms, *n,* ми́лостыня; ~*-house* бога́де́льня.

aloe, *n,* ало́э; *pl,* сабу́р.

aloft, *ad,* наверху́; наве́рх.

alone, *a,* оди́н; одино́кий; ¶ *ad,* то́лько; *let* ~ оставля́ть в поко́е; не говоря́ уже́ о.

along, *pr,* вдоль; по; ~ *the road* по доро́ге; ¶ *ad,* вперёд; с собо́й; *come* ~! идём!; *all* ~ всё вре́мя; ~*side* бок о́ бок, ря́дом.

aloof, *a,* отчуждённый; холо́дный, равноду́шный; ¶ *ad,* поо́даль, вдали́, в стороне́; *stand* ~ держа́ться в стороне́.

aloud, *ad,* вслух, гро́мко.

alphabet, *n,* алфави́т, а́збука; ~**ical,** *a,* алфави́тный.

Alpine, *a,* альпийский.

already, *ad,* уже́.

also, *ad,* та́кже, то́же.

altar, *n,* алта́рь.

alter, *v.t,* изменя́ть, переде́лывать; **~ation,** *n,* измене́ние, переме́на; переде́лка, перестро́йка.

altercate, *v.i,* ссо́риться; **altercation,** *n,* ссо́ра.

alternate, *a,* череду́ющийся, перемежа́ющийся; переме́нный; *on ~ days* че́рез день; ¶ *v.t. (& i.),* чередова́ть(ся); **alternation,** *n,* чередова́ние; **alternating,** *a,* перемежа́ющийся; переме́нный (ток); **alternative,** *a,* альтернати́вный; ¶ *n,* вы́бор, альтернати́ва.

although, *c,* хотя́; несмотря́ на то, что.

altitude, *n,* высота́.

altogether, *ad,* в це́лом, всецело, вполне́; соверше́нно; всего́.

alum, *n,* квасцы́.

aluminium, *n,* алюми́ний.

always, *ad,* всегда́.

amalgam, *n,* амальга́ма; смесь; **~ate,** *v.t. (& i.),* соединя́ть(ся); слива́ть(ся); **~ation,** *n,* слия́ние, амальгама́ция; смеше́ние; соедине́ние.

amanuensis, *n,* ли́чный секрета́рь.

amass, *v.t,* накопля́ть, собира́ть.

amateur, *n,* люби́тель; ¶ *a,* люби́тельский; **~ish,** *a,* дилета́нтский.

amatory, *a,* любо́вный.

amaze, *v.t,* удивля́ть, изумля́ть; **~ment,** *n,* удивле́ние, изумле́ние; **amazing,** *a,* удиви́тельный, изуми́тельный.

Amazon, *n,* амазо́нка.

ambassador, *n,* посо́л; посла́нец; **ambassadress,** *n,* жена́ посла́; же́нщина-посо́л, посла́нница.

amber, *n,* янта́рь; **ambergris,** *n,* а́мбра.

ambidextrous, *a,* одина́ково владе́ющий обе́ими рука́ми.

ambiguity, *n,* двусмы́сленность, неопределённость; **ambiguous,** *a,* двусмы́сленный, неопределённый.

ambit, *n,* сфе́ра; преде́лы.

ambition, *n,* честолю́бие; стремле́ние; **ambitious,** *a* честолюби́вый; сме́лый.

amble, *v.i,* идти́ и́ноходью *(horse);* проха́живаться.

ambrosia, *n,* амбро́зия; перга́.

ambulance, *n,* маши́на ско́рой по́мощи, ско́рая по́мощь; *air ~* санита́рный самолёт.

ambuscade, ambush, *n,* заса́да; *make an ~* устра́ивать заса́ду; **ambush,** *v.t,* напада́ть из заса́ды на.

ameliorate, *v.t,* улучша́ть; **amelioration,** *n,* улучше́ние; мелиора́ция.

amenable, *a,* отве́тственный; сгово́рчивый; поддаю́щийся.

amend, *v.t,* исправля́ть; **~ment,** *n,* исправле́ние (недоста́тков); попра́вка (к законопрое́кту, *etc.);* **~s,** *n,* возмеще́ние, компенса́ция; **make ~** загла́живать (вину́).

amenity, *n,* любе́зность; *pl.* удово́льствия, удо́бства.

amethyst, *n,* амети́ст.

amiability, *n,* любе́зность; дружелю́бие; **amiable,** *a,* любе́зный; дружелю́бный.

amicable, *a,* дру́жеский.

amid[st], *pr,* среди́, ме́жду.

amiss, *a. & ad,* не в поря́дке; нела́дно; *come ~* приходи́ть некста́ти; *take ~* обижа́ться.

ammonia, *n,* аммиа́к.

ammunition, *n,* боеприпа́сы.

amnesty, *n,* амни́стия.

among[st], *pr,* среди́, ме́жду.

amorous, *a,* влюбчивый; любо́вный.

amorphous, *a,* бесфо́рменный, амо́рфный.

amortization, *n,* амортиза́ция, погаше́ние; **amortize,** *v.t,* погаша́ть, амортизи́ровать.

amount, *n,* су́мма; коли́чество; ¶ *v.i:* **~** *to* составля́ть; равня́ться *(dat.);* быть равноси́льным/равнозна́чащим *(dat.).*

ampere, *n,* ампе́р.

amphibian, *n,* амфи́бия; **amphibious,** *a,* земново́дный.

amphitheatre, *n,* амфитеа́тр.

ample, *a,* доста́точный; оби́льный; обши́рный.

amplification, *n,* расшире́ние, увеличе́ние; усиле́ние; **amplifier,** *n,* усили́тель *(radio);* **amplify,** *v.t,* расширя́ть, увели́чивать; уси́ливать; **amplitude,** *n,* амплиту́да; полнота́; оби́лие; широта́.

amputate, *v.t,* ампути́ровать; **amputation,** *n,* ампута́ция.

amulet, *n,* амуле́т.

amuse, *v.t,* забавля́ть, развлека́ть; **~ment,** *n,* заба́ва, развлече́ние, увеселе́ние;*pl,*аттракцио́ны;**amusing,** *a,* заба́вный.

an, *indef. article: no equivalent in Russian.*

anachronism, *n,* анахрони́зм.

anaemia, *n,* анеми́я, малокро́вие; **anaemic,** *a,* анеми́чный, малокро́вный.

anagram, *n,* анагра́мма.

analogical, *a,* аналоги́ческий; **analogous,** *a,* аналоги́чный, схо́дный; **analogy,** *n,* анало́гия, схо́дство.

analyse, *v.t,* анализи́ровать; разлага́ть *(chem.);* разбира́ть *(gram.);* **analysis,** *n,* ана́лиз; разложе́ние; разбо́р; **analyst,** *n,* анали́тик; лабора́нт-хи́мик; **analytical,** *a,* аналити́ческий.

anarchic, *a,* анархи́ческий; **anarchist,** *n,* анархи́ст; **anarchy,** *n,* ана́рхия.

anathema, *n,* ана́фема.

anatomical, *a,* анатоми́ческий; **anatomy,** *n,* анато́мия.

ancestor, *n,* пре́док; **ancestral,** *a,* насле́дственный, родово́й; **ancestry,** *n,* пре́дки; происхожде́ние.

anchor, *n,* я́корь; ¶ *v.t,* ста́вить на я́корь; *v.i,* станови́ться на я́корь; **~age,** *n,* я́корная стоя́нка; порто́вый сбор; *(fig.)* прибе́жище.

anchorite, *n,* анахоре́т, отше́льник.

anchovy, *n,* анчо́ус.

ancient, *a,* дре́вний, анти́чный.

and, *c,* и; а; да.

anecdotal, *a,* анекдоти́ч|еский, -ный; **anecdote,** *n,* анекдо́т.

anemone, *n,* анемо́н.

anew, *ad,* сно́ва; за́ново.

angel, *n,* а́нгел; **~ic,** *a,* а́нгельский.

anger, *n,* гнев.

angle, *n,* у́гол; то́чка зре́ния; рыболо́вный крючо́к; ¶ *v.i,* уди́ть ры́бу; **~ for** напра́шиваться на; **~r,** *n,* рыболо́в; **angling,** *n,* ры́бная ло́вля.

Anglomania, *n,* англома́ния; **Anglophil[e],** *n,* англофи́л; **Anglophobe,** *n,* англофо́б; **Anglo-Saxon,** *n,* англоса́кс.

angrily, *ad,* серди́то; **angry,** *a,* серди́тый, гне́вный; *be* **~** *with* серди́ться на.

anguish, *n,* муче́ние, страда́ние, боль.

angular, *a,* углово́й; углова́тый.

aniline, *n,* анили́н.

animadversion, *n,* кри́тика, порица́ние; **animadvert,** *v.i,* критикова́ть, порица́ть.

animal, *a,* живо́тный; ¶ *n,* живо́тное.

animate, *v.t,* оживля́ть; вдохновля́ть; побужда́ть; **~d,** *p.p. & a,* оживлённый; бо́дрый; **~d cartoon(s)** мультиплика́ция; мультфи́льм; **animation,** *n,* оживле́ние.

animosity, *n,* вражде́бность, зло́ба; **animus,** *n,* неприя́знь; предубежде́ние.

aniseed, *n,* ани́с.

ankle, *n,* лоды́жка.

annals, *n,* анна́лы, ле́топись.

annex, *n,* приложе́ние; дополне́ние; пристро́йка, фли́гель; ¶ *v.t,* анекси́ровать; присоединя́ть; прилага́ть; **~ation,** *n,* анне́ксия; присоедине́ние.

annihilate, *v.t,* уничтожа́ть, истребля́ть; **annihilation,** *n,* уничтоже́ние.

anniversary, *n,* годовщи́на.

annotate, *v.t,* аннати́ровать; снабжа́ть примеча́ниями; **annotation,** *n,* аннота́ция; примеча́ние.

announce, *v.t,* объявля́ть, заявля́ть; докла́дывать (о прихо́де го́стя); **~ment,** *n,* объявле́ние, сообще́ние; **~r,** *n,* ди́ктор *(radio).*

annoy, *v.t,* досажда́ть *(dat.),* раздража́ть; **~ance,** *n,* доса́да, раздраже́ние; **~ing,** *a,* доса́дный.

annual, *a,* ежего́дный; годово́й; **annuitant,** *n,* получа́ющий ежего́дную ре́нту; **annuity,** *n,* ежего́дная ре́нта, ежего́дная пе́нсия.

annul, *v.t,* аннули́ровать, отменя́ть; **~ment,** *n,* аннули́рование, отме́на.

Annunciation, *n,* благове́щение.

anode, *n,* ано́д.

anodyne, *a,* болеутоля́ющий; ¶ *n,* болеутоля́ющее сре́дство.

anoint, *v.t,* нама́зывать; пома́зывать *(eccl.);* **~ed,** *n,* пома́занник.

anomalous, *a,* анома́льный, ненорма́льный; **anomaly,** *n,* анома́лия.

anon, *a,* сейча́с; ско́ро.

anonymous, *a,* анони́мный.

anorak, *n,* ку́ртка, анора́к.

another *a,* друго́й, ещё оди́н; *one* **~** друг дру́га, *etc.*

answer, *n,* отве́т; ¶ *v.t,* отвеча́ть *(dat.;* на); возража́ть (на обвине́ние); ~ *the bell* открыва́ть дверь на звоно́к; ~ *for* отвеча́ть за; руча́ться за; ~ *to (name)* отклика́ться на; ~ *back* дерзи́ть; ~able, *a*, отве́тственный.

ant, *n*, мураве́й.

antagonism, *n*, антагони́зм, вражда́; сопе́рничество; **antagonist**, *n*, антагони́ст, сопе́рник, проти́вник; **antagonize**, *v.t*, вызыва́ть вражду́/ антагони́зм у.

Antarctic, *a*, антаркти́ческий.

antecedent, *a*, предше́ствующий, пре-дыду́щий; ¶ *n*, предше́ствующее; пе́рвый член отноше́ния *(maths)*; *pl*, про́шлое.

antechamber, *n*, пере́дняя, прихо́жая.

antedate, *v.t*, дати́ровать за́дним число́м; предше́ствовать *(dat.)*.

antediluvian, *a*, допото́пный.

antelope, *n*, антило́па.

ante meridiem, *ad*, до полу́дня.

anterior, *a*, пере́дний; предше́ству-ющий.

ante-room, *n*, пере́дняя.

anthem, *n*, гимн; *national* ~ национа́льный/госуда́рственный гимн.

anthology, *n*, антоло́гия.

anthracite, *n*, антраци́т.

anthrax, *n*, сиби́рская я́зва.

anthropology, *n*, антрополо́гия.

anti-aircraft, *a*, противовозду́шный, зени́тный.

antibiotic, *n*, антибио́тик.

Antichrist, *n*, анти́христ.

anticipate, *v.t*, предви́деть; пред-чу́вствовать, ожида́ть; предвку-ша́ть; предупрежда́ть; де́лать ра́ньше вре́мени; **anticipation**, *n*, ожида́ние, предчу́вствие; пред-вкуше́ние.

anticlimax, *n*, паде́ние напряже́ния; упа́док, реа́кция.

antics, *n.pl*, ша́лости.

antidote, *n*, противоя́дие.

antifreeze, *n*, антифри́з.

antimony, *n*, сурьма́.

antipathetic, *a*, антипати́чный; **antipathy**, *n*, антипа́тия.

antipode, *n*, антипо́д; по́лная про-тивоположность.

antiquarian, antiquary, *n*, антиква́р, собира́тель дре́вностей; **antiquated**, *a*, старомо́дный, устаре́в-ший; **antique**, *a*, стари́нный; дре́вний; старомо́дный; ¶ *n*, антиква́рная вещь; **antiquity**, *n*,

дре́вность, старина́; *pl*, дре́в-ности.

antiseptic, *a*, антисепти́ческий; ¶ *n*, антисепти́ческое сре́дство.

antisubmarine, *a*, противолодо́ч-ный.

anti-tank. *a*, противота́нковый.

antithesis, *n*, антите́за, противопо-ло́жность.

antler, *n*, оле́ний рог.

anus, *n*, за́дний прохо́д.

anvil, *n*, накова́льня.

anxiety, *n*, беспоко́йство, трево́га; си́льное жела́ние; **anxious**, *a*, озабо́ченный, встрево́женный; беспоко́йный; трево́жный; *be* ~ *about* беспоко́иться о; *be* ~ *to* стра́стно жела́ть *(+ inf.).*

any, *a*, како́й-ли́бо, како́й-нибудь; любо́й, вся́кий; *have you* ~ *money?* есть ли у вас де́ньги?; *are you* ~ *better?* вам немно́го лу́чше?; ¶ *ad*, ско́лько-нибудь, не-ско́лько.

anybody, anyone, *pn*, кто́-нибудь, кто́-либо.

anyhow, *ad*, ка́к- нибудь; так и́ли ина́че; ко́е-ка́к; во вся́ком слу́-чае.

anything, *pn*, что́-нибудь, что́-либо; всё; ~ *but* далеко́ не, *if* ~ по-жа́луй.

anyway, *ad*, как уго́дно; во вся́ком слу́чае; как бы то ни́ было.

anywhere, *ad*, где́-нибудь, где́-либо; где́/куда́ уго́дно.

aorta, *n*, ао́рта.

apace, *n*, о́чень бы́стро.

apart, *ad*, отде́льно, в стороне́; в сто́рону; врозь; *joking* ~ шу́тки в сто́рону; ~ *from* кро́ме, не счита́я; *grow* ~ отдаля́ться друг от дру́га; *take* ~ разбира́ть на ча́сти.

apartheid, *n*, апарте́ид, ра́совая изоля́ция.

apartment, *n*, кварти́ра.

apathetic, *a*, безразли́чный, равно-ду́шный; **apathy**, *n*, безразли́чие, апа́тия.

ape, *n*, обезья́на; ¶ *v.t*, подража́ть *(dat.)*, обезья́нничать.

aperient, *n*, слаби́тельное.

aperture, *n*, отве́рстие, щель.

apex, *n*, верши́на; конёк кры́ши.

aphis, *n*, тля.

aphorism, *n*, афори́зм.

apiary, *n*, па́сека.

apiece, *ad*, на ка́ждого; за шту́ку; *he gave them 10 r.* ~ он дал им по деся́ти рубле́й.

apish, *a*, обезья́ний.

apocryphal, *a*, апокрифи́ческий; недостове́рный.

apogee, *n*, апоге́й.

apologetic, *a*, извиня́ющийся; примири́тельный; апологети́ческий; ~s, *n*, апологе́тика; apologize, *v.i*, извиня́ться; опра́вдываться; apologist, *n*, сторо́нник, апологе́т; apology, *n*, извине́ние; объясне́ние.

apoplectic, *a*, апоплекси́ческий; apoplexy, *n*, уда́р, парали́ч.

apostasy, *n*, отсту́пничество; apostate, *n*, отсту́пник; apostatize, *v.i*, отступа́ться.

apostle, *n*, апо́стол; apostolic[al], *a*, апо́стольский; па́пский.

apostrophe, *n*, апостро́ф; обраще́ние.

apothecary, *n*, апте́карь.

apotheosis, *n*, апофео́з.

appal, *v.t*, ужаса́ть; ~ling, *a*, ужа́сный, ужаса́ющий.

apparatus, *n*, аппара́т; прибо́р, инструме́нт; гимнасти́ческий снаря́д.

apparel, *n*, пла́тье, оде́жда; украше́ние на облаче́нии.

apparent, *a*, ви́димый, очеви́дный; я́вный; ~ly, *ad*, ви́димо, очеви́дно.

apparition, *n*, появле́ние; виде́ние; при́зрак.

appeal, *n*, призы́в, обраще́ние; про́сьба; привлека́тельность; апелля́ция *(law)*; ¶ *v.i*, апелли́ровать, обраща́ться, взыва́ть; подава́ть апелляцио́нную жа́лобу; привлека́ть.

appear, *v.i*, пока́зываться, появля́ться; выступа́ть (публи́чно); каза́ться; *he* ~*s to forget* ... он, ка́жется/по-ви́димому, забыва́ет ...; ~ance, *n*, появле́ние; вид, нару́жность; ви́димость.

appease, *v.t*, умиротворя́ть; успока́ивать; облегча́ть; ~ment, *n*, умиротворе́ние.

appellant, *n*, апелля́нт; appellation, *n*, и́мя, назва́ние.

append, *v.t*, приве́шивать; прибавля́ть, прилага́ть; ~age, *n*, прида́ток; приве́сок; приложе́ние; appendicitis, *n*, аппендици́т; ap-

pendix, *n*, аппе́ндикс; дополне́ние, приложе́ние.

appertain, *v.i*, принадлежа́ть, относи́ться.

appetite, *n*, аппети́т; скло́нность, влече́ние, потре́бность; appetizer, *n*, заку́ска; appetizing, *a*, аппети́тный; привлека́тельный.

applaud, *v.t*, аплоди́ровать *(dat.)*; одобря́ть; applause, *n*, аплодисме́нты; одобре́ние.

apple, *n*, я́блоко; ~ *of the eye* зени́ца о́ка; ~ *tree* я́блоня.

appliance, *n*, прибо́р; (пожа́рная) маши́на; примене́ние; applicable, *a*, примени́мый; подходя́щий; applicant, *n*, проси́тель; кандида́т; абитурие́нт *(in universities)*; application, *n*, заявле́ние, зая́вка; про́сьба; примене́ние; ~ *form* анке́та; apply, *v.t*, прилага́ть, прикла́дывать; применя́ть *(technique, etc.)*; *v.i*, обраща́ться *(to —* к) *(for —* за); ~ *for work* подава́ть заявле́ние на рабо́ту; ~ *oneself to* занима́ться *(inst.)*; принима́ться за.

appoint, *v.t*, назнача́ть; устра́ивать; снаряжа́ть; ~ment, *n*, назначе́ние; свида́ние; до́лжность.

apportion, *v.t*, распределя́ть, дели́ть; ~ment, *n*, распределе́ние.

apposite, *a*, уда́чный, уме́стный; apposition, *n*, прикла́дывание; приложе́ние.

appraise, *v.t*, оце́нивать; appraisal, *n*, оце́нка; appraiser, *n*, оце́нщик.

appreciable, *a*, заме́тный, ощути́мый; поддаю́щийся оце́нке; appreciate, *v.t*, оце́нивать; цени́ть; понима́ть; *v.i*, повыша́ться в це́нности; appreciation, *n*, оце́нка; понима́ние; призна́тельность; повыше́ние (це́нности); appreciative, *a*, призна́тельный.

apprehend, *v.t*, понима́ть; заде́рживать; опаса́ться *(gen.)*; apprehension, *n*, понима́ние; аре́ст; опасе́ние; apprehensive, *a*, по́лный стра́ха; восприи́мчивый.

apprentice, *n*, учени́к, подмасте́рье; ~ship, *n*, уче́ние, учени́чество.

apprise, *v.t*, извеща́ть, уведомля́ть.

approach, *v.t*, приближа́ться/подходи́ть к; обраща́ться к; де́лать предложе́ния *(dat.)*; ¶ *n*, приближе́ние; подхо́д; предложе́ние; ~able, *a*, досту́пный.

approbation, *n*, одобре́ние; согла́сие.

appropriate, *a*, сво́йственный; подходя́щий; ¶ *v.t*, присва́ивать; ассигнова́ть.

approval, *n*, одобре́ние; утвержде́ние; **approve**, *v.t*, одобря́ть; утвержда́ть; ~*d school* шко́ла для малоле́тних престу́пников.

approximate, *a*, приблизи́тельный; бли́зкий; ¶ *v.i*, приближа́ться; (почти́) соотве́тствовать; ~*ly*, *ad*, приблизи́тельно; **approximation**, *n*, приближе́ние; приблизи́тельная ци́фра.

apricot, *n*, абрико́с.

April, *n*, апре́ль; ¶ *a*, апре́льский.

apron, *n*, пере́дник, фа́ртук; площа́дка.

apropos, *ad*, кста́ти; по по́воду, относи́тельно.

apse, *n*, апси́да.

apt, *a*, скло́нный; подходя́щий; уда́чный; спосо́бный; **aptitude**, *n*, спосо́бность; скло́нность.

aqua fortis, *n*, концентри́рованная азо́тная кислота́.

aquarium, *n*, аква́риум.

aquatic, *a*, во́дный.

aqueduct, *n*, акведу́к.

aqueous, *a*, водяно́й, водяни́стый; осадочный *(geol.)*.

aquiline, *a*, орли́ный.

Arab, *n*, ара́б, ~ка; ара́бская ло́шадь; ¶ *a*, ара́бский; **arabesque**, *n*, арабе́ска; **Arabian**, *a*, ара́бский; **Arabic** *(language)*, *n*, ара́бский язы́к.

arable, *a*, па́хотный.

arbiter, *n*, арби́тр, трете́йский судья́; **arbitrary**, *a*, произво́льный, капри́зный; **arbitrate**, *v.t*, реша́ть трете́йским судо́м; **arbitration**, *n*, трете́йское реше́ние, арбитра́ж; **arbitrator**, *n*, арби́тр, трете́йский судья́.

arbor, *n*, *(tech.)* вал; де́рево.

arbour, *n*, бесе́дка.

arc, *n*, дуга́; ~ *lamp* дугова́я ла́мпа.

arcade, *n*, пасса́ж (с магази́нами); арка́да.

arch, *n*, а́рка; свод; дуга́; ¶ *v.t*, перекрыва́ть а́ркой; изгиба́ть (дуго́й); *v.i*, изгиба́ться; ¶ *a*, лука́вый; пе́рвый.

archaeological, *a*, археологи́ческий; **archaeologist**, *n*, архео́лог; **archaeology**, *n*, археоло́гия.

archaic, *a*, устаре́лый, архаи́ческий; **archaism**, *n*, архаи́зм, устаре́вшее выраже́ние/сло́во.

archangel, *n*, арха́нгел.

archbishop, *n*, архиепи́скоп; ~**ric**, *n*, архиепи́скопство.

archdeacon, *n*, архидиа́кон.

archduchess, *n*, эрцгерцоги́ня; **archduke**, *n*, эрцге́рцог.

arched, *a*, сво́дчатый; изо́гнутый.

archer, *n*, стрело́к из лу́ка; ~**y**, *n*, стрельба́ из лу́ка.

archipelago, *n*, архипела́г.

architect, *n*, архите́ктор; **architectural**, *a*, архитекту́рный; **architecture**, *n*, архитекту́ра.

archives, *n pl*, архи́в; **archivist**, *n*, архива́риус.

archway, *n*, прохо́д под а́ркой.

Arctic, *a*, аркти́ческий; ¶ *n*, А́рктика; ~ *Circle* Се́верный поля́рный круг.

ardent, *a*, горя́чий, пы́лкий; **ardour**, *n*, жар, пыл, рве́ние.

arduous, *a*, тру́дный.

area, *n*, пло́щадь; райо́н, зо́на.

argue, *v.t*, дока́зывать; обсужда́ть; аргументи́ровать; приводи́ть до́воды в по́льзу/про́тив; *v.i*, спо́рить; **argument**, *n*, спор; до́вод, аргуме́нт; ~**ation**, *n*, аргумента́ция; ~**ative**, *n*, люба́щий спо́рить.

arid, *a*, сухо́й, засу́шливый; беспло́дный; ~**ity**, *n*, су́хость.

aright, *ad*, пра́вильно.

arise, *v.i*, возника́ть; появля́ться; происходи́ть; встава́ть.

aristocracy, *n*, аристокра́тия; **aristocrat**, *n*, аристокра́т; ~**ic**, *a*, аристократи́ческий.

arithmetic, *n*, арифме́тика; ~**al**, *a*, арифмети́ческий; ~**ian**, *n*, арифме́тик.

ark, *n*, ковче́г; я́щик; *Noah's* ~ но́ев ковче́г.

arm, *n*, рука́; ру́чка (кре́сла); рука́в; ору́жие; ~ *in* ~ под руку; ¶ *v.t.* (& *i.*), вооружа́ть(ся); ~*chair* кре́сло; ~*ful* оха́пка; ~*-hole* про́йма; ~*less* безру́кий; ~*pit* подмы́шка.

armada, *n*, арма́да.

armament, *n*, вооруже́ние.

armistice, *n*, переми́рие.

armorial, *a*, ге́рбовый.

armour, *n*, броня́; бронеси́лы; вооруже́ние; доспе́хи; па́нцирь;

a, броневóй; ~ed, *a*, бронирóванный; ~er, *n*, оружéйник; ~y, *n*, склад орýжия, арсенáл, оружéйный завóд; вооружéние.

army, *n*, áрмия; ¶ *a*, армéйский; *join the* ~ вступáть в áрмию, поступáть на воéнную слýжбу.

aroma, *n*, аромáт, зáпах; ~tic, *a*, аромáт|ный; ~йческий, -йчный.

around, *pr*, вокрýг; за; óколо; по; ~ *the corner* за углóм; *walk* ~ *the town* гулять по гóроду; ¶ *ad*, всюду; кругóм ~ *here* неподалёку.

arouse, *v.t*, будйть; вызывáть, возбуждáть; пробуждáть.

arraign, *v.t*, обвинять, привлекáть к судý; ~ment, *n*, привлечéние к судý, обвинéние.

arrange, *v.t*, устрáивать; приводйть в порядок; договáриваться о; аранжйровать *(mus.)*; ~ment, *n*, устрóйство; приготовлéние; расположéние; приведéние в порядок; соглашéние; *(mus.)* аранжирóвка.

arrant, *a*, отъявленный, сýщий, ~ *nonsense* сýщий вздор.

array, *n*, (боевóй) порядок, строй; мáсса, мнóжество; наряд; ¶ *v.t*, выстрáивать; наряжáть, украшáть.

arrears, *n.pl*, задóлженность (по налóгам); недоймки; *be in* ~ имéть задóлженность.

arrest, *n*, арéст; задéржка, останóвка; ¶ *v.t*, арестóвывать; задéрживать, останáвливать; прикóвывать *(attention)*.

arrival, *n*, прибытие, приéзд; вновь прибывший; новорождённый; **arrive**, *v.i*, прибывáть, приезжáть, приходйть; наступáть.

arrogance, *n*, высокомéрие, надмéнность; **arrogant**, *a*, высокомéрный, надмéнный; **arrogate**, *v.t*, самонадéянно трéбовать, претендовáть на; без основáния приписывать.

arrow, *n*, стрелá.

arsenal, *n*, арсенáл.

arsenic, *n*, мышьяк; ~al, *a*, мышьякóвый.

arson, *n*, поджóг.

art, *n*, искýсство; ремеслó; умéние, лóвкость; *Faculty of Arts* гуманитáрный факультéт; ¶ *a*, худóжественный.

arterial, *a*, артериáльный; магистрáльный; ~ *road* магистрáль; **artery**, *n*, артéрия.

artesian well артезиáнский колóдец.

artful, *a*, хйтрый, лóвкий.

artichoke, *n*, артишóк.

article, *n*, статья; пункт; предмéт; член, артйкль *(gram.)*; ¶ *v.t*, отдавáть в учéние по контрáкту; предъявлять пýнкты (обвинéния).

articulate, *a*, ясный; членйстый; ¶ *v.t*, соединять; произносйть отчётливо; ~d, *p.p. & a*, шарнйрный; сочленённый; артикулйрованный; **articulation**, *n*, сочленéние; членораздéльное произношéние; артикуляция.

artifice, *n*, выдумка; продéлка; лóвкость; ~r, *n*, тéхник; ремéсленник; **artificial**, *a*, искýсственный.

Aryan, *n*, арй|ец, -йка; *a*, арййский.

artillery, *n*, артиллéрия; ~man, *n*, артиллерйст.

artisan, *n*, ремéсленник.

artist, *n*, худóжник; мáстер; артйст; ~ic, *a*, худóжественный, артистйческий.

artless, *a*, простóй, простодýшный.

as, *ad*, как, в кáчестве; ~ ... ~ ... так же ... как; ~ *far* ~ до; так далекó; ~ *for me* что касáется меня; ~ *far* ~ *I know* наскóлько мне извéстно; ~ *good* ~ всё равнó, что; ~ *much* ~ *you like* скóлько хотйте; ~ *well* тáкже; ¶ *c*, когдá; в то врéмя как; так как; как ни; ~ *if* как бýдто; ¶ *pr*, какóй, котóрый; что.

asbestos, *n*, асбéст.

ascend, *v.i*, подниматься, в(о)сходйть; *v.t*, поднимáться на; ~ancy, ~ency, *n*, превосхóдство; власть; госпóдство; ~ant, ~ent, *n*, восхождéние; преобладáние; *his star is in the* ~ его звездá восхóдит; ¶ *a*, восходящий; преобладáющий, госпóдствующий; **ascension**, *n*, восхождéние; подъём; *A~ Day* вознесéние; **ascent**, *n*, подъём, восхождéние.

ascertain, *v.t*, устанáвливать; выяснять.

ascetic, *a*, аскетйческий; ¶ *n*, аскéт; ~ism, *n*, аскетйзм.

ascribe, *v.t*, приписывать.

aseptic, *a*, асепти́ческое сре́дство.
ash, *n*, зола́; пе́пел; прах; я́сень *(tree)*.
ashamed, *a*, пристыжённый; *I feel* ~ мне сты́дно.
ashen, *a*, пе́пельный; бле́дный.
ashore, *ad*, на бе́рег, на берегу́, к бе́регу; *run* ~ наска́кивать на мель/бе́рег.
Asiatic, *a*, азиа́тский; ¶ *n*, азиа́т.
aside, *ad*, в стороне́; в сто́рону; отде́льно; ¶ *n*, слова́, произноси́мые в сто́рону.
asinine, *a*, осли́ный.
ask, *v.t*, спра́шивать; проси́ть; приглаша́ть; ~ *after* осведомля́ться о; ~ *a question* задава́ть вопро́с.
askance, *ad*, и́скоса; с подозре́нием.
askew, *ad*, и́скоса, кри́во.
aslant, *ad*, на́искось; попере́к.
asleep, *a*, спя́щий; затёкший; во сне; *be* ~ спать; *fall* ~ засыпа́ть.
asp, *n*, *(zool.)* гадю́ка, а́спид.
asparagus, *n*, спа́ржа.
aspect, *n*, аспе́кт, вид; выраже́ние; нару́жность; сторона́.
aspen, *n*, оси́на.
asperity, *n*, суро́вость; ре́зкость; шерохова́тость.
aspersion, *n*, обры́згивание; клевета́.
asphalt, *n*, асфа́льт; ¶ *v.t*, асфальти́ровать.
asphyxia, *n*, уду́шье; ~**te**, *v.t*, вызыва́ть уду́шье у; удуша́ть.
aspirant, *n*, претенде́нт; **aspirate**, *v.t*, произноси́ть с придыха́нием; **aspiration**, *n*, стремле́ние; придыха́ние; *aspire to* стреми́ться к; домога́ться *(gen.)*.
aspirin, *n*, аспири́н.
ass, *n*, осёл; *make an* ~ *of oneself* валя́ть дурака́.
assail, *v.t*, напада́ть на; забра́сывать (вопро́сами); ~**ant**, *n*, напада́ющий; напада́ющая сторона́; проти́вник.
assassin, *n*, уби́йца; ~**ate**, *v.t*, убива́ть; ~**ation**, *n*, уби́йство.
assault, *n*, штурм, ата́ка, нападе́ние; изнаси́лование; ~ *and battery* оскорбле́ние де́йствием; ¶ *v.t*, атакова́ть, напада́ть на; наси́ловать.
assay, *n*, испыта́ние, про́ба; ¶ *v.t*, испы́тывать, про́бовать; ~**er**, *n*, анали́тик.

assemblage, *n*, собра́ние; скопле́ние; **assemble**, *v.t*, собира́ть, созыва́ть; монти́ровать; *v.i*, собира́ться; **assembly**, *n*, собра́ние; ассамбле́я; агрега́т; монта́ж, сбо́рка; ¶ *a*, сбо́рочный.
assent, *n*, согла́сие; са́нкция; ¶ *v.i*, ~ *to* соглаша́ться/дава́ть согла́сие на; санкциони́ровать.
assert, *v.t*, утвержда́ть; отста́ивать; ~ *oneself* самоутвержда́ться; отста́ивать свои́ права́; быть напо́ристым; ~**ion**, *n*, утвержде́ние.
assess, *v.t*, оце́нивать; определя́ть су́мму (нало́га); облага́ть (нало́гом); ~**ment**, *n*, оце́нка; обложе́ние.
asset, *n*, *(fin.)* акти́в; досто́инство; *pl*, *(fin.)* акти́в, иму́щество.
asseverate, *v.t*, утвержда́ть.
assiduity, *n*, прилежа́ние, усе́рдие; **assiduous**, *a*, приле́жный, усе́рдный.
assign, *v.t*, (пред)назнача́ть; определя́ть; прикрепля́ть (к ме́сту, гру́ппе), ассигнова́ть; припи́сывать; ~**ation**, *n*, назначе́ние; усло́вленная встре́ча; ассигнова́ние; ~**ee**, *n*, уполномо́ченный; правопрее́мник; ~**ment**, *n*, назначе́ние; ассигнова́ние; переда́ча; припи́сывание; зада́ние.
assimilate, *v.t*, уподобля́ть; ассимили́ровать; усва́ивать; **assimilation**, *n*, уподобле́ние; ассимиля́ция; усвое́ние.
assist, *v.t*, помога́ть *(dat.)*, соде́йствовать *(dat.)*; ~**ance**, *n*, по́мощь; соде́йствие; ~**ant**, *n*, помо́щник; ассисте́нт.
assizes, *n. pl*, выездна́я се́ссия суда́.
associate, *n*, това́рищ, колле́га; мла́дший член, член-корреспонде́нт; ~ *professor* доце́нт ¶ *v.t*, соединя́ть, свя́зывать; *v.i*: ~ *with* обща́ться с; присоединя́ться к; **association**, *n*, о́бщество, ассоциа́ция; обще́ние.
assonance, *n*, созву́чие; ассона́нс.
assort, *v.t*, сортирова́ть; группирова́ть; ~**ment**, *n*, ассортиме́нт; сортиро́вка.
assuage, *v.t*, успока́ивать; облегча́ть; смягча́ть; утоля́ть *(hunger)*.
assume, *v.t*, брать на себя́; присва́ивать; принима́ть; допуска́ть; предполага́ть; ~*d name* вымышленное и́мя; **assuming**, *a*, само-

надеянный, высокомерный; **assumption**, *n*, принятие; присвоение; предположение; высокомерие; *the A~* успение.

assurance, *n*, заверение; гарантия; уверение; (само)уверенность; страхование; **assure**, *v.t*, уверять; обеспечивать; страховать; **~d**, *p.p. & a*, уверенный; обеспеченный; самоуверенный; застрахованный; **~dly**, *ad*, несомненно.

asterisk, *n*, звёздочка.

astern, *ad*, назад; на корме; за кормой.

asthma, *n*, астма; одышка; **~tic**, *a*, астматический.

astir, *ad*, на ногах; в движении; в возбуждении.

astonish, *v.t*, удивлять, изумлять; **~ing**, *a*, удивительный, изумительный; **~ment**, *n*, удивление, изумление.

astrakhan, *n*, каракуль.

astray, *ad· go ~* заблудиться *(pf.)*; сбиваться с пути; теряться; *lead ~* вводить в заблуждение.

astride, *ad*, верхом на.

astringent, *n*, вяжущее средство.

astrologer, *n*, астролог; **astrology**, *n*, астрология.

astronomer, *n*, астроном; **astronomical**, *a*, астрономический; **astronomy**, *n*, астрономия.

astute, *a*, проницательный; хитрый.

asunder, *ad*, порознь; отдельно; *tear ~* разрывать на куски.

asylum, *n*, убежище, приют; психиатрическая больница.

at, *pr*, у; около; в; на; за; *~ all* вообще; *~ best* в лучшем случае; *~ dawn* на рассвете; *~ dinner* за обедом; *~ first* сначала; *~ a gallop* галопом; *~ a high price* по высокой цене; *~ home* дома; *~ last* наконец; *~ least* по крайней мере; *~ night* ночью; *~ once* сразу; *~ present* в настоящее время; *~ 9 o'clock* в девять часов; *~ work* за работой.

atheist, *n*, атеист; **~ic**, *a*, атеистический.

athirst, *a*, жаждущий.

athlete, *n*, спортсмен, физкультурник; атлет; **athletic**, *a*, атлетический; спортивный; **~s**, *n.pl*, атлетика; физкультура; *track and field ~* лёгкая атлетика.

atlas, *n*, атлас.

atmosphere, *n*, атмосфера; **atmospheric**, *a*, атмосферный; **~s**, *n. pl*, атмосферные помехи.

atom, *n*, атом; ¶ *a*, атомный; **~ic**, *a*, атомный.

atone, *v.i*: *~ for* искупать, заглаживать; возмещать за; **~ment**, *n*, искупление; возмещение.

atonic, *a*, безударный; ослабевший.

atrocious, *a*, ужасный; скверный; зверский; **atrocity**, *n*, жестокость; зверство.

atrophy, *n*, атрофия; ослабление.

attach, *v.t*, прикреплять; присоединять; припаивать, придавать; *~ oneself* привязываться; **~é**, *n*, атташе; **~ment**, *n*, привязанность, преданность; прикрепление; приспособление, принадлежность.

attack, *n*, атака, наступление; нападение; *(fig.)* нападки; приступ *(of disease)*, припадок; ¶ *v.t*, атаковать; нападать на; поражать *(of disease)*.

attain, *v.t*, достигать *(gen.)*; добиваться *(gen.)*; **~able**, *a*, достижимый; **~ment**, *n*, достижение; приобретение; *pl*, (по)знания, навыки.

attempt, *n*, попытка, проба; покушение; *make an ~ on the life of* покушаться на; ¶ *v.i*, пытаться, стараться; *v.t*, предпринимать, пробовать.

attend, *v.t*, посещать *(lectures)*; присутствовать на; сопровождать; ухаживать за (больным); *~ to* быть внимательным к; заботиться о; следить за; заниматься (делом/вопросом); обслуживать; **~ance**, *n*, посещение; присутствие; посещаемость; уход, обслуживание; **~ant**, *n*, провожатый; слуга; обслуживающее лицо; ¶ *a*, сопровождающий; сопутствующий; **attention**, *n*, внимание; *pay ~* обращать внимание; **attentive**, *a*, внимательный; заботливый; вежливый.

attenuate, *v.t*, ослаблять, смягчать; истощать; разжижать; **attenuation**, *n*, разжижение.

attest, *v.t*, свидетельствовать, удостоверять; приводить к присяге; **~ation**, *n*, удостоверение; показание; приведение к присяге.

attic, *n*, чердак.

attire, *n*, наряд, платье; украшение; ¶ *v.t*, наряжать, одевать.

attitude, *n*, отношение; позиция; поза.

attorney, *n*, поверенный, адвокат; ~ *general* генеральный атторней/прокурор; министр юстиции; *letter of* ~ доверенность; *power of* ~ полномочие.

attract, *v.t*, привлекать, притягивать; пленять; ~**ion**, *n*, притяжение; привлекательность; ~**ive**, *a*, привлекательный.

attribute, *n*, свойство, характерный признак; атрибут;; определение; ¶ *v.t*, приписывать; относить; **attribution**, *n*, приписывание.

attrition, *n*, изнурение, истощение; изнашивание, (и)стирание.

attune, *v.t*, настраивать.

auburn, *a*, каштановый.

auction, *n*, аукцион; ¶ *v.t*, продавать с аукциона; ~**eer**, *n*, аукционист.

audacious, *a*, смелый; дерзкий; **audacity**, *n*, смелость; дерзость.

audible, *a*, слышный, слышимый; **audibly**, *ad*, вслух, внятно; **audience**, *n*, слушатели, зрители, публика, аудитория; аудиенция.

audit, *n*, проверка, ревизия; ¶ *v.t*, проверять *(accounts)*; ~**ion**, *n*, выслушивание, проба (голосов); ~**or**, *n*, ревизор, контролёр; ~**orium**, *n*, аудитория; зрительный зал.

auger, *n*, бурав, сверло.

aught, *n*, что-нибудь, что-то; *for* ~ *I know* насколько мне известно.

augment, *v.t*, увеличивать; прибавлять; *v.i*, увеличиваться; ~**ation**, *n*, увеличение, повышение, приращение.

augur, *n*, авгур, прорицатель; ¶ *v.t*, предсказывать, предвидеть; ~**y**, *n*, предсказание; предзнаменование.

august, *a*, августейший, величественный.

August, *n*, август; ¶ *a*, августовский.

aunt, *n*, тётя.

aureole, *n*, ореол.

auricular, *a*, ушной, слуховой; тайный.

aurora, *n*, аврора; ~ *borealis* северное сияние.

auspices, *n.pl*, покровительство; *under the* ~ *of* под покровительст-

вом, при содействии; **auspicious**, *a*, благоприятный.

austere, *a*, суровый; простой; аскетический; **austerity**, *n*, суровость; простота; аскетизм.

austral, *a*, южный.

Australian, *n*, австрал|иец, ~ийка; ¶ *a*, австралийский.

Austrian, *n*, австр|иец, ~ийка; ¶ *a*, австрийский.

authentic, *a*, подлинный; достоверный; ~**ate**, *v.t*, удостоверять, устанавливать подлинность *(gen.)*; ~**ity**, *n*, подлинность; достоверность.

author, *n*, автор; писатель; создатель; инициатор, виновник; ~**ess**, *n*, автор; писательница.

authoritative, *a*, авторитетный; властный; **authority**, *n*, авторитетный источник; авторитет; власть, полномочие; *pl*, власти; **authorization**, *n*, разрешение; уполномочивание; **authorize**, *v.t*, разрешать; уполномочивать.

authorship, *n*, авторство.

autobiography, *n*, автобиография.

autocracy, *n*, автократия, самодержавие; **autocrat**, *n*, самодержец; деспот; ~**ic**, *a*, самодержавный; деспотический.

autograph, *n*, автограф; оригинал рукописи.

automatic, *a*, автоматический; ¶ *n*, автомат; автоматическое оружие; **automaton**, *n*, автомат.

automobile, *n*, автомобиль.

autonomous, *a*, автономный; **autonomy**, *n*, автономия.

autopsy, *n*, вскрытие.

autumn, *n*, осень; ~**al**, *a*, осенний.

auxiliary, *a*, вспомогательный; ¶ *n*, помощник; *pl*, вспомогательные войска.

avail, *n*, выгода, польза; *of no* ~ бесполезный; ¶ *v.i*, быть полезным; ~ *oneself of* пользоваться *(inst.)*; ~**able**, *a*, имеющийся, наличный; доступный; *this ticket is* ~ *for one day* билет действителен только на один день.;

avalanche, *n*, лавина; снежный обвал.

avarice, *n*, жадность, скупость; **avaricious**, *a*, жадный, скупой.

avenge, *v.t*, мстить *(dat.)*; ~ *oneself* мстить за себя; ~**r**, *n*, мститель.

avenue, n, проспе́кт, авеню́; алле́я, доро́га; (fig) путь, сре́дство.

aver, v.t, утвержда́ть.

average, a, сре́дний; норма́льный; рядово́й; ¶ n, сре́днее число́; распределе́ние убы́тка (от ава́рии); on ~ в сре́днем; ¶ v.t, выводи́ть сре́днее число́ из; составля́ть в сре́днем.

averse, a, нерасполо́женный; несклонный; I am not ~ to ... ничего́ не име́ю про́тив ...; I am not ~ to doing this я непро́чь э́то сде́лать; aversion, n, отвраще́ние, антипа́тия; неохо́та.

avert, v.t, отвраща́ть (danger); отводи́ть (eyes).

aviary, n, пти́чник.

aviation, n, авиа́ция; aviator, n, лётчик.

avid, a, а́лчный, жа́дный; ~ity, n, жа́дность, а́лчность.

avocation, n, призва́ние, профе́ссия; побо́чное заня́тие.

avoid, v.t, избега́ть (gen.); уклоня́ться от; ~able, a, тако́й, кото́рого мо́жно избежа́ть; ~ance, n, уклоне́ние; избежа́ние; аннули́рование.

avow, v.t, признава́ть; заявля́ть; ~al, n, призна́ние; ~ed, p.p. & a, откры́то призна́нный.

await, v.t, ждать, ожида́ть.

awake, a, бо́дрствующий; (fig.) бди́тельный; ¶ v.t, буди́ть; v.i, просыпа́ться; ~n, v.t, пробужда́ть; ~ning, n, пробужде́ние.

award, n, награ́да; присужде́ние; стипе́ндия; пре́мия; ¶ v.t, присужда́ть; награжда́ть.

aware, a, сознаю́щий; зна́ющий; be ~ of сознава́ть; отдава́ть себе́ отчёт в.

awash, ad, покры́тый/смы́тый водо́й.

away, ad, прочь; в разъе́здах; go ~ уходи́ть, отходи́ть; уезжа́ть; take ~ убира́ть; far ~ далеко́; he is ~ from home он уе́хал.

awe, n, страх; благогове́ние; ~-struck поражённый/охва́ченный (благогове́йным) стра́хом; awful, a, ужа́сный; гро́зный.

awhile, ad, (на) не́которое вре́мя; ненадо́лго; wait ~ подожди́те немно́го!.

awkward, a, нело́вкий, неуклю́жий; an ~ situation щекотли́вое поло-

же́ние; ~ness, n, нело́вкость, неуклю́жесть.

awl, n, ши́ло.

awning, n, наве́с, тент.

awry, a, косо́й; криво́й; ¶ ad, непра́вильно, пло́хо; ко́со.

axe, n, топо́р; ¶ v.t, сокраща́ть; уре́зывать.

axiom, n, аксио́ма; ~atic, a, самоочеви́дный, не тре́бующий доказа́тельства.

axis, n, ось.

axle, n, ось, вал.

ay, int. & n, да; положи́тельный отве́т.

aye, ad, всегда́; навсегда́.

azalea, n, аза́лия.

azure, a, лазу́рный; ¶ n, лазу́рь.

B

babble, n, болтовня́; ле́пет; журча́ние; ¶ v.i, болта́ть; бормота́ть; журча́ть; ~r, n, болту́н.

babel, n, галдёж; вавило́нское столпотворе́ние.

baboon, n, бабу́йн.

baby, n, ребёнок, младе́нец; ¶ a, ма́лый, небольшо́й; де́тский; ~hood, n, младе́нчество; ~ish, a, ребя́ческий, де́тский.

Bacchanalian, a, вакхи́ческий.

bachelor, n, холостя́к; бакала́вр.

bacillus, n, баци́лла.

back, n, спина́; спи́нка (of chair, dress); корешо́к (of book); за́дняя часть; защи́тник (sport); be at the ~ of быть та́йной причи́ной (gen.); with one's ~ to the wall прижа́тый к стене́; ¶ a, за́дний; ста́рый (но́мер журна́ла); просро́ченный (платёж); ¶ ad, наза́д; обра́тно; тому́ наза́д (ago); ¶ v.t, подде́рживать; помога́ть (dat.), субсиди́ровать; v.i, отступа́ть; пя́титься; ~ down отступа́ться; уступа́ть; ~ out уклоня́ться (от).

backbite, v.t, клевета́ть на; backbiter, n, клеветни́к; backbiting, n, клевета́.

backbone, n, спинно́й хребе́т, позвоно́чник; осно́ва, суть; твёрдость.

back door, n, чёрный ход; за́дняя дверь; ¶ a, закули́сный.

backer, *n*, покрови́тель.

backgammon, *n*, игра́ в трикtpа́к.

background, *n*, фон, за́дний план; *stay in the* ~ остава́ться в тени́.

backside, *n*, за́дняя сторона́, зад.

backslide, *v.i*, не выполня́ть обеща́ний; не опра́вдывать наде́жд.

backward, *a*, обра́тный; отста́лый, отстаю́щий; ро́бкий; ¶ *ad*, наза́д; наоборо́т; за́дом напере́д; ~**ness**, *n*, отста́лость; запозда́лое разви́тие.

backwash, *n*, вода́, поднима́емая корабле́м; обра́тный пото́к; после́дствия.

backwater, *n*, запру́женная вода́; за́водь.

backwoods, *n*, глушь.

bacon, *n*, груди́нка, беко́н.

bacterium, *n*, бакте́рия.

bad, *a*, плохо́й, дурно́й; больно́й; си́льный *(pain); грубый *(mistake); go* ~ по́ртиться; *go from* ~ *to worse* ухудша́ться; *to the* ~ в убы́тке.

badge, *n*, значо́к; эмбле́ма; знак.

badger, *n*, барсу́к; ¶ *v.t*, трави́ть; раздража́ть, пристава́ть к.

badly, *ad*, пло́хо; си́льно; о́чень; **badness**, *n*, него́дность; вре́дность.

baffle, *v.t*, расстра́ивать; ста́вить в тупи́к/замеша́тельство.

bag, *n*, мешо́к; су́мка; добы́ча; ~ *and baggage* со все́ми пожи́тками; ¶ *v.t*, класть в мешо́к; убива́ть; лови́ть; собира́ть.

bagatelle, *n*, пустя́к, безде́лица; де́тский билья́рд.

baggage, *n*, бага́ж; ¶ *a*, бага́жный.

baggy, *a*, мешкова́тый.

bagpipe, *n*, волы́нка; ~r, *n*, волы́нщик.

bail, *n*, зало́г, поручи́тельство; поручи́тель; перекла́дина воро́т *(cricket); go* ~ *for* руча́ться за; ¶ *v.t*, брать на пору́ки; вычёрпывать *(water);* ~ *out* выбра́сываться с парашю́том.

bailiff, *n*, суде́бный при́став; управля́ющий име́нием.

bait, *n*, прима́нка; нажи́вка; паёк, еда́; корм; *swallow the* ~ попада́ться на у́дочку; ¶ *v.t*, трави́ть; изводи́ть; наса́живать на у́дочку.

baize, *n*, ба́йка.

bake, *v.t*, печь; обжига́ть *(bricks); v.i*, пе́чься; загора́ть на со́лнце;

~ **house**, ~**ry**, *n*, пека́рня; ~r, *n*, пе́карь; бу́лочник; ~ *'s shop* бу́лочная; **baking**, *n*, пече́ние, вы́печка.

balance, *n*, весы́; равнове́сие; бала́нс; ¶ *v.t*, уравнове́шивать; взве́шивать; балансировать, подводи́ть бала́нс *(gen.); v.i*, балансировать; сохраня́ть равнове́сие; ~-*sheet* бала́нс

balcony, *n*, балко́н.

bald, *a*, лы́сый; *(fig.)* неприкра́шенный; просто́й.

balderdash, *n*, вздор.

baldness, *n*, плеши́вость; лы́сина.

bale, *n*, тюк, ки́па; ¶ *v.l*, укла́дывать в тюки́/ки́пы.

baleful, *a*, па́губный, ги́бельный; мра́чный.

balk, *n*, ба́лка, брус; препя́тствие; ¶ *v.t*, препя́тствовать *(dat.)*, меша́ть *(dat.);* пропуска́ть; отка́зываться от.

ball, *n*, шар, мяч; бросо́к, уда́р *(sport);* пу́ля; клубо́к (ше́рсти); бал; *eye*~ глазно́е я́блоко; ~ *and socket* шарово́й шарни́р; ~-*point pen* ша́риковая ру́чка.

ballad, *n*, балла́да.

ballast, *n*, балла́ст; ¶ *v.t*, грузи́ть балла́стом.

ball-bearing, *n*, шарикоподши́пник.

ballet, *n*, бале́т.

balloon, *n*, возду́шный шар, аэроста́т; ¶ *v.t*, поднима́ться на возду́шном ша́ре; раздува́ться (как шар).

ballot, *n*, голосова́ние, баллотиро́вка; ~ *paper* избира́тельный бюллете́нь; ¶ *v.i*, голосова́ть; тяну́ть жре́бий.

balm, balsam, *n*, бальза́м; **balmy, balsamic**, *a*, души́стый; не́жный.

baluster, *n*, баля́сина; *pl*, балюстра́да; **balustrade**, *n*, балюстра́да, пери́ла.

bamboo, *n*, бамбу́к.

bamboozle, *v.t*, мистифици́ровать; обма́нывать.

ban, *n*, запреще́ние; ана́фема; ¶ *v.t*, запреща́ть.

banal, *a*, бана́льный.

banana, *n*, бана́н.

band, *n*, гру́ппа, ба́нда; орке́стр; о́бод, о́бруч; тесьма́, ле́нта; ¶ *v.t*, объединя́ть; свя́зывать; ~ *together* собира́ться, объединя́ться.

bandage, *n*, бинт, повя́зка.

bandit, *n*, банди́т.

bandoleer, *n*, патронта́ш.

bandsman, *n*, оркестра́нт.

bandy, *v.t*, обме́ниваться (слова́ми, уда́рами); **~-legged**, *a*, криво-но́гий.

bane, *n*, отра́ва; прокля́тие; ги́бель; **~ful**, *a*, ги́бельный; ядови́тый.

bang, *n*, уда́р, стук; звук вы́стрела; ¶ *v.t*, ударя́ть; стуча́ть, хло́пать (две́рью); *v.i*, ударя́ться; с шу́мом захло́пываться *(of door)*; гро́хнуть *(pf.)*.

bangle, *n*, брасле́т.

banish, *v.t*, изгоня́ть, высыла́ть; отгоня́ть *(thought)*; **~ment**, *n*, изгна́ние, вы́сылка.

banister, *n*, пери́ла.

banjo, *n*, ба́нджо.

bank, *n*, бе́рег; о́тмель; нано́с, зано́с; банк; *(avia.)* вира́ж, крен; ¶ *v.t*, класть в банк *(money)*; **~ up** наноси́ть; окружа́ть ва́лом; *v.i*, де́лать вира́ж, накреня́ться; **~ on** осно́вываться на; полага́ться на; **~er**, *n*, банки́р; **~ing**, *n*, ба́нковое де́ло; вира́ж, крен *(avia.)*.

bankrupt, *a*, несостоя́тельный; ¶ *n*, банкро́т; несостоя́тельный должни́к; *go* **~** обанкро́титься *(pf.)*; **~cy**, *n*, банкро́тство, несостоя́тельность.

banner, *n*, зна́мя, флаг, стяг; заго-ло́вок.

banns, *n.pl*, оглаше́ние имён всту-па́ющих в брак.

banquet, *n*, банке́т, пир.

banter, *v.t*, подшу́чивать над, под-дра́знивать.

baptism, *n*, креще́ние; **~al**, *a*, крес-ти́нный; **baptistry**, *n*, баптисте́рий; **baptize**, *v.t*, крести́ть.

bar, *n*, полоса́ (мета́лла); брусо́к; лом *(crow-bar)*; засо́в; прегра́да; о́тмель *(of river)*; сто́йка; бар; барье́р *(law)*; **~** *of chocolate* пли́тка шокола́да; **~** *of soap* кусо́к мы́ла; *be called to the B***~** получа́ть пра́во адвока́тской пра́ктики; ¶ *v.t*, запреща́ть; прегражда́ть; запира́ть на засо́в *(door)*.

barb, *n*, зубе́ц.

barbarian, *a*, ва́рварский; ¶ *n*, ва́рвар; **barbaric**, *a*, гру́бый; ва́рварский; **barbarism**, *n*, ва́р-варство; **barbarous**, *a*, ва́рвар-ский.

barbed wire колю́чая про́волока.

barber, *n*, парикма́хер; **~'s** *shop* парикма́херская.

bard, *n*, бард, певе́ц.

bare, *a*, го́лый; обнажённый; пус-то́й; бе́дный; неприкра́шенный; *a* **~** *majority* о́чень незначи́тель-ное большинство́; **~-footed** босо́й; **~-headed** с непокры́той голово́й; ¶ *v.t*, обнажа́ть; **~** *one's head* снима́ть шля́пу; **~ly**, *ad*, едва́, то́лько; про́сто; **~ness**, *n*, нагота́; бе́дность.

bargain, *n*, сде́лка; вы́годная по-ку́пка, дешёвка; *strike a* **~** заклю-ча́ть сде́лку; *into the* **~** в прида́чу, к тому́ же; ¶ *v.i*, торгова́ться.

barge, *n*, ба́ржа; речно́й трамва́й; **bargee**, *n*, ло́дочник.

baritone, *n*, барито́н.

bark, *n*, *(of tree)* кора́; *(of dog)* лай; *(boat)* ба́рка; ¶ *v.t*, сдира́ть кору́ с; *v.i*, ла́ять.

barley, *n*, ячме́нь.

barm, *n*, заква́ска.

barmaid, *n*, буфе́тчица, **barman**, *n*, буфе́тчик.

barn, *n*, амба́р; сара́й.

barnacle, *n*, морска́я у́точка.

barometer, *n*, баро́метр.

baron, *n*, баро́н **~ess**, *n*, бароне́сса; **~et**, *n*, бароне́т; **~ial**, *a*, баро́н-ский; **~y**, *n*, владе́ние/ти́тул баро́на.

baroque, *a*, в сти́ле баро́кко; при-чу́дливый; ¶ *n*, баро́кко.

barrack, *n*, бара́к; *pl*, каза́рмы; ¶ *v.t*, размеща́ть в бара́ках/каза́р-мах.

barrel, *n*, бо́чка; ду́ло *(of gun)*; *(tech.)* цили́ндр, бараба́н; ту́ло-вище *(of horse)*; **~-organ** шарма́н-ка.

barren, *a*, беспло́дный; неплодо-ро́дный; ску́чный; **~ness**, *n*, беспло́дие.

barricade, *n*, баррика́да; прегра́да; ¶ *v.t*, баррикади́ровать.

barrier, *n*, барье́р, заста́ва, шлаг-ба́ум; прегра́да.

barring, *pr*, за исключе́нием *(gen.)*.

barrister, *n*, адвока́т.

barrow, *n*, курга́н, холм; та́чка.

barter, *n*, товарообме́н; ¶ *v.t*, об-ме́ниваться (това́рами).

basalt, *n*, база́льт.

base, *a*, ни́зкий, ни́зменный; усло́в-ный; **~** *coin* фальши́вая моне́та; ¶ *n*, осно́ва; основа́ние; ба́за;

фунда́мент *(arch.)*; ¶ *v.i*, закла́дывать основа́ние *(gen.)*; осно́вывать; ~ *oneself on* осно́вываться на.

baseless, *a*, необосно́ванный.

basement, *n*, основа́ние, фунда́мент; подва́л, (полу)подва́льный эта́ж.

baseness, *n*, ни́зость, по́длость.

bashful, *a*, ро́бкий, засте́нчивый; ~ness, *n*, ро́бость, засте́нчивость.

basic, *a*, основно́й.

basilica, *n*, базили́ка.

basilisk, *n*, васили́ск.

basin, *n*, таз, ми́ска; бассе́йн, водоём.

basis, *n*, ба́зис, основа́ние; ба́за.

bask, *v.i*, гре́ться (на со́лнце); наслажда́ться.

basket, *n*, корзи́на; ку́зов; ~ful, *n*, по́лная корзи́на.

Basque, *a*, ба́скский; ¶ *n*, баск; ба́скский язы́к.

bas-relief, *n*, барельéф.

bass, *n*, *(mus.)* бас; *(fish)* морско́й о́кунь.

bassoon, *n*, фаго́т.

bastard, *n*, незаконорождённый, внебра́чный; *(fig.)* подде́льный; плохо́го ка́чества; ¶ *n*, внебра́чный ребёнок; ~y, *n*, рожде́ние вне бра́ка.

baste, *v.t*, смётывать *(sew.)*; полива́ть жи́ром *(meat)*; бить.

bastion, *n*, бастио́н.

bat, *n*, бита́ *(for games)*; уда́р; темп, шаг; *(zool.)* летучая мышь ¶ *v.i*, бить бито́й.

batch, *n*, вы́печка хле́ба; па́чка, ку́чка; гру́ппа.

bate, *v.t*, уменьша́ть; притупля́ть; *v.i*, слабе́ть; *with* ~*d breath* зата́йв дыха́ние.

bath, *n*, ва́нна; купа́ние; *pl*, ба́ня; *take a* ~ принима́ть ва́нну; *swimming* ~ (закры́тый) пла́вательный бассе́йн; ~ *house* ба́ня; ~ *robe* купа́льный хала́т; ~room ва́нная ко́мната; ~*tub* ва́нна.

bathe, *n*, купа́ние; ¶ *v.t*, купа́ть; омыва́ть (берега́); *v.i*, купа́ться; ~r, *n*, купа́ль|щик; ~щица; **bathing**, *n*, купа́ние; ~ *costume* купа́льный костю́м.

bathos, *n*, перехо́д от высо́кого сти́ля к коми́ческому.

baton, *n*, жезл; дирижёрская па́лочка; полице́йская дуби́нка; бато́н *(bread)*.

battalion, *n*, батальо́н.

batten, *n*, рéйка, доска́; ¶ *v.t*, закола́чивать до́сками; откáрмливать; *v.i*, откáрмливаться; процвета́ть (за счёт други́х).

batter, *n*, взби́тое те́сто; мя́тая гли́на; ¶ *v.t*, колоти́ть; разруша́ть; ~ing-ram, *n*, тара́н; ~y, *n*, батаре́я; *(law)* оскорбле́ние де́йствием.

battle, *n*, би́тва, сраже́ние; бой; борьба́; ¶ *a*, боево́й; ~ *field* по́ле бо́я; ~ship броненóсец, линкóр.

battledore, *n*, раке́та; ~ *and shuttlecock* игра́ в вола́н.

battlement, *n*, зубча́тая стена́; зубцы́ стен.

bauble, *n*, игру́шка; безделу́шка; *fool's* ~ жезл шута́.

bawdy, *a*, непристо́йный; ~ *house* публи́чный дом.

bawl, *v.i*, крича́ть, ора́ть.

bay, *n*, зали́в, бу́хта; лавр, лавро́вое де́рево; *(build)* пролёт; пане́ль; железнодоро́жная платфо́рма; лай; гнеда́я ло́шадь; *sick* ~ лазаре́т; *at* ~ в безвы́ходном положе́нии; ~ *window* ни́ша, "фона́рь"; ¶ *v.i*, ла́ять.

bayonet, *n*, штык.

bazaar, *n*, база́р; магази́н; *Christmas* ~ ёлочный база́р; благотвори́тельный база́р.

be, *v.i*, быть, существова́ть; находи́ться; происходи́ть, случа́ться; *how are you?* как вы пожива́ете?; *are you often in town?* вы ча́сто быва́ете в го́роде? *how much is it?* ско́лько э́то сто́ит?; ~ *about to* собира́ться (+ *inf*); ~ *away* отсу́тствовать; ~ *off* уходи́ть, уезжа́ть; ~ *out* не быть до́ма.

beach, *n*, пляж; ¶ *v.t*, выта́скивать на бе́рег; сади́ть на мель.

beacon, *n*, мая́к, бáкен, буй; сигна́льный огóнь.

bead, *n*, бу́сина, ша́рик; ка́пля; *(pl.)* бу́сы, чётки.

beadle, *n*, педль.

beagle, *n*, го́нчая (соба́ка); *(fig.)* сы́щик.

beak, *n*, клюв; но́сик *(of vessel)*; *(coll.)* судья́.

beaker, *n*, ча́ша; ку́бок; мензу́рка.

beam, *n*, ба́лка *(wood)*; луч *(light)*; коромы́сло *(scales)*; бимс, ширина́ *(of ship)* ¶ *v.t,* излуча́ть; *v.i,* свети́ть, сия́ть; ~**ing,** *a,* сия́ющий.

bean, *n,* боб; фасо́ль.

bear, *n,* медве́дь; ~ *cub* медвежо́нок; *Great (Little)* В Больша́я (Ма́лая) Медве́дица; ¶ *v.t,* носи́ть; перевози́ть; рожда́ть, производи́ть; рожа́ть; приноси́ть *(fruit);* подде́рживать; терпе́ть, выноси́ть; *v.i,* держа́ться; опира́ться; ~ *down* преодолева́ть; ~ *down on* брать направле́ние на; ~ *on* каса́ться *(gen.);* ~ *with* относи́ться терпели́во к; ~**able,** *a,* сно́сный, терпи́мый.

beard, *n,* борода́; ~**ed,** *a,* борода́тый; ~**less,** *a,* безборо́дый.

bearer, *n,* носи́тель; носи́льщик; пода́тель, предъяви́тель.

bearing, *n,* ноше́ние; мане́ра держа́ть себя́, поведе́ние; каса́тельство; *(tech.)* подши́пник; опо́ра; *lose one's* ~ заблуди́ться *(pf.); take one's* ~ ориенти́роваться.

beast, *n,* зверь, живо́тное; *(fig.)* скоти́на; ~**ly,** *a,* ско́тский, проти́вный.

beat, *n,* бой *(drum);* бие́ние *(heart);* такт; обхо́д; ¶ *v.t,* бить, ударя́ть; отбива́ть *(time);* выбива́ть *(carpet);* взбива́ть *(egg); v.i,* би́ться; ~ *back* отбива́ть; ~ *the air* перели́вать из пусто́го в поро́жнее; *the* ~*en track* проторённая доро́жка.

beatific, *a,* блаже́нный; **beatify,** *v.t,* канонизи́ровать; де́лать счастли́вым.

beating, *n,* битьё; пораже́ние; бие́ние *(of heart);* взма́хивание (кры́льями).

beatitude, *n,* блаже́нство.

beau, *n,* франт, щёголь; кавале́р (да́мы).

beautiful, *a,* краси́вый, прекра́сный; **beautify,** *v.t,* украша́ть; **beauty,** *n,* красота́; краса́вица; пре́лесть; ~ *parlour* институ́т красоты́; ~ *spot* му́шка (на лице́).

beaver, *n,* бобр; бобро́вы й мех, бобёр.

becalm, *v.t,* успока́ивать; штилева́ть *(ship);* ~**ed,** *p.p. & a,* заштиле́вший *(of ship).*

because, *c,* потому́ что; так как; из-за; всле́дствие.

beck, *n,* руче́й; **beckon,** *v.t,* кива́ть *(dat.);* подзыва́ть руко́й.

become, *v.i,* де́латься; станови́ться; случа́ться; *what has* ~ *of him?* что с ним ста́лось?; *this dress* ~*s you* э́то пла́тье вам о́чень идёт; **becoming,** *a,* подоба́ющий; иду́щий к лицу́ *(of dress).*

bed, *n,* посте́ль, крова́ть; ло́же; клу́мба; гря́дка; дно *(sea);* ру́сло *(river);* (*geol.*) пласт, слой; *make a* ~ стлать посте́ль; *go to* ~ ложи́ться спать; ~ *clothes* посте́льное бельё; ~ *head* изголо́вье; ~-*ridden* прико́ванный к посте́ли; ~*room* спа́льня; ~ *spread* покрыва́ло; ~-*sitting room* однокомна́тная кварти́ра; ~*time* вре́мя ложи́ться спать; ~**ding,** *n,* посте́льное бельё; *(build.)* основа́ние; *(geol.)* залега́ние.

bedeck, *v.t,* украша́ть.

bedew, *v.t,* покрыва́ть росо́й; обры́згивать.

bedlam, *n,* бедла́м; сумасше́дший дом.

bedraggled, *a,* гря́зный, запа́чканный.

bee, *n,* пчела́; ~*hive* у́лей; ~*keeping* пчелово́дство; ~*line* пряма́я ли́ния; *have a* ~ *in one's bonnet* быть с причу́дой.

beech, *n,* бук.

beef, *n,* говя́дина; ~*steak* бифште́кс.

beer, *n,* пи́во; ~ *house* пивна́я.

beet, *n,* свёкла.

beetle, *n,* жук; *(tech.)* трамбо́вка; кува́лда; **beetling,** *a,* нави́сший; ~ *brows* нави́сшие бро́ви.

beetroot, *n,* свёкла.

befall, *v.i,* случа́ться, приключа́ться, происходи́ть.

befit, *v.t,* подходи́ть *(dat.);* ~**ting,** *a,* подходя́щий.

before, *ad,* вперёд; вперёд; ра́ньше; уже́; ~ *long* ско́ро; *long* ~ задо́лго до; ¶ *pr,* пе́ред; пе́ред лицо́м; до; вперёд; *the day* ~ *yesterday* позавчера́; ¶ *c,* пре́жде чем; ~*hand,* *ad,* зара́нее; наперёд.

befriend, *v.t,* относи́ться дру́жески к; помога́ть *(dat.).*

beg, *v.t,* проси́ть, умоля́ть; ~ *pardon* проси́ть извине́ния; *v.i,* ни́щенствовать; служи́ть *(of dog).*

beget, *v.t,* рожда́ть; производи́ть; *(fig.)* порожда́ть.

beggar, *n,* ни́щий; попроша́йка; ¶ *v.t,* разоря́ть, доводи́ть до нищеты́; превосходи́ть; ~ *oneself* разоря́ться; ~ *description* не поддава́ться описа́нию; ~**liness**, *n*, нищета́; ни́щенство; ~**ly**, *a*, бе́дный, ни́щенский; жа́лкий; ~**y**, *n*, нищета́; ни́щенство.

begin, *v.t.* *(& i.)*, начина́ть(ся); *to* ~ *with* во-пе́рвых; ~**ner**, *n*, новичо́к; начина́ющий; ~**ning**, *n*, нача́ло; то́чка отправле́ния; исто́чник.

begone, *int*, убира́йся!.

begrime, *v.t*, па́чкать.

begrudge, *v.t*, зави́довать *(dat.);* жале́ть.

beguile, *v.t*, обма́нывать; развлека́ть; ~ *the time* корота́ть вре́мя.

behalf, *n: on* ~ *of* для; ра́ди; в по́льзу; от и́мени.

behave, *v.i*, вести́ себя́, поступа́ть; ~ *yourself!* веди́те себя́ прили́чно!; **behaviour**, *n*, поведе́ние.

behead, *v.t*, обезгла́вливать; ~**ing**, *n*, обезгла́вливание.

behest, *n*, приказа́ние.

behind, *ad*, сза́ди, позади́; по́сле; *leave* ~ оставля́ть позади́ себя́; ¶ *pr*, за, сза́ди, позади́; по́сле; ~ *the scenes* за кули́сами; ~ *the times* отста́лый.

behold, *v.t*, ви́деть; замеча́ть; ~**en** *a*, обя́занный; признательный.

behoof, *n*, по́льза, вы́года, интере́с.

behove, *v.t*, сле́довать/надлежа́ть *(dat.).*

being, *n* *(pers. & abstract)* существо́; челове́к; бытие́, существова́ние, жизнь; ¶ *a*, живу́щий, существу́ющий; *for the time* ~ на не́которое вре́мя; в да́нное вре́мя; ме́жду тем.

belabour, *v.t*, бить, колоти́ть.

belated, *a*, запозда́лый, по́здний; засти́гнутый но́чью.

belch, *n*, отры́жка; ¶ *v.i*, рыга́ть; *v.t*, отры́гивать; изверга́ть *(lava);* выбра́сывать *(fire).*

beleaguer, *v.t*, осажда́ть.

belfry, *n*, колоко́льня; ба́шня.

Belgian, *a*, бельги́йский; ¶ *n*, бельг|ие́ц, ~и́йка.

belie, *v.t*, оклевета́ть *(pf.);* опроверга́ть; изоблича́ть.

belief, *n*, ве́ра; дове́рие; убежде́ние; ве́рование; **believable**, *a*, вероя́тный; правдоподо́бный.

believe, *v.t*, ве́рить *(dat.),* доверя́ть *(dat.);* *v.i*, ду́мать, полага́ть; ~ *in* ве́рить в; ~**r** *n*, ве́рующий.

belittle, *v.t*, умаля́ть, преуменьша́ть, принижа́ть.

bell, *n*, ко́локол; колоко́льчик; звоно́к.

belladonna, *n*, белладо́нна.

belle, *n*, краса́вица.

bellicose, *a*, вои́нственный.

belligerent, *a*, вою́ющий; ¶ *n*, вою́ющая сторона́.

bellow, *v.i*, мыча́ть, реве́ть; ~**s**, *n*, кузне́чные мехи́.

belly, *n*, живо́т, брю́хо; ~**-band** подпру́га; ~**ful**, *n*, сы́тость; пресыще́ние; доста́точное коли́чество.

belong, *v.i*, принадлежа́ть, относи́ться; быть ро́дом из; ~**ings**, *n.pl*, пожи́тки, ве́щи, принадле́жности.

beloved, *a. & n*, возлю́бленный, люби́мый.

below, *ad*, ни́же; внизу́; ¶ *pr*, ни́же, под.

belt, *n*, по́яс, реме́нь; по́яс, зо́на; ¶ *v.t*, подпоя́сывать; опоя́сывать; поро́ть ремнём.

bemoan, *v.t*, опла́кивать.

bench, *n*, скамья́; ме́сто (в парла́менте); ме́сто (судьи́); верста́к, стано́к.

bend, *n*, изги́б; сгиб; ¶ *v.t*, сгиба́ть; изгиба́ть; гнуть; напряга́ть *(thoughts, etc.);* направля́ть *(steps); v.i*, сгиба́ться; изгиба́ться.

beneath, *ad*, внизу́; ¶ *pr*, под; ни́же.

benediction, *n*, благослове́ние.

benefaction, *n*, благодея́ние; ми́лость; **benefactor**, *n*, благоде́тель; **benefactress**, *n*, благоде́тельница.

benefice, *n*, бенефи́ций; прихо́д; ~**nce**, *n*, благодея́ние; благотвори́тельность; ~**nt**, *a*, благоде́тельный; благотво́рный.

beneficial, *a*, благотво́рный, целе́бный; вы́годный, поле́зный; **beneficiary**, *n*, владе́лец бенефи́ция; насле́дник; получа́ющий пе́нсию/ посо́бие.

benefit, *n*, вы́года; по́льза; при́быль; *(theat.)* бенефи́с; пе́нсия; посо́бие (по безрабо́тице, *etc);* ~ *society* ка́сса взаимопо́мощи; ¶ *v.t*, помога́ть *(dat.); v.i*, извлека́ть по́льзу.

benevolence, *n*, благожела́тельность, благоскло́нность; **benevolent**, *a*, благожела́тельный, благоскло́нный; ще́дрый.

benighted, *a,* засти́гнутый но́чью; *(fig.)* погружённый во мрак (невѣ́жества).

benign, *a,* до́брый; мя́гкий *(climate);* *(med.)* в лёгкой фо́рме.

benison, *n,* благослове́ние;

bent, *a,* изо́гнутый; ¶ *n,* изги́б; скло́нность.

benumb, *v.t,* приводи́ть в оцепене́ние; притупля́ть.

benzene, *n,* бензо́л.

benzine, *n,* бензи́н.

benzoin, *n,* бензо́йная смола́.

bequeath, *v.t,* завеща́ть; **bequest,** *n,* насле́дство; посме́ртный дар.

bereave, *v.t,* лиша́ть, отнима́ть; ~ment, *n,* тяжёлая утра́та.

beret, *n,* бере́т.

berry, *n,* я́года; зёрнышко *(caviar).*

berth, *n,* ко́йка, каю́та, (спа́льное) ме́сто; *(mar.)* я́корная стоя́нка; *give a wide ~ to* обходи́ть, избега́ть *(gen.);* ¶ *v.t,* предоставля́ть спа́льное ме́сто *(dat.);* ста́вить на я́корь.

beryl, *n,* бери́лл.

beseech, *v.t,* проси́ть, умоля́ть.

beset, *v.t,* окружа́ть, осажда́ть.

beside, *pr,* ря́дом с, о́коло, близ; по сравне́нию с; ми́мо; ~ *the point* некста́ти; ~ *oneself* вне себя́; ~s, *ad,* кро́ме того́, сверх того́.

besiege, *v.t,* осажда́ть; ~r, *n,* осажда́ющая сторона́.

besmear, *v.t,* мара́ть, па́чкать.

besom, *n,* ве́ник, метла́.

besotted, *a,* одуре́лый.

bespatter, *v.t,* забры́згивать (гря́зью), черни́ть.

bespeak, *v.t,* зака́зывать зара́нее; огова́ривать.

besprinkle, *v.t,* обры́згивать, осыпа́ть.

best, *a,* лу́чший, са́мый лу́чший; ~*man* ша́фер; ~*seller* хо́дкая кни́га, бестсе́ллер; ¶ *n,* са́мое лу́чшее; *at ~* в лу́чшем слу́чае; *all the ~* всего́ хоро́шего; *do one's ~* де́лать всё от себя́ зави́сящее; *to the ~ of one's ability* по ме́ре сил; ¶ *ad,* лу́чше всего́; бо́льше всего́.

bestial, *a,* ско́тский; ~ity, *n,* ско́тство; зве́рство.

bestir oneself встря́хиваться; бра́ться за де́ло.

bestow, *v.t,* дава́ть, дарова́ть; ~al, *n,* дар; награжде́ние.

bestride, *v.t,* сади́ться/сиде́ть верхо́м на; стоя́ть, расста́вив но́ги над.

bet, *n,* пари́; *make a ~* заключа́ть пари́; ¶ *v.i,* держа́ть пари́, би́ться об закла́д; ~ting, *n,* пари́; ~ter, *n,* держа́щий пари́.

betake oneself отправля́ться; прибега́ть к.

bethink oneself вспомина́ть; ду́мать.

betide, *v.t,* постига́ть; *v.i,* случа́ться.

betimes, *ad,* своевре́менно; ра́но.

betoken, *v.t,* означа́ть; предвеща́ть.

betray, *v.t,* предава́ть; изменя́ть *(dat.);* выдава́ть; обма́нывать; ~ *trust* не опра́вдывать дове́рия; ~al, *n,* преда́тельство, изме́на; ~er, *n,* преда́тель, изме́нник.

betroth, *v.t,* обруча́ть; ~al, *n,* обруче́ние, помо́лвка; ~ed, *a. & n,* обручённый, помо́лвленный.

better, *a,* лу́чший; *the ~ part* большинство́; *be ~ off* жить лу́чше; ¶ *ad,* лу́чше, бо́льше; *all the ~* тем лу́чше; *get the ~ of* брать верх над; ¶ *v.t,* улучша́ть; исправля́ть; ~ment, *n,* улучше́ние; исправле́ние.

between, *ad. & p,* ме́жду; ~ *you and me* ме́жду на́ми; ~ *times* ме́жду тем.

bevel, *n,* скос; ¶ *v.t,* ска́шивать.

beverage, *n,* напи́ток.

bevy, *n,* ста́я.

bewail, *v.t,* опла́кивать.

beware, *v.i,* бере́чься, остерега́ться; ~ *of dogs!* остерега́йтесь соба́к!; ~ *of trains!* береги́тесь по́езда!

bewilder, *v.t,* смуща́ть, сбива́ть с то́лку; ~ment, *n,* смуще́ние, замеша́тельство.

bewitch, *v.t,* очаро́вывать; заколдо́вывать; ~ing, *a,* очарова́тельный.

beyond, *ad,* вдали́; ¶ *pr,* по ту сто́рону; за; по́зже; вне; сверх; вы́ше; ¶ *n,* загро́бная жизнь; даль; *the back of ~* глушь.

bias, *n,* укло́н; пристра́стие; скло́нность; ¶ *v.t,* склоня́ть; ока́зывать влия́ние на; ~ed, *p.p. & a,* скло́нный; пристра́стный; предубеждённый; *be ~* име́ть предубежде́ние.

bib, *n,* нагру́дник.

Bible, *n,* би́блия; **biblical,** *a,* библе́йский.

bibliography, *n*, библиогра́фия.
bibliophile, *n*, библиофи́л.
bibulous, *a*, впи́тывающий вла́гу; пья́нствующий.
biceps, *n*, би́цепс.
bicker, *v.i*, спо́рить, пререка́ться; дра́ться.
bicycle, *n*, велосипе́д; **bicyclist**, *n*, велосипеди́ст.
bid, *n*, зая́вка; *(auction)* предложе́ние цены́; попы́тка; *make a* ~ предлага́ть це́ну; де́лать попы́тку; ¶ *v.t*, предлага́ть *(price)*; проси́ть; прика́зывать *(dat.)*; ~ *farewell* проща́ться; ~ *welcome* приве́тствовать; **bidding**, *n*, предложе́ние цены́; то́рги; приказа́ние.
bide, *v.i*, ждать благоприя́тного слу́чая, выжида́ть.
biennial, *a*, двухле́тний, двухгоди́чный.
bier, *n*, похоро́нные дро́ги.
bifurcated, *a*, раздво́енный; **bifurcation**, *n*, раздвое́ние; разветвле́ние.
big, *a*, большо́й; кру́пный; высо́кий; широ́кий; ва́жный; хвастли́вый; *talk* ~ хва́статься.
bigamist, *n*, двоеже́нец; двуму́жница; **bigamy**, *n*, бигами́я, двоеже́нство, двоему́жие.
bight, *n*, бу́хта; излу́чина (реки́).
bigness, *n*, величина́; высота́.
bigot, *n*, фана́тик, изуве́р; ~ed, *a*, фанати́ческий, нетерпи́мый; ~ry, *n*, фанати́зм; слепа́я приве́рженность.
big-wig, *n*, ва́жная персо́на, «ши́шка».
bilberry, *n*, черни́ка.
bile, *n*, жёлчь; *(fig.)* жёлчность, раздражи́тельность; **bilious**, *a*, жёлчный, раздражи́тельный.
bilge, *n*, дни́ще *(of ship)*; ~ *(water)* трю́мная вода́; *(fig.)* чепуха́, ерунда́.
bilingual, *a*, двуязы́чный; говоря́щий на двух языка́х.
bilk, *v.t*, обма́нывать; уклоня́ться от (упла́ты).
bill, *n*, законопрое́кт; билль; докуме́нт; счёт; ве́ксель; афи́ша, рекла́ма; банкно́та; ~ *of entry* тамо́женная деклара́ция; ~ *of health* каранти́нное свиде́тельство; ~ *poster* раскле́йщик афи́ш; афи́ша; *5 dollar* ~ биле́т в 5 до́л-

ларов; ¶ *v.t*, объявля́ть в афи́шах; раскле́ивать афи́ши; *v.i*, ласка́ться.
billet, *n*, о́рдер на посто́й; помеще́ние для посто́я; *pl*, кварти́ры; ¶ *v.t*, расквартиро́вывать.
billiard-ball, *n*, билья́рдный шар; **billiard-room**, *n*, билья́рдная; **billiards**, *n*, билья́рд.
billion, *n*, биллио́н; миллиа́рд.
billow, *n*, больша́я волна́, вал; *(fig.)* лави́на; ¶ *v.i*, вздыма́ться; ~y, *a*, вздыма́ющийся.
billy-goat, *n*, козёл.
bin, *n*, му́сорное ведро́; ларь, за́кром; корзи́на.
bind, *v.t*, свя́зывать; привя́зывать; переплета́ть *(book)*; обя́зывать; ~ *oneself* брать на себя́ обяза́тельство; *be bound to ...* быть вы́нужденным *(+ inf.)*; не мочь не *(+ inf.)*; ~er, *n*, переплётчик; свя́зывающее вещество́; *(agr.)* сноповяза́лка; ~ing, *a*, переплёт *(of book)*; обши́вка, око́вка (мета́ллом).
bindweed, *n*, вьюно́к.
binnacle, *n*, накто́уз.
binoculars, *n.pl*, бино́кль.
biographer, *n*, био́граф; **biographical**, *a*, биографи́ческий; **biography**, *n*, биогра́фия.
biological, *a*, биологи́ческий; **biologist**, *n*, био́лог; **biology**, *n*, биоло́гия.
biped, *n*, двуно́гое (живо́тное).
biplane, *n*, бипла́н.
birch, *n*, берёза; ро́зга; ¶ *v.t*, сечь ро́згой; ~ing, *n*, сече́ние ро́згой.
bird, *n*, пти́ца, пта́шка; ~'s *eye view* вид с пти́чьего полёта; ~ *of passage* перелётная пти́ца; ~*catcher* птицело́в; ~*watcher* люби́тель птиц.
birth, *n*, рожде́ние; происхожде́ние; ~ *certificate* ме́трика, свиде́тельство о рожде́нии; ~ *control* противозача́точные ме́ры; ~*day* день рожде́ния; ~*place* ме́сто рожде́ния; ро́дина; ~ *rate* рожда́емость.
biscuit, *n*, пече́нье.
bisect, *v.t*, разреза́ть/дели́ть попола́м.
bishop, *n*, епи́скоп; *(chess)* слон; ~ric, *n*, сан епи́скопа; епа́рхия.
bismuth, *n*, ви́смут.
bison, *n*, бизо́н.

bit, *n,* сверло; удила *(of horse);* частица; *a ~* немного; *not a ~* ничуть; *~ by ~* постепенно.

bitch, *n,* сука.

bite, *n,* укус; клёв *(of fish);* кусочек; *have a ~* перекусить *(pf.);* ¶ *v.t,* кусать; жалить; *v.i,* кусаться; клевать; **biting,** *a,* острый, едкий, язвительный.

bitter, *a,* горький; *(fig.)* горький, мучительный; резкий *(wind, words); ~ enemy* злейший враг; *~ly cold* ужасно холодно.

bittern, *n,* выпь.

bitterness, *n,* горечь; мучительность; резкость.

bitters, *n,* горькая настойка; горькое лекарство.

bitumen, *n,* битум; **bituminous,** *a,* битумный.

bivouac, *n,* бивак; ¶ *v.i,* располагаться биваком.

bizarre, *a,* странный; эксцентричный.

blab, *v.t,* разбалтывать; ¶ *v.i,* болтать.

black, *a,* чёрный; *~ and blue* в синяках; *~berry* ежевика; *~bird* чёрный дрозд; *~board* классная доска; *~ eye* подбитый глаз, синяк под глазом; *~leg* штрейкбрехер; *~ list* чёрный список; *~mail (n.)* шантаж; *(v.t.)* шантажировать; *~ market* чёрный рынок; *~ pudding* кровяная колбаса; *~ sheep* выродок; ¶ *n,* чёрный цвет; чёрная краска; чернота; траурное платье; негр.

blackamoor, *n,* негр; арап.

blacken, *v.t,* чернить; пачкать; *v.i,* чернеть.

blacking, *n,* вакса.

blackish, *a,* черноватый; **blackness,** *n,* чернота.

bladder, *n,* мочевой пузырь; *football ~* футбольная камера.

blade, *n,* лезвие, клинок; былинка *(of grass);* лопасть *(of oar, etc.).*

blame, *n* упрёк, порицание; вина; *take the ~* принимать вину на себя; ¶ *v.t,* упрекать, порицать; считать виновным; *he is to ~ for this* он виноват в этом; *~less, a,* невинный; *~worthy, a,* заслуживающий порицания.

blanch, *v.t,* белить, отбеливать; *v.i,* белеть; бледнеть.

bland, *a,* вежливый, ласковый; успокаивающий; *~ishment, n,* лесть; уговаривание.

blank, *a,* пустой; незаполненный, чистый *(cheque, etc.);* бессмысленный; *~ cartridge* холостой патрон; *~ wall* глухая стена; *~ verse* белый стих; ¶ *n,* пустое место; пробел; бланк *(form).*

blanket, *n,* одеяло.

blare, *n,* трубный звук; рёв; ¶ *v.i,* трубить; реветь.

blaspheme, *v.i,* поносить; богохульствовать; **blasphemous,** *a,* богохульный; **blasphemy,** *n,* богохульство.

blast, *n,* порыв (ветра); взрыв; звук; тяга; *~ furnace* доменная печь; домна; ¶ *v.t,* взрывать; разрушать *(hopes);* вредить *(dat.);* прокᴫинать; *(tech.)* продувать; *~ing, a,* взрывчатый; подрывной; ¶ *n,* порча; гибель; взрывные работы; дутьё.

blatant, *a,* крикливый; вопиющий.

blaze, *n,* пламя; яркий свет/цвет; вспышка; *in a ~* в огне; ¶ *v.i,* пылать, ярко гореть; *(fig.)* кипеть; *~ away* вести непрерывный огонь; *~ up* вспыхивать; *v.t,* делать знаки/зарубки на; *~ a trail* прокладывать путь.

blazer, *n,* спортивная куртка.

blazon, *v.t,* украшать гербами; объявлять, разглашать; *~ry, n,* гербы, геральдика.

bleach, *n,* хлорная известь; отбеливающее вещество; ¶ *v.t,* белить, отбеливать; обесцвечивать; *~er, n,* отбельщик; *~ing, n,* отбелка; обесцвечивание.

bleak, *a,* открытый, незащищённый (от ветра); оголённый; унылый.

bleary, *a,* затуманенный, смутный.

bleat, *n,* блеяние; ¶ *v.i,* блеять.

bleed, *v.i,* кровоточить; истекать кровью; *my heart ~s* сердце кровью обливается; *v.t,* пускать кровь *(dat.); (fig.)* вымогать деньги у; *~ing, a,* истекающий кровью; ¶ *n,* кровотечение, кровопускание.

blemish, *n,* позор, пятно; недостаток; ¶ *v.t,* пятнать; портить.

blend, *n,* смесь; ¶ *v.t,* смешивать; *v.i,* смешиваться; гармонировать.

bless, *v.t,* благословля́ть; осчаст-ли́вливать; **~ed,** *a,* блаже́нный; счастли́вый; **~edness,** *n,* блаже́нство; **~ing,** *n,* благослове́ние; бла́го, благодея́ние.

blight, *n,* скру́чивание *(plant disease);* парази́ты на расте́ниях; ги́бель; ¶ *v.t,* приноси́ть вред (расте́ниям); разбива́ть *(hopes).*

blind, *a,* слепо́й; тёмный; безрас-су́дный; **~** *alley* тупи́к; **~** *side* сла́бая стру́нка; слабо́е ме́сто; **~** *man's buff* жму́рки; ¶ *n,* што́ра; предло́г; отво́д глаз; *Venetian* **~** жалюзи́; ¶ *v.t,* ослепля́ть; затемня́ть; **~fold** *a,* с завя́занными глаза́ми; де́йствующий вслепу́ю; безрассу́дный; ¶ *v.t,* завя́зывать глаза́ *(dat.);* **~ly,** *ad,* сле́по; **~ness,** *n,* слепота́; ослепле́ние; безрассу́дство.

blink, *n,* мерца́ние; миг; ¶ *v.t,* закрыва́ть глаза́ на; мига́ть (глаза́ми); *v.i,* мерца́ть, мига́ть; **~ers,** *n.pl,* шо́ры, нагла́зники.

bliss, *n,* блаже́нство; **~ful,** *a,* блаже́нный.

blister, *n,* волды́рь, пузы́рь; ¶ *v.i,* покрыва́ться волдыря́ми; вызыва́ть пузыри́.

blithe, *a,* весёлый, жизнера́достный.

blizzard, *n,* бура́н, вью́га, пурга́.

bloat, *v.t,* копти́ть *(fish), become* **~ed** раздува́ться, пу́хнуть; **~er,** *n,* копчёная ры́ба/сельдь.

blob, *n,* ша́рик; ка́пля.

bloc, *n,* блок.

block, *n,* чурба́н, коло́да; глы́ба *(of stone);* кварта́л, жили́щный масси́в; пла́ха; прегра́да; зато́р *(of traffic);* **~** *of flats* жило́й дом; **~head** болва́н; **~** *letter* прописна́я бу́ква; ¶ *v.t,* прегражда́ть; заде́рживать; блоки́ровать.

blockade, *n,* блока́да; ¶ *v.t,* блоки́ровать.

blockage, *n,* прегра́да; зато́р; *(rly.)* блокиро́вка.

blond(e), *a,* белоку́рый, све́тлый; ¶ *n,* блонди́н, -ка.

blood, *n,* кровь; род, происхожде́ние, родство́; *cold* **~** хладно-кро́вие; *hot* **~** вспы́льчивость; **~hound** ище́йка; сы́щик; **~ letting** кровопуска́ние; **~poisoning** зараже́ние кро́ви; **~** *pressure* кровяно́е давле́ние; **~shed** кровопро-

ли́тие; **~shot** на́литый кро́вью; **~thirsty** кровожа́дный; **~** *transfusion* перелива́ние кро́ви; **~** *vessel* кровено́сный сосу́д; **~less,** *a,* бескро́вный; **~y,** *a,* крова́вый, окрова́вленный; *(coll.)* прокля́тый.

bloom, *n,* цвет; цвете́ние; расцве́т; ¶ *v.i,* цвести́, расцвета́ть; **~ing,** *a,* цвету́щий.

blossom, *n,* цвет; расцве́т; ¶ *v.i,* цвести́, расцвета́ть; распуска́ться.

blot, *n,* кля́кса; пятно́; ¶ *v.t,* па́чкать, пятна́ть; промока́ть (бума́гой).

blotch, *n,* кля́кса, пятно́.

blotter, blotting paper, *n,* промока́тельная бума́га.

blouse, *n,* блу́зка, ко́фточка.

blow, *n,* уда́р; дунове́ние; *at one* **~** одни́м уда́ром, сра́зу; *come to* **~s** вступа́ть в дра́ку; *take a* **~** подыша́ть *(pf.)* све́жим во́здухом; **~hole** ды́хало *(whale);* отду́шина; **~lamp** пая́льная ла́мпа; **~pipe** духова́я тру́бка; ¶ *v.t,* развева́ть, гнать; раздува́ть *(fire);* пуска́ть *(bubbles);* игра́ть на *(horn, etc.);* *v.i,* дуть; тяжело́ дыша́ть; пыхте́ть; звуча́ть; **~** *one's nose* сморка́ться; **~** *one's own trumpet* хва́статься; **~** *up* взрыва́ть; **~** *out* заду́вать *(candle);* **~** *one's brains out* пуска́ть пу́лю в лоб.

blubber, *n,* во́рвань *(whale);* ¶ *v.i,* реве́ть, рыда́ть.

bludgeon, *n,* дуби́нка; ¶ *v.t,* бить дуби́нкой.

blue, *a,* си́ний, голубо́й; уны́лый; **~bell** колоко́льчик; *B~ beard* Си́няя Борода́; **~** *bottle* си́няя му́ха; **~-eyed** голубогла́зый; *B~ Peter* флаг отплы́тия; **~** *print* си́нька, светопи́сная ко́пия; **~** *stocking* «си́ний чуло́к»; **~tit** сини́ца; ¶ *n,* си́ний цвет, си́няя кра́ска; си́нька; мо́ре; не́бо; консерва́тор; ¶ *v.t,* окра́шивать в си́ний цвет; подси́нивать.

bluff, *a,* круто́й, обры́вистый; прямо́й, ре́зкий; ¶ *n,* круто́й бе́рег, обры́в, утёс; блеф, обма́н; ¶ *v.t,* обма́нывать.

bluish, *a,* синева́тый, голубова́тый.

blunder, *n,* (гру́бая) оши́бка; ¶ *v.i,* дви́гаться о́щупью, спотыка́ться; гру́бо ошиба́ться.

blunderbuss, *n*, мушкетóн.

blunt, *a*, тупóй; прямóй, рéзкий;
¶ *v.t*, притупля́ть; **~ly**, *ad*,
тýпо; грýбо, рéзко; **~ness**, *n*,
тýпость; грýбость, прямотá, рéзкость.

blur, *n*, пятнó; кля́кса; нея́сное
очертáние; ¶ *v.t*, пáчкать; стáвить кля́ксы на; затумáнивать
(memory, etc.); пятнáть *(reputation)*.

blurt, *v.t*: **~** *out* сболтнýть *(pf.)*,
выпáливать.

blush, *n*, крáска стыдá/смущéния;
¶ *v.i*, краснéть от стыдá/смущé-
ния.

bluster, *n*, рёв бýри; хвастовствó;
угрóзы; ¶ *v.i*, бушевáть; ревéть
(of storm); шумéть, хвáстаться,
грозúться; **~er**, *n*, забия́ка; хвастýн.

boa, *n*, боá, горжéтка; **~** *constrictor*
удáв.

boar, *n*, бóров; *wild* **~** дúкий кабáн.

board, *n*, доскá; стол, питáние; прав-
лéние, совéт; *pl*, подмóстки,
сцéна *(theat.)*; *on* **~** на борт(ý);
B~ of Trade министéрство тор-
гóвли; ¶ *v.t*, настилáть (пол);
садúться (на корáбль, *etc.*);
with столовáться у; **~er**, *n*,
пансионéр; гость; **~ing**, *n*, пан-
сиóн, меблирóванные кóмнаты со
столóм; дóски; **~** *school* интер-
нáт.

boast, *n*, хвастовствó; ¶ *v.t*, хвáстаться *(inst.)*; гордúться *(inst.)*;
~er, *n*, хвастýн; **~ful**, *a*, хвас-
тлúвый.

boat, *n*, лóдка, сýдно, парохóд;
~hook багóр; **~house** навéс/сарáй
для лóдок; **~man** лóдочник;
¶ *v.i*, катáться на лóдке; **~ing**,
n, лóдочный спорт; **~swain**, *n*,
бóцман.

bob, *n*, мáятник; гúря; груз отвéса;
поплавóк; завитóк *(of hair)*;
¶ *v.i*, качáться, подскáкивать;
v.t, кóротко стричь.

bobbin, *n*, катýшка; веретенó; шпýль-
ка.

bobsleigh, *n*, бóбслей.

bobtail, *n*, обрéзанный хвост.

bode, *v.t*, предвещáть, сулúть.

bodice, *n*, корсáж; лиф.

bodiless, *a*, бестелéсный.

bodily, *a*, телéсный; физúческий; ¶
ad, лúчно; целикóм.

bodkin, *n*, шúло; шпúлька; кин-
жáл.

body, *n*, тéло; тýловище; глáвная
часть; кóрпус; óстов; *in a* **~** в
пóлном состáве; **~** *guard* телохра-
нúтель; **~** *work* кýзов.

bog, *n*, болóто, трясúна; *get bogged
down* завязáть.

bogey, *n*, телéжка; карéтка.

boggle, *v.i*, колебáться; пугáться;
останáвливаться.

boggy, *a*, болóтистый.

bogus, *a*, поддéльный, фиктúвный.

boil, *n*, кипéние; *(med.)* фурýнкул,
нары́в; *bring to the* **~** доводúть
до кипéния; ¶ *v.t*, кипятúть;
варúть; *v.i*, кипéть; варúться;
кипятúться; сердúться; **~** *away*
выкипáть; **~** *down* выпáривать-
(ся); **~** *over* перекипáть; *(fig.)*
кипéть негодовáнием; **~ed**, *a*,
варёный; кипячёный; **~er**, *n*,
котёл; кипятúльник; **~er** *house*
котéльная; **~ing**, *n*, кипéние;
кипячéние; ¶ *a*, кипя́щий; **~ing**
point тóчка кипéния.

boisterous, *a*, нейстовый, бýрный,
шумлúвый.

bold, *a*, смéлый; дéрзкий; самоувéренный; отчётливый; размá-
шистый *(writing)*; жúрный
(type); **~-faced** нáглый; *make*
~ осмéливаться; **~ness**, *n*, смé-
лость; нáглость; самоувéрен-
ность.

bole, *n*, ствол; пень.

bolster, *n*, вáлик (под подýшкой);
брус; поперéчина; *(tech.)* под-
клáдка; ¶ *v.t*, поддéрживать;
подклáдывать вáлик под по-
дýшку.

bolt, *n*, болт; засóв, задвúжка;
стрелá; мóлния, удáр грóма;
бéгство; сúто; ¶ *v.t*, запирáть на
засóв *(door)*; скрепля́ть бол-
тáми; просéивать; *v.i*, нестúсь
стрелóй; убегáть; понестú *(pf)*
(of horse); **~-upright**, *a*, прямóй;
как стрелá.

bolus, *n*, большáя пилю́ля.

bomb, *n*, бóмба, мúна; *atom* **~**
áтомная бóмба; **~proof** непро-
бивáемый бóмбами; **~thrower** бом-
бомёт; **~** *shelter* бомбоубéжище;
¶ *v.t*, бомбúть; **~ard**, *v.t*, бом-
бардировáть; засыпáть (вопрó-
сами); **~ardment**, *n*, бомбарди-
рóвка; **~er**, *n*, бомбардирóвщик

(avia.); ~**ing,** *n,* бомбёжка; бомбардировка.

bombast, *n,* напыщенность; ~**ic,** *a,* напыщенный.

bona fide, *a,* добросовестный; настоящий; ¶ *n,* добросовестность, честное намерение.

bond, *n,* связь; соединение; долговое обязательство; облигация *(fin.);* таможенная закладная; *pl,* оковы, узы; ¶ *v.t,* связывать; соединять; оставлять (товары на таможне до уплаты пошлины); ~**age,** *n,* рабство; зависимость; ~**ed goods** товары, хранящиеся на таможенных складах; ~**ed warehouse** склад для хранения товаров до уплаты пошлины.

bondholder, *n,* держатель облигаций/бон.

bondsman, *n,* крепостной; раб.

bone, *n,* кость; *pl.* скелет; костяк; игральные кости; кастаньеты; трещотки; ~ *of contention* яблоко раздора; ¶ *v.t,* снимать мясо с костей; ~**less,** *a,* бескостный; ~**setter,** *n,* костоправ.

bonfire, *n,* костёр.

bonnet, *n,* капор; дамская шляпа; детский чепчик; шотландская шапочка; капот (автомобиля).

bonny, *a,* красивый; здоровый.

bonus, *n,* премия, премиальные.

bony, *a,* костлявый; костистый.

booby, *n,* болван, дурак.

book, *n,* книга; ~**binder** переплётчик; ~ *case* книжный шкаф; ~ *collector* коллекционер редких книг; ~**keeper** бухгалтер, счетовод; ~**keeping** бухгалтерия; счетоводство; ~ *marker* закладка; ~**seller** продавец книг; ~**worm** книгоед; ¶ *v.t,* заказывать (билеты, *etc.);* принимать заказы (на билеты); регистрировать, записывать в книгу; приглашать; ~**ing,** *n,* заказ; приём/выдача заказов; ~ *clerk* кассир билетной/театральной кассы; ~ *office* билетная касса; бюро/стол заказов; ~**ish,** *a,* книжный; учёный; педантичный; ~**let,** *n,* брошюра.

boom, *n,* гул; бум (в торговле); большой спрос; заграждение; ¶ *v.i,* гудеть; быстро расти.

boomerang, *n,* бумеранг.

boon, *n,* благо благодеяние.

boor, *n,* грубиян, хам. ~**ish,** *a,* грубый, невоспитанный.

boot, *n,* ботинок; багажник *(of car);* high ~ сапог; ~**licker** подхалим; ~ *tree* сапожная колодка; *to* ~ в придачу; ~**black,** *n,* чистильщик обуви; ~**ee,** *n,* дамский ботинок; детский вязаный башмачок.

booth, *n,* будка; палатка; кабина; балаган (на ярмарке).

bootless, *a,* бесполезный; босоногий; без башмаков.

booty, *n,* добыча.

booze, *n,* выпивка, попойка; ¶ *v.i,* пьянствовать.

boracic, *a,* борнокислый; **borax,** *n,* бура.

border, *n,* граница; край, кайма; ~**land** пограничная полоса; ~**line** демаркационная линия, граница; ¶ *v.t,* окаймлять; обшивать; ~ *on* граничить с.

bore, *n,* высверленное отверстие; нудный человек; ~**hole** буровая скважина; ¶ *v.t,* буравить, сверлить; надоедать *(dat.); I am bored* мне надоело; ~**dom,** *n,* скука; ~**r,** *n,* бур, бурав, сверло; бурильщик, сверлильщик.

boric, *a,* борный; ~ *acid* борная кислота.

boring, *a,* сверлящий; скучный, надоедливый; ~ *machine* буровая машина; ¶ *n,* бурение, сверление; буровая скважина; надоедание.

born, *p.p. & a,* (при)рождённый; *be* ~ родиться.

borough, *n,* город(ок).

borrow, *v.t,* занимать; заимствовать.

bosh, *n,* вздор, болтовня.

bosom, *n,* грудь; пазуха; сердце; ~ *friend* закадычный друг.

boss, *n,* хозяин, предприниматель; босс; заправила; шишка; выступ; ¶ *v.t,* быть хозяином *(gen.);* распоряжаться *(inst.);* командовать *(inst.);* ~**y,** *a,* властный; любящий командовать.

botanic(al), *a,* ботанический; **botanist,** *n,* ботаник; **botanize,** *v.i,* ботанизировать; **botany,** *n,* ботаника.

botch, *n,* заплата; плохо сделанная работа, халтура; ¶ *v.t,* неумело латать; портить (работу); ~er, *n*, плохой работник, халтурщик.

both, *a. & pn,* оба; ~ . . . *and* как . . . так и; и . . . и.

bother, *n*, беспокойство; хлопоты; ¶ *v.t*, беспокоить; надоедать *(dat.)*; *v.i*, беспокоиться; волноваться; суетиться.

bottle, *n*, бутылка; ~ *feeding* искусственное вскармливание; ¶ *v.t*, разливать в бутылки; консервировать *(fruit)*; *(fig.)* сдерживать.

bottom, *n*, дно; низ; основание; фундамент; основа; зад; задняя часть; *(fig.)* причина; *be at the* ~ *of* быть причиной/зачинщиком; *from the* ~ *of my heart* от всей души; ¶ *a*, низкий; нижний; последний; основной; ~**less,** *a*, бездонный.

boudoir, *n*, будуар.

bough, *n*, сук, ветвь.

boulder, *n*, валун.

bounce, *n*, прыжок, отскок; упругость; хвастовство; ¶ *v.i*, подпрыгивать, отскакивать.

bound, *n*, граница, предел; прыжок, скачок; отскок *(of ball)*; ¶ *a*, связанный; обязанный; *be* ~ *for* направляться к/в; ¶ *v.t*, ограничивать; граничить с; *v.i*, прыгать, скакать; отскакивать; ~**ary,** *n*, граница, межа.

bounden, *a: in* ~ *duty* по чувству долга.

boundless, *a*, безграничный, беспредельный.

bounteous, bountiful, *a*, щедрый, обильный; **bounty,** *n*, щедрость; щедрый подарок; премия.

bouquet, *n*, букет, аромат.

bout, *n*, схватка; приступ *(of illness)*.

bovine, *a*, бычачий, бычий; тяжеловесный; тупой.

bow, *n*, лук; дуга; смычок *(of violin)*; бант.

bow, *n*, поклон; нос *(of ship)*; ¶ *v.t*, гнуть, сгибать; *v.i*, гнуться, сгибаться; кланяться; подчиняться.

bowdlerize, *v.t*, очищать (текст), вырезать (из книги).

bowels, *n.pl*, кишки; внутренности.

bower, *n*, беседка; жилище.

bowl, *n*, кубок, чаша; миска; ваза; шар; *pl*, игра в шары; ¶ *v.i*, играть в шары; подавать мяч

(in cricket); катиться; *v.t*, катить.

bowler (hat), *n*, котелок.

bowling-alley, bowling green, *n*, кегельбан.

bowman, *n*, стрелок из лука.

bowsprit, *n*, бушприт.

bow-wow, *n*, собачий лай; гав-гав.

box, *n*, коробка, ящик, сундук; ложа *(theatre)*; козлы (для кучера); удар; *ballot* ~ избирательная урна; ~ *office* театральная касса; ~ *wood* самшит; ~ *on ear* оплеуха; ¶ *v.t*, запирать/класть в ящик; бить кулаком; ~ing, боксировать; ~er, *n*, боксёр; ~ing, *n*, бокс; ~ *gloves* боксёрские перчатки.

boy, *n*, мальчик; молодой человек.

boycott, *n*, бойкот; ¶ *v.t*, бойкотировать.

boyhood, *n*, отрочество; **boyish,** *a*, мальчишеский; живой; отроческий.

brace, *n*, скоба, скрепа, подпорка; *pl*, подтяжки; ¶ *v.t*, связывать, скреплять; подпирать; укреплять, подкреплять.

bracelet, *n*, браслет.

bracing, *a*, свежий, живительный.

bracken, *n*, орляк.

bracket, *n*, скобка; подпорка; кронштейн; газовый рожок; ¶ *v.t*, ставить в скобки; ~ *together* ставить наряду с.

brackish, *a*, солоноватый.

brad, *n*, гвоздь без шляпки, штифтик; **bradawl,** *n*, шило.

brag, *n*, хвастовство; ¶ *v.i*, хвастаться; **braggadocio,** *n*, бахвальство; **braggart,** *n*, хвастун.

braid, *n*, коса *(hair)*; тесьма, шнурок; ¶ *v.t*, заплетать *(hair)*; плести; обшивать !тесьмой.

braille, *n*, азбука для слепых.

brain, *n*, мозг, ум; *pl*, умственные способности; мозги *(dish)*; ~ *drain* утечка мозгов; ~ *fever* воспаление мозга; ~*wash* «обрабатывать», «промывать мозги»; ~*washing* «умственная обработка», «промывание мозгов»; ~*wave* гениальная идея; ~ *work* умственная работа; ~**less,** *a*, безмозглый; ~**y,** *a*, с головой, умный.

braise, *v.t*, тушить.

brake, *n*, тормоз; трепало *(of flax)*; тестомешалка; борона; папоротник *(bot.)*; ¶ *v.t*, тормозить; трепать *(flax)*; месить *(dough)*; **brakesman**, *n*, тормозной кондуктор.

bramble, *n*, ежевика.

bran, *n*, отруби.

branch, *n*, ветвь; ветка; отрасль; филиал, отделение; линия (родства); рукав *(river)*; ответвление *(road)*; *(rly.)* железнодорожная ветка; ¶ *a*, филиальный; вспомогательный; боковой; ¶ *v.i*, раскидывать ветви; ~ *out* разветвляться; отходить.

brand, *n*, клеймо; фабричная марка; сорт; головня; ~ *new* новый, «с иголочки»; ¶ *v.t*, выжигать клеймо на; *(fig.)* клеймить; *it is ~ed on my memory* это врезалось мне в память.

brandish, *v.t*, махать/размахивать *(inst.)*.

brandy, *n*, коньяк; бренди.

brass, *n*, жёлтая медь, латунь; *the ~* духовые инструменты; ~ *band* духовой оркестр.

brassière, *n*, бюстгальтер, лифчик.

brat, *n*, пострел; выродок.

bravado, *n*, бравада, хвастовство.

brave, *a*, храбрый, смелый; ¶ *v.t*, бравировать *(inst.)*; презирать *(danger)*; ~**ry**, *n*, храбрость, мужество.

bravo!, *int*, браво!

brawl, *n*, ссора, скандал; ¶ *v.i*, ссориться, скандалить; ~**er**, *n*, скандалист.

brawn, *n*, мускулы, мускульная сила; ~**y**, *a*, сильный, мускулистый.

bray, *n*, крик осла; резкий звук; ¶ *v.i*, кричать *(of ass)*; издавать резкий звук.

brazen, *a*, медный; бронзовый ~-*faced* бесстыдный.

brazier, *n*, жаровня.

Brazilian, *a*, бразильский; ¶ *n*, бразил|ец, -иянка.

breach, *n*, пролом, отверстие, брешь, разрыв *(of relations)*; нарушение *(of law)*; ~ *of faith* измена; ~ *of peace* нарушение общественного порядка.

bread, *n*, хлеб *(also fig.)*; средства к существованию; *daily* ~ хлеб насущный; ~ *and butter* хлеб с маслом; пища; ~*winner* кормилец.

breadth, *n*, ширина; широта кругозора; размах; полотнище.

break, *n*, поломка; отверстие; прорыв; перерыв; разрыв; *lunch* ~ перерыв на обед; перемена (в школе); ~ *of day* рассвет; ¶ *v.t*, ломать; разбивать; разрушать; взламывать; нарушать *(law, promise)*; порывать *(relations)*; прерывать *(sleep)*; побить *(pf.) (record)*; сообщать *(news)*; *v.i*, светать; ломаться; прерываться *(of voice)*; разоряться; ~ *away* убегать; вырываться; ~ *down (v.t.)* разбивать; разбирать; *(v.i.)* ломаться; терпеть аварию; ~ *forth* вырываться; разражаться; ~ *(forth) into tears* расплакаться *(pf.)*; ~ *in (v.i)* врываться; вмешиваться в (разговор); *(v.t.)* укрощать; объезжать *(horses)*; ~*off* отламывать; прекращать; обрывать; ~ *out* вспыхивать *(of fire)*; убегать (из тюрьмы); появляться; разражаться; ~ *out laughing* расхохотаться *(pf.)*; ~ *through* прорываться(ся); ~ *up (n)* развал; распад; закрытие школы (на каникулы); *(v.t.)* разбивать (на куски); распускать на каникулы; *(v.i.)* разбиваться; расходиться *(of meeting)*; на крываться (на каникулы); меняться *(of weather)*; ~**able**, *a*, ломкий; хрупкий; ~**age**, *n*, ломка, поломка; авария; ~**down**, *n*, упадок сил; разруха; авария, поломка; разборка, расчленение; *nervous* ~ нервное расстройство.

breaker, *n*, бурун; *(wave)*; *ice* ~ ледокол.

breakfast, *n*, завтрак; ¶ *v.i*, завтракать.

breakneck, *a*, опасный; *at* ~ *speed* сломя голову.

breakthrough, *n*, прорыв.

breakwater, *n*, волнорез.

breast, *n*, грудь; *(fig.)* душа.

breath, *n*, дыхание; дуновение; жизнь; *be out of* ~ запыхаться *(pf.)*; задыхаться; *take* ~ передохнуть *(pf.)*, переводить дыхание; ~**e**, *v.i*, дышать; вздыхать; жить; *v.t*, тихо говорить; дышать *(inst.)*, выражать; ~**ing**, *n*, дыхание; дуновение; *(phon.)* придыхание; ~ *space* передышка; **~less**, *a*, запыхавшийся, задыхающийся; бездыханный; безветренный.

breech, *n*, казённая часть *(of gun)*; **~es**, *n.pl*, штаны; бриджи.

breed, *n*, порода; потомство; ¶ *v.t*, выводить, разводить *(animals)*; воспитывать; *(fig.)* порождать; *v.i*, размножаться; **~er**, *n*, производитель; *cattle* ~ скотовод, животновод; **~ing**, *n*, выведение, разведение; воспитание; *cattle* ~ скотоводство, животноводство.

breeze, *n*, лёгкий ветерок, бриз; овод; **breezy**, *a*, ветреный; живой.

brethren, *n.pl*, собратья.

breviary, *n*, конспект; *(eccl.)* требник.

brevity, *n*, краткость.

brew, *n*, варево; заварка *(of tea)*; ¶ *v.t*, варить *(beer, coffee)*; заваривать *(tea)*; приготовлять; смешивать; *v.i*, надвигаться *(of storm)*; **~er**, *n*, пивовар; **~ery**, *n*, пивоваренный завод.

briar, *n*, эрика; шиповник; трубка из эрики.

bribe, *n*, взятка; подкуп; ¶ *v.t*, давать взятку *(dat.)*; подкупать; **~ry**, *n*, взяточничество.

brick, *n*, кирпич; брусок *(of soap)*; *(pers.)* золотой человек; *pl*, *(toy)* кубики; ¶ *a*, кирпичный; **~layer** каменщик; **~work** кладка кирпича; **~yard** кирпичный завод.

bridal, *a*, свадебный; **bride**, *n*, невеста, новобрачная; **~groom** жених, новобрачный; *bridesmaid* подружка невесты.

bridge, *n*, мост; капитанский мостик; перемычка; переносица; кобылка (скрипки); бридж *(cards)*; **~head** плацдарм; ¶ *v.t*, соединять мостом; перекрывать; ликвидировать *(gap)*.

bridle, *n*, узда, уздечка; ~ *path* вьючная тропа; ¶ *v.t*, взнуздывать; обуздывать.

brief, *n*, сводка, резюме; *accept a* ~ принимать на себя ведение дела в суде; *in* ~ вкратце; ¶ *a*, краткий, сжатый; ¶ *v.t*, инструктировать; **~case**, *n*, портфель, чемоданчик; **~ly**, *ad*, кратко.

brig, **brigantine**, *n*, бриг, бригантина.

brigade, *n*, бригада; команда, отряд; **brigadier**, *n*, бригадир, командир бригады.

brigand, *n*, разбойник, бандит; **~age**, *n*, разбой, бандитизм.

bright, *a*, яркий; светлый; блестящий; прозрачный; полированный; умный, живой; ¶ *ad*, ярко; блестяще; **~en**, *v.t*, освещать; полировать; придавать блеск *(dat.)*; *v.i*, проясняться; улучшаться; оживляться; **~ness**, *n*, яркость; блеск; живость; весёлость.

brilliancy, *n*, яркость; блеск; великолепие; **brilliant**, *a*, блестящий; сверкающий; выдающийся.

brim, *n*, край; поля *(pl.)* *(of hat)*; *fill to the* ~ наполнять(ся) до краёв; *full to the* ~ полный до краёв.

brimstone, *n*, сера

brindled, *a*, пёстрый, полосатый.

brine, *n*, морская вода; рассол; **briny**, *a*, солёный.

bring, *v.t*, приносить, привозить, приводить; причинять; заставлять; ~ *about* осуществлять; вызывать; ~ *back* приносить обратно; вспоминать; ~ *down* снижать *(price)*; сбивать *(aeroplane)*; ~ *forth* производить; порождать; ~ *forward* выдвигать *(proposal)*; ~ *in* вводить; вносить *(bill)*; приносить *(income)*; ~ *into action* вводить в бой; приводить в действие; ~ *on* навлекать; ~ *out* выводить; выявлять; ~ *round* приводить в себя; переубеждать; ~ *to a close* доводить до конца; ~ *to life* приводить в чувство; ~ *to light* выяснять; выводить на чистую воду; ~ *up* воспитывать; поднимать *(question)*.

brink, *n*, край; крутой берег.

brisk, *a*, живой; оживлённый.

brisket, *n*, грудинка.

briskness, *n*, живость; свежесть.

bristle, *n*, щетина; ¶ *v.i*, ощетиниваться; подниматься дыбом; сердиться; ~ *with difficulties* изобиловать трудностями; **bristly**, *a* щетинистый; колючий.

British, *a*, (велико) британский, английский.

Briton, *n*, британец, англичанин; древний бритт.

brittle, *a*, хрупкий, ломкий.

broach, *n,* вёртел; шпиль *(of church);* *(tech.)* сверло, развёртка; ¶ *v.t,* прокалывать; буравить; развёртывать; *(fig.)* оглашать; начинать обсуждать *(question).*

broad, *a,* широкий; просторный; свободный; общий; грубый; *in ~ daylight* среди бела дня; *~cast (v.t.)* передавать по радио; *(n.)* радиопередача; *~casting* радиовещание; *~-minded* с широким кругозором; *~-shouldered* широкоплечий; *~side* орудия одного борта; бортовой залп; *(fig.)* брань; *give smb. a ~side* обрушиваться на; *~ly, ad,* широко; *~ speaking* в общих чертах; *~en, v.t. (& i.),* расширять(ся).

brocade, *n,* парча.

broken, *p.p. & a,* разбитый; сломанный; нарушенный; разорившийся; ломаный *(language);* прерывистый *(voice);* *~-hearted* убитый горем.

broker, *n,* маклер; комиссионёр; оценщик; *~age, n,* маклерство; комиссионное вознаграждение.

bromide, *n,* бромид; **bromine,** *n,* бром.

bronchial, *a,* бронхиальный; **bronchitis,** *n,* бронхит.

bronze, *n,* бронза; бронзовое изделие; ¶ *a,* бронзовый; ¶ *v.t,* покрывать бронзой.

brooch, *n,* брошь.

brood, *n,* выводок; семья; дети; стая; ¶ *v.i,* сидеть на яйцах; высиживать; *(fig.)* размышлять; *~y, a: ~ hen* насёдка.

brook, *n,* ручей; ¶ *v.t,* терпеть, выносить.

broom, *n,* метла, веник; *(bot.)* ракитник; *~stick, n,* метловище.

broth, *n,* суп, похлёбка; отвар.

brothel, *n,* публичный дом.

brother, *n,* брат; коллега; *~-in-arms* собрат по оружию; *~-in-law* зять; шурин; деверь; *~hood, n,* братство; *~ly, a,* братский; ¶ *ad,* по-братски.

brougham, *n,* двухместная карета.

brow, *n,* бровь; лоб; выступ *(of cliff);* край *(of hill);* *~beat, v.t,* запугивать; обращаться надменно с.

brown, *a,* коричневый; смуглый, загорелый; карий *(of eyes);* *~* bread серый хлеб; *~ paper* обёрточная бумага; *~ sugar* жёлтый сахарный песок; ¶ *v.t, & i,* делать(ся) коричневым; загорать; *~ish, a* бурый, коричневатый.

browse, *n,* молодые побеги; ¶ *v.i,* читать, рыться в книгах; *v.t,* ощипывать.

bruise, *n,* синяк; ушиб; ¶ *v.t,* ставить синяки *(dat.,* на); ушибать.

brunette, *n,* брюнётка.

brunt, *n,* главный удар.

brush, *n,* щётка, кисть; хвост *(of fox);* *~wood* хворост; ¶ *v.t,* чистить щёткой; причёсывать *(hair);* *~ off* смахивать; *~ up (fig.)* освежать (в памяти).

Brussels sprouts брюссельская капуста.

brutal, *a,* жестокий; грубый; *~ity, n,* жестокость; *~ize, v.t. (& i.)* делать(ся) грубым/жестоким.

brute, *n,* животное; жестокий человек; «скотина»; **brutish,** *a,* грубый, зверский.

bubble, *n,* пузырь, пузырёк; *(fig.)* «мыльный пузырь»; ¶ *v.i,* пузыриться; кипеть; *~ up* бить ключом.

buccaneer, *n,* пират.

buck, *n,* самец *(of deer, rabbit, etc.);* брыкание; *(mil.)* ~shot крупная дробь; *~skin* оленья кожа; ¶ *v.i,* становиться на дыбы; брыкаться.

bucket, *n,* ведро.

buckle, *n,* пряжка; ¶ *v.t,* застёгивать; гнуть, сгибать; *v.i,* сгибаться; *~ to* приниматься за дело; *~r, n,* щит; защита.

buckram, *n,* клеёнка.

buckthorn, *n,* крушина.

buckwheat, *n,* гречиха.

bucolic, *a,* сельский.

bud, *n,* почка; бутон; ¶ *v.i,* давать почки; развиваться.

Buddhism, *n,* буддизм; **Buddhist,** *a,* буддийский; ¶ *n,* буддист.

budge, *v.t,* шевелить; сдвигать с места; *v.i,* шевелиться.

budgerigar, *n,* попугайчик

budget, *n,* бюджет; ¶ *v.t: ~ for* предусматривать в бюджете.

buff, *n,* кожа буйвола/быка; ¶ *a,* тускло-жёлтый.

buffalo, *n,* буйвол.

buffer, *n,* бу́фер; амортиза́тор; глуши́тель; ~ *state* бу́ферное госуда́рство.

buffet, *n,* буфе́т; уда́р.

buffoon, *n,* шут, фигля́р; ¶ *a,* шутовско́й; ~**ery,** *n,* шутовство́; буффона́да.;

bug, *n,* клоп; ви́рус; *big* ~ ши́шка.

bugbear, *n,* пуга́ло; бу́ка.

bugle, *n,* охо́тничий рог; горн; сигна́льная труба́; ~**r,** *n,* горни́ст; сигнали́ст.

build, *n,* констру́кция; телосложе́ние; ¶ *v.t,* стро́ить; создава́ть; вить *(nest);* *well-built* хорошо́ сложённый; ~ *on* осно́вывать(ся) на; пристра́ивать; ~ *up* укрепля́ть; ~**er,** *n,* строи́тель; ~**ing,** *n,* зда́ние, постро́йка; строе́ние; строи́тельство; ¶ *a,* строи́тельный; ~ *engineer* инжене́р-строи́тель; ~ *society* жили́щно-строи́тельная коопера́ция.

bulb, *n,* электри́ческая ла́мпочка; ша́рик (термо́метра); лу́ковица *(bot.);* ~**ous,** *a,* лу́ковичный; луковицеобра́зный; вы́пуклый.

bulge, *n,* вы́пуклость; увеличе́ние; ¶ *v.i,* выдава́ться, выпя́чиваться.

bulk, *n,* объём; бо́льшая часть; ко́рпус (зда́ния), грома́да; груз; *sell in* ~ продава́ть гурто́м ~**head,** *n,* перебо́рка; ~**y,** *a,* объёмистый; громо́здкий; гру́зный.

bull, *n,* бык; саме́ц; (па́пская) бу́лла; ~ *calf* бычо́к; ~*dog* бульдо́г; ~*fight* бой быко́в; ~*finch* снеги́рь; ~*'s eye* слухово́е окно́; я́блоко мише́ни.

bullet, *n,* пу́ля; ~*proof* пуленепроница́емый.

bulletin, *n,* бюллете́нь; сво́дка; сообще́ние.

bullion, *n,* сли́ток зо́лота/серебра́.

bullock, *n,* вол.

bully, *n,* задира, забия́ка; хулига́н; сутенёр; ¶ *v.t,* дразни́ть; запу́гивать.

bulrush, *n,* камы́ш.

bulwark, *n,* вал; бастио́н; опло́т; фальшбо́рт *(of ship).*

bumble-bee, *n,* шмель.

bump, *n,* уда́р, толчо́к; ши́шка; вы́пуклость; ¶ *v.t,* ударя́ть, толка́ть; догоня́ть (пере́днюю ло́дку); *v.i,* ударя́ться, сту́каться; ~**er,** *a,* о́чень большо́й; ~

harvest небыва́лый урожа́й; ¶ *n,* бу́фер.

bumpkin, *n,* мужла́н, неотёсанный па́рень.

bumptious, *a,* самоуве́ренный; надме́нный.

bun, *n,* бу́лочка, сдо́ба; кекс; пучо́к; у́зел *(of hair).*

bunch, *n,* пучо́к, свя́зка; па́чка; буке́т; грозд *(of grapes);* свя́зка *(of keys);* гру́ппа, компа́ния; ¶ *v.t,* свя́зывать в пучки́, собира́ть; *v.i,* сбива́ться в ку́чу.

bundle, *n,* у́зел; паке́т; вяза́нка; ~ *of nerves* комо́к не́рвов; ¶ *v.t,* свя́зывать в у́зел; ~ *away/off* отсыла́ть; спрова́живать.

bung, *n,* про́бка; заты́чка; ¶ *v.t,* затыка́ть; заку́поривать.

bungalow, *n,* бу́нгало, одноэта́жный дом.

bungle, *n,* плоха́я рабо́та; пу́таница; ¶ *v.t,* по́ртить; ~**r,** *n,* плохо́й рабо́тник.

bunion, *n,* о́пухоль (на большо́м па́льце ноги́).

bunk, *n,* ко́йка.

bunker, *n,* бу́нкер; я́мка *(of golf);* убе́жище; блинда́ж; ~ *coal* бу́нкерный у́голь.

bunkum, *n,* болтовня́, чепуха́.

bunting, *n,* материа́л для фла́гов; фла́ги; овся́нка *(bird).*

buoy, *n,* буй, ба́кен; ве́ха; ¶ *v.t,* ста́вить ба́кены на; ~ *up* подде́рживать на пове́рхности; *(fig.)* подде́рживать; ~**ancy,** *n,* плаву́честь; жизнера́достность; ~**ant,** *a,* плаву́чий; жизнера́достный.

burden, *n,* но́ша, тя́жесть; груз; бре́мя; ¶ *v.t,* нагружа́ть; обременя́ть; ~**some,** *a,* обремени́тельный, тя́гостный.

burdock, *n,* лопу́х, репе́йник.

bureau, *n,* бюро́, отде́л, управле́ние; пи́сьменный стол, конто́рка; ~**cracy,** *n,* бюрокра́тия; бюрократи́зм; ~**crat,** *n,* бюрокра́т; ~**cratic,** *a,* бюрократи́ческий.

burglar, *n,* вор-взло́мщик; ~**y,** *n,* кра́жа со взло́мом; **burgle,** *v.t,* соверша́ть кра́жу со взло́мом.

burgundy, *n,* кра́сное бургу́ндское вино́.

burial, *n,* погребе́ние; ~ *ground* кла́дбище; ~ *place* ме́сто погребе́ния; ~ *service* заупоко́йная слу́жба.

burlesque, *n*, паро́дия, карика́тура; ¶ *a*, пароди́йный; ¶ *v.t*, пароди́ровать.

burly, *a*, здорове́нный; большо́й и си́льный.

burn, *n*, ожо́г; ¶ *v.t*, жечь, сжига́ть; *v.i*, горе́ть; сгора́ть; подгора́ть *(of food)*; get sun~t загора́ть; ~ down сжига́ть (сгора́ть) дотла́; ~ one's fingers обжёчься *(pf.)*; ~er, *n*, горе́лка *(gas)*; ~ing, *n*, горе́ние; о́бжиг; ¶ *a*, горя́чий; жгу́чий *(fig.)*.

burnish, *v.t*, полирова́ть; ~er, *n*, полиро́вщик; инструме́нт для полиро́вки; ~ing, *n*, полиро́вка.

burnt offering всесожже́ние.

burr, *n*, жужжа́ние, шум; заусе́нец *(of metal)*; ве́нчик (вокру́г луны́).

burrow, *n*, нора́, хо́д; ¶ *v.i*, рыть нору́; жить в норе́; ры́ться в кни́гах.

bursar, *n*, казначе́й; завхо́з; ~у, *n*, казначе́йство; стипе́ндия.

burst, *n*, взрыв *(of applause)*; разры́в *(shell)*; вспы́шка *(fire)*; ¶ *v.t*, взрыва́ть, разрыва́ть; разла́мывать; размыва́ть *(banks)*; *v.i*, взрыва́ться, разрыва́ться; ло́паться; разража́ться; ~ into blossom расцвета́ть; ~ into tears залива́ться слеза́ми; ~ into the room врыва́ться в ко́мнату; ~ open распа́хивать(ся); ~ out вырыва́ться; вспы́хивать; ~ with envy ло́паться от за́висти.

bury, *v.t*, хорони́ть; зарыва́ть; пря́тать; ~ one's face in one's hands закрыва́ть лицо́ рука́ми; ~ oneself in books зарыва́ться в кни́гах.

bus, *n*, авто́бус.

bush, *n*, куст, куста́рник; *(tech.)* вту́лка.

bushel, *n*, бу́шель (ме́ра ёмкости о́коло 36.3 ли́тра).

bushy, *a*, покры́тый куста́рником; густо́й *(beard)*; пуши́стый *(tail)*.

business, *n*, де́ло; заня́тие, профе́ссия; (торго́вое) предприя́тие; комме́рческая де́ятельность; сде́лка; обя́занность; on ~ по де́лу; big ~ кру́пный капита́л; ~ hours часы́ приёма/торго́вли; mean ~ бра́ться за де́ло реши́тельно; mind your own ~! не ва́ше де́ло!; ~like, *a*, делово́й; ~man, *n*, бизнесме́н, деле́ц.

buskin, *n*, коту́рн.

bust, *n*, бюст; грудь.

bustle, *n*, суета́, суматоха; ¶ *v.i*, суети́ться, торопи́ться.

busy, *a*, занято́й; де́ятельный; за́нятый; оживлённый; беспоко́йный; ¶ *v.t*, дава́ть рабо́ту *(dat.)*; занима́ть; ~body, *n*, хлопоту́н, ~ья.

but, *c*, но; а; одна́ко; тем не ме́нее; е́сли (бы) не; ~ then но с друго́й стороны́; но зато́; ¶ *ad*, то́лько; лишь; all ~ почти́; едва́ не; ¶ *pr*, кро́ме; за исключе́нием; anything ~ далеко́ не; всё, что уго́дно, то́лько не.

butcher, *n*, мясни́к; *(fig.)* уби́йца; пала́ч; ¶ *v.t*, убива́ть; *(fig.)* искажа́ть; ~у, *n*, бо́йня, резня́.

butler, *n*, дворе́цкий.

butt, *n*, бо́чка; мише́нь; прикла́д *(of weapon)*; уда́р (голово́й/рога́ми); стык; пе́тля *(of door)*; *(fig.)* предме́т (насме́шек); ¶ *pl*, стре́льбище, полиго́н; ¶ *v.t*, ударя́ть голово́й; бода́ть; *v.i*, выдава́ться; ~ into вма́киваться.

butter, *n*, ма́сло; ~ dish маслёнка; ¶ *v.t*, нама́зывать ма́слом; льстить *(dat.)*.

buttercup, *n*, лю́тик.

butterfly, *n*, ба́бочка.

buttock, *n*, я́годица.

button, *n*, пу́говица; кно́пка; ~hole пе́тля; ¶ *v.t*, застёгивать (на пу́говицы).

buttress, *n*, *(build.)* подпо́ра; *(fig.)* опо́ра, подде́ржка; ¶ *v.t*, подде́рживать; служи́ть опо́рой *(dat.)*.

buxom, *a*, миловидный; здоро́вый; по́лный *(of figure)*.

buy, *v.t*, покупа́ть, приобрета́ть; ~ in закупа́ть; ~ off откупа́ться от; ~ out выкупа́ть; ~ over подкупа́ть; ~ up скупа́ть; ~er, *n*, покупа́тель, ~ница; ~ing, *n*, поку́пка, приобрете́ние.

buzz, *n*, жужжа́ние; гул *(of voices)*; ¶ *v.i*, жужжа́ть; гуде́ть; лете́ть о́чень ни́зко *(of aircraft)*.

buzzard, *n*, каню́к.

by, *pr*, у; при; о́коло; вдоль; ми́мо; че́рез; посре́дством; ~ airmail авиапо́чтой; ~ and large в о́бщем; ~ law по зако́ну; ~ no means ни в ко́ем слу́чае; ~ 5 o'clock к пяти́ часа́м; ~ plane самолётом; ~ then к тому́ вре́мени; ~ the way кста́ти, между прочим; ¶ *ad*, близко; рядом; мимо.

by-election, *n*, дополнительные выборы.

bygone, *a*, прошлый.

by-law, *n*, постановление местной власти/организации.

by-pass, *n*, обход, обходная дорога; обходный канал.

bypath, *n*, боковая дорога/тропа.

by-product, *n*, побочный продукт.

bystander, *n*, свидетель, зритель.

byway, *n*, боковая/просёлочная дорога.

byword, *n*, поговорка; *be a* ~ быть притчей во языцех.

C

cab, *n*, наёмный экипаж, кэб; такси; кабина водителя *(of lorry)*; ~*man* извозчик; шофёр такси.

cabal, *n*, интрига; политический манёвр; политическая клика; ~-**istic**, *a*, каб(б)алистический; таинственный; мистический.

cabaret, *n*, кабаре, эстрадное представление.

cabbage, *n*, капуста; *head of* ~ кочан капусты.

cabin, *n*, кабина; будка; хижина; каюта; ~ *boy* юнга.

cabinet, *n*, кабинет; кабинет министров; шкатулка; комод; ~ *maker* столяр-краснодеревщик; ~ *work* тонкая столярная работа.

cable, *n*, кабель; канат, трос; якорная цепь; телеграмма; ¶ *v.t*, телеграфировать.

cabriolet, *n*, экипаж.

cache, *n*, тайник; тайный склад.

cackle, *n*, кудахтанье *(of hens)*; гоготанье *(of geese)*; хихиканье; болтовня; ¶ *v.i*, кудахтать; гоготать; хихикать; болтать; ~**r**, *n*, хохотун; болтун.

cactus, *n*, кактус.

cad, *n*, хам; грубиян.

cadaverous, *a*, трупный; смертельно бледный.

caddish, *a*, грубый, вульгарный.

caddy, *n*, человек, прислуживающий при игре в гольф; чайница.

cadence, *n*, ритм; модуляция; понижение голоса; *(mus.)* каденция.

cadet, *n*, курсант, кадет.

café, *n*, кафе.

cage, *n*, клетка; лифт; кабина; ¶ *v.t*, сажать в клетку.

cairn, *n*, каменная пирамида.

cajole, *v.t*, льстить *(dat.)*; обхаживать; обманывать; ~**ry**, *n*, лесть; обман.

cake, *n*, торт; пирожное; лепёшка *(also of mud)*; плитка, кусок, брусок; ~ *of soap* кусок мыла.

calabash, *n*, горлянка; бутылка из горлянки.

calamitous, *a*, пагубный; бедственный; **calamity**, *n*, бедствие.

calcareous, *a*, известковый.

calcine, *v.t*, обжигать; прокаливать; **calcium**, *n*, кальций.

calculable, *a*, измеримый, исчисляемый; **calculate**, *v.t*, вычислять, подсчитывать; рассчитывать; предполагать; **calculation**, *n*, вычисление, калькуляция; расчёт; предположение; **calculus**, *n*, *(med.)* камень; *(maths)* исчисление.

calendar, *n*, календарь; святцы; список.

calf, *n*, телёнок *(also fig.)*; оленёнок, слонёнок; икра *(of leg)*; ~ *skin* телячья кожа.

calibrate, *v.t*, калибровать; градуировать; проверять; **calibration**, *n*, калибрование; градуировка; **calibre**, *n*, калибр; диаметр; *(fig.)* значительность, достоинство, качество.

calico, *n*, коленкор; ситец.

caliph, *n*, халиф; ~**ate**, *n*, халифат.

call, *n*, зов; оклик; крик *(of bird, animal)*; призыв; сигнал; телефонный вызов; перекличка; призвание; визит; остановка *(of train)*; заход в порт *(of ship)*; ¶ *v.t*, звать; окликать; называть; вызывать, призывать; созывать; будить; *v.i*, приходить с визитом; заходить; ~ *at* останавливаться в, заходить в; ~ *back* звать обратно; ~ *for* требовать; заходить за; ~ *in* требовать назад; ~ *off* отзывать; отменять; прекращать; переносить; ~ *on* посещать, навещать; взывать; ~ *out* вызывать; ~ *over* делать перекличку; ~ *up* вызывать по телефону; призывать **на**

военную службу; **~er**, *n*, гость; посетитель; **~ing**, *n*, призвание; влечение; профессия.

callous, *a*, огрубелый; мозолистый; чёрствый.

callow, *a*, неоперившийся; неопытный.

calm, *n*, тишина; безветрие, штиль; ¶ *a*, спокойный; тихий; мирный; безветренный; ¶ *v.t*, успокаивать; **~ly**, *ad*, спокойно; хладнокровно; **~ness**, *n*, тишина; спокойствие.

calorie, *n*, калория.

calumniate, *v.t*, клеветать на, порочить; **calumny**, *n*, клевета.

calve, *v.i*, телиться; родить детёныша *(of elephant, whale)*.

Calvinist, *n*, кальвинист.

calyx, *n*, *(bot.)* чашечка; *(anat.)* чашевидная полость.

cambric, *n*, батист.

camel, *n*, верблюд.

camellia, *n*, камелия.

cameo, *n*, камея.

camera, *n*, фотоаппарат; **~man** фоторепортёр; кинооператор; телеоператор.

camomile, *n*, ромашка.

camouflage, *n*, маскировка, камуфляж; *(fig.)* хитрость; ¶ *v.t.* *(& i.)*, маскировать(ся).

camp, *n*, лагерь; привал; **~ bed** раскладушка; **~ stool** складной стул; ¶ *v.i*, располагаться лагерем; жить в палатке.

campaign, *n*, кампания, поход; ¶ *v.i*, проводить кампанию; участвовать в походе; **~er**, *n*, участник кампании; *old* **~** старый служака; *(fig.)* бывалый человек.

campanula, *n*, колокол. чик.

camphor, *n*, камфара.

can, *n*, бидон; жестяная банка/ коробка; банка консервов; ¶ *v.t*, консервировать; **~ned**, *a*, консервированный.

can, *v.aux*, мочь; уметь; иметь возможность/право.

Canadian, *a*, канадский; ¶ *n*, канад|ец, **~ка**.

canal, *n*, канал; **~ization**, *n*, канализация; система/устройство каналов; **~ize**, *v.t*, проводить канализацию/каналы в; направлять.

canary, *n*, канарейка.

cancel, *v.t*, отменять; аннулировать; вычёркивать; погашать *(stamp)*; *(maths)* сокращать дробь; **~lation**, *n*, отмена, аннулирование; вычёркивание; погашение; сокращение.

cancer, *n*, рак; *(fig.)* бич; **~ous**, *a*, раковый.

candelabrum, *n*, канделябр.

candid, *a*, честный; искренний; откровенный; **~** *camela* скрытая камера.

candidate, *n*, кандидат; **candidature**, *n*, кандидатура.

candied, *a*, засахаренный.

candle, *n*, свеча; **~stick** подсвечник.

Candlemas, *n*, праздник сретения.

candour, *n*, искренность; прямота.

cane, *n*, трость; палка; камыш; тростник; ¶ *v.t*, бить палкой.

canine, *a*, собачий.

canister, *n*, жестяная коробка.

canker, *n*, язва, червоточина; **~** *worm* плодовый червь; **~ous**, *a*, разъедающий; губительный.

cannibal, *n*, людоед, каннибал; ¶ *a*, людоедский, каннибальский; **~ism**, *n*, людоедство.

cannon, *n*, пушка; артиллерия; **~ball** пушечное ядро; **~ fodder** пушечное мясо; **~ shot** пушечный выстрел/снаряд; **~ade**, *n*, канонада, артиллерийский огонь; пушечная стрельба; ¶ *v.t*, обстреливать артиллерийским огнём.

canny, *a*, ловкий, хитрый, «себе на уме».

canoe, *n*, каноэ, челнок, байдарка.

canon, *n*, *(eccl.)* канон, святцы; правило; критерий; каноник; **~ical**, *a*, канонический; **~ization**, *n*, канонизация; **~ize**, *v.t*, канонизировать; **~ry**, *n*, должность каноника.

canopy, *n*, балдахин; навес, тент; купол (парашюта).

cant, *n*, косяк, наклон; лицемерие, ханжество; плаксивый тон (нищего); ¶ *v.t*, скашивать; наклонять.

cantankerous, *a*, сварливый, придирчивый.

cantata, *n*, кантата.

canteen, *n*, столовая; буфет; ящик.

canter, *n*, лёгкий галоп; ¶ *v.i*, ехать лёгким галопом.

Canterbury Bell колокольчик средний.

canticle, *n*, песнь, гимн.

canton, *n*, кантон, округ.

canvas, *n*, холст; парусина; канва; *under* ~ *(mar.)* под парусами; *(mil.)* в палатках.

canvass, *v.t*, обсуждать; собирать (голоса); агитировать; ~**er**, *n*, участник обсуждения; сборщик голосов, агитатор; ~**ing**, *n*, обсуждение; собирание голосов, агитация.

canyon, *n*, каньон, глубокое ущелье.

cap, *n*, шапка, фуражка, кепка; чепец; наконечник; крышка; головка; пистон, капсюль; *set one's* ~ *at* заигрывать с; ¶ *v.t*, перекрывать; перещеголять *(pf.)*.

capability, *n*, способность; умение; возможность; **capable**, *a*, способный; одарённый; умелый; ~ *of* способный на *(or inf.)*.

capacious, *a*, просторный; вместительный, объёмистый; **capacitate**, *v.t*, делать способным/правомочным; **capacity**, *n*, ёмкость, вместимость; способность; компетенция; положение; *(tech.)* мощность.

caparison, *n*, попона; убор, украшение; ¶ *v.t*, покрывать попоной; украшать.

cape, *n*, накидка, пелерина; *(geog.)* мыс.

caper, *n*, каперсовый куст; прыжок; шалость; ¶ *v.i*, делать прыжки; шалить.

capillary, *n*, капилляр; ¶ *a*, капиллярный.

capital, *n*, капитал, состояние; столица; *(arch.)* капитель; ¶ *a*, превосходный; главный; ~ *letter* заглавная буква; ~ *punishment* смертная казнь; ~**ism**, *n*, капитализм; ~**ist**, *n*, капиталист; ~**ic**, *a*, капиталистический; ~**ize**, *v.t*, капитализировать, превращать в капитал.

capitulate, *v.i*, капитулировать, сдаваться; **capitulation**, *n*, капитуляция.

capon, *n*, каплун.

caprice, *n*, каприз, причуда; непостоянство; **capricious**, *a*, капризный; непостоянный.

capsize, *v.t. (& i.)*, опрокидывать(ся).

capstan, *n*, кабестан, ворот.

capsule, *n*, капсюль; капсула, оболочка.

captain, *n*, капитан.

caption, *n*, заголовок *(in newspaper)*; титр *(in film, etc)*.

captious, *a*, придирчивый; каверзный; ~**ness**, *n*, придирчивость; каверзность.

captivate, *v.t*, пленять, очаровывать; **captivation**, *n*, пленительность, очарование; **captive**, *a*, пленный, взятый в плен; ¶ *n*, пленный, пленник; **captivity**, *n*, плен; **capture**, *n*, захват; добыча; взятие в плен; ¶ *v.t*, захватывать (силой), брать в плен.

Capuchin, *n*, капуцин; плащ с капюшоном.

car, *n*, машина, автомобиль; вагон; ~ *park* стоянка машин, автомобильный парк.

caramel, *n*, карамель.

caravan, *n*, караван; фургон; дом на колёсах.

caraway, *n*, тмин.

carbolic acid, *n*, карболовая кислота.

carbon, *n*, углерод; *(elec.)* угольный углерод; уголь; ~ *monoxide* угарный газ; ~ *paper* копирка; ~**iferous**, *a*, угленосный; каменноугольный; ~**ize**, *v.t*, обугливать, обжигать; коксовать.

carbuncle, *n*, карбункул.

carburettor, *n*, карбюратор.

carcass, *n*, каркас, остов; корпус; кузов; туша.

card, *n*, карта, карточка; билет (членский, пригласительный); *(tech.)* чесалка; ~*board* картон; ¶ *v.t*, чесать.

cardigan, *n*, кофточка.

cardinal, *n*, кардинал; ¶ *a*, главный, основной; *(gram.)* количественный.

care, *n*, забота; попечение, уход; внимание; осмотрительность; *take* ~! береги(те)сь!; *take* ~ *of* смотреть за, заботиться о; ~*taker* сторож; ~*worn* измученный заботами; ¶ *v.i*, заботиться; беспокоиться; ~ *to* иметь желание; *I don't* ~ мне всё равно.

careen, *v.t*, килевать, кренговать.

career, *n*, карьера; карьер, быстрый бег; ¶ *v.i*, быстро двигаться, нестись.

careful, a, забо́тливый; осторо́жный; внима́тельный, стара́тельный; ~ness, n, осторо́жность; внима́тельность.

careless, a, небре́жный; неосторо́жный; беззабо́тный ~ness, n, небре́жность; неосторо́жность; беззабо́тность.

caress, n, ла́ска; ¶ v.t, ласка́ть.

cargo, n, груз; ~ boat грузово́е су́дно, торго́вое су́дно.

caricature, n, карикату́ра; ¶ v.t, изобража́ть в карикату́рном ви́де; caricaturist, n, карикатури́ст.

carmine, n, карми́н.

carnage, n, бо́йня, резня́.

carnal, a, пло́тский, чу́вственный; половой.

carnation, n, гвозди́ка.

carnival, n, карнава́л.

carnivora, n.pl, плотоя́дные живо́тные; carnivorous, a, плотоя́дный.

carol, n, гимн.

carotid, n, со́нная арте́рия.

carousal, n, пиру́шка, попо́йка; carouse, v.i, пирова́ть.

carp, n, карп; ¶ v.i, придира́ться; критикова́ть; ~ing, a, придирчи́вый.

carpenter, n, пло́тник; ¶ v.i, пло́тничать; carpentry, n, пло́тничное де́ло.

carpet, n, ковёр; ¶ v.t, устила́ть коврами.

carriage, n, каре́та, экипа́ж; (rly.) ваго́н; перево́зка, пересы́лка; сто́имость перево́зки; оса́нка; поса́дка (головы); каре́тка (of typewriter); проведе́ние (of proposals); gun ~ лафе́т, оруди́йный стано́к; ~ free пересы́лка беспла́тно; ~ paid за пересы́лку упла́чено.

carrier, n, носи́льщик; посы́льный; (post.) почтальо́н; (mar.) авиано́сец; (med.) бациллоноси́тель; (tech.) держа́тель; кронште́йн; ~borne aircraft самолёты, де́йствующие с авиано́сца; luggage ~ бага́жник; ~ pigeon почто́вый го́лубь.

carrion, n, па́даль.

carrot, n, морко́вь, морко́вка.

carry, v.t, везти́, (пере)вози́ть; нести́, (пере)носи́ть; подде́рживать; проводи́ть (proposal); приноси́ть (profit); ~ away уноси́ть; (fig.) увлека́ть; ~ forward продвига́ть;

переноси́ть; ~ off уноси́ть; похища́ть; ~ on продолжа́ть; флирто́вать; ~ out, through доводи́ть до конца́; выполня́ть; ~ the day одержа́вать побе́ду; ~ weight (fig.) име́ть вес/влия́ние.

cart, n, теле́га; пово́зка; ~ horse ломова́я ло́шадь; ~load воз; ¶ v.t, везти́ в теле́ге; ~age, n, гужева́я перево́зка; сто́имость гужево́й перево́зки; ~er, n, возчи́к.

cartilage, n, хрящ.

cartoon, n, карикату́ра; мультфи́льм; ~ist, n, карикатури́ст.

cartridge, n, патро́н; ~belt патронта́ш; патро́нная ле́нта; ~ case патро́нная ги́льза; ~ pouch патро́нная су́мка.

carve, v.t, ре́зать; выреза́ть (по де́реву, ко́сти); вая́ть; высека́ть (из ка́мня); разде́лывать (meat); ~ up дели́ть, дроби́ть; ~r, n, ре́зчик по де́реву; нож (для мя́са); carving, n, резьба́ по де́реву; резна́я рабо́та.

cascade, n, водопа́д, каска́д.

case, n, слу́чай; обстоя́тельство; (суде́бное) де́ло; я́щик, коро́бка; футля́р, чехо́л, чемода́н; (gram.) паде́ж; ~shot карте́чь; in ~ в слу́чае; in any ~ во вся́ком слу́чае; ¶ v.t, класть в я́щик; вставля́ть в опра́ву; покрыва́ть; обрамля́ть.

case-hardened, a, закалённый.

casemate, n, каземат́.

casement, n, око́нный переплёт.

cash, n, де́ньги; нали́чные де́ньги; ~ book ка́ссовая кни́га; in ~ при деньга́х; нали́чными (деньга́ми); out of ~ не при деньга́х; ~ on delivery нало́женным платежо́м; ~ payment нали́чный расчёт; pay in ~ плати́ть нали́чными; ¶ v.t, получа́ть де́ньги по че́ку; ~ier, n, касси́р.

cashmere, n, кашеми́р.

casing, n, обши́вка; покры́шка.

cask, n, бочо́нок.

casket, n, шкату́лка; (U.S.) гроб.

casserole, n, кастрю́ля.

cassette, n, кассе́та.

cassock, n, ря́са, сута́на.

cast, n, бросо́к; броса́ние, мета́ние; фо́рма для отли́вки; ги́псовый слепо́к; образе́ц; (theat.) соста́в; ~ in the eye небольшо́е косогла́зие; ~ of features выраже́ние

лица́; ~ *of mind* склад ума́; ¶
v.t, броса́ть, кида́ть; меня́ть,
сбра́сывать *(skin)*; роня́ть *(leaves)*; распределя́ть (ро́ли); наз-
знача́ть на роль; отлива́ть *(metal)*;
~ *about for* обду́мывать; иска́ть;
~ *a glance* броса́ть взгляд; ~ *a
vote* голосова́ть; ~ *ashore* выбра́сы-
вать на бе́рег; ~ *down* сверга́ть;
разруша́ть; удруча́ть; ~ *loose*
освобожда́ть; ~ *lots* броса́ть
жре́бий; ~ *off* покида́ть; сбра́сы-
вать; зака́нчивать; ~ *out* вы-
гоня́ть; ~ *the net* заки́дывать
сеть; ~ *up* изверга́ть; вски́ды-
вать *(eyes, etc)*; ~ *iron, n,* чугу́н;
¶ *a,* чугу́нный; *(fig.)* непрек-
ло́нный, твёрдый.

castaway, *n,* потерпе́вший корабле-
круше́ние; *(fig.)* отве́рженный.

caste, *n,* ка́ста.

castellated, *a,* постро́енный в ви́де
за́мка.

castigate, *v.t,* нака́зывать; суро́во
критикова́ть, бичева́ть; **castiga-
tion,** *n,* наказа́ние; суро́вая кри́-
тика.

casting, *n,* литьё, отли́вка; *(theat.)*
распределе́ние роле́й; ~ *vote*
реша́ющий го́лос.

castle, *n,* за́мок; *(chess)* ладья́;
¶ *v.t, (chess)* рокирова́ть.

castor, *n,* судо́к; ро́лик, коле́-
сико *(on furniture)*; ~ *oil* касто́-
ровое ма́сло, касто́рка; ~ *sugar*
са́харная пу́дра.

castrate, *v.t,* кастри́ровать; **castra-
tion,** *n,* кастра́ция.

casual, *a,* случа́йный; непостоя́н-
ный; нерегуля́рный; небре́жный;
~ty, *n,* несча́стный слу́чай;
(pers.) пострада́вший; *(mil.)* ра́-
неный; уби́тый; *pl,* поте́ри; ~ *list*
спи́сок уби́тых, ра́неных и про-
ва́вших без ве́сти.

casuist, *n,* казуи́ст; ~ical, *a,* казу-
исти́ческий; ~ry, *n,* казуи́стика;
софи́стика.

cat, *n,* кот; ко́шка.

catcall, *n,* свист, осви́стывание;
¶ *v.t,* осви́стывать.

cataclysm, *n,* катакли́зм; перево-
ро́т.

catacombs, *n.pl,* катако́мбы, под-
земе́лье.

catafalque, *n,* катафа́лк.

catalogue, *n,* катало́г; ¶ *v.t,* вно-
си́ть в катало́г.

catapult, *n,* катапу́льта; рога́тка.

cataract, *n,* водопа́д; *(med.)* ката-
ра́кта.

catarrh, *n,* ката́р, просту́да.

catastrophe, *n,* катастро́фа; **catas-
trophic,** *a,* катастрофи́ческий.

catch, *n,* пои́мка, захва́т; уло́в
(fish); добы́ча; па́ртия; уло́в-
ка, хи́трость; загво́здка; защёлка, задви́жка *(of door)*; ¶
v.t, лови́ть *(also fig.)*; схва́ты-
вать *(also disease)*; заража́ться
(inst; disease); успева́ть на
(train); застава́ть; догоня́ть; за-
цепля́ть; *v.i,* цепля́ться; ~ *breath*
переводи́ть/затаи́ть *(pf.)* дыха́-
ние; ~ *cold* простужа́ться; ~ *fire*
загора́ться; ~ *hold of* ухва́ты-
ваться за; ~ *on* ухва́тываться за;
понима́ть; станови́ться мо́дным;
~ *the eye* лови́ть взгляд; попа-
да́ться на глаза́; ~ *up* подхва́ты-
вать *(also fig.)*; догоня́ть; ~-
ing, *a,* зарази́тельный; привле-
ка́тельный; захва́тывающий.

catechism, *n,* катехи́зис; **catechize,**
v.t, допра́шивать; излага́ть в
фо́рме вопро́сов и отве́тов.

categorical, *a,* категори́ческий; ре-
ши́тельный; безусло́вный; **category,** *n,* катего́рия.

cater, *v.i,* снабжа́ть прови́зией; пос-
тавля́ть; обслу́живать; ~er, *n,*
поставщи́к.

caterpillar, *n,* гу́сеница *(also tech.)*;
~ *tractor* гу́сеничный тра́ктор.

caterwaul, *v.i,* мяу́кать; ~ing, *n,*
коша́чий конце́рт.

catgut, *n,* струна́.

cathedral, *n,* собо́р.

catholic, *a,* католи́ческий; ¶ *n,*
като́лик; ~ism, *n,* католи́чество,
католици́зм.

catkin, *n,* серёжка.

cattle, *n,* рога́тый скот; ~ *raiser*
скотово́д; ~ *raising* скотово́д-
ство.

caucus, *n,* закры́тое собра́ние (ли́де-
ров); кли́ка.

cauldron, *n,* котёл.

cauliflower, *n,* цветна́я капу́ста.

caulk, *v.t,* конопа́тить, смоли́ть
(ships); затыка́ть, зама́зывать
(gaps).

causative, *a,* причи́нный; *(gram.)*
каузати́вный; **cause,** *n,* причи́на;
основа́ние, по́вод; де́ло *(also
law)*; ¶ *v.t,* причиня́ть, вызыва́ть;

заставлять; ~less, *a*, беспричинный, необоснованный.

causeway, *n*, мостовая; тротуар; дамба.

caustic, *a*, каустический; едкий; *(fig.)* язвительный; ¶ *n*, каустическое средство; едкое вещество; **cauterize**, *v.t*, прижигать; **cautery**, *n*, прижигание; прижигающее средство.

caution, *n*, осторожность; предостережение; ¶ *v.t*, предостерегать; **cautious**, *a*, осторожный, предусмотрительный.

cavalcade, *n*, кавалькада.

cavalier, *n*, всадник; кавалерист; *(coll.)* кавалер; *(hist.)* роялист.

cavalry, *n*, кавалерия, конница.

cave, *n*, пещера; полость; впадина; ~ *dweller* троглодит, пещерный человек; ¶ *v.t*, выдалбливать; ~ *in* оседать, опускаться; *(fig.)* сдаваться.

cavern, *n*, пещера; *(med.)* каверна; ~ous, *a*, похожий на пещеру; пещеристый.

caviar, *n*, икра.

cavil, *n*, придирка; ¶ *v.i*, придираться.

cavity, *n*, полость; впадина.

caw, *n*, карканье; ¶ *v.i*, каркать.

cease, *v.t*, прекращать; *v.i*, переставать, прекращаться; ~less, *a*, непрерывный, непрестанный; ~lessly, *ad*, непрестанно, непрерывно.

cedar, *n*, кедр.

cede, *v.t*, сдавать *(territory)*; уступать.

ceiling, *n*, потолок; перекрытие.

celebrant, *n*, священник; **celebrate**, *v.t*, праздновать; прославлять; служить (обедню); **celebrated**, *a*, знаменитый; прославленный; **celebration**, *n*, празднование; прославление; церковная служба; **celebrity**, *n*, известность, знаменитость.

celerity, *n*, быстрота.

celery, *n*, сельдерей.

celestial, *a*, небесный, божественный.

celibacy, *n*, безбрачие; обет безбрачия; **celibate**, *a*, холостой; давший обет безбрачия.

cell, *n*, тюремная камера; келья; ячейка; *(biol.)* клетка.

cellar, *n*, подвал; *wine* ~ винный погреб.

'cellist, *n*, виолончелист; **'cello**, *n*, виолончель.

cellular, *a*, клеточный.

celluloid, *n*, целлулоид.

cellulose, *n*, целлюлоза; клетчатка.

Celt, *n*, кельт; ~ic, *a*, кельтский.

cement, *n*, цемент; клей; *(fig.)* связь, союз; ¶ *v.t*, цементировать; крепко склеивать, скреплять *(also fig.)*.

cemetery, *n*, кладбище.

cenotaph, *n*, кенотафий.

cense, *v.t*, кадить; ~r, *n*, кадило; курильница.

censor, *n*, цензор; ¶ *v.t*, подвергать цензуре; ~ious, *a*, цензурный; строгий; ~ship, *n*, цензура; **censure**, *n*, осуждение; порицание; ¶ *v.t*, осуждать; порицать.

census, *n*, перепись.

cent, *n*, цент; сто; *per* ~ процент.

centenarian, *a*, столетний; ¶ *n*, человек ста лет; **centenary**, *a*, столетний; ¶ *n*, столетие, столетняя годовщина.

centipede, *n*, сороконожка.

central, *a*, центральный; главный; *C*~ *Asia* Средняя Азия; ~ *heating* центральное отопление; ~ization, *n*, централизация; ~ize, *v.t*, централизовать; **centre**, *n*, центр; середина; помещать в центре; концентрировать, сосредоточивать; **centrifugal**, *a*, центробежный; **centripetal**, *a*, центростремительный.

century, *n*, столетие, век.

ceramic, *a*, гончарный, керамический; ~s, *n*, керамика, гончарное дело.

cereal, *a*, хлебный, зерновой; ¶ *n*, крупа; хлебный злак; овсянка, зерновые хлопья *(breakfast)*.

cerebral, *a*, мозговой.

ceremonial, *a*, формальный; церемониальный; ¶ *n*, церемониал, обряд; ~ly, *ad*, формально; церемонно; **ceremonious**, *a*, церемониальный; церемонный, чопорный; **ceremony**, *n*, обряд, церемония; церемонность.

certain, *a*, определённый; некий, некоторый; уверенный; несомненный; *for* ~ наверняка; *make* ~ убеждаться; проверять; обеспечивать; ~ly, *ad*, конечно; непременно; несомненно; ~ty, *n*, уверенность; несомненность.

certificate, *n*, удостоверение; свидетельство; аттестат; ~ *of health* справка о состоянии здоровья; **certify**, *v.t*, удостоверять, заверять; ручаться за; свидетельствовать о.

cessation, *n*, прекращение, остановка; перерыв.

cession, *n*, уступка; передача.

cesspool, *n*, выгребная яма; сточный колодец.

chafe, *v.t*, тереть, растирать; раздражать; ¶ *v.i*, тереться; раздражаться, горячиться.

chaff, *n*, мякина; солома, отбросы; *(fig.)* подшучивание, поддразнивание; ¶ *v.t*, резать; *(fig.)* дразнить; подшучивать над.

chaffinch, *n*, зяблик.

chafing dish, *n*, жаровня.

chagrin, *n*, досада, огорчение.

chain, *n*, цепь; цепочка; *pl, (fig.)* оковы, узы; ~ *reaction* цепная реакция; ~ *of stores* цепь магазинов; ¶ *v.t*, заковывать; садить на цепь *(dog)*; *(fig.)* привязывать.

chair, *n*, стул; кафедра; председательское место; *take the* ~ председательствовать; ~**man**, *n*, председатель; ~**manship**, *n*, председательство.

chalice, *n*, чаша, кубок.

chalk, *n*, мел; мелок; ¶ *v.t*, писать/рисовать мелом; ~**y**, *a*, меловой; известковый.

challenge, *n*, вызов; *(law)* отвод; оклик (часового); ¶ *v.t*, вызывать (на соревнование/дуэль); сомневаться в; оспаривать; окликать *(of sentry)*; *(law)* давать отвод *(dat.)*; ~**r**, *n*, посылающий вызов; претендент.

chalybeate, *a*, железистый.

chamber, *n*, комната; помещение; палата (парламентская); *(tech.)* камера; ~-*maid* горничная; ~-*music* камерная музыка; ~-*of commerce* торговая палата; ~-*pot* ночной горшок.

chamberlain, *n*, камергер.

chameleon, *n*, хамелеон.

chamois, *n*, серна; замша; ~-*leather* замша; кусок замши.

champ, *v.t*, жевать; *v.i*, чавкать; ~ *at the bit* грызть удила; *(fig.)* быть в нетерпении.

champagne, *n*, шампанское.

champion, *n*, чемпион; победитель; защитник, поборник; ¶ *a*, первый; первоклассный; ¶ *v.t*, защищать; бороться за; ~**ship**, *n*, первенство, чемпионат; звание чемпиона; защита, поборничество.

chance, *a*, случайный; ¶ *n*, случай; случайность; шанс, возможность; риск; *by* ~ случайно; *take one's* ~ рисковать; *stand a* ~ иметь шанс/надежду; ¶ *v.i*, случаться; *v.t*, рисковать *(inst.)*; ~ *upon* случайно натыкаться на.

chancel, *n*, алтарь;

chancellery, *n*, канцелярия; **chancellor**, *n*, канцлер; первый секретарь посольства; президент университета; ~ *of the Exchequer* министр финансов.

chandelier, *n*, люстра; канделябр.

change, *n*, перемена; изменение; обмен; замена; смена *(of clothes)*; пересадка; сдача, мелкие деньги, мелочь; *for a* ~ для разнообразия; ¶ *v.t*, менять, изменять; обменивать; заменять; ~ *clothes* переодеваться; ~ *colour (fig.)* меняться в лице; ~ *hands* переходить из рук в руки; ~ *one's mind* раздумать *(pf.)*; передумывать; ~ *trains* делать пересадку; *v.i*, меняться, изменяться; ~**able**, *a*, непостоянный, изменчивый; ~**ableness**, *n*, непостоянство; изменчивость; ~**less**, *a*, неизменный, постоянный.

channel, *n*, пролив; канал *(also television)*; русло; проток; сток; путь; *English C*~ Ламанш; ¶ *v.t*, проводить канал через; пускать по каналу; направлять.

chant, *n*, песнь; песнопение; ¶ *v.t*, воспевать, петь; *v.i*, петь.

chaos, *n*, хаос; **chaotic**, *a*, хаотический.

chap, *n*, парень, малый; трещина; челюсть *(jaw)*; ¶ *v.i*, трескаться.

chapel, *n*, часовня, капелла.

chaperon, *n*, компаньонка; ¶ *v.t*, сопровождать.

chaplain, *n*, священник; капеллан.

chapter, *n*, глава; *(eccl.)* капитул.

char, *v.t*, обжигать, обугливать; *v.i*, обугливаться; работать уборщицей.

character, *n*, характер, личность; характеристика *(testimonial)*;

буква, иероглиф; *(lit.)* образ, герой, персонаж; ~ *actor* характерный актёр; ~**istic**, *a*, характерный, типичный; ¶ *n*, характерная черта/особенность; ~**ize** *v.t*, характеризовать; изображать.

charade, *n*, шарада.

charcoal, *n*, древесный уголь; ~ *drawing* рисунок углём; ~ *pencil* угольный карандаш.

charge, *n*, нагрузка; заряд; забота; попечение; питомец; обвинение; ответственность; предписание, поручение; требование; цена; *pl*, расходы; *(mil.)* атака; *take* ~ *of* брать на себя заботу/ответственность за; *be in* ~ *of* возглавлять; руководить *(inst.)*; ¶ *v.t*, заряжать; нагружать; поручать; предписывать; требовать; обременять; обвинять; брать с; назначать (цену); *(mil.)* атаковать; ~**able**, *a*, подлежащий оплате.

charger, *n*, *(mil.)* патронная обойма; строевая лошадь.

chariness, *n*, осторожность; заботливость.

charlot, *n*, колесница.

charitable, *a*, благотворительный; милосердный; щедрый; **charity**, *n*, благотворительность; милосердие; милостыня; ~ *ball* благотворительный бал.

charlatan, *n*, шарлатан; знахарь, обманщик.

charm, *n*, очарование, обаяние; *pl*, чары; амулет; ¶ *v.t*, очаровывать; зачаровывать; заклинать *(snake)*; ~**ing**, *a*, очаровательный; прелестный.

charnel house склеп.

chart, *n*, карта; диаграмма, схема, чертёж; ¶ *v.t*, наносить на карту; чертить карту *(gen.)*.

charter, *n*, хартия, грамота; право, привилегия; устав; фрахтовый договор; ¶ *v.t*, даровать привилегию *(dat.)*; фрахтовать; ~**er**, *n*, фрахтовщик.

charwoman, *n*, уборщица, подёнщица.

chary, *a*, осторожный; сдержанный, скупой (на слова).

chase, *n*, погоня, преследование; охота; ¶ *v.t*, преследовать, гнаться за; охотиться на.

chasm, *n*, глубокое ущелье; бездна, пропасть.

chassis, *n*, шасси, рама.

chaste, *a*, целомудренный; сдержанный.

chasten, *v.t*, наказывать; очищать.

chastize, *v.t*, наказывать; ~**ment**, *n*, наказание.

chastity, *n*, целомудрие, чистота.

chasuble, *n*, риза.

chat, *n*, болтовня; беседа, разговор; ¶ *v.i*, разговаривать.

chattels, *n.pl*, движимость.

chatter, *n*, болтовня; щебетание; ¶ *v.i*, болтать; щебетать; стучать (зубами); ~**box**, *n*, болтун, пустомеля; **chatty**, *a*, болтливый.

chauffeur, *n*, шофёр, водитель.

cheap, *a*, дешёвый; обесценённый; ~**en**, *v.t*, обесценивать; удешевлять; *v.i*, дешеветь; обесцениваться; ~**ness**, *n*, дешевизна.

cheat, *n*, обман, мошенничество; обманщик, мошенник; ¶ *v.t*, обманывать; *v.i*, мошенничать, плутовать; ~**ing**, *n*, мошенничество, обман.

check, *n*, задержка; остановка; контроль, проверка; (багажная) квитанция; номерок (в раздевалке); *(chess)* шах; чек; клетка; ~ *cloth* клетчатая ткань; ¶ *v.t*, проверять, контролировать; останавливать; сдерживать; *(chess)* объявлять шах *(dat.)*; ~**ing**, *n*, проверка, контроль; ~**mate**, *n*, шах и мат; полное поражение; ¶ *v.t*, объявлять мат *(dat.)*; наносить полное поражение *(dat.)*; расстраивать (планы).

cheek, *n*, щека; наглость, нахальство; ~-*bone* скула; ~**y**, *a*, нахальный, дерзкий.

cheep, *n*, писк; ¶ *v.i*, пищать.

cheer, *n*, одобрительное восклицание; ура; веселье; *pl*, аплодисменты; ¶ *int*, *pl*, за здоровье!; *good* ~ хорошее настроение; ¶ *v.t*, приветствовать; ободрять, поощрять; аплодировать *(dat.)*; ~ *up* подбодрять(ся); ~ *up!* не унывай(те)!; ~**ful**, *a*, бодрый, весёлый; ~**fulness**, *n*, бодрость, весёлость; ~**io**, *int*, пока!; ~**less**, *a*, унылый, мрачный.

cheese, *n*, сыр; ~ *dairy* сыроварня; ~ *monger* торговец молочными продуктами; ~-*paring* корка сыра; *(fig.)* скупость.

chemical, *a*, химический; ¶ *a*, химикат.

chemise, *n*, женская сорочка.

chemist, *n*, химик; аптекарь; ~'*s shop* аптека; ~**ry**, *n*, химия.

cheque, *n*, чек; ~ **book** чековая книжка.

chequer, *v.t*, чертить в клетку; располагать в шахматном порядке; разнообразить; ~**ed**, *a*, разнообразный; изменчивый.

cherish, *v.t*, лелеять *(hopes, etc.)*; хранить (в памяти); нежно любить.

cherry, *n*, вишня; ~ *stone* вишнёвая косточка.

cherub, *n*, херувим; ~**ic**, *a*, с розовыми щёчками, как херувим.

chess, *n*, шахматы; ~-*board* шахматная доска; ~-*man* шахматная фигура; ~ *player* шахматист.

chest, *n*, ящик, сундук; казна; фонд; *(anat.)* грудная клетка, грудь; ~ *of drawers* комод.

chestnut, *a*, каштановый; ¶ *n*, каштан; ~ *tree* каштан.

chevron, *n*, шеврон.

chew, *v.t*, жевать; *(coll.)* обдумывать; ~ *the cud* жевать жвачку; *(coll.)* пережёвывать старое; ~-*ing*, *n*, жвачка; ~ *gum* жевательная резинка.

chic, *a*, шикарный; модный; нарядный; ¶ *n*, шик.

chicane, *n*, придирка; крючкотворство; ¶ *v.t*, придираться к; *v.i*, заниматься крючкотворством; ~**ry**, *n*, крючкотворство; придирка; софистика.

chick, *n*, цыплёнок; ~**en**, *n*, курица; цыплёнок; птенец; ~-*hearted* трусливый, малодушный; ~-*pox* ветряная оспа, ветрянка; ~**weed**, *n*, алзина.

chicory, *n*, цикорий.

chide, *v.t*, бранить; упрекать.

chief, *a*, главный, основной; ¶ *n*, глава; начальник; руководитель; вождь; ~ *of staff* начальник штаба; ~**ly**, *ad*, главным образом, особенно; ~**tain**, *n*, вождь; атаман.

chiffon, *n*, шифон.

chilblain, *n*, обморожение обмороженное место.

child, *n*, ребёнок; дитя; *be with* ~ быть беременной; ~-*birth* роды; ~'*s play* пустяк; ~**hood**, *n*, детство; *since* ~ с детства; ~**ish**, *a*, детский; ребяческий; ~**ishness**, *n*, ребячество; ~**less**, *a*, бездетный; ~**like**, *a*, инфантильный, невинный, как ребёнок; ~**ren**, *n.pl*, дети.

Chilean, *a*, чилийский; ¶ *n*, чил|иец, ~ийка.

chill, *a*, холодный; прохладный; *(fig.)* бесчувственный, холодный; ¶ *n*, холод; прохлада; простуда; озноб; *(fig.)* холодность; *(tech.)* закалка; *cast a* ~ *over* расхолаживать; *catch a* ~ простудиться *(pf.)*; *take the* ~ *off* подогревать; ¶ *v.t*, охлаждать; студить; *(fig.)* расхолаживать; *(tech.)* закаливать; *v.i*, охлаждаться; холодеть; ~**iness**, *n*, прохлада; холодность; ~**y**, *a*, прохладный; зябкий; *(fig.)* холодный, сухой.

chime, *n*, колокола; колокольный звон; бой часов; гармония; согласие; ¶ *v.i*, звонить *(of bells)*; бить *(of clock)*; ~ *in with* соответствовать *(dat.)*; гармонировать с.

chimera, *n*, химера, дикая фантазия; **chimerical**, *a*, химерический, несбыточный.

chimney, *n*, труба; дымоход; камин; ~-*sweep* трубочист.

chimpanzee, *n*, шимпанзе.

chin, *n*, подбородок.

china[-ware], *n*, фарфор; фарфоровые изделия; ~ *cabinet* буфет.

Chinese, *a*, китайский; ¶ *n*, кита|ец, -янка.

chink, *n*, звон, звякание; трещина, щель; ¶ *v.i*, звенеть; трещать; *v.t*, позвякивать (монетами).

chintz, *n*, ситец.

chip, *n*, щепка; стружка; обломок *(of stone)*; осколок *(of glass)*; фишка *(gaming)*; ¶ *v.t*, стругать; обтёсывать; откалывать; *v.i*, откалываться, отламываться; биться.

chiropodist, *n*, педикюрша; мозольный оператор; **chiropody**, *n*, педикюр.

chirp, *n*, чириканье, щебетанье; ¶ *v.i*, чирикать, щебетать.

chisel, *n,* резе́ц, долото́, стаме́ска; ¶ *v.t,* вая́ть; высека́ть; долби́ть долото́м.

chit, *n,* ребёнок; кро́шка; запи́ска; ~ *of a girl* девчу́шка.

chit-chat, *n,* болтовня́.

chivalrous, *a,* ры́царский; **chivalry** *n,* ры́царство.

chive, *n,* лук-скорода́.

chlorate, *n,* хлора́т; **chloride,** *n,* хлори́д; **chlorine,** *n,* хлор; **chloroform,** *n,* хлорофо́рм; ¶ *v.t,* хлороформи́ровать.

chock, *n,* шокола́д; под-по́рка; ~-**full,** *a,* битко́м наби́тый, перепо́лненный.

chocolate, *n,* шокола́д; *pl,* шокола́дные конфе́ты; ~ *bar* пли́тка шокола́да.

choice, *a,* отбо́рный; ¶ *n,* вы́бор; отбо́р; альтернати́ва.

choir, *n,* хор; ~*master* хормей-стер.

choke, *v.t,* души́ть; загроможда́ть, заноси́ть, засоря́ть; *v.i,* задыха́ться; дави́ться.

cholera, *n,* холе́ра; **choleric,** *a,* холери́ческий; раздражи́тельный, жёлчный.

choose, *v.t,* выбира́ть, избира́ть; хоте́ть, реша́ть (+ *inf.*).

chop, *n,* уда́р; отбивна́я котле́та; ¶ *v.t,* руби́ть; кроши́ть; ~ *off* отруба́ть; ~ *and change* коле-ба́ться, меня́ть взгля́ды/пла́ны; ~ *about* изменя́ть(ся); ~*per, n,* нож (мясника́), коса́рь *(knife);* топо́р-колу́н; ~*ping block* пла́ха; ~*py, a,* неспоко́йный *(sea).*

choral, *a,* хорово́й; ~ *society* хорово́й кружо́к.

chord, *a,* струна́; *(anat.)* свя́зка; *(mus.)* акко́рд; *(maths.)* хо́рда.

chorister, *n,* Хори́ст; **chorus,** *n,* хор; припе́в; *in* ~ хо́ром; ~-*girl* хори́стка; ~-*singer* хори́ст.

Christ, *n,* Христо́с; ~**en,** *v.t,* кре-сти́ть; ~**endom,** *n,* христиа́н-ский мир; ~**ening,** *n,* кре-ще́ние; ~**ian,** *a,* христиа́нский; ¶ *n,* христиани́н|ин, -ка; ~ *name* и́мя; ~**ianity,** *n,* христиа́нство; ~**ianize,** *v.t,* обраща́ть в хри-стиа́нство.

Christmas, *n,* рождество́; *Father* ~ дед-моро́з; *A Merry* ~! с рождество́м!; ~ *carol* рожде́ственский гимн; ~ *Eve* кану́н Рождества́,

сочи́льник; ~ *tree* рожде́ствен-ская ёлка.

chromatic, *a,* цветно́й; *(mus.)* хро-мати́ческий.

chrome, *n,* хром; **chromium,** *n,* хром; ~ *steel* хро́мистая сталь; ~-*plated* хроми́рованный.

chronic, *a,* хрони́ческий.

chronicle, *n,* хро́ника; ле́топись; ¶ *v.t,* запи́сывать в ле́тописи/ дневнике́; ~**r,** *n,* хроникёр; лето-пи́сец.

chronological, *a,* хронологи́ческий; **chronology,** *n,* хроноло́гия; хро-нологи́ческая табли́ца.

chronometer, *n,* хроно́метр.

chrysalis, *n,* ку́колка (ба́бочки).

chubby, *a,* круглоли́цый, толсто-щёкий.

chuck, *n,* чурба́н, поле́но; *(tech.)* зажимно́й патро́н; ¶ *v.t,* швыря́ть, броса́ть; *(tech.)* зажима́ть; ~ *away* упуска́ть *(opportunity);* сори́ть (деньга́ми); ~ *out* выгоня́ть; вы-води́ть; ~ *under the chin* трепа́ть по подборо́дку; ~ *up* броса́ть.

chuckle, *n,* хихи́канье, смех; ¶ *v.i,* посме́иваться, хихи́кать.

chum, *n,* закады́чный друг, при-я́тель, това́рищ.

chump, *n,* чурба́н, коло́да; филе́йная часть *(meat).*

chunk, *n,* кусо́к, ломо́ть.

church, *n,* це́рковь; *C*~ *of England* англика́нская це́рковь; ~*man* церко́вник; ~ *services* богослу-же́ние, слу́жба; ~ *warden* цер-ко́вный ста́роста; ~ *yard* клад-би́ще.

churl, *n,* грубия́н; ~*ish, a,* гру́бый.

churn, *n,* маслобо́йка; ¶ *v.t,* сби-ва́ть *(butter);* взба́лтывать; вспе-нивать *(sea);* ~ *out* выпуска́ть/ производи́ть в большо́м коли-честве.

cider, *n,* сидр.

cigar, *n,* сига́ра.

cigarette, *n,* сигаре́та; папиро́са; ~-*case* портсига́р; ~-*end* оку́рок; ~-*holder* мундшту́к; ~-*lighter* за-жига́лка.

cinder, *n,* зола́; шлак; **Cinderella,** *n,* Зо́лушка.

cinema, *n,* кино́, кинотеа́тр; кине-матогра́фия; ~-*goer* кинозри́тель.

cineraria, *n,* цинера́рия.

cinerary, *a,* пе́пельный; ~ *urn* у́рна с пра́хом.

cinnabar, n, кѝноварь.

cinnamon, n, корѝца.

cipher, n, шифр; цѝфра; монограмма; нуль *(also fig.)*; ¶ *v.t*, зашифровывать; высчѝтывать.

circle, n, круг; окружность; кружок; *(theat.)* ярус; ¶ *v.t*, вращаться вокруг, кружѝться вокруг; окружать.

circuit, n, кругооборот; цикл; объезд; округ (судебный); *(elec.)* цепь; ~ous, a, окольный, окружный; circular, a, круглый; круговой; циркулярный; ~ *railway* окружная железная дорога; ¶ n, циркуляр; реклама; circulate, *v.t*, распространять; передавать; *v.i*, распространяться; обращаться *(of money)*; циркулѝровать; circulating, a, обращающийся; переходящий; circulation, n, циркуляция; тираж *(newspaper)*; (денежное) обращение; распространение.

circumcise, *v.t*, совершать обрезание; circumcision, n, обрезание.

circumference, n, окружность.

circumflex, a, диакритѝческий знак над гласной.

circumlocution, n, многословие, уклончивый разговор.

circumnavigate, *v.t*, совершать кругосветное плавание вокруг; circumnavigation, n, кругосветное плавание.

circumscribe, *v.t*, огранѝчивать; опѝсывать; circumscription, n, ограничение, предел; надпись по кругу/краям.

circumspect, a, осмотрѝтельный, осторожный; ~ion, n, осмотрѝтельность, осторожность.

circumstance, n, обстоятельство; случай; подробность, деталь; *in easy ~s* в хорошем материальном положении; circumstantial, a, подробный; обстоятельный; случайный; ~ *evidence* косвенные улѝки.

circumvent, *v.t*, обманывать, перехитрѝть *(pf.)*; расстраивать.

circus, n, цирк; круглая площадь.

cistern, n, цистерна, бак; резервуар.

citadel, n, крепость; цитадель; оплот.

citation, n, ссылка; цитата; цитѝрование; вызов в суд; cite, *v.t*, цитѝровать; ссылаться на; вызывать (в суд).

citizen, n, гражданѝн, подданный; горожанин; ~ship, n, гражданство, подданство.

citric, a, лимонный; citron, n, цитрон.

city, n, город; *the C~* Сѝти.

civic, a, гражданский; civil, a, гражданский; штатский; вежливый; ~ *defence* противовоздушная оборона; ~ *servant* государственный служащий; ~ *service* государственная гражданская служба; ~ian, a, штатский; ¶ n, штатский человек; pl, гражданское население; ~ity, n, любезность, вежливость.

civilization, n, цивилизация; civilize, *v.t*, цивилизовать; civilized, *p.p.* & a, цивилизованный.

clack, n, треск; щёлканье; болтовня; ¶ *v.i*, трещать; щёлкать; громко болтать.

clad, a, одетый, покрытый, обшѝтый.

claim, n, требование; претензия; *(law)* иск; утверждение; ~ *for damages* требование возмещения убытков; ¶ *v.t*, требовать *(gen.)*; претендовать на; утверждать, заявлять; *(law)* возбуждать иск о; ~ant, n, претендент; *(law)* истец.

clairvoyance, n, ясновѝдение; проницательность; clairvoyant, a, ясновѝдящий; проницательный; ¶ n, ясновѝдец.

clam, n, моллюск.

clamber, *v.i*, карабкаться.

clamminess, n, клейкость; лѝпкость; clammy, a, клейкий; лѝпкий; холодный и влажный.

clamorous, a, криклѝвый, шумный; clamour, n, шум; крѝки; ¶ *v.i*, кричать; ~ *for* шумно требовать.

clamp, n, зажѝм; скоба; ¶ *v.t*, скреплять; зажимать.

clan, n, клан, род; клѝка.

clandestine, a, тайный.

clang, clank, n, звон, лязг, бряцанье; ¶ *v.i*, лязгать, греметь, бряцать.

clannish, a, родовой; обособленный; привѐрженный к своему роду; ~ness, n, привѐрженность к своему роду; кружковщина.

clap, n, хлопанье; хлопок; удар *(of thunder)*; ¶ *v.t*, похлопывать (по спине, *etc.*); хлопать (в ладо́ши); *v.i,* аплоди́ровать; **~per,** *n,* язы́к *(of bell);* трещо́тка; **~ping,** *n,* хло́панье; аплоди- сме́нты.

claptrap, *n,* трескучая фра́за; ерунда́.

claret, *n,* кра́сное вино́.

clarification, *n,* выясне́ние; проясне́ние; **clarify,** *v.t,* выясня́ть, вноси́ть я́сность в.

clarinet, *n,* кларне́т; **~tist,** *n,* кларнети́ст.

clarion, *n,* горн; рожо́к.

clarity, *n,* я́сность; чистота́; прозра́чность.

clash, *n,* столкнове́ние; конфли́кт; лязг; ¶ *v.i,* ста́лкиваться, ударя́ться; греме́ть; расходи́ться *(of views).*

clasp, *n,* пря́жка, застёжка; рукопожа́тие; **~-knife** складно́й нож; ¶ *v.t,* застёгивать; сжима́ть; пожима́ть *(hands).*

class, *n,* класс; разря́д; сорт; **~mate** однокла́ссник; **~ room** кла́ссная ко́мната, класс; **~ war** кла́ссовая война́; ¶ *v.t,* классифици́ровать; распределя́ть.

classic, *a,* класси́ческий; ¶ *n,* кла́ссик; класси́ческое произведе́ние; **~al,** *a,* класси́ческий; **~ist,** *n,* специали́ст по класси́ческим языка́м.

classification, *n,* классифика́ция, **classify,** *v.t,* классифици́ровать.

clatter, *n,* стук, гро́хот; гул *(of voices);* ¶ *v.i,* стуча́ть, греме́ть; болта́ть.

clause, *n,* статья́; пункт; *(gram.)* предложе́ние.

claustrophobia, *n,* боя́знь закры́того простра́нства.

claw, *n,* ко́готь, ла́па, клешня́; *(tech.)* клещи; ¶ *v.t,* хвата́ть; цара́пать, рвать когтя́ми.

clay, *n,* гли́на; ил, ти́на; **~ pipe** гли́няная тру́бка; **~ey,** *a,* гли́нистый.

clean, *a,* чи́стый, опря́тный; чистопло́тный; **~-cut** ре́зко очерченный; я́сный, то́чный; **~-shaven** чистовы́бритый; ¶ *v.t,* чи́стить; очища́ть; **~ up** прибира́ть, приводи́ть в поря́док; **~er,** *n,* убо́рщик, убо́рщица; **~ing,** *n,* убо́рка, чи́стка; *spring* **~** генера́льная убо́рка; **~liness,** *n,* чистота́; чистопло́тность; опря́тность; **cleanse,**

v.t, чи́стить, очища́ть; дезинфици́ровать.

clear, *a,* я́сный; све́тлый; чи́стый; отчётливый; свобо́дный; поня́тный; це́лый, по́лный; *keep* **~** *of* острега́ться/сторони́ться *(gen.);* **~-sighted** дальнови́дный, проница́тельный; ¶ *v.t,* очища́ть, расчища́ть; опорожня́ть; перепры́гивать; распродава́ть; освобожда́ть; *v.i,* проясня́ться; станови́ться прозра́чным; рассе́иваться; **~** *away* убира́ть (со стола́); **~** *off* отде́лываться; удира́ть *(coll.);* **~** *out (v.t.)* опорожня́ть; *(v.i.)* уходи́ть; **~** *up (v.t.)* прибира́ть; выясня́ть *(mystery); (v.i.)* проясня́ться; **~ance,** *n,* очи́стка (от по́шлин); *(tech.)* зазо́р; **~** *sale* распрода́жа; **~ing,** *n,* расчи́щенный уча́сток ле́са; *polη:на:~house* расчётная пала́та; **~ness,** *n,* я́сность.

cleavage, *n,* раска́лывание; *(fig.)* расхожде́ние; вы́рез (пла́тья); **cleave,** *v.t,* раска́лывать; рассека́ть *(air, wave);* **~** *to* остава́ться ве́рным *(dat.);* **~r,** *n,* колу́н; нож мясника́.

clef, *n,* ключ.

cleft, *n,* рассе́лина; уще́лье.

clematis, *n,* ломоно́с.

clemency, *n,* милосе́рдие; мя́гкость *(of weather);* **clement,** *a,* милосе́рдный; мя́гкий.

clench, *v.t,* сжима́ть *(fist);* сти́скивать *(teeth);* зажима́ть.

clergy, *n,* духове́нство; **~man,** *n,* свяще́нник; **clerical,** *a,* клерика́льный *(eccl.);* **~** *error* канцеля́рская оши́бка; **~** *duties* канцеля́рская/конто́рская рабо́та; **~** *staff* конто́рские слу́жащие; **clerk,** *n,* клерк, конто́рский слу́жащий; пи́сарь; секрета́рь; **~** *of works* производи́тель рабо́т, делопроизводи́тель.

clever, *a,* у́мный; спосо́бный; ло́вкий, иску́сный; **~ness,** *n,* одарённость; ло́вкость; уме́ние, иску́сность.

cliché, *n,* клише́, штамп, изби́тая фра́за.

click, *n,* щёлканье; ¶ *v.t,* щёлкать *(inst.).*

client, *n,* клие́нт; покупа́тель; зака́зчик; **~èle,** *n,* клиенту́ра; клие́нты.

cliff, n, утёс.

climacteric, a, климактери́ческий; крити́ческий, опа́сный.

climate, n, кли́мат; **climatic,** a, климати́ческий.

climax, n, вы́сшая то́чка, кульмина́цио́нный пункт.

climb, n, подъём, восхожде́ние; *(avia.)* набо́р высоты́; ¶ v.t, поднима́ться/взбира́ться на; кара́бкаться на; v.i, ла́зить, лезть; ви́ться *(plants);* ~ *down* спуска́ться/слеза́ть с; *(fig.)* уступа́ть; ~**er,** n, альпини́ст; вью́щееся расте́ние; *(fig.)* карьери́ст.

clinch, v.t, прибива́ть гвоздя́ми; заклёпывать; заключа́ть *(deal);* реша́ть *(argument).*

cling, v.i, цепля́ться; прилипа́ть; льнуть; облега́ть *(of dress).*

clinic, n, кли́ника; ~**al,** a, клини́ческий.

clink, n, звон; ¶ v.t, звене́ть *(inst.);* **clinker,** n, кли́нкерный кирпи́ч; шлак.

clip, n, прико́лка *(hair);* скре́пка *(paper);* скоба́, зажи́м; ¶ v.t, скрепля́ть; зажима́ть; стричь *(sheep);* обреза́ть; пробива́ть *(ticket);* ~**per,** n, *(mar.)* кли́пер; pl, но́жницы; *(tech.)* куса́чки; маши́нка для стри́жки; ~**ping,** n, вы́резка из газе́ты; обре́зок; обре́зывание; стри́жка.

clique, n, кли́ка.

cloak, n, плащ; ма́нтия; *(fig.)* покро́в; предло́г; ма́ска; ¶ v.t, покрыва́ть плащо́м; *(fig.)* скрыва́ть; ~**room** раздева́лка, гардеро́б; ка́мера хране́ния.

clock, n, часы́; стре́лка *(on stocking);* ~ *face* цифербла́т; ~**maker** часовщи́к; ~**work** часово́й механи́зм.

clod, n, ком, глы́ба; ~**hopper** дереве́нщина, о́лух.

clog, n, башма́к на деревя́нной подо́шве; коло́дка; препя́тствие; ¶ v.t, меша́ть/препя́тствовать *(dat.);* засоря́ть; v.i, засоря́ться.

cloister, n, монасты́рь; *(arch.)* кры́тая арка́да; ¶ v.t, заточа́ть в монасты́рь; **cloistral,** a, монасты́рский; уедине́нный.

close, a, ду́шный; те́сный; скры́тый; бли́зкий; густо́й, пло́тный; при́стальный *(look);* то́чный *(translation);* сжа́тый *(handwriting);*

~-*fisted* скупо́й; ~-*fitting* облега́ющий; ~-*up* кру́пным пла́ном *(photo);* ¶ v.t, закрыва́ть; зака́нчивать; v.i, закрыва́ться; зака́нчиваться; сближа́ться; ~ *in (v.t.)* огора́живать, окружа́ть; *(v.i.)* приближа́ться; ~ *up (v.t.)* закрыва́ть; *(v.i.)* смыка́ть ряды́; ~ *with* вступа́ть в борьбу́ с; заключа́ть сде́лку с; ¶ n, оконча́ние; заключе́ние; огоро́женное ме́сто; ~**ness,** n, бли́зость духоты́; пло́тность; то́чность; **closet,** n, чула́н; кабине́т; убо́рная; *be* ~*ed with* совеща́ться наедине́ с; **closing,** n, закры́тие; смыка́ние; ~ *down* ликвида́ция; остано́вка рабо́ты; **closure,** n, закры́тие; прекраще́ние пре́ний *(parl.).*

clot, n, сгу́сток; комо́к; ¶ v.i, свёртываться, сгуща́ться, запека́ться.

cloth, n, ткань; сукно́; ска́терть; тря́пка (для пы́ли); духо́вный сан; ~**e,** v.t, одева́ть; *(fig.)* облека́ть; покрыва́ть; ~**es,** n. pl, пла́тье; оде́жда; бельё; ~-*brush* платяна́я щётка; ~-*hanger* пле́чики; ~-*horse* складна́я ра́ма для су́шки белья́; ~-*line* бельева́я верёвка; ~-*moth* моль; ~-*peg* зажи́мка; **clothier,** n, фабрика́нт суко́н; торго́вец мануфакту́рой; портно́й; **clothing,** n, оде́жда; *(mil.)* обмундирова́ние; *(tech.)* обши́вка.

cloud, n, о́блако; ту́ча; *(fig.)* пятно́; *be up in the* ~*s* вита́ть в облака́х; ~-*burst* ли́вень; ¶ v.t, завола́кивать; омрача́ть; ~ *over* завола́киваться; ~**less,** a, безо́блачный; ~**y,** a, о́блачный; му́тный; тума́нный *(also fig.).*

clout, n, лоску́т, тря́пка; затре́щина; ¶ v.t, ударя́ть, дава́ть затре́щину *(dat.).*

clove, n, гвозди́ка; до́лька *(чеснока́).*

cloven, a, раско́лотый; ~ *hoof* раздво́енное копы́то.

clover, n, кле́вер; *in* ~ припева́ючи, «как сыр в ма́сле».

clown, n, кло́ун, шут; ~**ery,** n, клоуна́да; шутки́; ~**ish,** a, шутовско́й.

cloy, v.t, пресыща́ть; ~**ing,** a, сентимента́льный, слаща́вый.

club, n, дуби́нка; *(sport)* клю́шка; клуб; *(cards)* pl, тре́фы; ~-*foot* изуро́дованная ступня́; ¶ v.t, бить дубинкой/прикладом; ~ *together* собираться вместе, устраивать складчину.

cluck, *v.i*, кудахтать; ~ing, *n*, кудахтанье.

clue, *n*, ключ (к разгадке).

clump, *n*, глыба; группа (деревьев); топот (ног); толстая подошва.

clumsiness, *n*, неуклюжесть; грубость; топорность; бестактность; clumsy, *a*, неуклюжий, неповоротливый; грубый; топорный: бестактный.

cluster, *n*, кисть; гроздь; пучок; группа; ¶ *v.i*, расти пучками/гроздьями/группами; собираться группами.

clutch, *n*, сжатие; хватка; *(tech.)* зубцы, муфта; яйца (наседки); выводок; *fall into the* ~s *(of)* попадать в лапы/когти; ¶ *v.t*, схватывать; зажимать; стискивать; выводить *(chicks)*; ~ *at* хвататься за.

clutter, *n*, суматоха; хаос; беспорядок; ¶ *v.t*: ~ *up* заваливать, загромождать.

coach, *n*, карета; *(rly.)* вагон; автобус; тренер, инструктор; репетитор; ~ *builder* вагоностроитель; ~ *building* вагоностроение; ~-house каретный сарай; ~man кучер; ~ *work* кузов; ¶ *v.t*, тренировать, подготавливать, coadjutor, *n*, помощник.

coagulate, *v.t*, коагулировать; *v.i*, свёртываться; сгущаться; coagulation, *n*, свёртывание; коагуляция.

coal, *n*, (каменный) уголь; ~-cellar подвал/погреб для угля; ~-field залежи каменного угля; ~-heaver угольщик; ~ *merchant* торговец углём; ~-mine (каменноугольная) шахта; ~ *mining* каменноугольная промышленность; ~ *scuttle* ведёрко для угля; ~-tar каменноугольная смола; ~ *yard* угольная база; ¶ *v.i*, грузить углём.

coalesce, *v.i*, объединяться; срастаться; coalition, *n*, коалиция.

coarse, *a*, грубый; необработанный; крупный; ~ness, *n*, грубость; необработанность; вульгарность.

coast, *n*, побережье; ~-defence *ship* судно береговой охраны; *the* ~ *is clear* путь свободен; ¶ *v.i*, плавать вдоль берега; ~er, *n*, каботажное судно; ~ing, *n*, каботажное судоходство.

coat, *n*, пальто; пиджак, жакет; шерсть *(of animal)*; слой *(of paint)*; ~ *of arms* герб; ~ *of mail* кольчуга; *turn one's* ~ менять свои убеждения; ¶ *v.t*, покрывать краской; облицовывать; ~ing, *n*, слой (краски) *(tech.)* обшивка; облицовка; материал на пальто.

coax, *v.t*, упрашивать, уговаривать; задабривать; ~ *out of* добиваться *(gen.)* от; ~ing, *n*, уговоры, упрашивание.

cob, *n*, глыба, ком; лебедь-самец; низкая верховая лошадь; крупный орех; кукурузный початок; *(build.)* смесь глины с соломой.

cobalt, *n*, кобальт.

cobble, *n*, булыжник; ¶ *v.t*, мостить булыжником; чинить *(footwear)*; ~r, *n*, сапожник; плохой мастер.

cobra, *n*, кобра, очковая змея.

cobweb, *n*, паутина.

cocaine, *n*, кокаин.

cochineal, *n*, кошениль.

cock, *n*, петух; кран; курок *(of gun)*; стог; ~-a-doodle-doo кукареку; ~-and-bull *story* небылица; ~-crow пение петухов на рассвете; ~ *of the walk* главная фигура; хозяин положения; ~'s *comb* гребешок; ¶ *v.t*, поднимать; настораживать *(ears)*; возводить курок *(gen)*; ~ed *hat* треуголка.

cockade, *n*, кокарда.

cockatoo, *n*, какаду.

cockchafer, *n*, майский жук.

cockerel, *n*, петушок.

cockle, *n*, *(bot.)* куколь; раковина.

cockpit, *n*, арена для петушиных боёв; *(mar.)* кубрик; *(avia.)* кабина.

cockroach, *n*, таракан.

cocktail, *n*, коктейль; ~-shaker прибор для приготовления коктейля.

cocky, *a*, дерзкий, нахальный; самоуверенный.

cocoa, *n*, какао.

coconut, *n*, кокосовый орех; ~ *tree* кокосовая пальма.

cocoon, *n*, кокон.

cod, *n*, треска; ~-liver *oil* рыбий жир.

coddle, *v.t*, баловать, изнеживать; кутать.

code, *n*, кодекс; код, шифр; система сигналов; ¶ *v.t*, шифровать по коду, кодировать; **codicil**, *n*, приписка (к завещанию); **codification**, *n*, кодификация; **codify**, *v.t*, составлять кодекс *(gen.)*, кодифицировать; систематизировать; шифровать.

coeducation, *n*, совместное обучение; ~*al school* школа совместного обучения.

coefficient, *n*, коэффициент; содействующий фактор.

coerce, *v.t*, заставлять, принуждать; **coercion**, *n*, принуждение, насилие; **coercive**, *a*, принудительный.

co-exist, *v.i*, сосуществовать; ~**ence**, *n*, сосуществование.

coffee, *n*, кофе; ~ *bean* кофейное зерно; ~ *cup* кофейная чашка; ~-*grounds* кофейная гуща; ~-*mill* кофейная мельница, кофемолка; ~-*plantation* кофейная плантация; ~-*pot* кофейник; ~ *tree* кофейное дерево.

coffer, *n*, сундук; *pl*, казна.

coffin, *n*, гроб.

cog, *n*, зубец; ~ *in a machine* «винтик», маленький человек; ~ *wheel* зубчатое колесо.

cogency, *n*, убедительность; неоспоримость; **cogent**, *a*, убедительный; неоспоримый.

cogitate, *v.i*, обдумывать; размышлять; **cogitation**, *n*, обдумывание; размышление.

cognate, *a*, родственный; близкий; сходный.

cognition, *n*, знание; познание; познавательная способность.

cognizance, *n*, знание; узнавание; компетенция; подсудность; **cognizant**, *a*, знающий; осознавший; познавший.

cohabit, *v.i*, сожительствовать; ~**ation**, *n*, сожительство.

cohere, *v.i*, быть связанным/сцепленным; согласовываться; быть связным; **coherence**, *n*, связность; **coherent**, *a*, связный; последовательный; понятный; **cohesion**, *n*, связь; сплочённость; **cohesive**, *a*, способный к сцеплению; связующий.

coil, *n*, кольцо; спираль; *(mar.)* бухта (троса); *(elec.)* катушка; ¶ *v.t*, свёртывать кольцом/спиралью; наматывать; *(mar.)* укладывать в бухту; *v.i*, свёртываться кольцом/спиралью; ~ *up* извиваться.

coin, *n*, монета; *pay in his own* ~ отплачивать той же монетой; ¶ *v.t*, чеканить; *(fig.)* фабриковать, измышлять; создавать *(new words)*; ~*age*, *n*, чеканка монеты; монетная система.

coincide, *v.i*, совпадать; ~**nce**, *n*, совпадение.

coiner, *n*, чеканщик монеты; фальшивомонетчик.

coke, *n*, кокс.

colander, *n*, дуршлаг.

cold, *a*, холодный; равнодушный; неприветливый; слабый; *I am* ~ мне холодно; *it is* ~ холодно; *in* ~ *blood* хладнокровно; ~-*blooded* хладнокровный; невозмутимый; ~ *cream* кольдкрем; ~*shoulder* холодный приём; ~ *steel* холодное оружие; ~ *storage* хранение в холодильнике; ¶ *n*, холод; простуда; насморк; ~**ness**, *n* холодность; равнодушие; неприветливость.

coleoptera, *n.pl*, жесткокрылые (насекомые); **coleopterous**, *a*, жесткокрылый.

colic, *n*, колики, резкая боль.

collaborate, *v.i*, сотрудничать; **collaboration**, *n*, сотрудничество; **collaborator**, *n*, сотрудник; коллаборационист.

collapse, *n*, обвал, падение; крушение, крах *(of hopes, plans)*; провал; гибель; изнеможение, упадок сил; ¶ *v.i*, рушиться, обваливаться; терпеть крах; падать духом; падать от слабости; **collapsible**, *a*, складной; откидной.

collar, *n*, воротник; ошейник *(of dog)*; хомут *(also fig.)*; ~-*bone* ключица; ~-*stud* запонка; ¶ *v.t*, хватать за ворот; надевать хомут *(dat.)*; *(coll.)* захватывать.

collate, *v.t*, сравнивать; сопоставлять; сличать.

collateral, *a*, второстепенный, побочный; параллельный.

collation, *n*, сравнивание, сличение; лёгкий ужин.

Colleague, n, коллéга; сослужи́вец.
Collect, n, крáткая моли́тва; ¶ v.t,
собирáть; коллекциони́ровать; за-
ходи́ть за; v.i, собирáться, скоп-
ля́ться; ~ oneself овладевáть
собóй; сосредотóчиваться; собирáться с мы́слями; ~ed, a,
сóбранный; сосредотóченный;
спокóйный; ~ion, n, коллéкция;
сбор (дéнежный); собирáние;
скоплéние; ~ive, a, коллекти́в-
ный; (gram.) собирáтельный; ~
farm колхóз; ~ farmer колхóзник;
~ivization, n, коллективизáция;
~or, n, сбóрщик; коллекционéр.
college, n, коллéдж; университéт;
коллéгия; **collegian,** n, член/
студéнт коллéджа; **collegiate** ,a,
университéтский; академи́чес-
кий; коллегиáльный.
collide, v.i, стáлкиваться.
collie, n, кóлли, шотлáндская ов-
чáрка.
collier, n, углекóп; шахтёр; (mar.)
ýгольщик; ~y, n, (каменноугóль-
ная) шáхта.
collision, n, столкновéние; противо-
рéчие.
colloquial, a, разговóрный; ~ism, n,
разговóрное выражéние; просто-
рéчие; **colloquy,** n, разговóр;
бесéда.
collusion, n, тáйный сгóвор, тáй-
ное сотрудничество.
colon, n, двоетóчие.
colonel, n, полкóвник.
colonial, a, колониáльный; **colonist,**
n, колони́ст, поселéнец; **colonize,**
v.t, колонизи́ровать, заселя́ть.
colonnade, n, коллоннáда.
colony, n, колóния.
colossal, a, колоссáльный; гранди-
óзный; громáдный; **colossus,** n,
колóсс.
colour, n, цвет; крáска; румя́нец
(of face); колори́т; (mil.) знáмя;
~-blind страдáющий дальтони́з-
мом; ~-blindness дальтони́зм; ~
prejudice рáсовая дискримина́-
ция; under ~ of под предлóгом;
под ви́дом; ¶ v.t, раскрáшивать;
окрáшивать; приукрáшивать; v.i,
окрáшиваться; краснéть; ~ed,
p.p. & a, цветнóй; раскрáшенный;
~ful, a, крáсочный; ~ing, n,
колори́т; раскрáска; окрáска;
~less, a, бесцвéтный; блéдный.
colt, n, жеребёнок.

coltsfoot, n, мáть-и-мáчеха.
columbine, n, водосбóр.
column, n, колóнна; стóлб(ик);
столбéц (newspaper); графá; ~ist,
n, журнали́ст; фельетони́ст.
coma, n, кóма; ~tose, a, комá-
тóзный.
comb, n, расчёска, гребёнка; грé-
бень; ¶ v.t, чесáть, расчёсывать;
~ out вычёсывать; разы́скивать.
combat, n, бой, сражéние; ¶ v.t,
сражáться/борóться с; ~ant, a,
боевóй; ¶ n, боéц; побóрник;
~ive, a, боевóй, войнственный;
~iveness, n, боевóй дух, войн-
ственность.
combination, n, сочетáние; соеди-
нéние; сою́з, объединéние; pl,
комбинáция; **combine,** n, (agr.)
комбáйн; комбинáт, синдикáт;
объединéние; ¶ v.t, (& i.),
сочетáть(ся); объединя́ть(ся);
смéшивать(ся).
combustible, a, горю́чий, воспла-
меня́емый; ¶ n, горю́чее, тóпливо;
combustion, n, горéние; сго-
рáние.
come, v.i, приходи́ть, прибывáть;
приезжáть; происходи́ть; ~ about
случáться; ~ across случáйно
встречáться с; натáлкиваться на;
~ back возвращáться; ~ by про-
ходи́ть ми́мо; достигáть (gen.);
достáвать; ~ down спускáться;
пáдать; переходи́ть по тради́-
ции; ~ down in the world теря́ть
состоя́ние/положéние; опускáться; ~ forward выходи́ть вперёд;
выдвигáться; откликáться; ~
home возвращáться домóй; ~ in
входи́ть; прибывáть; вступáть
(в дóлжность); ~ in! войди́(те)!
~ in useful пригоди́ться (pf.);
~ into one's head приходи́ть в
гóлову; ~ near приближáться;
~ off отрывáться (button); от-
чищáться (stain); удавáться; про-
исходи́ть; ~ on наступáть; приближáться; преуспевáть; расти́;
~ out выходи́ть; обнару́живать-
ся; распускáться (leaf); ~ out
with выступáть с; ~ round за-
ходи́ть; поправля́ться; изменя́ть-
ся к лýчшему; ~ to доходи́ть до;
составля́ть; приходи́ть в себя́;
~ to an agreement приходи́ть к
соглашéнию; ~ to blows доходи́ть
до рукопáшной; ~ to light об-

нару́живаться; ~ *to pass* происхо́дить, случа́ться; ~ *up* подни́ма́ться; возника́ть; всходи́ть *(plant)*; ~ *up to* подходи́ть к; равня́ться с; ~ *upon* ната́лкиваться на; ~ *undone* развя́зываться; ~ *what may!* будь что бу́дет!.

comedian, *n*, ко́мик; комедиа́нт; **comedy**, *n*, коме́дия.

comeliness, *n*, милови́дность.

comely, *a*, милови́дный, хоро́шенький.

comet, *n*, коме́та.

comfort, *n*, утеше́ние, подде́ржка; поко́й; комфо́рт, удо́бство; ¶ *v.t*, утеша́ть, успока́ивать; **~able**, *a*, удо́бный, комфорта́бельный; ую́тный; споко́йный; утеши́тельный; **~er**, *n*, утеши́тель; тёплый шарф; **~ing**, *a*, утеши́тельный, успокои́тельный.

comic, *a*, коми́ческий; смешно́й; коме́дийный; ~ *opera* коми́ческая о́пера; ~ *part* коми́ческая/коме́дийная роль; ¶ *n*, *(pers.)* ко́мик; ко́микс *(paper)*; **~al**, *a*, смешно́й, поте́шный.

coming, *a*, бу́дущий; наступа́ющий; многообеща́ющий ¶ *n*, прихо́д; прие́зд; прибы́тие; **~s** *and goings* постоя́нная ходьба́ туда́ и обра́тно; ~ *out* дебю́т; вы́ход; вы́воз *(of goods)*.

comma, *n*, запята́я.

command, *n*, прика́з; распоряже́ние; кома́нда, кома́ндование; госпо́дство; владе́ние; вое́нный о́круг; ¶ *v.t*, прика́зывать *(dat.)*; кома́ндовать/управля́ть *(inst.)*; госпо́дствовать над; владе́ть *(inst.)*; внуша́ть *(respect)*; **~ant**, *n*, команди́р; нача́льник; коменда́нт; **~eer**, *v.t*, принуди́тельно набира́ть (в а́рмию); реквизи́ровать; **~er**, *n*, команди́р; нача́льник; кома́ндующий; **~-in-chief** главнокома́ндующий; **~ment**, *n*, прика́з; за́поведь.

commemorate, *v.t*, пра́здновать, отмеча́ть; служи́ть напомина́нием *(gen.)*; **commemoration**, *n*, пра́зднование.

commence, *v.t*, начина́ть; *v.i*, начина́ться; **~ment**, *n*, нача́ло; а́ктовый день.

commend, *v.t*, хвали́ть; рекомендова́ть; вверя́ть, поруча́ть; **~-**

~able, *a*, похва́льный; **~ation**, *n*, похвала́; рекоменда́ция.

commensurate, *a*, соотве́тственный; соразме́рный.

comment, *n*, примеча́ние; толкова́ние; коммента́рий; замеча́ние; ¶ *v.i*, комменти́ровать; де́лать замеча́ние; замеча́ть; **~ary**, *n*, коммента́рий; **~ator**, *n*, коммента́тор.

commerce, *n*, торго́вля, комме́рция; **commercial**, *a*, комме́рческий, торго́вый; ~ *traveller* коммивояжёр; **~ism**, *n*, торга́шеский дух.

commiserate, *v.i*, сочу́вствовать, выража́ть соболе́знование; **commiseration**, *n*, сочу́вствие, соболе́знование.

commissariat, *n*, комиссариа́т; интенда́нтство; **commissary**, *n*, комисса́р; уполномо́ченный; интенда́нт.

commission, *n*, поруче́ние; полномо́чие; коми́ссия; комиссио́нная прода́жа; комиссио́нное вознагражде́ние; ¶ *v.t*, поруча́ть *(dat.)*; уполномо́чивать; назнача́ть на до́лжность; подготовля́ть к пла́ванию *(ship)*; **~ed** *officer* офице́р, произведённый в чин прика́зом короля́/президе́нта; **~er**, *n*, уполномо́ченный; комисса́р; член коми́ссии.

commit, *v.t*, соверша́ть *(crime, suicide)*; предава́ть (огню́, суду́); ~ *to memory* зау́чивать, запомина́ть; ~ *to prison* заключа́ть в тюрьму́; ~ *to writing* запи́сывать; ~ *oneself* подверга́ть себя́ ри́ску; свя́зывать себя́; **~ment**, *n*, заключе́ние под стра́жу; обяза́тельство.

committee, *n*, комите́т; коми́ссия.

commodious, *a*, просто́рный; удо́бный; **~ness**, *n*, просто́рность.

commodity, *n*, това́р; предме́т потребле́ния.

common, *a*, о́бщий; обще́ственный; обыкнове́нный, заря́дный; распространённый; вульга́рный; ~ *herd* чернь; ~ *land* обще́ственный вы́гон, общи́нная земля́; ~ *law* обы́чное пра́во; непи́саный зако́н; *the* ~ *people* обыкнове́нные лю́ди; ~ *sense* здра́вый смысл; *the* ~ *weal* о́бщее бла́го; *in* ~ совме́стно; *have nothing in* ~ не име́ть ничего́ о́бщего; **~ness**, *n*, обычность, обыденность; вульгарность; ~place, a, банальный, избитый; ¶ n, общее место, банальность; ~s, n.pl, третье сословие (народ); ~wealth, n, государство, республика; федерация; общее благосостояние; British C~ Британское Содружество Наций.

commotion, n, волнение; смятение; суматоха.

communal, a, общинный; коммунальный; commune, n, община; коммуна; ¶ v.i, общаться; communicant, n, (eccl.) причастник, причастница; communicate, v.t, сообщать; передавать; v.i, сообщаться; (eccl.) причащаться; communication, n, сообщение; коммуникация; связь; средство сообщения; общение; communicative, a, общительный; communion, n, общение; (eccl.) причастие; communism, n, коммунизм; communist, a, коммунистический; ¶ n, коммунист; community, n, община, общество; общность.

commutable, a, заменимый; commutation, n, замена; смягчение (of punishment); (elec.) переключение; commute, v.t, заменять; смягчать (punishment); переключать (elec.); ездить регулярно.

compact, a, компактный; плотный; сжатый; ¶ n, соглашение, договор; прессованная пудра; пудреница; ~ness, n, компактность, сжатость, плотность.

companion, n, товарищ; спутник, попутчик; собеседник; компаньон(ка); справочник; ~able, a, общительный, компанейский; ~ship, n, товарищеские отношения; компания.

company, n, компания, общество; (mil.) рота; (theat.) труппа; ship's ~ экипаж корабля; present ~ excepted о присутствующих не говорят.

comparable, a, сравнимый; comparative, a, сравнительный; относительный; ¶ n, сравнительная степень; compare, v.t, сравнивать; v.i, сравниться (pf.); поддаваться сравнению; comparison, n, сравнение; сходство.

compartment, n, отделение; купе.

compass, n, круг; объём, обхват; диапазон; предел(ы); (mar.) компас; pl, циркуль; ¶ v.t, достигать (gen.); осуществлять; замышлять; окружать.

compassion, n, сострадание, жалость; ~ate, a, сострадательный, жалостливый.

compatibility, n, совместимость; compatible, a, совместимый.

compatriot, n, соотечественник.

compel, v.t, вынуждать, заставлять.

compendious, a, краткий, сжатый; compendium, n, конспект; резюме; краткое руководство.

compensate, v.t, возмещать (losses), компенсировать; вознаграждать; compensation, n, возмещение, компенсация; вознаграждение.

compete, v.i, конкурировать; соревноваться, состязаться.

competence, n, способность, умение; компетентность; достаток; (law) компетенция, правомочность; competent, a, компетентный; достаточный; (law) правомочный; умелый, способный.

competition, n, конкуренция; соревнование, состязание; конкурс; competitive, a, конкурирующий; соревнующийся; конкурсный; competitor, n, конкурент; соперник; участник конкурса.

compilation, n, компиляция; собирание; compile, v.t, компилировать; собирать (материал); составлять.

complacence, -cy, n, самодовольство; благодушие; complacent, a, самодовольный; благодушный.

complain, v.i, жаловаться; выражать недовольство; ~t, n, жалоба; недовольство; недомогание.

complaisance, n, вежливость; услужливость; complaisant, a, услужливый, уступчивый.

complement, n, дополнение (also gram.); комплект; ~ary, a, дополнительный, добавочный.

complete, a, полный; законченный; совершённый; ¶ ad, совершенно, вполне, полностью; ¶ v.t, завершать, заканчивать, пополнять; комплектовать; completion, n, окончание, завершение.

complex, *a*, сло́жный; ко́мплекс-
ный; ¶ *n*, ко́мплекс.
complexion, *n*, цвет лица́; *(fig.)*
вид; аспе́кт.
complexity, *n*, сло́жность; запу́тан-
ность.
compliance, *n*, согла́сие; усту́пчи-
вость; уго́дливость; compliant, *a*,
усту́пчивый; уго́дливый.
complicate, *v.t*, усложня́ть; ~d, *a*,
сло́жный, запу́танный; compli-
cation, *n*, сло́жность; запу́тан-
ность; усложне́ние; complicity,
n, соуча́стие (в преступле́нии).
compliment, *n*, комплиме́нт; любе́з-
ность; *pl*, поздравле́ние; покло́н,
приве́т; ¶ *v.t*, поздравля́ть; при-
ве́тствовать; говори́ть компли-
ме́нт *(dat.)*; льстить *(dat.)*; ~ary,
a, ле́стный; поздрави́тельный;
беспла́тный.
comply, *v.i*, исполня́ть (про́сьбу,
жела́ние); уступа́ть; ~ *with*
соглаша́ться с; подчиня́ться
(dat.).
component, *a*, составно́й; состав-
ля́ющий; ¶ *n*, компоне́нт; сос-
тавна́я часть.
comport oneself вести́ себя́; comport-
ment, *n*, поведе́ние; мане́ры.
compose, *v.t*, составля́ть; сочиня́ть
(music); успока́ивать; ~ oneself успока́иваться; be ~d of
состоя́ть из; ~d, *a*, споко́йный,
сде́ржанный; ~r, *n*, компози́-
тор; composite, *a*, составно́й;
сло́жный; composition, *n*, сос-
тавле́ние; сочине́ние (шко́льное);
произведе́ние *(lit., mus.)*; по-
строе́ние; соста́в; compositor, *n*,
набо́рщик.
compost, *n*, компо́ст.
composure, *n*, споко́йствие; само-
облада́ние.
compound, *a*, составно́й; сло́жный;
(gram.) сложносочинённый; ¶
n, смесь; составно́е сло́во; огоро́-
женное ме́сто; ¶ *v.t*, сме́шивать;
соединя́ть; составля́ть; *v.i*, при-
ходи́ть к соглаше́нию/компро-
ми́ссу.
comprehend, *v.t*, понима́ть; охва́ты-
вать; comprehensible, *a*, поня́тный;
comprehension, *n*, понима́ние; по-
ня́тливость; comprehensive, *a*,
всесторо́нний, исче́рпывающий;
~ *school* общеобразова́тельная
шко́ла.

compress, *n*, компре́сс; ¶ *v.t*, сжи-
ма́ть; сда́вливать; ~ion, *n*, сжа́-
тие; сда́вливание; *(tech.)* ком-
пре́ссия; ~or, *n*, компре́ссор.
comprise, *v.t*, охва́тывать; заклю-
ча́ть в себе́; содержа́ть.
compromise, *n*, компроми́сс; ¶ *v.t*,
компромети́ровать; *v.i*, идти́ на
компроми́сс.
compulsion, *n*, принужде́ние; *under*
~ вы́нужденный; compulsorily,
ad, в обяза́тельном поря́дке;
compulsory, *a*, обяза́тельный; при-
нуди́тельный.
compunction, *n*, сожале́ние; угры-
зе́ние со́вести.
computation, *n*, вычисле́ние; расчёт; compute, *v.t*, подсчи́тывать;
вычисля́ть; ~r, *n*, вычисли́тель-
ная маши́на, компью́тер.
comrade, *n*, това́рищ; ~ship, *n*,
това́рищеские отноше́ния.
con, *v.t*, зубри́ть; зау́чивать наизу́сть.
concave, *a*, во́гнутый; впа́лый; con-
cavity, *n*, во́гнутая пове́рхность;
во́гнутость.
conceal, *v.t*, скрыва́ть, ута́ивать;
~ment, *n*, ута́ивание; та́йное
убе́жище.
concede, *v.t*, уступа́ть; допуска́ть;
признава́ть.
conceit, *n*, самомне́ние; тщесла́вие;
самодово́льство; ~ed, *a*, само-
дово́льный; тщесла́вный.
conceivable, *a*, мы́слимый; пости-
жи́мый; возмо́жный; conceive,
v.t, представля́ть себе́; понима́ть;
заду́мывать; *(biol.)* зача́ть *(pf.)*.
concentrate, *v.t*, сосредото́чивать,
концентри́ровать; *(chem.)* вы-
па́ривать, сгуща́ть; *v.i*, сосредо-
то́чиваться, концентри́роваться;
concentration, *n*, концентра́ция;
сосредото́чение; сгуще́ние; ~
camp концентрацио́нный ла́герь,
концла́герь.
concentric, *a*, концентри́ческий.
concept, *n*, поня́тие; о́бщее пред-
ставле́ние; ~ion, *n*, понима́ние;
истолкова́ние; поня́тие; кон-
це́пция; за́мысел; *(biol.)* зача́тие.
concern, *n*, интере́с; забо́та; бес-
поко́йство; де́ло, отноше́ние; зна-
че́ние, ва́жность; предприя́тие,
конце́рн; *it is no* ~ *of mine* э́то
меня́ не каса́ется; *meddle in
other people's* ~s вме́шиваться в
чужи́е дела́; ¶ *v.t*, каса́ться

(gen.), относи́ться к; интересо-
ва́ть; ~ *oneself* интересова́ться;
занима́ться; ~ed, *p.p. & a*, за́ня-
тый; заинтересо́ванный; озабо́-
ченный; *as far as I am* ~ что
каса́ется меня́; ~ing, *pr*, отно-
си́тельно, каса́тельно.

concert, *n*, конце́рт; согла́сие; ¶ *v.t*,
сгова́риваться/договариваться о;
согласо́вывать; ~ina, *n*, концерт-
и́но; ~o, *n*, конце́рт.

concession, *n*, усту́пка; конце́с-
сия.

conch, *n*, ра́ковина.

concierge, *n*, консье́рж, ~ка.

conciliate, *v.t*, примиря́ть; распола-
га́ть к себе́; **conciliation**, *n*, при-
мире́ние; **conciliatory**, *a*, прими-
ри́тельный; примире́нческий.

concise, *a*, кра́ткий; сжа́тый; ~ness,
n, кра́ткость; сжа́тость.

conclave, *n*, совеща́ние; *(eccl.)* кон-
кла́в.

conclude, *v.t. & i*, заключа́ть; де́-
лать вы́вод; зака́нчивать(ся);
conclusion, *n*, заключе́ние; вы́вод;
оконча́ние; исхо́д, результа́т;
conclusive, *a*, реша́ющий; убе-
ди́тельный.

concoct, *v.t*, (со)стря́пать *(also fig.)*;
приду́мывать; составля́ть; ~ion,
n, ва́рево; стряпня́; *(coll.)* не-
были́ца, «ба́сни».

concomitant, *a*, сопу́тствующий, ¶
n, сопу́тствующее обстоя́тель-
ство.

concord, *n*, согла́сие; согласова́ние
(also gram.); соглаше́ние; до-
гово́р; ~ance, *n*, согла́сие; со-
отве́тствие; ~at, *n*, конкорда́т,
догово́р.

concourse, *n*, толпа́; скопле́ние.

concrete, *a*, конкре́тный, реа́льный;
бето́нный; ¶ *n*, бето́н.

concubinage, *n*, сожи́тельство; **concubine**, *n*, нало́жница.

concupiscence, *n*, похотли́вость,
вожделе́ние; **concupiscent**, *a*, по-
хотли́вый.

concur, *v.i*, совпада́ть; соглаша́ться;
де́йствовать совме́стно; ~rence,
n, совпаде́ние; стече́ние (обстоя́-
тельств); согла́сие; ~rent, *a*,
совпада́ющий; де́йствующий сов-
ме́стно.

concussion, *n*, сотрясе́ние; толчо́к;
конту́зия; ~ *of the brain* сотря-
се́ние мо́зга.

condemn, *v.t*, осужда́ть, приго-
ва́ривать; бракова́ть; призна-
ва́ть него́дным; ~ation, *n*, осуж-
де́ние; пригово́р; *condemned man*
приговорённый к сме́рти, сме́рт-
ник.

condensation, *n*, сгуще́ние; конден-
са́ция; сжа́тость *(of style)*; **con-
dense**, *v.t*, сгуща́ть *(milk, etc.)*;
конденси́ровать; сжа́то выра-
жа́ть; ~r, *n*, конденса́тор; холо-
ди́льник.

condescend, *v.i*, снисходи́ть; снис-
хо́дить; **condescension**, *n*, снис-
ходи́тельность; снисхожде́ние.

condign, *a*, заслу́женный *(of punishment)*.

condiment, *n*, припра́ва.

condition, *n*, усло́вие; состоя́ние;
pl, обстоя́тельства; обще́ствен-
ное положе́ние; *on* ~ *that* при
усло́вии, что; ¶ *v.t*, обу-
сло́вливать; кондициони́ровать
(air); *be* ~ *ed by* обусло́вли-
ваться *(inst.)*; ~al, *a*, усло́вный
(also gram.); ¶ *n*, усло́вное
наклоне́ние; ~ed, *p.p. & a*, обус-
ло́вленный; усло́вный; кондицио-
ни́рованный.

condole, *v.i*, сочу́вствовать, выра-
жа́ть соболе́знование; ~nce, *n*,
соболе́знование, сочу́вствие.

condone, *v.t*, проща́ть; *(eccl.)* от-
пуска́ть (грехи́).

conduce, *v.i*, спосо́бствовать; при-
води́ть к; **conducive**, *a*, способствующий; благоприя́тный.

conduct, *n*, поведе́ние; веде́ние;
руково́дство; ¶ *v.t*, вести́; руко-
води́ть/управля́ть *(inst.)*; со-
провожда́ть; *(mus.)* дирижи́ро-
вать; ~or, *n*, руководи́тель;
(mus.) дирижёр; конду́ктор *(of
bus)*; проводни́к *(also elec.)*.

conduit, *n*, трубопрово́д; водопро-
во́дная труба́.

cone, *n*, ко́нус; *(bot.)* ши́шка; моро́-
женое в стака́нчике.

confection, *n*, конди́терское из-
де́лие; ~er, *n*, конди́тер; ~'s
shop конди́терская; ~y, *n*, кон-
ди́терская; конди́терские изде́-
лия.

confederacy, *n*, конфедера́ция; сою́з
госуда́рств; **confederate**, *a*, со-
ю́зный; федерати́вный; ¶ *n*,
член конфедера́ции, сою́зник; кон-
федера́т; сообщник; ¶ *v.i*, всту-

пать в союз, составлять федерацию; **confederation**, *n*, федерация, союз.

confer, *v.t*, даровать; присуждать *(degree)*; присваивать *(title)*; *v.i*, совещаться; **~ence**, *n*, совещание, конференция.

confess, *v.t. (& i.)*, признавать(ся); исповедовать(ся); **~edly**, *ad*, по личному/общему признанию; **~ion**, *n*, признание; исповедь; **~ional**, *n*, исповедальня; **~or**, *n*, духовник; исповедник.

confidant, *n*, доверенное лицо; наперсник; **confide**, *v.t*, доверять, вверять; сообщать по секрету; **confidence**, *n*, доверие; уверенность; конфиденциальное сообщение; **confident**, *a*, уверенный; самоуверенный; **confidential**, *a*, секретный, конфиденциальный; доверительный; **~ly**, *ad*, по секрету, конфиденциально; **confiding**, *a*, доверяющий; доверительный.

configuration, *n*, конфигурация; форма.

confine, *n*, предел; граница; ¶ *v.t*, ограничивать; заключать в тюрьму; *be ~ed* рожать; *be ~ to bed* быть прикованным к постели; **~ment**, *n*, ограничение; тюремное заключение; роды.

confirm, *v.t*, подтверждать; утверждать; подкреплять; **~ation**, *n*, подтверждение;утверждение;подкрепление; *(eccl.)* конфирмация; **~ative**, **~atory**, *a*, подтверждающий; подкрепляющий.

confiscate, *v.t*, конфисковать; **confiscation**, *n*, конфискация.

conflagration, *n*, пожар; сожжение.

conflict, *n*, конфликт; столкновение; противоречие; ¶ *v.i*, сталкиваться, быть в конфликте; противоречить; **~ing**, *a*, противоречивый.

confluence, *n*, слияние *(of streams)*; пересечение *(of roads)*; стечение народа; **confluent**, *a*, сливающийся.

conform, *v.t*, приводить в соответствие; сообразовать; приспосабливать; *v.i*, подчиняться (правилам); сообразоваться; соответствовать; **~able**, *a*, соответствующий; подчиняющийся; **~ation**, *n*, устройство; приспособление; подчинение; **~ist**, *n*, конфор-

мист; **~ity**, *n*, соответствие; подчинение; ортодоксальность.

confound, *v.t*, смешивать, спутывать; поражать, смущать; разрушать *(plans)*; **~ed**, *p.p. & a*, смешанный; смущённый; удивлённый; проклятый.

confraternity, *n*, братство.

confront, *v.t*, стоять лицом к лицу с; смотреть в лицо *(dat.)*; устраивать *(dat.)* очную ставку; сопоставлять; сличать; **~ation**, *n*, очная противостоять *(dat.)*; сопоставление.

confuse, *v.t*, смешивать; перепутывать; смущать; **~d**, *p.p. & a*, смущённый; перепутанный; беспорядочный; **confusion**, *n*, смущение, замешательство; путаница; беспорядок.

confute, *v.t*, опровергать.

congeal, *v.t*, замораживать; *v.i*, замерзать, застывать.

congenial, *a*, близкий по духу; подходящий; благоприятный.

congenital, *a*, прирождённый; врождённый.

conger eel, *n*, морской угорь.

congest, *v.t*, перегружать; переполнять; скоплять; *v.i*, переполняться; скопляться; **~ion**, *n*, теснота; перенаселённость; перегруженность, затор (движения); *(med.)* закупорка.

conglomerate, *n*, конгломерат; ¶ *v.t. (& i.)*, собирать(ся); скоплять(ся); **conglomeration**, *n*, скопление; конгломерация.

congratulate, *v.t*, поздравлять; **congratulation**, *n*, поздравление; **congratulatory**, *a*, поздравительный.

congregate, *v.t*, собирать; *v.i*, собираться; скопляться; сходиться; **congregation**, *n*, скопление; собрание; сходка; *(eccl.)* конгрегация; община.

congress, *n*, конгресс; съезд.

congruity, *n*, соответствие; согласованность; совпадение; **congruous**, *a*, соответствующий; гармонирующий; подходящий.

conic(al), *a*, конический; конусообразный.

conifer, *n*, хвойное дерево; **~ous**, *a*, хвойный.

conjectural, *a*, предположительный; **conjecture**, *n*, догадка; предположение; ¶ *v.t*, предполагать.

conjoin, v.t, соединять; ~t, a, соединённый; объединённый; общий.

conjugal, a, супружеский; брачный.

conjugate, v.t, спрягать; conjugation, n, спряжение.

conjunction, n, соединение; связь; (gram.) союз; conjuncture, n, стечение обстоятельств; конъюнктура.

conjuration, n, заклинание; колдовство; conjure, v.t, заклинать; v.i, заниматься магией; колдовать; показывать фокусы; ~ away изгонять (ghost); ~ up вызывать (ghost); вызывать в воображении; conjurer, conjuror, n, волшебник; фокусник; conjuring, n, фокусы; показывание фокусов; ~ trick фокус.

connect, v.t. (& i.), соединять(ся); связывать(ся); сочетать(ся); ~ed, p.p. & a, связанный; соединённый; связный; ~ing rod шатун; ~ion, connexion, n, связь, соединение; родство; родственник; pl, согласованность расписания (поездов); in ~ with в связи с; have good ~s иметь хорошие связи/знакомства.

conning tower, n, боевая рубка.

connivance, n, потворство; попустительство; connive, v.i, потворствовать, смотреть сквозь пальцы.

connoisseur, n, знаток.

connote, v.t, иметь дополнительное значение; означать.

connubial, a, супружеский, брачный.

conquer, v.t, завоёвывать, покорять; побеждать; ~or, n, завоеватель, победитель; conquest, n, завоевание, покорение, победа.

consanguineous, a, родственный, единокровный; consanguinity, n, родство.

conscience, n, совесть; conscientious, a, совестливый; добросовестный; ~ness, n, добросовестность.

conscious, a, сознающий; ощущающий; сознательный; ~ly, ad, сознательно; ~ness, n, сознание; сознательность.

conscript, n, призывник, новобранец; ¶ v.t, призывать на военную службу; ~ion, n, воинская повинность; набор (в армию).

consecrate, v.t, посвящать; освящать; consecration, n, посвящение; освящение.

consecutive, a, последовательный.

consensus, n, согласованность; согласие, единодушие.

consent, n, согласие; разрешение; by common ~ с общего согласия; ¶ v.i, соглашаться; уступать; разрешать.

consequence, n, следствие, последствие; значение, важность; consequent, a, последовательный; вытекающий; ~ly, ad, следовательно; поэтому.

conservation, n, сохранение; консервирование; conservative, a, консервативный; умеренный; охранительный; ¶ n, консерватор; conservatory, n, оранжерея; консерватория; conserve, v.t, сохранять; консервировать.

consider, v.t, рассматривать; обсуждать; принимать во внимание; считаться с; обдумывать; v.i, считать, полагать; ~able, a, значительный; важный; ~ate, a, внимательный к другим, предупредительный; чуткий; ~ation, n, рассмотрение; обсуждение; размышление; соображение; внимание; предупредительность; уважение; in ~ of принимая во внимание; ввиду того, что; that is a ~ это важное соображение/обстоятельство; take into ~ принимать во внимание; under ~ на рассмотрении, рассматриваемый; ~ing, pr, относительно; принимая во внимание.

consign, v.t, передавать; поручать; (пред)назначать; отправлять (goods); ~ee, n, грузополучатель; ~ment, n, груз; отправка товаров; ~ note накладная.

consist, v.i: ~ of состоять из; ~ in заключаться в; ~ence, -cy, n, консистенция, плотность, густота; последовательность; постоянство; согласованность; ~ent, a, последовательный; стойкий; плотный; ~ with совместимый с; согласующийся с; ~ory, n, консистория; коллегия кардиналов.

consolation, n, утешение; ~ prize утешительный приз; console, v.t, утешать; ¶ n, консоль; пульт (управления).

consolidate, *v.t,* укрепля́ть; утвержда́ть; объединя́ть; *(fin.)* консолиди́ровать; *v.i,* укрепля́ться; объединя́ться; затвердева́ть; **consolidation,** *n,* консолида́ция; укрепле́ние; затвердева́ние.

consoling, *a,* утеши́тельный.

consonance, *n,* созву́чие; *(mus.)* консона́нс; **consonant,** *a,* согла́сный; созву́чный; ~ *with* совмести́мый с; ¶ *n,* согла́сный звук.

consort, *n,* супру́г, супру́га; ¶ *v.i,* обща́ться; ~*ium,* *n,* консо́рциум.

conspicuous, *a,* ви́дный, заме́тный; *make oneself* ~ обраща́ть на себя́ внима́ние

conspiracy, *n,* за́говор, конспира́ция; **conspirator,** *n,* заго́ворщик; **conspire,** *v.i,* устра́ивать за́говор; та́йно догова́риваться.

constable, *n,* консте́бль, полице́йский; **constabulary,** *n,* поли́ция.

constancy, *n,* постоя́нство; ве́рность; тве́рдость; **constant,** *a,* постоя́нный; ве́рный; твёрдый; ¶ *n,* постоя́нная величина́, конста́нта.

constellation, *n,* созве́здие; *(fig.)* плея́да.

consternation, *n,* беспоко́йство; трево́га.

constipate, *v.t.* вызыва́ть запо́р у; **constipation,** *n,* запо́р.

constituency, *n,* избира́тели; избира́тельный о́круг; клиенту́ра; **constituent,** *a,* составно́й; избира́ющий; ~ *assembly* учреди́тельное собра́ние ¶ *n,* составна́я часть; избира́тель; **constitute,** *v.t,* составля́ть, образо́вывать; осно́вывать; учрежда́ть; **constitution,** *n,* конститу́ция; устро́йство; составле́ние; учрежде́ние; склад (ума́); телосложе́ние; ~**al,** *a,* конституцио́нный; *(med.)* органи́ческий; ¶ *n,* моцио́н, прогу́лка.

constrain, *v.t,* принужда́ть, вынужда́ть; сде́рживать; стесня́ть; **constraint,** *n,* принужде́ние; принуждённость; ско́ванность; стесне́ние.

constrict, *v.t,* сжима́ть; стя́гивать; сужа́ть; **constringent,** *a,* сжима́ющий; стя́гивающий.

construct, *v.t,* стро́ить, сооружа́ть; создава́ть; ~**ion,** *n,* строи́тельство; стро́йка; строе́ние; сооруже́ние; *(gram.)* констру́кция; ~**ional,** *a,* строи́тельный, конструкти́вный; структу́рный; ~**ive,** *a,* конструкти́вный; строи́тельный; тво́рческий, созида́тел.ный; ~**or,** *n,* констру́ктор; строи́тель.

construe, *v.t,* объясня́ть, толкова́ть; разбира́ть.

consul, *n,* ко́нсул; ~**ar,** *a,* ко́нсульский; ~**ate,** *n,* ко́нсульство.

consult, *v.t,* сове́товаться с; консульти́роваться с; совеща́ться с; справля́ться (по кни́ге); учи́тывать; ~**ation,** *n,* консульта́ция; совеща́ние; *(med.)* конси́лиум; ~**ing,** *a,* консульти́рующий; ~ *room* кабине́т врача́.

consume, *v.t,* потребля́ть; расхо́довать; поглоща́ть; ~**r,** *n,* потреби́тель; ~**r goods** това́ры широ́кого потребле́ния; ширпотре́б.

consummate, *a,* соверше́нный; зако́нченный; ¶ *v.t,* заверша́ть, доводи́ть до конца́; соверше́нствовать; **consummation,** *n,* заверше́ние; коне́ц; соверше́нство.

consumption, *n,* потребле́ние; расхо́д; *(med.)* туберкулёз лёгких, чахо́тка; **consumptive,** *a,* туберкулёзный, чахо́точный; ¶ *n,* больно́й туберкулёзом.

contact, *n,* соприкоснове́ние; конта́кт; ¶ *v.t,* устана́вливать связь/ конта́кт с; соприкаса́ться с.

contagion, *n,* зара́за, инфе́кция; зара́зная боле́знь; *(fig.)* вре́дное влия́ние; **contagious,** *a,* зара́зный, инфекцио́нный; *(fig.)* зарази́тельный; ~**ness,** *n,* зарази́тельность.

contain, *v.t,* содержа́ть, вмеща́ть; сде́рживать; *he could not* ~ *himself for joy* он не мог сдержа́ть себя́ от ра́дости; *this box will not* ~ *it all* э́тот я́щик не вмести́т всего́; ~**er,** *n,* конте́йнер; я́щик; резервуа́р.

contaminate, *v.t,* загрязна́ть; по́ртить; оскверня́ть; заража́ть; **contamination,** *n,* загрязне́ние; по́рча; заражение; оскверне́ние.

contemn, *v.t,* презира́ть; пренебрега́ть *(inst.).*

contemplate, *v.t. & i,* созерца́ть; размышля́ть; обду́мывать; предполага́ть, намерева́ться (+ *inf.);* **contemplation,** *n,* созерца́ние; размышле́ние; рассмотре́ние; предположе́ние; contemplative, *a*, созерца́тельный.

contemporaneous, contemporary, *a*, совреме́нный; одновреме́нный; **contemporary,** *n*, совреме́нник; све́рстник.

contempt, *n*, презре́ние; ~ *of court* неуваже́ние к суду́; ~ible *a*, презри́тельный; ~uous, *a*, презри́тельный.

contend, *v.t.* & *i*, утвержда́ть, заявля́ть; ~ *with* боро́ться с; спо́рить с.

content, *a*, дово́льный; ¶ *v.t*, удовлетворя́ть; ~ *oneself with* дово́льствоваться *(inst.)*; ¶ *n*, удовлетворе́ние; дово́льство; объём; вмести́мость; *pl*, содержа́ние; содержи́мое; *table of* ~s оглавле́ние; ~ed, *p.p.* & *a*, дово́льный, удовлетворённый; ~edly, *ad*, дово́льно, удовлетворённо.

contention, *n*, борьба́; спор; соревнова́ние; утвержде́ние; *my* ~ *is that* . . . я утвержда́ю, что . . .; **contentious,** *a*, спо́рный; придирчивый.

contentment, *n*, удовлетворённость, дово́льство.

contest, *n*, спор; соревнова́ние; состяза́ние; ко́нкурс; ¶ *v.t*, оспа́ривать, опроверга́ть; добива́ться (пре́мии, ме́ста); уча́ствовать (в вы́борах).

context, *n*, конте́кст.

contiguity, *n*, сме́жность; соприкоснове́ние; бли́зость; **contiguous,** *a*, сме́жный; соприкаса́ющийся, прилега́ющий.

continence, *n*, сде́ржанность; воздержа́ние; целому́дрие; **continent,** *a*, сде́ржанный; возде́ржанный; целому́дренный; ¶ *n*, матери́к, контине́нт; ~al, *a*, континента́льный; ~ly, *ad*, сде́ржанно.

contingency, *n*, случа́йность; слу́чай; **contingent,** *a*, случа́йный; усло́вный; зави́сящий (от); ¶ *n*, континге́нт.

continual, *a*, постоя́нный; беспреста́нный; **continuance,** *n*, продолжи́тельность, дли́тельность; продолже́ние; **continuation,** *n*, продолже́ние; возобновле́ние; **continue,** *v.t*, продолжа́ть; *v.i*, продолжа́ться; тяну́ться; остава́ться; **continuity,** *n*, непреры́вность; прее́мственность; **continuous,** *a*, не-

преры́вный; постоя́нного де́йствия; дли́тельный *(also gram.)*.

contort, *v.t*, искривля́ть; искажа́ть; ~ion, *n*, искривле́ние; искаже́ние; ~ionist, *n*, акроба́т.

contour, *n*, ко́нтур, очерта́ние; ~ *line* горизонта́ль.

contraband, *n*, контраба́нда; ¶ *a*, контраба́ндный; ~ist, *n*, контрабанди́ст.

contraception, *n*, примене́ние противозача́точных средств; **contraceptive,** *n*, противозача́точное сре́дство.

contract, *n*, контра́кт, догово́р; ¶ *v.t*, сжима́ть; сокраща́ть; хму́рить *(brows)*; схвати́ть *(pf.) (illness)*; заключа́ть *(marriage)*; де́лать *(debts)*; *v.i*, сжима́ться; сокраща́ться; ~ing, *a* : ~ *party* догова́ривающаяся сторона́; ~ion, *n*, сжа́тие; сокраще́ние; *(philol.)* контракту́ра; ~or, *n*, подря́дчик; *(anat.)* стя́гивающая мы́шца; ~ual, *a*, догово́рный.

contradict, *v.t*, противоре́чить *(dat.)*; опроверга́ть; ~ion, *n*, противоре́чие; опроверже́ние; ~ory, *a*, противоре́чащий; несовмести́мый; противоречи́вый.

contralto, *n*, контра́льто.

contraption, *n*, нови́нка, устро́йство.

contrariety, *n*, противоречи́вость, противополо́жность; **contrarily,** *ad*, напро́тив, наоборо́т; **contrariness,** *n*, упря́мство, своево́лие; **contrary,** *a*, противополо́жный; проти́вный *(wind)*; неблагоприя́тный; упря́мый; ¶ *n*, противополо́жность; *on the* ~ наоборо́т; ~ *to* вопреки́; про́тив.

contrast, *n*, контра́ст; противоположность; сопоставле́ние; ¶ *v.t*, противопоставля́ть; *v.i*, контрасти́ровать.

contravene, *v.t*, наруша́ть; **contravention,** *n*, наруше́ние.

contribute, *v.t*, соде́йствовать/спосо́бствовать *(dat.)*; же́ртвовать *(money)*; ~ *to* вноси́ть вклад (в нау́ку, *etc.)*; сотру́дничать (в газе́те); **contribution,** *n*, соде́йствие; вклад; сотру́дничество (в газе́те, *etc.)*; статья́; поже́ртвование; взнос; нало́г; контрибу́ция; **contributor,** *n*, соуча́стник; жéртвователь; сотрýдник газéты/журнáла; **contributory**, *a*, содéйствующий, способствующий.

contrite, *a*, кáющийся, сокрушáющийся; **contrition**, *n*, раскáяние.

contrivance, *n* приспособлéние; изобретéние; изобретáтельность; **contrive**, *v.t*, придýмывать; изобретáть; затевáть; ~ *to* ухитряться, умудряться.

control, *n*, контрóль, провéрка; управлéние; регулирование; сдéржанность; *under* ~ под контрóлем; *in* подчинéнии; *be out of* ~ выходить из подчинéния; ¶ *v.t*, контролировать, проверять; управлять *(inst.)*; регулировать; сдéрживать *(feelings); (tech.)* настрáивать; ~ *oneself* сдéрживаться; **controller**, *n*, контролёр; инспéктор; *(tech.)* контрóллер; регулятор.

controversial, *a*, спóрный; **controversy**, *n*, спор, полéмика; **controvert**, *v.t*, оспáривать; полемизировать с; возражáть *(dat.)*.

contumacious, *a*, непокóрный; упóрный; упрямый; **contumacy**, *n*, неповиновéние, неподчинéние; упóрство; упрямство.

contumelious, *a*, оскорбительный; дéрзкий; **contumely**, *n*, оскорблéние; дéрзость; бесчéстье.

contuse. *v.t*, контýзить; **contusion**, *n*, контýзия; ушиб.

conundrum, *n*, загáдка, головолóмка.

convalesce, *v.i*, выздорáвливать, попрáвляться; **~nce**, *n*, выздорáвливание; **~nt**, *a*, выздорáвливающий.

convene, *v.t*, созывáть; *v.i*, собирáться.

convenience, *n*, удóбство; выгода; пригóдность; убóрная; *pl*, удóбства, комфóрт; *at your earliest* ~ как/когда вам бýдет удóбно; **convenient**, *a*, удóбный; подходящий; пригóдный; **~ly**, *ad*, удóбно; подходяще.

convent, *n*, монастырь.

convention, *n*, собрáние, съезд; договóр; конвéнция; обычай; услóвность; **~al**, *a*, услóвный; общепринятый, обычный; подчиняющийся услóвностям, старомóдный; **~ality**, *n*, услóвность.

conventual, *a*, монастырский.

converge, *v.i*, сходиться в однóй тóчке; **~nce**, *n*, схождéние в однóй тóчке; конвергéнция; **~nt**, *a*, сходящийся в однóй тóчке.

conversant, *a*, знакóмый, свéдущий.

conversation, *n*, разговóр; **~al**, *a*, разговóрный; **converse**, *a*, обрáтный; перевёрнутый; ¶ *n*, разговóр, бесéда; общéние; обрáтное положéние/утверждéние; ¶ *v.i*, разговáривать, бесéдовать; общáться; **~ly**, *ad*, обрáтно, наоборóт.

conversion, *n*, превращéние; обращéние (в другýю вéру); **convert**, *n*, новообращённый; ¶ *v.t*, превращáть; обращáть (в другýю вéру); *become* ~ed принимáть другýю вéру; переходить в другýю пáртию; **~ible**. *a*, обратимый; заменимый; откиднóй.

convex, *a*, выпуклый; выгнутый; **~ity**, *n*, выпуклость; выгнутость.

convey, *v.t*, перевозить, транспортировать; сообщáть; выражáть *(idea); (law)* передавáть *(property)*; **~ance**, *n*, перевóзка; достáвка; перевóзочное срéдство; *(law)* передáча *(of property)*; **~er**, *n*, конвéйер; транспортёр.

convict, *n*, осуждённый; кáторжник; ¶ *v.t*, признавáть виновным, осуждáть; **~ion**, *n*, осуждéние; судимость; убеждéние; увéренность.

convince, *v.t*, убеждáть; **convincing**, *a*, убедительный.

convivial, *a*, прáздничный; весёлый; **~ity**, *n*, весёлость; прáздничное настроéние.

convocation, *n*, созыв; собрáние; *(eccl.)* собóр; **convoke**, *v.t*, созывáть, собирáть.

convolvulus, *n*, вьюнóк.

convoy, *n*, сопровождéние, конвóй; ¶ *v.t*, сопровождáть; вести под конвóем, конвоировать.

convulse, *v.t*, потрясáть; вызывáть сýдороги/конвýльсии у; *be* ~*d with laughter* сýдорожно смеяться; **convulsion**, *n*, конвýльсия, сýдорога; потрясéние; колебáние; **convulsive**, *a*, сýдорожный, конвульсивный.

coo, *v.i*, воркóвать; **~ing**, *n*, воркóвание.

cook, *n*, повар; кухарка; кок *(on ship)*; ¶ *v.t*, готовить, стряпать, варить; *v.i*, вариться; ~er, *n*, плита, печь; ~ery, *n*, кулинария; ~ book поваренная книга; ~ing, *n*, приготовление пищи, стряпня; кухня.

cool, *a*, прохладный; спокойный; хладнокровный; равнодушный; неприветливый; нахальный; ¶ *n*, прохлада; хладнокровие; ¶ *v.t*, охлаждать; *v.i*, охлаждаться; остывать; ~ down *(fig.)* успокаиваться; ~er, *n*, холодильник; ведёрко для охлаждения; ~ness, *n*, прохлада; хладнокровие; спокойствие; равнодушие; холодок *(of voice);* охлаждение *(of relationship).*

coop, *n*, клетка; курятник; ¶ *v.t*, сажать в клетку; ~ *up* держать взаперти; набивать битком.

cooper, *n*, бондарь; ~age, *n*, бондарный промысел; бондарня.

co-operate, *v.i*, сотрудничать; содействовать; объединяться; кооперироваться; co-operation, *n*, сотрудничество; кооперация; co-operative, *a*, услужливый, объединённый; кооперативный; ~ *society* кооператив.

co-ordinate, *v.t*, координировать; согласовывать; co-ordination, *n*, координация; согласование.

coot, *n*, лысуха.

cope, *n*, *(eccl.)* риза; ¶ *v.t*, крыть, покрывать; обменивать; ~ *with* справляться/совладать с; *I can't* ~ *with him* я не могу справиться с ним; coping, *n*, перекрывающая плита; гребень (плотины).

copious, *a*, обильный; ~ness, *n*, обилие.

copper, *n*, медь; медная монета; медный котёл; *(coll.)* полицейский; ~-coloured цвета меди; ~ *plate* медная гравировальная доска; ¶ *v.t*, покрывать медью; ~smith, *n*, медник; котельщик.

coppice, copse, *n*, роща, подлесок.

copulate, *v.i*, спариваться; copulation, *n*, копуляция, спаривание.

copy, *n*, копия; экземпляр; репродукция; образец; ~-book тетрадь; тетрадь с прописями; *make a fair* ~ *of* переписывать начисто;

¶ *v.t*, снимать копию с; копировать; списывать; переписывать; подражать *(dat.)*; ~ing, *n*, копирование; переписывание; подражание; ~ist, *n*, копировщик; переписчик; подражатель.

copyright, *n*, авторское право.

coquet, *v.i*, кокетничать; ~ry, *n*, кокетство; coquette, *n*, кокетка; coquettish, *a*, кокетливый.

coral, *n*, коралл; ~ *reef* коралловый риф.

cord, *n*, верёвка, шнур; струна; umbilical ~ пуповина; *vocal* ~s голосовые связки; ¶ *v.t*, связывать верёвкой; ~age, *n*, верёвки; снасти, такелаж.

cordial, *a*, сердечный; радушный; ¶ *n*, стимулирующее сердечное средство; освежающий напиток; ~ity, *n*, сердечность; радушие.

cordon, *n*, кордон.

corduroy, *n*, вельвет; *pl*, вельветовые брюки.

core, *n*, сердцевина; внутренность; ядро; *(fig.)* центр; суть; ¶ *v.t*, вырезать сердцевину из.

cork, *n*, пробка; поплавок; ~screw *(n.)* штопор; *(a.)* спиральный, винтообразный; ~ *tree* пробковый дуб; ¶ *v.t*, затыкать пробкой; закупоривать.

cormorant, *n*, баклан.

corn, *n*, зерно; хлеба; пшеница; кукуруза, маис; мозоль *(on foot)*; ~ *chandler* торговец хлебом и фуражом; ~-cob кукурузный початок; ~field (кукурузное) поле; ~-flour кукурузная мука; ~-flower василёк.

corned beef солонина.

corner, *n*, угол; закоулок; часть; район; неловкое положение, затруднение; ~-stone *(fig.)* краеугольный камень; ¶ *v.t*, загонять в угол; *(com.)* скупать (товары); ~ *the market* овладевать рынком.

cornet, *n*, *(mus.)* корнет; корнетист.

cornice, *n*, карниз.

corolla, *n*, венчик.

corollary, *n*, вывод, заключение; следствие.

coronation, *n*, коронация.

coronet, *n*, корона; диадема; венок.

corporal, *a*, телесный; физический; ¶ *n*, капрал; corporate, *a*, корпоративный; общий; **corporation,** *n,* корпорация; муниципалитет; **corporeal,** *a,* телесный; материальный; вещественный.

corps, *n, (mil.)* корпус; служба.

corpse, *n,* труп.

corpulence, *n,* дородность, тучность; **corpulent,** *a,* дородный, тучный.

corpuscle, *n,* частица; *pl, (blood)* красные (белые) кровяные шарики.

correct, *a,* правильный; точный; корректный; ¶ *v.t,* исправлять; поправлять, корректировать; делать замечание/выговор *(dat.);* наказывать; ~ion, *n,* исправление, (по)правка; наказание; ~ive, *a,* исправительный; ¶ *n,* корректив; поправка; ~ness, *n,* правильность; точность; корректность.

correlative, *a,* соотносительный, соответственный.

correspond, *v.i,* соответствовать; переписываться; ~ence, *n,* соответствие; корреспонденция, переписка; ~ courses заочные курсы; ~ent, *n,* корреспондент; ~ing, *a,* соответствующий, соответственный; переписывающийся.

corridor, *n,* коридор.

corroborate, *v.t,* подтверждать, подкреплять; **corroboration,** *n,* подтверждение; **corroborative,** *a,* подтверждающий; укрепляющий.

corrode, *v.t,* разъедать *(also fig.);* *v.i,* ржаветь; подвергаться действию коррозии; **corrosion,** *n,* коррозия; **corrosive,** *a,* едкий.

corrugate, *v.t,* морщить; гофрировать *(metal);* ~d iron рифлёное железо.

corrupt, *a,* испорченный, развращённый; продажный; ¶ *v.t,* портить, развращать; подкупать; *v.i,* портиться; разлагаться; развращаться; ~ible, *a,* портящийся; подкупной; ~ion, *n,* испорченность; развращение; разложение *(also* моральное); продажность.

corsair, *n,* пират, корсар; капер.

corset, *n,* корсет.

coruscate, *v.i,* сверкать, блистать; **coruscation,** *n,* сверкание, блеск.

corvette, *n,* корвет.

cosily, *ad,* уютно.

cosmetic, *a,* косметический; ¶ *n,* косметика.

cosmic, *a,* космический.

cosmonaut, *n,* космонавт.

cosmopolitan, *a,* космополитический; ¶ *n,* космополит.

cost, *n,* стоимость; цена; *pl,* издержки; *(law)* судебные издержки; ~ *of living* стоимость жизни; ~ *price* себестоимость; *at all* ~s любой ценой; во что бы то ни стало; ¶ *v.i,* стоить.

coster, *n,* уличный торговец.

costliness, *n,* дороговизна; **costly,** *a,* дорогой, ценный.

costume, *n,* костюм; ~*-piece* историческая пьеса.

cosy, *a,* уютный.

cot, *n,* детская кроватка; койка.

coterie, *n,* кружок; избранный круг.

cottage, *n,* коттедж; загородный дом.

cotton, *n,* хлопок; бумажная ткань; нитка; ~ *cloth* хлопчатобумажная ткань; ~ *mill* хлопкопрядильная фабрика; ~ *plant* хлопчатник; ~ *waste* хлопковые отбросы; ~*-wool* вата; хлопок-сырец.

couch, *n,* кушетка; ложе; ¶ *v.t,* излагать, выражать *(words);* *v.i,* лежать; притаиться *(pf.).*

couch-grass, *n,* пырей.

cough, *n,* кашель; ¶ *v.i,* кашлять; ~ *up* отхаркивать.

council, *n,* совет; совещание; *(eccl.)* собор; ~lor, *n,* советник; член совета.

counsel, *n,* совещание, обсуждение; совет; адвокат; *take* ~ совещаться; ¶ *v.t,* советовать; ~lor, *n,* советник, консультант; адвокат.

count, *n,* счёт, подсчёт; итог; граф; ¶ *v.t,* считать, подсчитывать; принимать во внимание; *v.i,* иметь значение; идти в расчёт; ~ *on* рассчитывать на; *that does not* ~ это не считается.

countenance, *n,* выражение лица; лицо; *out of* ~ в замешательстве; ¶ *v.t,* одобрять, разрешать.

counter, *n,* прилавок; фишка, шашка; отражение удара; *(tech.)* счётчик; ¶ *a,* противоположный; встречный; ¶ *v.t,* противостоять *(dat.);* наносить *(dat.)* встречный уда́р; возража́ть на; ¶ *ad,* напро́тив; обра́тно; *run ~ to* проги́воре́чить *(dat.);* идти́ наперекор *(dat.).*

counteract, *v.t,* противоде́йствовать *(dat.);* нейтрализова́ть; **~ion,** *n,* противоде́йствие.

counter-attack, *n,* контрата́ка, контрнаступле́ние.

counterbalance, *n,* противове́с; ¶ *v.t,* уравнове́шивать.

counter-claim, *n,* встре́чный иск.

counterfeit, *a,* подде́льный; подло́жный; ¶ *n,* подде́лка, подло́г; ¶ *v.t,* подде́лывать; **~er,** *n,* фальшивомоне́тчик.

counterfoil, *n,* корешо́к.

countermand, *v.t,* отменя́ть *(order);* отзыва́ть.

counterpane, *n,* покрыва́ло; стёганое одея́ло.

counterpart, *n,* ко́пия; дублика́т; двойни́к.

counterpoint, *n,* контрапу́нкт.

counterpoise, *n,* противове́с; равнове́сие; ¶ *v.t,* уравнове́шивать.

counter-revolution, *n,* контрреволю́ция.

countersign, *n,* паро́ль; скре́па, контрассигна́ция; ¶ *v.t,* скрепля́ть по́дписью; ста́вить втору́ю по́дпись на.

countess, *n,* графи́ня.

counting-house, *n,* конто́ра, бухгалте́рия.

countless, *a,* бесчи́сленный, несчётный.

countrified, *a,* дереве́нский; **country,** *n,* страна́; ро́дина; дере́вня, се́льская ме́стность; пейза́ж; **~-house** за́городный дом; да́ча; поме́щичий дом; **~** *life* се́льская жизнь; **~man** соотве́тственник, земля́к; се́льский жи́тель; **~side** се́льская ме́стность; приро́да; дере́вня; **~** *town* провинциа́льный го́род; **~** *woman* соотве́чественница, земля́чка; крестья́нка.

county, *n,* гра́фство; о́круг; **~** *town* гла́вный го́род гра́фства/о́круга.

couple, *n,* па́ра; *married ~* супру́ги, чета́; *engaged ~* жени́х и неве́ста; ¶ *v.t,* соединя́ть; свя́зывать; спа́ривать; *(rly.)* сцепля́ть; **~t,** *n,* двусти́шие; купле́т; **coupling,** *n,* соедине́ние; спа́ривание; *(tech.)* му́фта; сцепле́ние.

courage, *n,* хра́брость, сме́лость; му́жество; **~ous,** *a,* хра́брый, сме́лый.

courier, *n,* курье́р, на́рочный; аге́нт.

course, *n,* курс; направле́ние; ход *(of events);* тече́ние *(of time);* курс (ле́кций); ли́ния (поведе́ния); блю́до; скаковой круг; *in due ~* в до́лжное вре́мя; *matter of ~* не́что само́ собо́й разуме́ющееся; *of ~* коне́чно; *take its ~* идти́ свои́м чередо́м; ¶ *v.t,* пресле́довать; гна́ться за; **coursing,** *n,* охо́та с го́нчими.

court, *n,* двор; суд; *(sport)* корт; площа́дка; **~-martial** вое́нный трибуна́л; **~s** *of justice* суд; **~yard** двор; *pay ~ to* уха́живать за; ¶ *v.t,* уха́живать за; иска́ть *(gen.) (favour, etc.);* наклика́ть *(disaster).*

courteous, *a,* ве́жливый, учти́вый.

courtesan, *n,* куртиза́нка.

courtesy, *n,* ве́жливость, учти́вость; реве́ранс.

courtier, *n,* придво́рный; **courtly,** *a,* ве́жливый; изы́сканный; льсти́вый.

courtship, *n,* уха́живание.

cousin, *n,* кузе́н, кузи́на; *first ~* двою́родный брат; двою́родная сестра́; *second ~* трою́родный брат, трою́родная сестра́.

cove, *n,* бу́хта; *(arch.)* свод.

covenant, *n,* соглаше́ние; догово́р; ¶ *v.i,* заключа́ть соглаше́ние.

cover, *n,* (по)кры́шка; покрыва́ло; чехо́л; конве́рт; переплёт; покро́в, укры́тие; убе́жище; ши́рма; предло́г; *under ~* в укры́тии, под защи́той; ¶ *v.t,* закрыва́ть; покрыва́ть, прикрыва́ть, скрыва́ть; охва́тывать; распространя́ться на; освеща́ть *(radio, press, etc.);* ~ *oneself* скрыва́ться; **~age,** *n,* освеще́ние по ра́дио/в печа́ти; **~ing,** *n,* покры́шка; чехо́л; обши́вка; **~let,** *n,* покрыва́ло; одея́ло.

covert, *a,* скры́тый, та́йный; **~ly,** *ad,* та́йно, укра́дкой.

covet, *v.t,* жа́ждать *(gen.);* домога́ться *(gen.);* зави́довать *(dat.);* **~ous,** *a,* жа́дный; а́лчный; зави́стливый; **~ousness,** *n,* жа́дность; а́лчность; за́висть.

cow, *n,* коро́ва; **~boy** пасту́х: ковбо́й; **~herd** пасту́х; **~hide** воло́вья

кóжа; плеть (из волóвьей кóжи);
~shed хлев, корóвник; ¶ v.t,
запýгивать; усмирять.
coward, n, трус; ~ice, n, трýсость,
малодýшие; ~ly, a, труслúвый,
малодýшный.
cower, v.i, пригибáться; сжимáться,
съёживаться.
cowl, n, мáнтия с капюшóном; капюшóн; колпáк (дымовóй трубы́).
cowslip, n, барáнчик.
coxcomb, n, щёголь, хлыщ, фат.
coxswain, n, старшинá шлю́пки;
рулевóй.
coy, a, застéнчивый, скрóмный;
~ness, n, застéнчивость, скрóмность.
cozen, v.t, надувáть, морóчить;
~age, n, надувáтельство, обмáн.
crab, n, краб; Рак (zodiac); ~-apple
дúкое яблоко; ~-apple tree дúкая
яблоня; catch a ~ «поймáть (pf.)
лещá»; ~bed, a, раздражúтельный, ворчлúвый; мéлкий и неразбóрчивый (handwriting).
crack, n, трéщина, щель; треск;
щёлканье; удáр; ¶ a, замечáтельный, первоклáссный, зна-
менúтый; ~-brained слабоýм-
ный, помéшанный; неразýмный;
¶ v.t, щёлкать (хлыстóм); колóть
(nuts); раскáлывать; v.i, трéскаться; раскáлываться; ломáться
(voice); ~ed, p.p. & a, трéснув-
ший; пошатнýвшийся (reputation);
надтрéснутый (voice); по-
мéшанный; ~er, n, хлопýшка;
сухóе печéнье, крéкер; щипцы́
для орéхов.
crackle, n, треск, потрéскивание;
хруст; ¶ v.i, потрéскивать; хру-
стéть; crackling, n, треск; хруст;
хрустящая кóрочка.
cradle, n, колыбéль, лю́лька; (fig.)
начáло, истóки; ¶ v.t, убаю́ки-
вать.
craft, n, ремеслó; лóвкость, умéние;
сýдно; самолёт; ~ily, ad, хúтро;
обмáнным путём; ~iness, n,
хúтрость; лукáвство; ~sman, n,
мáстер; ремéсленник; ~smanship,
n, мастерствó; ~y, a, лóвкий,
хúтрый.
crag, n, скалá, утёс; ~gy, a, ска-
лúстый; крутóй.
cram, v.t, впúхивать; набивáть;
пúчкать, откáрмливать; натáски-

вать (к экзáмену); ~-full битко́м
набúтый.
cramp, n, сýдорога, спáзма; (tech.)
скобá; ¶ v.t, сводúть сýдорогой;
свя́зывать, стесня́ть; (tech.)
скрепля́ть скобóй.
cranberry, n, клю́ква.
crane, n, жýравль; (tech.) подъёмный кран; ~-fly долгонóжка; ¶
v.t: ~ one's neck вытя́гивать шéю.
cranium, n, чéреп.
crank, n, рукоя́тка, рýчка; (tech.)
кривоши́п, колéно; (pers.) чудáк;
~-shaft колéнчатый вал; ¶ v.t,
сгибáть; заводúть рукоя́ткой; ~y,
a, шáткий, расшáтанный; чу-
дакóватый.
cranny, n, щель, трéщина.
crape, n, креп; (fig.) трáур.
crash, n, треск, грóхот; крах,
банкрóтство; авáрия, крушéние;
¶ v.i, пáдать; рýшиться с трéс-
ком/грóхотом; разбивáться; терпéть авáрию/крушéние; терпéть
крах; v.t, разбивáть, разрушáть.
crass, a, грýбый; совершéнный,
полнéйший.
crate, n, корзúна, я́щик; рáма
(стекóльщика).
crater, n, крáтер (вулкáна); ворóнка
от снаря́да.
cravat, n, гáлстук.
crave, v.t, просúть, умоля́ть; ~ for
жáждать/стрáстно желáть (gen.).
craven, a, малодýшный, труслúвый.
craving, n, стрáстное желáние,
стремлéние.
crawl, v.i, пóлзать, ползтú; тащúться;
пресмыкáться; ~ with кишéть
(inst.).
crayfish, n, речнóй рак; лангýста.
crayon, n, цветнóй карандáш/мелóк;
пастéль; ¶ v.t, рисовáть цветны́м
карандашóм/мелкóм.
craze, n, мáния; мóда, повáльное
увлечéние; crazy, a, сумасшéдший; помéшанный; ~ pavement
мостовáя из кáмня различной
фóрмы; drive ~ сводúть с умá.
creak, n, скрип; ¶ v.i, скрипéть.
cream, n, слúвки; крем; ~ cheese
сыркóвая мáсса; слúвочный сыр;
~ery, n, маслобóйня; сыровáр-
ня; молóчная; ~y, a, слúвочный; крéмовый.
crease, n, склáдка; загúб; ¶ v.t,
мять; загибáть; дéлать склáдки
на; v.i, мя́ться.

create, *v.t*, творить, создавать; возводить в звание; **creation,** *n*, создание, творёние; сотворёние мира; мироздание; произведёние (науки/искусства); возведёние в звание; **creative,** *a*, творческий; **creator,** *n*, творёц, создатель, созидатель; **creatress,** *n*, создательница; **creature,** *n*, создание; живое существо, тварь.

crèche, *n*, детские ясли.

credence, *n*, вёра, довёрие; *letter of* ~ рекомендательное письмо; *give* ~ *to* вёрить *(dat.);* **credentials,** *n.pl*, верительные грамоты; **credibility,** *n*, вероятность, правдоподобие; **credible,** *a*, вероятный; заслуживающий довёрия.

credit, *n*, довёрие; честь; крёдит, долг; ~ *note* обмённый чек; *on* ~ в долг, в крёдит; *give* ~ *to* предоставлять крёдит *(dat.);* вёрить *(dat.),* оказывать честь *(dat.);* *give* ~ *for* отдавать *(dat.)* должное; считать заслугой *(gen.);* *take* ~ *for* присваивать себё честь; ставить себё в заслугу; ¶ *v.t*, вёрить/повёрять *(dat.);* предоставлять крёдит *(dat.);* записывать в крёдит; ~ *with* приписывать; ~**able,** *a*, похвальный, дёлающий честь; ~**or,** *n*, кредитор.

credulity, *n*, довёрчивость, легковёрие; **credulous,** *a*, довёрчивый, легковёрный.

creed, *n*, вероучёние; крёдо.

creek, *n*, бухта, залив; устье реки.

creep, *v.i*, ползать, виться *(plant);* содрогаться (от страха); ~ *in,* ~ *up* красться, подкрадываться; *it made my flesh* ~ у меня мурашки забёгали по тёлу; ~*ing paralysis* прогрессивный паралич; ~**er,** *n*, ползучее растёние; пресмыкающееся живóтное.

cremate, *v.t*, кремировать; **cremation,** *n*, кремация; **crematorium,** *n*, крематорий.

creole, *n*, креол, ~ка.

creosote, *n*, креозот.

crepitate *v.i*, хрустёть; хрипёть.

crescendo, *a*, в бурном тёмпе; нарастая; ¶ *n*, крещёндо.

crescent, *a*, нарастающий; в форме полумёсяца, серповидный; ¶ *n*, полумёсяц; серп луны; полукруг.

cress, *n*, кресс.

crest, *n*, гребешóк *(of cock);* хохолóк *(of bird);* грива *(mane);* грёбень *(of helmet, of wave);* конёк *(of roof);* ~-*fallen* упавший духом, унылый; ~**ed,** *a*, украшенный грёбнем/хохолкóм.

cretonne, *n*, кретóн.

crevice, *n*, щель, расщёлина.

crew, *n*, экипáж (судна); комáнда; бригáда, артёль рабóчих.

crib, *n*, дётская кровáтка; ясли, кормушка; ларь, закром; шпаргалка; плагиáт; ¶ *v.t*, запирáть; списывать (тайкóм).

crick, *n*, растяжёние мышц.

cricket, *n*, сверчóк; *(sport)* крикет; ~ *bat* битá.

crier, *n*, крикун, глашáтай.

crime, *n*, преступлёние, злодеяние; **criminal,** *a*, престýпный; уголóвный; ¶ *n*, престýпник; ~**ity,** *n*, престýпность; винóвность; **criminate,** *v.t*, обвинять в преступлёнии; осуждáть.

crimp, *v.t*, завивáть; гофрировáть.

crimson, *a*, áлый; малиновый; ¶ *n*, малиновый цвет; румянец.

cringe, *v.i*, раболёпствовать, низкопоклóнничать; съёживаться (от страха); **cringing,** *a*, раболёпный; ¶ *n*, раболёпие, низкопоклóнство.

crinkle, *n*, изгиб, извилина, складка, морщина; ¶ *v.t*, морщить; *v.i*, мóрщиться; извивáться.

crinoline, *n*, кринолин.

cripple, *n*, калёка, инвалид; ¶ *v.t*, калёчить, урóдовать; *(fig.)* приводить в негóдность; ~**d,** *p.p. & a*, искалёченный, изурóдованный.

crisis, *n*, кризис; перелóм.

crisp, *a*, хрустящий; живительный; бодрящий *(air);* кудрявый *(hair);* рёзкий *(manner);* ¶ ~**s,** *n*, чипсы.

criterion, *n*, критёрий.

critic, *n*, критик; ~**al,** *a*, критический; перелóмный; разбóрчивый; ~**ism,** *n*, критика; ~**ize,** *v.t*, критиковáть; **critique,** *n*, критический разбóр, рецёнзия.

croak, *n*, кáрканье, квáканье; ¶ *v.i*, кáркать, квáкать.

crochet, *n*, вязáние крючкóм; ~ *hook* вязáльный крючóк; ¶ *v.i*, вязáть крючкóм.

crockery, n, посуда.
crocodile, n, крокодил.
crocus, n, крокус.
crone, n, старуха, старая карга;
crony, n, закадычный друг.
crook, n, крюк; посох; изгиб (реки,
дороги); жулик, мошенник; ¶
v.t, сгибать; изгибать; искривлять; v.i, сгибаться; скрючивать-
ся; горбиться; ~ed, a, изогну-
тый, кривой; (coll.) нечестный;
~edness, n, кривизна; (coll.)
нечестность, жульничество.
croon, v.i, напевать, мурлыкать.
crop, n, урожай, жатва; культура;
зоб (of bird); стрижка; коротко
остриженные волосы; pl, посевы;
¶ v.t, собирать урожай с; засе-
вать; подстригать, обрезать; ~ up
неожиданно обнаруживаться;
возникать.
croquet, n, крокет.
crosier, n, епископский посох.
cross, n, крест; распятие; скрещивание (of breeds); помесь, гибрид; ¶ v.i, пересекать; переходить, переезжать; скрещивать;
препятствовать (dat.); противоречить (dat.); v.i, разминуться
(pf, letters); скрещиваться; ~
one's path встречаться; становиться поперек дороги; ~ out
вычеркивать; ~ oneself крестить-
ся; ~ over переходить, переправляться; it ~ed my mind мне
пришло в голову; ¶ a, попереч-
ный, пересекающийся; пере-
крёстный; неблагоприятный;
противоположный; сердитый,
раздражённый; ~-bar попере-
чина; штанга; ~-bones череп и
кости; ~-bow самострел; ~-bred
гибридный, смешанный; ~-exa-
mine подвергать перекрёстному
допросу; ~-examination перекрёс-
тный допрос; ~-eyed косой, ко-
соглазый; ~-grained свилеватый
(wood); упрямый, ворчливый; ~-
patch ворчун; ~ purpose недоразумение; be at ~ purposes действовать наперекор друг другу;
~-road перекрёсток; ~-section
поперечное сечение; ~-word (puzzle) кроссворд; ~ing, n, пересечение, скрещивание; переход;
перекрёсток; переправа (rly.)
переезд; ~ly, ad, сердито; ~ness,
n, раздражительность, сварли-

вость; ~wise, ad, крестообразно,
крест-накрест.
crotchet, n, крючок; ~y, a, капризный; сварливый.
crouch, v.i, сгибаться.
croup, n, круп.
croupe, n, зад, круп (лошади).
crow, n, ворона; пение петуха;
~-bar лом; ~ foot лютик; ~'s
foot морщинки у глаз; ~'s nest
воронье гнездо; (mar.) наблю-
дательная вышка; as the ~ flies
по прямой (линии); ¶ v.i, кричать, петь; ликовать; ~ over
торжествовать над.
crowd, n, толпа; давка; множество,
масса; ¶ v.t, теснить; вытеснять;
v.i, толпиться; протискиваться;
~ed, a, переполненный; битком
набитый; ~ with полный, напол-
ненный.
crown, n, венец, корона; верхушка
(of tree); макушка (of head);
тулья (of hat); коронка (of
tooth); венок (of flowers); крона
(coin); ~ prince наследник престола; ¶ v.i, короновать, венчать;
завершать, увенчивать; ~ing, a,
завершающий; ¶ n, увенчание.
crucial, a, решающий; критический.
crucible, n, тигель; (fig.) суровое
испытание, горнило.
crucifix, n, распятие; ~ion, n,
распятие на кресте; crucify, v.t,
распинать.
crude, a, сырой; незрелый; необработанный; грубый (manner);
голый (fact); кричащий (colour);
~ness, crudity, n, незрелость;
необработанность; грубость.
cruel, a, жестокий, безжалостный;
мучительный; ~ty, n, жестокость.
cruet, n, графинчик, бутылочка;
~-stand, n, судок.
cruise, n, морская прогулка; плавание; рейс; ¶ v.i, совершать
рейс, крейсировать; ~missile
крылатая ракета; ~ r, n, крей-
сер.
crumb, n, крошка; мякиш.
crumble, v.t, крошить; толочь;
v.i, крошиться; осыпаться; обваливаться; разрушаться; crum-
bly, a, рассыпчатый, рых-
лый.
crumple, v.t, мять; комкать; сгибать;
v.i, мяться; морщиться; падать
духом.

crunch, *v.t,* грызть; *v.i,* хрустеть; трещать; скрипеть (под ногами); ¶ *n,* хруст; треск; скрип.

crusade, *n,* крестовый поход; кампания; **~r,** *n,* крестоносец; участник кампании; борец.

crush, *n,* давка, толкотня; толпа; сокрушительный удар; ¶ *v.t,* давить; толочь; дробить; подавлять *(resistance);* уничтожать, сокрушать; **~ing,** *a,* сокрушительный; уничтожающий.

crust, *n,* корка; земная кора; ¶ *v.t. (& i.),* покрывать(ся) корой/коркой.

crustacean, *a. & n,* ракообразный.

crustily, *ad,* сварливо, раздражительно; **crustiness,** *n,* сварливость, раздражительность; **crusty,** *a,* покрытый корой/коркой; твёрдый; сварливый.

crutch, *n,* костыль.

crux, *n,* затруднение; трудный вопрос; суть (дела).

cry, *n,* крик; плач; боевой клич; лозунг; **~-baby** плакса; ¶ *v.i,* кричать; плакать; *v.t,* оглашать, объявлять; **~** *down* заглушать (криками); **~** *one's heart out* горько рыдать; **~** *out* выкрикивать; **~ing,** *a,* кричащий, плачущий; вопиющий, возмутительный; ¶ *n,* плач, крик.

crypt, *n,* склеп; **~ic,** *a,* загадочный, таинственный, сокровенный.

crystal, *a,* хрустальный; кристаллический; *(fig.)* кристальный, прозрачный; чистый; **~-glass** хрусталь; ¶ *n,* хрусталь; кристалл; **~line,** *a,* кристальный; прозрачный, чистый; **~** *lens* хрусталик (глаза); **~lization,** *n,* кристаллизация; **~lize,** *v.t. (& i.),* кристаллизовать(ся); засахариваться(ся) *(fruits).*

cub, *n,* детёныш, щенок; *(fig.)* молокосос, юнец; новичок.

cube, *n,* куб; **~-root** корень кубический; **~** *sugar* пилёный сахар; ¶ *v.t,* возводить в куб; вычислять кубический объём *(gen.);* **cubiform,** *a,* кубовидный.

cubicle, *n,* клетушка.

cubism, *n,* кубизм **cubist,** *a,* кубистский; ¶ *n,* кубист.

cuckoo, *n,* кукушка.

cucumber, *n,* огурец.

cud, *n,* жвачка.

cuddle, *n,* объятия *(pl.);* ¶ *v.t,* прижимать к себе; *v.i,* прижиматься; свёртываться калачиком.

cudgel, *n,* дубина; *take up the* **~s** *for* заступаться за; ¶ *v.t,* бить палкой; **~** *one's brains* ломать себе голову; **~ling,** *n,* избиение.

cue, *n,* намёк; *(theat.)* реплика; кий (бильярдный); косичка.

cuff, *n,* манжета; удар рукой; **~-links** запонки; ¶ *v.t,* бить рукой, колотить.

cuirass, *n,* кираса, панцирь; **~ier,** *n,* кирасир.

cul-de-sac, *n,* тупик.

culinary, *a,* кулинарный, кухонный.

cull, *v.t,* собирать; отбирать.

culminate, *v.i,* достигать высшей точки; **culminating,** *a,* наивысший, кульминационный; **culmination,** *n,* наивысшая точка, кульминационный пункт, кульминация.

culpability, *n,* виновность; **culpable,** *a,* виновный, преступный; **culprit,** *n,* обвиняемый, преступник, виновник.

cult, *n,* культ.

cultivate, *v.t,* обрабатывать; возделывать; культивировать; разводить *(talents);* **cultivation,** *n,* обработка; возделывание; разведение, культура *(of plants);* развитие, культивирование; **cultivator,** *n,* земледелец; культиватор; **culture,** *n,* культура; **~d,** *a,* культурный.

culvert, *n,* дренажная труба.

cumber, *v.t,* затруднять, обременять; **~some,** **cumbrous,** *a,* затруднительный, обременительный; громоздкий.

cumulative, *a,* совокупный, накопленный.

cunning, *a,* ловкий, искусный; хитрый; коварный; ¶ *n,* ловкость; умение; хитрость; коварство.

cup, *n,* чашка; кубок; чаша; чашечка (цветка); **~-bearer** виночерпий; ¶ *v.t,* *(med.)* ставить банки *(dat.);* складывать рупором *(hands); cupping glass (med.)* банка.

cupboard, *n,* шкаф.

Cupid, *n,* Купидо́н.

cupidity, *n,* а́лчность, жа́дность.

cupola, *n,* ку́пол.

cur, *n,* дворня́жка; *(fig.)* наха́л; негодя́й.

curable, *a,* излечи́мый.

curacy, *n,* сан свяще́нника; прихо́д (церко́вный); **curate,** *n,* помо́щник прихо́дского свяще́нника.

curative, *a,* целе́бный, цели́тельный; ¶ *n,* целе́бное сво́йство.

curator, *n,* храни́тель (музе́я/библиоте́ки); член правле́ния (университе́та).

curb, *n,* узда́; обузда́ние; обо́чина, край (тротуа́ра); ¶ *v.t,* надева́ть узду́ (на ло́шадь); обу́здывать; сгиба́ть.

curd, *n,* творо́г; **curdle,** *v.i,* свёртываться *(milk);* ~ *the blood* ледени́ть кровь.

cure, *n,* лека́рство, сре́дство; лече́ние; ¶ *v.t,* лечи́ть, исцеля́ть, вылечивать; консерви́ровать.

curfew, *n,* коменда́нтский час.

curing, *n,* лече́ние, исцеле́ние; консерви́рование.

curiosity, *n,* любопы́тство, любозна́тельность; ре́дкость; стра́нность; ~ *shop* антиква́рный магази́н, «ла́вка дре́вностей»; **curious,** *a,* любопы́тный; любозна́тельный; стра́нный; *the ~ thing is that* ... стра́нно, что ...

curl, *n,* ло́кон; зави́вка; завито́к; спира́ль; кольцо́ *(of smoke);* ¶ *v.t,* завива́ть; крути́ть; криви́ть *(lips); v.i,* завива́ться, ви́ться *(of hair);* клуби́ться *(of smoke);* ~ *up* смо́рщиваться, скру́чиваться.

curlew, *n,* кро́ншнеп.

curliness, *n,* курча́вость; **curling,** *n,* зави́вка; скру́чивание; ~ *tongs* щипцы́ для зави́вки; **curly,** *a,* кудря́вый, вью́щийся; волни́стый.

curmudgeon, *n,* грубия́н, скря́га.

currant, *n,* кори́нка; *black (red)* ~ чёрная (кра́сная) сморо́дина.

currency, *n,* де́нежное обраще́ние; валю́та; распространённость; **curent,** *a,* теку́щий *(of time, event);* находя́щийся в обраще́нии; ходя́чий; распространённый; общепри́нятый; ¶ *n,* пото́к, струя́; тече́ние, ход; *(elec.)* то́к; ~ *affairs*

теку́щие собы́тия; *alternating* ~ переме́нный ток; *direct* ~ постоя́нный ток.

curriculum, *n,* програ́мма, уче́бный план.

curry, *n,* ка́рри; ¶ *v.t,* чи́стить скребни́цей; выде́лывать *(leather);* ~*-comb* скребни́ца; ~ *favour with* заи́скивать пе́ред, подли́зываться к.

curse, *n,* прокля́тие; руга́тельство; ¶ *v.t,* проклина́ть; *v.i,* руга́ться; ~**d,** *a,* прокля́тый, окая́нный; отврати́тельный.

cursive, *a,* скорописный; рукопи́сный; ¶ *n,* ско́ропись; рукопи́сный шрифт.

cursorily, *ad,* бе́гло; поверхностно; **cursory,** *a,* бе́глый; поверхностный.

curt, *a,* кра́ткий, сжа́тый; сухо́й *(of answer).*

curtail, *v.t,* сокраща́ть, уре́зывать, укора́чивать; ~**ment,** *n,* сокраще́ние, уре́зывание.

curtain, *n,* занаве́ска, што́ра; *(theat)* за́навес; *(mil.)* заве́са; ~*-ring* кольцо́ для занаве́сок; ~*-rod* (металли́ческий) прут для занаве́сок; *drop the* ~ опуска́ть за́навес; *raise the* ~ поднима́ть за́навес; *(fig.)* приподнима́ть заве́су; ¶ *v.t,* за(на)ве́шивать; ~ *off* отделя́ть за́навесом.

curtness, *n,* кра́ткость, сжа́тость; сухость.

curtsy, *n,* реvера́нс, приседа́ние; ¶ *v.i,* де́лать реvера́нс, приседа́ть.

curvature, *n,* кривизна́; изги́б; ~ *of the spine* искривле́ние позвоно́чника; **curve,** *n,* крива́я ли́ния; изги́б; лека́ло; ¶ *v.t,* гнуть, сгиба́ть; изгиба́ть; *v.i,* изгиба́ться; ~**d,** *a,* криво́й, изо́гнутый; **curvilinear,** *a,* криволине́йный.

cushion, *n,* поду́шка (дива́нная); ~*-cover* чехо́л для поду́шки; ¶ *v.t,* смягча́ть *(shock, etc.);* обкла́дывать поду́шками защища́ть.

custard, *n,* заварно́й крем, со́ус.

custodian, *n,* страж; храни́тель (музе́я); опеку́н; **custody,** *n,* опе́ка, попече́ние; охра́на; заключе́ние, аре́ст; *in* ~ под стра́жей, под надзо́ром.

custom, *n,* обы́чай; привы́чка; зака́зы; ~**arily,** *ad,* обы́чно; привы́чно; ~ary, *a*, обы́чный; привы́чный; ~er, *n*, покупа́тель; зака́зчик; клие́нт; *awkward* ~ чуда́к; тяжёлый челове́к.

customs, *n.pl*, тамо́женные по́шлины; ~*-house* тамо́жня; ~ *officer* тамо́женник; ~ *tariff* тамо́женный тари́ф.

cut, *n*, разре́з; поре́з; резна́я ра́на; зару́бка; отре́зок; вы́резка (из кни́ги); покро́й *(of dress)*; сокраще́ние, сниже́ние *(of prices)*; гравю́ра (на де́реве); ¶ *v.t* ре́зать; разреза́ть; отреза́ть; стричь; руби́ть *(wood)*; жать, коси́ть; высека́ть (из ка́мня); уре́зывать, сокраща́ть; снижа́ть *(prices)*; пропуска́ть *(lecture)*; проре́зываться *(of teeth)*; пересека́ть *(of roads, lines)*; ~ *and dried* зара́нее гото́вый; зара́нее решённый; ~ *away* среза́ть; ~ *down* руби́ть *(trees)*; сокраща́ть *(expenses)*; ~ *in* вме́шиваться (в разгово́р); *(elec.)* включа́ть; ~ *off* отреза́ть; прерыва́ть; отреза́ть *(mil.)*; выключа́ть *(water, electricity)*; лиша́ть (насле́дства); ~ *oneself off from the world* отреза́ть себя́ от всего́ ми́ра; ~ *out* выреза́ть; кро́ить *(dress)*; вытесня́ть; *(elec.)* выключа́ть; *be* ~ *out for* быть сло́вно со́зданным для; ~ *short* прерыва́ть, обрыва́ть; ~*throat* головоре́з; ~*throat razor* опа́сная бри́тва; ~ *up* разруба́ть, разреза́ть на куски́; *he is very* ~ *up about it* он о́чень расстро́ен э́тим; ~ *up rough* возмуща́ться.

cutaneous, *a*, ко́жный.

cute, *a*, у́мный, сообрази́тельный; остроу́мный; преле́стный.

cuticle, *n*, ко́жа; *(bot.)* ко́жица.

cutlass, *n*, абордажная са́бля.

cutler, *n*, ножо́вщик; ~y, *n*, ножевы́е изде́лия.

cutlet, *n*, отбивна́я котле́та.

cutter, *n*, резе́ц; ре́жущий стано́к; ре́зчик (по де́реву/ка́мню); закро́йщик; *(mar.)* ка́тер; **cutting**, *a*, ре́жущий; о́стрый, ре́зкий; язви́тельный *(remark)*; ¶ *n*, ре́зка; ру́бка; газе́тная вы́резка; кро́йка *(of clothes)*; *pl*, обре́зки, стру́жки; *railway* ~ вы́емка железнодоро́жного пути́.

cuttle-fish, *n*, карака́тица.

cybernetics, *n*, киберне́тика.

cyclamen, *n*, цикламе́н.

cycle, *n*, цикл, круг; велосипе́д; ¶ *v.i*, е́здить на велосипе́де; **cyclic, cyclical**, *a*, цикли́ческий; **cycling**, *n*, езда́ на велосипе́де; **cyclist**, *n*, велосипеди́ст.

cyclone, *n*, цикло́н.

cygnet, *n*, молодо́й ле́бедь.

cylinder, *n*, цили́ндр; ва́лик; га́зовый балло́н; бараба́н револьве́ра; **cylindrical**, *a*, цилиндри́ческий.

cymbals, *n.pl*, таре́лки.

cynic, *n*, ци́ник; ~**al**, *a*, цини́чный; ~**ism**, *n*, цини́зм.

cynosure, *n*, созве́здие Ма́лой Медве́дицы; поля́рная звезда́; *(fig.)* путево́дная звезда́.

cypher, *n*, *see* **cipher**.

cypress, *n*, кипари́с.

cyst, *n*, киста́.

czar, *n*, царь.

Czech, *a*, че́шский; ¶ *n*, чех, че́шка; че́шский язы́к; **Czecho-Slovak**, *a*, чехослова́цкий; ¶ *n*, жи́тель Чехослова́кии.

D

dab, *n*, лёгкий уда́р; прикоснове́ние; мазо́к (ки́стью); пятно́ (кра́ски); ¶ *v.t*, слегка́ ударя́ть; прикаса́ться к; прикла́дывать; нама́зывать; покрыва́ть (кра́ской).

dabble, *v.i*, плеска́ться, бара́хтаться; ~ *in* занима́ться пове́рхностно *(inst.)*; ~ *in politics* политика́нствовать; ~r, *n*, люби́тель, дилета́нт.

dace, *n*, еле́ц.

dad(dy), *n*, па́па, па́почка; ~*-long-legs* долгоно́жка.

dado, *n*, цо́коль; пьедеста́л; пане́ль (стены́).

daffodil, *n*, бле́дно-жёлтый нарци́сс.

daft, *a*, сумасше́дший, глу́пый.

dagger, *n*, кинжа́л.

dahlia, *n*, георги́н.

daily, *a*, ежедне́вный; повседне́вный; су́точный; ¶ *ad*, ежедне́вно; ¶ *n*, ежедне́вная газе́та; приходя́щая рабо́тница.

dainties, *n.pl*, делика́тесы; **daintily** *ad*, изы́сканно; утончённо; вку́сно; **daintiness**, *n*, изы́сканность; утончённость; **dainty**, *a*, утончён-

ный, изысканный; изящный;
вкусный, лакомый; разборчивый;
¶ n, лакомство; деликатес.
dairy, n, молочная; маслодельня;
сыроварня; ~ farm молочная
ферма; ~ man молочник; работник молочной фермы; ~ maid
молочница; доярка.
dais, n, помост, возвышение.
daisy, n, маргаритка.
dale, n, долина.
dalliance, n, праздное времяпре-
провождение; развлечение;
флирт; **dally**, v.i, болтаться без
дела; зря терять время; развлекаться; кокетничать, флиртовать.
Dalmatian, n, далматский; ¶ n,
далматский дог.
dam, n, дамба, плотина; матка
(of animals); ¶ v.t, запру-
живать.
damage, n, повреждение; убыток;
ущерб; pl, (law) убытки; компенсация за убытки; ¶ v.t,
повреждать, портить; наносить
ущерб (dat.); ~able, a, легко
портящийся; **damaging**, a, при-
носящий вред, вредный.
damask, a, камчатный; сделанный
из дамасской стали; ~ steel булат;
¶ n, камчатное полотно; дамас-
ская сталь.
dame, n, госпожа; дама.
damn, n, проклятие; I don't care a
~ я совершенно не интересуюсь,
мне наплевать; ¶ v.t, проклинать;
осуждать; ~able, a, ужасный,
отвратительный; ~ably, ad, ужасно; чёртовски; очень; ~ation
n, проклятие; осуждение.
damp, a, сырой, влажный; ~ proof
водонепроницаемый; ¶ n, сырость, влажность; ¶ v.t, смачивать; делать влажным; (fig.)
угнетать; обескураживать; тушить (fire); заглушать (sound);
~er, n, увлажнитель; демпфер
(piano); (tech.) глушитель; за-
слонка; ~ness, n, сырость,
влажность.
damsel, n, девица.
damson, n, тернослив.
dance, n, танец; танцевальный вечер; ~ frock бальное платье; ~
hall танцевальный зал, дансинг;
¶ v.i, танцевать, плясать; прыгать; ~ attendance on ходить на

задних лапках перед; **dancer**, n,
танцовщик; танцовщица; балерина; **dancing**, n, танцы; пляска;
~-master учитель танцев; ~
partner партнёр, ~ша.
dandelion, n, одуванчик.
dandle, v.t, качать; ласкать; баловать.
dandruff, n, перхоть.
dandy, n, денди, щёголь.
Dane, n, датчанин; ~ка; great D~
датский дог.
danger, n, опасность; ~ous, a,
опасный.
dangle, v.t, покачивать; v.i, качаться; свисать; болтаться.
Danish, a, датский; ¶ n, датский
язык.
dank, a, сырой, влажный.
dapper, a, одетый с иголочки, опрятный; изящный.
dapple, a, пёстрый, пятнистый;
~-grey horse серая в яблоках
лошадь; ¶ v.t, испещрять.
dare, v.i, сметь, отваживаться, осмеливаться; v.t, рисковать
(inst.); подзадоривать; I ~ say
полагаю; вероятно; ~-devil (a)
отважный, безрассудный; (n)
смельчак, сорвиголова; **daring**,
a, смелый, отважный, дерзкий;
¶ n, смелость, отвага, бесстра-
шие.
dark, a, тёмный; смуглый; темно-
волосый; ~ ages раннее средневе-
ковье; ~ lantern потайной фонарь;
~ room тёмная комната; it is
getting ~ темнеет; ¶ n, темнота,
тьма; невежество; неведение;
тень (в живописи); in the ~ (fig.)
в неведении; ~en, v.t, затемнять;
делать тёмным; омрачать; v.i,
темнеть, становиться тёмным;
омрачаться; ~ly, ad, мрачно;
загадочно; неясно; ~ness, n,
темнота, мрак.
darling, a, дорогой, милый, любимый; ¶ n, любимый, любимая;
голубчик; my ~ мой дорогой,
моя дорогая.
darn, n, штопка; заштопанное место;
¶ v.t, штопать; ~er, n, штопаль|-
щик, ~щица; «гриб для штопки»;
~ing, n, штопанье, штопка; ~
needle штопальная игла.
dart, n, стрела, стрелка, дротик;
стремительное движение; ¶ v.t,
мчаться стрелой; устремляться;

рйнуться *(pf.)*; *v.t*, метáть, бросáть *(glance)*.

dash, *n,* стремйтельное движéние; порыв; удáр, толчóк; тирé, чёрточка; штрих, набрóсок; прймесь; ~-*board* крылó (экипáжа); прибóрная доскá; ~ *of a pen* штрих; рóсчерк; *cut a* ~ рисовáться, пускáть пыль в глазá; ¶ *v.t,* бросáть, швырять; брызгать/плескáть *(inst.)*; разбавлять; смéшивать; разбивáть; *v.i,* бросáться, мчáться; бйться *(waves)*; ~ *off* быстро набросáть *(pf.)*; ~ *out* выбегáть из; ~*ing*, *a,* стремйтельный; лихóй.

dastardly, *a,* труслйвый; пóдлый.

data, *n.pl,* дáнные; фáкты.

date, *n,* дáта, числó; срок, свидáние; *(bot.)* фйник; *out of* ~ устарéлый; *up to* ~ современный, новéйший; ~ *palm* фйниковая пáльма; ¶ *v.t,* датйровать; ~ *back to* отноойться к; вестй начáло от.

dative, *a,* дáтельный; ¶ *n,* дáтельный падéж.

daub, *n,* обмáзка; мазня, пачкотня; ¶ *v.t,* мáзать; малевáть, пáчкать; ~*er,* *n,* плохóй худóжник, мазйлка.

daughter, *n,* дочь; ~-*in-law* невéстка; снохá; ~*ly,* *a,* дочéрний.

daunt, *v.t,* устрашáть, запýгивать; обескурáживать; ~*less,* *a,* ... ... устрашймый, бесстрáшный.

dauphin, *n,* дофйн.

daw, *n,* гáлка.

dawdle, *v.i,* бездéльничать, болтáться без дéла; копáться; ~*r,* *n,* бездéльник; копýша.

dawn, *n,* рассвéт, заря; *(fig.)* начáло, зарождéние; ¶ *v.i,* (рас)светáть; появляться; начинáться; проясняться; ~ *on one* приходйть в гóлову *(dat.)*; ~*ing,* *n,* рассвéт; проясирéние.

day, *n,* день; сýтки; *all* ~ *long* весь день, день-дéньскóй; *by* ~ днём; ~-*book* дневнйк; журнáл; ~-*break* рассвéт; ~ *by* ~ день за днём, с кáждым днём; ~-*dream(s)* грёзы, мечты; ~-*labourer* подéнщик; ~ *light* дневнóй свет; *in broad* ~ *light* средь бéла дня; ~ *off* выходнóй день; ~ *school* шкóла для приходящих ученикóв; ~-*star* ýтренняя звездá;

good ~*!* дóбрый день!; всегó хорóшего!; *work* ~ рабóчий день; *the* ~ *after tomorrow* послезáвтра; *the* ~ *before* наканýне; *the* ~ *before yesterday* позавчерá; *in* ~*s to come* в бýдущем; *on the next* ~ на слéдующий день; *one* ~ однáжды; *some* ~ когдá-нибудь; *the other* ~ недáвно, на днях.

daze, *n,* изумлéние; ¶ *v.t,* изумлять, ошеломлять.

dazzle, *n,* ослеплéние; ослепйтельный блеск; ¶ *v.t,* ослеплять; поражáть; **dazzling,** *a,* ослепйтельный; поразйтельный.

deacon, *n,* дьякон.

dead, *a,* мёртвый; дóхлый *(animals)*; увядший *(flowers, etc.)*; неподвйжный; безжйзненный; унылый; онемéвший *(fingers, etc.)*; пóлный, совершéнный; ~ *beat* смертéльно устáлый; ~ *calm(a.)* совершéнно спокóйный; *(n.)* мёртвая тишинá; ~ *certainty* пóлная увéренность; вéрное дéло; ~ *drunk* мертвéцки пьяный; ~ *end* тупйк; ~ *letter* недостáвленное письмó; *remain a* ~ *letter* остáвáться без послéдствий; ~*lock* мёртвая тóчка; тупйк; затóр, «прóбка»; ~ *march* похорóнный марш; ~ *shot* мéткий выстрел; мéткий стрелóк; ~ *tired* до смéрти устáлый; ¶ *n.pl,* мёртвые; ~*en,* *v.t,* лишáть сйлы/рáдости *(etc.)*, дéлать нечувствйтельным; ослаблять, заглушáть; ~*ly,* *a,* смертéльный; смертонóсный; беспощáдный; ужáсный; ~ *sin* смéртный грех.

deaf, *a,* глухóй *(also fig.)*; ~-*mute* глухонемóй; *turn a* ~ *ear* не обращáть внимáния на; ~*en,* *v.t,* оглушáть; ~*ening,* *a,* оглушйтельный; заглушáющий; ~*ness,* *n,* глухотá.

deal, *n,* колйчество; дóля; сдéлка; соглашéние; сдáча *(cards)*; *a good* ~ мнóго; *make a* ~ *with* заключáть сдéлку с; ¶ *v.t,* сдавáть *(cards)*; наносйть *(blow)*; ~ *out* распределять, раздавáть; ~ *with* обходйться с; поступáть с; общáться с, имéть дéло с; борóться с; *(com.)* быть клиéнтом у; вестй торгóвые делá с; ~ *in* торговáть *(inst.)*; ~*er,* *n,* торго́вец, торго́вый аге́нт; ~ing, *n*, поведе́ние, посту́пок; *pl*, дела́, деловы́е отноше́ния.

dean, *n*, дека́н; настоя́тель собо́ра; ~ery, *n*, декана́т; дом настоя́теля; церко́вный о́круг.

dear, *a*, дорого́й; ми́лый, сла́вный; ~ me! бо́же мой!; D~ Sir, ми́лостивый госуда́рь; *my* ~ мой ми́лый; ~ly, *ad*, до́рого *(also fig.)*; не́жно; ~ness, *n*, дороговизна.

dearth, *n*, го́лод; недоста́ток, нехва́тка.

death, *n*, смерть; коне́ц, ги́бель; ~ *bed* сме́ртное ло́же; предсме́ртные мину́ты; ~ *blow* смерте́льный/роково́й уда́р; ~ *certificate* свиде́тельство о сме́рти; ~'s *head* че́реп; мёртвая голова́ *(butterfly);* ~ *rate* сме́ртность; ~ *roll* спи́сок уби́тых; ~-*throes* предсме́ртная аго́ния; ~ *toll* похоро́нный звон; число́ уби́тых; ~ *warrant* распоряже́ние о приведе́нии в исполне́ние сме́ртной ка́зни; *on pain of* ~ под стра́хом сме́ртной ка́зни; *put to* ~ казни́ть; ~less, *a*, бессме́ртный; ~ly, *a*, смерте́льный; ~ *silence* гробово́е молча́ние.

debar, *v.t*, воспреща́ть; лиша́ть (пра́ва).

debase, *v.t*, унижа́ть; понижа́ть *(quality, etc.);* по́ртить; подде́лывать *(coin);* ~ment, *n*, униже́ние; сниже́ние це́нности/ка́чества; подде́лка (де́нег).

debatable, *a*, спо́рный, дискуссио́нный; оспа́риваемый; **debate**, *n*, деба́ты; пре́ния; диску́ссия; спор; ¶ *v.t*, обсужда́ть; дебати́ровать; обду́мывать; *v.i*, дискути́ровать; спо́рить; ~r, *n*, уча́стник деба́тов/пре́ний; спо́рщик.

debauch, *v.t*, развраща́ть; обольща́ть; ~ee, *n*, развра́тник; ~ery, *n*, разврат; распу́щенность.

debenture, *n*, долгово́е обяза́тельство; ~ *bonds* облига́ции акционе́рного о́бщества.

debilitate, *v.t*, ослабля́ть, расслабля́ть; **debility**, *n*, сла́бость, бесси́лие.

debit, *n*, де́бет; ¶ *v.t*, вноси́ть в де́бет.

debouch, *v.i*, выходи́ть на пове́рхность *(river);* *(mil.)* дебуши́ровать.

debris, *n*, оско́лки; обло́мки, разва́лины.

debt, *n*, долг; *run into* ~ влеза́ть в долг; ~or, *n*, должни́к; ~'s *prison* долгова́я тюрьма́.

début, *n*, дебю́т; *make one's* ~ дебюти́ровать; ~ante, *n*, дебюта́нтка.

decade, *n*, десятиле́тие.

decadence, *n*, упа́док; упа́дничество, декаде́нтство; **decadent**, *a*, упа́дочный, декаде́нтский; ¶ *n*, декаде́нт.

decalogue, *n*, де́сять за́поведей.

decamp, *v.i*, снима́ться с ла́геря, выступа́ть из ла́геря; удира́ть.

decant, *v.t*, перелива́ть (вино́) из буты́лки в графи́н; сце́живать, фильтрова́ть; ~er, *n*, графи́н.

decapitate, *v.t*, обезгла́вливать; **decapitation**, *n*, обезгла́вливание.

decay, *v.i*, гнить, разлага́ться; по́ртиться; приходи́ть в упа́док; распада́ться ¶ *n*, гние́ние; разложе́ние, упа́док; распа́д; расстро́йство *(of health);* разруше́ние *(of building).*

decease, *n*, смерть, кончи́на; ¶ *v.i*, сконча́ться *(pf.);* ~d, *a*, поко́йный, уме́рший; ¶ *n*, поко́йник.

deceit, *n*, обма́н; лжи́вость; хи́трость; ~ful, *a*, обма́нчивый; лжи́вый; **deceive**, *v.t*, обма́нывать; вводи́ть в заблужде́ние; ~r, *n*, обма́нщик, лгун.

December, *n*, дека́брь.

decency, *n*, прили́чие; поря́дочность, благопристо́йность; **decent**, *a*, прили́чный; поря́дочный; скро́мный; сла́вный.

decennial, *a*, десятиле́тний.

decentralize, *v.t*, децентрализова́ть.

deception, *n*, обма́н, ложь; **deceptive**, *a*, обма́нчивый, вводя́щий в заблужде́ние.

decide, *v.t. & i*, реша́ть, принима́ть реше́ние; ~d, *a*, реши́тельный; бесспо́рный, определённый; ~dly, *ad*, реши́тельно; несомне́нно, я́вно.

deciduous, *a*, опада́ющий *(leaves);* ли́ственный.

decimal, *a*, десяти́чный; ~ *fraction* десяти́чная дробь; ~ *point* то́чка в десяти́чной дро́би.

decimate, *v.t*, взима́ть десяти́ну с; казни́ть ка́ждого деся́того; *(fig.)* уничтожа́ть, «коси́ть»; decimation, *n*, взимание десятины; казнь каждого десятого; *(fig.)* ~ мор, опустошение, уничтожение.

decipher, *v.t*, расшифровывать; разбирать; ~able, *a*, поддающийся расшифровке/чтению.

decision, *n*, решение; решимость; **decisive**, *a*, решающий; решительный; ~ly, *ad*, решительно; ~ness, *n*, решимость; решительность.

deck, *n*, палуба; крыша; верх; колода *(cards);* ~ *chair* шезлонг; ~ *hand* матрос; *on* ~ на палубе; под рукой; *quarter* ~ шканцы; ют; ¶ *v.t*, настилать палубу; убирать, украшать.

declaim, *v.i*, декламировать; говорить с пафосом; ~er, *n*, декламатор; оратор; **declamation**, *n*, декламация; торжественная речь; **declamatory**, *a*, декламационный; ораторский; напыщенный.

declaration, *n*, заявление, декларация; объявление *(of war);* **declare**, *v.t*, объявлять, провозглашать; предъявлять *(goods); v.i:* ~ *for/ against* высказываться за/против.

declension, *n*, отклонение; *(gram.)* склонение.

decline, *n*, падение, упадок; ухудшение *(of health);* склон; закат *(of life);* ¶ *v.t*, отклонять; отказываться от; *(gram.)* склонять; *v.i*, наклоняться, склоняться, подходить к концу; уменьшаться; ухудшаться *(of health);* приходить в упадок.

declivity, *n*, покатость; склон, уклон.

decoction, *n*, вываривание; (лечебный) отвар.

décolleté, *a*, декольтированный; ~ *dress* платье декольте.

decompose, *v.t*, разлагать на составные части; анализировать; *v.i*, разлагаться; гнить; **decomposition**, *n*, разложение; распад, гниение.

decontaminate, *v.t*, обеззараживать; дегазировать.

decorate, *v.t*, украшать; отделывать *(house);* награждать знаком отличия; **decoration**, *n*, украшение; отделка *(of house);* знак отличия; **decorative**, *a*, декоративный; **decorator**, *n*, декоратор; маляр; обойщик.

decorous, *a*, приличный, пристойный· **decorum**, *n*, приличие, декорум.

decoy, *n*, западня, ловушка; приманка; ¶ *v.t*, заманивать в ловушку; завлекать.

decrease, *n*, уменьшение, убыль; ¶ *v.t*, уменьшать; *v.i*, уменьшаться, убывать.

decree, *n*, декрет, указ; постановление, решение ; ¶ *v.t*, издавать декрет/указ о; постановлять.

decrepit, *a*, дряхлый *(pers.);* ветхий; ~ude, *n*, дряхлость; ветхость.

decry, *v.t*, осуждать, порицать; принижать.

dedicate, *v.t*, посвящать; надписывать *(book);* **dedication**, *n*, посвящение; преданность; **dedicatory**, *a*, посвятительный.

deduce, *v.t*, выводить; делать вывод о.

deduct, *v.t*, вычитать, отнимать; удерживать; ~ion, *n*, вычитание; вычет, удержание; скидка; вычитаемое; вывод, заключение.

deed, *n*, дело, поступок; действие; подвиг; *(law)* документ, акт.

deem, *v.t*, полагать, считать.

deep, *a*, глубокий; серьёзный; погружённый (в); таинственный; густой *(colour);* низкий *(sound);* ~*-sea fishing* лов рыбы в глубоких водах; ~*-seated* укоренившийся; затаённый *(feeling);* крепкий *(belief);* ¶ *n*, пучина, бездна, пропасть; ~en, *v.t. (& i.),* углублять(ся), усиливать(ся); сгущать(ся) *(colour);* понижать(ся) *(voice);* ~ly, *ad*, глубоко; ~ness, *n*, глубина *(also fig.).*

deer, *n*, олень.

deface, *v.t*, портить, марать; стирать; ~ment, *n*, порча, маранье; стирание.

de facto, *ad*, на деле, фактически, де-факто.

defalcate, *v.i*, присваивать чужие деньги; **defalcation**, *n*, растрата.

defamation, *n*, клевета; **defamatory**, *a*, бесчестящий; клеветнический; **defame**, *v.t*, клеветать на; порочить, поносить.

default, *n*, недостаток, отсутствие; невыполнение обязательств; неплатёж; неявка в суд; ¶ *v.i*, не выполнять обязательств; пре-

кращáть платежú; ~er, n, не
вúполнивший свойх обязá-
тельств; банкрóт; растрáтчик;
не явúвшийся в суд.
defeat, n, поражéние, разгрóм;
расстрóйство *(of plans)*; крушéние *(of hopes)*; ¶ *v.t*, побеждáть;
разбивáть; расстрáивать *(plans)*;
разрушáть *(hopes)*; провáливать
(bill); ~ism, n, поражéнчество.
defecate, *v.t*, очищáть; *v.i*, очищáть-
ся; *(med.)* испражнáться.
defect, n, недостáток; дефéкт; недочёт; неисправность; ~ion, n,
нарушéние *(of duty)*; дезертúр-
ство; отступничество; ~ive, a,
несовершéнный; неисправный;
повреждённый; *(gram.)* недос-
тáточный.
defence, n оборóна, защúта; ~less,
a, беззащúтный; необороняéмый;
defend, *v.t*, защищáть *(also law)*;
оборонять; ~ant, n, *(law)* подсудúмый, обвиняемый; ~er, n,
защúтник; **defensible,** a, удóбный
для оборóны; защитúмый; **defen-**
sive, a, оборонú-
тельный; оборóнный; ¶ n, оборóна; оборонúтельная позúция.
defer, *v.t*, отклáдывать, отсрóчи-
вать; *v.i*, мéдлить, мéшкать;
тянýть; ~ *to* считáться с; уступ-
áть; ~ence, n, уважéние, поч-
тúтельное отношéние; ~en-
tial, a, почтúтельный; ~ment,
n, отсрóчка, отклáдывание.
defiance, n, вúзов; открúтое неповиновéние, пренебрежéние;
defiant, a, вызывáющий; непо-
винýющийся.
deficiency, n, недостáток, отсýт-
ствие; **deficient,** a, недостáточ-
ный; непóлный; *be* ~ *in* быть
лишённым *(gen.)*; **deficit,** n,
дефицúт, недочёт; нехвáтка; *cash*
~ недосдáча.
defile, n, теснúна, ущéлье; ¶ *v.t*,
загрязнять; осквернять; развра-
щáть; *v.i*, проходúть ýзкой ко-
лóнной; ~ment, n, загрязнéние;
осквернéние; развращéние.
definable, a, определúмый; **define,**
v.t, определять; устанáвливать;
definite, a, определённый; úсный,
тóчный; ~ly, ad, определённо;
úсно, тóчно; ~ness, n, определён-
ность; тóчность, úсность; **defi-**
nition, n, определéние; úсность,

тóчность; **definitive,** a, окончáтельный.
deflate, *v.t*, выкáчивать, выпускáть
вóздух из; *(fig.)* сбивáть спесь с;
разрушáть; *v.i*, сплющиваться;
проводúть дефляцию *(fin.)*; **de-**
flation, n, выкáчивание, выпус-
кáние; *(fin.)* дефляция.
deflect, *v.t. (& i.)*, отклонять(ся);
преломлять(ся); ~ion, n, отклонéние; *(optic.)* преломлéние.
defloration, n, лишéние дéвствен-
ности; **deflower,** *v.t*, лишáть дéв-
ственности, насúловать.
deforest, *v.t*, вырубáть лесá; обез-
лéсить *(pf.)*.
deform, *v.t*, урóдовать, обезобрá-
живать; деформúровать; ~ation, n,
урóдование; деформáция; ~ed,
a, изурóдованный; деформúро-
ванный; ~ity, n, урóдливость;
урóдство; урóд.
defraud, *v.t*, обмáнывать; обмáном
лишáть; ~er, n, обмáнщик; ~ing,
n, обмáн.
defray, *v.t*, оплáчивать.
deft, a, лóвкий; искýсный; ~ness,
n, лóвкость.
defunct, a, умéрший.
defy, *v.t*, вызывáть (на спор/борьбý);
дéйствовать наперекóр *(dat.)*;
не поддавáться (решéнию/опи-
сáнию).
degeneracy, n, вырождéние, деге-
нерáция; **degenerate,** a, вырож-
дáющийся, дегенератúвный; ¶
n, вúродок, дегенерáт; ¶ *v.i*,
вырождáться; ухудшáться.
degradation, n, упáдок, деградáция;
понижéние; унижéние; *(biol.)*
вырождéние; **degrade,** *v.t*, по-
нижáть; разжáловать *(pf.)*; унижáть; **degrading,** a, унизúтельный.
degree, n, ступéнь; стéпень; учёная
стéпень; положéние, ранг; грáдус; кáчество, сорт; *(gram.)*
стéпень сравнéния; *by* ~s по-
степéнно; *take a* ~ получáть учё-
ную стéпень.
dehydrate, *v.t*, обезвóживать.
deification, n, обожествлéние; **deify,**
v.t, обожествлять; боготворúть.
deign, *v.i*, соизволять, соблагово-
лúть *(pf.)*.
deism, n, деúзм; **deist,** n, деúст;
deity, n, божествó.
deject, *v.t*, удручáть, угнетáть
~ion, n, унúние.

de jure, *ad*, юриди́чески, де-ю́ре.

delay, *n*, заде́ржка; промедле́ние; отсро́чка; ¶ *v.t*, заде́рживать; откла́дывать, отсро́чивать; *v.i*, ме́длить; опа́здывать.

delectable, *a*, услади́тельный; преле́стный; **delectation**, *n*, наслажде́ние, удово́льствие.

delegate, *n*, делега́т, представи́тель; ¶ *v.t*, посыла́ть делега́том; назнача́ть; уполномо́чивать; **delegation**, *n*, делега́ция.

delete, *v.t*, вычёркивать, стира́ть; *(fig.)* уничтожа́ть.

deleterious, *a*, вре́дный.

deletion, *n*, вычёркивание, стира́ние; уничтоже́ние.

deliberate, *a*, (пред)наме́ренный; умы́шленный; обду́манный; неторопл
́ивый; ¶ *v.i*, обду́мывать, обсужда́ть; *v.i*, размышля́ть; совеща́ться; ~ly, *ad*, наро́чно, умы́шленно; осторо́жно; **deliberation**, *n*, обсужде́ние; размышле́ние; нетороплᴎ́вость; **deliberative**, *a*, совеща́тельный.

delicacy, *n*, делика́тность; утончённость; не́жность; ла́комство *(food)*; **delicate**, *a*, делика́тный; изя́щный, то́нкий; щекотли́вый *(situation)*; сла́бый *(health)*.

delicious, *a*, вку́сный; восхити́тельный

delight, *n*, восто́рг; удово́льствие; наслажде́ние; ¶ *v.t*, восхища́ть, приводи́ть в восто́рг; *be ~ed* восхища́ться; ~*ed to meet you* о́чень рад познако́миться с ва́ми; ~*ful*, *a*, восхити́тельный, очарова́тельный; ~*fully*, *ad*, восхити́тельно.

delimit, *v.t*, определя́ть грани́цы *(gen.)*; разграни́чивать; ~*ation*, *n*, определе́ние грани́ц; разграниче́ние.

delineate, *v.t*, обрисо́вывать; изобража́ть, опи́сывать; **delineation**, *n*, очерта́ние; описа́ние, изображе́ние.

delinquency, *n*, просту́пок; правонаруше́ние; престу́пность; **delinquent**, *a*, вино́вный; ¶ *n*, правонаруши́тель, хулига́н.

delirious, *a*, находя́щийся в бреду́/ исступле́нии; бредово́й; бессвя́зный *(speech)*; ~ *with joy* вне себя́ от ра́дости; *be ~* бре́дить;

delirium, *n*, бред; исступле́ние; ~ *tremens* бе́лая горя́чка.

deliver, *v.t*, доставля́ть, вруча́ть; разноси́ть *(letters)*; освобожда́ть, избавля́ть; наноси́ть *(blow)*; произноси́ть *(speech)*; чита́ть *(lecture)*; ~ *over* передава́ть; ~ *up* сдава́ть; ~ *oneself up* сдава́ться; *be ~ ed (med.)* разреша́ться от бре́мени, рожа́ть; ~**ance**, *n*, освобожде́ние, избавле́ние; заявле́ние; ~**er**, *n*, разно́счик; поста́вщи́к; освободи́тель; ~**y**, *n*, доста́вка; поста́вка; разно́ска *(of letters)*; переда́ча, вруче́ние; ро́ды; речь, ди́кция; пода́ча *(of ball)*; ~ *van* фурго́н для доста́вки зака́зов на дом.

dell, *n*, лощи́на.

delta, *n*, де́льта.

delude, *v.t*, обма́нывать, вводи́ть в заблужде́ние.

deluge, *n*, пото́п; наводне́ние; ¶ *v.t*, затопля́ть; наводня́ть *(also fig.)*.

delusion, *n*, заблужде́ние; иллю́зия; обма́н; **delusive**, *a*, обма́нчивый, иллюзо́рный.

delve, *v.t (& i.)*, копа́ть(ся), ры́ть(ся).

demagogue, *n*, демаго́г.

demand, *n* тре́бование; потре́бность; запро́с; *(com.)* спрос; *in steady ~* в большо́м спро́се; *на́ он ~* опла́та по предъявле́нию; ¶ *v.t*, тре́бовать *(gen.)*; нужда́ться в.

demarcate, *v.t*, разграни́чивать; проводи́ть демаркацио́нную ли́нию ме́жду; **demarcation**, *n*, разграниче́ние; демарка́ция.

demean oneself роня́ть своё досто́инство; **demeanour**, *n*, мане́ра держа́ться.

demented, *a*, сумасше́дший; **dementia**, *n*, слабоу́мие.

demerit, *n*, недоста́ток.

demesne, *n*, владе́ние; поме́стье.

demi *[prefix]* полу-.

demigod, *n*, полубо́г.

demijohn, *n*, больша́я буты́ль.

demise, *n*, переда́ча по насле́дству; сда́ча в аре́нду; кончи́на; ¶ *v.t*, передава́ть по насле́дству; сдава́ть в аре́нду.

demobilize, *v.t*, демобилизо́вывать.

democracy, *n*, демокра́тия; **democrat**, *n*, демокра́т; **democratic**, *a*, демократи́ческий.

demolish, *v.t,* разрушáть; сносúть *(building);* **demolition,** *n,* разрушéние; снос.

demon, *n,* дéмон; **~iacal,** *a,* одержúмый; дья́вольский.

demonstrable, *a,* доказу́емый; очевúдный, нагля́дный; **demonstrate,** *v.t,* демонстрúровать; доказывать; проявля́ть *(feeling); v.i,* учáствовать в демонстрáции; **demonstration,** *n,* демонстрúрование; доказáтельство; проявлéние *(of feeling);* демонстрáция; **demonstrative,** *a,* нагля́дный; демонстратúвный; несдéржанный; *(gram.)* указáтельный; **demonstrator,** *n,* демонстрáнт, учáстник демонстрáции; демонстрáтор.

demoralization, *n,* деморализáция; **demoralize,** *v.t,* деморализовáть; **demoralizing,** *a,* деморализу́ющий.

demur, *v.l,* возражáть; сомневáться, колебáться; ¶ *n,* возражéние; колебáние.

demure, *a,* скрóмный, сдéржанный; **~ness,** *n,* скрóмность, сдéржанность.

demurrage, *n,* простóй.

den, *n,* лóговище, берлóга; клéтка; кабинéт.

denial, *n,* отрицáние; откáз.

denim, *n,* деним.

denizen, *n,* жúтель, обитáтель.

denominate, *v.t,* называ́ть, именовáть; **denomination,** *n,* название; наименовáние; вероисповéдание; сéкта; достóинство *(of coin).*

denote, *v.t,* обозначáть, означáть.

dénouement, *n,* развя́зка *(of story);* исхóд.

denounce, *v.t,* разоблачáть; осуждáть, обвиня́ть; доносúть на; денонсúровать *(treaty).*

dense, *a,* плóтный; густóй; глу́пый, тупóй; **density,** *n,* плóтность; густотá.

dent, *n,* вы́емка, впáдина; ¶ *v.t,* вдáвливать, оставля́ть след в/на.

dental, *a,* зубнóй; **~** *surgeon* зубнóй хиру́рг; **dentifrice,** *n,* зубнóй порошóк, зубнáя пáста; **dentist,** *n,* зубнóй врач; **~ry,** *n,* зуболечéние; **dentition,** *n,* прорéзывание зубóв; расположéние зубóв; **denture,** *n,* зубнóй протéз; вставнáя чéлюсть.

denudation, *n,* обнажéние, оголéние; **denude,** *v.t,* обнажáть, оголя́ть; лишáть.

denunciation, *n,* разоблачéние; обвинéние; денонсúрование *(of treaty).*

deny, *v.t,* отрицáть; откáзывать в; откáзываться от.

deodorant, *a,* уничтожáющий (зáпах); ¶ *n,* дезодорáтор; **deodorize,** *v.t,* уничтожáть дурнóй зáпах *(gen.).*

depart, *v.i,* уходúть, уезжáть; отправля́ться; отступáть; умирáть; **~ed,** *a. & n,* бы́лой, мину́вший; покóйный.

department, *n,* отдéл; вéдомство; министéрство, департáмент; факультéт, отделéние; цех; óкруг; **~** *store* универмáг; **~al,** *a,* вéдомственный.

departure, *n,* отъéзд, ухóд; отправлéние; смерть; отклонéние, отступлéние.

depend, *v.i,* завúсеть; полагáться, рассчúтывать; *it all* **~***s* как сказáть; *смотря́* по обстоя́тельствам; **~able,** *a,* надёжный; заслу́живающий довéрия; **~ant** *n,* иждивéнец, -éнка; **~ence,** *n,* завúсимость; подчинéние; довéрие; **~ency,** *n,* завúсимость; *foreign* **~** завúсимая странá, колóния; **dependent,** *a,* завúсимый; подчинённый; *be* **~** *on* находúться на иждивéнии; завúсеть от.

depict, *v.t,* изображáть, опúсывать.

deplete, *v.t,* истощáть, исчéрпывать; **depletion,** *n,* истощéние, исчéрпывание.

deplorable, *a,* плачéвный, прискóрбный; **deplore,** *v.t,* оплáкивать; сожалéть о; считáть предосудúтельным.

deploy, *v.t,* развёртывать; **~ment,** *n,* развёртывание.

deponent, *n, (law)* свидéтель; *(gram.)* отложúтельный глагóл.

depopulate, *v.t,* истребля́ть населéние *(gen.),* обезлю́дить *(pf.);* **depopulation,** *n,* истреблéние населéния; безлю́дье.

deport, *v.t,* высылáть, ссылáть; **~ation,** *n,* вы́сылка, ссы́лка; **~ment,** *n,* поведéние, манéра держáться.

depose, *v.t,* смещáть (с дóлжности); свергáть (с престóла); *v.i, (law)* свидéтельствовать.

deposit, *n*, вклад в банк; задаток; залог; осадок, отложение; *(geol.)* месторождение, залежь; ~ *account* депозит; ¶ *v.t*, класть (в банк); отдавать на хранение/под залог; давать в задаток; отлагать; давать осадок в виде *(gen.)*; ~ion, *n*, свержение (с престола); показание под присягой; отложение, осадок; ~or, *n*, вкладчик; ~ory, *n*, склад, хранилище.

depot, *n*, *(rly.)* депо; склад; *(U.S.)* железнодорожная станция; сборный пункт.

depravation, *n*, развращение; ухудшение, порча; **deprave**, *v.t*, развращать; портить; ~d, *p.p. & a*, развращённый; испорченный; **depravity**, *n*, развращённость; испорченность; порочность.

deprecate, *v.t*, возражать/выступать против, осуждать.

depreciate, *v.t. (& i.)*, обесценивать(ся); **depreciation**, *n*, обесценение; снижение; амортизация, **depreciatory**, *a*, обесценивающий; умаляющий.

depredation, *n*, грабёж, расхищение; опустошение.

depress, *v.t*, подавлять, угнетать, удручать; понижать; ~ed, *p.p. & a*, подавленный, угнетённый, удручённый; ~ing, *a*, гнетущий, тягостный, унылый; ~ion, *n*, уныние; угнетённое состояние; *(econ.)* депрессия; низина, ложбина *(on surface)*.

deprivation, *n*, лишение; потеря; **deprive**, *v.t*, лишать.

depth, *n*, глубина, глубь; густота *(of colour)*; *in the* ~ *of night* глубокой ночью; *in the* ~ *of winter* в разгар зимы; *the* ~s *of the wood* чаща леса.

deputation, *n*, делегация, депутация; **depute**, *v.t*, делегировать; уполномочивать; назначать; **deputize**, *v.i*, замещать; представлять; **deputy**, *n*, депутат; делегат; представитель; заместитель, помощник.

derail, *v.t*, вызывать крушение *(gen.)*; пускать под откос; *v.i* сходить с рельсов; ~ment, *n*, крушение.

derange, *v.t*, приводить в беспорядок; выводить из строя *(machine)*; расстраивать *(plans, etc.)*; сводить с ума; ~d, *a*, перепутанный, беспорядочный; помешанный; ~ment, *n*, беспорядок; расстройство; психическое расстройство.

derelict, *a*, покинутый, брошенный; беспризорный; ¶ *n*, брошенное имущество/судно *(etc.)*; ~ion, *n*, заброшенность; нарушение долга; упущение.

deride, *v.t*, высмеивать, осмеивать, насмехаться над; ~r, *n*, насмешник; **derision**, *n*, высмеивание; осмеяние; посмешище; **derisive**, *a*, насмешливый; смехотворный; **derisory**, *a*, *see* derisive.

derivation, *n*, источник; происхождение; этимология *(of word)*; словопроизводство; деривация; *(med.)* отвлечение; **derivative**, *a*, производный; ¶ *n*, *(gram.)* производное слово; **derive**, *v.t*, получать; извлекать; производить; *be* ~d *from* происходить от.

derogate, *v.i*, унижать себя, терять своё достоинство; ~ *from* умалять *(merit)*; нарушать *(rights)*; порочить *(reputation)*; **derogatory**, *a*, умаляющий; нарушающий; унизительный.

derrick, *n*, подъёмный кран; буровая вышка.

dervish, *n*, дервиш.

descant, *n*, песня, напев, мелодия; дискант; рассуждение; ¶ *v.i*, петь; ~ *upon* рассуждать/распространяться о.

descend, *v.t*, спускаться/сходить с; *v.i*, происходить; переходить (по наследству); обрушиваться; ~ *to* падать/опускаться до; унижаться до; ~ant, *n*, потомок; **descent**, *n*, спуск; склон; происхождение; десант; внезапное нападение (с моря).

describe, *v.t*, описывать *(also circle)*; изображать; **description**, *n*, описание; изображение; вид, род, **descriptive**, *a*, описательный; образный.

descry, *v.t*, замечать.

desecrate, *v.t*, осквернять; оскорблять; **desecration**, *n*, осквернение, профанация.

desert, *a*, необитаемый; пустынный; ¶ *n*, пустыня; ¶ *v.t*, покидать, оставлять; бросать; *v.i*, дезертировать; ~ed, *p.p. & a*, покинутый; пустынный; заброшенный; **~er**, *n*, дезертир, перебежчик; **~ion**, *n*, оставление; дезертирство; заброшенность.

deserts, *n.pl*, заслуги; **deserve**, *v.t*, заслуживать; **deservedly**, *ad*, по заслугам, заслуженно; **deserving**, *a*, заслуживающий, достойный.

desiccate, *v.t*, высушивать; **desiccation**, *n*, сушка; сухость.

desideratum, *n*, пробел; (что-то) желаемое; *pl*, пожелания, дезидераты.

design, *n*, замысел, план; намерение, умысел; проект; чертёж; конструкция; рисунок, узор; эскиз; *by* **~** (пред)намеренно; *have* **~s** *on* злоумышлять против; ¶ *v.t*, замышлять; предназначать; составлять план *(gen.)*; конструировать; проектировать; рисовать; делать эскизы (костюмов, *etc.*).

designate, *v.t*, (пред)назначать; назначать на должность; обозначать, определять; указывать; **designation**, *n*, предназначение, цель; назначение на должность; указание.

designer, *n*, проектировщик; конструктор; чертёжник; художник-декоратор; **designing**, *a*, проектирующий, планирующий; *n*, проектирование, конструирование.

desirable, *a*, желательный; желанный; **desire**, *n*, желание; предмет желания; **~** *v.t*, желать, просить, требовать; **desirous**, *a*, желающий, жаждущий.

desist, *v.i*, прекращать, переставать.

desk, *n*, контора, письменный стол, парта; *cash* **~** касса.

desolate, *a*, заброшенный, запущенный; безлюдный; ¶ *v.t*, опустошать, разорять; обезлюдить *(pf.)*; **desolation**, *n*, опустошение, разорение; запустение, запущенность.

despair, *n*, отчаяние; безнадёжность; *drive to* **~** доводить до отчаяния; ¶ *v.i*, отчаиваться; **~ingly**, *ad*, безнадёжно, в отчаянии.

despatch, *n*, отправка (курьера почты); депеша; официальное донесение; быстрота; **~** *box* сумка

курьера; **~** *rider* курьер; ¶ *v.t*, отправлять, посылать; быстро справляться с; отправлять на тот свет.

desperado, *n*, сорвиголова; разбойник; **desperate**, *a*, отчаянный, безнадёжный; доведённый до отчаяния; **~ly**, *ad*, в отчаянии; безнадёжно; отчаянно; **desperation**, *n*, отчаяние.

despicable, *a*, презренный; **despise**, *v.t*, презирать.

despite, *pr*, несмотря на, вопреки; ¶ *n*, злоба, гнев.

despoil, *v.t*, грабить, обирать; **~er**, *n*, грабитель.

despondency, *n*, подавленность, уныние; **despondent**, *a*, подавленный, унылый.

despot, *n*, деспот; **~ic**, *a*, деспотический; **~ism**, *n*, деспотизм.

dessert, *n*, десерт, сладкое.

destination, *n*, назначение, предназначение; место назначения; **destine**, *v.t*, назначать, предназначать, предопределять; **destiny**, *n*, судьба, удел.

destitute, *a*, сильно нуждающийся, неимущий; **destitution**, *n*, лишения *(pl.)*; нужда, нищета.

destroy, *v.t*, разрушать; уничтожать; **~er**, *n*, разрушитель; эсминец *(warship)*; **destruction**, *n*, разрушение; уничтожение; **destructive**, *a*, разрушительный; вредный.

desultory, *a*, несвязный, бессвязный; отрывочный, беспорядочный.

detach, *v.t*, отделять; *(mil.)* отряжать; **~able**, *a*, отделимый; съёмный; заменяемый; **~ed**, *a*, отдельный; обособленный; беспристрастный; *(mil.)* откомандированный; **~** *house* особняк, отдельный дом; **~ment**, *n*, отделение; обособленность; беспристрастность; *(mil.)* отряд; откомандирование.

detail, *n*, подробность; деталь; *(mil.)* наряд; команда; *in* **~** подробно; ¶ *v.t*, подробно рассказывать; вдаваться в подробности *(gen.)*; *(mil.)* откомандировывать; назначать в наряд; **~ed**, *a*, подробный, детальный.

detain, *v.t*, задерживать; содержать под арестом; удерживать *(money)*.

detect, *v.t*, обнару́живать, откры-
ва́ть; ~**ion**, *n*, откры́тие, обнару́-
жение; ~**ive**, *n*, сы́щик; ~ *story*
детекти́в; ~**or**, *n*, *(radio)* детéк-
тор; *(chem.)* индика́тор.

detention, *n*, задержа́ние; содер-
жа́ние под аре́стом.

deter, *v.t*, уде́рживать, отгова́ри-
вать; отпу́гивать.

deteriorate, *v.t. (& i.)*, ухудша́ть(ся);
по́ртить(ся); **deterioration**, *n*, ухуд-
ще́ние; по́рча.

determinate, *a*, определённый, уста-
но́вленный; оконча́тельный; **determination**, *n*, установле́ние; ре-
ше́ние; реши́тельность; реши́-
мость; **determine**, *v.t*, определя́ть,
устана́вливать; реша́ть; ~**d**, *a*,
реши́тельный; **determinism**, *n*,
детермини́зм.

deterrent, *n*, сре́дство устраше́ния.

detest, *v.t*, ненави́деть, пита́ть от-
враще́ние к; ~**able**, *a*, отврати́-
тельный; ~**ation**, *n*, отвраще́ние;
не́нависть.

dethrone, *v.t*, сверга́ть с престо́ла;
~**ment**, *n*, сверже́ние с пре-
сто́ла.

detonate, *v.i*, взрыва́ть; детони́ро-
вать; *v.i*, взрыва́ться; **detonation**,
n, взрыв; детона́ция; **detonator**,
n, детона́тор.

detour, *n*, око́льный путь, обхо́д,
объе́зд.

detract, *v.t*, умаля́ть; уменьша́ть;
поро́чить, клевета́ть на; ~**ion**, *n*,
умале́ние; уменьше́ние; клевета́;
~**or**, *n*, клеветни́к; зави́стник.

detriment, *n*, вред, уще́рб; убы́ток;
~**al**, *a*, вре́дный; убы́точный.

deuce, *n*, дво́йка, два очка́; ¶ *int.*
черт!

devaluation, *n*, обесце́нение; деваль-
ва́ция; **devalue**, *v.t*, обесце́нивать;
проводи́ть девальва́цию *(gen.).*

devastate, *v.t*, опустоша́ть, разоря́ть;
devastation, *n*, опустоше́ние, разо-
ре́ние.

develop, *v.t*, развива́ть; разраба́ты-
вать *(resources)*; соверше́нство-
вать; *(phot.)* проявля́ть; *v.i*,
развива́ться; ~**er**, *n*, *(phot.)*
прояви́тель; ~**ment**, *n*, разви́тие;
разрабо́тка *(of resources)*; строй-
тельство; усоверше́нствование;
(phot.) проявле́ние.

deviate, *v.i*, отклоня́ться; уклоня́ть-
ся; **deviation**, *n*, отклоне́ние;

(polit.) укло́н; ~ *of the compass*
девиа́ция ко́мпаса.

device, *n*, сре́дство, спо́соб, приём;
деви́з, эмбле́ма; *(tech.)* приспо-
собле́ние; механи́зм; устро́й-
ство.

devil, *n*, дья́вол, чёрт; *lucky* ~ счаст-
ли́вец; *poor* ~ бедня́га; *between
the* ~ *and the deep blue sea* ме́жду
двух огне́й; *The* ~! чёрт возьми́!;
~**ish**, *a*, дьяво́льский; а́дский;
~**ishly**, *ad*, чёртовски; ~**ment**,
n, чёрная ма́гия; чертовщи́на;
жесто́кость; зло́ба; прока́зы, ша́-
лости.

devious, *a*, изви́листый, око́льный;
хи́трый.

devise, *v.t*, изобрета́ть, выду́мывать;
(law) завеща́ть; ~**e**, *n*, насле́д-
ник; ~**r**, *n*, изобрета́тель; *(law)*
завеща́тель; **devisor**, *n*, *(law)*
завеща́тель.

devoid, *a*: ~ *of* лишённый *(gen.)*;
свобо́дный от.

devolution, *n*, переда́ча; перехо́д;
devolve, *v.t*, передава́ть; *v.i*, пере-
ходи́ть.

devote, *v.t*, посвяща́ть; уделя́ть
(time); ~**d**, *p.p. & a*, пре́данный;
посвящённый; увлека́ющийся; **de-
votee**, *n*, пре́данный; энтузиа́ст
своего́ де́ла; **devotion**, *n*, пре́дан-
ность; привя́занность; набо́ж-
ность; **devotional**, *a*, набо́жный,
благочести́вый.

devour, *v.t*, пожира́ть; поглоща́ть.

devout, *a*, благогове́йный; набо́ж-
ный; пре́данный; ~**ness**, *n*, на-
бо́жность; благочести́вость; пре́-
данность.

dew, *n*, роса́; ка́пля дождя́; ¶ *v.t*,
покрыва́ть росо́й; ороша́ть; об-
ры́згивать; ~**drop** ка́пля росы́,
роси́нка.

dewy, *a*, покры́тый росо́й; роси́-
тый, вла́жный.

dexterity, *n*, прово́рство, ло́вкость;
снаро́вка; одарённость; **dexte-
rous**, *a*, прово́рный, ло́вкий; одарённый, спосо́бный.

diabetes, *n*, диабе́т, са́харная бо-
ле́знь; **diabetic**, *a*, диабети́ческий.

diabolical, *a*, дья́вольский; жесто́-
кий; злой.

diadem, *n*, диаде́ма; коро́на.

diaeresis, *n*, диэре́за, трема́.

diagnose, *v.t*, ста́вить диа́гноз *(gen.)*;
diagnosis, *n*, диа́гноз; **diagnostic**, *a*,

диагности́ческий; ¶ *n*, симпто́м; **diagnostics**, *n*, диагно́стика.

diagonal, *a*, диагона́льный; ¶ *n*, диагона́ль; ~ly, *ad*, по диагона́ли.

diagram, *n*, диагра́мма; чертёж, схе́ма.

dial, *n*, диск набо́ра *(telephone)*; шкала́; *sun*~ со́лнечные часы́; *watch* ~ цифербла́т; ¶ *v.t*, набира́ть (но́мер по телефо́ну).

dialect, *n*, диале́кт, наре́чие, го́вор.

dialectics, *n*, диале́ктика.

dialogue, *n*, диало́г; разгово́р.

diameter, *n*, диа́метр; **diametrical**, *a*, диаметра́льный; ~ly, *ad*, диаметра́льно.

diamond, *n*, алма́з; бриллиа́нт; *pl*, бу́бны *(cards)*; ~ *cutter* алма́з для ре́зки стекла́; ~ *wedding* бриллиа́нтовая сва́дьба.

diapason, *n*, диапазо́н.

diaper, *n*, узо́рчатое полотно́; ромбови́дный узо́р; ¶ *v.t*, украша́ть ромбови́дным узо́ром.

diaphanous, *a*, прозра́чный, просве́чивающий.

diaphragm, *n*, диафра́гма; мембра́на.

diarrhoea, *n*, поно́с.

diarist, *n*, веду́щий дневни́к; **diary**, *n*, дневни́к; записна́я кни́жка.

diatonic, *a*, диатони́ческий.

diatribe, *n*, обличи́тельная речь; ре́зкая кри́тика; дли́нная диску́ссия.

dice, *n.pl*, игра́ в ко́сти; игра́льные ко́сти.

dickens: *the* ~ чёрт.

dicky, *n*, мани́шка; вста́вка; де́тский нагру́дник; ~ *seat* сиде́нье для ку́чера.

dictaphone, *n*, диктофо́н; **dictate**, *v.t*, диктова́ть; предпи́сывать; ¶ *n*, предписа́ние; *(polit.)* дикта́т; **dictation**, *n*, дикта́нт, дикто́вка; предписа́ние; **dictator**, *n*, дикта́тор; ~ial, *a*, дикта́торский; ~ship, *n*, диктату́ра.

diction, *n*, ди́кция; стиль, мане́ра выраже́ния.

dictionary, *n*, словарь.

dictum, *n*, изрече́ние, афори́зм; официа́льное заявле́ние; *(law)* мне́ние судьи́.

didactic, *a*, дидакти́ческий; поучи́тел ный.

die, *v.i*, умира́ть; увяда́ть *(plants)*; до́хнуть *(animals)*; сконча́ться *(pf.)*; томи́ться жела́нием, до́ смерти хоте́ть; конча́ться, исчеза́ть; ~ *away* увяда́ть; замира́ть *(sound)*; ~ *down* отмира́ть; затиха́ть *(wind)*; ~ *out* вымира́ть; заглохнуть *(pf.)* *(engine)*.

die, *n*, игра́льная кость; штамп; штемпель; ма́трица; *the* ~ *is cast* жре́бий бро́шен.

diehard, *n*, твердоло́бый.

diet, *n*, дие́та; пи́ща, стол; режи́м; парла́мент; ¶ *v.t*, держа́ть на дие́те; *v.i*, соблюда́ть дие́ту; ~ary, *n*, дие́та; паёк; ¶ *a*, диети́ческий; ~etics, *n*, диете́тика.

differ, *v.i*, различа́ться, отлича́ться; расходи́ться (во мне́ниях); ~ence, *n*, ра́зница, разли́чие, отли́чие; разногла́сие; ссо́ра; *(maths)* ра́зность; ~ent, *a*, друго́й; ра́зный, разли́чный; необы́чный; **differential**, *a*, отличи́тельный; *(maths)* дифференциа́льный; ¶ *n*, *(tech.)* дифференциа́л; ~entiate, *v.t*, *(& i.)*, различа́ть(ся), отлича́ть(ся); дифференци́ровать(ся); ~ently, *ad*, разли́чно; ина́че.

difficult, *a*, тру́дный, затрудни́тельный, тяжёлый; ~y, *n*, тру́дность; затрудне́ние.

diffidence, *n*, засте́нчивость, неуве́ренность в себе́; **diffident**, *n*, засте́нчивый, неуве́ренный в себе́.

diffuse, *a*, распространённый; расплы́вчатый; рассе́янный; ¶ *v.t*, распространя́ть; рассе́ивать *(light, warmth)*; **diffusion**, *n*, распростране́ние; *(phys.)* диффу́зия.

dig, *n*, толчо́к; раско́пки; *(fig.)* насме́шка; *live in* ~s жить на кварти́ре; ¶ *v.t. & i*, толка́ть, ты́кать *(poke)*; копа́ть, рыть; ~ *out*, ~ *up* выка́пывать; разы́скивать.

digest, *n*, кра́ткий обзо́р/сбо́рник, кра́ткое изложе́ние, дайдже́ст; ¶ *v.t*, перева́ривать *(food)*; усва́ивать; ~ible, *a*, удобоваримый; легко́ усва́иваемый; ~ion, *n*, пищеваре́ние; усвое́ние ~ive, *a*, пищевари́тельный; помога́ющий пищеваре́нию.

digger, *n*, тот, кто копа́ет; землеко́п; **digging**, *n*, копа́ние; земляны́е рабо́ты; *pl*, *(coll.)* жильё. е

digit, *n*, па́лец; ци́фра; однозна́чно число́.

dignified, *a*, с чу́вством со́бственного досто́инства; досто́йный; велича́вый; ва́жный; **dignify**, *v.t*, облагора́живать; удоста́ивать; велича́ть; **dignitary**, *n*, сано́вник; церко́вный де́ятель; **dignity**, *n*, досто́инство; чу́вство со́бственного досто́инства; зва́ние, сан.

digress, *v.i*, отступа́ть; отклоня́ться; **~ion**, *n*, отступле́ние; отклоне́ние; **~ive**, *a*, отступа́ющий, отклоня́ющийся.

dike, *n*, да́мба, плоти́на; ров; огра́да; *(geol.)* да́йка; ¶ *v.t*, окружа́ть рвом; защища́ть да́мбой.

dilapidated, *a*, ве́тхий, полуразвали́вшийся; разорённый; **dilapidation**, *n*, обветша́ние; упа́док; разоре́ние.

dilate, *v.t. (& i.)*, расширя́ть(ся); распространя́ть(ся); **~d**, *a*, широко́ раскры́тый.

dilatoriness, *n*, медли́тельность; **dilatory**, *a*, ме́дленный, медли́тельный.

dilemma, *n*, диле́мма;

dilettante, *n*, дилета́нт, люби́тель.

diligence, *n*, прилежа́ние; усе́рдие, стара́ние; **diligent**, *a*, приле́жный, усе́рдный, стара́тельный.

dill, *n*, укро́п.

dilly-dally, *v.i*, колеба́ться, ме́шкать.

dilute, *v.t*, разбавля́ть, разводи́ть; **~d**, *p.p. & a*, разба́вленный; разведённый; **dilution**, *n*, разбавле́ние.

diluvial, *a*, дилювиа́льный.

dim, *a*, ту́склый; нея́сный; ма́товый; сла́бый *(sight)*; сму́тный, тума́нный; тупо́й; ¶ *v.t*, де́лать ту́склым; затума́нивать; затемня́ть; *v.i*, тускне́ть; затума́ниваться.

dimension, *n*, измере́ние; величина́; объём.

diminish, *v.t*, уменьша́ть, убавля́ть; унижа́ть; *v.i*, уменьша́ться; **diminution**, *n*, уменьше́ние; сокраще́ние; уба́вле́ние; **diminutive**, *a*, ма́ленький, миниатю́рный; *(gram.)* уменьши́тельный.

dimity, *n*, кисея́ для занаве́сок.

dimly *ad*, ту́скло; нея́сно; сму́тно, тума́нно; **dimness**, *n*, ту́склость; нея́сность; сму́тность.

dimple, *n*, я́мочка *(cheek)*; рябь *(water)*; впа́дина.

din, *n*, шум, гро́хот.

dine, *v.i*, обе́дать; *v.t*, угоща́ть обе́дом; **~r**, *n*, обе́дающий; *(rly.)* ваго́н-рестора́н.

dinghy, *n*, шлю́пка, я́лик.

dingy, *a*, ту́склый; тёмный.

dining-car, *n*, ваго́н-рестора́н; **dining-room**, *n*, столо́вая; **dinner**, *n*, обе́д; **~** *jacket* смо́кинг; **~** *party* зва́ный обе́д; **~** *service* обе́денный серви́з; **~** *table* обе́денный стол; **~** *time* вре́мя обе́да.

dint, *n*, след от уда́ра; уда́р; си́ла; *by* **~** *of* посре́дством; путём.

diocesan, *a*, епархиа́льный; **diocese**, *n*, епа́рхия.

dioxide, *n*, двуо́кись.

dip, *n*, погруже́ние; ныря́ние; укло́н, отко́с; *take a* **~** искупа́ться *(pf.)*; ¶ *v.t*, погружа́ть, окуна́ть; спуска́ть *(flag, sail)*; наклоня́ть *(head)*; *v.i*, погружа́ться, окуна́ться; ныря́ть; наклоня́ться; опуска́ться.

diphtheria, *n*, дифтери́я.

diphthong, *n*, дифто́нг.

diploma, *n*, дипло́м; свиде́тельство. **diplomacy**, *n*, диплома́тия; **diplomat**, *n*, диплома́т; **~ic**, *a*, дипломати́ческий; дипломати́чный; такти́чный; **~ist**, *n*, *see* diplomat.

dipsomania, *n*, алкоголи́зм.

dire, *a*, ужа́сный, стра́шный.

direct, *a*, прямо́й; по́лный, диаметра́льный; то́чный; *(elec.)* постоя́нный; ¶ *v.t*, направля́ть; ука́зывать доро́гу *(dat.)*; адресова́ть; управля́ть/руководи́ть *(inst.)*; ста́вить *(play)*; прика́зывать *(dat. + inf.)*; **~ion**, *n*, направле́ние; управле́ние; руково́дство; указа́ние; инстру́кция; директи́ва; постано́вка *(of play)*; **~ly**, *ad*, пря́мо; непосре́дственно; неме́дленно; **~or**, *n*, дире́ктор; режиссёр; дирижёр (орке́стра); **~orate**, *n*, дире́кция; правле́ние; дире́кторство; **~ory**, *n*, спра́вочник; а́дресная кни́га.

dirge, *n*, панихи́да; погреба́льная песнь.

dirt, *n*, грязь; земля́, грунт; по́длость, га́дость; **~iness**, *n*, грязь; неопря́тность; **~y**, *a*, гря́зный; непристо́йный, неприли́чный; нече́стный; нена́стный *(weather)*; ¶ *v.t*, па́чкать, загрязня́ть.

disability, *n*, неспосо́бность, бесси́лие; **disable**, *v.t*, де́лать неспо-

со́бным; де́лать нетрудоспосо́б-
ным; лиша́ть возмо́жности/пра́ва;
(mil.) выводи́ть из стро́я; ~d,
p.p. & a, нетрудоспосо́бный;
вы́веденный из стро́я; ~ *soldier*
инвали́д войны́; ~ment, *n,* не-
трудоспосо́бность; инвали́дность;
выведе́ние из стро́я.

disabuse, *v.t,* выводи́ть из заблуж-
де́ния.

disadvantage, *n,* неудо́бство; не-
вы́года, невы́годное положе́ние;
уще́рб, вред; ~ous, *a,* невы́год-
ный, неблагоприя́тный.

disaffected, *a,* недово́льный; не-
лоя́льный; **disaffection**, *n,* недо-
во́льство; нелоя́льность.

disagree, *v.i,* не соглаша́ться, рас-
ходи́ться во мне́ниях; ссо́риться;
противоре́чить друг дру́гу; не
совпада́ть; не подходи́ть; быть
вре́дным *(food, climate)* ; ~able, *a,*
неприя́тный; ~ment, *n,* разно-
гла́сие; расхожде́ние во мне́ниях;
разла́д, ссо́ра.

disallow, *v.t,* отверга́ть; отка́зы-
вать; запреща́ть.

disappear, *v.i,* исчеза́ть, пропада́ть,
скрыва́ться; ~ance, *n,* исчезно-
ве́ние.

disappoint, *v.t,* разочаро́вывать; рас-
стра́ивать; обма́нывать *(hope)* ;
~ing, *a,* разочаро́вывающий; ~-
ment, *n,* разочарова́ние; неприя́т-
ность; доса́да.

disapproval, *n,* неодобре́ние; **dis-
approve**, *v.t:* ~ *of* не одоб-
ря́ть;

disarm, *v.t,* обезору́живать; разо-
ружа́ть; *(fig.)* умиротворя́ть; *v.i,*
разоружа́ться; ~ament, *n,* разо-
руже́ние.

disarrange, *v.t,* расстра́ивать, при-
води́ть в беспоря́док; дезоргани-
зо́вывать.

disarray, *n,* беспоря́док; смяте́ние,
замеша́тельство; ¶ *v.t,* приводи́ть
в беспоря́док; приводи́ть в смя-
те́ние.

disaster, *n,* бе́дствие, катастро́фа;
несча́стье; **disastrous**, *a,* бе́дствен-
ный, ги́бельный.

disavow, *v.t,* отрица́ть; отрека́ться/
отка́зываться от; ~al, *n,* отрица́-
ние; отрече́ние, отка́з.

disband, *v.t,* распуска́ть, расформи-
ро́вывать; *v.i,* разбега́ться, рас-
се́иваться.

disbelief, *n,* неве́рие, недове́рие;
disbelieve, *v.t,* не ве́рить *(dat.)* ;
не доверя́ть *(dat.)* ; ~r, *n,* неве́-
рующий.

disburden, *v.t,* разгружа́ть; снима́ть
тя́жесть с; ~ *oneself* отво́дить
ду́шу.

disburse, *v.t,* плати́ть; ~ment, *a,*
отпла́та, распла́та.

disc, *n,* диск, круг.

discard, *n,* что́-то нену́жное; сбро́-
шенная ка́рта; ¶ *v.t,* выбра́сы-
вать; увольня́ть; сбра́сывать
(cards) .

discern, *v.t,* ви́деть, различа́ть; ~ible,
a, види́мый, различи́мый, заме́т-
ный; ~ing, *a,* проница́тельный;
уме́ющий различа́ть; ~ment, *n,*
проница́тельность; уме́ние раз-
лича́ть.

discharge, *n,* разгру́зка; освобожде́-
ние, увольне́ние; *(law)* оправ-
да́ние; исполне́ние *(of duties)* ;
(com.) платёж; *(mil.)* разря́д;
вы́стрел; *(med.)* выделе́ние; ¶
v.t, разгружа́ть; выстре́ли́ть *(pf.)* ;
освобожда́ть; увольня́ть; демо-
билизо́вывать; выпи́сывать из
больни́цы; *(elec.)* разряжа́ть; вы-
пла́чивать *(debts)* ; выполня́ть
(duties) ; выпуска́ть; *v.i,* впада́ть
(of river) ; *(med.)* прорыва́ться.

disciple, *n,* учени́к, после́дователь;
(eccl.) апо́стол.

disciplinarian, *n,* сторо́нник дис-
ципли́ны; **disciplinary**, *a,* дисци-
лина́рный, исправи́тельный; **dis-
cipline**, *n,* дисципли́на, поря́док;
дисциплини́рованность; наказа́-
ние; ¶ *v.t,* дисциплини́ровать;
нака́зывать.

disclaim, *v.t,* отрека́ться/отка́зы-
ваться от; ~er, *n,* отрече́ние, от-
ка́з.

disclose, *v.t,* раскрыва́ть, обнару́жи-
вать, разоблача́ть; **disclosure**, *n,*
раскры́тие, откры́тие, разобла-
че́ние.

discoloration, *n,* измене́ние цве́та;
обесцве́чивание; **discolour**, *v.t,* из-
меня́ть цвет *(gen.)* ; обесцве́чи-
вать; ~ed, *p.p. & a,* обесцве́тив-
шийся, вы́цветший.

discomfit, *v.t,* смуща́ть, приводи́ть
в замеша́тельство; расстра́ивать
пла́ны *(gen.)* ; ~ure, *n,* замеша́-
тельство, смуще́ние; расстро́й-
ство пла́нов.

discomfort, *n,* неудо́бство; нело́вкость; беспоко́йство.

discompose, *v.t,* расстра́ивать; **discomposure,** *n,* беспоко́йство, волне́ние, замеша́тельство.

disconcert, *v.t,* смуща́ть, приводи́ть в замеша́тельство; расстра́ивать *(plans).*

disconnect, *v.t,* разъединя́ть, разобща́ть; *(elec.)* выключа́ть; ~ed, *p.p. & a,* разъединённый; бессвя́зный, отры́вистый.

disconsolate, *a,* неуте́шный, печа́льный.

discontent, *n,* недово́льство; неудовлетворённость; ¶ *v.t,* вызыва́ть недово́льство *(gen.);* ~ed, *a,* недово́льный.

discontinuance, *n,* прекраще́ние, переры́в; **discontinue,** *v.t,* прерыва́ть, прекраща́ть; **discontinuous,** *a,* преры́вистый.

discord, *n,* разногла́сие, разла́д; раздо́р; *(mus.)* диссона́нс; ~ance, *n,* разноголо́сица; ~ant, *a,* несогла́сный, разноголо́сый; противоречи́вый; диссони́рующий.

discount, *n,* ски́дка; учёт векселе́й; ¶ *v.t,* де́лать ски́дку на; учи́тывать *(bills);* не принима́ть в расчёт.

discountenance, *v.t,* не одобря́ть.

discourage, *v.t,* расхола́живать, отбива́ть охо́ту у, отгова́ривать; обескура́живать, ~ment, *n,* обескура́живание; обескура́женность; отгова́ривание.

discourse, *n,* ле́кция, речь; рассужде́ние; ¶ *v.i,* выступа́ть с ре́чью/ ле́кцией; рассужда́ть.

discourteous, *a,* гру́бый, неве́жливый, невоспи́танный; **discourtesy,** *n,* гру́бость, невоспи́танность, неве́жливость.

discover, *v.t,* открыва́ть, обнару́живать; ~er, *n,* соверши́вший откры́тие; ~y, *n,* откры́тие.

discredit, *n,* дискредита́ция; ¶ *v.t,* дискредити́ровать; позо́рить; не доверя́ть *(dat.);* ~able, *a,* дискредити́рующий, позо́рный.

discreet, *a,* осторо́жный, благоразу́мный; сде́ржанный.

discrepancy, *n,* разногла́сие; противоре́чие; расхожде́ние; разли́чие.

discretion, *n,* осторо́жность, осмотри́тельность; благоразу́мие; свобо́да де́йствий; *at your* ~ на ва́ше усмотре́ние; ~ary, *a,* предоста́вленный на усмотре́ние; де́йствующий по своему́ усмотре́нию; *full* ~ *power* дискрецио́нная власть.

discriminate, *v.t,* отлича́ть; различа́ть; распознава́ть; ~ *against* относи́ться по-ра́зному к; дискриминѝ́ровать; **discriminating,** *a,* отличи́тельный (при́знак); хорошо́ разбира́ющийся, проница́тельный; **discrimination,** *n,* дискримина́ция; неодина́ковое отноше́ние; предпочте́ние; уме́ние разбира́ться, проница́тельность.

discursive, *a,* разбро́санный, непосле́довательный.

discus, *n,* диск.

discuss, *v.t,* обсужда́ть; дискути́ровать; ~ion, *n,* обсужде́ние, диску́ссия; пре́ния, перегово́ры *(pl.).*

disdain, *n,* пренебреже́ние, презре́ние; ¶ *v.t,* пренебрега́ть *(inst.),* презира́ть; ~ful, *a,* презри́тельный, пренебрежи́тельный.

disease, *n,* боле́знь; ~d, *a,* больно́й.

disembark, *v.t. (& v.i.),* выгружа́ть(ся) *(goods);* выса́живать(ся) на бе́рег; ~ation, *n,* вы́грузка; высадка на бе́рег.

disembodied, *a,* расформиро́ванный; бестеле́сный; **disembody,** *v.t,* расформиро́вывать, распуска́ть.

disembogue, *v.i,* впада́ть, влива́ться.

disembowel, *v.t,* потроши́ть.

disenchant, *v.t,* освобожда́ть от иллю́зий/ча́р.

disencumber, *v.t,* освобожда́ть от препя́тствий/бре́мени; снима́ть но́шу с.

disengage, *v.t,* освобожда́ть; отвя́зывать; разобща́ть; ~d, *a,* свобо́дный.

disentangle, *v.t,* распу́тывать, высвобожда́ть; ~ *oneself* выпу́тываться; ~ment, *n,* освобожде́ние.

disestablish, *v.t,* отделя́ть це́рковь от госуда́рства; отменя́ть; ~ment, *n,* отделе́ние це́ркви от госуда́рства.

disfavour, *n,* неми́лость; неодобре́ние; ¶ *v.t,* не одобря́ть.

disfigure, *v.t,* обезобра́живать, уро́довать, искажа́ть; ~ment, *n,* обезобра́живание, искаже́ние; уро́дство.

disfranchise, *v.t*, лиша́ть гражда́нских прав; ~ment, *n*, лише́ние гражда́нских прав.

disgorge, *v.t*, изверга́ть *(lava)*; изрыга́ть *(food)*; выбра́сывать; разгружа́ть; *(fig.)* возвраща́ть; *v.i*, впада́ть *(river)*.

disgrace, *n*, позо́р, бесче́стье; неми́лость; ¶ *v.t*, позо́рить; разжа́ловать; ~ful, *a*, позо́рный, посты́дный; бесче́стный.

disgruntled, *a*, недово́льный.

disguise, *n*, маскиро́вка; переодева́ние; *(fig.)* ма́ска; ¶ *v.t*, переодева́ть; маскирова́ть; скрыва́ть; ~d, *p.p. & a*, переоде́тый; замаскиро́ванный; скры́тый.

disgust, *n*, отвраще́ние, омерзе́ние; ¶ *v.t*, внуша́ть отвраще́ние *(dat.)*; ~ing, *a*, отврати́тельный.

dish, *n*, блю́до; таре́лка; ку́шанье; *pl*, посу́да; ~ *cloth* посу́дное полоте́нце; ~ *washer* судомо́йка; посу́дник; маши́на для мытья́ посу́ды; ~ *water* помо́и; ¶ *v.t*, класть на блю́до; подава́ть; сервирова́ть; обма́нывать.

dishearten, *v.t*, приводи́ть в уны́ние.

dishevelled, *a*, растрёпанный, взъеро́шенный, всклоко́ченный.

dishonest, *a*, нече́стный; недобросо́вестный; ~y, *n*, нече́стность; обма́н; недобросо́вестность.

dishonour, *n*, позо́р; бесче́стие; неупла́та по ве́кселю; ¶ *v.t*, позо́рить, бесче́стить, оскорбля́ть; ~ed bill ве́ксель, неупла́ченный в срок; ~able, *a*, бесче́стный, позо́рный; ни́зкий, по́длый.

disillusion, *v.t*, разочаро́вывать; разруша́ть иллю́зии *(gen.)*; ~ment, *n*, разочарова́ние.

disinclination, *n*, несклóнность; нежела́ние, неохóта; **disincline**, *v.t*, не чу́вствовать склóнности к; отбива́ть охóту/жела́ние у.

disinfect, *v.t*, дезинфици́ровать; ~ant, *a*, дезинфици́рующий; ¶ *n*, дезинфици́рующее сре́дство; ~ion, *n*, дезинфе́кция.

disingenuous, *a*, нейскренний, хи́трый; нече́стный.

disinherit, *v.t*, лиша́ть насле́дства.

disintegrate, *v.t*, разлага́ть, разделя́ть на составны́е ча́сти, раздробля́ть; *v.i*, разлага́ться; распада́ться, разруша́ться; **disinteg-**

ration, *n*, разложе́ние; распа́д, разруше́ние.

disinter, *v.t*, выка́пывать; *(fig.)* отка́пывать.

disinterested, *a*, бескоры́стный; беспристра́стный; незаинтересо́ванный; ~ness, *n*, бескоры́стие; беспристра́стие; незаинтересо́ванность.

disinterment, *n*, выка́пывание; отка́пывание.

disjoin, *v.t*, разъединя́ть; разобща́ть.

disjoint, *v.t*, расчленя́ть, разделя́ть; ~ed, *a*, несвя́зный *(speech)*; вы́вихнутый; расчленённый.

dislike, *n*, неприя́знь; отвраще́ние; ¶ *v.t*, не люби́ть; пита́ть отвраще́ние к.

dislocate, *v.t*, вы́вихнуть *(pf.)*; наруша́ть; расстра́ивать; сдвига́ть; **dislocation**, *n*, вы́вих; расстро́йство; неувя́зка; *(geol., med.)* дислока́ция, наруше́ние.

dislodge, *v.t*, смеща́ть, вытесня́ть; выгоня́ть *(animal)*; выбива́ть *(enemy)*.

disloyal, *a*, нелоя́льный; вероло́мный; преда́тельский; ~ty, *n*, нелоя́льность; вероло́мство, преда́тельство.

dismal, *a*, мра́чный, уны́лый.

dismantle, *v.t*, разбира́ть *(machine)*; демонти́ровать; разоружа́ть, расснаща́ть *(ship)*; срыва́ть *(fortress)*.

dismast, *v.t*, снима́ть/сноси́ть ма́чты.

dismay, *n*, страх, испу́г; уны́ние; ¶ *v.t*, пуга́ть; обескура́живать; беспоко́ить.

dismember, *v.t*, расчленя́ть, разделя́ть на ча́сти.

dismiss, *v.t*, отпуска́ть; увольня́ть; распуска́ть; освобожда́ть; гнать от себя́ *(thought)*; *(law)* прекраща́ть; ~al, *n*, увольне́ние; ро́спуск; освобожде́ние.

dismount, *v.t*, разбира́ть *(machine)*; вынима́ть, снима́ть; *v.i*, спе́шиваться;

disobedience, *n*, непослуша́ние, неповинове́ние; **disobedient**, *a*, непослу́шный; **disobey**, *v.t*, не слу́шаться; ослу́шаться *(pf.)* *(gen.)*.

disobliging, *a*, нелюбе́зный, неуслу́жливый.

disorder, *n*, беспоря́док; *(med.)* расстро́йство; ¶ *v.t*, приводи́ть в беспорядок; расстраивать; ~ly, a, беспорядочный; неаккуратный; распущенный.

disorganization, n, дезорганизация; расстройство; беспорядок; **disorganize**, v.t, дезorganизовывать; расстраивать.

disown, v.t, не признавать, отказываться от.

disparage, v.t, говорить пренебрежительно о; умалять; ~ment, a, пренебрежительное отношение; умаление; **disparagingly**, ad, пренебрежительно; унизительно.

disparity, n, неравенство, несоответствие, несоразмерность.

dispassionate, a, бесстрастный; беспристрастный.

dispatch see despatch.

dispel, v.t, разгонять; рассеивать.

dispensary, n, аптека; амбулатория; **dispensation**, n, раздача, распределение; освобождение (от обязательства); воля провидения; **dispense**, v.t, раздавать, распределять; приготовлять (medicine); ~ with обходиться без.

dispersal, n, рассеивание; рассыпание; распространение; **disperse**, v.t, разгонять; рассеивать; разбрасывать; рассыпать; v.i, рассеиваться; рассыпаться; расходиться.

dispirit, v.t, удручать, расстраивать.

displace, v.t, перемещать; переставлять, перекладывать; замещать, вытеснять; смещать, увольнять; ~ed person перемещённое лицо; ~ment, n, смещение; перемещение; перестановка; (mar.) водоизмещение; (chem.) замещение; (geol.) сдвиг.

display, n, показ; выставка; проявление; выставление напоказ, хвастовство; ~ type особый шрифт; ¶ v.t, выставлять, показывать; проявлять, обнаруживать; хвастаться (inst.); выделять особым шрифтом.

displease, v.t, раздражать, сердить; не нравиться (dat.); **displeasing**, a, неприятный, противный; **displeasure**, n, неудовольствие, недовольство; досада.

disport oneself развлекаться, веселиться.

disposable, a, такой, которым можно распоряжаться/который можно выбрасывать; **disposal**, n, расположение, размещение; распоряжение; передача; продажа; **dispose**, v.t, располагать, размещать, расставлять; склонять; ~ of распоряжаться (inst.); отделываться/избавляться от; ~d, p.p. & a, расположенный, склонный; **disposition**, n, расположение, размещение; распоряжение; склонность; характер, нрав; (mil.) диспозиция; pl, приготовления.

dispossess, v.t, лишать собственности/права владения; выселять.

disproportion, n, непропорциональность, несоразмерность; ~ate, a, непропорциональный, несоразмерный.

disprove, v.t, опровергать.

dispute, n, диспут, обсуждение; полемика, спор; пререкания (pl.); ¶ v.t, обсуждать; оспаривать.

disqualification, n, дисквалификация, лишение права; **disqualified**, p.p. & a, дисквалифицированный; негодный; **disqualify**, v.t, дисквалифицировать, лишать права; делать/признавать негодным.

disquiet, n, беспокойство, волнение, тревога; ¶ v.t, беспокоить, тревожить; ~ing, a, беспокойный, тревожный.

disquisition, n, исследование, изыскание; следствие, дознание.

disregard, n, невнимание; пренебрежение; игнорирование; ¶ v.t, не обращать внимания на, игнорировать; пренебрегать (inst.); ~ful, a, равнодушный; игнорирующий.

disrepair, n, плохое состояние, ветхость.

disreputable, a, имеющий плохую репутацию, позорный; **disrepute**, n, дурная слава, плохая репутация; позор.

disrespect, n, неуважение; непочтительность; ~ful, a, непочтительный.

disrobe, v.t, (& i.), раздевать(ся); разоблачать(ся).

disrupt, v.t, разрывать, разрушать; подрывать; ~ion, n, разрыв, разрушение; подрыв; ~ive, a, разрушительный; подрывной.

dissatisfaction, *n,* неудовлетворён-ность, недовольство; **dissatisfy,** *v.t,* не удовлетворять.

dissect, *v.t,* вскрывать, анатомиро-вать; рассекать; *(fig.)* анализиро-вать, разбирать; **~ion,** *n,* вскры-тие; рассечение; *(fig.)* анализ, разбор.

dissemble, *v.t,* скрывать; не замечать; умалчивать; *v.i,* притворяться, лицемерить.

disseminate, *v.t,* рассеивать; раз-брасывать *(seeds);* распростра-нять *(learning);* сеять *(discon-tent);* **dissemination,** *n,* рассеи-вание; разбрасывание.

dissension, *n,* разногласие; разлад; раздор; **dissent,** *n,* разногласие; *(eccl.)* сектантство, раскол; ¶ *v.i,* расходиться во взглядах/мне-ниях; *(eccl.)* отступать от взгля-дов церкви; **~er,** *n,* раскольник, сектант; **~ient,** *a,* раскольничес-кий; инакомыслящий; несог-ласный; ¶ *n,* инакомыслящий; голос против.

dissertation, *n,* диссертация.

disservice, *n,* плохая услуга; ущерб, вред.

dissever, *v.t,* разъединять, отделять.

dissimilar, *a,* непохожий, несход-ный; **~ity,** *n,* несходство.

dissimulate, *v.t,* диссимилировать; **dissimulation,** *n,* диссимиляция.

dissipate, *v.t,* рассеивать, разгонять *(fog, cloud);* расточать; прома́ты-вать *(money);* **dissipation,** *n,* рассеивание; расточение; бес-путный образ жизни.

dissociate, *v.t,* разъединять, отделять; разобщать; **~** *oneself* отмежёвы-ваться; **dissociation,** *n,* разъеди-нение; разобщение; отмежевание.

dissoluble, *a,* растворимый; растор-жимый.

dissolute, *a,* распущенный, беспут-ный; **dissolution,** *n,* растворение; разложение (на части) расторже-ние *(of treaty, etc.);* роспуск *(of parliament);* **dissolve,** *v.t,* раство-рять; разлагать; расторгать; рас-пускать; *v.i,* растворяться; таять; разлагаться (на части) **dissolvent,** *a,* растворяющий; ¶ *n,* раство-ритель.

dissonance, *n,* неблагозвучие, дис-сонанс; **dissonant,** *a,* нестройный *(sound);* противоречивый.

dissuade, *v.t,* отговаривать, отсове-товать, разубеждать; **dissuasion,** *n,* отговаривание, разубеждение; **dissuasive,** *a,* разубеждающий.

distaff, *n,* прялка.

distance, *n,* расстояние; дистанция; даль; промежуток *(of time);* **at a ~** вдали; **keep one's ~** из-бегать; **distant,** *a,* дальний, далё-кий, отдалённый; холодный, сдер-жанный; **~** *relative* дальний род-ственник.

distaste, *n,* отвращение; **~ful,** *a,* противный, неприятный.

distemper, *n,* темпера; живопись темперой; клеевая краска; не-здоровье; душевное расстройство; собачья чума; ¶ *v.i,* писать тем-перой; красить клеевой крас-кой.

distend, *v.t. (& i.),* надувать(ся); раздувать(ся); растягивать(ся); **distension,** *n,* растяжение; рас-ширение.

distil, *v.t,* дистиллировать; очищать; опреснять *(water);* перегонять *(spirit);* *v.i,* сочиться, капать; **~lation,** *n,* дистилляция; пере-гонка; **~lery,** *n,* винокурен-ный завод; перегонный завод.

distinct, *a,* отчётливый; ясный; от-дельный; особый; отличный (от других); определённый; **~ion,** *n,* различие; отличие; знак от-личия; известность; **~ive,** *a,* отличительный; **~ly,** *ad,* ясно, отчётливо; определённо; **~ness,** *n,* ясность, отчётливость; опреде-лённость.

distinguish, *v.t,* различать, отличать; **~** *oneself* отличиться *(pf.);* **~able,** *a,* различимый, отличимый; **~ed,** *a,* выдающийся, изве-стный.

distort, *v.t,* искривлять; искажать; извращать *(facts);* **~ion,** *n,* ис-кривление; искажение; извра-щение.

distract, *v.t,* отвлекать; рассеивать; смущать; расстраивать; **~ed,** *p.p. & a,* обезумевший; отчаявшийся; рассеянный; **~ion,** *n,* развлече-ние; отвлечение внимания; от-чаяние; безумие; раздражение; рассеянность.

distrain, *v.t,* описывать (имущест-во); **~t,** *n,* опись имущества.

distraught, *a,* обезумевший.

distress, n, го́ре; беда́; бе́дствие; недомога́ние; истоще́ние; *(law)* о́пись иму́щества; ¶ *v.t*, огорча́ть; му́чить; истоща́ть; ~ed, *p.p. & a*, огорчённый, расстро́енный; ~ing, *a*, огорчи́тельный, печа́льный.

distribute, *v.t*, распределя́ть, раздава́ть; распространя́ть; **distribution**, n, распределе́ние, разда́ча; распростране́ние; **distributive**, *a*, распредели́тельный; *(gram.)* раздели́тельный; **distributor**, n, распредели́тель.

district, n, райо́н, о́круг.

distrust, n, недове́рие, сомне́ние, подозре́ние; ¶ *v.t*, не доверя́ть *(dat.)*, сомнева́ться в; ~ful, *a*, недове́рчивый, подозри́тельный.

disturb, *v.t*, беспоко́ить; наруша́ть *(order, peace)*; расстра́ивать *(plans)*; волнова́ть, трево́жить; ~ance, n, беспоко́йство; волне́ние; трево́га; наруше́ние *(of order, peace)*; *(riot)* волне́ния, беспоря́дки; ~ing, *a*, трево́жный, беспоко́йный.

disunion, n, разделе́ние; разобще́ние; **disunite**, *v.t*, раздсля́ть; разобща́ть; разъединя́ть.

disuse, n, неупотребле́ние.

disyllabic, *a*, двусло́жный.

ditch, n, кана́ва; ров; транше́я; ¶ *v.t*, ока́пывать (рвом); чи́стить кана́ву; *(coll.)* броса́ть.

ditto, n, то же; тако́й же.

ditty, n, пе́сенка.

diuretic, *a*, мочего́нный.

diurnal, *a*, дневно́й; ежедне́вный.

divan, n, дива́н.

dive, n, прыжо́к (в во́ду); *(avia.)* пики́рование; прито́н; ¶ *v.i*, ныря́ть; броса́ться в во́ду; ныма́ть; *(avia.)* пики́ровать; ~bomber пики́рующий бомбардиро́вщик; ~r, n, водола́з; *(bird)* гага́ра.

diverge, *v.i*, расходи́ться; отклоня́ться; ~nce, n, расхожде́ние; отклоне́ние; ~ nt, *a*, расходя́щийся.

diverse, *a*, разли́чный; ино́й; разнообра́зный; **diversify**, *v.t*, разнообра́зить; **diversion**, n, отклоне́ние; отвлече́ние; развлече́ние; *(mil.)* диве́рсия; объе́зд; **diversity**, n, разнообра́зие; разли́чие.

divert, *v.t*, отводи́ть; отвлека́ть;

развлека́ть; ~ing, *a*, развлека́ющий; занима́тельный.

divest, *v.t*, раздева́ть; снима́ть; лиша́ть.

divide, *v.t*, дели́ть; разделя́ть; отделя́ть; градуи́ровать; *v.i*, дели́ться, *etc.*; расходи́ться.

dividend, n, *(maths)* дели́мое; *(fin.)* дивиде́нд.

divider, n, тот, кто де́лит; *pl*, ци́ркуль; **dividing**, *a*, разделя́ющий.

divination, n, гада́ние; предсказа́ние.

divine, *a*, боже́ственный; превосхо́дный; ¶ n, богосло́в; ¶ *v.t*, проро́чествовать; предска́зывать; ~r, n, проро́к; предсказа́тель.

diving, n, ныря́ние; прыжки́ (в во́ду); ~ *bell* водола́зный ко́локол; ~ *suit* скафа́ндр.

divinity, n, боже́ственность; божество́; богосло́вие.

divisibility, n, дели́мость; **divisible**, *a*, дели́мый; **division**, n, деле́ние; перегоро́дка; часть; отде́л; *(mil.)* диви́зия; **divisor**, n, *(maths)* дели́тель.

divorce, n, разво́д; разъедине́ние; разры́в; ¶ *v.t*, разводи́ть; отделя́ть; разъединя́ть; разводи́ться с.

divulge, *v.t*, разглаша́ть.

dizziness, n, головокруже́ние; **dizzy**, *a*, чу́вствующий головокруже́ние; головокружи́тельный.

do, *v.t*, де́лать; выполня́ть; гото́вить *(food)*; *(cheat)* обма́нывать; ~ *a room* убира́ть ко́мнату; ~ *one's hair* причёсываться; де́лать причёску; ~ *harm* причиня́ть вред; *he will ~ for us* он нам подойдёт; *that will ~!* хва́тит!; дово́льно!; ~ *away with* уничтожа́ть; поко́нчить *(pf.)* с; ~ *up* прибира́ть; приводи́ть в поря́док; застёгивать; завя́зывать; ~ *without* обходи́ться без; *how do you ~?* здра́вствуйте!; ~ *well* поправля́ться; процвета́ть; де́лать успе́хи; *well-to-*~ зажи́точный; *make ~ (with)* удовлетворя́ться *(inst.)*; обходи́ться *(inst.)*.

docile, *a*, послу́шный; **docility**, n, послуша́ние.

dock, n, док; при́стань; скамья́ подсуди́мых; щаве́ль *(bot.)*; *dry~* сухо́й док; ¶ *v.t*, ста́вить (су́дно) в док; *v.i*, входи́ть в док; стыкова́ться; ~ er, n, до́кер.

docket, *n*, ярлы́к; этике́тка; квита́н-
ция; на́дпись; ¶ *v.t*, накле́ивать
этике́тку на; де́лать на́дпись на.
docking, *n*, стыко́вка *(in space).*
dockyard, *n*, верфь.
doctor, *n*, врач, до́ктор; ¶ *v.t*, ле-
чи́ть; подде́лывать; фальсифи-
ци́ровать *(food);* ремонти́ро-
вать, чини́ть; ~ate, *v.t*, до́ктор-
ская сте́пень.
doctrinaire, *a*, доктринёрский; ¶ *n*,
доктринёр; **doctrinal,** *a*, относя́-
щийся к доктри́не; **doctrine,** *n*,
уче́ние; доктри́на.
document, *n*, докуме́нт; свиде́тель-
ство; ¶ *v.t*, подтвержда́ть доку-
ме́нтами; ~ary, *a*, документа́ль-
ный; ¶ *n*, документа́льный фильм.
dodge, *n*, уло́вка; уве́ртка; хи́т-
рость; ¶ *v.t*, избега́ть *(gen.);*
увёртываться от; *v.i*, пря́таться;
увиливать; ~r, *n*, хитре́ц.
doe, *n*, са́мка *(deer, etc.).*
doer, *n*, исполни́тель.
doff, *v.t*, снима́ть.
dog, *n*, соба́ка; пёс; кобе́ль; ~ *fox*
саме́ц лиси́цы; ~-*collar* оше́йник;
~ *ear* за́гнутый уголо́к (страни́-
цы); ~ *in the manger* соба́ка на
се́не; ~ *Latin* испо́рченная/ло́-
маная латы́нь; ~*rose* шипо́вник;
~*star* Си́риус; *under*~ неуда́ч-
ник; сла́бый; ¶ *v.t*, ходи́ть по
пята́м за; высле́живать; пресле́-
довать; ~ged, *a*, упря́мый; на-
сто́йчивый; ~ness, *n*, упря́м-
ство; упо́рство.
doggerel, *n*, плохи́е стихи́; ви́рши.
dogma, *n*, до́гма; до́гмат; ~tic, *a*,
догмати́ческий.
doings, *n.pl*, де́йствия; де́ятель-
ность. посту́пки.
do-it-yourself shop, "сде́лай сам".
doldrums, *n.pl*, полоса́ штиле́й;
плохо́е настрое́ние; депре́ссия;
be in the ~ хандри́ть.
dole, *n*, пода́чка; посо́бие по без-
рабо́тице; ¶ *v.t:* ~*out* выдава́ть;
раздава́ть.
doleful, *a*, ско́рбный, печа́льный.
doll, *n*, ку́кла.
dollar, *n*, до́ллар.
dolly, *n*, ку́колка.
dolphin, *n*, дельфи́н.
dolt, *n*, болва́н; ~ish, *a*, тупо́й; при-
дуркова́тый.
domain, *n*, владе́ние; террито́рия;
(fig.) о́бласть.

dome, *n*, ку́пол; свод.
domestic, *a*, дома́шний; семе́йный;
вну́тренний *(trade);* ручно́й; ¶ *n*,
прислу́га; ~ate, *v.t*, прируча́ть
(animals); привя́зывать к до́му;
~ity, *n*, семе́йная/дома́шняя
жизнь; любо́вь к семе́йной
жи́зни.
domicile, *n*, постоя́нное местожи́-
тельство; **domiciliary,** *a*, дома́ш-
ний; по ме́сту жи́тельства.
dominant, *a*, госпо́дствующий; пре-
облада́ющий; **dominate,** *v.t*, гос-
по́дствовать над; име́ть влия́ние
на; подавля́ть; *v.i*, домини́ровать;
преоблада́ть; **domination,** *n*, гос-
по́дство; преоблада́ние; **domineer,**
v.i, вла́ствовать; держа́ть себя́
высокоме́рно; ~ing, *a*, вла́стный;
высокоме́рный; возвыша́ющийся
(над ме́стом).
dominion, *n*, влады́чество; домини́-
о́н.
domino(es), *n*, домино́.
don, *n*, дон; преподава́тель; член
колле́джа; ¶ *v.t*, надева́ть.
donate, *v.t*, дари́ть; дарова́ть; **donation,** *n*, дар; де́нежное поже́рт-
вование.
done, *p.p. & a*, сде́ланный; хорошо́
пригото́вленный; прожа́ренный;
~ *for* ко́нченый; разорённый;
~ *up* измучённый; уста́лый; за-
стёгнутый.
donkey, *n*, осёл; ~ *engine* неболь-
шо́й дви́гатель.
donor, *n*, же́ртвователь; *(med.)*
до́нор.
doom, *n*, рок; судьба́; ги́бель; *crack
of* ~ тру́бный глас; ¶ *v.t*, обре-
ка́ть; ~sday, *n*, день стра́шного
суда́.
door, *n*, дверь; две́рца; ~ *bell* двер-
но́й звоно́к; ~*man* швейца́р;
привра́тник; ~*mat* полови́к (для
вытира́ния ног); ~ *plate* доще́чка
на дверя́х; ~-*post* дверно́й коса́к;
~*step* поро́г; ~*way* дверно́й проём; проле́т две́ри.
dope, *n*, нарко́тик; дурма́н; ¶ *v.t*,
дава́ть нарко́тики *(dat.); (fig.)*
одурма́нивать.
Doric, *a*, дори́ческий.
dormant, *a*, дре́млющий; спя́щий;
безде́йствующий; потенциа́ль-
ный; мёртвый *(capital).*
dormer window, *n*, мансáрдное
окно́.

dormitory, *n*, óбщая спáльня.

dormouse, *n*, сóня.

dorsal, *a*, дорсáльный; спиннóй.

dose, *n*, дóза; приём; *(fig.)* пóрция; дóля; ¶ *v.t*, давáть лекáрство *(dat.)*.

dot, *n*, тóчка; крóшка *(small child)*; ¶ *v.t*, стáвить тóчки; отмечáть пунктúром; усéивать; *dotted line* пунктúрная лúния.

dotage, *n*, стáрческое слабоýмие; **dote**, *v.i*, впадáть в дéтство; ~ *on* любúть до безýмия.

double, *a*, двойнóй; двоякий; двóйственный; ~-*barrelled* двуствóльный; ~ *bass* контрабáс; ~ *bed* двуспáльная кровáть; ~-*bedded room* кóмната на двоúх; ~-*breasted* двубóртный; ~ *chin* двойнóй подбородок; ~-*dealing* *(n)* двурýшничество; *(a)* двурýшнический; ~-*decker*, двухэтáжный автóбус; ~-*edged* обоюдоóстрый; ~-*faced* двулúчный; двустороний; ~-*tracked* двухколéйный; ¶ *ad*, вдвойнé; вдвóе; ¶ *n*, двойнóе колúчество; двойнúк; дубликáт; *at the* ~ бéглым шáгом; *doubles (game)* пáрные úгры; *(mixed)* úгра смéшанных пар; ¶ *v.t*, удвáивать; склáдывать вдвóе; исполнять две рóли; *v.i*, удвáиваться; двигáться бéглым шáгом; ~ *back* идтú обрáтно по сóбственным следáм; ~ *up* скрючивать(ся); сгибáть(ся); разделять (кóмнату).

doublet, *n*, дубликáт; корóткий камзóл.

doubloon, *n*, дублóн.

doubly, *ad*, вдвойнé; вдвóе.

doubt, *n*, сомнéние; *without* ~ несомнéнно; ¶ *v.t*, сомневáться в; не доверять *(dat.)*; ~*ful*, *a*, сомнúтельный; пóлный сомнéний; ~*less*, *ad*, несомнéнно.

douche, *n*, душ; промывáние; ¶ *v.t*, поливáть (из дýша); обливáть водóй.

dough, *n*, тéсто; ~*nut*, *n*, пóнчик, **doughty**, *a*, смéлый, хрáбрый.

dour, *a*, сурóвый.

douse, *v.t*, окунáть; погружáть в вóду.

dove, *n*, гóлубь; ~-*cote* голубятня; ~-*tail*, *n*, *(tech.)* лáсточкин хвост, лáпа; ¶ *v.t*, вязáть в лáпу; подгонять; согласóвывать; *v.i*, совпадáть.

dowager, *n*, вдовá; велúчественная дáма; ¶ *a*, вдóвствующая.

dowdy, *a*, неэлегáнтный, безвкýсный.

dower, *n*, вдóвья часть; придáное; *(fig.)* прирóдный дар.

down, *pr*, вниз; вниз по; вдоль по; ¶ *ad*, вниз; внизý; *cash* ~ дéньги на бóчку; ~ *stream* вниз по течéнию; ~ *with* долóй!; ¶ *a*, напрáвленный кнúзу; ~ *grade* уклóн (железнодорóжного путú); *(fig.)* упáдок; ~ *train* пóезд, идýщий из большóго гóрода; ¶ *v.t*, опускáть; сбивáть *(person, aircraft)* ~ *tools* прекращáть рабóту.

down, *n*, пух; пушóк; холм; возвышенность.

down, *comps*, ~*cast* потýпленный *(gaze)*; подáвленный *(pers.)*; ~*fall* падéние; гúбель; разорéние; лúвень; снегопáд; ~*hearted* упáвший дýхом; ~*hill* *(a)* наклóнный; покáтый; *(ad)* вниз, под гóру; ~*pour* лúвень; потóк; ~*right*, *(a)* прямóй; откровéнный; совершéнный; *(ad)* совершéнно; ~*stairs (ad)* вниз; внизý; *go* ~*stairs* спускáться вниз; ~*stairs (floor)* нúжний этáж; низ; ~*trodden* угнетённый; ~*ward* спускáющийся; ~*wards* вниз; кнúзу.

dowry, *n*, придáное.

doze, *n*, дремóта; ¶ *v.i*, дремáть.

dozen, *n*, дюжина; *baker's* ~ чёртова дюжина.

drab, *a*, тýскло-корúчневый; *(fig.)* скýчный; бесцвéтный; ¶ *n*, тýскло-корúчневый цвет.

draft, *n*, чертёж; план; черновúк; проéкт, набрóсок; сквозняк; чек; *(tech.)* тяга, дутьё; *(mil.)* набóр; ~ *animals* рабóчий скот; ¶ *v.t*, дéлать чертёж *(gen.)*; составлять проéкт *(gen.)*; набрáсывать черновúк *(gen.)*; *(mil.)* отбирáть; ~*sman*, *n*, чертёжник, рисовáльщик.

drag, *n*, дрáга; землечерпáлка; тормóжение; *(fig.)* обýза; ~*net* брéдень; ¶ *v.t*. *(&i.)*, тащúть(ся), волочúть(ся), тянýть(ся); чúстить дно дрáгой; буксúровать.

dragon, *n*, дракóн; ~*fly* стрекóза.

dragoon, *n*, драгýн; ¶ *v.t*, принуждáть.

drain, *n*, дренажная канава; водоотвод, водосток; *pl*, канализация; *(fig.)* утечка, расход, истощение; ~*-pipe* водосточная труба; ¶ *v.t*, дренировать; осушать *(ground)*; сушить; фильтровать; истощать *(strength)*; *v.i*, стекать; сочиться; ~**age**, *n*, дренаж; осушение; сток; канализация; ~*ing board* сушильная доска.

drake, *n*, селезень.

dram, *n*, драхма; глоток спиртного.

drama, *n*, драма; ~**tic**, *a*, драматический; драматичный; ~**tist**, *n*, драматург; ~**tize**, *v.t*, драматизировать; инсценировать.

drape, *v.t*, драпировать; ~**r**, *n*, торговец мануфактурными товарами; ~**y**, *n*, драпировка; магазин тканей.

drastic, *a*, сильно действующий; решительный.

draught, *n*, тяга; сквозняк; глоток; нацеживание; набросок, черновик; водоизмещение *(mar.)*; *(pl.)* шашки; *drink at a* ~ пить залпом; ~ *board* шашечная доска; ~**sman**, *n*, чертёжник; рисовальщик; ~**y**, *a*, на сквозняке.

draw, *n*, вытягивание; жеребьёвка, лотерея; приманка; ничья (в игре); *in a* ~ вничью; ¶ *v.t*, тащить, тянуть; писать, рисовать; выписывать *(cheque)*; брать *(money)*; выводить *(conclusions)*; вызывать *(tears)*; задёргивать *(curtain)*; кончать (игру) вничью; обнажать *(sword)*; привлекать *(attention)*; потрошить *(fowl)*; пускать *(blood)*; тянуть *(lots)*; черпать *(water)*; *v.i*, иметь тягу; настаиваться *(tea)*; ~ *aside* отводить в сторону; ~ *away (v.t.)* уводить; *(v.i.)* удаляться; ~ *back (v.t.)* тянуть назад; *(v.i.)* отступать; выходить из дела; ~ *near* приближаться; ~ *on (v.t.)* натягивать; *(v.i.)* наступать; ~ *out (v.t.)* вытягивать, вытаскивать; *(v.i.)* удлиняться; ~ *up v.t. (& i.)* составлять; останавливать(ся); *(mil.)* выстраивать(ся).

drawback, *n*, препятствие, помеха; недостаток.

drawbridge, *n*, подъёмный/разводной мост.

drawee, *n*, трассат.

drawer, *n*, чертёжник; рисовальщик; (выдвижной) ящик; *pl*, кальсоны.

drawing, *n*, рисование; рисунок; *(wire)* волочение; *(tech.)* вытягивание -~ *board* чертёжная доска; ~ *paper* рисовальная/чертёжная бумага; ~ *pen* рейсфедер; ~ *pin* чертёжная кнопка; ~*-room* гостиная.

drawl, *n*, протяжное произношение; медлительность речи; ¶ *v.i*, растягивать слова.

drawn, *(p.p. of draw)* ~ *face* бледное, усталое лицо; ~ *game* игра, кончившаяся вничью; ~ *sword* обнажённый меч.

dray, *n*, подвода, ломовая телега; ~*man* ломовой извозчик.

dread, *n*, страх, боязнь, опасение; ¶ *a*, страшный, грозный; ¶ *v.t*, страшиться/бояться/опасаться *(gen.)*; ~**ful**, *a*, страшный, ужасный; ~**nought**, *n*, дредноут.

dream, *n*, сон, сновидение; мечта; видение; ¶ *v.t*, видеть во сне: мечтать о; воображать; *v.i*, мечтать; видеть сон; ~ *up* выдумывать; ~**er**, *n*, мечтатель; фантазёр; ~**ily**, *ad*, мечтательно; ~**y**, *a*, мечтательный; непрактичный.

dreariness, *n*, мрачность; тоскливость; **dreary**, *a*, мрачный; скучный.

dredge, *n*, драга; землечерпалка; ¶ *v.t*, драгировать; углублять; ~**r**, *n*, землечерпалка; экскаватор; сосуд для посыпания (сахаром *etc.*).

dregs, *n.pl*, осадок; отбросы; ~ *o society* подонки общества.

drench, *v.t*, промачивать; орошать; ~*ed to the skin* насквозь промокший; ~*ing rain* проливной дождь.

dress, *n*, платье; одежда; *(fig.)* одеяние; ~ *circle* бельэтаж; ~ *coat* фрак; ~*maker* портниха; ~*making* шитьё дамского платья; ~*-protector* подмышник; ~ *rehearsal* генеральная репетиция; ¶ *v.t*, одевать; наряжать; украшать; выравнивать *(mil.)*; выделывать *(skins)*; обтёсывать *(wood)*; перевязывать *(wound)*; приготовлять *(food)*; приправлять *(salad)*; причёсывать *(hair)*; разделывать *(carcass)*; убирать *(windows)*;

шлифовать *(stone)*; *v.i,* одеваться; *(mil.)* выравниваться; ~ *up* изысканно одевать(ся); надевать маскарадный костюм.

dresser, *n,* костюмер, -ша *(theat.);* хирургическая сестра *(med.);* кухонный шкаф;

dressing, *n,* одевание; отделка; *(med.)* перевязочный материал; *(cook.)* приправа, соус; *(mil.)* равнение; шлифовка; ~ *case* несессер; санитарная сумка; ~ *gown* халат; ~ *room* туалетная комната; ~ *table* туалетный столик.

dribble, *v.i,* капать; пускать слюни; вести мяч; **driblet,** *n,* капелька; небольшая сумма, небольшое количество.

dried, *a,* сушёный.

drift, *n,* течение; направление; тенденция; стремление; сугроб *(snow)*; наносы; *(mar.)* дрейф; *(fig.)* бездействие; ~-*net* плавная сеть; ~*wood* сплавной лес; лес, прибитый к берегу моря; ¶ *v.t,* относить/наносить (ветром/течением); *v.i,* плыть по течению; дрейфовать; скопляться *(snow, sand).*

drill, *n,* тренировка; упражнение; *(mil.)* муштра; сверло, бур; борозда; сеялка; ¶ *v.t,* сверлить, бурить; обучать; тренировать; муштровать; сеять, сажать рядами; *v.i,* проходить строевое обучение, тренироваться; ~*ing,* *n,* обучение; высверливание, бурение; ~ *machine* сверлильная машина.

drink, *n,* питьё; напиток; *hard* ~*s* спиртные напитки; *soft* ~*s* безалкогольные напитки; *have a* ~ выпить, попить *(pf.)*; ¶ *v.t,* пить; *v.i,* пьянствовать; ~ *off* выпивать залпом; ~ *his health* пить за его здоровье; ~*able,* *a,* годный для питья; питьевой; ~*er,* *n,* пьющий; пьяница; ~*ing,* *n,* питьё; пьянство; ~ *bout* запой; ~ *song* застольная песня; ~ *water* питьевая вода.

drip, *n,* капанье; капля; ¶ *v.i,* капать; ~*ping,* *n,* капанье; жир; ~ *pan* сковорода, противень.

drive, *n,* поездка, прогулка; подъездная дорога; преследование *(hunt);*

сила, энергия; спешка *(work);* гонка *(armaments);* передача, привод *(tech.);* плоский удар *(tennis, etc.);* ¶ *v.t,* гнать; преследовать; вбивать *(nail);* везти *(pers.);* водить *(car);* править *(inst.) (car, horse);* прокладывать *(road);* ударять *(ball);* *v.i,* ехать, кататься; нестись; ~ *at* клонить к; ~ *away (v.t.)* прогонять, рассеивать; *(v.i.)* уезжать; ~ *in (v.t.)* загонять; *(v.i.)* въезжать; ~ *into a corner* загонять в угол; ~ *out (v.t.)* выбивать, выгонять; *(v.i.)* выезжать; ~ *mad* сводить с ума; ~ *a bargain* заключать сделку.

drivel, *n,* слюни; *(fig.)* бессмыслица, чушь; ¶ *v.i,* распускать слюни/ сопли; пороть чушь.

driver, *n,* водитель, шофёр; кучер; машинист *(engine)*; погонщик скота; **driving,** *n,* катание; езда; вождение (автомобиля); ¶ *a,* энергичный; *(tech.)* движущий.

drizzle, *n,* мелкий дождь; ¶ *v.i,* моросить.

droll, *a,* забавный, смешной; ~*ery,* *n,* юмор; шутки.

dromedary, *n,* одногорбый верблюд.

drone, *n,* трутень *(also fig.)*; жужжание, гудение; ¶ *v.i,* жужжать, гудеть; *(fig.)* бубнить; петь монотонно.

droop, *v.i,* свисать, поникать; изнемогать; опускаться; унывать; *v.t,* понурить *(pf.) (head);* потупить *(pf.) (eyes);* ~*ing,* *a,* поникший; понурый.

drop, *n,* капля; глоток *(drink):* леденец *(sweet);* серьга *(earring);* падение, понижение; *pl, (med.)* капли; ~ *curtain* падающий занавес; ~ *kick* удар с полулёта; ~ *scene* заключительная сцена; ¶ *v.t,* ронять; проливать *(tears);* бросать *(habit);* покидать *(friends);* понижать *(voice);* прекращать *(work);* пропускать *(letters);* проронить *(pf.) (words);* подвозить (до дома); сбрасывать (с самолёта); *v.i,* падать; снижаться; капать; ~ *a line* черкнуть *(pf.)* несколько слов; ~ *in* заходить, забегать; ~ *off (v.i.)* уменьшаться; засыпать; умирать; *(v.t.)* высаживать; сбрасывать;

~ *out (v.i.)* исчезáть; выпадáть; *(v.t.)* выбрáсывать.

droppings, *n.pl,* кáпли (дождя́, жи́ра, *etc.)*; помёт живóтных.

dropsy, *n,* водя́нка.

dross, *n,* отбрóсы; *(fig.)* подóнки;

drought, *n,* зáсуха.

drove, *n,* стáдо, гурт; толпá; ~r, *n,* гуртовщи́к; скотопромы́шленник.

drown, *v.t,* топи́ть; затопля́ть; залива́ть; заглушáть *(sound/sorrow)*; *v.i,* тонýть; топи́ться.

drowse, *v.i,* дремáть; **drowsiness,** *n,* дремóта; сонли́вость; **drowsy,** *a,* сóнный, дремóтный; снотвóрный.

drub, *v.t,* бить, колоти́ть; ~bing, *n,* битьё, побóи.

drudge, *n,* раб, рабы́ня; ~ry, *n,* тяжёлая рабóта.

drug, *n,* медикамéнт; лекáрство; наркóтик, дурмáн; ~ *store* аптéка; ~ *addict* наркомáн; ¶ *v.t,* подмéшивать наркóтики/яд (в пи́щу); давáть наркóтики *(dat.)*; ~gist, *n,* аптéкарь.

druid, *n,* друи́д.

drum, *n,* барабáн; ~ *beat* барабáнный бой; ~*head* барабáнная перепóнка; кóжа на барабáне; ~*head court martial* воéнно-полевóй суд; ~ *major* стáрший барабáнщик; ~*stick* барабáнная пáлочка; ¶ *v.i,* бить в барабáн; барабáнить (пáльцами); ~mer, *n,* барабáнщик.

drunk, *a,* пья́ный; вы́питый; *(fig.)* опьянённый; *get~* напи́ться *(pf.)*; ~ard, *n,* пья́ница; ~en, *a,* пья́ный; ~enness, *n,* пья́нство.

dry, *a,* сухóй *(also fig.)*; вы́сохший, засóхший; неинтерéсный; иронúческий; ~ *cleaning* химчи́стка; ~ *dock* сухóй док; ~ *goods* мануфактýра; ~ *land* сýша; ~ *rot* сухáя гниль; ¶ *v.t,* сушúть; вытирáть; *v.i,* сушúться; сóхнуть; ~ *up (v.t.)* высýшивать; осушáть; *(v.i.)* высыхáть; ~ing, *n,* сýшка; сушéние; ¶ *a,* сушúльный; сушúтельный; ~ *room* сушúльня; ~ness, *n,* сýхость, сушь; засýшливость.

dual, *a,* двóйственный; двойнóй.

dub, *v.t,* посвящáть в ры́цари; давáть прóзвище *(dat.)*; дубли́ровать *(film)*.

dubious, *a,* сомни́тельный; подозри́тельный; сомневáющийся; ~-

ness, *n,* сомни́тельность; подозри́тельность.

ducal, *a,* герцогский.

ducat, *n,* дукáт.

duchess, *n,* герцоги́ня; **duchy,** *n,* гéрцогство.

duck, *n,* ýтка; *(cloth)* парусúна; ¶ *v.t,* наклоня́ть; окунáть; увéртываться от; *v.i,* ныря́ть; окунáться; нагибáться; ~ling, *n,* утёнок.

duct, *n,* протóк, канáл; трубá.

ductile, *a,* эласти́чный; кóвкий, тягýчий *(metal)*; подáтливый *(person)*; **ductility,** *n,* эласти́чность; кóвкость, тягýчесть.

dud, *a,* поддéльный; негóдный.

dudgeon, *n,* оби́да; возмущéние; рукоя́тка кинжáла; *in high* ~ в глубóком возмущéнии.

duds, *n.pl,* лохмóтья.

due, *a,* дóлжный; причитáющийся; обуслóвленный/вы́званный *(to-inst.)*; ~ *to (pr.)* благодаря́; вслéдствие; *in* ~ *course* дóлжным поря́дком; *in* ~ *time* в своё врéмя; *the train is* ~ *west* пóезд дóлжен прибы́ть; ~ *west* пря́мо на зáпад; ¶ *n,* дóлжное; то, что причитáется; *pl,* сбóры, налóги, пóшлины; члéнские взнóсы; *give smb. his~* отдавáть дóлжное.

duel, *n,* дуэ́ль, поеди́нок; борьбá, состязáние; ¶ *v.i,* дрáться на дуэ́ли; ~list, *n,* дуэля́нт.

duet, *n,* дуэ́т.

duffer, *n,* тупи́ца.

dug, *n,* сосóк, вы́мя.

dug-out, *n,* челнóк *(canoe)*; земля́нка; *(mil.)* убéжище, блиндáж.

duke, *n,* гéрцог; ~dom, *n,* гéрцогство; ти́тул гéрцога.

dulcet, *a,* слáдкий, нéжный.

dulcimer, *n,* цимбáлы.

dull, *a,* тупóй, глýпый; скýчный; тýсклый *(light)*; нея́сный; пáсмурный *(weather)*; уны́лый; ¶ *v.t,* притупля́ть; дéлать тупы́м/тýсклым, *etc.;* ~ard, *n,* тупи́ца; ~ness, *n,* тýпость, глýпость.

duly, *ad,* дóлжным óбразом; в дóлжное врéмя.

dumb, *a,* немóй; молчали́вый; *deaf and* ~ глухонемóй; ~ *show* пантоми́ма; ~ *waiter* вращáющийся стóлик; откры́тая этажéрка для закýсок; я́щик с пóлками для блюд; лифт на кýхне; ~found, *v.t,* ошеломля́ть; ~ness, *n,* немотá.

dummy, *a*, поддéльный; фиктúвный; подставнóй; учéбный *(cartridge)*; ¶ *n*, манекéн; макéт; марионéтка; *baby's* ~ сóска, пустýшка; *tailor's* ~ манекéн; *(fig.)* франт.

dump, *n*, свáлка; кýча хлáма/мýсора; нáсыпь; *be in the* ~*s* быть в унынии; ¶ *v.t*, сбрáсывать, свáливать; разгружáть; *(econ.)* устрáивать дéмпинг *(gen.)*; ~ing, *n*, дéмпинг; разгрýзка.

dumpling, *n*, клёцка.

dumpy, *a*, тóлстенький.

dun, *a*, серовáто-корúчневый; булáный; ¶ *n*, серовáто-корúчневый цвет; назóйливый кредитóр; ¶ *v.t*, трéбовать (уплáты дóлга); надоедáть *(dat.)*.

dunce, *n*, тупúца.

dunderhead, *n*, болвáн.

dune, *n*, дюнa.

dung, *n*, помёт; навóз; удобрéние.

dungarees, *n.pl*, рабóчие брюки.

dungeon, *n*, темнúца, подзéмная тюрьмá.

dupe, *n*, простофúля; ¶ *v.t*, обмáнывать.

duplicate, *n*, дубликáт; кóпия; *in* ~ в двух экземплярáх; ¶ *a*, двойнóй; удвóенный; запаснóй *(part)*; ¶ *v.t*, снимáть кóпию с; удвáивать; дублúровать.

durability, *n*, прóчность; длúтельность; **durable**, *a*, прóчный; длúтельный; долговрéменный.

durance, *n*, заточéние.

duration, *n*, продолжúтельность.

duress, *n*, лишéние свобóды; *(law)* принуждéние.

during, *pr*, в течéние, в продолжéние, во врéмя.

dusk, *n*, сýмерки; ~y, *a*, сýмеречный, тёмный; смýглый.

dust, *n*, пыль; *(bot.)* пыльцá; прах; ~-*bin* мýсорный ящик; ~-*cart* телéга для мýсора; ~-*jacket* суперобложка; ~-*man* мýсорщик; ~-*pan* совóк для сóра; ¶ *v.t*, стирáть пыль с; чúстить; пылúть; посыпáть (сáхарной пýдрой, *etc.*); ~er, *n*, пыльная тряпка; ~y, *a*, пыльный.

Dutch, *a*, голлáндский; ~ *courage* хрáбрость во хмелю; ¶ *n*, голлáндский язык; ~*man*, ~*woman* голлáндец, голлáндка.

dutiable, *a*, подлежáщий обложéнию пóшлиной.

dutiful, *a*, с сознáнием дóлга; покóрный; *duty*, *n*, долг; обязанность; дежýрство; пóшлина; *be on* ~ дежýрить; ~ *free* свобóдный (от дежýрства); не подлежáщий обложéнию пóшлиной; *do one's* ~ исполнять долг; ¶ *a*, дежýрный.

dwarf, *n*, кáрлик; ¶ *a*, кáрликовый; ¶ *v.t*, останáвливать развúтие *(gen.)*; мешáть рóсту *(gen.)*; уменьшáть размéры *(gen.)*; возвышáться над.

dwell, *v.i*, жить, пребывáть; обитáть; ~ *upon* останáвливаться на; ~er, *n*, жúтель, обитáтель; ~ing *n*, жилúще, дом; ~ *house* жилóй дом; ~ *place* местожúтельство.

dwindle, *v.i*, уменьшáться; сокращáться.

dye, *n*, крáска; красúтель; ~ *works* красúльня; ¶ *v.t*, крáсить, окрáшивать; ~*d in the wool* хорошó пропúтанный крáской; убеждённый; ~ing, *n*, покрáска, крáшение; красúльное дéло; ~*r*, *n*, красúльщик.

dying, *a*, умирáющий; предсмéртный.

dynamic, *a*, динамúческий; актúвный; дéйствующий; **dynamics**, *n*, динáмика; дéйствующие сúлы.

dynamite, *n*, динамúт.

dynamo, *n*, динáмо, динамомашúна.

dynastic, *a*, династúческий; **dynasty**, *n*, динáстия.

dysentery, *n*, дизентерúя.

dyspepsia, *n*, расстрóйство пищеварéния, диспéпсия; **dyspeptic**, *a*, страдáющий диспéпсией; раздражúтельный.

E

E, *n*, *(mus.)* ми.

each, *a. & pn*, кáждый; всякий; ~ *of us* кáждый из нас; ~ *other* друг дрýга.

eager, *a*, жáдный; усéрдный; пылкий; горячий; *be* ~ *to* горéть желáнием (+ *inf.)*; ~ly, *ad*, пылко; охóтно; ~ness, *n*, пыл, рвéние; усéрдие; жáдность.

eagle, *n*, орёл; ~-*eyed* с зóрким глáзом; ~t, *n*, орлёнок.

ear, *n,* у́хо; слух; ушко́; *(corn)* ко́-
лос; ¶ *v.i,* колоси́ться; ~*ache*
боль в у́хе; ~ *flaps* наушники;
~ *mark (n.)* клеймо́ на у́хе; от-
личи́тельный при́знак; *(v.t.)* клей-
ми́ть; ассигнова́ть; (пред)назна-
ча́ть; ~ *piece* ра́ковина телефо́н-
ной тру́бки; ~*-ring* серьга́; ~
trumpet слуховая́ тру́бка; *be all*
~*s* превраща́ться в слух; *turn
a deaf* ~ *to* не обраща́ть внима́ния
на.

earl, *n,* граф; ~**dom,** *n,* гра́фство;
ти́тул гра́фа.

early, *a,* ра́нний; преждевре́мен-
ный; ~ *bird* ра́нняя пта́шка;
¶ *ad,* ра́но; заблаговре́менно;
~ *in the year* в нача́ле го́да; *come
2 hours* ~ приходи́ть на два часа́
ра́ньше.

earn, *v.t,* зараба́тывать; заслу́жи-
вать.

earnest, *a,* серьёзный; ва́жный;
и́скренний; ре́вностный; *in* ~
всерьёз; ¶ *n,* зада́ток; зало́г; ~*ly,*
ad, серьёзно, всерьёз; ре́вностно;
~**ness,** *n,* серьёзность; и́скрен-
ность; ре́вностность.

earnings, *n.pl,* за́работок; при́-
быль.

earth, *n,* земля́; земно́й шар; су́ша;
по́чва; нора́ *(of animals); (elec.)*
заземле́ние; *what on* ~ *is wrong?*
в чём же де́ло? ~*-born* сме́ртный,
челове́ческий; ~*quake* землетря-
се́ние; ~*work* земляно́е укрепле́-
ние; земляны́е рабо́ты; ~*-worm*
земляно́й червь; ¶ *v.t, (elec.)* за-
земля́ть; ~ *up* зака́пывать; оку́-
чивать *(plants);* ~**en,** *a,* земля-
но́й; гли́няный; ~**enware,** *n,*
гли́няная посу́да, кера́мика; ~*ly,*
a, земно́й; жите́йский; ~*y,* *a,*
земляно́й; земли́стый; гру́бый.

earwig, *n,* уховёртка.

ease, *n,* поко́й; досу́г; лёгкость; непринуждённость; *with* ~ с лёг-
костью; *at* ~ свобо́дно; непри-
нуждённо; во́льно!; *ill at* ~ не-
ло́вко; ¶ *v.t,* облегча́ть *(pain,
burden);* растя́гивать *(boots);* вы-
пуска́ть *(clothes).*

easel, *n,* мольбе́рт.

easily, *ad,* легко́; свобо́дно; **easiness,**
n, лёгкость.

east, *n,* восто́к; ¶ *a,* восто́чный.

Easter, *n,* па́сха; ¶ *a,* пасха́льный.

eastern, *a,* восто́чный; **eastwards,** *ad,*
на восто́к, к восто́ку.

easy, *a,* лёгкий; удо́бный; непринуждённый; ~ *chair* кре́сло; ~
going добродушный; беззабо́тный;
~ *to get on with* покла́дистый.

eat, *v.t,* есть, ку́шать; ~ *away* разъ-
еда́ть; ~ *into* въеда́ться в; рас-
тра́чивать; ~ *up* пожира́ть; по-
глоща́ть; ~**able,** *a,* съедо́бный;
~**ables,** *n,* съестно́е; пи́ща; ~**ing
house,** *n,* столо́вая; рестора́н.

eau de Cologne, *n,* одеколо́н.

eaves, *n.pl,* карни́з; стреха́; ~**drop,**
v.i, подслу́шивать; ~**dropper,** *n,*
подслу́шивающий.

ebb, *n,* отли́в; *(fig.)* упа́док; ~ *tide*
отли́в; ¶ *v.i,* отлива́ть, убыва́ть;
ослабева́ть.

ebonite, *n,* эбони́т; **ebony,** *n,* чёрное/
эбе́новое де́рево.

ebullient, *a,* кипя́щий; *(fig.)* кипу́-
чий; запа́льчивый.

eccentric, *a,* эксцентри́чный; стра́н-
ный; ¶ *n,* чуда́к, оригина́л;
~**ity,** *n,* эксцентри́чность.

ecclesiastic, *n,* духо́вное лицо́; ¶ *a,*
церко́вный; духо́вный.

echo, *n,* э́хо; отголо́сок; ¶ *v.t,* вто́-
рить/подража́ть *(dat.);* *v.i,* от-
дава́ться э́хом; отража́ться.

eclectic, *a,* эклекти́ческий; ~**ism,** *n,*
эклекти́зм; экле́ктика.

eclipse, *m,* затме́ние; *(fig.)* потус-
кне́ние; упа́док; ~ *of the moon/
sun* лу́нное/со́лнечное затме́ние;
¶ *v.t,* затмева́ть *(also fig.);* за-
слоня́ть.

economic, *a,* экономи́ческий; хозя́й-
ственный; ~**al,** *a,* эконо́мный; бе-
режли́вый; ~**s,** *n,* эконо́мика,
наро́дное хозя́йство; **economist,** *n,*
экономи́ст; **economize,** *v.i,* эко-
но́мить; **economy,** *n,* хозя́йство;
эконо́мия, бережли́вость.

ecstasy, *n,* экста́з; исступле́ние;
ecstatic, *a,* исступлённый; восто́р-
женный.

ecumenical, *a,* вселе́нский.

eczema, *n,* экзе́ма.

eddy, *n,* водоворо́т; вихрь; клуб
(smoke); (tech.) вихрево́е дви-
же́ние; ¶ *v.i,* крути́ться в водо-
воро́те; клуби́ться.

edelweiss, *n,* эдельве́йс.

Eden, *n,* Эде́м; рай.

edge, *n,* край; кро́мка; грань; ле́з-
вие; опу́шка *(forest); on* ~ взвол-

нóванный; *set one's teeth on* ~ действовать на нéрвы; набить *(pf.)* оскóмину; ¶ *v.t*, окаймлять; обрезáть края *(gen.)*; ~ways, *ad*, острием; крáем, бóком; edging, *n*, каймá, бордюр *(wallpaper)*.

edible, *a*, съедóбный.

edict, *n*, эдúкт, укáз.

edification, *n*, назидáние, наставлéние.

edifice, *n*, здáние; сооружéние, пострóйка.

edify, *v.t*, поучáть; ~ing, *a*, назидáтельный.

edit, *v.t*, редактúровать; приготовлять к печáти; монтúровать *(film.)*; ~ing, *n*, редактúрование; монтáж; ~ion, *n*, издáние; ~or, *n*, редáктор; ~orial, *a*, редáкторский; редакциóнный; ¶ *n*, передовáя статья, передовúца; ~ *staff* редакциóнная коллéгия.

educate, *v.t*, давáть образовáние *(dat.)*; воспúтывать; тренировáть; education, *n*, образовáние; обучéние; ~al, *a*, образовáтельный; учéбный; воспитáтельный; educator, *n*, воспитáтель; педагóг.

cel, *n*, угóрь.

eerie, *a*, жýткий; мрáчный.

efface, *v.t*, изглáживать; вычёркивать; стирáть.

effect, *n*, резýльтáт; дéйствие, влияние; эффéкт; прои̇звéдение *pl*, имýщество; *in* ~ в действúтельности; *in* сýщности; *of no* ~ безрезультáтный; *take* ~ дéйствовать; вступáть в сúлу; ¶ *v.t*, производúть; осуществлять; выполнять; ~ive, *a*, эффектúвный; эффéктный; ~ual, *a*, действенный; успéшный.

effeminacy, *n*, изнéженность; effeminate, *a*, изнéженный; женоподóбный.

effervesce, *v.i*, пузыриться; пéниться; шипéть; *(fig.)* кипéть; ~nce, *n*, шипéние; *(fig.)* пылкость; ~nt, *a*, шипýчий; *(fig.)* кипýчий.

effete, *a*, истощённый; упáдочный.

efficacious, *a*, эффектúвный; производúтельный; efficiency, *n*, эффектúвность; умéлость; производúтельность, работоспосóбность; efficient, *a*, дéльный, работоспосóбный; эффектúвный; производúтельный.

effigy, *n*, изображéние; óбраз.

efflorescence, *n*, цветéние; расцвéт.

effluvium, *n*, испарéние.

effort, *n*, усúлие; напряжéние.

effrontery, *n*, нáглость, дéрзость.

effulgence, *n*, лучезáрность, блеск; effulgent, *a*, лучезáрный.

effusion, *n*, излияние; effusive, *a*, экспансúвный.

egg, *n*, яйцó; ~-cup рюмка для яйцá; ~shell яúчная скорлупá; ¶ *v.t:* ~ *on* подстрекáть.

ego, *n*, эго, моё, «я»; самомнéние; ~ism, *n*, эгоúзм; ~ist, *n*, эгоúст; ~tism, *n*, эготúзм; самомнéние.

egregious, *a*, отъявленный; вопиющий; необыкновéнный.

egress, *n*, выход; истóк.

Egyptian, *a*, египетский; ¶ *n*, египтян|ин, -ка; Egyptologist, *n*, египтóлог.

eiderdown, *n*, пухóвое одеяло; гагáчий пух.

eight, *num*, вóсемь; ~een, *num*, восемнáдцать; ~eenth, *ord. num*, восемнáдцатый; ~h, *ord. num*, восьмóй; ~ieth, *ord. num*, восьмидесятый; ~y, *num*, вóсемьдесят.

either, *pn. & a*, одúн из двух; тот úли другóй; óба; ¶ *c*, úли; лúбо; ~ ... *or* ... úли ... úли ...; лúбо ... лúбо ...; ¶ *ad* и так и эáк; во всяком слýчае.

ejaculate, *v.t*, восклицáть; извергáть; ejaculation, *n*, восклицáние; извержéние.

eject, *v.t*, изгонять; выселять; извергáть; выбрáсывать; ~ion, *n*, изгнáние; выселéние; извержéние.

eke out, *v.t*, восполнять; удлинять; ~one's existence перебивáться кóе-кáк.

elaborate, *a*, подрóбный; прострáнный *(explanation)*; искýсный *(lie)*; ¶ *v.t*, тщáтельно разрабáтывать; развивáть; уточнять; elaboration, *n*, разрабóтка; уточнéние.

elapse, *v.i*, проходúть.

elastic, *a*, эластúчный *(also fig.)*; упрýгий; ¶ *n*, резúнка; лáстик; ~ity, *n*, эластúчность; упрýгость.

elate, *v.t*, подбодрять; ~d, *a*, в востóрге; elation, *n*, востóрг; припóднятое настроéние.

elbow, *n*, ло́коть; *(tech.)* коле́но; ~ *room* просто́р; ¶ *v.t*, толка́ть локтя́ми; ~ *one's way* прота́лкиваться.

elder, *a*, ста́рший; ¶ *n*, ста́рший; ста́рец; *(bot.)* бузина́; ~*berry* я́года бузины́; ~*ly*, *a*, пожило́й; **eldest**, *a*, са́мый ста́рший.

elect, *a*, и́збранный; ¶ *n*, избра́нник; ¶ *v.t*, избира́ть, выбира́ть; назнача́ть; реша́ть; ~*ion*, *n*, вы́боры; избра́ние; ~ *campaign* избира́тельная кампа́ния; ~*ive*, *a*, вы́борный; ~*or*, *n*, избира́тель; вы́борщик; ~*oral*, *a*, избира́тельный.

electric, *a*, электри́ческий; *(fig.)* наэлектризо́ванный; ~*al*, *a*, электри́ческий; ~ *engineer* инжене́р-электроте́хник; ~*ian*, *n*, электромонтёр; электроте́хник; ~*ity*, *n*, электри́чество; **electrify**, *v.t*, электрифици́ровать; *(fig.)* электризова́ть; **electrocute**, *v.t*, убива́ть электри́ческим то́ком; казни́ть на электри́ческом сту́ле; **electrolysis**, *n*, электро́лиз; **electromagnet**, *n*, электромагни́т; **electron**, *n*, электро́н; **electroplate**, *v.t*, покрыва́ть гальвани́ческим спо́собом; **electroplating**, *n*, гальванопокры́тие; **electrotype**, *n*, гальванопла́стика; электроти́пия.

elegance, *n*, элега́нтность, изя́щество; **elegant**, *a*, элега́нтный; изя́щный.

elegiac, *a*, элеги́ческий; гру́стный; **elegy**, *n*, эле́гия.

element, *n*, элеме́нт; стихи́я; стихи́я; *pl*, осно́вы; ~*ary*, *a*, элемента́рный; первонача́льный; нача́льный *(education, school)*.

elephant, *n*, слон; ~*ine*, *a*, слоно́вый; *(fig.)* слоноподо́бный.

elevate, *v.t*, поднима́ть, повыша́ть; ~*d*, *a*, возвы́шенный *(also fig.)*; по́днятый; **elevation**, *n*, подня́тие; возвы́шенность; высота́; *(tech.)* про́филь; фаса́д; **elevator**, *n*, лифт; элева́тор; грузоподъёмник.

eleven, *num*, оди́ннадцать; ~*th*, *ord. num*, оди́ннадцатый.

elf, *n*, эльф; ~*in*, *a*, волше́бный; миниатю́рный; ~*ish*, *a*, ма́ленький; прока́зливый.

elicit, *v.t*, извлека́ть; вызыва́ть; ~ *a reply* добива́ться отве́та.

elide, *v.t*, выпуска́ть; ума́лчивать.

eligibility, *n*, пра́во на избра́ние, избира́емость; прие́млемость; **eligible**, *a*, могу́щий быть и́збранным; подходя́щий.

eliminate, *v.t*, устраня́ть; ликвиди́ровать; **elimination**, *n*, устране́ние; ликвида́ция.

elision, *n*, эли́зия.

elite, *n*, цвет (о́бщества); эли́та, лу́чшие.

elixir, *n*, эликси́р.

elk, *n*, лось.

ellipse, *n*, э́ллипс; ова́л; **ellipsis**, *n*, э́ллипс(ис); **elliptical**, *a*, эллипти́ческий.

elm, *n*, вяз.

elocution, *n*, ора́торское иску́сство; ди́кция; ~*ist*, *n*, ора́тор; учи́тель ди́кции.

elongate, *v.t*, *(& i.)*, растя́гивать(ся); удлиня́ть(ся).

elope, *v.i*, бежа́ть (с возлю́бленным); ~*ment*, *n*, та́йное бе́гство.

eloquence, *n*, красноре́чие; **eloquent**, *a*, красноречи́вый.

else, *ad*, ещё; кро́ме; *what* ~? что ещё?; *who* ~? кто ещё?; *nobody* ~ никто́ бо́льше; *nothing* ~ ничто́ (ничего́) бо́льше; *or* ~ ина́че; а то; ¶ *pn*, друго́й; *somebody* ~ кто́-нибудь друго́й; ~*where*, *ad*, где́-нибудь в друго́м ме́сте.

elucidate, *v.t*, объясня́ть; пролива́ть свет на; **elucidation**, *n*, разъясне́ние.

elude, *v.t*, избега́ть *(gen.)*; уклоня́ться от; ускольза́ть от; **elusive**, *a*, неулови́мый; укло́нчивый.

Elysian fields, *n*, Елисе́йские поля́.

emaciate, *v.t*, истоща́ть, изнуря́ть; ~*d*, *p.p. & a*, истощённый; **emaciation**, *n*, истоще́ние; изнуре́ние; худоба́.

emanate, *v.i*, исходи́ть, истека́ть; ~ *from* происходи́ть от; **emanation**, *n*, эмана́ция; истече́ние; излуче́ние; происхожде́ние.

emancipate, *v.t*, освобожда́ть; эмансипи́ровать; **emancipation**, *n*, освобожде́ние; эмансипа́ция.

emasculate, *v.t*, кастри́ровать; *(fig.)* обесси́ливать; изне́живать.

embalm, *v.t*, бальзами́ровать; *(fig.)* храни́ть от забве́ния.

embankment, *n*, на́бережная; на́сыпь, да́мба.

embargo, *n*, эмба́рго; запреще́ние.

embark, *v.t*, грузи́ть; сажа́ть (на кора́бль, *etc.*); *v.i*, грузи́ться; сади́ться (на кора́бль, *etc.*); ~ *upon* начина́ть, пуска́ться в; ~ation, *n*, поса́дка; погру́зка.

embarrass, *v.t*, смуща́ть; стесня́ть; затрудня́ть; *be* ~*ed* быть смущённым; запу́тываться в долга́х; ~ment, *n*, смуще́ние.

embassy, *n*, посо́льство.

embattle, *v.t*, возводи́ть зубцы́ (на сте́нах); ~d, *a*, гото́вый к бою.

embed, *v.t*, вставля́ть; вде́лывать.

embellish, *v.t*, украша́ть; ~ment, *n*, украше́ние.

embers, *n*, горя́чая зола́.

embezzle, *v.t*, присва́ивать; растра́чивать; похища́ть; ~ment, *n*, растра́та; похище́ние.

embitter, *v.t*, озлобля́ть; огорча́ть; отравля́ть.

emblazon, *v.t*, распи́сывать герб;

emblem, *n*, эмбле́ма; си́мвол; ~atic, *a*, символи́ческий.

embodiment, *n*, воплоще́ние; объедине́ние; **embody**, *v.t*, воплоща́ть, олицетворя́ть; объединя́ть.

embolden, *v.t*, ободря́ть; поощря́ть.

emboss, *v.t*, выбива́ть; чека́нить; гофрирова́ть; украша́ть релье́фом.

embrace, *n*, объя́тие; ¶ *v.t*, обнима́ть; охва́тывать; включа́ть, содержа́ть; принима́ть *(faith, theory); v.i*, обнима́ться.

embrasure, *n*, проём; *(mil.)* амбразу́ра.

embrocation, *n*, мазь; растира́ние.

embroider, *v.t*, вышива́ть; приукра́шивать; ~ess, *n*, вышива́льщица; ~y, *n*, вышива́ние; вы́шивка; украше́ние; прикра́са; ~ *frame* пя́льцы.

embroil, *v.t*, запу́тывать *(affair);* впу́тывать *(pers.);* ~ *with* ссо́рить с.

embryo, *n*, эмбрио́н, заро́дыш; **embryonic**, *a*, эмбриона́льный, заро́дышевый.

emend, *v.t*, исправля́ть; ~ment, *n*, исправле́ние; попра́вка.

emerald, *n*, изумру́д; изумру́дный цвет.

emerge, *v.i*, появля́ться; всплыва́ть; выходи́ть; выясня́ться; возника́ть; ~nce, *n*, вы́ход; появле́ние; ~ncy, *n*, крити́ческое положе́ние; кра́йность; ава́рия;

in case of ~ при кра́йней необходи́мости; ¶ *a*, вспомога́тельный; запасно́й; авари́йный; ~ *brake* запасно́й то́рмоз; ~ *exit* запа́сный вы́ход; ~ *landing* вынужденная поса́дка; ~ *store* неприкоснове́нный запа́с; ~ *powers* чрезвыча́йные полномо́чия; ~nt, *a*, развива́ющийся.

emery, *n*, нажда́к; ~ *paper* нажда́чная бума́га.

emetic, *a*, рво́тный; ¶ *n*, рво́тное.

emigrant, *n*, эмигра́нт; переселе́нец; **emigrate**, *v.i*, эмигри́ровать; переселя́ться; **emigration**, *n*, эмигра́ция; переселе́ние.

eminence, *n*, высота́; возвы́шенность; знамени́тость высокопреосвяще́нство *(title);* **eminent**, *a*, выдаю́щийся, замеча́тельный; возвы́шенный.

emir, *n*, эми́р.

emissary, *n*, эмисса́р; аге́нт; по́сланный; **emission**, *n*, выделе́ние; распростране́ние; излуче́ние; эми́ссия; **emit**, *v.t*, испуска́ть; выделя́ть; издава́ть *(sound);* выпуска́ть *(currency).*

emollient, *a*, смягча́ющий; ¶ *n*, смягча́ющее сре́дство.

emolument, *n*, за́работок, жа́лованье; дохо́д.

emotion, *n*, волне́ние; чу́вство, эмо́ция; ~al, *a*, эмоциона́льный; чувстви́тельный.

emperor, *n*, импера́тор.

emphasis, *n*, ударе́ние; си́ла; вырази́тельность; **emphasize**, *v.t*, подчёркивать; придава́ть осо́бое значе́ние *(dat.);* де́лать осо́бое ударе́ние на; **emphatic**, *a*, вырази́тельный; подчёркнутый; реши́тельный.

empire, *n*, импе́рия.

empiric(al), *a*, эмпири́ческий; **empiricism**, *n*, эмпири́зм.

employ, *n*, слу́жба; ¶ *v.t*, держа́ть на слу́жбе; нанима́ть, принима́ть на рабо́ту; применя́ть, испо́льзовать; *be* ~*ed by* рабо́тать у; ~ee, *n*, слу́жащий; рабо́чий; ~er, *n*, работода́тель; хозя́ин; ~ment, *n*, наём; рабо́та, слу́жба; заня́тие; примене́ние, испо́льзование; *(econ.)* за́нятость; ~ *bureau* бюро́ на́йма.

emporium, *n*, торго́вый центр; большо́й магази́н.

empower, v.t, уполномо́чивать.

empress, n, императри́ца; цари́ца.

emptiness, n, пустота́; **empty,** a, пусто́й; поро́жний; свобо́дный (seat); голо́дный; (tech.) холосто́й; ~-handed с пусты́ми рука́ми; ~-headed пустоголо́вый; ¶ n, пуста́я буты́лка, etc.; pl, порожня́к; ¶ v.t, опорожня́ть; осуша́ть (glass); вылива́ть, высыпа́ть; выпуска́ть; v.i, пусте́ть; опорожня́ться; впада́ть (river).

empyrean, a, небе́сный; неземно́й; заобла́чный.

emu, n, э́му.

emulate, v.t, соревнова́ться с; сопе́рничать с; **emulation,** n, соревнова́ние; сопе́рничество.

emulsion, n, эму́льсия.

enable, v.t, дава́ть возмо́жность (dat.); приспоса́бливать; де́лать го́дным.

enact, v.t, постановля́ть; вводи́ть (law); ста́вить на сце́не; be ~ed разы́грываться; происходи́ть; ~ment, n, введе́ние зако́на; зако́н; ука́з.

enamel, n, эма́ль; глазу́рь; ¶ v.t, покрыва́ть эма́лью/глазу́рью.

enamour, v.t, очаро́вывать; ~ed, p.p: ~ by, with влюблённый в; увлечённый (inst.).

encamp, v.i, располага́ться ла́герем; ~ment, n, ла́герь.

encase, v.t, упако́вывать/класть в я́щик.

encaustic, a, обожжённый.

enchain, v.t, зако́вывать; сажа́ть на цепь; (fig.) ско́вывать.

enchant, v.t, очаро́вывать; околдо́вывать; ~er, n, чароде́й; обворожи́тель; ~ing, a, очарова́тельный; преле́стный; ~ment, n, очарова́ние; ~ress, n, чароде́йка; обворожи́тельница.

encircle, v.t, окружа́ть.

enclose, v.t, огора́живать; окружа́ть; заключа́ть; прилага́ть, вкла́дывать (with letter); **enclosure,** n, огоро́женное ме́сто; огра́да; вложе́ние, приложе́ние.

encomium, n, панеги́рик.

encompass, v.t, окружа́ть (also fig.); заключа́ть.

encore, n, вы́зов на бис; ¶ int. бис!; ¶ v.t, вызыва́ть на бис; тре́бовать повторе́ния (gen.).

encounter, n, встре́ча; столкнове́ние; ¶ v.t, встреча́ть; ста́лкиваться с; ната́лкиваться на.

encourage, v.t, ободря́ть, поощря́ть; подстрека́ть; ~ment, n, ободре́ние, поощре́ние; подстрека́тельство.

encroach, v.i: ~ on вторга́ться в; покуша́ться на; ~ment, n, вторже́ние.

encrust, v.t, инкрусти́ровать.

encumber, v.t, загроможда́ть; затрудня́ть; меша́ть (dat.); обременя́ть; **encumbrance,** n, затрудне́ние; бре́мя; обу́за.

encyclical, n, энци́клика.

encyclopaedia, n, энциклопе́дия.

end, n, коне́ц; оконча́ние; оста́ток; обло́мок; край; грани́ца; цель; результа́т; смерть; ~ on концо́м к себе́; in the ~ в конце́ концо́в; on ~ стойма́; дыбом; 3 days on ~ три дня подря́д; make ~s meet своди́ть концы́ с конца́ми; no ~ of мно́го, ма́сса; чуде́сный; ¶ v.t. (& i.), конча́ть(ся), зака́нчивать(ся).

endanger, v.t, подверга́ть опа́сности.

endear, v.t, де́лать дороги́м; ~ing, a, ла́сковый; ~ment, n, ла́ска; привя́занность.

endeavour, n, попы́тка, стара́ние; стремле́ние; ¶ v.i, пыта́ться, стара́ться.

ending, n, оконча́ние (also gram.); коне́ц.

endive, n, энди́вий.

endless, a, бесконе́чный, бесчи́сленный.

endorse, v.t, подпи́сывать; (fig.) подтвержда́ть; одобря́ть; ~ment, ne индоссаме́нт; подтвержде́ние.

endow, v.t, обеспе́чивать постоя́нным дохо́дом; завеща́ть постоя́нный дохо́д (dat.); наделя́ть; b-~ed with быть одарённым (inst.); ~ment, n, вклад, поже́ртвование; дар, дарова́ние; дохо́д.

endue, v.t, наделя́ть; одаря́ть; об, лача́ть.

endurable, a, прие́млемый; про́чный; **endurance,** n, выно́сливость, терпе́ние; про́чность; сто́йкость; **endure,** v.t, выноси́ть, терпе́ть; v.i, дли́ться, продолжа́ться.

enema, n, кли́зма.

enemy, n, враг; проти́вник; ¶ a; вражде́бный; вра́жеский.

energetic, *a,* энергичный; **energy,** *n,* энергия; сила.

enervate, *v.t,* обессиливать; расслаблять.

enfeeble, *v.t,* ослаблять.

enfilade, *v.t,* обстреливать (продольным огнём).

enfold, *v.t,* обнимать, обхватывать; завёртывать, закутывать.

enforce, *v.t,* принуждать; настаивать на; заставлять; проводить в жизнь; **~ment,** *n,* давление; принуждение.

enfranchise, *v.t,* предоставлять избирательные права *(dat.);* освобождать.

engage, *v.t,* нанимать; привлекать; *(tech.)* зацеплять; обязывать, связывать; **~** *in* вступать (в сражение/разговор); *be* **~d** быть занятым; быть помолвленным; **~d,** *a. & p.p,* занятый; поглощённый; помолвленный; **~ment,** *n,* дело, занятие; приглашение; свидание; обязательство; помолвка; *(mil.)* бой, стычка; **~** *ring* обручальное кольцо; **engaging,** *a,* привлекательный.

engender, *v.t,* порождать, вызывать, возбуждать.

engine, *n,* мотор, двигатель; машина; локомотив; **~** *driver* машинист; **~er,** *n,* инженер; механик; машинист; ¶ *v.t,* устраивать; проводить; **~ering,** *n,* техника; машиностроение.

English, *a,* английский; ¶ *n,* английский язык; *the* **~,** *n,* англичане; **~man, ~woman,** *n,* англичанин, англичанка.

engrave, *v.t,* гравировать; резать; запечатлевать (в памяти); **~r,** *n,* гравёр; **engraving,** *n,* гравирование; гравюра.

engross, *v.t,* поглощать; писать крупным почерком; *be* **~ed** быть поглощённым.

engulf, *v.t,* поглощать.

enhance, *v.t,* повышать; увеличивать; усиливать.

enigma, *n,* загадка; **~tic,** *a,* загадочный.

enjoin, *v.t,* предписывать; приказывать.

enjoy, *v.t,* получать удовольствие от; обладать *(inst);* пользоваться *(inst.);* **~** *oneself* наслаждаться; **~able,** *a,* приятный;

~ment, *n,* наслаждение; удовольствие; обладание.

enlarge, *v.t. (& i.),* увеличивать(ся) *(also phot.);* расширять(ся); **~ment,** *n,* расширение; увеличение.

enlighten, *v.t,* просвещать; осведомлять; **~ed,** *a,* просвещённый; **~ment,** *n,* просвещение; просвещённость.

enlist, *v.t,* вербовать (на военную службу); привлекать; *v.i,* поступать на военную службу; **~ment,** *n,* поступление на военную службу.

enliven, *v.t,* оживлять, подбодрять.

enmesh, *v.t,* опутывать.

enmity, *n,* вражда, неприязнь.

ennoble, *v.t,* облагораживать; жаловать дворянством.

enormity, *n,* ужас; гнусность; чудовищное преступление; **enormous,** *a,* громадный, огромный.

enough, *a,* достаточный; ¶ *n,* достаточное количество; ¶ *ad,* достаточно, довольно; **~** *and to spare* больше, чем нужно.

enquire, *v.i,* спрашивать; наводить справки; осведомляться, справляться; **~** *into* исследовать, разузнавать; **enquiry,** *n,* вопрос; справка; расследование; следствие, исследование; **~** *office* справочное бюро.

enrage, *v.t,* бесить.

enrapture, *v.t,* восхищать.

enrich, *v.t,* обогащать; удобрять *(soil) ;* украшать; **~ment,** *n,* обогащение; украшение.

enrol, *v.t,* вносить в список, зачислять, регистрировать; *(mil.)* вербовать; *v.i,* поступать (на военную службу, *etc.).*

ensconce, *v.t,* укрывать; устраивать удобно; **~** *oneself* устраиваться; усаживаться.

enshrine, *v.t,* помещать в раку; *(fig.)* хранить.

enshroud, *v.t,* закутывать.

ensign, *n,* знамя, флаг; младший лейтенант.

enslave, *v.t,* порабощать; **~ment,** *n,* порабощение.

ensnare, *v.t,* ловить в западню; *(fig.)* заманивать.

ensue, *v.i,* следовать; происходить; получаться в результате.

ensure, v.t, обеспéчивать, гаранти́ровать; страховáть.

entail, n, (law) акт, закрепля́ющий наслéдование земли́; майорáт; ¶ v.t, влечь за собóй; вызывáть; (law) определя́ть наслéдование земли́.

entangle, v.t, запýтывать; ~ment, n, запýтанность; затрудни́тельное положéние; заграждéние.

enter, v.t. & i, входи́ть (в); приходи́ть (в гóлову); поступáть (в áрмию/институ́т); вступáть (в); вноси́ть (в кни́гу); регистри́ровать; вступáть (в перегово́ры, etc.).

enteric, a, брюшнóй, **enteritis,** n, воспалéние тóнких кишóк, энтери́т.

enterprise, n, предприя́тие; предприи́мчивость, инициати́ва; **enterprising,** a, предприи́мчивый, инициати́вный.

entertain, v.t, развлекáть; занимáть; принимáть (guests); питáть (hopes); лелéять (dreams); ~ing, a, забáвный, занимáтельный, развлекáтельный; ~ment, n, развлечéние, увеселéние; приём.

enthral, v.t, порабощáть; очарóвывать; ~ling, a, увлекáтельный, захвáтывающий.

enthrone, v.t, возводи́ть на престóл; ~ment, n, возведéние на престóл.

enthusiasm, n, энтузиáзм, востóрг; **enthusiast,** n, энтузиáст; ~ic, a востóрженный; пóлный энтузиáзма.

entice, v.t, соблазня́ть; замáнивать; увлекáть; ~ment, n, замáнивание; примáнка; соблáзн.

entire, a, пóлный; совершéнный; цéлый; весь; сплошнóй; ~ly, ad, пóлностью, всецéло, вполнé, совершéнно; ~ty, n, полнотá; цéльность; óбщая сýмма; in its ~ в цéлом.

entitle, v.t, называ́ть; озаглáвливать; давáть прáво (dat.); be ~ed имéть прáво.

entity, n, бытиé; сýщность.

entomb, v.t, погребáть; (fig.) укрывáть.

entomologist, n, энтомóлог; **entomology,** n, энтомолóгия.

entrails, n.pl, внýтренности, кишки́.

entrance, n, вход; вступлéние; (theat.) вы́ход; ~ examination вступи́тельный экзáмен; ~ hall вестибю́ль.

entrance, v.t, восхищáть; приводи́ть в состоя́ние трáнса; **entrancing,** a, чарýющий; очаровáтельный.

entreat, v.t, умоля́ть; ~y, n, мольбá, прóсьба.

entrench, v.t, окружáть окóпами, укрепля́ть; ~ment, n, окóп, полевóе укреплéние.

entrust, v.t, вверя́ть; возлагáть на; поручáть.

entry, n, вход, въезд; вступлéние; зáпись, статья́; (theat.) вы́ход; вестибю́ль; no ~ проéзда нет.

entwine, v.t, сплетáть; обвивáть.

enumerate, v.t, перечисля́ть; **enumeration,** n, перечислéние; пéречень.

enunciate, v.t, объявля́ть; формули́ровать (theory); произноси́ть; **enunciation,** n, возвещéние; формулирóвка; произношéние, ди́кция.

envelop, v.t, завора́чивать; закýтывать; окýтывать; ~e, n, конвéрт; оболóчка; покры́шка.

envenom, v.t, отравля́ть.

enviable, a, зави́дный; **envious,** a, зави́стливый.

environment, n, средá; окружéние; окружáющая обстанóвка; **environs,** n, окрéстности.

envisage, v.t, смотрéть (dat.) пря́мо в глазá (of danger, etc.); предусмáтривать.

envoy, n, послáнник; агéнт.

envy, n, зáвисть; ¶ v.t, зави́довать (dat.).

epaulet(te), n, эполéт.

ephemeral, a, эфемéрный; недолговéчный.

epic, a, эпи́ческий; ¶ n, эпи́ческая поэ́ма.

epicure, n, эпикурéец.

epidemic, a, эпидеми́ческий; ¶ n, эпидéмия.

epigram, n, эпигрáмма.

epilepsy, n, эпилéпсия; **epileptic,** a, эпилепти́ческий.

epilogue, n, эпилóг.

Epiphany, n, богоявлéние; крещéние.

episcopacy, n, епи́скопство; **episcopal,** a, епи́скопский; епископáльный; **episcopate,** *n,* сан епи́скопа; епа́рхия.

episode, *n,* эпизо́д; **episodic,** *a,* эпизоди́ческий; случа́йный.

epistle, *n,* посла́ние; **epistolary,** *a,* эпистоля́рный.

epitaph, *n,* эпита́фия; на́дпись на надгро́бном па́мятнике.

epithet, *n,* эпи́тет.

epitome, *n,* конспе́кт, сокраще́ние; *(fig.)* изображе́ние в миниатю́ре; воплоще́ние; **epitomize,** *v.t,* конспекти́ровать; сокраща́ть; воплоща́ть.

epoch, *n,* эпо́ха; перио́д.

equable, *a,* уравнове́шенный; равноме́рный; ро́вный.

equal, *a,* ра́вный; одина́ковый; *be~ to a task* справля́ться с зада́чей; *be on ~ terms with* быть на ра́вных нача́лах с; ¶ *n,* ра́вный; ро́вня; ¶ *v.t,* равня́ться *(dat.);* прира́внивать, ура́внивать; **~ity,** *n,* ра́венство; равнопра́вие; **~ization,** *n,* ура́внивание; уравне́ние; **~ize,** *v.t,* ура́внивать; уравнове́шивать; **~ly,** *ad,* ра́вно.

equanimity, *n,* хладнокро́вие; невозмути́мость.

equation, *n,* выра́внивание; *(math.)* уравне́ние.

equator, *n,* эква́тор; **~ial,** *a,* экватори́альный.

equerry, *n,* ко́нюший; **equestrian,** *a,* ко́нный.

equidistant, *a,* равноотстоя́щий.

equilibrate, *v.t,* уравнове́шивать; **equilibrium,** *n,* равнове́сие.

equine, *a,* ко́нский, лошади́ный.

equinox, *n,* равноде́нствие.

equip, *v.t,* снаряжа́ть; обору́довать; снабжа́ть (зна́ниями); **~ment,** *n,* обору́дование; снаряже́ние.

equipoise, *n,* равнове́сие; противове́с.

equitable, *a,* справедли́вый; беспристра́стный; **equity,** *n,* справедли́вость, беспристра́стность.

equivalence, *n,* эквивале́нтность; равноце́нность; **equivalent,** *a,* равноце́нный; равноси́льный; ¶ *n,* эквивале́нт.

equivocal, *a,* двусмы́сленный; сомни́тельный; **equivocate,** *v.i,* говори́ть двусмы́сленно; увиливать; **equivocation,** *n,* увиливание; укло́нчивость.

era, *n,* э́ра, эпо́ха.

eradicate, *v.t,* искореня́ть; **eradication,** *n,* искорене́ние.

erase, *v.t,* стира́ть; подчища́ть; *(fig.)* стира́ть; изгла́живать; **~r,** *n,* рези́нка, ла́стик; **erasure,** *n,* подчи́стка; соска́бливание; уничтоже́ние.

ere, *pr,* до; пе́ред; *~ long* вско́ре; ¶ *c,* пре́жде чем; скоре́е чем.

erect, *a,* прямо́й; вертика́льный; по́днятый; ¶ *v.t,* сооружа́ть; воздвига́ть; *(fig.)* создава́ть, возвыша́ть; **~ion,** *n,* выпрямле́ние; сооруже́ние; строе́ние.

ermine, *n,* горноста́й.

erode, *v.t,* разъеда́ть; разруша́ть; *(geol.)* выве́тривать, размыва́ть; **erosion,** *n,* разъеда́ние; *(geol.)* эро́зия.

erotic, *a,* эроти́ческий, любо́вный.

err, *v.i,* ошиба́ться, заблужда́ться; греши́ть.

errand, *n,* поруче́ние; *~ boy* ма́льчик на посы́лках; рассы́льный.

errant, *a,* стра́нствующий; блужда́ющий *(thoughts);* сби́вшийся с пути́.

erratic, *a,* блужда́ющий; рассе́янный; оши́бочный.

erratum, *n,* опеча́тка; опи́ска; **erring,** *a,* заблу́дший, гре́шный; **erroneous,** *a,* оши́бочный; **error,** *n,* оши́бка, заблужде́ние; погре́шность.

eructate, *v.i,* отры́гивать; изрыга́ть; изверга́ть; **eructation,** *n,* отры́жка; изверже́ние.

erudite, *a,* учёный; **erudition,** *n,* эруди́ция; начи́танность.

erupt, *v.i,* изверга́ться; прорыва́ться; проре́зываться *(teeth);* **~ion,** *n,* изверже́ние; *(fig.)* взрыв; *(med.)* сыпь, высыпа́ние.

escalade, *n,* штурм; ¶ *v.t,* штурмова́ть (с по́мощью ле́стниц).

escalator, *n,* эскала́тор.

escape, *n,* бе́гство; побе́г; *(fig.)* ухо́д (от действи́тельности); спасе́ние; уте́чка; выделе́ние; *(tech.)* вы́ход, вы́пуск; ¶ *v.t,* избега́ть *(gen.);* избавля́ться от; ускольза́ть от; *v.i,* бежа́ть (из тюрьмы́); дава́ть уте́чку; улету́чиваться; вырыва́ться *(groan, etc.).*

escarpment, *n,* эска́рп; *(geol.)* вертика́льное обнаже́ние поро́ды.

eschew, *v.t,* избегать/сторониться *(gen.).*

escort, *n,* охрана, конвой; эскорт; ¶ *v.t,* конвоировать, эскортировать; сопровождать.

escutcheon, *n,* щит герба; *a blot on one's* ~ пятно позора.

eskimo, *a,* эскимосский; ¶ *n,* эскимос.

esoteric, *a,* тайный; особенный.

especial, *a,* особенный; специальный; ~ly, *ad,* особенно; главным образом.

espionage, *n,* шпионаж, шпионство.

esplanade, *n,* эспланада; площадка для прогулок.

espousal, *n,* свадьба; обручение; *(fig.)* поддержка; espouse, *v.t,* выдавать замуж; жениться на; *(fig.)* отдаваться (делу); поддерживать.

espy, *v.t,* замечать; видеть издалека.

esquire, *n,* эсквайр.

essay, *n,* сочинение, очерк, эссе; попытка; проба; ¶ *v.t, & i,* подвергать испытанию; пытаться (+ *inf.);* ~ist, *n,* очеркист, эссеист.

essence, *n,* сущность; существо; эссенция; духи.

essential, *a,* существенный; необходимый; ~s, *n.pl,* предметы первой необходимости; ~ly, *ad,* по существу.

establish, *v.t,* устанавливать; основывать; учреждать; упрочивать *(reputation, etc.);* ~ed, *p.p. & a,* учреждённый; установленный; авторитетный; *E* ~ed *Church* государственная церковь; ~ment, *n,* основание; учреждение, заведение; штат; хозяйство; *the* ~ власти.

estate, *n,* имение; имущество; сословие; ~ *agent* агент по продаже домов; управляющий имением; *personal* ~ движимость; *real* ~ недвижимость.

esteem, *n,* уважение; ¶ *v.t,* уважать, почитать; считать; estimable, *a,* достойный уважения.

estimate, *n,* оценка; смета; калькуляция; ¶ *v.t,* оценивать; составлять смету *(gen.);* определять глазомером; подсчитывать приблизительно; estimation, *n,* оценка; мнение; вычисление; подсчёт.

estrange, *v.t,* отдалять, отчуждать; *be* ~ed быть в ссоре; ссориться; отдаляться; ~ment, *n,* отчуждение; холодок (в отношениях); ссора.

estuary, *n,* устье реки.

etcetera, etc. и так далее; и тому подобное; и т.д.; и т.п.

etch, *v.t,* гравировать; травить на металле; ~er, *n,* гравёр; ~ing, *n,* гравировка; гравюра; вытравливание.

eternal, *a,* вечный, неизменный; eternity, *n,* вечность.

ether, *n,* эфир; ~eal, *a,* эфирный.

ethical, *a,* этический, этичный; ethics, *n,* этика.

Ethiopian, *a,* эфиопский; ¶ *n,* эфиоп.

ethnic, *a,* этнический; ethnography, *n,* этнография; ethnologist, *n,* этнолог; ethnology, *n,* этнология.

etiquette, *n,* этикет.

Etruscan, *a,* этрусский; ¶ *n,* этруск; этрусский язык.

etymological, *a,* этимологический; etymologist, *n,* этимолог; etymology, *n,* этимология.

eucalyptus, *n,* эвкалипт.

Eucharist, *n,* евхаристия; причастие.

eugenics, *n,* евгеника.

eulogist, *n,* панегирист; ~ic, *a,* хвалебный, панегирический; eulogize, *v.t,* превозносить; eulogy, *n,* панегирик.

eunuch, *n,* евнух.

euphemism, *n,* эвфемизм; euphemistic, *a,* эвфемистический.

euphonious, *a,* благозвучный; euphony, *n,* благозвучие.

European, *a,* европейский; ¶ *n,* европеец.

evacuate, *v.t,* эвакуировать; вывозить; опорожнять; evacuation, *n,* эвакуация.

evade, *v.t,* ускользать от; избегать *(gen.);* уклоняться от; обходить *(law).*

evaluate, *v.t,* оценивать; evaluation, *n,* оценка.

evanescent, *a,* мимолётный; *(math.)* бесконечно малый.

evangelical, *a,* евангельский; evangelist, *n,* евангелист.

evaporate, *v.t,* выпаривать; сгущать; *v.i,* испаряться; исчезать; evaporation, *n,* испарение.

evasion, *n*, уклоне́ние; увёртка; отгово́рка; **evasive**, *a*, укло́нчивый; неулови́мый.

eve, *n*, кану́н; *on the* ~ накану́не.

even, *a*, ро́вный; гла́дкий; ра́вный; одина́ковый; споко́йный *(temperament)*; чётный *(number)*; *be* ~ *with* своди́ть счёты с; ¶ *ad*, ро́вно; да́же; ~ *if* да́же е́сли; хотя́ бы; ~ *now* да́же сейча́с; ¶ *v.t*, выра́внивать; сгла́живать; равня́ть; уравнове́шивать.

evening, *n*, ве́чер; *good* ~! до́брый ве́чер!; ¶ *a*, вече́рний; ~ *dress* вече́рний туале́т; смо́кинг; фрак; вече́рнее пла́тье; ~ *party* вечери́нка.

evenly, *ad*, ро́вно, по́ровну; одина́ково, равноме́рно; справедли́во; споко́йно; **evenness**, *n*, ро́вность.

event, *n*, собы́тие, происше́ствие, слу́чай; *(sport)* соревнова́ние, но́мер (в програ́мме); исхо́д; *at all* ~s во вся́ком слу́чае; *in the* ~ *of* в слу́чае; ~**ful**, *a*, по́лный собы́тий; знамена́тельный; ~**ual**, *a*, возмо́жный; коне́чный; ~**uality**, *n*, возмо́жность; случа́йность; ~**ually**, *ad*, в конце́ концо́в.

ever, *ad*, всегда́; когда́-либо; ~ *since* с тех пор; *for* ~ *and* ~ навсегда́; наве́чно; *hardly* ~ едва́ ли когда́-нибудь; весьма́ ре́дко.

evergreen, *a*, вечнозелёный; ¶ *n*, вечнозелёное расте́ние.

everlasting, *a*, ве́чный; постоя́нный; про́чный.

evermore, *ad*, наве́ки; навсегда́.

every, *a*, ка́ждый; вся́кий; ~**body**, ка́ждый; вся́кий; все; ~ *day (ad)* ка́ждый день; *(a)* ежедне́вный, повседне́вный; обы́чный; ~*day clothes* оде́жда для постоя́нной но́ски; ~ *now and then* вре́мя от вре́мени; то и де́ло; ~ *other day* че́рез день; ~*thing* всё; ~*where* везде́; всю́ду.

evict, *v.t*, выселя́ть; изгоня́ть; ~**ion**, *n*, выселе́ние; изгна́ние; *(law)* лише́ние иму́щества.

evidence, *n*, доказа́тельство; *(law)*ули́ка; свиде́тельское показа́ние; *give* ~ свиде́тельствовать, дава́ть показа́ния; ¶ *v.t*, дока́зывать; **evident**, *a*, очеви́дный, я́сный; ~**ly**, *ad*, очеви́дно, я́сно.

evil, *a*, злой; вре́дный; ¶ *n*, зло; вред; бе́дствие; ~*doer* престу́п-

ник, злоде́й; гре́шник; ~ *eye* дурно́й глаз; ~-*minded* злонаме́ренный.

evince, *v.t*, проявля́ть.

eviscerate, *v.t*, потроши́ть; *(fig.)* выхола́щивать, лиша́ть содержа́ния.

evoke, *v.t*, вызыва́ть.

evolution, *n*, эволю́ция; разви́тие; *(math.)* извлече́ние ко́рня; ~**ary**, *a*, эволюцио́нный; **evolve**, *v.t*, развива́ть; *v.i*, развива́ться; развёртываться; эволюциони́ровать.

ewe, *n*, овца́.

ewer, *n*, кувши́н.

exacerbate, *v.t*, обостря́ть, усили́вать; раздража́ть.

exact, *a*, то́чный; аккура́тный; стро́гий; ¶ *v.t*, тре́бовать *(gen.)*; взы́скивать; вымога́ть; ~**ing**, *a*, тре́бовательный; суро́вый; изнуря́ющий; ~**ion**, *n*, вымога́тельство; взы́скивание; ~**ly**, *ad*, то́чно; как раз; и́менно; ~**ness**, *n*, то́чность.

exaggerate, *v.t*, преувели́чивать; **exaggeration**, *n*, преувеличе́ние.

exalt, *v.t*, возвыша́ть; превозноси́ть; ~**ation**, *n*, возвыше́ние; восто́рг; ~*ed*, *a*, высокопоста́вленный.

examination, *n*, экза́мен; осмо́тр; иссле́дование; *(law)* допро́с; **examine**, *v.t*, экзаменова́ть; осма́тривать; иссле́довать; *(law)* допра́шивать; **examinee**, *n*, экзаменую́щийся; **examiner**, *n*, экзамина́тор.

example, *n*, приме́р; образе́ц; *for* ~ наприме́р.

exasperate, *v.t*, раздража́ть; **exasperation**, *n*, раздраже́ние.

excavate, *v.t*, выка́пывать; *(archaeol.)* производи́ть раско́пки *(gen.)*; **excavation**, *n*, выка́пывание; раско́пки; экскава́ция, земляны́е рабо́ты; вы́рытая я́ма; **excavator**, *n*, экскава́тор; землеко́п.

exceed, *v.t*, превыша́ть; превосходи́ть; ~**ing**, *a*, безме́рный; чрезвыча́йный; ~**ingly**, *ad*, чрезвыча́йно.

excel, *v.t*, превосходи́ть; *v.i*, выдава́ться; отлича́ться; ~**lence**, *a*, превосхо́дство; высо́кое ка́чество; **E~lency**, *n*, превосходи́тельство; ~**lent**, *a*, превосхо́дный.

except, excepting, *pr*, за исключе́нием; исключа́я; кро́ме; ¶ *c*, е́сли не; ¶ *v.t*, исключа́ть; *(law)* отводи́ть;

~ion, *n*, исключе́ние; *(law)* отво́д; *take* ~ *at* обижа́ться на; *take* ~ *to* возража́ть про́тив; ~ional, *a*, исключи́тельный; необы́чный.

excerpt, *n*, отры́вок, вы́держка.

excess, *n*, изли́шек, избы́ток; невоздержанность; эксце́сс; ~ *luggage* бага́ж вы́ше но́рмы; ~ *fare* допла́та; ~ *profit* сверхприбыль; *to* ~ до кра́йности.

exchange, *n*, обме́н; разме́н; би́ржа; *bill of* ~ ве́ксель; ~able, *a*, мено́вой; *(tech.)* сме́нный.

exchequer, *n*, казначе́йство; казна́; ресу́рсы; ~ *bill* креди́тный биле́т.

excise, *n*, акци́з; ¶ *v.t*, выреза́ть; excision, *n*, выреза́ние, отреза́ние.

excitability, *n*, возбуди́мость; возбужда́емость; excitable, *a*, возбуди́мый; excite, *v.t*, возбужда́ть, волнова́ть; пробужда́ть *(interest)*; вызыва́ть *(hate, etc.)*; ~ment, *n*, возбужде́ние; волне́ние; exciting, *a*, захва́тывающий.

exclaim, *v.i*, восклица́ть; exclamation *n*, восклица́ние.

exclude, *v.t*, исключа́ть; не впуска́ть; не включа́ть; exclusion, *n*, исключе́ние; exclusive, *a*, исключи́тельный; еди́нственный; недосту́пный.

excommunicate, *v.t*, отлуча́ть от це́ркви; excommunication, *n*, отлуче́ние от це́ркви.

excrement, *n*, экскреме́нты.

excrescence, *n*, разраста́ние; наро́ст; *(fig.)* отро́сток.

excruciating, *a*, мучи́тельный.

exculpate, *v.t*, опра́вдывать; exculpation, *n*, оправда́ние; реабилита́ция.

excursion, *n*, экску́рсия; пое́здка; экскурс; ~ *ticket* биле́т на экску́рсию; ~*train* экскурсио́нный по́езд; ~ist, *n*, экскурса́нт, тури́ст.

excusable, *a*, извини́тельный; прости́тельный; excuse, *n*, извине́ние; оправда́ние; предло́г, отгово́рка; ¶ *v.t*, извиня́ть, проща́ть; освобожда́ть (от обя́занности); ~ *me!* извини́те!, прости́те!

execrable, *a*, отврати́тельный; execrate, *v.t*, ненави́деть; проклина́ть.

execute, *v.t*, исполня́ть, выполня́ть; казни́ть; *(law)* оформля́ть; exe-cution, *n*, выполне́ние, исполне́ние; казнь; *(law)* оформле́ние; ~er, *n*, пала́ч; executive, *a*, исполни́тельный; администрати́вный; ¶ *n*, исполни́тельный о́рган; исполни́тельная власть; executor, *n*, душеприка́зчик; суде́бный исполни́тель.

exegesis, *n*, толкова́ние.

exemplary, *a*, образцо́вый; приме́рный; exemplify, *v.t*, приводи́ть приме́р *(gen.)*; служи́ть приме́ром *(gen.)*.

exempt, *a*, освобождённый, изъя́тый; ¶ *v.t*, освобожда́ть; изыма́ть; ~ion, *n*, освобожде́ние.

exercise, *n*, упражне́ние; трениро́вка; физи́ческая заря́дка, моцио́н; проявле́ние; ¶ *v.t*, упражня́ть; тренирова́ть; прогу́ливать *(dog etc.)*; испо́льзовать, по́льзоваться *(inst. rights, power)*; проявля́ть *(patience)*; беспоко́ить *(mind)*; *v.i*, упражня́ться; *(mil.)* проводи́ть уче́ние.

exert, *v.t*, напряга́ть *(strength)*; ока́зывать *(pressure)*; ~ *oneself* напряга́ться, де́лать уси́лия; ~ion, *n*, напряже́ние; уси́лие.

exfoliate, *v.i*, распуска́ться; лупи́ться, шелуши́ться; отсла́иваться.

exhalation, *n*, выдыха́ние; испаре́ние; exhale, *v.t*, выдыха́ть; выделя́ть.

exhaust, *n*, вы́хлоп; вы́пуск; ~ *pipe* выхлопна́я труба́; ¶ *v.t*, истоща́ть; изнуря́ть; исче́рпывать; ~ed, *a. & p.p*, истощённый, изнурённый; измученный; ~ion, *n*, истоще́ние; изнеможе́ние; ~ive, *a*, исче́рпывающий.

exhibit, *n*, экспона́т; *(law)* веще́ственное доказа́тельство; ¶ *v.t*, пока́зывать; проявля́ть; выставля́ть, экспони́ровать; ~ion, *n*, вы́ставка; пока́з; проявле́ние; стипе́ндия; ~ioner, *n*, стипендиа́т; ~ionist, *n*, эксгибициони́ст; ~or, *n*, экспоне́нт.

exhilarate, *v.t*, весели́ть; оживля́ть; exhilarating, *a*, оживля́ющий; весёлый; exhilaration, *n*, оживле́ние; увеселе́ние.

exhort, *v.t*, увещева́ть; призыва́ть; ~ation, *n*, увещева́ние; про́поведь.

exhume, *v.t*, выка́пывать.

exigence, -cy, n, крайняя необходимость; exigent, a, срочный; требовательный.

exiguous, a, скудный, малый.

exile, n, изгнание; ссылка; изгнанник; ¶ v.t, изгонять; ссылать.

exist, v.i, существовать; находиться; ~ence, n, существование; наличие; ~ent, ~ing, a, существующий; наличный.

exit, n, выход; (theat.) уход со сцены; (fig.) смерть; ¶ v.i, уходить; ~ visa выездная виза.

exodus, n, массовый отъезд, массовое переселение.

exonerate, v.t, снимать бремя вины с; реабилитировать; exoneration, n, оправдание; реабилитация.

exorbitant, a, непомерный; чрезмерный.

exorcism, n, заклинание/изгнание духов; exorcize, v.t, заклинать/изгонять духов.

exordium, n, вступление, введение.

exotic, a, экзотический; иноземный.

expand, v.t. (& i.), расширять(ся), увеличивать(ся); распускать(ся); растягивать(ся); развивать(ся).

expanse, n, пространство; протяжение; expansion, n, расширение; растяжение; экспансия; (tech.) раскатка.

expansive, a, расширительный, экспансивный, открытый.

expatiate, v.i, распространяться о.

expatriate, v.t, экспатриировать.

expect, v.t, ожидать (gen.); рассчитывать на, надеяться на; полагать; ~ancy, n, ожидание; надежда; предвкушение; вероятность; ~ant, n, ожидающий; выжидательный; ~ mother беременная женщина

expectorate, v.t, отхаркивать, откашливать; expectoration, n, отхаркивание; мокрота.

expediency, n, целесообразность; выгодность; expedient, a, подходящий, целесообразный, соответствующий; ¶ n, средство (для достижения цели); приём; expedite, v.t, ускорять, быстро выполнять; облегчать; отправлять; expedition, n, экспедиция; поспешность; ~ary, a, экспедиционный; expeditious, a, быстрый.

expel, v.t, исключать; выгонять.

expend, v.t, тратить; расходовать; ~iture, n, трата, расход; expense, n, цена; pl, расходы; at his ~ за его счёт; expensive, a, дорогой.

experience, n, (жизненный) опыт; переживание; стаж (работы); мастерство, (по)знания; ¶ v.t, испытывать; переживать.

experiment, n, опыт, эксперимент; ¶ v.i, производить опыты, экспериментировать.

expert, a, опытный, искусный; квалифицированный; ¶ n, знаток, специалист, эксперт.

expiate, v.t, искупать; expiation, n, искупление; expiatory, a, искупительный.

expiration, n, выдыхание, выдох; истечение; expire, v.i, выдыхать; угасать, умирать; истекать, кончаться.

explain, v.t, объяснять; толковать; оправдывать; explanation, n, объяснение; толкование; explanatory, a, объяснительный.

expletive, n, вставное слово; бранное слово.

explicit, a, ясный; определённый; точный; категорический.

explode, v.t, взрывать; подрывать (theory, etc.); v.i, взрываться; (fig.) разражаться (гневом).

exploit, n, подвиг; ¶ v.t, эксплуатировать; разрабатывать (mines); ~ation, n, эксплуатация.

exploration, n, исследование; explore, v.t, исследовать; изучать; (geol.) разведывать; ~r, n, исследователь; путешественник.

explosion, n, взрыв; (fig.) вспышка; explosive, a, взрывчатый; (fig.) вспыльчивый; взрывной (sound); ¶ n, взрывчатое вещество.

exponent, n, представитель; истолкователь; исполнитель (mus.); образец; (maths) показатель степени.

export, n, экспорт, вывоз; предмет вывоза; ¶ v.t, экспортировать, вывозить; ~ation, n, экспортирование, вывоз; ~er, n, экспортёр.

expose, v.t, выставлять; подвергать (to danger, etc.); разоблачать; (phot.) делать выдержку; exposition, n, изложение, толкование; выставка.

expostulate, *v.i*, спо́рить; протесто-ва́ть; ~ *with* увещева́ть; **expostulation**, *n*, увещева́ние.

exposure, *n*, выставле́ние; подверга́ние; разоблаче́ние; *(phot.)* экспози́ция, вы́держка.

expound, *v.t*, излага́ть; разъясня́ть.

express, *n*, сро́чное (почто́вое) отправле́ние; ~ *messenger* курье́р, наро́чный; ~ *train* экспре́сс, курье́рский по́езд; ¶ *a*, определённый, я́сно вы́раженный; сро́чный; курье́рский; ¶ *v.t*, выража́ть; отправля́ть сро́чной по́чтой; ~ *oneself* выража́ться; выска́зываться; ~ion, *n*, выраже́ние; вырази́тельность; ~ive, *a*, вырази́тельный; ~ly, *ad*, наро́чно, специа́льно; то́чно, я́сно.

expropriate, *v.t*, экспроприи́ровать; отчужда́ть; **expropriation**, *n*, экспроприа́ция; отчужде́ние; конфиска́ция.

expulsion, *n*, изгна́ние; исключе́ние (из шко́лы).

expunge, *v.t*, вычёркивать; уничтожа́ть.

expurgate, *v.t*, вычёркивать; очища́ть; **expurgation**, *n*, вычёркивание; очище́ние.

exquisite, *a*, изы́сканный, утончённый; преле́стный; ~ *pain* о́страя боль.

ex-serviceman, *n*, демобилизо́ванный.

extant, *a*, сохрани́вшийся; существу́ющий.

extempore, *a*, неподгото́вленный, импровизи́рованный; ¶ *ad*, без подгото́вки, экспро́мтом; **extemporize**, *v.i*, импровизи́ровать.

extend, *v.t*, выта́гивать, протя́гивать; расширя́ть, продолжа́ть *(road);* удлиня́ть *(period);* выска́зывать *(sympathy);* распространя́ть; *v.i*, простира́ться; тяну́ться; **extension**, *n*, выта́гивание; протяже́ние; расшире́ние; распростране́ние; продле́ние; пристро́йка; *(rly.)* ве́тка; *(telephone)* доба́вочный (но́мер); **extensive**, *a*, простра́нный; обши́рный; **extent**, *n*, протяже́ние, простра́нство; *to what* ~ до како́й сте́пени; наско́лько; *to a certain* ~ до не́которой сте́пени; *to a great* ~ в значи́тельной сте́пени; *to the full* ~ в по́лную ме́ру.

extenuate, *v.t*, ослабля́ть; уменьша́ть; служи́ть извине́нием *(gen.);* *extenuating circumstances* смягча́ющие (вину́) обстоя́тельства; **extenuation**, *n*, изнуре́ние, истоще́ние; ослабле́ние; извине́ние, оправда́ние.

exterior, *a*, вне́шний, нару́жный; ¶ *n*, вне́шность; вне́шний вид; экстерье́р.

exterminate, *v.t*, истребля́ть; искореня́ть; **extermination**, *n*, уничтоже́ние, истребле́ние; искорене́ние.

external, *a*, нару́жный, вне́шний; ~ *trade* вне́шняя торго́вля; ~ly, *ad*, вне́шне; с вне́шней/нару́жной стороны́.

extinct, *a*, поту́хший *(volcano);* вы́мерший; уга́сший; ~ion, *n*, туше́ние; угаса́ние; вымира́ние; прекраще́ние.

extinguish, *v.t*, гаси́ть, туши́ть; *(fig.)* затмева́ть; уничтожа́ть; ~er, *n*, гаси́тель; огнетуши́тель.

extirpate, *v.t*, искореня́ть, вырыва́ть с ко́рнем; истребля́ть **extirpation**, *n*, искорене́ние, истребле́ние.

extol, *v.t*, превозноси́ть.

extort, *v.t*, вымога́ть *(money);* вы́пытывать *(secret);* ~ion, *n*, вымога́тельство; граби́тельство; ~ionate, *a*, вымога́тельский; граби́тельский; ~ioner, *n*, вымога́тель; граби́тель.

extra, *a*, доба́вочный; дополни́тельный; экстренный; сверх-; ~ *charge* допла́та; ¶ *ad*, осо́бо, осо́бенно; дополни́тельно; ¶ *n*, (что-то) дополни́тельное; экстренный вы́пуск *(newspaper);* *(theat.)* стати́ст; припла́та.

extract, *n*, вы́держка *(of book);* *(chem.)* экстра́кт; ¶ *v.t*, удаля́ть *(tooth);* выжима́ть *(juice);* вырыва́ть *(agreement);* *(maths)* извлека́ть; выбира́ть; ~ion, *n*, извлече́ние; добыва́ние; происхожде́ние; экстра́кт.

extradite, *v.t*, выдава́ть; **extradition**, *n*, вы́дача.

extraneous, *a*, чу́ждый; посторо́нний.

extraordinary, *a*, чрезвыча́йный; необы́чный; удиви́тельный.

extravagance, *n*, расточи́тельность; сумасбро́дство; изли́шество; **extravagant**, *a*, расточи́тельный; сумасбро́дный; преувели́ченный.

extreme, *a*, крайний; чрезвычайный; последний; ¶ *n*, крайность; крайняя степень; **~ly**, *ad*, чрезвычайно, крайне; очень; **extremist**, *n*, экстремист; максималист; сторонник крайних мер; **extremity**, *n*, конец, край; крайность; *pl*, конечности.

extricate, *v.t*, выводить (из затруднительного положения); распутывать; **~** *oneself* выпутываться.

extrinsic, *a*, внешний; посторонний; несвойственный.

exuberance, *n*, жизнерадостность; изобилие; богатство; **exuberant**, *a*, жизнерадостный; обильный; пышно растущий; плодовитый.

exude, *v.t*, выделять; *v.i*, выделяться; проступать сквозь поры.

exult, *v.i*, радоваться; ликовать; торжествовать; **~ant**, *n*, ликующий; **~ation**, *a*, ликование; торжество.

eye, *n*, глаз; зрение; взгляд; глазок *(in door)*; ушко *(needle)*; *(bot.)* глазок; **~ball** глазное яблоко; **~brow** бровь; **~-glass** линза; монокль; *pl*, очки; пенсне; **~lash** ресница; **~lid** веко; **~shade** козырёк от солнца; **~sight** зрение; **~sore** (что-то) оскорбительное для глаза *(fig.)*; бельмо на глазу; **~-tooth** глазной зуб; **~-witness** очевидец; свидетель; *one-~d* одноглазый; *keep an* **~** *on* следить за; *see* **~** *to* **~** *with* сходиться во взглядах с; *shut one's* **~s** *to* закрывать глаза на; ¶ *v.t*, рассматривать; наблюдать; **~let**, *n*, ушко, петелька; глазок (для наблюдения).

eyrie, *n*, орлиное гнездо.

F

F, *n*, *(mus.)* фа.

fable, *n*, басня; небылица; фабула.

fabric, *n*, ткань, материя; материал; устройство; структура; сооружение; **~ate**, *v.t*, выдумывать; подделывать; фабриковать; изготовлять; **~ation**, *n*, выдумка; подделка; производство, фабрикация.

fabulist, *n*, баснописец; выдумщик; **fabulous**, *a*, баснословный; легендарный.

face, *n*, лицо; гримаса; внешний вид; лицевая сторона *(cloth)*; фасад; циферблат; наглость; **~ cream** крем для лица; *make* **~s** гримасничать; **~** *value* номинальная стоимость; ¶ *v.t*, быть обращённым к; выходить на/в; смело встречать; сталкиваться с; отделывать *(dress)*; облицовывать; **~** *the facts* смотреть правде в лицо.

facet, *n*, грань, фацет; *(fig.)* аспект.

facetious, *a*, шутливый; игривый.

facial, *a*, лицевой.

facile, *a*, лёгкий; свободный *(pers.)* покладистый; **facilitate**, *v.t*, облегчать; продвигать; содействовать *(dat.)*; **facility**, *n*, лёгкость; способность; плавность (речи); льгота; *pl*, удобства; средства.

facing, *pr*, лицом к; ¶ *n*, облицовка; (лицевая) отделка.

facsimile, *n*, факсимиле.

fact, *n*, факт; обстоятельство; *in* **~** в действительности; *as a matter of* **~** в самом деле; *the* **~** *is that* дело в том, что . . .

faction, *n*, фракция; клика; раздор; **factious**, *a*, фракционный, раскольнический.

factitious, *a*, поддельный, искусственный.

factor, *n*, фактор; момент; особенность; *(com.)* агент; *(maths)* множитель.

factory, *n*, фабрика, завод.

factotum, *n*, фактотум; мастер на все руки.

factual, *a*, фактический, действительный.

faculty, *n*, дар, способность; факультет.

fad, *n*, прихоть, причуда; конёк; мания.

fade, *v.t*, обесцвечивать; *v.i*, вянуть, увядать; линять; выгорать; стираться *(colours)*; замирать *(sound)*; постепенно исчезать; **~d**, *a. & p.p*, увядший; поблёклый; **fading**, *n*, затухание *(radio)*.

fag, *n*, тяжёлая работа; младший ученик; папироса, сигаретка; **~** *end* окурок; ¶ *v.i*, трудиться; *be* **~ged** *out* утомляться; **~** *for* оказывать услуги *(dat.)*.

faggot, *n*, вязанка/охапка хвороста.

fail, *v.t*, обманывать ожидания *(gen.)*, подводить; изменять *(dat.);* покида́ть; прова́ливать *(of exam); I will never ~ you* я никогда́ вас не подведу́; *v.i,* прова́ливаться *(in exam);* недо-става́ть; не удава́ться; банкро́титься; ослабева́ть; *don't ~ to* не забу́дьте; *without ~* непреме́нно; обяза́тельно; во что бы то ни ста́ло; **~ing,** *n,* недоста́ток; сла́бость; ¶ *a,* хи́лый; ¶ *pr,* за неиме́нием; в слу́чае отсу́тствия; **~ure,** *n,* неуда́ча; неуда́чник.

fain, *a,* гото́вый; ¶ *ad,* охо́тно; с ра́достью.

faint, *a,* сла́бый, вя́лый; ту́склый; бле́дный; ¶ *n,* о́бморок; поте́ря созна́ния; ¶ *v.i,* па́дать в о́бморок; **~-hearted** ро́бкий; малоду́шный; **~ness,** *n,* сла́бость; дурнота́; ту́склость, бле́дность.

fair, *a,* краси́вый; че́стный, справедли́вый; све́тлый; белоку́рый; поря́дочный; *~ amount* изря́дное коли́чество; *~ complexion* бе́лый цвет лица́; *~ copy* чистови́к; **~-haired person** блонди́н, -ка; *by ~ means* че́стным путём; *~ to middling* нева́жный; так себе́; *~ wind* попу́тный ве́тер; *~ play* че́стная игра́; че́стный посту́пок; *play ~* игра́ть по пра́вилам; игра́ть че́стно; *it's not ~* это несправедли́во; ¶ *n,* я́рмарка; благотвори́тельный база́р; **~ly,** *ad,* справедли́во; дово́льно; *~ well* непло́хо.

fairy, *n,* фе́я; волше́бница; ¶ *a,* волше́бный; ска́зочный; *~ tale* ска́зка.

faith, *n,* ве́ра; дове́рие; рели́гия; *in good ~* добросо́вестно; **~ful,** *a,* ве́рный, пре́данный; то́чный; ¶ *n: the ~* ве́рующие; **~fully,** *ad,* ве́рно; че́стно; то́чно; *yours ~* с почте́нием, с и́скренним уваже́нием; **~fulness,** *n,* ве́рность, пре́данность; **~less,** *a,* неве́рующий; вероло́мный; **~lessness,** *n,* безве́рие; вероло́мство.

fake, *n,* подде́лка; фальши́вка; обма́нщик; ¶ *v.t,* подде́лывать, фабрикова́ть.

fakir, *n,* факи́р.

falcon, *n,* со́кол; **~er,** *n,* соколи́ный охо́тник, соко́льничий; **~ry,** *n,* соколи́ная охо́та.

fall, *n,* паде́ние; сниже́ние; о́сень; водопа́д; склон; *a heavy ~ of*

rain ли́вень; ¶ *v.i,* па́дать; опуска́ться; понижа́ться; обва́ливаться; наступа́ть *(night);* стиха́ть *(wind);* его́ день рожде́ния прихо́дится на...; *~ asleep* засыпа́ть; *~ back* отступа́ть; *~ back on* прибега́ть к; *~ behind* отстава́ть; *~ down* па́дать; *~ due* подлежа́ть упла́те; *~ in* впада́ть в; прова́ливаться; *(mil.)* стро́иться; *~ in with* ста́лкиваться с; соглаша́ться с; *~ in love with* влюбля́ться в; *~ off* отпада́ть; уменьша́ться; *~ out* ссо́риться; выпада́ть; *~ sick* заболева́ть; *~ through (fig.)* прова́ливаться; терпе́ть неуда́чу.

fallacious, *a,* оши́бочный; ло́жный; **fallacy,** *n,* заблужде́ние; оши́бка; ло́жное заключе́ние.

fallen, *p.p. & a,* па́дший; (о)па́вший.

fallibility, *n,* оши́бочность; погре́шность; **fallible,** *a,* подве́рженный оши́бкам.

falling, *a,* па́дающий; понижа́ющийся; *~ star* па́дающая звезда́.

fall-out, *n,* радиоакти́вные выпаде́ния.

fallow, *a, (agr.)* вспа́ханный под пар; *(fig.)* неразвито́й; коричнева́то-жёлтый; *~ deer, n,* лань.

false, *a,* ло́жный, оши́бочный; фальши́вый; лжи́вый; подде́льный; иску́сственный; **~-bottomed** с двойны́м дном; **~hood,** *n,* ложь, непра́вда; фальшь; **~ness,** *n,* оши́бочность; фальши́вость; лжи́вость; **~tto,** *n,* фальце́т; **falsify,** *v.t,* фальсифици́ровать, подде́лывать; искажа́ть; обма́нывать.

falter, *v.i,* шата́ться; запина́ться *(in speech);* дрожа́ть; колеба́ться; **~ing,** *a,* нереши́тельный; запина́ющийся; *~ voice* дрожа́щий го́лос.

fame, *n,* сла́ва; репута́ция; **~d,** *a,* изве́стный, знамени́тый.

familiar, *a,* знако́мый; бли́зкий; фамилья́рный; ¶ *n,* бли́зкий друг; бес; **~ity,** *n,* дру́жественные отноше́ния; бли́зость; фамилья́рность; осведомлённость; **~ize,** *v.t,* ознакомля́ть.

family, *n,* семья́, семе́йство; род; содру́жество; ¶ *a,* семе́йный; фами́льный; *~ tan* семе́йный

человéк, домосéд; ~ *tree* родослóвное дéрево.
famine, *n,* гóлод; недостáток.
famish, *v.t,* морить гóлодом; *be* ~*ing* голодáть; быть голóдным; ~*ed, p.p,* изголодáвшийся.
famous, *a,* знаменйтый, извéстный; замечáтельный.
fan, *n,* вéер; вентиля́тор; *(agr.)* вéялка; энтузиáст, поклóнник; болéльщик; ~ *light* веерообрáзное окнó; ~ *mail* письма почитáтелей; ~ *shaped* веерообрáзный; ¶ *v.t,* вéять; обмáхивать; обвевáть; раздувáть *(fire);* ~ *the flame (fig.)* разжигáть стрáсти; ~ *oneself* обмáхиваться вéером.
fanatic, *n,* фанáтик; ~*al, a,* фанатйческий.
fancied, *p.p. & a,* воображáемый; **fancier,** *n,* знатóк; любйтель; **fanciful,** *a,* причýдливый; фантастйческий; капрйзный; **fancy,** *a,* орнаментáльный; разукрáшенный; мóдный; ~ *urticles* мóдные товáры; галантерéя; безделýшки; ~ *dress* маскарáдный костю́м; ~ *dress ball* маскарáд, костюмирóванный бал; ~ *work* вышйвка; ¶ *n,* воображéние, фантáзия; прйхоть, причýда; каприз; конёк; склóнность; *take a* ~ *to* увлекáться *(inst.);* привя́зываться к; ¶ *v.t,* представля́ть себé; полагáть; хотéть.
fanfare, *n,* фанфáра.
fang, *n,* клык; ядовйтый зуб; кóрень зýба.
fantasia, *n,* фантáзия; **fantastic,** *a,* фантастйческий; причýдливый; **fantasy,** *n,* воображéние, фантáзия; иллю́зия.
far, *a,* дáльний, далёкий, отдалённый; ¶*ad,*далекó; на большóм расстоя́нии; *as* ~ *as I know* насколько мне извéстно; *by* ~ намнóго; ~ *and away* несравнéнно, горáздо; ~ *and wide* повсю́ду; ~ *better* горáздо лýчше; ~*-fetched* «с натя́жкой», натя́нутый, неестéственный; ~ *from* далекó от; ~ *from it* отню́дь нет; ~ *off (a)* дáльний, далёкий; *(ad)* далекó; ~*-reaching* имéющий большйе послéдствия; ~*-seeing* дальновйдный; *so* ~ до сих пор; *in so* ~ *as* поскóльку; *go too* ~ заходйть

слйшком далекó; ~ *East* Дáльний Востóк.
farce, *n,* фарс; шýтка; **farcical,** *a,* фáрсовый; смехотвóрный.
fare, *n,* плáта за проéзд; пассажйр; пйща, стол; *bill of* ~ меню́.
farewell, *n,* прощáние; *say* ~ прощáться; ¶ *int,* до свидáния!; дóбрый путь!; ¶ *a,* прощáльный.
farinaceous, *a,* мучнйстый, мучнóй.
farm, *n,* фéрма; хýтор, хозя́йство; питóмник; ~*hand* сельскохозя́йственный рабóчий; батрáк; ~*house* дом на фéрме; ~*yard* двор фéрмы; ¶ *v.t,* обрабáтывать зéмлю; быть фéрмером; ~ *out* выдавáть; сдавáть в арéнду; ~*er, n,* фéрмер; ~*ing, n,* заня́тие сéльским хозя́йством; фéрмерство.
farrago, *n,* смесь; вся́кая вся́чина.
farrier, *n,* кузнéц; ~*y, n,* кýзница.
farrow, *n,* опорóс; поросёнок.
farther, *a,* бóлее отдалённый; дальнéйший; дополнйтельный; *until* ~ *notice* впредь до нóвого уведомлéния; ¶ *ad,* дáльше; тáкже; **farthest,** *a,* сáмый дáльний; ¶ *ad,* дáльше всегó.
farthing, *n,* фáртинг.
fascinate, *v.t,* очарóвывать; **fascinating,** *a,* очаровáтельный; интерéснейший; **fascination,** *n,* очаровáние.
fascism, *n.* фашйзм; **fascist,** *a,* фашйстский; ¶ *n,* фашйст.
fashion, *n,* мóда; стиль, фасóн; манéра; *be in* ~ быть в мóде; *out of* ~ старомóдный; ¶ *v.t,* придавáть фóрму *(dat); (tech.)* формовáть; лепйть; ~*able, n,* мóдный; свéтский.
fast, *a,* быстрый, скóрый; прóчный *(colour);* беспýтный, фривóльный; крéпкий; *be* ~ спешйть; ~ *and loose* непостоя́нный; измéнчивый; *make* ~ закрепля́ть; прикрепля́ть; запирáть; ¶ *ad,* крéпко; прóчно; *be* ~ *asleep* крéпко спáть; ¶ *v.t,* постйться; ¶ *n,* пост; *break one's* ~ разговля́ться.
fasten, *v.t,* прикрепля́ть; привя́зывать; зажимáть; запирáть; застёгивать; ~*er, n,* запóр; задвйжка; застёжка *(dress);* зажйм.
fastidious, *a,* придйрчивый; разбóрчивый.

fastness, *n*, прочность; стойкость; быстрота; твердыня; оплот.

fat, *a*, жирный, сальный *(food)*; толстый; обильный; ¶ *n*, жир; сало.

fatal, *a*, роковой; фатальный; смертельный; пагубный; ~ism, *n*, фатализм; ~ist, *n*, фаталист; ~ity, *n*, фатальность; несчастный случай; смерть.

fate, *n*, судьба, рок; жребий; the Fates Парка; ~d, *a*, обречённый; предопределённый; ~ful, *a*, роковой; важный.

father, *n*, отец; родоначальник; ~-in-law свёкор *(of wife)*; тесть *(of husband)*; ¶ *v.t*, быть отцом *(gen.)*; порождать; производить; быть автором *(gen.)*; отечески заботиться о; усыновлять; ~ *upon* возлагать ответственность на; ~hood, *n*, отцовство; ~land, *n*, отечество; ~less, *a*, оставшийся без отца; ~ly, *a*, отеческий.

fathom, *n*, морская сажень; ¶ *v.t*, измерять глубину *(gen.)*; *(fig.)* постигать, проникать в суть.

fatigue, *n*, усталость, утомление; ~ *duty (mil.)* внестроевой наряд; ~ *party (mil.)* команда солдат, назначенных в наряд; ¶ *v.t*, утомлять, изнурять.

fatness, *n*, упитанность; тучность; fatten, *v.t*, откармливать (на убой); *v.i*, жиреть, толстеть; ~ing, *n*, откармливание; fatty, *a*, жирный; тучный; жировой; ¶ *n*, толстяк.

fatuity, *n*, тупоумие; бессмысленность; fatuous, *a*, глупый; пустой; бесполезный.

fault, *n*, недостаток; ошибка; проступок; вина; *(geol.)* разрыв, сдвиг; *(elec.)* замыкание; *(tech.)* дефект, неисправность; повреждение; *be at* ~ быть виновным; ~-finder придира; ~iness, *n*, ошибочность; испорченность; ~less, *a*, безупречный; безошибочный; ~y, *a*, испорченный; повреждённый.

faun, *n*, фавн.

fauna, *n*, фауна.

favour, *n*, благосклонность; одобрение; одолжение; пристрастие; покровительство; *(com.)* письмо; *in* ~ *of* в пользу; *be in* ~ *of* стоять за; *out of* ~ в немилости;

¶ *v.t*, быть благосклонным к; покровительствовать *(dat.)*; предпочитать; ~able, *a*, благоприятный; подходящий; благосклонный; ~ite, *a*, любимый, излюбленный; ¶ *n*, любимец, фаворит; ~itism, *n*, фаворитизм.

fawn, *a*, желговато-коричневый; ¶ *n*, молодой олень; ~ *upon* подлизываться к; ~ing, *a*, раболепный; ¶ *n*, раболепие.

fealty, *n*, верность.

fear, *n*, страх; боязнь; опасение; *for* ~ *of* из боязни *(gen.)*; ¶ *v.t*, бояться/опасаться *(gen.)*; ~ful, *a*, страшный; испуганный; ~less, *a*, бесстрашный, неустрашимый; ~some, *a*, грозный; страшный.

feasibility, *n*, возможность, выполнимость, осуществимость; feasible *a*, возможный, выполнимый, осуществимый.

feast, *n*, банкет, пир; праздник; ¶ *v.t*, угощать; принимать; праздновать; ~ *one's eyes on* любоваться *(inst.)*; *v.i*, пировать; *(fig.)* наслаждаться.

feat, *n*, подвиг; достижение.

feather, *n*, перо; *(tech.)* выступ; шпонка; *birds of a* ~ птицы одного полёта; одного поля ягода; ~-bed перина; ~-brained ветреный; ~ *stitch* шов «в ёлочку»; ~weight полулёгкий вес, «вес пера»; ¶ *v.t*, покрывать перьями; устанавливать во флюгерное положение *(avia.)*; ~ *one's nest* нагревать руки; набивать карман; ~y, *a*, похожий на перо; пушистый, лёгкий как пёрышко.

feature, *n*, особенность; свойство; черта; ~ *film* художественный фильм; ¶ *v.t*, изображать; показывать; *v.i*, участвовать; featuring с участием *(gen.)* *(in film)*.

febrile, *a*, лихорадочный.

February, *n*, февраль; ¶ *a*, февральский.

fecund, *a*, плодородный; плодовитый; ~ate, *v.t*, оплодотворять; ~ity, *n*, плодородность; плодовитость.

federal, *a*, федеральный; союзный; ~ist, *n*, федералист; federate, *v.t.* *(& i.)*, объединять(ся) на федеративных началах; federation, *n*, федерация.

fee, *n*, гонора́р, вознагражде́ние; чле́нский взнос; пла́та (за уче́ние).

feeble, *a*, сла́бый; хи́лый; ~-*minded*, слабоу́мный; ~*ness*, *n*, сла́бость.

feed, *n*, пита́ние, кормле́ние; пи́ща; корм; *(tech.)* пода́ча материа́ла; ~ *pump* пита́тельный насо́с; ¶ *v.t*, пита́ть; корми́ть; пасти́; снабжа́ть; подава́ть; *v.i*, пита́ться; пасти́сь, корми́ться; *I am fed up* мне надое́ло; ~*er*, *n*, едо́к; де́тский нагру́дник; *(tech.)* пита́тель; **feeding**, *n*, пита́ние; кормле́ние; ~ *bottle* де́тский рожо́к.

feel, *n*, чутьё; ощуще́ние; ¶ *v.t*, чу́вствовать; испы́тывать; ощуща́ть, щу́пать; полага́ть; предчу́вствовать; *v.i*, чу́вствовать себя́; *I* ~ *cold* мне хо́лодно; ~ *for* нащу́пывать; сочу́вствовать *(dat.)*; ~*er*, *n*, щу́пальце, у́сик; *(fig.)* про́ба; ~*ing*, *n*, чу́вство; ощуще́ние; эмо́ция; настрое́ние; впечатле́ние; отноше́ние; сочу́вствие; ¶ *a*, чувстви́тельный; прочу́вствованный.

feign, *v.t*, выду́мывать; *v.i*, притворя́ться.

feint, *n*, притво́рство; манёвр, ло́жный вы́пад; ¶ *v.i*, де́лать ло́жный вы́пад/манёвр.

felicitation, *n*, поздравле́ние; **felicitous**, *a*, уда́чный; счастли́вый; **felicity**, *n*, сча́стье; ме́ткость; уме́ние.

feline, *a*, коша́чий.

fell, *a*, беспоща́дный; ¶ *n*, шку́ра; гора́; ¶ *v.t*, руби́ть; сбива́ть с ног.

felloe, *n*, о́бод.

fellow, *n*, това́рищ; па́рень; па́рная вещь; член о́бщества/колле́джа; ~-*citizen* согражда́нин; ~-*countryman* соoте́чественник; ~ *feeling* сочу́вствие; ~-*student* това́рищ по университе́ту; ~-*traveller* попу́тчик; *nice* ~ сла́вный ма́лый; ~*ship*, *n*, това́рищество; бра́тство; корпора́ция; зва́ние чле́на (колле́джа/о́бщества); стипе́ндия.

felon, *n*, уголо́вный престу́пник; ~*ious*, *a*, престу́пный; ~*y*, *n*, уголо́вное преступле́ние.

felt, *n*, во́йлок, фетр.

female, *a*, же́нский; ¶ *n*, же́нщина; *(zool.)* са́мка; **feminine**, *a*, же́нский; же́нственный; **feminist**, *n*, фемини́ст.

femur, *n*, бедро́.

fen, *n*, боло́то; боло́тистая ме́стность

fence, *n*, забо́р, и́згородь; огражде́ние; *(tech.)* предохрани́тель; ¶ *v.t*, загора́живать, огора́живать; *v.i*, фехтова́ть; пари́ровать; ~*r*, *n*, фехтова́льщик; **fencing**, *n*, фехтова́ние; и́згородь; огора́живание.

fend [**off**], *v.t*, отража́ть; пари́ровать; ~ *for oneself* перебива́ться; забо́титься о себе́.

fender, *n*, решётка; щит; крыло́ *(car)*.

fennel, *n*, укро́п.

ferment, *n*, броже́ние; заква́ска; ¶ *v.t*, вызыва́ть броже́ние в; *(fig.)* возбужда́ть; *v.i*, броди́ть; *(fig.)* возбужда́ться; ~*ation*, *n*, броже́ние.

fern, *n*, па́поротник.

ferocious, *a*, ди́кий; свире́пый; лю́тый; **ferocity**, *n*, ди́кость; свире́пость; лю́тость.

ferret, *n*, хорёк; ¶ *v.t*: ~ *out* выгоня́ть из норы́; выню́хивать; разы́скивать; *v.i*: ~ *about* ры́ться; разню́хивать.

ferrous, *a*, желе́зистый, ferruginous, *a*, ржа́вый; желе́зистый.

ferrule, *n*, о́бруч; наконе́чник.

ferry, *n*, паро́м; ~ *charge* пла́та за перепра́ву; ~*man* перево́зчик, паро́мщик; ¶ *v.t*, перевози́ть; *v.i*, переезжа́ть.

fertile, *a*, плодоро́дный, изоби́льный; **fertility**, *n*, плодоро́дие; **fertilize**, *v.t*, удобря́ть; *(biol.)* оплодотворя́ть; **fertilizer**, *n*, удобре́ние.

fervency, *n*, горя́чность; рве́ние; **fervent**, *a*, горя́чий; пы́лкий; **fervour**, *n*, жар, пыл; усе́рдие.

festal, *a*, пра́здничный; весёлый.

fester, *v.i*, гнои́ться; *(fig.)* му́чить *(of envy, etc.)*.

festival, *n*, пра́зднество; фестива́ль; **festive**, *a*, пра́здничный; весёлый; **festivity**, *n*, весе́лье; *pl*, пра́зднества, торжества́.

festoon, *n*, гирля́нда; фесто́н; ¶ *v.t*, украша́ть гирля́ндами.

fetch, *v.t*, приноси́ть; сходи́ть *(pf.)* за; выруча́ть *(price)*.

fête, n, пра́зднество, пра́здник; ¶ v.t, пра́здновать; че́ствовать.

fetid, a, злово́нный.

fetish, n, фети́ш, амуле́т; *(fig.)* куми́р.

fetlock, n, щётка.

fetter, v.t, зако́вывать; спу́тывать *(horse); (fig.)* свя́зывать по рука́м и нога́м; ~s, n, кандалы́, око́вы; *(fig.)* пу́ты, у́зы.

fettle, n, состоя́ние.

feud, n, (кро́вная) вражда́; междоусо́бица; феода́льное поме́стье.

feudal, a, феода́льный; ~ism, n, феодали́зм.

fever, n, жар, лихора́дка; ~ish, a, лихора́дочный; возбуждённый.

few, a, pr, немно́гие; ма́ло; a ~ немно́го; не́сколько; ~ and far between ре́дкие; ~er, a, ме́ньше.

fez, n, фе́ска.

fiancé, n, жени́х; **fiancée,** n, неве́ста.

fiasco, n, прова́л, фиа́ско.

fiat, n, декре́т, ука́з.

fib, n, вы́думка; ¶ v.i, выду́мывать, врать; **fibber,** n, выду́мщик, враль.

fibre, n, фи́бра; нить; волокно́; *(fig.)* хара́ктер; **fibrous,** a, фибро́зный; волокни́стый.

fickle, a, непостоя́нный; ~ness, n, непостоя́нство.

fiction, n, вы́думка; беллетри́стика; **fictitious,** a, вы́мышленный; фикти́вный; взя́тый из беллетри́стики.

fiddle, n, скри́пка; *(coll.)* проде́лка; ¶ v.i, игра́ть на скри́пке; ~ with игра́ть с; ~r, n, скрипа́ч; ~stick, n, смычо́к; ~sl вздор!; **fiddling,** a, пусто́й; пустяко́вый.

fidelity, n, ве́рность, пре́данность; то́чность.

fidget, n, егоза́, непосе́да; ¶ v.i, ёрзать; волнова́ться; ~ with не́рвно игра́ть с; не́рвно перебира́ть; ~y, a, непосе́дливый, беспоко́йный.

fief, n, феода́льное поме́стье.

field, n, по́ле; о́бласть, сфе́ра; по́прище; спорти́вная площа́дка; *(geol.)* месторожде́ние; ¶ a, полево́й; ~ artillery лёгкая артилле́рия; ~ day *(fig.)* знамена́тельный день; ~ glasses (полево́й) бино́кль; ~ hospital полево́й го́спиталь; ~ marshal фельдма́ршал; ~ mouse полева́я мышь.

fiend, n, дья́вол, де́мон; и́зверг; ~ish, a, дья́вольский.

fife, n, ду́дка, фле́йта.

fifteen, num, пятна́дцать; ~th, ord. num, пятна́дцатый; **fifth,** ord. num, пя́тый; ¶ n, пя́тая часть; *(mus.)* кви́нта.

fiftieth, ord. num, пятидеся́тый; ¶ n, пятидеся́тая часть; **fifty,** num, пятьдеся́т; ~ ~ fifty пополáм, по́ровну.

fig, n, инжи́р, фи́га, смо́ква; фи́говое де́рево, смоко́вница; ~ leaf фи́говый лист; I don't care a ~ мне наплева́ть.

fight, n, бой; дра́ка; *(fig.)* борьба́, спор; задо́р; ¶ v.t, дра́ться/сража́ться/боро́ться с; ~ a duel дра́ться на дуэ́ли; ~ a case отста́ивать де́ло; ~ shy of избега́ть *(gen.)*; ~ a way through пробира́ться; прокла́дывать себе́ доро́гу; ~er, n, бое́ц; *(avia.)* истреби́тель; ~ pilot лётчик-истреби́тель; ~ing, a, боево́й; ¶ n, сраже́ние, бой; дра́ка.

figment, n, вы́мысел, фи́кция; плод воображе́ния.

figurative, a, фигура́льный, перено́сный; изобрази́тельный; in the ~ sense в перено́сном смы́сле.

figure, n, фигу́ра; о́браз; ли́чность; чертёж; *(maths)* ци́фра; цена́; ~ of speech риторическая фигу́ра; ¶ v.t, изобража́ть; воображáть; v.i, фигури́ровать; игра́ть ви́дную роль; ~ out вычисля́ть; разга́дывать; ~ up подсчи́тывать; ~d, a, фигу́рный; узо́рчатый; ~head, n, носово́е украше́ние; *(fig.)* номина́льный нача́льник.

filament, n, нить; волокно́, воло́сок.

filch, v.t, красть; ворова́ть.

file, n, напи́льник; пи́лочка *(manicure)*; регистра́тор *(for papers)*; па́пка; подши́вка *(of newspapers)*; картоте́ка; де́ло; ряд, шере́нга; ¶ v.t, пили́ть, подпи́ливать; *(fig.)* шлифова́ть; подшива́ть; регистри́ровать *(papers)*; v.i, идти́ гусько́м/ шере́нгой.

filial, a, сыно́вний, доче́рний.

filibuster, n, филибусте́р; обструкциони́ст.

filigree, n, филигра́нь.

filing, n, пи́лка; регистра́ция, хране́ние *(of documents)*; подши́вка бума́г к де́лу; *pl*, опи́лки, стру́жки; ~ *cabinet* шкаф для хране́ния докуме́нтов.

fill, *n*, доста́точное коли́чество; *eat one's* ~ наеда́ться до́сыта; ¶ *v.t*, наполня́ть; заполня́ть *(gap)*; пломбирова́ть *(tooth)*; занима́ть *(post)*; удовлетворя́ть; *v.i*, наполня́ться, ~ *in* заполня́ть *(form)*; ~ *in one's name* впи́сывать своё и́мя.

fillet, *n*, филе́; повя́зка; ¶ *v.t*, приготовля́ть филе́ из.

filling, *n*, наполне́ние; погру́зка; пло́мба *(dental)*; фарш, начи́нка.

fillip, *n*, щелчо́к; толчо́к, сти́мул.

filly, *n*, молода́я кобы́ла.

film, *n*, фильм; (фото)плёнка; обо́лочка; перепо́нка; ды́мка; ~ *camera* кинока́мера; ~ *star* кинозвезда́; ~ *test* кинопро́ба; ¶ *v.t*, производи́ть киносъёмку *(gen.)*; экранизи́ровать; покрыва́ть оболо́чкой/плёнкой; ~у, *a*, покры́тый плёнкой; тума́нный.

filter, *n*, фильтр; цеди́лка; ¶ *v.t*, фильтрова́ть, проце́живать; *v.i*, проса́чиваться; проника́ть.

filth, *n*, грязь; *(fig.)* непристо́йность; ~у, *a*, гря́зный; ме́рзкий; непристо́йный.

fin, *n*, плавни́к; *(avia.)* киль.

final, *a*, коне́чный, фина́льный; после́дний; оконча́тельный; ¶ *(sport)* фина́л; ~е, *n*, фина́л; заключе́ние; ~ity, *n*, оконча́тельность; ~ly, *ad*, в конце́ концо́в; оконча́тельно.

finance, *n*, фина́нсы; дохо́ды; фина́нсовые опера́ции; ¶ *v.t*, финанси́ровать.

finch, *n*, зя́блик.

find, *n*, нахо́дка; ¶ *v.t*, находи́ть, обнару́живать; снабжа́ть; *(law)* устана́вливать; ~ *out* узнава́ть; ~er, *n*, *(tech.)* иска́тель, определи́тель; ~ing, *n*, нахожде́ние; обнару́жение; *(law)* реше́ние, пригово́р.

fine, *a*, превосхо́дный; то́нкий, изя́щный; я́сный; о́стрый; высокопро́бный; ме́лкий; ~ *arts* изобрази́тельные иску́сства, изя́щные иску́сства; *that's* ~! прекра́сно!; ¶ *n*, штраф; ¶ *v.t*, штрафова́ть; ~ness, *n*, то́нкость; изя́щество; высокопро́бность; мелкозерни́стость; ~ry, *n*, (пы́шный) наря́д.

finesse, *n*, иску́сность; хи́трость.

finger, *n*, па́лец; ~ *board* клавиату́ра; ~ *print (n)* отпеча́ток па́льца; *(v.t.)* снима́ть отпеча́тки па́льцев у; ~ *stall* напа́лок; *index* ~ указа́тельный па́лец; *little* ~ мизи́нец; *have a* ~ *in the pie* быть заме́шанным в де́ле; *have at one's* ~ *tips* знать как свои́ пять па́льцев; ¶ *v.t*, тро́гать; перебира́ть па́льцами; ~ing, *n*, апплика-ту́ра.

finical, finicky, *a*, приди́рчивый, разбо́рчивый.

finish, *n*, коне́ц, оконча́ние; *(sport)* фи́ниш; отде́лка; ¶ *v.t*, конча́ть, ока́нчивать; заверша́ть; доеда́ть; ~ *off* отде́лывать; прика́нчивать; *v.i*, конча́ться; ~ing touch после́дний штрих.

finite, *a*, ограни́ченный; *(gram.)* ли́чный.

Finn, *n*, финн, фи́нка; ~ish, *a*, фи́нский; ¶ *n*, фи́нский язы́к.

fir, *n*, пи́хта; ель; ~ *cone* ело́вая ши́шка.

fire, *n*, ого́нь; пожа́р; пыл; ~ *alarm* пожа́рная трево́га; ~*arm* огнестре́льное ору́жие; ~*brand* головня́; *(fig.)* подстрека́тель; ~ *brigade* пожа́рная кома́нда; ~*damp* руди́чный газ; ~ *eater* пожира́тель огня́; *(fig.)* смутья́н; ~ *engine* пожа́рная маши́на; ~ *escape* пожа́рная ле́стница; ~ *extinguisher* огнетуши́тель; ~*fly* светля́к; ~*guard* ками́нная решётка; ~*lighter* расто́пка; ~*place* ками́н; оча́г; ~*proof* огнеупо́рный; ~*side* ме́сто о́коло ками́на; *(fig.)* дома́шний оча́г; ~*wood* дрова́; ~*works* фейерве́рк; *be on* ~ горе́ть; *make a* ~ разводи́ть ого́нь; топи́ть ками́н/печь; *set* ~ *to* поджига́ть; ¶ *v.t*, зажига́ть; обжига́ть *(bricks)*; увольня́ть; воодушевля́ть *(inspire, etc.)*; стреля́ть из; *v.i*, стреля́ть; загора́ться; ~*ing*, *n*, стрельба́; о́бжиг; *execution by* ~*-squad* расстре́л.

firkin, *n*, бочо́нок.

firm, *a*, твёрдый, кре́пкий; непоколеби́мый; насто́йчивый; ¶ *n*, фи́рма.

firmament, *n*, небе́сный свод.

firmness, *n*, твёрдость; усто́йчивость; непоколеби́мость; реши́тельность.

first, *a*, пе́рвый; ра́нний; выдаю́-
щийся; ~ *aid* ско́рая по́мощь;
~*born* пе́рвенец; ~ *floor* второ́й
эта́ж; ~ *hand* из пе́рвых рук; ~
night премье́ра; ~*-rate* перво-
кла́ссный; ¶ *ad*, сперва́, снача́ла;
впервы́е; ~ *of all* пре́жде всего́;
~ *and foremost* в пе́рвую о́чередь;
the ~ *of January* пе́рвое января́;
~ly, *ad*, во-пе́рвых.

firth, *n*, зали́в; у́стье реки́.

fiscal, *a*, фиска́льный; фина́нсо-
вый.

fish, *n*, ры́ба; ¶ *a*, ры́бный; ~*hook*
рыболо́вный крючо́к; ~*monger*
торго́вец ры́бой; ~ *pond* ры́бный
пруд; ~*wife* торго́вка ры́бой; ¶
v.i, лови́ть/уди́ть ры́бу; ~ *out*
выста́скивать; ~*erman*, *n*, ры-
ба́к; рыболо́в; ~*ing*, *n*, ры́бная
ло́вля; ~ *line* ле́ска; ~ *net* рыбо-
ло́вная сеть; ~ *rod* уди́лище,
у́дочка; ~ *tackle* рыболо́вная
снасть; ~*y*, *a*, ры́бный; ры́бий;
(fig.) подозри́тельный; *there's
something* ~ здесь что́-то ни то.

fission, *n*, расщепле́ние *(also phys.)*;
деле́ние кле́ток *(biol.)*.

fissure, *n*, тре́щина; изло́м; ¶ *v.i*,
тре́снуть *(pf.)*.

fist, *n*, кула́к; ~*icuffs*, *n.pl*, кула́ч-
ный бой.

fistula, *n*, фистула́, свищ.

fit, *a*, го́дный, подходя́щий; гото́-
вый; досто́йный; здоро́вый; в хоро́-
шей фо́рме *(of sportsman)*; ~ *to
drink* го́дный для питья́; ¶ *n*,
припа́док, при́ступ; *(tech.)* при-
го́нка; *by* ~*s and starts* поры́вами,
уры́вками; *fainting* ~ о́бморок;
~ *of coughing* при́ступ ка́шля; *be
a good* ~ хорошо́ сиде́ть; ¶ *v.t*,
прила́живать, приспоса́бливать;
устана́вливать; монти́ровать; *v.i*,
быть впо́ру; соотве́тствовать; го-
ди́ться; ~ *in* приспоса́бливать-
(ся); приноравливать(ся); под-
ходи́ть; ~ *out* снаряжа́ть, снаб-
жа́ть; обору́довать; ~**ful**, *a*, пре-
ры́вистый; непостоя́нный; ~**ness**,
n, (при)го́дность; соотве́тствие;
хоро́шая фо́рма *(sportsman)*; ~
ter, *n*, меха́ник; монтёр; монта́ж-
ник; ~**ting**, *a*, подходя́щий, го́д-
ный; досто́йный; надлежа́щий; ¶
n, приме́рка; прила́живание;
сбо́рка, монта́ж; *pl*, принадле́ж-
ности; ~*-room* приме́рочная.

five, *num*, пять; ¶ *n*, пятёрка.

fix, *n*, диле́мма; затрудни́тельное
положе́ние; ¶ *v.t*, закрепля́ть,
прикрепля́ть; устана́вливать; на-
знача́ть *(price, time)*; устра́ивать;
остана́вливать *(attention)*; *(phot.)*
фикси́ровать; чини́ть; ~ *upon*
выбира́ть; остана́вливаться на;
~**ed**, *p.p. & a*, неподви́жный; неиз-
ме́нный; постоя́нный; устано́влен-
ный; ~**ture**, *n*, армату́ра; (что-то)
неподви́жное; дви́жимость, про-
дава́емая вме́сте с до́мом; назна́-
ченная встре́ча.

fizz[le], *n*, шипе́ние; ¶ *v.i*, шипе́ть;
~ *out* конча́ться неуда́чей.

flabbergast, *v.t*, поража́ть, ошелом-
ля́ть; ~**ed**, *a*, поражённый, ошеломлённый.

flabbiness, *n*, вя́лость; мягкоте́лость;
(fig.) сла́бость; **flabby**, *a*, вя́лый;
мягкоте́лый; сла́бый.

flaccid, *a*, вя́лый, сла́бый; нереши́-
тельный.

flag, *n*, флаг, зна́мя; ~ *ship* фла́г-
манский кора́бль; ~*staff* флаг-
што́к; ~*stone* плита́ (для моще́ния);
lower the ~ сдава́ться; ¶ *v.i*,
сигнализи́ровать фла́гом; ослабе-
ва́ть; повиснуть *(pf.)*.

flagellate, *v.t*, бичева́ть, поро́ть·
flagellation, *n*, бичева́ние.

flagon, *n*, графи́н.

flagrant, *a*, сканда́льный, вопию́-
щий.

flail, *n*, цеп.

flair, *n*, чутьё; уме́лость.

flake, *n*, слой; чешу́йка; снежи́нка;
pl, хло́пья; ¶ *v.i*, рассла́иваться;
flaky, *a*, сло́истый; чешу́йчатый;
хлопьеви́дный.

flamboyant, *a*, я́ркий.

flame, *n*, пла́мя; страсть; предме́т
любви́; ~ *thrower* огнемёт; ¶ *v.i'*,
пламене́ть, пыла́ть; **flaming**, *a*
пламене́ющий; ~ *row* шу́мная
ссо́ра.

flamingo, *n*, флами́нго.

flange, *n*, вы́ступ, борт; *(tech.)* фла́-
нец.

flank, *n*, бок, сторона́; *(mil.)* фланг;
¶ *v.t. (& i.)*, располага́ть(ся)
сбо́ку/на фла́нге; фланки́ровать.

flannel, *n*, флане́ль.

flap, *n*, взмах; хлопо́к; кла́пан; пола́;
откидна́я две́рца; ¶ *v.t*, взма́хи-
вать (кры́льями); хло́пать; *v.i*,
развева́ться; свиса́ть; болта́ться.

flare, *n*, вспы́шка; сия́ние; сигна́льная раке́та; ¶ *v.i*, вспы́хивать; я́рко горе́ть.

flash, *n*, вспы́шка, про́блеск; ~*light* карма́нный фона́рь; *(phot.)* вспы́шка ма́гния; ~ *of lightning* сверка́ние мо́лнии; *in a* ~ в мгнове́ние о́ка; ~ *in the pan* неожи́данная (непро́чная) уда́ча; ~ *of wit* блеск остроу́мия; ¶ *a*, показно́й, крича́щий; ¶ *v.i*, сверка́ть; вспы́хивать; мелька́ть; *v.t*, передава́ть (по телегра́фу, *etc.*).

flask, *n*, фля́жка; буты́ль; ко́лба.

flat, *a*, пло́ский, ро́вный; скучный; уны́лый; вя́лый *(market)*; *(mus.)* бемо́льный; ~*-bottomed* плоскодо́нный; ~ *denial* категори́ческий отка́з; ~ *nose* приплю́снутый нос; ~ *race* ска́чки без препя́тствий; ¶ *n*, кварти́ра; равни́на, низи́на; о́тмель; пло́скость; *(mus.)* бемо́ль; ~ *of hand* ладо́нь; ~*ly*, *ad*, пло́ско; реши́тельно; ~*ness*, *n*, пло́скость; скука; вя́лость; ~**ten**, *v.t*, де́лать ро́вным; выра́внивать; плю́щить.

flatter, *v.t*, льстить *(dat.)*; прикра́шивать; ласка́ть; ~ *oneself* те́шить себя́; ~**er**, *n*, льстец; ~**ing**, *a*, льсти́вый, ле́стный; ~**y**, *n*, лесть.

flatulence, *n*, скопле́ние га́зов; **flatulent,** *a*, страда́ющий от га́зов; *(fig.)* напы́щенный.

flaunt, *v.t*, размахивать *(inst.)*, выставля́ть; щеголя́ть *(inst.)*.

flautist, *n*, флейти́ст.

flavour, *n*, при́вкус, вкус; арома́т; за́пах; ¶ *v.t*, приправля́ть; придава́ть вкус *(dat.)*; ~**less**, *a*, безвкусный.

flaw, *n*, изъя́н, недоста́ток, брак; тре́щина; ~**less**, *a*, безупре́чный; безукори́зненный.

flax, *n*, лён; ~**en**, *a*, льняно́й; соло́менный *(hair)*.

flay, *v.t*, сдира́ть ко́жу с; чи́стить; *(fig.)* критикова́ть беспоща́дно.

flea, *n*, блоха́; ~ *bite* блоши́ный укус; *(fig.)* ма́ленькая неприя́тность; *a* ~ *in one's ear* ре́зкое замеча́ние.

fleck, *n*, пятно́, кра́пинка; ¶ *v.t*, покрыва́ть кра́пинками.

fledged: *become* ~ опери́ться; *(fig.)* станови́ться незави́симым; **fledgeling,** *n*, опери́вшийся птене́ц.

flee, *v.i*, бежа́ть; спаса́ться бе́гством.

fleece, *n*, руно́; ове́чья шерсть; ¶ *v.t*, обира́ть; вымога́ть; **fleecy,** *a*, покры́тый ше́рстью; ~ *clouds* кудря́вые облака́, бара́шки.

fleet, *n*, флот, флоти́лия; ¶ *a*, бы́стрый; ~*-footed* быстроно́гий; ~**ing**, *a*, мимолётный; бе́глый; ~**ness**, *n*, быстрота́; мимолётность.

Fleming, *n*, флама́ндец; **Flemish,** *a*, флама́ндский; ¶ *n*, флама́ндский язы́к.

flesh *n*, мя́со; плоть; мя́коть; ~ *wound* лёгкое ране́ние; ~ *and blood* челове́ческая приро́да; плоть и кровь; *one's own* ~ *and blood* своя́ родня́; ~**y**, *a*, мяси́стый; то́лстый.

flexibility, *n*, ги́бкость; податли́вость; приспособля́емость; **flexible,** *a*, ги́бкий; податливый; легко́ приспособля́ющийся; **flexion,** *n*, сгиб; фле́ксия *(gram.)*.

flick, *n*, щелчо́к (па́льцем); лёгкий уда́р; ¶ *v.t*, стега́ть; щёлкать; сма́хивать.

flicker, *n*, мерца́ние; колыха́ние; ¶ *v.i*, мерца́ть, колыха́ться; ~**ing**, *a*, мерца́ющий.

flight, *n*, полёт *(also fig.)*; перелёт; ста́я *(birds)*; пролёт *(stairs)*; бе́гство; ~**y**, *a*, ве́треный.

flimsiness, *n*, непро́чность; неосно́вательность; **flimsy,** *a*, непро́чный, то́нкий; неоснова́тельный.

flinch, *v.i*, вздра́гивать; уклоня́ться; *without* ~*ing* не дро́гнув.

fling, *v.t*, кида́ть, швыря́ть; ~ *down/off* сбра́сывать; ¶ *n*, бросо́к; стреми́тельный та́нец; *have one's* ~ перебеси́ться *(pf.)*.

flint *n*, креме́нь; ~*-hearted* жестокосе́рдый; ~**y**, *a*, кремни́стый; *(fig.)* твёрдый как ка́мень.

flippancy, *n*, легкомы́слие, ве́треность; **flippant,** *a*, ве́треный.

flirt, *n*, коке́тка; ¶ *v.i*, коке́тничать, флиртова́ть; ~**ation**, *n*, флирт.

flit, *v.i*, перелета́ть, порха́ть.

float *n*, поплаво́к; буй; плот, паро́м; макет; ¶ *v.t*, подде́рживать на пове́рхности; спуска́ть (на во́ду); сплавля́ть *(timber)*; распространя́ть *(rumour)*; выпуска́ть, размеща́ть *(fin.)*; *v.i*, пла́вать; плыть *(on water, in air)*; проноси́ться; ~**ing**, *a*, пла́вающий; плаву́чий; изме́нчивый.

flock, *n*, ста́до *(sheep)*; ста́я *(birds)*; толпа́; ~ *mattress* матра́с из очёсков; ¶ *v.i*, собира́ться толпо́й, толпи́ться; собира́ться.

floe, *n*, плаву́чая льди́на.

flog, *v.t*, поро́ть, сечь; **flogging**, *n*, по́рка.

flood, *n*, наводне́ние, пото́п; разли́в; прили́в; *(fig.)* пото́к; ~-*gate* шлюз; ¶ *v.t*, затопля́ть, наводня́ть; *v.i*, выходи́ть из берего́в.

floor, *n*, пол; эта́ж; дно; *(fig.)* пра́во сло́ва; ~ *board* полови́ца; ~ *cloth* полова́я тря́пка; *take the* ~ выступа́ть, брать сло́во; ¶ *v.t*, настила́ть пол *(gen.)*; вали́ть на́ пол; *(fig.)* смуща́ть; одолева́ть; ~ing, *n*, насти́л; насти́лка поло́в; половы́е до́ски.

flop, *n*, шлёпанье, хло́панье; *(fig.)* прова́л; ¶ *v.i*, шлёпаться; *(fig.)* прова́ливаться; опуска́ться.

flora, *n*, фло́ра; **floral**, *a*, цвето́чный; **florescence**, *n*, цвете́ние.

florid, *a*, цвети́стый; крича́щий; румя́ный.

florin, *n*, флори́н.

florist, *n*, торго́вец цвета́ми; цветово́д.

flotilla, *n*, флоти́лия.

flotsam, *n*, пла́вающие обло́мки.

flounce, *n*, обо́рка; ¶ *v.t*, отде́лывать обо́рками; *v.i*, броса́ться.

flounder, *n*, ка́мбала; ¶ *v.i*, бара́хтаться; пу́таться.

flour, *n*, мука́; ~ *mill* мукомо́льный заво́д; ¶ *v.t*, посыпа́ть муко́й.

flourish, *n*, ро́счерк; разма́хивание; процвета́ние; фанфа́ры *(mus.)* ~ *of trumpets* туш; ¶ *v.i*, процвета́ть; пы́шно расти́; *v.t*, разма́хивать *(inst.)*; ~ing, *a*, процвета́ющий; цвету́щий.

floury, *a*, мучни́стый.

flout, *v.t*, пренебрега́ть *(inst.)*; попира́ть.

flow, *n*, тече́ние; пото́к; прили́в; ¶ *v.i*, течь, ли́ться, струи́ться; ~ *from* проистека́ть от/из; ~ *into* впада́ть в; ~ *with* изоби́ловать *(inst.)*.

flower, *n*, цвет, цвето́к; ~ *bed* клу́мба; ~ *bud* буто́н; ~ *garden* цветни́к; ~ *girl* цвето́чница; ~ *pot* цвето́чный горшо́к; ~ *shop* цвето́чный магази́н; ~ *show* вы́ставка цвето́в; ¶ *v.i*, цвести́; ~ed,

a, укра́шенный цвето́чным узо́ром; ~y, *a*, цвети́стый; покры́тый цвета́ми.

flowing, *a*, теку́щий; пла́вный *(style)*; мя́гкий.

fluctuate, *v.i*, колеба́ться; изменя́ться; **fluctuation**, *n*, колеба́ние; неусто́йчивость.

flue, *n*, дымохо́д.

fluency, *n*, бе́глость, пла́вность; **fluent**, *a*, бе́глый, пла́вный; ~ly, *ad*, бе́гло.

fluff, *n*, пух, пушо́к; ~y *a*, пуши́стый.

fluid, *a*, жи́дкий, теку́чий; ¶ *n*, жи́дкость; ~ity, *n*, жи́дкое состоя́ние; теку́честь.

fluke, *n*, ла́па *(anchor)*; счастли́вая случа́йность.

flunky, *n*, лаке́й.

fluorescent, *a*, флуоресце́нтный.

flurry, *n*, шквал; беспоко́йство; ¶ *v.t*, волнова́ть.

flush, *a*, изоби́лующий; по́лный; *be* ~ *with money* име́ть мно́го де́нег; ¶ *n*, прили́в; румя́нец; ¶ *v.t*, промыва́ть; затопля́ть; наполня́ть; *v.i*, бить струёй; вспы́хивать, красне́ть.

fluster, *n*, суета́; волне́ние; ¶ *v.t*, волнова́ть; сбива́ть с то́лку.

flute, *n*, фле́йта; *(arch.)* канелю́ра, желобо́к; вы́емка; ¶ *v.t*, де́лать вы́емки в/на; ~d, *a*, с канелю́рами.

flutter, *n*, порха́ние; маха́ние; волне́ние; тре́пет; *(coll.)* *have a* ~ ста́вить ста́вку; ¶ *v.i*, маха́ть кры́льями; порха́ть; колыха́ться; трепета́ть; неро́вно би́ться *(pulse)*.

fluvial, *a*, речно́й.

flux, *n*, тече́ние; пото́к; флюс; разжижи́тель; *in a state of* ~ в состоя́нии измене́ния.

fly, *n*, му́ха; ширина́ (в брю́ках); ~*catcher* мухоло́вка; ~ *wheel* махово́е колесо́; ¶ *v.i*, лета́ть; спеши́ть; развева́ться *(flag)*; *v.t*, управля́ть (самолётом); доставля́ть по во́здуху; ~ *a kite* пуска́ть зме́я; ~ *at* напада́ть на; ~ *into* влета́ть в; ~ *into a rage* впада́ть в я́рость; ~ *off* улета́ть; убега́ть; отска́кивать; ~ *open* распа́хиваться; *let* ~ *at* стреля́ть в; броса́ть в; напада́ть на; ~ing, *a*, лета́ющий; летя́чий; лётный; бы́стрый; ~*boat* лета́ющая ло́дка;

~ *column* летучий отря́д; ~ *visit* мимолётный визи́т.

foal, *n,* жеребёнок; ослёнок; ¶ *v.i.* жеребиться.

foam, *n,* пе́на; мы́ло *(on horse);* ¶ *v.i,* пе́ниться; взмы́ливаться *(horse).*

fob, *n,* карма́шек для часо́в; ¶ *v.t:* ~ *off sth. on smb.* навя́зывать что-то кому́-то.

focal, *a,* фо́кусный; центра́льный; **focus,** *n,* фо́кус; центр; ¶ *v.t,* помеща́ть в фо́кусе; сосредото́чивать.

fodder, *n,* корм, фура́ж.

foe, *n,* враг, проти́вник.

foetus, *n,* заро́дыш, утро́бный плод.

fog, *n,* густо́й тума́н, мгла; *(phot.)* тума́н, вуа́ль; ~ *horn* сигна́льная сире́на; ¶ *v.t,* затума́нивать; озада́чивать; ~**gy,** *a,* тума́нный; *(phot.)* нея́сный.

foible, *n,* сла́бость; недоста́ток.

foil, *n,* фо́льга; *(sport)* рапи́ра; *(fig.)* контра́ст; ¶ *v.t,* ста́вить в тупи́к; расстра́ивать *(plans);* срыва́ть.

foist, *v.t,* всо́вывать; ~ *oneself* втира́ться; ~ *oneself on* навя́зываться *(dat.).*

fold, *n,* скла́дка, сгиб; застёжка; ство́р *(door);* заго́н *(sheep);* ¶ *v.t,* скла́дывать; сгиба́ть; скре́щивать *(arms);* обхва́тывать; ~ *in* завёртывать; *(bookbind.)* фальцева́ть; ~**er,** *n,* па́пка; скоросшива́тель; брошю́ра *(pers.)* фальцо́вщик; ~**ing,** *a,* складно́й; откидно́й; ство́рчатый; ~ *bed* раскладу́шка; ~ *chair* складно́й стул; ~ *screen* ши́рма.

foliage, *n,* листва́; **foliate,** *a,* ли́ственный; листообра́зный; **foliation,** *n,* листва́; сло́йстость.

folio, *n,* фолиа́нт; лист.

folk, *n,* лю́ди; наро́д; *own* ~*(s)* родня́; ~*lore* фолькло́р; ~ *song* наро́дная пе́сня.

follow, *v.t,* сле́довать/идти́ за; следи́ть за; пресле́довать; провожа́ть (взгля́дом); приде́рживаться *(gen.);* подде́рживать; *v.i,* сле́довать; вытека́ть; *as* ~*s* как сле́дует ни́же; ~ *suit* ходи́ть в масть ~ *up* упо́рно пресле́довать, доводи́ть до конца́; ~**er,** *n,* после́дователь; покло́нник; ~**ing,** *a,* сле́дующий, после́дую-

щий; ¶ *n,* после́дователи; сви́та; *the* ~ сле́дующее.

folly, *n,* глу́пость; безу́мие; капри́з.

foment, *v.t,* класть припа́рки на; *(fig.)* раздува́ть, разжига́ть; ~**ation,** *n,* припа́рка; *(fig.)* возбужде́ние.

fond, *a,* не́жный, лю́бящий; безрассу́дный; *be* ~ *of* люби́ть; быть привя́занным к.

fondle, *v.t,* ласка́ть.

fondly, *ad,* не́жно; безрассу́дно; **fondness,** *n,* любо́вь, привя́занность.

font, *n,* купе́ль.

food, *n,* пи́ща; пита́ние; корм; ~ *stuffs* пищевы́е проду́кты; продово́льствие.

fool, *n,* дура́к, глупе́ц; шут; кисе́ль *(cook.); make a* ~ *of* одура́чивать; *make a* ~ *of oneself* ста́вить себя́ в глу́пое положе́ние; *play the* ~ валя́ть дурака́; ¶ *v.t,* дура́чить; обма́нывать; *v.i,* дура́читься; шути́ть; ~**ery,** *n,* дура́чество; глу́пый посту́пок; ~**hardiness,** *n,* безрассу́дство; риско́ванность; ~**hardy,** *a,* безрассу́дно отва́жный; ~**ish,** *a,* глу́пый; ~**ishness,** *n,* глу́пость; безрассу́дство; ~**proof,** *a,* несло́жный; безопа́сный; ~**scap,** *n,* шутовско́й колпа́к; большо́й форма́т бума́ги.

foot, *n,* нога́; ступни́; похо́дка, фут *(measure); (mil.)* пехо́та; подно́жие *(of hill);* но́жка *(of furniture);* ~*ball* футбо́л; футбо́льный мяч; ~*baller* футболи́ст; ~*board* подно́жка; ~*fall* по́ступь; ~*hold* опо́ра для ноги́; то́чка опо́ры; ~ *lights* ра́мпа; ~*man* лаке́й; ~*note* примеча́ние; сно́ска; ~*pad* граби́тель; ~*path* доро́жка, тропи́нка; тротуа́р; ~*plate* площа́дка маши́ниста *(rly.);* ~*print;* ~*step* след; ~*sore* со стёртыми нога́ми; ~*step* след; шаг; звук шаго́в; ~*stool* скаме́ечка для ног; ~*wear* о́бувь; *from head to* ~ с головы́ до ног; *on* ~ пешко́м; *put one's* ~ *in it* сади́ться в лу́жу; *set on* ~ пуска́ть в ход; *trample under* ~ попира́ть; притесня́ть; ~**ing,** *n* фунда́мент; опо́ра; *be on equal* ~ быть на ра́вной ноге́.

fop, *n,* фат, щёголь; ~**pery,** *n,* фатовство́, щегольство́; ~**pish,** *a,* фатова́тый, пусто́й.

for, *pr,* для, ради; за; к, в направлении; вместо; от; ~ *joy* от радости; ~ *fear* из страха; ~ *a few minutes* (на) несколько минут; ~ *an hour* в течение часа; *medicine* ~ *a cough* лекарство от кашля; *as* ~ *me* что касается меня; ~ *all I know* насколько я знаю; ~ *all that* несмотря на всё это; ~ *good* навсегда; *what* ~? зачём?; ¶ *c,* йбо, потому что.

forage, *n,* фураж, корм; ~*cap* фуражка; ¶ *v.i,* фуражировать; разыскивать.

forasmuch as ввиду того, поскольку.

foray, *n,* набег.

forbear, *v.i,* воздёрживаться; быть терпеливым; ~*ance, n,* воздержанность; терпеливость.

forbid, *v.t,* запрещать; не позволять; *God* ~! избави Боже!; ~*ding, a,* грозный, страшный; отталкивающий.

force, *n,* сила; насилие; принуждёние; смысл; *pl, (mil.)* вооружённые войска; *by* ~ силой; *by* ~ *of circumstances* в силу обстоятельств; *in* ~ в силе, в действии; в полном составе; *motive* ~ движущая сила; ~ *pump* нагнетательный насос; ¶ *v.t,* заставлять, принуждать; взламывать *(lock)*; форсировать *(pace)*; напрягать; выводить *(plants)*; ~ *in* втискивать; продавливать; ~ *one's way* прокладывать себё дорогу; ~*d, p.p. & a,* вынужденный; натянутый *(smile)*; ~*ful, a,* сильный; убедительный.

forcemeat, *n,* фарш.

forceps, *n.pl,* хирургические щипцы́, пинцёт.

forcible, *a,* насильственный; вёский; **forcing,** *n,* насилие; принуждёние; выгонка *(of plants)*; ~ *bed* парник.

ford, *n,* брод; ¶ *v.t,* переходить вброд.

fore, *a,* передний; *(mar.)* носовой; ~ *and aft* на носу и на кормё; ¶ *ad,* впереди.

forearm, *n,* предплечье; ¶ *v.t,* заранее вооружать.

forebear, *n,* прёдок.

forebode, *v.t,* предвещать; **foreboding,** *n,* предчувствие; предзнаменование.

forecast, *n,* предсказание; прогноз; ¶ *v.i,* предсказывать.

forecastle, *n,* бак, полубак.

foreclose, *v.i,* лишать прав пользования/выкупа; предрешать; **foreclosure,** *n,* лишение права выкупа.

forefather, *n,* прёдок, праотец.

forefinger, *n,* указательный палец.

forefront, *n,* передовая линия; передний план.

foregoing, *a,* предшёствующий; **foregone,** *a,* принятый заранее: ~ *conclusion* заранее известное решение; неизбёжный результат.

foreground, *n,* передний план; авансцёна.

forehead, *n,* лоб.

foreign, *a,* иностранный; внёшний; чужой; чуждый; ~ *policy* внёшняя политика; ~ *office* министёрство иностранных дел; ~ *trade* внёшняя торговля; ~*er, n,* иностранец; чужой человёк.

foreknowledge, *n,* предвидение; предуведомление.

foreland, *n,* мыс; прибрёжная полоса.

forelock, *n,* вихор, чуб.

foreman, *n,* мастер, старший рабочий; прораб; старшина (присяжных).

foremast, *n,* фок-мачта.

foremost, *a,* передний, передовой; главный.

forensic, *a,* судёбный.

forerunner, *n,* предтёча; предвёстник.

foresail, *n,* фок.

foresee, *v.t,* предвидеть.

foreshadow, *v.t,* предзнаменовать.

foreshore, *n,* береговая полоса.

foreshortening, *n,* сокращение.

foresight, *n,* предвидение, предусмотрительность; *(gun)* мушка.

forest, *n,* лес; ¶ *v.t,* засаживать лёсом.

forestall, *v.t,* предупреждать; *(com.)* скупать товары.

forester, *n,* леснйк, лесничий.

foretaste, *n,* предвкушёние.

foretell, *v.t,* предсказывать.

forethought, *n,* предусмотрительность.

forewarn, *v.t,* предостерегать.

foreword, *n,* предисловие.

forfeit, *n,* штраф; фант *(games)*; *pl,* игра в фанты; ¶ *v.t,* платиться *(inst.);* терять право на; ~ure, *n,* потеря; конфискация.

forgather, *v.i,* собираться.

forge *n,* кузница; горн; ¶ *v.t,* ковать; подделывать *(money);* ~ *ahead* двигаться вперёд.

forger, *n,* фальшивомонетчик; подделыватель; ~y, *n,* подделка.

forget, *v.t,* забывать; ~ful, *a,* забывчивый; ~-me-not, *n,* незабудка.

forgive, *v.t,* прощать; ~ness, *n,* прощение; **forgiving,** *a.* всепрощающий.

forgo, *v.t,* отказываться от; воздерживаться от.

fork, *n,* вилка; *(agr.)* вилы; разветвление, развилина; ¶ *v.i,* работать вилами; разветвляться; ~ed, *a,* разветвлённый; вилкообразный; ~ *lightning* зигзагообразная молния.

forlorn, *a,* несчастный; унылый; ~ *hope* слабая надежда.

form, *n,* форма; очертание; фигура; формальность; бланк, анкета; класс; вид, разновидность; скамья; *in* ~ в форме; в ударе; *bad/ good* ~ дурной/хороший тон; *for* ~'s *sake* для вида; для чистой формальности; ¶ *v.t,* придавать форму *(dat.);* составлять; формировать; образовывать; воспитывать; *v.i,* образовываться, формироваться; принимать форму.

formal, *a,* формальный; официальный; ~ *letter* официальное письмо; ~ *visit* официальный визит; ~ity, *n,* формальность; ~ly, *ad,* формально.

formation, *n,* образование; составление; формирование; формация.

former, *a,* прежний, бывший; *the* ~ первый; ~ly, *ad,* прежде, раньше.

formidable, *a,* грозный; громадный.

formula, *n,* формула; рецепт; ~te, *v.t,* формулировать.

fornicate, *v.i,* прелюбодействовать; **fornication,** *n,* блуд.

forsake, *v.t,* оставлять, покидать; отказываться от.

forsooth, *ad,* поистине.

forswear, *v.t,* отрекаться от.

fort, *n,* форт.

forth, *ad,* вперёд; дальше; наружу; *back and* ~ взад и вперёд; туда и сюда; *and so* ~ и так далее; ~coming предстоящий, грядущий, будущий; ~with немедленно.

fortieth, *ord, num,* сороковой; ¶ *n,* сороковая часть.

fortification, *n,* фортификация; спиртование *(wine);* укрепление; **fortify,** *v.t,* укреплять; *(fig.)* подкреплять; добавлять спирт к.

fortitude, *n,* мужество, постоянство.

fortnight, *n,* две недели; ~ly, *a* двухнедельный; выходящий раз в две недели; ¶ *ad,* раз в две недели.

fortress, *n,* крепость.

fortuitous, *a,* случайный.

fortunate, *a,* счастливый, удачный; ~ly, *ad,* к счастью; **fortune,** *n,* счастье, удача; судьба; состояние; *tell* ~s гадать; *make a* ~ богатеть; ~-*hunter* авантюрист, -ка; искатель(-ница) богатых невест (женихов); ~-*teller* гадалка; ~-*telling* гадание.

forty, *num,* сорок.

forum, *n,* форум; *(fig.)* суд.

forward, *a,* передний; передовой; дерзкий; ~-*looking* дальновидный, предусмотрительный; прогрессивный; ¶ *ad,* вперед; *look* ~ *to* предвкушать; ¶ *v.t,* ускорять; способствовать *(dat.);* отправлять, пересылать; ~ness, *n,* раннее развитие; развязность.

fossil, *a,* окаменелый, ископаемый; *(fig.)* допотопный; ¶ *n,* окаменелость,ископаемое;~ize,*v.t.(& i.),* превращать(ся) в окаменелость; *(fig.) v.i,* коснеть.

foster, *v.t,* воспитывать; питать, лелеять; поощрять; ~-*brother* молочный брат; ~-*child* приёмыш; ~-*mother* приёмная мать; ~-*sister* молочная сестра.

foul, *a,* грязный; отвратительный; скверный; непристойный; ~-*blow* запрещённый удар; нарушение правил; ~-*mouthed* сквернословящий; ~ *play* нечестная игра; мошенничество; преступное деяние; *fall* ~ *of* ссориться/сталкиваться с; ¶ *n, (sport)* нарушение правил; запрещённый удар/ход; ¶ *v.t,* пачкать, засорять; нечестно играть с; создавать затор *(gen);* ~ness, *n,* грязь; испорченность.

found, *v.t,* основывать; закладывать; плавить; отливать; *be* ~ed *on* основываться на; ~ation, *n,* основание; основа; фундамент;

учреждéние; ~-stone фундáментный кáмень; (fig.) краеугóльный кáмень; ~er, n, основáтель; литéйщик; ¶ v.i, идти ко дну; погибáть; ~ing, n, литéйное дéло, литьё; основáние.

foundling, n, найдёныш.

foundry, n, литéйный завóд/цех.

fountain, n, фонтáн; истóчник; ~head истóчник; первоистóчник; ~ pen «вéчная» рýчка, авторýчка.

four, num., четы́ре; ¶ n, четвёрка; on all ~s на четверéньках; ~footed четвероногий; ~fold (a.) четырёхкратный; (ad) вчéтверо; ~square квадрáтный; основáтельный; ~teen, num., четы́рнадцать; ~th, ord. num., четы́рнадцатый; ¶ n, четы́рнадцатая часть; **fourth**, ord. num., четвёртый; ¶ n, чéтверть; ~ly, ad. в-четвёртых.

fowl, n, дичь; домáшняя птúца; ~ house птúчник; курятник; ~er, n, птицелóв; ~ing, n, охóта за дúчью; лóвля птиц; ~ piece охóтничье ружьё.

fox, n, лисá, лисúца; ~-brush лúсий хвост; ~glove наперстянка; ~hound порáтая гóнчая; ~-hunt охóта на лисý; ~trot фокстрóт; ~y, a, лúсий; (fig.) хúтрый.

foyer, n, фойé.

fraction, n, дробь; частúца; облóмок; ~al, a, дрóбный; частúчный; незначúтельный.

fractious, a, раздражúтельный.

fracture, n, перелóм; излóм, трéщина; ¶ v.t, ломáть; раздроблять; v.i, ломáться.

fragile, a, хрýпкий; слáбый; **fragility**, n, хрýпкость; слáбость.

fragment, n, отры́вок, облóмок, оскóлок, фрагмéнт; ~ary, a, фрагментáрный, отры́вочный.

fragrance, n, аромáт; **fragrant**, a, аромáтный, благоухáющий.

frail, a, хрýпкий; хúлый, болéзненный; ~ty, n, хрýпкость; хúлость.

frame, n, рáма; рáмка; óстов; скелéт; тéло; кадр (film.); ~ of mind настроéние; ¶ v.t, вставлять в рáму; обрамлять; стрóить; выражáть; подстрáивать лóжное обвинéние прóтив; ~work, n,

óстов; решётка; обрамлéние; (fig.) структýра; ~ of society общéственный строй.

franc, n, франк.

franchise, n, прáво учáстия в вы́борах.

frank, a, úскренний, откровéнный; ¶ v.t, франкúровать.

frankincense, n, лáдан.

frankly, ad, откровéнно.

frantic, a, нестовый, безýмный.

fraternal, a, брáтский; **fraternity**, n, брáтство; общúна; **fraternize**, v.i, братáться; **fratricidal**, a, братоубúйственный; **fratricide**, n, братоубúйство; братоубúйца.

fraud, n, обмáн; поддéлка; обмáнщик; ~ulent, a, обмáнный, мошéннический.

fraught, a, пóлный, чревáтый.

fray, n, дрáка; протёршееся мéсто; ¶ v.i, протирáться, изнáшиваться; (fig.) истрёпываться.

freak, n, капрúз, причýда; чудáк; урóд; ~ish, a, капрúзный; чудаковáтый, стрáнный; необыкновéнный.

freckle, n, веснýшка; ~d, a, веснýшчатый.

free, a, свобóдный; независúмый; добровóльный; неощущéнный; бесплáтный; ~ and easy непринуждённый; ~ city вóльный гóрод; ~hand drawing рисýнок от рукú; ~lance независúмый; внештáтный сотрýдник; ~ list спúсок беспóшлинных товáров; ~ on board с погрýзкой на сýдно; ~ school бесплáтная шкóла; ~ thinker вольнодýмец; ~thinking свободомы́слие; ~ trade беспóшлинная торгóвля; ~ will свобóда вóли; of one's own ~ will добровóльно; ¶ v.t, освобождáть; выпускáть; развязывать; ~dom, n, свобóда, вóльность; ~ of speech свобóда слóва; ~ of worship свобóда сóвести; ~hold, n, земéльная сóбственность; ~ly, ad, свобóдно.

freemason, n, масóн; ~ry, n, масóнство.

freeze, v.t, морáживать; ~ wages заморáживать зарáботную плáту; v.i, замерзáть, мёрзнуть; (fig.) застывáть; it is freezing морóзит; ~r, n, холодúльник; морóженица; **freezing**, a, леденящий;

заморáживающий; ~ *point* тóчка замерзáния.

freight, *n,* груз; ~ *train* товáрный пóезд; ¶ *v.t,* грузи́ть; **~age,** *n,* стóимость перевóзки; фрахтóвка; **~er,** *n,* грузовóе сýдно, грузовóй самолёт; фрахтóвщик.

French, *a,* францýзский; ~ *beans* фасóль; ~ *leave* ухóд без прощáния/разрешéния; ~ *window* ствóрчатое окнó (доходя́щее до пóла); ¶ *n,* францýзский язы́к; **~man, ~woman** францýз, францýженка.

frenzied, *a,* взбéшенный; **frenzy,** *n,* безýмие; бéшенство; неи́стовство.

frequency, *n,* частотá; чáстое повторéние; *high* ~ высóкая частотá; **frequent,** *a,* чáстый; ¶ *v.t,* чáсто посещáть; **~er,** *n,* постоя́нный посети́тель; завсегдáтай; **~ly,** *ad,* чáсто.

fresco, *n,* фрéска.

fresh, *a,* свéжий; нóвый; бóдрый; неóпытный; нáглый; ~ *air* свéжий вóздух; ~ *from school* пря́мо со шкóльной скамьи́; ~ *water* *(n)* прéсная водá; *(a)* пресновóдный; **~en,** *v.t,* освежáть; *v.i,* свежéть; **~ly,** *ad,* свежó; недáвно; **~man,** *n,* первокýрсник; **~ness,** *n,* свéжесть; бóдрость; неóпытность.

fret, *n,* раздражéние; лад *(guitar)*; орнáмент, и́зморось; **~saw** лóбзик; ¶ *v.t,* разъедáть; беспокóить; *(arch.)* украшáть резнóй рабóтой; *v.i,* тосковáть; беспокóиться; **~ful,** *a,* тоскли́вый; раздражи́тельный; **~fulness,** *n,* раздражи́тельность; **~work,** *n,* резнóе/лепнóе украшéние; ажýрная рабóта.

friable, *a,* ры́хлый; лóмкий.

friar, *n,* монáх; **~y,** *n,* мужскóй монасты́рь.

fricassée, *n,* фрикасé.

friction, *n,* трéние; *(fig.)* трéния.

Friday, *n,* пя́тница.

friend, *n,* друг, прия́тель; товáрищ; квáкер; *boy* ~ друг, «молодóй человéк»; *girl* ~ дéвушка, подрýга; **~less,** *a,* одинóкий; **~liness,** *n,* дружелю́бие; **~ly,** *a,* дрýжеский, дружелю́бный; дрýжественный; ~ *society* óбщество взаимопóмощи; **~ship,** *n,* дрýжба.

frieze, *n,* фриз; бордю́р.

frigate, *n,* фрегáт.

fright, *n,* испýг; страши́лище; **~en,** *v.t,* пугáть; ~ *away* спýгивать; **~ful,** *a,* стрáшный; **~fully,** *ad,* стрáшно; ужáсно.

frigid, *a,* холóдный *(also fig.);* **~ity,** *n,* хóлодность; морóзность; мерзлотá.

frill, *n,* обóрка, сбóрка; *pl,* (ненýжные) украшéния; *without* **~s** прóсто; ¶ *v.t,* гофри́ровать.

fringe, *n,* бахромá; каймá, край; чёлка *(hair);* *on the* ~ *of the wood* на опýшке лéса.

frippery, *n,* мишурá, безделýшки; ¶ *a,* мишýрный.

frisk, *v.i,* резви́ться, пры́гать; *v.t,* обы́скивать; **~y,** *a,* игри́вый.

fritter, *n,* олáдья; ¶ *v.t:* ~ *away* растрáчивать по мелочáм.

frivolity, *n,* легкомы́слие, фривóльность; **frivolous,** *a,* легкомы́сленный; повéрхностный; пустя́чный.

frizzle, *n,* зави́вка; ¶ *v.t,* завивáть; **~d,** *a,* вы́сохший.

fro, *ad: to and* ~ взад и вперёд; тудá и сюдá.

frock, *n,* плáтье; **~-coat** сюртýк.

frog, *n,* лягýшка.

frolic, *n,* шáлость, шýтка; ¶ *v.i,* резви́ться; **~some,** *a,* игри́вый, рéзвый.

from, *pr,* от, из, с; ~ *above* свéрху; ~ *afar* издали́, издалекá издали́; ~ *among* из среды́/ числá; ~ *behind* из-за; ~ *earliest times* и́здавна, с дáвних времён; ~ *memory* по пáмяти; ~ *nature* с натýры; ~ *now on* с э́тих пор, отны́не; ~ *time to time* врéмя от врéмени; ~ *under* из-под.

front, *n,* передня́я сторонá; фасáд; *(mil.)* фронт; *in* ~ *of* перёд; впереди́; ¶ *a,* передний; ~ *door* парáдный вход; передня́я дверь; ~ *garden* палисáдник; ~ *line* передовáя ли́ния (фрóнта); ~ *page* ти́тульный лист; пéрвая полосá *(newspaper);* **~age,** *n,* передний фасáд; протяжéние фасáда; **~al,** *a,* лобный; *(mil.)* лобовóй; *(build.)* фронтáльный.

frontier, *n,* грани́ца; ¶ *a,* пограни́чный.

frontispiece, *n,* фронтиспи́с.

frost, *n,* морóз; **~bitten** обморóженный; **~ed glass** мáтовое стеклó; **~y,** *a,* морóзный; *(fig.)* холóдный.

froth, *n,* пе́на; *(fig.)* пусты́е слова́; ¶ *v.i,* пе́ниться; ~у, *a,* пе́нистый.

frown, *n,* хму́рый взгляд; ¶ *v.i,* хму́рить бро́ви, хму́риться; ~ *at* смотре́ть с неодобре́нием на.

frowsy, *a,* неря́шливый; за́тхлый.

frozen, *p.p. & a,* замёрзший; заморо́женный.

frugal, *a,* бережли́вый, эконо́мный; скро́мный; ~ity, *n,* бережли́вость; уме́ренность.

fruit, *n,* плод; фрукт(ы); ~ *tree* фрукто́вое де́рево; *candied* ~ заса́харенные фру́кты; *dried* ~ сушёные фру́кты; *preserved* ~ консерви́рованные фру́кты; ~erer, *n,* торго́вец фру́ктами; ~ful, *a,* плодови́тый, плодоро́дный; *(fig.)* плодотво́рный; ~fulness, *n,* плодови́тость; плодотво́рность; ~ion, *n,* осуществле́ние; ~less, *a,* беспло́дный; ~у, *a,* вку́сный; арома́тный; похо́жий на фру́кты.

frump, *n,* пло́хо оде́тая же́нщина; ста́рая карга́.

frustrate, *v.t,* расстра́ивать, срыва́ть; **frustration,** *n,* расстро́йство; круше́ние; тще́тность.

fry, *n,* ме́лкая рыбёшка; ¶ *v.t.* *(& i.),* жа́рить(ся); ~ing *pan* сковорода́.

fuchsia, *n,* фу́ксия.

fuddle, *v.t,* спа́ивать; одурма́нивать; ~ed, *a,* пья́ный; одуре́лый.

fudge, *n,* пома́дка.

fuel, *n,* то́пливо; горю́чее; ¶ *v.t,* заправля́ть горю́чим.

fugitive, *a,* бе́глый; мимолётный; ¶ *n,* бегле́ц; бе́женец.

fugue, *n,* фу́га.

fulcrum, *n,* то́чка опо́ры/враще́ния.

fulfil, *v.t,* выполня́ть, исполня́ть; осуществля́ть; ~ment, *a,* выполне́ние, исполне́ние; осуществле́ние.

full, *a,* по́лный; сы́тый; це́лый; бога́тый; свобо́дный *(dress);* ~ *back* защи́тник; ~-*blooded* полнокро́вный; ~-*blown* вполне́ распусти́вшийся; ~ *dress* пара́дная фо́рма; ~-*faced (a.)* полноли́цый; *(ad.)* анфа́с;~-*length* во всю длину́; во весь рост; ~ *moon* полнолу́ние; ~ *powers* полномо́чия; ~ *stop* то́чка; ~ *time* по́лный рабо́чий день; коне́ц игры́; ~ *well* о́чень хорошо́; ¶ *v.t,* валя́ть; ~er, *n,* валя́льщик, сукнова́л;

~ing *mill,* *n.* сукнова́льня; ~ness, *n,* полнота́; *in the* ~ *of time* в надлежа́щее вре́мя; ~у, *ad,* вполне́, по́лностью.

fulminant, *a,* молниено́сный.

fulminate, *n:* ~ *of mercury* грему́чая ртуть; ¶ *v.i,* сверка́ть; взрыва́ться; ~ *against* обру́шиваться на.

fulsome, *a,* рабо́лепный; нейскре́нний; ~ *praise* гру́бая лесть.

fumble, *v.i,* нело́вко брать; неуме́ло обраща́ться с; нащу́пывать; ~ *with* верте́ть в рука́х.

fume, *n,* испаре́ние; за́пах; ¶ *v.i,* испаря́ться; кипе́ть (от зло́сти).

fumigate, *v.t,* оку́ривать; **fumigation,** *n,* оку́ривание.

fuming, *a,* кипя́щий от зло́сти.

fun, *n,* весе́лье, заба́ва; *have* ~ весели́ться; *for* ~ в шу́тку; *make* ~ *of* высме́ивать.

function, *n,* фу́нкция; обя́занности; торжество́; ¶ *v.i,* де́йствовать, функциони́ровать; ~al, *a,* функциона́льный; ~ary, *n,* до́лжностно́е лицо́.

fund, *n,* запа́с; фонд; *pl,* де́нежные сре́дства; госуда́рственные проце́нтные бума́ги.

fundamental, *a,* основно́й.

funeral, *n,* по́хороны; похоро́нная проце́ссия; ~ *service* заупоко́йная слу́жба, панихи́да; ¶ *a,* похоро́нный; мра́чный.

fungous, *a,* гу́бчатый, плодрева́тый; **fungus,** *n,* гриб; пле́сень; древе́сная гу́бка.

funk, *n,* испу́г; ¶ *v.t,* уклоня́ться от; боя́ться *(gen.).*

funnel, *n,* дымова́я труба́, дымохо́д; воро́нка.

funny, *a,* заба́вный, смешно́й; стра́нный.

fur, *n,* мех; шерсть; шку́ра; налёт *(on tongue);* на́кипь *(in kettle);* ~ *coat* шу́ба.

furbelow, *n,* обо́рка.

furbish, *v.t,* полирова́ть; ~ *up* подновля́ть.

furious, *a,* взбешённый; я́ростный.

furlong, *n,* восьма́я часть ми́ли.

furlough, *n,* о́тпуск.

furnace, *n,* печь; оча́г; горн.

furnish, *v.t,* меблирова́ть, обставля́ть; снабжа́ть; представля́ть; ~ed, *p.p. & a,* меблиро́ванный; ~er, *n,* поставщи́к (ме́бели); **furniture,** *n,* ме́бель; обору́дование.

furrier, *n,* скорня́к; мехо́вщик.

furrow, *n,* борозда́; жёлоб; глубо́кая морщи́на; ¶ *v.t,* борозди́ть; морщи́нить; ~ed, *a,*морщи́нистый.

further, *a,* дальне́йший; доба́вочный; *till* ~ *notice* впредь до дальне́йшего уведомле́ния; ¶ *ad,* да́льше; да́лее; зате́м; кро́ме того́; ¶ *v.t,* спосо́бствовать/соде́йствовать *(dat.);* продвига́ть; ~ance,*n,* продвиже́ние; ~more, *ad,* к тому́ же; **furthest,** *a,* са́мый да́льний; ¶ *ad,* да́льше всего́.

furtive, *a,* скры́тый, та́йный; ~ *glance* взгляд укра́дкой.

fury, *n,* я́рость, нейсто́вство; *(myth.)* фу́рия.

furze, *n,* дрок.

fuse, *n,* фити́ль; запа́л; взрыва́тель; *(elec.)* предохрани́тель; *time* ~ дистанцио́нный взрыва́тель; ¶ *v.t,* пла́вить, сплавля́ть; вставля́ть взрыва́тель в; *v.i,* пла́виться; перегора́ть; *the bulb is* ~d ла́мпочка перегоре́ла; **fusible,** *a,* пла́вкий.

fuselage, *n,* фюзеля́ж.

fusillade,, *n,* стрельба́; расстре́л.

fusion, *n,* пла́вка; сплав; слия́ние.

fuss, *n,* суета́; *make a* ~ *about* суети́ться, поднима́ть шум (вокру́г); ¶ *v.i,* хлопота́ть; пристава́ть с пустяка́ми; ~y, *a,* суетли́вый.

fustian, *n,* бума́зея; *(fig.)* напы́щенный стиль; ¶ *a,* наду́тый.

futile, *a,* бесполе́зный, тще́тный; **futility,** *n,* тще́тность, пустота́.

future, *a,* бу́дущий; ¶ *n,* бу́дущее; бу́дущность; ~ *tense* бу́дущее вре́мя; *in* ~ в бу́дущем.

fuzzy, *a,* курча́вый.

G

G, *(mus.),* соль.

gab, *n,* болтовня́; *gift of the* ~ дар сло́ва.

gabardine, *n,* габарди́н.

gabble, *n,* бормота́ние; ¶ *v.i,* бормота́ть; гогота́ть; ~r, *n,* болту́н.

gad about, *v.i,* шата́ться, весели́ться; **gadabout,** *n,* праздношата́ющийся.

gadfly, *n,* о́вод, слепе́нь.

gadget, *n,* приспособле́ние; (техни́ческая) нови́нка.

gaff, *n,* острога́; ¶ *v.i,* багри́ть.

gaffe, *n,* опло́шность.

gaffer, *n,* стари́к; хозя́ин.

gag, *n,* кляп; *(theat.)* шу́тка; *(coll.)* обма́н; ¶ *v.t,* вставля́ть кляп/заты́ка́ть рот *(dat.); v.i,* отпуска́ть шу́тки.

gage, *n,* зало́г; ¶ *v.t,* дава́ть в зало́г.

gaiety, *n,* весёлость; весе́лье.

gaily, *ad,* ве́село; я́рко.

gain, *n,* при́быль, вы́года; вы́игрыш; увеличе́ние; ¶ *v.t,* получа́ть; достига́ть *(gen.);* добива́ться *(gen.);* ~ *on* нагоня́ть; ~ *ground* продвига́ться вперёд; ~ *time* выи́грывать вре́мя; *my watch* ~s мои́ часы́ иду́т вперёд, мои́ часы́ спеша́т; ~ful, *a,* дохо́дный, при́быльный; опла́чиваемый; ~s, *n,* дохо́д, за́работок; вы́игрыш.

gainsay, *v.t,* отрица́ть; противоре́чить *(dat.).*

gait, *n,* похо́дка; шаг.

gaiter, *n,* гама́ша.

gala, *n,* пра́зднество; ~ *day* пра́здник.

galaxy, *n,* гала́ктика, Мле́чный путь; *(fig.)* плея́да.

gale, *n,* шторм; бу́ря; си́льный ве́тер.

gall, *n,* жёлчь; жёлчный пузы́рь; *(fig.)* жёлчность; ~stone жёлчный ка́мень; ¶ *v.t,* раздража́ть.

gallant, *a,* хра́брый; гала́нтный; ¶ *n,* све́тский челове́к; кавале́р; ~ry, *n,* хра́брость; гала́нтность.

gallery, *n,* галере́я; *(theat.)* галёрка; *(geol.)* штрек; *play to the* ~ подла́живаться под вкус толпы́.

galley, *n,* гале́ра; ка́мбуз; *the* ~s ка́торжные рабо́ты; ~ *proof* гра́нка; ~ *slave* ка́торжник на гале́ре.

Gallic, *a,* га́лльский; ~ism, *n,* галлици́зм.

galling, *a,* раздражи́тельный.

gallon, *n,* галло́н.

galloon, *n,* галу́н.

gallop, *n,* гало́п; *at full* ~ во весь опо́р; ¶ *v.i,* скака́ть гало́пом; *v.t,* пуска́ть гало́пом.

gallows, *n.pl.,* ви́селица; ~ *bird* ви́сельник.

galore, *ad,* в изоби́лии.

galosh, *n,* гало́ша.

galvanic, *a,* гальвани́ческий; **galvanism,** *n,* гальвани́зм; **galvanize,**

v.t, гальванизи́ровать; оцинко́-
вывать.

gambit, *n*, гамби́т; пе́рвый шаг.

gamble, *n*, аза́ртная игра́; риско́-
ванное предприя́тие; *military* ~
вое́нная авантю́ра; ¶ *v.t*, про-
и́грывать; *v.i*, игра́ть (в аза́рт-
ные и́гры); ~ *with* рискова́ть
(inst.); ~r, *n*, игро́к, картёжник; **gambling**, *n*, аза́ртная
игра́; ~ *house* игро́рный дом.

gambol, *n*, прыжо́к; ¶ *v.i*, пры́гать,
р звви́ться.

game, *n*, игра́; шу́тка; дичь; ~ *bag*
ягдта́ш; ~ *of chance* аза́ртная
игра́; ~*keeper* лесни́к (охраня́ю-
щий дичь); *play the* ~ игра́ть
че́стно/по пра́вилам; *(fig.)* посту-
па́ть благоро́дно; ¶ *a*, сме́лый;
задо́рный; бо́дрый; ~ster, *n*, иг-
ро́к; *gaming table* иго́рный
стол.

gammon, *n*, о́корок.

gamut, *n*, га́мма; диапазо́н.

gander, *n*, гуса́к.

gang, *n*, брига́да; ша́йка, ба́нда;
кли́ка; ~*plank* схо́дни.

gangrene, *n*, гангре́на.

gangster, *n*, га́нгстер, банди́т.

gangway, *n*, прохо́д (ме́жду ряда́ми);
схо́дни.

gaol, *n*, тюрьма́; ~*bird* ареста́нт,
уголо́вник; ¶ *v.t*, заключа́ть в
тюрьму́; ~er, *n*, тюре́мщик.

gap, *n*, брешь, пробе́л, проло́м,
проры́в; разры́в; промежу́ток;
уще́лье; *fill a* ~ заполня́ть про-
бе́л.

gape, *v.i*, широко́ раскрыва́ть рот;
зия́ть; ~ *at* глазе́ть на.

garage, *n*, гара́ж.

garb, *n*, оде́жда; одея́ние.

garbage, *n*, му́сор.

garble, *v.t*, искажа́ть; подтасо́вы-
вать.

garden, *n*, сад; ~ *bed* гря́дка,
клу́мба; ~ *frame* парнико́вая
ра́ма; ~ *hose* садо́вый шланг;
nursery ~ пито́мник; ~er, *n*,
садо́вник.

gardenia, *n*, гарде́ния.

gardening, *n*, садово́дство.

gargle, *n*, полоска́ние; ¶ *v.i*, полос-
ка́ть го́рло.

garish, *a*, крича́щий, я́ркий.

garland, *n*, гирля́нда, вено́к.

garlic, *n*, чесно́к.

garment, *n*, предме́т оде́жды.

garner, *n*, амба́р; храни́лище; ¶
v.t, скла́дывать в амба́р; запа-
са́ть.

garnet, *n*, грана́т.

garnish, *n*, гарни́р; украше́ние; ¶
v.t, гарни́ровать; украша́ть.

garret, *n*, черда́к; манса́рда.

garrison, *n*, гарнизо́н; ¶ *v.t*, ста́вить
гарнизо́н (в/на.).

garrulity, *n*, болтли́вость; **garrulous**,
a, болтли́вый.

garter, *n*, подвя́зка; *Order of the* ~
о́рден Подвя́зки.

gas, *n*, газ; *(U.S.)* бензи́н, горю́чее;
~ *burner* га́зовая горе́лка; ~
chamber га́зовая ка́мера; ~ *cooker*
га́зовая пе́чка/плита́; ~ *fire* га́зо-
вый ками́н; ~ *mask* противога́з;
~ *meter* га́зовый счётчик; ~ *ring*
конфо́рка; ~*works* га́зовый за-
во́д; *coal* ~ свети́льный газ; ¶
v.t, отравля́ть га́зом; *v.i*, *(coll.)*,
болта́ть; хва́стать.

gash, *n*, глубо́кая ра́на; разре́з; ¶
v.t, наноси́ть глубо́кую ра́ну
(dat.); ре́зать.

gasolene, *n*, газоли́н; *(U.S.)* бензи́н.

gasp, *n*, вы́дох; ¶ *v.i*, дыша́ть с тру-
до́м, задыха́ться; ~ *out* говори́ть
задыха́ясь; ~ *for breath* лови́ть
во́здух.

gastric, *a*, желу́дочный; **gastritis**, *n*,
гастри́т; **gastronome**, *n*, гастро-
но́м; **gastronomic**, *a*, гастрономи́-
ческий; **gastronomy**, *n*, гастроно́-
мия; кулина́рия.

gate, *n*, кали́тка; воро́та; шлагба́ум;
~*keeper* привра́тник; ~*way* во-
ро́та; вход.

gather, *v.t*, собира́ть; рвать *(flowers)*;
мо́рщить *(brows)*; собира́ть в
сбо́рки *(dress)*; ~ *speed* уско-
ря́ть ход, набира́ть ско́рость; ~
strength накопля́ть си́лы; *v.i*, соби-
ра́ться, скопля́ться; *(med.)* нары-
ва́ть; предполага́ть; ~s, *n.pl*,
сбо́рки; ~ing, *n*, сбор; соби-
ра́ние; собра́ние *(people)*; *(med.)*
нагное́ние.

gaudiness, *n*, я́ркость; безвку́сица;
gaudy, *a*, я́ркий, крича́щий.

gauge, *n*, ме́ра; кали́бр; *(rly.)* ко-
ле́я; измери́тельный прибо́р; *(fig.)*
крите́рий; ¶ *v.t*, измеря́ть; оце́ни-
вать.

gaunt, *a*, исхуда́лый.

gauntlet, *n*, рукави́ца; *fling down
the* ~ броса́ть вы́зов/«перча́тку»;

run the ~ проходи́ть сквозь строй;
(fig.) подверга́ться опа́сности/
ре́зкой кри́тике.
gauze, *n*, газ, ма́рля.
gavotte, *n*, гаво́т.
gawky, *a*, неуклю́жий; засте́нчивый.
gay, *a*, весёлый; я́ркий; пёстрый;
~ *dog* весельча́к.
gaze, *n*, взгляд; ¶ *v.i*, смотре́ть.
gazelle, *n*, газе́ль.
gazette, *n*, (официа́льная) газе́та; ¶
v.t, опубли́ковывать в официа́льной газе́те; ~er, *n*, географи́ческий
спра́вочник.
gear, *n*, прибо́р; приспособле́ние;
(tech.) шестерня́, переда́ча; обо-
ру́дование; ~ *box* коро́бка ско-
росте́й; *in* ~ включённый, действующий; *out of* ~ вы́ключен-
ный; *(fig.)* дезорганизо́ванный;
change ~ переключа́ть переда́чу;
three-speed ~ переда́ча для трёх
скросте́й.
gee, *int*, но!
gelatine, *n*, желати́н; ¶ *a*, желати́-
новый.
geld, *v.t*, кастри́ровать; ~ing, *n*,
кастра́ция; ме́рин.
gem, *n*, драгоце́нный ка́мень; *(fig.)*
драгоце́нность; *She is a* ~ она́
пре́лесть.
Gemini, *n.pl*, Близнецы́.
gemma, *n*, по́чка.
gender, *n*, род.
genealogical, *a*, генеалоги́ческий;
genealogy, *n*, генеало́гия; родос-
ло́вная.
general, *a*, о́бщий, всео́бщий; гене-
ра́льный; обы́чный; *G* ~ *Assembly*
Генера́льнаяАссамбле́я; ~ *impression* о́бщее впечатле́ние; ~ *election*
всео́бщие вы́боры; ~ *post office*
гла́вный почта́мт; ~ *practitioner*
врач о́бщей пра́ктики; ~ *strike*
всео́бщая забасто́вка; *in* ~вообще́;
¶ *n*, генера́л; ~issimo, *n*, гене-
рали́ссимус; ~ity, *n*, всео́бщность;
большинство́; *pl*, о́бщие места́;
~ization, *n*, обобще́ние; ~ize, *v.t*,
обобща́ть; *v.i*, говори́ть неопреде-
лённо; ~ly, *ad*, вообще́; обы́чно;
бо́льшей ча́стью; ~ship, *n*, гене-
ра́льский чин; вое́нное иску́сство;
руково́дство.
generate, *v.t*, порожда́ть; производи́ть; вызыва́ть; *(elec.)* генери́ро-
вать; **generation**, *n*, поколе́ние;

порожде́ние; **generator**, *n*, гене-
ра́тор.
generic, *a*, родово́й; о́бщий.
generosity, *n*, ще́дрость; велико-
ду́шие; **generous**, *a*, ще́дрый;
великоду́шный; оби́льный.
genesis, *n*, происхожде́ние, ге́незис;
Book of G~ кни́га Бытия́; **genetics**, *n*, гене́тика.
genial, *a*, прия́тный; приве́тливый;
мя́гкий; ~ity, *n*, общи́тельность;
доброду́шие; мя́гкость.
genista, *n*, дрок.
genital, *a*, половой; ~s, *n*, половы́е
о́рганы.
genitive (case), *n*, роди́тельный
паде́ж.
genius, *n*, ге́ний; дух; *(man of)* ~
гениа́льный челове́к.
genteel, *a*, благоро́дный; благовос-
пи́танный; изя́шный.
gentian, *n*, горева́вка.
Gentile, *n*, не евре́й.
gentility, *n*, элега́нтность; аристок-
рати́чность; ве́жливость.
gentle, *a*, мя́гкий; не́жный; ла́ско-
вый; кро́ткий; сла́бый; ~folk,
n.pl, благоро́дные лю́ди; ~man,
n, господи́н; джентльме́н; ~ *farmer* фе́рмер-джентльме́н; ~*-in-
waiting* камерге́р; ~manly, *a*,
джентльме́нский; корре́ктный; ~-
ness, *n*, мя́гкость; доброта́, ~wo-
man, *n*, да́ма; ле́ди; **gently**, *ad*,
мя́гко; не́жно; осторо́жно; спо-
ко́йно; ¶ *int*, ти́ше!.
genuflect, *v.i*, преклоня́ть коле́на;
~flexion, *n*, коленопреклоне́ние.
genuine, *a*, по́длинный, настоя́щий;
и́скренний; ~ly, *ad*, и́скренне; ~-
ness, *n*, по́длинность; и́скрен-
ность.
genus, *n*, род; вид; класс.
geographer, *n*, гео́граф; **geographical**,
a, географи́ческий; **geography**, *n*,
геогра́фия.
geological, *a*, геологи́ческий; **geologist**, *n*, гео́лог; **geology**, *n*, гео-
ло́гия.
geometrical, *a*, геометри́ческий; **geo-
metrician**, *n*, гео́метр; **geometry**,
n, геоме́трия.
Georgian, *a*, грузи́нский; гео́ргиев-
ский; ¶ *n*, грузи́н, ~ка; грузи́н-
ский язы́к.
geranium, *n*, гера́нь.
germ, *n*, микро́б; заро́дыш; *(bot.)*
за́вязь.

German, *a*, неме́цкий, герма́нский;
¶ *n*, не́мец, не́мка; неме́цкий
язы́к; ~ *measles* красну́ха.

germane, *a*, уме́стный, подходя́щий.

Germanic, *a*, герма́нский.

germicide, *n*, вещество́, убива́ю-
щее бакте́рии; **germinate**, *v.t*,
порожда́ть; *v.i*, зарожда́ться, про-
раста́ть; **germination**, *n*, прораста́-
ние; *(fig.)* разви́тие.

gerund, *n*, геру́ндий; дееприча́стие.

gesticulate, *v.i*, жестикули́ровать;
gesticulation, *n*, жестикуля́ция.

gesture, *n*, жест.

get, *v.t*, получа́ть; достава́ть; дости-
га́ть *(gen.)*; добива́ться *(gen.)*;
приноси́ть; понима́ть; *v.i*, прихо-
ди́ть; де́латься; ~ *about* ходи́ть;
выходи́ть; распространя́ться; ста-
нови́ться изве́стным; ~ *along*
пожива́ть; де́лать успе́хи; ~ *at*
добира́ться до; напада́ть на; ~
away уходи́ть; убира́ться прочь;
~ *back (v.t.)* получа́ть обра́тно;
(v.i.) возвраща́ться; ~ *better*
поправля́ться; ~ *down* спуска́ться;
слеза́ть; ~ *down to* принима́ться
за; ~ *left behind* отстава́ть; ~
married жени́ться; выходи́ть за́-
муж; ~ *in (v.t.)* собира́ть; *(v.i.)*
входи́ть; ~ *off* сходи́ть, слеза́ть;
спаса́ться; отде́лываться; ~ *on*
сади́ться в *(train)*; продвига́ться
вперёд; преуспева́ть; ~ *on with*
ла́дить с; ~ *out (v.t.)* вынима́ть;
(v.i.) выходи́ть; ~ *out of hand*
выходи́ть из-под контро́ля; ~ *out
of order* по́ртиться; ~ *out of the
way* уходи́ть в сто́рону/с доро́ги;
~ *over* преодолева́ть; переходи́ть;
~ *through* проходи́ть че́рез; выде́р-
живать экза́мен; ~ *ready* гото́-
вить(ся); ~ *rid of* избавля́ться
от; ~ *up (v.t.)* поднима́ть; под-
гото́вля́ть; ста́вить *(play)* наря-
жа́ть; *(v.i.)* поднима́ться, вста-
ва́ть; *I have got to* . . . я до́лжен . . .;
~ *it right* находи́ть пра́вильное
реше́ние; понима́ть пра́вильно.

getaway, *n*, бе́гство.

get-up, *n*, оде́жда.

gewgaw, *n*, безделу́шка.

geyser, *n* ге́йзер; га́зовая коло́нка.

ghastly, *a*, ужа́сный, стра́шный.

gherkin, *n*, корнишо́н.

ghost, *n*, привиде́ние, при́зрак; дух;
тень; *give up the* ~ испуска́ть дух;
~**ly**, *n*, при́зрачный.

ghoul, *n*, вампи́р.

giant, *n*, велика́н, гига́нт.

gibber, *v.i*, тарато́рить; ~**ish**, *n*,
тараба́рщина.

gibbet, *n*, ви́селица.

gibe, *n*, насме́шка; ¶ *v.i*: ~ *at* насме-
ха́ться над.

giblets, *n.pl*, потроха́.

giddily, *ad*, легкомы́сленно, ве́трено;
giddiness, *n*, головокруже́ние;
легкомы́слие, ве́треность; **giddy**,
a, головокружи́тельный; легко-
мы́сленный, ве́треный; *I feel* ~
у меня́ кру́жится голова́.

gift, *n*, пода́рок; дар, тала́нт; спо-
со́бность; ~**ed**, *a*, одарённый, та-
ла́нтливый.

gig, *n, (mar.)* ги́чка; кабриоле́т.

gigantic, *a*, гига́нтский.

giggle, *n*, хихи́канье; ¶ *v.i*, хихи́-
кать.

gild, *v.t*, золоти́ть; ~**ing**, *n*, позо-
ло́та; золоче́ние.

gill, *n*, жа́бра; че́тверть пи́нты; *be
green about the* ~*s* вы́глядеть боль-
ны́м.

gilly flower, *n*, левко́й.

gilt, *a*, золочёный, позоло́ченный;
¶ *n*, позоло́та; ~*-edged* с золоты́м
обре́зом; ~*-edged securities* надёж-
ные це́нные бума́ги.

gimcrack, *a*, мишу́рный; пло́хо сде́-
ланный; него́дный.

gimlet, *n*, бура́вчик.

gimmick, *n*, трюк; рекла́мная
шту́чка.

gin, *n*, джин; западня́; хлопкоочи-
сти́тельная маши́на.

ginger, *a*, имби́рный; ры́жий; ¶ *n*,
имби́рь; ¶ *v.t*: ~ *up* подстёги-
вать; ~ *beer* имби́рный лимона́д;
~ *bread* имби́рный пря́ник; ~**ly**,
ad, осторо́жно; ~**y**, *a*, имби́р-
ный; рыжева́тый.

gipsy, *a*, цыга́нский; ¶ *n*, цыга́н, -ка.

giraffe, *n*, жира́ф.

gird, *v.t*, опоя́сывать; окружа́ть; ~**er**,
n, ба́лка; брус; ~**le**, *n*, по́яс;
(tech.) кольцо́; ¶ *v.t*, подпоя́сы-
вать; кольцева́ть; окружа́ть.

girl, *n*, де́вочка; де́вушка; ~**hood**,
n, деви́чество; ~**ish**, *a*, деви́ческий;
похо́жий на де́вушку.

girth, *n*, подпру́га *(horse)*; обхва́т.

gist, *n*, суть; су́щность.

give, *v.t*, дава́ть; доставля́ть *(pleasure)*; причиня́ть *(pain)*; *v.i*, по-
дава́ться; сгиба́ться; ~ *away*

отдавать; выдавать; проговариваться; ~ back возвращать; ~ birth to родить; ~ in (v.i) сдаваться, уступать; (v.t.) вручать; ~ out (v.t.) выдавать; издавать; (v.i.) иссякать; ~ up отдавать; отказываться от; бросать; ~ oneself up сдаваться; ~ oneself to предаваться (dat.); given to данный (dat.); склонный к; ~r, n, дающий.

gizzard, n, глотка.

glacial, a, ледниковый; ледяной: glacier, n, ледник.

glad, a, радостный; I am ~ я рад; be ~ радоваться; ~den, v.t, радовать.

glade, n, прогалина, поляна; просека.

gladiator, n, гладиатор.

gladiolus, n, гладиолус.

gladly, ad, охотно; с удовольствием; gladness, n, радость.

glamorous, a, очаровательный; шикарный.

glamour, n, обаяние; очарование; ~ girl шикарная девушка.

glance, n, (быстрый) взгляд; at first ~ с первого взгляда; ¶ v.i, взглядывать; ~ off скользить, отскакивать; ~ through бегло просматривать.

gland, n, железа.

glare, n, пристальный взгляд; ослепительный блеск; яркий свет; ¶ v.i, пристально смотреть; ослепительно сверкать; glaring, a, яркий, ослепительный; ~ mistake грубая ошибка.

glass, n, стеклянный; ¶ n, стекло; стакан, рюмка; стеклянная посуда; зеркало; pl, очки; ~ cutter резец; ~ fibre стекловолокно; ~ house, теплица; карцер; ~ y, a, зеркальный; тусклый (look).

glaze, n, глазурь, глянец; ¶ v.t, застеклять; покрывать глазурью; ~d, p.p. & a, застеклённый; глазированный; glazier, n, стекольщик; гончар-глазировщик.

gleam, n, свет; отблеск; проблеск; ¶ v.i, светиться; ~ing, a, мерцающий.

glean, v.t, собирать колосья; (fig.) собирать; ~ings, n.pl, собранные колосья; собранные факты.

glee, n, ликование; радость; ~ful, a, ликующий, радостный.

glen, n, долина, лощина.

glib, a, бойкий на язык.

glide, n, скольжение; (avia.)планирование; горка для катания; ¶ v.i, скользить; незаметно проходить; планировать; ~r, n, планёр; hang ~ дельтоплан.

glimmer, n, мерцание; тусклый свет; (fig.) проблеск; ¶ v.i, мерцать; ~ing, a, мерцающий; тусклый.

glimpse, n, взгляд; мелькание; ¶ v.t, видеть мельком.

glint, n, блеск; вспышка; ¶ v.i, сверкать; вспыхивать.

glisten, v.i, блестеть, сиять.

glitter, n, сверкание, блеск; ¶ v.i, сверкать, блистать, блестеть.

gloaming, n, сумерки.

gloat, v.i, злорадствовать; ~ over пожирать глазами.

globe, n, земной шар; шар: глобус; ~-trotter страстный путешественник; globular, a, сферический, шаровидный; globule, n, шарик.

gloom, n, мрак; мрачность; уныние; ~y, a, мрачный; угрюмый.

glorification, n,прославление;glorify, v.t, прославлять; glorious, a, славный; великолепный; glory, n, слава, ¶ v.i, ликовать, торжествовать.

gloss, n, лоск, глянец; (comment) толкование; ¶ v: ~ over благоприятно истолковывать; ~ary, n, словарь, глоссарий; ~y, a, блестящий, лоснящийся, глянцевитый.

glove, n, перчатка; be hand in ~ with быть в тесной дружбе с; ~r, n, перчаточник.

glow, n, зарево, заря; свечение; румянец; пыл; ~-worm светляк; evening ~ вечерняя заря; ¶ v.i, сверкать; сиять; пылать.

glower, v.i, сердито смотреть.

glowing, a, ярко блестящий; раскалённый докрасна; пылающий; ~ with health пышущий здоровьем.

glucose, n, глюкоза.

glue, n, клей; ¶ v.t, клеить, приклеивать; ~y, a, клейкий, липкий.

glum, a, угрюмый.

glut, n, пресыщение; избыток; затоваривание (рынка); ¶ v.t, пресыщать; затоваривать.

glutinous, a, клейкий.

glutton, n, обжора; ~ous, a, прожорливый; ~y, n, обжорство.

glycerine, *n*, глицерин.

gnarled, *a*, шишковатый; угловатый.

gnash, *v.t*, скрежетать (зубами).

gnat, *n*, комар; мошка.

gnaw, *v.t*, грызть; глодать; *(fig.)* беспокоить.

gnome, *n*, гном, карлик.

gnostic, *n*, гностик.

go, *v.i*, идти, ходить; ехать, ездить; исчезать; работать; *(suit)* подходить; ~ *about* расхаживать; браться за *(work)*; ~ *after* искать; следовать за; ~ *ahead* двигаться вперёд; идти впереди; продолжать; ~ *astray* сбиваться с пути, заблудиться *(pf.)*; ~ *away* уходить; уезжать; ~ *back* возвращаться; ~ *by* проходить мимо; проходить *(time)*; ~ *down* спускаться, сходить; садиться *(sun)*; стихать *(wind)*; ~ *for* идти за *(inst.)*; стремиться к; ~ *in for* заниматься *(inst.)*; ~ *in for an exam* экзаменоваться; ~ *into* входить в; вступать в; ~ *off* уходить; проходить *(inst.)*; стрелять *(gun)*; портиться; ~ *on* идти дальше; продолжать; ~ *out* выходить; гаснуть; ~ *over* переходить; повторять; ~ *through* проходить; испытывать; подвергаться *(dat.)*; обыскивать; ~ *through with* доводить до конца; ~ *together* сочетаться; гармонировать; ~ *under* подходить под; погибать; ~ *up* всходить; подниматься; взрываться; ~ *with* сопровождать; гармонировать с; ~ *without* обходиться без; *let* ~ освобождать; отпускать; выпускать из рук; ¶ *n*, движение; попытка; энергия; *full of* ~ полон энергии; *have a* ~ попытаться *(pf.)*; *be on the* ~ быть в движении; *it's no* ~ это бесполезно.

goad, *n*, стрекало; *(fig.)* стимул; ¶ *v.t*, подгонять; побуждать, подстрекать.

go-ahead, *a*, предприимчивый.

goal, *n*, цель; *(sport)* финиш; гол; ворота; *score a* ~ забивать гол; ~*keeper* вратарь.

goat, *n*, коза, козёл; *young* ~ козлёнок; ~*herd* козий пастух; ~*ee*, *n*, козлиная бородка.

gobble, *v.t*, проглатывать; жадно есть; *v.i*, кулдыкать.

go-between, *n*, посредник.

goblet, *n*, кубок; бокал.

goblin, *n*, домовой.

god, *n*, бог, божество; кумир; *my* ~*!* боже мой!; *thank* ~*!* слава Богу!; ~ *forbid!* избави Бог!; ~*fearing* богобоязненный; ~*-forsaken* заброшенный, захолустный; ~*child* крест|ник, ~ница; ~*-father* крёстный отец; ~*-mother* крёстная мать; ~*-send* неожиданное счастье, находка; ~*ess*, *n*, богиня; ~*less*, *a*, безбожный; ~*lessness*, ~*less*, *n*, безбожие; ~*-like*, *a*, богоподобный; ~*liness*, *n*, набожность; ~*ly*, *a*, набожный.

goffer, *n*, щипцы для гофрировки; ¶ *v.t*, гофрировать.

goggle(s), *n.pl*, защитные очки; ~*eyed* пучеглазый; ¶ *v.t*, выпучивать глаза.

going, *n*, ходьба; отъезд; ~ *concern* дело на полном ходу; *set* ~ приводить в движение; *be* ~ *to* *(+ inf.)* собираться, намереваться *(+ inf.)*.

goings-on, *n.pl*, действия, поступки; козни.

goitre, *n*, зоб.

gold, *n*, золото; ~*-digger* золотоискатель; *(fig.)* авантюристка; ~*-dust* золотоносный песок; ~*field* золотоносный участок; золотые прииски; ~*finch* щегол; ~*fish* золотая рыбка; ~ *lace* золотой галун; ~ *leaf* тонкое листовое золото; ~ *mine* золотой рудник; *(fig.)* золотое дно; ~ *mining* золотопромышленность; добыча золота; ~*smith* ювелир; золотых дел мастер; ¶ *a*, золотой; ~*en*, *a*, золотистый; золотой; ~ *mean* золотая середина; ~ *wedding* золотая свадьба.

golf, *n*, гольф; ~ *course* поле для игры в гольф; ~*er*, *n*, игрок в гольф.

gondola, *n*, гондола; корзина (воздушного шара); **gondolier**, *n*, гондольёр.

gone, *p.p*, ушедший, уехавший; потерянный; мёртвый; *be* ~ *on* быть влюблённым в.

good, *a*, хороший; добрый; милый; умелый; *as* ~ *as* всё равно что; почти; ~ *afternoon(evening)!* добрый день (вечер)!; ~ *breeding* хорошие манеры; воспитанность; ~*-bye* до свидания!; прощайте!;

say ~*-bye* прощáться; *a* ~ *deal* мнóго; значи́тельное коли́чество; ~ *Friday* страстнáя пя́тница; ~*-for-nothing* бездéльник; ни на что не спосóбный; ~ *heavens!* гóсподи!; ~*-looking* краси́вый, хорóш собóй; прия́тный; ~ *morning!* дóброе ýтро!; ~*-natured* добродýшный; ~ *night!* спокóйной нóчи!; ~ *sense* здрáвый смысл; *in* ~ *time* своеврéменно; ~*will* дóбрая вóля, доброжелáтельство; *(com.)* клиентýра и репутáция фи́рмы; *be* ~ *at* быть спосóбным к; *be so* ~ будьте добры́ . . .; *for* ~ навсегдá; *make* ~ возмещáть; исполня́ть *(promise);* ¶ *n,* блáго, добрó; пóльза; *for the* ~ *of* для, рáди; *it is no* ~ бесполéзно; ~*ies,* *n.pl,* слáдости, конфéты; ~*ly,* *a,* значи́тельный; добрóтный; прекрáсный; ~*ness,* *n,* добротá; великодýшие; *for* ~ *sake!* гóсподи!

goods, *n.pl,* товáры; имýщество, вéщи; ~ *train* товáрный пóезд.

goose, *n,* гусь, гусы́ня; *(coll.)* простофи́ля; ~ *flesh* гуси́ная кóжа.

gooseberry, *n,* крыжóвник.

gore, *n,* кровь; клин; ¶ *v.l,* бодáть; вшивáть клин в.

gorge, *n,* глóтка, гóрло; пасть; *(geol.)* ущéлье; ¶ *v.i, v.t,* глотáть, поглощáть; *v.t,* насыщáть пó гóрло.

gorgeous, *a,* великолéпный; пы́шный.

gorilla, *n,* гори́лла.

gormandize, *v.i,,* объедáться; ~*r,* *n,* обжóра.

gory, *a,* окровáвленный; кровопроли́тный.

goshawk, *n,* я́стреб-тетеревя́тник.

gosling, *n,* гусёнок.

gospel, *n,* евáнгелие; ~ *truth* и́стинная прáвда.

gossamer, *n,* тóнкая ткань; паути́на.

gossip, *n,* сплéтня, болтовня́; *(pers.)* сплéт|ник, ~ница; ¶ *v.i,* сплéтничать; болтáть.

Goth, *n,* гот; ~*ic,* *a,* гóтский; готи́ческий.

gouge, *n,* полукрýглое долотó; вы́емка; ¶ *v.t,* выдáлбливать; выкáлывать.

gourd, *n,* ты́ква.

gourmet, *n,* гурмáн.

gout, *n,* подáгра; ~*y,* *a,* подагри́ческий.

govern, *v.t,* управля́ть/прáвить *(inst.);* ~*able,* *a,* послýшный; ~*ess,* *n,* гувернáнтка; ~*ment,* *n,* прави́тельство; управлéние; ~*mental,* *a,* прави́тельственный; ~*or,* *n,* губернáтор; комендáнт; *(coll.)* хозя́ин.

gown, *n,* плáтье (жéнское); мáнтия; *dressing* ~ халáт.

grab, *n,* захвáт; *(tech.)* автомати́ческий ковш; экскавáтор; ¶ *v.t,* хватáть; захвáтывать.

grace, *n,* грáция; любéзность; ми́лость; *the* ~*s* Грáции; *Your* ~ вáша ми́лость; ¶ *v.t,* удостáивать; ~ *with* украшáть; ~*ful,* *a,* грациóзный; изя́щный; прия́тный.

gracious, *a,* милосéрдный, ми́лый; *good* ~*!* бóже мой!; ~*ness,* *n,* добротá, ми́лость.

gradation, *n,* градáция; постепéнный перехóд.

grade, *n,* грáдус; стéпень; сорт; класс; *(rly.)* уклóн; *down* ~ скат, спуск; *up* ~ подъём; ¶ *v.t,* располагáть по степеня́м/клáссам; сортировáть; **gradient,** *n,* уклóн; наклóн; **grading,** *n,* расположéние; сортирóвка; **gradual,** *a,* постепéнный; **graduate,** *n,* окóнчивший университéт/вы́сшую шкóлу, выпускни́к; ¶ *v.i,* кончáть университéт/вы́сшую шкóлу; *v.t,* градуи́ровать, наноси́ть делéния на.

graft, *n,* взя́точничество; *(bot.)* приви́вка; пересáдка ткáни; ¶ *v.t,* прививáть *(bot.);* пересáживать *(surg.).*

grain, *n,* зернó; крупи́нка; песчи́нка; структýра *(of wood, etc.); against the* ~ прóтив шéрсти; не по нутрý; ¶ *v.t,* крáсить под дéрево/мрáмор.

grammar, *n,* граммáтика; ~ *school* срéдняя (класси́ческая) шкóла; ~*ian,* *n,* граммáтик; **grammatical,** *a,* граммати́ческий.

gramm(e), *n,* грамм.

gramophone, *n,* граммофóн, патефóн; ~ *record* граммофóнная пласти́нка.

grampus, *n,* сéверный дельфи́н.

granary, *n,* амбáр, жи́тница, зернохрани́лище.

grand, *a,* величественный; превосходный; великолепный; великий; важный; ~*daughter* внучка; ~*father* дед, дедушка; ~*master* гроссмейстер; ~*mother* бабушка; ~ *piano* рояль; ~*son* внук; ~*stand* трибуна; ~*eur,* *n,* величие; грандиозность; ~*iloquent,* *a,* высокопарный; ~*iose,* *a,* грандиозный, напыщенный.

grange, *n,* ферма, усадьба.

granite, *n,* гранит.

granny, *n,* бабушка.

grant, *n,* субсидия, дотация; стипендия; дар; ¶ *v.t,* дарить; давать; предоставлять; удовлетворять *(request);* допускать; соглашаться на/с; *take for* ~*ed* считать само собой разумеющимся; относиться небрежно к.

granulate, *v.t,* дробить, мельчить, гранулировать; ~*d sugar* сахарный песок.

grape, *n,* виноград; ~*fruit* грейпфрут; ~ *shot* картечь.

graph, *n,* график, диаграмма; ~*ic,* *a,* графический; наглядный.

graphite, *n,* графит.

grapple, *n,* *(tech.)* крюк, захват; ¶ *v.t,* схватывать; зацеплять; ~ *with* сражаться с; бороться с; ломать голову над; ~*-iron* абордажный крюк.

grasp, *n,* схватывание; хватка; *(fig.)* власть; *beyond one's* ~ выше понимания: вне пределов досягаемости; ¶ *v.t,* схватывать *(also fig.);* зажимать; понимать; ~ *at* хвататься за; ~*ing,* *a,* жадный.

grass, *n,* трава; ~*hopper* кузнечик; ~*land* луг, пастбище; прерия, степь; ~ *plot* газон; лужайка; ~ *snake* уж; ~ *widow* соломенная вдова; ~*y,* *a,* травяной; травянистый; покрытый травой.

grate, *n,* (каминная) решётка; ¶ *v.t,* тереть; скрести; скрежетать (зубами); *v.i,* тереться; ~ *on* раздражающе действовать на.

grateful, *a,* благодарный.

grater, *n,* тёрка.

grating, *n,* решётка; ¶ *a,* скрипучий; раздражающий.

gratis, *ad,* бесплатно, даром.

gratitude, *n,* благодарность.

gratuitous, *a,* даровой; добровольный; беспричинный; необосно-

ванный; **gratuity,** *n,* денежное пособие; чаевые.

grave, *a,* серьёзный; важный; ¶ *n,* могила; ~*digger* могильщик; ~*stone* надгробный памятник, могильная плита; ~*yard* кладбище.

gravel, *n,* гравий; *(med.)* мочевые камни; ~ *walk* гравийная дорожка; ¶ *v.t,* посыпать гравием.

gravely, *ad,* серьёзно; важно; мрачно.

graven, *a,* высеченный; выгравированный.

graver, *n,* гравёр; *(tool)* резец.

gravitate, *v.i,* тяготеть; притягиваться; **gravitation,** *n,* тяготение, притяжение; **gravity,** *n,* серьёзность, важность; *(phys.)* сила тяжести; *specific* ~ удельный вес.

gravy, *n,* подливка, соус; ~ *boat* соусник.

gray *see* **grey.**

grayling, *n,* хариус.

graze, *n,* царапина; ¶ *v.t,* пасти; задевать; натирать *(skin); v.i,* пастись; **grazier,** *n,* скотовод; *grazing land* пастбище.

grease, *n,* сало; жир; смазка; мазь; ¶ *v.t,* смазывать; замасливать; *(fig.)* подмазывать; ~*r,* *n,* смазчик; **greasiness,** *n,* сальность, жирность; *(fig.)* приторность; **greasy,** *a,* сальный, жирный; скользкий; приторный.

great, *a,* великий; большой; прекрасный; долгий; ~ *oat* пальто; шинель; *a* ~ *deal* много; ~*-grandchildren* правнуки; ~ *-granddaughter* ~*-grandfather* прадед; ~*-grandson* правнук; *a* ~ *many* множество; *a* ~ *while* долгое время; ~*est,* *a,* величайший; самый замечательный; ~*ly,* *ad,* очень; значительно; ~*ness,* *n,* величие.

Grecian, *a,* греческий.

greed, greediness, *n,* жадность, алчность; **greedy,** *a,* жадный; алчный.

Greek, *a,* греческий; ¶ *n,* грек; гречанка; греческий язык.

green, *a,* зелёный; неопытный; незрелый; ~*finch* зеленушка; ~*eyed* *(fig.)* ревнивый; завистливый; ~*gage* ренклод; ~*grocer* зеленщик; ~*horn* новичок, молокосос; ~*house* теплица, оранжерея; ¶ *n*, зелёный цвет; луг; *pl*, зéлень, óвощи; ~ery, *n*, растительность, зéлень; ~ish, *a*, зеленовáтый.

greet, *v.t*, привéтствовать; здорóваться с; клáняться *(dat.)*; ~ing, *n*, привéтствие; поклóн.

gregarious, *a*, живýщий стадáми/ стáями; стáдный; общúтельный.

Gregorian, *a*, грегориáнский.

grenade, *n*, гранáта; **grenadier**, *n*, гренадёр; **grenadine**, *n*, грснадúн.

grey, *a*, сéрый; седóй *(hair)*; пáсмурный *(weather)*; *go* ~ седéть; ~hound борзáя; ~ *hair* седина; ¶ *n*, сéрый цвет; ~ing, *a*, седéющий; ~ish, *a*, серовáтый; седовáтый; с прóседью.

grid, *n*, решётка; сéтка; ~*iron* рáшпер.

grief, *n*, гóре, печáль; *come to* ~ попадáть в бедý.

grievance, *n*, обúда; жáлоба; **grieve**, *v.t*, огорчáть; опечáливать; *v.i*, (~ *for*) горевáть (о); **grievous**, *a*, тяжёлый, мучúтельный; гóрестный; ~ly, *ad*, мучúтельно; гóрестно.

grill, *n*, жáреное мясо; решётка, рáшпер; ¶ *v.t. (& i.)*, жáрить(ся); жечь; *(coll.)* допрáшивать.

grille, *n*, решётка.

grim, *a*, мрáчный, угрюмый; жестóкий; стрóгий.

grimace, *n*, гримáса, ужúмка; ¶ *v.i*, гримáсничать.

grime, *n*, грязь; сáжа.

grimness, *n*, мрáчность, угрюмость; жестóкость; стрóгость.

grimy, *a*, грязный; закоптéлый.

grin, *n*, усмéшка; оскáл зубóв; ¶ *v.i*, скáлить зýбы; усмехáться.

grind, *v.t*, молóть, толóчь; скрежетáть (зубáми); точúть; шлифовáть; *v.i*, терéться; ~ *at* усéрдно рабóтать над; ~stone жёрнов; точúльный станóк; ~er, *n*, точúльщик; ~ing, *a*, шлифовáльный, точúльный; ¶ *n*, помóл; толчéние; тóчка.

grip, *n*, схвáтывание; сжáтие; пожáтие (рукú); власть; рукоятка; *(bag)* саквояж; ¶ *v.t*, схвáтывать; сжимáть; овладевáть (внимáнием).

gripes, *n*, кóлики.

grisly, *a*, стрáшный, ужáсный.

grist, *n*, зернó для помóла; *bring* ~ *to the mill* приносúть дохóд.

gristle, *n*, хрящ; **gristly**, *a*, хрящевáтый.

grit, *n*, песóк; грáвий; *(fig.)* твёрдость харáктера; ~ty, *a*, песчáный; твёрдый.

grizzled, *a*, седóй; **grizzly**, *a*, сéрый; ¶ *n*, сéрый медвéдь, грúзли.

groan, *n*, стон; вздох; ¶ *v.i*, стонáть; óхать.

groats, *n.pl*, крупá.

grocer, *n*, бакалéйщик; ~'s *shop* бакалéйный магазúн; ~ies бакалéя.

grog, *n*, грог, пунш; ~gy, *a*, пьяный; шáткий, нетвёрдый на ногáх.

groin, *n*, пах; *(arch.)* крестóвый свод.

groom, *n*, грум, кóнюх; женúх; ¶ *v.t*, ходúть за (лóшадью), чúстить *(horse)*; *(fig.)* воспúтывать; *well* ~ed выхоленный; ~sman шáфер.

groove, *n*, жёлоб; выемка; паз; рутúна; ¶ *v.t*, желобúть; дéлать выемку в.

grope, *v.i*, идтú óщупью; ~ *for* искáть (óщупью).

gross, *a*, огрóмный; тóлстый; валовóй; óптовый; ~ *income* валовóй дохóд; ~ *weight* вес брýтто; ¶ *n*, гросс (12 дюжин); мáсса; *by the* ~ óптом; гýртом; ~ly, *ad*, грýбо; чрезвычáйно.

grotesque, *a*, гротéскный; нелéпый.

grotto, *n*, грот, пещéра.

ground, *n*, земля, пóчва; мéстность; спортúвная площáдка; фон; *pl*, парк; осáдок, гýща; основáние; ~ *floor* пéрвый этáж; ~nut земляной орéх; арáхис; ~-rent земéльная рéнта; ~work основáние; фундáмент; *break* ~ поднимáть целинý; *(fig.)* проклáдывать нóвые путú; *gain* ~ продвигáться вперёд; *(fig.)* дéлать успéхи; *lose* ~ отступáть; *stand one's* ~ держáться; стоять на своём; *on the* ~s *of* по причúне; на основáнии; ¶ *v.t*, оснóвывать; обоснóвывать; опускáть на зéмлю; *(avia.)* запрещáть полёты; *v.i*, опускáться на зéмлю; наскáкивать на мель/бéрег; ¶ *a*, молóтый; отшлифóванный; ~ *glass* мáтовое стеклó; ~ *rice* рúс-сéчка.

groundsel, *n*, крестóвник.

group, *n,* гру́ппа; авиапо́лк; ¶ *v.t. (& i.),* группирова́ть(ся).

grouse, *n,* (шотла́ндская) куропа́тка; те́терев; *(fig.)* ворчу́н.

grove, *n,* ро́ща; *(geol.)* штолᴨня.

grovel, *v.i,* пресмыка́ться; унижа́ться; **~ler,** *n,* подхали́м.

grow, *v.t,* выра́щивать; разводи́ть; культиви́ровать; отра́щивать *(beard, etc.); v.i,* расти́, выраста́ть; увели́чиваться; **~** *cold* холоде́ть; **~** *dark* темне́ть, смерка́ться; **~** *little* уменьша́ться; **~** *old* старе́ть; **~** *up* выраста́ть, станови́ться взро́слым; **~er,** *n,* садово́д; **~ing,** *a,* расту́щий; ¶ *n,* рост; выра́щивание, разведе́ние.

growl, *n,* рост, рыча́ние; гро́хот; ¶ *v.i,* ворча́ть; рыча́ть.

grown-up, *n. & a,* взро́слый.

growth, *n,* рост, разви́тие; увеличе́ние; по́росль; *(med.)* о́пухоль.

grub, *n,* личи́нка; еда́; ¶ *v.i,* ры́ться; **~** *up* выкорчёвывать; **~ber,** *n,* корчева́тель **~by,** *a,* гря́зный.

grudge, *n,* зло́ба; *have a* **~** *against* име́ть зуб про́тив; ¶ *v.t,* неохо́тно дава́ть; жале́ть; зави́довать *(dat.);* **grudgingly,** *ad,* неохо́тно.

gruel, *n,* жи́дкая ка́ша.

gruesome, *a,* ужаса́ющий; отврати́тельный.

gruff, *a,* хри́плый; грубова́тый; **~ness,** *n,* грубова́тость.

grumble, *n,* ворча́ние, ро́пот; ¶ *v.i,* ворча́ть, жа́ловаться; **~r,** *n,* ворчу́н; **grumpy,** *a,* серди́тый, сварли́вый.

grunt, *n,* хрю́канье; брюзжа́ние; ¶ *v.i,* хрю́кать; брюзжа́ть.

guarantee, *n,* гара́нтия; зало́г; поручи́тель(ство); поручи́тель; ¶ *v.t,* гаранти́ровать; руча́ться за; **guarantor,** *n,* поручи́тель.

guard, *n,* охра́на; конво́й; карау́л; часово́й; сто́рож; конво́йр; проводни́к *(rly.);* гва́рдия; бди́тельность; *advance* **~** аванга́рд; *be off one's* **~** быть недоста́точно бди́тельным; *be on* **~** быть насторо́же/начеку́; *changing of the* **~** сме́на часовы́х; *mount* **~** вступа́ть в карау́л; *relieve the* **~** сменя́ть карау́л; **~-room** карау́льное помеще́ние, гауптва́хта; ¶ *v.t,* охраня́ть; сторожи́ть, стере́чь; **~** *against* остерега́ться *(gen.);* **~ed,** *a,* осторо́жный; **~ian,**

n, опеку́н; попечи́тель; храни́тель; **~ship,** *n,* опе́ка; опеку́нство; **~sman,** *n,* гварде́ец.

gudgeon, *n,* пеcка́рь; *(tech.)* болт.

guerrilla, *n,* партиза́н; **~** *warfare* партиза́нская война́.

guess, *n,* предположе́ние, дога́дка; ¶ *v.t,* уга́дывать, отга́дывать; *v.i,* дога́дываться; предполага́ть; *(coll.)* счита́ть.

guest, *n,* гость, го́стья; **~-house** гости́ница; **~room** ко́мната для госте́й.

guffaw, *n,* хо́хот, го́гот; ¶ *v.i,* хохота́ть.

guidance, *n,* руково́дство; **guide,** *n,* гид, экскурсово́д; проводни́к; руководи́тель; *(book)* путеводи́тель, руково́дство; **~-post** указа́тельный столб; ¶ *v.t,* руководи́ть *(inst.);* вести́.

guild, *n,* ги́льдия; цех; сою́з; **~hall** ра́туша.

guile, *n,* обма́н; хи́трость; **~ful,** *a,* кова́рный, хи́трый; **~less,** *a,* простоду́шный; **~lessness,** *n,* простоду́шие.

guillotine, *n,* гильоти́на; ¶ *v.t,* отруба́ть го́лову *(dat.).*

guilt, *n,* вина́, вино́вность; **~less,** *a,* неви́нный, невино́вный; **~y,** *a,* вино́вный.

guinea, *n,* гине́я; **~-fowl** цеса́рка; **~** *pig* морска́я сви́нка; *(fig.)* «подо́пытный кро́лик».

guise, *n,* вид; личи́на, ма́ска; предло́г; *under the* **~** *of* под ви́дом; *in this* **~** в тако́м ви́де.

guitar, *n,* гита́ра; **~ist,** *n,* гитари́ст.

gulch, *n,* уще́лье.

gulf, *n,* зали́в; *(fig.)* бе́здна; **~** *Stream* Гольфстри́м.

gull, *n,* ча́йка; *(pers.)* проста́к; ¶ *v.t,* дура́чить.

gullet, *n,* пищево́д; гло́тка.

gullibility, *n,* легкове́рие; **gullible,** *a,* дове́рчивый.

gully, *n,* овра́г; водосто́чная кана́ва.

gulp, *n,* глото́к; ¶ *v.t,* глота́ть.

gum, *n,* десна́; каме́дь, гу́мми; клей; **~boil** флюс; **~boots** рези́новые сапоги́; ¶ *v.t,* скле́ивать; **~my,** *a,* кле́йкий; смоли́стый.

gumption, *n,* смышлёность.

gun, *n,* ружьё, винто́вка; ору́дие, пу́шка; револьве́р; *double-barrelled* **~** двуство́лка; **~boat** каноне́рка; **~carriage** лафе́т; **~** *cotton* пироксилйн; ~*fire* орудйиный огóнь; ~*-metal* пýшечный метáлл; ~*powder* пóрох; ~*-running* незакóнный ввоз орýжия; ~*shot* орудйиный вы́стрел; *within* ~*-shot* на расстоя́нии пýшечного вы́стрела; ~*smith* оружéйный мáстер; ~*ner*, *n*, артиллерйст; пулемётчик; ~*y*, *n*, артиллéрия.

gunwale, *n*, планшúр.

gurgle, *n*, бýльканье; ¶ *v.i*, бýлькать.

gush, *n*, сúльный потóк; излия́ние; ¶ *v.i*, хлы́нуть *(pf.)*; разливáться; изливáться; ~*ing*, *a*, слащáвый.

gusset, *n*, встáвка, клин.

gust, *n*: ~ *of wind* поры́в вéтра.

gusto, *n*, удовóльствие; смак.

gusty, *a*, поры́вистый; бýрный.

gut, *n*, кишкá; струнá из кишкú; *pl*, внýтренности; мýжество; ¶ *v.t*, потрошúть; опустошáть; ломáть внýтренность (дóма); ~*led* вы́горевший внутрú.

gutta-percha, *n*, гуттапéрча.

gutter, *n*, стóчная канáва; водостóчный жёлоб; ~*snipe* ýличный мальчúшка; подлéц; ~ *press* бульвáрная прéсса.

guttural, *a*, гортáнный, горлоóвй.

guy, *n*, пáрень; чучело; ¶ *v.t*, выставля́ть на посмéшище.

guzzle, *v.t*, пропивáть, проедáть; жáдно глотáть.

gymnasium, *n*, гимнастúческий зал; гимнáзия; **gymnast**, *n*, гимнáст, -ка; ~*ic*, *a*, гимнастúческий; ~*ics*, *n*, гимнáстика.

gynaecologist, *n*, гинекóлог; **gynaecology**, *n*, гинекология.

gyrate, *v.i*, вращáться по крýгу; двúгаться по спирáли; **gyration**, *n*, вращéние; **gyroscope**, *n*, гироскóп.

H

haberdasher, *n*, галантерéйщик; ~*'s shop* галантерéйный магазúн; ~*y*, *n*, галантерéя.

habiliment, *n*, одея́ние, одéжда.

habit, *n*, привы́чка; обы́чай; свóйство; одéжда; *be in the* ~ имéть обыкновéние.

habitable, *a*, гóдный для жилья́; обитáемый; **habitat**, *n*, жилúще, жильё; местожúтельство.

habitual, *a*, обы́чный; привы́чный **habituate**, *v.t*, приучáть.

hack, *n*, наёмная лóшадь; кля́ча; писáка; зарýбка; ¶ *v.t*, рубúть; подрезáть; ~*ing cough* сухóй кáшель.

hackney carriage, *n*, наёмный экипáж.

hackneyed, *a*, банáльный, избúтый.

haddock, *n*, пúкша.

Hades, *n*, Гáдес.

haemorrhage, *n*, кровоизлия́ние.

haemorrhoids, *n. pl*, геморрóй.

haft, *n*, рукоя́тка.

hag, *n*, каргá.

haggard, *a*, измождённый, осýнувшийся.

haggle, *v.i*, торговáться; придирáться.

hail, *n*, град; приветствие; ~*stone* грáдина; ~*storm* лúвень с грáдом; *within* ~*ing distance* на расстоя́нии слы́шимости гóлоса; ¶ *v.t*, приветствовать; оклúкать; ~ *from* происходúть из.

hair, *n*, вóлос(ы); шерсть *(animal)*; *to a* ~ тóчь-в-тóчь; ~ *brush* щётка для волóс; ~*cut* стрúжка; ~*dresser* парикмáхер, -ша; ~*dresser's* парикмáхерская; ~ *drier* сушúлка для волóс; ~*net* сéтка для волóс; ~*pin* шпúлька; ~*pin bend* крутóй поворóт; ~ *splitting* педантúчность; ~ *spring* волосóк; ~*less*, *a*, безволóсый, лы́сый; ~*y*, *a*, волосáтый; ворсúстый.

hake, *n*, мерлýза.

halcyon, *a*, я́сный.

hale, *a*, здорóвый, крéпкий.

half, *n*, половúна; *do by halves* дéлать кое-кáк; *better* ~ дражáйшая половúна, женá; ¶ *a*, половúнный; ¶ *ad*, наполовúну, полу-; ~*-back* полузащúтник; ~*-brother* свóдный брат; ~*-caste* метúс, человéк смéшанной рáсы; *go halves* делúть пополáм; ~ *an hour* полчасá; *an hour and a* ~ полторá часá; *leave* ~*-done* доделывать; ~*-length portrait* поясной портрéт; ~*-mast* приспущенный (флаг); ~ *moon* полумéсяц; ~ *pay* половúнный оклáд; ~*penny* полпéнни; ~ *price* полценá; *at* ~ *price* за полценý; ~*-seas-over* подвы́пивший; ~*-way* на полпутú; *meet* ~*-way* идтú навстречу/на уступки; ~-*witted* слабоумный; ~ *year* полгода; ~-*yearly (a.)* полугодовой; *(ad.)* раз в полгода.

halibut, *n*, палтус.

hall, *n*, зал, холл; передняя, вестибюль; столовая; большой (помещичий) дом; *fig.)* отличительный признак; ~ *porter* коридорный; ~*way* передняя, прихожая.

hallo, *int*, алло!; здорово!; **haloo**, *v.t*, натравливать (собак); *(fig.)* подстрекать.

hallucination, *n*, галлюцинация.

halo, *n*, ореол, нимб.

halt, *n*, остановка; привал; *(rly.)* полустанок; ¶ *a*, хромой; ¶ *v.t*, останавливать, задерживать; *v.i*, останавливаться; делать привал; ¶ *int*, стой!.

halter, *n*, повод, недоуздок; петля.

halve, *v.t*, делить пополам; сокращать наполовину.

halyard, *n*, фал.

ham, *n*, ветчина; окорок; ляжка; плохой актёр.

hamlet, *n*, деревушка.

hammer, *n*, молоток; курок *(gun)*; ¶ *v.t*, вбивать, прибивать; ковать; бить; ~ *at* колотить в; *(fig.)* приставать к; упорно работать над; ~*ing*, *n*, ковка; удары.

hammock, *n*, гамак.

hamper, *n*, корзина с крышкой; ¶ *v.t*, мешать *(dat.)*; затруднять.

hamster, *n*, хомяк.

hand, *n*, рука; почерк; ладонь *(measure)*; стрелка *(clock)*; участие; работник; *at* ~ под рукой, наготове; *by* ~ от руки; *in* ~ в подчинении; в исполнении; ~ *in* рука об руку; *on* ~ имеющийся в распоряжении/в наличии/налицо; *on one* ~ с одной стороны; *from* ~ *to mouth* со дня на день; ~*-to*~ рукопашный (бой); ~*bag* сумка; ~*ball* гандбол; ~*-bell* колокольчик; ~*bill* рекламный листок; ~*book* справочник; ~*cart* ручная тележка; ~*cuff (n.)* наручник; *(v.t.)* надевать наручники *(dat.)*; ~ *in glove with* в тесной дружбе с; заодно с; ~*kerchief* носовой платок; ~*made* ручной работы; ~*maid* служанка; ~*rail* перила;

~*saw* ручная пила; ~*shake* рукопожатие; ~*writing* почерк; ~*s off!* руки прочь!; *all* ~*s on deck!* все наверх!; ~*s up!* руки вверх!; *get the upper* ~ брать верх над; *hold one's* ~ воздерживаться от вмешательства; *off one's* ~*s* с рук долой; *on* ~*s and knees* на четвереньках; *under one's* ~ собственноручно; ¶ *v.t*, передавать, вручать; ~ *down* подавать сверху; передавать (потомству); ~ *in* подавать; возвращать; ~ *over* передавать; сдавать; ~*ful*, *n*, пригоршня, горсть; маленькая кучка.

handicap, *n*, гандикап *(sport)*; *(fig.)* помеха; ¶ *v.t*, ставить в невыгодное положение; ~*ped* страдающий физическим недостатком.

handicraft, *n*, ремесло; ручная работа; искусство; ~ *industry* кустарное производство; ~*sman*, *n*, ремесленник; кустарь; **handi-work**, *n*, ручная работа; дело рук.

handle, *n*, ручка, рукоятка; ~*bar* руль; ¶ *v.t*, держать в руках, перебирать руками; обращаться с; управлять *(inst.)*; трактовать *(theme)*; иметь дело с *(com.)*; вести; грузить; **handling**, *n*, обхождение; трактовка; управление; погрузка.

handsome, *a*, красивый; щедрый.

handy, *a*, удобный; легко управляемый; (имеющийся) под рукой; *(pers.)* умелый, способный; *come in* ~ пригодиться *(pf.)*; ~*man* на все руки мастер.

hang, *v.t*, вешать; развешивать; оклеивать (обоями); *v.i*, висеть; сидеть *(dress)*; ~ *about* слоняться, шляться; надвигаться; ~ *back* колебаться; ~ *down* свисать; ~ *in the balance* висеть на волоске; ~ *on* держаться; упорствовать; ~ *out (v.t.)* вывешивать; *(v.i.)* высовываться (из окна).

hangar, *n*, ангар.

hanger, *n*, вешалка; ~*-on* прихлебатель; **hanging**, *a*, висячий; подвесной; ¶ *n*, вешание, повешение *(execution)*; ~*s*, *n*, портьеры, драпировки; **hangman**, *n*, палач.

hank, *n*, моток.

hanker after, страстно желать, жаждать *(gen.);* **hankering,** *n,* страстное желание.

hansom, *n,* двухколёсный экипаж.

haphazard, *a,* случайный; ¶ *ad,* случайно;

hapless, *a,* несчастный; злополучный.

happen, *v.i,* случаться; происходить; ~ *to be* случайно оказываться; *whatever* ~s что бы ни случилось; ~**ing,** *n,* случай, событие.

happily, *ad,* счастливо; к счастью; **happiness,** *n,* счастье; **happy,** *a,* счастливый; удачный; довольный; ~-*go-lucky* беспечный.

harangue, *n,* речь; ¶ *v.i,* произносить речь.

harass, *v.t,* беспокоить.

harbinger, *n,* предвестник; ¶ *v.t,* предвещать.

harbour, *n,* гавань, порт; *(fig.)* убежище; ~ *dues* портовые сборы.

hard, *a,* твёрдый, жёсткий; крепкий; тяжёлый; суровый; упорный; ~ *and fast* твёрдый; строго определённый; ~-*boiled egg* яйцо вкрутую; ~*bitten* стойкий, упорный; ~ *cash* наличные деньги; ~-*headed* практичный, трёзвый; ~-*hearted* жестокосердный; ~-*heartedness* жестокосердие; ~ *labour* каторжные работы, каторга; ~-*pressed* в тяжёлом положении; ~*ware* металлические изделия; ~ *water* жёсткая вода; ¶ *ad,* твёрдо; крепко; сильно; усердно, упорно; сурово; *breathe* ~ тяжело дышать; *drink* ~ сильно пить; *work* ~ много работать; ~ *by* близко; ~ *of hearing* тугой на ухо; ~-*up* имеющий мало денег; ~**en,** *v.t,* делать твёрдым; закаливать *(metal);* ожесточать *(pers.); (fig.)* закалять; *v.i,* твердеть; застывать; ~**hood,** *n,* смелость; ~**iness,** *n,* крепость, выносливость; ~**ily,** *ad,* со стойкостью, смело; ~**ly,** *ad,* едва; едва ли; с трудом ~**y,** *a,* стойкий, выносливый.

hare, *n,* заяц; ~*bell* колокольчик; ~-*brained* безрассудный; ~ *lip* заячья губа.

harem, *n,* гарем.

haricot beans, *n.pl,* фасоль стручковая.

hark, *int,* слушай!; ¶ *v.t,* слушать; ~ *back to* возвращаться к.

harlequin, *n,* арлекин; шут; ~**ade,** *n,* арлекинада.

harlot, *n,* проститутка, шлюха.

harm, *n,* вред; ущерб; зло; ¶ *v.t,* вредить *(dat.);* повреждать; обижать; ~**ful,** *a,* врёдный; ~**less,** *a,* безврёдный; ~**lessness,** *n,* безврёдность.

harmonic, *a,* гармонический; ~**s,** *a,* гармоника; ~**a,** *n,* губная гармоника; **harmonious.** *a,* гармонический; гармоничный, дружный; **harmonium,** *n,* фисгармония; **harmonize,** *v.t,* гармонизировать; согласовывать; *v.i,* гармонировать; **harmony,** *n,* гармония, созвучие; согласие.

harness, *n,* упряжь, сбруя; ¶ *v.t,* запрягать, впрягать; использовать.

harp, *n,* арфа; ¶ *v.i:* ~ *on* твердить одно и то же, заводить волынку; ~**ist,** *n,* арфист, -ка.

harpoon, *n,* гарпун; острога; ¶ *v.t,* бить гарпуном.

harpsichord, *n,* клавикорды.

harpy, *n,* гарпия.

harridan, *n,* старая карга.

harrow, *n,* борона; ¶ *v.t,* боронить; *(fig.)* мучить; ~**ing,** *a,* ужасающий.

harry, *v.t,* опустошать; изводить.

harsh, *a,* жёсткий; суровый; грубый; ~**ness,** *n,* жестокость; суровость; грубость.

hart, *n,* олень.

harum-scarum, *a,* безрассудный.

harvest, *n,* жатва; урожай; *(fig.)* плоды; ¶ *v.ta,* жать, собирать урожай *(gen.);* ~**er,** *n,* уборочная машина; жнец.

hash, *n,* рубленое мясо; *(fig.)* путаница; *make a* ~ *of* портить; ¶ *v.t,* рубить, крошить.

hassock, *n,* подушечка; кочка.

haste, *n,* спешка; поспешность; опрометчивость; ~**n,** *v.t,* торопить; ускорять; *v.i,* спешить, торопиться; **hastily,** *ad,* поспешно; необдуманно; **hasty,** *a,* поспешный; необдуманный; опрометчивый; вспыльчивый.

hat, *a,* шляпа; шапка; ~ *box* картонка; ~ *rack* вешалка для шляп; ~ *shop* шля́пный магази́н;

hatch, *n,* вы́водок; люк; ¶ *v.t,* выси́живать; штрихова́ть; *(plot)* замышля́ть; *v.i,* вылу́пливаться (из яйца́); рожда́ться.

hatchet, *n,* топо́рик; *bury the* ~ заключа́ть мир.

hatching, *n,* выведе́ние *(chicks);* штрихо́вка.

hatchment, *n,* герб.

hatchway, *n,* люк.

hate *(& hatred), n,* не́нависть; ¶ *v.t,* ненави́деть.

haughtily, *ad,* надме́нно; **haughtiness,** *n,* надме́нность, высокоме́рие; **haughty,** *a,* надме́нный, высокоме́рный.

haul, *n,* тя́га; перево́зка; уло́в *(fish);* добы́ча; ¶ *v.t,* тащи́ть, тяну́ть; букси́ровать; перевози́ть; ~ *down* спуска́ть; ~**age,** *n,* перево́зка.

haunch, *n,* ля́жка, бедро́; за́дняя нога́.

haunt, *n,* ча́сто посеща́емое ме́сто; ¶ *v.t,* ча́сто посеща́ть; явля́ться (как при́зрак) *(dat.);* упо́рно возвраща́ться к; пресле́довать; ~*ed house* дом с привиде́ниями; ~*ed look* испу́ганный взгляд.

hautboy, *n,* гобо́й.

have, *v.t,* име́ть; облада́ть *(inst.); I* ~ у меня́ есть . . .; *I* ~ *not* у меня́ нет . . .; ~ *a nice time* прия́тно проводи́ть вре́мя; ~ *a walk* прогу́ливаться; *I* ~ *to* я до́лж|ен, -на́; ~ *on* быть в *(clothing); you had better* . . . вам лу́чше бы . . . ~*s and* ~*-nots* иму́щие и неиму́щие.

haven, *n,* га́вань; *(fig.)* убе́жище, прию́т.

haversack, *n,* вещево́й мешо́к.

havoc, *n,* разруше́ние, опустоше́ние.

haw, *n,* я́года боя́рышника; ~*thorn* боя́рышник; ¶ *v.i,* бормота́ть, запина́ться.

hawk, *n,* я́стреб; *(fig.)* хи́щник; ~*-eyed* с о́стрым гла́зом; ¶ *v.t,* торгова́ть в разно́с *(inst.);* отка́шливать; *v.i,* охо́титься с я́стребом; отка́шливаться; ~**er,** *n,* разно́счик, у́личный торго́вец.

hawser, *n,* (стально́й) трос.

hay, *n,* се́но; ~ *fever* сенна́я лихора́дка; ~ *loft* сенова́л; ~*maker* коса́рь; сеноубо́рочная маши́на; ~*making* сеноко́с; ~*stack* стог се́на.

hazard, *n,* опа́сность, риск; аза́ртная игра́; препя́тствие; ¶ *v.t,* рискова́ть *(inst.),* ста́вить на ка́рту; осме́ливаться на *(or inf.);* ~*ous,* *a,* риско́ванный.

haze, *n,* тума́н, ды́мка; ¶ *v.t,* зату́манивать.

hazel, *a,* ка́рий, све́тло-кори́чневый; ¶ *n,* оре́шник; ~*-nut* оре́х.

hazy, *a,* тума́нный; сму́тный.

he, *pn,* он; ¶ *n,* мужчи́на; саме́ц; ~*-goat* козёл.

head, *n,* голова́; глава́, вождь; руководи́тель; дире́ктор (шко́лы); нача́льник *(firm);* изголо́вье *(bed);* копна́ *(hair);* коча́н *(cabbage);* шля́пка *(nail);* ~*ache* головна́я боль; ~ *of cattle* голова́ скота́; ~ *cook* шеф-по́вар; ~*dress* головно́й убо́р; ~*land* мыс; ~*light* фа́ра; ~*line* заголо́вок; ~*long (a)* опроме́тчивый; *(ad.)* очертя́ го́лову; ~*master* дире́ктор шко́лы; ~*mistress* директри́са; ~ *office* правле́ние; ~*phones* нау́шники; ~*quarters* штаб, штаб-кварти́ра; центр, гла́вное управле́ние; ~*stone* краеуго́льный ка́мень; надгро́бная плита́; ~*waiter* метрдоте́ль; ~*way* движе́ние вперёд; *(fig.)* успе́х, прогре́сс; *(mar.)* поступа́тельное движе́ние; ~ *wind* встре́чный ве́тер; *from* ~ *to foot* с головы́ до ног; ~ *over heels in love* по́ уши влюблённый; ~ *over heels* вверх торма́шками; *bring to a* ~ обостря́ть; *come to a* ~ достига́ть крити́ческой ста́дии; *hit the nail on the* ~ попада́ть в то́чку; ~*s or tails* орёл и́ли ре́шка; ¶ *v.t,* возглавля́ть; озагла́вливать *(article, etc.);* ударя́ть голово́й (по мячу́); *v.i,* держа́ть курс; ~*er,* *n,* прыжо́к вниз голово́й; ~*ing,* *n,* загла́вие, заголо́вок; курс; ~*y,* *a,* опроме́тчивый; кре́пкий *(wine).*

heal, *v.t,* изле́чивать; исцеля́ть; *v.i,* зажива́ть; ~*er,* *n,* исцели́тель; ~*ing,* *a,* лече́бный, целе́бный.

health, *n,* здоро́вье; тост; *officer of* ~ санита́рный врач; ~*-resort* курорт; ~у, а, здоровый; полезный для здоровья.

heap, n, куча, груда; масса; ¶ v.t, нагромождать; ~ up накоплять; ~ with нагружать.

hear, v.t, слышать; выслушивать; (law) слушать; ~ of слышать, узнавать о; ~ from получать известия/письмо от; ~ing, n, слух; (law) слушание, разбор дела; hard of ~ тугой на ухо; within~ в пределах слышимости.

hearken, v.t, слушать.

hearsay, n, слух, молва.

hearse, n, катафалк.

heart, n, сердце; (fig.) душа; мужество; сердцевина; ядро; сущность; (pl., card) черви; at ~ в глубине души; by ~ наизусть; ~ and soul всей душой; ~ and soul of the party душа общества; ~-breaking душераздирающий; ~-broken убитый горем; с разбитым сердцем; ~burn изжога: ~ disease болезнь сердца; take to ~ принимать близко к сердцу; ~en, v.t, ободрять; ~felt, а, сердечный, искренний.

hearth, n, очаг, камин; (fig.) домашний очаг; (tech.) горн; ~rug коврик перед камином.

heartily, ad, сердечно; охотно, усердно; с аппетитом; **heartless**, a, бессердечный, безжалостный; **hearty**, a, сердечный, искренний; обильный (food); здоровый.

heat, n, жара; жар; тепло; пыл, гнев; (phys.) теплота; период течки (of animals); ~ stroke солнечный удар; white ~ белое каление; (fig.) бешенство; ¶ v.t, (& i.), нагревать(ся), разогревать(ся); топить(ся); накаливать(ся); ~er, n, грелка; радиатор; печь; кипятильник.

heath, n, степь, пустошь; ~-cock тетерев.

heathen, a, языческий; ¶ n, язычник; ~ish, a, варварский; ~ism, a, язычество.

heather, n, вереск.

heating, n, отопление; нагревание; накаливание.

heave, v.t, поднимать; грузить; тянуть; ~ a sigh тяжело вздыхать; v.i, вздыматься (waves, etc.); поворачиваться; ~ to останавливаться.

heaven, n, небо, рай; ~ly, a, небесный; божественный; ~ body небесное светило.

heaver, n, грузчик; (tech.) рычаг.

heavily, ad, тяжело; сильно; **heaviness**, n, тяжесть; инертность; **heavy**, a, тяжёлый; сильный (rain); бурный (sea); мрачный (sky); ~ traffic сильное движение; ~weight тяжеловес.

Hebraic, a, древнееврейский; ¶ n, еврей; древнееврейский язык.

hecatomb, n, гекатомба.

heckle, v.t, прерывать вопросами/криками.

hectic, a, лихорадочный; чахоточный.

hector, v.t, задирать; оскорблять.

hedge, n, живая изгородь; ограда; (fig.) препятствие; ~hog ёж; ¶ v.t, огораживать изгородью; ограничивать; v.i, уклоняться; ~ round окружать.

heed, n, внимание; осторожность; ¶ v.t, обращать внимание на; следить за; ~ful, a, внимательный; заботливый; ~less, a, небрежный; необдуманный.

heel, n, пятка; пята; каблук (of shoe); dig one's ~s in укрепляться; занимать позицию; down at ~ стоптанный; (fig.) жалкий; take to one's ~ удирать; on the ~s (of) по пятам.

hefty, a, дюжий, здоровенный.

hegemony, n, гегемония.

heifer, n, тёлка.

height, n, высота; вышина, рост; возвышенность; (fig.) верх; ~ of folly предел глупости; at the ~ of summer в разгар лета; ~en, v.t. (& i.), повышать(ся); усиливать(ся).

heinous, a, ужасный, гнусный.

heir, n, наследник; ~ess, n, наследница; ~loom наследственная вещь; наследие.

helicopter, n, вертолёт.

heliograph, n, гелиограф.

heliotrope, n, гелиотроп.

helix, n, спираль; (tech.) винт.

hell, n, ад.

Hellenic, a, эллинский.

hellish, a, адский.

hello, int, алло!; здравствуйте!

helm, n, руль; штурвал; (fig.) бразды правления.

helmet, n, шлем; каска.

helmsman, *n*, рулевой, кормчий.

help, *n*, помощь; помощник; прислуга; *call for* ~ звать на помощь; *there's no* ~ *for it* этому нельзя помочь; ¶ *v.t*, помогать *(dat.)*, способствовать *(dat.)*; угощать *(at table)*; ~ *yourself!* берите, пожалуйста!; угощайтесь!; *I can't* ~ *it* я ничего не могу поделать; *I can't* ~ *saying* я не могу не сказать; ¶ *int*, помоги(те)!; ~**er**, *n*, помощник; ~**ful**, *a*, полезный, готовый помочь; ~**fulness**, *n*, полезность; готовность помочь; ~**ing**, *n*, порция; ~**less**, *a*, беспомощный.

helter-skelter, *ad*, как попало; сломя голову.

helve, *n*, черенок; ручка, рукоятка.

hem, *n*, рубец; кайма ¶ *v.t*, подрубать, окаймлять; ~ *in* ограничивать; окружать; ¶ *int*, гм!.

hemisphere, *n*, полушарие.

hemistich, *n*, полустишие.

hemlock, *n*, болиголов.

hemp, *n*, конопля; пенька; ¶ *a*, конопляный; пеньковый.

hen, *n*, курица; ~ *house* курятник; ~-*pecked* (находящийся) под башмаком у жены.

henbane, *n*, белена.

hence, *ad*, отсюда; следовательно; *ten years* ~ через десять лет; ~**forth**, *ad*, с этих пор; отныне.

henchman, *n*, приверженец, ставленник.

henna, *n*, хна.

her, *pn*, её, *etc.*; свой.

herald, *n*, герольд; вестник; предвестник; ¶ *v.t*, возвещать; предвещать; ~**ic**, *n*, геральдический; ~**ry**, *n*, геральдика.

herb, *n*, трава, растение; ~**age**, *n*, травы; ~**al**, *a*, травяной; ¶ *n*, травник; ~**alist**, *n*, специалист по травам; торговец лечебными травами; ~**arium**, *n*, гербарий; ~**ivorous**, *a*, травоядный.

herculean, *a*, геркулесовский; исполинский.

herd, *n*, стадо; ¶ *v.t*, пасти; *v.i*, толпиться; ~**sman**, *n*, пастух.

here, *ad*, здесь, тут; сюда; вот; ~ *goes!* начнём!; пошли!; ~ *and there* там и сям; ~'*s to you!* (за) ваше здоровье!; ~ *you are!* вот, пожалуйста!; *look* ~! послушай-

(те)!; ~**abouts**, *ad*, поблизости; ~**after**, *ad*, в будущем; ~**by**, *ad*, настоящим; при сём; таким образом.

hereditary, *a*, наследственный; **heredity**, *n*, наследственность.

herein, *ad*, при сём; в этом; ~**after**, *ad*, ниже, в дальнейшем; **hereof**, *ad*, об этом; этого; отсюда.

heresy, *n*, ересь; **heretic**, *n*, еретик; ~**al**, *a*, еретический.

hereto, *ad*, к этому, к тому; ~**fore**, *ad*, прежде; до этого; **hereupon**, *ad*, после этого; вследствие этого; **herewith**, *ad*, настоящим; при сём, при этом.

heritage, *n*, наследство; наследие.

hermaphrodite, *n*, гермафродит.

hermetic, *a*, герметический.

hermit, *n*, отшельник; ~ *crab* рак-отшельник; ~**age**, *n*, келья; пустынь; убежище.

hernia, *n*, грыжа.

hero, *n*, герой; ~**ic**, *a*, геройческий; ~**ine**, *n*, героиня; ~**ism**, *n*, героизм.

heron, *n*, цапля.

herring, *n*, сельдь.

hers, *pn*, её; свой; ~**elf**, *pn*, себя; сама.

hesitant, *a*, нерешительный; колеблющийся; **hesitate**, *v.i*, колебаться; не решаться; запинаться; **hesitation**, *n*, нерешительность; колебание.

heterodox, *a*, иноверный; ~**y**, *n*, иноверие.

heterogeneous, *a*, разнородный.

hew, *v.t*, рубить, разрубать; ~ *down* срубать; ~ *out* высекать, вытёсывать; ~**er**, *n*, дровосек; забойщик *(coal)*.

hexagon, *n*, шестиугольник; ~**al**, *a*, шестиугольный; **hexameter**, *n*, гекзаметр.

heyday, *n*, расцвет; зенит.

hi!, *int*, эй!, привет!

hiatus, *n*, зияние; пробел, пропуск.

hibernate, *v.i*, находиться в зимней спячке, зимовать; *(fig.)* бездействовать; **hibernation**, *n*, зимняя спячка, зимовка.

hiccup, *n*, икота; ¶ *v.i*, икать.

hickory, *n*, гикори.

hidden, *p.p. & a*, спрятанный; скрытый; **hide**, *v.t. (& i.)*, скрывать(ся), прятать(ся); ~ *and seek* (игра́ в) пря́тки; ~-*out* убе́жище, укры́тие.

hide, *n,* шку́ра, ко́жа; ~-*bound* у́зкий, ограни́ченный.

hideous, *a,* безобра́зный, уро́дливый; отврати́тельный.

hiding, *n,* по́рка; скрыва́ние; ~ *place* потаённое ме́сто, убе́жище; *go into* ~ скрыва́ться.

hierarchy, *n,* иера́рхия.

hieroglyph, *n,* иеро́глиф.

higgledy-piggledy, *ad,* как попа́ло, беспоря́дочно.

high, *a,* высо́кий; возвы́шенный; вы́сший, лу́чший; си́льный (*wind*); испо́рченный (*meat*); большо́й (*speed*); ~ *and low* (лю́ди) вся́кого зва́ния; ~ *and dry* вы́брошенный на бе́рег; (*fig.*) поки́нутый; ~-*born* зна́тного происхожде́ния; ~*brow* интеллектуа́льный; ~ *Command* верхо́вное кома́ндование; ~-*flown* напы́щенный; ~-*handed* своево́льный; вла́стный; ~ *hat* цили́ндр; ~ *jump* прыжо́к в высоту́; ~*land* го́рный райо́н; ~*lander* (шотла́ндский) го́рец; ~-*light* светово́й эффе́кт; ~-*pitched* ре́зкий; ~ *priest* жрец; ~ *school* сре́дняя шко́ла; ~ *sea* откры́тое мо́ре; ~ *society* вы́сшее о́бщество; ~-*speed* скоростно́й; быстроре́жущий; ~-*spirited* пы́лкий; ~ *tide* прили́в, по́лная вода́; ~*way* больша́я доро́га, шоссе́; (*fig.*) столбова́я доро́га; ~*wayman* разбо́йник с большо́й доро́ги; ¶ *ad,* высоко́; си́льно; ~ *and low* повсю́ду; ~*ly,* *ad,* о́чень, весьма́; ~*ness,* *n,* высота́; высо́чество (*title*).

hijack, *v.t,* угоня́ть (*aeroplane, etc.*); ~*er,* *n,* налётчик, «возду́шный пира́т».

hike, *v.i,* ходи́ть в похо́д, ходи́ть пешко́м; ¶ *n,* похо́д, экску́рсия; путеше́ствие пешко́м; ~*r,* *n,* путеше́ственник, экскурса́нт.

hilarious, *a,* весёлый; **hilarity,** *n,* весе́лье; весёлость.

hill, *n,* холм, возвы́шенность; ~*ock,* *n,* хо́лмик, буго́р; ~*side,* *n,* склон горы́; ~*y,* *a,* холми́стый.

hilt, *n,* рукоя́тка; *up to the* ~ по рукоя́тку; (*fig.*) вполне́; до конца́.

him, *pn,* его́, ему́, *etc.*; ~*self,* *pn,* себя́; сам.

hind, *n,* лань.

hind(er), *a,* за́дний.

hinder, *v.t,* меша́ть/препя́тствовать (*dat.*).

hindmost, *a,* са́мый за́дний; са́мый отдалённый; **hindquarters,** *n.pl,* за́дняя часть.

hindrance, *n,* препя́тствие, поме́ха.

Hindu, *a,* инду́сский; ¶ *n,* инду́с; язы́к хиндуста́ни.

hinge, *n,* пе́тля; шарни́р; ¶ *v.t,* прикрепля́ть на пе́тлях; *v.i,* враща́ться/висе́ть на пе́тлях; ~ *on* зави́сеть от; враща́ться вокру́г.

hint, *n,* намёк; ¶ *v.t:* ~ *at* намека́ть на.

hinterland, *n,* глубина́ страны́; райо́н вглубь от грани́цы/побере́жья; райо́н, тяготе́ющий к це́нтру; (*mil.*) глубо́кий тыл.

hip, *n,* бедро́; (*bot.*) я́года шипо́вника; ~ *bath* поясна́я ва́нна; ~ *bone* подвздо́шная кость; ~ *pocket* за́дний карма́н.

hippodrome, *n,* ипподро́м.

hippopotamus, *n,* гиппопота́м.

hire, *n,* наём; прока́т; наёмная пла́та; ~ *purchase* прода́жа/поку́пка в рассро́чку; ¶ *v.t,* нанима́ть; брать напрока́т (*thing*); снима́ть (*room*); ~ *out* сдава́ть внаём, дава́ть напрока́т; ~*d,* *p p. & a,* на́нятый; взя́тый напрока́т; ~*ling,* *n,* наёмник; ~*r,* *n* нанима́тель.

hirsute, *a,* волоса́тый, косма́тый.

his, *pn,* его́; свой.

hiss, *v.t,* освисты́вать; *v.i,* свисте́ть; шипе́ть; ¶ *n,* свист, шипе́ние.

hist, *int,* ти́ше!; тсс!.

historian, *n,* исто́рик; **historic(al),** *a,* истори́ческий; **history,** *n* исто́рия.

histrionic, *a,* актёрский, сцени́ческий; театра́льный.

hit, *n,* уда́р, толчо́к; попада́ние; успе́х, уда́ча; гвоздь сезо́на; вы́пад; ~ *or miss* науга́д; как попа́ло; *make a* ~ име́ть успе́х, производи́ть сенса́цию; ¶ *v.t,* бить, ударя́ть; попада́ть в цель; попада́ть в то́чку; ~ *it off with* ла́дить с; ~ *against/upon* ударя́ться о; натыка́ться на; *it* ~*s you in the eye* э́то броса́ется в глаза́.

hitch, *n,* толчо́к; заце́пка; заде́ржка; поме́ха; (*mar.*) у́зел, пе́тля; *without a* ~ гла́дко; как по ма́слу; ¶ *v.t,* зацепля́ть; запряга́ть.

hitch-hike, *v.i,* путеше́ствовать автосто́пом, «голосова́ть» на доро́ге.

hither, *ad,* сюда; ~ *and thither* туда и сюда; ~most, *a,* ближайший; ~to, *ad,* до сих пор.

hive, *n,* улей; рой пчёл; ¶ *v.i,* ройться; ~ *off* отделять(ся).

hoard, *n,* запас; хранилище; клад; ¶ *v.t,*запасать; откладывать;хранить; ~ing, *n,* хранение; временный забор; щит для наклейки афиш.

hoar-frost, *n,* иней.

hoarse, *a,* хриплый, охрипший; ~ness, *n,* хрипота.

hoary, *a,* седой; древний.

hoax, *n,* злая шутка, обман; мистификация; ¶ *v.t,* мистифицировать; ~er, *n,* обманщик, мистификатор.

hob, *n,* плита, полка в камине.

hobble. *v.t,* стреножить; *v.i,* хромать; ¶ *n,* прихрамывание; путы *(for horse).*

hobby, *n,* любимое занятие, конёк, хобби; ~-horse лошадка, палочка с лошадиной головой.

hobgoblin, *n,* домовой.

hobnail, *n,* гвоздь с большой шляпкой.

hob-nob with водить дружбу с, водиться с.

hock, *n,* рейнвейн; *(horse)* поджилки.

hockey, *n,* хоккей; ~ *stick* клюшка.

hocus-pocus, *n,* фокус; надувательство.

hod, *n,* лоток; ведёрко.

hoe, *n,* мотыга; ¶ *v.t,* мотыжить.

hog, *n,* свинья; боров; ~gish, *a,* свинский; ~shead, *n* большая бочка.

hoist, *n,* подъём; поднятие; подъёмник; лебёдка; ¶ *v.t,* поднимать.

hold, *n,* захват; власть; *(ship)* трюм; ¶ *v.t,* держать; владеть *(inst.);* вмещать; содержать в себе; занимать *(office);* проводить, вести *(meeting, etc.); v.i,* держаться; ~ *back* сдерживать(ся); воздерживать(ся); ~ *down* держать в подчинении; ~ *fast to* придерживаться *(gen.);* ~ *forth* рассуждать; ~ *in* сдерживать; ~ *on to* держаться за; ~ *on!* стой!, подожди!;~*one's own* держаться; сохранять свои позиции; ~ *one's tongue* держать язык за зубами; ~ *out (v.t.)* протягивать; предлагать; *(v.i.)* держаться до конца; ~ *over* откладывать; ~ *up* задер-

живать; поддерживать; останавливать и грабить; ~er, *n,* владелец; держатель; предъявитель; оправа; ручка; *(tech.)* обойма; патрон; ~ing, *n,* держание; владение; участок земли.

hole, *n,* дыра; отверстие; нора *(of animal);* захолустье; ¶ *v.t,* продырявливать; прорывать; ~-and-corner секретный.

holiday, *n,* праздник, отдых; отпуск; выходной день; *(pl.)* каникулы; ~ *camp* туристский лагерь; ~ *resort* курорт; дом отдыха; ~maker отдыхающий.

holiness, *n,* святость; *your* ~ ваше святейшество.

holland, *n,* холст, полотно.

hollow, *a,* пустой, полый; впалый *(cheek);* глухой *(sound);* ~ *tree* дуплистое дерево·; ¶ *n,* дупло *(in tree);* лощина; выбоина; ¶ *v.t:* ~ *out* выдалбливать.

holly, *n,* остролист.

hollyhock, *n,* мальва.

holocaust, *n,* всесожжение; *(fig.)* массовое уничтожение.

holster, *n,* кобура.

holy, *a,* священный, святой; *H* ~ *Spirit* Святой дух; ~ *Office* инквизиция; ~ *Week* Страстная неделя; ~ *Writ* Священное писание.

homage, *n,* почтение; *pay* ~ свидетельствовать почтение; *(fig.)* отдавать должное.

home, *n,* дом; жилище; родина; *at* ~ дома; ¶ *a,* домашний; родной *(town, etc.);* внутренний *(trade etc.);* ¶ *ad,* домой; в цель; *go* ~ идти домой; *feel at* ~ чувствовать себя как дома; *make yourself at* ~ будьте как дома!; *strike* ~ попадать в цель; ~-*made* домашнего производства; самодельный; ~ *Office* министерство внутренних дел; ~ *rule* автономия; ~-*sickness* тоска по родине; ~spun домотканый; ~ *truth* горькая истина; ~*work* домашняя работа; ~less, *a,* бездомный, бесприютный; ~ly, *a,* простой, скромный; уютный; ~stead, *n,* усадьба; участок; ~ward, *ad,* домой, к дому; ~ *bound* возвращающийся домой.

homicidal, *a,* убийственный; одержимый мыслью об убийстве; homicide, *n,* убийство.

homily, *n*, пропóведь.
homing pigeon, *n*, почтóвый гóлубь.
homoeopath, *n*, гомеопáт; ~у, *n*, гомеопáтия.
homogeneous, *a*, одноpóдный.
homonym, *n*, омóним.
hone, *n*, точи́льный кáмень; ¶ *v.t*, точи́ть.
honest, *a*, чéстный; и́скренний; настоя́щий; ~ly, *ad*, чéстно; и́скренне; ~у, *a*, чéстность.
honey, *n*, мёд; *(pers.)* ми́л|ый, -ая; ~ *bee* (рабóчая) пчелá; ~comb медóвые сóты; ~moon медóвый мéсяц; ~suckle жи́молость; ~ed, *a*, слáдкий, медóвый.
honorarium, *n*, гонорáр; honorary, почётный; honour, *n*, честь; слáва; почёт; уважéние; *pl*, пóчести; *on my* ~ чéстное слóво; *point of* ~ вопрóс чéсти; *your* ~ вáша честь; ¶ *v.t*, почитáть; чтить; *(com.)* плати́ть в срок; ~ *with* удостáивать; ~able, *a*, чéстный; почтéнный; *Right* ~ достопочтéнный.
hood, *n*, капюшóн; кáпор; верх; *(tech.)* кры́шка, колпáк; ~wink, *v.t*, обмáнывать; завя́зывать глазá *(dat.).*
hoof, *n*, копы́то; ~ed, *a*, копы́тный·
hook, *n*, крючóк; крюк; багóр; *(fig.)* ловýшка; ~ *and eye* крючóк с петлёй; ~ *nose* крючкóватый нос; *by* ~ *or by crook* всéми прáвдами и непрáвдами; ¶ *v.t*,зацепля́ть; лови́ть (на ýдочку).
hookah, *n*, калья́н.
hooked, *a*, кривóй, крючковáтый.
hooligan, *n*, хулигáн.
hoop, *n*, óбруч; ги́канье; ¶ *v.t*, скрепля́ть óбручем; *v.i*, ги́кать.
hoot, *n*, крик совы́; ги́канье; ¶ *v.i*, кричáть; ги́кать; гудéть; *v.t*, осв

и́стывать; ~er, *n*, гудóк, сирéна.
hop, *v.i*, пры́гать; скакáть; хромáть; *v.t*, перепры́гивать; ¶ *n*, прыжóк; *(coll.)* тáнцы; *(bot.)* хмель; ~scotch «клáссы».
hope, *n*, надéжда; ¶ *v.i*, надéяться; ~ful, *a*, надéющийся; настрóенный оптимисти́чески; подаю́щий надéжды; ~less, *a*, безнадёжный; ~lessness, *n*, безнадёжность, безвы́ходность.
horde, *n*, ордá; вáтага.
horizon, *n*, горизóнт; кругозóр; ~tal, *a*, горизонтáльный.

horn, *n*, рог; рýпор; гудóк, сирéна *(motor)*; *(mus.)* рожóк; ~ *of plenty* рог изоби́лия; ~ed, *a*, рогáтый.
hornet, *n*, шéршень; *stir up a* ~*s' nest* растревóжить *(pf.)* оси́ное гнездó.
hornpipe, *n*, волы́нка.
horny, *a*, роговóй; мозóлистый.
horoscope, *n*, гороскóп.
horrible, *a*, ужáсный; стрáшный; отврати́тельный; horribly, *ad*, ужáсно, стрáшно; horrid, *a*, проти́вный; horrific, *a*, ужасáющий; horror, *n*, ýжас; отвращéние.
horse, *n*, лóшадь; конь; кавалéрия, кóнница; кóзлы *(trestle)*; ¶ *a*, лошади́ный, кóнский; *on* ~*back* верхóм; ~ *chestnut* кóнский каштáн; ~ *collar* хомýт; ~ *dealer* торгóвец лошадьми́; ~ *flesh* кони́на; ~ *fly* слепéнь; ~*hair* кóнский вóлос; ~*man* всáдник, наéздник; ~*manship* иск ýсство верховóй езды́; ~*power* лошади́ная си́ла; ~*radish* хрен;~ *race* скáчки; ~*shoe* подкóва; ~*whip* хлыст; ~*woman* всáдница, наéздница; horsy, *a*, лошади́ный.
horticultural, *a*, садóвый; horticulture, *n*, садовóдство; horticulturist, *n*, садовóд.
hose, *n*, рукáв; шланг; чулки́; *half* ~ гóльфы; hosier, *n*, торгóвец трикотáжем; ~у, *n*, трикотáж, чулóчные издéлия.
hospice, *n*, гости́ница, прию́т; hospitable, *a*, гостеприи́мный; hospitably, *ad*, радýшно; hospital, *n* больни́ца; *(mil.)* гóспиталь; ~ *ship* плавýчий гóспиталь; ~ *train* санитáрный пóезд; hospitality, *n*, гостеприи́мство, радýшие.
host, *n*, хозя́ин (дóма); мнóжество; вóйско *(army)*.
hostage, *n*, залóжник.
hostel, *n*, общежи́тие; ~ry, *n*, гости́ница.
hostess, *n*, хозя́йка(дóма); проводни́ца; бортпроводни́ца.
hostile, *a*, враждéбный; врáжеский; hostility, *n*, враждéбность; *pl*, воéнные дéйствия.
hot, *a*, горя́чий; жáркий; *(spiceso* óстрый; ~*bed* парни́к; *(fig.)* очáг; ~*-blooded* пы́лкий; ~*-fot)*

поспе́шно; ~-headed опроме́тчивый; вспы́льчивый; ~house тепли́ца, оранжере́я; ~-water bottle гре́лка; it is ~ жа́рко (weather); горячо́ (object).

hotchpotch, n, рагу́; вся́кая вся́чина.

hotel, n, гости́ница, оте́ль.

hotly, ad, горячо́.

hough, n, поджи́лки.

hound, n, го́нчая; охо́тничья соба́ка; ¶ v.t, трави́ть; ~ on натра́вливать, подстрека́ть.

hour, n, час; ~ glass песо́чные часы́; ~ hand часова́я стре́лка.

houri, n, гу́рия.

hourly, a, ежеча́сный; ad, ежеча́сно.

house, n, дом; пала́та (парла́мента); торго́вая фи́рма; пу́блика (audience); сеа́нс (cinema); семья́; дина́стия; keep ~ вести́ хозя́йство; ~ agent аге́нт по прода́же и сда́че внаём домо́в; ~breaker взло́мщик; ~-dog сторожево́й пёс; full ~ по́лный сбор (theatre); ~hold семья́, дома́шние; дома́шнее хозя́йство; ~holder владе́лец до́ма; съёмщик до́ма; ~keeper эконо́мка; ~maid го́рничная; ~ of Commons пала́та общи́н; ~ of Lords пала́та ло́рдов; ~-painter маля́р; ~-warming новосе́лье; ~-wife дома́шняя хозя́йка; ~work дома́шняя рабо́та; ¶ v.t, предоставля́ть жили́ще (dat.), обеспе́чивать жильём; поселя́ть; приюти́ть (pf.); housing, n, обеспе́чение жильём; жили́щное строи́тельство; ~ problem жили́щная пробле́ма.

hovel, n, лачу́га, хиба́рка.

hover, v.i, пари́ть; нависа́ть (cloud); колеба́ться; сло́нться; ~craft, n, хо́веркра́фт, кора́бль/ка́тер на возду́шной поду́шке; ~ing, n, паре́ние; колеба́ние.

how, ad, как, каки́м о́бразом; ~ far как далеко́; ~ long как до́лго; ~ much many? ско́лько?; ~ do you do? здра́вствуйте!; как пожива́ете?; however, ad, как бы ни; ¶ c, одна́ко; ~ much ско́лько бы ни, как бы ни.

howitzer, n, га́убица.

howl, n, вой, завыва́ние; рёв; ¶ v.i, выть, завыва́ть; стона́ть

(wind); реве́ть (child); ~er, n, (coll.) грубе́йшая оши́бка.

hoyden, n, девчо́нка-сорване́ц.

hub, n, сту́пица, вту́лка; (fig.) центр.

hubbub, n, шум, гул.

huckster, n, разно́счик, торга́ш; ¶ v.i, торгова́ть в разно́с.

huddle, v.t, сва́ливать в ку́чу; v.i, жа́ться, тесни́ться, толпи́ться; ~ up свора́чиваться «кала́чиком»; ¶ n, ку́ча; толпа́.

hue, n, отте́нок, цвет; ~ and cry пого́ня; кри́ки.

huff, n, раздраже́ние; чу́вство оскорбле́ния; take the ~ обижа́ться; ~y, a, раздражи́тельный.

hug, n, объя́тие; хва́тка; ¶ v.t, обнима́ть; держа́ться (gen.); ~ the coast держа́ться близ бе́рега.

huge, a, огро́мный, грома́дный; ~ly, ad, о́чень; ~ness, n, огро́мность, грома́дность.

hulk, n, ко́рпус корабля́; грома́да; ~ing, a, грома́дный; неуклю́жий.

hull, n, шелуха́, кожура́, скорлупа́; ко́рпус (ship); ¶ v.t, очища́ть (от кожуры), шелуши́ть.

hullabaloo, n, гам, шум.

hullo see hello.

hum, n, жужжа́ние, гуде́ние; ¶ v.i, жужжа́ть, гуде́ть; напева́ть.

human, a, челове́ческий; ¶ n, челове́к; ~e, a, гума́нный, челове́чный; гуманита́рный; ~ism, n, гумани́зм; ~ist, n, гумани́ст; ~itarian, a, гуманита́рный; ~ity, n, челове́чество; гума́нность; ~ize, v.t, очелове́чивать; смягча́ть.

humble, a, просто́й; поко́рный; бе́дный; ¶ v.t, унижа́ть; ~ness, n, поко́рность; humbly, ad, поко́рно.

humbug, n, обма́н; претенцио́зность; вздор.

humdrum, a, ску́чный; бана́льный.

humerus, n, плечо́.

humid, a, вла́жный, сыро́й; ~ity, n, вла́жность, сы́рость.

humiliate, v.t, унижа́ть; **humiliation,** n, униже́ние; **humility,** n, смире́ние; скро́мность.

humming-bird, n, коли́бри.

humming-top, n, волчо́к, юла́.

hummock, n, буго́р; ледяно́й торо́с.

humorist, n, юмори́ст; **humorous,** a, юмористи́ческий; заба́вный; **hu-**

mour, *n,* юмор; настроéние; ¶ *v.t,* потакáть *(dat.);* ублажáть.
hump, *n,* горб; бугóр; ~*back* горб; горбýн; ~*backed* горбáтый.
humus, *n,* перегнóй.
hunch, *n,* горб; ломóть; *(coll.)* предчýвствие, подозрéние; ~*back* горбýн; ~*backed* горбáтый.
hundred, *n,* сто; сóтня; ~*fold* стократный; ~*th, ord. num,* сóтый; ¶ *n,* сóтая часть; ~*weight, n,* цéнтнер.
Hungarian, *a,* венгéрский; ¶ *n,* венгр, венгéр|ец; ~ка; венгéрский язык.
hunger, *n,* гóлод; *(fig.)* жáжда; ~ *strike* голодóвка; ¶ *v.i:* ~ *after* жáждать *(gen.),* сильно желáть; **hungrily,** *ad,* жáдно; **hungry,** *a,* голóдный, голодáющий; *(fig.)* жáждущий.
hunk, *n,* ломóть.
hunt, *n,* охóта; пóиски; ¶ *v.t,* охóтиться на; травить; ~ *for* искáть; ~ *out* отыскивать; ~*er, n,* охóтник; охóтничья лóшадь; кармáнные часы с крышкой; ~*ing, n,* охóта; ¶ *a,* охóтничий; ~ *lodge* охóтничий дóмик; ~*ress, n,* жéнщина-охóтник; ~*sman, n,* охóтник.
hurdle, *n,* загорóдка; *(fig.)* препятствие, барьéр; ~*race* барьéрный бег; скáчки с препятствиями.
hurdy-gurdy, *n,* шармáнка.
hurl, *v.t,* швырять.
hurly-burly, *n,* переполóх.
hurrah, *int,* урá!.
hurricane, *n,* урагáн.
hurry, *n,* спéшка, тороплйвость; *in a* ~ второпях; ¶ *v.t,* торопить; *v.i,* спешить, торопиться; ~ *away (v.t.)* поспéшно увозить/уводить; *(v.i.)* поспéшно уезжáть/уходить; ~ *up* скорéе!.
hurt, *n,* вред, ущéрб; повреждéние; обида; боль; ¶ *v.t,* причинять боль *(dat.);* ушибáть; вредить *(dat.); (fig.)* задевáть; обижáть; *v.i,* болéть; ~*ful, a,* врéдный; оскорбительный.
husband, *n,* муж; ¶ *v.t,* управлять *(inst.);* экономить; ~*man, n,* земледéлец; ~*ry, n,* земледéлие; хозяйство; бережливость.
hush, *n,* тишинá; молчáние; ¶ *v.t,* водворять тишинý; успокáивать;

v.i, молчáть; утихáть; ~ *up* замáлчивать; заминáть; ~*-money* взятка за молчáние; ¶ *int,* тише!.
husk, *n,* шелухá, скорлупá; оболóчка; ¶ *v.t,* очищáть (от шелухи); ~*y, a,* хриплый, сиплый; ¶ *n,* лáйка.
hussar, *n,* гусáр.
hussy, *n,* шкатýлка; *(pers.)* нахáльная дéвка.
hustle, *v.t,* толкáть; торопить; *v.i,* толкáться; торопиться.
hut, *n,* хижина; барáк.
hutch, *n,* клéтка; ящик.
hyacinth, *n,* гиацинт.
hybrid, *a,* гибридный; смéшанный; ¶ *n,* гибрид; пóмесь.
hydra, *n,* гидра.
hydrangea, *n,* гортéнзия.
hydrant, *n,* водоразбóрный кран.
hydrate, *v.t,* гидратировать; ¶ *n,* гидрáт.
hydraulic, *a,* гидравлический; ~*s, n,* гидрáвлика.
hydrocarbon, *n,* углеводорóд.
hydrochloric *a,* хлористоводорóдный.
hydrogen, *n,* водорóд; ~ *bomb* водорóдная бóмба.
hydropathic, *a,* водолечéбный.
hydrophobia, *n,* водобоязнь.
hydroplane, *n,* гидроплáн.
hydrostatics, *n,* гидростáтика.
hyena, *n,* гиéна.
hygiene, *n,* гигиéна; **hygienic,** *a,* гигиенический.
hymen, *n,* дéвственная плевá.
hymn, *n,* гимн; ~*al, n,* сбóрник гимнов.
hyperbola, *n,* гипéрбола; **hyperbole,** *n,* гипéрбола, преувеличéние.
hypercritical, *a,* придирчивый.
hyphen, *n,* дефис.
hypnotic, *a,* гипнотический; **hypnotism,** *n,* гипнотизм; **hypnotize** *v.t,* гипнотизировать.
hypochondria, *n,* ипохóндрия; ~*c, a,* страдáющий ипохóндрией; ¶ *n,* ипохóндрик.
hypocrisy, *n,* лицемéрие; **hypocrite,** *n,* лицемéр; **hypocritical,** *a,* лицемéрный; притвóрный.
hypodermic, *a,* подкóжный; ~ *syringe* шприц.
hypothesis, *n,* гипóтеза; **hypothetical,** *a,* гипотетический.
hysteria, *n,* истéрия; **hysterical,** *a,* истерический; **hysterics,** *n,* истéрика, истерический припáдок.

I

I, *pn,* я.

iambic, *a,* ямби́ческий; ¶ *n,* ямби́ческий стих.

Iberian, *a,* ибери́йский; ~*Peninsular,* Пирене́йский полуо́стров; ¶ *n,* ибе́р; язы́к дре́вних ибе́ров.

ibex, *n,* ка́менный козёл.

ibis, *n,* и́бис.

ice, *n,* лёд; моро́женое; ~ *Age* леднико́вый пери́од; ~ *axe* ледору́б; ~*berg* а́йсберг; ~*-bound* ско́ванный льдом *(river);* затёртый льда́ми; ~*-box* холоди́льник; ~*-breaker* ледохо́д; ~*-cream* моро́женое; ~ *field* ледяно́е по́ле; ~ *floe* плаву́чая льди́на; ¶ *v.t,* заморо́живать; покрыва́ть са́харной глазу́рью.

Icelandic, *a,* исла́ндский; ¶ *n,* исла́ндский язы́к.

icicle, *n,* сосу́лька.

icing, *n,* са́харная глазу́рь.

icon, *n,* ико́на; ~*oclast, n,* иконобо́рец.

icy, *a,* ледяно́й.

idea, *n,* иде́я; мысль; поня́тие; наме́рение; план; *bright* ~ блестя́щая иде́я; ~l, *a,* идеа́льный; ¶ *n,* идеа́л; ~*lism, n,* идеали́зм; ~*list, n,* идеали́ст; ~*listic, a,* идеалисти́ческий; ~*lize, v.t,* идеализи́ровать.

identical, *a,* одина́ковый, иденти́чный, тожде́ственный; тот же са́мый; **identification,** *n,* опозна́ние, установле́ние ли́чности; **identify,** *v.t,* отождествля́ть; опознава́ть, устана́вливать ли́чность *(gen.);* **identity,** *n,* тожде́ственность; то́ждество; ли́чность; ~ *card* удостовере́ние ли́чности; ~ *disc* ли́чный (опознава́тельный) знак.

ideology, *n,* идеоло́гия.

idiocy, *n,* идиоти́зм; *(coll.)* идио́тство.

idiom, *n,* идио́ма; диале́кт, го́вор; ~*atic, a,* идиомати́ческий.

idiosyncracy, *n,* идиосинкра́зия.

idiot, *n,* идио́т; ~*ic, a,* идио́тский.

idle, *a,* пра́здный; лени́вый; тще́тный; пусто́й *(tech.)* безде́йствующий, холосто́й; ~ *time* просто́й (маши́ны); переры́в в рабо́те; ¶ *v.i,* лени́ться, безде́льничать; ~-

ness, *n,* пра́здность; лень; ~*r, n,* лентя́й; **idly,** *ad,* лени́во.

idol, *n,* и́дол; куми́р; ~*ater, n,* идолопокло́нник; обожа́тель; ~*atrous, a,* идолопокло́ннический; ~*atry, n,* идолопокло́нство; обожа́ние; ~*ize, v.t,* боготвори́ть; обожа́ть.

idyll, *n,* иди́ллия; ~*ic, a,* идилли́ческий.

if, *c,* е́сли; е́сли бы; ли; *as* ~ как бу́дто; *even* ~ е́сли да́же; ~ *only* е́сли (бы) то́лько.

igloo, *n,* и́глу.

igneous, *a,* о́гненный, огнево́й; вулкани́ческого происхожде́ния; **ignis fatuus,** *n,* блужда́ющий ого́нь; **ignite,** *v.t,* зажига́ть; *v.i,* загора́ться; **ignition,** *n,* зажига́ние; вспы́шка.

ignoble, *a,* по́длый, ни́зкий.

ignominious, *a,* позо́рный, бесче́стный; **ignominy,** *n,* позо́р, бесче́стие.

ignoramus, *n,* неве́жда; **ignorance,** *n,* неве́жество; незна́ние; **ignorant,** *a,* неве́жественный; несве́дущий; *be* ~ *of* не знать; **ignore,** *v.t,* игнори́ровать; *(law)* отклоня́ть.

iguana, *n,* игуа́на.

ill, *a,* больно́й; дурно́й; ¶ *n,* зло, вред; *(pl.)* несча́стья; *fall* ~ заболева́ть; *feel* ~ чу́вствовать себя́ ду́рно; ~ *at ease* не по себе́; ~*advised* неблагоразу́мный; ~*-bred* невоспи́танный; ~*-contrived* неуда́чно заду́манный; не в ду́хе; ~*-famed* по́льзующийся дурно́й сла́вой; ~*-fated* злополу́чный; несча́стливый; ~*-favoured* некраси́вый; ~ *feeling* неприя́знь; ~*-founded* необосно́ванный; ~*-gotten* полу́ченный нече́стным путём; ~*-humoured* в дурно́м настрое́нии; ~*-natured* гру́бый; дурно́го нра́ва; ~*-omened* злове́щий; ~*-starred* несча́стливый; ~*-tempered* раздражи́тельный; ~*-timed* несвоевре́менный; ~*-treat* пло́хо обраща́ться с; ~ *will* недоброжела́тельство.

illegal, *a,* нелега́льный, незако́нный; ~*ity, n,* нелега́льность, незако́нность.

illegible, *a,* неразбо́рчивый.

illegitimacy, *n,* незаконнорождённость; **illegitimate,** *a,* незаконнорождённый; незако́нный.

illiberal, *a*, непросвещённый; нетерпи́мый; скупо́й; ~ity, *n*, непросвещённость; нетерпи́мость; ску́пость.

illicit, *a*, незако́нный, запрещённый.

illiteracy, *n*, негра́мотность; **illiterate,** *a*, негра́мотный.

illness, *n*, боле́знь.

illogical, *a*, нелоги́чный.

illuminate, *v.t*, освеща́ть; украша́ть; разъясня́ть; **illumination,** *n*, освеще́ние; иллюмина́ция; украше́ние; **illumine,** *v.t*, освеща́ть; просвеща́ть; иллюстри́ровать.

illusion, *n*, иллю́зия; мира́ж; **illusory,** *a*, иллюзо́рный.

illustrate, *v.t*, иллюстри́ровать; поясня́ть; **illustration,** *n*, иллюстра́ция; иллюстри́рование; поясне́ние; **illustrative,** *a*, иллюстрати́вный; поясни́тельный.

illustrious, *a*, знамени́тый, сла́вный.

image, *n*, о́браз; отраже́ние *(mirror)*; подо́бие; ~ry, *n*, о́бразы; о́бразность; **imaginable,** *a*, вообрази́мый; **imaginary,** *a*, вообража́емый; мни́мый; **imagination,** *n*, воображе́ние; фанта́зия; **imaginative,** *a*, облада́ющий бога́тым воображе́нием; оригина́льный; **imagine,** *v.t*, вообража́ть; представля́ть себе́; предполага́ть.

imbecile, *a*, слабоу́мный; **imbecility,** *n*, слабоу́мие.

imbibe, *v.t*, впи́тывать; вдыха́ть.

imbricated, *a*, чешу́йчатый.

imbroglio, *n*, пу́таница.

imbrue, *v.t*, мочи́ть.

imbue, *v.t*, насыща́ть; пропи́тывать; внуша́ть.

imitate, *v.t*, подража́ть *(dat.)*; ими́тировать; подде́лывать; **imitation,** *n*, подража́ние; имита́ция; подде́лка; ¶ *a*, иску́сственный; подде́льный; **imitator,** *a*, подража́тельный; **imitator,** *n*, подража́тель; имита́тор.

immaculate, *a*, незапя́тнанный, чи́стый; безупре́чный.

immanent, *a*, прису́щий; имма́нентный.

immaterial, *a*, невеще́ственный; бестеле́сный; несуще́ственный.

immature, *a*, незре́лый.

immeasurable, *a*, неизмери́мый.

immediate, *a*, непосре́дственный; неме́дленный; ~ly, *ad*, непосре́дственно; неме́дленно.

immemorial, *a*, незапа́мятный.

immense, *a*, безме́рный; необъя́тный; **immensity,** *n*, необъя́тность, грома́дность.

immerse, *v.t*, погружа́ть; **immersion,** *n*, погруже́ние.

immigrant, *n*, иммигра́нт, -ка; **immigrate,** *v.i*, иммигри́ровать; **immigration,** *n*, иммигра́ция.

imminence, *n*, бли́зость; **imminent,** *a*, бли́зкий, грозя́щий.

immobile, *a*, неподви́жный; **immobility,** *n*, неподви́жность; **immobilize,** *v.t*, де́лать неподви́жным; изыма́ть из обраще́ния.

immoderate, *a*, неуме́ренный; ~ly, *ad*, неуме́ренно.

immodest, *a*, бессты́дный, непри-ли́чный; на́глый; ~y, *n*, бессты́дство; на́глость.

immolate, *v.t*, приноси́ть в же́ртву; *(fig.)* же́ртвовать *(inst.)*; **immolation,** *n*, жертвоприноше́ние, же́ртва.

immoral, *a*, безнра́вственный; **immorality,** *n*, безнра́вственность.

immortal, *a*, бессме́ртный; ве́чный; ~ity, *n*, бессме́ртие; ве́чность; ~ize, *v.t*, обессме́ртить *(pf.)*; увекове́чивать; **immortelle,** *n*, бессме́ртник.

immovable, *a*, неподви́жный; недви́жимый; непоколеби́мый; ~s, *n,pl*, недви́жимость.

immune, *n*, невоспри́мчивый (к боле́зни); свобо́дный; **immunity,** *n*, невоспри́мчивость; свобо́да; иммуните́т; **immunize,** *v.t*, иммунизи́ровать.

immure *v.t*, зато́чать, замуро́вывать; ~ *oneself* запира́ться в четырёх стена́х.

immutability, *n* неизме́нность; **immutable,** *a*, неизме́нный.

imp, *n*, чертёнок; прока́зник.

impact, *n*, уда́р; столкнове́ние; влия́ние.

impair, *v.t*, поврежда́ть; ухудша́ть; ослабля́ть.

impale, *v.t*, прока́лывать, пронза́ть; сажа́ть на кол.

impalpable, *a*, неосяза́емый, неощути́мый.

impart, *v.t*, придава́ть; сообща́ть.

impartial, *a*, беспристра́стный, справедли́вый; ~ity, *n*, беспристра́стие, справедли́вость.

impassable, *a,* непроходи́мый, непроézжий.

impasse, *n,* тупи́к; *(fig.)* безвы́ходное положе́ние.

impassive, *a,* нечувстви́тельный; споко́йный, бесстра́стный.

impassioned, *a,* стра́стный, пы́лкий.

impatience, *n,* нетерпе́ние; **impatient,** *a,* нетерпели́вый; **~ly,** *ad,* нетерпели́во.

impeach, *v.t,* обвиня́ть, привлека́ть к суду́; **~ment,** *n,* привлече́ние к суду́.

impeccability, *n,* безупре́чность; **impeccable,** *a,* безупре́чный.

impecunious, *a,* безде́нежный, бе́дный.

impede, *v.t,* препя́тствовать *(dat.),* меша́ть *(dat.);* заде́рживать; **impediment,** *n,* препя́тствие, поме́ха, заде́ржка; **~** *in speech* заика́ние.

impel, *v.t,* побужда́ть; принужда́ть; приводи́ть в движе́ние.

impending, *a,* предстоя́щий, надвига́ющийся.

impenetrable, *a,* непроходи́мый; непроница́емый; непромока́емый; непостижи́мый.

impenitence, *n,* нераска́янность; **impenitent,** *a,* нераска́явшийся.

imperative, *a,* повели́тельный; **¶** *n,* повели́тельное наклоне́ние.

imperceptible, *a,* незаме́тный.

imperfect, *a,* несоверше́нный; непо́лный; **~ion,** *n,* несоверше́нство; недоста́ток; **~ive aspect** несоверше́нный вид.

imperial, *a,* импе́рский, импера́торский; **¶** *n,* эспаньо́лка *(beard);* **~ism,** *n,* империали́зм; **~ist,** *n,* империали́ст.

imperil, *v.t,* подверга́ть опа́сности.

imperious, *a,* вла́стный; **~ness,** *n,* вла́стность.

imperishable, *a,* непо́ртящийся; ве́чный.

impermeable, *a,* непроница́емый.

impersonal, *a,* безли́чный.

impersonate, *v.t,* выдава́ть себя́ за; *(theat.)* исполня́ть роль *(gen.);* олицетворя́ть; имити́ровать; **impersonation,** *n,* самозва́нство; исполне́ние ро́ли; имита́ция; **impersonator,** *n,* самозва́нец; имита́тор.

impertinence, *n,* де́рзость; **impertinent,** *a,* де́рзкий.

imperturbable, *a,* невозмути́мый.

impervious, *a,* непроница́емый; глухо́й (к).

impetuosity, *n,* пы́лкость; **impetuous,** *a,* пы́лкий; стреми́тельный.

impetus, *n,* стреми́тельность; побужде́ние; дви́жущая си́ла.

impiety, *n,* нечести́вость.

impinge, *v.t:* **~** *upon* ударя́ться о, па́дать на; покуша́ться на.

impious, *a,* нечести́вый.

impish, *a,* прока́зливый.

implacable, *a,* неумоли́мый.

implant, *v.t,* насажда́ть; внедря́ть.

implement, *n,* ору́дие, инструме́нт; *pl,* у́тварь; инвента́рь; **¶** *v.t,* выполня́ть, осуществля́ть.

implicate, *v.t,* впу́тывать, вовлека́ть, заме́шивать; **implication,** *n,* заме́шанность; вовлече́ние; (подразумева́емое) значе́ние.

implicit, *a,* подразумева́емый; безогово́рочный; **~ly,** *ad,* безогово́рочно; сле́по; **implied,** *p.p. & a,* подразумева́емый.

implore, *v.t,* умоля́ть.

imply, *v.t,* зна́чить; подразумева́ть.

impolite, *a,* неве́жливый; **~ness,** *n,* неве́жливость.

impolitic, *a,* неполити́чный.

imponderable, *a,* невесо́мый; не поддаю́щийся учёту; **¶** *n,* не́что невесо́мое/неопределёмое.

import, *v.t,* ввози́ть, импорти́ровать; **¶** *n,* ввоз, и́мпорт; ввози́мые това́ры; значе́ние; **~** *duty* ввозна́я/и́мпортная по́шлина.

importance, *n,* ва́жность, значе́ние; **important,** *a,* ва́жный, значи́тельный.

importation, *n,* ввоз, и́мпорт; **importer,** *n,* импортёр.

importunate, *a,* насто́йчивый; назо́йливый; **importune,** *v.t,* пристава́ть к; **importunity,** *n,* назо́йливость.

impose, *v.t,* налага́ть; навя́зывать; **~** *upon* злоупотребля́ть (дове́рием); навя́зываться *(dat.);* **imposing,** *a,* внуши́тельный; **imposition,** *n,* наложе́ние; обложе́ние; бре́мя; штрафна́я рабо́та.

impossibility, *n,* невозмо́жность; **impossible,** *a,* невозмо́жный; несбы́точный; невыноси́мый.

impost, *n,* нало́г, по́дать.

impostor, *n,* самозва́нец; **imposture,** *n,* обма́н.

impotence, *n,* бесси́лие, сла́бость; *(med.)* импоте́нция; **impotent,** *a,* бесси́льный; *(med.)* импоте́нтный.

impound, *v.t,* загоня́ть *(cattle);* конфискова́ть.

impoverish, *v.t,* доводи́ть до нищеты́; истоща́ть; ~ed, *p.p. & a,* убо́гий; истощённый; ~ment, *n,* обнища́ние; истоще́ние.

impracticability, *n,* невыполни́мость; **impracticable,** *a,* невыполни́мый; него́дный.

imprecate, *v.t,* проклина́ть; **imprecation,** *n,* прокля́тие.

impregnable, *a,* непреодоли́мый, непристу́пный.

impregnate, *v.t,* оплодотворя́ть; насыща́ть, пропи́тывать; ~d, *p.p. & a,* оплодотворённый; пропи́танный.

impresario, *n,* импреса́рио; антрепренёр.

impress, *v.t,* производи́ть си́льное впечатле́ние на; поража́ть; штампова́ть; ¶ *n,* отпеча́ток; печа́ть; ~ion, *n,* впечатле́ние; отпеча́ток; след; изда́ние; ~ionable, *a,* впечатли́тельный; ~ionism, *n,* импрессиони́зм; ~ive, *a,* импоза́нтный; порази́тельный; производя́щий впечатле́ние.

imprint, *n,* отпеча́ток; штамп; *(fig.)* след; *printer's* ~ выходны́е све́дения; ¶ *v.t,* запечатлева́ть, оставля́ть след в/на; отпеча́тывать.

imprison, *v.t,* заключа́ть в тюрьму́; заточа́ть; ~ment, *n,* заключе́ние, заточе́ние.

improbability, *n,* невероя́тность; неправдоподо́бие; **improbable,** *a,* невероя́тный; неправдоподо́бный.

impromptu, *a,* импровизи́рованный; ¶ *n,* импровиза́ция, экспро́мт.

improper, *a,* неприли́чный; неподходя́щий; **impropriety,** *n,* неприли́чие.

improve, *v.t. (& i.),* улучша́ть(ся), соверше́нствовать(ся); ~ment, *n,* улучше́ние; *(agr.)* мелиора́ция.

improvidence, *n,* непредусмотри́тельность; расточи́тельность; **improvident,** *a,* расточи́тельный.

improvise, *v.t,* импровизи́ровать.

imprudence, *n,* неблагоразу́мие; неосторо́жность; **imprudent,** *a,* неблагоразу́мный; неосторо́жный.

impudence, *n,* бессты́дство; де́рзость; **impudent,** *a,* бессты́дный; де́рзкий.

impugn, *v.t,* оспа́ривать; ~able, *a,* спо́рный.

impulse, *&* **impulsion,** *n,* толчо́к; побужде́ние; и́мпульс; **impulsive,** *a,* импульси́вный.

impunity, *n,* безнака́занность; *with* ~ безнака́занно.

impure, *a,* нечи́стый; сме́шанный; **impurity,** *n,* нечистота́; при́месь; засоре́ние.

impute, *v.t,* ста́вить в вину́; припи́сывать.

in, *pr,* в, на; во вре́мя; че́рез; ¶ *ad,* внутри́; внутрь; ~ *all* всего́; вообще́; ~ *a few days* че́рез/в не́сколько дней; ~ *a week's time* че́рез неде́лю; ~ *a week* за неде́лю; ~ *the day* днём; ~ *due course* в своё вре́мя; до́лжным поря́дком; ~ *the morning* у́тром; *7 o'clock* ~ *the morning* 7 часо́в утра́; ~ *my opinion* по моему́ мне́нию; ~ *order that* для того́, что́бы; ~ *print* в печа́ти; в прода́же; ~ *so far as* постольку, поско́льку; ~ *the sun* на со́лнце; ~ *the rain* под дождём; ~ *time* во́-время; ~ *writing* в пи́сьменной фо́рме; *be* ~ быть до́ма/внутри́; *one* ~ *six* оди́н на шесть; *2 shillings* ~ *the pound* два ши́ллинга на фунт; *be well* ~ быть в хоро́ших отноше́ниях с; *now we are* ~ *for it!* тепе́рь нам доста́нется!; *ins and outs* все вхо́ды и вы́ходы.

inability, *n,* неспосо́бность.

inaccessible, *a,* недосту́пный, непристу́пный.

inaccuracy, *n,* нето́чность; **inaccurate,** *a,* нето́чный.

inaction, *n,* безде́йствие; **inactive,** *a,* безде́ятельный; ине́ртный; **inactivity,** *n,* безде́ятельность.

inadequacy, *n,* несоотве́тствие тре́бованиям; недоста́точность; **inadequate,** *a,* не отвеча́ющий тре́бованиям; недоста́точный.

inadmissible, *a,* недопусти́мый.

inadvertently, *ad,* невнима́тельно; небре́жно.

inalienable, *a,* неотчужда́емый, неотъе́млемый.

inane, *a,* пусто́й, глу́пый.

inanimate, *a,* неодушевлённый; безжи́зненный.

inanition, *n,* изнуре́ние, истоще́ние.

inanity, *n,* пустота́; глу́пость.

inapplicable, *a*, неприменимый; не-подходящий.

inapposite, *a*, неуместный.

inappreciable, *a*, незаметный; не-значительный; неоценимый.

inappropriate, *a*, неподходящий, не-уместный.

inapt, *a*, неподходящий; ~itude, *n*, неспособность; несоответствие;

inarticulate, *a*, невнятный; не спо-собный выражаться ясно.

inasmuch as, *ad*, поскольку.

inattention, *n*, невнимательность; inattentive, *a*, невнимательный.

inaudible, *a*, неслышимый.

inaugural, *a*, вступительный; in-augurate, *v.t*, торжественно вво-дить в должность; торжественно открывать; inauguration, *n*, тор-жественное вступление в долж-ность; торжественное откры-тие.

inauspicious, *a*, неблагоприятный; зловещий.

inborn, *a*, врождённый, природ-ный.

incalculable, *a*, несчётный, неисчис-лимый.

incandescent, *n*, раскалённый; ~ lamp лампа накаливания.

incantation, *n*, заклинание.

incapability, *n*, неспособность; in-capable, *a*, неспособный; incapa-citate, *v.t*, делать неспособным; *(mil.)* выводить из строя; in-capacity, *n*, неспособность.

incarcerate, *v.t*, заключать в тюрь-му; incarceration, *n*, заключение в тюрьму.

incarnate, *n*, воплощённый; incar-nation, *n*, воплощение.

incautious, *a*, неосторожный.

incendiarism, *n*, поджог; *(fig.)* под-стрекательство; incendiary, *a*, за-жигательный; подстрекающий; ¶ *n*, поджигатель.

incense, *n*, ладан, фимиам; ~-burner курильница; ¶ *v.t*, сердить; кадить.

incentive, *n*, побуждение; стимул.

inception, *n*, неопределённость; не-уверенность.

incessant, *a*, непрерывный; ~ly, *ad*, непрерывно.

incest, *n*, кровосмешение; ~uous, *a*, кровосмесительный.

inch, *n*, дюйм; every ~ целиком; с головы до ног; ~ by ~ мало-

-помалу; within an ~ of на воло-сок от.

incidence, *n*, падение; *(avia.)* угол атаки; количество; incident, *a*, случайный; *(phys.)* падающий; ¶ *n*, случай, происшествие; ин-цидент; ~al, *a*, случайный; ~ expenses побочные расходы; ~ally, *ad*, случайно; между прочим.

incinerate, *v.t*, сжигать; испепелять; incineration, *n*, сжигание; inci-nerator, *n*, мусоросжигательная печь/станция; кремационная печь.

incipient, *a*, начинающийся, зарож-дающийся.

incise, *v.t*, надрезать; incision, *n*, надрез; incisive, *a*, режущий; проницательный; incisor, *n*, ре-зец *(also tech.).*

incite, *v.t*, подстрекать; побуждать; ~ment, *n*, подстрекательство.

incivility, *n*, невежливость.

inclemency, *n*, суровость; inclement, *a*, суровый.

inclination, *n*, склонность; склон; incline, *v.t. (& i.)*, наклонять(ся), склонять(ся); inclined, *p.p. & a*, склонный; ~ plane наклонная плоскость.

include, *v.t*, содержать в себе, вклю-чать; including, *p*, включая; в том числе; inclusive, *a*, включаю-щий; ~ly, *ad*, включительно.

incognito, *ad*, инкогнито.

incoherence, *n*, бессвязность; in-coherent, *a*, бессвязный.

incombustible, *a*, несгораемый; ог-нестойкий.

income, *n*, доход; заработок; ~ tax подоходный налог.

incoming, *a*, прибывающий; следую-щий; поступающий.

incommensurable, *a*, несоизмеримый; *(maths)* иррациональный; in-commensurate, *a*, несоразмерный.

incommode, *v.t*, мешать *(dat.);* incommodious, *a*, тесный, неудоб-ный.

incommunicable, *a*, несообщаемый, непередаваемый.

incommunicative, *a*, необщитель-ный.

incomparable, *a*, несравнимый, не-сравнённый; incomparably, *ad*, несравненно.

incompatibility, *n*, несовместимость; incompatible, *a*, несовместимый.

incompetence, *n*, неспособность; *(law)* неправоспособность; incompetent, *a*, неспособный; некомпетентный.

incomplete, *a*, неполный; незавершённый; несовершённый.

incomprehensible, *a*, непонятный, непостижимый.

inconceivable, *a*, невообразимый.

inconclusive, *a*, неубедительный; нерешающий.

incongruity, *n*, несоответствие; неуместность; incongruous, *a*, несоответственный; неуместный.

inconsequent(ial), *a*, непоследовательный; незначительный.

inconsiderate, *a*, невнимательный; необдуманный.

inconsistency, *n*, непоследовательность; несообразность; непостоянство; inconsistent, *a*, непоследовательный; несообразный; непостоянный.

inconsolable, *a*, неутешный.

inconspicuous, *a*, незаметный.

inconstancy, *n*, непостоянство; нерегулярность; inconstant, *a*, непостоянный; нерегулярный.

incontestable, *a*, неоспоримый.

incontinence, *n*, *(med.)* недержание; incontinent, *a*, несдержанный; *(med.)* страдающий недержанием.

incontrovertible, *a*, неопровержимый.

inconvenience, *n*, неудобство; беспокойство; inconvenient, *a*, неудобный; затруднительный.

inconvertible, *a*, не подлежащий обмену, неразменный.

incorporate, *v.t.* *(& i.)*, соединять(ся), объединять(ся); принимать; включать; incorporation, *n*, объединение; корпорация.

incorporeal, *a*, бестелесный; невещественный.

incorrect, *a*, неправильный; неточный; ~ness, *n*, неправильность; неточность.

incorrigible, *a*, неисправимый.

incorruptibility, *n*, неподкупность; неповреждённость; incorruptible, *a*, неподкупный; непортящийся.

increase, *n*, увеличение; рост; ¶ *v.t*, увеличивать; усиливать; *v.i*, увеличиваться; усиливаться; расти.

incredibility, *n*, невероятность; incredible, *a*, невероятный.

incredulity, *n*, недоверчивость; incredulous, *a*, недоверчивый.

increment, *n*, увеличение; прирост; прибавка.

incriminate, *v.t*, обвинять в преступлении; вовлекать в преступление; incrimination, *n*, инкриминация; вовлечение в преступление.

incrust, *v.t*, покрывать корой; покрывать инкрустацией; ~ation, *n*, образование коры; кора, корка; инкрустация.

incubate, *v.t*, высиживать *(chicks)*; выращивать *(germ)*; incubation, *n*, высиживание; инкубация; *(med.)* инкубационный период.

incubus, *n*, злой дух; кошмар.

inculcate, *v.t*, внедрять, вселять.

inculpate, *v.t*, изобличать; обвинять.

incumbent. *a*, лежащий, возложенный; ¶ *n*, имеющий приход; *it is ~ on you* на вас лежит обязанность.

incur, *v.t*, подвергаться *(dat.)*; навлекать на себя; ~ *debts* наделать *(pf.)* долгов; ~ *losses* терпеть убытки; *(mil.)* нести потери.

incurable, *a*, неизлечимый; неисцеримый.

incurious, *a*, нелюбопытный.

incursion, *n*, вторжение, набег.

indebted, *a*, (находящийся) в долгу; обязанный; ~ness, *n*, задолженность; чувство обязанности.

indecency, *n*, неприличие, непристойность; indecent, *a*, неприличный, непристойный.

indecision, *n*, нерешительность; indecisive, *a*, нерешительный; неопределённый.

indecorous, *a*, неприличный; безвкусный.

indeed, *ad*, в самом деле, действительно.

indefatigable, *a*, неутомимый.

indefensible, *a*, беззащитный; несостоятельный; не могущий быть оправданным.

indefinable, *a*, неопределимый; indefinite, *a*, неопределённый.

indelible, *a*, неизгладимый.

indelicacy, *n*, неделикатность; бестактность; indelicate, *a*, неделикатный; бестактный.

indemnification, *n*, возмещение, компенсация; indemnify, *v.t*, возмещать, компенсировать; indemnity, *n*, компенсация; контрибуция.

indent, *v.t*, зазубривать; *(print.)* делать абзац/отступ; ~ *for* реквизировать; ~ *upon* предъявлять требование; ~ation, *n*, зубец; отступ; вмятина.

indenture, *n*, контракт, договор.

independence, *n*, независимость, самостоятельность; independent, *a*, независимый, самостоятельный; *person of* ~ *means* человек с самостоятельным доходом; ~ly, *ad*, независимо самостоятельно.

indescribable, *a*, неописуемый.

indestructible, *a*, неразрушимый.

indeterminate, *a*, неопределённый.

index, *n*, указатель; индекс; показатель; *card* ~ картотека; ~ *finger* указательный палец; ¶ *v.t*, заносить в указатель; снабжать указателем.

Indian, *a*, индийский; индейский; ¶ *n*, индиец; индеец *(American)*; ~ *corn* майс, кукуруза; ~ *ink* (китайская) тушь; ~ *summer* бабье лето; ~ *woman* индианка.

indiarubber, *n*, резина; резинка.

indicate, *v.t*, указывать; indication, *n*, указание; симптом, знак; indicative, *a*, указывающий; *(gram.)* изъявительный; ¶ *n*, *(gram.)* изъявительное наклонение; indicator, *n*, указатель; счётчик; стрелка.

indict, *v.t*, обвинять; ~ment, *n*, обвинительный акт.

indifference, *n*, равнодушие, безразличие; indifferent, *a*, равнодушный, безразличный; посредственный.

indigence, *n*, нужда, бедность.

indigenous, *a*, туземный; местный.

indigent, *a*, бедный.

indigestible, *a*, неудобоваримый; indigestion, *n*, расстройство желудка.

indignant, *a*, негодующий, возмущённый; indignation, *n*, негодование, возмущение; indignity, *n*, унижение.

indigo, *n*, индиго; синий свет.

indirect, *a*, косвенный, побочный; непрямой.

indiscipline, *n*, непослушание.

indiscreet, *a*, неосторожный; неблагоразумный; indiscretion, *n*, неосторожность; неблагоразумный поступок.

indiscriminate, *a*, неразборчивый; беспорядочный; ~ly, *ad*, неразборчиво; беспорядочно.

indispensable, *a*, необходимый; незаменимый.

indispose, *v.t.:* ~ *towards*, восстанавливать против; indisposed, *p.p. &a*, нездоровый; нерасположенный; indisposition, *n*, недомогание; нерасположение.

indisputable, *a*, неоспоримый; бесспорный.

indissoluble, *a*, нерастворимый; *(fig.)* неразрывный.

indistinct, *a*, неясный; невнятный.

indistinguishable, *a*, неразличимый.

individual, *a*, личный; индивидуальный; отдельный; ¶ *n*, индивидуум; личность; человек; ~ity, *n*, индивидуальность; ~ly, *ad*, индивидуально; отдельно.

indivisible, *a*, неделимый.

indocile, *a*, непокорный.

indoctrinate, *v.t*, навязывать/внушать доктрину *(dat.)*; indoctrination, *n*, навязывание доктрины.

Indo-European, *a*, индоевропейский.

indolence, *n*, леность; indolent, *a*, ленивый.

indomitable, *a*, неукротимый.

indoor, *a*, (находящийся) внутри дома; комнатный; внутренний; ~s, *ad*, внутри (дома); в помещении.

indubitable, *a*, несомненный; indubitably, *ad*, несомненно.

induce, *v.t*, убеждать; побуждать; *(elec.)* индуктировать; ~ment, *n*, побуждение; приманка; induction, *n*, индукция; *(eccl.)* введение в должность; inductive, *a*, индуктивный.

indulge, *v.t*, баловать *(child, etc.)*; снисходить к; потворствовать *(dat.)*; ~ *in* предаваться *(dat.)*; indulgence, *n*, снисходительность; потворство; потакание; indulgent, *a*, снисходительный; терпимый.

industrial, *a*, промышленный, индустриальный; ~ist, *n*, промышленник; ~ize, *v.t*, индустриализировать; industrious, *a*, трудолюбивый, прилёжный; **industry**, *n*, промышленность; отрасль промышленности; прилежание.

inebriate, *v.t*, опьянять; ~**d**, *a*, пьяный; **inebriation**, *n*, опьянение.

inedible, *a*, несъедобный.

ineffable, *a*, невыразимый.

ineffaceable, *a*, неизгладимый.

ineffective, ineffectual, *a*, безрезультатный; безуспешный.

inefficiency, *n*, неспособность; неэффективность; **inefficient**, *a*, неспособный; неэффективный; непроизводительный.

inelegant, *a*, неизящный; безвкусный; неотделанный *(style)*.

inept, *a*, неспособный; неподходящий; неуместный; **ineptitude**, *n*, неспособность; неуместность.

inequality, *n*, неравенство.

inequitable, *a*, несправедливый.

inert, *a*, инертный; вялый; ~**ia**, *n*, инёрция; инёртность.

inestimable, *a*, неоценимый.

inevitable, *a*, неизбёжный, неминуемый; **inevitably**, *ad*, неизбёжно.

inexact, *a*, неточный.

inexcusable, *a*, непростительный.

inexhaustible, *a*, неистощимый

inexorable, *a*, неумолимый.

inexpedient, *a*, нецелесообразный, невыгодный.

inexpensive, *a*, недорогой.

inexperience, *n*, неопытность; ~**d**, *a*, неопытный.

inexpert, *a*, неумёлый.

inexpiable, *a*, неискупимый.

inexplicable, *a*, необъяснимый.

inexpressible, *a*, невыразимый; **inexpressive**, *a*, невыразительный.

inextinguishable, *a*, неугасимый.

inextricable, *a*, запутанный; неразрешимый.

infallibility, *n*, непогрешимость; безошибочность; **infallible**, *a*, непогрешимый; безошибочный.

infamous, *a*, позорный; бесчестный; **infamy**, *n*, позор, бесчестие.

infancy, *n*, раннее детство, младенчество; *(law)* несовершеннолётие; **infant**, *n*, младенец, ребёнок; ~ *school* детский сад; **infanticide**, *n*, детоубийство; детоубийца; **infantile**, *a*, младенческий; инфантильный.

infantry, *n*, пехота; ~**man**, *n*, пехотинец.

infatuate, *v.t*, вскружить *(pf.)* голову *(dat.)*, увлекать; **infatuation**, *n*, слепое увлечение.

infect, *v.t*, заражать; ~**ion**, *n*, заражёние; инфёкция, зараза: ~**ious**, *a*, заразный; *(fig.)* заразительный.

infer, *v.t*, заключать; подразумевать; ~**ence**, *n*, вывод, заключёние.

inferior, *a*, низший; плохой, худший; ¶ *n*, подчинённый; ~**ity**, *n*, низшее положёние; худшее качество; ~ *complex* комплекс неполноцённости.

infernal, *a*, адский; **inferno**, *n*, ад.

infertile, *a*, неплодородный; бесплодный.

infest, *v. t*, наводять; *be* ~ *ed with* кишёть *(inst.)*.

infidel, *a*, невёрующий; ¶ *n*, невёрующий; язычник; ~**ity**, *n*, невёрность.

infiltrate, *v.t*, фильтровать; *v.i*, проникать; **infiltration**, *n*, проникновёние.

infinite, *a*, бесконёчный; безграничный; *(gram.)* неопределённый; ~**ly**, *ad*, бесконёчно; ~**simal**, *a*, бесконёчно малый; **infinitive (mood)**, *n*, неопределённое наклонёние, инфинитив: **infinity**, *n*, бесконёчность.

infirm, *a*, дряхлый, слабый; ~**ary**, *n*, больница; ~**ity**, *n*, нёмощь, дряхлость.

inflame, *v.t*, воспламенять; возбуждать; ~**d**, *p.p. & a. (med.)* палённый; возбуждённый; **inflammable**, *a*, легко воспламеняющийся; легко возбудимый; **inflammation**, *n, (med.)* воспалёние.

inflate, *v.t*, надувать; вздувать *(prices)*; **inflation**, *n*, надувание; *(fin.)* инфляция.

inflect, *v.t*, гнуть; *(gram.)* изменять; ~**ion**, *n*, сгибание, изгиб; *(gram.)* флёксия; *(mus.)* модуляция голоса.

inflexibility, *n*, негибкость; непреклонность; **inflexible**, *a*, негибкий; непреклонный.

inflict, *v.t*, наносить; причинять *(pain)*; налагать *(penalty)*; ~**ion**, *n*, наложёние; причинёние.

inflow, *n*, приток, наплыв.

influence, *n*, влия́ние; де́йствие; ¶ *v.t*, влия́ть на; influential, *a*, влия́тельный.

influenza, *a*, грипп.

influx, *n*, впаде́ние, прито́к; на-плы́в.

inform, *v.t*, сообща́ть, информи́ровать, осведомля́ть; ~ *against* доноси́ть на.

informal, *a*, неформа́льный, не-официа́льный; ~ity, *n*, несоблю-де́ние форма́льностей, непринуж-дённость; отсу́тствие церемо́ний.

informant, *n*, осведоми́тель; обви-ни́тель; information, *n*, инфор-ма́ция, све́дения; informative, *a*, поучи́тельный; поле́зный; infor-med, *p.p. & a*, осведомлённый; просвещённый; informer, *n*, до-но́счик; осведоми́тель.

infraction, *n*, наруше́ние.

infrequent, *a*, ре́дкий; ~ly, *ad*, ре́дко.

infringe, *v.t*, наруша́ть; ~ment, *n*, наруше́ние; ~r, *n*, наруши́тель.

infuriate, *v.t*, разъяря́ть.

infuse, *v.t*, влива́ть; *(fig.)* внуша́ть; зава́ривать *(tea);* infusion, *n*, влива́ние; внуше́ние; зава́рка.

ingenious, *a*, изобрета́тельный; ис-ку́сный; ingenuity, *n*, изобрета́-тельность; остроу́мие.

ingenuous, *a*, бесхи́тростный, про-стоду́шный.

ingle-nook, *n*, ме́сто у ками́на.

inglorious, *a*, бессла́вный.

ingoing, *a*, входя́щий; ¶ *n*, вход.

ingot, *n*, сли́ток; брусо́к.

ingrained, *a*, про́чно укорени́вший-ся; ~ *dirt* въе́вшаяся грязь.

ingratiate oneself *(with him)* втира́ть-ся (к нему́) в ми́лость.

ingratitude, *n*, неблагода́рность.

ingredient, *n*, составна́я часть.

ingress, *n*, вход, до́ступ.

ingrowing, *a*, враста́ющий.

inhabit, *v.t*, населя́ть, жить в/на; ~able, *a*, обита́емый, го́дный для жилья́; ~ant, *n*, обита́тель, жи́-тель.

inhalant, *n*, ингаля́цио́нное сре́д-ство; inhalation, *n*, вдыха́ние; *(med.)* ингаля́ция.

inhale, *v.t*, вдыха́ть; затя́гиваться (ды́мом).; ~r, *n*, ингаля́тор.

inharmonious, *a*, негармони́чный.

inherent. *a*, врождённый; прису́-щий.

inherit, *v.t*, насле́довать; ~ance, *n*, насле́дство; *(fig.)* насле́дие.

inhibit, *v.t*, сде́рживать, подавля́ть; заде́рживать, тормози́ть; ~ed, *p.p. & a*, сде́ржанный; стесни́-тельный; ~ion, *n*, сде́рживание; заде́рживание; *(biol.)* торможе́-ние; ко́мплекс.

inhospitable, *a*, негостеприи́мный; суро́вый; inhospitality, *n*, негосте-прии́мность; суро́вость.

inhuman, *a*, бесчелове́чный; нече-лове́ческий; ~ity, *n*, бесчелове́ч-ность.

inhume, *v.t*, предава́ть земле́.

inimical, *a*, враждебный; неблаго-прия́тный.

inimitable, *a*, неподража́емый, не-сравнённый.

iniquitous, *a*, несправедли́вый; ini-quity, *n*, несправедли́вость.

initial, *a*, первонача́льный; ~ *expen-diture* предвари́тельные рас-хо́ды; ¶ *n*, нача́льная бу́ква; *(pl.)* инициа́лы; ¶ *v.t*, ста́вить инициа́лы.

initiate, *v.t*, начина́ть; быть ини-циа́тором *(gen.);* посвяща́ть (в та́йну); принима́ть (в о́бщество); initiation, *n*, введе́ние; initiative, *n*, инициати́ва; initiator, *n*, ини-циа́тор.

inject, *v.t*, впры́скивать; вводи́ть; ~ion, *n*, впры́скивание; инъе́к-ция, уко́л.

injudicious, *a*, неблагоразу́мный.

injunction, *n*, предписа́ние; *(law)* постановле́ние суда́.

injure, *v.t*, вреди́ть *(dat.);* ушиба́ть, ра́нить; оскорбля́ть; injurious, *a*, вре́дный; оскорби́тельный; in-jury, *n*, вред; поврежде́ние; ра-не́ние; оскорбле́ние.

injustice, *n*, несправедли́вость.

ink, *n*, черни́ла *(pl.); printer's* ~ типогра́фская кра́ска; ~*pot* черни́льница; ¶ *v.t*, покры-ва́ть черни́лами; отмеча́ть черни́-лами.

inkling, *n*, намёк, подозре́ние.

inland, *a*, вну́тренний; располо́-женный внутри́ страны́; ¶ *ad*, внутрь/внутри́ страны́.

inlay, *v.t*, покрыва́ть инкруста́цией; вставля́ть; ¶ *n*, инкруста́ция; мо-заи́чная рабо́та.

inlet, *n*, зали́в, бу́хта; *(tech.)* впуск, вход.

inmate, *n*, жилец; заключённый (в тюрьме); больной.

inmost, *a*, сокровенный; самый внутренний.

inn, *n*, гостиница; трактир; постоялый двор; ~*keeper* хозяин гостиницы; трактирщик; ~*s of court* коллегии адвокатов.

innate, *a*, врождённый.

inner, *a*, внутренний; скрытый; ~most, *a*, глубочайший.

innings, *n*, очередь; уборка урожая; *(fig.)* период пребывания у власти *a good*; ~ счастливая/долгая жизнь.

innocuous, *a*, безвредный; безобидный.

innovation, *n*, нововведение; новшество; innovator, *n*, новатор.

innuendo, *n*, намёк; инсинуация.

innumerable, *a*, бесчисленный, несметный.

inobservance, *n*, несоблюдение; невнимательность.

inoculate, *v.t*, делать прививку *(dat.);* inoculation, *n*, прививка.

inoffensive, *a*, безвредный, безобидный.

inoperative, *a*, недействующий.

inopportune, *a*, несвоевременный, неподходящий; ~ly, *ad*, несвоевременно.

inordinate, *a*, чрезмерный, неумеренный.

inorganic, *a*, неорганический; чуждый.

in-patient, *n*, стационарный больной.

inquest, *n*, *(law)* следствие, дознание.

inquietude, *n*, беспокойство.

inquire *see* enquire

inquisition, *n*, расследование; Инквизиция; inquisitive, *a*, любознательный, пытливый; inquisitor, *n*, инквизитор; следователь.

inroad, *n*, набег; *(fig.)* вторжение.

insane, *a*, безумный; душевнобольной; insanity, *n*, умопомешательство, безумие.

insatiable, *a*, ненасытный.

inscribe, *v.t*, надписывать; вырезать; посвящать; inscription, *n*, надпись; посвящение.

inscrutable, *a*, непроницаемый; загадочный.

insect, *n*, насекомое; ~ *powder* порошок от насекомых; ~icide, *n*, инсектицид.

insecure, *a*, непрочный; небезопасный; insecurity, *n*, небезопасность; неуверенность.

insemination, *n*, оплодотворение; *artificial* ~ искусственное осеменение.

insensate, *a*, бесчувственный; нечувствительный; бессмысленный.

insensibility, *n*, нечувствительность; безразличие; потеря сознания; insensible, *a*, нечувствительный; потерявший сознание; insensitive, *a*, нечувствительный.

inseparable, *a*, неотделимый; неразлучный.

insert, *v.t*, вставлять; помещать *(in newspaper);* включать; ~ion, *n*, вставление, помещение, включение; вставка; объявление.

inset, *n*, вкладка, вклейка; вставка *(in dress).*

inshore, *a*, прибрежный; ¶ *ad*, близко от берега/к берегу.

inside, *a*, внутренний; секретный; ~ *track (sport)* внутренняя сторона беговой дорожки; ¶ *n*, внутренняя сторона; внутренность; изнанка; ¶ *ad*, внутри, внутрь; ~ *out* наизнанку; ¶ *pr*, внутри, в.

insidious, *a*, коварный; подкрадывающийся.

insight, *n*, проницательность, интуиция.

insignia, *n.pl*, знаки отличия.

insincere, *a*, нейскренний; insincerity, *n*, нейскренность.

insinuate, *v.t*, инсинуировать, намекать; ~ *oneself into* пробираться в; вкрадываться в; insinuation, *n*, инсинуация; намёк.

insipid, *a*, безвкусный; скучный.

insist, *v.i*, настаивать; утверждать; требовать; ~ence, *n*, настойчивость; утверждение.

insobriety, *n*, нетрезвость.

insolation, *n*, инсоляция.

insolence, *n*, наглость, дерзость; insolent, *a*, наглый, дерзкий.

insoluble, *a*, нерастворимый; неразрешимый.

insolvency, *n*, банкротство, несостоятельность; insolvent, *a*, не-

состоя́тельный; *become* ~ обанк-
ро́титься *(pf.).*
insomnia, *n*, бессо́нница.
insomuch, *ad:* ~ *as* насто́лько...
что.
inspect, *v.t*, осма́тривать; инспекти́-
ровать; ~ion, *n*, смотр, осмо́тр;
инспе́кция; ~or, *n*, инспе́ктор;
контролёр.
inspiration, *n*, вдохнове́ние; вооду-
шевле́ние; **inspire**, *v.t*, вдохнов-
ля́ть; внуша́ть.
inspirit, *v.t*, воодушевля́ть; обод-
ря́ть.
instability, *n*, неусто́йчивость.
install, *v.t*, помеща́ть, водворя́ть;
вводи́ть в до́лжность; *(tech.)*
устана́вливать; *(elec. etc.)* про-
води́ть; ~ation, *n*, введе́ние в
до́лжность; устано́вка; монта́ж,
прово́дка; *pl*, сооруже́ния.
instalment, *n*, очередно́й взнос;
(of story) вы́пуск; *pay by* ~s вы-
пла́чивать в рассро́чку.
instance, *n*, приме́р; слу́чай; *(law)*
инста́нция; *for* ~ наприме́р;
¶ *v.t*, приводи́ть в ка́честве при-
ме́ра; **instant**, *a*, неме́дленный;
теку́щий; ¶ *n*, мгнове́ние, мо-
ме́нт; *the* ~ *(that)* как то́лько...;
instantaneous, *a*, мгнове́нный, не-
ме́дленный; одновреме́нный; **in-
stantly**, *ad*, неме́дленно.
instead, *ad*, вме́сто, взаме́н; ~ *of*...
вме́сто *(+ gen)*; вме́сто того́,
что́бы *(+ inf.).*
instep, *n*, подъём.
instigate, *v.t*, побужда́ть, подстре-
ка́ть; **instigation**, *n*, подстрекательство; **instigator**, *n*, подстре-
ка́тель; поджига́тель.
instil, *v.t*, внуша́ть.
instinct, *n*, инсти́нкт; чутьё; ~ive,
a, инстинкти́вный, бессозна́тель-
ный.
institute, *n*, институ́т, учрежде́ние;
¶ *v.t*, учрежда́ть; устана́вливать;
institution, *n*, установле́ние; у-
чрежде́ние, заведе́ние; *(pl.)* об-
ще́ственные организа́ции.
instruct, *v.t*, обуча́ть, инструкти́ро-
вать; прика́зывать *(dat.);* ~ion,
n, обуче́ние; директи́ва; *pl*, ука-
за́ния, инстру́кции; ~ive, *a*,
поучи́тельный; ~or, *n*, инстру́к-
тор; учи́тель.
instrument, *n*, инструме́нт; прибо́р;
ору́дие *(also fig.);* докуме́нт,

догово́р; ¶ *v.t*, проводи́ть в жизнь;
~al, *a*, инструмента́льный; слу́-
жащий ору́дием; *be* ~ *in* способствовать *(dat.);* ~ *case* твори́-
тельный паде́ж; ~alist, *n*, инстру-
ментали́ст; ~ation, *n*, инстру-
менто́вка.
insubordinate, *a*, непослу́шный, не-
подчиня́ющийся; **insubordination**,
n, неподчине́ние, неповино-
ве́ние.
insufferable, *a*, невыноси́мый; не-
стерпи́мый.
insufficiency, *n*, недоста́точность;
insufficient, *a*, недоста́точный.
insular, *a*, островно́й; *(fig.)* ограни́-
ченный; за́мкнутый; **insulate**, *v.t*,
изоли́ровать; **insulator**, *n*, изо-
ля́тор; **insulation**, *n*, изоля́ция.
insulin, *n*, инсули́н.
insult, *n*, оскорбле́ние, оби́да; ¶ *v.t*,
оскорбля́ть, обижа́ть; ~ing, *a*,
оскорби́тельный.
insuperable, *a*, непреодоли́мый.
insupportable, *a*, нестерпи́мый; ко-
то́рого невозмо́жно содержа́ть.
insurance, *n*, страхова́ние; *fire* ~
страхова́ние от пожа́ра; ~ *company* страхова́я компа́ния; ~
policy страхово́й по́лис; ~ *premium* страхова́я пре́мия; **insure**,
v.t, страхова́ть; обеспе́чивать; ~d,
p.p. & a, застрахо́ванный; ~r,
n, страхово́е о́бщество; страхо́в-
щик.
insurgent, *a*, восста́вший, мяте́ж-
ный; ¶ *n*, повста́нец.
insurmountable, *a*, непреодоли́мый.
insurrection, *n*, восста́ние, бунт.
intact, *a*, нетро́нутый; неповреждённый; це́лый.
intake, *n*, впуск, вход; набо́р.
intangible, *a*, неосяза́емый; *(fig.)*
непостижи́мый, неулови́мый.
integer, *n*, це́лое число́; **integral**, *a*,
неотъе́млемый; составно́й;
(maths) интегра́льный; це́лый.
integrate, *v.t*, объединя́ть; сос-
тавля́ть це́лое из; *(maths.)* ин-
тегри́ровать; **integration**, *n*,
(maths.) интегра́ция; объедине́-
ние в одно́ це́лое; слия́ние.
integrity, *n*, прямота́, че́стность;
це́лостность.
intellect, *n*, интелле́кт, ум; ~ual, *a*,
интеллектуа́льный; у́мственный;
¶ *n*, интеллиге́нт; *pl*, интелли-
ге́нция.

intelligence, *n*, ум, разум; смышлёность; понятливость *(of animals)*; информация; разведка; ~ *service* разведка; intelligent, *a*, умный; смышлёный, понятливый; intelligible, *a*, понятный.

intemperance, *n*, невоздержанность; пьянство; intemperate, *a*, невоздержанный; сильно пьющий.

intend, *v.t*, намереваться; предназначать; ~ed, *p.p. & a*, предназначенный; ¶ *n*, жених, невеста.

intense, *a*, напряжённый; интенсивный; пылкий; сильный; intensify, *v.t. (& i.)*, усиливать(ся); intensity, *n*, интенсивность; напряжённость; сила; intensive, *a*, интенсивный; *(gram.)* усилительный.

intent, *n*, намерение; цель; *to all* ~s *and purposes* фактически; ¶ *a*, внимательный; ~ *on* стремящийся к; погружённый в; ~ion, *n*, намерение; ~ional, *a*, намеренный, умышленный; ~ionally, *ad*, намеренно, умышленно; ~ness, *n*, внимательность.

inter, *v.t*, хоронить, погребать.

intercalate, *v.t*, вставлять; intercalation, *n*, вставка.

intercede, *v.i*, ходатайствовать, вступаться.

intercept, *v.t*, перехватывать; пересекать; выключать.

intercession, *n*, заступничество, посредничество, ходатайство; intercessor, *n*, заступник ходатай.

interchange, *n*, обмен; смена; перестановка; ¶ *v.t. (& i.)*, обменивать(ся); чередовать(ся); ~able, *a*, взаимозаменяемый; равнозначный.

intercourse, *n*, общение; связь; отношения; сношения.

interdependence, *n*, взаимозависимость; interdependent, *a*, взаимозависимый.

interdict, *n*, запрещение, запрет; *(eccl.)* отлучение; ¶ *v.t*, запрещать; ~ion, *n*, запрещение; отлучение.

interest, *n*, интерес; заинтересованность; выгода; процент; *bear* ~ приносить прибыль; *compound* ~ сложные проценты; *controlling* ~ контроль; *in your* ~ в ваших интересах; *life* ~ пожизненное владение; *rate of* ~ норма процента; *simple* ~ простые проценты; ~-*bearing* прибыльный; ¶ *v.t*, интересовать; заинтересовывать; ~ *oneself in* интересоваться *(inst.)*; ~ing, *a*, интересный.

interfere, *v.i*, вмешиваться; ~ *with* мешать *(dat.)*; приставать к; ~псе, *n*, вмешательство; препятствие; *(radio)* помехи.

interim, *a*, временный, промежуточный; ¶ *n*, промежуток времени;

interior, *a*, внутренний; ¶ *n*, внутренность, внутренняя сторона; интерьер; внутренние области страны.

interject, *v.t*, вставлять; ~ion, *n*, восклицание; *(gram.)* междометие.

interlace, *v.t. (& i.)*, переплетать(ся).

interlard, *v.t*, шпиговать; *(fig.)* пересыпать; подмешивать.

interleave, *v.t*, прокладывать между листами книги; прослаивать.

interline, *v.t*, вписывать между строк.

interlink, *v.t*, связывать, сцеплять.

interlock, *v.t. (& i.)*, сцеплять(ся), соединять(ся).

interlocutor, *n*, собеседник.

interloper, *n*, человек, вмешивающийся в чужие дела; пришлый человек, незнакомец.

interlude, *n*, антракт; интермедия; *(mus.)* интерлюдия.

intermarriage, *n*, брак между людьми разных рас; брак между родственниками; intermarry, *v.i*, вступать в брак с человеком другой расы; родниться.

intermediary, *a*, промежуточный; ¶ *n*, посредник.

interment, *n*, погребение.

intermezzo, *n*, интермедия; *(mus.)* интермеццо.

interminable, *a*, бесконечный.

intermingle, *v.t. (& i.)*, перемешивать(ся), смешивать(ся).

intermission, *n*, перерыв, пауза; *(theat.)* антракт; intermittent, *a*, перемежающийся, прерывистый; с перебоями.

intern, *v.t*, интернировать.

internal, *a*, внутренний; комнатный; ~-*combustion engine* двигатель внутреннего сгорания; ~ly, *ad*, внутренне.

international, *a,* международный; интернациональный; сборный *(team);* ~ism, *n,* интернационализм; ~ize, *v.t,* делать интернациональным.

internecine, *a,* междоусобный.

internment, *n,* интернирование; ~ *camp* лагерь для интернированных.

interplay, *n,* взаимодействие.

interpolate, *v.t,* вставлять; интерполировать.

interpose, *v.t,* вставлять; ставить между; *v.i,* вмешиваться; прерывать; становиться между.

interpret, *v.t,* толковать; переводить; ~ation, *n,* толкование; перевод; ~er, *n,* толкователь; переводчик.

interregnum, *n,* междуцарствие; перерыв.

interrogate, *v.t,* допрашивать; опрашивать; **interrogation,** *n,* допрос; вопрос; опрос; **interrogative,** *a,* вопросительный; **interrogator,** *n,* следователь.

interrupt, *v.t,* прерывать; мешать *(dat.);* ~er, *n,* прерыватель; ~ion, *n,* прерывание; перерыв; остановка; *(tech.)* разрыв.

intersect, *v.t. (& i.),* пересекать(ся), скрещивать(ся); ~ion, *n,* пересечение.

intersperse, *v.t,* рассыпать; пересыпать; перемешивать.

interstice, *n,* промежуток; щель.

intertwine, *v.t. (& i.),* переплетать(ся).

interval, *n,* промежуток; перерыв, пауза; *(theat.)* антракт; перемена *(school).*

intervene, *v.i,* вмешиваться; происходить; **intervention,** *n,* интервенция; вмешательство.

interview, *n,* беседа, встреча; интервью *(press);* ¶ *v.t,* иметь беседу с; интервьюировать; ~er, *n,* интервьюёр.

interweave, *v.t,* воткать *(pf.); (fig.)* переплетать.

intestate, *a,* скончавшийся без завещания.

intestinal, *a,* кишечный; **intestine,** *n,* кишечник; ¶ *a,* внутренний; междоусобный.

intimacy, *n,* близость, интимность.

intimate, *a,* близкий, интимный; ¶ *v.t,* намекать; конфиденциально

сообщать; ~ly, *ad,* близко; тесно; интимно.

intimation, *n,* намёк; сообщение.

intimidate, *v.t,* запугивать; **intimidation,** *n,* запугивание.

into, *pr,* в, во; на; ~ *the bargain* в придачу; к тому же.

intolerable, *a,* невыносимый, нестерпимый; **intolerance,** *n,* нетерпимость; **intolerant,** *a,* нетерпимый.

intonation, *n,* интонация; модуляция; **intone,** *v.t,* интонировать.

intoxicant, *n,* опьяняющий напиток; **intoxicate,** *v.t,* опьянять; возбуждать; **intoxication,** *n,* опьянение.

intractable, *a,* неподатливый; трудный (для воспитания); труднообрабатываемый.

intransigent, *a,* непримиримый, непреклонный.

intransitive, *a,* непереходный.

intrepid, *a,* неустрашимый; ~ity, *n,* неустрашимость.

intricacy, *n,* сложность, запутанность; **intricate,** *a,* сложный, запутанный.

intrigue, *n,* интрига; любовная связь; ¶ *v.i,* интриговать; ~ *against* строить козни против; ~r, *n,* интриган; **intriguing,** *a,* занимательный; интригующий.

intrinsic, *a,* внутренний; присущий; существенный; ~ally, *ad,* существенно; внутренне.

introduce, *v.t,* представлять, знакомить; вводить; вносить; ~ *oneself* представиться *(pf);* **introduction,** *n,* представление; введение, предисловие; внесение; **introductory,** *a,* вступительный, вводный.

introspection, *n,* самоанализ; интроспекция; **introspective,** *a,* интроспективный.

intrude, *v.i,* вторгаться; входить без приглашения; ~ *upon* навязываться *(dat.);* ~r, *n,* незваный гость; навязчивый человек; **intrusion,** *n,* вторжение; **intrusive,** *a,* навязчивый.

intuition, *n,* интуиция; **intuitive,** *a,* интуитивный.

inundate, *v.t,* наводнять, затоплять; **inundation,** *n,* наводнение.

inure, *v.t,* приучать; ~d, *p.p. & a,* приученный; привычный.

invade, *v.t,* вторгаться в/на; посягать на; ~r, *n,* захватчик; посягатель.

invalid, *a*, больнóй; нетрудоспосóбный; недействительный; ¶ *n*, больнóй, инвалид; ¶ *v.t*, освобождáть от службы по инвалидности; дéлать инвалидом; ~ate, *v.t*, дéлать недействительным.

invaluable, *a*, неоценимый, бесцéнный.

invariable, *a*, неизмéнный, неизменяемый.

invasion, *n*, вторжéние, нашéствие; посягáтельство.

invective, *n*, брань, ругáтельства *(pl.)*; **inveigh**, *v.i*: ~against нападáть на, ругáть.

inveigle, *v.t*, замáнивать; соблазнять.

invent, *v.t*, изобретáть; выдýмывать; ~ion, *n*, изобретéние; выдумка; ~ive, *a*, изобретáтельный; ~or, *n*, изобретáтель; выдумщик.

inventory, *n*, инвентáрь, óпись имýщества; ¶ *v.t*, составлять óпись (имýщества).

inverse, *a*, обрáтный; противополóжный; ~ly, *ad*, обрáтно; **inversion**. *n*, перестанóвка; *(gram.)* инвéрсия; **invert**, *v.t*, переставлять, переворáчивать; ~ed commas кавычки.

invertebrate, *a*, беспозвонóчный; *(fig.)* бесхребéтный; ¶ *n*, беспозвонóчное животное.

invest, *v.t*, вклáдывать, помещáть *(capital)*; облекáть *(with power, etc.)*; *(mil.)* осаждáть.

investigate, *v.t*, исслéдовать, расслéдовать; **investigation**, *n*, исслéдование; *(law)* расслéдование; **investigator**, *n*, исслéдователь; *(law)* слéдователь.

investiture, *n*, облачéние; введéние в дóлжность; награждéние.

investment, *n*, (капитало)вложéние; вклад; *(mil.)* осáда; **investor**, *n*, вклáдчик.

inveterate, *a*, закоренéлый, заядлый.

invidious, *a*, завидный; враждéбный; несправедливый.

invigorate, *v.t*, придавáть силы *(dat.)*; укреплять; бодрить; стимулировать; **invigorating**, *a*, подкрепляющий; бодрящий.

invincible, *a*, непобедимый.

inviolability, *n*, неприкосновéнность; нерушимость; **inviolable**, *a*, неприкосновéнный; нерушимый; **inviolate**, *a*, ненарýшенный.

invisibility, *n*, невидимость; **invisible**, *a*, невидимый; незамéтный; ~ ink симпатические чернила.

invitation, *n*, приглашéние; **invite**, *v.t*, приглашáть; привлекáть; **inviting**, *a*, привлекáтельный; манящий.

invocation, *n*, призыв; заклинáние.

invoice, *n*, фактýра, накладнáя; ¶ *v.t*, писáть фактýру/накладнýю на.

invoke, *v.t*, призывáть; применять *(law, etc)*; заклинáть.

involuntarily, *ad*, невóльно, нечáянно; **involuntary**, *a*, невóльный.

involve, *v.t*, вовлекáть; замéшивать; запýтывать; влечь за собóй.

invulnerability, *n*, неуязвимость; **invulnerable**, *a*, неуязвимый.

inward, *a*, внýтренний; ~ly, *ad*, внутри; в душé; ~s, *ad*, внутрь.

iodine, *n*, йод.

ion, *n*, иóн.

Ionic, *a*, ионический.

I.O.U., *n*, долговáя расписка.

irascibility, *n*, раздражительность; **irascible**, *a*, раздражительный.

irate, *a*, гнéвный, разгнéванный; **ire**, *n*, гнев.

iridescence, *n*, рáдужность; **iridescent**, *a*, рáдужный.

iris, *n*, *(bot.)* ирис; рáдужная оболóчка (глáза).

Irish, *a*, ирлáндский; ¶ *n*, ирлáндский язык; ~man, ~ woman ирлáндец, ирлáндка.

irk, *v.t*, раздражáть; надоедáть *(dat.)*; ~some, *a*, скýчный.

iron, *n*, желéзо; утюг; желéзное издéлие; *(pl.)* кандалы; ¶ *a*, желéзный; *strike while the ~ is hot* куй желéзо, покá горячó; ~ *foundry* чугунолитéйный завóд; ~*monger* торгóвец желéзными/ скобяными издéлиями; ~ *ore* желéзная рудá; ~ *ration* неприкосновéнный запáс; ~*works* чугуноплавильный завóд; ¶ *v.t*, глáдить, утюжить; ~ *out* сглáживать; ~clad, *n*, броненóсец; ~er, *n*, гладильщица.

ironic(al), *a*, иронический.

ironing, *n*, утюжка, глáженье; бельё для глáженья; глáженое бельё; ~ board, гладильная доскá.

irony, *n*, ирóния.

irradiate, *v.t*, освещáть; излучáть; испускáть лучи; **irradiation**, *n*, освеще́ние;   лучеиспуска́ние; *(phys.)* иррада́ция.

irrational, *a,* нерациона́льный; *(maths.)* иррациона́льный.

irreclaimable, *a,* невозвра́тный; него́дный для обрабо́тки; неисправи́мый.

irreconcilable, *a,* непримири́мый.

irrecoverable, *a,* невозвра́тный.

irredeemable, *a,* неисправи́мый; *(com.)* не подлежа́щий вы́купу.

irreducible, *a,* несокраща́емый; неизме́нный.

irrefutable, *a,* неопровержи́мый.

irregular, *a,* нерегуля́рный; беспоря́дочный; непра́вильный; несимметри́чный; неро́вный; **~ity,** *n,* нерегуля́рность; непра́вильность.

irrelevance, *n,* неуме́стность; **irrelevant,** *a,* неуме́стный.

irreligious, *a,* нерелиги́озный, неве́рующий.

irremediable, *a,* непоправи́мый; неизлечи́мый.

irreparable, *a,* непоправи́мый.

irreproachable, *a,* безукори́зненный, безупре́чный.

irresistible, *a,* неотрази́мый.

irresolute, *a,* нереши́тельный.

irrespective, *a:* **~ of** незави́симый от; безотноси́тельный.

irresponsibility, *n,* безотве́тственность; **irresponsible,** *a,* безотве́тственный.

irretrievable, *a,* невозмести́мый; непоправи́мый.

irreverence, *n,* непочти́тельность; **irreverent,** *a,* непочти́тельный.

irrevocable, *a,* безвозвра́тный.

irrigate, *v.t,* ороша́ть; *(med.)* промыва́ть; **irrigation,** *n,* ороше́ние, ирига́ция.

irritability, *n,* раздражи́тельность; **irritable,** *a,* раздражи́тельный; **irritant,** *a,* вызыва́ющий раздраже́ние; ¶ *n,* раздража́ющее сре́дство; **irritation,** *n,* раздраже́ние.

irruption, *n,* вторже́ние.

isinglass, *n,* ры́бий клей.

Islam, *n,* исла́м.

island, *n,* о́стров; ¶ *a,* островно́й; **~er,** *n,* островитя́нин; **islet,** *n,* острово́к.

isolate, *v.t,* отделя́ть; изоли́ровать; **~d,** *p.p. & a,* отде́льный; отдалённый; изоли́рованный; **isolation,** *n,* одино́чество; изоля́ция; ~

hospital инфекцио́нная больни́ца’ изоля́тор; **~ism,** *n,* изоляциони́зм.

Israeli(te), *a,* изра́ильский; ¶ *n,* израильтя́нин, -ка.

issue, *n,* вы́ход; исхо́д; изда́ние; вы́пуск; предме́т обсужде́ния; пото́мство; *(fin.)* эми́ссия; *be at* ~ быть предме́том обсужде́ния; *bring to a successful* ~ разреши́ть *(pf.)* вопро́с; ¶ *v.i,* выходи́ть, вытека́ть, происходи́ть; *v.t,* выпуска́ть; выдава́ть.

isthmus, *n,* переше́ек.

it, *pn,* он, она́, оно́; *who is* ~? кто там?; ~ *is said that* говоря́т, что . . .

Italian, *a,* италья́нский; ¶ *n,* италья́н|ец, -ка; италья́нский язы́к.

italic, *a,* итали́йский; *(print.)* курси́вный; **~s,** *n,pl,* курси́в; **~ize,** *v.t,* выделя́ть курси́вом.

itch, *n,* зуд, чесо́тка; *(fig.)* жа́жда, жела́ние; ¶ *v.i,* зуде́ть, чеса́ться; *(fig.)* нетерпели́во жела́ть; *my hand* **~es** у меня́ че́шется рука́; **~y,** *a,* зудя́щий.

item, *n,* пункт; статья́; предме́т; но́мер (програ́ммы); вопро́с.

iterate, *v.t,* повторя́ть; **iteration,** *n,* повторе́ние.

itinerant, *a,* стра́нствующий; **itinerary,** *n,* маршру́т, путь; путевы́е заме́тки; путеводи́тель.

its, *pn,* его́, её; свой; **itself,** *pn,* себя́; сам, сама́, само́; *she is virtue* ~ она́ сама́ доброде́тель.

ivory, *n,* слоно́вая кость; ¶ *a,* из слоно́вой ко́сти; цве́та слоно́вой ко́сти.

ivy, *n,* плющ.

J

jab, *n,* толчо́к, уда́р; ¶ *v.t,* толка́ть, пиха́ть; коло́ть.

jabber, *v.i,* болта́ть.

jack, *n,* *(tech.)* домкра́т; рыча́г; *(cards)* вале́т; **~boot** сапо́г; **~-in-the-box** попрыгу́нчик; **~-in-office** чину́ша; **~-knife** складно́й нож; ~ *of all trades* ма́стер на все ру́ки; **~-o'-lantern** блужда́ющий огонёк; **~-plane** руба́нок; ~ *tar* матро́с.

jackal, *n,* шака́л.

jackanapes, *n,* выско́чка; щёголь.

jackass, *n,* осёл.

jackdaw, *n*, га́лка.

jacket, *n*, жаке́т; ку́ртка; пиджа́к; кожура́ *(potato);* (супер)обло́жка *(book);* чехо́л.

jade, *n*, *(min.)* нефри́т; *(horse)* кля́ча; *(woman)* шлю́ха; ~d, *a*, изнурённый, изму́ченный.

jagged, *a*, зубча́тый, зазу́бренный.

jaguar, *n*, ягуа́р.

jail, *n*, тюрьма́: ~*bird* ареста́нт.

jam, *n*, варе́нье, джем; *(coll.)* да́вка; ¶ *v.t*, жать, дави́ть; прищемля́ть; впи́хивать; загромож-да́ть; *(radio)* заглуша́ть; *v.i*, оста-на́вливаться, заеда́ть.

jamb, *n*, коса́к.

jangle, *n*, лязг, звон; ¶ *v.i*, ля́згать; звене́ть.

janitor, *n*, привра́тник, швейца́р; сто́рож; дво́рник.

January, *n*, янва́рь; ¶ *a*, янва́рский.

japan, *n*, чёрный лак; ¶ *v.t*, покры-ва́ть чёрным ла́ком.

Japanese, *a*, япо́нский; ¶ *n*, япо́н|ец, ~ка; япо́нский язы́к.

jar, *n*, ба́нка; кру́жка, кувши́н; сотрясе́ние; шок, потрясе́ние; ¶ *v.t*, сотряса́ть; раздража́ть; *v.i*, де́йствовать на не́рвы; дребез-жа́ть.

jardinière, *n*, жардинье́рка.

jargon, *n*, жарго́н.

jarring, *a*, дребезжа́щий; раздража́-ющий.

jasmine, *n*, жасми́н.

jasper, *n*, я́шма.

jaundice, *n*, желту́ха; *(fig.)* жёлч-ность; за́висть; ~d, *a*, больно́й желту́хой; *(fig.)* жёлчный, за-ви́стливый.

jaunt, *n*, увесели́тельная прогу́лка/ экску́рсия; ~y, *a*, беспе́чный; самодово́льный.

javelin, *n*, мета́тельное копьё.

jaw, *n*, че́люсть; *(pl.)* пасть; *pl*, *(tech.)* тиски́; ~ *bone* челюстна́я кость.

jay, *n*, со́йка; ~*walker* неосторо́ж-ный пешехо́д.

jazz, *n*, джаз; ¶ *a*, джа́зовый; ~ *band* джаз-ба́нд, джаз-орке́стр.

jealous, *a*, ревни́вый, зави́стливый; ре́вностный; ~y, *n*, ре́вность, за́висть.

jean, *n*, бума́жная ткань; *(pl.)* джи́нсы (-ов).

jeer, *n*, насме́шка; ¶ *v.i:* ~ *at* насме-ха́ться над; высме́ивать.

jejune, *a*, ску́дный; ску́чный.

jelly, *n*, желе́; сту́день; ~-*fish* меду́за.

jemmy, *n*, отмы́чка.

jeopardize, *v.t*, подверга́ть опа́сности, рискова́ть *(inst.);* **jeopardy**, *n*, опа́сность, риск.

jerk, *n*, толчо́к; подёргивание; ¶ *v.t*, дёргать; *v.i*, дви́гаться ре́зкими толчка́ми; вздра́гивать.

jerkin, *n*, коро́ткая ку́ртка.

jerky, *a*, тря́ский; отры́вистый.

jerry-built, *a*, постро́енный на ско́-рую ру́ку.

jersey, *n*, сви́тер; вя́заная ткань; ~ *dress* вя́заное пла́тье.

jest, *n*, шу́тка; остро́та; ¶ *v.i*, шути́ть; остри́ть; ~er, *n*, шут, шутни́к.

Jesuit, *n*, иезуи́т; ~ic(al), *a*, иезуи́т-ский; *(fig.)* кова́рный.

Jesus, *n*, Иису́с.

jet, *n*, струя́; *(min.)* ага́т; жиклёр; ~ *plane* реакти́вный самолёт; ~-*black* чёрный как смоль; ~ *propulsion* реакти́вное движе́ние.

jetsam, *n*, груз, приби́тый к бе́регу (по́сле ава́рии).

jettison, *v.t*, выбра́сывать за борт; сбра́сывать; *(fig.)* отверга́ть.

jetty, *n*, при́стань.

Jew, *n*, евре́й; ~'*s harp* варга́н.

jewel, *n*, драгоце́нный ка́мень; юве-ли́рное изде́лие; ~-*case* футля́р для ювели́рных изде́лий; **jeweller**, *n*, ювели́р; **jewellery**, *n*, ювели́р-ные изде́лия.

Jewess, *n*, евре́йка; **Jewish**, *a*, евре́й-ский; **Jewry**, *n*, евре́йство.

jib, *n*, стрела́ (кра́на); попере́чина; кли́вер; ¶ *v.i*, упира́ться; вне-за́пно остана́вливаться.

jiffy, *n*, миг, мгнове́ние.

jig, *n*, джи́га *(dance);* *(print.)* ма́т-рица; ~*saw puzzle* составна́я карти́нка-зага́дка, головоло́мка.

jilt, *v.t*, броса́ть.

jingle, *n*, звя́канье, бряца́нье; ¶ *v.i*, звя́кать, бряца́ть.

jingo, *n*, шовини́ст; ~*ism*, *n*, шови-ни́зм.

job, *n*, рабо́та, слу́жба; ме́сто; зада́-ние, зада́ча; ~ *lot* разро́зненные това́ры, продаю́щиеся о́птом; ~ *work* сде́льная рабо́та; *it's a good* ~ *that* ... хорошо́, что ...; ~*ber*, *n*, ма́клер, комиссионе́р; сде́ль-ный рабо́чий; ~*bery*, *n*, злоупотребле́ние служе́бным положе́нием; спекуля́ция; ~bing, n, случа́йная рабо́та; торго́вля а́кциями.

jockey, n, жоке́й; ¶ v.i: ~ for position пробива́ться на вы́годную пози́цию.

jocose & **jocular**, a, шутли́вый; **jocund**, a, весёлый.

jog, v.t, подта́лкивать; v.i, бежа́ть ме́лкой рысцо́й; ~ along дви́гаться вперёд; ¶ n, толчо́к; ~-trot (ме́лкая) рысца́.

join, v.t, соединя́ть; вступа́ть в; впада́ть в (river); ~ the army поступа́ть в а́рмию; ~ battle вступа́ть в бой; v.i, соединя́ться; грани́чить с; ~er, n, столя́р; ~ery, n, столя́рная рабо́та; столя́рная мастерска́я; ~t, n, ме́сто соедине́ния, стык; суста́в (finger, etc.); сочлене́ние; кусо́к мя́са; out of ~ вы́вихнутый; (fig.) не в поря́дке; ¶ a, о́бщий, соединённый; совме́стный; ~ account о́бщий счёт; ~ authors соа́вторы; ~ heir сонасле́дник; ~ stock акционе́рный капита́л; ~-stock company акционе́рное о́бщество; ¶ v.t, сочленя́ть, соединя́ть; ~tly, ad, совме́стно; сообща́.

joist, n, ба́лка, перекла́дина.

joke, n, шу́тка; анекдо́т; остро́та; (pers.) посме́шище; practical ~ гру́бая шу́тка; ¶ v.i, шути́ть; ~r, n, шутни́к, насме́шник; дополни́тельная ка́рта, джо́кер; **jokingly**, ad, шутли́во, в шу́тку.

jollification, n, весе́лье, увеселе́ние; **jolly**, a, весёлый.

jolt, v.t, трясти́, подбра́сывать; v.i, трясти́сь; ¶ n. & ~ing, n, тря́ска.

jonquil, n, нарци́сс-жонки́ль; бле́дно-жёлтый цвет.

joss-stick, n, аромати́ческая свеча́.

jostle, n, толкотня́; ¶ v.t. (& i), толка́ть(ся).

jot, n, йо́та; not a ~ ни на йо́ту; ¶ v.t: ~ down бы́стро запи́сывать; ~tings, n.pl, кра́ткие за́писи.

journal, n, журна́л; дневни́к; протоко́л заседа́ния; ~ism, n, журнали́стика; ~ist, n, журнали́ст; ~istic, a, журна́льный.

journey, n, путеше́ствие, пое́здка; рейс; ¶ v.i, соверша́ть пое́здку; путеше́ствовать; ~man, n, поденщик.

joust, n, турни́р; ¶ v.i, би́ться на турни́ре/поеди́нке.

jovial, a, общи́тельный, весёлый; ~ity, n, общи́тельность, весёлость.

jowl, n, че́люсть; щека́.

joy, n, ра́дость; ~ful, a, ра́достный; ~less, a, безра́достный.

jubilant, a, лику́ющий; **jubilation**, n, ликова́ние.

jubilee, n, юбиле́й; годовщи́на.

Judaic, a, иуде́йский, евре́йский.

judge, n, судья́; цени́тель, знато́к; ¶ v.t, суди́ть; выноси́ть пригово́р (dat.); осужда́ть; оце́нивать; реша́ть; ~ment, n, реше́ние суда́; сужде́ние; ка́ра; ~ seat судье́йское ме́сто; day of ~ день стра́шного суда́.

judicature, n, соверше́ние правосу́дия; **judicial**, a, суде́бный; суде́йский; **judiciary**, n, суде́йская корпора́ция.

judicious, a, рассуди́тельный.

jug, n, кувши́н; ¶ v.t, туши́ть (cook.).

juggle, v.t, подтасо́вывать; v.i, жонгли́ровать; ~r, n, жонглёр; ~y, n, обма́н; **juggling**, n, жонгли́рование.

jugular, a, ше́йный.

juice, n, сок; (fig.) су́щность; **juiciness**, n, со́чность; **juicy**, n, со́чный; (fig.) пика́нтный.

ju-jitsu, n, джи́у-джи́тсу.

July, n, июль; ¶ a, ию́льский.

jumble, n, пу́таница; беспоря́док; барахло́; ~ sale дешёвый благотвори́тельный база́р; ¶ v.t, сме́шивать, перепу́тывать.

jump, n, прыжо́к, скачо́к; ski ~ прыжо́к с трампли́на; ¶ v.i, пры́гать; скака́ть; повыша́ться; ~ at ухва́тываться за; ~ over перепры́гивать; ~ the rails сходи́ть с ре́льсов; ~er, n, прыгу́н; скаку́н; (garment) дже́мпер; jumping-off point исхо́дный пункт; (mil.) плацда́рм; **jumpy**, a, не́рвный.

junction, n, соедине́ние; скреще́ние; перекрёсток; (rly.) у́зел; слия́ние рек.

juncture, n, соедине́ние; стече́ние обстоя́тельств; at this ~ в э́тот моме́нт.

June, n, июнь; ¶ a, ию́ньский.

jungle, n, джу́нгли.

junior, *n. & a*, мла́дший; *John Smith* ~ Джон Смит мла́дший.

juniper, *n*, можжеве́льник.

junk, *n*, джо́нка; хлам; ути́ль-сырьё; ~ *shop* ла́вка старьёвщика.

junket, *n*, сла́дкий тво́рог; пиру́шка.

juridical, *a*, юриди́ческий; судéбный; **jurisdiction**, *n*, правосу́дие; юрисди́кция; **jurisprudence**, *n*, юриспруде́нция; **jurist**, *n*, юри́ст.

juror, *n*, прися́жный; член жюри́; **jury**, *n*, прися́жные; жюри́.

just, *a*, справедли́вый; ¶ *ad*, то́чно; как раз; то́лько что; ~ *as* как то́лько, едва́; ~ *in case* на вся́кий слу́чай; ~ *now* сейча́с; то́лько что; ~**ice**, *n*, справедли́вость; правосу́дие; судья́; ~ *of the peace* мирово́й судья́; *do* ~ *to* отдава́ть до́лжное *(dat.);* отдава́ть честь *(dat.).*

justifiable, *a*, могу́щий быть опра́вданным; прости́тельный; зако́нный; **justification**, *n*, оправда́ние; **justify**, *v.t*, опра́вдывать; **justly**, *ad*, справедли́во.

jut, *v.i*, выдава́ться, выступа́ть.

jute, *n*, джут.

juvenile, *a*, ю́ный, ю́ношеский; ~ *delinquent* малоле́тний престу́пник; ¶ *n*, ю́ноша, подро́сток.

juxtapose, *v.t*, сопоставля́ть; помеща́ть ря́дом; **juxtaposition**, *n*, сопоставле́ние; расположе́ние бок о бок.

К

kale, *n*, кудря́вая капу́ста.

kaleidoscope, *n*, калейдоско́п.

kangaroo, *n*, кенгуру́.

keel, *n*, киль; ¶ *v.i:* ~ *over* опроки́дываться.

keen, *a*, о́стрый; ре́зкий проница́тельный; энерги́чный; си́льно жела́ющий; *be* ~ *on* си́льно жела́ть *(gen. inf.);* стра́стно увлека́ться *(inst.);* ~**ness**, *n*, острота́; ре́зкость; усе́рдие; си́льное жела́ние.

keep, *v.t*, держа́ть; храни́ть, сохраня́ть; соблюда́ть *(rule);* содержа́ть; име́ть; пра́здновать; вести́ *(diary, etc.);* *v.i*, сохраня́ться; ~ *aloof* держа́ться в стороне́; ~ *away* держа́ть(ся) в отдале́нии,

не подпуска́ть бли́зко; ~ *back* заде́рживать; скрыва́ть; ~ *down* подавля́ть; не позволя́ть встава́ть/расти́; ~ *house* вести́ дома́шнее хозя́йство; ~ *in* не выпуска́ть; ~ *off* не подпуска́ть; не тро́гать; ~ *on* оставля́ть; продолжа́ть; ~ *out (v.t.)* не впуска́ть; *(v.i.)* не входи́ть; ~ *out of* избега́ть *(gen.);* ~ *a secret* не выдава́ть та́йну; ~ *up (v.t.)* подде́рживать; продолжа́ть; *(v.i.)* бо́дро держа́ться; ~ *him waiting* заставля́ть его́ ждать; ~ *well* хорошо́ сохраня́ться; облада́ть хоро́шим здоро́вьем; ~ *one's word* держа́ть сло́во; ¶ *n*, содержа́ние, пи́ща; ба́шня за́мка; ~**er**, *n*, храни́тель; сто́рож; ~**ing**, *n*, содержа́ние; хране́ние; согла́сие; *in his* ~ на его́ попече́нии; *in safe* ~ в надёжных рука́х; *be in* ~ *with* согласо́вываться/гармони́ровать с; ~**sake**, *n*, пода́рок на па́мять.

keg, *n*, бочо́нок.

ken, *n*, зна́ние.

kennel, *n*, конура́; *pl*, соба́чий пито́мник.

kerb, *n*, край тротуа́ра; обо́чина; бордю́рный ка́мень.

kerchief, *n*, плато́к, косы́нка.

kernel, *n*, зерно́; зёрнышко; ядро́ (оре́ха); *(fig.)* суть.

kerosene, *n*, кероси́н.

kestrel, *n*, пустельга́.

ketch, *n*, кеч.

kettle, *n*, ча́йник; котело́к; *a pretty* ~ *of fish* хоро́шенькое де́ло; ~*drum* лита́вра.

key, *n*, ключ *(also fig.);* собра́ние отве́тов, подстро́чный перево́д; кла́виша; ~*board* клавиату́ра; *(telephone)* коммута́тор; ~*hole* замо́чная сква́жина; ~ *industries* веду́щие о́трасли промы́шленности; ~*note* основна́я но́та; *(fig.)* преоблада́ющий тон, основна́я мысль; ~*ring* кольцо́ для ключе́й; ~*stone* краеуго́льный ка́мень;

khaki, *n*, ха́ки.

khan, *n*, хан.

kick, *n*, уда́р ного́й, пино́к; брыка́нье; отда́ча (ружья́); ¶ *v.t*, ударя́ть ного́й, пина́ть; ляга́ть; *v.i*, брыка́ться, ляга́ться; отдава́ть *(gun);* ~ *against* проти́виться *(dat.);* ~ *against the pricks* лезть на рожо́н; ~ *off* начина́ть игру́ (в футбо́л); ~ *out* выгоня́ть; *free* ~ штрафно́й уда́р.

kid, *n*, козлёнок; ла́йка; ребёнок; ~ *glove* ла́йковая перча́тка; ¶ *v.t*, обма́нывать, надува́ть; ~dy, *n*, малы́ш, ребёнок.

kidnap, *v.t*, похища́ть; ~per, *n*, похити́тель; ~ping, *n*, похище́ние.

kidney, *n*, по́чка; *(fig.)* тип; ~ *beans* фасо́ль.

kill, *v.t*, убива́ть; ре́зать *(cattle)*; си́льно поража́ть; ~ *time* убива́ть вре́мя; ~er, *n*, уби́йца; ~ing, *a*, уби́йственный; умори́тельный; ¶ *n*, уби́йство; убо́й (скота́).

kiln, *n*, печь.

kilometre, *n*, кило́метр.

kilowatt, *n*, килова́тт.

kilt, *n*, ю́бка (шотла́ндца).

kimono, *n*, кимоно́.

kin, *n*, род, семья́; ро́дственники, родня́; родство́; *next of* ~ ближа́йший ро́дственник.

kind, *a*, до́брый, любе́зный; ~ *regards* серде́чный приве́т; ¶ *n*, род, сорт, вид; разнови́дность; поро́да; ~ *of* как бу́дто, вро́де; *in* ~ нату́рой; подо́бным о́бразом.

kindergarten, *n*, де́тский сад.

kindle, *v.t*, зажига́ть; *v.i*, загора́ться.

kindliness, *n*, доброта́, серде́чность; **kindly**, *a*, до́брый; благоприя́тный; ~ *tell me* бу́дьте добры́, скажи́те мне . . .; **kindness**, *n*, доброта́; любе́зность; одолже́ние.

kindred, *a*, ро́дственный, схо́дный; ¶ *n*, ро́дственники; *(fig.)* схо́дство.

king, *n*, коро́ль, царь; *(draughts)* да́мка; *(chess)* коро́ль; ~-*bolt* ось, шкво́рень; ~*fisher* зиморо́док; ~dom, *n*, короле́вство, ца́рство; ~ly, *a*, короле́вский, ца́рский; вели́чественный.

kink, *n*, изги́б; пе́тля; *(fig.)* причу́да; ¶ *v.t.* *(& i.)*, свёртывать(ся) в пе́тлю; перекру́чивать(ся); ~y, *a*, курча́вый *(hair)*; *(fig.)* стра́нный; причу́дливый.

kinship, *n*, родство́; схо́дство; **kinsman**, *n*, ро́дствен|ник, -ница.

kiosk, *n*, кио́ск.

kipper, *n*, копчёная селёдка; ¶ *v.t*, копти́ть.

kiss, *n*, поцелу́й; ¶ *v.t*, целова́ть.

kit, *n*, костю́м; снаряже́ние; компле́кт инструме́нтов; ~*bag* вещево́й мешо́к; *model* ~ сбо́рная моде́ль.

kitchen, *n*, ку́хня; ~ *garden* огоро́д; ~ *maid* судомо́йка; ~ *range* плита́; ~ *utensils* ку́хонная посу́да.

kite, *n*, возду́шный змей; ко́ршун; *fly a* ~ пуска́ть змея́; *(fig.)* пуска́ть про́бный шар.

kith and kin, *n*, знако́мые и родня́.

kitten, *n*, котёнок; ¶ *v.i*, коти́ться.

kleptomania, *n*, клептома́ния; ~c, *n*, клептома́н.

knack, *n*, уме́ние, сноро́вка.

knapsack, *n*, ра́нец, рюкза́к.

knave, *n*, моше́нник; *(cards)* вале́т; ~ry, *n*, моше́нничество; **knavish**, *a*, моше́ннический.

knead, *v.t*, меси́ть, заме́шивать; *(fig.)* формирова́ть; ~ing, *n*, заме́шивание; ~-*trough* квашня́.

knee, *n*, коле́но ~-*breeches* бри́джи; ~-*cap* коле́нная ча́шка; наколе́нник; ~-*deep*, ~-*high* по коле́но; ~-*joint* коле́нный суста́в; ~l, *v.i*, станови́ться на коле́ни; ~ *to* стоя́ть на коле́нях пе́ред; ~ling, *a*, на коле́нях.

knell, *n*, похоро́нный звон.

knickerbockers, *n.pl*, бри́джи.

knickers, *n.pl*, панталоны.

knick-knack, *n*, безделу́шка.

knife, *n*, нож; ~-*edge* остриё ножа́; ~-*grinder* точи́льщик; ¶ *v.t*, ударя́ть ножо́м.

knight, *n*, ры́царь; *(chess)* конь; ~-*errant* стра́нствующий ры́царь; ¶ *v.t*, дава́ть зва́ние «*knight*» *(dat.)*; ~-*hood*, *n*, зва́ние «*knight*»; ры́царское досто́инство; ~ly, *a*, ры́царский.

knit, *v.t*, вяза́ть; соединя́ть; ~ *brows* хму́рить бро́ви; *v.i*, соединя́ться, сраста́ться; ~ted, *a*, вя́заный, трикота́жный; ~ter, *n*, вяза́ль|щик, -ица; трикота́жная маши́на; ~ting, *n*, вяза́ние; вя́заные ве́щи; ~ *needle* вяза́льная игла́, спи́ца; ~wear, *n*, вя́заные ве́щи, трикота́жные изде́лия.

knob, *n*, ши́шка; кру́глая ру́чка (две́ри); набалда́шник.

knock, *n*, стук; уда́р; ¶ *v.t*, бить, ударя́ть; *v.i*, стуча́ться; ~ *at the door* стуча́ть в дверь; ~ *about (v.t.)* колоти́ть; *(fig.)* *(v.i)* болта́ться по све́ту; ~ *down* сбива́ть; ~-*kneed* с вы́вернутыми внутрь коле́нями; ~ *in* вбива́ть; ~ *off* сбива́ть; сма́хивать; сбавля́ть; ~ *off work* прекраща́ть рабо́ту; ~

out выбивáть; выбивáть из стрóя; побеждáть; нокаутировать *(sport)*; ~ *together (v.t.)* скола́чивать; *(v.i.)* ста́лкиваться; ~ *to pieces* разбива́ть вдре́безги; ~ *up* уда́ром подбра́сывать вверх; на́скоро скола́чивать; буди́ть; ~er, *n*, дверно́й молото́к, дверно́е кольцо́.

knoll, *n*, бугоро́к.

knot, *n*, у́зел; бант; сучо́к *(in wood)*; наро́ст (*on plant*); гру́ппа, ку́чка; *(fig.)* затрудне́ние; ¶ *v.t*, завя́зывать узло́м, свя́зывать; ~ty, *a*, узлова́тый; сучкова́тый; *(fig.)* сло́жный, запу́танный.

know, *v.t*, знать; быть знако́мым с; ~-*all* всезна́йка; ~ *how to* уме́ть; *be in the* ~ быть в ку́рсе де́ла; ~ing, *a*, хи́трый; ~ingly, *ad*, созна́тельно, наме́ренно; ло́вко, хи́тро; ~ledge, *n*, зна́ние; позна́ние; нау́ка; эруди́ция; знако́мство; изве́стие; *it came to my* ~ мне ста́ло изве́стно; *to my* ~ наско́лько мне изве́стно; *without my* ~ без моего́ ве́дома; ~ledge-able, *a*, хорошо́ осведомлённый; ~n, *a*, изве́стный.

knuckle, *n*, суста́в (па́льца); но́жка *(pig's, etc.)*; *(tech.)* шарни́р; ~duster кастéт; ~ *bones* игра́ в ба́бки; ¶ *v.i*, ~ *under* уступа́ть, подчиня́ться.

kolkhoz, *n*, колхо́з.

Koran, *n*, кора́н.

kosher, *n*, ко́шер; ~*food* коше́рная пища.

kowtow, *v.i*, раболе́пствовать; ни́зко кла́няться.

kremlin, *n*, кремль.

kudos, *n*, сла́ва.

L

label, *n*, ярлы́к; этике́тка; би́рка; ¶ *v.t*, накле́ивать ярлы́к на; относи́ть к катего́рии.

labial, *a*, губно́й.

laboratory, *n*, лаборато́рия.

laborious, *a*, тру́дный; трудоёмкий; трудолюби́вый; **labour**, *n*, труд; рабо́та; рабо́чие; ро́ды; уси́лие; ~ *crisis* трудово́й кри́зис; ~ *pains* родовы́е схва́тки; ~ *Party* лейбори́стская па́ртия; ~-*saving* эко-

но́мящий труд; рационализа́торский; ¶ *v.i*, труди́ться; *v.t*, подро́бно рассма́тривать/разраба́тывать; ~ed, *a*, тяжелове́сный; затруднённый; вы́мученный; ~er, *n*, чернорабо́чий.

laburnum, *n*, золото́й дождь.

labrador *n*, лаг ра́до́рская соба́ка.

labyrinth, *n*, лабири́нт.

lac, *n*, кра́сная смола́; лак.

lace, *n*, кру́жево; *(shoe)* шнуро́к; ¶ *v.t*, шнурова́ть; отде́лывать кру́жевом; подбавля́ть спиртны́е напи́тки к.

lacerate, *v.t*, раздира́ть; терза́ть; ~*d wound* рва́ная ра́на.

lachrymal, *a*, слёзный; **lachrymatory**, *a*, слезоточи́вый; **lachrymose**, *a*, слезли́вый.

lack, *n*, недоста́ток; отсу́тствие; ¶ *v.t*, испы́тывать недоста́ток в; нужда́ться в; *he is lacking in* . . . ему́ недостаёт/ему́ не хвата́ет *(gen.)*; ~*lustre* ту́склый.

lackadaisical, *a*, то́мный, мечта́тельный.

lackey, *n*, лаке́й.

laconic, *a*, лакони́чный, -и́ческий.

lacquer, *n*, лак; глазу́рь; ¶ *v.t*, покрыва́ть ла́ком/глазу́рью, лакирова́ть.

lactation, *n*, выделе́ние молока́.

lacuna, *n*, пробе́л; впа́дина.

lad, *n*, па́рень.

ladder, *n*, ле́стница; *(mar.)* трап; спусти́вшаяся пе́тля *(stocking)*; *extension* ~ выдвижна́я ле́стница.

lade, *v.t*, грузи́ть; *bill of lading* коносаме́нт.

ladle, *n*, ковш, черпа́к; *soup* ~ поло́вник; ¶ *v.t*, че́рпать.

lady, *n*, да́ма; ле́ди; *young* ~ де́вушка; ба́рышня; *our* ~ Богома́терь ; ~*bird* бо́жья коро́вка; ~ *Day* Благове́щение; ~*killer* сердцее́д; ~*love* возлю́бленная; ~*'s man* кавале́р; ~*-in-waiting* фре́йлина; ~*like* изя́щный, воспи́танный; ~*ship* ти́тул ле́ди.

lag, *n*, отстава́ние, запа́здывание; ¶ *v.t*, покрыва́ть терми́ческой изоля́цией; *v.i*, отстава́ть; ~**gard**, *a*, медли́тельный.

lagoon, *n*, лагу́на.

lair, *n*, берло́га, ло́говище.

laity, *n*, миря́не *(pl.)*.

lake, *n*, о́зеро; ~ *District* Озёрный край.

lama, *n,* ла́ма.

lamb, *n,* ягнёнок, бара́шек; *(meat)* бара́нина; *(fig.)* а́гнец, ове́чка; ¶ *v.i,* ягни́ться.

lambent, *a,* игра́ющий; сия́ющий; лучи́стый.

lame, *a,* хромо́й; неубеди́тельный, сла́бый; *be* ~ хрома́ть; ¶ *v.t,* калéчить, увéчить; ~**ness,** *n,* хромота́.

lament, *n,* жа́лоба; плач; ¶ *v.t,* опла́кивать; *v.i,* пла́кать, горева́ть; ~**able,** *c,* печа́льный; жа́лкий; ~**ation,** *n,* плач; жа́лоба.

lamina, *n,* то́нкая пласти́нка; то́нкий слой, лист; ~**te,** *v.t,* расщепля́ть на то́нкие слои́; прока́тывать в листы́; ~**d,** *a,* листово́й, сло́йстый.

lamp, *n,* ла́мпа, фона́рь; фа́ра *(of car)*; ~**black** ла́мповая ко́поть; ~**lighter** фона́рщик; ~ *post* фона́рный столб; ~ *shade* абажу́р.

lampoon, *n,* па́сквиль.

lamprey, *n,* мино́га.

lance, *n,* пи́ка; копьё; *(med.)* ланце́т; ¶ *v.t,* пронза́ть пи́кой/копьём; *(med.)* вскрыва́ть ланце́том; ~**r,** *n,* ула́н; *pl,* лансье́ *(dance);* ~**t,** *n,* ланце́т.

land, *n,* земля́; су́ша; по́чва; страна́; *by* ~ сухи́м путём; ~ *agent* земéльный агéнт, комиссионéр по прода́же земéльной со́бственности; ~ *forces* сухопу́тные си́лы; ~*lady* хозя́йка; ~*lord* хозя́ин; лендло́рд, помéщик~*-locked* окружённый су́шей; ~*mark* межево́й знак, вéха; ориенти́р; *(fig.)* вéха; ~*owner* землевладéлец; ~*scape* ландша́фт, пейза́ж; ~*scape gardener* ландша́фтный архитéктор; ~*scape painter* пейзажи́ст; ~*slide* обва́л, о́ползень; сокруши́тельная побéда на вы́борах; ¶ *v.t,* выса́живать на бéрег; выта́скивать на бéрег *(fish);* сади́ть *(aircraft);* ~ *a blow* наноси́ть уда́р; *v.i,* выса́живаться на бéрег; приземля́ться.

landau, *n,* ландо́.

landed, *a,* земéльный; владéющий земéльной со́бственностью; **landing,** *n,* вы́садка; *(avia.)* поса́дка; *(mil.)* деса́нт; лéстничная площа́дка; ~ *gear* шасси́; ~ *ground* поса́дочная площа́дка; ~ *stage* при́стань.

lane, *n,* просёлочная доро́га; тропи́нка; переу́лок; прохо́д.

language, *n,* язы́к; ~ *laboratory* лингафо́нный кабинéт; *bad* ~ брань.

languid, *a,* вя́лый, то́мный; **languish,** *v.i,* томи́ться; тоскова́ть; ча́хнуть; ~**ing,** *a,* сла́бый, вя́лый; тоску́ющий; **languor,** *n* то́мность, уста́лость; сла́бость; ~**ous,** *a,* то́мный; томи́тельный.

lank, *a,* худо́й, то́щий; прямо́й *(hair);* ~**y,** *a,* долговя́зый.

lantern, *n,* фона́рь; *(mar.)* светова́я ка́мера маяка́; *magic* ~ волшéбный фона́рь; ~ *jaws* впа́лые щёки; ~*-slide* диапозити́в.

lanyard, *n,* та́лреп; шнур; ремéнь.

lap, *n,* пола́, фа́лда; колéни; *(fig.)* ло́но; *(sport)* круг, эта́п; ~*-dog* ко́мнатная соба́чка; ¶ *v.t,* завёртывать; лака́ть; *v.i,* плеска́ться *(waves);* ~ *over* перекрыва́ть; ~ *up* лака́ть; *(fig.)* упива́ться *(inst.).*

lapel, *n,* отворо́т; ла́цкан.

lapidary, *a,* грани́льный; вы́гравированный на ка́мне; ¶ *n,* грани́льщик.

lapis lazuli, *n,* ля́пис-лазу́рь.

Laplander, *n,* лапла́ндец, лопа́рь.

lapse, *n,* оши́бка, просту́пок; *(moral)* падéние; течéние *(of time);* истечéние; ¶ *v.i,* па́дать; истека́ть; проходи́ть.

lapwing, *n,* чи́бис.

larceny, *n,* воровство́.

larch, *n,* ли́ственница.

lard, *n,* свино́е са́ло; ¶ *v.t,* шпигова́ть; сма́зывать са́лом; уснаща́ть; ~**er,** *n,* кладова́я.

large, *a,* большо́й; кру́пный; оби́льный; *at* ~ на свобо́де; простра́нно; ~**ly,** *ad,* в значи́тельной стéпени; ~**ness,** *n,* большо́й размéр; огро́мность.

largesse, *n,* щéдрый дар; щéдрость.

lark, *n,* жа́воронок; *(coll.)* шу́тка.

larva, *n,* личи́нка.

laryngitis, *n,* ларинги́т; **larynx,** *n,* гло́тка, горта́нь.

lascivious, *a,* похотли́вый, ~**ness,** *n,* похотли́вость.

laser, *n,* ла́зер.

lash, *n,* бич, плеть; уда́р бичо́м/плéтью; ¶ *v.t,* хлеста́ть; *(fig.)* бичева́ть; ~ *together* свя́зывать; ~ *out* внеза́пно лягну́ть *(pf.);*

ударя́ть сплеча́; разража́ться (бра́нью).

lass, *n,* де́вушка, де́вочка.

lassitude, *n,* уста́лость, утомле́ние.

lasso, *n,* арка́н, лассо́; ¶ *v.t,* лови́ть арка́ном/лассо́.

last, *a,* после́дний, про́шлый; кра́йний; ~ *but one* предпосле́дний; ~ *night* вчера́ ве́чером/но́чью; ~ *week* на про́шлой неде́ле; *be on one's* ~ *legs* быть при после́днем издыха́нии; быть на гра́ни разоре́ния; ~ *time* в про́шлый раз; в после́дний раз; ¶ *ad,* по́сле всех; в после́дний раз; ¶ *n,* коне́ц; после́днее; коло́дка; *at* ~ наконе́ц; ¶ *v.i,* продолжа́ться, дли́ться; сохраня́ться; быть доста́точным; носи́ться *(clothing);* ~ing, *a,* про́чный; дли́тельный; ~ly, *ad,* в заключе́ние, наконе́ц.

latch, *n,* щеко́лда, защёлка, задви́жка; ¶ *v.t,* запира́ть.

late, *a,* по́здний; неда́вний; поко́йный; бы́вший; *he is* ~ он опа́здывает; *it is* ~ по́здно; *be* ~ *for a train* опа́здывать на по́езд; ~ly, *ad,* неда́вно; за после́днее вре́мя; ~ness, *n,* запозда́лость; опозда́ние; ~r, *a,* бо́лее по́здний; *a,* по́зже, поздне́е, пото́м; ~st, *a,* са́мый по́здний, са́мый после́дний; *at the latest* са́мое поздне́е.

latent, *n,* скры́тый.

lateral, *a,* боково́й.

lath, *n,* пла́нка, дра́нка.

lathe, *n,* тока́рный стано́к.

lather, *n,* (мы́льная) пе́на; ¶ *v.t,* намы́ливать.

Latin, *a,* лати́нский; рома́нский; ¶ *n,* лати́нский язы́к, латы́нь.

latitude, *n,* широта́; *(fig.)* свобо́да; обши́рность.

latrine, *n,* отхо́жее ме́сто.

latter, *a,* после́дний; ~ly, *a,* неда́вно; под коне́ц.

lattice, *n,* решётка.

laud, *v.t,* хвали́ть, превозноси́ть; ~able, *a,* похва́льный.

laudanum, *n,* тинкту́ра о́пия.

laudatory, *a,* хвале́бный.

laugh, *n,* смех; ¶ *v.i,* смея́ться (над); ~ *off* сме́хом отде́лываться от; ~ *out loud* хохота́ть; *burst out* ~ing рассмея́ться *(pf.),* расхохота́ться *(pf.);* ~able, *a,* смешно́й; ~ing stock посме́шище;

~ingly, *ad,* смея́сь; ~ter, *n,* смех.

launch, *n,* барка́с, ка́тер; спуск су́дна на́ воду; ¶ *v.t,* спуска́ть на́ воду; запуска́ть *(rocket);* пуска́ть (в ход); броса́ть; начина́ть; ~ *out* пуска́ться (в путь); сори́ть деньга́ми; ~ing, *n,* спуск на́ воду; за́пуск *(of rocket).*

launder, *v.t,* стира́ть и гла́дить; **laundress,** *n,* пра́чка; **laundry,** *n,* пра́чечная; бельё для сти́рки/ из сти́рки.

laureate, *n,* лауреа́т.

laurel, *n,* лавр; *rest on one's* ~s почива́ть на ла́врах.

lava, *n,* ла́ва.

lavatory, *n,* убо́рная.

lavender, *n,* лава́нда.

lavish, *a,* ще́дрый; оби́льный; ¶ *v.t,* расточа́ть; ~ *care on* окружа́ть забо́той; ~ness, *n,* ще́дрость; оби́лие.

law, *n,* зако́н, пра́вило; пра́во, юриспруде́нция; *by* ~ по зако́ну; *go to* ~ подава́ть в суд; начина́ть суде́бный проце́сс; ~-abiding уважа́ющий зако́ны; ~ breaker правонаруши́тель; ~ court суд; ~giver, ~maker законода́тель; ~ and order правопоря́док; ~ful, *a,* зако́нный; ~less, *a,* беззако́нный; ~lessness, *n,* беззако́ние.

lawn, *n,* лужа́йка, газо́н; *(cloth)* бати́ст; ~mower газонокоси́лка.

lawsuit, *n,* проце́сс, тя́жба; **lawyer,** *n,* адвока́т, юри́ст.

lax, *a,* сла́бый; нестро́гий; неря́шливый; неопределённый; ~ative, *n,* слаби́тельное.

lay, *v.t,* класть *(also eggs);* закла́дывать *(foundation);* накрыва́ть (на стол); успока́ивать *(fears); v.i,* нести́сь *(of hen);* ~ *bets* держа́ть пари́; ~ *aside* откла́дывать; ~ *by* запаса́ть; ~ *claim to* претендова́ть на; *требовать (gen.);* ~ *down* класть; устана́вливать; предпи́сывать; оставля́ть, отка́зываться от *(gen.);* слага́ть с себя́; ~ *down one's arms* капитули́ровать; ~ *hands on* схва́тывать; присва́ивать; поднима́ть ру́ку на; ~ *hold of* завладева́ть *(inst.);* ~ *in* запаса́ть; ~ *off (v.t.)* увольня́ть; *(v.i.)* прекраща́ть рабо́ту; переставать; ~ *on* накла́дывать; налага́ть; заготовля́ть; снабжа́ть;

~ *open* открыва́ть; ~ *out* выкла́дывать; разбива́ть *(garden)*; выводи́ть из стро́я; *be laid up* лежа́ть больны́м; ¶ *a*, све́тский; непрофессиона́льный; ¶ *n*, балла́да, пе́сня; положе́ние.

layer, *n*, слой, пласт; *(hen)* несу́шка; *(bot.)* отво́док; ¶ *v.t*, насла́ивать; *(bot.)* разводи́ть отво́дками.

layette, *n*, прида́ное новорождённого.

laying, *n*, кла́дка (яи́ц).

layman, *n*, миря́нин; непрофессиона́л, люби́тель.

layout, *n*, план; маке́т; расположе́ние; набо́р инструме́нтов.

lazaretto, *n*, лепрозо́рий.

laze, *v.i*, безде́льничать; **lazily**, *ad*, лени́во; **laziness**, *n*, ле́ность, лень; **lazy**, *a*, лени́вый; ~ *bones* лентя́й.

lea, *n*, пар; луг.

lead, *n*, свине́ц; гри́фель; *(mar.)* лот; *pl*, *(print.)* шпо́ны; ~**en**, *a*, графи́товый каранда́ш; ~**en**, *a*, свинцо́вый; тяжёлый.

lead, *n*, руково́дство; инициати́ва; приме́р; при́вязь, поводо́к; гла́вная роль; пе́рвое ме́сто, ли́дерство *(sport)*; пе́рвый ход *(games)*; *(elec.)* про́вод; ~*-in (elec.)* вводно́й про́вод; ¶ *v.t*, вести́, води́ть; кома́ндовать *(inst.)*; возглавля́ть; заставля́ть, побужда́ть; *v.i*, идти́ пе́рвым, опережа́ть; ~ *astray* сбива́ть с пути́ и́стинного; ~ *off* уводи́ть; начина́ть; ~ *out* выводи́ть; ~ *to trouble* приводи́ть к беде́/неприя́тности; ~ *up to* подготовля́ть; приводи́ть к; наводи́ть разгово́р на; ~ *a good life* вести́ хоро́шую жизнь.

leader, *n*, руководи́тель, вождь; ли́дер; дирижёр, веду́щий музыка́нт; передова́я статья́; ~**ship**, *n*, руково́дство; *(polit.)* ли́дерство; **leading**, *a*, веду́щий; передово́й; ~ *lady* исполни́тельница гла́вной ро́ли; ~ *question* наводя́щий вопро́с; ~*-reins* помо́чи; ~*-reins* помо́чи;

leaf, *n*, лист; страни́ца; ство́рка две́ри; опускна́я пола́ (стола́); *turn over a new* ~ начина́ть но́вую жизнь; ¶ *v.t*: ~ *through* перели́стывать; ~**age**, *n*, листва́; ~**let**, *n*, листо́вка; ~**y**, *a*, покры́тый ли́стьями; листово́й.

league, *n*. ли́га, сою́з; ли́га *(measure)*.

leak, *n*, течь; уте́чка; *there was a press* ~ в пре́ссу просочи́лось; ¶ *v.i*, дава́ть течь; пропуска́ть во́ду; ~ *out* проса́чиваться; *(fig.)* станови́ться изве́стным; ~**age**, *n*, течь, уте́чка; проса́чивание; ~**y**, *a*, име́ющий течь.

lean, *a*, то́щий; по́стный *(meat)*; ску́дный; ¶ *n*, по́стная часть (мя́са); ¶ *v.t. (& i.)*, наклоня́ть(ся); прислоня́ть(ся); ~ *against* опира́ться на, прислоня́ться к; ~ *back* отклоня́ться наза́д; ~ *one's elbows on* облока́чиваться на; ~ *out of* высо́вываться из; ~ *upon* опира́ться на; *(fig.)* полага́ться на; ~ *towards* склоня́ться к; ~**ing**, *n*, скло́нность; ~**ness**, *n*, худоща́вость; по́стность; ску́дность; ~*-to*, *n*, пристро́йка, наве́с.

leap, *n*, прыжо́к, скачо́к; ~*-frog* чехарда́; ~ *year* високо́сный год; ¶ *v.i*, пры́гать, скака́ть; си́льно би́ться *(heart)*; *v.t*, перепры́гивать.

learn, *v.t*, учи́ть; узнава́ть; *v.i*, учи́ться; ~**ed**, *a*, учёный; ~**er**, *n*, уча́щийся, учени́к; ~**ing**, *n*, уче́ние; учёность, эруди́ция.

lease, *n*, аре́нда; сда́ча в аре́нду; догово́р об аре́нде; ~*hold* арендо́ванная земля́; ~*holder* арендда́тор; откупщи́к; ¶ *v.t*, сдава́ть/ брать в аре́нду.

leash, *n*, сво́ра, при́вязь.

least, *a*, наиме́ньший, мале́йший; ¶ *ad*, ме́нее всего́/всех; ¶ *n*, наиме́ньшее коли́чество; наиме́ньшая сте́пень; *at* ~ по кра́йней ме́ре; *not in the* ~ ничу́ть.

leather, *n*, ко́жа; ~**ette**, *n*, иску́сственная ко́жа; ~**y**, *a*, похо́жий на ко́жу; жёсткий.

leave, *n*, разреше́ние; о́тпуск; проща́ние; *by your* ~ с ва́шего разреше́ния; *on* ~ в о́тпуске; *take one's* ~ проща́ться; ~*-taking* проща́ние; ¶ *v.t*, оставля́ть, покида́ть; предоставля́ть; *v.i*, уходи́ть, уезжа́ть; ~*behind* оставля́ть позади́; забыва́ть; превосходи́ть; ~ *off* перестава́ть; остана́вливаться; ~ *out* пропуска́ть.

leaven, *n*, дро́жжи, заква́ска; ¶ *v.t*, ста́вить (те́сто), заква́шивать; *(fig.)* пропи́тывать.

leavings, *n.pl*, оста́тки, отбро́сы.

lecherous, *a*, распу́тный; **lechery,** *n*, развра́т.

lectern, *n*, анало́й.

lecture, *n*, ле́кция; нота́ция; ~ *room* аудито́рия; ¶ *v.i*, чита́ть ле́кцию; преподава́ть; *v.t*, де́лать вы́говор *(dat.)*; чита́ть нота́цию *(dat.)*; ~r, *n*, преподава́тель; ле́ктор.

ledge, *n*, вы́ступ, край; риф; по́лка.

ledger, *n*, гла́вная кни́га, кни́га счето́в; попере́чная ба́лка.

lee, *n*, защи́та, укры́тие; подве́тренная сторона́; ¶ *a*, подве́тренный.

leech, *n*, пия́вка; *(fig.)* кровопи́йца; *(coll.)* ле́карь.

leek, *n*, лук-поре́й.

leer, *n*, хи́трый/похотли́вый взгляд; ¶ *v.i*, смотре́ть хи́тро/зло́бно/с вожделе́нием.

lees, *n.pl*, оса́док; подо́нки.

leeward, *n*, подве́тренная сторона́; **leeway,** *n*, дрейф (в подве́тренную сто́рону); снос (самолёта).

left, *a*, ле́вый; ¶ *n*, ле́вая сторона́; *on the* ~, *to the* ~ нале́во, сле́ва; ~-*handed* де́лающий всё ле́вой руко́й; *(fig.)* неуклю́жий; лицеме́рный; *he is* ~-*handed* он левша́; ~-*wing* ле́вый; ~ist, *n*, ле́вый, член ле́вой па́ртии.

left, *p.p*, оста́вленный; ~-*luggage office* ка́мера хране́ния; ~-*overs* оста́тки.

leg, *n*, нога́; но́жка *(of chair, etc.)*; подста́вка; ~ *of mutton* бара́нья нога́; *trouser* ~ штани́на; *pull s.o's* ~ моро́чить го́лову *(dat.)*.

legacy, *n*, насле́дство.

legal, *a*, зако́нный; юриди́ческий; правово́й; ~ *adviser* юрисконсу́льт; ~ *aid* юриди́ческая по́мощь; ~ *claim* зако́нное притяза́ние; ~ *entity* юриди́ческое лицо́; *by* ~ *means* зако́нным путём; *take* ~ *action* возбужда́ть суде́бное де́ло; ~ *tender* зако́нное платёжное сре́дство; ~ity, *n*, зако́нность, лега́льность; ~ize, *v.t*, узако́нивать, легализи́ровать.

legate, *n*, лега́т, па́пский посо́л; ~e, *n*, насле́дник; **legation,** *n*, дипломати́ческая ми́ссия.

legend, *n*, леге́нда; ~ary, *a*, легенда́рный.

legerdemain, *n*, ло́вкость рук; фо́кусы.

leggings, *n.pl*, гама́ши, кра́ги; по́лзунки *(for child)*.

legible, *a*, разбо́рчивый, чёткий.

legion, *n*, легио́н; мно́жество; ~ary, *n*, легионе́р.

legislate, *v.i*, издава́ть зако́ны; **legislation,** *n*, законода́тельство; **legislative,** *a*, законода́тельный; **legislator,** *n*, законода́тель; **legislature,** *n* законода́тельные учрежде́ния.

legitimacy, *n*, зако́нность; **legitimate,** *a*, зако́нный; законнорождённый; **legitimize,** *v.t*, узако́нивать.

leguminous, *a*, стручко́вый, бобо́вый.

leisure, *n*, досу́г; *at* ~ на досу́ге; ~ly, *a*, нетороплйвый.

leitmotiv, *n*, лейтмоти́в.

lemon, *n*, лимо́н; ~ *juice* лимо́нный сок; ~ *squeezer* соковыжима́лка; ~ade, *n*, лимона́д.

lend, *v.t*, дава́ть взаймы́, ода́лживать; придава́ть; ока́зывать; ~ *oneself* предава́ться; поддава́ться; ~er, *n*, заимода́вец, даю́щий взаймы́; ~ing, *n*, ода́лживание; ~ *library* библиоте́ка с вы́дачей книг на́ дом.

length, *n*, длина́; расстоя́ние; продолжи́тельность, долгота́; отре́з *(cloth)*; *at* ~ простра́нно; ~en, *v.t. (& i.)*, удлиня́ть(ся); ~ening, *n*, удлине́ние; ~wise, *ad*, в длину́; ~y, *a*, дли́нный, растя́нутый.

leniency, *n*, мя́гкость, снисходи́тельность; **lenient,** *a*, мя́гкий, снисходи́тельный.

lens, *n*, ли́нза, объекти́в; хруста́лик гла́за; *contact* ~ конта́ктная ли́нза.

Lent, *n*, Вели́кий пост; ~en, *a*, великопо́стный; по́стный.

lentil, *n*, чечеви́ца.

leonine, *a*, льви́ный.

leopard, *n*, леопа́рд.

leper, *n*, прокажённый; **leprosy,** *n*, прока́за; **leprous,** *a*, прокажённый.

lesion, *n*, повреждё́ние.

less, *a*, ме́ньший; ¶ *ad*, ме́нее, ме́ньше; *grow* ~ уменьша́ться; *more or* ~ бо́лее и́ли ме́нее.

lessee, *n*, аренда́тор, съёмщик.

lessen, *v.t. (& i.)*, уменьша́ть(ся); **lesser,** *a*, ме́ньший.

lesson, *n*, уро́к; нота́ция.

lessor, n, сдающий в аре́нду.
lest, c, чтобы не.
let, v.t, позволя́ть (dat.); пуска́ть; дава́ть; сдава́ть внаём; ~'s have tea! дава́йте пить чай!; house to ~ дом сдаётся; to ~ alone оставля́ть в поко́е; ~ alone не говоря́ уже́ о; ~ down опуска́ть; подводи́ть; разочаро́вывать; ~ fall роня́ть; ~ go выпуска́ть; отпуска́ть, освобожда́ть; ~ know дава́ть знать; ~ in впуска́ть; ~ loose выпуска́ть; ~ off выстрелить (pf.); проща́ть, отпуска́ть; ~ out выпуска́ть; выдава́ть; сдава́ть внаём; ¶ n, сда́ча внаём; without ~ or hindrance беспрепя́тственно.
lethal, a, смерте́льный, смертоно́сный.
lethargic, a, летарги́ческий, вя́лый; **lethargy,** n, летарги́я, вя́лость.
letter, n, бу́ква; письмо́; (print.) ли́тера; pl, литерату́ра; ~ box почто́вый я́щик; ~ card письмо́-секре́тка; ~ of credit аккредити́в; ~ paper почто́вая бума́га; to the ~ буква́льно; в то́чности; ¶ v.t, помеча́ть бу́квами; вытесня́ть бу́квы; ~ed, a, с тиснёными бу́квами; образо́ванный; ~ing, n, тисне́ние, на́дпись.
letting, n, сда́ча внаём.
lettuce, n, сала́т.
levee, n, приём; да́мба, при́стань.
level, a, ро́вный; горизонта́льный; на одно́м у́ровне; одина́ковый; ~ crossing перее́зд; ~-headed уравнове́шенный; be on the ~ быть че́стным; do one's ~ best де́лать всё от себя́ зави́сящее; ¶ n, у́ровень; высота́; равни́на; нивели́р; ватерпа́с; ¶ ad, вро́вень; ро́вно; ¶ v.t, выра́внивать; ура́внивать; ~ at направля́ть про́тив; ~ling, n, выра́внивание; ура́внивание.
lever, n, рыча́г; ¶ v.t, поднима́ть рычаго́м; ~age, n, де́йствие рыча́га; подъёмная си́ла.
leveret, n, зайчо́нок.
levity, n, ве́треность, легкомы́слие.
levy, n, сбор, взима́ние; набо́р; ¶ v.t, взима́ть (tax); набира́ть (recruits).
lewd, a, развра́тный; непристо́йный; ~ness, n, развра́т; непристо́йность.

lexicographer, n, лексико́граф, соста́витель словаре́й; **lexicon,** n, слова́рь, лексико́н.
liability, n, отве́тственность; обяза́тельство; подве́рженность; without ~ безотве́тственно; **liable,** a, отве́тственный; обя́занный; подве́рженный; подлежа́щий; вероя́тный, возмо́жный.
liaison, n, связь; любо́вная связь; ~ officer офице́р свя́зи.
liar, n, лгун.
libation, n, возлия́ние.
libel, n, клевета́; па́сквиль; ¶ v.t, клевета́ть на; ~ler, n, клеветни́к; ~lous, a, клеветни́ческий.
liberal, a, либера́льный; ще́дрый; оби́льный; ¶ n, либера́л; ~ism, n, либерали́зм.
liberate, v.t, освобожда́ть; **liberation,** n, освобожде́ние.
libertine, n, распу́тник.
liberty, n, свобо́да; во́льность; бесцеремо́нность; at ~ на свобо́де; take liberties позволя́ть себе́ во́льности.
libidinous, a, развра́тный; порнографи́ческий.
librarian, n, библиоте́карь; **library,** n, библиоте́ка.
librettist, n, а́втор либре́тто; **libretto,** n, либре́тто.
Libyan, a, ливи́йский.
licence, n, разреше́ние; пра́во; пате́нт; лице́нзия; во́льность; распу́щенность; driving ~ (води́тельские) права́; license v.t, разреша́ть; дава́ть пра́во/пате́нт (dat.); **licentiate,** n, лициниа́т; име́ющий дипло́м; **licentious,** a, распу́щенный; ~ness, n, распу́щенность.
lichen, n, лиша́й.
licit, a, зако́нный.
lick, n, лиза́ние; кусо́чек; ¶ v.t, лиза́ть; (coll.) колоти́ть; превосходи́ть.
lid, n, кры́шка.
lie, n, ложь, обма́н; ¶ v.i, лгать.
lie, n, положе́ние; расположе́ние; ~ of the land релье́ф ме́стности; (fig.) положе́ние веще́й; ¶ v.i, лежа́ть; находи́ться; ~ down ложи́ться; ~ in wait подстерега́ть, сиде́ть в заса́де.
liege, a, васса́льный; ¶ n, васса́л.
lien, n, пра́во наложе́ния аре́ста на иму́щество должника́; зало́г.
lieu: in ~ of вме́сто.

lieutenant, *n*, лейтена́нт; ~ *colonel* подполко́вник; ~ *commander* капита́н-лейтена́нт; ~ *general* генера́л-лейтена́нт.

life, *n*, жизнь; существова́ние; о́браз жи́зни; биогра́фия; жи́вость; срок (слу́жбы/маши́ны), долгове́чность; ~ *annuity* пожи́зненная пе́нсия; ~ *belt* спаса́тельный по́яс; ~*boat* спаса́тельная ло́дка; ~*guard* слу́жащий спаса́тельной ста́нции; член спаса́тельной кома́нды; L~ *Guards* лейб-гва́рдия; ~ *insurance* страхова́ние жи́зни; ~*like* сло́вно живо́й; ~*-line* спаса́тельная верёвка; доро́га жи́зни; ~ *size* натура́льная величина́; *for* ~ на всю жизнь; *from* ~ с нату́ры; ~*less*, *a*, безжи́зненный; ску́чный; ~*time*, *n*, (це́лая) жизнь; продолжи́тельность жи́зни.

lift, *n*, подня́тие, подъём; лифт, подъёмная маши́на; ~*tap* лифтёр; *give a* ~ *to* подвози́ть; *(coll.)* подбодря́ть; ¶ *v.t*, поднима́ть, возвыша́ть; *v.i*, поднима́ться; рассе́иваться *(clouds)*.

light, *n*, свет, освеще́ние; ла́мпа, фа́ра, фона́рь; ого́нь; светило *(also fig.)*; *pl*, *(traffic)* светофо́р; *at first* ~ на рассве́те; *against the* ~ про́тив све́та; *bring to* ~ выясня́ть; *throw* ~ *on* пролива́ть свет на; ¶ *a*, све́тлый; лёгкий; незначи́тельный; ~*-footed* прово́рный; ~*-headed* легкомы́сленный; чу́вствующий головокруже́ние; *в* бреду́; ~*-hearted* безабо́тный, весёлый; ~*house* мая́к; ~ *opera* опере́тта; ~*ship* плаву́чий мая́к; ~ *soil* рыхлая по́чва; ~ *wave* световолна́; ~*weight* лёгкий вес, легкове́с; ¶ *v.t. (& i.)*, освеща́ть(ся); зажига́ть(ся); заку́ривать; оживля́ть(ся); ~ *upon* неожи́данно ната́лкиваться на; опуска́ться на.

lighten, *v.t*, освеща́ть; облегча́ть; смягча́ть; *v.i*, светле́ть, сверка́ть.

lighter, *n*, ли́хтер; зажига́лка; ~*man* рабо́чий на ли́хтере.

lighting, *n*, освеще́ние.

lightly, *ad*, слегка́; чуть; беспе́чно; легко́; lightness, *n*, лёгкость.

lightning, *n*, мо́лния; ~ *conductor* громоотво́д.

lights, *n.pl*, лёгкие (живо́тных).

ligneous, *a*, деревяни́стый; lignite, *n*, бу́рый у́голь.

likeable, *a*, прия́тный, симпати́чный, ми́лый; like, *a*, похо́жий, подо́бный; одина́ковый; ра́вный; ¶ *ad*, подо́бно, похо́же; так; как; ¶ *n*, не́что подо́бное/ра́вное; ро́вня; ~*s and dislikes* симпа́тии и антипа́тии; *and the* ~ и тому́ подо́бное; *be as* ~ *as two peas* быть похо́жими как две ка́пли воды́; *be* ~ быть похо́жим на; *in* ~ *manner* подо́бным же о́бразом; *it's not* ~ *him* э́то не похо́же на него́; *what is he* ~? что он за челове́к? ¶ *v.t*, люби́ть; *I* ~ *it* мне э́то нра́вится; *as you* ~ как вам уго́дно; *I should* ~ я хоте́л бы . . .

likelihood, *n*, вероя́тность; likely, *a*, вероя́тный; подходя́щий, подаю́щий наде́жды; ¶ *ad*, вероя́тно.

liken, *v.t*, уподобля́ть; сра́внивать; likeness, *n*, схо́дство; подо́бие; о́браз; портре́т.

likewise, *ad*, подо́бно; та́кже.

liking, *n*, вкус, скло́нность, симпа́тия; любо́вь.

lilac, *n*, сире́нь; ¶ *a*, сире́невый.

lilliputian, *a*, ка́рликовый, кро́шечный.

lily, *n*, ли́лия; ~ *of the valley* ла́ндыш.

limb, *n*, член; сук.

limber, *a*, ги́бкий; ¶ *v.i: up* размина́ться; ~ *ness*, *n*, ги́бкость.

limbo, *n*, преддве́рие а́да; *(fig.)* забве́ние.

lime, *n*, и́звесть; род лимо́на; ~ *juice* лимо́нный сок; ~ *kiln* печь для о́бжига и́звести; *be in the* ~*light* быть на виду́, быть в це́нтре внима́ния; ~*stone* изве́стняк; ~ *tree* ли́па; ¶ *v.t*, бели́ть и́звестью; удобря́ть и́звестью.

limit, *n*, грани́ца, преде́л; *it is the* ~! э́то перехо́дит все грани́цы!; ¶ *v.t*, ограни́чивать; ~*ation*, *n*, ограниче́ние; огово́рка; ~*ed*, *p.p. & a*, ограни́ченный; ~ *company* акционе́рная компа́ния с ограни́ченной отве́тственностью; ~*less*, *a*, безграни́чный; беспреде́льный.

limousine, *n*, лимузи́н.

limp, *a*, мя́гкий, сла́бый; безво́льный; ¶ *n*, хромота́; ¶ *v.i*, хрома́ть; ковыля́ть.

limpet, *n*, блю́дечко.

limpid, *a*, прозра́чный; ~ity, *n*, прозра́чность.

linchpin, *n*, чека́.

linden(tree), *n*, ли́па.

line, *n*, ли́ния; черта́, штрих; морщи́на; строка́; верёвка; ле́ска *(fishing)*; стих *(poetry)*; о́чередь, ряд; па́ртия *(of goods)*; о́бласть де́ятельности; направле́ние; *the* ~ эква́тор; *hard* ~*s* несча́стная судьба́; ¶ *v.t*, проводи́ть ли́нии на, линова́ть; окаймля́ть; подбива́ть; ~ *one's stomach* набива́ть желу́док; ~ *up* выстра́ивать(ся) в ли́нию; станови́ться в о́чередь; ~age, *n*, происхожде́ние; родосло́вная; ~eal, *a*, происходя́щий по прямо́й ли́нии, лине́йный; родово́й; ~ament, *n*, черта́; очерта́ние; ~ear, *a*, лине́йный.

linen, *n*, полотно́; бельё; ~ *goods* льняны́е това́ры.

liner, *n*, ла́йнер, ре́йсовый парохо́д/самолёт.

linesman, *n*, лине́йный монтёр; *(rly.)* путево́й сто́рож; *(sport)* судья́ на ли́нии.

ling, *n*, *(bot.)* ве́реск; морска́я щу́ка *(fish)*.

linger, *v.i*, ме́длить, заде́рживаться; затя́гиваться; ~ing, *a*, медли́тельный; затяжно́й.

lingo, *n*, язы́к; жарго́н.

linguist, *n*, лингви́ст, языкове́д; ~ic, *a*, лингвисти́ческий; ~ics, *n*, лингви́стика, языкозна́ние.

liniment, *n*, жи́дкая мазь.

lining, *n*, подкла́дка; оби́вка.

link, *n*, звено́; связь, соедине́ние; *(tech.)* шарни́р; ¶ *v.t*, соединя́ть, свя́зывать; сцепля́ть; ~ *up (of spacecraft) (n.)* стыко́вка.

links, *n.pl*, по́ле для игры́ в гольф.

linnet, *n*, конопля́нка.

linoleum, *n*, лино́леум.

linotype, *n*, линоти́п.

linseed, *n*, льняно́е се́мя; ~ *oil* льняно́е ма́сло.

lint, *n*, ко́рпия.

lintel, *n*, перемы́чка (окна́/две́ри).

lion(ess), *n*, лев, (льви́ца); *(fig.)* знамени́тость; ~'*s share* льви́ная до́ля.

lip, *n*, губа́; край; ~-*service* пусты́е слова́; ~*stick* губна́я пома́да.

liquefaction, *n*, сжиже́ние; плавле́ние; **liquefy**, *v.t. (& i.)*, превраща́ть(ся) в жи́дкое состоя́ние, разжижа́ть(ся); расплавля́ть(ся).

liqueur, *n*, ликёр.

liquid, *a*, жи́дкий; пла́вный *(sound)*; непостоя́нный; *(com.)* легко́ реализу́емый; ¶ *n*, жи́дкость.

liquidate, *v.t*, ликвиди́ровать; выпла́чивать *(debt)*; **liquidation**, *n*, ликвида́ция; вы́плата до́лга.

liquor, *n*, напи́ток.

liquorice, *n*, лакри́ца, лакри́чник.

lisp, *n*, ле́пет, шепеля́вость; ¶ *v.i*, лепета́ть; шепеля́вить; ~ing, *a*, шепеля́вый.

lissom, *a*, ги́бкий.

list, *n*, спи́сок, пе́речень; крен, накло́н; *pl*, аре́на; ¶ *v.t*, вноси́ть в спи́сок; ¶ *i*, крени́ться, наклоня́ться.

listen, *v.i. & t:* ~ *to* слу́шать; ~ *in* слу́шать ра́дио; подслу́шивать; ~er, *n*, слу́шатель.

listless, *a*, апати́чный, вя́лый; ~ness, *n*, апати́чность, вя́лость.

lit, *p.p*, освещённый.

litany, *n*, моле́бствие.

literal, *a*, буква́льный; бу́квенный; ~ly, *ad*, буква́льно, досло́вно.

literary, *a*, литерату́рный; **literate**, *a*, гра́мотный; **literature**, *n*, литерату́ра.

lithe, *a*, ги́бкий.

lithograph, *n*, литогра́фия; ¶ *v.t*, литографи́ровать; ~er, *n*, литогра́ф; ~y, *n*, литогра́фия.

litigant, *n*, сторона́ (в тя́жбе): **litigate**, *v.i*, суди́ться; **litigation**, *n*, тя́жба; **litigious**, *a*, сутя́жнический.

litmus, *n*, ла́кмус.

litre, *n*, литр.

litter, *n*, носи́лки; припло́д *(of young)*; сор; подсти́лка; ¶ *v.t*, разбра́сывать; подстила́ть.

little, *a*, ма́ленький; коро́ткий; незначи́тельный; ~ *finger* мизи́нец; ~ *ones* де́ти; ~ *Red Riding Hood* Кра́сная ша́почка; ¶ *n*, немно́гое; ~-*by*-~ ма́ло-пома́лу; ¶ *ad*, немно́го, ма́ло; ~ness, *n*, ма́лая величина́; ме́лочность.

littoral, *n*, побере́жье.

liturgy, *n*, литурги́я.

live, *a*, живо́й; реа́льный; де́йствующий; энерги́чный; актуа́льный;

~wire, n, *(fig.)*, энергичный человек, огонь.

live, *v.i,* жить; обитать; ~ *from hand to mouth* жить впроголодь, перебиваться; ~ *up to* жить согласно (принципам, *etc.).*

livelihood, n, средства к жизни.

liveliness, n, живость, оживление; lively, a, живой, оживлённый; яркий; сильный.

liver, n, печень; *(cook.)* печёнка.

livery, n, ливрея; ~ *stables* платная конюшня.

livestock, n, скот, живой инвентарь.

livid, n, мёртвенно-бледный; *(coll.)* очень сердитый.

living, a, живой; жилой; ~ *room* гостиная, общая комната; ~ *wage* прожиточный минимум; *within* ~ *memory* на памяти живущих; ¶ n, средства к жизни; жизнь; пища; *earn a* ~ зарабатывать на жизнь.

lizard, n, ящерица.

llama, n, лама.

lo, *int,* вот!.

load, n, груз, нагрузка; *(fig.)* бремя, тяжесть; воз, вагон, судно; ¶ *v.t,* грузить; обременять; заряжать *(gun);* осыпать *(with presents, etc.);* ~er, n, грузчик; ~ing, n, погрузка; заряжание.

loadstar, n, полярная звезда; *(fig.)* путеводная звезда.

loadstone, n, магнитный железняк, магнетит.

loaf, n, хлеб; буханка (хлеба); голова (сахару); ~ *sugar* кусковой сахар; ¶ *v.i,* бездельничать, слоняться; ~er, n, бездельник.

loam, n, жирная глина; *clay* ~ суглинок.

loan, n, заём, ссуда: займствование; *raise a* ~ раздобывать деньги взаймы; ¶ *v.t,* давать взаймы, ссужать.

loath: *be* ~ *to* не хотеть; ¶ a, неохотный.

loathe, *v.t,* чувствовать отвращение к; не терпеть; loathing, n, отвращение, ненависть; loathsome, n, отвратительный.

lob, n, высоко подброшенный мяч.

lobby, n, вестибюль, прихожая, фойе; кулуары; группа членов; ~ing, n, воздействие на членов (конгресса, *etc.).*

lobe, n, мочка *(ear);* доля.

lobster, n, омар, морской рак.

local, a, местный; ~ *train* пригородный поезд; ~ity, n, местность; местоположение; ~ize, *v.t,* локализовать; ~ly, *ad,* в местном масштабе; в определённом месте; locate, *v.t,* определять местонахождение *(gen.);* обнаруживать; размещать; поселять; location, n, определение места; местожительство; размещение; *on* ~ на натуре *(filming).*

loch, n, озеро; залив.

lock, n, локон *(hair);* замок *(also of gun);* затор; шлюз; ~ *gate* шлюзные ворота; ~ *jaw* столбняк; ~*nut* контргайка; ~*smith* слесарь; ~*-up* арестантская камера; тюрьма; *spring* ~ пружинный затвор; *under* ~ *and key* под замком; ¶ *v.t,* запирать на замок; сжимать; стискивать; ~ *in* запирать (и не выпускать); ~ *out* не впускать; объявлять локаут *(dat.);* ~ *up* запирать, заключать; locker, n, шкафчик, ящик.

locket, n, медальон.

locomotion, n, передвижение; locomotive, a, движущий(ся); ¶ n, локомотив; паровоз, тепловоз, электровоз.

locum tenens, n, временный заместитель.

locust, n, саранча.

locution, n, выражение.

lode, n, рудная жила; ~*star* полярная звезда; ~*stone* магнетит.

lodge, n, домик; сторожка; ложа *(masonic);* помещение привратника; ¶ *v.t,* поселять; давать на хранение; подавать; *v.i,* снимать квартиру; ~r, n, жилец, жилица; квартирант, -ка; lodging, n, жилище; квартира; *board and* ~ квартира и стол, пансион; ~ *house* гостиница, меблированные комнаты.

loft, n, чердак; сеновал; голубятня; ~iness, n, возвышенность; надменность; ~y, a, высокий, возвышенный; надменный.

log, n, колода, бревно; чурбан; *(mar.)* лаг; ~ *book* вахтенный журнал; ~ *cabin* бревенчатый дом.

loganberry, n, логанова ягода.

logarithm

414   lorry

logarithm, *n*, логари́фм; ~ic, *a*, логарифми́ческий.

loggerheads: *be at* ~ ссо́риться.

logic, *n*, ло́гика; ~ical, *a*, логи́ческий; ~ian, *n*, ло́гик.

loin, *n*, филе́йная часть; *pl*, поясни́ца; ~-*cloth* набе́дренная повя́зка.

loiter, *v.i*, ме́длить, слоня́ться.

loll, *v.i*, сиде́ть разваля́сь; стоя́ть в лени́вой по́зе; ~ *out* высо́вываться.

lollipop, *n*, ледене́ц.

London, *a*, ло́ндонский; ~er, *n*, ло́ндонец.

loneliness, *n*, одино́чество; уедине́нность; **lonely**, & **lonesome**, *a*, одино́кий; уединённый.

long, *a*, дли́нный; до́лгий; ~*boat* барка́с; ~*-legged* длинноно́гий; ~*-lived* долгове́чный; ~*-playing* долгоигра́ющий; ~*-sighted* дальнозо́ркий; *(fig.)* дальнови́дный; ~*-term* долгосро́чный; ~*-winded* многоречи́вый; *for a* ~ *time* до́лго; давно́; *how* ~ *is this string?* како́й длины́ э́та верёвка?; *one metre* ~ длино́й в оди́н метр; *one hour* ~ продолжа́ющийся час; *in the* ~ *run* в конце́ концо́в; *it is a* ~ *way* э́то далеко́; ¶ *ad* до́лго; давно́; *as* ~ *as* пока́; до тех пор, пока́; ~ *ago (ad.)* давно́; *(n.)* далёкое про́шлое; ~ *before this* задо́лго до э́того; ~ *since* давно́; *all day* ~ весь день напролёт; ¶ *v.i*: ~ *for* стра́стно жела́ть *(gen.)*; томи́ться по; ~er, *ad*: *no* ~ бо́льше не.

longevity, *n*, долгове́чность.

longing, *n*, стра́стное жела́ние; томле́ние.

longish, *a*, долгова́тый.

longitude, *n*, долгота́; **longitudinal**, *a*, продо́льный; по долготе́.

longshoreman, *n*, порто́вый гру́зчик.

look, *v.i*, смотре́ть, гляде́ть; вы́глядеть; каза́ться; ~ *after* забо́титься о, присма́тривать за; ~ *at* смотре́ть на; ~ *bad* вы́глядеть пло́хо; ~ *down* смотре́ть све́рху вниз; смотре́ть свысока́; ~ *for* иска́ть; ~ *forward to* ожида́ть *(gen.)*, предвкуша́ть; ~ *here!* послу́шай(те)!; ~ *in* загля́дывать; ~ *into* иссле́довать; ~ *like* вы́глядеть как, быть похо́жим на; ~ *on* наблюда́ть; смотре́ть на;

~ *on to* выходи́ть на/в; ~ *out (v.t.)* разы́скивать; *(v.i.)* остере́гаться, быть насторо́же; ~ *out!* береги́сь!, осторо́жнее!; ~ *over* просма́тривать; ~ *round (v.t.)* осма́тривать; *(v.i.)* огля́дываться; ~ *through* просма́тривать; ~ *up (v.t.)* справля́ться (по кни́ге) о; *(v.i.)* смотре́ть вверх; улучша́ться; ~ *well* вы́глядеть хорошо́; *he is fifty, but does not look it* он вы́глядит моло́же свои́х пяти́десяти лет; ¶ *n*, взгляд; вид; вне́шность; *good* ~s красота́; *take a* ~ *at* посмотре́ть *(pf.)* на; ~er-on, *n*, зри́тель, наблюда́тель; ~ing glass. *n*, зе́ркало; ~-out, *n*, наблюда́тель; наблюда́тельный пункт; *be on the* ~ быть насторо́же.

loom, *n*, тка́цкий стано́к; ¶ *v.i*, мая́чить, нея́сно вырисо́вываться.

loop, *n*, пе́тля; *(avia.)* мёртвая пе́тля; *(rly.)* ве́тка; ~*hole* бойни́ца; *(fig.)* лазе́йка; ¶ *v.t*, де́лать пе́тлю.

loose, *a*, свобо́дный; широ́кий, просто́рный; нето́чный; неприкреплённый; распу́щенный; ~ *cover* чехо́л; *at a* ~ *end* без де́ла; *be* ~ болта́ться; шата́ться; *break* ~ вырыва́ться на свобо́ду; срыва́ться с це́пи; *come* ~ открепля́ться; отвя́зываться; ¶ *v.t*, & ~n, освобожда́ть; развя́зывать; ~ness, *n*, широта́; нето́чность; сла́бость.

loot, *n*, добы́ча; ¶ *v.t*, гра́бить; ~er, *n*, граби́тель.

lop, *v.t*, подреза́ть; уре́зывать; ~*-eared* вислоу́хий; ~*-sided* криво́бо́кий; наклонённый.

loquacious, *a*, болтли́вый; **loquacity**, *n*, болтли́вость.

lord, *n*, лорд; господи́н; *the Lord (God)*, Госпо́дь Бог; *the Lords* пала́та ло́рдов; ~ *Mayor* лорд-мэр; *the* ~'s *Prayer* О́тче наш; ¶ *v.t*: ~ *it over* вести́ себя́ самовла́стно по отноше́нию к; ~liness, *n*, великоле́пие; высокоме́рие; ба́рство; ~ly, *a*, ба́рский; великоле́пный; высокоме́рный; *your Lordship* ва́ша све́тлость.

lore, *n*, зна́ние.

lorgnette, *n*, лорне́т.

lorry, *n*, грузови́к.

lose, *v.t,* терять; лишаться *(gen.);* проигрывать; *v.i,* отставать *(clock);* ~ *heart* падать духом; ~ *one's temper* терять самооблада́ние, серди́ться; ~r, *n,* теря́ющий, потеря́вший; прои́грыва-ющий, проигра́вший; **loss,** *n,* поте́ря, утра́та; *(com.)* убы́ток; про́игрыш; *be at a* ~ быть в затрудне́нии/недоуме́нии; *sell at a* ~ продава́ть в убы́ток.

lost, *p.p. & a,* потеря́нный; утра́чен-ный; поги́бший; ~-*property office* бюро́ нахо́док.

lot, *n,* жре́бий; *(fig.)* у́часть, судьба́; уча́сток земли́; па́ртия *(goods);* вещь, ве́щи *(at auction);* a ~ *of* мно́го; *a bad* ~ плохо́й челове́к.

loth: *be* ~ не хоте́ть.

lotion, *n,* примо́чка; лосьо́н.

lottery, *n,* лотере́я.

lotus, *n,* ло́тос.

loud, *a,* гро́мкий, зву́чный; шу́м-ный; крича́щий *(colour);* ~ness, *n,* гро́мкость; ~speaker, *n,* гром-коговори́тель.

lounge, *n,* ко́мната о́тдыха; ~ *suit* пиджа́чный костю́м; ¶ *v.i,* сиде́ть развали́сь; ~ *about* безде́льничать.

louse, *n,* вошь; **lousy,** *a,* вши́вый; *(coll.)* ме́рзкий, парши́вый.

lout, *n,* неуклю́жий челове́к; гру-бия́н; ~ish, *a* гру́бый, неотёсан-ный.

lovable, *a,* ми́лый, привлека́тель-ный; **love,** *n,* любо́вь; возлюб-ленн|ый, -ая; *(sport)* нуль; *be in* ~ *with* быть влюблённым в; *fall in* ~ влюбля́ться в; *not for* ~ *or money* ни за что на све́те; ~ *affair* рома́н; ~ *bird* попуга́й; ~-*in-a--mist* садо́вая черну́шка; ~-*letter* любо́вное письмо́; ~-*making* уха́-живание; физи́ческая бли́зость; ~-*match* брак по любви́; ~-*sick* изныва́ющий от любви́; ~ *story* любо́вная исто́рия; ~-*token* пода́-рок в знак любви́; ¶ *v.t,* люби́ть; жела́ть.

loveliness, *n,* красота́, пре́лесть; **lovely,** *a,* преле́стный; ми́лый; чуде́сный.

lover, *n,* любо́вник; возлюбленн|ый, -ая; люби́тель; **loving,** *a,* любя́-щий; не́жный.

low, *a,* ни́зкий; сла́бый; ти́хий; по́длый *(fig);* ску́дный; ¶ *ad.,* ни́зко;~*frequency;* ни́зкая частота́;

~ *gear* переда́ча для ма́лой ско́-рости; ~ *neck* глубо́кий вы́рез; ~-*necked* декольти́рованный; ~ *pressure* ни́зкое давле́ние; ~ *spi-rits* пода́вленность; *in a* ~ *voice* ти́хим го́лосом; ~ *water* ма́лая вода́, отли́в.

low, *v.i,* мыча́ть.

lower, *a,* ни́зший; ни́жний; ¶ *ad,* ни́же; ¶ *v.t,* понижа́ть; снижа́ть; опуска́ть *(eyes);* спуска́ть *(flag).*

lower, *v.i,* хму́риться; темне́ть; ~ing, *a,* мра́чный.

lowest, *a,* са́мый ни́жний.

lowing, *n,* мыча́ние.

lowland, *n,* ни́зменность, доли́на.

lowliness, *n,* скро́мность; **lowly,** *a,* скро́мный.

lowness, *n,* ни́зость.

loyal, *a,* ве́рный, лоя́льный; ~ty, *n,* ве́рность, лоя́льность.

lozenge, *n,* ромб; табле́тка.

lubricant, *n,* сма́зочный; ¶ *n,* сма́-зочное сре́дство; **lubricate,** сма́зы-вать; **lubrication,** *n,* сма́зка; **lubri-cator,** *n,* сма́зчик; лубрика́тор.

lucerne, *n,* люце́рна.

lucid, *a,* я́сный; прозра́чный; ~ity, *n,* я́сность; прозра́чность.

luck, *n,* сча́стье; уда́ча; везе́ние; слу́чай; судьба́; *bad* ~! неуда́ча, не везёт!; *good* ~! счастли́вой уда́чи!, в до́брый путь!; *I am in (out of)* ~ мне везёт (не везёт); *try one's* ~ попыта́ть *(pf.)* сча́стья; ~ily, *ad,* к сча́стью; ~less, *a,* несча́стный; невезу́чий; ~y, *a,* счастли́вый, уда́чный; везу́чий.

lucrative, *a,* при́быльный; **lucre,** *n,* при́быль; де́ньги; *filthy* ~ през-ре́нный мета́лл.

ludicrous, *a,* смешно́й, неле́пый.

lug, *n,* ушко́, глазо́к; ¶ *v.t,* тащи́ть, волочи́ть, дёргать.

luggage, *n,* бага́ж; *excess* ~ бага́ж вы́ше но́рмы; ~ *boot* бага́жник; ~ *rack* се́тка/по́лка для веще́й; ~ *van* бага́жный ваго́н.

lugger, *n,* лю́гер.

lugubrious, *a,* мра́чный, печа́льный.

lukewarm, *a,* теплова́тый; *(fig.)* равноду́шный.

lull, *n,* зати́шье; переры́в; ¶ *v.t,* убаю́кивать; усыпля́ть; ~aby, *n,* колыбе́льная пе́сня.

lumbago, *n,* простре́л.

lumber, *n,* хлам; лесоматериа́лы; ~*jack* лесору́б; ~ *room* чула́н; ~

yard лесно́й склад; ¶ *v.t*, загромождáть; *v.i*, двигаться тяжело́.

luminary, *n*, свети́ло.

luminous, *a*, светя́щийся, све́тлый.

lump, *n*, кусо́к; о́пухоль, ши́шка; комо́к (в го́рле); чурбáн; ~ *sugar* пилёный сáхар, рафинáд; ~ *sum* о́бщая су́мма, кру́пная су́мма; ¶ *v.t:* ~ *together* брать о́птом; брать без разбо́ра; смéшивать в ку́чу; ~ish, *a*, неуклю́жий; ~y, *a*, комковáтый.

lunacy, *n*, безу́мие; *(law)* невменя́емость; **lunatic**, *n. & a*, сумасшéдший, безу́мный; ~ *asylum* психиатри́ческая больни́ца.

lunch, ~eon, *n*, второ́й зáвтрак, обéд; ¶ *v.i*, обéдать.

lung, *n*, лёгкое.

lunge, *n*, удáр, вы́пад; толчо́к; прыжо́к; ¶ *v.i*, дéлать вы́пад, чуть не пáдать; бросáться вперёд.

lupin, *n*, лупи́н.

lupus, *n*, *(med.)* волчáнка.

lurch, *n*, крен; *leave in the* ~ покидáть в бедé; ¶ *v.i*, идти шатáясь; *(mar.)* крен́иться; ~er, *n*, собáка-ищéйка.

lure, *n*, примáнка; обая́ние; ¶ *v.t*, примáнивать; завлекáть.

lurid, *a*, мрáчный, стрáшный.

lurk, *v.i*, скрывáться в засáде; прятáться.

luscious, *a*, со́чный, слáдкий.

lush, *a*, со́чный; пы́шный.

lust, *n*, вожделéние, по́хоть; ¶ *v.i:* ~ *after* стрáстно желáть; испы́тывать физи́ческое влечéние к; ~ful, *a*, похотли́вый.

lustily, *ad*, с си́лой, бо́дро.

lustre, *n*, гля́нец; блеск; лю́стра; **lustrous**, *a*, глянцеви́тый; блестя́щий.

lusty, *a*, здоро́вый, живо́й.

lute, *n*, лю́тня; замáзка, масти́ка.

Lutheran, *a*, лютерáнский; ¶ *n*, лютерáнин.

luxuriance, *n*, пы́шность; **luxuriant**, *a*, пы́шный; цвети́стый.

luxurious, *a*, роско́шный; **luxury**, *n*, ро́скошь; удово́льствие.

lyceum, *n*, лицéй.

lye, *n*, щёлок.

lying, *a*, ло́жный, лжи́вый; распо-ло́женный; лежáщий; ¶ *n*, лжи́вость, ложь.

lying-in, *n*, ро́ды.

lymph, *n*, ли́мфа; ~atic, *a*, лимфати́ческий.

lynch, *v.t*, линчевáть.

lynx, *n*, рысь; ~-*eyed* вострогля́зый.

lyre, *n*, ли́ра.

lyric(al), *a*, лири́ческий; **lyric**, *n*, лири́ческое стихотворéние; ~ism, *n*, лири́зм.

M

macabre, *a*, ужáсный.

macadam, *n*, макадáм, щéбень для мощéния доро́г; ¶ *v.t*, мости́ть щéбнем.

macaroni, *n*, макаро́ны.

macaroon, *n*, миндáльное пиро́жное.

macaw, *n*, макáо.

mace, *n*, булавá; жезл.

machiavellian, *a*, маккиавелисти́ческий.

machination, *n*, махинáция, ко́зни.

machine, *n*, маши́на; механи́зм; инструмéнт; аппарáт; ¶ *a*, маши́нный; ~ *gun* пулемёт; ~-*made* маши́нного произво́дства; ~ *tool* механи́ческий стано́к; *adding* ~ счётная маши́на; ¶ *v.t*, подвергáть механи́ческой обрабо́тке; шить на маши́не; ~ry, *n*, маши́ны, механи́змы; **machinist**, *n*, слéсарь; механ́ик.

mackerel, *n*, макрéль, ску́мбрия.

mackintosh, *n*, макинто́ш, непромокáемое пальто́.

mad, *a*, сумасшéдший, безу́мный; бéшеный *(dog)*; ~*cap* сорви́-голова́; ~*house* сумасшéдший дом; ~*man* сумасшéдший; *be* ~ *about* быть помéшанным на; *go* ~ сходи́ть с умá.

madam, *n*, мадáм.

madden, *v.t*, своди́ть с умá; раздражáть; беси́ть; ~ing, *a*, раздражáющий.

madder, *n*, марéна.

made, *p.p*, сдéланный; ~ *out to bearer* вы́писанный предъяви́телю; ~ *to order* сдéланный на закáз; ~ *up* вы́думанный; загримиро́ванный; накрáшенный; иску́сственный.

madeira, *n*, мадéра.

madly, *ad*, безу́мно; **madness**, *n*, сумасшéствие; бéшенство; безу́мие.

madrigal 417 make

madrigal, *n,* мадригал.
magazine, *n,* журнал; склад; пороховой погреб.
maggot, *n,* личинка; ~у, *a,* червивый.
magic, *a,* волшебный, магический; ~ *wand* волшебная палочка; ¶ *n,* магия, волшебство; *as if by* ~ как по волшебству; ~al, *a,* волшебный, магический; ~ian, *n,* волшебник; фокусник.
magisterial, *a,* повелительный, авторитетный; судебный; **magistracy,** *n,* должность судьи; магистрат; **magistrate,** *n,* судья; член городского магистрата.
magnanimity, *n,* великодушие; **magnanimous,** *a,* великодушный.
magnate, *n,* магнат.
magnesia, *n,* окись магния; магнезия; **magnesium,** *n,* магний.
magnet, *n,* магнит; ~ic, *a,* магнитный; *(fig.)* притягивающий; ~ism, *n,* магнетизм; *(fig.)* обаяние; ~ize, *v.t,* намагничивать; **magneto,** *n,* магнето.
magnificence, *n,* великолепие; **magnificent,** *a,* великолепный.
magnify, *v.t,* увеличивать; *(fig.)* преувеличивать; ~ing glass увеличительное стекло, лупа.
magniloquence, *n,* высокопарность; **magniloquent,** *a,* высокопарный.
magnitude, *n,* величина; значительность.
magnolia, *n,* магнолия.
magpie, *n,* сорока.
magus, *n,* маг, волхв.
maharajah, *n,* магараджа.
mahogany, *n,* красное дерево.
maid, *n,* девица; девушка; служанка, горничная; ~ *of honour* фрейлина; ~en, *n,* девица, дева; ¶ *a,* незамужний; девичий; девственный; первый; ~ *name* девичья фамилия; ~enhood, *n,* девичество; девственность; ~enly, *a,* девический.
mail, *n,* почта; кольчуга, броня; ~bag почтовая сумка; ~ coach почтовый вагон; ~ train почтовый поезд; ¶ *v.t,* посылать почтой, сдавать на почту; ~ed fist бронированный кулак.
maim, *v.t,* калечить, увечить.
main, *a,* главный основной; ~ *chance* личные цели; ~ *deck* верхняя палуба; ~ *drain* главная труба; ~land материк; берег; ~

line главная линия, магистраль; ~mast грот-мачта; ~ *road* большая дорога, шоссе; ~spring часовая пружина; *(fig.)* главная движущая сила; ~ *street* главная улица; ~stay грот-штаг; *(fig.)* главная поддержка/опора; *the* ~ *thing* главное; ¶ *n,* магистраль; открытое море; главная труба; *in the* ~ в основном; ~ly, *ad,* главным образом, большею частью.
maintain, *v.t,* поддерживать; содержать; утверждать; отстаивать; продолжать; **maintenance,** *n,* поддержка; содержание; *(tech.)* ремонт; уход.
maisonette, *n,* квартира.
maize, *n,* майс, кукуруза.
majestic, *a,* величественный; **majesty,** *n,* величие; величество *(title).*
major, *a,* больший; более важный; главный; старший; *(mus.)* мажорный; ¶ *n,* майор; *(age)* совершеннолетний; ~-general генерал-майор.
majordomo, *n,* мажордом.
majority, *n,* большинство; совершеннолетие.
make, *n,* производство, работа; марка, модель, тип; ~-believe *(n.)* фантазия; *(a.)* воображаемый; ~-shift замена; временное средство/устройство; ~-up грим; косметика; состав; склад характера; *(print.)* верстка; ~weight довесок; противовес; ¶ *v.t,* делать, производить, изготовлять; производить *(speech);* образовывать; равняться *(dat.);* заставлять; становиться *(inst.);* ~ *as if* делать вид, что...; ~ *a bed* стелить постель; ~ *away with* покончить *(pf.)* с; ~ *do with* довольствоваться *(inst.);* ~ *faces* гримасничать; ~ *for* способствовать *(dat.);* направляться к; ~ *fun of* высмеивать; ~ *good* вознаграждать; преуспевать; ~ *haste* спешить; ~ *enquiries* наводить справки; ~ *light of* не принимать всерьёз, не придавать значения; ~ *money* зарабатывать деньги; ~ *the most of* использовать наилучшим образом; ~ *much of* высоко ценить; ~ *off* убегать; ~ *one's way* продвигаться, пробираться; ~ *out* разбирать; понимать; доказывать; составлять; выписывать *(cheque);*

~ *over* передавáть; ~ *sure (of)* обеспéчивать; убеждáться (в); ~ *up v.t. (& i)*, выдýмывать; *(theat.)* гримировáть(ся); *(of face)* крáсить(ся); навёрстывать *(time)*; возмещáть *(losses); (v.i)* мирíться; ~ *up one's mind* решáть(ся); ~ *up to* заúскивать пéред; ~ *use of* испóльзовать; ~r, *n*, создáтель; *making, n*, создáние; произвóдство; становлéние; *pl*, задáтки.

malachite, *n*, малахúт.

maladjustment, *n*, плохóе приспособлéние.

maladministration, *n*, плохóе управлéние; злоупотреблéние.

maladroit, *a*, нелóвкий.

malady, *n*, болéзнь; расстрóйство.

malaise, *n*, недомогáние.

malaria, *n*, малярúя; ~l, *a*, малярúйный.

Malay(an), *a*, малáйский; ¶ *n*, малá|ец, -йка; малáйский язы́к.

malcontent, *n*, недовóльный (человéк).

male, *a*, мужскóй; ~ *dog* кобéль; ~ *screw* винт; ¶ *n*, мужчúна; самéц *(animal)*.

malediction, *n*, проклятие.

malefactor, *n*, престýпник, злодéй.

malevolent, *a*, недоброжелáтельный; злорáдный.

malformation, *n*, урóдство.

malice, *n*, злóба; ехúдство; *(law)* злой ýмысел; **malicious**, *a*, злóбный, ехúдный; предумы́шленный.

malign, *a*, пáгубный; *(med.)* злокáчественный; ¶ *v.t.* клеветáть на; ~ant, *a*, злóбный; злокáчественный.

malinger, *v.i*, притворяться больны́м; ~er, *n*, симулянт.

malleable, *a*, кóвкий; *(fig.)* подáтливый.

mallet, *n*, деревянный молотóк.

mallow, *n*, мáльва.

malnutrition, *n*, недостáточное питáние, недоедáние.

malt, *n*, сóлод.

Maltese, *a*, мальтúйский; ¶ *n*, мальтúец.

maltreat, *v.t*, жестóко обращáться с.

mamma, *n*, мáма.

mammal, *n*, млекопитáющее; ~ia, *n.pl*, грудны́е сóски.

mammoth, *n*, мáмонт; ¶ *a*, гигáнтский.

man, *n*, человéк; мужчúна; рабóчий; слугá; ~ *and wife* муж и женá; ~-*eater* людоéд; ~*hole* лаз, люк; ~-*o'-war* воéнный корáбль; ~ *in the street* пéрвый встрéчный; рядовóй человéк; ~*slaughter* человекоубúйство; *(law)* непредумы́шленное убúйство; ~ *of the world* свéтский человéк; человéк с жúзненным óпытом; ¶ *v.t*, укомплектóвывать лúчным состáвом; занимáть.

manacle, *v.t*, надевáть нарýчники *(dat.)*; ~s, *n.pl*, нарýчники, кандалы́.

manage, *v.t*, руководúть/управлять/ завéдовать *(inst.)*; владéть *(inst.)*; справляться с; сумéть *(pf.)* *(+ inf.)*; ~able, *a*, послýшный; выполнúмый; ~ment, *n*, управлéние; правлéние, дирéкция; ~r, (~ress), *n*, завéдующ|ий, управляющ|ий, -ая; дирéктор; мéнаджер; ~rial, *a*, дирéкторский.

mandarin, *n*, мандарúн.

mandarin(e) (orange), *n*, мандарúн.

mandatary, -ory, *n*, мандатáр|ий; **mandate**, *n*, мандáт; предписáн|е; **mandatory**, *a*, обязáтельный.

mandible, *n*; нúжняя чéлюсть; жвáло *(of insect)*.

mandolin(e), *n*, мандолúна.

mandrake, *n*, мандрагóра.

mandrill, *n*, мандрúл.

mane, *n*, грúва; *(fig.)* кóсмы.

manège, *n*, манéж; искýсство верховóй езды́.

manful, *a*, мýжественный; ~ly, *ad*, мýжественно.

manganese, *n*, мáрганец.

mange, *n*, чесóтка.

manger, *n*, ясли, кормýшка.

mangle, *n*, катóк (для бельá); ¶ *v.t*, рубúть; калéчить; искажáть; катáть.

mango, *n*, мáнго.

mangy, *a*, паршúвый.

manhandle, *v.t*, передвигáть/грузúть вручнýю; грýбо обращáться с.

manhole, *n*, лаз, люк.

manhood *n*, возмужáлость; зрéлость.

mania, *n*, мáния; ~c, *n*, маньяк; ~cal, *a*, маниакáльный.

manicure, *n*, маникю́р; ¶ *v.t*, дéлать маникю́р; ~ist, *n*, маникю́рша.

manifest, *a*, явный; ¶ *n*, декларáция; ¶ *v.t*, проявлять; ~ation, *n*, проявлéние; ~o, *n*, манифéст.

manifold, *a*, разнообра́зный; много-
чи́сленный.
manikin, *n*, челове́чек; мане-
ке́н.
manipulate, *v.t*, манипули́ровать
(inst.); подта́со́вывать; **manipula-
tion**, *n*, манипуля́ция; подта-
со́вка.
mankind, *n*, челове́чество.
manliness, *n*, му́жественность;
manly, *a*, му́жественный; му-
жеподо́бный.
manna, *n*, ма́нна небе́сная.
mannequin, *n*, манеке́н, манеке́н-
щица.
manner, *n*, спо́соб, о́браз; мане́ра,
ме́тод; *(pl.)* мане́ры; нра́вы, обы́-
чаи; *he has no* ~s он не уме́ет
вести́ себя́; *in this* ~ таки́м о́бра-
зом; ~**ed**, *a*, мане́рный; ~**ism**, *n*,
мане́рность; *(art)* маньери́зм; ~**ly**,
a, ве́жливый.
mannish, *a*, мужеподо́бная.
manoeuvre, *n*, манёвр; ¶ *v.i*, манев-
ри́ровать . . .
manometer, *n*, мано́метр.
manor, *n*, поме́стье; ~ *house* поме́-
щичий дом; ~**ial**, *a*, манориа́ль-
ный.
manse, *n*, дом па́стора.
mansion, *n*, большо́й особня́к.
mantelpiece, -**shelf**, *n*, по́лка над
ками́ном.
mantilla, *n*, манти́лья.
mantle, *n*, ма́нтия; *(fig.)* покро́в;
(tech.) кожу́х; *(gas)* кали́льная
се́тка.
manual, *a*, ручно́й; ~ *labour* физи́-
ческий труд; ¶ *n*, руково́дство,
уче́бник.
manufacture, *n*, произво́дство; фаб-
рика́ция; фабрика́т, изде́лие; ¶
v.t, производи́ть; *(fig.)* фабрико-
ва́ть; ~**r**, *n*, фабрика́нт; изгото-
ви́тель; **manufacturing**, *n*, произ-
во́дство; обраба́тывающая про-
мы́шленность.
manure, *n*, наво́з, удобре́ние; ¶ *v.t*,
удобря́ть.
manuscript, *n*, ру́копись; ¶ *a*,
рукопи́сный.
Manx, *a*, с о́строва Мэн; ~ *cat*
бесхво́стая ко́шка.
many, *a*, мно́го; мно́гие, многочи́с-
ленные; ~ *a time* ча́сто; ~-*coloured*
многоцве́тный; ~-*sided* многосто-
ро́нний; *a great* ~ мно́жество;
how ~? ско́лько?; *be one too* ~

for быть сильне́е/умне́е *(gen.); so*
~ так мно́го.
map, *n*, ка́рта, план; ¶ *v.t*, наноси́ть
на ка́рту; ~ *out* плани́ровать.
maple, *n*, клён.
mar, *v.t*, по́ртить.
maraud, *v.i*, мароде́рствовать; ~**er**,
n, мароде́р; ~**ing**, *n*, мароде́рство.
marble, *n*, мра́мор; *pl*, игра́ в ша́рики;
¶ *a*, мра́морный; ¶ *v.t*, распи́сы-
вать под мра́мор.
March, *n*, март; ¶ *a*, ма́ртовский.
march, *n*, марш; *(fig.)* ход; *day's* ~
дневно́й перехо́д; ~ *past* прохож-
де́ние церемониа́льным ма́ршем;
quick ~ ско́рый шаг; ¶ *v.i*, мар-
широва́ть; ~ *in* вступа́ть; ~ *off*
выступа́ть, уходи́ть; ~ *past* про-
ходи́ть; ~**ing**, *n*, марширо́вка; ~
order похо́дный поря́док; *pl*, при-
ка́з о выступле́нии; увольне́ние;
~ *song* похо́дная пе́сня.
marchioness, *n*, марки́за.
mare, *n*, кобы́ла.
margarine, *n*, маргари́н.
margin, *n*, край, грани́ца; по́ле *(of
page)*; опу́шка; *(fig.)* резе́рв,
запа́с; ~**al**, *a*, кра́йний; ~ *note*
заме́тка на поля́х страни́цы.
marigold, *n*, ноготки́.
marine, *a*, морско́й; ¶ *n*, флот;
солда́т морско́й пехо́ты; ~**r**, *n*,
моря́к, матро́с.
marionette, *n*, марионе́тка.
marital, *a*, бра́чный, супру́жеский.
maritime, *a*, примо́рский, морско́й.
marjoram, *n*, майора́н.
mark, *n*, знак; ме́тка; при́знак;
цель; след; балл, отме́тка; ма́рка
(coin); *hit the* ~ попада́ть в цель;
make one's ~ отлича́ться; *up to
the* ~ на до́лжной высоте́; ¶ *v.t*,
отмеча́ть; обознача́ть; ме́тить;
ста́вить балл/отме́тку (за, *or
dat.)*; ~ *out* размеча́ть; ~ *time*
маршрова́ть на ме́сте; *(fig.)*
топта́ться на ме́сте; ~**ed**, *p.p. &
a*, поме́ченный; заме́тный; изве́ст-
ный; ~**er**, *n*, закла́дка *(in book)*;
знак; указа́тель.
market, *n*, ры́нок, база́р; сбыт, про-
да́жа; ¶ *a*, ры́ночный; ~ *day*
база́рный день; ~ *garden* огоро́д;
~ *place* ры́ночная пло́щадь; ~
price ры́ночная цена́; *money* ~
де́нежный ры́нок; ¶ *v.t*, продава́ть
на ры́нке; сбыва́ть; ~**able**, *a*,
хо́дкий; ~ **ing**, *n*, ма́ркетинг.

marking, n, расцве́тка; ме́тка; маркиро́вка; отме́тки.

marksman, n, (ме́ткий) стрело́к; **~ship**, n, стрельба́.

marl, n, ме́ргель, изве́стко́вая гли́на; **~y**, a, ме́ргельный.

marmalade, n, мармела́д, апельси́новый джем.

marmoset, n, марты́шка.

marmot, n, суро́к.

maroon, a, кашта́нового цве́та; ¶ n, кашта́новый цвет; ¶ v.t, выса́живать (на необита́емом о́строве); покида́ть, броса́ть.

marquee, n, больша́я пала́тка. ·

marquess see **marquis**.

marquetry, n, маркетри́.

marquis, n, марки́з.

marriage, n, брак, заму́жество; жени́тьба, сва́дьба; (fig.) те́сное едине́ние; **~** lines/licence свиде́тельство о бра́ке; **~** settlement бра́чный контра́кт; **~able**, a, взро́слый; **married**, p.p. & a, жена́тый, заму́жняя; супру́жеский; **~** couple супру́жеская чета́; newly-**~** couple чета́ новобра́чных; be **~** быть жена́тым/заму́жем; get **~** (to) жени́ться (на), выходи́ть за́муж (за).

marrow, n, ко́стный мозг; (fig.) су́щность; (bot.) кабачо́к; **~-bone** мозгова́я кость; **~fats** горо́х мозгово́й.

marry, v.t, жени́ть; выдава́ть за́муж; жени́ться на; выходи́ть за́муж за.

Mars, n, Марс.

Marseillaise, n, марселье́за.

marsh, n, боло́то, топь; **~mallow** (bot.) алте́й лека́рственный; зефи́р (sweets); **~-marigold** калу́жница.

marshal, n, ма́ршал; организа́тор, руководи́тель; церемонийме́йстер; нача́льник; ¶ v.t, выстра́ивать; располага́ть, размеща́ть; marshalling yard сортиро́вочная ста́нция.

marshy, a, боло́тистый, то́пкий.

marsupial, n, су́мчатое живо́тное.

mart, n, ры́нок, торго́вый центр.

Martian, n, марсиа́нин.

marten, n, куни́ца.

martial, a, вое́нный, вои́нственный; **~** law вое́нное положе́ние.

martin, n, городска́я ла́сточка.

martinet, n, сторо́нник стро́гой дисципли́ны.

martyr, n, му́че|ник, **~ница**; ¶ v.t, му́чить; **~dom**, n, му́ченичество; (fig.) му́ка.

marvel, n, чу́до, ди́во; ¶ v.i: **~** at удивля́ться (dat.), восхища́ться (inst.); **~lous**, a, чуде́сный.

Marxist, a, маркси́стский; ¶ n, маркси́ст.

marzipan, n, марципа́н.

mascot, n, талисма́н.

masculine, a, мужско́й, му́жественный; мужеподо́бная; ¶ n, мужско́й род (gram.); **masculinity**, n, му́жественность.

mash, n, пюре́; меша́ни́на, смесь; по́йло; ¶ v.t, размина́ть, де́лать пюре́ из; **~ed** potatoes карто́фельное пюре́.

mask, n, ма́ска; (fig.) личи́на; ¶ v.t, маскирова́ть, скрыва́ть; **~ed** ball бал-маскара́д.

mason, n, ка́менщик; масо́н; **~ic**, a, масо́нский; **~** lodge масо́нская ло́жа; **~ry**, n, ка́менная/кирпи́чная кла́дка; масо́нство.

masquerade, n, маскара́д; ¶ v.i: **~** as выдава́ть себя́ за.

mass, n, ма́сса; мно́жество; (eccl.) ме́сса, обе́дня; **~** production ма́ссовое/сери́йное произво́дство; in the **~** в це́лом; ¶ v.t. (& i.), собира́ть(ся), концентри́ровать(ся).

massacre, n, резня́; ¶ v.t, убива́ть, ре́зать.

massage, n, масса́ж; ¶ v.t, масси́ровать; **masseur**, n, массажи́ст, -ка.

massive, a, масси́вный, кру́пный.

mast, n, ма́чта.

master, n, хозя́ин, владе́лец, нача́льник; ма́стер; учи́тель; маги́стр; head **~** дире́ктор шко́лы; M**~** of Arts маги́стр гуманита́рных нау́к; **~-key** отмы́чка; **~** mind руководи́тель; **~piece** шеде́вр; **~-stroke** ма́стерской уда́р/ход; **~** of ceremonies конферансье́; ¶ v.t, овладева́ть (inst.); одолева́ть; справля́ться с; **~ful**, a, вла́стный; **~ly**, a, ма́стерской; in a **~** way ма́стерски; **~y**, n, соверше́нное владе́ние; госпо́дство; ма́стерство́.

mastic, n, масти́ка.

masticate, v.t, жева́ть; **mastication**, n, жева́ние.

mastiff, n, масти́ф.

mastodon, n, мастодо́нт.

mat, *n,* ко́врик; полови́к, рого́жа, цыно́вка; подсти́лка *(table);* ¶ *a,* ма́товый; **matted,** *a,* спу́танный.

match, *n,* спи́чка; па́ра, ро́вня; брак; матч, состяза́ние; **~-**box спи́чечная коро́бка; **~-**maker сват, сва́ха; *a good* **~** хоро́шая па́ртия; *meet one's* **~** встреча́ть досто́йного проти́вника; ¶ *v.t,* подбира́ть под па́ру, сочета́ть; гармони́ровать с; противопоставля́ть; состяза́ться с; **~less,** *a,* несравне́нный.

mate, *n,* това́рищ; супру́г, супру́га; саме́ц, са́мка *(animal);* помо́щник; *(chess)* мат; ¶ *v.t,* спа́ривать; *(chess)* де́лать мат *(dat.).*

material, *n,* материа́л; мате́рия *(cloth); building* **~**s строи́тельные материа́лы; ¶ *a,* материа́льный; суще́ственный; **~ism,** *n,* материали́зм; **~ist,** *n,* материали́ст; **~istic,** *a,* материалисти́ческий; **~ize,** *v.t,* материализова́ть(ся); осуществля́ть(ся); **~ly,** *ad,* материа́льно, суще́ственно.

maternal, *a,* матери́нский; с матери́нской стороны́; **maternity,** *n,* матери́нство; **~** *home* роди́льный дом.

mathematical, *a,* математи́ческий; **mathematician,** *n,* матема́тик; **mathematics,** *n,* матема́тика.

matinée, *n,* дневно́й спекта́кль/конце́рт/сеа́нс.

matins, *n.pl,* зау́треня.

matriarchy, *n,* матриарха́т.

matriculate, *v.t,* зачисля́ть в вы́сшее уче́бное заведе́ние; **matriculation,** *n,* зачисле́ние в вуз.

matrimonial, *a,* супру́жеский; **matrimony,** *n,* супру́жество, брак.

matrix, *n,* ма́тка; *(tech.)* ма́трица.

matron, *n,* замужняя же́нщина; заве́дующая хозя́йством, сестра́-хозя́йка.

matter, *n,* вещество́; де́ло; *(philos.)* мате́рия; *(med.)* гной; содержа́ние; *what is the* **~***?* в чём де́ло?; *what's the* **~** *with you?* что с ва́ми?; **~** *of course* я́сное де́ло; *as a* **~** *of course* есте́ственным о́бразом; **~***-of-course* есте́ственный; **~***-of-fact* прозаи́чный, сухо́й; *as a* **~** *of fact* факти́чески, в су́щности; на са́мом де́ле; *no* **~** *what happens* что бы то ни́ было; *it's a* **~** *of taste* э́то де́ло вку́са; ¶ *v.i,*

име́ть значе́ние; *it doesn't* **~** нева́жно, ничего́.

matting, *n,* рого́жа, цыно́вка; материа́л для цыно́вок.

mattock, *n,* моты́га.

mattress, *n,* матра́ц, тюфя́к.

mature, *a,* зре́лый, спе́лый; созре́вший; хорошо́ обду́манный; ¶ *v.t,* доводи́ть до зре́лости; *v.i,* созрева́ть; *(com.)* наступа́ть; **maturity,** *n,* зре́лость; *(com.)* срок платежа́.

maudlin, *a,* слезли́вый, сентимента́льный.

maul, *v.t,* уве́чить, избива́ть; *(fig.)* жесто́ко критикова́ть.

Maundy Thursday, *a,* Вели́кий четве́рг.

mausoleum, *n,* мавзоле́й.

mauve, *a,* розова́то-лило́вый.

maw, *n,* утро́ба; *(fig.)* бе́здна.

mawkish, *a,* прито́рный, слезли́вый.

maxim, *n,* сенте́нция, афори́зм; пра́вило.

maximum, *n,* ма́ксимум; ¶ *a,* макси́мальный.

May, *n,* май; *M~ Day* пра́здник Пе́рвого ма́я; **~***fly* ма́йская му́ха; **~***pole* ма́йское де́рево.

may, *n,* цвето́к боя́рышника.

may, *v. aux,* мочь, име́ть возмо́жность; *It* **~** *be that* возмо́жно, что . . .; *I* **~** *go* мо́жет быть, я пойду́; **~** *I come in?* мо́жно войти́?; **~***be,* *ad,* мо́жет быть.

mayonnaise, *n,* майоне́з.

mayor, *n,* мэр; **~ess,** *n,* жена́ мэ́ра; же́нщина-мэр.

maze, *n,* лабири́нт; *(fig.)* пу́таница.

mazurka, *n,* мазу́рка.

me, *pn,* меня́, мне, *etc.*

mead, *n,* мёд.

meadow, *n,* луг; **~***-sweet* таво́лга.

meagre, *a,* худо́й, то́щий; ску́дный; бе́дный; **~ness,** *n,* худоба́; ску́дность; бе́дность.

meal, *n,* еда́; мука́ (кру́пного помо́ла); **~** *time* вре́мя еды́; **~y,** *a,* мучно́й, мучни́стый; **~***-mouthed* сладкоречи́вый.

mean, *a,* ни́зкий, по́длый; скро́мный; скупо́й; сре́дний; *in the* **~***time* ме́жду тем; ¶ *n,* середи́на; *(maths)* сре́днее число́; **~s,** *n,* сре́дство, спо́соб; сре́дства, состоя́ние; *by all* **~** коне́чно; *by* **~** *of* посре́дством, путём, при по́мощи; *by no* **~** нико́им о́бразом; ¶ *v.t*

зна́чить; подразумева́ть; намере-
ва́ться (+ inf.).
meander, n, изви́лина; ¶ v.i, изви-
ва́ться; ~ing, a, изви́листый.
meaning, a, многозначи́тельный; ¶
n, значе́ние, смысл; double ~
двоя́кое значе́ние; ~less, a, бес-
смы́сленный.
meanness, n, ни́зость, по́длость;
убо́жество; ску́пость.
meantime, -while, ad, ме́жду тем,
тем вре́менем.
measles, n, корь; фи́нны (in animals).
measly, a, ничто́жный.
measurable, a, измери́мый; значи́-
тельный; **measure,** n, ме́ра, ме́рка;
разме́р (стиха́); такт (mus.);
крите́рий; beyond ~ чрезме́рно;
dry ~s ме́ры сыпу́чих тел; in
great ~ в значи́тельной сте́пени;
liquid ~s ме́ры жи́дкостей; made
to ~ сде́ланный на зака́з; take ~s
принима́ть ме́ры; take smb's~
снима́ть ме́рку; ¶ v.t, ме́рить,
измеря́ть; снима́ть ме́рку с; оце́-
нивать; име́ть разме́ры в; ~ out
отмеря́ть; распределя́ть; he ~d
his length on the floor он растяну́лся
во весь рост на полу́; ~d, p.p. &
a, изме́ренный; ритми́чный, ме́р-
ный; взве́шенный; ~ment, n, из-
мере́ние; pl, разме́ры.
meat, n, мя́со; ¶ a, мясно́й; minced
~ мясно́й фарш; ~ ball котле́та;
~ pie пиро́г с мя́сом; ~-safe холо-
ди́льник; ~y, a, мяси́стый; содер-
жа́тельный.
mechanic, n, меха́ник; ~al, a, меха-
ни́ческий; маши́нный; (fig.) ма-
шина́льный; ~s, n, меха́ника;
mechanism, n, механи́зм, устро́й-
ство; **mechanize,** v.t, механизи́ро-
вать.
medal, n, меда́ль; **medallion,** n,
медальо́н.
meddle, v.i, вме́шиваться; ~r, n,
вме́шивающийся во всё челове́к;
навя́зчивый челове́к.
mediaeval, a, средневеко́вый.
mediate, v.i, посре́дничать; **mediation,** n, посре́дничество; **mediator,**
n, посре́дник.
medical, a, медици́нский; враче́б-
ный; ~ examination медици́нский
осмо́тр; ~ school медици́нский
институ́т/факульте́т; ~ service ме-
дици́нское обслу́живание; **medica-**

ment, n, медикаме́нт; лека́рство;
medicate, v.t, пропи́тывать лека́р-
ствами; **medicinal,** a, лека́рствен-
ный, целе́бный; **medicine,** n, меди-
ци́на; лека́рство; ~-chest дома́ш-
няя апте́чка; ~-man зна́харь,
шама́н.
mediocre, a, посре́дственный; **medio-
crity,** n, посре́дственность.
meditate, v.i, размышля́ть; v.t, замыш-
ля́ть; **meditation** .n, размышле́ние,
созерца́ние; **meditative,** a, созер-
ца́тельный; заду́мчивый.
Mediterranean, a, средиземномо́р-
ский; ¶ n, Средизе́мное мо́ре.
medium, n, сре́дство, спо́соб; (phys.)
среда́; ме́диум (spiritualist); по-
сре́дник; ¶ a, сре́дний; уме́рен-
ный; ~-sized сре́днего разме́ра.
medley, n, смесь, сброд; ¶ a, сме́-
шанный, разнообра́зный.
meek, a, кро́ткий, поко́рный; ~ness,
n, кро́тость, поко́рность.
meerschaum, n, морска́я пе́нка.
meet, v.t, встреча́ть; знако́миться
с; соединя́ться с; удовлетворя́ть
(wishes); v.i, встреча́ться; соби-
ра́ться; ~ half way идти́ навстре́чу
(dat.); ~ in, встре́ча; со́-
ра́ние; ми́тинг, заседа́ние; сли-
я́ние; call a ~ созыва́ть собра́ние;
hold a ~ проводи́ть собра́ние;
~-place ме́сто встре́чи.
megaphone, n, ру́пор.
melancholia, n, меланхо́лия; **melancholy,** a, гру́стный, уны́лый; ¶ n,
грусть, уны́ние.
mellifluous, a, медоточи́вый; слад-
козву́чный.
mellow, a, спе́лый; вы́держанный
(wine); мя́гкий; добро́ду́шный,
умудрённый; ¶ v.t, смягча́ть;
де́лать спе́лым; v.i, созрева́ть;
смягча́ться; ~ness, n, спе́лость,
зре́лость; мя́гкость.
melodious, a, мелоди́чный.
melodrama, n, мелодра́ма.
melody, n, мело́дия.
melon, n, ды́ня.
melt, v.t, пла́вить; растворя́ть;
(fig.) смягча́ть; v.i, та́ять; пла́-
виться; (fig.) смягча́ться; ~ in
tears расчу́вствоваться (pf.) до
слёз; ~ing, n, пла́вка, плавле́ние;
та́яние; ~-pot ти́гель, плави́ль-
ный котёл; ~ point то́чка плав-
ле́ния; ¶ a, пла́вкий; плави́ль-
ный.

member, *n,* член; ~**ship,** *n,* членство; количество членов; ~ *card* членский билет.

membrane, *n,* *(med.)* перепонка; плёнка; *(tech.)* мембрана.

memento, *n,* напоминание; подарок на память.

memoir, *n,* краткая биография; *pl,* мемуары, воспоминания.

memorable, *a,* памятный, незабвенный; **memorandum,** *n,* памятная записка; меморандум; заметка; **memorial,** *n,* памятник; петиция; ¶ *a,* мемориальный; **memorize,** *v.t,* запоминать; **memory,** *n,* память.

menace, *n,* угроза; опасность; ¶ *v.t,* угрожать *(dat.).*

menagerie, *n,* зверинец.

mend, *v.t,* исправлять, чинить; ремонтировать; штопать *(darn); v.i,* поправляться; улучшаться; *on the* ~ на поправку.

mendacious, *a,* лживый; **mendacity,** *n,* лживость.

mender, *n,* ремонтный мастер.

mendicancy, *n,* нищенство; **mendicant,** *a. & n,* нищий.

mending, *n,* починка, ремонт.

menial, *a,* низкий, лакейский; ¶ *n,* слуга; лакей.

meningitis, *n,* менингит.

menstruation, *n,* менструация.

mensuration, *n,* измерение.

mental, *a,* умственный, мысленный; психический; ~ *arithmetic* счёт в уме; ~ *home* психиатрическая больница; ~ *specialist* психиатр; ~**ity,** *n,* склад ума; ~**ly,** *ad,* мысленно.

mention, *n,* упоминание, ссылка; ¶ *v.t,* упоминать, ссылаться на; *don't* ~ *it!* не стоит!; нé за что!

mentor, *n,* наставник.

menu, *n,* меню.

mephitic, *a,* зловонный; ядовитый.

mercantile, *a,* торговый; коммерческий; ~ *marine* торговый флот.

mercenary, *a,* корыстный; наёмный; ¶ *n,* наёмник.

mercer, *n,* торговец.

merchandise, *n,* товары; **merchant,** *n,* купец, торговец; ¶ *a,* торговый, коммерческий; ~**man,** ~**ship,** торговое судно.

merciful, *a,* милосердный; **merciless,** *a,* беспощадный.

mercurial, *a,* ртутный; *(fig.)* живой, подвижный; **mercury,** *n,* ртуть.

mercy, *n,* милосердие, милость; пощада; *at the* ~ *of* во власти; *beg for* ~ просить пощады; *have* ~ *on* щадить, миловать.

mere, *a,* простой; сущий; *a* ~ *nothing* сущий пустяк; ~**ly,** *ad,* только.

mere, *n,* озеро, пруд.

meretricious, *a,* показной, мишурный.

merge, *v.t. (& i.),* сливать(ся), соединять(ся); ~**r,** *n,* объединение.

meridian, *n,* меридиан; полдень; зенит; высшая точка; **meridional,** *a,* меридиональный.

meringue, *n,* меренга.

merit, *n,* заслуга; достоинство; ¶ *v.t,* заслуживать, быть достойным *(gen.);* **meritorious,** *a,* похвальный.

merlin, *n,* кречет.

mermaid, *n,* русалка; **merman,** *n,* водяной, тритон.

merrily, *ad,* весело; **merriment,** *n,* веселье; **merry,** *a,* весёлый; ~*-go-round* карусель; ~*-making* веселье, потеха; *make* ~ веселиться.

mesh, *n,* петля; ячейка; сеть; *(fig.)* западня; *(tech.)* зацепление; меш.

mesmerism, *n,* гипнотизм, гипноз; **mesmerize,** *v.t,* гипнотизировать.

mess, *n,* беспорядок; путаница; сор; беда; столовая; месиво; ~*mate* однокашник; *make a* ~ *of* перепутывать, портить; ¶ *v.t,* пачкать, грязнить; ~ *up* портить.

message, *n,* сообщение; поручение; **messenger,** *n,* вестник, посыльный, курьер.

Messiah, *n,* мессия.

messy, *a,* грязный; беспорядочный.

metal, *n,* металл; щебень; *pl,* *(rly.)* рельсы; ~ *worker* металлист; *leave the* ~s сходить с рельсов; ¶ *a. &* ~**lic** металлический; ~**lurgy,** *n,* металлургия.

metamorphose, *v.t,* превращать, изменять; **metamorphosis,** *n,* метаморфоза.

metaphor, *n,* метафора; ~**ical,** *a,* метафорический.

metaphysics, *a,* метафизический; **metaphysician,** *n,* метафизик; **metaphysics,** *n,* метафизика.

mete (out), *v.t,* назначать, отмерять.

meteor, *n*, метео́р; ~**ite**, *n*, метеори́т; ~**ological**, *a*, метеорологи́ческий; ~**ology**, *n*, метеороло́гия.

meter, *n*, счётчик.

method, *n*, ме́тод, спо́соб, систе́ма; ~**ical**, *a*, методи́ческий; системати́ческий.

Methodism, *n*, методи́зм; **Methodist**, *n*, методи́ст.

methylated spirit, *n*, мети́ловый спирт.

meticulous, *a*, дото́шный, аккура́тный.

metre, *n*, метр; разме́р, ритм; **metric**, *a*, метри́ческий; **metrics**, *n*, ме́трика.

metronome, *n*, метроно́м.

metropolis, *n*, столи́ца; метропо́лия; **metropolitan**, *a*, столи́чный.

mettle, *n*, темпера́мент, хара́ктер; пыл; хра́брость; *put him on his* ~ заставля́ть его́ сде́лать всё, что в его́ си́лах; ~**some**, *a*, сме́лый.

mew, *n*, мяу́канье; ча́йка; кле́тка; ¶ *v.i*, мяу́кать.

mews, *n*, коню́шня.

Mexican, *a*, мексика́нский; ¶ *n*, мексика́н|ец, ~ка.

mezzanine, *n*, антресо́ли.

mezzotint, *n*, ме́ццо-ти́нто.

miaow, *n*, мяу́канье; ¶ *v.i*, мяу́кать.

miasma, *n*, миа́змы, вре́дные испаре́ния.

mica, *n*, слюда́.

Michaelmas, *n*, Миха́йлов день.

microbe, *n*, микро́б.

microphone, *n*, микрофо́н.

microscope, *n*, микроско́п; **microscopic**, *a*, микроскопи́ческий.

mid, *a*, сре́дний, середи́нный; *in* ~ *air* высоко́ в во́здухе; *in* ~ *winter* в середи́не зимы́.

midday, *n*, по́лдень.

middle, *n*, середи́на; та́лия; ¶ *a*, сре́дний; ~*-aged* пожило́й, сре́дних лет; ~ *class* сре́дняя буржуази́я; ~ *finger* сре́дний па́лец; ~*man* комиссионе́р; посре́дник; ~*-sized* сре́дних разме́ров.

Middle Ages сре́дние века́
Middle East Сре́дний Восто́к.

middling, *a*, сре́дний, посре́дственный; ¶ *ad*, так себе́; сно́сно.

midge, *n*, кома́р; мо́шка.

midget, *n*, ка́рлик, лилипу́т.

midnight, *n*, по́лночь.

midriff, *n*, диафра́гма.

midshipman, *n*, ми́чман; курса́нт вое́нно-морско́го учи́лища.

midst, *n*, середи́на; ¶ *pr*, среди́, посреди́, ме́жду.

midsummer, *n*, середи́на ле́та; *Midsummer's day* Ива́нов день.

midway, *ad*, на полпути́.

midwife акуше́рка; *midwifery* акуше́рство.

mien, *n*, ми́на, выраже́ние лица́.

might, *n*, могу́щество, мощь, си́ла; *with* ~ *and main* изо всех сил; ~**iness**, *n*, мо́щность, вели́чие; ~**y**, *a*, могу́щественный, мо́щный; ¶ *ad*, чрезвыча́йно.

mignonette, *n*, резеда́.

migraine, *n*, мигре́нь.

migrant, *a*, перелётный *(bird)*; кочу́ющий; **migrate**, *v.i*, соверша́ть перелёт; пересели́ться; **migration**, *n*, перелёт; переселе́ние; **migratory**, *a*, перелётный; *(med.)* блужда́ющий; кочу́ющий.

milch cow, *n*, до́йная коро́ва.

mild, *a*, мя́гкий; ти́хий; не́жный; сла́бый (на вкус).

mildew, *n*, пле́сень, ми́льдью.

mildly, *ad*, мя́гко, ти́хо; споко́йно; **mildness**, *n*, мя́гкость; не́жность; сла́бость.

mile, *n*, ми́ля; ~*stone* верстово́й ка́мень; *(fig.)* ве́ха; ~**age**, *n*, расстоя́ние в ми́лях; число́ про́йденных миль.

militant, *a*, вои́нствующий, вои́нственный; **militarism**, *n*, милитари́зм; **militarist**, *n*, милитари́ст; **militarize**, *v.t*, милитаризи́ровать; **military**, *a*, вое́нный; во́инский; *the* ~ вое́нные, солда́ты; **militate**, *v.i*: ~ *against* свиде́тельствовать про́тив; препя́тствовать *(dat.)*; **militia**, *n*, мили́ция; ~**man**, *n* милиционе́р.

milk, *n*, молоко́; мле́чный сок; ¶ *a*, моло́чный; ~*-and-water* безво́льный; ~ *chocolate* моло́чный шокола́д; ~*maid* доя́рка; моло́чница; ~*man* продаве́ц молока́, моло́чник; доя́льщик; ~*sop* тря́пка; ¶ *v.t*, дои́ть; ~**er**, *n*, доя́рка, дои́льщик; дои́льная маши́на; ~**ing**, *n*, дое́ние; ~**y**, *a*, моло́чный; *M~ Way* Мле́чный путь.

mill, *n*, ме́льница; заво́д; прока́тный стан; стано́к; фре́за: ~ *pond* ме́льничный пруд; ~ *race* ме́льничный лото́к; ~*stone* жёрнов; ~ *wheel* ме́льничное колесо́; *go through the* ~ проходи́ть суро́вую шко́лу; ¶ *v.t*, моло́ть; дроби́ть; валя́ть *(cloth)*; обраба́тывать на станке́, фрезерова́ть; ~ *about* копоши́ться; дви́гаться круго́м; ~*ed edge* зазу́бренный край.

millenary, *a,* тысячеле́тний; **millennium,** *n,* тысячеле́тие.

miller, *n,* ме́льник; фрезеро́вщик.

millet, *n,* про́со.

milliard, *n,* миллиа́рд.

milliner, *n,* моди́стка; ~у, *n,* да́мские шля́пы; магази́н да́мских шляп.

milling, *n,* размо́л; валя́ние *(of cloth)*; обрабо́тка на станке́, фрезерова́ние; ~ *cutter* фре́за, фре́зер; ~ *machine* фре́зерный стано́к.

million, *n,* миллио́н; ~aire, *n,* миллионе́р; ~th, *a,* миллио́нный.

milt, *n,* моло́ки.

mime, *n,* мим, пантоми́ма; ¶ *v.t,* изобража́ть мими́чески; *v.i,*исполня́ть роль без слов; **mimic,** *n,* подража́тель, имита́тор; ¶ *v.t,* имити́ровать; **mimicry,** *n,* ми́мика; имити́рование; *(biol.)* мимикри́я.

mimosa, *n,* мимо́за.

minaret, *n,* минаре́т.

mince, *n,* фарш; ~*meat* сла́дкий фарш; ¶ *v.t,* кроши́ть, руби́ть; *v.i,* говори́ть жема́нно; семени́ть нога́ми; *not to* ~ *words* говори́ть без обиняко́в.

mind, *n,* ум, ра́зум; па́мять; мне́ние; *have a* ~ *to* хоте́ть; *bear in* ~ име́ть в виду́; *of one* ~ одного́ и того́ же мне́ния; *of sound* ~ здравомы́слящий; *go out of one's* ~ сходи́ть с ума́; ¶ *v.t,* не хоте́ть, име́ть что́-нибудь про́тив; смотре́ть за; бере́чься *(gen.)*; по́мнить; *I don't* ~ я не про́тив; ~*!* береги́сь!; ~ *your own business!* не вме́шивайтесь в чужи́е дела́!; *never* ~*!* ничего́!, не беспоко́йтесь!; ~ed, *a,* располо́женный, скло́нный; ~er, *n,* смотря́щий за *(inst.)*; ~ful, *a,* по́мнящий, забо́тливый.

mine, *pn,* мой, моя́, моё, мой; свой, своя́, своё, свои; *this book is* ~ э́та кни́га моя́; *a friend of* ~ мой друг.

mine, *n,* ша́хта, рудни́к; *(mil.)* ми́на; *(fig.)*; исто́чник; ~*sweeper* ми́нный тра́льщик; ¶ *v.t,* добыва́ть; мини́ровать *(mil.)*; *v.i,* производи́ть го́рные рабо́ты; **miner,** *n,* шахтёр; горня́к.

mineral, *n,* минера́л; ¶ *a,* минера́льный; ~ *water* минера́льная вода́; ~ogical, *a,* минералоги́ческий; ~ogist, *n,* минерало́г; ~ogy, *n,* минерало́гия.

mingle, *v.t. (& inst.),* сме́шивать(ся); ~ *in society/company* враща́ться в о́бществе.

miniature, *n,* миниатю́ра; ¶ *a,* миниатю́рный.

minimize, *v.t.* доводи́ть до ми́нимума; преуменьша́ть; **minimum,** *a,* минима́льный; ¶ *n,* ми́нимум.

mining, *n,* го́рное де́ло, го́рная промы́шленность; *(mil.)* мини́рование; ~ *engineer* го́рный инжене́р.

minion, *n,* люби́мец, фавори́т.

minister, *n,* мини́стр; посла́нник; свяще́нник; ¶ *v.i,* служи́ть; помога́ть; ~ial, *a,* министе́рский; **ministration,** *n,* по́мощь; *(eccl.)* богослуже́ние; **ministry,** *n,* министе́рство; кабине́т мини́стров; служе́ние; духове́нство.

mink, *n,* но́рка.

minnow, *n,* пескарь; *(fig.)* мелюзга́.

minor, *a,* ме́ньший; мла́дший; незначи́тельный; *(mus.)* мино́рный; второстепе́нный; ¶ *n,* несоверше́ннолетний; ~ity, *n,* меньшинство́; несовершенноле́тие.

minster, *n,* собо́р.

minstrel, *n,* менестре́ль; певе́ц.

mint, *n,* моне́тный двор; мя́та; мя́тная конфе́та; *a* ~ *of money* ку́ча де́нег; ¶ *v.t,* чека́нить; ~er, *n,* чека́нщик.

minuet, *n,* менуэ́т.

minus, *pr,* без, ми́нус; ~ *quantity* отрица́тельная величина́; ~ **[sign]** ми́нус; знак ми́нуса.

minute, *n,* мину́та; па́мятная запи́ска; *pl,* протоко́л; ~ *hand* мину́тная стре́лка; ¶ *a,* кро́шечный; подро́бный; ¶ *v.t,* заноси́ть в протоко́л; ~ness, *n,* ма́лость; то́чность; **minutiae,** *n.pl,* ме́лочи; мельча́йшие подро́бности.

minx, *a,* коке́тка; шалу́нья.

miracle, *n,* чу́до; ~ *play* мисте́рия; **miraculous,** *a,* сверхъесте́ственный; чуде́сный.

mirage, *n,* мира́ж.

mire, *n,* тряси́на, грязь.

mirror, *n,* зе́ркало; ¶ *v.t,* отража́ть.

mirth, *n,* весе́лье '~ful. *a* ,весёлый, ра́достный.

miry, *a,* то́пкий, гря́зный.

misadventure, *n,* несча́стье, несча́стный слу́чай.

misalliance, *n,* нера́вный брак, меза́льянс.

misanthrope, *n,* человеконенави́стник, мизантро́п; **misanthropic,** *a,* мизантропи́ческий; **misanthropy,** *n,* мизантро́пия.

misapplication, *n,* непра́вильное испо́льзование; злоупотребле́ние; **misapply,** *v.t,* непра́вильно испо́льзовать; злоупотребля́ть *(inst.).*

misapprehend, *v.t,* поня́ть *(pf.)* оши́бочно/превра́тно; **misapprehension,** *n,* недоразуме́ние.

misappropriate, *v.t,* незако́нно присва́ивать.

misbehave, *v.i,* ду́рно вести́ себя́; **misbehaviour,** *n,* дурно́е поведе́ние.

miscalculate, *v.i,* ошиба́ться в расчёте, просчи́тываться; **miscalculation,** *n,* оши́бка, просчёт.

miscarriage, *n,* вы́кидыш, або́рт; оши́бка; ~ *of justice* суде́бная оши́бка; **miscarry,** *v.i,* де́лать вы́кидыш; терпе́ть неуда́чу; не доходи́ть.

miscellaneous, *a,* сме́шанный; разнообра́зный; **miscellany,** *n,* смесь; сбо́рник.

mischance, *n,* несча́стный слу́чай, неуда́ча.

mischief, *n,* зло, беда́; поврежде́ние, вред; озорство́, ша́лость; ~ *maker* интрига́н, смутья́н; **mischievous,** *a,* озорно́й; злонаме́ренный.

misconceive, *v.t,* непра́вильно поня́ть *(pf.);* непра́вильно проекти́ровать; **misconception,** *n,* непра́вильное представле́ние.

misconduct, *n,* дурно́е поведе́ние.

misconstruction, *n,* непра́вильное построе́ние/истолкова́ние; **misconstrue,** *v.t,* непра́вильно истолко́́вывать.

miscreant, *n,* злоде́й.

misdeed, *n,* злодея́ние.

misdemeanour, *n,* просту́пок.

misdirect, *v.t,* непра́вильно направля́ть, непра́вильно адресова́ть.

miser, *n,* скря́га, скупе́ц.

miserable, *a,* жа́лкий; несча́стный; убо́гий.

miserly, *a,* скупо́й.

misery, *n,* несча́стье; нищета́.

misfire, *v.i,* дава́ть осе́чку.

misfit, *n,* пло́хо сидя́щее пла́тье; *(fig.)* неприспосо́бленный к жи́зни челове́к.

misfortune, *n,* несча́стье; неуда́ча.

misgiving, *n,* опасе́ние.

misgovern, *v.t,* пло́хо управля́ть *(inst.);* ~ment, *n,* плохо́е управле́ние.

misguide, *v.t,* вводи́ть в заблужде́ние; непра́вильно направля́ть.

mishap, *n,* неуда́ча.

misinform, *v.t,* непра́вильно информи́ровать, дезориенти́ровать; ~ation, *n,* дезинформа́ция.

misinterpret, *v.t,* неве́рно истолко́вывать; ~ation, *n,* неве́рное/непра́вильное истолкова́ние.

misjudge, *v.t,* непра́вильно суди́ть о; недооце́нивать; ~ment, *n,* непра́вильное сужде́ние, недооце́нка.

mislay, *v.t,* класть не на ме́сто, теря́ть.

mislead, *v.t,* вводи́ть в заблужде́ние.

mismanage, *v.t,* по́ртить; пло́хо управля́ть *(inst.);* ~ment, *a,* плохо́е управле́ние.

misname, *v.t,* непра́вильно называ́ть; **misnomer,** *n,* ло́жное назва́ние.

misogynist, *n,* женоненави́стник.

misplace, *v.t,* класть не на ме́сто; *have* ~d *confidence* доверя́ться ненадёжному челове́ку, *etc.*

misprint, *n,* опеча́тка.

mispronounce, *v.t,* непра́вильно произноси́ть.

misquotation, *n,* непра́вильное цити́рование; непра́вильная цита́та; **misquote,** *v.t,* непра́вильно цити́ровать.

misrepresent, *v.t,* представля́ть в ло́жном ви́де, искажа́ть; ~ation, *n,* искаже́ние.

misrule, *n,* плохо́е управле́ние.

miss, *n,* мисс; де́вушка.

miss, *v.i,* промахну́ться *(pf.),* не попада́ть; *v.t,* упуска́ть; опа́здывать на; не замеча́ть; избега́ть *(gen.);* скуча́ть по; ~ *out* пропуска́ть; *be missing* отсу́тствовать; недоставать; ¶ *n*, промах.

missal, *n*, католический требник.

missel thrush, *n*, деряба.

misshapen, *a*, уродливый.

missile, *n*, метательный снаряд; ракета.

missing, *a*, отсутствующий; недостающий; без вести пропавший.

mission, *n*, миссия; поручение; командировка; призвание; ~ary, *n*, миссионер; **missive**, *n*, послание.

misspell, *v.t*, неправильно писать/ произносить по буквам; ~ing, *n*, орфографическая ошибка.

misstatement, *n*, неправильное/ложное заявление/показание.

mist, *n*, туман, дымка, мгла; ¶ *v.t*, затуманивать.

mistake, *n*, ошибка, заблуждение, недоразумение; ¶ *v.t:* ~ *for* принимать за; ~n, *a*, ошибочный; неуместный; *be* ~ ошибаться, заблуждаться.

mister, *n*, мистер, господин.

mistletoe, *n*, омела.

mistranslate, *v.t*, неправильно переводить; **mistranslation**, *n*, неправильный перевод.

mistress, *n*, хозяйка (дома); учительница; любовница; миссис, госпожа; *she is her own* ~ она сама себе хозяйка.

mistrust, *n*, недоверие; подозрение; ¶ *v.t*, не доверять *(dat.)*, подозревать; ~ful, *a*, недоверчивый, подозрительный.

misty, *a*, туманный; неясный.

misunderstand, *v.t*, неправильно понимать; ~ing, *n*, недоразумение; размолвка.

misuse, *n*, неправильное употребление; злоупотребление; ¶ *v.t*, злоупотреблять *(inst.);* дурно обращаться с.

mite, *n*, скромная лепта, полушка; маленькое существо; клещ.

mitigate, *v.t*, смягчать; уменьшать; *mitigating circumstances* смягчающие дело обстоятельства); **mitigation**, *n*, смягчение, уменьшение.

mitre, *n*, митра; срез, скос под углом.

mitt[en], *n*, рукавица, варежка.

mix, *v.t*, мешать, смешивать; *v.i*, смешиваться, соединяться; сходиться, общаться; ~ *up* (хорошо) перемешивать; путать ; ~ed, *p.p.*

& *a*, смешанный; разнородный; ~ *school* смешанная школа; *get* ~ *up in* быть замешанным в; ~er, *n*, миксер; ~ture, *n*, смесь.

mizzen, *n*, бизань.

mizzle, *n*, изморось; ¶ *v.i: it* ~*s* моросит.

moan, *n*, стон; ¶ *v.i*, стонать; *v.t*, оплакивать; жаловаться на.

moat, *n*, ров.

mob, *n*, толпа, сборище; ~ *law* самосуд; ¶ *v.t*, толпой нападать на; окружать.

mobile, *a*, подвижный; мобильный; лёгкий; гибкий; ~ *library* передвижная библиотека; **mobility**, *n*, подвижность, мобильность; **mobilization**, *n*, мобилизация; **mobilize**, *v.t*, мобилизовать.

mock, *v.t*, высмеивать, осмеивать; передразнивать; издеваться над; ¶ *a*, поддельный; ложный; искусственный; ~er, *n*, насмешник; ~ery, *n*, издевательство, насмешка; пародия; ~ing, *a*, насмешливый; ~ *bird* пересмешник.

mode, *n*, способ, метод, мода.

model, *a*, образцовый, примерный; ¶ *n*, модель, макет; образец; пример; точная копия; манекенщица; натурщик; ~щица; ¶ *v.t*, моделировать; лепить; демонстрировать ; ~ *for* позировать для; ~ *on* создавать по образцу; **modeller**, *n*, лепщик; модельер.

moderate, *a*, умеренный; средний, посредственный; достучный; ¶ *v.t*, умерять, смягчать; сдерживать ; *v.i*, становиться умеренным; стихать; ~ly, *ad*, умеренно; **moderation**, *n*, умеренность; **moderator**, *n*, арбитр, посредник; экзаменатор; регулятор; председатель.

modern, *a*, современный; ~ *languages* новые языки; ~ism, *n*, модернизм; ~ist, *n*, модернист; ~ity, *n*, современность; ~ize, *v.t*, модернизировать.

modest, *a*, скромный; умеренный; ~y, *n*, скромность.

modicum, *n*, чуточка.

modification, *n*, (видо)изменение; модификация; **modify**, *v.t*, (видо)изменять.

modish, *a*, модный.

modulate, *v.t*, модулировать; **modulation**, *n*, модуляция.

mohair, *n*, ангóрская шерсть, мохéр.
Mohammedan, *a*, магометáнский; ¶ *n*, магометáн/ин, -ка.
moiety, *n*, половúна.
moist, *n*, влáжный, сырóй; ~en, *v.t*, мочúть, увлажнять; ~ure, *n*, влáга, влáжность, сýрость.
molar, *n*, кореннóй зуб.
molasses, *n*, пáтока.
mole, *n*, *(zool.)* крот; рóдинка; мол, дáмба *(jetty)*; ~hill кротóвина; ~skin кротóвый мех.
molecular, *a*, молекулярный; molecule, *n*, молéкула.
molest, *v.t*, приставáть к; надоедáть *(dat.)*; ~ation, *n*, приставáние.
mollify, *v.t*, смягчáть; успокáивать.
mollusc, *n*, моллюск.
molly-coddle, *n*, нéженка; ¶ *v.t*, изнéживать.
molten, *a*, расплáвленный.
moment, *n*, миг, мгновéние; момéнт; значéние; ~arily, *ad*, на мгновéние; ~ary, *a*, моментáльный; преходящий; ~ous, *a*, вáжный; momentum, *n*, инéрция, механúческий момéнт.
monarch, *n*, монáрх, монáрхиня; ~ic, *a*, монархúческий; ~ist, *n*, монархúст; ~y, *n*, монáрхия.
monastery, *n*, монастырь; monastic, *a*, монáшеский, монастырский.
Monday, *n*, понедéльник.
monetary, *a*, дéнежный; money, *n*, дéньги; ~-bag дéнежный мешóк; ~-box копúлка; ~ *changer* меняла; ~-grubber стяжáтель, скряга; ~-lender ростовщúк; ~ *order* дéнежный перевóд; *make* ~ зарабáтывать дéньги; составлять себé состояние; moneyed, *a*, богáтый.
monger, *n*, торгóвец, продавéц.
Mongol, *a*, монгóльский; ¶ *n*, монгóл, -ка; монгóльский язык.
mongoose, *n*, мангýста.
mongrel, *a*, смéшанный, нечистокрóвный; ¶ *n*, пóмесь; дворняжка.
monitor, *n*, стáроста клáсса; *(mar.)* монитóр; *(zool.)* варáн; ¶ *v.t*, производúть контрóльный приём *(gen.)*.
monk, *n*, монáх; ~hood, *n*, монáшество; ~'s-hood *(bot.)* аконúт.
monkey, *n*, обезьяна; ~ *nut* земляной орéх; ~ *tricks* глýпые выходки; ~-wrench раздвижнóй гáечный ключ.

monochrome, *n*, одноцвéтное изображéние.
monocle, *n*, монóкль.
monogamy, *n*, единобрáчие.
monogram, *n*, моногрáмма.
monograph, *n*. моногрáфия.
monolith, *n*, монолúт; ~ic, *a*, монолúтный.
monologue, *n*. монолóг.
monoplane, *n*, моноплáн.
monopolize, *v.t*, монополизúровать.
monopoly, *n*, монопóлия.
monosyllabic, *a*, однослóжный; monosyllable, *n*, однослóжное слóво.
monotonous, *a*, монотóнный; однообрáзный; monotony, *n*, монотóнность; однообрáзие.
monoxide, *n*, óкись (с áтомом кислорóда).
monsoon, *n*, муссóн.
monster, *n*, чудóвище; урóд; ¶ *a*, громáдный.
monstrance, *n*, дароносúца.
monstrosity, *n*, чудóвищность; чудóвище; урóдство; monstrous, *a*, чудóвищный; безобрáзный; громáдный.
month, *n*, мéсяц; ~ly, *a*, ежемéсячный; ¶ *ad*, ежемéсячно; ¶ *n*, ежемéсячный журнáл.
monument, *n*, пáмятник, монумéнт; ~al, *a*, монументáльный.
moo, *n*, мычáние; ¶ *v.i*, мычáть.
mood, *n*, настроéние; *(gram.)* наклонéние; ~y, *a*, капрúзный; в дурнóм настроéнии.
moon, *n*, лунá; мéсяц; ~beam полосá лýнного свéта; ~light лýнный свет; ~lit залúтый лýнным свéтом; ~shine вздор; ~struck помéшанный.
Moor, *n*, мавр.
moor, *n*, пýстошь, зарóсшая вéреском; вéресковая мéстность; ~hen бéлая куропáтка.
moor, *v.t*, причáливать, пришвартóвывать; ~ing, *n*, причáл; *(pl.)* якорные цéпи.
Moorish, *a*, мавритáнский.
moose, *n*, американский лось.
moot, *a*, спóрный; ¶ *v.t*, стáвить на обсуждéние.
mop, *n*, швáбра; копнá (волóс); ¶ *v.t*, мыть швáброй; вытирáть; ~ *up* вытирáть; ликвидúровать, уничтожáть.
mope, *v.i*, хандрúть, быть унылым.

moral, *a*, морáльный, нрáвственный; нравоучúтельный; ¶ *n*, морáль; *pl*, нрáвы; нрáвственность; ~e, *n*, морáльное состоя́ние; ~ist, *n*, моралúст; ~ity, *n*, морáль, нрáвственность; нравоучéние; ~ize, *v.i*, морализúровать; ~ly, *ad*, морáльно, в нрáвственном отношéнии; в сýщности.

morass, *n*, болóто, трясúна.

moratorium, *n*, моратóрий.

Moravian, *a*, морáвский; ¶ *n*, жúтель Морáвии.

morbid, *a*, болéзненный, нездорóвый.

mordant, *a*, кóлкий, éдкий; ¶ *n*, протрáва.

more, *ad*, бóльше; ещё; опя́ть; *never* ~ никогдá бóльше; *once* ~ ещё раз; ~ *and* ~ ещё и ещё; всё бóльше; *all the* ~ тем бóльше; *the* ~ ... *the* ~ ... чем бóльше ... тем бóльше ...; ~over, *ad*, крóме тогó.

morganatic, *a*, морганатúческий.

moribund, *a*, умирáющий.

morning, *n*, ýтро; *good* ~! дóброе ýтро!; *tomorrow* ~ зáвтра ýтром; ¶ *a*, ýтренний; ~ *glory* вьюнóк; *M*~ *star* ýтренняя звездá.

Moroccan, *a*, мороккáнский; **Morocco leather**, *n*, сафья́н.

morose, *a*, угрю́мый.

morphia, morphine, *n*, мóрфий.

morrow, *n*, ýтро; зáвтрашний день; *on the* ~ *of* на слéдующий день пóсле.

morsel, *n*, кусóчек.

mortal, *a*, смéртный; смертéльный; ¶ *n*, смéртный; ~ity, *n*, смéртность; ~ly, *ad*, смертéльно.

mortar, *n*, стýпка; известкóвый раствóр; *(mil.)* мортúра.

mortgage, *n*, заклáд; закладнáя; *pay off a* ~ выплáчивать по закладнóй; ¶ *v.t*, заклáдывать; ~e, *n*, кредитóр по закладнóй; ~r, *n*, должнúк по закладнóй.

mortician, *n*, гробовщúк.

mortification, *n*, унижéние, огорчéние; умерщвлéние; *(med.)* омертвéние, гангрéна; **mortify**, *v.t*, огорчáть; умерщвля́ть *(the flesh)*; *v.i, (med.)* мертвéть.

mortise, -ice, *n*, паз, гнездó шипá; углублéние; ~ *lock* врезнóй замóк; ¶ *v.t*, вставля́ть в гнездó.

mortuary, *n*, морг, покóйницкая.

mosaic, *n*, мозáика.

Moslem, *a*, мусульмáнский; ¶ *n*, мусульмáн|ин, ~ка.

mosque, *n*, мечéть.

mosquito, *n*, комáр, москúт; ~-*net* сéтка от комарóв.

moss, *n*, мох; ~y, *a*, мшúстый.

most, *a*, наибóльший; ~ *people* большинствó людéй; *for the* ~ *part* бóльшею чáстью; ¶ *ad*, бóльше всегó; наибóлее; *at the* ~ сáмое бóльшее; ~ly, *ad*, глáвным óбразом.

mote, *n*, пылúнка, сорúнка.

motel, *n*, мотéль.

moth, *n*, моль, мотылёк; ~-*eaten* изъéденный мóлью.

mother, *n*, мать; ~ *country* рóдина; метрополúя; ~-*in-law* тёща; свекрóвь; ~-*of-pearl* перламýтровый; ~ *of pearl* перламýтр; ~ *tongue* роднóй язы́к; ~ *wit* смекáлка; ¶ *v.t*, усыновля́ть; относúться по-матерúнски к; ~hood, *n*, матерúнство; ~ly, *a*, матерúнский.

motion, *n*, движéние; ход; жест; предложéние; *(picture)* фильм, кинокартúна; ¶ *v.i*, дéлать знак, покáзывать жéстом; ~less, *a*, неподвúжный; **motive**, *a*, движýщий; двúгательный; ~ *power* движущая сúла; ¶ *n*, мотúв, побуждéние; пóвод; **motivation**, *n*, мотивирóвка.

motley, *a*, разноцвéтный, пёстрый; ¶ *n*, шутовскóй костю́м.

motor, *n*, мотóр, двúгатель; ~ *boat* мотóрная лóдка; ~ *bus* автóбус; ~-*car* автомобúль; ~ *coach* автóбус; ~ *cycle*, мотоцúкл; ~ *cyclist* мотоциклúст; ~ *lorry* грузовúк; ¶ *v.i*, éздить/éхать на автомобúле; ~ing, *n*, eздá на автомобúле; автомобúльное дéло; автомобúльный спорт; ~ist, *n*, автомобилúст.

mottled, *a*, испещрённый, в крáпинку.

motto, *n*, девúз; эпúграф.

mould, *n*, плéсень; литéйная фóрма; шаблóн; мáтрица *(print.)*; фóрмочка *(cook.)*; харáктер, склад; взрыхлённая земля́; ¶ *v.t*, отливáть в фóрму; дéлать по шаблóну; *(fig.)* формовáть; ~er **[away]**, *v.i*, разлагáться, рассыпáться; ~iness, *n*, плéсень; ~ing, *n*, отлúвка, формóвка; *(arch.)* лепнóе украшéние, карнúз; ~y,

a, заплéсневелый; *(fig.)* старомóдный.

moult, *v.i,* линя́ть; ¶ *n,* ли́нька;
~**ing,** *a,* линю́чий.

mound, *n,* нáсыпь; холм.

mount, *n,* холм, горá; верховáя
лóшадь; ¶ *v.t,* вскáкивать на
(horse); поднимáться на; мон-
ти́ровать; вставля́ть в опрáву;
наклéивать на картóн; ~ *guard*
вступáть в караýл.

mountain, *n,* горá; *(fig.)* кýча,
мáсса; ~ *ash* ряби́на; ~ *chain*
гóрная цепь; ~ *ridge* гóрный
хребéт; ~*side* склон горы́; ~*eer,*
n, альпи́ст; гóрец; ~*eering, n,*
альпини́зм; ~*ous, a,* гори́стый;
(fig.) громáдный.

mountebank, *n,* фигля́р; шарлатáн.

mourn, *v.t,* оплáкивать; *v.i,* горевáть, носи́ть трáур; ~*er, n,*
прису́тствующий на похоронáх;
~*ful, a,* печáльный; трáурный;
~*ing, n,* трáур; *be in* ~ быть в
трáуре.

mouse, *n,* мышь; ~ *coloured, a,*
мыши́ного цвéта; ~*trap* мыше-
лóвка; ~*ousy, a,* мыши́ный.

moustache, *n,* усы́.

mouth, *n,* рот; отвéрстие, вход;
гóрлышко *(of bottle);* у́стье *(of
river);* make one's ~ *water* разжигáть аппети́т; *it made my* ~
water у меня́ потекли́ слю́нки;
~*organ* губнáя гармóшка; ~*piece*
мундшту́к; *(pers.)* глашáтай; микрофóн; ~*wash* полоскáние рта;
¶ *v.t,* произноси́ть, изрекáть;
v.i, гримáсничать; ~*ful, n,* ку-
сóк, глотóк.

movable, *a,* дви́жимый; подвижнóй,
передвижнóй; ~*s, n.pl,* дви́жи-
мость, дви́жимое иму́щество; **move,** *n,* движéние; ход *(in game);*
перемéна мéста; *(fig.)* шаг;
whose ~ *is it?* чей ход?; ¶ *v.t,*
дви́гать; передвигáть; трóгать;
вноси́ть *(proposal);* *v.i,* дви́гать-
ся; вращáться; идти́, развивáться; ~ *(house)* переезжáть; ~ *away*
удаля́ть(ся); отодвигáть; уезжáть; ~ *back* дви́гать(ся) назáд;
~ *in (v.t.)* вдвигáть; *(v.i.)* въез-
жáть; ~ *on!* проходи́те дáльше!;
~ *out (v t.)* выдвигáть; *(v.i.)*
выезжáть; ~*ment, n,* движéние;
жест; *(tech.)* ход; *(mus.)* часть;
темп; ~*r, n,* дви́гатель; *(fig.)*

инициáтор; **movies,** *n.pl,* кинó;
фи́льмы; **moving,** *a,* дви́жущийся;
подвижнóй; трóгательный; ¶ *n,*
(пере)движéние; переéзд.

mow, *v.t,* коси́ть, жать; ~*er, n,*
косéц, жнец; *(machine)* коси́лка,
жнéйка.

Mr. *see* Mister; **Mrs.** *see* mistress.

much, *a,* мнóго; ¶ *ad,* óчень; горáздо;
as ~ *as* стóлько же; *how* ~*?* скóлько?; *so* ~ *the better* тем лýчше; *too* ~
сли́шком; *very* ~ óчень; ~ *the
same* почти́ то же сáмое; *make* ~ *of*
высокó цени́ть; ~ *ado about
nothing* мнóго шýма из ничегó;
it is too ~ *for you* это вам не под
си́лу.

mucilage, *n,* клéйкое вещество́.

muck, *n,* навóз; грязь; ~*y, a,*
грязный.

mucous, *a,* сли́зистый; ~ *membrane*
сли́зистая оболóчка; **mucus,** *n,*
слизь.

mud, *n,* грязь; ~*guard* крылó/щит
от грязи; ~*lark* у́личный маль-
чи́шка.

muddle, *n,* пу́таница, неразберúха;
¶ *v.t,* спу́тывать; ~ *through* кóе-
-кáк доводи́ть дéло до концá.

muddy, *a,* гря́зный, му́тный; ¶ *v.t,*
пáчкать.

muezzin, *n,* муэдзи́н.

muff, *n,* му́фта.

muffle, *n,* *(tech.)* му́фель; глуши́-
тель; ¶ *v.t,* закýтывать; заглушáть; ~*d, p.p. & a,* заглушённый;
~*r, n,* кашнé, шарф; *(tech.)*
глуши́тель.

mufti, *n,* штáтское плáтье.

mug, *n,* крýжка.

muggy, *a,* удýшливый, тёплый и
влáжный.

mulatto, *n,* мулáт, -ка.

mulberry, *n,* шелкови́ца, ту́товое
дéрево.

mulch, *n,* прéлая солóма, прéлые
ли́стья.

mulct, *v.t,* штрафовáть; лишáть.

mule, *n,* мул; *(tech.)* мюль-маши́на;
(fig.) упря́мый осёл; **muleteer,**
n, погóнщик му́лов; **mulish,** *n,*
упря́мый как осёл.

mull, *v.t,* подогревáть с пря́ностями;
~ *over* обду́мывать.

mullet, *n,* кефáль.

mullion, *n,* срéдник.

multicoloured, *a,* цветнóй; разноцвéтный.

multifarious, *a,* разнообра́зный.

multi-millionaire, *n,* мультимиллионе́р.

multiple, *a,* сло́жный; многокра́тный, многочи́сленный; ¶ *n,* кра́тное число́: **multiplicand,** *n,* мно́жимое; **multiplication,** *n,* умноже́ние; увеличе́ние; **multiplicity,** *n,* разнообра́зие; сло́жность; многочи́сленность; **multiplier,** *n,* мно́житель; коэффицие́нт; **multiply,** *v.t,* умножа́ть; увели́чивать; *v.i,* увели́чиваться.

multitude, *n,* мно́жество; ма́сса; **multitudinous,** *a,* многочи́сленный.

mum: *keep* ~ пома́лкивать; ~'s *the word!* об э́том ни гугу́!

mumble, *v.i,* бормота́ть, мя́млить.

mummer, *n,* уча́стник пантоми́мы; ря́женый; ~у, *n,* пантоми́ма.

mummify, *v.t,* мумифици́ровать; **mummy,** *n,* му́мия; ма́ма.

mumps, *n,* сви́нка.

munch, *v.t,* жева́ть.

mundane, *a,* све́тский, мирско́й; прозаи́ческий.

municipal, *a,* городско́й, муниципа́льный; ~**ity,** *n,* го́род (с самоуправле́нием); муниципалите́т.

munificence, *n,* ще́дрость; **munificent,** *a,* ще́дрый.

munitions, *n.pl,* вое́нные запа́сы; снаряже́ние.

mural, *a,* стенно́й; ¶ *n,* стенна́я жи́вопись.

murder, *n,* уби́йство; ¶ *v.t,* убива́ть; *(fig.)* по́ртить; кове́ркать; ~**er,** *n,* уби́йца; ~**ous,** *a,* уби́йственный; крова́вый.

murky, *a,* тёмный; па́смурный.

murmur, *n,* журча́ние; ше́лест; шёпот; глухо́й шум, ро́пот; ¶ *v.i,* журча́ть; шелесте́ть; шепта́ть, ропта́ть.

murrain, *n,* чума́.

muscat, *n,* муска́т.

muscle, *n,* му́скул, мы́шца; **muscular,** *a,* му́скульный; му́скулистый.

Muscovite, *n,* москви́ч, -ка; ¶ *a,* моско́вский; ру́сский.

Muse, *n,* му́за.

muse, *v.i,* размышля́ть, заду́мываться; говори́ть заду́мчиво.

museum, *n,* музе́й.

mush, *n,* ка́ша.

mushroom, *n,* гриб; ¶ *a,* грибно́й.

music, *n,* му́зыка; но́ты; ~ *hall* мю́зик-хо́лл; ~ *stand* пюпи́тр;

~ *stool* табуре́т для роя́ля; ~**al,** *a,* музыка́льный; мелоди́чный; ~ *comedy* опере́тта, музыка́льная коме́дия; ~**ian,** *n,* музыка́нт; компози́тор.

musing, *n,* размышле́ние, заду́мчивость.

musk, *n,* му́скус; ~**-rat** онда́тра.

musket, *n,* мушке́т; ~**eer,** *n,* мушкетёр.

muslin, *n,* мусли́н.

musquash, *n,* онда́тра.

mussel, *n,* двуство́рчатая ра́ковина.

must, *v.aux,* до́лжен, должна́, *etc.; he* ~ *have gone* должно́ быть, он ушёл; *he* ~ *have missed the train* он, должно́ быть, опозда́л на по́езд.

must, *n,* пле́сень; молодо́е вино́.

mustard, *n,* горчи́ца; ¶ *a,* горчи́чный; ~ *plaster* горчи́чник; ~ *pot* горчи́чница.

mustiness, *n,* за́тхлость; **musty,** *a,* за́тхлый.

mutability, *n,* переме́нчивость; **mutation,** *n,* измене́ние, переме́на; *(biol.)* мута́ция; *(phon.)* перегласо́вка.

mute, *a,* немо́й; безмо́лвный; ¶ *n,* немо́й; *(mus.)* сурди́нка; ~**d,** *p.p. & a,* приглушённый.

mutilate, *v.t,* уве́чить; искажа́ть; **mutilation,** *n,* уве́чье; искаже́ние.

mutineer, *n,* мяте́жник; **mutinous,***a,* мяте́жный; **mutiny,** *n,* мяте́ж, восста́ние; ¶ *v.i,* восстава́ть.

mutter, *v.t,* бормота́ть; *v.i,* ворча́ть; ¶ *n, &* ~**ing,** бормота́ние; ворча́ние.

mutton, *n,* бара́нина; *leg of* ~ бара́нья нога́; ~ *chop* бара́нья котле́та.

mutual, *a,* взаи́мный, обою́дный; о́бщий; ~ *account* о́бщий счёт; ~ *friend* о́бщий друг; ~ *relations* взаимоотноше́ния; *to* ~ *advantage* взаимовы́годно; ~**ly,** *ad,* взаи́мно.

muzzle, *n,* мо́рда; намо́рдник *(for dog); (of gun);* ~ *loading* заря́дка с ду́ла; ¶ *v.t,* надева́ть намо́рдник на; заставля́ть молча́ть.

my, *a,* мой, моя́, моё, мой.

myopia, *n,* близору́кость.

myriad, *n,* несме́тное число́, мириа́да.

myrmidon, *n*, прислу́жник.
myrrh, *n*, ми́рра.
myrtle, *n*, мирт.
myself, *pn*, *(refl.)*, себя́, себе́, *etc;* *(emphatic)* сам, сама́; *I see ~ in a mirror* я ви́жу себя́ в зе́ркале; *I ~ saw it* я сам ви́дел э́то.
mysterious, *a*, таи́нственный; непостижи́мый; **mystery**, *n*, та́йна; ~ *play* мисте́рия; **mystic**, *n*, ми́стик; ~**al**, *a*, мисти́ческий; таи́нственный; ~**ism**, *n*, мистици́зм; **mystification**, *n*, мистифика́ция; **mystify**, *v.t*, мистифици́ровать; озада́чивать.
myth, *n*, миф; ~**ical**, *a*, мифи́ческий; ~**ological**, *a*, мифологи́ческий; ~**ology**, *n*, мифоло́гия.

N

nab, *v.t*, *(coll.)* аресто́вывать, лови́ть.
nadir, *n*, са́мая ни́зкая то́чка; упа́док.
nag, *n*, кля́ча; ¶ *v.t*, *(coll.)* пили́ть **nagging**, *n*, нытьё.
naiad, *n*, найя́да.
nail, *n*, но́готь; ко́готь; гвоздь; ~ *brush* щёточка для ногте́й; ~ *file* пи́лочка для ногте́й; *on the* *(fig.)* неме́дленно, сра́зу; *hit the* ~ *on the head* попада́ть в то́чку; ¶ *v.t*, прибива́ть; пригвожда́ть; ~ *down* прибива́ть; *(fig.)* прижима́ть к стене́; ~ *up* закола́чивать.
naive, *a*, наи́вный; безыску́сственный; ~**ty**, *n*, наи́вность; безыску́сственность.
naked, *a*, го́лый, наго́й, обнажённый; ~ *eye* невооружённый глаз; ~ *sword* обнажённый меч; ~ *truth* неприкра́шенная пра́вда; ~ *wire* неизоли́рованный про́вод; ~**ness**, *n*, нагота́, обнажённость.
namby-pamby, *a*, изне́женный; жема́нный.
name, и́мя; фами́лия; назва́ние; репута́ция; *by* ~ по и́мени; *in God's* ~*!* ра́ди бо́га!; *in the* ~ *of* во и́мя; *от и́мени; call* ~*s* руга́ть, обзыва́ть; *make a* ~ *for os.* создава́ть себе́ и́мя; ~*-day* имени́ны; ~*-plate* доще́чка с и́менем; ~*sake* тёзка; *what is your* ~? как вас зову́т?; ¶ *v.t*, называ́ть; наз-

нача́ть; ~**less**, *a*, безымя́нный; анони́мный; неизве́стный; ~**ly**, *ad*, и́менно, то́ есть.
nankeen, *n*, на́нка; *pl*, на́нковые брю́ки.
nanny, *n*, ня́ня; ~*-goat* коза́.
nap, *n*, коро́ткий сон; ворс *(on fabric);* *have a* ~ вздремну́ть *(pf.);* *catch napping* застига́ть враспло́х.
nape [*of neck*], *n*, заты́лок.
napery, *n*, столо́вое бельё.
naphtha, *n*, нефть; кероси́н; ~**lene**, *n*, нафтали́н.
napkin, *n*, салфе́тка; пелёнка; ~*ring* кольцо́ для салфе́тки.
narcissus, *n*, нарци́сс.
narcotic, *a*, наркоти́ческий; ¶ *n*, нарко́тик.
narrate, *v.t*, расска́зывать; повествова́ть о; **narration**, *n*, расска́з; повествова́ние; **narrative**, *a*, повествова́тельный; ¶ *n*, расска́з, повествова́ние; **narrator**, *n*, расска́зчик.
narrow, *a*, у́зкий; те́сный; ограни́ченный *(minded);* ~*-gauge* узкоколе́йный; ~ *v.t.* *(& i.),* су́живать(ся); уменьша́ть(ся); ~**ly**, *ad*, чуть; при́стально; ~**ness**, *n*, у́зость; ограни́ченность.
nasal, *a*, носово́й; гнуса́вый; ~**ize**, *v.t*, говори́ть в нос.
nascent, *a*, возника́ющий, рожда́ющийся.
nastiness, *n*, га́дость; отврати́тельность.
nasturtium, *n*, насту́рция.
nasty, *a*, га́дкий, отврати́тельный.
natal, *a*, относя́щийся к рожде́нию.
natation, *n*, пла́вание.
nation, *n*, на́ция, наро́д; госуда́рство; ~**al**, *n*, по́дданный; ¶ *a*, национа́льный, наро́дный; госуда́рственный; ~ *anthem* госуда́рственный гимн; ~ *economy* наро́дное хозя́йство; ~**alism**, *n*, национали́зм; ~**alist**, *n*, национали́ст; ¶ *a*, националисти́ческий; ~**ality**, *n*, национа́льность; гражда́нство, по́дданство; ~**alization**, *n*, национализа́ция; ~**alize**, *v.t*, национализи́ровать.
native, *a*, родно́й, оте́чественный; прирождённый, приро́дный; тузе́мный, ме́стный; ~ *land* ро́дина; ~ *tongue* родно́й язы́к; ¶ *n*,

тузе́мец; уроже́нец; **nativity,** n, рожде́ние; *(eccl.)* Рождество́.

natty, a, мо́дный, изя́щный.

natural, a, есте́ственный; приро́дный; норма́льный; непринуждённый; прису́щий; внебра́чный *(child);* ¶ n, *(mus.)* ключ С, бека́р; саморо́док; идио́т; ~**ist,** n, естествоиспыта́тель; натура́лист; ~**ization,** n, натурализа́ция; акклиматиза́ция; ~**ize,** v.t, натурализова́ть; акклиматизи́ровать; ~**ly,** ad, коне́чно; есте́ственно; по приро́де; ~**ness,** n, есте́ственность; непринуждённость; **nature,** n, приро́да, естество́; хара́ктер; род; *from* ~ с нату́ры.

naught, n, ничто́; ноль.

naughtiness, n, непослуша́ние, шаловли́вость; **naughty,** a, непослу́шный, шаловли́вый; де́рзкий.

nausea, n, тошнота́; отвраще́ние; ~**te,** v.t, вызыва́ть отвраще́ние у; ~**ting,** n, отврати́тельный.

nautical, a, морско́й, морехо́дный; ~ *mile* морска́я ми́ля.

nautilus, n, наути́лус.

naval, a, вое́нно-морско́й, морско́й.

nave, n, неф, кора́бль *(church);* ступи́ца колеса́.

navel, n, пупо́к, пуп; ~ *cord* пупови́на.

navigable, a, судохо́дный; управля́емый; **navigate,** v.t, управля́ть (су́дном/самолётом); v.i, пла́вать; лета́ть; **navigation,** n, навига́ция; аэронавига́ция; судохо́дство; пла́вание; **navigator,** n, морепла́ватель; штурма́н.

navvy, n, чернорабо́чий, землеко́п; *work like a* ~ рабо́тать как вол.

navy, n, вое́нно-морско́й флот; ~ *blue* тёмно-си́ний; ~ *list* спи́сок офице́ров вое́нно-морско́го фло́та; ~ *yard* вое́нная верфь.

nay, *neg.particle* нет; да́же, ма́ло того́.

Nazi, n, наци́ст.

Neapolitan, a, неаполита́нский.

neap tide, n, квадрату́рный прили́в.

near, pr, во́зле, о́коло, у; бли́зко от; ¶ ad, бли́зко; почти́, чуть не; ¶ a, бли́зкий; сосе́дний; скупо́й; ~ *relative* бли́зкий ро́дственник; ~ *side* ле́вая/пра́вая сторона́; ~ *sighted* близору́кий; *N*~ *East*

Бли́жний Восто́к; ~ *at hand* под руко́й; ¶ v.i, приближа́ться; ~**ly,** ad, почти́, чуть не; приблизи́тельно; *I* ~ *fell* я чуть не упа́л; ~**ness,** n, бли́зость; скупость.

neat, a, опря́тный; аккура́тный; то́чный; чёткий; ло́вкий; чи́стый *(spirits);* ¶ n, бык, коро́ва; ~*'s leather* воло́вья ко́жа; ~**ness,** n, опря́тность; чёткость.

nebulous, a, сму́тный, тума́нный, о́блачный.

necessaries, n.pl, предме́ты пе́рвой необходи́мости; **necessarily,** ad, неизбе́жно. **necessary,** a, необходи́мый; ну́жный; неизбе́жный; ¶ n, необходи́мое; **necessitate,** v.t, де́лать необходи́мым; тре́бовать; **necessitous,** a, нужда́ющийся; **necessity,** n, необходи́мость; неизбе́жность; pl, предме́ты пе́рвой необходи́мости.

neck, n, ше́я; го́рлышко *(of bottle);* гриф *(of violin);* воротни́к; *(geogr.)* переше́ек; ~ *or nothing* ли́бо пан, ли́бо пропа́л; *break one's* ~ сверну́ть *(pf.)* себе́ ше́ю; *get it in the* ~ получи́ть *(pf.)* по ше́е; ~*band* во́рот; ~*erchief* плато́к; ~*lace* ожере́лье; ~ *and* ~ *(ad.)* голова́ в го́лову; *(fig.)* в ра́вном положе́нии.

necrology, n, некроло́г.

necromancer, n, колду́н.

necromancy, n, чёрная ма́гия.

necropolis, n, некро́поль.

nectar, n, некта́р; ~**ine,** n, гла́дкий пе́рсик.

need, n, нужда́; на́добность, потре́бность; *if* ~ *be* е́сли ну́жно; ¶ v.t, нужда́ться в; име́ть потре́бность в; *it* ~ *s to be done* на́до э́то сде́лать *(pf.);* ~**ful,** a, ну́жный, необходи́мый.

needle, n, игла́, иго́лка; спи́ца *(knitting);* стре́лка *(compass);* ~*-case* иго́льник; ~*woman* швея́; ~*work* шитьё; вы́шивка.

needless, a, нену́жный, изли́шний; ~ *to say* не прихо́дится и говори́ть; коне́чно; **needy,** a, нужда́ющийся.

ne'er-do-well, n, безде́льник, него́дник; ¶ a, никуда́ не го́дный.

nefarious, a, ни́зкий, гну́сный, бесче́стный.

negation, n, отрица́ние; **negative,** a, отрица́тельный: *(phot.)* негати́вный; ¶ *n*, отрицáние, отрицáтельный отвéт; *(phot.)* негатúв; ¶ *v.t*, отрицáть; налагáть вéто на; отвергáть.

neglect, *n*, пренебрежéние; забрóшенность, запýщенность; *fall into* ~ приходúть в состоя́ние запýщенности; ¶ *v.t*, пренебрегáть *(inst.);* запускáть; не забóтиться о; упускáть; ~ *one's duties* не выполня́ть своúх обя́занностей; **~ful**, *a*, невнимáтельный, нерадúвый; **negligée**, *n*, дáмский халáт; **negligence**, *n*, небрéжность; халáтность; нерадúвость; **negligent**, *a*, небрéжный, халáтный, нерадúвый; **negligible**, *a*, незначúтельный.

negotiable, *a*, реализýемый; проходúмый; **negotiate**, *v.t*, договáриваться о; реализовáть; преодолевáть; *v.i*, вестú переговóры; **negotiation**, *n*, переговóры; обсуждéние; *enter into* ~ вступáть в переговóры; **negotiator**, *n*, учáстник переговóров; посрéдник.

negress, *n*, негритя́нка; **negro**, *a*, негритя́нский; ¶ *n*, негр; **negroid**, *n*, негрóидный.

neigh, *n*, ржáние; ¶ *v.i*, ржать.

neighbour, *n*, сосéд, -ка; *love one's* ~ любúть блúжнего; **~hood**, *n*, окрéстности; **~ing**, *a*, сосéдний, смéжный; **~ly**, *a*, добрососéдский.

neither, *a. & pn*, никакóй; ни тот, ни другóй; ¶ *c*, ни; ~ ... *nor* ... ни ... ни ...; ¶ *ad*, тáкже/тóже не.

Nemesis, *n*, немезúда.

neo-, *prefix*, нео- **neologism**, *n*, неологúзм.

neon, *n*, неóн.

neophyte, *n*, неофúт, новообращённый.

nephew, *n*, племя́нник.

nepotism, *n*, кумовствó.

nerve, *n*, нерв; хладнокрóвие; *(coll.)* нахáльство; *(bot.)* жúлка; *pl*, нéрвность, нéрвы; ¶ *v*: ~ *oneself* собирáться с силами; **~less**, *a*, не имéющий нéрвной систéмы; вя́лый; бесстрáшный; **nervous**, *a*, нéрвный; *be* ~ *about* волновáться/нéрвничать о; ~ *breakdown* нéрвное расстрóйство; **nervy**, *a*, нéрвный.

nest, *n*, гнездó; **~-egg** пóдкладень; *(fig.)* сбережéния; ¶ *v.i*, гнездúться; **~le**, *v.i*, ую́тно устрáиваться; ~ *up to* прижимáться к; **~ling**, *n*, птенéц.

net, [*& network*], *n*, сеть; сéтка; тенёта; ¶ *a*, чúстый, нéтто; ~ *cost* себестóимость; ~ *price* ценá без скúдки; ~ *profit* чúстый дохóд; ~ *weight* вес нéтто; ¶ *v.t*, ловúть сéтью/сéткой; покрывáть сéтью; плестú; получáть/приносúть чúстый дохóд.

nether, *a*, нúжний, бóлее нúзкий; ~ *regions* ад. **Netherlander**, *n*, голлáндец; **Netherlands**, *a*, нидерлáндский, голлáндский.

nethermost, *a*, сáмый нúжний/зáдний.

netting, *n*, сеть, сéтка; плетéние сетéй.

nettle, *n*, крапúва; **~rash** крапúвная лихорáдка; ¶ *v.t*, раздражáть, уязвля́ть.

network see **net**.

neuralgia, *n*, невралгúя; **neuralgic**, *a*, невралгúческий; **neurasthenia**, *n*, неврастенúя; **neurasthenic**, *a*, неврастенúческий; **neuritis**, *n*, неврúт; **neurologist**, *n*, неврóлог; **neurology**, *n*, невролóгия; **neurosis**, *n*, неврóз; **neurotic**, *a*, невротúческий, нéрвный.

neuter, *a*, срéднего рóда; ¶ *n*, срéдний род; **neutral**, *a*, нейтрáльный; **~ity**, *n*, нейтралитéт; **~ize**, *v.t*, нейтрализовáть; обезврéживать.

never, *ad*, никогдá; **~-ending** бесконéчный; ~ *fear!* не беспокóйтесь!; ~ *mind!* ничегó!; ~ *more* никогдá бóльше; **~theless**, *ad. & c*, тем не мéнее, однáко.

new, *a*, нóвый; свéжий; **~-born** новорождённый **~comer** приéзжий, новоприбы́вший; новичóк; **~-fangled** новомóдный; **N~foundland dog** ньюфáундлéнд; **~-laid** свежеснесённое (яйцó); **~-mown** свежескóшенный; **N~ Year** нóвый год; **N~ Year's Day** пéрвое января́; **N~ Year gift** новогóдний подáрок.

newel, *n*, стéржень винтовóй лéстницы; стóйка перúл.

newly, *ad*, вновь; недáвно; **~-weds** новобрáчные; **newness**, *n*, новизнá.

news, n, но́вость, изве́стие; кино-
журна́л; ~agent газе́тчик; ~-boy
продаве́ц/разно́счик газе́т; ~ bulletin бюллете́нь после́дних из-
ве́стий; ~ items но́вости; ~monger
спле́тник; ~paper газе́та; ~print
газе́тная бума́га; ~ theatre кино-
теа́тр хроника́льных и докумен-
та́льных фи́льмов; ~reel кино-
журна́л, кинохро́ника; ~-stand
газе́тный кио́ск; stop-press ~
э́кстренные сообще́ния.

newt, n, трито́н.

next, a, сле́дующий; бу́дущий; сосе́д-
ний, ближа́йший; ~-door neigh-
bour ближа́йший сосе́д; ~ door to
ря́дом с, по сосе́дству с; on the ~
day на сле́дующий день; the ~
life загро́бная жизнь; ~ of kin
ближа́йший ро́дственник; ¶ ad,
пото́м, по́сле; в сле́дующий раз;
~ to ря́дом с; what ~? что же
да́льше?.

nexus, n, связь; звено́.

nib, n, остриё пера́.

nibble, n, обгрыза́ние; ¶ v.t, грызть,
обгрыза́ть; щипа́ть; клева́ть (of
fish).

nice, a, прия́тный; любе́зный, ми́-
лый; делика́тный; a ~ question
делика́тный вопро́с; it is ~ and
warm дово́льно тепло́; ~ly, ad,
хорошо́; прия́тно; ~ness, n, прия́т-
ность; любе́зность; ~ty, n, то́ч-
ность; pl, то́нкости; to a ~ то́чно,
как сле́дует.

niche, n, ни́ша.

nick, n, зару́бка, засе́чка; in the ~
of time как раз во́-время; ¶ v.t,
де́лать зару́бку в/на.

nickel, n, ни́кель; моне́та в 5 це́нтов;
¶ a, ни́келевый; ~-plated никели-
ро́ванный.

nick-nack, n, безделу́шка.

nickname, n, про́звище; ¶v.t, дава́ть
про́звище (dat.).

nicotine, n, никоти́н.

niece, n, племя́нница.

niggardliness, n, ску́пость; ску́д-
ность; **niggardly,** a, скупо́й; ску́д-
ный.

nigh, ad, бли́зко, ря́дом; почти́; ¶ a,
бли́зкий.

night, n, ночь; ве́чер; at ~ но́чью,
ве́чером; good ~! споко́йной но́чи!;
last ~ вчера́ ве́чером; the ~ before
last позавчера́ ве́чером; ~cap
ночно́й колпа́к; (fig.) стака́нчик

спиртно́го на́ ночь; ~club ноч-
но́й клуб; ~dress ночна́я руба́шка;
~fall су́мерки; ~-light ночни́к;
~mare кошма́р; ~ school вече́рняя
шко́ла; ~shade (bot.) паслён; ~-
watchman ночно́й сто́рож.

nightingale, n, солове́й.

nightly, a, ежено́щный; ¶ ad, по
ноча́м, ка́ждую ночь.

nihilism, n, нигили́зм; **nihilist,** n,
нигили́ст.

nil, n, ноль, ничего́.

nimble, a, прово́рный, ло́вкий; ги́б-
кий (mind); живо́й; ~-footed
лёгкий на́ ногу; ~ness, n, про-
во́рность; ло́вкость; ги́бкость;
жи́вость.

nimbus, n, нимб, орео́л.

nincompoop, n, простофи́ля.

nine, num, де́вять; ¶ n, девя́тка; ~
pins ке́гли; dressed to the ~s рас-
франчённый; ~teen, num, дев-
ятна́дцать; ~teenth, ord.num, дев-
ятна́дцатый; ~tieth, ord.num, девя-
но́стый; ~ty, num, девяно́сто.

ninny, n, простофи́ля.

ninth, ord.num, девя́тый; ¶ n, дев-
я́тая часть; девя́тое число́.

nip, n, щипо́к; глото́чек; кусо́чек;
¶ v.t, щипа́ть; куса́ть; (tech.)
зажима́ть; поби́ть (pf.) (of frost);
~ in the bud пресека́ть в ко́рне;
~per, n, клешня́; (coll.) маль-
чи́шка, дитя́; pl, щипцы́, остро-
гу́бцы.

nipple, n, сосо́к; (tech.) ни́ппель.

nit, n, гни́да.

nitrate, n, нитра́т; **nitre,** n, сели́тра;
nitric, a, азо́тный; **nitro-glycerine,**
n, нитроглицери́н; **nitrogen,** n,
азо́т; **nitrous,** n, азо́тистый.

no, ad, нет; ¶ n, отка́з; отрица́ние;
¶ a, никако́й; ~ admittance вход
воспрещён; ~ doubt несомне́нно;
~ entry прое́зда нет; въезд воспрещён; it is ~ good бесполе́зно; ~
longer до́льше/бо́льше не; ~ matter безразли́чно; нева́жно; by ~
means ни в ко́ем слу́чае; ~ more
нечего/ничего́ бо́льше; бо́льше
нет; ~ one никто́; ~ smoking! не
кури́ть!; ~ sooner едва́; как
то́лько; ~ thoroughfare прямо́го
прое́зда нет; ~ wonder, that неу-
диви́тельно, что . . .

Noah's Ark, n, но́ев ковче́г.

nobility, n, дворя́нство; знать; бла-
горо́дство.

noble, *a,* благоро́дный; вели́чественный; зна́тный; дворя́нский; **~man,** *n,* дворяни́н; пэр *(in G. B.);* **~ness,** *n,* благоро́дство.

nobody, *pn,* никто́; *a* ~ ничто́жество.

nocturnal, *a,* ночно́й; **nocturne,** *n,* ноктю́рн.

nod, *n,* киво́к; ¶ *v.i,* кива́ть голово́й; наклоня́ться; дрема́ть; *nodding acquaintance* ша́почное знако́мство.

node, *n,* у́зел; *(med.)* наро́ст, утолще́ние; **nodule,** *n,* узело́к; *(med.)* узелко́вое утолще́ние.

noise, *n,* шум; ¶ *v.i:* ~ *abroad* распространя́ть, разглаша́ть; **~less,** *a,* бесшу́мный; **noisily,** *ad,* шу́мно; **noisiness,** *n,* шуми́вость.

noisome, *a,* вре́дный; злово́нный; отврати́тельный.

noisy, *a,* шу́мный.

nolens volens, во́лей-нево́лей.

nomad, *n,* коче́вник; **~ic,** *a,* коче-во́й.

no-man's land, *n,* ничья́ земля́.

nomenclature, *n,* номенклату́ра.

nominal, *a,* номина́льный; именно́й; ~ *sentence* усло́вный пригово́р.

nominate, *v.t,* называ́ть, выставля́ть кандида́том; назнача́ть; **nomination,** *n,* выставле́ние кандидату́ры; назначе́ние; **nominative-(case),** *n,* имени́тельный паде́ж; **nominee,** *n,* кандида́т.

non-, *prefix,* не-, без-; **~-acceptance** непри́нятие; **~-alcoholic** безалко́гольный; **~-appearance** нея́вка; **~-attendance** непосеще́ние заня́тий, прогу́л; **~-combatant** нестроево́й; **~-commissioned officer** у́нтер-офице́р; **~-committal** укло́нчивый; **~-existent** несуществу́ющий; **~-intervention** невмеша́тельство; **~-payment** неплатёж, неупла́та; **~-slip** нескользя́щий; **~-stop** безостано́вочный; *(avia.)* беспоса́дочный.

nonagenarian, *n,* девяностоле́тн|ий стари́к, -яя стару́ха.

nonce: *for the* ~ пока́, в да́нное вре́мя.

nonchalance, *n,* беззабо́тность; безразли́чие; **nonchalant,** *a,* беззабо́тный; безразли́чный.

nonconformist, *a,* оппозицио́нно настро́енный, инакомы́слящий; сек-

та́нтский; ¶ *n,* оппозицио́нно настро́енный челове́к; секта́нт.

nondescript, *a,* неопределённый; ничём не выдаю́щийся.

none, *pn,* никто́; ничто́; никако́й; ~ *of that!* хва́тит!; ¶ *ad,* ниско́лько, совсе́м не; *he was* ~ *the worse* он был ничу́ть не ху́же; ~ *the less* тем не ме́нее.

nonentity, *n,* ничто́жество; небытие́.

nonplus, *v.t,* смуща́ть, приводи́ть в замеша́тельство; ста́вить в тупи́к.

nonsense, *n,* вздор, ерунда́; бессмы́слица; пустяки́; глу́пости; ¶ *int,* вздор!; **nonsensical,** *a,* глу́пый; бессмы́сленный.

noodle, *n,* глупе́ц, балда́; *pl,* лапша́.

nook, *n,* у́гол; укро́мный уголо́к.

noon, *n,* по́лдень; ¶ *a,* полу́денный.

noose, *n,* пе́тля; аркан; лову́шка.

nor, *c,* и не, та́кже не, ни.

Nordic, *a,* скандина́вский.

norm, *n,* но́рма; образе́ц; **~al,** *a,* норма́льный, обыкнове́нный; **~ality,** *n,* норма́льность, норма́льное состоя́ние; **~alize,** *v.t,* нормализова́ть.

Norman, *a,* норма́ндский; ¶ *n,* норма́ндец.

Norse, *a,* норве́жский; древнескандина́вский; ¶ *n,* дре́вний скандина́в; норве́жец.

north, *n,* се́вер; ¶ *ad,* на се́вер, к се́веру; ¶ *a,* се́верный; ~ *east* се́веро-восто́к; *(mar.)* норд-о́ст; **~-eastern** се́веро-восто́чный; ~ *west* се́веро-за́пад; *(mar.)* норд-ве́ст; **~-western** се́веро-за́падный; **~erly,** *a,* се́верный; обращённый к се́веру; **~ern,** *a,* се́верный; ~ *lights* се́верное сия́ние; **~erner,** *n,* северя́нин; **~wards,** *ad,* на се́вер, к се́веру.

Norwegian, *a,* норве́жский; ¶ *n,* норве́ж|ец, **~ка;** норве́жский язы́к.

nose, *n,* нос; чутьё, нюх; обоня́ние; *speak through the* ~ говори́ть в нос; *turn one's* ~ *up at* задира́ть нос пе́ред; вороти́ть нос от; *have a good* ~ *for* име́ть чутьё на; **~-bag** то́рба; **~-dive** *(n.)* пики́рование; *(v.i.)* пики́ровать; **~gay** буке́т; ¶ *v.t. & i:* ~ *about* вы́искивать; ~ *forward* осторо́жно продвига́ться вперёд; ~ *out* выве́дывать, разню́хивать.

nostalgia, *n*, ностальгия, тоска (по родине); **nostalgic**, *a*, тоскливый.

nostril, *n*, ноздря.

nostrum, *n*, панацея от всех болезней; излюбленный приём.

not, *ad*, не, ни; ~ *at all* нисколько (не), ничуть (не); вовсе не; не стоит (благодарности); нисколько; ~ *yet* ещё не(т); *she sings well, does she* ~? она хорошо поёт, не правда ли?.

notability, *n*, знаменитость; известность; **notable**, *a*, заметный; значительный; **notably**, *ad*, особенно; значительно.

notary, *n*, нотариус.

notation, *n*, запись; примечание.

notch, *n*, зарубка; ¶ *v.t*, делать зарубку в/на.

note, *n*, записка, заметка; замечание, примечание; банковый билет; *(mus.)* нота; дипломатическая нота; тон; ~*-book* записная книжка; ~*-case* бумажник; ~ *paper* почтовая бумага; ¶ *v.t*, замечать, отмечать; записывать; ~**d**, *a*, знаменитый; ~**worthy**, *a*, достойный внимания; достопримечательный.

nothing, *pn*, ничто, ничего; ¶ *n*, пустяк: *(maths)* нуль; *that is* ~ *to* мэто меня не касается; *for* ~ напрасно, зря; даром; из-за пустяка; *come to* ~ кончаться ничем; *sweet* ~*s* нежности, любезности; ~**ness**, *n*, ничто; небытие.

notice, *n*, уведомление; объявление; внимание; наблюдение; увольнение; *at a moment's* ~ немедленно, по первому требованию; *escape* ~ ускользать от внимания; *give* ~ предупреждать (об увольнении); *(at) short* ~ (в/за) короткий срок; *take* ~ *of* обращать внимание на; ~ *board* доска для объявлений; ¶ *v.t*, замечать; ~**able**, *a*, заметный; **notification**, *n*, извещение; **notify**, *v.t*, извещать, уведомлять.

notion, *n*, понятие, представление; ~**al**, *a*, воображаемый; умозрительный.

notoriety, *n*, известность; дурная слава; **notorious**, *a*, известный; пресловутый.

notwithstanding, *pr*, несмотря на; ¶ *ad*, тем не менее; ¶ *c*, хотя.

nougat, *n*, нуга.

nought, *n*, ничто; ноль.

noun, *n*, имя существительное; *common* ~ имя нарицательное; *proper* ~ имя собственное.

nourish, *v.t*, питать; ~**ing**, *a*, питательный; ~**ment**, *n*, питание, пища.

novel, *n*, роман; ¶ *a*, новый; необыкновенный; ~**ette**, *n*, новелла; ~**ist**, *n*, романист; ~**ty**, *n*, новизна; новость; новшество; новинка.

November, *n*, ноябрь; ¶ *a*, ноябрьский.

novice, *n*, новичок; послуш|ник, ~ница.

now, *ad*, теперь; сейчас; ~ ... ~ .... то ... то ...; ~ *and again* время от времени; *just* ~ только что; сейчас; ~ *then!* ну!; ~ *and then* иногда; ~ *that* теперь, когда; *from* ~ *on* впредь; в дальнейшем; ~**adays**, *ad*, в наши дни.

nowhere, *ad*, нигде, никуда.

nowise, *ad*, никоим образом; вовсе нет.

noxious, *a*, вредный, пагубный.

nozzle, *n*, носик; выпускное отверстие.

nuance, *n*, нюанс.

nuclear, *a*, ядерный; **nucleus**, *n*, ядро; ячейка; центр.

nude, *a*, нагой, голый; ¶ *n*, обнажённая фигура.

nudge, *n*, лёгкий толчок; ¶ *v.t*, слегка подталкивать.

nudity, *n*, нагота.

nugatory, *a*, напрасный; пустячный.

nugget, *n*, самородок.

nuisance, *n*, досада, неприятность; надоедливый человек; *what a* ~! какая досада!.

null, *a*, недействительный; потерявший законную силу; ~**ify**, *v.t*, аннулировать; делать недействительным; ~**ity**, *n*, недействительность; ничтожество.

numb, *a*, онемелый; окоченелый (от холода); ¶ *v.t*, вызывать онемение/окоченение у/в.

number, *n*, число, количество; номер; выпуск; ~ *plate* номерная дощечка; *a* ~ *of* ряд; *quite a* ~ довольно много; *in large* ~*s* в большом количестве; ¶ *v.t*, нумеровать; причислять; насчитывать; ~**ing**, *n*, нумерация; ~**less**, *a*, бесчисленный.

numbness, *n*, окоченéлость; оцепенéние.

numeral, *a*, числовóй; цифровóй; ¶ *n*, имя числи́тельное; **numerator**, *n*, числи́тель; *(tech.)* нумерáтор; **numerical**, *a*, числовóй; цифровóй; **numerous**, *a*, многочи́сленный.

numismatics, *n*, нумизмáтика.

numskull, *n*, болвáн.

nun, *n*, монáхиня

nuncio, *n*, пáпский нýнций.

nunnery, *n*, жéнский монасты́рь.

nuptial, *a*, брáчный, свáдебный; ~s, *n.pl*, свáдьба.

nurse, *n*, меди́цинская сестрá; сидéлка; нáня; корми́лица; ¶ *v.t*, ухáживать за; нáнчить; *(fig.)* лелéять, таи́ть; ~ry, *n*, дéтская; я́сли: питóмник, ~ *rhymes* дéтские стишки́; ~ *school* дéтский сад; **nursing**, *n*, ухóд; выкáрмливание: рабóта/профéссия медсестры́; ~ *home* чáстная лечéбница.

nurture, *v.t*, питáть; воспи́тывать; вырáщивать.

nut, *n*, орéх; гáйка; *pl*, мéлкий ýголь; ~-*brown* орéхового цвéта; ~*crackers* щипцы́ для орéхов; ~*shell* орéховая скорлупá; *in a* ~ в двух словáх; ~-*tree* орéшник.

nutmeg, *n*, мускáтный орéх.

nutriment, *n*, пи́ща; питáтельное вещество́; **nutritious**, *a*, питáтельный.

nutty, *a*, имéющий вкус орéха.

nuzzle, *v.t*, ню́хать; рыть (нóсом/ры́лом); ~ *into* совáть нос в; прижимáться к.

nylon, *n*, нейлóн; *pl*, нейлóновые чулки́.

nymph, *n*, ни́мфа.

O

O!, *int*, о!; ~ *my!* бóже мой!

oaf, *n*, óлух.

oak, *n*, дуб; ~-*apple* черни́льный орéшек; ~ *grove* дубрáва; ~en, *a*, дубóвый.

oakum, *n*, пáкля.

oar, *n*, веслó; ~sman, *n*, гребéц.

oasis, *n*, оáзис.

oast, *n*, суши́льная печь.

oats, *n.pl*, овёс: **oatmeal** овся́нка.

oath, *n*, кля́тва; прися́га; *on* ~ под прися́гой; *take an* ~ давáть кля́тву/прися́гу.

obduracy, *n*, упря́мство; **obdurate**, *a*, упря́мый; чёрствый.

obedience, *n*, послушáние, повиновéние; покóрность; **obedient**, *a*, послýшный; покóрный; **obeisance**, *n*, реверáнс, глубóкий поклóн; уважéние.

obelisk, *n*, обели́ск.

obese, *a*, тýчный; **obesity**, *n*, тýчность, полнотá.

obey, *v.t*, слýшаться *(gen.)*, повиновáться *(dat.)*; подчиня́ться *(dat.)*.

obituary, *n*, некролóг; спи́сок умéрших; ¶ *a*, некрологи́ческий, похорóнный.

object, *n*, предмéт, вещь; цель; *(gram.)* дополнéние; *(philos.)* объéкт; ~ *lesson* нагля́дный урóк; ¶ *v.i*, возражáть, протестовáть; не люби́ть; ~ion, *n*, возражéние, протéст: *I have no* ~ я не прóтив; ~ionable, *a*, неприя́тный; нежелáтельный; ~ive, *a*, объекти́вный; ¶ *n*, цель; ~ivity, *n*, объекти́вность.

objurgate, *v.t*, попрекáть; **objurgation**, *n*, упрёк.

oblation, *n*, пожéртвование, жéртва.

obligate, *v.t*, обя́зывать; **obligation**, *n*, обязáтельство; обя́занность, долг; *be under an* ~ *to* быть в долгý пéред; **obligatory**, *a*, обязáтельный; **oblige**, *v.t*, обя́зывать; заставля́ть; дéлать одолжéние *(dat.)*; *be* ~d быть обя́занным; быть благодáрным; **obliging**, *a*, любéзный, услýжливый.

oblique, *a*, косóй, наклóнный; *(gram.)* кóсвенный; **obliquity**, *n*, наклóнность; отклонéние от прямóго пути́.

obliterate, *v.t*, вычёркивать; стирáть; **obliteration**, *n*, вычёркивание; стирáние.

oblivion, *n*, забвéние; **oblivious**, *a*, забы́вчивый.

oblong, *a*, продолговáтый; ¶ *n*, продолговáтая фигýра.

obloquy, *n*, поношéние; позóр.

oboe, *n*, гобóй; **oboist**, *n*, гобои́ст.

obscene, *a*, непристóйный, бессты́дный; **obscenity**, *n*, непристóйность, бессты́дство.

obscure, *a*, нея́сный; мýтный; тýсклый; ¶ *v.t*, затемня́ть; дéлать неясным; делать невидным; **obscurity**, *n*, неизвестность; неясность; непонятность.

obsequies, *n.pl*, похороны.

obsequious, *a*, подобострастный; ~ness, *n*, подобострастие.

observable, *a*, заметный, различимый; **observance**, *n*, соблюдение; ритуал; **observant**, *a*, наблюдательный; **observation**, *n*, наблюдение; замечание; ~ *post* наблюдательный пункт; **observatory**, *n*, обсерватория; **observe**, *v.t*, наблюдать; соблюдать *(rules)*; замечать; ~**r**, *n*, наблюдатель.

obsess, *v.t*, преследовать; овладевать *(inst.)*; ~*ed by* поглощённый *(inst.)*; одержимый *(inst.)*; ~**ion**, *n*, навязчивая идея; одержимость.

obsolescent, *a*, выходящий из употребления, отживающий; **obsolete**, *a*, устарелый, отживший.

obstacle, *n*, препятствие, помеха.

obstetric(al), *a*, акушерский; **obstetrics**, *n*, акушерство.

obstinacy, *n*, упрямство; **obstinate**, *a*, упрямый.

obstreperous, *a*, буйный, шумный.

obstruct, *v.t*, заграждать, преграждать; препятствовать *(dat.)*; ~ *the view* заслонять вид; ~**ion**, *n*, заграждение; препятствие.

obtain, *v.t*, получать; доставать; добывать; достигать *(gen.)*; *v.i*, существовать; ~**able**, *a*, доступный, достижимый.

obtrude, *v.i*, вторгаться; *v.t*, навязывать; ~ *oneself* навязываться; **obtrusive**, *a*, навязчивый.

obtuse, *a*, глупый, тупой.

obverse, *n*, лицевая сторона.

obviate, *v.t*, избегать *(gen.)*; устранять.

obvious, *a*, очевидный, явный; ~**ly**, *ad*, очевидно.

occasion, *n*, случай; событие; возможность; повод; основание; *have* ~ *for complaint* иметь основание для жалобы; *give* ~ *for* давать повод для; *on the* ~ *of* по случаю; ¶ *v.t*, вызывать; причинять; служить поводом для; ~**al**, *a*, случайный; ~**ally**, *ad*, изредка, иногда.

occident, *n*, запад; ~**al**, *a*, западный.

occult, *a*, тайный; таинственный; оккультный; ~**ism**, *n*, оккультизм.

occupancy, *n*, аренда; завладение; занятие; **occupant**, *n*, житель; арендатор; занимающий (должность); оккупант; **occupation**, *n*, занятие; профессия; пользование; оккупация; **occupier**, *n*, жилец, арендатор; **occupy**, *v.t*, занимать; арендовать; оккупировать; *be occupied in* ~ заниматься *(inst.)*.

occur, *v.i*, происходить, случаться; встречаться; приходить на ум/в голову; *it* ~*red to me that* мне пришло в голову, что ...; ~**rence**, *n*, случай, событие, происшествие; местонахождение.

ocean, *n*, океан; *an* ~ *of tears* море слёз; ~ *liner* океанский пароход.

ochre, *n*, охра.

o'clock: *at five* ~ в пять часов; *at about one* ~ около часа.

octagon, *n*, восьмиугольник; ~**al**, *a*, восьмиугольный.

octave, *n*, октава.

octet, *n*, октет.

October, *n*, октябрь; ¶ *a*, октябрьский.

octogenarian, *a*, восьмидесятилетний. ¶ *n*, восьмидесятилет|ний старик, -яя старуха.

octopus, *n*, осьминог, спрут.

ocular, *a*, глазной; **oculist**, *n*, окулист.

odd, *a*, нечётный; непарный; случайный; странный; ~ *job* случайная работа; *at* ~ *times* между делом; *twenty* ~ двадцать с лишним; ~**ity**, *n*, странность; *(pers.)* чудак; ~**ly**, *ad*, странно; ~**ments**, *n.pl*, разрозненные предметы; остатки; ~ *sale* распродажа разрозненных товаров; ~**ness**, *n*, странность, необычность; ~**s**, *n.pl*, шансы; ~ *and ends* обрезки, остатки; хлам; *be at* ~ быть в ссоре; *fight against* ~ бороться против значительно превосходящих сил.

ode, *n*, ода.

odious, *a*, отвратительный; **odium**, *n*, позор; ненависть.

odoriferous, & **odorous**, *a*, благоухающий; **odour**, *n*, запах, аромат; ~**less**, *a*, без запаха.

Odyssey, *n*, Одиссея.

of, *pr*, *expressed by genitive case or various prepositions;* ~ *course* конечно; ~ *late* за последнее время; *one* ~ *them* один из них;

smell ~ *flowers* па́хнуть цвета́ми; *think* ~ ду́мать о; *be afraid* ~ боя́ться *(gen.); be proud* ~ горди́ться *(inst.); a piece* ~ *bread* кусо́к хле́ба.

off, *pr,* с, от; *be* ~ уходи́ть, уезжа́ть; *hands* ~ ру́ки прочь (от); ~ *hand (ad)* бесцеремо́нно; невнима́тельно; *(a)* бесцеремо́нный, невнима́тельный; *a mile* ~ в одно́й ми́ле от; *be badly* ~ быть бе́дным; ~ *and on* вре́мя от вре́мени; нерегуля́рно; *it's all* ~ всё отменя́ется; ~*side* пра́вая (ле́вая) сторона́; *(sport)* (положе́ние) вне игры́; ~ *season* мёртвый сезо́н.

offal, *n,* требуха́, потроха́; па́даль; отбро́сы.

offence, *n,* просту́пок, преступле́ние; оби́да, оскорбле́ние; *take* ~ *at* обижа́ться на; **offend,** *v.t,* обижа́ть; ~ *against* наруша́ть (зако́н); ~**er,** *n,* правонаруши́тель, престу́пник; оби́дчик; **offensive,** *a,* оскорби́тельный; отврати́тельный; ¶ *n,* наступле́ние.

offer, *n,* предложе́ние; *on* ~ в прода́же; ¶ *v.t,* предлага́ть; ока́зывать; *v.i,* предоставля́ться; ~ *to help him* вызыва́ться помо́чь ему́; ~**ing,** *n,* предложе́ние; подноше́ние; пожертвование; же́ртва; ~**tory,** *n,* церко́вные поже́ртвования.

office, *n,* конто́ра; канцеля́рия; ве́домство, министе́рство; управле́ние; бюро́; обря́д, слу́жба; услу́га; до́лжность; *be in* ~ быть у вла́сти; ~ *worker* слу́жащий; *good* ~*s* услу́ги.

officer, *n,* офице́р; заве́дующий; *medical* ~ врач; *medical* ~ *of health* санита́рный врач; *staff* ~ штабно́й офице́р; **official,** *a,* официа́льный; форма́льный; ~ *duties* служе́бные обя́занности; ~ *circles* официа́льные круги́; ¶ *n,* должностно́е лицо́, слу́жащий; чино́вник; ~**dom,** *n,* бюрократи́зм; чино́вничество; **officiate,** *v.i,* исполня́ть обя́занности; соверша́ть богослуже́ние; **officious,** *a,* назо́йливый; официо́зный.

offing, *n,* морска́я даль; *in the* ~ вдали́ от бе́рега; в недалёком бу́дущем.

offscourings, *n.pl,* отбро́сы; подо́нки.

offset, *n,* возмеще́ние; побе́г; ответвле́ние; отво́д; ¶ *a,* сдви́нутый; *(print.)* офсе́тный; ¶ *v.t,* возмеща́ть; сдвига́ть; печа́тать офсе́тным спо́собом.

offshoot, *n,* побе́г, ответвле́ние; о́трыск.

offspring, *n,* пото́мок, о́трыск; плод.

often, *ad,* ча́сто.

ogle, *v.t,* стро́ить гла́зки *(dat.)*.

ogre, *n,* велика́н-людое́д.

oh, *int,* о!

ohm, *n,* ом.

oil, *n,* ма́сло; нефть; *pl,* ма́сляные кра́ски; ~*can* маслёнка; ~*cloth* клеёнка; ~*field* месторожде́ние не́фти; нефтяно́й про́мысел; ~ *lamp* кероси́новая ла́мпа; ~ *painting* карти́на, напи́санная ма́сляными кра́сками; ~*skins* клеёнчатый костю́м; ~ *stove* кероси́нка; ~ *tanker* нефтеналивно́е су́дно, та́нкер; ~ *well* нефтяна́я сква́жина; ¶ *v.t,* сма́зывать; пропи́тывать ма́слом; ~ *the wheels (fig.)* подма́зывать; ~**y,** *a,* масляни́стый; еле́йный, льсти́вый.

ointment, *n,* мазь.

old, *a,* ста́рый; стари́нный; *how* ~ *are you?* ско́лько вам лет?; *I know him of* ~ я зна́ю его́ и́здавна; ~ *age* ста́рость; ~*-age pension* пе́нсия по ста́рости; ~ *boy (of school)* бы́вший учени́к; ~ *clothes* поно́шенные ве́щи; ~*-established* давно́ устано́вленный; ~*-fashioned* старомо́дный; ~ *maid* ста́рая де́ва; ~ *man* стари́к; ~ *master (art)* ста́рый ма́стер; ~ *offender* рециди́вист; ~ *salt* морско́й волк; *the same* ~ *story* ста́рая пе́сня; *O*~ *Testament* Ве́тхий заве́т; ~ *timer* старожи́л; ~ *woman* стару́ха.

olden, *a: in* ~ *times* в старину́; **older,** *a,* бо́лее ста́рый; **oldish,** *a,* старова́тый; пожило́й.

oleaginous, *a,* масляни́стый; жи́рный.

oleander, *n,* олеа́ндр.

olfactory, *a,* обоня́тельный.

oligarchy, *n,* олига́рхия.

olive, *n,* масли́на, оли́ва; ~ *(tree)* оли́ва, оли́вковое де́рево; ~ *coloured* оли́вкового цве́та; ~ *oil* оли́вковое ма́сло.

Olympic games, *n.pl,* Олимпи́йские и́гры.

omega, *n,* оме́га.

omelet[te], *n*, омлет, яичница.
omen, *n*, предзнаменование, примета; **ominous**, *a*, зловещий.
omission, *n*, пропуск; упущение; **omit**, *v.t*, пропускать.
omnibus, *n*, автобус.
omnipotence, *n*, всемогущество; **omnipotent**, *a*, всемогущий.
omniscience, *n*, всеведение; **omniscient**, *a*, всеведущий.
on, *pr*, на; в; о, относительно; ¶ *ad*, вперёд, дальше; ~ *and* ~ всё дальше; не останавливаясь; ~ *arrival* по прибытии; ~ *foot* пешком; ~ *hand* на руках; в наличности; налицо; ~ *Monday* в понедельник; ~ *Mondays* по понедельникам; ~ *my part* с моей стороны; ~ *sale* в продаже; ~ *November 2nd* второго ноября; ~ *the way to* по пути в; ~ *this condition* при этом условии; *she had a coat* ~ она была в пальто.
once, *ad*, (один) раз, однажды; некогда, когда-то; ~ *for all* раз (и) навсегда; *at* ~ сразу, сейчас же; ~ *upon a time* давным давно; жил(и)-был(и).
one, *num*, один; единый, единственный; ~ *after another* один за другим; ~*day* однажды; ~*eyed* одноглазый; ~*sided* однобокий; *(fig.)* односторонний; ~*storey* одноэтажный; ~*way street* улица с односторонним движением; *it is all* ~ *to me* мне совершенно безразлично; *love* ~ *another* любить друг друга; *the* ~ *who* тот самый, кто ...; *he is* ~ *of us* он один из нас; ~ *never knows* никогда не знаешь; ~**ness**, *n*, единство; неизменяемость.
onerous, *a*, обременительный; тягостный.
oneself, *pn*, *(reflexive)* себя; *(emphatic)* сам, сама.
onion, *n*, лук; луковица.
onlooker, *n*, зритель, наблюдатель.
only, *ad*, только; ¶ *a*, единственный; ¶ *c*, но; *if* ~ если бы только ...; *the* ~ *thing* единственное.
onomatopoeia, *n*, звукоподражание; **onomatopoeic**, *a*, звукоподражательный.
onrush, & **onset**, *n*, нападение; начало.
onslaught, *n*, атака, нападение.
onus, *n*, бремя, ответственность.

onward, *a*, продвигающийся, идущий вперёд; ¶ *ad*, вперёд, далее.
onyx, *n*, оникс.
ooze, *v.i*, просачиваться; медленно течь; выделять влагу; ~ *away* утекать; ¶ *n*, ил; тина; **oozy**, *a*, илистый, тинистый.
opacity, *n*, непрозрачность; *(fig.)* неясность.
opal, *n*, опал; ~**ine**, *a*, опаловый.
opaque, *a*, непрозрачный; неясный; ~**ness**, *n*, непрозрачность; неясность.
open, *v.t. (& i.)*, открывать(ся), раскрывать(ся); начинать(ся); ~ *into* вести в; сообщаться с; ~ *on* выходить на; ~ *out*, ~ *up* развёртывать(ся): раскрывать(ся); ¶ *a*, открытый; откровенный; доступный; *lay oneself* ~ *to* давать основания для; *in the* ~ *air* на открытом воздухе; ~ *question* открытый вопрос; ~*handed* щедрый; ~*mouthed* разинув(ший) рот; жадный; ~ *sea* открытое море; ~ *work* ажурная работа; ~**er**, *n*, ключ, нож, открывалка; ~**ing**, *n*, отверстие, щель; вакансия; открытие; ¶ *a*, начальный; вступительный, первый; ~**ness**, *n*, откровенность.
opera, *n*, опера; ~ *glasses* театральный бинокль; ~ *singer* оперный певец.
operate, *v.t*, управлять *(inst.)*; приводить в действие; эксплуатировать; *v.i*, действовать, работать; ~ *on (surg.)* оперировать.
operatic, *a*, оперный.
operating, *a*, операционный; ~ *costs* эксплуатационные расходы; ~ *theatre* операционная; **operation**, *n*, действие; операция *(also surg.)*; управление; *put into* ~ вводить в действие; **operative**, *a*, действующий; оперативный; ¶ *n*, рабочий-станочник, ремесленник; **operator**, *n*, механик, станочник; телефонист; делец.
operetta, *n*, оперетта.
ophthalmia, *n*, офтальмия; **ophthalmic**, *a*, глазной.
opiate, *n*, опиат; наркотик; ~**d**, *a*, наркотический.
opine, *v.i*, полагать, высказывать мнение; **opinion**, *n*, мнение; *in*

my ~ по моему мнению; ~ated, *a*, чересчур самоуверенный.

opium, *n*, опиум.

opossum, *n*, опоссум.

opponent, *n*, противник; оппонент; ¶ *a*, противоположный.

opportune, *a*, своевременный; ~ness, *n*, своевременность; **opportunism**, *n*, оппортунизм; **opportunist**, *n*, оппортунист; **opportunity**, *n*, удобный случай, возможность.

oppose, *v.t*, противопоставлять; быть против *(gen.)*; сопротивляться *(dat.)*; мешать *(dat.)*; ~d, *p.p. & a*, враждебный; противоположный; **opposing**, *a*, выступающий против; **opposite**, *a*, противоположный; обратный; ¶ *pr*, против, напротив; ¶ *ad*, напротив; ¶ *n*, противоположность; *quite the* ~ совсем наоборот; **opposition**, *n*, сопротивление; оппозиция; контраст.

oppress, *v.t*, притеснять, угнетать; удручать; ~ion, *n*, притеснение, угнетение, гнёт; подавленность; ~ive, *a*, гнетущий, угнетающий; тягостный; душный; деспотический; ~or, *n*, притеснитель; угнетатель.

opprobrious, *a*, позорный; **opprobrium**, *n*, позор.

opt, *v.t*, выбирать.

optic, *a*, глазной; ~al, *a*, оптический; ~ *illusion* оптический обман; ~ian, *n*, глазной врач; оптик; ~s, *n*, оптика.

optimism, *n*, оптимизм; **optimist**, *n*, оптимист; ~ic, *a*, оптимистический.

option, *n*, выбор; ~al, *a*, факультативный; необязательный.

opulence, *n*, богатство; изобилие; **opulent**, *a*, богатый; обильный; пышный.

opus, *n*, опус.

or, *c*, или; ~ *else* иначе.

oracle, *n*, оракул; прорицание; **oracular**, *a*, пророческий; догматический; двусмысленный.

oral, *a*, устный; словесный; ~ *examination* устный экзамен.

orange, *n*, апельсин; ¶ *a*, апельсиновый; оранжевый; ~ *blossom* померанцевый цвет; ~-*coloured* оранжевого цвета; ~ *peel* апель-синовая корка; ~ade, *n*, оранжад; ~ry, *n*, оранжерея.

orang-outang, *n*, орангутанг.

oration, *n*, речь; **orator**, *n*, оратор; ~ical, *a*, ораторский; риторический; **oratorio**, *n*, оратория; **oratory**, *n*, красноречие, риторика; *(eccl.)* молельня.

orb, *n*, шар; сфера; **orbit**, *n*, орбита; *(anat.)* глазная впадина.

orchard, *n*, фруктовый сад.

orchestra, *n*, оркестр; ~ *stalls* партер; ~l, *a*, оркестровый; ~te, *v.t*, оркестровать; ~tion, *n*, оркестровка.

orchid, *n*, орхидея.

ordain, *v.t*, предопределять; предписывать; *(eccl.)* посвящать в духовный сан.

ordeal, *n*, тяжёлое испытание.

order, *n*, порядок; последовательность; приказ; заказ; ордер, разрешение; орден *(award, religious, etc.)*; *(mil.)* строй; *call to* ~ призывать к порядку; открывать собрание; *in* ~ *that/to* для того, чтобы . . .; с тем, чтобы . . .; ~ *book* книга заказов; *out of* ~ в неисправности; ~ *form* бланк заказа/требования; ~ *of the day* повестка дня; *in working* ~ в исправности; ¶ *v.t*, приказывать *(dat. + inf.)*; заказывать; ~ *about* командовать *(inst.)*, помыкать *(inst.)*; ~ly, *a*, опрятный, аккуратный; регулярный; дисциплинированный; ~ *officer* дежурный офицер; ¶ *n*, ординарец; санитар *(in hospital)*.

ordinal, *a*, порядковый; ¶ *n*, порядковое числительное.

ordinance, *n*, декрет, постановление.

ordinarily, *ad*, обыкновенно, обычно; обыкновенным путём; **ordinary**, *a*, обыкновенный, обычный; заурядный.

ordination, *n*, посвящение в духовный сан.

ordnance, *n*, артиллерия.

ore, *n*, руда.

organ, *n*, орган; *(mus.)* орган; ~grinder шарманщик; ~ *loft* галерея для органа, хоры.

organdie, *n*, кисея, органди.

organic, *a*, органический; **organism**, *n*, организм.

organist, *n*, органи́ст.
organization, *n*, организа́ция; устро́йство; **organize**, *v.t*, организо́вывать; устра́ивать; **~r**, *n*, организа́тор.
orgy, *n*, о́ргия.
oriel, *n*, алько́в; закры́тый балко́н.
orient, *n*, Восто́к, стра́ны Восто́ка; **~al**, *a*, восто́чный; **~[ate]**, *v.t*, ориенти́ровать; определя́ть местонахожде́ние *(gen.)*; *v.i.* ориенти́роваться; **~ation**, *n*, ориента́ция.
orifice, *n*, отве́рстие.
origin, *n*, нача́ло; исто́чник, происхожде́ние; **~al**, *a*, первонача́льный; оригина́льный; самобы́тный; ¶ *n*, оригина́л, по́длинник; чуда́к; **~ality**, *n*, оригина́льность; по́длинность; **~ally**, *ad*, первонача́льно; оригина́льно; **~ate**, *v.t*, порожда́ть, дава́ть нача́ло *(dat.)*; *v.i*, происходи́ть, брать нача́ло; **~ator**, *n*, инициа́тор, а́втор.
oriole, *n*, и́волга.
ornament, *n*, украше́ние, орна́мент; ¶ *v.t*, украша́ть; **~al**, *a*, декорати́вный; орнамента́льный; **~ation**, *n*, украше́ние; **ornate**, *a*, разукра́шенный; витиева́тый.
ornithologist, *n*, орнито́лог; **ornithology**, *n*, орнитоло́гия.
orphan, *a*, сиро́тский; ¶ *n*, сирота́; **~age**, *n*, сиро́тский прию́т.
orthodox, *a*, ортодокса́льный; общепри́нятый; *(eccl.)* правосла́вный; **~y**, *n*, ортодокса́льность; правосла́вие.
orthography, *n*, орфогра́фия, правописа́ние.
orthopaedic, *a*, ортопеди́ческий; **orthopaedist**, *n*, ортопе́д; **orthopaedy**, *n*, ортопе́дия.
oscillate, *v.i*, кача́ться, колеба́ться *(also fig.)*; вибри́ровать; **oscillation**, *n*, кача́ние, колеба́ние; вибра́ция; **oscillatory**, *a*, колеба́тельный.
osier, *n*, и́ва; лоза́; ¶ *a*, и́вовый.
osprey, *n*, скопа́.
osseous, *a*, кости́стый; ко́стный; **ossification**, *n*, окостене́ние; **ossify**, *v.t*, превраща́ть в кость; *v.i*, превраща́ться в кость, костене́ть.
ostensible, *a*, мни́мый; очеви́дный; я́вный; официа́льный; **ostensibly**, *ad*, очеви́дно; на вид.

ostentation, *n*, показно́е поведе́ние; хвастовство́; **ostentatious**, *a*, показно́й.
ostler, *n*, ко́нюх.
ostracism, *n*, изгна́ние из о́бщества; **ostracize**, *v.t*, изгоня́ть из о́бщества.
ostrich, *n*, стра́ус.
other, *a*, друго́й, ино́й; *every ~ day* че́рез день; *the ~ day* на днях, неда́вно; *on the ~ hand* с друго́й стороны́; ¶ *pn*, друго́й; *each ~* друг дру́га/дру́гу, *etc.*; *none ~ than* никто́ ино́й, как; **~wise**, *ad*, ина́че; по-друго́му;
otter, *n*, вы́дра.
Ottoman, *a*, оттома́нский, туре́цкий; ¶ *n*, оттома́н, ту́рок; **ottoman**, *n*, оттома́нка, дива́н.
ought, *v.aux*, до́лжен, до́лжен бы; сле́довало бы; *she ~ to know* она́ должна́ (бы) знать; *it ~ to be so* так должно́ быть; ¶ *n*, ноль.
ounce, *n*, у́нция; *(fig.)* чу́точка.
our, *a*, & **ours**, *pn*, наш, на́ша, *etc.;* свой, своя́, *etc.* **~selves**, (мы) са́ми; себя́ *etc.*
oust, *v.t*, вытесня́ть.
out, *ad*, нару́жу, вон; *take ~* вынима́ть; *go ~* выходи́ть; *he is ~* его́ нет до́ма; *the fire is ~* ого́нь поту́х; *~-and-~* отъявле́нный, соверше́нный.
out of, *pr*, из, вне; за; *~ action* вы́веденный из стро́я; *~ date* старомо́дный, устаре́вший; *~ doors* на откры́том во́здухе; *~ envy* из за́висти; *~ favour* в неми́лости; *~ hand* без подгото́вки, сра́зу; *get ~ hand* отбива́ться от рук; *~ order* неиспра́вный; *~ place* неуме́стный; *be ~ pocket* быть в убы́тке; не име́ть де́нег; *~ print* распро́данный; *~ shape* непра́вильной фо́рмы; *~ sight* скры́тый из ви́ду; *be ~ sorts* пло́хо себя́ чу́вствовать; *~ town* за́ го́род(ом); *~ tune* не в тон; расстро́енный; *~-the-way* отдалённый; необы́чный; *~ work* безрабо́тный; *~ use* вы́шедший из употребле́ния.
outbalance, *v.t*, переве́шивать.
outbid, *v.t*, перебива́ть.
outbreak, *n*, взрыв, вспы́шка; нача́ло; появле́ние.
outbuilding, *n*, надво́рное строе́ние.
outburst, *n*, взрыв, в спы́шка.

outcast, *n*, изгнанник.

outcome, *n*, исход, результат.

outcrop, *n*, *(geol.)* обнажение пород; *(fig.)* выявление.

outcry, *n*, протест.

outdistance, *v.t*, обгонять, перегонять.

outdo, *v.t*, превосходить.

outdoor, *a*, на открытом воздухе.

outer, *a*, внешний, наружный; ~**most**, *a*, крайний.

outfit, *n*, снаряжение; оборудование; наряд, обмундирование, костюм; набор инструментов; *(U.S.A.)* компания; ~**ter**, *n*, поставщик снаряжения/обмундирования; торговец одеждой.

outflank, *v.t*, обходить с фланга; *(fig.)* перехитрить *(pf.)*.

outflow, *n*, истечение; исток.

outgoing, *a*, уходящий, отбывающий; исходящий *(post)*; ~**s**, *n.pl*, издержки.

outgrow, *v.t*, вырастать из; перерастать; отделываться от; *he has* ~*n his clothes* он вырос из своей одежды.

outhouse, *n*, надворное строение.

outing, *n*, экскурсия, прогулка.

outlandish, *a*, диковинный; чужеземный.

outlast, *v.t*, продолжаться дольше, чем; переживать.

outlaw, *n*, человек вне закона; изгнанник; разбойник; ¶ *v.t*, объявлять вне закона; изгонять из общества.

outlay, *n*, издержки, расходы.

outlet, *n*, выпускное отверстие; выход, отдушина; ~ *pipe* выпускная труба.

outline, *n*, очертание, контур; конспект; набросок; *give an* ~ *of* набрасывать в общих чертах; ¶ *v.t*, описывать в общих чертах; рисовать контур *(gen.)*.

outlive, *v.t*, переживать; отживать.

outlook, *n*, кругозор; точка зрения; мировоззрение; вид.

outlying, *a*, далёкий, отдалённый.

outnumber, *v.t*, превосходить численно.

out-patient, *n*, амбулаторный больной.

outpost, *n*, аванпост; застава.

output, *n*, выпуск; продукция; *(tech.)* мощность, производительность.

outrage, *n*, насилие; жестокое преступление; беззаконие; надругательство; ¶ *v.t*, надругаться над; насиловать; ~**ous**, *a*, возмутительный; жестокий.

outright, *a*, прямой; совершённый; ¶ *ad*, совершённо, полностью; напрямик, открыто; раз и навсегда.

outrival, *v.t*, превосходить.

outset, *n*, начало; отправление.

outshine, *v.t*, затмевать.

outside, *a*, наружный, внешний; крайний; посторонний; ¶ *n*, наружная сторона; внешность; крайность; *at the* ~ в крайнем случае; ¶ *ad*, извне, снаружи; наружу; на улице, на открытом воздухе; ¶ *pr*, вне, за; ~**r**, *n*, посторонний; отщепенец, аутсайдер.

outsize[d], *a*, больше обычного размера; нестандартный.

outskirts, *n.pl*, окраина, окрестность; опушка.

outspoken, *a*, искренний, откровенный; ~**ness**, *n*, искренность, откровенность.

outspread, *a*, разостланный, распростёртый.

outstanding, *a*, выдающийся; невыполненный, неразрешённый; неуплаченный.

outstretched, *a*, распростёртый, протянутый; растянувшийся.

outstrip, *v.t*, обгонять, опережать; превосходить.

outward, *a*, внешний, наружный; ~ *bound* отплывающий; ~**ly**, *ad*, внешне, на вид; ~**s**, *ad*, наружу.

outweigh, *v.t*, перевешивать, превосходить в весе.

outwit, *v.t*, перехитрить *(pf.)*.

outworks, *n.pl*, внешние укрепления.

outworn, *a*, изношенный; изнурённый; устарелый.

ouzel, *n*, дрозд.

oval, *a*, овальный; ¶ *n*, овал.

ovary, *n*, *(anat.)* яичник; *(bot.)* завязь.

ovation, *n*, овация.

oven, *n*, печь; духовка.

over, *pr*, над, через; по; за; более, свыше; ¶ *ad*, сверх, слишком; *all* ~ повсюду; сплошь; *all* ~ *the country* по всей стране; *be left* ~ оставаться; быть отложенным;

~ *and above all this* сверх всего;
be ~ *(ended)* быть окóнченным;
it is all ~ всё кóнчено; ~ *and* ~
again снóва и снóва; ~ *26* за 26;
twice ~ два рáза; в два рáза больше; ~ *the way* через дорóгу.

overact, *v.t,* переигрывать.

overall, *a,* óбщий; всеохвáтывающий;
~**[s],** *n,* спецодéжда; комбине-
зóн; халáт.

overawe, *v.t,* внушáть благоговéйный страх *(dat.).*

overbalance, *v.t,* персвéшивать; *v.i,*
терять равновéсие, пáдать.

overbearing, *a,* влáстный, повелительный.

overboard, *ad,* зá борт, за бóртом;
man ~! человéк за бóртом!.

overburden, *v.t,* перегружáть; отя-
гощáть.

overcast, *a,* покрытый облакáми;
мрáчный.

overcharge, *v.t,* брать/запрáшивать
слишком высóкую цéну.

overcoat, *n,* пальтó, шинéль.

overcome, *v.t,* преодолевáть; пересиливать; ¶ *p.p,* обессиленный;
be ~ растрóгаться *(pf.).*

overcrowd, *v.t,* переполнять; ~**ed,**
p.p, & a, переполненный.

overdo, *v.t,* преувеличивать, утри-
ровать; пережáривать; ~ *it* пере-
стáраться *(pf.).* перебáрщивать;
overdone, *p.p, & a,* преувели-
ченный, утрированный; пере-
жаренный.

overdose, *n,* чрезмéрная дóза.

overdraft, *n,* превышéние крéдита;
overdraw, *v.t,* превышáть крéдит
(в бáнке).

overdressed, *a,* разодéтый.

overdrive, *v.t,* переутомлять; загонять; ¶ *n,* ускоряющая пере-
дáча.

overdue, *a,* запоздáлый; просрóчен-
ный; *the train is 2 hours* ~ пóезд
опáздывает на 2 часá.

overeat, *v.i,* объедáться, переедáть.

overestimate, *v.t,* переоцéнивать.

overexcite, *v.t,* (чересчур) возбуждáть.

overexposure, *n, (phot.)* передéрж-
ка.

overfatigue, *v.t,* переутомлять; ¶ *n,*
переутомлéние.

overfeed, *v t,* перекáрмливать.

overflow, *n,* переливáние чéрез край,
вытекáние; разлив; избыток; слив-

нáя трубá; ¶ *v.i,* переливáться
чéрез край, вытекáть; разливáться; *v.t,* заливáть, затоплять; ~**ing,**
a, льющийся чéрез край; бьющий
чéрез край; переполненный; ~
with kindness преисполненный
добрóты.

overgrow, *v.t,* заглушáть *(of plants);*
v.i, вытягиваться; ~**n,** *p.p, & a,*
зарóсший.

overhang, *v.t,* нависáть над, выступáть над; *v.i,* свéшиваться.

overhaul, *v.t,* капитáльно ремонтировать; реконструировать; до-
гонять.

overhead, *a,* вéрхний; ~ *charges*
накладные расхóды; ¶ *ad,* наверху, над головóй; на нéбе.

overhear, *v.t,* подслушивать; случáйно слышать.

overheat, *v.t,* перегревáть; пере-
кáливать.

overindulgence, *n,* чрезмéрное увлечéние, злоупотреблéние.

overjoyed, *a,* вне себя от рáдости.

overladen, *a,* перегруженный.

overland, *a,* сухопýтный; ¶ *ad,* по
сýше, на сýше.

overlap, *v.t,* частично покрывáть;
частично совпадáть с; пере-
крывáть.

overlay, *v.t,* покрывáть; ¶ *n,* по-
крышка.

overleaf, *ad,* на обрáтной сторонé.

overload, *v.t,* перегружáть.

overlook, *v.t,* не замечáть, проглядывать,
пропускáть; возвышáться
над; выходить на *(of window).*

overmuch, *ad,* слишком мнóго;
чрезмéрно.

overnight, *ad,* нóчью; нá ночь; *stay*
~ ночевáть.

overpay, *v.t,* переплáчивать.

overpower, *v.t,* пересиливать; подавлять; ~**ing,** *a,* подавляющий.

overproduction, *n,* перепроизвóдство.

overrate, *v.t,* переоцéнивать.

overreach, *v.t,* превышáть, выходить
за предéлы *(gen.);* перехитрить
(pf.); ~ *oneself* просчитáться.

override, *v.t,* задавить *(pf.);* загонять *(horse);* отвергáть, отменять.

overripe, *a,* перезрéлый.

overrule, *v.t,* отвергáть; отменять;
госпóдствовать над.

overrun, *v.t,* переливáться чéрез
край; оккупировать; *be* ~

(with) кишéть (муравья́ми, *etc.*); зараста́ть.

overseas, *a,* замо́рский; ¶ *ad,* зá морем, чéрез мо́ре.

overseer, *n,* надзира́тель.

overshadow, *v.t,* затемня́ть; затмева́ть.

overshoe, *n,* гало́ша.

overshoot, *v.i,* прома́хиваться; заходи́ть сли́шком далеко́; *v.t,* превосходи́ть, превыша́ть.

oversight, *n,* недосмо́тр, опло́шность.

oversleep, *v.i,* просыпа́ть; заспа́ться *(pf.).*

overspread, *v.t,* покрыва́ть.

overstate, *v.t,* преувели́чивать.

overstep, *v.t,* переступа́ть, перешáгивать; ~ *the mark* переходи́ть грани́цы.

overstock, *v.t,* дéлать сли́шком большо́й запа́с; забива́ть това́ром.

overstrain, *n,* переутомлéние; чрезмéрное напряжéние; ¶ *v.t,* переутомля́ть, перенапряга́ть.

overtake, *v.t,* догоня́ть; перегоня́ть.

overtax, *v.t,* брать чрезмéрный нало́г с; перенапряга́ть; ~ *oneself* переутомля́ться.

overthrow, *v.t,* опроки́дывать; *(fig.)* сверга́ть.

overtime, *n,* сверхуро́чное врéмя; *work* ~ рабо́тать сверхуро́чно.

overtop, *v.t,* превыша́ть, превосходи́ть.

overture, *n,* увертю́ра; предложéние.

overturn, *v.t,* опроки́дывать; опровергáть; *v.i,* опроки́дываться.

overweening, *a,* высокомéрный.

overweight, *n,* перевéс, изли́шек вéса.

overwhelm, *v.t,* овладевáть *(inst.);* потрясáть; сокрушáть; переполня́ть; забрáсывать; ~ing, *a,* подавля́ющий; непреодоли́мый.

overwork, *v.t,* заставля́ть сли́шком мно́го рабо́тать, переутомля́ть; ¶ *n,* чрезмéрная рабо́та, перегру́зка.

overwrought, *a,* переутомлённый, напряжённый.

ovine, *a,* овéчий.

oviparous, *a,* яйцено́сный.

owe, *v.t,* быть до́лжным; быть обя́занным; *I* ~ *him 4 roubles* я дол-

жен ему́ пять рублéй; *I* ~ *him everything* я всем обя́зан ему́; *owing to* по причи́не, вслéдствие.

owl, *n,* совá.

own, *a,* свой, со́бственный; родно́й; *of one's* ~ *free will* по своéй со́бственной во́ле; ¶ *v.t,* владéть *(inst.);* признавáть; ~ *up to* признавáться в; ~er, *n,* владéлец, со́бственник, хозя́ин; ~ership, *n,* владéние; пра́во со́бственности.

ox, *n,* бык, вол; ~*-eye daisy* попо́вник, рома́шка.

oxide, *n,* о́кись; **oxidize,** *v.t,* окисля́ть, оксиди́ровать.

oxygen, *n,* кислоро́д; **oxygenate,** *v.t,* окисля́ть; **oxygenation,** *n,* окислéние.

oyster, *n,* у́стрица; ~ *bed* у́стричный садо́к.

ozone, *n,* озо́н.

P

pace, *n,* ско́рость, темп; шаг, похо́дка; *keep* ~ *with* идти́ наравнé с; ¶ *v.i,* шагáть; *v.t,* измеря́ть шагáми; задавáть темп *(dat.).*

pachyderm, *n,* толстоко́жее (живо́тное).

pacific, *a,* споко́йный, ти́хий, ми́рный; *the P*~ *Ocean* Ти́хий океáн; **pacification,** *n,* умиротворéние; усмирéние; **pacifist,** *n,* пацифи́ст; **pacify,** *v.t,* умиротворя́ть; усмиря́ть.

pack, *n,* тюк; свя́зка, у́зел; пáчка, пакéт; *(mil.)* рáнец; сво́ра *(hounds);* стáя *(wolves);* коло́да *(cards);* ~ *horse* вьючная ло́шадь; ~ *ice* пáковый лёд; ~ *of lies* сплошнáя ложь; ¶ *v.t,* упако́вывать, уклáдывать; уплотня́ть; набивáть; *v.i,* уклáдываться; ~ *up* упако́вываться; ~age, *n,* пакéт, посы́лка; ~ed, *p.p. & a,* наби́тый; ~er, *n,* упако́вщик; ~et, *n,* пакéт; пáчка (сигарéт); ~-*boat* почто́вый парохо́д; ~ing, *n,* уклáдка, упако́вка; уплотнéние; упако́вочный материáл; ~ *case* я́щик для упако́вки.

pact, *n,* пакт, догово́р.

pad, *n,* поду́шка; поду́шечка; мя́гкая проклáдка; блокно́т; ¶ *v.t,* подбивáть; **padding,** *n,* наби́вка, набивочный материал; *(fig.)* «вода».

paddle, *n*, (короткое) весло; лопасть *(of wheel)*; ~ *steamer* колёсный пароход; ~ *wheel* гребное колесо; ¶ *v.t. (& i.)*, грести одним веслом; плескаться в воде.

paddock, *n*, загон.

padlock, *n*, висячий замок; ¶ *v.t*, запирать на висячий замок.

paean, *n*, пеан; песнь.

pagan, *a*, языческий; ¶ *n*, язычник; ~ism, *n*, язычество.

page, *n*, страница; паж, мальчик-слуга.

pageant, *n*, карнавальное шествие; пышное зрелище; ~ry, *n*, помпа, великолепие.

paginate, *v.t*, нумеровать страницы *(gen.)*.

pagoda, *n*, пагода.

paid, *p.p*, оплачиваемый; выплаченный; оплаченный; ~-*up shares* полностью оплаченные акции; *put* ~ *to* положить *(pf.)* конец *(dat.)*.

pail, *n*, ведро; ~ful, *n*, полное ведро.

pain, *n*, боль; *pl*, страдания; усилия; *on* ~ *of death* под страхом смертной казни; *where do you feel* ~? где вам больно?; ¶ *v.t*, причинять боль *(dat.)*; огорчать; *v.i*, болеть; ~ed, *p.p. & a*, огорчённый; ~ful, *a*, болезненный, больной; мучительный; тягостный; ~less, *a*, безболезненный; ~staking, *a*, старательный, тщательный.

paint, *n*, краска; *coat of* ~ слой краски; ~ *brush* кисть; ¶ *v.i*, писать красками; заниматься живописью; *v.t*, красить; писать красками; описывать; ~ed *white* покрашенный в белый цвет; ~er, *n*, художник; маляр; ~ing, *n*, картина; живопись; окраска.

pair, *n*, пара; чета; ~ *of scales* весы; ~ *of scissors* ножницы; ~ *of spectacles* очки; ~ *of steps* стремянка; ¶ *v.t. (& i.)*, соединять(ся) по двое; подбирать под пару; спаривать(ся); ~ *off* разделять(ся) на пары.

pal, *n*, товарищ, приятель.

palace, *n*, дворец.

palatable, *a*, приятный; вкусный; **palatal**, *a*, нёбный; **palatalize**, *v.t*,

палатализовать, смягчать; **palate**, *n*, нёбо; вкус.

palatial, *a*, великолепный.

palaver, *n*, совещание; переговоры; болтовня.

pale, *a*, бледный; слабый; *grow* ~ бледнеть; тускнеть; ¶ *n*, кол; предел, граница; черта оседлости; *beyond the* ~ *of* за пределами; ~ness, *n*, бледность; тусклость.

paleography, *n*, палеография.

paleology, *n*, палеология.

paleontology, *n*, палеонтология.

palette, *n*, палитра; ~-*knife* мастихин.

palfrey, *n*, верховая лошадь.

palimpsest, *n*, палимпсест.

palisade, *n*, частокол, палисад.

palish, *a*, бледноватый.

pall, *n*, покров; завеса; ¶ *v.i*, надоедать.

palliasse, *n*, соломенный тюфяк.

palliate, *v.t*, облегчать; смягчать; **palliative**, *a*, смягчающий, паллиативный; ¶ *n*, паллиатив, смягчающее средство; полумера.

pallid, *a*, бледный.

pallium, *n*, плащ; *(zool.)* мантия.

pallor, *n*, бледность.

palm, *n*, пальма; ладонь *(hand)*; *Palm Sunday* Вербное воскресенье; ~ *tree* пальма; ¶ *v.t*, прятать в руке; ~ *off* подсовывать, всучивать; ~ist, *n*, хиромант; ~istry, *n*, хиромантия.

palmy, *a*, пальмовый; счастливый; цветущий.

palpable, *a*, осязаемый; явный.

palpitate, *v.i*, биться, пульсировать; трепетать; **palpitating**, *a*, *(fig.)* животрепещущий; **palpitation**, *n*, сердцебиение; дрожь, трепет.

palsied, *a*, парализованный; **palsy**, *n*, паралич; ¶ *v.t*, парализовать.

paltry, *a*, мелкий, ничтожный, жалкий.

pampas, *n.pl*, пампасы.

pamper, *v.t*, изнеживать; баловать.

pamphlet, *n*, памфлет, брошюра; ~eer, *n*, памфлетист.

pan, *n*, кастрюля; миска; чашка (весов); *(tech.)* лоток; ¶ *pan out well* удаваться.

panacea, *n*, панацея.

panache, *n*, рисовка, щегольство.

panama[hat], *n*, панама.

Pan-American, *a*, панамериканский.

pancake, *n,* блин, блинчик; оладья.
pancreas, *n,* поджелудочная железа.
panda, *n,* панда.
pandemonium, *n,* гвалт, столпотворение.
pander, *v.i:* ~ *to* потворствовать *(dat.).*
panegyric, *n,* панегирик.
panel, *n,* панель; филёнка; щит, доска; *(law)* список присяжных; жюри; ¶ *v.t,* обшивать панелями; ~**ling,** *n,* панельная обшивка.
pang, *n,* острая боль; мучение; ~*s of conscience* угрызения совести.
panic, *n,* паника; ~-*monger* паникёр; ~-*stricken* охваченный паникой.
pannier, *n,* корзина; короб.
panoply, *n,* доспехи; полное вооружение.
panorama, *n,* панорама; **panoramic,** *a,* панорамный.
pansy, *n, (bot.)* анютины глазки.
pant, *v.i,* тяжело дышать, задыхаться, пыхтеть; ~ *after* страстно желать *(gen.).*
pantechnicon, *n,* мебельный склад; ~ *van* фургон для мебели.
pantheism, *n,* пантеизм; **pantheon,** *n,* пантеон.
panther, *n,* пантера.
panting, *a,* задыхающийся, пыхтящий.
pantomime, *n,* пантомима.
pantry, *n,* кладовая, чулан.
pants, *n.pl,* кальсоны; брюки; штаны.
pap, *n,* кашка; полужидкая масса; сосок.
papa, *n,* папа.
papacy, *n,* папство; **papal,** *a,* папский.
paper, *n,* бумага; газета; научный доклад, статья; экзаменационная бумага; документ; ¶ *a,* бумажный; ~*back* книга в бумажной обложке; ~ *chase* (бумажный) кросс; ~ *clip* скрепка для бумаг; ~*hanger* обойщик; ~ *knife* разрезной нож; ~ *money* ассигнации, бумажные деньги; ~ *weight* пресс-папье; ¶ *v.t,* оклеивать обоями.
papier mâché, *n,* папье-маше.
papyrus, *n,* папирус.
par, *n,* равенство; *at* ~ по номинальной стоимости; *I feel below* ~ я себя плохо чувствую; *be on a* ~

with быть наравне/на равных началах с.
parable, *n,* притча.
parabola, *n,* парабола.
parachute, *n,* парашют; ~ *jump* прыжок с парашютом; **parachutist,** *n,* парашютист.
parade, *n,* парад; ~-*ground* плац-парад; учебный плац; ¶ *v.i,* проходить строем, маршировать; строиться; *v.t,* строить; выставлять напоказ.
paradise, *n,* рай.
paradox, *n,* парадокс; ~**ical,** *a,* парадоксальный.
paraffin, *n,* парафиновое масло, керосин.
paragon, *n,* образец; *(print.)* парагон.
paragraph, *n,* параграф; абзац; газетная заметка; ¶ *v.t,* разделять на абзацы.
Paraguayan, *a,* парагвайский; ¶ *n,* парагв|аец, ~айка.
parakeet, *n,* длиннохвостый попугай.
parallel, *a,* параллельный; аналогичный; ¶ *n,* параллель; параллельная линия; сравнение; *(elec.)* параллельное соединение; ~ *bars* параллельные брусья; *without* ~ бесподобный; ~**ogram,** *n,* параллелограмм.
paralyse, *v.t,* парализовать; **paralysis,** *n,* паралич; **paralytic,** *a,* параличный; ¶ *n,* паралитик.
paramount, *a,* высший; верховный.
paramour, *n,* любовн|ик, -ица.
parapet, *n,* парапет; перила.
paraphernalia, *n.pl,* принадлежности.
paraphrase, *n,* парафраза; ¶ *v.t,* парафразировать.
parasite, *n,* паразит, тунеядец; **parasitic,** *a,* паразитический, паразитный.
parasol, *n,* зонтик (от солнца).
paratrooper, *n,* парашютист.
parcel, *n,* пакет, посылка, свёрток; участок; партия; ~ *post* почтово-посылочная служба; ¶ *v.t:* ~ *out* делить, разделять.
parch, *v.t,* иссушать, палить; *I am* ~*ed with thirst* у меня пересохло в горле от жажды.
parchment, *n,* пергамент.
pardon, *n,* извинение, прощение; *(law)* помилование; *I beg your* ~!

извини́те!; *general* ~ амни́стия; ¶ *v.t*, извиня́ть, проща́ть; *(law)* поми́ловать; ~able, *a*, прости́тельный.

pare, *v.t*, подстрига́ть *(nails)*; обреза́ть; *(fig.)* сокраща́ть, уре́зывать.

paregoric, *a*, болеутоля́ющий.

parent, *n*, оте́ц, мать; *pl*, роди́тели; *(fig.)* исто́чник; ¶ *a*, роди́тельский; ~age, *n*, происхожде́ние; родосло́вная; ~al, *a*, роди́тельский.

parenthesis, *n*, вво́дное сло́во/предложе́ние; *pl*, кру́глые ско́бки; **parenthetic(al)**, *a*, вво́дный; *(fig.)* вста́вленный мимохо́дом.

parenthood, *n*, отцо́вство, матери́нство.

pariah, *n*, па́рия.

paring, *n*, подстрига́ние; сре́зывание; *pl*, обре́зки.

parish, *n*, церко́вный прихо́д; о́круг; ¶ *a*, прихо́дский; ~ *register* метри́ческая кни́га; ~ioner, *n*, прихожа́н|ин, -ка.

Parisian, *a*, пари́жский; ¶ *n*, парижа́н|ин, -ка

parity, *n*, ра́венство; параллели́зм; *(com.)* парите́т.

park, *n*, парк; запове́дник; ¶ *v.t*, ста́вить (маши́ну); ~ing, *n*, стоя́нка.

parlance, *n*, язы́к; мане́ра выраже́ния.

parley, *n*, перегово́ры; ¶ *v.i*, вести́ перегово́ры.

parliament, *n*, парла́мент; ~arian, *n*, парламента́рий; ~ary, *a*, парла́ментский; парламента́рный.

parlour, *n*, гости́ная; приёмная; ~ *maid* го́рничная.

parochial, *a*, прихо́дский; *(fig.)* ограни́ченный, ме́стный.

parody, *n*, паро́дия; ¶ *v.t*, пароди́ровать.

parole, *n*, че́стное сло́во; обеща́ние; *(mil.)* паро́ль; ¶ *v.t*, освобожда́ть под че́стное сло́во.

paroxysm, *n*, парокси́зм.

parquet, *n*, парке́т.

parricidal, *a*, отцеуби́йственный; **parricide**, *n*, отцеуби́йца; отцеуби́йство.

parrot, *n*, попуга́й.

parry, *n*, пари́рование, отраже́ние уда́ра; уве́ртка; ¶ *v.t*, пари́ро-

вать, отража́ть; ~ *a question* увёртываться от отве́та.

parse, *v.t*, де́лать граммати́ческий разбо́р *(gen.)*.

Parsee, *n*, парс.

parsimonious, *a*, бережли́вый; скупо́й; **parsimony**, *n*, бережли́вость; ску́пость.

parsley, *n*, петру́шка.

parsnip, *n*, пастерна́к.

parson, *n*, свяще́нник, па́стор; ~age, *n*, дом свяще́нника, пастора́т.

part, *n*, часть; уча́стие; *(theat.)* роль; *(mus.)* па́ртия; *pl*, края́; ~ *of speech* часть ре́чи; ~-*owner* совладе́лец; ~-*timer* рабо́чий, за́нятый непо́лный рабо́чий день; *for my* ~ с мое́й стороны́; ¶ *v.t. (& i.)*, разделя́ть(ся); отделя́ть(ся); разнима́ть; разлуча́ть(ся); ~ *from* расстава́ться с; ~ *one's hair* расчёсывать во́лосы на пробо́р; ~ *with* отдава́ть; отпуска́ть.

partake, *v.t*, принима́ть уча́стие; ку́шать; ~r, *n*, уча́стник.

partial, *a*, части́чный, непо́лный; пристра́стный; ~ly, *ad*, части́чно; ~ity, *n*, пристра́стие; скло́нность.

participate, *v.i*, уча́ствовать; разделя́ть; **participation**, *n*, уча́стие; разделе́ние; **participator**, *n*, уча́стн|ик, -ица.

participle, *n*, прича́стие; *past* ~ прича́стие проше́дшего вре́мени.

particle, *n*, части́ца; кру́пица.

particular, *a*, осо́бенный, осо́бый; определённый; тща́тельный; разбо́рчивый; *in* ~ в осо́бенности; ¶ *n*, подро́бность; осо́бенность; *pl*, обстоя́тельства; подро́бный отчёт; ~ity, *n*, осо́бенность; ~ize, *v.t*, подро́бно остана́вливаться на; ~ly, *ad*, осо́бенно; о́чень; в ча́стности.

parting, *n*, расстава́ние, разлу́ка; пробо́р *(of hair)*; ~ *of ways* перепу́тье.

partisan, *a*, партиза́нский; пристра́стный; ¶ *n*, партиза́н; приве́рженец, сторо́нник.

partition, *n*, разде́л, разделе́ние; отделе́ние; перегоро́дка, вну́тренняя стена́; ¶ *v.t*, дели́ть, разделя́ть; ~ *off* отгора́живать перегоро́дкой; **partitive**, *a*, раздели́тельный.

partner, *n*, (со)уча́стник, компаньо́н; това́рищ; партнёр, -ша *(in* dance/game); супру́г(а); *sleeping* ~ номина́льный компаньо́н; ~ship, *n*, уча́стие; това́рищество; ме́сто/права́ компаньо́на.

partridge, *n*, куропа́тка.

party, *n*, па́ртия; гру́ппа; ве́чер, вечери́нка; *(law)* сторона́; уча́стник; *interested* ~ заинтере́сованная сторона́; ~ *member* член па́ртии, парти́ец; ~ *wall* о́бщая стена́.

paschal, *a*, пасха́льный.

pasha, *n*, паша́.

pass, *v.t*, передава́ть; выноси́ть *(decision);* принима́ть *(law);* выде́рживать *(exam);* проводи́ть *(time);* проходи́ть/проезжа́ть ми́мо; переходи́ть че́рез; обгоня́ть; *v.i*, проходи́ть, проезжа́ть; протека́ть; пасова́ть *(cards);* ~ *away* сконча́ться *(pf.);* исчеза́ть; ~ *by* пропуска́ть; проходи́ть ми́мо; ~ *for* счита́ться/слыть *(inst.);* быть при́нятым за; ~ *over* упуска́ть; обходи́ть молча́нием; *come to* ~ происходи́ть; ¶ *n*, перева́л; про́пуск; беспла́тный биле́т; разреше́ние; удовлетвори́тельная оце́нка *(exam);* вы́пад *(fencing); a pretty* ~ крити́ческое положе́ние; *make a* ~ *at* пристава́ть к; ~ *book* расчётная кни́жка; ~ *key* отмы́чка; ~ *word* паро́ль; ~able, *a*, проходи́мый; сно́сный, удовлетвори́тельный; ~age, *n*, прохо́д, прое́зд; коридо́р; рейс; путь; отры́вок; утвержде́ние *(of law).*

passenger, *n*, пассажи́р.

passer-by, *n*, прохо́жий; **passing**, *a*, мимолётный, преходя́щий; случа́йный; ¶ *n*, перехо́д; протека́ние, прохожде́ние; смерть; *in* ~ мимохо́дом; ~ *fancy* мимолётное увлече́ние.

passion, *n*, страсть; увлече́ние; я́рость; пыл; ~ *flower* страстоцве́т; ~ate, *a*, стра́стный; вспы́льчивый; пы́лкий; ~ately, *ad*, стра́стно, горячо́.

passive, *a*, пасси́вный; инéртный; поко́рный; *(gram.)* страда́тельный; ~ *voice* страда́тельный зало́г; **passivity**, *n*, пасси́вность, инéртность, поко́рность.

Passover, *n*, Евре́йская па́сха.

passport, *n*, па́спорт.

password, *n*, паро́ль; ло́зунг.

past, *a*, про́шлый; *(gram.)* проше́дший; ~ *president* бы́вший президе́нт; ¶ *n*, про́шлое; *(gram.)* проше́дшее вре́мя; ¶ *pr*, ми́мо; по́сле, за; свы́ше; *half* ~ *three* полови́на четвёртого.

paste, *n*, па́ста; те́сто; кле́йстер; ¶ *v.t*, накле́ивать, скле́ивать; ~ *with* обкле́ивать; ~board карто́н.

pastel, *n*, пасте́ль; ¶ *a*, пасте́льный.

pasteurization, *n*, пастериза́ция; **pasteurize**, *v.t*, пастеризова́ть.

pastille, *n*, лепёшка, табле́тка.

pastime, *n*, времяпрепровожде́ние, развлече́ние.

pastor, *n*, па́стырь; *(eccl.)* па́стор; ~al, *a*, пастора́льный; ~ale, *n*, пастора́ль.

pastry, *n*, пече́нье, пиро́жное; те́сто; ~ *cook* конди́тер; ~ *shop* конди́терская.

pasturage, *n*, па́стбище; подно́жный корм; **pasture**, *n*, вы́гон, па́стбище; ¶ *v.t*, пасти́.

pasty, *a*, тестообра́зный; одутлова́тый; ¶ *n*, паште́т.

pat, *a*, уме́стный; уда́чный; ¶ *n*, похло́пывание, хлопо́к; кусо́к; ¶ *v.t*, похло́пывать, хло́пать.

patch, *n*, запла́та; уча́сток земли́; пятно́; му́шка *(on face);* ¶ *v.t*, чини́ть; лата́ть; ~ *up* чини́ть на ско́рую ру́ку; ула́живать *(quarrel);* ~work лоску́тная рабо́та; вещь из лоскуто́в; *(fig.)* меша́нина; ~work quilt стёганое одея́ло из лоскуто́в; ~ed, *a*, запла́танный, с запла́тами; ~y, *a*, пятни́стый; обры́вочный *(of knowledge);* неро́вный.

pate, *n*, *(coll.)* башка́, маку́шка.

pâté, *n*, паште́т.

paten, *n*, диск.

patent, *n*, очеви́дный, я́вный; откры́тый; патенто́ванный; ~ *leather* лаки́рованная ко́жа; ~ *medicine* патенто́ванное лека́рство; ¶ *n*, пате́нт; дипло́м; *letters* ~ жа́лованная гра́мота; ~ *of nobility* при́знак благоро́дства; ~ *office* бюро́ пате́нтов; *sole* ~ *rights* исключи́тельные права́; ¶ *v.t*, патентова́ть; брать пате́нт на.

paternal, *a*, оте́ческий; отцо́вский; ро́дственный по отцу́; **paternity**, *n*, отцо́вство.

path, *n*, тропи́нка, доро́жка; путь; траекто́рия.
pathetic, *a*, тро́гательный; жа́лкий; патети́ческий.
pathless, *a*, бездоро́жный.
pathological, *a*, патологи́ческий; **pathologist**, *n*, пато́лог; **pathology**, *n*, патоло́гия.
pathos, *n*, чу́вство; тро́гательность; па́фос.
pathway, *n*, доро́жка, тропи́нка; мостки́; тротуа́р.
patience, *n*, терпе́ние; пасья́нс; **patient**, *a*, терпели́вый; упо́рный; ¶ *n*, пацие́нт, больно́й.
patina, *n*, пати́на.
patriarch, *n*, патриа́рх; глава́; ~**al**, *a*, патриа́рший; *(fig.)* патриарха́льный.
patrician, *a*, патрициа́нский, аристократи́чский.
patrimony, *n*, насле́дие; во́тчина.
patriot, *n*, патрио́т; ~**ic**, *a*, патриоти́ческий; ~**ism**, *n*, патриоти́зм.
patrol, *n*, патру́ль, дозо́р; патрули́рование; *on* ~ в дозо́ре; ¶ *v.t*, патрули́ровать.
patron, *n*, покрови́тель, засту́пник; патро́н; ~**age**, *n*, покрови́тельство; ~**ize**, *v.t*, покрови́тельствовать *(dat.);* поддержа́ть; ~**izing**, *a*, покрови́тельственный; снисходи́тельный.
patronymic, *n*, о́тчество.
patter, *n*, стук; скорогово́рка; болтовня́; ¶ *v.i*, бараба́нить, стуча́ть; говори́ть скорогово́ркой.
pattern, *n*, образе́ц, приме́р; моде́ль; вы́кройка *(of dress);* узо́р.
patty, *n*, пирожо́к.
paucity, *n*, ма́лое коли́чество.
paunch, *n*, брю́хо, пу́зо.
pauper, *n*, бедня́к, ни́щий; ~**ism**, *n*, нищета́.
pause, *n*, па́уза, переры́в; остано́вка; ¶ *v.i*, де́лать па́узу/переры́в.
pave, *v.t*, мости́ть; ~ *the way for* прокла́дывать путь для; ~**ment**, *n*, тротуа́р, мостова́я.
pavilion, *n*, павильо́н; пала́тка.
paving, *n*, мостова́я; ~ *stone* брусча́тка; булы́жник.
paw, *n*, ла́па; ¶ *v.t*, тро́гать ла́пой; бить копы́том.
pawn, *n*, пе́шка *(chess, & fig.);* закла́д; ~**broker** ростовщи́к; хозя́ин ломба́рда; ~**shop** ломба́рд;

¶ *v.t*, закла́дывать; отдава́ть в зало́г.
pay, *n*, пла́та; зарпла́та, жа́лованье; ~ *day* день зарпла́ты; *on half* ~ на полуста́вке; ~ *office* ка́сса; ~ *roll* платёжная ве́домость; ¶ *v.t*, плати́ть; опла́чивать; *v.i*, приноси́ть дохо́д; быть вы́годным; окупа́ться; ~ *attention* обраща́ть внима́ние; ~ *back* возвраща́ть; отпла́чивать; ~ *in cash* плати́ть нали́чными; ~ *a compliment* де́лать комплиме́нт; ~ *for* плати́ть за, опла́чивать; ~ *off* распла́чиваться с; ~ *respects* свиде́тельствовать почте́ние; ~ *a visit* посеща́ть; наноси́ть визи́т; ~ *out* выпла́чивать; *I'll* ~ *you out for this* я вам отплачу́ за э́то; ~**able**, *a*, подлежа́щий опла́те; ~ *to bearer* с упла́той на предъяви́теля; ~**ee**, *n*, получа́тель; предъяви́тель че́ка; ~**er**, *n*, плате́льщик; ~**ing**, *a*, вы́годный, дохо́дный; ~**ment**, *n*, упла́та, платёж; пла́та; ~ *in advance* пла́та вперёд; ~ *in full* пла́та по́лностью.
pea, *n*, горо́шина; *pl*, горо́х; *sweet* ~ души́стый горо́шек; *they are as like as two* ~s они́ похо́жи как две ка́пли воды́.
peace, *n*, мир; споко́йствие; ~**maker** примири́тель, миротво́рец; ~ *offering* искупи́тельная же́ртва; ~**able**, & ~**ful**, *a*, ми́рный, споко́йный; ~**fulness**, *n*, споко́йствие, тишина́.
peach, *n*, пе́рсик; ~ *tree* пе́рсиковое де́рево.
peacock, *n*, павли́н; **peahen**, *n*, па́ва.
peak, *n*, пик, верши́на; козырёк *(of cap);* вы́сшая то́чка.
peal, *n*, звон, трезво́н; ~ *of laughter* взрыв сме́ха; ~ *of thunder* раска́т гро́ма; ¶ *v.i*, звони́ть, трезво́нить.
peanut, *n*, ара́хис, земляно́й оре́х.
pear, *n*, гру́ша; ~*-shaped* груше-ви́дный; ~ *tree* гру́шевое де́рево.
pearl, *n*, же́мчуг; жемчу́жина; перл; ~ *barley* перло́вая крупа́; ~ *button* перламу́тровая пу́говица; ~ *oyster* жемчу́жная ра́ковина; ~**y**, *a*, жемчу́жный; укра́шенный же́мчугом.
peasant, *n*, крестья́нин; ~**ry**, *n*, крестья́нство.

peat, *n,* торф; ~ *bog* торфянóе болóто; ~у, *а,* торфянóй.

pebble, *n,* гáлька; **pebbly,** *a,* покрытый гáлькой.

peccadillo, *n,* грешóк.

peck, *n,* клевóк; пек *(measure);* ¶ *v.t,* клевáть; *be* ~*ish* быть голóдным.

pectoral, *a,* груднóй; нагрýдный.

peculate, *v.i,* растрáчивать, расхищáть; **peculation,** *n,* растрáта, расхищéние; казнокрáдство.

peculiar, *a,* осóбенный, своеобрáзный; стрáнный; ~ *to* свóйственный *(dat.);* ~**ity,** *n,* осóбенность; стрáнность; свóйство.

pecuniary, *a,* дéнежный.

pedagogue, *n,* педагóг; **pedagogy,** *n,* педагóгика.

pedal, *n,* педáль; ¶ *v.i,* нажимáть педáли; éхать на велосипéде.

pedant, *n,* педáнт; ~**ic,** *a,* педантúчный; ~**ry,** *n,* педантúчность.

peddle, *v.t,* торговáть вразнóс *(inst.);* *(fig.)* перескáзывать.

pedestal, *n,* пьедестáл; поднóжие; подстáвка.

pedestrian, *n,* пешехóд; ~ *crossing* перехóд; ¶ *a,* пéший, пешехóдный; прозаúческий.

pedigree, *n,* родослóвная; происхождéние; ¶ *a,* порóдистый; ~ *cattle* племеннóй скот.

pediment, *n,* фронтóн.

pedlar, *n,* разнóсчик, коробéйник.

peel, *n,* кóжица, кожурá, кóрка, шелухá; ¶ *v.t,* чúстить; шелушúть; *v.i,* шелушúться, лупúться; ~**er,** *n,* обдúрочная машúна; ~**ing,** *n,* кóжа, кóрка, шелухá; *potato* ~**s** картóфельные очúстки.

peep, *n,* взгляд украдкой; писк; ~*-hole* глазóк, смотровóе отвéрстие; ¶ *v.i,* загля́дывать; выгля́дывать; подгля́дывать; прогля́дывать; пищáть, чирúкать.

peer, *n,* пэр, лорд; рóвня; ¶ *v.i,* глядéть; выгля́дывать; ~ *into* всмáтриваться в.

peerage, *n,* звáние пэра; знать; **peerless,** *a,* несравнéнный, бесподóбный.

peevish, *a,* раздражúтельный, сварлúвый; ~**ness,** *n,* раздражúтельность, сварлúвость.

peg, *n,* кóлышек; деревя́нный гвоздь; крючóк (вéшалки); ~*-top* волчóк, юлá; *buy clothes off the* ~

покупáть готóвое плáтье; *take down a* ~ осáживать, сбивáть спесь с; ¶ *v.t,* прикреплять (кóлышком); ~ *prices* держáть цéны на однóм ýровне; ~ *away* упóрно рабóтать.

Pekinese, *a,* пекúнский; ¶ *n,* китáйский мопс.

pelican, *n,* пеликáн.

pellet, *n,* кáтышек; пýля, дробúнка; пилюля.

pellicle, *n,* кóжица, плёнка.

pell-mell, *ad,* как попáло, беспорядочно.

pellucid, *a,* прозрáчный, я́сный.

pelt, *n,* кóжа, шкýра; ¶ *v.t,* забрáсывать (камня́ми/вопрóсами); *v.i,* барабáнить, лить *(of rain);* ~*ing rain* проливнóй дождь.

pelvis, *n,* таз.

pen, *n,* перó, рýчка; загóн; ~*holder* рýчка; ~*knife* перочúнный нож; ~*manship* каллигрáфия; пóчерк; ~*-name* псевдонúм; *slip of the* ~ опúска; ¶ *v.t,* запирáть; загоня́ть.

penal, *a,* уголóвный; карáтельный; ~ *servitude* кáторжные рабóты; ~**ize,** *v.t,* накáзывать; штрафовáть; ~**ty,** *n,* наказáние; взыскáние, штраф *(also sport);* *under* ~ *of* под стрáхом *(gen.);* **penance,** *n,* епитимья́.

Penates, *n.pl,* пенáты.

pencil, *n,* карандáш; ~ *sharpener* точúлка для карандашéй; ¶ *v.t,* писáть/рисовáть карандашóм.

pendant, *a,* вися́чий; нерешённый; ¶ *n,* подвéска, кулóн; *(mar.)* вы́мпел; **pending,** *a,* незакóнченный, нерешённый; ¶ *pr,* в ожидáнии *(gen.).*

pendulum, *n,* мáятник.

penetrate, *v t,* прони́зывать; пропúтывать; ~ *into* проникáть в; **penetrating,** *a,* пронзúтельный, проницáтельный; **penetration,** *n,* проникновéние; проницáтельность.

penguin, *n,* пингвúн.

penicillin, *n,* пенициллúн.

peninsula, *n,* полуóстров; ~**r,** *a,* полуостровнóй.

penitence, *n,* раскáяние; покая́ние; **penitent,** *a,* раскáивающийся; кáющийся; ¶ *n,* кáющийся грéшник; ~**ial,** *a,* покáянный; ~**iary,** *n,* исправúтельный дом.

pennant, *n,* вы́мпел, знáмя; подвéска-

penniless, *a*, без гроша; безденежный, бедный; **penny**, *n*, пенни; ~**worth**, *n*, небольшое количество (получаемое за одно пенни); ¶ *a*, грошовый.

pension, *n*, пенсия, пособие; пансион; *old age* ~ пенсия по старости; ¶ *v.t.:* ~ *off* увольнять на пенсию; ~**er**, *n*, пенсионер.

pensive, *a*, задумчивый.

pentagon, *n*, пятиугольник; ~**al**, *a*, пятиугольный.

Pentecost, *n*, пятидесятница.

pent-house, *n*, навес; квартира на верхнем этаже.

pent-up, *a*, сдерживаемый.

penultimate, *a*, предпоследний.

penumbra, *n*, полутень.

penurious, *a*, скупой; бедный; **penury**, *n*, бедность.

peony, *n*, пион.

people, *n*, народ; люди; родные, родители; *some* ~ некоторые люди; *young* ~ молодёжь; ¶ *v.t*, заселять, населять.

pepper, *n*, перец; ~**corn** зёрнышко перца; ~**mill**, *n*, перечница; ~**mint** перечная мята; мятная лепёшка; ¶ *v.t*, перчить; осыпать; ~**y**, *a*, наперченный; *(fig.)* вспыльчивый; едкий.

per, *pr*, в, на; по; ~ *annum* в год; ~ *cent* процент, на сотню.

perambulate, *v.i*, расхаживать; **perambulator**, *n*, детская коляска.

perceive, *v.t*, ощущать; понимать; воспринимать.

percentage, *n*, процент.

perceptibility, *n*, ощутимость; воспринимаемость; **perceptible**, *a*, ощутимый, заметный; **perception**, *n*, восприятие, понимание; **perceptive**, *a*, восприимчивый.

perch, *n*, окунь *(fish)*; насест; мера длины (= 5,03 м.); высокое положение; ¶ *v.i*, садиться; взгромождаться.

perchance, *ad*, случайно; возможно.

percolate, *v.t*, процеживать, фильтровать; *v.i*, просачиваться; **percolator**, *n*, фильтр; ситечко; кофейник с ситечком; кофеварка.

percussion, *n*, столкновение, удар; *(med.)* выстукивание; ~ *cap* пистон, капсюль; ~ *instrument* ударный инструмент; **percussive**, *a*, ударный.

perdition, *n*, гибель, погибель.

peregrinate, *v.i*, странствовать; **peregrination**, *n*, странствие; **peregrine [falcon]**, *n*, сапсан.

peremptory, *a*, безапелляционный; повелительный, властный.

perennial, *a*, вечный; *(bot.)* многолетний; ¶ *n*, многолетнее растение.

perfect, *a*, совершённый; безупречный; ¶ *v.t*, совершенствовать; завершать; ~**ion**, *n*, совершенство, безупречность; ~**ly**, *ad*, совершенно, вполне.

perfidious, *a*, вероломный, предательский; **perfidy**, *n*, вероломство, предательство.

perforate, *v.t*, просверливать, пробивать; **perforation**, *n*, просверливание, пробивание; отверстие; *(med.)* прободение.

perforce, *ad*, волей-неволей, по необходимости.

perform, *v.t*, выполнять *(duty)*; исполнять *(role)*; играть; совершать; представлять; *v.i*, играть, делать трюки; ~**ance**, *n*, выполнение; исполнение; *(theat.)* представление; ходовые качества *(of car, etc.)*; лётные данные *(of aircraft)*; ~**er**, *n*, исполнитель; актёр.

perfume, *n*, аромат; духи; ¶ *v.t*, душить; ~**ry**, *n*, парфюмерия.

perfunctory, *a*, небрежный; поверхностный.

pergola, *n*, беседка, аллея.

perhaps, *ad*, может быть, возможно.

peril, *n*, опасность; риск; ~**ous**, *a*, опасный, рискованный.

perimeter, *n*, периметр.

period, *n*, период; эпоха; круг, цикл; *(U.S.)* точка; ~**ic**, *a*, периодический; ~**ical**, *n*, периодическое издание, журнал; ~**icity**, *n*, периодичность.

periphery, *n*, периферия, окружность.

periphrasis, *n*, перифраз(а).

periscope, *n*, перископ.

perish, *v.i*, погибать, умирать; пропадать; портиться; ~**able**, *a*, скоропортящийся; бренный, тленный.

peristyle, *n*, перистиль.

peritonitis, *n*, воспаление брюшины.

periwig, *n*, парик.

periwinkle, *n*, *(bot.)* барвинок; *(zool.)* литорина.

perjure oneself лжесвиде́тельствовать; **perjurer**, n, лжесвиде́тель; **perjury**, n, лжесвиде́тельство; наруше́ние кля́твы.

perk up оживля́ться; воспря́нуть (*pf.*) ду́хом; **perky**, a, бо́йкий.

permanence, n, про́чность, неизме́нность; **permanent**, a, постоя́нный, неизме́нный; ~ *wave* пермане́нт.

permanganate, n, пермангана́т.

permeable, a, проница́емый; **permeate**, v.t, проника́ть в; пропи́тывать;

permissible, a, позволи́тельный, допусти́мый; **permission**, n, разреше́ние, позволе́ние; **permissive**, a, дозволя́ющий, позволя́ющий, допуска́ющий; ~ *society* о́бщество, в кото́ром всё дозво́лено; **permissiveness**, n, дозво́ленность; **permit**, n, про́пуск; разреше́ние; ¶ v.t, допуска́ть; разреша́ть, позволя́ть.

permutation, n, переме́на; перестано́вка.

pernicious, a, вре́дный, па́губный.

peroration, n, заключе́ние ре́чи.

peroxide, n, пе́рекись; ~ *blonde* кра́шеная блонди́нка.

perpendicular, a, перпендикуля́рный, отве́сный; ¶ n, перпендикуля́р.

perpetrate, v.t, соверша́ть; **perpetrator**, n, вино́вник, престу́пник.

perpetual, a, ве́чный, бесконе́чный; ~ *motion* ве́чное движе́ние; **perpetuate**, v.t, увекове́чивать; **perpetuity**, n, ве́чность, бесконе́чность; *in* ~ навсегда́, наве́ки.

perplex, v.t, смуща́ть, приводи́ть в недоуме́ние; ~ed, p.p. & a, расте́рянный, сби́тый с то́лку; ~ing, a, сло́жный, затрудни́тельный; ~ity, n, недоуме́ние, расте́рянность.

perquisite, n, при́работок; случа́йный дохо́д.

perry, n, гру́шевый сидр.

persecute, v.t, пресле́довать, подверга́ть гоне́ниям; надоеда́ть (dat.); **persecution**, n, пресле́дование, гоне́ние; **persecutor**, n, пресле́дователь, гони́тель.

perseverance, n, упо́рство; насто́йчивость; **persevere**, v.i, проявля́ть

упо́рство; **persevering**, a, упо́рный; насто́йчивый.

Persian, a, перси́дский; ¶ n, перс, -ия́нка.

persist, v.i, упо́рствовать; ~ence, n, упо́рство, насто́йчивость; ~ent, a, упо́рный, насто́йчивый.

person, n, челове́к; лицо́, осо́ба; вне́шность; *in* ~ ли́чно; ~age, n, выдаю́щаяся ли́чность; де́йствующее лицо́; ~al, a, ли́чный, ча́стный; ~ality, n, ли́чность, индивидуа́льность; ~ally, ad, сам, ли́чно; ~ate, v.t, выдава́ть себя́ за; ~ification, n, олицетворе́ние, воплоще́ние; ~ify, v.t, олицетворя́ть, воплоща́ть; ~nel n, персона́л, ли́чный соста́в.

perspective, n, перспекти́ва; ¶ a, перспекти́вный.

perspicacious, a, проница́тельный; **perspicacity**, n, проница́тельность; **perspicuity**, n, я́сность; прозра́чность.

perspiration, n, пот, испа́рина; поте́ние; **perspire**, v.i, поте́ть; **perspiring**, a, вспоте́вший.

persuade, v.t, убежда́ть, угова́ривать; ~ *from* отгова́ривать от; **persuasion**, n, убежде́ние; вероиспове́дание; **persuasive**, a, убеди́тельный.

pert, a, бо́йкий; де́рзкий.

pertain, v.i: ~ *to* принадлежа́ть к, име́ть отноше́ние к.

pertinacious, a, упря́мый; **pertinacity**, n, упря́мство.

pertinent, a, уме́стный, подходя́щий.

pertness, n, бо́йкость; де́рзость.

perturb, v.t, беспоко́ить, волнова́ть; ~ation, n, волне́ние, беспоко́йство; ~ing, a, волну́ющий.

peruke, n, пари́к.

perusal, n, чте́ние, рассма́тривание; **peruse**, v.t, (внима́тельно) чита́ть, рассма́тривать.

Peruvian, a, перуа́нский; ¶ n, перуа́н|ец, -ка; ~ *bark* хи́нная ко́рка.

pervade, v.t, проника́ть в; пропи́тывать; **pervasive**, a, проника́ющий.

perverse, a, упря́мый; капри́зный; **perversion**, n, извраще́ние; искаже́ние; **perversity**, n, упря́мство, несгово́рчивость; **pervert**, n, извращённый челове́к; ¶ v.t,

извраща́ть; развраща́ть; ~ed, *p.p.*
& *a*, развра́тный; извращённый.
pervious, *a*, проница́емый, прохо-
ди́мый.
pessimism, *n*, пессими́зм; **pessimist**,
n, пессими́ст; ~ic, *a*, пессимисти́-
ческий.
pest, *n*, я́зва; вреди́тель, парази́т;
эпидеми́ческое заболева́ние.
pester, *v.t*, надоеда́ть *(dat.)*, при-
става́ть к.
pestiferous, *a*, зара́зный; вре́дный;
pestilence, *n*, чума́, мор; эпиде́мия;
pestilential, *a*, зара́зный; па́губный;
надое́дливый.
pestle, *n*, пе́стик; ¶ *v.t*, толо́чь.
pet, *n*, ко́мнатное живо́тное; ба́ло-
вень, люби́мец; раздраже́ние; *be
in a* ~ ду́ться; ~ *name* ласка́тель-
ное и́мя; ¶ *v.t*, ласка́ть; ба́ловать.
petal, *n*, лепесто́к.
peter, *v.i*: ~ *out* истоща́ться, исся-
ка́ть.
petition, *n*, проше́ние, петйция,
хода́тайство; ¶ *v.t*, подава́ть
проше́ние *(dat.)*; ~ *for* хода́тай-
ствовать о; ~er, *n*, проси́тель.
petrel, *n*, буреве́стник.
petrifaction, *n*, окамене́ние; окамене́-
лость; **petrify**, *v.t*, превраща́ть в
ка́мень, *(fig.)* ошеломля́ть; *v.i*,
превраща́ться в ка́мень, каме-
не́ть; *be petrified* столбене́ть от
у́жаса.
petrol, *n*, бензи́н; ~-*tank* бензоба́к;
~eum, *n*, нефть, петро́леум.
petticoat, *n*, ни́жняя ю́бка; де́т-
ская ю́бочка.
pettifoggery, *n*, крючкотво́рство, кля-
узничество; **pettifogging**, *a*, кля-
узный, ме́лочный.
pettiness, *n*, ме́лочность; малова́ж-
ность; **pettish**, *a*, обидчивый;
petty, *a*, ме́лкий; ме́лочный; мало-
ва́жный; ~ *officer* старшина́.
petulance, *n*, раздражи́тельность,
обидчивость; **petulant**, *a*, раздра-
жи́тельный, обидчивый.
pew, *n*, церко́вная скамья́.
pewter, *n*, о́лово; сплав о́лова со
свинцо́м; оловя́нная посу́да.
phaeton, *n*, фаэто́н.
phalanx, *n*, фала́нга.
phantasm, *n*, иллю́зия; **phantom**, *n*,
при́зрак.
pharisaical, *a*, фарисе́йский; ха́н-
жеский; **Pharisee**, *n*, фарисе́й;
ханжа́.

pharmaceutical, *a*, фармацевти́чес-
кий; **pharmacist**, *n*, фармаце́вт;
pharmacology, *n*, фармаколо́гия;
pharmacy, *n*, апте́ка; фарма́ция.
pharyngitis, *n*, фаринги́т; **pharynx**,
гло́тка.
phase, *n*, фа́за, ста́дия.
pheasant, *n*, фаза́н.
phenacetin, *n*, фенаце́тин.
phenomenal, *a*, феномена́льный, не-
обыкнове́нный; **phenomenon**, *n*,
явле́ние; фено́мен.
phial, *n*, скля́нка, пузырёк.
philander, *v.i*, флиртова́ть; ~er, *n*,
волоки́та, ухажёр.
philanthropic, *a*, филантропи́ческий;
philanthropist, *n*, филантро́п; **philanthropy**, *n*, филантро́пия.
philatelist, *n*, филатели́ст; **philately**,
n, филателия.
philharmonic, *a*, филармони́ческий.
philippic, *n*, фили́ппика.
Philippine, *a*, филиппи́нский; ¶ *n*,
филиппи́н|ец, *pl.* ~ка.
Philistine, *n*, филистер, обыва́тель;
¶ *a*, фили́стерский, обыва́тель-
ский.
philological, *a*, филологи́ческий; **phi-
lologist**, *n*, фило́лог; **philology**, *n*,
филоло́гия.
philosopher, *n*, фило́соф; **philoso-
phic(al)**, *a*, филосо́фский; **philosophy**, *n*, филосо́фия.
philtre, *n*, любо́вный напи́ток, зе́лье.
phlebitis, *n*, флеби́т.
phlegm, *n*, мокро́та; флегма, хлад-
нокро́вие; ~atic, *a*, флегмати́ч-
ный.
phlox, *n*, флокс.
Phoenician, *a*, финики́йский; ¶ *n*,
финики́ян|ин, *pl.* -ка; финики́йский
язы́к.
phoenix, *n*, фе́никс.
phonetic, *a*, фонети́ческий; ~s, *n*,
фоне́тика.
phosphate, *n*, фосфа́т; **phosphorescence**, *n*, фосфоресце́нция, све-
че́ние; **phosphorescent**, *a*, фосфо-
ресци́рующий, светя́щийся; **phosphorus**, *n*, фо́сфор.
photograph, *n*, фотогра́фия, сни́мок;
¶ *v.t*, фотографи́ровать, снима́ть;
~er, *n*, фото́граф; ~ic, *a*, фото-
графи́ческий; ~y, *n*, фотогра́фия,
фотографи́рование; **photogravure**,
n, фотогравю́ра.
phrase, *n*, фра́за *(also mus.)*, выра-
же́ние; идио́ма; ¶ *v.t*, выража́ть;

(mus.) фразировать; **phraseology,** *n,* фразеология.

phrenology, *n,* френология.

physic, *n,* медицина; лекарство; ~**al,** *a,* физический; телесный; ~**ian,** *n,* врач, доктор; ~**ist,** *n,* физик; ~**s,** *n,* физика.

physiognomy, *n,* физиономия.

physiology, *n,* физиология.

physique, *n,* телосложение.

pianist, *n,* пианист; **piano,** *n,* форте-пьяно; *upright* ~ пианино; ~ *stool* табурет для рояля/пианино; **pianola,** *n,* пианола.

piccaninny, *n,* негритёнок.

piccolo, *n,* пикколо.

pick, *n,* выбор; лучшая часть; кирка, мотыга; ~ *axe* кирка, мотыга; ~*-те-ир* возбуждающее средство; ~ *pocket* карманный вор; ¶ *v.t,* выбирать; рвать, собирать; обгладывать *(bone);* открывать отмычкой *(lock);* ковырять (в зубах); ~ *a quarrel* напрашиваться на ссору; ~ *off* отрывать; пере-стреливать; ~ *up* поднимать; выздоравливать; заезжать за; знакомиться случайно с; *have a bone to* ~ *with* иметь счёты с.

pick-a-back, *ad,* на спине, за плечами.

picked, *p.p. & a,* отобранный; отборный.

picket, *n,* кол; пикет; пикётчик; *(mil.)* сторожевая застава; ¶ *v.t,* пикетировать.

picking, *n,* собирание, сбор; выбор; *pl,* мелкий заработок; остатки, объедки.

pickle, *n,* рассол; *pl,* маринад, пикули; *a pretty* ~ затруднительное положение; ¶ *v.t,* мариновать, солить.

picnic, *n,* пикник; *по* ~ нелёгкое дело; ¶ *v.i,* принимать участие в пикнике.

pictorial, *a,* изобразительный; живо-писный; иллюстрированный **pic-ture,** *n,* картина; портрет; копия *(also fig.);* фильм; ~*-frame* рама; ~ *gallery* картинная галерея; ~ *postcard* художественная открыт-ка; ~ *theatre* кинотеатр; ¶ *v.t,* описывать; представлять себе; **picturesque,** *a,* живописный; образный *(of language).*

pie, *n,* пирог; *have a finger in the* ~ быть замешанным в деле.

piebald, *a,* пегий; *(fig.)* разнош-ёрстный.

piece, *n,* кусок; часть; произведе-ние, пьеса; монета; штука; учас-ток; предмет; ~ *of furniture* мебель; ~ *of ground* участок земли; ~ *of news* новость; ~ *of work* работа; ~ *work* сдельная работа; *come to* ~*s* разваливаться; разбиваться вдребезги; *go to* ~*s* портиться; пропадать; *take to* ~*s* разбирать (на части); ¶ *v.t:* ~ *together* собирать воедино; ~*meal,* *ad,* по частям; постепенно.

pied, *a,* пёстрый.

pier, *n,* мол; пристань; свая, столб; бык *(of bridge);* простёнок.

pierce, *v.t,* пронзать, прокалывать; проходить/прорываться сквозь; **piercing,** *a,* пронзительный *(cry);* острый *(look, pain);* пронизы-вающий; ¶ *n,* прокол.

piety, *n,* благочестие, набож-ность.

pig, *n,* свинья; *(tech.)* болванка, чушка; ~*-headed* упрямый, глу-пый; ~ *iron* чугун (в чушках); ~*skin* свиная кожа; ~*sty* свинар-ник; ~*tail* косичка; *buy a* ~ *in a poke* покупать кота в мешке.

pigeon, *n,* голубь; ~*-hole* ящик; от-деление письменного стола; ~ *loft* голубятня.

pigment, *n,* пигмент.

pike, *n, (fish)* щука; пика, копьё; ~*staff* древко пики; *as plain as a* ~*staff* ясный как день.

pilaster, *n,* пилястра.

pilchard, *n,* сардинка.

pile, *n,* куча, груда, кипа *(paper);* погребальный костёр; громада (зданий); свая, столб; *(elec.)* батарея; ворс *(on cloth); pl, (med.)* геморрой; *atomic* ~ ядерный реактор; ~ *of books* стопка книг; ~*-driver* копёр; ¶ *v.t,* складывать/ сваливать в кучу; ~ *up* нагро-мождать, накоплять.

pilfer, *v.t,* воровать; ~**ing,** *n,* мел-кая кража.

pilgrim, *n,* паломник, пилигрим; ~**age,** *n,* паломничество, стран-ствие.

pill, *n,* пилюля, таблетка.

pillage, *n,* грабёж; ¶ *v.t,* грабить.

pillar, *n,* столб, колонна; *(fig.)* опора, столп; ~ *box* почтовый ящик.

pillion, *n*, да́мское седло́; за́днее сиде́нье (мотоци́кла).

pillory, *n*, позо́рный столб; ¶ *v.t*, ста́вить/ *(fig.)* пригвожда́ть к позо́рному столбу́.

pillow, *n*, поду́шка; ~ *case*, ~ *slip* на́волочка; ¶ *v.t*, класть (го́лову на).

pilot, *n*, *(avia.)* пило́т, лётчик; *(mar.)* ло́цман; проводни́к; ~ *boat* ло́цманский кора́бль; ~ *scheme* о́пытный прое́кт; ¶ *v.t*, вести́; управля́ть *(inst.)*; пилоти́ровать.

pimp, *n*, сво́дник; сутенёр; ¶ *v.i*, сво́дничать.

pimpernel, *n*, о́чный цвет.

pimple, *n*, пры́щик.

pin, *n*, була́вка; шпи́лька; *(tech.)* болт; ~ *cushion* поду́шечка для була́вок; ~ *money* де́ньги на ме́лкие расхо́ды; ¶ *v.t*, зака́лывать; прика́лывать була́вкой.

pinafore, *n*, пере́дник, фа́ртук.

pincers, *n.pl*, щипцы́, щи́пчики; кле́щи; пинце́т.

pinch, *n*, щипо́к; щепо́тка *(of salt, etc.)*; нужда́; *at a* ~ в кра́йнем слу́чае; ¶ *v.t*, щипа́ть; щеми́ть; жать *(of shoe)*; красть; *know where the shoe ~es* знать в чём загво́здка.

pine, *n*, сосна́; ~ *cone* сосно́вая ши́шка; ~ *needle* сосно́вая хво́я.

pine, *v.i*: ~ *away* ча́хнуть; изныва́ть; ~ *for* тоскова́ть по.

pineapple, *n*, анана́с.

pining, *n*, тоска́.

pinion, *n*, оконе́чность пти́чьего крыла́, крыло́; *(tech.)* шестерня́, зубча́тое колесо́; ¶ *v.t*, подреза́ть кры́лья *(dat.)*; *(fig.)* свя́зывать ру́ки *(dat.)*.

pink, *a*, ро́зовый; ¶ *n*, гвозди́ка; ро́зовый цвет; *in the* ~ в отли́чном состоя́нии.

pinnace, *n*, ка́тер.

pinnacle, *n*, шпиц; *(fig.)* верши́на, верх.

pint, *n*, пи́нта.

pioneer, *n*, пионе́р; инициа́тор; *(mil.)* сапёр.

pious, *a*, благочести́вый, на́божный.

pip, *n*, зёрнышко, ко́сточка; звёздочка *(on epaulette)*; очко́ *(on card)*.

pipe, *n*, труба́; (кури́тельная) тру́бка; ду́дка, свире́ль; *pl*, волы́нка;

~ *clay* бе́лая гли́на; ~*line* трубопрово́д; ¶ *v.i*, игра́ть на свире́ли, *etc.*; петь, свисте́ть; *v.t*, игра́ть; пуска́ть по тру́бам; ~*r*, *n*, волы́нщик; **piping**, *n*, игра́ (на свире́ли); тру́бы; кант *(on dress)*; ~ *hot* о́чень горя́чий; соверше́нно но́вый/све́жий.

pipkin, *n*, гли́няный горшо́чек.

pippin, *n*, пепи́н.

piquancy, *n*, пика́нтность; **piquant**, *a*, пика́нтный.

piqué, *n*, пике́.

pique, *n*, заде́тое самолю́бие, доса́да; ¶ *v.t*, коло́ть; задева́ть самолю́бие *(gen.)*.

piracy, *n*, пира́тство; наруше́ние а́вторского пра́ва; **pirate**, *n*, пира́т; наруши́тель а́вторского пра́ва; ¶ *v.t*, гра́бить; незако́нно перепеча́тывать; **piratical**, *a*, пира́тский.

pistol, *n*, пистоле́т, револьве́р.

piston, *n*, по́ршень; ~ *rod* шату́н.

pit, *n*, я́ма; впа́дина; ша́хта, копь; ряби́на *(on face)*; за́дние ряды́ партёра *(on face)*; ме́сто для орке́стра; *in the* ~ *of the stomach* под ло́жечкой; ¶ *v.t*, противопоставля́ть; ~ *one's strength against* сража́ться с.

pit-a-pat: *go* ~ трепета́ть.

pitch, *n*, смола́; дёготь; высота́ *(of sound)*; сте́пень; килева́я ка́чка *(of boat)*; укло́н; *(sport)* по́ле, площа́дка; пода́ча; *black as* ~ чёрный как смоль; *(fig.) darkness* тьма кроме́шная; ¶ *v.t*, смоли́ть; ста́вить *(tent)*; разбива́ть *(camp)*; броса́ть, подава́ть; *(mus.)* дава́ть основно́й тон *(dat.)*; *v.i*, па́дать; испы́тывать килеву́ю ка́чку; ~ *into* набра́сываться на; ~*ed battle* реши́тельное сраже́ние; *high-~ed voice* высо́кий го́лос.

pitcher, *n*, кувши́н; *(sport)* подаю́щий мяч.

pitchfork, *n*, ви́лы.

pitching, *n*, *(mar.)* килева́я ка́чка; пода́ча.

piteous, *a*, жа́лкий, жа́лобный.

pitfall, *n*, во́лчья я́ма; *(fig.)* западня́, лову́шка.

pith, *n*, сердцеви́на; спинно́й мозг; суть, су́щность; ~*y*, *a*, с сердцеви́ной; содержа́тельный; сжа́тый *(style)*.

pitiable & **pitiful**, *a*, жа́лкий, несча́стный; жа́лостливый; **pitiless**, *a*, безжа́лостный.

pittance, *n*, скудное жа́лованье; жа́лкие гроши.

pitted, *a*, рябо́й *(with smallpox)*; уха́бистый.

pituitary, *a*, сли́зистый.

pity, *n*, жа́лость, сожале́ние, сострада́ние; *for* ~'*s sake!* ра́ди бо́га!; *what a* ~! как жа́лко!; ¶ *v.t*, жале́ть.

pivot, *n*, ось, сте́ржень; то́чка враще́ния; *(fig.)* центр; ¶ *v.i*, враща́ться (вокру́г оси́).

pixie, pixy, *n*, фе́я, эльф.

placard, *n*, плака́т, афи́ша, объявле́ние; ¶ *v.t*, покрыва́ть объявле́ниями; реклами́ровать.

placate, *v.t*, успока́ивать, умиротворя́ть.

place, *n*, ме́сто; положе́ние; до́лжность; *take* ~ име́ть ме́сто, состоя́ться; *in* ~ *of* вме́сто; *out of* ~ не на ме́сте, неуме́стный; ¶ *v.t*, помеща́ть, класть, ста́вить.

placid, *a*, споко́йный; ~**ity**, *n*, споко́йствие.

plagiarism, *n*, плагиа́т; **plagiarist**, *n*, плагиа́тор; **plagiarize**, *v.t*, займствовать.

plaice, *n*, ка́мбала.

plaid, *n*, плед.

plain, *a*, просто́й; я́сный; некраси́вый; одноцве́тный; ~ *clothes* шта́тское пла́тье; ~ *dealing* прямота́; ~ *speaking* разгово́р в откры́тую; *in* ~ *English* без обиняко́в; ¶ *n*, равни́на; пло́скость; ~**ness**, *n*, простота́; некраси́вость; очеви́дность.

plaint, *n*, иск; жа́лоба; плач; ~**iff**, *n*, исте́ц; ~**ive**, *a*, жа́лобный, заунывный.

plait, *n*, коса́; ¶ *v.t*, заплета́ть.

plan, *n*, план; схе́ма; прое́кт; *rough* ~ набро́сок, эски́з; ¶ *v.t*, плани́ровать, проекти́ровать; замышля́ть; *v.i*, намерева́ться.

plane, *n*, пло́скость; самолёт; *(tool)* руба́нок; ~ *tree* плата́н; ¶ *v.t*, строга́ть.

planet, *n*, плане́та; ~**arium**, *n*, планета́рий; ~**ary**, *a*, плане́тный.

plank, *n*, доска́, пла́нка; ¶ *v.t*, выстила́ть до́сками; ~**ing**, *n*, насти́л.

plant, *n*, *(bot.)* расте́ние; заво́д; устано́вка; *(coll.)* лову́шка; ¶ *v.t*, сажа́ть; *(fig.)* насажда́ть; ~ *on* подсо́вывать; ~ *out* расса́живать.

plantain, *n*, подоро́жник.

plantation, *n*, планта́ция; **planter**, *n*, планта́тор; *(agr.)* сажа́лка.

plaque, *n*, диск, стенна́я таре́лка; табли́чка.

plasma, *n*, пла́зма.

plaster, *n*, *(med.)* пла́стырь; *(build.)* штукату́рка; ¶ *a*, ги́псовый; штукату́рный; ~ *of Paris* гипс; алеба́стр; ~**er**, *n*, штукату́р; ~**ing**, *n*, оштукату́ривание, штукату́рная рабо́та.

plastic, *a*, пласти́ческий, пластма́ссовый; ~ *surgery* пласти́ческая хирурги́я; ¶ *n*, пластма́сса.

plate, *n*, таре́лка; пласти́нка; доще́чка; лист *(of metal)*; фотопласти́нка; гравю́ра; иллюстра́ция; вставна́я че́люсть *(dental)*; золота́я/сере́бряная посу́да; ~ *glass* зерка́льное стекло́; ~ *rack* суши́лка для посу́ды; ¶ *v.t*, брони́ровать; золоти́ть, никелирова́ть, серебри́ть.

plateau, *n*, плато́, плоского́рье.

plateful, *n*, по́лная таре́лка.

platform, *n*, платфо́рма, перро́н; трибу́на, помо́ст; площа́дка *(of coach)*.

plating, *n*, золоче́ние, никелиро́вка, серебре́ние.

platinum, *n*, пла́тина.

platoon, *n*, взвод.

platter, *n*, *(деревянная)* таре́лка; доска́ для хле́ба.

plaudit, *n*, рукоплеска́ние, аплодисме́нты.

plausibility, *n*, правдоподо́бие, вероя́тность; уме́ние внуша́ть дове́рие; **plausible**, *a*, правдоподо́бный, вероя́тный.

play, *n*, игра́; пье́са, спекта́кль; *(tech.)* зазо́р; ~ *actor* актёр; ~*bill* афи́ша; програ́мма; ~*goer* театра́л; ~*ground* площа́дка для игр; ~*house* теа́тр; ~*mate* друг де́тства; ~*time* вре́мя игры́; ~*thing* игру́шка; ~*wright* драмату́рг; ¶ *v.t*, игра́ть (роль); игра́ть на *(instrument)*; игра́ть в *(game)*; ~ *ball* игра́ть в мяч; ~ *a trick on* разы́грывать; *v.i*, игра́ть, забавля́ться; бить *(of fountain)*; переливаться *(of colours)*; ~ up, *(v.t.)* дразни́ть; *(v.i.)* игра́ть энерги́чно; капри́зничать; ~er, *n*, актёр; игро́к; музыка́нт; ~ful, *a*, игри́вый, шутли́вый.

plea, *n*, мольба́, про́сьба; заявле́ние (подсуди́мого); ~d, *v.i*, умоля́ть; ~ *a case* защища́ть де́ло; ~ *guilty* признава́ть себя́ вино́вным; ~ding, *n*, мольба́; хода́тайство; защи́та.

pleasant, *a*, прия́тный; ~ry, *n*, шу́тка; **please**, *v.t*, нра́виться *(dat.)*, угожда́ть *(dat.)*; *do as you* ~ де́лайте, что вам уго́дно; ¶ *imper*, пожа́луйста!; ~d, *a*, ~ *(with)* дово́льный *(inst.)*; ~ *to meet you* о́чень прия́тно познако́миться с ва́ми; *we are* ~ *to inform you* мы ра́ды сообщи́ть вам; **pleasing**, *a*, прия́тный; **pleasure**, *n*, удово́льствие; развлече́ние; во́ля; ~ *ground* парк; ~ *trip* увесели́тельная пое́здка.

pleat, *n*, скла́дка; ¶ *v.t*, плиссирова́ть, де́лать скла́дки на.

plebeian, *a*, плебе́йский; **plebiscite**, *n*, плебисци́т.

pledge, *n*, зало́г; обе́т, обеща́ние; обяза́тельство; ¶ *v.t*, закла́дывать; ~ *one's word* дава́ть сло́во; ~ *oneself* брать на себя́ обяза́тельство.

plenary, *a*, плена́рный; по́лный; **plenipotentiary**, *n*, уполномо́ченный; **plenitude**, *n*, полнота́, изоби́лие; **plenteous**, **plentiful**, *a*, оби́льный; **plenty**, *n*, доста́ток; изоби́лие; ~ *of* доста́точно; мно́го; **plenum**, *n*, пле́нум.

pleonasm, *n*, плеона́зм.

plethora, *n*, *(med.)* полнокро́вие; *(fig.)* избы́ток, изоби́лие; **plethoric**, *a*, полнокро́вный.

pleurisy, *n*, плеври́т.

plexus, *n*, сплете́ние.

pliable, **pliant**, *a*, ги́бкий; пода́тливый; **pliancy**, *n*, ги́бкость; пода́тливость.

pliers, *n*, щипцы́, плоскогу́бцы.

plight, *n*, тяжёлое положе́ние; ¶ *v.t:* ~ *one's troth* дава́ть обеща́ние (при обруче́нии).

plinth, *n*, пли́нтус.

plod, *v.i*, брести́, тащи́ться; ~ *at* корпе́ть над; ~der, *n*, рабо́тя́га, труже́ник.

plot, *n*, за́говор, интри́га; сюже́т; фа́була; уча́сток земли́; ¶ *v.t*, замышля́ть; *v.i*, устра́ивать за́говор, интригова́ть; ~ *a course* определя́ть курс; ~ter, *n*, заго́ворщик, интрига́н.

plough, *n*, плуг; ~man па́харь; ~share ле́мех; ¶ *v.t*, паха́ть; прова́ливать (на экза́мене); ~ *through* продвига́ться с трудо́м; одолева́ть *(work, etc.)*; ~ing, *n*, вспа́шка.

plover, *n*, ржа́нка.

pluck, *n*, му́жество; потроха́, ли́вер; ¶ *v.t*, рвать; ощи́пывать *(fowl)*; перебира́ть *(strings)*; дёргать; ~ *up courage* собира́ться с ду́хом; ~y, *a*, сме́лый.

plug, *n*, вту́лка, заты́чка, про́бка; *(elec.)* ште́псель, ви́лка; ¶ *v.t*, затыка́ть; заку́поривать; *(coll.)* назо́йливо реклами́ровать; ~ *in* вставля́ть ште́псель.

plum, *n*, сли́ва; ~ *tree* сли́вовое де́рево; ~ *pudding* пу́динг с изю́мом; рожде́ственский пу́динг.

plumage, *n*, опере́ние.

plumb, *a*, вертика́льный; *(fig.)* абсолю́тный; ¶ *n*, & ~ *line* отве́с, ватерпа́с; лот; ¶ *v.t*, измеря́ть глубину́ *(gen.)*; ста́вить по отве́су; *(fig.)* проника́ть в глубь (та́йны, *etc.)*; погружа́ться в глубину́ *(gen.)*; ~ er, *n*, водопрово́дчик; ~ing, *n*, водопрово́дное де́ло; водопрово́д.

plume, *n*, перо́; султа́н; ¶ *v.t*, украша́ть пе́рьями; ~ *oneself on* кичи́ться *(inst.)*.

plummet, *n*, ги́рька отве́са, отве́с; лот; ¶ *v.i*, па́дать отве́сно.

plump, *a*, по́лный, пу́хлый; ¶ *v.i:* ~ *for* голосова́ть за; выбира́ть; ~ness, *n*, полнота́.

plunder, *n*, грабёж; добы́ча; ¶ *v.t*, гра́бить; расхища́ть.

plunge, *n*, ныря́ние; погруже́ние; ¶ *v.t*, погружа́ть, окуна́ть; *v.i:* ныря́ть, погружа́ться, па́дать, броса́ться; ~r, *n*, плу́нжер.

pluperfect, *n*, давнопроше́дшее вре́мя.

plural, *a*, мно́жественный; ¶ *n*, мно́жественное число́. ~ity, *n*, мно́жественность; большинство́.

plus, *pr*, плюс; ¶ *a*, положи́тельный; ~*fours* брю́ки «гольф».

plush, n, плюш, плис; ¶ a, плюше-
вый, плисовый.

plutocrat, n, плутократ.

ply, n, сгиб, складка; слой; three-
~ трёхслойный; трёхпрядный
(wool); ~wood фанера; ¶ v.t,
угощать; засыпать (with ques-
tions); заниматься (inst., a trade);
v.i, курсировать.

pneumatic, a, пневматический.

pneumonia, n, воспаление лёгких,
пневмония.

poach, v.t, варить без скорлупы
(eggs); незаконно охотиться на;
займствовать, перенимать; v.i,
браконьерствовать; ~er, n, браконьер.

pock, n, óспина; ~-marked рябой.

pocket, n, карман; (avia.) воздуш-
ная яма; луза (billiards); be in
~ быть в выигрыше; be out of
~ быть в убытке; не иметь денег;
~-money карманные деньги; ¶ v.t,
класть в карман; прикармáни-
вать.

pod, n, стручок; шелуха; ¶ v.t,
лущить, шелушить.

podgy, a, короткий и толстый, пух-
лый.

poem, n, поэма; poet, n, поэт; ~ess,
n, поэтесса; ~ic, a, поэтический;
поэтичный; ~ry, n, поэзия, стихи;
поэтичность.

poignancy, n, острота; горькость;
мучительность; poignant, a, острый; горький; мучительный.

point, n, точка, пункт; кончик,
остриё; место; момент; очко (rly.)
стрелка; (geog.) мыс; (fig.) глáв-
ное, суть; ~-blank прямой; ~-
duty регулирование движения;
дежурство на посту; ~ of honour
дело чести; ~ of view точка зрения; be beside the ~ быть нек-
стáти, быть неуместным; be on the
~ of doing собираться сделать;
come to the ~ доходить до сути
дела; speak to the ~ говорить по
существу; ¶ v.t, точить, заост-
рять; ~ at показывать/указывать
на; наводить на (gun); ~ed,
p.p. & a, остроконечный, заострённый; колкий (of remark, etc.);
~er, n, указатель; стрелка (of
clock, etc.); указка; пойнтер
(dog); ~less, a, бесцельный, бессмысленный; ~sman, n стре-
лочник.

poise, n, равновесие; осанка; ¶ v.t,
уравновешивать; взвешивать; ~
oneself балансировать; ~d (to)
готовый (к, or inf.); самоуверенный.

poison, n, яд, отрава; ¶ v.t, отравлять; (fig.) портить; ~er, n,
отравитель; ~ing, n, отравление;
порча; ~ous, a, ядовитый.

poke, n, тычок, толчок; ¶ v.t, тыкать,
толкать; совать; мешать (with
poker); ~ about любопытствовать;
рыться; ~ fun at подшучивать
над; ~ one's nose in совать нос
в чужие дела; ~r, n, кочерга;
(cards) покер; roky, a, тесный.

polar, a, полярный; ~ bear белый
медведь; ~ize, v.t, поляризовáть.

pole, n, столб, шест; (geog. & elec.)
полюс; (punt) багор; ~-axe се-
кира; резак; ~-cat хорёк; ~ star
полярная звезда; ~ vault прыжок с шестом.

Pole, n, поляк, полька.

polemic, n, полемика; ~al, a, поле-
мический.

police, n, полиция; милиция; ~man
полицейский, милиционер; ~ station полицейский участок; ¶ v.t,
охранять.

policy, n, политика; страховой
полис; ~-holder держатель стра-
хового полиса.

Polish, a, польский; ¶ n, польский
язык.

polish, n, политура; крем для обуви;
глянец; (fig.) лоск; ¶ v.t, полировать, шлифовать (also fig.);
чистить (shoes); ~ off быстро
справляться с; покончить (pf.)
с; ~ed, p.p. & a, (от)полированный;
гладкий, блестящий; изысканный; ~er, n, полировщик, шли-
фовщик; машина/инструмент для
полирования/шлифования.

polite, a, вежливый; ~ly, ad, веж-
ливо; ~ness, n, вежливость.

politic, a, политичный, обдуманный;
~al, a, политический; ~ economy
политэкономия; ~ian, n, политик,
политический деятель; ~s, n,
политика; политические убеждения; polity, n, политическое устройство.

polka, n, полька.

polka-dot, n, крапинка.

poll, n, баллотировка; голосовáние; число голосов; опрос насе-

ле́ния; *pl*, вы́боры; ~ *tax* поду́ш-
ный нало́г; ¶ *v.t. & i*, голосова́ть;
получа́ть (голоса́); *polling booth*
каби́на для голосова́ния; *polling
station* избира́тельный пункт.

pollard, *n*, подстри́женное де́рево;
безро́гое живо́тное.

pollen, *n*, пыльца́; **pollinate**, *v.t*,
опыля́ть.

pollute, *v.t*, загрязня́ть; **pollution**, *n*,
загрязне́ние.

polo, *n*, по́ло.

polonaise, *n*, полоне́з·

poltroon, *n*, трус.

polyanthus, *n*, первоцве́т высо́кий.

polygamist, *n*, полига́мист; **poly-
gamy**, *n*, полига́мия, многобра́-
чие.

polyglot, *a*, многоязы́чный; говоря́-
щий на мно́гих языка́х; ¶ *n*,
полигло́т.

polygon, *n*, многоуго́льник.

polypus, *n*, поли́п.

polystyrene, *n*, полистро́л..

polysyllabic, *a*, многосло́жный.

polytechnic, *a*, политехни́ческий; ¶
n, полите́хникум.

polytheism, *n*, политеи́зм, много-
бо́жие.

pomade, *n*, пома́да.

pomegranate, *n*, грана́т; ~ *tree*
грана́товое де́рево.

pommel, *n*, пере́дняя лука́ *(on
saddle)*; голо́вка *(of sword)*; ¶
v.t, колоти́ть.

pomp, *n*, великоле́пие, пы́шность;
~**osity**, *n*, напы́щенность; ~**ous**,
a, напы́щенный.

pond, *n*, пруд; водоём.

ponder, *v.t*, обду́мывать, взве́ши-
вать; *v.i*, размышля́ть; ~**able**, *a*,
весо́мый; ве́ский; ~**ous**, *a*, тяжёлый, тяжелове́сный.

poniard, *n*, кинжа́л.

pontiff, *n*, ри́мский па́па; архиере́й;
pontifical, *a*, па́пский; еписко-
па́льный; **pontificate**, *n*, понтифи-
ка́т; ¶ *v.i*, говори́ть категори́-
чески/напы́щенно.

pontoon, *n*, понто́н; *(cards)* два́д-
цать одно́; ~ *bridge* понто́нный
мост.

pony, *n*, по́ни.

poodle, *n*, пу́дель.

pooh, *int*, тьфу!; ~**-pooh**, *v.t*, отно-
си́ться с пренебреже́нием к.

pool, *n*, лу́жа; бассе́йн; фонд;
пу́лька *(cards)*; *football* ~ фут-

бо́льная лотере́я; *typing* ~ маши́н-
ное бюро́; ¶ *v.t*, объединя́ть в
о́бщий фонд.

poor, *a*, бе́дный; несча́стный; пло-
хо́й; сла́бый; ~ *thing!* бедня́жка!;
~*man* бедня́к; несча́стный; ¶ *n*,
the ~ беднота́; ~**ly**, *a*, нездоро́вый;
he is ~ ему́ нездоро́вится; ¶ *ad*,
пло́хо, неуда́чно.

pop, *n*, отры́вистый звук; вы́стрел;
шипу́чий напи́ток; ~ *art* поп-
а́рт; ~*corn* жа́реные кукуру́зные
хло́пья; ~*-gun* пуга́ч; ~ *music*
поп-му́зыка; ¶ *v.t. & i*, хло́пать,
выстре́ливать; *(coll.)* закла́ды-
вать; ~ *the question* сде́лать *(pf.)*
предложе́ние о бра́ке; ~ *in* загля́-
дывать, забега́ть; ~ *out* выбега́ть;
выгля́дывать.

pope, *n*, ри́мский па́па; ~**ry**, *n*,
папи́зм.

popinjay, *n*, фат.

popish, *a*, папи́стский.

poplar, *n*, то́поль.

poplin, *n*, попли́н.

poppy, *n*, мак.

populace, *n*, населе́ние; ма́ссы; **popular**, *a*, популя́рный; наро́дный;
~**ity**, *n*, популя́рность; ~**ize**, *v.t*,
популяризи́ровать; **populate**, *v.t*,
заселя́ть, населя́ть; **population**, *n*,
населе́ние; **populous**, *a*, лю́дный.

porcelain, *n*, фарфо́р; ¶ *a*, фарфо́ро-
вый.

porch, *n*, крыльцо́; вера́нда.

porcupine, *n*, дикобра́з.

pore, *n*, по́ра; ¶ *v.i*: ~ *over* размыш-
ля́ть над; сосредото́ченно смот-
ре́ть на/изуча́ть.

pork, *n*, свини́на; ~**er**, *n*, отко́рм-
ленная на убо́й свинья́.

pornography, *n*, порногра́фия.

porosity, *n*, по́ристость; **porous**, *a*,
по́ристый; гу́бчатый; ноздрева́-
тый.

porphyry, *n*, порфи́р.

porpoise, *n*, бу́рый дельфи́н.

porridge, *n*, ка́ша; **porringer**, *n*,
ми́сочка.

port, *n*, порт, га́вань; ле́вый борт;
отве́рстие; портве́йн; ~ *hole* амб-
разу́ра; иллюмина́тор; ~ *of call*
порт назначе́ния; ~ *arms!* на
грудь!.

portable, *a*, портати́вный. перено́с-
ный, передвижно́й.

portage, *n*, перево́зка; сто́имость
перево́зки.

portal, n, портал; ворота.

portcullis, n, опускная решётка.

portend, v.t, предвещать; portent, n, предзнаменование; ~ous, a, знаменательный; зловещий.

porter, n, швейцар; носильщик, грузчик; портер (beer); ~'s lodge швейцарская; ~age, n, переноска груза; плата носильщику.

portfolio, n, портфель; папка; «дело».

portico, n, портик, галерея.

portion, n, часть, доля; порция; надел; приданое; участь; ¶ v.t, делить на части; разделять.

portliness, n, тучность; portly, a, полный, тучный, представительный.

portrait, n, портрет; portray, v.t, изображать, описывать; ~al, n, изображение, описание.

Portuguese, a, португальский; ¶ n, португал|ец, -ка; португальский язык.

pose, n, поза; ¶ v.t, ставить (question); ставить в позу; v.i, позировать; ~ as выдавать себя за; position, n, положение; позиция; место; состояние; ¶ v.t, ставить, определять положение (gen.).

positive, a, положительный; уверенный; positivism, n, позитивизм.

posse, n, полицейский отряд; отряд вооружённых людей.

possess, v.t, владеть/обладать (inst.); иметь; ~ed, a, одержимый; ~ion, n, владение, обладание; pl, имущество; ~ive, a, собственнический; (gram.) притяжательный; ~ person собственник; ~or, n, владелец.

possibility, n, возможность; possible, a, возможный; as soon as ~ как можно скорее; possibly, ad, возможно; he can't ~ он никак не может.

post, n, почта; пост, должность; (mil.) пост; столб; ~card открытка; ~free без почтовой оплаты; ~man почтальон; ~mark почтовый штемпель; ~ master почтмейстер; начальник почтового отделения; P~master General министр почт; ~ office почта, почтовое отделение, почтамт; ~ office savings bank сберегательная касса при почтовом отделении; ~-paid с оплаченными почтовыми расходами; from pillar to ~ туда и

сюда; ¶ v.t, отправлять по почте, опускать в почтовый ящик; вывешивать; (mil.) назначать; ~age, n, почтовая оплата, почтовые расходы; ~ stamp почтовая марка; ~al, a, почтовый; ~ order почтовый перевод.

postdate, v.t, датировать более поздним числом.

poste restante, ad, до востребования.

poster, n, афиша, плакат.

posterior, a, задний; последующий; ¶ n, зад.

posterity, n, потомство, потомки.

postern, n, задняя дверь, боковой вход.

postgraduate, n, аспирант.

post-haste, ad, сломя голову.

posthumous, a, посмертный.

postillion, n, форейтор.

post meridiem, p.m., ad, после полудня.

post mortem, n, вскрытие трупа; ¶ a, посмертный.

postpone, v.t, откладывать, отсрочивать; ~ment, n, отсрочка.

postscript, n, постскриптум.

postulant, n, кандидат; postulate, v.t, принимать без доказательства; предполагать.

posture, n, поза, положение; ¶ v.i, позировать.

postwar, a, послевоенный.

posy, n, букет; девиз.

pot, n, горшок; ~-bellied пузатый; ~hole выбоина, рытвина; пещера; ¶ v.t, класть в горшок; сажать в горшок.

potable, a, годный для питья, питьевой.

potash, n, поташ.

potassium, n, калий.

potato, n, картофелина; pl, картофель.

potency, n, сила, могущество.

potent, a, сильный, крепкий; сильнодействующий; ~ate, n, властитель; ~ial, a, потенциальный, возможный; ¶ n, потенциал, ~iality, n, возможность.

pother, n, суматоха.

pothook, n, крюк (над очагом).

pothouse, n, пивная, кабак.

potion, n, доза лекарства/яда.

potter, n, гончар; ~'s clay гончарная глина; ~'s wheel гончарный круг; ¶ v.i, бездельничать; ~y, *n*, глиняные изделия; керамика; гончарня *(place)*.

pouch, *n*, сумка; мешочек; кисет *(tobacco)*; ~у, *a*, мешковатый.

poulterer, *n*, торговец домашней птицей.

poultice, *n*, припарка.

poultry, *n*, домашняя птица; птицеводство; ~ *yard* птичник.

pounce, *n*, внезапный прыжок, наскок; ¶ *v.i*, набрасываться, обрушиваться.

pound, *n*, фунт; фунт стерлингов; загон; ¶ *v.i*, толочь, колотить; обстреливать; бомбить; *v.i*, сильно биться; ~age, *n*, процент с фунта.

pour, *v.t.* *(& i.)*, лить(ся); сыпать(ся); *it's* ~*ing* идёт проливной дождь.

pout, *v.i*, надувать губы.

poverty, *n*, бедность, нищета; скудность; ~-*stricken* бедный.

powder, *n*, порох, порошок; пудра; ~ *compact* пудреница; ~ *magazine* пороховой погреб; ~*puff* пуховка; ~ *room* дамская туалетная комната; ¶ *v.t*, пудрить; посыпать; превращать в порошок; ~ed, *a*, порошкообразный; ~ *milk* молочный порошок.

power, *n*, сила; мощность; энергия; могущество, власть; держава; *(maths.)* степень; *great* ~s великие державы; *horse* ~ лошадиная сила; *purchasing* ~ покупательная способность; *the* ~*s that be* власти предержащие; ~ *boat* моторный катер; ~ *house* электростанция; ~ *shovel* экскаватор; ~ful, *a*, сильный; могущественный; ~less, *a*, бессильный.

practicable, *a*, осуществимый; **practical,** *a*, практический; практичный; ~ *joke* грубая шутка; ~ly, *ad*, практически; фактически; почти; **practice,** *n*, практика; упражнение; привычка; тренировка, учение; *in* ~ на деле; *put into* ~ осуществлять; **practise,** *v.t*, практиковать, упражнять; заниматься *(inst.)*; *v.i*, упражняться, тренироваться; **practitioner,** *n*, практикующий врач/юрист.

pragmatic, *a*, прагматический.

prairie, *n*, прерия, степь.

praise, *n*, похвала; восхваление; ¶ *v.t*, хвалить; ~worthy, *a*, похвальный.

pram, *n*, детская коляска.

prance, *v.i*, становиться на дыбы; гарцевать; задаваться.

prank, *n*, выходка, шалость; *play* ~s шалить.

prate, *v.i*, болтать, пустословить.

prattle, *n*, лепет; болтовня; ¶ *v.i*, лепетать; болтать.

prawn, *n*, креветка.

pray, *v.i*, молиться; ~er, *n*, молитва; мольба.

preach, *v.t.* *& i*, проповедовать; ~er, *n*, проповедник; ~ing, *n*, проповедование; проповедь.

preamble, *n*, преамбула; вступление.

prearrange, *v.t*, заранее подготавливать/планировать; ~d, *p.p. & a*, заранее подготовленный/назначенный.

precarious, *a*, опасный.

precaution, *n*, предосторожность; ~ary, *a*, предупредительный.

precede, *v.t*, предшествовать *(dat.)*; ~nce, *n*, первенство, старшинство; ~nt, *n*, прецедент; **preceding,** *a*, предшествующий.

precept, *n*, правило, наставление; *(law)* предписание; ~or, *n*, наставник.

precinct, *n*, огороженное место; предел; *(U.S.A.)* избирательный/полицейский участок; *pl*, окрестности.

precious, *a*, драгоценный, изысканный; ~ness, *n*, изысканность.

precipice, *n*, пропасть, обрыв; **precipitate,** *a*, опрометчивый; ¶ *n*, осадок; ¶ *v.t*, низвергать; ускорять; *(chem.)* осаждать; **precipitation,** *n*, низвержение; ускорение; осаждение; осадки; стремительность; **precipitous,** *a*, обрывистый.

precise, *a*, точный; аккуратный; педантичный; ~ly, *ad*, точно; именно; **precision,** *n*, точность; меткость; ~ *instrument* прецизионный инструмент.

preclude, *v.t*, предотвращать; ~ *from* мешать.

precocious, *a*, развитой не по годам; скороспелый; **precocity,** *n*, раннее развитие; скороспелость.

preconceived, *a*, предвзятый; **preconception,** *n*, предвзятое мнение.

precursor, *n*, предтеча; предшественник.

predatory, *a*, хищный.

predecessor, *n*, предшественник.

predestination, *n*, предопределение; predestine, *v.t*, предопределять.

predetermine, *v.t*, предрешать; предопределять.

predicament, *n*, затруднительное положение.

predicate, *n*, сказуемое, предикат *(gram.)*; утверждение *(logic)*; ¶ *v.t*, утверждать; predicative, *a*, предикативный.

predict, *v.t*, предсказывать; ~ion, *n*, предсказание.

predilection, *n*, пристрастие; склонность.

predispose, *v.t*, предрасполагать; predisposition, *n*, предрасположение.

predominance, *n*, превосходство, преобладание; predominant, *a*, преобладающий; господствующий; predominate, *v.i*, преобладать, господствовать.

pre-eminence, *n*, превосходство; pre-eminent, *a*, выдающийся.

preen, *v.t*, чистить (клювом); ~ oneself прихорашиваться; задаваться.

pre-existence, *n*, предсуществование.

prefabricate, *v.t*, изготовлять заводским способом; изготовлять заранее; ~d *house* сборный/стандартный дом.

preface, *n*, предисловие, вступление; ¶ *v.t*, писать предисловие к; начинать; prefatory, *a*, вступительный.

prefect, *n*, префект; старший ученик; ~ure, *n*, префектура.

prefer, *v.t*, предпочитать; продвигать; подавать *(complaint)*; выдвигать *(claim)*; ~able, *a*, предпочтительный; ~ence, *n*, предпочтение; ~ *shares* привилегированные акции; ~ential, *a*, пользующийся предпочтением; льготный; ~ment, *n*, повышение, продвижение по службе.

prefix, *n*, префикс, приставка; ¶ *v.t*, ставить префикс к; предпосылать.

pregnancy, *n*, беременность; pregnant, *a*, беременная; *(fig.)* чреватый.

prehensile, *a*, цепкий, хватательный.

prehistoric, *a*, доисторический.

prejudge, *v.t*, осуждать заранее; предрешать.

prejudice, *n*, предрассудок, предубеждение; ущерб; *without* ~ *to* без ущерба для; ¶ *v.t*, предубеждать; наносить ущерб *(dat.)*; prejudicial, *a*, вредный.

prelacy, *n*, прелатство; prelate, *n*, прелат.

preliminary, *a*, предварительный; подготовительный; preliminaries, *n.pl*, предварительные мероприятия/переговоры.

prelude, *n*, прелюдия; вступление; ¶ *v.t*, служить вступлением к.

premature, *a*, преждевременный.

premeditate, *v.t*, обдумывать/продумывать заранее; ~d, *a*, преднамеренный; premeditation, *n*, преднамеренность.

premier, *a*, первый; ¶ *n*, премьер-министр; ~ship, *n*, должность премьер-министра.

première, *n*, премьера.

premise, *n*, (пред)посылка; *pl*, помещение; ¶ *v.t*, предпосылать.

premium, *n*, награда, премия; *at a* ~ выше нормальной стоимости; в большом спросе.

premonition, *n*, предчувствие.

preoccupation, *n*, озабоченность; preoccupy, *v.t*, поглощать (внимание).

preordain, *v.t*, предопределять.

preparation, *n*, приготовление; подготовка; препарат; preparatory, *a*, подготовительный; prepare, *v.t* *(& i.)*, готовить(ся), подготавливать(ся); preparedness, *n*, подготовленность, готовность.

prepay, *v.t*, платить вперёд; франкировать.

preponderance, *n*, перевес, превосходство; preponderant, *a*, преобладающий; preponderate, *v.i*, превосходить.

preposition, *n*, предлог; ~al, *a*, предложный.

prepossess, *v.t*, располагать к себе; ~ing, *a*, располагающий, привлекательный.

preposterous, *a*, абсурдный, нелепый.

prerogative, *n*, прерогатива.

presage, *n*, предсказание, предзнаменование; ¶ *v.t*, предсказывать, предзнаменовать.

Presbyterian, *a*, пресвитерианский; ¶ *n*, пресвитериан/ин, -ка.

prescience, *n*, предвидение; **prescient**, *a*, предвидящий.

prescribe, *v.t*, предписывать; прописывать *(med.)*; **prescription**, *n*, предписание; *(med.)* рецепт.

presence, *n*, присутствие; наличие; ~ *of mind* присутствие духа.

present, *a*, присутствующий; настоящий, нынешний; *at* ~ в настоящее время; *for the* ~ пока; *be* ~ *at* присутствовать на; ¶ *n*, подарок; настоящее время *(also gram.)*; ¶ *v.t*, дарить, преподносить; подавать *(petition)*; ставить *(play)*; давать; ~**able**, *a*, приличный; презентабельный; ~**ation**, *n*, подношение (подарка); подарок; представление *(also theat.)*.

presentiment, *n*, предчувствие.

presently, *ad*, вскоре, сейчас.

preservation, *n*, сохранение; сохранность; **preservative**, *a*, предохранительный; ¶ *n*, консервант; **preserve**, *v.t*, сохранять; консервировать; хранить; ¶ *n*, заповедник; *pl*, консервы; **preserved**, *p.p. & a*, (хорошо) сохранившийся; консервированный.

preside, *v.i*, председательствовать; ~**псу**, *n*, председательство; президентство; ~**nt**, *n*, председатель; президент; ректор; ~**ntial**, *a*, президентский.

press, *n*, *(tech.)* пресс; печать, пресса; типография; шкаф; давка; ~ *agency* агентство печати; ~ *cutting* газетная вырезка; ~ *conference* пресс-конференция; ~ *stud* кнопка; ¶ *v.t*, жать, нажимать; давить; гладить; прессовать *(tech.)*; насильно вербовать; убеждать; ~ *for* настаивать на; ~ *forward* проталкивать; ~**ing**, *a*, неотложный; настоятельный; ~**man**, *n*, журналист; прессовщик.

pressure, *n*, давление, нажим; ~ *cooker* герметическая кастрюля; ~ *gauge* манометр.

prestige, *n*, престиж.

presumable, *a*, вероятный; **presumably**, *ad*, предположительно; **presume**, *v.t*, предполагать; полагать; осмеливаться *(+ inf.)*; **presumption**, *n*, предположение; самонадеянность; **presumptive**, *a*, предполагаемый, предположи-

тельный; **presumptuous**, *a*, самонадеянный, нахальный.

presuppose, *v.t*, предполагать.

pretence, *n*, притворство; обман; **pretend**, *v.i*, притворяться, делать вид; ~ *to* претендовать на; **pretender**, *n*, претендент; притворщик; **pretension**, *n*, претензия; претенциозность; **pretentious**, *a*, претенциозный.

preterite, *n*, прошедшее время.

preternatural, *a*, сверхъестественный.

pretext, *n*, предлог, отговорка.

prettiness, *n*, миловидность; **pretty**, *a*, хорошенький, миловидный; ¶ *ad*, довольно.

prevail, *v.i*, преобладать, господствовать; ~ *over* побеждать; преобладать над; ~ *on* уговаривать; ~**ing**, *a*, господствующий, преобладающий; широко распространённый; **prevalence**, *n*, преобладание; **prevalent**, *a*, преобладающий.

prevaricate, *v.i*, говорить уклончиво, увиливать; **prevarication**, *n*, уклончивость, увиливание.

prevent, *v.t*, предотвращать, предупреждать; мешать/препятствовать *(dat.)*; ~**ion**, *n*, предотвращение, предупреждение; *is better than cure* предупреждение лучше лечения; ~**ive**, *a*, предупредительный; *(med.)* профилактический.

previous, *a*, предыдущий; ~**ly**, *ad*, заранее, предварительно.

prevision, *n*, предвидение.

prey, *n*, добыча; *(fig.)* жертва; *beast of* ~ хищное животное; ¶ *v.i*: ~ *on* охотиться на; грабить; мучить.

price, *n*, цена; ~ *cutting* снижение цен; ~ *list* прейскурант; ¶ *v.t*, назначать цену *(gen.)*; спрашивать о цене *(gen.)*; ~**less**, *a*, бесценный.

prick, *n*, укол; шип; игла; ¶ *v.t*, колоть; задевать; ~ *up one's ears* навострить *(pf.)* уши; ~**le**, *n*, шип, колючка; игла; ¶ *v.t*, колоть; ~**ly**, *a*, колючий; *(fig.)* раздражительный.

pride, *n*, гордость; спесь; ¶ ~ *oneself on* гордиться *(inst.)*.

priest, *n*, священник; жрец; ~**ess**, *n*, жрица; ~**hood**, *n*, духовен-

ство; свящéнство; ~ly, a, свя-
щéннический.
priggish, a, самодовóльный.
prim, a, опря́тный; чóпорный.
primacy, n, пéрвенство.
prima donna, n, примадóнна.
primal, a, первобы́тный.
primarily, ad, первоначáльно; глáвным óбразом; **primary**, a, первúч-
ный; (перво)начáльный; ~ colours
основны́е цветá; ~ school начáль-
ная шкóла; **primate**, n, примáс; (zool.) примáт; **prime**, a,
глáвный; основнóй; пéрвый; ~
minister премьéр-минúстр; ~ number простóе числó; ¶ n, расцвéт;
in the ~ of life во цвéте лет; ¶
v.t, (mil.) затрáвливать пóрохом;
грунтовáть (painting); подго-
тáвливать; **primer**, n, буквáрь;
начáльный учéбник; запáл; грунтóвка; **primeval**, a, первобы́тный;
priming, n, грунтóвка; заправка;
подготóвка; **primitive**, a, примú-
тúвный; **primogeniture**, n, перво-
рóдство; **primordial**, a, искóнный.
primrose, n, прúмула; the ~ path
путь наслаждéний.
prince, n, принц; князь; ~ly, a,
цáрственный, кня́жеский; великолéпный; ~ss, n, принцéсса;
княжнá, княгúня.
principal, a, глáвный, основнóй;
¶ n, начáльник, -ица; главá;
дирéктор; патрóн; капитáл; ~ity,
n, кня́жество; ~ly, ad, глáвным
óбразом.
principle, n, прúнцип, прáвило;
оснóва; (chem.) элемéнт.
prink, v.i, чúстить пéрья; прихорá-
шиваться.
print, n, óттиск; отпечáток; шрифт;
печáть; гравю́ра; фотокáрточка;
сúтец; in ~ в продáже; out of ~
распрóданный; ¶ v.t, печáтать;
отпечáтывать (photo, etc.); (textile) набивáть; ~ed, a, печáтный;
набивнóй; ~er, n, печáтник,
типóграф; (textile) набóйщик;
~ing, n, печáтание; тирáж; (textile) набúвка; ~ frame свето-
копировáльный аппарáт; ~ press
печáтный станóк; ~ office типогрáфия; ~ type шрифт.
prior, a, предшéствующий, прéжний;
~ claim бóлее вéская претéнзия;
~ to this рáньше э́того; ¶ n,
настоя́тель монастыря́; ~ess, n,

настоя́тельница; ~ity, n, прио-
ритéт, старшинствó; поря́док оче-
рéдности; преимýщество; ~y, n,
монасты́рь.
prism, n, прúзма; ~atic, a, призматú-
ческий.
prison, n, тюрьмá; ~ camp лáгерь
для (воéнно)плéнных; ~er, n,
плéнный; заключённый; ~ of war
военноплéнный.
pristine, a, дрéвний, первобы́тный.
privacy, n, уединéние, уединённость;
private, a, чáстный, лúчный; тáйный; уединённый; конфиденци-
áльный; ~ secretary лúчный сек-
ретáрь; ~ (soldier) рядовóй; in
~ наединé; по секрéту; **privateer**,
n, кáпер; капитáн кáпера; **priva-
tely**, ad, конфиденциáльно; в тáйне.
privation, n, лишéние, нуждá.
privilege, n, привилéгия; ~d, a,
привилегирóванный.
privy, a, тáйный; чáстный; ~ to
причáстный к; ~ council тáйный
совéт; ~ seal мáлая государственная печáть; ¶ n, (coll.)
убóрная.
prize, n, прéмия, приз; награ́да;
трофéй; (mar.) захвáченное сýдно;
~ court призóвый суд; ~ fight
состязáние в бóксе на приз; ~
giving вручéние прéмий/прúзов;
award a ~ присуждáть прéмию;
draw a ~ получáть приз; ¶ v.t,
высокó ценúть; вскрывáть.
probability, n, вероя́тность; правдоподóбие; in all ~ по всей вероя́т-
ности; **probable**, a, вероя́тный;
правдоподóбный; **probably**, ad,
вероя́тно.
probate, n, официáльное утверждé-
ние завещáния; **probation**, n,
испытáние, стажирóвка; (law)
услóвное освобождéние на порýки; (eccl.) послýшничество; on
~ на порýках; прохóдящий испытáтельный стаж; ~ officer инспéктор услóвно осуждённых (несо-
вершеннолéтних) престýпников;
probationary, a, испытáтельный;
~ sentence услóвный приговóр;
probationer, n, стажёр; кандидáт
в члéны; (law) услóвно осуждённый престýпник; (eccl.) послýшник.
probe, n, зонд; расслéдование; зон-
дúрование; ¶ v.t, зондúровать;
расслéдовать.

probity, *n,* чéстность, неподкýпность.

problem, *n,* проблéма, вопрóс, задáча; ~**atic(al),** *a,* проблематичный; спóрный.

proboscis, *n,* хóбот; хоботóк.

procedure, *n,* процедýра; óбраз дéйствия; процéсс; **proceed,** *v.i,* продолжáть(ся); отправлáться дáльше; приступáть к дéлу; ~ *against* преслéдовать в судéбном порядке; ~ *from* происходить от; **proceeding,** *n,* постýпок; *(pl.)* протокóлы, трудьi; мероприятия; **proceeds,** *n.pl,* дохóд, вырýчка; **process,** *n,* процéсс; движéние; течéние; ~**ion,** *n,* процéссия.

proclaim, *v.t,* провозглашáть, объявлять; **proclamation,** *n,* провозглашéние, объявлéние; воззвáние.

proclivity, *n,* склóнность.

procrastinate, *v.i,* мéшкать; **procrastination,** *n,* отклáдывание.

procreate, *v.t,* порождáть.

proctor, *n,* прóктор.

procurable, *a,* достýпный; **procurator,** *n,* прокурóр; прокурáтор; **procure,** *v.t,* доставáть, доставлять; *v.i,* сводничать.

prod, *n,* тычóк; шило; ¶ *v.t,* тыкать, толкáть; *(fig.)* подгонять.

prodigal, *a,* расточительный; ~ *son* блýдный сын; ¶ *n,* мот; ~**ity,** *n,* расточительность.

prodigious, *a,* изумительный; громáдный; **prodigy,** *n,* чýдо; *child* ~ вундеркинд.

produce, *n,* продýкция; урожáй; ¶ *v.t,* производить; доставáть; предъявлять; *(theat.)* стáвить; ~**r,** *n,* производитель; *(theat.)* режиссёр; продюсер; **product,** *n,* продýкт, издéлие, фабрикáт; *(fig.)* результáт; ~**ion,** *n,* производство *(also film, etc.);* постанóвка (пьéсы); произведéние *(literary);* ~**ive,** *a,* производительный; плодорóдный; ~**ivity,** *n,* производительность.

profanation, *n,* профанáция, осквернéние; **profane,** *a,* свéтский; богохýльный; **profanity,** *n,* богохýльство.

profess, *v.t,* исповéдовать *(faith);* занимáться *(inst.);* уверять; признавáть; *v.i,* притворяться; ~**ed,** *a,* мнимый; ~**edly,** *ad,* открыто, явно; ~**ion,** *n,* профéссия; люди (однóй профéссии); признáние; увéрение; вероисповéдание; ~**ional,** *a,* профессионáльный; ¶ *n,* профессионáл; ~**or,** *n,* профéссор; ~**orial,** *a,* профéссорский.

proffer, *v.t,* предлагáть.

proficiency, *n,* умéние, óпытность; **proficient,** *a,* умéлый, искýсный, óпытный.

profile, *n,* прóфиль, очертáние.

profit, *n,* пóльза, выгода; прибыль, дохóд; ¶ *v.i,* извлекáть пóльзу; приносить пóльзу; ~**able,** *a,* прибыльный; полéзный; ~**eer,** *n,* спекулянт.

profligacy, *n,* распýтство; расточительность; **profligate,** *a,* распýтный; расточительный; ¶ *n,* распýтник; расточитель.

profound, *a,* глубóкий; **profundity,** *n,* глубинá.

profuse, *a,* изобильный; щéдрый; **profusion,** *n,* изобилие.

progenitor, *n,* основáтель рóда; прародитель; **progeny,** *n,* потóмок; потóмство.

prognathous, *a,* с выдающимися чéлюстями.

prognosis, *n,* прогнóз; **prognosticate,** *v.t,* предскáзывать; **prognostication,** *n,* предсказáние.

programme, *n,* прогрáмма; план; **programming,** *n,* программировáние.

progress, *n,* прогрéсс, развитие; продвижéние; успéхи; *make* ~ дéлать успéхи; ¶ *v.i,* продвигáться; развивáться; дéлать успéхи; ~**ion,** *n,* прогрéссия; ~**ive,** *a,* прогрессивный.

prohibit, *v.t,* запрещáть; ~**ion,** *n,* запрещéние; «сухóй закóн»; ~**ive,** *a,* запретительный.

project, *n,* проéкт, план; нóвое предприятие; ¶ *v.t,* проектировать; отбрáсывать; бросáть; *v.i,* выдавáться, выступáть; ~**ile,** *n,* снаряд, пуля; ¶ *a,* метáтельный; ~**ion,** *n,* проектировáние; проéкция; бросáние; выступ; ~**or,** *n,* проéктор, проекциóнный фонáрь; проектирóвщик.

proletarian, *a,* пролетáрский; ¶ *n,* пролетáрий; **proletariat,** *n,* пролетариáт.

prolific, *a,* плодорóдный; плодовитый.

prolix, *a,* многослóвный.

prologue, n, пролог.

prolong, v.t, продлевать; затягивать; ~ation, n, продление; затягивание; отсрочка.

promenade, n, прогулка; место для гуляния; дорога вдоль пляжа; набережная; ¶ v.i, прогуливаться.

prominence, n, выступ; выпуклость; (fig.) превосходство; выдающееся положение; prominent, a, выдающийся, видный; выступающий; выпуклый.

promiscuous, a, разнородный; неразборчивый; распутный.

promise, n, обещание; ¶ v.t, обещать; подавать надежды на; ~d land земля обетованная; promising, a, подающий надежды, многообещающий; promissory note долговое обязательство; вексель.

promontory, n, мыс.

promote, v.t, повышать (в чине), производить (в чин); способствовать (dat.); представлять; ~r, n, покровитель; антрепренёр; promotion, n, повышение, производство; содействие; антреприза.

prompt, a, немедленный; ~ payment наличный расчёт; ¶ n, подсказка; ¶ v.t, побуждать; подсказывать; (theat.) суфлировать (dat.); ~er, n, (theat.) суфлёр; ~itude, n, быстрота; ~ly, ad, быстро, немедленно.

promulgate, v.t, объявлять, провозглашать; опубликовывать; promulgation, n, опубликование, обнародование.

prone, a, распростёртый; наклонный; be ~ to быть склонным к.

prong, n, зубец; шпенёк; (fig.) ветка, ответвление.

pronominal, a, местоимённый; pronoun, n, местоимение.

pronounce, v.t, произносить; объявлять; ~d, a, резко выраженный; ясный; ~ment, n, объявление; pronunciation, n, произношение.

proof, n, доказательство; испытание; корректура, гранка; ¶ a, установленного градуса; ~ against непроницаемый для; не поддающийся (dat.); ~-reader корректор; ~-reading читка корректуры; ¶ v.t, делать непроницаемым.

prop, n, подпорка; (fig.) опора; pl, (theat.) бутафория; ¶ v.t, подпирать; поддерживать.

propaganda, n, пропаганда; propagandist, n, пропагандист; propagate, v.t, размножать; разводить; распространять; propagation, n, размножение, разведение; распространение.

propel, v.t, продвигать, приводить в движение; ~ler, n, пропеллер, винт; ~ling pencil автоматический карандаш.

propensity, n, склонность; пристрастие.

proper, a, надлежащий, пристойный; правильный; (gram.) собственный; (coll.) настоящий; ~ly, ad, должным образом, как следует; (coll.) здорово;

property, n, собственность, имущество; свойство, качество; pl, (theat.) бутафория.

prophecy, n, пророчество; prophesy, v.t, пророчить, предсказывать; prophet, n, пророк; prophetess, n, пророчица; pro hetic, a, пророческий.

prophylactic, a, профилактический; prophylaxis, n, профилактика.

propinquity, n, близость; родство.

propitiate, v.t, примирять; умиротворять; propitiatory, a, примирительный; propitious, a, благоприятный.

proportion, n, пропорция; соразмерность; часть; in ~ to соразмерно с; ¶ v.t, соразмерять; ~al, a, пропорциональный; ~ate, a, соразмерный.

proposal, n, предложение; propose, v.t, предлагать; представлять; v.i, делать предложение (о браке); намереваться (+ inf.); proposition, n, предложение; (maths.) теорема.

propound, v.t, выдвигать.

proprietary, a, собственнический; proprietor, ~tress, n, собственн|ик, -ица; propriety, n, пристойность, приличие.

propulsion, n, движение (вперёд); propulsive force движущая сила.

prorogation, n, перерыв (в работе парламента); отсрочка; prorogue, v.t, назначать перерыв в работе (gen.); отсрочивать.

prosaic, *a,* прозаический; прозайчный.

proscenium, *n,* авансцена.

proscribe, *v.t,* объявлять вне закона; запрещать; **proscription,** *n,* объявление вне закона; запрещение; проскрипция.

prose, *n,* проза; ~ *writer* прозаик.

prosecute, *v.t,* преследовать судебным порядком; вести, проводить; **prosecution,** *n,* судебное преследование; обвинение; ведение, выполнение; **prosecutor,** *n,* обвинитель; *public* ~ прокурор.

proselyte, *n,* новообращённый.

prosody, *n,* просодия.

prospect, *n,* перспектива; вид; *pl,* виды на будущее; ¶ *v.t,* разведовать; ~**ing,** *n,* разведка; ~**or,** *a,* разведчик; золотоискатель.

prospectus, *n,* проспект.

prosper, *v.i,* процветать, преуспевать; ~**ity,** *n,* благосостояние; ~**ous,** *a,* процветающий, зажиточный.

prostitute, *n,* проститутка; ¶ *v.t,* проституировать; **prostitution,** *n,* проституция.

prostrate, *a,* распростёртый; обессиленный; ¶ *v.t,* повергать ниц; ~ *oneself* падать ниц; унижаться; **prostration,** *n,* распростёртое положение; изнеможение.

prosy, *a,* прозаический; прозайчный.

protagonist, *n,* поборник; главный герой.

protect, *v.t,* защищать, охранять; покровительствовать *(dat.);* ~**ion,** *n,* защита; покровительство; ~**ive,** *a,* защитный; ~**or,** *n,* защитник; покровитель; *(tech.)* предохранитель; ~**orate,** *n,* протекторат.

protein, *n,* протеин, белок.

protest, *n,* протест; ¶ *v.i,* протестовать, возражать; *v.t,* опротестовывать.

Protestant, *n,* протестант; ~**ism,** *n,* протестантство.

protestation, *n,* заявление; протест.

protocol, *n,* протокол.

prototype, *n,* прототип.

protract, *v.t,* тянуть; ~**ed,** *a,* длительный; ~**or,** *n,* транспортёр.

protrude, *v.t. & i,* высовывать(ся); выдаваться; **protrusion,** *n,* выступ.

protuberance, *n,* выпуклость; опухоль; **protuberant,** *a,* выпуклый.

proud, *a,* гордый; *be* ~ *of* гордиться *(inst.).*

prove, *v.t,* доказывать; пробовать; удостоверять; *v.i,* оказываться.

provenance, *n,* источник.

provender, *n,* корм; фураж.

proverb, *n,* пословица, поговорка; ~**ial,** *a,* вошедший в поговорку.

provide, *v.t,* давать, снабжать; ~ *against* принимать меры против; ~ *for* обеспечивать; предусматривать;~*d that* при условии, что . . .; ~**nce,** *n,* предусмотрительность; Провидение; ~**nt,** *a,* предусмотрительный; ~**ntial,** *a,* провиденциальный; ~**r,** *n,* поставщик.

province, *n,* провинция, область; компетенция; **provincial,** *a,* провинциальный.

provision, *n,* снабжение, обеспечение; приготовление; условие; *pl,* запасы, провизия; ~**al,** *a,* временный, условный; ~**ally,** *ad,* условно.

proviso, *n,* условие; оговорка.

provocation, *n,* провокация; раздражение; **provocative,** *a,* вызывающий, провокационный; возбуждающий; **provoke,** *v.t,* вызывать; раздражать; провоцировать.

provost, *n,* ректор; мэр; ~ *marshal* начальник военной полиции.

prow, *n,* нос.

prowess, *n,* доблесть.

prowl, *v.i,* красться; ~**er,** *n,* мародёр.

proximate, *a,* ближайший; **proximity,** *n,* близость.

proxy, *n,* полномочие; доверенность; уполномоченный, заместитель; *by* ~ по доверенности.

prude, *n,* чересчур щепетильная женщина.

prudence, *n,* благоразумие; предусмотрительность; **prudent,** *a,* благоразумный; предусмотрительный.

prudery, *n,* излишняя щепетильность/чопорность; **prudish,** *a,* чересчур щепетильный/стыдливый.

prune, *n,* чернослив; ¶ *v.t,* подрезать; *(fig.)* сокращать; **pruning,** *n,* подрезка; ~ *shears* садовые ножницы.

pruriency, *n,* похотли́вость; **prurient,** *a,* похотли́вый.

Prussian, *a,* пру́сский; ~ *blue* берли́нская лазу́рь; ¶ *n,* прусса́к.

prussic, *a:* ~ *acid* сини́льная кислота́.

pry, *v.i,* подгля́дывать; сова́ть нос; ~*ing, a,* любопы́тный.

psalm, *n,* псало́м; ~*ist, n,* псало́мщик; **psalter,** *n,* псалты́рь.

pseudo, *prefix,* псе́вдо-, ло́жно-; ~*nym, n,* псевдони́м.

psychiatrist, *n,* психиа́тр; **psychiatry,** *n,* психиатри́я; **psychic,** *a,* психи́ческий; **psycho-analysis,** *n,* психоана́лиз; **psychological,** *a,* психологи́ческий; **psychologist,** *n,* психо́лог; **psychology,** *n,* психоло́гия.

ptarmigan, *n,* бе́лая куропа́тка.

ptomaine, *n,* птома́ин.

pub, *n,* пивна́я, каба́к.

puberty, *n,* полова́я зре́лость.

public, *a,* публи́чный; обще́ственный; общедосту́пный; ~ *assistance* госуда́рственные посо́бия; ~ *health* здравоохране́ние; ~ *house* пивна́я; ~ *school* ча́стная сре́дняя шко́ла; ~ *service* коммуна́льные услу́ги; *make* ~ опубликова́ть; ¶ *n,* пу́блика, о́бщество; *in* ~ публи́чно; ~*an, n,* тракти́рщик; ~*ation, n,* опубликова́ние, оглаше́ние; изда́ние; ~*ity, n,* гла́сность; ~ *agent* аге́нт по рекла́ме; ~*ize, v.t,* разглаша́ть; реклами́ровать; **publish,** *v.t,* издава́ть, опублико́вывать; ~*er, n,* изда́тель; ~*ing, n,* изда́тельское де́ло; ~ *house* изда́тельство.

puce, *a,* краснова́то-кори́чневый.

puck, *n,* эльф; *(sport)* ша́йба.

pucker, *n,* морщи́на; *(sew.)* сбо́рка, скла́дка; ¶ *v.t. (& i.),* мо́рщить(ся); собира́ть в сбо́рку.

pudding, *n,* пу́динг.

puddle, *n,* лу́жа.

puerile, *a,* ребя́ческий; **puerility,** *n,* ребя́чество.

puff, *n,* дунове́ние (ве́тра); поры́в *(air);* клуб *(smoke);* пухо́вка (для пу́дры); сло́йка, слоёный пирожо́к; буф *(on dress);* ~ *pastry* слоёное те́сто; ¶ *v.i,* пыхте́ть; дыми́ть, пуска́ть клубы́ ды́ма; ~ *up with pride* чва́ниться, кичи́ться; *puffed up* надме́нный.

puffin, *n,* ту́пик.

pug, *n,* мопс *(dog);* ~*-nose* приплю́снутый нос.

pugilism, *n,* бокс; **pugilist,** *n,* боксёр; **pugnacious,** *a,* драчли́вый.

puke, *v.i,* рвать.

pule, *v.i,* хны́кать.

pull, *n,* тя́га; рыво́к; влия́ние; ¶ *v.t,* тащи́ть, тяну́ть; дёргать; нажима́ть *(trigger);* грести́; ~ *faces* грима́сничать; ~ *back (v.t.)* оття́гивать наза́д; *(v.i.)* отступа́ть; ~ *down* тяну́ть вниз; сноси́ть *(building);* ~ *in* втя́гивать; ~ *off* стя́гивать; снима́ть; выи́грывать *(prize);* ~ *off the road* съезжа́ть с доро́ги; ~ *out (v.t.)* выта́скивать; удаля́ть *(tooth); (v.i.)* отходи́ть; ~ *the strings* пуска́ть в ход свои́ свя́зи; стоя́ть за спино́й *(gen);* ~ *to pieces* разрыва́ть на куски́; *(fig.)* разноси́ть; ~ *through (v.t.)* прота́скивать; *(v.i.)* выжива́ть (по́сле боле́зни); выпу́тываться из беды́; ~ *together (v.t.)* стя́гивать; *(v.i.)* рабо́тать дру́жно; ~ *oneself together* брать себя́ в ру́ки; ~ *up* подтя́гивать; остана́вливать(ся).

pullet, *n,* моло́дка.

pulley, *n,* блок; шкив.

pullman, *n,* пу́льмановский ваго́н.

pullulate, *v.i,* прораста́ть; кише́ть.

pulmonary, *a,* лёгочный.

pulp, *n,* мя́коть; бума́жная ма́сса; мя́гкая ма́сса.

pulpit, *n,* ка́федра.

pulsate, *v.i,* пульси́ровать, би́ться; **pulsation,** *n,* пульса́ция; **pulse,** *n,* пульс, бие́ние *(also fig.); (bot.)* бобо́вые расте́ния.

pulverize, *v.t,* превраща́ть в порошо́к; *(fig.)* сокруша́ть; ~*r, n,* пульвериза́тор.

puma, *n,* пу́ма.

pumice stone, *n,* пе́мза.

pump, *n,* насо́с; (лакиро́ванная) ту́фля; ¶ *v.t,* кача́ть; ~ *out* выка́чивать; ~ *up* нака́чивать.

pumpkin, *n,* ты́ква.

pun, *n,* каламбу́р; ¶ *v.i,* каламбу́рить.

punch, *n,* уда́р кулако́м; *(tech.)* пробо́йник; компо́стер; пунш; ~ *ball* боксёрская гру́ша; ¶ *v.t,* ударя́ть кулако́м; пробива́ть; штампова́ть, компости́ровать.

Punch, *n,* «Петру́шка».

punctilio, *n,* форма́льность; ~*us, a,* педанти́чный, щепети́льный.

punctual, *a*, пунктуа́льный, то́чный; **~ity**, *n*, пунктуа́льность, то́чность.

punctuate, *v.t*, ста́вить зна́ки препина́ния в; прерыва́ть; **punctuation**, *n*, пунктуа́ция; **~ marks** зна́ки препина́ния.

puncture, *n*, проко́л; пробо́й; ¶ *v.t*, прока́лывать; пробива́ть; *v.i*, ло́паться.

pundit, *n*, панди́т; экспе́рт.

pungency, *n*, е́дкость; **pungent**, *a*, е́дкий.

punish, *v.t*, нака́зывать; **~able**, *a*, наказу́емый; **~ment**, *n*, наказа́ние; **punitive**, *a*, кара́тельный.

punt, *n*, плоскодо́нная ло́дка, плоскодо́нка; уда́р ного́й; ¶ *v.i*, плыть на плоскодо́нке; *v.t*, подава́ть ного́й *(a ball)*; **~er**, *n*, игро́к.

puny, *a*, ма́ленький, хи́лый.

pup, *n*, щено́к.

pupa, *n*, ку́колка.

pupil, *n*, учени́к; зрачо́к *(of eye)*.

puppet, *n*, марионе́тка, ку́кла; **~ government** марионе́точное прави́тельство; **~ theatre** ку́кольный теа́тр.

puppy, *n*, щено́к; *(fig.)* молокосо́с.

purchase, *n*, поку́пка; приобрете́ние; *(tech.)* рыча́г; вы́игрыш в си́ле; ¶ *v.t*, покупа́ть; поднима́ть рычаго́м; **~r**, *n*, покупа́тель.

pure, *a*, чи́стый; непоро́чный; беспри́месный; **~ly**, *ad*, чи́сто, соверше́нно; **~ness**, *n*, чистота́.

purgative, *n*, слаби́тельное; **purgatory**, *n*, чисти́лище; **purge**, *n*, *(med.)* очище́ние; чи́стка; ¶ *v.t*, очища́ть, прочища́ть; искупа́ть *(guilt)*; *(polit.)* проводи́ть чи́стку в.

purification, *n*, очище́ние; **purify**, *v.t*, очища́ть; **purist**, *n*, пури́ст; **puritan**, *n*, пурита́нин; **~ical**, *a*, пурита́нский; **purity**, *n*, чистота́; непоро́чность; беспри́месность.

purl, *n*, журча́ние; вяза́ние с наки́дкой; ¶ *v.i*, журча́ть; вяза́ть с наки́дкой.

purloin, *v.t*, ворова́ть, похища́ть.

purple, *a*, пурпу́рный; ¶ *n*, пурпу́рный цвет; порфи́ра.

purport, *n*, смысл; цель; ¶ *v.t*, означа́ть; утвержда́ть.

purpose, *n*, цель, наме́рение; *on* **~** наро́чно; *to no* **~** напра́сно; *to*

some **~** не напра́сно; ¶ *v.i*, намерева́ться; **~ful**, *a*, целеустремлённый; преднаме́ренный; **~ly**, *ad*, наро́чно.

purr, *n*, мурлы́канье; ¶ *v.i*, мурлы́кать.

purse, *n*, кошелёк; *public* **~** казна́; ¶ *v.t*, поджима́ть *(lips)*; **~r**, *n*, казначе́й.

pursuance, *n*, выполне́ние, исполне́ние; пресле́дование; **pursuant to** согла́сно *(dat.)*; **pursue**, *v.t*, гна́ться за, пресле́довать; продолжа́ть; занима́ться *(inst.)*; проводи́ть *(policy)*; **~r**, *n*, пресле́дователь; **pursuit**, *n*, пресле́дование, пого́ня; заня́тие.

purulent, *a*, гно́йный.

purvey, *v.t*, поставля́ть; **~or**, *n*, поставщи́к.

purview, *n*, кругозо́р; компете́нция.

pus, *n*, гной.

push, *n*, толчо́к; нажи́м; наступле́ние, ата́ка; эне́ргия, предприи́мчивость; **~-button** кно́пка; **~-cart** (ручна́я) теле́жка; ¶ *v.t*, толка́ть; нажима́ть; прота́лкивать *(business)*; торопи́ть; реклами́ровать; **~ away** отта́лкивать; **~ forward** продвига́ть(ся) вперёд; **~ off** отта́лкивать(ся); *(coll.)* убира́ться; **~ out** *(v.t.)* выпуска́ть; выжима́ть; *(v.i.)* выдава́ться; **~ing**, *a*, предприи́мчивый, «пробивно́й».

pusillanimous, *a*, малоду́шный.

puss[y], *n*, ко́шечка, ки́ска.

pustule, *n*, прыщ.

put, *v.t*, класть, ста́вить; задава́ть *(question)*; выража́ть; толка́ть; **~ at** оце́нивать в; **~ away** убира́ть; откла́дывать; **~ back** ста́вить на ме́сто; заде́рживать; отводи́ть наза́д *(clock)*; возвраща́ть(ся); **~ by** откла́дывать (на чёрный день); **~ down** подавля́ть; запи́сывать; припи́сывать; *(animal)* умертви́ть *(pf)*; **~ forth** пуска́ть *(shoots, etc.)*; **~ in** вкла́дывать, вставля́ть; проводи́ть (вре́мя) за; подава́ть *(request)*; предъявля́ть *(claim)*; **~ into operation** пуска́ть в де́йствие; **~ off** откла́дывать; отгова́ривать от; снима́ть; **~ on** надева́ть; ста́вить на сце́не; прибавля́ть; **~ on weight** толсте́ть; **~ out** выкла́дывать, выставля́ть; туши́ть *(fire)*; раздража́ть; выходи́ть (в мо́ре); **~ through** выполнять; проводить; соединять (по телефону); ~ *a stop to* прекращать; положить *(pf.)* конéц *(dat.)*; ~ *to death* казнить; ~ *to flight* обращать в бéгство; ~ *to a vote* стáвить на голосовáние; ~ *to music* класть (словá) на мýзыку; ~ *together* сопоставлять, соединять; ~ *heads together* совещáться; ~ *up* поднимáть; приютить *(pf.)*; упакóвывать; выставлять *(notice)*; стрóить; ~ *up with* терпéть; ~ *upon (fig.)* обременять.

putative, *a*, предполагáемый, мнимый.

putrefaction, *n*, гниéние; разложéние; **putrefy,** *v.i*, гнить, разлагáться; **putrid,** *a*, гнилóй; вонючий.

putty, *n*, замáзка; шпаклёвка.

puzzle, *n*, загáдка, головолóмка; недоумéние; ¶ *v.t*, стáвить втупик, озадáчивать; ~ *one's brains over* ломáть себé гóлову над; ~ *out* разбирáться в.

pygmy, *n*, пигмéй.

pyjamas, *n.pl*, пижáма.

pylon, *n*, пилóн; мáчта.

pyramid, *n*, пирамида; ~**al,** *a*, пирамидáльный.

pyre, *n*, погребáльный костёр.

pyrites, *n*, колчедáн.

pyrotechnics, *n*, пиротéхника.

python, *n*, питóн.

Q

quack, *n*, крякáнье; знáхарь; шарлатáн; ¶ *v.i*, крякáть.

quadrangle, *n*, четырёхугóльник; **quadrangular,** *a*, четырёхугóльный.

quadrant, *n*, квадрáнт.

quadrilateral, *n*, четырёхугóльник; ¶ *a*, четырёхсторóнний.

quadrille, *n*, кадриль.

quadroon, *n*, квартерóн.

quadruped, *n*, четверонóгое.

quadruple, *a*, четвернóй; учетверённый; ~**ts,** *n.pl*, четверня.

quaff, *v.t*, пить большими глоткáми.

quagmire, *n*, болóто, трясина.

quail, *n*, пéрепел; ¶ *v.i*, трýсить.

quaint, *a*, причýдливый; живопúсный; оригинáльный.

quake, *v.i*, дрожáть, трястúсь.

Quaker, *n*, квáкер.

qualification, *n*, квалификáция; оговóрка, ограничéние; избирáтельный ценз; **qualified,** *p.p. & a*, квалифицúрованный; ограничéнный; правомóчный; **qualify,** *v.t*, квалифицúровать, дéлать правомóчным; ограничивать; видоизменять; **qualifying,** *a*, квалификациóнный.

qualitative, *a*, кáчественный; **quality,** *n*, кáчество; достóинство; *the* ~ вышее óбщество.

qualm, *n*, тошнотá; сомнéние ~**s of conscience** угрызéния сóвести.

quandary, *n*, затруднéние, недоумéние.

quantitative, *a*, количественный; **quantity,** *n*, количество; **quantum,** *n*, количество; *(phys.)* квант.

quarantine, *n*, карантúн.

quarrel, *n*, ссóра; ¶ *v.i*, ссóриться; ~**some,** *a*, придúрчивый, драчлúвый.

quarry, *n*, каменолóмня, карьéр; добыча; преслéдуемый зверь; *(fig.)* намéченная жéртва; ¶ *v.t*, добывáть (из карьéра); *v.i*, разрабáтывать карьéр.

quart, *n*, квáрта.

quarter, *n*, чéтверть; квартáл; сторонá; пощáда; *pl*, *(mil.)* квартúры; ~ *day* пéрвый день квартáла; ~*-deck* шкáнцы; ~*master* квартирмéйстер; начáльник хозяйственной чáсти; ~ *past five* чéтверть шестóго; ~ *to five* без чéтверти шесть; *at close* ~**s** бок ó бок; при ближáйшем рассмотрéнии; *(mil.)* с ближáйшего расстояния; ~**ly,** *a*, квартáльный, трёхмесячный; ¶ *ad*, раз в квартáл.

quartet,, *n*, квартéт.

quarto, *n*, чéтверть листá; ¶ *a*, в чéтвертую дóлю.

quartz, *n*, кварц.

quash, *v.t*, аннулúровать, отменять; подавлять.

quasi-, *prefix* квáзи-.

quatrain, *n*, четверостúшие.

quaver, *n*, дрожáние (гóлоса); *(mus.)* восьмáя нóты; ¶ *v.i*, дрожáть.

quay, *n*, нáбережная, причáл.

queasy, *n*, слáбый *(stomach)*; испытывающий тошнотý.

queen, *n*, королéва; *(cards)* дáма; *(chess)* ферзь; ~ *bee* мáтка.

queer, *a*, стра́нный; подозри́тельный; *feel* ~ чу́вствовать недомога́ние.

quell, *v.t*, подавля́ть.

quench, ~, *v.t*, утоля́ть *(thirst)*; туши́ть; подавля́ть.

querulous, *a*, ворчли́вый.

query, *n*, вопро́с; вопроси́тельный знак; ¶ *v.t*, спра́шивать о; подверга́ть сомне́нию; **quest**, *n*, по́иски; **question**, *n*, вопро́с; сомне́ние; ~ *mark* вопроси́тельный знак; ¶ *v.t*, спра́шивать; (д)опра́шивать; сомнева́ться в; **questionable**, *a*, сомни́тельный; **questioner**, *n*, спра́шивающий; сле́дователь; интервьюёр; **questionnaire**, *n*, анке́та, вопро́сник.

quibble, *n*, уве́ртка; софи́зм; ме́лочь; ¶ *v.i*, уклоня́ться от прямо́го отве́та.

quick, *a*, бы́стрый, ско́рый; неме́дленный; прово́рный; ~*-change artist* трансформа́тор; ~*lime* негашёная и́звесть; ~ *march* ско́рый шаг; ~ *sand* сыпу́чий песо́к; ~ *silver* ртуть; ~*tempered* вспы́льчивый; ~*-witted* остроу́мный; *be* ~ спеши́ть; ¶ *n* «живо́е мя́со», чувстви́тельное ме́сто; *the* ~ *and the dead* живы́е и мёртвые; *cut to the* ~ задева́ть за живо́е; ~**en**, *v.t. (& i.)*, ускоря́ть(ся); оживля́ть(ся); ~**ly**, *ad*, бы́стро, ско́ро; ~**ness**, *n*, быстрота́.

quid, *n*, кусо́к жева́тельного таба́ка; *(com.)* фунт; ~ *pro quo* компенса́ция, услу́га за услу́гу.

quiescence, *n*, споко́йствие; неподви́жность; **quiescent**, *a*, споко́йный; неподви́жный; пасси́вный.

quiet, *a*, ти́хий, споко́йный; ми́рный; ¶ *int*. ти́ше!; *keep smth.* ~ ума́лчивать; ¶ *n*, тишина́; споко́йствие; *on the* ~ тайко́м; ~**ly**, *ad*, ти́хо, споко́йно.

quill, *n*, перо́; игла́ *(porcupine)*; *(textile)* шпу́лька.

quilt, *n*, стёганое одея́ло; ¶ *v.t*, стега́ть; подбива́ть ва́той.

quince, *n*, айва́.

quinine, *n*, хини́н.

quinquennial, *a*, пятиле́тний.

quinsy, *n*, анги́на.

quintessence, *n*, квинтэссе́нция.

quintet(te), *n*, квинте́т.

quip, *n*, эпигра́мма, остро́та.

quire, *n*, десть бума́ги.

quirk, *n*, причу́да; уве́ртка.

quit, *v.t*, покида́ть; броса́ть; *give notice to* ~ предупрежда́ть об ухо́де; *be* ~*s with* быть в расчёте с.

quite, *ad*, совсе́м, вполне́; ~ *a lot* дово́льно мно́го.

quittance, *n*, квита́нция; опла́та; освобожде́ние от пла́ты.

quiver, *n*, тре́пет; колча́н; ¶ *v.i*, трепета́ть, дрожа́ть.

quixotic, *a*, донкихо́тский.

quiz, *n*, (прове́рочные) вопро́сы, опро́с; викторина; ¶ *v.t*, задава́ть вопро́сы *(dat.)*; ~**zical**, *a*, насме́шливый.

quoit, *n*, мета́тельное кольцо́; *(pl.)* мета́ние коле́ц в цель.

quondam, *a*, бы́вший.

quorum, *n*, кво́рум.

quota, *n*, кво́та.

quotation, *n*, цита́та; *(com.)* котиро́вка; ~ *marks* кавы́чки; **quote**, *v.t*, цити́ровать; *(com.)* назнача́ть (це́ну).

quotient, *n*, коэффицие́нт, ча́стное.

R

rabbi, *n*, равви́н; **rabbinical**, *a*, равви́нский.

rabbit, *n*, кро́лик; ~ *hutch* кле́тка (для кро́ликов); ~ *warren* кро́личий садо́к.

rabble, *n*, толпа́, сброд.

rabid, *a*, нейстовый; бе́шеный; **rabies**, *n*, бе́шенство; водобоя́знь.

race, *n*, ра́са, род; состяза́ние в ско́рости; го́нка; бы́строе тече́ние; *(tech.)* го́нка; обо́йма подши́пника; *pl*, бега́, ска́чки; *arms* ~ го́нка вооруже́ний; ~ *course* ипподро́м; ~ *horse* скакова́я ло́шадь; ~ *track* бегова́я доро́жка; *human* ~ род челове́ческий; ¶ *v.i*, состяза́ться в ско́рости, уча́ствовать в ска́чках; мча́ться; *v.t*, гнать *(engine)*; состяза́ться с; ~**r**, *n*, го́нщик; скакова́я ло́шадь; го́ночный автомоби́ль; **racial**, *a*, ра́совый; **raciness**, *n*, колори́тность; **racing**, *n*, ска́чки, бега́.

rack, *n*, ве́шалка, подста́вка; по́лка/ се́тка для веще́й *(in coach, etc.)*; решётка; кормушка; *(hist.)* ды́ба/ *(tech.)* зу́бчатая ре́йка; *(fig.)* пы́тка; *go to* ~ *and ruin* разоря́ться; ¶ *v.t,* мучить, пытать; ~ *one's brains* ломать себе голову.

racket, *n,* гам, суета; вымогательство; *(sport)* ракетка.

racoon, *n,* енот.

racy, *a,* простой, колоритный.

radar, *n,* радиолокация; радар.

radiance, *n,* сияние; **radiant,** *a,* лучезарный; лучистый; **radiate,** *v.t,* излучать; *v.i,* расходиться из центра; **radiation,** *n,* излучение; радиация; **radiator,** *n,* радиатор, батарея.

radical, *a,* коренной, радикальный; корневой; ¶ *n,* радикал; *(maths.)* корень; ~ly, *ad,* в корне, полностью.

radio, *n,* радио; ~ *set* радиоприёмник; радиоаппарат.

radioactive, *a,* радиоактивный.

radiogram, *n,* радиограмма.

radiography, *n,* радиография.

radiolocation, *n,* радиолокация.

radiology, *n,* радиология.

radiotherapy, *n,* радиотерапия.

radish, *n,* редиска.

radium, *n,* радий.

radius, *n,* радиус.

raffia, *n,* рафия.

raffle, *n,* лотерея; ¶ *v.t,* разыгрывать в лотерее.

raft, *n,* паром, плот.

rafter, *n,* стропило.

rag, *n,* тряпка; студенческий капустник; ~-*and-bone man* старьёвщик; *in* ~*s* в лохмотьях; ~**amuffin,** *n,* оборванец.

rage, *n,* гнев, ярость; *all the* ~ последний крик моды; ¶ *v.i,* беситься; свирепствовать *(epidemic, etc.).*

ragged, *a,* оборванный, истрёпанный; неотделанный, небрежный.

raging, *a,* яростный; бушующий.

raglan, *n,* пальто-реглан.

raid, *n,* облава, налёт; набег, рейд; ¶ *v.t,* делать налёт на.

rail, *n,* перила, поручни; перекладина; *(rly.)* рельс; *by* ~ по железной дороге; ¶ *v.t,* обносить перилами/забором; ~ *off* отгораживать; ~**ing,** *n,* ограда; перила.

raillery, *n,* добродушное подшучивание.

railway, *n,* железная дорога; ¶ *a,* железнодорожный; ~ *bed* железнодорожное полотно; ~ *strike* забастовка железнодорожных ра-

бочих; ~ *timetable* расписание поездов; *cable* ~ канатная дорога, фуникулёр; *narrow-gauge* ~ узкоколейная железная дорога.

raiment, *n,* одеяние.

rain, *n,* дождь; ~*bow* радуга; ~ *cloud* дождевое облако; ~*coat* плащ; ~*fall* количество осадков; ~-*gauge* дождемер; ~-*proof* непромокаемый, непроницаемый для дождя; ~-*water* дождевая вода; ¶ *v.t. (& i.),* сыпать(ся), лить(ся); *it is* ~*ing hard* идёт сильный дождь; *it is* ~*ing cats and dogs* дождь льёт как из ведра; ~y, *a,* дождливый.

raise, *v.t,* поднимать; воздвигать *(building);* воспитывать *(children);* выращивать *(plants);* разводить *(animals, etc.);* повышать *(standard, pay);* добывать *(money);* вызывать *(a laugh);* возбуждать *(hopes);* ~**d,** *a,* рельефный; приподнятый.

raisin, *a,* изюмина; *pl,* изюм.

rajah, *n,* раджа.

rake, *n,* грабли; скребок; кочерга; наклон; *(pers.)* распутник, повеса; ¶ *v.t,* сгребать; равнять граблями; ~ *up* сгребать, собирать; ~**ish,** *a,* распущенный.

rally, *n,* слёт, массовый митинг; собрание; ралли; ¶ *v.t. (& i.),* собирать(ся) вновь; оживлять(ся); оправляться от болезни.

ram, *n,* баран; таран; ¶ *v.t,* таранить; ~ *in* вбивать.

ramble, *n,* прогулка; ¶ *v.i,* бродить; говорить бессвязно; ползти *(plant);* ~**r,** *n,* празднношатающийся; вьющаяся роза; **rambling,** *a,* бессвязный; ползучий.

ramification, *n,* разветвление; **ramify,** *v.i,* разветвляться.

rammer, *n,* трамбовка; прибойник.

ramp, *n,* скат, уклон; ~**ant,** *a,* необузданный; буйно разросшийся; сильно распространённый; *(heraldry)* стоящий на задних лапах.

rampart, *n,* вал; *(fig.)* оплот.

ramrod, *n,* шомпол.

ramshackle, *a,* ветхий.

ranch, *n,* ранчо, ферма; ~**er,** *n,* хозяин или работник на ранчо.

rancid, *a,* прогорклый.

rancorous, *a,* злобный; **rancour,** *n,* злоба.

random, *a*, случа́йный; беспоря́дочный; вы́бранный науга́д; *at ~* науга́д, наобу́м.

range, *n*, разма́х, диапазо́н; цепь *(mountains)*; полиго́н, тир; ку́хонная плита́; обши́рное па́стбище; да́льность, досяга́емость; *(mil.)* дальнобо́йность; *~ of vision* по́ле зре́ния; ¶ *v.t*, выстра́ивать в ряд; *v.i*, простира́ться; колеба́ться; скита́ться; *~-finder* дальноме́р; *~r*, *n*, лесни́чий; *pl*, *(mil.)* деса́нтно-диверсио́нные ча́сти.

rank, *n*, ряд; шере́нга; зва́ние, ранг, чин; катего́рия, класс; *~ and file* рядово́й соста́в; ¶ *v.t*, классифици́ровать, оце́нивать; *v.i*, стоя́ть; ¶ *a*, прого́рклый; воню́чий; проти́вный; отъя́вленный.

rankle, *v.i*, причиня́ть боль, му́чить.

ransack, *v.t*, гра́бить; ры́ться в.

ransom, *n*, вы́куп; ¶ *v.t*, выкупа́ть.

rant, *v.i*, деклами́ровать.

rap, *v.t*, стуча́ть; слегка́ ударя́ть; ¶ *n*, стук; *I don't give a ~* мне наплева́ть.

rapacious, *a*, жа́дный, хи́щный; **rape**, *n*, изнаси́лование; *(bot.)* суре́пица; ¶ *v.t*, наси́ловать; похища́ть.

rapid, *a*, бы́стрый; круто́й; *pl*, поро́ги (реки); *~ity*, *n*, быстрота́.

rapier, *n*, рапи́ра.

rapine, *n*, грабёж.

rapt, *a*, поглощённый; восхищённый; *~ure*, *n*, восто́рг, экста́з; *~urous*, *a*, восто́рженный.

rare, *a*, ре́дкий; исключи́тельный; недожа́ренный; **rarefy**, *v.t*, разрежа́ть; **rarity**, *n*, ре́дкость; разрежённость.

rascal, *n*, негодя́й, моше́нник; *~ly*, *a*, моше́ннический.

rash, *a*, необду́манный; опроме́тчивый; ¶ *n*, сыпь.

rasher, *n*, ло́мтик (ветчины).

rasp, *n*, напи́льник, тёрка; скре́жет; ¶ *v.t*, подпи́ливать; *v.i*, скрежета́ть.

raspberry, *n*, мали́на; ¶ *a*, мали́новый.

rat, *n*, кры́са; *~race* конкуре́нция; *~-trap* крысоло́вка; ¶ *v.i*: *~ on* предава́ть.

ratchet, *n*, храпови́к.

rate, *n*, нало́г; ста́вка, но́рма; цена́; ско́рость, темп; *~ of exchange* валю́тный курс; *at any ~* во вся́ком слу́чае; *bank ~* учётная ста́вка ба́нка; ¶ *v.t*, оце́нивать; счита́ть; брани́ть, руга́ть; *~payer*, *n*, налогоплате́льщик.

rather, *ad*, скоре́е, верне́е; дово́льно, не́сколько; предпочти́тельно; лу́чше.

ratification, *n*, ратифика́ция; **ratify**, *v.t*, ратифици́ровать.

rating, *n*, оце́нка, классифика́ция; обложе́ние нало́гом; *(mar.)* специа́льность, матро́с; «статья́» матро́са; класс; вы́говор, нагоня́й.

ratio, *n*, отноше́ние; коэффицие́нт.

ration, *n*, паёк, рацио́н; *pl*, продово́льствие; *~ card* продово́льственная/промтова́рная ка́рточка; ¶ *v.t*, норми́ровать, разделя́ть.

rational, *a*, разу́мный, рациона́льный; *~ism*, *n*, рационали́зм; *~ization*, *n*, рационализа́ция; рационалисти́ческое объясне́ние.

rationing, *n*, норми́рование.

rattle, *n*, гро́хот; дребезжа́ние; *(toy)* погрему́шка; трещо́тка; *~snake* гремуча́я змея́; ¶ *v.t*, трясти́; *v.i*, треща́ть, грохота́ть, дребезжа́ть; *~ off* «отбараба́нивать».

raucous, *a*, хри́плый.

ravage, *v.t*, опустоша́ть.

rave, *v.i*, бре́дить; неи́стовствовать; бушева́ть.

ravel, *v.t*, запу́тывать.

raven, *n*, во́рон.

ravenous, *a*, прожо́рливый; хи́щный.

ravine, *n*, уще́лье.

raving, *n*, бред; ¶ *a*, бредово́й; сумасше́дший.

ravish, *v.t*, наси́ловать; похища́ть; *~ing*, *a*, восхити́тельный; *~ment*, *n*, изнаси́лование; похище́ние; восхище́ние.

raw, *a*, сыро́й; необрабо́танный; нео́пытный; *~ cotton* хло́пок-сыре́ц; *~ hide* недублёная ко́жа; *~ material* сырьё.

ray, *n*, луч; *(fig.)* про́блеск; скат *(fish)*.

raze, *v.t*, разруша́ть до основа́ния; *(fig.)* стира́ть.

razor, *n*, бри́тва.

reach, *n*, преде́л досяга́емости; охва́т; протяже́ние; *out of ~* вне преде́лов досяга́емости; недосту́пный; ¶ *v.t.* *(& i.)*, протя́гивать(-ся); дотя́гиваться до; доходи́ть до; достига́ть *(gen.)*; простира́ть-(ся).

react, *v.i,* реаги́ровать; **~ion,** *n,* реа́кция; **~ionary,** *a,* реакцио́н-ный; ¶ *n,* реакционе́р.

read, *v.t,* чита́ть; пока́зывать *(of instrument);* снима́ть показа́ния *(gen.);* отсчи́тывать; изуча́ть; *v.i,* гласи́ть; чита́ться; **~able,** *a,* чёт-кий; интере́сный.

readdress, *v.t,* переадресо́вывать.

reader, *n,* чита́тель; корре́ктор; ста́рший преподава́тель; хресто-ма́тия.

readily, *ad,* охо́тно; легко́; **readiness,** *n,* гото́вность.

reading, *n,* чте́ние; вариа́нт те́кста; показа́ние прибо́ра; **~-desk** пю-пи́тр; **~** *room* чита́льный зал.

re-adjust, *v.t,* переде́лывать; изме-ня́ть.

ready, *a,* гото́вый; **~-made** гото́вый; **~** *money* нали́чные де́ньги; **~** *reckoner* табли́цы гото́вых рас-чётов.

reaffirm, *v.t,* вновь подтвержда́ть.

reagent, *n,* реакти́в.

real, *a,* настоя́щий, действи́тель-ный; по́длинный; недви́жимый *(estate);* **~ism,** *n,* реали́зм; **~istic,** *a,* реалисти́ческий, тре́звый; **~ity,** *n,* действи́тельность; **~ization,** *n,* осуществле́ние; осозна́ние; **~ize,** *v.t,* осуществля́ть; понима́ть; реа-лизова́ть; **~ly,** *ad,* в са́мом де́ле, действи́тельно.

realm, *n,* короле́вство; *(fig.)* о́б-ласть, сфе́ра.

ream, *n,* стопа́.

reanimate, *v.t,* оживля́ть, возвра-ща́ть к жи́зни.

reap, *v.t,* жать; *(fig.)* пожина́ть; **~er,** *n,* жнец, жни́ца; жа́твенная маши́на; **~ing,** *n,* жа́тва; **~** *hook* серп.

reappear, *v.i,* сно́ва появля́ться; **~ance,** *n,* возвраще́ние, но́вое появле́ние.

rear, *n,* тыл; за́дняя сторона́; зад; ¶ *a,* за́дний; *in the* **~** позади́, в тылу́; *bring up the* **~** замыка́ть ше́ствие; **~-admiral** контр-адми-ра́л; **~guard** арьерга́рд; ¶ *v.t,* поднима́ть; воспи́тывать; выра́-щивать; разводи́ть; *v.i,* стано-ви́ться на дыбы́; вы́ситься.

reason, *n,* ра́зум, рассу́док; основа́-ние, причи́на; *by* **~** *of* по причи́не;

¶ *v.i,* рассужда́ть; **~** *out* проду́-мывать до конца́; **~able,** *a,* (благо)разу́мный; уме́ренный; прие́млемый; **~ableness,** *n,* рас-сужде́ние; аргумента́ция.

reassure, *v.t,* успока́ивать; вновь уверя́ть; **reassuring,** *a,* успока́и-вающий.

rebate, *n,* ски́дка, усту́пка.

rebel, *n,* бунтовщи́к, повста́нец; ¶ *v.i,* восстава́ть, бунтова́ть; **~-lion,** *n,* восста́ние, мяте́ж; **~-lious,** *a,* мяте́жный.

rebirth, *n,* перерожде́ние.

rebound, *n,* отда́ча; отско́к; рико-ше́т; ¶ *v.i,* отска́кивать.

rebuff, *n,* отпо́р, ре́зкий отка́з; ¶ *v.t,* дава́ть отпо́р/отка́зывать на-отре́з *(dat.).*

rebuild, *v.t,* отстра́ивать за́ново, восстана́вливать.

rebuke, *n,* упрёк, вы́говор; ¶ *v.t,* упрека́ть.

rebut, *v.t,* опроверга́ть; дава́ть отпо́р *(dat.);* **~tal,** *n,* опроверже́ние; отпо́р.

recalcitrance, *n,* непоко́рность, упо́р-ство; **recalcitrant,** *a,* непоко́рный; упо́рный.

recall, *n,* о́тзыв *(of envoy, etc.);* призы́в верну́ться; ¶ *v.t,* отзы-ва́ть; призыва́ть обра́тно; вспо-мина́ть; напомина́ть; отменя́ть.

recant, *v.i,* отрека́ться; **~ation,** *n,* отрече́ние.

recapitulate, *v.t,* перечисля́ть; резю-ми́ровать; **recapitulation,** *n,* пере-числе́ние; резюме́.

recapture, *n,* взя́тие обра́тно; ¶ *v.t,* брать/захва́тывать обра́тно.

recast, *v.t,* придава́ть но́вую фо́рму *(dat.),* переде́лывать.

recede, *v.i,* отступа́ть; па́дать.

receipt, *n,* квита́нция, распи́ска; получе́ние; *pl,* прихо́д; ¶ *v.t,* дава́ть распи́ску в получе́нии *(gen.);* **receive,** *v.t,* получа́ть; при-нима́ть; **receiver,** *n,* получа́тель; телефо́нная тру́бка; радиоприём-ник; укрыва́тель кра́деного; су-де́бный исполни́тель.

recent, *a,* неда́вний, но́вый, све́жий, совреме́нный; **~ly,** *ad,* неда́вно.

receptacle, *n,* вмести́лище; храни́-лище; **reception,** *n,* приём; получе́-ние; восприя́тие; **~** *room* при-ёмная, гости́ная; **receptive,** *a,* воспри́мчивый.

recess, *n,* перерыв в занятиях, каникулы; ниша, углубление; *in the secret* ~*es* в тайниках; ~**ion,** *n,* удаление; углубление; падение.

recipe, *n,* рецепт; средство.

recipient, *n,* получатель.

reciprocal, *a,* взаимный; ответный; **reciprocate,** *v.t,* отвечать (взаимностью); обмениваться *(inst.);* **reciprocity,** *n,* взаимность.

recital, *n,* чтение, декламация; концерт; **recitation,** *n,* декламация; **recite,** *v.t,* декламировать, читать наизусть; перечислять; отвечать урок.

reckless, *a,* безрассудный, опрометчивый; ~ *driving* пренебрежение правилами езды.

reckon, *v.t,* подсчитывать; считать; *v.i,* думать, считать; ~ *on* рассчитывать на; ~ *with* принимать в расчёт; рассчитываться с; ~**ing,** *n,* расчёт, подсчёт; расплата.

reclaim, *v.t,* требовать обратно; восстанавливать, исправлять; поднимать, осваивать *(agr.).*

recline, *v.t,* откидывать; *v.i,* облокачиваться, откидываться назад; полулежать.

recluse, *n,* затвор|ик, отшельн|ик, -ица.

recognition, *n,* узнавание; признание; одобрение; **recognize,** *v.t,* узнавать; признавать.

recoil, *n,* отдача *(gun);* ¶ *v.i,* отдавать *(gun);* отскакивать; отшатываться.

recollect, *v.t,* вспоминать; ~**ion,** *n,* воспоминание; память.

recommence, *v.t,* снова начинать.

recommend, *v.t,* рекомендовать; советовать; представлять (к награде); поручать попечению; ~**ation,** *n,* рекомендация; совет.

recompense, *n,* вознаграждение; компенсация; ¶ *v.t,* вознаграждать.

reconcile, *v.t,* примирять; **reconciliation,** *n,* примирение.

recondite, *a,* тёмный, неясный.

recondition, *v.t,* ремонтировать, переделывать.

reconnaissance, *n,* разведка; **reconnoitre,** *v.t,* разведовать.

reconsider, *v.t,* пересматривать.

reconstruct, *v.t,* перестраивать; восстанавливать; ~**ion,** *n,* пере-

стройка, реконструкция; восстановление.

record, *n,* запись, протокол; (граммофонная) пластинка; репутация; личное дело; *(sport)* рекорд; ¶ *a,* рекордный; *break a* ~ побить *(pf.)* рекорд; *off the* ~ неофициально; ~*-player* проигрыватель; ~ *office* государственный архив; ~**er,** *n,* регистратор; городской судья; звукозаписывающий аппарат; *(mus.)* дудка.

re-count, *n,* пересчёт голосов; ¶ *v.t,* пересчитывать; пересказывать.

recoup, *v.t,* возмещать.

recourse, *n: have* ~ *to* прибегать к помощи.

re-cover, *v.t,* перекрывать; **recover,** *v.t,* получать обратно; восстанавливать; *v.i,* поправляться, выздоравливать; ~**y,** *n,* возмещение; возвращение; выздоровление.

recreant, *n,* трус; отступник.

re-create, *v.t,* воссоздавать.

recreation, *n,* отдых, развлечение; ~ *ground* площадка для игр.

recriminate, *v.t,* обвинять друг друга; **recrimination,** *n,* взаимное обвинение.

recruit, *n,* рекрут, новобранец; *(fig.)* новичок; ¶ *v.t,* вербовать, набирать; ~**ment,** *n,* вербовка.

rectangle, *n,* прямоугольник; **rectangular,** *a,* прямоугольный.

rectification, *n,* исправление; *(elec.)* выпрямление; **rectify,** *v.t,* исправлять; выпрямлять.

rectilinear, *a,* прямолинейный.

rectitude, *n,* честность.

rector, *n,* ректор; пастор; ~**y,** *n,* дом пастора.

recumbent, *a,* лежащий.

rectum, *n,* прямая кишка.

recuperate, *v.t. (& i.),* выздоравливать; восстанавливать(ся); **recuperation,** *n,* выздоровление; восстановление.

recur, *v.i,* повторяться; ~**rence,** *n,* повторение; возвращение; ~**ring,** *a,* повторяющийся.

red, *a,* красный; *turn* ~ краснеть; ~*breast* малиновка; *R*~ *Cross* Красный Крест; ~ *deer* благородный олень; ~*-haired* рыжий; ~*-handed* с поличным; на месте преступления; ~ *herring* отвлекающий манёвр; ~ hot раскалённый докрасна; ~ lead свинцо́вый су́рик; ~-letter day пра́здничный/ счастли́вый день; R~ Sea Кра́сное мо́ре; ~skin краснокожий, индеец; ~ tape бюрократизм, канцеля́рщина, волоки́та; redden, v.t, окра́шивать в кра́сный цвет; v.i, красне́ть.

redeem, v.t, выкупа́ть; выпла́чивать (debt); спаса́ть; искупа́ть (sins); ~er, n, спаси́тель; **redemption,** n, вы́куп, вы́плата; спасе́ние; искупле́ние.

redness, n, краснота́.

redolent, a, арома́тный.

redouble, v.t. (& i.), удва́ивать(ся).

redoubt, n, реду́т; ~able, a, гро́зный.

redound, v.i: ~ to способствовать (dat.); ~ upon возвраща́ться к; па́дать на.

redress, n, возмеще́ние, удовлетворе́ние; ¶ v.t, исправля́ть; возмеща́ть; ~ a wrong загла́живать оби́ду.

reduce, v.t, понижа́ть, уменьша́ть; снижа́ть (price); сокраща́ть; v.i, худе́ть; ~ to доводи́ть до; ~ to the ranks разжа́ловать (pf.) в рядовы́е; ~d circumstances стеснённые обстоя́тельства; **reduction,** n, пониже́ние, уменьше́ние; сниже́ние; сокраще́ние.

redundancy, n, избы́ток, изли́шество; чрезме́рность; нену́жность; безрабо́тица; **redundant,** a, изли́шний, ли́шний, чрезме́рный; нену́жный.

re-echo, v.i, отдава́ться э́хом.

reed, n, тростни́к, камы́ш; (mus.) язычо́к; ~-mace рого́з.

reef, n, риф; ~-knot ри́фовый у́зел.

reek, n, вонь; дым; ¶ v.i, воня́ть; па́хнуть; дыми́ть.

reel, n, кату́шка; (tech.) бараба́н; бы́стрый та́нец; ¶ v.i, кружи́ться; шата́ться; ~ on нама́тывать.

re-elect, v.t, переизбира́ть; ~ion, n, переизбра́ние.

re-embark, v.i, сно́ва сади́ться на кора́бль; сно́ва начина́ть.

re-establish, v.t, восстана́вливать.

re-examine, v.t, пересма́тривать; вновь экзаменова́ть.

refectory, n, столо́вая; тра́пезная (monastery).

refer, v.t, отсыла́ть, направля́ть; ~ to относи́ться к; ссыла́ться на; ~ee, n, трете́йский судья́; (sport) судья́; ~ence, n, ссы́лка; упомина́ние; рекоменда́ция; ~ library спра́вочная библиоте́ка; ~endum, n, референду́м.

refill, n, дополне́ние, пополне́ние; ¶ v.t, вновь наполня́ть; заправля́ть (горю́чим).

refine, v.t, очища́ть, рафини́ровать; де́лать бо́лее утончённым/изя́щным; ~d, p.p. & a, очи́щенный, рафини́рованный; утончённый, изя́щный; ~ment, n, очище́ние, рафини́рование; обрабо́тка; изы́сканность; ~ry, n, рафини́ровочный заво́д.

refit, v.t, снаряжа́ть за́ново; ремонти́ровать.

reflect, v.t, отража́ть; ~ on (fig.) броса́ть тень на; v.i, разду́мывать, размышля́ть; ~ion, n, отраже́ние; размышле́ние; ~or, n, отража́тель, рефле́ктор; **reflex,** a, рефлекто́рный; ~ action непроизво́льное де́йствие; ¶ n, рефле́кс.

reform, n, рефо́рма, преобразова́ние; ¶ v.t, реформи́ровать; исправля́ть; v.i, исправля́ться; ~ation, n, преобразова́ние; исправле́ние; Реформа́ция; ~atory, n, исправи́тельный дом; ~er, n, преобразова́тель.

refract, v.t, преломля́ть; ~ion, n, преломле́ние; ~oriness, n, стропти́вость, непоко́рность; (tech.) огнеупо́рность, тугопла́вкость; ~ory, n, стропти́вый, непоко́рный; (tech.) огнеупо́рный, тугопла́вкий.

refrain, n, припе́в; ¶ v.i, возде́рживаться.

refresh, v.t, освежа́ть; подкрепля́ть; ~ing, a, освежи́тельный; ~ment, n, о́тдых, подкрепле́ние; pl, заку́ски, напи́тки; ~ room буфе́т.

refrigerate, v.t, замора́живать; **refrigeration,** n, замора́живание, охлажде́ние; **refrigerator,** n, холоди́льник; конденса́тор; ~-car ваго́н-холоди́льник.

refuge, n, убе́жище; прибе́жище; **refugee,** n, бе́женец, эмигра́нт.

refulgent, a, блестя́щий, сверка́ющий.

refund, *n*, уплата; возвращение, возмещение; ¶ *v.t*, возвращать, возмещать.

refurnish, *v.t*, вновь обставлять мебелью.

refusal, *n*, отказ; **refuse**, *v.t*, отказывать *(smb-dat., sth.*-в); отвергать; отказываться от; ¶ *n*, отбросы; мусор; ~ *dump* мусорная свалка.

refutation, *n*, опровержение; **refute**, *v.t*, опровергать.

regain, *v.t*, вновь приобретать, вновь достигать *(gen);* ~ *consciousness* приходить в чувство.

regal, *a*, царственный, королевский; величественный; ~e, *v.t*, угощать, потчевать; услаждать; ~ia, *n.pl*, регалии.

regard, *n*, уважение; внимание; взгляд; *pl*, поклон, привет; *kindest* ~s сердечный привет; *with* ~ *to* относительно; ¶ *v.t*, смотреть на; считать; относиться к; *as* ~s что касается; ~ing, *pr*, относительно, о(б); ~less, *a*, равнодушный; ~ *of* не считаясь с.

regatta, *n*, регата.

regency, *n*, регентство.

regenerate, *v.t*, возрождать; восстанавливать; *(tech.)* регенерировать; **regeneration**, *n*, возрождение; регенерация, восстановление.

regent, *n*, регент.

regicide, *n*, цареубийство; цареубийца.

regime, *n*, режим; ~n, *n*, режим; ~nt, *n*, полк; ~ntal, *a*, полковой.

region, *n*, край; область *(also fig.);* *in the* ~ *of* поблизости; приблизительно; ~al, *a*, областной.

register, *n*, журнал; список; метрическая книга; *(mus.)* регистр; ¶ *v.t*, регистрировать; записывать; отправлять заказным *(letter);* сдавать *(luggage); v.i*, регистрироваться; *(fig.)* запечатлеваться; ~ed *letter* заказное письмо; **registrar**, *n*, регистратор; **registration**, *n*, регистрация; запись; **registry**, *n*, регистратура.

regret, *n*, сожаление; раскаяние; *to our* ~ к нашему сожалению; ¶ *v.t*, сожалеть о, раскаиваться в; ~table, *a*, прискорбный.

regular, *a*, регулярный; правильный; нормальный; очередной;

постоянный; *(coll.)* настоящий; ¶ *n*, солдат регулярной армии; завсегдатай; ~ity, *n*, регулярность; порядок; **regulate**, *v.t*, регулировать, упорядочивать; приспосабливать; **regulation**, *n*, регулирование; правило; *pl*, устав; ¶ *a*, установленный; положенный; **regulator**, *n*, регулировщик; *(tech.)* регулятор.

rehabilitate, *v.t*, реабилитировать; восстанавливать (в правах); **rehabilitation**, *n*, реабилитация; восстановление.

rehearsal, *n*, репетиция; *dress* ~ генеральная репетиция; **rehearse**, *v.t*, репетировать; повторять.

rehouse, *v.t*, переселять.

reign, *n*, царствование; ¶ *v.i*, царствовать; *(fig.)* царить.

reimburse, *v.t*, возмещать; ~ment, *n*, компенсация, возмещение.

rein, *n*, повод, вожжа; ~s *of government* бразды правления *give* ~ *to* давать волю *(dat.).*

reincarnation, *n*, перевоплощение.

reindeer, *n*, северный олень.

reinforce, *v.t*, усиливать, подкреплять; армировать *(concrete);* ~d *concrete* железобетон; ~ment, *n*, усиление, укрепление; *(mil.)* подкрепление; *(tech.)* арматура.

reinstate, *v.t*, восстанавливать.

reinsurance, *n*, перестраховка; **reinsure**, *v.t*, перестраховывать.

reiterate, *v.t*, повторять; **reiteration**, *n*, повторение.

reject, *v.t*, отвергать; отклонять; отказываться от; извергать; ~ion, *n*, отказ; отклонение; извержение.

rejoice, *v.t*, радовать; *v.i*, радоваться *(at-dat.);* **rejoicing**, *n*, веселье.

rejoin, *v.i*, возвращаться; отвечать, возражать; ~der, *n*, ответ, возражение.

rejuvenate, *v.t*, омолаживать.

relapse, *n*, рецидив; ¶ *v.i*, снова впадать; снова заболевать.

relate, *v.t*, рассказывать; устанавливать связь *(gen.); v.i*, относиться к; *be* ~d *to* состоять в родстве/быть связанным с; **relation**, *n*, родственн|ик, -ица; отношение; связь; ~ship, *n*, родство; отношение; связь; **relative**, *a*, относи-

тельный; ¶ *n*, ро́дственн/ик, -ица;
relativity, *n*, относи́тельность;
реляти́визм.
relax, *v.t*, ослабля́ть, смягча́ть;
v.i, ослабля́ться, смягча́ться; от-
дыха́ть; ~**ation**, *n*, ослабле́ние;
о́тдых; ~**ing**, *a*, смягча́ющий;
расслабля́ющий *(climate, etc.);*
relay, *n*, сме́на; *(radio)* трансля́ция;
(sport) эстафе́та; ¶ *v.t*, сно́ва
класть; передава́ть; трансли́ро-
вать; ~ *race* бег с эстафе́той.
release, *n*, освобожде́ние; сбра́сы-
вание *(bombs); (tech.)* разъеди-
не́ние; расцепле́ние; ¶ *v.t*, осво-
божда́ть; отпуска́ть; выпуска́ть
(film, etc.); (tech.) расцепля́ть;
сбра́сывать.
relegate, *v.t*, передвига́ть; отсыла́ть;
relegation, *n*, передвиже́ние; вы́-
сылка.
relent, *v.i*, смягча́ться; ~**less**, *a*,
безжа́лостный.
relevance, *n*, уме́стность; целесо-
обра́зность; **relevant**, *a*, уме́ст-
ный; целесообра́зный.
reliability, *n*, надёжность; про́ч-
ность; достове́рность; **reliable**, *a*,
надёжный; про́чный; достове́р-
ный; **reliance**, *n*, дове́рие.
relic, *n*, оста́ток; *pl*, оста́нки; ре-
ли́квии.
relief, *n*, облегче́ние; посо́бие, по́-
мощь; сме́на; сня́тие (оса́ды);
релье́ф *(art & geol.);* ~ *train* до-
полни́тельный по́езд; **relieve**, *v.t*,
облегча́ть; выруча́ть; сменя́ть;
снима́ть оса́ду с; освобожда́ть;
лиша́ть.
religion, *n*, рели́гия; **religious**, *a*,
религио́зный.
relinquish, *v.t*, оставля́ть; отка́зы-
ваться от.
relish, *n*, вкус, при́вкус; припра́ва;
удово́льствие, наслажде́ние; ¶
v.t, получа́ть/предвкуша́ть удо-
во́льствие от.
reluctance, *n*, неохо́та, нежела́ние;
reluctant, *a*, неохо́тный; не жела́-
ющий *(+ inf.).*
rely, *v.i:* ~ *on* полага́ться на.
remain, *v.i*, остава́ться; ~**der**, *n*,
оста́ток; ~**ing**, *a*, оста́вшийся;
друго́й, ли́шний; ~**s**, *n.pl*, оста́т-
ки; оста́нки *(of deceased);* рели́к-
вии; руи́ны; посме́ртные произ-
веде́ния.
remake, *v.t*, переде́лывать.

remand, *n*, отсы́лка под стра́жу;
person on ~ подсле́дственный;
¶ *v.t*, отсыла́ть под стра́жу;
(mil.) отчисля́ть.
remark, *n*, замеча́ние; ¶ *v.t*, заме-
ча́ть, отмеча́ть; ~**able**, *a*, заме-
ча́тельный.
remedy, *n*, сре́дство; лека́рство;
возмеще́ние уще́рба; ¶ *v.t*, ис-
правля́ть; выле́чивать.
remember, *v.t*, по́мнить, вспомина́ть;
~ *me to him* переда́йте ему́ приве́т
от меня́; **remembrance**, *n*, воспо-
мина́ние, па́мять.
remind, *v.t*, напомина́ть; ~**er**, *n*,
напомина́ние.
reminiscence, *n*, воспомина́ние; **re-
miniscent**, *a*, напомина́ющий.
remiss, *a*, небре́жный, невнима́-
тельный; ~**ion**, *n*, смягче́ние
(пригово́ра), проще́ние; **remit**, *v.t*,
смягча́ть; проща́ть; пересыла́ть;
remittance, *n*, пересы́лка де́нег;
де́нежный перево́д.
remnant, *n*, оста́ток, отре́зок.
remodel, *v.t*, переде́лывать.
remonstrance, *n*, проте́ст, увеща́ние;
remonstrate, *v.i*, протестова́ть;
~ *with* увеща́ть.
remorse, *n*, раска́яние, угрызе́ние
со́вести; ~**less**, *a*, безжа́лост-
ный.
remote, *a*, отдалённый, уединённый;
маловероя́тный; ~**ness**, *n*, от-
далённость, уединённость.
removable, *a*, передвига́емый, под-
вижно́й; сменя́емый; **removal**, *n*,
перемеще́ние; перее́зд; смеще́ние;
убо́рка; ~ *van* фурго́н для пере-
во́зки ме́бели; **remove**, *v.t*, уби-
ра́ть; удаля́ть; устраня́ть; пере-
вози́ть; передвига́ть; *v.i*, пере-
езжа́ть.
remunerate, *v.t*, вознагражда́ть, оп-
ла́чивать; **remuneration**, *n*, воз-
награжде́ние, опла́та; **remune-
rative**, *a*, вы́годный; хорошо́
опла́чиваемый.
renaissance, *n*, возрожде́ние.
rend, *v.t. (& i.)*, раздира́ть(ся), раз-
рыва́ть(ся).
render, *v.t*, воздава́ть; ока́зывать
(help); передава́ть; переводи́ть;
исполня́ть (роль); топи́ть *(fat);*
~ *an account* представля́ть счёт
к опла́те; дава́ть отчёт; ~**ing**, *n*,
переда́ча; исполне́ние; выта́пли-
вание.

rendezvous, *n,* свида́ние; ме́сто встре́чи.

renegade, *n,* ренега́т, изме́нник.

renew, *v.t,* обновля́ть; возобновля́ть; *(com.)* продлева́ть; ~al, *n,* обновле́ние, возобновле́ние; продле́ние.

renounce, *v.t,* отка́зываться от; отрека́ться от; ~ment, *n,* отка́з; отрече́ние.

renown, *n,* сла́ва; ~ed, *a,* изве́стный, знамени́тый.

rent, *n,* аре́ндная/кварти́рная пла́та; ре́нта; дыра́, проре́ха; ¶ *v.t,* снима́ть, нанима́ть; сдава́ть в аре́нду; брать напрока́т; ~al, *n,* аре́ндная пла́та; ~er, *n,* аренда́тор, съёмщик.

renunciation, *n,* отка́з, отрече́ние.

reopen, *v.t. (& i.),* открыва́ть(ся) сно́ва.

reorganization, *n,* реорганиза́ция; **reorganize,** *v.t,* реорганизо́вывать.

rep, *n,* репс.

repair, *n,* почи́нка, ремо́нт; ¶ *v.t,* чини́ть, исправля́ть, ремонти́ровать; *v.i,* направля́ться; прибега́ть (к); ~able, *a,* поправи́мый; **reparation,** *n,* репара́ция, возмеще́ние.

repartee, *n,* остроу́мный отве́т; остроу́мие.

repast, *n,* еда́, тра́пеза.

repatriate, *v.t,* репатрии́ровать; **repatriation,** *n,* репатриа́ция.

repay, *v.t,* отдава́ть; оплача́ивать; возмеща́ть; ~able, *a,* подлежа́щий упла́те/возмеще́нию; ~ment, *n,* отпла́та; возмеще́ние.

repeal, *n,* отме́на, аннули́рование; ¶ *v.t,* отменя́ть, аннули́ровать.

repeat, *n,* повторе́ние; ¶ *v.t. (& i.),* повторя́ть(ся); ~edly, *ad,* неоднокра́тно, повто́рно; ~er, *n,* магази́нная винто́вка; часы́ с репети́цией.

repel, *v.t,* отта́лкивать; отража́ть; ~lent, *a,* отта́лкивающий, отврати́тельный.

repent, *v.t,* раска́иваться в, сожале́ть о; ~ance, *n,* раска́яние, сожале́ние; ~ant, *a,* ка́ющийся.

repercussion, *n,* отда́ча; о́тзвук, отраже́ние *(fig.).*

repertoire, *n,* репертуа́р.

repertory, *n,* храни́лище; сбо́рник, катало́г; ~ *theatre* теа́тр с ча́сто меня́ющимся репертуа́ром.

repetition, *n,* повторе́ние.

repine, *v.i,* жа́ловаться, ропта́ть.

replace, *v.t,* класть/ста́вить обра́тно на ме́сто; заменя́ть; ~ment, *n,* заме́на, замеще́ние; сме́на.

replay, *n,* переигро́вка.

replenish, *v.t,* сно́ва наполня́ть; пополня́ть.

replete, *a,* насы́щенный, пресы́щенный; **repletion,** *n,* пресыще́ние.

replica, *n,* ре́плика; то́чная ко́пия.

reply, *n,* отве́т; ~ *paid* с опла́ченным отве́том; ¶ *v.i,* отвеча́ть.

report, *n,* докла́д; о́тзыв, характери́стика; *(mil.)* донесе́ние; звук взры́ва/вы́стрела; ¶ *v.t,* докла́дывать; сообща́ть; *(mil.)* доноси́ть о; *v.i,* явля́ться; дава́ть отчёт; ~age, *n,* репорта́ж; ~er, *n,* репортёр.

repose, *n,* поко́й; о́тдых; ¶ *v.i,* поко́иться.

repository, *n,* склад, храни́лище.

reprehend, *v.t,* де́лать *(dat.)* вы́говор, порица́ть; **reprehensible,** *a,* досто́йный порица́ния.

represent, *v.t,* представля́ть; изобража́ть; символизи́ровать; быть представи́телем *(gen.);* ~ation, *n,* представи́тельство; ~ative, *n,* представи́тель, уполномо́ченный; ¶ *a,* представи́тельный; символизи́рующий.

repress, *v.t,* подавля́ть; сде́рживать; ~ion, *n,* подавле́ние, репре́ссия; сде́рживание; ~ive, *a,* репресси́вный.

reprieve, *n,* отме́на/отсро́чка пригово́ра; поми́лование; переды́шка; ¶ *v.t,* откла́дывать/отменя́ть исполне́ние пригово́ра *(dat.).*

reprimand, *n,* вы́говор; ¶ *v.t,* де́лать вы́говор *(dat.).*

reprisal, *n,* репресса́лия.

reproach, *n,* упрёк, уко́р; ¶ *v.t,* упрека́ть, укоря́ть; ~ful, *a,* укори́зненный.

reprobate, *n,* негодя́й; **reprobation,** *n,* осужде́ние, порица́ние.

reproduce, *v.t,* воспроизводи́ть; де́лать ко́пию с; *v.i,* размножа́ться; **reproduction,** *n,* воспроизведе́ние; размноже́ние; *(art, photo.)* репроду́кция.

reproof, *n,* порица́ние; вы́говор; **reprove,** *v.t,* порица́ть, укоря́ть.

reptile, *n,* пресмыка́ющееся; *(fig.)* подхали́м.

republic, *n,* респу́блика; **~an,** *n,* республика́нец; ¶ *a,* республика́нский.

republish, *v.t,* переиздава́ть.

repudiate, *v.t,* отверга́ть; отка́зываться от; отрека́ться от; отрица́ть; **repudiation,** *n,* отка́з, отрече́ние; отрица́ние.

repugnance, *n,* отвраще́ние; **repugnant,** *a,* отврати́тельный.

repulse, *n,* отпо́р; ¶ *v.t,* отража́ть; опроверга́ть; отверга́ть; **repulsive,** *a,* отта́лкивающий.

reputable, *a,* почётный; **reputation,** *n,* репута́ция, сла́ва; **reputed: ~** *to be* счита́ющийся *(inst.);* **~ly,** *ad,* по о́бщему мне́нию.

request, *n,* про́сьба; *on* **~** по про́сьбе, по тре́бованию; ¶ *v.t,* проси́ть.

requiem, *n,* ре́квием.

require, *v.t,* тре́бовать; нужда́ться в; прика́зывать; **~ment,** *n,* тре́бование; потре́бность; **requisite,** *a,* необходи́мый; **~s,** *n.pl,* всё необходи́мое; **requisition,** *n,* реквизи́ция; зая́вка; ¶ *v.t,* реквизи́ровать; представля́ть зая́вку на.

requital, *n,* вознагражде́ние; отпла́та; возме́здие; **requite,** *v.t,* вознагражда́ть; мстить *(dat.).*

resale, *n,* перепрода́жа.

rescind, *v.t,* аннули́ровать, отменя́ть.

rescript, *n,* рескри́пт.

rescue, *n,* спасе́ние; освобожде́ние; ¶ *v.t,* спаса́ть; освобожда́ть; **~r,** *n,* спаси́тель.

research, *n,* иссле́дование; **~** *worker* нау́чный рабо́тник.

resemblance, *n,* схо́дство; **resemble,** *v.t,* походи́ть на.

resent, *v t,* негодова́ть на; обижа́ться на; **~ful,** *a,* оби́женный; злопа́мятный; **~ment,** *n,* негодова́ние; оби́да.

reservation, *n,* огово́рка; зака́занное зара́нее ме́сто, бро́ня резерва́ция (для инде́йцев); **reserve,** *n,* запа́с, резе́рв; *(sport)* запасно́й игро́к; заповедник; сде́ржанность, скры́тность; *in* **~** в запа́се; *with* **~** с огово́ркой; ¶ *v.t,* сберега́ть; откла́дывать; брони́ровать; зака́зывать зара́нее; **~** *one's strength* бере́чь си́лы; **~** *the right* сохраня́ть пра́во; **reserved,** *p.p. & a,* сде́ржанный; зака́занный зара́нее; **reservist,** *n,* запасно́й; **reservoir,** *n,* резервуа́р; запа́с.

reside, *v.i,* прожива́ть, пребыва́ть; **~nce,** *n,* местожи́тельство; прожива́ние; резиде́нция; **~nt,** *n,* прожива́ющий; постоя́нный жи́тель; *residential quarter* райо́н жилы́х домо́в.

residuary, *a,* остаю́щийся, оста́вшийся; **residue,** *n,* оста́ток; оса́док; *(law)* насле́дство, очи́щенное от долго́в и нало́гов.

resign, *v.i,* отка́зываться от до́лжности, уходи́ть в отста́вку; **~** *oneself to* покоря́ться *(dat.);* **~ation,** *n,* отка́з от до́лжности; отста́вка; заявле́ние об отста́вке; смире́ние, поко́рность; **~ed,** *a,* смире́нный, поко́рный.

resilience, *n,* упру́гость; **resilient,** *a,* упру́гий.

resin, *n,* смола́; **~ous,** *a,* смоли́стый.

resist, *v.t. & i,* проти́виться/сопротивля́ться *(dat.);* **~ance,** *n,* сопротивле́ние; сопротивля́емость.

resolute, *a,* реши́тельный; **resolution,** *n,* реше́ние, резолю́ция; реши́мость, реши́тельность; **resolve,** *n,* реши́мость; ¶ *v.t,* реша́ть; разреша́ть *(doubts, problems);* раство쇼ря́ть.

resonance, *n,* резона́нс; **resonant,** *a,* резони́рующий, звуча́щий.

resort, *n,* прибе́жище; куро́рт; *last* **~** после́днее сре́дство; ¶ *v.i:* **~** *to* прибега́ть к.

resound, *v.i,* звуча́ть; раздава́ться.

resource, *n,* ресу́рс; сре́дство; нахо́дчивость; спо́соб; **~ful,** *a,* нахо́дчивый, изобрета́тельный.

respect, *n,* уваже́ние; отноше́ние; *pl,* почте́ние; *in all* **~s** во всех отноше́ниях; ¶ *v.t,* уважа́ть, почита́ть; **~ability,** *n,* почте́нность, респекта́бельность; **~able,** *a,* почте́нный, поря́дочный; респекта́бельный; **~ful,** *a,* почти́тельный; **~ing,** *pr,* относи́тельно; **~ive,** *a,* соотве́тственный; **~ively,** *ad,* в ука́занном поря́дке, соотве́тственно.

respiration, *n,* дыха́ние; **respirator,** *n,* противога́з, респира́тор; **respiratory,** *a,* дыха́тельный.

respite, *n,* переды́шка; отсро́чка.

resplendence, *n,* блеск; **resplendent,** *a,* блестя́щий.

respond, *v.i,* отвеча́ть; реаги́ровать, отзыва́ться; **~ent,** *n,* отве́тчик; **response,** *n,* отве́т; о́тклик; **respon-**

sibility, *n*, ответственность, обязанность; **responsible**, *a*, ответственный; виновный; **responsive**, *a*, отзывчивый.

rest, *n*, отдых, покой; подставка; остаток, остальное, остальные; ¶ *v.i*, отдыхать; покоиться, опираться, прислоняться; *v.t*, давать отдых *(dat.)*; опираться (рукой, *etc.*); прислонять.

restaurant, *n*, ресторан; ~ *car* вагон--ресторан; **restaurateur**, *n*, владелец ресторана.

restful, *a*, успокоительный, спокойный; **resting place** место отдыха.

restitution, *n*, возмещение (убытка); восстановление.

restive, *a*, беспокойный; норовистый *(horse)*; **restless**, *a*, беспокойный, неспокойный.

re-stock, *v.t*, пополнять запасы *(of shop)*.

restoration, *n*, реставрация; восстановление; **restorative**, *n*, укрепляющее средство; **restore**, *v.t*, реставрировать; восстанавливать; возвращать; ~**r**, *n*, реставратор.

restrain, *v.t*, сдерживать, удерживать, обуздывать; ~**t**, *n*, сдержанность, самообладание; обуздание; задержание; заключение; *put under* ~ подвергать заключению.

restrict, *v.t*, ограничивать; ~**ion**, *n*, ограничение; ~**ive**, *a*, ограничительный.

result, *n*, результат; ¶ *v.i:* ~ *in* кончаться *(inst.)*; приводить к; ~ *from* происходить из-за/от; ~**ant**, *a*, получающийся в результате.

resume, *v.t*, возобновлять, продолжать; **résumé**, *n*, резюме; **resumption**, *n*, возобновление.

resurgence, *n*, возрождение.

resurrect, *v.t*, воскрешать; ~**ion**, *n*, воскресение; *(eccl.)* воскресение.

resuscitate, *v.t*, воскрешать.

retail, *n*, розничная продажа; ~ *price* розничная цена; ¶ *v.t*, продавать в розницу; ~**er**, *n*, розничный торговец.

retain, *v.t*, сохранять, удерживать; нанимать *(lawyer)*; ~**er**, *n*, предварительный гонорар; слуга.

retake, *v.t*, брать обратно; вновь занимать.

retaliate, *v.i*, отвечать тем же самым; сопротивляться; **retaliation**, *n*, ответ, отплата, возмездие; **retaliatory**, *a*, ответный.

retard, *v.t*, задерживать.

retch, *v.i*, рыгать; ~**ing**, *n*, рвота.

retention, *n*, сохранение, удерживание; задержание; **retentive**, *a*, удерживающий.

reticence, *n*, сдержанность, скрытность; **reticent**, *a*, сдержанный, скрытный.

reticule, *n*, сумочка, ридикюль.

retina, *n*, сетчатка.

retinue, *n*, свита.

retire, *v.t*, увольнять; *v.i*, уходить в отставку; удаляться; ложиться спать; *(mil.)* отступать; ~**d**, *a*, отставной; ~**ment** *n*, отставка; **retiring**, *a*, застенчивый.

retort, *n*, возражение, резкий ответ; отместка; *(chem.)* реторта; ¶ *v.t*, возражать, отвечать.

retouch, *v.t*, ретушировать.

retrace, *v.t*, прослеживать; ~ *one's steps* возвращаться по пройденному пути.

retract, *v.t*, втягивать; брать назад; ~**able**, *a*, способный втягиваться.

retreat, *n*, отступление; приют, убежище; ¶ *v.i*, отступать; уходить.

retrench, *v.t*, сокращать, урезывать; ~**ment**, *n*, сокращение расходов, экономия.

retribution, *n*, возмездие, кара.

retrievable, *a*, восстановимый; поправимый; **retrieve**, *v.t*, возвращать; восстанавливать; исправлять; **retriever**, *n*, охотничья собака.

retrograde, *a*, ретроградный; **retrogression**, *n*, обратное движение; регресс.

retrospect, *n*, взгляд назад; *in* ~ ретроспективно; ~**ive**, *a*, ретроспективный.

return, *n*, возвращение; *(com.)* прибыль; *by* ~ *of post* обратной почтой; *in* ~ в обмен; в ответ; *tax* ~ налоговая декларация; *many happy* ~*s!* (поздравляю) с днём рождения!; ~ *ticket* обратный билет; билет туда и обратно; ¶ *v.t*, возвращать; отдавать; избирать; выносить *(verdict)*; *v.i*, возвраща́ться; повторя́ться; ~ *a visit* отвеча́ть визи́том на визи́т; ~able, *a*, возврати́мый.

reunion, *n*, воссоедине́ние; встре́ча, сбор; reunite, *v.t. (& i.)*, воссоединя́ть(ся).

reveal, *v.t*, обнару́живать, открыва́ть; выдава́ть *(secret)*.

reveille, *n*, подъём.

revel, *n*, весе́лье; пиру́шка; ¶ *v.i*, пирова́ть; ~ *in* наслажда́ться *(inst.)*.

revelation, *n*, открове́ние; *(eccl.)* Апока́липсис.

reveller, *n*, пиру́ющий; revelry, *n*, пиру́шка; весе́лье.

revenge, *n*, месть, мще́ние; рева́нш; ¶ *v.t*, мстить *(dat.)*; ~ful, *a*, мсти́тельный.

revenue, *n*, (госуда́рственный) дохо́д; *pl*, дохо́дные статьи́; ~ *officer* тамо́женный чино́вник.

reverberate, *v.i*, отдава́ться; отража́ться; reverberation, *n*, о́тзвук; отраже́ние.

revere, *v.t*, уважа́ть; благогове́ть пе́ред; ~nce, *n*, почте́ние; благогове́ние; ~nt, *a*, почте́нный; ~nd, *a*, почти́тельный; благогове́йный.

reverie, *n*, мечта́тельность, мечты́.

reversal, *n*, измене́ние; отме́на; reverse, *n*, противополо́жное; обра́тная сторона́; неуда́ча; за́дний/обра́тный ход; *quite the* ~ совсе́м наоборо́т; ~ *gear* реверси́вный механи́зм; ¶ *v.t*, изменя́ть; перевёртывать; переставля́ть; *(law)* отменя́ть; *(tech.)* дава́ть за́дний ход *(dat.)*; reversible, *a*, обрати́мый; одина́ковый с двух сторо́н; *(tech.)* реверси́рование; re-version, *n*, возвраще́ние; revert, *v.i*, возвраща́ться; *(law)* переходи́ть к пре́жнему владе́льцу.

review, *n*, обзо́р, обозре́ние; журна́л; реце́нзия; просмо́тр; *(law)* пересмо́тр; *(mil.)* смотр; ¶ *v.t*, обозрева́ть; рецензи́ровать; проверя́ть, просма́тривать; *(law)* пересма́тривать; ~er, *n*, реценэе́нт, обозрева́тель.

revile, *v.t*, руга́ть.

revise, *n*, втора́я корректу́ра; ¶ *v.t*, пересма́тривать; перераба́тывать; повторя́ть; revision, *n*, пересмо́тр; повторе́ние.

revisionism, *n*, ревизиони́зм; revisionist, *n*, ревизиони́ст.

revival, *n*, возрожде́ние; оживле́ние; *(theat.)* возобновле́ние; revive, *v.t*, приводи́ть в чу́вство; оживля́ть; восстана́вливать, воскреша́ть; *v.i*, приходи́ть в чу́вство; ожива́ть, воскреса́ть.

revoke, *v.t*, отменя́ть; брать наза́д.

revolt, *n*, восста́ние, мяте́ж; ¶ *v.i*, восстава́ть; *v.t*, отта́лкивать; возмуща́ть; ~ing, *a*, отта́лкивающий; отврати́тельный.

revolution, *n*, револю́ция; враще́ние, оборо́т; ~ary, *n*, революционе́р; ¶ *a*, революцио́нный.

revolve, *v.t. (& i)*, враща́ть(ся), верте́ть(ся); ~r, *n*, револьве́р; revolving, *a*, враща́ющийся.

revue, *n*, обозре́ние.

revulsion, *n*, отвраще́ние: внеза́пное измене́ние.

reward, *n*, награ́да; вознагражде́ние; ¶ *v.t*, награжда́ть; вознагражда́ть; ~ing, *a*, прино́ся́щий по́льзу/ удовлетворе́ние.

rewrite, *v.t*, перепи́сывать.

rhapsody, *n*, рапсо́дия.

rhetoric, *n*, рито́рика; ~al, *a*, ритори́ческий; ~ian, *n*, ри́тор; краснобай.

rheumatic, *a*, ревмати́ческий; rheumatism, *n*, ревмати́зм.

Rhine wine, *n*, ре́йнское вино́, ре́йнвейн.

rhinoceros, *n*, носоро́г.

rhododendron, *n*, рододе́ндрон.

rhomb[us], *n*, ромб.

rhubarb, *n*, реве́нь.

rhyme, *n*, ри́фма; *without* ~ *or reason* без смы́сла; ¶ *v.t*, рифмова́ть.

rhythm, *n*, ритм; разме́р *(стиха́)*; ~ic[al], *a*, ритми́ч|еский, ~ный.

rib, *n*, ребро́ *(also tech.)*; *(mar.)* шпанго́ут.

ribald, *a*, непристо́йный; ~ry, *n*, непристо́йное поведе́ние; скверносло́вие.

ribbed, *a*, ребри́стый; полоса́тый; ~ *stockings* чулки́ в рези́нку.

ribbon, riband, *n*, ле́нта.

rice, *n*, рис; ~ *field* ри́совое по́ле; ~ *paper* ри́совая бума́га.

rich, *a*, бога́тый; жи́рный, сдо́бный *(food)*; глубо́кий *(tone)*; густо́й *(colour)*; плодоро́дный *(soil)*; ~es, *n.pl*, бога́тство; ~ly, *ad*, вполне; **~ness,** *n,* бога́тство; жи́рность; я́ркость; плодоро́дие.

rick, *n,* скирда́, стог.

rickets, *n,* рахи́т; **rickety,** *a,* рахити́чный; хру́пкий; ша́ткий.

ricochet, *n,* рикоше́т; ¶ *v.i,* де́лать рикоше́т.

rid, *v.t,* избавля́ть, освобожда́ть; *get ~ of* отде́лываться/избавля́ться от; **~dance,** *n,* избавле́ние.

riddle, *n,* зага́дка; решето́; ¶ *v.t,* просе́ивать; изреше́чивать.

ride, *n,* прогу́лка; езда́, пое́здка; *go for a ~* прокати́ться *(pf.);* ¶ *v.t,* е́здить/е́хать верхо́м на; *v.i,* е́здить/е́хать, ката́ться; **~r,** *n,* вса́дн|ик, нае́здн|ик, -ица; дополне́ние.

ridge, *n,* гре́бень; го́рный хребе́т; конёк *(of roof); (agr.)* борозда́, гря́дка.

ridicule, *n,* осмея́ние; ¶ *v.t,* осме́ивать; **ridiculous,** *a,* неле́пый, смехотво́рный.

riding, *n,* (верхова́я) езда́; *~ breeches* рейту́зы; *~ habit* амазо́нка; *~ school* шко́ла верхово́й езды.

rife, *a,* широко́ распространённый.

riff-raff, *n,* подо́нки.

rifle, *n,* винто́вка; ¶ *v.t,* обы́скивать, гра́бить; наре́зать *(barrel);* **~man,** *n,* стрело́к.

rift, *n,* тре́щина, скважина; разрыв, раздо́р.

rig, *n,* осна́стка; снаряже́ние; ¶ *v.t,* оснаща́ть; вооружа́ть; *~ out* снаряжа́ть; **~ging,** *n,* сна́сти, такела́ж.

right, *n,* пра́во; справедли́вость; пра́вая сторона́; *~ of way* пра́во прохо́да/прое́зда; ¶ *a,* пра́вый; справедли́вый; пра́вильный; подходя́щий, уме́стный; *~ angle* прямо́й у́гол; *~ hand [man]* пра́вая рука́; *~-minded* благоразу́мный, уравнове́шенный; ¶ *ad,* пра́вильно; напра́во; о́чень; *~ and left* спра́ва и сле́ва; во все сто́роны; *~ away* неме́дленно, сейча́с; *~ honourable* достопочте́нный; *R~ Reverend* его́ высокопреподо́бие; ¶ *int.* ла́дно! хорошо́!.

righteous, *a,* пра́ведный; справедли́вый; **~ness,** *n,* пра́ведность; справедли́вость.

rightful, *a,* зако́нный; **~ly,** *ad,* зако́нно, по пра́ву; **rightly,** *ad,* пра́вильно; справедли́во.

rigid, *a,* жёсткий, неги́бкий; негну́щийся; **~ity,** *n,* жёсткость, неги́бкость.

rigmarole, *n,* пустосло́вие, вздор.

rigorous, *a,* стро́гий, суро́вый; **rigour,** *n,* стро́гость, суро́вость.

rill, *n,* ручеёк.

rim, *n,* край; о́бод(о́к); опра́ва *(spectacles).*

rime, *n,* и́ней.

rind, *n,* кора́, ко́рка, кожура́.

ring, *n,* круг; кольцо́; ринг *(boxing);* аре́на; кли́ка; горе́лка *(cooker);* звон, звуча́ние; *~ finger* безымя́нный па́лец; **~-shaped** кольцеобра́зный; ¶ *v.t,* звони́ть в; *v.i,* звене́ть, звуча́ть; раздава́ться; *~ up* звони́ть/вызыва́ть по телефо́ну; **~let,** *n,* коле́чко; ло́кон; **~worm,** *n,* стригу́щий лиша́й.

rink, *n,* като́к.

rinse, *v.t,* полоска́ть; **rinsing,** *n,* полоска́ние.

riot, *n,* бунт; разгу́л; беспоря́док; ¶ *v.i,* бунтова́ть; подыма́ть шум; **~er,** *n,* бунтовщи́к; **~ous,** *a,* бу́йный, шу́мный.

rip, *n,* разры́в, разре́з; *(pers.)* шалу́н; ¶ *v.t,* рвать; разреза́ть; пили́ть; *~ off* сдира́ть.

riparian, *a,* прибре́жный.

ripe, *a,* зре́лый, спе́лый; **~n** *v.t,* де́лать зре́лым; *v.i,* зреть; **~ness** *n,* зре́лость, спе́лость; **~ning** *n,* созрева́ние.

ripple, *n,* зыбь, рябь; ¶ *v.i,* покрыва́ться ря́бью, струи́ться.

rise, *n,* подъём; повыше́ние; увеличе́ние, приба́вка; восхо́д *(of sun);* *give ~ to* дава́ть по́вод к; ¶ *v.i,* поднима́ться, возвыша́ться; повыша́ться; встава́ть; начина́ться; **rising,** *n,* восста́ние; встава́ние; восхо́д *(of sun);* ¶ *a,* поднима́ющийся; *~ generation* подраста́ющее поколе́ние.

risk, *n,* риск; ¶ *v.t,* рискова́ть *(inst.);* отва́живаться на; **~y,** *a,* риско́ванный, опа́сный.

rissole, *n,* котле́та.

rite, *n,* обря́д; церемо́ния; **ritual,** *n,* ритуа́л; ¶ *a,* ритуа́льный, обря́довый.

rival, *n,* сопе́рник; конкуре́нт; ¶ *a,* сопе́рничающий; конкури́рующий; ¶ *v.t,* сопе́рничать/конкури́ровать с; **~ry,** *n,* сопе́рничество, конкуре́нция.

river, *n*, река́; *down* ~ вниз по тече́нию реки́; ~**side**, *n*, бе́рег реки́, прибре́жная полоса́; ¶ *a*, прибре́жный.

rivet, *n*, заклёпка; ¶ *v.t*, клепа́ть, заклёпывать; *(fig.)* прико́вывать.

rivulet, *n*, руче́й.

road, *n*, доро́га, путь; ~ *hog* лиха́ч; ~ *house* придоро́жная заку́сочная; ~ *map* ка́рта автомоби́льных доро́г; ~*man* доро́жный рабо́чий; ~*side (n.)* край/обо́чина доро́ги; *(a.)* придоро́жный;~*sign* доро́жный знак; ~*way* проéзжая часть доро́ги; *high* ~ шоссé; *(fig.)* столбова́я доро́га; ~**stead**, *n*, *(nar.)* рейд.

roam, *v.i*, броди́ть, скита́ться.

roan, *a*, ча́лый.

roar, *n*, рёв; шум; ~ *of laughter* взрыв хо́хота; ¶ *v.i*, реве́ть; ора́ть; грохота́ть; ~ *with laughter* хохота́ть во всё го́рло; ~*ing*, *a*, реву́щий; бу́рный; грохо́чущий.

roast, *n*, жарко́е; ¶ *v.t. (& i.)*, жа́рить(ся), печь(ся); ~ *beef* ро́стбиф; ~**er**, *n*, жаро́вня.

rob, *v.t*, обкра́дывать, гра́бить; лиша́ть; ~**ber**, *n*, граби́тель, разбо́йник; ~**bery**, *n*, кра́жа, грабёж.

robe, *n*, мужско́е пла́тье; ¶ *v.t. (& i.)*, облача́ть(ся).

robin redbreast, *n*, мали́новка.

robot, *n*, ро́бот.

robust, *a*, здоро́вый, кре́пкий; си́льный.

rock, *n*, скала́, утёс; го́рная поро́да; ка́мень; ~ *crystal* го́рный хруста́ль; ~ *drill* перфора́тор, бура́в; ~ *garden* сад камне́й; ¶ *v.t. (& i.)*, кача́ть(ся); трясти́(сь).

rocket, *n*, раке́та.

rocking, *n*, кача́ние; ¶ *a*, кача́ющийся; ~ *chair* кре́сло-кача́лка; ~ *horse* ло́шадь-кача́лка.

rocky, *a*, скали́стый, камени́стый; твёрдый; *R*~ *Mountains* Скали́стые го́ры.

rococo, *n*, стиль рококо́; ¶ *a*, в сти́ле рококо́; вы́чурный.

rod, *n*, прут; у́дочка; сте́ржень; ре́йка.

rodent, *n*, грызу́н.

roe, *n*, косу́ля; *(fish)* икра́ *(hard)*, моло́ки *(soft)*; ~*buck* саме́ц косу́ли.

rogation, *n*, моле́бствие.

rogue, *n*, жу́лик, моше́нник, плут; ~**ry**, *n*, моше́нничество, плутовство́; **roguish**, *a*, плутова́тый.

role, *n*, роль.

roll, *n*, свёрток, сви́ток; руло́н; бу́лочка; ка́чка; похо́дка вразва́лку; раска́т *(thunder)*, гро́хот *(drums)*; спи́сок; ~ *call* перекли́чка; ~ *of honour* спи́сок уби́тых на войнé; ~*-top desk* стол-бюро́ с раздвижно́й кры́шкой; ¶ *v.t*, ката́ть, кати́ть; прока́тывать *(metal)*; ука́тывать *(road, lawn)*; скру́чивать *(cigarette)*; враща́ть (глаза́ми); *v.i*, ката́ться, кати́ться; враща́ться; идти́ пока́чиваясь; ~ *up* завёртывать(ся), свёртывать(ся); *rolled gold* накладно́е зо́лото; ~**er**, *n*, като́к; ро́лик; вал *(tech., also wave)*; ~ *skates* ро́ликовые коньки́; ~ *towel* полоте́нце на ро́лике.

rollick, *v.i*, весели́ться; ~**ing**, *a*, весёлый, шу́мный.

rolling, *n*, прока́тывание; ка́чка *(at sea)*; ¶ *a*, холми́стый; ~ *mill* прока́тный стан; ~*-pin* ска́лка; ~ *stock* подвижно́й соста́в; ~ *stone* перекати́-по́ле.

Roman, *n*, ри́млянин; ¶ *a*, ри́мский; ~ *Catholic (n.)* като́лик; *(a.)* католи́ческий; ~ *Catholicism* католи́чество.

romance, *n*, рома́н; *(mus.)* рома́нс; ¶ *v.i*, фантази́ровать.

Romance, *a*, рома́нский; **Romanesque**, *a*, рома́нский.

romantic, *n*, рома́нтик; ¶ *a*, романти́|ческий, -ный; ~*ism*, *n*, романти́зм.

Romany, *n*, цыга́н, -ка; цыга́нский язы́к; ¶ *a*, цыга́нский.

romp, *n*, шу́мная игра́, возня́; ¶ *v.i*, вози́ться.

rood, *n*, че́тверть а́кра; крест.

roof, *n*, кры́ша; *(fig.)* кров; ~ *of mouth* нёбо; ~ *tile* черепи́ца; ¶ *v.t*, крыть, покрыва́ть; ~*ing*, *n*, кро́вельный материа́л; покры́тие кры́ши; ~ *felt* кро́вельный карто́н.

rook, *n*, грач; *(chess)* ладья́; ¶ *v.t, (coll.)*, обма́нывать; ~**ery**, *n*, грачо́вник.

room, *n*, ко́мната; но́мер *(hotel)*; ме́сто, простра́нство; *make* ~ сторони́ться; освобожда́ть ме́сто;

~у, *а*, просто́рный, вмести́тельный.

roost, *n*, насе́ст; *rule the* ~ задава́ть тон, кома́ндовать; ¶ *v.i,* уса́живаться на насе́ст; ~er, *n*, пету́х.

root, *n*, ко́рень; *take* ~ пуска́ть ко́рни, укореня́ться; ¶ *v.i,* укореня́ться; ры́ться; ~ *out* вырыва́ть с ко́рнем, искореня́ть; ~ed, *p.p. & a*, укорени́вшийся; про́чный; ~ *to the spot* остолбене́лый, пригвождённый к ме́сту.

rope, *n*, верёвка; кана́т, трос; ~ *ladder* верёвочная ле́стница; ~*-walker* канатохо́дец; *know the* ~s хорошо́ ориенти́роваться в де́ле; ¶ *v.i,* привя́зывать кана́том.

rosary, *n*, чётки; **rose,** *n*, ро́за; ро́зовый цвет; розе́тка *(elec.);* разбры́згиватель; ~*bay* иван-ча́й; ~*bud* буто́н ро́зы; ~ *nursery* роза́рий; ~ *tree* ро́зовый куст; ~*wood* палиса́ндровое де́рево; **roseate,** *a*, ро́зовый; **rosemary,** *n*, розмари́н; **rosette,** *n*, розе́тка.

rosin, *n*, канифо́ль, смола́.

roster, *n*, расписа́ние дежу́рств, спи́сок.

rostrum, *n*, ка́федра; трибу́на.

rosy, *a*, ро́зовый; румя́ный; благоприя́тный.

rot. *n*, гниль; гние́ние; *(coll.)* вздор; ¶ *v.i,* гнить, по́ртиться; *(fig.)* разлага́ться.

rota, *n*, расписа́ние дежу́рств; ~**ry** *a*, враща́тельный, ротацио́нный; ~**te,** *v.t. (& i.),* враща́ть(ся); чередова́ть(ся); ~**tion,** *n*, враще́ние; чередова́ние; *in* ~ по о́череди, попереме́нно.

rotten, *a*, гнило́й; испо́рченный; *(coll.)* гну́сный; **rotter,** *n*, дрянь.

rotund, *a*, кру́глый; по́лный, то́лстый; ~**a,** *n*, рото́нда; ~**ity,** *n*, округлённость; полнота́.

rouge, *n*, румя́на; ¶ *v.i,* румя́ниться.

rough, *a*, гру́бый, неро́вный; шерша́вый; бу́рный *(sea);* неотде́ланный, черново́й; тру́дный; приблизи́тельный *(estimate);* ~ *cast* гру́бая штукату́рка; ~ *copy* черновик; ~ *diamond* неотшлифо́ванный алма́з; ~ *sketch* набро́сок; ~ *and tumble* возня́; ~ *wine* те́рпкое вино́; *ride* ~*shod over* самоупра́вно поступа́ть с; ~**en,** *v.t,* де́лать гру́бым; шерша́вым ~**ly,** *ad*, гру́бо; приблизи́тельно; ~**ness,**

n, гру́бость: неро́вность, шерша́вость; бу́рность.

roulette, *n*, руле́тка.

Roumanian, *a*, румы́нский; ¶ *n*, румы́н, -ка; румы́нский язы́к.

round, *n*, обхо́д; *(sport)* ра́унд, тур; ло́мтик; патро́н, вы́стрел; ¶ *a*, кру́глый; по́лный; ~*-shouldered* суту́лый; ~ *sum* кру́глая су́мма; ¶ *ad*, вокру́г, круго́м; обра́тно; *the year* ~ кру́глый год; ~ *and* вокру́г, круго́м; ¶ *v.t:* ~ *off* округля́ть; конча́ть; ~ *up* сгоня́ть; аресто́вывать; ~*-up* заго́н, обла́ва; ~**about,** *n*, карусе́ль; ¶ *a*, око́льный; ~**ly,** *ad*, основа́тельно; ~**ness,** *n*, круглота́.

rouse, *v.t*, буди́ть, побужда́ть; вспу́гивать.

rout, *n*, разгро́м; ра́ут; ¶ *v.t*, обраща́ть в бе́гство.

route, *n*, маршру́т, курс; доро́га, путь; ~ *march* марш в тылу́; *en* ~ по пути́.

routine, *n*, рути́на, заведённый поря́док; ¶ *a*, очередно́й; устано́вленный.

rove, *v.i,* скита́ться; блужда́ть *(of glance);* ~**r,** *n*, скита́лец; **roving,** *a*, стра́нствующий; блужда́ющий.

row, *n*, ряд; прогу́лка на ло́дке; ~ *boat* гребна́я ло́дка; ¶ *v.t*, грести́; перевози́ть в ло́дке.

row, *n*, ссо́ра; сканда́л; гам, шум; ¶ *v.i,* ссо́риться; сканда́лить; ~**dy,** *n*, хулига́н; ¶ *a*, бу́йный, шу́мный.

rowel, *n*, колёсико шпо́ры.

rower, *n*, гребе́ц; **rowing,** *n*, гре́бля; ~ *boat* гребна́я ло́дка; **rowlock,** *n*, уклю́чина.

royal, *a*, короле́вский, ца́рский; великоле́пный; ~**ist,** *n*, рояли́ст; ~**ty,** *n*, член(ы) короле́вской семьи́; аре́ндная пла́та, а́вторский гонора́р.

rub, *n*, тре́ние; затрудне́ние, препя́тствие; ка́мень преткнове́ния; ¶ *v.t*, тере́ть, натира́ть; копи́ровать рису́нок с; ~ *against* тере́ть(ся) о; ~ *shoulders with* обща́ться с; ~ *one's hands* потира́ть ру́ки; ~ *off* стира́ть; ~ *up the wrong way* гла́дить про́тив ше́рсти; ~**ber,** *n*, каучу́к; рези́на; рези́нка; *(cards)* ро́ббер; тря́пка; гу́бка (для вытира́ния доски́, *etc.);* ¶ *a*, каучу́ковый; рези́новый; ~ *stamp (n.)* штемпель; *(v.t)* ставить печать на; ~ *tree* каучуковое дерево; ~bing, *n*, трение, натирание; копированный рисунок.

rubbish, *n*, мусор, хлам; вздор.

rubble, *n*, щебень.

rubicund, *a*, румяный.

rubric, *n*, рубрика, заголовок.

ruby, *n*, рубин.

rucksack, *n*, рюкзак.

rudder, *n*, руль.

ruddy, *a*, румяный, красноватый.

rude, *a*, грубый; неотделанный; ~ly, *ad*, грубо; ~ness, *n*, грубость.

rudiments, *n.pl*, зачатки, начатки; элементарные знания; **rudimentary**, *a*, рудиментарный; элементарный.

rue, *v.t*, раскаиваться в; сожалеть о; ~ful, *a*, печальный.

ruff, *n*, рюш; ёрш *(fish)*.

ruffian, *n*, головорез, хулиган.

ruffle, *v.t*, ерошить *(hair)*; беспокоить; гофрировать; рябить.

rug, *n*, коврик; плед.

rugby, *n*, регби.

rugged, *a*, суровый, грубый; крепкий; ~ *terrain* пересечённая местность.

ruin, *n*, гибель; разорение; развалина, руина; ¶ *v.t*, губить; разорять; разрушать; ~ous, *a*, губительный; разорительный.

rule, *n*, правило; норма; власть; господство; правление; *as a* ~ как правило; *work to* ~ отказываться от сверхурочной работы; ¶ *v.t*, править/управлять *(inst.)*; графить, линовать; *v.i*, постановлять, решать; ~ *out* исключать; ~ *over* господствовать над; ~r, *n*, правитель; линейка; **ruling**, *n*, постановление, решение; ¶ *a*, правящий; господствующий.

rum, *n*, ром.

rumble, *n*, громыхание, грохотанье; ¶ *v.i*, громыхать, грохотать.

ruminant, *n*, жвачное животное; **ruminate**, *v.i*, жевать жвачку; размышлять.

rummage, *v.i*, рыться; обыскивать.

rumour, *n*, молва, слух; *it is* ~ed *that* ходят слухи, что . . .

rump, *n*, огузок; ~ *steak* ромштекс.

rumple, *v.t*, мять; ерошить *(hair)*.

rumpus, *n*, гам, суматоха.

run, *n*, бег; пробег; короткая поездка; петля на чулке; ход, действие; продолжение; ряд; спрос; *a heavy* ~ *on goods* огромный спрос на товары; *in the long* ~ в конечном счёте; ~ *on the bank* массовые требования о возвращении вкладов из банка; ¶ *v.t*, управлять *(inst.)*; вести *(affairs)*; гнать; *v.i*, бегать, бежать; течь; курсировать; работать *(of machine)*; идти *(play)*; ~ *about* бегать туда-сюда; ~ *across* перебегать через; случайно встречать; ~ *after (fig.)* ухаживать за; преследовать; ~ *against* сталкиваться с; ~ *aground* садиться на мель; ~ *away* убегать; ~ *between* курсировать между; ~ *into* вбегать в; случайно встречать; доходить до; ~ *in the family* быть в роду, быть наследственным; ~ *out* выбегать; вытекать; истекать; кончаться; ~ *out of* истощать свой запас *(gen.)*; ~ *over (v.t.)* перебегать; давить; просматривать, повторять; *(v.i.)* переливаться через край; ~ *through* пробегать, бегло просматривать; мотать *(money)*; прокалывать; ~ *to* доходить до, достигать *(gen.)*; ~ *to seed* идти в семена; *(fig.)* опускаться; ~ *up against* натыкаться на; ~away, *n*, беглец, дезертир; ¶ *a*, беглый, убежавший.

rung, *n*, ступенька.

runner, *n*, бегун/, -ья; посыльный ; *(tech.)* бегунок, рабочее колесо; полоз *(sledge)*; **running**, *n*, беганье; действие, работа, ход; *be in the* ~ иметь шансы (на успех); ¶ *a*, бегущий; беговой; ~ *commentary* (радио)репортаж; ~ *eyes* слезящиеся глаза; ~ *knot* затяжной узел; ~ *water* проточная вода; водопровод; *three days* ~ три дня подряд; **runway**, *n*, стартовая дорожка.

rupee, *n*, рупия.

rupture, *n*, перелом; разрыв; *(med.)* грыжа; ¶ *v.t*, прорывать; порывать *(links)*.

rural, *a*, деревенский, сельский.

ruse, *n*, уловка, хитрость.

rush, *n*, наплыв; натиск; стремительное движение; *(bot.)* тростник; ~ *hour* часы «пик»; ¶ *v.t*, торопить; *(mil.)* брать стремительным нáтиском; *v.i*, торопи́ться; мчáться, бросáться.

rusk, *n*, сухáрь.

russet, *a*, краснова́то-кори́чневый.

Russian, *a*, ру́сский; ¶ *n*, ру́сск|ий, -ая; ру́сский язы́к.

rust, *n*, ржáвчина; ¶ *v.i*, ржáветь.

rustic, *a*, дереве́нский; неотёсанный; грубый; ¶ *n*, се́льский жи́тель, крестья́нин; ~ate, *v.t*, вре́менно исключáть из университе́та.

rustle, *n*, ше́лест, шо́рох, шуршáние; ¶ *v.i*, шелесте́ть, шуршáть.

rusty, *a*, ржáвый, заржáвленный; запущенный; *my Russian is* ~ я подзабы́л ру́сский язы́к.

rut, *n*, жёлоб; борозда́; те́чка *(of animals); be in a* ~ прозябáть.

ruthless, *a*, безжáлостный.

rye, *n*, рожь; ~*-bread* ржанóй хлеб.

S

sabbath, *n*, суббóта *(Jewish);* воскресе́нье *(Christian);* шáбаш (ведьм).

sable, *n*, сóболь; собóлий мех.

sabotage, *n*, саботáж; ¶ *v.t*, саботи́ровать.

sabre, *n*, сáбля.

sac, *n*, мешóчек, су́мка.

saccharine, *n*, сахари́н; ¶ *a*, сáхарный, сáхаристый.

sacerdotal, *a*, свяще́ннический, жре́ческий.

sachet, *n*, мешóчек; **sack**, *n*, мешóк; *get the* ~ быть уво́ленным; ~*cloth* дерю́га, холст; ¶ *v.t*, ссыпáть в мешóк; *(coll.)* увольня́ть; ~ful, *n*, мешóк; ~ing, *n*, мешкови́на.

sacrament, *n*, причáстие; *receive the* ~ причащáться.

sacred, *a*, свято́й, свяще́нный; неприкосновéнный.

sacrifice, *n*, же́ртва, жертвоприноше́ние; ¶*v.t*, приноси́ть в же́ртву; же́ртвовать *(inst.);* **sacrificial**, *a*, же́ртвенный.

sacrilege, *n*, кощу́нство, святотáтство; **sacrilegious**, *a*, кощу́нственный, святотáтственный.

sacristy, *n*, ри́зница; **sacrosanct**, *a*, свяще́нный.

sad, *a*, гру́стный, печáльный; *be* ~ печáлиться; **sadden**, *v.t*, печáлить.

saddle, *n*, седлó; ~*-bag* седéльный вьюк; ~*-cloth* чепрáк; ¶ *v.t*, седлáть; *(fig.)* обременя́ть; ~r, *n*, седéльный мáстер, шóрник.

sadism, *n*, сади́зм; **sadistic**, *a*, сади́стский.

sadly, *ad*, гру́стно, печáльно; **sadness**, *n*, грусть, печáль.

safe, *a*, невреди́мый; безопáсный; надёжный; ~ *arrival* благополу́чное прибы́тие; ~ *conduct* охрáнное свиде́тельство; ~ *keeping* сохрáнность; ~ *and sound* цéл(ый) и невреди́м(ый); ¶ *n*, сейф, несгорáемый шкаф; холоди́льник; ~guard, *n*, гарáнтия; охрáна; предохрани́тель; предосторóжность; ¶ *v.t*, гаранти́ровать; охраня́ть; ~ly, *ad*, благополу́чно; безопáсно; ~ty, *n*, безопáсность; ~ *belt* привязнóй ремéнь; ~ *match* безопáсная спи́чка, ~ *measures* мéры предосторóжности; ~ *pin* англи́йская булáвка; ~ *razor* безопáсная бри́тва; ~ *valve* предохрани́тельный клáпан; *(fig.)* отду́шина.

saffron, *n*, шафрáн; ¶ *a*, шафрáнный.

sag, *n*, провéс, проги́б; оседáние; ¶ *v.i*, обвисáть, проги́бáться; оседáть.

saga, *n*, сáга, сказáние.

sagacious, *a*, смышлёный, у́мный, проницáтельный; **sagacity**, *n*, проницáтельность.

sage, *a*, му́дрый; ¶ *n*, мудре́ц; *(bot.)* шалфéй.

sago, *n*, сáго.

said, **(the)**, *a*, (вы́ше)упомя́нутый.

sail, *n*, пáрус; плáвание; крылó *(windmill);* ~*cloth* пару́си́на; *set* ~ отправля́ться в плáвание; ¶ *v.t*, управля́ть (кораблём); пускáть (корáблики); *v.i*, идти́ под парусáми; плáвать; отплывáть; ~ *close to the wind* идти́ вплотну́ю прóтив вéтра; *(fig.)* зарывáться, рисковáть; ~ing, *n*, плáвание: пáрусный спорт; ~ *boat* пáрусная лóдка; ~ *ship* пáрусное су́дно; *plain* ~ *(fig.)* лёгкий путь; ~or, *n*, матрóс, моря́к.

saint, *n*, свято́й; *St. Bernard dog* сенбернáр; ~liness, *n*, свя́тость, безгрéшность; ~ly, *a*, свято́й, безгрéшный.

sake, n: for the ~ of ради бога; for God's ~ ради бога.

salaam, n, селям; ¶ v.i, приветствовать.

salacious, a, сладострастный; непристойный.

salad, n, салат; ~ bowl салатница; ~ dressing заправка к салату; ~ oil прованское масло.

salamander, n, саламандра.

salami, n, копчёная колбаса.

salaried, p.p. & a, получающий жалованье; salary, n, жалованье, оклад.

sale, n, продажа; распродажа; be for ~ продаваться; bill of ~ закладная, купчая; ~sman, n, продавец; ~swoman, n, продавщица.

salient, a, выдающийся, выпуклый; заметный; ¶ n, выступ.

saline, a, соляной.

saliva, n, слюна; ~te, v.i, выделять слюну.

sallow, a, желтоватый.

sally, n, вылазка; острота; ¶ v.i, делать вылазку.

salmon, n, лосось; лососина; сёмга; ¶ a, желтовато-розовый.

saloon, n, зал; салон; бар, пивная; ~ car легковой автомобиль.

salt, n, соль; ~ cellar солонка; ~ mine соляная копь; ~-water морской; ~ works солеварня; ¶ v.t, солить; ~ing, n, засол; ~petre, n, селитра; ~y, a, солёный.

salubrious, a, здоровый, целебный; salutary, a, благотворный, целительный.

salute, n, приветствие; салют; ¶ v.t, приветствовать; салютовать (dat.); (mil.) отдавать честь (dat.).

salvage, n, спасение имущества; спасённое имущество; ¶ v.t, спасать; salvation, n, спасение; S~ Army Армия спасения.

salve, n, целебная мазь; успокаивающее средство; ¶ v.t, смазывать мазью; (fig.) успокаивать.

salver, n, поднос.

salvo, n, залп.

same, a, тот же (самый); одинаковый; the ~ thing одно и то же; it's all the ~ to me мне всё равно; all the ~ всё-таки; ~ness, n, тождество; однообразие.

sample, n, образец, шаблон; проба; ¶ v.t, пробовать, испытывать.

sanatorium, n, санаторий.

sanctification, n, освящение; sanctify, v.t, освящать; sanctimonious, a, ханжеский; sanctimony, n, ханжество; sanction, n, санкция; разрешение; pl, карательные меры; ¶ v.t, санкционировать; sanctuary, n, святилище, убежище; sanctum, n, святая святых.

sand, n, песок; (pl.) пляж; отмель; ~bank песчаная отмель; ~ hill дюна; ~paper наждачная бумага; ~piper болотный кулик; ~ pit песчаный карьер; площадка с песком (for children); ~stone песчаник; ~storm самум; ¶ v.t, посыпать песком; чистить песком.

sandal, n, сандаловое дерево; сандалия.

sandwich, n, бутерброд; ~-man человек-реклама; ¶ v.t, вставлять между, помещать посередине.

sandy, a, песчаный; рыжеватый.

sane, a, нормальный, здравый.

sang-froid, n, хладнокровие; sanguinary, a, кровопролитный; sanguine, a, сангвинический, оптимистический.

sanitary, a, санитарный, гигиенический; ~ inspector санитарный инспектор; ~ towel гигиеническая подушка; sanitation, n, оздоровление, санитария.

sanity, n, здравый ум, здравомыслие; нормальная психика.

Santa Claus, n, дед Мороз.

sap, n, сок; (fig.) жизненные силы; (mil.) крытая траншея; сапа; ~wood заболонь; ¶ v.t, истощать; (mil.) подводить сапу под, подкапывать (под).

sapience, n, мудрость; sapient, a, мудрый.

sapling, n, молодое дерево.

sapper, n, сапёр.

sapphire, n, сапфир; ¶ a, сапфирный; тёмно-синий.

Saracen, n, сарацин.

sarcasm, n, сарказм; sarcastic, a, саркастический.

sarcophagus, n, саркофаг.

sardine, n, сардин(к)а.

Sardinian, a, сардинский.

sardonic, a, сардонический.

sarsaparilla, n, сассапарель.

sash, *n*, кушак, шарф; оконная рама; ~ *window* подъёмное окно.

Satan, *n*, сатана; ~**ic**, *a*, сатанинский.

satchel, *n*, ранец, сумка.

sate, *v.t*, насыщать, пресыщать.

sateen, *n*, сатин.

satellite, *n*, спутник, сателлит; приспешник.

satiate, *v.t*, насыщать; пресыщать; **satiety**, *n*, насыщение; пресыщение.

satin, *n*, атлас; ~*у*, *a*, шелковистый.

satire, *n*, сатира; **satirical**, *a*, сатирический; **satirist**, *n*, сатирик; **satirize**, *v.t*, высмеивать.

satisfaction, *n*, удовлетворение; **satisfactory**, *a*, удовлетворительный; **satisfy**, *v.t*, удовлетворять; утолять *(hunger)*; ~ *oneself that* убеждаться в том, что . . .

satrap, *n*, сатрап.

saturate, *v.t*, насыщать, пропитывать; **saturation**, *n*, насыщение, насыщенность.

Saturday, *n*, суббота.

Saturn, *n*, Сатурн; ~**alian**, *a*, разгульный; ~**ine**, *a*, мрачный.

satyr, *n*, сатир.

sauce, *n*, соус; *(coll.)* наглость; ~*boat* соусник; ~*pan* кастрюля; ~*r*, *n*, блюдце; **saucy**, *a*, дерзкий; модный; весёлый.

saunter, *v.i*, прогуливаться.

sausage, *n*, колбаса; сосиска.

savage, *a*, дикий; жестокий; ¶ *n*, дикарь; ~*ry*, *n*, жестокость.

save, *v.t*, спасать; беречь; копить; экономить; ~ *trouble* избавлять(ся) от хлопот; ¶ *pr*, кроме, за исключением; **saving**, *n*, спасение; экономия; *pl*, сбережения; ~*s bank* сберегательная касса; ¶ *pr*, исключая, кроме; **saviour**, *n*, спаситель.

savour, *n*, вкус, привкус; аромат; ¶ *v.t*, смаковать; ~*y*, *a*, вкусный; острый на вкус.

saw, *n*, пила; поговорка; ~*dust* опилки; ~*fish* пила-рыба; ~*mill* лесопилка; ¶ *v.t*, пилить; ~*yer*, *n*, пильщик.

Saxon, *a*, саксонский; ¶ *n*, саксонец.

saxophone, *n*, саксофон.

say, *v.t*, говорить; *it is said that* . . . говорят, что . . .; *that is to* ~ то

есть; *I* ~! послушайте!; *to* ~ *nothing of* не говоря о; ¶ *n*, слово, мнение; ~*ing*, *n*, поговорка; *it goes without* ~ само собой разумеется.

scab, *n*, струп; *(vet.)* парша; *(coll.)* штрейкбрехер.

scabbard, *n*, ножны.

scabby, *a*, покрытый струпьями, паршивый.

scaffold, *n*, эшафот; ~*ing*, *n*, леса; помост, подмостки.

scald, *n*, ожог; ¶ *v.t*, обваривать.

scale, *n*, чешуя *(fish)*; шелуха; накипь; масштаб, шкала, линейка; *(mus.)* гамма; *(maths)* система счисления; чаша весов; *pl*, весы; *on a large* ~ в большом масштабе; ¶ *v.t*, чистить, соскабливать; подниматься на; ~ *down* понижать.

scallop, *n*, гребешок *(shell)*; фестон; ¶ *v.t*, украшать фестонами.

scalp, *n*, скальп; ¶ *v.t*, скальпировать.

scalpel, *n*, скальпель.

scaly, *a*, чешуйчатый; покрытый накипью.

scamp, *n*, шалун.

scamper, *v.i*, бегать, бежать.

scan, *v.t*, внимательно разглядывать, изучать; скандировать *(verse)*.

scandal, *n*, скандал, позор; сплетни; ~*monger* сплетник; ~*ize*, *v.t*, шокировать; ~*ous*, *a*, скандальный, позорный.

Scandinavian, *a*, скандинавский; ¶ *n*, скандинав, -ка.

scansion, *n*, скандирование.

scant(y), *a*, недостаточный, скудный.

scapegoat, *n*, козёл отпущения.

scapegrace, *n*, повеса.

scar, *n*, рубец, шрам.

scarab, *n*, скарабей.

scarce, *a*, редкий, скудный; дефицитный; ~*ly*, *ad*, едва; только что; едва ли; ~*ness*, *n*, недостаток, нехватка; редкость.

scare, *n*, испуг, паника; ~*crow* пугало; ¶ *v.t*, пугать; ~ *away* отпугивать.

scarcity, *n*, нехватка; голод; редкость.

scarf, *n*, шарф.

scarify, *v.t*, *(surg.)* делать насечки на.

scarlet, *a*, (*& n.*), áлый (цвет); ~ *fever* скарлатина.

scarp, *n*, крутóй откóс; *(mil.)* эскáрп.

scatheless, *a*, невредимый; **scathing**, *a*, éдкий, язвительный.

scatter, *v.t*, разбрáсывать, разгонять, рассéивать; рассыпáть; *v.i*, рассыпáться *(etc.);* разбегáться; разбивáться; ~ *brained* рассéянный; легкомысленный.

scavenge, *v.i*, убирáть мýсор; искáть пáдаль; ~r, *n*, мýсорщик; живóтное, питáющееся пáдалью.

scenario, *n*, сценáрий.

scene, *n*, мéсто дéйствия; *(theat.)* сцéна, явлéние; декорáции; зрéлище; картина; *(coll.)* сцéна; ~ *painter* худóжник-декорáтор; ~ *shifter* рабóчий сцéны; *behind the* ~s за кулисами; *make a* ~ устрáивать сцéну; ~ry, *n*, декорáции; пейзáж; scenic, *a*, сценичный.

scent, *n*, зáпах; след; нюх; духи; *throw off the* ~ сбивáть со слéда; ¶ *v.t*, чýять; душить; ~ed, *p.p. & a*, надýшенный; душистый.

sceptre, *n*, скипетр.

schedule, *n*, расписáние; список; ¶ *v.t*, составлять расписáние *(gen.);* планировать.

scheme, *n*, схéма; план, проéкт; интрига; ¶ *v.i*, замышлять, интриговáть; ~r, *n*, интригáн.

schism, *n*, раскóл; ~atic, *a*, раскóльнический; ¶ *n*, раскóльник.

scholar, *n*, учёный; ученик; стипендиáт; ~ly, *a*, учёный, эрудированный; ~ship, *n*, учёность; стипéндия; scholastic, *a*, схоластический; шкóльный; **school**, *n*, шкóла; ¶ *a*, шкóльный; ~ *book* учéбник; ~boy, ~girl, шкóль|ник, -ница; ~leaver выпуск|ник, -ница; ~teacher учитель, -ница; ¶ *v.t*, учить; обучáть; **schooling**, *n*, образовáние, обучéние.

schooner, *n*, шхýна.

sciatic, *a*, седáлищный; ~a, *n*, ишиáс.

science, *n*, наýка; естéственные наýки; **scientific**, *a*, наýчный; **scientist**, *n*, учёный, естествоиспытáтель.

scintillate, *v.i*, мерцáть, сверкáть.

scion, *n*, óтпрыск, потóмок; *(bot.)* побéг.

scissors, *n*, нóжницы.

sclerosis, *n*, склерóз.

scoff, *v.i*, издевáться, насмехáться; ~er, *n*, насмéшник; ~ing, *n*, издевáтельство.

scold, *v.t*, бранить; ~ing, *n*, нагоняй.

sconce, *n*, подсвéчник; *(mil.)* редýт.

scone, *n*, лепёшка.

scoop, *n*, ковш, черпáк; совóк; ~ *shovel* экскавáтор; ¶ *v.t*, выкáпывать, вычéрпывать.

scope, *n*, простóр; сфéра; кругозóр.

scorch, *v.t*, обжигáть, палить; ¶ *v.i*, обжигáться; ~ing, *a*, палящий; знóйный; *(fig.)* сурóвый.

score, *n*, счёт *(also sport);* зарýбка, мéтка; *(mus.)* партитýра; два десятка; *pl*, мнóжество; *settle old* ~s сводить стáрые счёты; ¶ *v.t*, выигрывать, получáть; дéлать зарýбки на; *(mus.)* оркестровáть; *v.i*, вести счёт; ~r, *n*, маркёр, счётчик.

scorn, *n*, презрéние; ¶ *v.t*, презирáть; ~ful, *a*, презрительный.

scorpion, *n*, скорпиóн.

Scot, *n*, шотлáнд|ец, -ка; **Scotch**, *a*, шотлáндский.

scotch, *v.t*, выводить из стрóя; надрéзать; расстрáивать.

scot-free, *a*, ненакáзанный; невредимый.

Scottish, *a*, шотлáндский.

scoundrel, *n*, негодяй, подлéц.

scour, *v.t*, отчищáть, прочищáть, чистить; ~ *about* рыскать; ~er, *n*, металлическая мочáлка.

scourge, *n*, бич; бéдствие; кáра; ¶ *v.t*, бичевáть; *(fig.)* карáть.

scout, *n*, развéдчик; *boy* ~ бойскáут; ~master вожáтый отряда бойскáутов; ¶ *v.i*, развéдывать.

scowl, *n*, хмýрый вид/взгляд; ¶ *v.i*, хмýриться, смотрéть сердито.

scrabble, *n*, карáкули; ¶ *v.i*, царáпать.

scraggy, *a*, сухопáрый, тóщий.

scramble, *n*, карáбканье; свáлка, схвáтка; ¶ *v.i*, карáбкаться; *v.t*, перемéшивать; ~ *for* дрáться за захвáт *(gen.);* ~d *eggs* яичница-болтýнья.

scrap, *n*, клочóк, лоскутóк; брак; лом; *pl*, остáтки, отбрóсы; ~book альбóм газéтных вырезок; ~ *iron* металлолóм, утильсырьё; ¶ *v.t*, выбрáсывать; браковáть; отдавáть в утиль; *v.i*, дрáться.

scrape, *n*, царапина; скобление; чистка; неприятное положение; ¶ *v.t*, скоблить, скрести; шаркать (ногами); ~ *off* отскабливать; ~ *through* éле выдерживать *(exam)*; ~ *together* наскребать; ~**r**, *n*, скребок; **scraping**, *n*, соскабливание; *pl*, обрезки.

scratch, *n*, царапина; почёсывание; ¶ *a*, случайный, разношёрстный; ¶ *v.t*, царапать; чесать; *v.i*, чесаться; скрипеть.

scrawl, *n*, каракули; ¶ *v.i*, писать каракулями.

scrawny, *a*, худой.

scream, *n*, вопль, крик; визг; ¶ *v.i*, вопить, кричать; визжать.

screech, *n*, крик: скрип; ~*owl* сова-сипуха; ¶ *v.i*, кричать.

screed, *n*, разглагольствование.

screen, *n*, экран *(cinema, etc.)*; ширма; перегородка; *(mil.)* завеса, прикрытие; ¶ *v.t*, загораживать; прикрывать; просеивать через сито; демонстрировать на экране; тщательно проверять.

screw, *n*, винт; ~*driver* отвёртка; ~ *nut* гайка; *put the* ~ *on (coll.)* нажимать на; ¶ *v.t*, завинчивать, привинчивать; ~ *out (of smb.)* вымогать (у); ~ *up one's face* морщить лицо; ~ *up one's eyes* щуриться.

scribble, *n*, каракули; ¶ *v.i*, писать каракулями/небрежно; ~**r**, *n*, писака; **scribe**, *n*, писец, переписчик.

scrimmage, *n*, свалка.

scrip, *n*, сума; *(fin.)* квитанция о подписке на акции.

script, *n*, почерк; рукопись; *(film)* сценарий; ~ *writer* сценарист; **Scripture**, *n*, священное писание.

scrivener, *n*, нотариус.

scrofula, *n*, золотуха; **scrofulous**, *a*, золотушный.

scroll, *n*, свиток; *(arch.)* завиток.

scrub, *n*, кустарник, поросль; ¶ *v.t*, скрести, тереть; чистить щёткой; ~**bing**, *n*, чистка щёткой; ~ *brush* жёсткая щётка, скребница.

scruff, *n*, шиворот; *take by the* ~ *of the neck* брать за шиворот.

scruple, *n*, сомнение; угрызение совести; ¶ *v.i*, колебаться; **scrupulous**, *a*, скрупулёзный, добросовестный.

scrutinize, *v.t*, тщательно рассматривать; **scrutiny**, *n*, тщательное рассмотрение/исследование; испытующий взгляд; проверка.

scud, *v.i*, скользить; *(mar.)* идти под ветром.

scuffle, *n*, драка; ¶ *v.i*, драться.

scull, *n*, кормовое весло; парное весло; ¶ *v.i*, грести парными вёслами.

scullery *n*, помещение для мытья посуды, судомойка, **scullion**, *n*, судомойка; поварёнок.

sculptor, *n*, скульптор, **sculptural**, *a*, скульптурный; **sculpture**, *n*, скульптура; ¶ *v.t*, ваять, лепить.

scum, *n*, накипь, пена; *(fig.)* негодяй; подонки.

scupper, *n*, шпигат.

scurf, *n*, перхоть.

scurrilous, *a*, непристойный.

scurvy, *n*, цинга; ¶ *a*, гнусный.

scutcheon, *n*, щит герба.

scuttle, *n*, ведро для угля; *(mar.)* люк; ¶ *v.t*, топить; *v.i*, удирать.

scythe, *n*, коса; ¶ *v.t*, косить.

sea, *n*, море; *at* ~ в открытом море; *(fig.)* в недоумении; *by* ~ морем; *heavy* ~*s* сильное волнение; ¶ *a*, морской; ~*board* побережье, приморье; ~ *bream* морской лещ; ~ *dog* «морской волк»; ~*gull* чайка; ~*horse* морской конёк; ~ *kale* морская капуста; ~*legs*: *find one's* ~ привыкать к морской качке; ~ *level* уровень моря; ~ *lion* морской лев; ~*man* матрос, моряк; ~*manship* искусство мореплавания; ~ *plane* гидросамолёт; ~ *port* морской порт, портовый город; ~*scape* морской пейзаж; ~*shore* морской берег; *be* ~*sick* страдать морской болезнью; ~*side* берег моря; ~ *voyage* морское путешествие; ~ *wall* дамба; ~*ward* (направленный) к морю; ~ *water* морская вода; ~*weed* морская водоросль; ~*worthy* годный для плавания.

seal, *n*, печать; пломба; тюлень; морской котик; ~*skin* котиковый мех; ¶ *v.t*, запечатывать; скреплять печатью; ~**ed**, *p.p. & a*, запечатанный; *a* ~*ed book* книга за семью печатями; ~**ing** *wax* сургуч.

seam, *n*, шов; рубец; *(geol.)* пласт; ~*less*, *a*, без шва, бесшовный;

~stress, *n*, швея; *the seamy side* изнанка.

seance, *n*, заседание, сеанс.

sear, *v.t*, опалять, прижигать; *(fig.)* притупля́ть.

search, *n*, поиски; обыск; исследование; ~*light* прожектор; ~ *warrant* ордер на обыск; ¶ *v.t*, обыскивать; осматривать; *(surg.)* зондировать; ~ *for* искать; ~**er**, *n*, искатель; ~**ing**, *a*, тщательный *(enquiry);* испытующий *(look);* пронизывающий *(wind).*

season, *n*, время года; сезон; период; *close* ~ время запрета на охоту; *hunting* ~ охотничий сезон; ~ *ticket* сезонный билет; ¶ *v.t*, приправля́ть *(food);* выдерживать *(wine);* ~**able**, *a*, своевременный; по сезону; ~**al**, *a*, сезонный; ~**ing**, *n*, приправа.

seat, *n*, сиденье; место *(also theat.);* стул, скамейка; *country* ~ имение; *take a* ~ садиться; ¶ *v.t*, сажать; *four-seater* четырёхместный автомобиль; *seating capacity* места для сидения.

secede, *v.i*, отделя́ться; **secession**, *n*, отделение; раскол.

seclude, *v.t*, отделя́ть; изоли́ровать; ~**d**, *a*, уединённый, укромный; **seclusion**, *n*, уединение; укромность.

second, *a*, второй; ~*-class* второклассный, второсортный; ~*hand* подержанный; из вторых рук; ~*hand bookshop* букинистический магазин; ~*-rate* второразря́дный, второсортный; ~ *sight* ясновидение; *on* ~ *thoughts* по зрелом размышлении; ~ *to none* непревзойдённый; *in the* ~ *place* во-вторых; ¶ *n*, секунда; секундант, помощник; *pl*, товар второго сорта; ¶ *v.t*, голосовать за, поддерживать; ~**ary**, *a*, вторичный, побочный; ~ *school* средняя школа; ~**ly**, *ad*, во-вторых.

secrecy, *n*, скрытность, секретность; **secret**, *n*, секрет, тайна; ¶ *a*, секретный, тайный.

secretaire, *n*, секретер, письменный стол; **secretarial**, *a*, секретарский; **secretariat**, *n*, секретариат; **secretary**, *n*, секретарь, -ша; министр; *Foreign* ~ министр иностранных дел; *Home* ~ министр внутренних дел.

secrete, *v.t*, выделя́ть; пря́тать; **secretion**, *n*, выделение, секреция; **secretive**, *a*, скрытный.

sect, *n*, секта; ~**arian**, *n*, сектант; ¶ *a*, сектантский.

section, *n*, разрез, сечение; профиль; отдел; квартал, район; *(mil.)* отделение; ~**al**, *a*, секционный; местный; данный в разрезе; **sector**, *n*, сектор, участок.

secular, *a*, мирской, светский; вековой, происходящий раз в сто лет; ~**ization**, *n*, секуляризация; ~**ize**, *v.t*, секуляризовать.

secure, *a*, прочный; безопасный; верный; уверенный; ¶ *v.t*, закреплять; запирать; охранять; доставать; обеспечивать, гарантировать; **security**, *n*, безопасность; гарантия, залог; *pl*, ценные бумаги; *social* ~ социальное обеспечение.

sedan-chair, *n*, портшез; паланкин.

sedate, *a*, спокойный, степенный; **sedative**, *a*, успокаивающий, снотворный; болеутоляющий; ¶ *n*, успокаивающее/болеутоляющее средство.

sedentary, *a*, сидячий.

sedge, *n*, камыш, осока.

sediment, *n*, осадок; гуща; *(geol.)* осадочная порода; ~**ary**, *a*, осадочный.

sedition, *n*, мятеж; призыв к мятежу; **seditious**, *a*, мятежный.

seduce, *v.t*, соблазня́ть, обольщать; ~**r**, *n*, соблазнитель; **seduction**, *n*, обольщение; **seductive**, *a*, соблазнительный.

sedulous, *a*, прилежный; ~**ness**, *n*, прилежание.

see, *n*, епархия; *Holy* **S**~ папский престол.

see, *v.t*, видеть, смотреть, осматривать; понимать; видеться с; ~ *about* (по)заботиться о; ~ *into* рассматривать; ~ *off* провожать; ~ *to* заботиться о; присматривать за; ~ *through!* видеть насквозь; доводить до конца; *let me* ~*!* дайте мне подумать!; ~ *home* провожать домой; ~ *you later!* до скорой встречи!.

seed, *n*, семя; зерно; зародыш; ракета; ~ *bed* парник; ~ *corn* посевное зерно; ~ *drill* рядовая сеялка; ~*sman* торговец семенами; ~

time вре́мя посе́ва; *go to* ~ идти́ в семена́; *(fig.)* переставáть разви́ва́ться, опуска́ться; *~ed player* отбóрный игрóк; ¶ *v.t*, се́ять; засева́ть; *(sport)* отбира́ть; *v.i*, роня́ть семена́; идти́ в семена́; *seeding machine* се́ялка; **~ling**, *n*, се́янец; *(pl.)* расса́да; **~у**, *a*, нездорóвый; обóрванный.

seeing, *n*, ви́дение; зре́ние; ~ *is believing* пока́ не уви́жу, не повéрю; ~ *that* ввиду́ тогó, что.

seek, *v.t*, иска́ть, разы́скивать; тре́бовать *(gen.)*; добива́ться *(gen.)*; **~er**, *n*, иска́тель.

coom, *v.i*, каза́ться; *it ~s to me* мне ка́жется; **~ingly**, *ad*, по-ви́ди́мому.

seemly, *a*, подоба́ющий, прили́чный.

seep, *v.i*, проса́чиваться.

seer, *n*, прови́дец, прорóк.

seesaw, *n*, каче́ли; ¶ *v.i*, кача́ться на доске́; *(fig.)* колеба́ться.

seethe, *v.i*, кипéть.

segment, *n*, отре́зок; часть; *(math.)* сегмéнт.

segregate, *v.t*, отделя́ть(ся); **segregation**, *n*, отделе́ние; сегрега́ция.

seismic, *a*, сейсми́ческий; **seismograph**, *n*, сейсмóграф.

seize, *v.t*, хвата́ть, схва́тывать; захва́тывать; конфискова́ть; аресто́вывать; ~ *the opportunity* пóльзоваться слу́чаем; **seizure**, *n*, захва́т, конфиска́ция; *(med.)* уда́р.

seldom, *ad*, ре́дко.

select, *a*, и́збранный, отбóрный; ¶ *v.t*, выбира́ть; отбира́ть; **~ion**, *n*, вы́бор; подбóр; *natural* ~ есте́ственный отбóр; **~ive**, *a*, отбóрный.

self, *n*, со́бственная ли́чность; ¶ *pn*, сам; *reflex pn.* себя́; **~-centred** эгоцентри́чный; **~-confidence** самоуве́ренность; **~-conscious** засте́нчивый; **~-contained** за́мкнутый; самостоя́тельный; отде́льный; **~-control** самооблада́ние; **~-defence** самооборо́на; самозащи́та; **~-denial** самоотрече́ние; **~-esteem** чу́вство со́бственного достóинства; **~-evident** самоочеви́дный; **~-government** самоуправле́ние; **~-made** обя́занный всем самому́ себе́; **~-portrait** автопортре́т; **~-possession** само-

облада́ние; **~-regulating** автомати́ческий **~-respect** = *self-esteem*; **~-sacrifice** самопожéртвование; **~-same** тот же са́мый; **~-service** самообслу́живание; **~-styled** самозва́нный; **~-sufficient** самостоя́тельный; самодовлéющий; **~-willed** своевóльный.

selfish, *a*, эгоисти́чный; **~ness**, *n*, эгои́зм.

sell, *v.t*, продава́ть; торгова́ть *(inst.)*; *v.i*, продава́ться; ~ *off* распродава́ть (со ски́дкой); ~ *out* продава́ть всё; ~ *up* продава́ть с торгóв; **~er**, *n*, продавéц; **~ing**, *n*, прода́жа; ~ *price* прода́жная цена́.

selvage, *n*, кайма́, крóмка.

semantic, *a*, семанти́ческий; **~s**, *n*, сема́нтика.

semaphore, *n*, семафóр.

semblance, *n*, вид, ви́димость, подóбие.

semester, *n*, семéстр.

semi-, *prefix*, полу-; наполови́ну; **~-circle** полукру́г; **~-colon** тóчка с запятóй; **~-conductor** полупровóдник; **~-detached** *(house)* дом на две полови́ны; **~-vowel** полугла́сный.

seminarist, *n*, семинари́ст; **seminary**, *n*, семина́рия.

semite, *n*, семи́т; **semitic**, *a*, семи́тический.

semolina, *n*, ма́нная крупа́.

senate, *n*, сена́т; совéт; **senator**, *n*, сена́тор; **senatorial**, *a*, сена́торский; **senatorship**, *n*, дóлжность сена́тора.

send, *v.t*, посыла́ть; отправля́ть; ~ *away* высыла́ть, усыла́ть; прогоня́ть; ~ *down* исключа́ть из университе́та; ~ *for* посыла́ть за; отзыва́ть; ~ *in* подава́ть *(application)*, представля́ть; ~ *off* отсыла́ть; провожа́ть; ~ *out* высыла́ть; выпуска́ть; отправля́ть; ~ *up* направля́ть вверх; **~er**, *n*, отправи́тель.

Senegalese, *a*, сенега́льский; ¶ *n*, сенега́лец.

seneschal, *n*, сенеша́ль.

senile, *a*, ста́рческий; дря́хлый; **senility**, *n*, ста́рость; дря́хлость.

senior, *a*, ста́рший; ¶ *n*, ста́рший; старшеку́рсник; **~ity**, *n*, старшинствó.

senna, *n*, александри́йский лист.

sensation, *n,* ощущéние; сенсáция; ~al, *a,* сенсациóнный.

sense, *n,* ощущéние, чýвство; рáзум; смысл, значéние; *be out of one's* ~s быть не в своём умé; *in a* ~ в извéстном смысле; *talk* ~ говорить дéло; ¶ *v.t,* ощущáть, чýвствовать; сознавáть; ~less, *a,* бессмысленный; бесчувственный; **sensibility,** *n,* чувствительность; **sensible,** *a,* (благо)разýмный; замéтный; **sensibly,** *ad,* (благо)разýмно; **sensitive,** *a,* чувствительный; воспримчивый; нéжный; обидчивый; ~ *paper* светочувствительная бумáга.

sensual, *a,* чувственный; сладострáстный; ~ist, *n,* сластолюбец; ~ity, *n,* чувственность; сладострáстие; **sensuous,** *a,* чувственный.

sentence, *n,* приговóр; решéние; *(gram.)* предложéние; ¶ *v.t,* осуждáть, приговáривать; **sententious,** *a,* нравоучительный; сентенциóзный.

sentient, *a,* ощущáющий, чýвствующий.

sentiment, *n,* чýвство; мнéние; ~al, *a,* сентиментáльный; ~ality, *n,* сентиментáльность.

sentinel, sentry, *n,* часовóй; *(poet.)* страж; ~-box карáульная бýдка; *stand on* ~ стоять на часáх.

separate, *a,* отдéльный, осóбый; самостоятельный; уединённый; ¶ *v.t,* отделять, разделять, разлучáть; *v.i,* отделяться; разлучáться; расходиться; ~ly, *ad,* отдéльно; самостоятельно; **separation,** *n,* отделéние, разделéние; разложéние на чáсти; разлýка; развóд; **separatism,** *n,* сепаратизм; **separator,** *n,* сепарáтор.

sepia, *n,* сéпия.

sepoy, *n,* сипáй.

September, *n,* сентябрь; ¶ *a,* сентябрьский.

septet, *n,* септéт.

septic, *a,* септический; ~aemia, *n,* сéпсис, заражéние крóви.

septuagenarian, *n,* семидесятилéтний человéк.

sepulchral, *a,* могильный; **sepulchre,** *n,* могила, гробница.

sequel, *n,* продолжéние; послéдствие; **sequence,** *n,* порядок; послéдовательность.

sequestered, *a,* изолированный, уединённый.

sequester, *v.t,* секвестровáть; **sequestration,** *n,* секвéстр.

sequin, *n,* блёстка.

seraglio, *n,* серáль.

seraph, *n,* серафим; ~ic, *a,* áнгельский.

Serb, *n,* серб, -ка; ~ian, *a,* сéрбский.

serenade, *n,* серенáда; ¶ *v.t,* петь серенáду *(dat.).*

serene, *a,* спокóйный; ясный; **serenity,** *n,* спокóйствие.

serf, *n,* крепостнóй; ~dom, *n,* крепостнóе прáво.

serge, *n,* сáржа.

sergeant, *n,* сержáнт; ~-at-arms парлáментский пристав.

serial, *a,* серийный; выходящий выпусками; послéдовательный; ¶ *n,* ромáн в нéскольких частях; фильм в нéскольких сéриях; **series,** *n,* сéрия, ряд.

serious, *a,* серьёзный; вáжный; ~ly *ad,* серьёзно; *take* ~ принимáть всерьёз.

sermon, *n,* прóповедь; поучéние; ~ize, *v.t,* проповéдовать.

serpent, *n,* змея; ~ine, *a,* змеевидный; ¶ *n,* серпантин.

serrated, *a,* зазýбренный; зубчáтый.

serried, *a,* сóмкнутый.

serum, *n,* сыворотка.

servant, *n,* слугá, прислýга; **serve,** *v.t,* служить *(dat.);* обслýживать; подавáть *(meal); v.i,* удовлетворять; *(sport)* подавáть мяч; ~ *as* служить *(inst.); it* ~s *him right!* так емý и нáдо!; ~ *time* отбывáть срок; **server,** *n,* подавáльщик, -ица; **service,** *n,* слýжба; обслýживание; услýга; сервиз; подáча; *active* ~ учáстие в боях; действительная воéнная слýжба; *at your* ~ к вáшим услýгам; *national* ~ вóинская (or трудовáя) повинность; ¶ *a,* служéбный; **serviceable,** *a,* пригóдный, полéзный.

serviette, *n,* салфéтка.

servile, *a,* подобострáстный, раболéпный; **servility,** *n,* подобострáстие, раболéпие; **servitude,** *n,* рáбство.

set, *n,* комплéкт, набóр; грýппа; *(theat.)* декорáция; *(tennis)* сет; сáженец *(plant);* сервиз; аппарáт; ~ *of teeth* ряд зубóв; ~ *of* *lectures* цикл лекций; ~*back* задержка; ~*-to* драка, схватка; ¶ *v.t*, класть, ставить; сажать *(plants)*; вставлять в раму/оправу; вправлять *(bone)*; *(print)* набирать; задавать *(task)*; подавать *(example)*; *v.i*, садиться *(sun)*; твердеть, застывать; ~ *against* противопоставлять; *(fig.)* восстанавливать против; ~ *one's face against* решительно противиться *(dat.)*; ~ *aside* отделять; откладывать; ~ *in* наступать; ~ *off (v.t.)* оттенять; *(v.i.)* отправляться; ~ *out (v.t.)* выставлять (напоказ); *(v.i.)* отправляться; ~ *right* приводить в порядок, исправлять; ~ *up* воздвигать; учреждать; начинать; поднимать *(noise)*; ¶ *p.p. & a*, отвердевший; застывший *(also of gaze)*; неподвижный; установленный; установившийся *(weather)*.

settee, *n*, диван, тахта.

setter, *n*, установщик; сеттер *(dog)*; **setting**, *n*, оправа *(of jewel)*; заход *(of sun)*; окружающая обстановка; музыка на слова; *(theat.)* постановка, декорации и костюмы; ~ *up* монтаж; сборка.

settle, *v.i*, поселять; заселять; решать; улаживать; оплачивать *(debt)*; *v.i*, поселяться; усаживаться; оседать; ~ *down* поселяться; успокаиваться; ~*d*, *a*, определённый, устойчивый; ~**ment**, *n*, поселение; расчёт, уплата; решение; ~**r,n**,посел нец; **settling**, *n*, оседание; осаждение.

seven, *num*, семь; ¶ *n*, семёрка; ~**teen**, *num*, семнадцать; ~**teenth**, *ord.num*, семнадцатый; ~**th**, *ord.num*, седьмой; ¶ *n*, седьмая часть; ~**tieth**, *ord.num*, семидесятый; ~**ty**, *num*, семьдесят.

sever, *v.t*, разрезать, рассекать; отрубать; рвать; разъединять; *v.i*, рваться; отделяться; ~**ance**, *n*, отделение, разрыв.

severe, *a*, строгий, суровый; *catch a* ~ *cold* сильно простудиться *(pf.)*; **severity**, *n*, строгость, суровость.

sew, *v.t*, шить; ~ *on* пришивать.

sewage, *n*, сточные воды; **sewer**, *n*, канализационная труба; ~**age**, *n*, канализация.

sewing, *n*, шитьё; ~ *machine* швейная машина.

sex, *n*, пол, секс; ~ *appeal* физическая привлекательность; *the fair* ~ прекрасный пол.

sextant, *n*, секстант.

sexton, *n*, церковный сторож, пономарь.

sexual, *a*, половой, сексуальный.

shabby, *a*, оборванный, потрёпанный; жалкий, подлый.

shack, *n*, лачуга, хибарка.

shackle, *n. pl*, кандалы; *(fig.)* оковы; ¶ *v.t*, заковывать в кандалы; *(fig.)* стеснять, сковывать.

shade, *n*, тень; оттенок: штора; призрак; ¶ *v.t*, заслонять (от света), затемнять; тушевать; **shadow**,*n*,тень;полумрак;призрак; ¶ *v.t*, бросать тень на; следовать за; выслеживать; **shadowy**, *a*, теннистый; неясный; призрачный; **shady**, *a*, тенистый; *(fig.)* сомнительный.

shaft, *n*, древко *(of spear, etc.)*; рукоятка, ручка; ствол (шахты); оглобля *(of cart)*; луч *(light)*; *(tech.)* вал, ось.

shag, *n*, махорка *(tobacco)*; баклан хохлатый *(bird)*; ~**gy**, *a*, косматый, лохматый.

shake, *n*, встряска; сотрясение; потрясение; *(mus.)* трель; ¶ *v.t*, трясти, сотрясать; колебать; *v.i*, трястись, сотрясаться; дрожать; ~ *hands* пожимать руки; ~ *one's head* качать головой; **shaking**, *n*, тряска; сотрясение; **shaky**, *a*, шаткий, трясущийся; сомнительный.

shale, *n*, глинистый сланец.

shall — *expressed by future tenses*.

shallot, *n*, шалот.

shallow, *a*, мелкий; *(fig.)* поверхностный; ~**s**, *n.pl*, (от)мель, мелководье.

sham, *n*, обман, притворство; притворщик; ¶ *a*, притворный, фальшивый; ¶ *v.i*, притворяться.

shamble, *v.i*, тащиться; ~**s**, *n*, мясной рынок, бойня; полный беспорядок.

shame, *n*, стыд; позор; ~ *on you!* как вам не стыдно! *what a* ~! какая досада!; ¶ *v.t*, стыдить, позорить, срамить; ~**faced**, *a*, стыдли́вый; ~less, *a*, бессты́д-ный; ~lessness, *n*, бессты́дство.

shampoo, *n*, шампу́нь; мытьё голо-вы́; ¶ *v.t*, мыть го́лову.

shamrock, *n*, трили́стник.

shank, *n*, го́лень; нога́; ствол, сте́ржень.

shape, *n*, фо́рма; очерта́ние; вид, о́браз; *(coll.)* состоя́ние; ¶ *v.t*, придава́ть фо́рму *(dat.)*; обра-зо́вывать; ~less, *a*, бесфо́рмен-ный; ~ly, *a*, хорошо́ сло́жен-ный.

share, *n*, до́ля, часть; уча́стие; *(com.)* а́кция, пай; *(plough)* ле́мех; ~holder акционе́р, пай-щик; ~ and ~ alike на ра́вных права́х, по́ровну; ¶ *v.t*, дели́ть, разделя́ть; уча́ствовать в; сов-ме́стно владе́ть *(inst.)*; ~ a room жить/рабо́тать в одно́й ко́мнате; ~ out раздава́ть; **sharing**, *n*, де-лёж.

shark, *n*, аку́ла *(also fig.)*.

sharp, *a*, о́стрый; остроконе́чный; отчётливый; круто́й *(turn)*; ед-кий *(taste)*; ре́зкий *(pain)*; то́н-кий *(hearing)*; проница́тельный *(mind)*; раздражи́тельный *(cha-racter)*; язви́тельный, ко́лкий *(re-mark)*; бы́стрый; *(mus.)* сли́ш-ком высо́кий; look ~! живе́й!; береги́сь!; ¶ *ad*, ро́вно, то́чно; four o'clock ~ ро́вно четы́ре часа́; ¶ *n*, *(mus.)* дие́з; ~en, *v.t*, точи́ть, заостря́ть; *(fig.)* обостря́ть; ~ener, *n*, точи́лка *(pencil)*; точи́ло; ~er, *n*, жу́лик, шу́лер; ~ly, *ad*, о́стро; отчётливо; кру́то, ре́зко; ~ness, *n*, острота́; отчётливость; проница́тельность; ~shooter, *n*, ме́ткий стрело́к.

shatter, *v.i*, разбива́ть вдре́безги, раздробля́ть; расша́тывать *(health)*; разруша́ть *(hopes)*; рас-стра́ивать *(plans)*.

shave, *v.t*, брить; скобли́ть; *v.i*, бри́ться; ~r, *n*, тот, кто бре́ется; *(coll.)* парснёк; **shaving**, *n*, бритьё; *pl*, стру́жки; ~ brush ки́сточка для бритья́.

shawl, *n*, шаль.

she, *pn*, она́; ¶ *n*, же́нщина; са́мка *(animal)*; ~ goat коза́.

sheaf, *n*, сноп *(corn)*; вя́зка, па́чка.

shear, *v.t*, стричь; ре́зать; *(coll.)* обира́ть; ~er, *n*, механи́ческие но́жницы; *(pers.)* стрига́ль; ~-

ing, *n*, стри́жка; ~s, *n*, но́ж-ницы.

sheath, *n*, но́жны; футля́р; *(med.)* оболо́чка; **sheathe**, *v.t*, вкла́ды-вать в но́жны.

sheave, *n*, блок, шкив; кату́шка.

shed, *n*, сара́й, наве́с; ¶ *v.t*, роня́ть, теря́ть *(hair, leaves)*; пролива́ть *(tears)*; сбра́сывать *(clothing, skin)*; броса́ть, излуча́ть *(light)*.

sheen, *n*, блеск, сия́ние.

sheep, *n*, овца́, бара́н; ¶ *dog* ов-ча́рка; ~fold овча́рня; ~skin овчи́на; ~skin coat дублёнка; ~ish, *a*, засте́нчивый, стыдли́-вый.

sheer, *a*, отве́сный, перпендикуля́р-ный; прозра́чный *(cloth)*; абсо-лю́тный, су́щий; by ~ force одно́й то́лько си́лой; ¶ *v.i*, *(mar.)* от-клоня́ться от ку́рса; ~ off уда-ля́ться.

sheet, *n*, простыня́ *(bed)*; лист *(paper, metal)*; широ́кая полоса́; пове́рхность; ~ anchor запасно́й я́корь; ~ iron листово́е желе́зо; ~ lightning зарни́ца; ~ing, *n*, (защи́тное) покры́тие; мета́лл в листа́х.

sheikh, *n*, шейх.

shekel, *n*, си́кель; *pl*, де́ньги.

sheldrake, *n*, пега́нка.

shelf, *n*, по́лка; вы́ступ *(geol.)*; мель, риф.

shell, *n*, ра́ковина; скорлупа́ *(nut)*; па́нцирь *(tortoise)*; *(mil.)* снаря́д; о́стов; ~fish моллю́ск; ~proof брони́рованный; ~-shock кон-ту́зия; ¶ *v.t*, чи́стить, снима́ть скорлупу́ с; *(mil.)* обстре́ливать (снаря́дами); ~ing, *n*, артиллери́й-ский обстре́л, бомбардиро́вка.

shelter, *n*, прию́т; убе́жище; при-кры́тие, укры́тие; ¶ *v.t*, прию-ти́ть *(pf.)*; прикрыва́ть, укры-ва́ть; служи́ть прикры́тием/убе́-жищем *(dat.)*; *v.i*, приюти́ться *(pf.)*; укрыва́ться; ~ed, *a*, по-крови́тельствуемый; live a ~ life жить вдали́ от мирски́х забо́т, жить «под кры́лышком»; ~less, *a*, без кро́ва, бесприю́тный.

shelve, *v.t*, ста́вить на по́лку; снаб-жа́ть по́лками; *(fig.)* откла́ды-вать, класть в до́лгий я́щик; *v.i*, отло́го спуска́ться; **shelving**, *n*, стелла́ж; откла́дывание; ¶ *a*, отло́гий.

shepherd, n, пастух; пастырь; ~ boy пастушок; ¶ v.t, пасти; смотреть за; ~ess, n, пастушка.

sherbet, n, шербет.

sheriff, n, шериф.

sherry, n, херес.

shield, n, щит; (fig.) защита; защитник; ¶ v.t, защищать, заслонять.

shift, n, сдвиг; изменение, перемена; смена; платье-рубашка (dress); ¶ v.t. (& i.), перемещать(ся); менять(ся); двигать(ся); ~ for oneself обходиться без посторонней помощи; ~ the blame on to сваливать вину на; ~ing, a, непостоянный; движущийся; ~y, a, изворотливый, хитрый.

shilling, n, шиллинг.

shilly-shally, v.i, колебаться.

shimmer, n, мерцание; ¶ v.i, мерцать.

shin, n, голень; ¶ v.i: ~ up карабкаться на.

shindy, n, скандал; свалка.

shine, n, свет; сияние; блеск, глянец; ¶ v.t, полировать; чистить (shoes); v.i, блестеть, светить(ся), сиять; (fig.) блистать.

shingle, n, галька; (кровельная) дранка; ¶ v.t, крыть; коротко стричь.

shingles, n.pl, (med.) опоясывающий лишай.

shining, a, блестящий, сияющий; ¶ n, блеск, сияние; **shiny**, a, блестящий, лоснящийся.

ship, n, корабль, судно; ~'s boy юнга; ~builder кораблестроитель; ~load судовой груз; ~owner судовладелец; ~shape в полном порядке; ~wreck кораблекрушение; be ~wrecked терпеть кораблекрушение; ~wright корабельный плотник; ~yard верфь; ¶ v.t, грузить, перевозить; класть в лодку (oars); ~ment, n, груз; погрузка; ~per, n, грузоотправитель; ~ping, n, торговый флот; перевозка груза; погрузка; ~ articles договор о найме на судно.

shire, n, графство.

shirk, v.t, увиливать/уклоняться от; ~er, n, лентяй.

shirt, n, рубашка; блузка; ~ front манишка; in ~ sleeves без пиджака.

shiver, n, дрожь, трепет; ¶ v.i' дрожать, вздрагивать, трястись; v.t, разбивать вдребезги.

shoal, n, стая (рыб); масса, толпа; (mar.) мель.

shock, n, потрясение, шок; удар; копна (волос); ~-headed всклокоченный; ¶ v.t, потрясать; шокировать, возмущать; ~ing, a, возмутительный.

shoddy, a, дрянной; ¶ n, шодди, материя из шерстяных тряпок.

shoe, n, ботинок, туфля; подкова (horse); (tech.) башмак, колодка; ~black чистильщик сапог; ~ horn рожок для обуви; ~ lace шнурок для ботинок; ~maker сапожник; ~ shop обувной магазин; ~ polish крем для чистки обуви; ¶ v.t, обувать; подковывать (horse).

shoot, n, росток, побег; охота; состязание в стрельбе; наклонный жёлоб; ¶ v.t, стрелять; расстреливать; снимать (film); фотографировать; задвигать (bolt); проноситься через (rapids); v.i, мчаться, нестись; посылать мяч; ~ down сбивать; ~er, n, стрелок; ~ing, n, стрельба; охота; съёмка (of film); ~ gallery тир; ~ pain внезапная острая боль; ~ star падающая звезда.

shop, n, магазин, лавка; мастерская, цех; ~ assistant продавец, -щица; ~keeper лавочник; ~lifting мелкое воровство; ~ steward цеховой староста; ~walker дежурный администратор универмага; ~ window витрина; ¶ v.i, делать покупки; ~per, n, покупатель; ~ping, n, покупки; go ~ ходить за покупками.

shore, n, берег; крепление, подпорка; go on ~ высаживаться на берег; ¶ v.t, подпирать.

short, a, короткий; низкого роста; недостаточный; cut ~ прерывать; fall ~ не хватать; уступать; ~ of breath запыхавшийся; I am ~ of money у меня не хватает денег; ~bread песочное печенье; ~ circuit короткое замыкание; ~coming недостаток; ~ cut сокращение пути/времени; кратчайший путь; ~hand стенография; ~ hand typist стенографистка;

~*sighted* близору́кий; *(fig.)* недальнови́дный; ~ *story* расска́з; ~*-tempered* вспы́льчивый; ~*-winded* страда́ющий оды́шкой; ~**age**, *n*, недоста́ток, нехва́тка; ~**en**, *v.t. (& i.)*, сокраща́ть(ся); укора́чивать(ся); ~**ly**, *ad*, вско́ре; незадо́лго; коро́тко; ре́зко; ~**ness**, *n*, кра́ткость; недоста́точность; ~**s**, *n.pl*, шо́рты.

shot, *n*, вы́стрел; пу́шечное ядро́; дробь; *(pers.)* стрело́к; *(sport)* ядро́; *(fig.)* уда́р; ~ *gun* дробови́к; *not by a long* ~ отню́дь не; ¶ *a*, перели́вчатый; с отли́вом (серебри́стым, *etc.*).

should, *v.aux*, *expressed by future tense or conditional;* I ~ *go* я до́лжен идти́; *If I knew them, I should speak to them* е́сли бы я знал их, я бы поговори́л с ни́ми.

shoulder, *n*, плечо́; ~ *blade* лопа́тка; ~ *strap* плечико; пого́н; ¶ *v.t*, взва́ливать на пле́чи; брать на себя́; ~ *arms* брать к плечу́.

shout, *n*, крик; ¶ *v.i*, крича́ть; ~**ing**, *n*, во́згласы, кри́ки.

shove, *n*, толчо́к; ¶ *v.t*, толка́ть; ~ *off from* отта́лкиваться от.

shovel, *n*, лопа́та; сово́к; *steam* ~ землечерпа́лка; ¶ *v.t*, копа́ть; сгреба́ть.

show, *n*, пока́з; пока́зывание; ви́димость; зре́лище; спекта́кль; вы́ставка; ~*case, window* витри́на; ~*man* хозя́ин цирка/аттракцио́на; балага́нщик; ~*manship* уме́ние вы́ставить, показа́ть, *etc.*; показу́ха; ¶ *v.t*, пока́зывать, демонстри́ровать, выставля́ть; дока́зывать; *v.i*, пока́зываться, появля́ться; ~ *in* вводи́ть; ~ *off* пока́зывать в вы́годном све́те; рисова́ться; щеголя́ть *(inst.);* ~ *up (v.t.)* изоблича́ть; смуща́ть; *(v.i.)* выделя́ться (на фо́не).

shower, *n*, ли́вень; град *(hail, & fig.);* снегопа́д; ~*-bath* душ; ¶ *v.t*, лить; полива́ть; осыпа́ть; *v.i*, ли́ться; сы́паться; ~**y**, *a*, дождли́вый.

showy, *a*, я́ркий; показно́й; эффе́ктный.

shrapnel, *n*, шрапне́ль.

shred, *n*, клочо́к, лоскуто́к; ¶ *v.t*, кромса́ть, ре́зать; рвать; ~**ded**, *a*, дроблёный.

shrew, *n*, *(zoo.)* землеро́йка; *(pers.)* сварли́вая же́нщина.

shrewd, *a*, проница́тельный; ~**ness**, *n*, проница́тельность.

shrewish, *a*, сварли́вый.

shriek, *n*, пронзи́тельный крик, визг; ¶ *v.i*, пронзи́тельно крича́ть, визжа́ть.

shrill, *a*, пронзи́тельный, ре́зкий.

shrimp, *n*, креве́тка.

shrine, *n*, гробни́ца.

shrink, *v.i*, сади́ться *(cloth);* сокраща́ться, уменьша́ться; ~ *from* уклоня́ться от; не реша́ться (+ *inf.* or на); *v.t*, сокраща́ть, уменьша́ть, сжима́ть; ~**age**, *n*, сокраще́ние, сжа́тие; уса́дка; усу́шка.

shrivel, *v.i*, смо́рщиваться, ссыха́ться; съёживаться.

shroud, *n*, са́ван; *(fig.)* покро́в; ¶ *v.t*, оку́тывать.

Shrovetide, *n*, ма́сленица.

shrub, *n*, куст; ~**bery**, *n*, куста́рник.

shrug, *n*, пожима́ние плеча́ми; ¶ ~ *one's shoulders* пожима́ть плеча́ми.

shudder, *n*, дрожь, содрога́ние; ¶ *v.i*, вздра́гивать, содрога́ться.

shuffle, *v.t*, тасова́ть *(cards);* переме́шивать; перемеща́ть; ша́ркать (нога́ми); ~ *along* волочи́ть но́ги; ~**shuffling**, *n*, тасо́вка; ша́рканье.

shun, *v.t*, избега́ть *(gen.).*

shunt, *v.t*, *(rly.)* переводи́ть (на запасно́й путь); перебра́сывать; откла́дывать; ¶ *n*, перево́д на запасно́й путь, сортиро́вка.

shut, *v.t. (& i.)*, закрыва́ть(ся), затворя́ть(ся), запира́ть(ся); ~ *off* выключа́ть *(current, etc.);* ~ *out* исключа́ть, не допуска́ть; ~ *up* забива́ть, зака́лачивать; заключа́ть (в тюрьму́); ~ *up!* замолчи́!; ~**ter**, *n*, ста́вень; задви́жка; *(phot.)* затво́р.

shuttle, *n*, челно́к; ~*-cock* вола́н; ¶ *v.i*, дви́гаться взад и вперёд; курси́ровать.

shy, *a*, засте́нчивый, ро́бкий; ¶ *v.t*, броса́ть; *v.i*, броса́ться в сто́рону; ~**ness**, *n*, засте́нчивость.

Siamese, *a*, сиа́мский; ¶ *n*, сиа́м|ец, -ка; сиа́мский язы́к.

Siberian, *a*, сиби́рский; ¶ *n*, сибиря́к, -я́чка.

sibilant, *a*, свистя́щий, шипя́щий.

sibyl, *n*, сиви́лла, предсказа́тельница.

Sicilian, *a*, сицили́йский; ¶ *n*, жи́тель Сици́лии.

sick, *a*, больно́й; *I feel* ~ меня́ тошни́т; *I am* ~ *of it* мне э́то надое́ло; ~ *headache* мигре́нь, головна́я боль; ~ *leave* о́тпуск по боле́зни; ~en, *v.t*, вызыва́ть тошноту́/отвраще́ние у; ~ening, *a*, тошнотво́рный, отврати́тельный.

sickle, *n*, серп.

sickly, *a*, боле́зненный; **sickness**, *n*, боле́знь; тошнота́.

side, *n*, сторона́; бок; край; склон (горы́); *(mar.)* борт; ~ *by* ~ бок о́ бок; ря́дом; *on the* ~ попу́тно; тайко́м; ме́жду про́чим; *on the left hand* ~ по ле́вую сто́рону; *on all* ~s со всех сторо́н; ~*board* буфе́т; ~*-car* коля́ска мотоци́кла; ~ *door* бокова́я дверь; ~ *glance* косо́й взгляд; ~ *light* боково́й фона́рь; *(fig.)* побо́чные све́дения; ~*line* побо́чная рабо́та; ~ *saddle* да́мское седло́; ~*-track* (*n.*) запасно́й путь; *(v.t.)* отвлека́ть; ~ *view* вид сбо́ку; про́филь; ~*walk* тротуа́р; ~*ways* бо́ком; ко́свенно; ~ *whiskers* бакенба́рды; ~ *with* примыка́ть к; быть на стороне́ *(gen.)*; **siding**, *n*, запасно́й путь, разъе́зд, бокова́я сте́нка.

sidle up подходи́ть бочко́м.

siege, *n*, оса́да; *lay* ~ *to* осажда́ть.

sieve, *n*, решето́, си́то; ¶ *v.t*, просе́ивать.

sift, *v.t*, просе́ивать; *(fig.)* тща́тельно иссле́довать; ~ings, *n*, вы́севки.

sigh, *n*, вздох; ¶ *v.i*, вздыха́ть.

sight, *n*, зре́ние; вид; зре́лище; *(gun)* прице́л; *pl*, достопримеча́тельности; *at (the)* ~ *(of)* при ви́де *(gen.)*; *at first* ~ с пе́рвого взгля́да; *in* ~ в по́ле зре́ния; *in* ~ *of* в виду́ *(gen.)*; *know by* ~ знать в лицо́; *lose* ~ *of* теря́ть из ви́ду; забыва́ть; *see the* ~s осма́тривать достопримеча́тельности; ¶ *v.t*, уви́деть *(pf.)*.

sign, *n*, знак; при́знак; си́мвол; зна́мение, след; ~*board* вы́веска; ~*post* указа́тельный столб; ¶ *v.t*, подпи́сывать; *v.i*, де́лать знак.

signal, *n*, сигна́л; знак; ~*man* сигна́льщик; ¶ *v.i*, сигнализи́ровать; ~ize, *v.t*, отмеча́ть; ознамено́вывать; ~ly, *ad*, заме́тно.

signatory, *n*, сторона́, подписа́вшая догово́р; подписа́вший; **signature**, *n*, по́дпись; *(mus.)* ключ; **signet**, *n*, печа́тка, печа́ть.

significance, *n*, ва́жность, значе́ние; **significant**, *a*, значи́тельный; **signify**, *v.t*, зна́чить, означа́ть; *v.i*, име́ть значе́ние.

silence, *n*, молча́ние; тишина́; ¶ *int*, ти́ше!; молча́ть!; ¶ *v.t*, заставля́ть замолча́ть; заглуша́ть; ~r, *n*, глуши́тель; *(mus.)* сурди́нка; **silent**, *a*, безмо́лвный, молчали́вый; ти́хий; бесшу́мный; ~ *film* немо́й фильм; ~ молча́ть.

silhouette, *n*, силуэ́т; *be* ~*d* вырисо́вываться (на фо́не).

silica, *n*, кремнезём; **silicon chip**, кре́мниевая пласти́на.

silk, *n*, шёлк; ¶ *a*, шёлковый; *raw* ~ шёлк-сыре́ц; *spun* ~ шёлко́вая пря́жа; *shot* ~ шёлк с отли́вом; ~*worm* шелкови́чный червь; ~ *hat* цили́ндр; ~en, ~y, *a*, шелкови́стый; мя́гкий, не́жный.

sill, *n*, подоко́нник.

silliness, *n*, глу́пость; **silly**, *a*, глу́пый; слабоу́мный.

silo, *n*, си́лос.

silt, *n*, ил, оса́док; ¶ *v.t. (& i.)*: ~ *up* засоря́ть(ся) и́лом.

silver, *n*, серебро́; ¶ *a*, сере́бряный; серебри́стый; седо́й *(hair)*; ~ *fox* чернобу́рая лиси́ца; ~ *plate* (*n.*) сере́бряная посу́да; *(v.t.)* покрыва́ть серебро́м; ¶ *v.t*, серебри́ть; покрыва́ть ртутью *(mirror)*; ~y, *a*, серебри́стый.

similar, *a*, подо́бный, похо́жий, схо́дный; ~ity, *n*, схо́дство; подо́бие; ~ly, *ad*, подо́бным о́бразом; так же.

simile, *n*, сравне́ние.

simmer, *v.i*, закипа́ть; кипе́ть (на ме́дленном огне́); *v.t*, кипяти́ть (на ме́дленном огне́).

simper, *n*, притво́рная улы́бка; ¶ *v.i*, притво́рно улыба́ться; жема́ниться.

simple, *a*, просто́й; неразложи́мый; **simpleton**, *n*, проста́к; **simplicity**, *n*, простота́; простоду́шие; **simplification**, *n*, упроще́ние; **simplify**, *v.t*, упроща́ть; **simply**, *ad*, про́сто, легко́.

simulacrum, *n*, подо́бие; **simulate**, *v.t*, симули́ровать; **simulation**, *n*, симуля́ция.

simultaneous, *a*, одновре́менный.

sin, *n*, грех; ¶ *v.i*, греши́ть.

since, *ad*, с тех пор; тому́ наза́д; *ever* ~ с тех пор; *some months* ~ не́сколько ме́сяцев тому́ наза́д; *long* ~ давно́; ¶ *c*, с тех пор как; так как; *it is an hour since he left* с тех пор как он ушёл, прошёл час; ¶ *pr*, с; по́сле.

sincere, *a*, и́скренний; sincerity, *n*, и́скренность.

sine, *n*, *(maths)* си́нус.

sinecure, *n*, синеку́ра.

sinew, *n*, сухожи́лие.

sinful, *a*, гре́шный, грехо́вный; ~ness, *n*, грехо́вность.

sing, *v.t. & i.*, петь; ~ *of* воспева́ть; ~ *out* выклика́ть; ~ *out of tune* фальши́вить; ~ *to sleep* убаю́кивать пе́нием.

singe, *v.t*, пали́ть, опаля́ть.

singer, *n*, певе́ц, певи́ца; singing, *n*, пе́ние; ~ *bird* пе́вчая пти́ца.

single, *a*, оди́н; еди́нственный; отде́льный; холосто́й; ~ *bed* односпа́льная крова́ть; ~-*breasted* однобо́ртный; ~-*handed* (рабо́тающий) в одино́чку; ~ *life* холоста́я жизнь; ~-*minded* пре́данный де́лу, целеустремлённый; ~ *room* ко́мната на одного́ челове́ка; ~ *ticket* биле́т в оди́н коне́ц; ¶ *v.t*: ~ *out* выбира́ть; выдвига́ть; выделя́ть; ~ness, *n*: ~ *of purpose* целеустремлённость; ~t, *n*, фуфа́йка; singly, *ad*, отде́льно, поодино́чке.

singsong, *n*, пе́ние, пе́сни; ¶ *a*, моното́нный.

singular, *a*, еди́нственный *(gram.)*; необы́чный, стра́нный; ~ity, *n*, необы́чность, стра́нность.

sinister, *a*, злове́щий.

sink, *n*, ра́ковина; сто́чная труба́; *(fig.)* клоа́ка; ¶ *v.t*, опуска́ть, погружа́ть; топи́ть *(ship)*; рыть *(well)*; *v.i*, опуска́ться, погружа́ться; оседа́ть; тону́ть *(ship)*; ослабева́ть; заходи́ть *(sun)*; ~er, *n*, грузи́ло; ~ing, *n*, опуска́ние, погруже́ние; потопле́ние; ~ *fund* амортизацио́нный фонд.

sinner, *n*, гре́шник.

sinuous, *a*, изви́листый; волни́стый.

sinus, *n*, па́зуха.

sip, *n*, ма́ленький глото́к; *take a* ~ пригуби́ть *(pf.)*; ¶ *v.t*, пить ма́ленькими глотка́ми.

siphon, *n*, сифо́н.

sir, сэр; господи́н; *Dear* ~ Ми́лостивый госуда́рь; *Dear* ~s уважа́емые господа́.

sire, *n*, оте́ц, пре́док; ва́ше вели́чество; производи́тель *(animal)*; ¶ *v.t*, быть производи́телем *(gen., animal)*.

siren, *n*, сире́на *(also myth.)*

sirloin, *n*, филе́й.

sister, *n*, сестра́; ~hood сестри́нская общи́на; ро́дственная связь сестёр; ~-*in-law* неве́стка; золо́вка; своя́ченица; ~ly, *a*, сестри́нский.

sit, *v.i*, сиде́ть; *v.t*, сажа́ть; ~ *down* сади́ться; ~-*down strike* сидя́чая забасто́вка; ~ *for* пози́ровать для; представля́ть (в парла́менте); ~ *up* приподнима́ться; не ложи́ться спать.

site, *n*, ме́сто, уча́сток; *building* ~ строи́тельная площа́дка, стро́йка.

sitting, *n*, заседа́ние; сеа́нс; *at one* ~ в оди́н присе́ст; ~ *room* гости́ная.

situated, *a*, располо́женный; situation, *n*, ме́сто, положе́ние, местоположе́ние; щекотли́вое положе́ние.

six, *num*, шесть; ~teen, *num*, шестна́дцать; ~teenth, *ord.num*, шестна́дцатый; ~th *ord.num*, шесто́й; ¶ *n*, шеста́я часть; ~ *of June* шесто́е ию́ня; ~tieth, *ord. num*, шестидеся́тый; ~ty, *num*, шестьдеся́т.

sizable, *a*, поря́дочного разме́ра; size, *n*, разме́р, величина́; объём; форма́т; но́мер *(gloves)*; клей *(glue)*; ¶ *v.t*, сортирова́ть по величине́; прокле́ивать; ~ *up* определя́ть разме́р *(gen.)*; составля́ть мне́ние о.

sizzle, *v.i*, шипе́ть.

skate, *n*, конёк; скат; *(fish)*; ¶ *v.i*, ката́ться на конька́х; ~r, *n*, конькобе́жец; *skating rink* като́к.

skein, *n*, мото́к.

skeleton, *n*, скеле́т; о́стов, карка́с; набро́сок; ~ *key* отмы́чка; ~ *in the cupboard* семе́йная та́йна.

sketch, *n*, набро́сок, эски́з; о́черк; *(theat.)* скетч; ¶ *v.t, & i*, де́лать набро́сок; оче́рчивать; ~y, *a*, отры́вочный.

skewer, *n*, ве́ртел; ¶ *v.t*, наса́живать на ве́ртел; пронза́ть.

ski, *n*, лы́жа; ¶ *v.i*, ката́ться на лы́жах; ~er, *n*, лы́жник.

skid, *n*, скольже́ние колёс, буксова́ние; тормозно́й башма́к; ¶ *v.i*, буксова́ть, скользи́ть.

skiff, *n*, я́лик.

skilful, *a*, иску́сный, уме́лый; **skill**, *n*, мастерство́, иску́сство, уме́ние; ~ed, *a*, иску́сный, квалифици́рованный.

skim, *v.t*, снима́ть *(milk, etc.)*; ~ *over* скользи́ть по; едва́ каса́ться *(gen.)*; ~ *through* бе́гло просма́тривать.

skimp, *v.t*, уре́зывать; *v.i*, эконо́мить.

skin, *n*, ко́жа; шку́ра *(animal)*; кожура́ *(fruit, etc.)*; мех *(for wine)*; ¶ *v.t*, сдира́ть ко́жу шку́ру, кожуру́) с; *v.i*, покрыва́ться ко́жей; ~flint скря́га; ~ner, *n*, скорня́к; ~ny, *a*, то́щий, худо́й.

skip, *n*, прыжо́к, скачо́к; ¶ *v.i*, пры́гать, скака́ть; *v.t*, пропуска́ть; переска́кивать.

skipper, *n*, шки́пер, капита́н.

skipping rope скака́лка.

skirmish, *n*, перестре́лка, сты́чка; ¶ *v.i*, сража́ться.

skirt, *n*, ю́бка; подо́л по́ла; ¶ *v.t*, идти́ вдоль кра́я *(gen.)*; обходи́ть; окаймля́ть; ~ing board пли́нтус.

skit, *n*, сати́ра, шу́тка.

skittish, *a*, игри́вый, капри́зный.

skittles, *n*, ке́гли.

skulk, *v.i*, пря́таться, скрыва́ться; кра́сться.

skull, *n*, че́реп; ~-cap ермо́лка, тюбете́йка.

skunk, *n*, скунс; *(fig.)* подле́ц.

sky, *n*, не́бо, небеса́; ~ *blue* лазу́рный; ~lark жа́воронок; ~light стекля́нная кры́ша, окно́ в кры́ше; светово́й люк; ~line горизо́нт; ~scraper небоскрёб.

slab, *n*, плита́; *(coll.)* ломо́ть.

slack, *a*, свобо́дный, ненатя́нутый, неприкреплённый; сла́бый; вя́лый; небре́жный; ¶ *n*, у́гольная пыль; ¶ *v.i*, безде́льничать; *v.t*, гаси́ть; ~en, *v.t*, отвя́зывать; освобожда́ть; ослабля́ть; *v.i*, слабе́ть, сла́бнуть; стиха́ть; ~er, *n*, ло́дырь; ~s, *n*, брю́ки.

slag, *n*, шлак.

slate, *v.t*, утоля́ть; гаси́ть *(lime)*.

slam, *n*, хло́панье (две́рью); *(cards)* шлем; ¶ *v.t*, хло́пать (две́рью, etc.).

slander, *n*, клевета́; ¶ *v.t*, клевета́ть на; ~er, *n*, клеветни́к; ~ous, *a*, клеветни́ческий.

slang, *n*, слэнг, жарго́н.

slant, *n*, склон, укло́н; взгляд, то́чка зре́ния; ¶ *v.t*, наклоня́ть; *(fig.)* искажа́ть; *v.i*, наклоня́ться, идти́ вкось; ~ing, *a*, накло́нный; косо́й.

slap, *n*, шлепо́к; ~ *in the face* пощёчина; ¶ *v.t*, хло́пать, шлёпать; дава́ть пощёчину *(dat.)*; ~dash, *a*, поспе́шный; неря́шливый.

slash, *n*, разре́з; ру́бка, уда́р сплеча́; ¶ *v.t*, руби́ть.

slat, *n*, пла́нка.

slate, *n*, сла́нец, ши́фер; грифельная доска́; ¶ *v.t*, крыть ши́фером; *(fig.)* критикова́ть; ~r, *n*, кро́вельщик; **slating**, *n*, ши́ферное покры́тие; *(fig.)* суро́вая кри́тика.

slattern, *n*, неря́ха; ~ly, *a*, неря́шливый.

slaughter, *n*, резня́; убо́й *(cattle)*; ¶ *v.t*, ре́зать, убива́ть; ~-house бо́йня.

Slav, *a*, славя́нский; ¶ *n*, славя́н|ин, ~ка.

slave, *n*, раб; ~-driver надсмо́трщик над раба́ми; эксплуата́тор; ~ *trade* работорго́вля; ¶ *v.i*, рабо́тать как раб; ~r, *n*, работорго́вец; нево́льничье су́дно.

slaver, *n*, слюна́; ¶ *v.i*, пуска́ть слюну́.

slavery, *n*, ра́бство; **slavish**, *a*, ра́бский; ~ness, *n*, ра́бская поко́рность.

Slavonic, *a*, славя́нский.

slay, *v.t*, убива́ть; ~er, *n*, уби́йца.

sledge, *n*, са́ни, са́нки; ~ *hammer* кува́лда, кузне́чный мо́лот; **sledging**, *n*, езда́/ката́нье на саня́х.

sleek, *a*, гла́дкий; лосня́щийся; прили́занный; ¶ *v.t*: ~ *down* приглажи́вать, прили́зывать.

sleep, *n*, сон; ~ *walker* луна́тик; *go to* ~ засыпа́ть; *put to* ~ укла́дывать спать; усыпля́ть *(animal)*; ¶ *v.i*, спать; ~ *like a log* спать как уби́тый; ~ *on it* откла́дывать рассмотре́ние до утра́; ~er, *n*, спя́щий; *(rly.)* шпа́ла; спа́льный ваго́н; ~ily, *ad*, со́нливо, со́нно;

~iness, *n*, сонли́вость; ~ing, *a*, спя́щий; ~ *Beauty* Спя́щая краса́вица; ~ *car* спа́льный ваго́н; ~ *draught* снотво́рное; ~less, *a*, бессо́нный; ~ness, *n*, бессо́нница; ~у, *a*, со́нный, сонли́вый; *be* ~ хоте́ть спать.

sleet, *n*, дождь со сне́гом.

sleeve, *n*, рука́в; (*tech.*) му́фта; ~ *link* за́понка; *laugh up one's* ~ смея́ться укра́дкой; *he wears his heart on his* ~ у него́ душа́ нараспа́шку.

sleigh, *n*, са́ни; ~ *bell* бубе́нчик.

sleight, *n*, ло́вкость; фо́кус; ~-*of-hand* ло́вкость рук, жонглёрство.

slender, *a*, то́нкий, стро́йный; ску́дный; сла́бый.

sleuth, *n*, сы́щик; ~ *hound* соба́ка-ище́йка.

slice, *n*, ло́мтик, ломо́ть; (то́нкий) слой; широ́кий нож, лопа́тка; (*sport*) непра́вильный уда́р; ¶ *v.t*, ре́зать ло́мтиками; (*sport*) сре́зать (*pf.*).

slide, *n*, скольже́ние; го́рка для ката́ния, като́к; ледяна́я гора́/доро́жка; диапозити́в; предме́тное стекло́ (*microscope*); ~ *projector* диапрое́ктор; ~ *rule* логарифми́ческая лине́йка; ¶ *v.i*, скользи́ть; ката́ться с го́рки; кати́ться (по льду); *v.t*, задвига́ть; сова́ть; ~ *by* незаме́тно проходи́ть; *let things* ~ относи́ться к де́лу спустя́ рукава́; sliding, *a*, скользя́щий; выдвижно́й; ~ *door* раздвижна́я дверь; ~ *scale* скользя́щая шкала́; ¶ *n*, скольже́ние.

slight, *a*, лёгкий, незначи́тельный; сла́бый; то́нкий; *not in the* ~*est* ни на йо́ту; ¶ *n*, неуваже́ние, пренебреже́ние; ¶ *v.t*. пренебрега́ть (*inst.*). трети́ровать; обижа́ть; ~ingly, *ad*, пренебрежи́тельно; ~ly, *ad*, слегка́.

slim, *a*, стро́йный, то́нкий; сла́бый; ¶ *v.i*, худе́ть.

slime, *n*, ли́пкая грязь, ил; слизь; slimy, *a*, и́листый, гря́зный; вя́зкий; сли́зистый.

sling, *n*, (*surg.*) пе́ревязь; праща́ (*weapon*); (*mar.*) строп; кана́т; ¶ *v.t*, мета́ть, швыря́ть; ве́шать (че́рез плечо́).

slink, *v.i*, идти́ краду́чись.

slip, *n*, скольже́ние; сдвиг; (*fig.*) оши́бка, про́мах; комбина́ция;

ни́жняя ю́бка, листо́к; (*bot.*) побе́г; (*mar.*) э́ллинг; ~ *knot* скользя́щий у́зел; ~*shod* небре́жный; ~ *, the pen* опи́ска; ~ *of the tongue* огово́рка; *give the* ~ ускольза́ть от; ¶ *v.i*, скользи́ть; ~ *away* ускольза́ть; ~ *off* соска́льзывать; ускольза́ть; ~ *one's memory* вы́скочить (*pf.*) из па́мяти; slipper, *n*, ко́мнатная ту́фля; slipper *, a*, ско́льзкий; увёртливый.

slit, *n*, щель; про́резь; (продо́льный) разре́з; ¶ *v.t*, разреза́ть, де́лать ра́зрез в.

slither, *v.i*, скользи́ть; ска́тываться.

sliver, *n*, ще́пка, лучи́на.

slobber, *n*, слюни́; ¶ *v.i*, пуска́ть слю́ни; ~ing, *a*, слюня́вый.

sloe, *n*, тёрн.

slog, *v.i*, упо́рно рабо́тать, корпе́ть.

slogan, *n*, ло́зунг.

sloop, *n*, шлюп.

slop, *n*, пере́дник; (широ́кая) спецоде́жда; *pl*, помо́и; ¶ *v.t*, (*& i.*), пролива́ть(ся); ~ *pail* помо́йное ведро́.

slope, *n*, накло́н, склон; косого́р; (*rly.*) отко́с; ¶ *v.t* (*& i.*), наклоня́ть(ся); sloping, *a*, накло́нный, пока́тый.

sloppy, *a*, мо́крый, гря́зный; неря́шливый.

slot, *n*, отве́рстие, проре́з, щель; ~ *machine* автома́т.

sloth, *n*, лень; (*zool.*) лени́вец; ~ful, *a*, лени́вый.

slouch, *n*, суту́лость; лени́вая похо́дка/по́за; ~ *hat* шля́па с широ́кими опу́щенными поля́ми; ¶ *v.i*, суту́литься; неуклю́же держа́ться.

slough, *n*, боло́то, тряси́на; о́мут; ¶ *v.i*, линя́ть; шелуши́ться; *v.t*, сбра́сывать; ~ *off* избавля́ться от.

Slovak, *a*, слова́цкий; ¶ *n*, словя́к, -а́чка.

sloven, *n*, неря́ха; ~liness, *n*, неря́шливость; ~ly, *a*, неря́шливый.

slow, *a*, ме́дленный, медли́тельный; тупо́й; ску́чный: *the clock is* ~ часы́ отстаю́т; ¶ *v.t*, (*& i.*): ~ *down* замедля́ть(ся); ~ly, *ad*, ме́дленно, ти́хо; ~ness, *n*, ме́дленность, медли́тельность; ту́пость.

sludge, *n*, ти́на, ил.

slug, *n*, слизня́к; пу́ля; (*print*) отли́тая на линоти́пе строка́.

sluggard, *n*, лежебо́ка, лентя́й; **sluggish**, *a*, медли́тельный; вя́лый, ине́ртный.

sluice, *n*, шлюз; промы́вка; промыва́льный жёлоб; ~ *gate* шлю́зные воро́та; ¶ *v.t*, залива́ть; промыва́ть.

slum, *n*, трущо́ба.

slumber, *n*, сон, дремо́та; ¶ *v.i*, спать, дрема́ть.

slump, *n*, ре́зкое паде́ние спро́са/ цен; ¶ *v.i*, ре́зко па́дать; тяжело́ опуска́ться.

slur, *n*, пятно́; сли́ние (овуко́в); *(mus.)* лега́то; ¶ *v.i*, нея́сно произноси́ть; неразбо́рчиво писа́ть; ~ *over* сма́зывать.

slush, *n*, сля́коть; ~у, *a*, сля́котный.

slut, *n*, неря́ха; девчо́нка; **sluttish**, *a*, неря́шливый.

sly, *a*, лука́вый, хи́трый; лицеме́рный; *on the* ~ тайко́м; ~**ness**, *n*, лука́вство; лицеме́рие.

smack, *n*, шлепо́к, уда́р; звук уда́ра; чмо́канье *(of lips)*; зво́нкий поцелу́й; вкус, при́вкус; однома́чтовое рыболо́вное су́дно, смэк; ¶ *v.t*, хло́пать, шлёпать; чмо́кать (губа́ми); ~ *of* отдава́ть/па́хнуть *(inst.)*

small, *a*, ма́ленький, ма́лый, ме́лкий; ~ *beer* мелкота́; ~ *change* ме́лочь; ~ *fry* мелюзга́, мелкота́; ~*holder* ме́лкий со́бственник; ~ *hours* глубо́кая ночь; ~*pox* о́спа; ~ *talk* све́тский разгово́р; *feel* ~ чу́вствовать себя́ унизи́тельно; *look* ~ име́ть глу́пый вид; ~ *of the back* поясни́ца; ~**ness**, *n*, ма́ленький разме́р, миниатю́рность; незначи́тельность.

smart, *a*, мо́дный, наря́дный, элега́нтный; ре́зкий, бы́стрый; остроу́мный; ¶ *n*, ре́зкая боль; ¶ *v.i*, боле́ть; ~**en**, *v.t*, прихора́шивать; ~**ly**, *ad*, наря́дно, с ши́ком; прово́рно; ~**ness**, *n*, наря́дность, шик; быстрота́; остроу́мие.

smash, *n*, столкнове́ние; катастро́фа; сокруши́тельный уда́р; гро́хот; *(fin.)* банкро́тство; ¶ *v.t. (& i.)*, разбива́ть(ся), лома́ть(ся); ~ *into* ста́лкиваться с; ~**er**, *n*, не́что сногсшиба́тельное; ~**ing**, *n*, битьё вдре́безги; разгро́м; ¶ *a*, сокруши́тельный; *(coll.)* сногсшиба́тельный.

smattering, *n*, пове́рхностное зна́ние.

smear, *n*, пятно́; клевета́; ¶ *v.t*, ма́зать, па́чкать.

smell, *n*, за́пах; обоня́ние, нюх; ¶ *v.t*, чу́вствовать за́пах *(gen.)*, ню́хать; *v.i*, па́хнуть; ~ *out* разню́хивать; ~ *a rat* чу́ять недо́брое; ~*ing salts* ню́хательная соль.

smelt, *n*, распла́вленный мета́лл, пла́вка; ¶ *v.t*, пла́вить *(ore)*, выплавля́ть *(metal)*; ~**ing**, *n*, плавле́ние; вы́плавка; ~ *works* пла́вильня, пла́вильный заво́д.

smile, *n*, улы́бка; ¶ *v.i*, улыба́ться; **smiling**, *a*, улыба́ющийся.

smirch, *n*, пятно́; ¶ *v.t*, па́чкать, пятна́ть.

smirk, *n*, самодово́льная улы́бка; ¶ *v.i*, ухмыля́ться.

smite, *v.t*, удара́ть; поража́ть.

smith, *n*, кузне́ц; ~у, *n*, ку́зница.

smitten, *p.p.*: ~ *with fear* охва́ченный стра́хом; ~ *with love* влюблённый.

smock, *n*, (де́тский) хала́т; же́нская руба́шка; рабо́чий хала́т.

smoke, *n*, дым; ¶ *v.t*, кури́ть; копти́ть; окури́вать; *v.i*, кури́ть; дыми́ть; копти́ть; ~ *out* выку́ривать; ~**less**, *a*, безды́мный; **smoker**, *n*, куря́щий; *(carriage)* ваго́н для куря́щих; **smoking**, *n*, куре́ние; *no* ~ кури́ть воспреща́ется.

smooth, *a*, гла́дкий, ро́вный; пла́вный; споко́йный; вкра́дчивый, льсти́вый; нете́рпкий *(wine)*; ~*faced* гла́дко вы́бритый; ~*tongued* сладкоре́чивый; ¶ *v.t*, пригла́живать; сгла́живать; де́лать ро́вным; полирова́ть, шлифова́ть; ~ *over* смягча́ть; успока́ивать; ~**ly**, *ad*, гла́дко; пла́вно; ~**ness**, *n*, гла́дкость, ро́вность; пла́вность.

smother, *v.t*, души́ть; туши́ть; подавля́ть.

smoulder, *v.i*, тлеть.

smudge, *n*, гря́зное пятно́; ¶ *v.t*, ма́зать, па́чкать.

smug, *a*, самодово́льный.

smuggle, *v.t*, нелега́льно ввози́ть; ~**r**, *n*, контрабанди́ст; **smuggling**, *n*, контраба́нда.

smut, *n*, са́жа, грязь; **smutty**, *a*, гря́зный; непристо́йный.

snack, *n*, заку́ска; ~ *bar* заку́сочная, буфе́т.

snag, *n*, коря́га; пенёк; *(fig.)* заг-
во́здка.

snail, *n*, ули́тка; *at a ~'s pace* чере-
па́шьим ша́гом.

snake, *n*, змея́; **snaky,** *a*, змеи́ный;
изви́листый.

snap, *n*, щёлканье, треск; защёлка,
щеко́лда; *(phot.)* момента́льный
сни́мок; *(tech.)* зажи́м; *cold ~*
внеза́пное похолода́ние; ¶ *v.t*,
щёлкать *(inst.)*; защёлкивать;
куса́ть; лома́ть; *(phot.)* снима́ть;
v.i, щёлкать; лома́ться; *~ at*
огрыза́ться на; *~dragon* льви́ный
зев; *~pish*, *a*, куса́ющийся
(dog); раздражи́тельный; *~shot*,
n, вы́стрел без прице́ла; момен-
та́льный сни́мок.

snare, *n*, западня́, лову́шка; ¶ *v.t*,
лови́ть в лову́шку.

snarl, *n*, ворча́ние; рыча́ние; ¶ *v.i*,
ворча́ть; рыча́ть.

snatch, *n*, хвата́нье, рыво́к; обры́-
вок, отры́вок; ¶ *v.t*, хвата́ть,
схва́тывать.

sneak, *n*, проны́ра; подле́ц; я́бед-
ник; *~thief* вори́шка; ¶ *v.i*,
кра́сться; доноси́ть, я́бедничать;
~ away ускольза́ть.

sneer, *n*, усме́шка; насме́шка; ¶ *v.i*,
усмеха́ться; насме́шливо улы-
ба́ться; *~ at* насмеха́ться над.

sneeze, *n*, чиха́нье; ¶ *v.i*, чиха́ть.

sniff, *n*, вдох; сопе́ние; (презри́-
тельное) фы́рканье; ¶ *v.t*, нюха́ть;
v.i, сопе́ть; презри́тельно фы́р-
кать.

snigger, *n*, хихи́канье; ¶ *v.i*, хихи́-
кать.

snip, *n*, надре́з, разре́з; отре́зок; ¶
v.t, ре́зать (но́жницами).

snipe, *n*, бека́с.

sniper, *n*, сна́йпер.

snippet, *n*, отре́зок; обры́вок *(information)*.

snivel, *v.i*, хны́кать; пуска́ть со́пли;
~ler, *n*, ню́ня.

snob, *n*, сноб; *~bish*, *a*, сноби́ст-
ский; *~bery*, *n*, сноби́зм.

snooze, *n*, коро́ткий сон; ¶ *v.i*,
вздремну́ть *(pf.)*, спать.

snore, *n*, храп; ¶ *v.i*, храпе́ть.

snort, *n*, фы́рканье; ¶ *v.i*, фы́ркать.

snout, *n*, ры́ло, мо́рда.

snow, *n*, снег; *~ball* снежо́к, снежный ком; *~blind* ослеплённый
сверка́ющим сне́гом; *~bound* за-
несённый сне́гом; *~capped* пок-
ры́тый сне́гом; *~drift* сугро́б; *~-
drop* подсне́жник; *~fall* снегопа́д;
~flake снежи́нка; *pl*, хло́пья
сне́га; *~man* снежная ба́ба; *~-
plough* снегоочисти́тель; *~storm*
мете́ль, бура́н; *~white* белосне́ж-
ный; ¶ *v.i*: *it ~s* идёт снег; *~y*,
a, снежный.

snub, *n*, оскорбле́ние, пренебрежи́-
тельное обхожде́ние; вы́говор;
отка́з; ¶ *a*, вздёрнутый; ¶ *v.t*,
оскорбля́ть; отка́зывать *(dat.)*;
оса́живать, де́лать вы́говор *(dat.)*.

snuff, *n*, ню́хательный таба́к; нага́р
на свече́; *~box* табаке́рка; ¶ *v.t*,
туши́ть; снима́ть нага́р (со свечи́)

snuffle, *n*, сопе́ние; ¶ *v.i*, сопе́ть.

snug, *a*, ую́тный; *~gle*, *v.i*, при-
жима́ться, ую́тно устра́иваться,
уку́тываться.

so, *ad. & c*, так; таки́м о́бразом;
насто́лько; ита́к, поэ́тому; *~ as
to* с тем что́бы; *~ far* насто́лько;
in ~ far поско́льку; *~ long!*
пока́!; *~ that* с тем что́бы; *~
that's* так-то вот; *and ~ on*
и так да́лее; *~ be it* быть по сему́;
if ~ раз так, в тако́м слу́чае; *~
much ~* до тако́й сте́пени; *and
~ тако́й-то*; *~ ~* так себе́, ничего́
осо́бенного; *I don't think ~* я не
ду́маю; *a month or ~* о́коло ме́сяца;
~-called так называ́емый.

soak, *n*, прома́чивание, мо́чка; ¶
v.t, мочи́ть; нама́чивать, выма́чи-
вать, прома́чивать; *v.i*, пропи́ты-
ваться; *~ up* впи́тывать, вса́сы-
вать; *I am ~ing wet* я промо́к
наскво́зь.

soap, *n*, мы́ло; *~ bubble* мы́льный
пузы́рь; *~ dish* мы́льница; *~
suds* мы́льная пе́на; ¶ *v.t*, намы́-
ливать; *~y*, *a*, мы́льный.

soar, *v.i*, пари́ть, высоко́ лета́ть;
плани́ровать.

sob, *n*, рыда́ние; ¶ *v.i*, рыда́ть.

sober, *a*, тре́звый; рассуди́тельный;
споко́йный; ¶ *v.t. (& i.)*, про-
трезвля́ть(ся); *(fig.)* отрезвля́ть;
sobriety, *n*, тре́звость.

sobriquet, *n*, кли́чка, про́звище.

soccer, *n*, футбо́л.

sociable, *a*, общи́тельный.

social, *a*, обще́ственный, социа́ль-
ный; ¶ *n*, ве́чер, собра́ние, вече-
ри́нка; *~ism*, *n*, социали́зм; *~ist*, *n*,
социали́ст; ¶ *a*, социалисти́чес-
кий; *~ization*, *n*, обобществле́ние;

социализа́ция; ~ize, *v.t,* обоб-ществля́ть, социализи́ровать; **society,** *n,* о́бщество; обще́ствен-ность; «свет», све́тское о́бщество; **sociology,** *n,* социоло́гия.

sock, *n,* носо́к.

socket, *n,* углубле́ние, гнездо́; впа́-дина *(eye);* (light) патро́н; *(plug)* розе́тка; *(tech.)* му́фта.

sod, *n,* дёрн.

soda, *n,* со́да; ~ *fountain* сатура́тор; ~ *water* со́довая вода́.

sodden, *a,* промо́кший; сыро́й.

sodium, *n,* на́трий.

sofa, *n,* дива́н, софа́.

soft, *a,* мя́гкий; не́жный; нея́ркий *(colour);* ти́хий *(sound);* ги́бкий, ко́вкий *(metal);* (coll.) придурко-ва́тый; ~-*boiled egg* яйцо́ всмя́тку; ~ *goods* тексти́льные изде́лия; ~-*hearted* мягкосерде́чный; ~ *water* мя́гкая вода́; ~en, *v.t.* (& *i.*), смягча́ть(ся); ~ening, *n,* смяг-че́ние; ~ness, *n,* мя́гкость; не́ж-ность; ги́бкость, ко́вкость.

soggy, *a,* мо́крый, сыро́й.

soil, *n,* по́чва; *native* ~ ро́дина; ¶ *v.t,* грязни́ть, па́чкать; *(fig.)* зап-ятна́ть *(pf.);* ~ed, *a,* гря́зный, запя́тнанный.

soirée, *n,* вечери́нка, ве́чер.

sojourn, *n,* пребыва́ние; ¶ *v.i,* вре́-менно жить, прожива́ть.

solace, *n,* утеше́ние; ¶ *v.t,* утеша́ть.

solar, *a,* со́лнечный.

solder, *n,* припо́й, спа́йка; ¶ *v.t,* пая́ть, спа́ивать; ~ing, *n,* па́йка; ~ *iron* пая́льник.

soldier, *n,* солда́т, вое́нный; ~ing, *n,* вое́нная слу́жба; ~ly, *a,* во́ин-ский, хра́брый; ~y, *n,* солда́ты, вое́нные.

sole, *a,* еди́нственный, исключи́тель-ный; ~ *agent* еди́нственный аге́нт; ~ *right* исключи́тельное пра́во; ¶ *n,* подо́шва, подмётка *(shoe);* морско́й язы́к *(fish).*

solecism, *n,* солеци́зм.

solely, *ad,* еди́нственно, то́лько, исключи́тельно.

solemn, *a,* торже́ственный; ва́жный; серьёзный; ~ity, *n,* торжество́, торже́ственность, ва́жность; ~ize, *v.t,* торже́ственно отмеча́ть, пра́зд-новать.

sol-fa, *n,* сольфе́джио.

solicit, *v.t,* проси́ть, выпра́шивать; хода́тайствовать о; пристава́ть

к; ~ation, *n,* про́сьба, хода́тайст-во; пристава́ние; ~or, *n,* адвока́т, стря́пчий; ~ *General* гла́вный прокуро́р; ~ous, *a,* забо́тливый; ~ude, *n,* забо́тливость.

solid, *a,* твёрдый; соли́дный; убе-ди́тельный; сплошно́й; ¶ *n,* твёр-дое те́ло; *(maths)* геометри́ческое те́ло; твёрдая пи́ща; ~arity, *n,* солида́рность, сплочённость; ~ify, *v.t,* де́лать твёрдым; *v.i,* тверде́ть, застыва́ть; ~ity, *n,* твёрдость; ~ly, *ad,* твёрдо.

soliloquize, *v.i,* говори́ть с сами́м собо́й; произноси́ть моноло́г; **soli-loquy,** *n,* моноло́г.

solitaire, *n,* солите́р; пасья́нс; **soli-tary,** *a,* одино́кий, уединённый; ~ *confinement* одино́чное заклю-че́ние; **solitude,** *n,* одино́чество; уедине́ние.

solo, *n,* со́ло; ~ist, *n,* соли́ст.

solstice, *n,* солнцестоя́ние.

soluble, *a,* раствори́мый; разреши́-мый; **solution,** *n,* раство́р; реше́-ние, разреше́ние; **solve,** *v.t,* ре-ша́ть.

solvency, *n,* платёжеспосо́бность; **solvent,** *a,* платёжеспосо́бный; растворя́ющий; ¶ *n,* раствори́-тель.

sombre, *a,* мра́чный.

some, *a,* како́й-либо, како́й-нибудь, како́й-то; не́который; не́сколько; ~ *people* не́которые лю́ди; ~ *time ago* не́которое вре́мя тому́ наза́д, неда́вно; ~ *two thousand men* о́коло двух ты́сяч челове́к; ¶ *pn,* не́ко-торые; не́которое коли́чество; ~ ... *others* ... одни́ ... дру-ги́е ...; **somebody** & **someone,** *pn,* кто́-нибудь, кто́-то; *be* ~ быть ва́жной персо́ной; **some-how,** *ad,* ка́к-нибудь; ка́к-то; почему́-то.

somersault, *n,* прыжо́к кувырко́м; *(fig.)* по́лный переворо́т; ¶ *v.i,* кувырка́ться.

something, *pn,* что́-либо, что́-нибудь, что́-то, не́что, ко́е-что; ~ *else* что́-нибудь/что́-то друго́е.

sometime, *ad,* когда́-нибудь, когда́-то; не́когда; ~s *иногда́.*

somewhat, *ad,* до не́которой сте́-пени, не́сколько.

somewhere, *ad,* где́-нибудь, где́-то; куда́-нибудь, куда́-то; ~ *else* где́-нибудь/где́-то в друго́м ме́сте.

somnambulism, *n*, лунати́зм; **somnambulist**, *n*, луна́тик; **somnolent**, *a*, сонли́вый, дре́млющий.

son, *n*, сын; ~-*in-law* зять.

sonata, *n*, сона́та.

song, *n*, пе́сня; пе́ние; *for a* ~ за бесце́нок; ~**ster**, *n*, певе́ц; пе́вчая пти́ца.

sonnet, *n*, соне́т.

sonorous, *a*, звучный.

soon, *ad*, вско́ре, ско́ро; ра́но; *as* ~ *as* как то́лько; *as* ~ *as possible* как мо́жно скоре́е; ~*er or later* ра́но и́ли по́здно.

soot, *n*, са́жа, ко́поть.

soothe, *v.t*, успока́ивать; облегча́ть *(pain)*; **soothing**, *a*, успокои́тельный, успока́ивающий.

soothsayer, *n*, предска́зате́ль.

sooty, *a*, закопчённый; покры́тый са́жей; чёрный как са́жа.

sop, *n*, кусо́чек; *(fig.)* пода́чка.

sophism, *n*, софи́зм; **sophist**, *n*, софи́ст; **sophisticated**, *a*, изощрённый, утончённый; искушённый в жите́йских дела́х.

soporific, *a*, усыпля́ющий; ¶ *n*, снотво́рное.

soprano, *n*, сопра́но.

sorcerer, *n*, волше́бник, колду́н; **sorceress**, *n*, колду́нья; **sorcery**, *n*, колдовство́.

sordid, *a*, гря́зный, по́длый; жа́лкий; ~**ness**, *n*, по́длость; убо́жество.

sore, *a*, больно́й; чувстви́тельный; оби́женный; *I have a* ~ *throat* у меня́ боли́т го́рло; ¶ *n*, боля́чка, я́зва.

sorrel, *n*, гнедо́й; ¶ *n*, гнеда́я ло́шадь; *(bot.)* щаве́ль.

sorrow, *n*, го́ре, печа́ль, скорбь; *to my* ~ к моему́ сожале́нию; ¶ *v.i*, горева́ть; ~**ful**, *a*, ско́рбный, печа́льный; ~**fully**, *ad*, печа́льно; **sorry**, *a*, сожале́ющий; жа́лкий; ~ *sight* жа́лкое зре́лище; *be* ~ (со)жале́ть; *I am so* ~ *for them* мне так жаль их; *I am* ~*!* прости́те!; винова́т!.

sort, *n*, сорт, вид, род; *a good* ~ сла́вный ма́лый; ¶ *v.t*, сортирова́ть; классифици́ровать; разбира́ть; ~**er**, *n*, сортиро́вщик.

sortie, *n*, вы́лазка.

sot, *n*, го́рький пья́ница; ~**tish**, *a*, отупе́вший от пья́нства.

sought-after, *a*, популя́рный.

soul, *n*, душа́; челове́к, существо́; ~ *of (fig.)* воплоще́ние; *upon my* ~ че́стное сло́во!; ~**ful**, *a*, эмоциона́льный; ~**less**, *a*, безду́шный.

sound, *n*, звук, шум; *(mar.)* узкий проли́в; *(med.)* зонд; ¶ *a*, звуково́й, здоро́вый, кре́пкий, про́чный; ~ *barrier* звуково́й барье́р; ¶ *v.t*, звони́ть (в ко́локол); бить *(alarm)*; высту́кивать, выслу́шивать *(med.)*; измеря́ть глубину́ *(gen.)*; зонди́ровать *(also fig.)*; ~**ing**, *a*, звуча́щий, зво́нкий; ¶ *n*, измере́ние глубины́; зонди́рование; ~ *board* резона́тор; ~ *lead* лот; ~**ly**, *ad*, кре́пко; про́чно; ~**ness**, *n*, кре́пкость; про́чность.

soup, *n*, суп; ~-*plate* глубо́кая таре́лка; ~-*tureen* су́пница; *in the* ~ в затрудне́нии.

sour, *a*, ки́слый *(also fig.)*; раздражи́тельный; *turn* ~ проки́снуть; ~ *grapes!* зе́лен виногра́д!; ¶ *v.t*, озлобля́ть.

source, *n*, исто́чник *(also fig.)*; верхо́вье, исто́к; *have from a good* ~ получа́ть из надёжного исто́чника.

sourness, *n*, кислота́; раздражи́тельность.

souse, *v.t*, маринова́ть солить; окуна́ть.

soutane, *n*, сута́на.

south, *n*, юг; ¶ *a*, ю́жный; ~-*east* юго-восто́к; ~-*west* юго-за́пад; ~**erly**, & ~**ern**, *a*, ю́жный; ~**erner**, *n*, южа́н|ин, -ка; ~**ward**, *ad*, к ю́гу, на юг.

souvenir, *n*, сувени́р, па́мятка.

sou'-wester, *n*, юго-за́падный ве́тер.

sovereign, *n*, мона́рх/, -иня; совере́н *(coin)*; ¶ *a*, верхо́вный, суверѐнный; ~**ty**, *n*, суверените́т; верхо́вная власть.

Soviet, *a*, сове́тский; ~ *Union* Сове́тский Сою́з; ¶ *n*, сове́т.

sovkhoz, *n*, совхо́з.

sow, *n*, свинья́.

sow, *v.t*, се́ять; засева́ть; ~ *one's wild oats* перебеси́ться *(pf.)*; бу́рно проводи́ть вре́мя; ~**er**, *n*, се́ятель; се́ялка; ~**ing**, *n*, посе́в; засе́в; ~ *time* сев.

soya bean, *n*, со́евый боб.

spa, *n*, куро́рт.

space, *n*, простра́нство; расстоя́ние; промежу́ток *(also time)*; *(print.)* шпа́ция; ¶ *v.t*, оставля́ть промежу́тки/пробе́лы в; расставля́ть с промежу́тками; **spacious**, *a*, просто́рный, обши́рный, широ́кий; **spaciousness**, *n*, просто́р(ность), обши́рность.

spade, *n*, лопа́та; за́ступ; *(pl, cards.)* пи́ки; *call a ~ a ~* называ́ть ве́щи свои́ми имена́ми.

spaghetti, *n*, спаге́тти.

span, *n*, пядь; расстоя́ние; промежу́ток вре́мени; проле́т *(of bridge)*; *(rly.)* перего́н; разма́х *(wings)*; ¶ *v.t*, измеря́ть; охва́тывать; перекрыва́ть; *~ a river* стро́ить мост че́рез ре́ку.

spangle, *n*, блёстка; *~d*, *a*, укра́шенный блёстками, блестя́щий.

Spaniard, *n*, испа́н|ец, -ка.

spaniel, *n*, спанье́ль.

Spanish, *a*, испа́нский; ¶ *n*, испа́нский язы́к.

spank, *v.t*, шлёпать; ¶ *n*, шлепо́к; *~ing*, *n*, шлёпание, трёпка.

spanner, *n*, га́ечный ключ; перекла́дина; *adjustable ~* раздвижно́й га́ечный ключ.

spar, *n*, *(mar.)* перекла́дина; *(avia.)* лонжеро́н; *(min.)* шпат; ¶ *v.i*, бокси́ровать; *(fig.)* перепира́ться.

spare, *a*, запасно́й, запа́сный, резе́рвный; ли́шний; свобо́дный; худоща́вый; *~ room* ко́мната для госте́й; *~ time* свобо́дное вре́мя; *~ wheel* запасно́е колесо́; ¶ *v.t*, щади́ть; жале́ть; уделя́ть *(time)*; **sparing**, *a*, ску́дный, недоста́точный; бережли́вый, уме́ренный.

spark, *n*, и́скра; вспы́шка, про́блеск; *~ of life* при́знаки жи́зни; ¶ *v.i*, искри́ться, вспы́хивать; *~ing plug* запа́льная свеча́; *~le*, *n*, и́скорка, сверка́ние; ¶ *v.i*, искри́ться, сверка́ть; *~ling*, *a*, искри́стый, сверка́ющий.

sparrow, *n*, воробе́й; *~-hawk* я́стреб-перепеля́тник.

sparse, *a*, ре́дкий.

Spartan, *a*, спарта́нский.

spasm, *n*, спа́зма, судоро́га; *(fig.)* при́ступ; *~odic*, *a*, спазмати́ческий; преры́вистый.

spate, *n*, внеза́пное наводне́ние, внеза́пный разли́в.

spatial, *a*, простра́нственный.

spats, *n.pl*, ге́тры.

spatter, *n*, бры́зги, бры́зганье; ¶ *v.t*, бры́згать, забры́згивать.

spatula, *n*, лопа́точка, шпа́тель.

spavin, *n*, шпат.

spawn, *n*, икра́; пото́мство; ¶ *v.i*, мета́ть икру́; плоди́ться, размножа́ться; *~ing*, *n*, не́рест.

speak, *v.t. & i*, говори́ть; выска́зывать; выступа́ть с ре́чью; *~ for itself* говори́ть само́ за себя́; *~ one's mind* выска́зываться открове́нно; *so to ~* так сказа́ть; *~er*, *n*, ора́тор, докла́дчик; *(radio)* ди́ктор; *(parl.)* спи́кер; *speaking trumpet* ру́пор; *speaking tube* перегово́рная тру́бка.

spear, *n*, копьё; гарпу́н; *~mint* мя́та (курча́вая); мя́тная конфе́та; ¶ *v.t*, пронза́ть (копьём).

special, *a*, специа́льный, осо́бый, осо́бенный; экстренный, сро́чный; *~ delivery* сро́чная доста́вка; *~ist*, *n*, специали́ст; *~ity*, *n*, специа́льность; *~ize*, *v.i*, специализи́роваться; *~ly*, *ad*, специа́льно, осо́бенно.

specie, *n*, зво́нкая моне́та.

species, *n*, вид, род, поро́да; **specific**, *a*, осо́бый, специфи́ческий; *(phys.)* уде́льный; ¶ *n*, специфи́ческое ка́чество; *~ally*, *ad*, осо́бо, специфи́чески; *~ation*, *n*, специфика́ция; техни́ческие усло́вия/ тре́бования; инстру́кция; дета́ль; **specify**, *v.t*, то́чно определя́ть, уточня́ть; устана́вливать техни́ческими усло́виями.

specimen, *n*, образе́ц, обра́зчик; экземпля́р.

specious, *a*, благови́дный, показно́й.

speck, *n*, кра́пинка, пя́тнышко; *(in eye)* сори́нка; ¶ *v.t*, пятна́ть, испещря́ть; **speckled**, *a*, кра́пчатый.

spectacle, *n*, зре́лище, спекта́кль; *pl*, очки́; **spectacular**, *a*, эффе́ктный; **spectator**, *n*, зри́тель, наблюда́тель.

spectral, *a*, при́зрачный; *(phys.)* спектра́льный; **spectre**, *n*, при́зрак.

spectrum, *n*, спектр.

speculate, *v.i*, размышля́ть; стро́ить дога́дки; спекули́ровать; **speculation**, *n*, размышле́ние, предположе́ние; спекуля́ция; **speculative**, *a*, умозри́тельный; спекуляти́вный; **speculator**, *n*, спекуля́нт.

speech, *n*, речь; го́вор; ди́кция; *make a ~* произноси́ть речь; *~-day* áктовый/торже́ственный день; ~-less, *a*, безмо́лвный, немо́й; ошело́мленный.

speed, *n*, ско́рость, быстрота́; *at full* ~ на по́лной ско́рости; по́лным хо́дом; ¶ *v.t*, ускоря́ть; подгоня́ть; соде́йствовать *(dat.)*; *v.i*, спеши́ть; е́хать сли́шком бы́стро; ~ily, *ad*, бы́стро, поспе́шно; ~iness, *n*, быстрота́, поспе́шность; прово́рность; ~ometer, *n*, спидо́метр; ~y, *a*, бы́стрый.

spell, *n*, заклина́ние; обая́ние; *under a* ~ зачаро́ванный; ~*bound* очаро́ванный; *short* ~ коро́ткий промежу́ток вре́мени; ¶ *v.t*, чита́ть по склада́м, произноси́ть по бу́квам; ~ing, *n*, правописа́ние, орфогра́фия; ~ *book* орфографи́ческий спра́вочник; а́збука.

spend, *v.t*, тра́тить, расхо́довать; проводи́ть *(time)*; ~*thrift*, *n*, мот, транжи́р; ¶ *a*, расточи́тельный; **spent**, *p.p. & a*, истощённый, израсхо́дованный.

sperm, *n*, спе́рма; ~-*whale* кашало́т; ~*aceti*, *n*, спермаце́т; ~*atozoon*, *n*, сперматозо́ид.

spew, *v.t*, блева́ть, изрыга́ть.

sphere, *n*, шар; глóбус; сфе́ра, о́бласть; **spherical**, *a*, шарообра́зный, сфери́ческий.

sphinx, *n*, сфинкс.

spice, *n*, пря́ность; *(fig.)* при́вкус, пика́нтность; ¶ *v.t*, приправля́ть; придава́ть пика́нтность *(dat.)*.

spick and span, *a*, опря́тный, с иго́лочки.

spicy, *a*, пря́ный; *(fig.)* пика́нтный.

spider, *n*, пау́к; ~'*s web* паути́на.

spike, *n*, остриё; гвоздь, шип; ¶ *v.t*, *(mil.)* забива́ть ершо́м; ~ *(someone's) guns* расстра́ивать за́мыслы *(gen.)*; **spiky**, *a*, заострённый, остроконе́чный; покры́тый остри́ями.

spill, *n*, паде́ние, несча́стный слу́чай; лучи́на; ¶ *v.t. (& i.)* прилива́ть(ся), разлива́ть(ся); рассыпа́ть(ся).

spin, *n*, круже́ние; прогу́лка (на маши́не); ~-*dryer* суши́лка; ¶ *v.t*, прясть; верте́ть, крути́ть; *v.i*, верте́ться, враща́ться, крути́ться; ~ *out* растя́гивать.

spinach, *n*, шпина́т.

spinal, *a*, спинно́й

spindle, *n*, веретено́; *(tech.)* вал, ось, шпи́ндель; ~-*legged* долговя́зый.

spine, *n*, спинно́й хребе́т; корешо́к *(book)*; *(bot.)* игла́, шип; ~less, *a*, беспозвоно́чный; *(fig.)* мягкоте́лый.

spinet, *n*, спине́т.

spinner, *n*, пряди́ль/щик, ~щица; пряди́льная маши́на.

spinney, *n*, ро́ща.

spinning, *n*, пряде́ние; ~ *mill* пряди́льная фа́брика; ~ *top* волчо́к; ~ *wheel* пря́лка.

spinster, *n*, незаму́жняя же́нщина

spiral, *a*, винтово́й, винтообра́зный, спира́льный; ¶ *n*, спира́ль; ~ *staircase* винтова́я ле́стница.

spire, *n*, шпиль, шпиц.

spirit, *n*, дух; душа́; привиде́ние; оживле́ние, задо́р; *pl*, спиртны́е напи́тки; ~ *lamp* спирто́вка; ~ *level* спиртово́й у́ровень; *high* ~s припо́днятое настрое́ние; ¶ *v.t*: ~ *away* та́йно убира́ть/похища́ть; ~ed, *a*, живо́й, энерги́чный, горя́чий *(horse)*; ~ual, *a*, духо́вный; одухотворённый; ~ualism, *n*, спиритуали́зм; ~ualist, *n*, спирити́ст; ~uality, *n*, духо́вность; одухотворённость. ~ually, *ad*, духо́вно.

spit, *n*, ве́ртел; плево́к, плева́ние; *(geog.)* коса́, о́тмель; ¶ *v.i*, плева́ть; шипе́ть *(cat)*; треща́ть *(fire)*; мороси́ть *(rain)*.

spite, *n*, зло́ба, злость; *in* ~ *of* вопреки́, несмотря́ на; ¶ *v.t*, досажда́ть *(dat.)*; ~ful, *a*, злора́дный, недоброжела́тельный.

spitfire, *n*, злю́чка.

spittle, *n*, плево́к, слюна́; **spittoon**, *n*, плева́тельница.

splash, *n*, плеск; бры́зганье, бры́зги; пятно́; ~*board* крыло́; ¶ *v.t*, бры́згать, забры́згивать; плеска́ть на; *v.i*, бры́згаться, плеска́ться; шлёпать (по воде́); ~ *into* бултыхну́ться *(pf.)* в.

spleen, *n*, *(med.)* селезёнка; сплин, зло́ба.

splendid, *a*, великоле́пный, роско́шный; **splendour**, *n*, великоле́пие, ро́скошь.

splice, *n*, *(mar.)* спле́сень; *(build.)* стык, соедине́ние внакро́й; ¶ *v.t*, *(mar.)* спле́снивать; сра́щивать, соединя́ть внакро́й.

splint, *n*, лубо́к; ши́на.

splinter, *n*, оско́лок, ще́пка; зано́за; ¶ *v.t.* *(& i.)* раска́лывать(ся), расщепля́ть(ся).

split, *n*, тре́щина, щель; раско́л; ¶ *v.t*, коло́ть, раска́лывать; расщепля́ть; дели́ть на ча́сти; *v.i*, раска́лываться, расщепля́ться, тре́скаться; ~ one's sides laughing надрыва́ться от хо́хота; my head is ~ting у меня́ голова́ раска́лывается от бо́ли.

splutter, *n*, бры́зги; лопота́нье; ¶ *v.i*, бры́згать слюно́й; лопота́ть; треща́ть.

spoil, *n*, добы́ча, награ́бленное добро́; ¶ *v.t*, по́ртить; балова́ть *(child)*; расстра́ивать; *v.i*, по́ртиться; ~ sport тот, кто по́ртит удово́льствие; ~t, *p.p.* & *a*, испо́рченный; избало́ванный.

spoke, *n*, спи́ца *(wheel)*; перекла́дина; put a ~ in his wheel ста́вить ему́ па́лки в колёса.

spokesman, *n*, ора́тор, представи́тель.

spoliation, *n*, грабёж, захва́т; *(law)* уничтоже́ние/искаже́ние докуме́нта.

sponge, *n*, гу́бка; ~ cake бискви́тный торт; throw in the ~ призна-ва́ть себя́ побеждённым; ¶ *v.t*, вытира́ть/мыть гу́бкой; *v.i*, жить на чужо́й счёт; ~r, *n*, парази́т, нахле́бник; **spongy**, *a*, гу́бчатый, по́ристый.

sponsor, *n*, поручи́тель; крёстн|ый оте́ц, -ая мать; организа́тор; фи́рма, субсиди́рующая ра́дио/телеви́дение; ¶ *v.t*, руча́ться за; подде́рживать, субсиди́ровать; организо́вывать.

spontaneity, *n*, непосре́дственность; стихи́йность, самопроизво́льность; **spontaneous**, *a*, непосре́дственный; стихи́йный, самопроизво́льный.

spook, *n*, привиде́ние.

spool, *n*, кату́шка, шпу́лька.

spoon, *n*, ло́жка; ¶ *v.t*, че́рпать ло́жкой; ~ful по́лная ло́жка.

spoor, *n*, след.

sporadic, *a*, споради́ческий.

sport, *n*, спорт; развлече́ние; *pl*, спорти́вные состяза́ния; *(bot.)* сла́вный ма́лый; *(bot.)* отклоне́ние; make ~ of высме́ивать; ¶ *v.t*, выставля́ть/носи́ть напока́з; *v.i*, игра́ть, весели́ться; резви́ться;

~ing, *a*, спорти́вный; охо́тничий; ~ive, *a*, игри́вый; ~sman, *n*, спортсме́н; охо́тник; рыболо́в; ~swoman, *n*, спортсме́нка.

spot, *n*, пятно́, кра́пинка; пры́щик; ме́сто; on the ~ на ме́сте; ¶ *v.t*, пятна́ть, па́чкать; замеча́ть; ~less, *a*, без еди́ного пя́тнышка; незапя́тнанный; безупре́чный; ~light, *n*, проже́ктор; *(fig.)* центр внима́ния; ¶ *v.t*, освеща́ть; ста́вить в центр внима́ния; ~ted, *p.p.* & *a*, пятни́стый, кра́пчатый; запя́тнанный; ~ter, *n*, наво́дчик; ~ty, *a*, пятни́стый; прыща́вый.

spouse, *n*, супру́г, супру́га.

spout, *n*, но́сик *(kettle)*; водосто́чная труба́, жёлоб; струя́; ¶ *v.t*, пуска́ть струёй; изверга́ть; *v.i*, бить струёй, струи́ться; разглаго́льствовать.

sprain, *n*, растяже́ние; ¶ *v.t*, растя́гивать.

sprat, *n*, ки́лька, шпрот.

sprawl, *v.i*, растя́гиваться, па́дать; сиде́ть разваля́сь.

spray, *n*, ве́тка, побе́г; бры́зги, водяна́я пыль; жи́дкость для пульвериза́ции; распыли́тель, пульвериза́тор; ¶ *v.t*, обры́згивать, опыля́ть; распыля́ть; ~er, *n*, распыли́тель, пульвериза́тор.

spread, *n*, распростране́ние; разма́х *(wings)*; угоще́ние, пир; па́ста; ¶ *v.t.* *(& i.)*, развёртывать(ся), распространя́ть(ся), расстила́ть(ся); нама́зывать.

spree, *n*, весе́лье, кутёж; go on a ~ кути́ть.

sprig, *n*, ве́точка; гвоздь, шти́фтик; *(fig.)* о́тпрыск.

sprightly, *a*, оживлённый, живо́й.

spring, *n*, весна́; прыжо́к; пружи́на, рессо́ра; упру́гость; исто́чник, родни́к, ключ; ¶ *a*, весе́нний; пружи́нный; ~board трампли́н; ~ mattress пружи́нный матра́ц; ~ tide сизиги́йный прили́в; ¶ *v.i*, пры́гать; пружи́нить; тре́скаться, коро́биться; ~ from брать нача́ло от, происходи́ть от; ~ a leak дава́ть течь; ~ up возника́ть; ~ a surprise де́лать сюрпри́з; ~y, *a*, упру́гий; пружи́нный.

sprinkle, *v.t*, бры́згать, обры́згивать; посыпа́ть; ~r, *n*, опры́скиватель, разбры́згиватель; **sprinkling**, *n*, обры́згивание; поли́вка.

sprint, *n*, бег на короткую дистанцию, спринт; ¶ *v.i*, бегать на короткую дистанцию, спринтовать; ~er, *n*, спринтер.

sprite, *n*, эльф.

sprout, *n*, отросток, побег; *pl*, брюссельская капуста; ¶ *v.i*, пускать ростки, расти.

spruce, *a*, нарядный, опрятный; ¶ *n*, ель.

spry, *a*, живой, проворный.

spud, *n*, мотыга; *(coll.)* картошка.

spume, *n*, пена; накипь; ¶ *v.i*, пениться.

spunk, *n*, мужество, пыл.

spur, *n*, шпора; *(geol.)* отрог, вершина; *(arch.)* выступ, контрфорс; *(fig.)* стимул; on the ~ of the moment под влиянием минуты; ¶ *v.t*, пришпоривать; ~ on подстрекать.

spurious, *a*, поддельный, подложный.

spurn, *v.t*, презрительно отказываться *(dat. or от)*; отталкивать.

spurt, *n*, струя; внезапное усилие, рывок; ¶ *v.i*, бить струёй; делать внезапное усилие; рвануться *(pf.)*.

sputum, *n*, слюна, мокрота.

spy, *n*, шпион; ~-glass подзорная труба; ~-hole глазок; ¶ *v.t*, замечать, видеть; *v.i*, шпионить; ~ on следить за; ~ out выслеживать, разведывать.

squabble, *n*, ссора; ¶ *v.i*, ссориться.

squad, *n*, группа; *(mil.)* отряд; отделение.

squadron, *n*, *(avia.)* эскадрилья; *(mar.)* эскадра; *(mil.)* эскадрон.

squalid, *a*, грязный; убогий.

squall, *n*, шквал; ¶ *v.i*, визжать, вопить; ~y, *a*, бурный, порывистый.

squalor, *n*, грязь; убожество.

squander, *v.t*, проматывать, расточать; ¶ *n*, мот, расточитель.

square, *n*, квадрат, прямоугольник; площадь, сквер; клетка; ¶ *a*, квадратный, прямоугольный; плотный *(meal)*; прямой, честный; *(coll.)* старомодный; ~-built коренастый; ~ foot квадратный фут; ~ root квадратный корень; two metres ~ два метра в длину и два в ширину; ¶ *v.t*, делать квадратным; оплачивать *(bill)*; согласовывать; *(maths)* возводить в

квадрат; *v.i*, согласовываться; ~ly, *ad*, прямо.

squash, *n*, давка, толпа; пюре, сок; игра в мяч (вроде тённиса); ¶ *v.t*, раздавливать, расплющивать, сжимать; *(fig.)* заставлять молчать.

squat, *a*, коренастый, приземистый; ¶ *v.i*, сидеть на корточках; припадать к земле; незаконно селиться на чужой земле, незаконно вселяться в дом.

squaw, *n*, индианка.

squawk, *n*, пронзительный крик; ¶ *v.i*, пронзительно кричать.

squeak, *n*, писк; скрип; ¶ *v.i*, пищать; скрипеть.

squeal, *n*, визг; ¶ *v.i*, визжать.

squeamish, *a*, брезгливый, щепетильный.

squeeze, *n*, сжатие; пожатие; давка, сдавливание; ¶ *v.t*, давить, сжимать; пожимать *(hand)*; ~ in впихивать, втискивать; ~ out выжимать, выдавливать; ~ through протискивать(ся).

squib, *n*, запал; петарда; пасквиль.

squid, *n*, каракатица, сепия.

squint, *n*, косоглазие; ~-eyed косой; ¶ *v.i*, косить, смотреть искоса.

squire, *n*, сквайр, помещик.

squirm, *v.i*, корчиться.

squirrel, *n*, белка.

squirt, *n*, струя; шприц; ¶ *v.t*, пускать струю на; спринцевать; *v.i*, бить струёй.

stab, *n*, удар (ножом); внезапная острая боль; ¶ *v.t*, колоть, ударять (ножом).

stability, *n*, устойчивость, прочность; стабильность; **stabilize**, *v.t*, стабилизировать; делать устойчивым; **stable**, *a*, устойчивый, прочный; стабильный; уравновешенный; ¶ *n*, конюшня, хлев; ~-man конюх; ¶ *v.t*, ставить в конюшню/хлев; держать в конюшне/хлеву.

stack, *n*, скирда, стог *(hay)*; куча, кипа *(paper, etc.)*; *(chimney)* дымовая труба; хранилище; *pl*, *(coll.)* масса; ¶ *v.t*, складывать в стог/кучу.

stadium, *n*, стадион.

staff, *n*, штат, личный состав, персонал; *(mil.)* штаб; посох, жезл; *(mus.)* нотные линейки; on the ~ в штате.

stag, *n*, олень-самец; ~-beetle жук-олень.

stage, *n*, сцена, подмостки, эстрада; платформа; стадия, фаза, этап; ~-manager режиссёр; go on the ~ делаться актёром; ¶ *v.t*, инсценировать, ставить; old stager бывалый человек.

stagger, *v.i*, шататься, идти шатаясь, качаться; *v.t*, шатать; ошеломлять; располагать в шахматном порядке; распределять с промежутками; ¶ *n*, шатание; ~ing, *a*, шатающийся; потрясающий.

stagnant, *a*, стоячий; инертный, косный; stagnate, *v.i*, застаиваться (water); (fig.) коснеть; stagnation, *n*, застой; (fig.) косность.

staid, *a*, благоразумный, степенный.

stain, *n*, пятно (also fig.); краска; ¶ *v.t*, пачкать, пятнать (also fig.); красить, окрашивать; ~ed glass цветное стекло; ~less, *a*, незапятнанный; ~ steel нержавеющая сталь.

stair, *n*, ступенька (лестницы); pl, лестница; ~case лестница; ~-rail лестничные перила; ~-rod стержень для укрепления лестничного ковра; flight of ~s лестничный марш.

stake, *n*, кол, столб; заклад, ставка (bet); pl, приз; (sport.) доля капитала; be at ~ быть поставленным на карту; burn at the ~ сжигать на костре.

stalactite, *n*, сталактит; **stalagmite**, *n*, сталагмит.

stale, *a*, чёрствый (bread); затхлый, несвежий; (fig.) избитый.

stalemate, *n*, пат; (fig.) тупик.

stalk, *n*, стебель; кочерыжка (cabbage); ¶ *v.t*, подкрадываться к; идти крадучись за; ~ing horse заслонная лошадь; (fig.) предлог.

stall, *n*, стойло (for horse); ларёк, прилавок; (theat.) кресло в партере; ¶ *v.t*, ставить в стойло; останавливать; *v.i*, застревать; мешкать; терять скорость.

stallion, *n*, жеребец.

stalwart, *a*, дюжий; стойкий; ¶ *n*, стойкий член (партии, etc.).

stamen, *n*, тычинка.

stamina, *n*, выносливость, жизненная энергия.

stammer, *n*, заикание; ¶ *v.t*, произносить заикаясь; *v.i*, заикаться; ~er, *n*, заика.

stamp, *n*, (почтовая) марка; штамп, штемпель; отпечаток; топанье, топот; (kind) род; ~ duty гербовый сбор; bear the ~ of походить на; ¶ *v.t*, наклеивать марку на; ставить штамп на; топтать (ногой); (fig.) характеризовать; *v.i*, топать ногой; ~ out подавлять, ликвидировать.

stampede, *n*, паническое бегство; ¶ *v.t*. (& i.), обращать(ся) в паническое бегство.

stamping, *n*, штамповка; топанье.

stand, *n*, место, позиция; стоянка; подставка, пьедестал; стойка, стэнд, киоск; трибуна; остановка; ¶ *v.t*, ставить; выдерживать, терпеть; *v.i*, стоять; вставать; находиться; оставаться в силе; ~ back держаться позади, ~ by присутствовать; быть наготове; ~ down уходить; снимать свою кандидатуру; ~ in the way of мешать (dat.); ~ off держаться на расстоянии; ~ on end подниматься дыбом; ~ out выделяться; ~ security ручаться; служить гарантией; ~ up вставать; as things ~ при настоящем положении вещей.

standard, *n*, стандарт; норма; мерило, образец; знамя, флаг; ~ of living жизненный уровень; ¶ *a*, стандартный, нормальный, образцовый; ~ gauge нормальная колея; ~ size стандартный размер; ~ization, *n*, стандартизация; ~ize, *v.t*, стандартизировать.

standing, *n*, вес, положение; продолжительность, стаж; ¶ *a*, стоящий; постоянный; ~ army постоянная армия; ~ order приказ-инструкция; pl, устав; ~ room место для стояния.

stand-offish, *a*, сдержанный, неприветливый.

standpoint, *n*, точка зрения.

standstill, *n*, остановка; бездействие; at a ~ остановившийся на мёртвой точке.

stanza, *n*, станс.

staple, *n*, крюк, скоба; главный продукт/предмет торговли; ¶ *a*, главный, основной.

star, *n*, звезда; звёздочка; ¶ *v.t*, украшать звёздами; отмечать звёздочкой; *v.i*, играть главную роль.

starboard, *n*, правый борт.

starch, *n*, крахмал; ¶ *v.t*, крахмалить; ~у, *a*, крахмалистый; накрахмаленный; *(fig.)* чопорный.

stare, *n*, пристальный взгляд; ¶ *v.i*, пристально смотреть, глазеть; *it* ~s *you in the face* это бросается в глаза.

stark, *a*, окоченевший; абсолютный; ~ *mad* совсем сумасшедший; ~ *naked* совершённо голый.

starling, *n*, скворец.

starry, *a*, звёздный; лучистый.

start, *n*, начало; отправление; *(sport)* старт; преимущество; вздрагивание; *at the* ~ в начале; *by* ~s урывками; ¶ *v.t*, начинать; открывать; браться за; пускать *(machine)*; вспугивать; *v.i*, начинаться; отправляться; открываться; *(sport)* стартовать; вздрагивать; ~er, *n*, стартер, пусковой прибор; диспетчер; участник соревнования; ~ing, *a*: ~ *handle* пусковой рычаг; ~ *point* отправной пункт; ~-post стартовый столб.

startle, *v.t*, пугать; поражать; **startling,** *a*, поразительный, потрясающий.

starvation, *n*, голод, голодная смерть; истощение; **starve,** *v.i*, голодать; умирать от голода; *v.t*, морить голодом; **starving,** *a*, голодный, голодающий.

state, *n*, государство, штат; состояние; великолепие; *lie in* ~ покоиться в открытом гробу; ¶ *a*, государственный; парадный; ~ *room* парадный зал; ¶ *v.t*, заявлять; излагать; констатировать; ~d, *p.p. & a*, назначенный; сформулированный; ~ly, *a*, величавый, величественный; ~ment, *n*, заявление; ~sman, *n*, государственный деятель.

static, *a*, неподвижный, статический; ~s, *n*, статика.

station, *n*, вокзал, станция; остановка *(bus, coach)*; место, пункт; общественное положение; ~-master начальник станции; ¶ *v.t*, ставить, помещать; *(mil.)* раз-

мещать; ~agу, *a*, неподвижный; стационарный.

stationer, *n*, торговец канцелярскими товарами; ~у, *n*, канцелярские товары; писчебумажный магазин.

statistical, *a*, статистический; **statistician,** *n*, статистик; **statistics,** *n*, статистика.

statuary, *n*, скульптура; **statue,** *n*, статуя; **statuette,** *n*, статуэтка.

stature, *n*, рост, стан; *(fig.)* вес.

status, *n*, статус, положение.

statute, *n*, статут, закон; *pl*, устав; ~ *law* писаный закон; **statutory,** *a*, установленный законом.

staunch, *a*, верный, прочный; ¶ *v.t*, останавливать (кровотечение).

stave, *n*, (бочарная) доска; *(poet.)* строфа; *pl, (mus.)* нотные линейки; ¶ ~ *off* предотвращать; отсрочивать.

stay, *n*, пребывание; остановка; задержка, преграда; поддержка, опора; *(law)* отсрочка; *(mar.)* штаг; *pl*, корсет; ¶ *v.t*, останавливать; задерживать; отсрочивать; *v.i*, оставаться, гостить, жить; ~-at-home домосед; ~ *up* не ложиться спать.

stead, *n*: *in my* ~ вместо меня, за меня.

steadfast, *a*, твёрдый, прочный.

steady, *n*, устойчивый, твёрдый; постоянный; ровный, уравновешенный; ¶ *v.t*, делать устойчивым; *v.i*, становиться устойчивым; приходить в равновесие.

steak, *n*, кусок мяса/рыбы; бифштекс.

steal, *v.t*, воровать, красть; *v.i*, красться, подкрадываться; ~ *a glance* взглядывать украдкой; ~ *a march on* опережать; ~ *away* незаметно ускользать; ~ing, *n*, воровство, кража; ~th: *by* ~ втихомолку, украдкой; ~thy, *a*, бесшумный; тайный.

steam, *n*, пар; испарение; ¶ *a*, паровой; ~*boat* пароход; ~ *boiler* паровой котёл; ~ *engine* паровая машина; паровоз; ¶ *v.t*, парить; варить на пару; *v.i*, выпускать пар; идти под парами; запотевать *(windows)*; ~er, *n*, пароход; котёл для варки на пару; ~у, *a*, парообразный; испаряющийся; запотевший.

steed, *n*, конь.

steel, *n*, сталь; точи́ло; ¶ *a*, сталь-но́й; ¶ *v.t*, покрыва́ть ста́лью; закаля́ть; ~works, *n.pl*, сталели-те́йный заво́д; ~у, *a*, твёрдый как сталь.

steep, *a*, круто́й; чрезме́рный, сли́ш-ком высо́кий; ¶ *n*, круча, стремни́на; ¶ *v.t*, погружа́ть, пропи́тывать; *v.i*, пропи́тываться; мо́кнуть; *be* ~ed *in* уходи́ть с голово́й в, погряза́ть в.

steeple, *n*, шпиль; колоко́льня.

steeplechase, *n*, бег/ска́чки с пре-пя́тствиями.

steepness, *n*, крутизна́.

steer, *n*, бычо́к, молодо́й вол; ¶ *v.t*, пра́вить/управля́ть *(inst.)*; на-правля́ть; ~ *clear of* избега́ть; ~age, *n*, управле́ние; ~ *ticket* биле́т в четвёртый класс; ~ing, *n*, управле́ние; ~ *wheel* руль; *(mar.)* штурва́л; ~sman, *n*, руле-во́й, штурман.

stellar, *a*, звёздный.

stem, *n*, сте́бель, ствол; *(gram.)* осно́ва; *(tech.)* вал, сте́ржень; ¶ *v.t*, заде́рживать, запру́живать; ~ *from* происходи́ть от.

stench, *n*, вонь, злово́ние.

stencil, *n*, трафаре́т, шабло́н; ¶ *v.t*, кра́сить/печа́тать по трафаре́ту.

stenographer, *n*, стеногра́фист, -ка; **stenography**, *n*, стеногра́фия.

stentorian, *a*, громово́й.

step, *n*, шаг; по́ступь, похо́дка; *(dancing)* па; ступе́нька, под-но́жка; вы́ступ; *(fig.)* шаг, ме́ра; *pl*, стремя́нка; ~brother сво́д-ный брат; ~daughter па́дчерица; ~father о́тчим; ~mother ма́чеха; ~sister сво́дная сестра́; ~son па́сынок; *march in* ~ шага́ть в но́гу; *take* ~s принима́ть ме́ры; ¶ *v.i*, ступа́ть, шага́ть; ~ *aside* сторони́ться; *(fig.)* уступа́ть до-ро́гу; ~ *back* отступа́ть; ~ *in* входи́ть; ~ *on* наступа́ть на; **stepping-stone** ка́мень в воде́; *(fig.)* сре́дство к достиже́нию це́ли.

steppe, *n*, степь.

stereoscope, *n*, стереоско́п.

stereotype, *n*, стереоти́п; ¶ *v.t*, печа́-тать со стереоти́па; создава́ть по шабло́ну; ~d, *a*, стереоти́пный, трафаре́тный.

sterile, *a*, беспло́дный, стери́ль-ный; **sterility**, *n*, беспло́дие, сте-

ри́льность; **sterilize**, *v.t*, стерили-зова́ть.

sterling, *a*, полновесный, полно-це́нный; надёжный; *pound* ~ фунт сте́рлингов.

stern, *a*, стро́гий, суро́вый; ¶ *n*, корма́; зад.

stethoscope, *n*, стетоско́п.

stevedore, *n*, порто́вый гру́зчик.

stew, *n*, тушёное мя́со; ¶ *v.t. (& i.)*, вари́ть(ся), туши́ть(ся); ~ed, *a*, тушёный; ~ *fruit* компо́т.

steward, *n*, управля́ющий, заве́ду-ющий хозя́йством; *(mar.)* офи-циа́нт; *(avia.)* бортпроводни́к; ~ess, *n*, *(avia.)* стюарде́сса, борт-проводни́ца; *(mar.)* го́рничная.

stick, *n*, па́лка, трость; ко́лышек, па́лочка; ве́тка; ¶ *v.t*, втыка́ть; коло́ть; кле́ить; *v.i*, ли́пнуть, при-кле́иваться; остава́ться; вя́знуть; ~ *to (fig.)* приде́рживаться *(gen.)*; ~ *at nothing* ни пе́ред чем не остана́вливаться; ~ *in-the-mud* отста́лый челове́к; ~ *out* вы-со́вывать(ся); ~iness, *n*, кле́й-кость, ли́пкость; *sticking plaster* ли́пкий пла́стырь; ~у, *a*, кле́й-кий, ли́пкий; *(coll.)* тру́дный, неприя́тный.

stiff, *a*, туго́й, неги́бкий, жёсткий; засты́вший, окочене́вший; на-тя́нутый, чо́порный; тру́дный, чрезме́рный; кре́пкий; *I have a* ~ *neck* мне наду́ло ше́ю; ~en, *v.t*, де́лать жёстким; *v.i*, де́латься жёстким; деревене́ть; коченеть; ~ness, *n*, жёсткость; окочене́ние; *(fig.)* натя́нутость, чо́порность.

stifle, *v.t*, души́ть; подавля́ть; *v.i*, задыха́ться; **stifling**, *a*, ду́шный.

stigma, *n*, позо́р, пятно́; *(bot.)* ры́ль-це; ~tize, *v.t*, бесче́стить, клей-ми́ть.

stile, *n*, перела́з.

stiletto, *n*, стиле́т; ~heel гвозди́к.

still, *a*, ти́хий; неподви́жный; ~born мертворождённый; ~ *life* на-тюрмо́рт; ¶ *ad*, до сих пор, всё ещё; одна́ко; ~ *better* ещё лу́чше; ¶ *n*, перего́нный куб, дестилля́-тор; кадр; ¶ *v.t*, успока́ивать; ~ness, *n*, тишина́, безмо́лвие; не-подви́жность.

stilt, *n*, ходу́ля; ~ed, *a*, ходу́льный напы́щенный.

stimulant, *n*, возбужда́ющее сре́д-ство, спиртно́е; **stimulate**, *v.t*, стимули́ровать, возбужда́ть; побужда́ть; **stimulus**, *n*, сти́мул, побуди́тель.

sting, *n*, жа́ло; уку́с; ожо́г (крапи́вой); *(fig.)* ко́лкость; ¶ *v.t*, жа́лить; обжига́ть; уязвля́ть; *v.i*, жечь; си́льно боле́ть.

stinginess, *n*, ску́пость; **stingy**, *a*, скупо́й.

stink, *n*, вонь, злово́ние; ¶ *v.i*, воня́ть; ~ing, *a*, воню́чий.

stint, *n*, преде́л; уро́чная рабо́та; ¶ *v.t*, уре́зывать, ограни́чивать; скупи́ться на; эконо́мить.

stipend, *n*, жа́лованье; стипе́ндия.

stipple, *v.t*, рисова́ть пункти́ром; кра́сить то́чками.

stipulate, *v.t*, ста́вить усло́вием; обусло́вливать; **stipulation**, *n*, усло́вие; обусло́вливание.

stir, *n*, движе́ние, оживле́ние; суета́, сумато́ха; ¶ *v.t. (& i.)*, шевели́ть(ся), дви́гать(ся); меша́ть, разме́шивать; ~ *up* разме́шивать; возбужда́ть; раздува́ть; ~ring, *a*, волну́ющий.

stirrup, *n*, стре́мя; ~ *leather* стремя́нный реме́нь.

stitch, *n*, стежо́к, пе́тля; шов; *I have a* ~ *in my side* у меня́ ко́лет в боку́; ¶ *v.t*, шить, стега́ть, стро́чить; ~ *up* зашива́ть; ~ing, *n*, сшива́ние.

stiver, *n*, грош.

stoat, *n*, горноста́й.

stock, *n*, ствол; руже́йная ло́жа; подпо́ра; род, семья́ *(descent)*; *(biol.)* поро́да; *(reserve)* запа́с, фонд, сырьё; *(cattle)* скот, пого́ловье скота́; *(com.)* акционе́рный капита́л, а́кция *(cook.)* бульо́н; *pl*, коло́дки; ~-*breeder* животново́д; ~-*breeding* животново́дство; ~-*broker* биржево́й ма́клер; ~ *exchange* фо́ндовая би́ржа; ~*fish* вя́леная треска́; ~*holder* акционе́р; ~-*jobbing* биржевы́е сде́лки; ~-*still* неподви́жный; как вко́панный; ~*taking* переучёт това́ров, инвентариза́ция; ~*yard* скотоприго́нный двор; ¶ *v.t*, име́ть на скла́де; снабжа́ть.

stockade, *n*, частоко́л.

stocking, *n*, чуло́к.

stocky, *a*, корена́стый, призе́мистый.

stodgy, *a*, тяжёлый; ску́чный.

Stoic, *n*, сто́ик; ~al, *a*, стои́ческий; ~ism, *n*, стоици́зм.

stoke, *v.t*, топи́ть; подде́рживать (ого́нь); ~-*hole* кочега́рка; ~r, *n*, кочега́р, истопни́к.

stole, *n*, шарф; мехова́я наки́дка.

stolid, *a*, флегмати́чный; про́чный; тупо́й.

stomach, *n*, желу́док, живо́т; аппети́т; вкус; ¶ *v.t*, перева́ривать; терпе́ть; прогла́тывать; ~ic, *a*, желу́дочный.

stone, *n*, ка́мень; ко́сточка *(in fruit)*; зёрнышко *(grape)*; сто́ун *(weight)*; *(med.)* ка́мень; ¶ *a*, ка́менный; ~ *deaf* соверше́нно глухо́й; ~-*fruit* костя́нка; ~ *quarry* каменоло́мня; ~-*mason* ка́менщик; ~'s *throw* рассто́яние, на кото́рое мо́жно бро́сить ка́мень; ~*ware* гли́няная посу́да; ~*work* ка́менная кла́дка; ка́менные рабо́ты; ¶ *v.t*, побива́ть камня́ми; вынима́ть ко́сточки из; **stony**, *a*, камени́стый; твёрдый; мёртвый.

stool, *n*, табуре́тка; сту́льчик; *(med.)* стул.

stoop, *n*, суту́лость; ¶ *v.i*, суту́литься, наклоня́ться; ~ *to* снисходи́ть до.

stop, *n*, остано́вка; заде́ржка; прекраще́ние; переры́в; ~-*gap* вре́менная ме́ра; *(pers.)* вре́менный замести́тель; ~ *press* экстренное сообще́ние; ~ *watch* секундоме́р; *put a* ~ *to* положи́ть *(pf.)* коне́ц *(dat.)*; ¶ *v.t*, остана́вливать, прекраща́ть, конча́ть; заде́лывать, заде́лывать; пломбирова́ть *(tooth)*; *v.i*, остана́вливаться, прекраща́ться, конча́ться; гости́ть; ¶ *int*, стой!; ~*page*, *n*, заде́ржка, прекраще́ние рабо́ты; вы́чет; ~*per*, *n*, про́бка, заты́чка; ~*ping*, *n*, зубна́я пло́мба.

storage, *n*, хране́ние; *(elec.)* аккумули́рование; **store**, *n*, запа́с; склад; магази́н, универма́г; ~*house* склад, амба́р; *(fig.)* сокро́вищница; ~*keeper* ла́вочник; кладо́вщик; ~-*room* кладова́я; ¶ *v.t*, храни́ть (на скла́де); запаса́ть, откла́дывать.

storey, *n*, эта́ж; я́рус; *three-*~ трёхэта́жный.

stork, *n*, áист.

storm, *n*, бýря, грозá; *(mar.)* шторм; *(mil.)* штурм; ¶ *v.t*, штурмовáть; брать прúступом; *v.i*, бушевáть, свирéпствовать; нейстовствовать; ~у, *a*, бýрный; нейстовый.

story, *n*, рассκáз, пóвесть; истóрия; скáзка; сюжéт, фáбула; *(coll.)* выдумка; ~-*teller* рассκáзчик, скáзочник; выдумщик.

stoup, *n*, бокáл.

stout, *a*, плóтный, прóчный; отвáжный, сúльный; стóйкий; пóлный, дорóдный; ¶ *n*, крéпкий пóртер.

stove, *n*, пéчка, печь, плитá.

stow, *v.t*, уклáдывать, склáдывать; грузúть; ~*age*, *n*, уклáдка, склáдывание; погрýзка; ~*away*, *n*, безбилéтный пассажúр, «зáяц».

straddle, *v.t*, сидéть верхóм на; *v.i*, ширóко расставлять нóги.

straggle, *v.i*, отставáть; идтú враз-брóд; ~*r*, *n*, отстáвший; отстáвшее сýдно; **straggling**, *a*, беспорядочный, разбрóсанный.

straight, *a*, прямóй; прáвильный; чéстный; ¶ *ad*, прямо; ~*away*, *ad*, немéдленно, срáзу; ~*en*, *v.t. (& i.)*, выпрямлять(ся); выправлять(ся); ~*forward*, *a*, прямóй, чéстный; простóй; ~*forwardness*, *n*, прямотá, чéстность; простотá. ~*ness*, *n*, прямизнá, прáвильность.

strain, *n*, напряжéние; натяжéние, растяжéние; переутомлéние; порóда, род; *(mus.)* мелóдия, напéв; ¶ *v.t*, напрягáть; натягивать, растягивать; переутомлять; процéживать, фильтровáть; *v.i*, напрягáться; переутомляться; ~*ed*, *p.p. & a*, натянутый; ~*er*, *n*, сúто, цедúлка, фильтр.

strait, *a*, ýзкий, тéсный; ~*s*, *n.pl*, пролúв; *(fig.)* затруднúтельное положéние; *in dire* ~ в ужáсной нуждé; ~*jacket*, *n*, смирúтельная рубáшка; ~*laced*, *a*, стрóгий, пуритáнский.

strand, *n*, бéрег, прибрéжная полосá; прядь *(of hair)*; чертá, сторонá; ¶ *v.t*, сажáть на мель.

strange, *a*, стрáнный; чужóй; незнакóмый, неизвéстный; ~*ness*, *n*, стрáнность; ~*r*, *n*, незнакóмец; чужóй/посторóнний человéк.

strangle, *v.t*, душúть; *(fig.)* подавлять; **strangulation**, *n*, удушéние; *(med.)* зажимáние.

strap, *n*, ремéнь, ремешóк, пóяс; полóска; ¶ *v.t*, стягивать ремнéм, скреплять ремнями; бить ремнéм; ~*ping*, *a*, рóслый.

stratagem, *n*, хúтрость; **strategic**, *a*, стратегúческий; **strategist**, *n*, стратéг; **strategy**, *n*, стратéгия.

stratosphere, *n*, стратосфéра.

stratum, *n*, пласт, слой.

straw, *n*, солóма; солóминка; *that's the last* ~ это послéдняя кáпля; ~-*coloured* солóменного цвéта.

strawberry, *n*, землянúка, клубнúка.

stray, *a*, заблудúвшийся; бездóмный; случáйный: ~ *bullet* шальнáя пýля; ¶ *v.i*, сбивáться с путú; блуждáть.

streak, *n*, полосá, полóска, прослóйка; *(fig.)* чертá; ¶ *v.t*, проводúть полосы на; испещрять; *v.i*, проносúться; ~*y*, *a*, полосáтый.

stream, *n*, потóк, ручéй; струя; течéние; ~*lined* обтекáемый; ¶ *v.i*, струúться, течь; *v.t*, разделять; ~*er*, *n*, длúнная лéнта; вымпел.

street, *n*, ýлица; ~*car* трамвáй; ~*urchin* беспризóрник; ~*walker* проститýтка.

strength, *n*, сúла; крéпость, прóчность; ~*en*, *v.t. (& i.)*, усилúвать(ся), укреплять(ся).

strenuous, *a*, напряжённый, энергúчный.

stress, *n*, напряжéние, давлéние, нажúм; *(gram.)* ударéние; ¶ *v.t*, подчёркивать; *(gram.)* стáвить ударéние на.

stretch, *n*, растягивание; прострáнство, протяжéние; промежýток врéмени; *at a* ~ в одúн присéст; ¶ *v.t*, вытягивать, растягивать; натягивать; ~ *one's legs* размúнáть нóги; *v.i*, растягиваться; простирáться; ~ *oneself* потягиваться; ~*er*, *n*, носúлки; приспособлéние для растягивания.

strew, *v.t*, разбрáсывать; посыпáть; усыпáть.

striated, *a*, полосáтый.

stricken, *a*, поражённый, охвáченный.

strict, *a*, стрóгий; трéбовательный; тóчный; ~*ness*, *n*, стрóгость;

требовательность; то́чность; ~-ure, *n*, стро́гая кри́тика, осужде́ние; *(med.)* суже́ние.

stride, *n*, шаг; *make great* ~s де́лать успе́хи; ¶ *v.i*, шага́ть.

strident, *a*, ре́зкий, скрипу́чий.

strife, *n*, борьба́; раздо́р.

strike, *n*, забасто́вка, ста́чка; откры́тие; ¶ *a*, забасто́вочный ~-breaker штрейкбре́хер; ¶ *v.t*, бить, ударя́ть; зажига́ть *(match)*; спуска́ть *(flags)*; чека́нить *(coins)*; убира́ть *(sail)*; открыва́ть *(oil)*; заключа́ть *(bargain)*; подводи́ть *(balance)*; *(fig.)* поража́ть; *v.i*, бастова́ть; бить *(clock)*; ~ *at* наноси́ть уда́р *(dat.)*; напада́ть на; ~ *down* вали́ть/сбива́ть с ног; ~ *off* вычёркивать; вычита́ть; ~ *out on one's own* начина́ть поступа́ть/де́йствовать самостоя́тельно; ~ *up* начина́ть; завя́зывать *(friendship)*; ~ *upon* па́дать на; напада́ть на *(thought)*; ~r, *n*, забасто́вщик; *(tech.)* язычо́к; **striking**, *a*, порази́тельный.

string, *n*, верёвка, шнуро́к; *(mus.)* струна́; тетива́ *(of bow)*; ряд, верени́ца; ~ *of pearls* ни́тка жемчуга́; ~ *instrument* стру́нный инструме́нт; ¶ *v.t*, нани́зывать; ~ *together* свя́зывать; ~ed, *a*, стру́нный.

stringent, *a*, стро́гий; то́чный.

stringy, *a*, волокни́стый.

strip, *n*, полоса́, поло́ска; лоску́т; ¶ *v.t*, обдира́ть, сдира́ть; раздева́ть; обнажа́ть; разбира́ть (на ча́сти); *v.i*, раздева́ться.

stripe, *n*, полоса́; *(mil.)* наши́вка; лампа́с; ~d, *a*, полоса́тый.

stroke, *n*, уда́р; ро́счерк *(of pen)*; взмах *(of oar, etc)*; штрих, погла́живание; бой часо́в; *(move)* приём, ход; *(med.)* уда́р; ~ *of luck* уда́ча; *at one* ~ одни́м уда́ром, сра́зу; ¶ *v.t*, гла́дить.

stroll, *n*, прогу́лка; *take a* ~ прогу́ливаться; ¶ *v.i*, гуля́ть, прогу́ливаться; ~ing, *a*, бродя́чий; стра́нствующий.

strong, *a*, си́льный, кре́пкий, про́чный; твёрдый; здоро́вый; ~-box сейф; ~hold кре́пость, тверды́ня, опло́т; ~point опо́рный пункт.

strop, *n*, реме́нь; ¶ *v.t*, пра́вить *(razor)*.

structural, *a*, структу́рный; строи́тельный; **structure**, *n*, структу́ра; устро́йство.

struggle, *n*, борьба́; уси́лие; ¶ *v.i*, боро́ться; би́ться; стара́ться изо всех сил.

strum, *v.i*, бренча́ть.

strumpet, *n*, проститу́тка.

strut, *n*, подпо́ра, сто́йка; ва́жная похо́дка; ¶ *v.i*, ходи́ть с ва́жным ви́дом; *v.t*, подпира́ть.

strychnine, *n*, стрихни́н.

stub, *n*, пень; обло́мок; огры́зок *(of pencil)*; оку́рок *(of cigarette)*; корешо́к *(of cheque)*; ¶ *v.t*, выкорчёвывать; ~ *out* гаси́ть; ~ *one's foot on* ударя́ться ного́й обо.

stubble, *n*, жнивьё; щети́на, небри́тая борода́.

stubborn, *a*, упря́мый, упо́рный; ~ness, *n*, упря́мство, упо́рство.

stucco, *n*, штукату́рка.

stuck-up, *a*, высокоме́рный.

stud, *n*, гвоздь (с большо́й шля́пкой); кно́пка; за́понка; ко́нный заво́д; ¶ *v.t*, обива́ть (гвоздя́ми); усыпа́ть, усе́ивать.

student, *n*, студе́нт, -ка, уча́щийся; учёный; **studied**, *a*, обду́манный, преднаме́ренный; **studio**, *n*, ателье́, мастерска́я, сту́дия; **studious**, *a*, приле́жный, усе́рдный; начи́танный; **study**, *n*, изуче́ние, иссле́дование; нау́чные заня́тия, нау́ка; о́черк, этю́д; кабине́т; ¶ *v.t*, изуча́ть, иссле́довать; *v.i*, занима́ться, учи́ться; гото́виться.

stuff, *n*, вещество́, материа́л; ¶ *v.t*, набива́ть; де́лать чу́чело из; начиня́ть, фарширова́ть; засо́вывать, затыка́ть; заका́рмливать; *v.i*, объеда́ться; ~ing, *n*, наби́вка; начи́нка; ~y, *a*, ду́шный, спёртый; щепети́льный; ко́сный.

stultify, *v.t*, своди́ть на нет; выставля́ть в смешно́м ви́де.

stumble, *v.i*, спотыка́ться запина́ться; *stumbling block* ка́мень преткнове́ния.

stump, *n*, пень; обру́бок; огры́зок; ¶ *v.t*, ста́вить в тупи́к; корчева́ть; *v.i*, ковыля́ть; тяжело́ ступа́ть; ~y, *a*, корена́стый; призе́мистый.

stun, *v.t*, оглуша́ть, ошеломля́ть.

stunt, *n*, трюк, фо́кус; *(avia.)* фигу́ра вы́сшего пилота́жа; ¶ *v.t*, задéрживать рост; ~ed, *a*, низкорóслый.

stupefy, *v.t*, притупля́ть *(feelings);* изумля́ть.

stupendous, *a*, изуми́тельный; громáдный.

stupid, *a*, глу́пый, тупóй; ~ity, *n*, глу́пость; **stupor**, *n*, оцепенéние, столбня́к.

sturdy, *a*, здорóвый; крéпкий, твёрдый.

sturgeon, *n*, осётр.

stutter, *n*, заикáние; ¶ *v.i*, заикáться, запинáться; *v.t*, произноси́ть заикáясь; ~er, *n*, зáика.

sty[e], *n*, свинáрник; ячмéнь (на глазу́)

style, *n*, стиль, слог; манéра; направлéние, шкóла; мóда, фасóн, покрóй; шик; ти́тул; ¶ *v.t*, титуловáть, величáть.

stylish, *a*, мóдный, шикáрный.

stylograph, *n*, стилогрáф; вéчная ру́чка.

suave, *a*, обходи́тельный, учти́вый; **suavity**, *n*, обходи́тельность.

subaltern, *n*, млáдший офицéр.

sub-committee, *n*, подкоми́ссия.

subconscious, *a*, подсознáтельный; ~ness, *n*, подсознáние.

subcutaneous, *a*, подкóжный.

subdivide, *v.t*, подразделя́ть.

subdue, *v.t*, подчиня́ть, покоря́ть, подавля́ть; ~d, *p.p. & a*, подчинённый; понижéнный; приглушённый.

sub-editor, *n*, помóщник редáктора.

subject, *a*, подчинённый, подвéрженный, подвлáстный; подлежáщий; ~ *to* при услóвии; допускáя, éсли; ¶ *n*, пóдданный; предмéт; тéма, сюжéт; субъéкт; человéк; *(gram.)* подлежáщее; ¶ *v.t*, подчиня́ть, покоря́ть; подвергáть; ~ion, *n*, подчинéние; покорéние; ~ive, *a*, субъекти́вный.

subjoined, *a*, добáвленный.

subjugate, *v.t*, подчиня́ть, покоря́ть.

subjunctive, *n*, сослагáтельное наклонéние.

sub-let, *v.t*, передавáть в субарéнду.

sublime, *a*, возвы́шенный; величéственный; ¶ *n*, возвы́шенное; **sublimity**, *n*, возвы́шенность.

sublunar, *a*, подлу́нный, земнóй.

submarine, *a*, подвóдный; ¶ *n*, подвóдная лóдка.

submerge, *v.t*, затопля́ть, погружáть; *v.i*, погружáться.

submission, *n*, подчинéние, покóрность; представлéние, предложéние; **submissive**, *a*, покóрный, смирéнный; **submit**, *v.t*, представля́ть (на рассмотрéние); *v.i*, подчиня́ться.

subordinate, *a*, подчинённый; второстепéнный; ¶ *v.t*, подчиня́ть.

suborn, *v.t*, подкупáть; ~ation, *n* пóдкуп; ~er, *n*, взяткодáтель.

subpoena, *n*, вы́зов в суд; ¶ *v*. вызывáть в суд.

subscribe, *v.i*: ~ *to* подпи́сываться на; жéртвовать дéньги на; при соединя́ться к; ~r, *n*, подпи́счик, абонéнт; жéртвователь; **subscription**, *n*, подпи́ска.

subsequent, *a*, послéдующий; ~ly, *ad*, впослéдствии, потóм.

subservience, *n*, рабóлепие; содéйствие; подчинённость; **subservient**, *a*, содéйствующий; подчинённый.

subside, *v.i*, пáдать, убывáть; осе дáть *(soil);* ~nce, *n*, падéние; осе дáние *(foundation);* осáдка *(of soil).*

subsidiary, *a*, вспомогáтельный, дополни́тельный; филиáл.

subsidize, *v.t*, субсиди́ровать; **subsidy**, *n*, субси́дия, дотáция.

subsist, *v.i*, существовáть, жить; добывáть пропитáние; ~ence, *n*, существовáние; пропитáние; срéдства к существовáнию.

sub-soil, *n*, подпóчва.

substance, *n*, веществó, матéрия, субстáнция; суть, су́щность; иму́щество, состоя́ние; **substantial**, *a*, вещéственный; существéнный, значи́тельный; прóчный, надёжный; ~ly, *ad*, в основнóм; **substantiate**, *v.t*, докáзывать, подтверждáть.

substantive, *a*, независи́мый, самостоя́тельный; ¶ *n*, и́мя существи́тельное.

substitute, *n*, замести́тель; замени́тель, суррогáт; ¶ *v.t*, замещáть, заменя́ть; **substitution**, *n*, замещéние, замéна; *(maths)* подстанóвка.

substructure, *n*, основáние, фундáмент.

sub-tenant, *n*, субарендáтор.

subterfuge, *n*, увёртка.

subterranean, *a.* подзе́мный.

subtilize, *v.t.* утонча́ть; *v.i.* вдава́ться в то́нкости.

sub-title, *a.* подзаголо́вок.

subtle, *a.* то́нкий, неулови́мый; утончённый; ло́вкий, хи́трый; ~ty, *n.* то́нкость, утончённость; хи́трость.

subtract, *v.t.* вычита́ть; ~ion, *n.* вычита́ние.

suburb, *n.* при́город; *pl.* предме́стья, окре́стности; ~an, *a.* при́городный.

subversion, *n.* сверже́ние; **subversive**, *a.* разруши́тельный; ~ activity подрывна́я де́ятельность; **subvert**, *v.t.* сверга́ть.

subway, *n.* тунне́ль; подзе́мный перехо́д; метрополите́н.

succeed, *v.i.* име́ть успе́х, удава́ться; ~ to насле́довать; *v.t.* сле́довать за; сменя́ть.

success, *n.* уда́ча, успе́х; ~ful, *a.* уда́чный, успе́шный; *(pers.)* преуспева́ющий; ~ion, *n.* после́довательность; прее́мственность; пра́во насле́дования; ряд; *in* ~ подря́д; ~ive, *a.* после́довательный, после́дующий; сле́дующий оди́н за други́м; ~or, *n.* прее́мник, насле́дник.

succinct, *a.* кра́ткий, сжа́тый.

succour, *n.* по́мощь; ¶ *v.t.* помога́ть *(dat.),* подде́рживать.

succulent, *a.* со́чный.

succumb, *v.i.* быть побеждённым, уступа́ть; умира́ть.

such, *a.* тако́й; ~ *as* как наприме́р; тако́й, как; ¶ *pr.* таково́й.

suck, *v.t.* соса́ть; ~ *up* вса́сывать; поглоща́ть; ~er, *n.* сосуно́к; *(bot.)* отро́сток; *(zool.)* присо́сок; *(tech.)* по́ршень насо́са; *(coll.)* простофи́ля; ~*ing pig* моло́чный поросёнок; ~le, *v.t.* корми́ть гру́дью; ~lirg, *n.* грудно́й ребёнок; **suction**, *n.* соса́ние; ~ *pump* вса́сывающий насо́с.

sudden, *a.* внеза́пный, неожи́данный; *all of a* ~ внеза́пно, вдруг; ~ly, *ad.* внеза́пно, неожи́данно, вдруг.

suds, *n.pl.* мы́льная пе́на, мы́льная вода́.

sue, *v.t.* пресле́довать суде́бным поря́дком; возбужда́ть де́ло про́тив.

suède, *n.* за́мша; ¶ *a.* за́мшевый.

suet, *n.* по́чечное/нутряно́е са́ло.

suffer, *v.t.* испы́тывать *(pain);* терпе́ть, выноси́ть; нести́ *(loss);* позволя́ть; *v.i.* страда́ть; ~able, *a.* терпи́мый; ~ance, *n.* терпе́ние; попусти́тельство *he is here on* ~ его́ здесь те́рпят; ~er, *n.* страда́лец; пострада́вший; ~ing, *n.* страда́ние; ¶ *a.* страда́ющий.

suffice, *v.i.* быть доста́точным, хвата́ть; удовлетворя́ть; ~ *it to say* доста́точно сказа́ть; **sufficiency**, *n.* доста́ток; доста́точность; **sufficient**, *a.* доста́точный.

suffix, *n.* су́ффикс.

suffocate, *v.t.* души́ть, удуша́ть; *v.i.* задыха́ться; **suffocating**, *a.* ду́шный, удушли́вый; **suffocation**, *n.* удуше́ние; уду́шье.

suffragan, *n.* вика́рный епи́скоп.

suffrage, *n.* пра́во го́лоса; избира́тельное пра́во; ~tte, *n.* суфражи́стка.

suffuse, *v.t.* залива́ть *(with tears);* покрыва́ть *(with colour);* **suffusion**, *n.* покры́тие; кра́ска.

sugar, *n.* са́хар; ~ *bowl* са́харница; ~ *beet* са́харная свёкла; ~ *cane* са́харный тростни́к; ~ *plum* леденёц; ~ *tongs* щи́пчики для са́хара; ¶ *v.t.* подсла́щивать, оса́харивать; ~y, *a.* са́харный, сла́дкий; *(fig.)* льсти́вый; сла́щавый.

suggest, *v.t.* предлага́ть; вызыва́ть *(idea);* ~ion, *n.* предложе́ние; внуше́ние; ~ive, *a.* наводя́щий на мысль; соблазни́тельный.

suicide, *n.* самоуби́йство; *(pers.)* самоуби́йца; *commit* ~ соверша́ть самоуби́йство, поко́нчить с собо́й *(pf.).*

suit, *n.* костю́м; компле́кт; проше́ние; *(law)* иск, тя́жба; уха́живание; *(cards)* масть; ~*case* чемода́н; ¶ *v.t.* приспоса́бливать; устра́ивать, быть удо́бным *(dat.);* удовлетворя́ть тре́бованиям *(gen.);* быть к лицу́ *(dat.);* *v.i.* годи́ться, подходи́ть; ~ability, *n.* го́дность; ~able, *a.* го́дный, подходя́щий, соотве́тствующий.

suite, *n.* сви́та; компле́кт; *(mus.)* сюи́та; ~ *of furniture* ме́бельный гар иту́р; ~ *of rooms* анфила́да ко́мнат; но́мер в не́сколько ко́мнат.

suiting, *n.* материа́л для костю́мов.

suitor, *n*, проси́тель; *(law)* исте́ц; покло́нник, ухажёр.

sulk, *v.i*, ду́ться; ~у, *a*, наду́тый, угрю́мый.

sullen, *a*, за́мкнутый, угрю́мый; ~**ness**, *n*, за́мкнутость, угрю́мость.

sully, *v.t*, па́чкать, пятна́ть.

sulphate, *n*, сульфа́т; **sulphide**, *n*, сульфи́д; **sulphite**, *n*, сульфи́т; **sulphur**, *n*, се́ра; ~**ous**, *a*, серни́стый.

sultan, *n*, султа́н; ~**a**, *n*, султа́нша; изюм без ко́сточек.

sultry, *a*, ду́шный, зно́йный.

sum, *n*, су́мма, коли́чество; ито́г; арифмети́ческая зада́ча; *do* ~**s** реша́ть зада́чи; ¶ *v.t*: ~*up* резюми́ровать; подводи́ть ито́г *(dat.)*; ~**marize** *v.t*, резюми́ровать, сумми́ровать; ~**mary**, *a*, сумма́рный; ско́рый; ¶ *n*, конспе́кт, резюме́ сво́дка

summer, *n*, ле́то; ¶ *a*, ле́тний; ~ *holidays* ле́тние кани́кулы, ле́тний о́тпуск; ~ *house* бесе́дка.

summing-up, *n*, сумми́рование, подведе́ние ито́гов.

summit, *n*, верши́на; *(fig.)* преде́л, верх; ~ *conference* совеща́ние на вы́сшем у́ровне.

summon, *v.t*, призыва́ть, вызыва́ть, созыва́ть; ~ *up courage* собира́ться с ду́хом; ~**s**, *n*, призы́в; вы́зов (в суд); суде́бная пове́стка; ¶ *v.t*, вызыва́ть в суд пове́сткой.

sumptuous, *a*, пы́шный, роско́шный.

sun, *n*, со́лнце; ~*blind* наве́с, тент; ~*burn* зага́р; ~*burnt* загоре́лый; ~ *dial* со́лнечные часы́; ~*flower* подсо́лнечник, подсо́лнух; ~*light* со́лнечный свет; ~*rise* восхо́д со́лнца; ~*set* захо́д со́лнца, зака́т; ~*shade* зо́нтик от со́лнца; наве́с; ~*shine* со́лнечный свет; *in the* ~*shine* на со́лнце; ~*stroke* со́лнечный уда́р; ¶ *v.i*, гре́ться на со́лнце.

Sunday, *n*, воскресе́нье; ¶ *a*, воскре́сный; ~ *best* лу́чший костю́м, лу́чшее пла́тье.

sunder, *v.t*, разлуча́ть, разъединя́ть.

sundries, *n.pl*, вся́кая вся́чина, ра́зное; **sundry**, *a*, ра́зный; *all and* ~ все без исключе́ния.

sunken, *a*, затону́вший; погружённый; впа́лый *(cheeks)*.

sunless, *a*, без со́лнца; **sunny**, *a*, со́лнечный; *(fig.)* ра́достный.

sup, *v.i*, у́жинать; *v.t*, отхлёбывать.

superabundant, *a*, изоби́льный.

superannuated, *a*, престаре́лый; уста́ре́лый; **superannuation**, *n*, преде́льный во́зраст; увольне́ние по ста́рости; пе́нсия за вы́слугу лет.

superb, *a*, великоле́пный.

supercargo, *n*, заве́дующий гру́зом.

supercilious, *a*, высокоме́рный, презри́тельный.

superficial, *a*, пове́рхностный, вне́шний; **superficies**, *n*, пове́рхность.

superfine, *a*, вы́сшего ка́чества; (чрезме́рно) утончённый.

superfluity, *n*, избы́точность, избы́ток, оби́лие; **superfluous**, *a*, (из)ли́шний, ненужный.

superheat, *v.t*, перегрева́ть.

superhuman, *a*, сверхчелове́ческий.

superimpose, *v.t*, накла́дывать.

superintend, *v.t*, заве́довать/управля́ть *(inst.)*; надзира́ть за; смотре́ть за; ~**ence**, *n*, надзо́р, управле́ние; ~**ent**, *n*, заве́дующий, управля́ющий; ста́рший (полице́йский) офице́р.

superior, *a*, вы́сший, ста́рший, лу́чший; превосхо́дный; превосходя́щий; ¶ *n*, нача́льник, ста́рший; настоя́тель, -ница.

superlative, *a*, превосхо́дный; ¶ *n*, *(gram.)* превосхо́дная сте́пень.

superman, *n*, сверхчелове́к.

supermarket, *n*, универса́м.

supernatural, *a*, сверхъесте́ственный.

supernumerary, *a*, сверхшта́тный, ли́шний; ¶ *n*, сверхшта́тный рабо́тник; *(theat.)* стати́ст, -ка.

supersede, *v.t*, заменя́ть; вытесня́ть.

supersonic, *a*, сверхзвуково́й.

superstition, *n*, суеве́рие; **superstitious**, *a*, суеве́рный.

superstructure, *n*, надстро́йка.

supertax, *n*, нало́г на сверхпри́быль.

supervene, *v.t*, сле́довать за; вытека́ть из.

supervise, *v.t*, смотре́ть/наблюда́ть за; руководи́ть *(inst.)*; надзира́ть за; **supervision**, *n*, наблюде́ние, надзо́р; руково́дство; **supervisor**, *n*, надсмо́трщик, надзира́тель; руководи́тель; контролёр.

supine, *a*, лежа́щий на́взничь; лени́вый, безразли́чный.

supper, n, ýжин; *have* ~ ýжинать.

supplant, v.t, выживáть, вытеснять.

supple, a, гибкий, подáтливый.

supplement, n, добавлéние, дополнéние; приложéние; ¶ v.t, добавлять, дополнять; ~ary, a, дополнительный.

suppleness, n, гибкость, подáтливость.

suppliant, a, умоляющий; ¶ n, просйтель; supplicate, v.t, просйть, умолять; supplication, n, прóсьба, мольба.

supplier, n, поставщйк, агéнт по снабжéнию; supply, n, постáвка, снабжéние; pl, запáсы, продовóльствие; ~ *and demand* предложéние и спрос; ¶ v.t, поставлять, снабжáть: удовлетворять (*needs*).

support, n, поддéржка; опóра, оплóт; подпóра; кормйлец; ¶ v.t, поддéрживать; содержáть; ~ *oneself* кормйть себя; ~er, n, сторóнник, привéрженец.

suppose, v.t, полагáть, предполагáть; *let's* ~ предположим, допýстим; ~d, *p.p. & a*, предполагáемый, мнймый; supposition, n, предположéние; suppositious, a, поддéльный, подлóжный.

suppress, v.t, подавлять; запрещáть; сдéрживать; замáлчивать (*truth*); ~ion, n, подавлéние; запрещéние; замáлчивание.

suppurate, v.i, гнойться; suppuration, n, нагноéние.

supremacy, n, главéнство; верхóвная власть; supreme, a, вýсший, верхóвный; критйческий.

surcharge, n, перегрýзка; приплáта, доплáта; ¶ v.t, перегружáть; взыскивать.

sure, a, увéренный; несомнéнный; вéрный, надёжный; *make* ~ *of* удостоверяться в, убеждáться в; обеспéчивать; *he is* ~ *to come* он обязáтельно придёт; ~ly, *ad*, несомнéнно, конéчно; ~ness, n, увéренность; надёжность; ~ty, n, порýка; (*pers.*) поручйтель; *stand* ~ *for* ручáться за.

surf, n, прибóй; бурýн; ¶ v.i, катáться на волнáх.

surface, n, повéрхность.

surfeit, n, излйшество; пресыщéние; ¶ v.t, перекáрмливать; пресыщáть; v.i, передáть.

surge, n, прилйв; вóлны; ¶ v.i, вздымáться; волновáться.

surgeon, n, хирýрг; воéнный врач; surgery, n, хирургйя; приёмная врачá, кабинéт врачá; ~ *hours* часы приёма (пациéнтов); surgical, a, хирургйческий.

surging a вздымáющийся; волнýющийся.

surly, a, грýбый, угрюмый.

surmise, n, предположéние, догáдка; ¶ v.t, предполагáть, подозревáть.

surmount, v.t, преодолевáть.

surname, n, фамйлия.

surpass, v.t, превосходйть, превышáть.

surplice, n, стихáрь.

surplus, a, излйшний, избýточный; ¶ n, излйшек, остáток; ~ *value* прибáвочная стóимость.

surprise, n, удивлéние; неожйданность; сюрпрйз; ~ *attack* неожйданное нападéние; ¶ v.t, удивлять; заставáть врасплóх; surprising, a, удивйтельный; неожйданный.

surrender, n, сдáча, капитуляция; откáз; ~ *value* сýмма, причитáющаяся отказáвшемуся от страховóго пóлиса; ¶ v.t, сдавáть; откáзываться от; v.i, сдавáться, капитулйровать.

surreptitious, a, тáйный, сдéланный тайкóм/ украдкой.

surrogate, n, заменйтель, суррогáт; (*pers.*) заместйтель.

surround, v.t, окружáть, обступáть; ~ing, a, окружáющий, сосéдний; ~ings, *n.pl*, окружéние; средá; *окр. стности.*

surtax, n, добáвочный налóг.

surveillance, n, наблюдéние, надзóр.

survey, n, обозрéние, осмóтр; топографйческая съёмка; межевáние; ¶ v.t, обозревáть, осмáтривать; дéлать съёмку (*gen.*), межевáть; ~or, n, землемéр, топóграф; инспéктор.

survival, n, выживáние, пережйток; ~ *of the fittest* естéственный отбóр.

survive, v.t, переживáть (*contemps.*); переносйть, выдéрживать; v.i, оставáться в живых, выживáть; survivor, n, уцелéвший, остáвшийся в живых.

susceptible, a, восприймчивый, впечатлйтельный; чувствйтельный.

suspect, *a*, подозреваемый; подозрительный; ¶ *v.t*, подозревать; не доверять *(dat.)*; *v.i*, полагать.

suspend, *v.t*, вешать, подвешивать; приостанавливать; временно отстранять от должности; **~ers**, *n.pl*, подвязки; **suspense**, *n*, ожидание, беспокойство; неизвестность; *in* **~** в состоянии неизвестности; **suspension**, *n*, подвешивание; приостановка; временная отставка; **~** *bridge* висячий мост; **suspensory**, *a*, поддерживающий; подвешивающий; **~** *bandage* суспензорий.

suspicion, *n*, подозрение; *not even a* **~** *of* ни чуточки; **suspicious**, *a*, подозрительный.

sustain, *v.t*, поддерживать; выносить; **~** *injury* потерпеть *(pf.)* увечье; **sustenance**, *n*, питание; пища; средства к существованию; поддержка.

suture, *n*, шов; наложение шва.

suzerain, *n*, сюзерен, феодальный властитель; **~ty**, *n*, власть сюзерена, сюзеренитет.

swab, *n*, швабра; *(med.)* тампон.

swaddling clothes, *n.pl*, пелёнки.

swag, *n*, *(coll.)* добыча, награбленное добро.

swagger, *v.i*, важничать, чваниться; **~er**, *n*, щёголь; хвастун.

swain, *n*, деревенский парень, пастух.

swallow, *n*, глоток; ласточка *(bird)*: ¶ *v.t*, глотать, проглатывать; **~** *up* поглощать.

swamp, *n*, болото, топь; ¶ *v.t*, заливать, затоплять; заваливать *(e.g. with correspondence)*; **~y**, *a*, болотистый.

swan, *n*, лебедь; **~'s** *down* лебяжий пух; **~** *song* лебединая песня.

swap, *n*, обмен; ¶ *v.t*, менять; обмениваться *(inst.)*.

sward, *n*, газон; дёрн.

swarm, *n*, рой; масса, толпа; ¶ *v.i*, роиться; толпиться; кишеть.

swarthy, *a*, смуглый, тёмный.

swastika, *n*, свастика.

swathe, *v.t*, бинтовать; закутывать, обматывать.

sway, *n*, качание, колебание; власть; ¶ *v.t*, качать; склонять (на свою сторону); иметь влияние на; *v.i*, качаться.

swear, *v.i*, клясться; ручаться; ругаться; присягать; **~** *in* приводить к присяге.

sweat, *n*, пот, испарина; ¶ *v.i*, потеть; *v.t*, эксплуатировать; **~er**, *n*, свитер; **~ing**, *n*, потение; **~** *system* потогонная система; **~y**, *a*, потный, в поту.

swede, *n*, брюква.

Swede, *n*, швед, -ка; **Swedish**, *a*, шведский; ¶ *n*, шведский язык.

sweep, *n*, выметание; взмах, размах; изгиб *(of road)*; протяжение; охват; *(pers.)* трубочист; ¶ *v.t*, мести, выметать; чистить; *(mar.)* тралить; охватывать, окидывать (взглядом); *v.i*, мчаться, нестись; простираться; **~** *away* сметать, смывать; уничтожать; **~** *past* проноситься; **~er**, *n*, подметальщик; машина для чистки улиц; **~ing**, *n*, подметание, уборка; *pl*, мусор; ¶ *a*, широкий; **~** *statements* огульные утверждения; **~stake**, *n*, пари (на скачках), тотализатор.

sweet, *a*, сладкий; душистый; мелодичный; милый, приятный; **~breads** сладкое мясо; **~** *briar* шиповник; **~** *herbs* душистые травы; **~meats** конфеты, сласти; **~** *potato* батат; **~-scented** душистый; *have a* **~** *tooth* быть сластёной; S**~** *William* турецкая гвоздика; ¶ *n*, конфета; сладкое; **~en**, *v.t*, подслащивать; **~ness**, *n*, сладость.

swell, *n*, выпуклость, возвышение; *(mar.)* зыбь, волнение; *(coll.)* щёголь; ¶ *a*, *(coll.)* шикарный; прекрасный; ¶ *v.t*, надувать, увеличивать; *v.i*, пухнуть, разбухать; надуваться; увеличиваться; **~ing**, *n*, опухоль; разбухание.

swelter, *v.i*, изнемогать от зноя.

swerve, *n*, отклонение; изгиб; ¶ *v.i*, отклоняться (от прямого пути), сворачивать в сторону.

swift, *a*, быстрый, скорый; ¶ *n*, стриж; **~ness**, *n*, быстрота, стремительность.

swig, *n*, глоток; ¶ *v.t*, потягивать.

swill, *n*, полоскание; пойло; помои; ¶ *v.t*, полоскать; жадно пить.

swim, *n*, плавание; *go for a* **~** идти плавать; *be in the* **~** быть в курсе дел; ¶ *v.i*, плавать, плыть; кружиться *(of head)*; *v.t*, переплы-

ва́ть; ~ming, *n*, пла́вание; ~ *bath| pool* плавательный бассе́йн; ~ *costume* купа́льный костюм.
swindle, *n*, надува́тельство, обма́н; ¶ *v.t*, надува́ть, обма́нывать; ~r, *n*, моше́нник, плут.
swine, *n*, свинья́; ~*herd* свинопа́с.
swing, *n*, кача́ние, колеба́ние; взмах; разма́х; каче́ли; *in full* ~ в по́лном разга́ре; ~ *bridge* поворо́тный мост; ~ *door* враща́ющаяся дверь; ¶ *v.t. (& i.)* кача́ть(ся), колеба́ть(ся); ~ *one's arms* разма́хивать рука́ми.
swirl, *n*, вихрь; круже́ние; водоворо́т; ¶ *v.i*, кружи́ться.
swish, *n*, свист; ¶ *v.i*, свисте́ть, рассека́ть во́здух со сви́стом.
Swiss, *a*, швейца́рский; ¶ *n*, швейца́р|ец, -ка.
switch, *n*, прут, хлыст; *(elec.)* выключа́тель, переключа́тель; *(rly.)* стре́лка; ~*back* америка́нские го́ры; ~*board* распредели́тельный щит; коммута́тор; ¶ *v.t*, переключа́ть; переводи́ть на другой путь; направля́ть в другу́ю сто́рону; ~ *off* выключа́ть; ~ *on* включа́ть.
swivel, *n*, вертлю́г, шарни́рное соедине́ние; ~ *chair* винтя́щийся стул; ¶ *v.t. (& i.)*, враща́ть(ся).
swollen, *a*, взду́тый, разду́тый.
swoon, *n*, о́бморок; ¶ *v.i*, па́дать в о́бморок.
swoop, *n*, налёт, внеза́пное нападе́ние; ¶ *v.i*, броса́ться, устремля́ться.
sword, *n*, меч, шпа́га, са́бля; ~*belt* портупе́я; ~*fish* меч-ры́ба; ~ *stick* трость с вкладно́й шпа́гой; *put to the* ~ предава́ть мечу́; ~*sman*, *n*, фехтова́льщик; ~*ship*, *n*, иску́сство фехтова́ния.
Sybarite, *n*, сибари́т.
sycamore, *n*, сикомо́р, плата́н.
sycophant, *n*, льстец, подхали́м.
syllabize, *v.t*, произноси́ть по слога́м; разделя́ть на сло́ги; **syllable**, *n*, слог.
syllabus, *n*, програ́мма.
syllogism, *n*, силлоги́зм.
sylph, *n*, сильф, сильфи́да.
sylvan, *a*, лесно́й, леси́стый.
symbol, *n*, си́мвол; ~*ic*, *a*, символи́ческий; ~*ize*, *v.t*, символизи́ровать.

symmetrical, *a*, симметри́чный; **symmetry**, *n*, симме́трия.
sympathetic, *a*, по́лный сочу́вствия; симпати́чный; **sympathize**, *v.i*, сочу́вствовать; **sympathy**, *n*, сочу́вствие, сострада́ние; симпа́тия.
symphony, *n*, симфо́ния.
symptom, *n*, симпто́м, при́знак; ~*atic*, *a*, симптомати́ческий.
synagogue, *n*, синаго́га.
synchronize, *v.t*, координи́ровать; согласо́вывать во вре́мени; *v.i*, совпада́ть во вре́мени; **synchronous**, *a*, одновреме́нный, синхро́нный.
syncopate, *v.t*, сокраща́ть; *(mus.)* синкопи́ровать.
syndicate, *n*, синдика́т.
synod, *n*, сино́д; собо́р духове́нства.
synonym, *n*, сино́ним; ~*ous*, *a*, синоними́ч|еский, ~ный.
synopsis, *n*, конспе́кт, сино́псис.
syntax, *n*, си́нтаксис.
synthesis, *n*, си́нтез; **synthetic**, *a*, синтети́ческий.
syphilis, *n*, си́филис; **syphilitic**, *a*, сифилити́ческий.
syphon, *n*, сифо́н.
Syrian, *a*, сири́йский; ¶ *n*, сир|и́ец, -и́йка.
syringa, *n*, сире́нь.
syringe, *n*, шприц; пожа́рный насо́с; ¶ *v.t*, спринцева́ть, впры́скивать.
syrup, *n*, сиро́п; *golden* ~ све́тлая па́тока; ~*y*, *a*, густо́й, как сиро́п.
system, *n*, систе́ма; сеть; ~*atic*, *a*, системати́ческий; ~*atize*, *v.t*, систематизи́ровать.

T

T, *n*: *to a* ~ точь-в-то́чь; ~*-square* та́вро́вый уго́льник.
tab, *n*, пе́телька; петли́ца; ве́шалка; ушко́.
tabby cat, *n*, пёстрая ко́шка.
tabernacle, *n*, шатёр; моли́твенный дом.
table, *n*, стол; доска́; табли́ца; расписа́ние; ~*cloth* ска́терть; ~ *companion* сосе́д по столу́; ~ *d'hôte* табльдо́т; ~ *knife* столо́вый нож; ~*land* плоского́рье, плато́; ~ *napkin* салфе́тка; ~ *runner* на-

стольная дорожка; ~ *spoon* столовая ложка; ~ *talk* застольная беседа; ~ *wate* посуда; ножи, вилки, ложки; ~ *water* минеральная вода; ¶ *v.t*, класть на стол; предлагать, представлять; *turn the* ~s меняться ролями.

tableau, *n*, живая картина; живописное изображение.

tablet, *n*, таблетка; блокнот; дощечка; кусок *(of soap)*.

taboo, *n*, табу; ¶ *v.t*, объявлять табу на.

tabular, *a*, табличный; плоский; слоистый; **tabulate**, *v.t*, вносить в таблицу; **tabulator**, *n*, табулятор; *(pers.)* составитель таблиц.

tacit, *a*, молчаливый; подразумеваемый; ~**urn**, *a*, молчаливый; ~**urnity**, *n*, молчаливость.

tack, *n*, гвоздик, кнопка; *(mar.)* галс; *(fig.)* курс; *pl,(sew.)* намётка; ¶ *v.t*, прибивать, прикреплять; *(sew.)* смётывать на живую нитку; *v.i*, поворачивать на другой галс; *(fig.)* лавировать.

tackle, *n*, принадлежности, снасть; оборудование *(mar.)* такелаж; полиспаст, система блоков; ¶ *v.t*, закреплять; браться за *(task, etc.)*.

tacky, *a*, клейкий, липкий.

tact, *n*, такт, тактичность; ~**ful**, *a*, тактичный; ~**less**, *a*, бестактный.

tactical, *a*, тактический; **tactician**, *n*, тактик; **tactics**, *n*, тактика.

tactile, *a*, осязаемый, осязательный.

tadpole, *n*, головастик.

taffeta, *n*, тафта.

tag, *n*, ярлык, этикетка, бирка; ушко; наконечник; ¶ *v.t*, прикреплять ярлык к; присоединять наконечник к.

tail, *n*, хвост; пола, фалда; коса *(of hair)*; обратная сторона; ~ *coat* фрак; ~ *light* задний фонарь; *(rly.)* буферный фонарь; ~ *wind* попутный ветер; *turn* ~ убегать, удирать; ¶ *v.t*, отрубать хвост; *(gen.)* следить за; ~ *after* следовать за, тащиться за; ~ *away* отставать; убывать; ~**less**, *a*, бесхвостый.

tailor, *n*, портной; ~-*made suit* костюм, сделанный на заказ, ~**ing**, *n*, портняжное дело.

taint, *n*, пятно, порок; налёт; ¶ *v.t*, портить; заражать; ~**ed**, *p.p. & a*, испорченный.

take, *v.t*, брать; захватывать; овладевать *(inst.)*; принимать *(steps, medicine)*; есть, пить; занимать *(place, time)*; считать, полагать; реагировать на; примиряться с; *v.i*, иметь успех; действовать; ~ *aback* захватывать врасплох; ошеломлять; ~ *advantage of* воспользоваться *(pf.)*; ~ *away* отнимать, удалять; вычитать; ~ *charge of* брать на себя заботу о/ответственность за; ~ *cover* укрываться; ~ *down* снимать; сносить; разбирать *(engine)*; записывать; ~ *in* брать на дом *(work)*; принимать *(guest)*; получать *(paper)*; ушивать *(dress)*; обманывать; понимать; ~ *into consideration* учитывать; ~ *off (v.t.)* снимать; вычитать; подражать *(dat.)*; имитировать; *(v.i.)* взлетать; ~ *on* принимать (на службу); предпринимать; бороться с; ~ *out* вынимать; приглашать (в театр, *etc.)*; выводить (на прогулку); выписывать; ~ *over* завладевать *(inst.)*, принимать (должность) от; ~ *part in* принимать участие в, участвовать в; ~ *place* иметь место, случаться; ~ *the chair* председательствовать; ~ *the trouble* брать на себя труд; ~ *to heart* принимать близко к сердцу; ~ *to pieces* разбирать на части; ~ *to task* призывать к ответу; ~ *up* поднимать; занимать *(time)*; браться за; ~ *up the thread* возвращаться к начатому; *he* ~s *after his father* он походит на отца; ¶ *n*, улов, добыча; *(filming)* снятая сцена, съёмка; ~-*off* взлёт; ~**r**, *n*, берущий; **taking**, *a*, привлекательный; ¶ *n*, захват; *pl*, барыши.

talc, **talcum powder**, *n*, тальк.

tale, *n*, рассказ, повесть, сказка; выдумка, сплетня; *tell* ~s сплетничать; ~-*bearer* сплетник, ябедник.

talent, *n*, талант; ~**ed**, *a*, талантливый, одарённый.

talisman, *n*, талисман.

talk, *n*, разговор, беседа; слух; доклад; ¶ *v.i*, говорить; сплетничать; ~ *into* убеждать, уговаривать; ~ *to* говори́ть с; ~ative, *a*, разгово́рчивый; болтли́вый; ~er, *n*, говоря́щий: болту́н; ора́тор; ~ing, *a*, говоря́щий, разгово́рчивый; ~ *film* звуково́й фильм; *give a* ~ *to* де́лать вы́говор *(dat.)*.

tall, *a*, высо́кий; ~ness, *n*, высота́; высо́кий рост.

tallow, *n*, жир, са́ло; ~y, *a*, жи́рный, са́льный.

tally, *n*, би́рка, ярлы́к; дублика́т, ко́пия; ¶ *v.i*, совпада́ть, соотве́тствовать.

talon, *n*, ко́готь; тало́н.

tambour, *n*, бараба́н; пя́льцы; ~ine, *n*, бу́бен.

tame, *a*, ручно́й, приручённый; поко́рный; ску́чный; ¶ *v.t*, прируча́ть, дрессирова́ть; усмиря́ть; укроща́ть; ~ness, *n*, приручённость; поко́рность; ~r, *n*, укроти́тель, дрессиро́вщик; усмири́тель.

tam-o'-shanter, *n*, (шотла́ндский) бере́т.

tamp, *v.t*, трамбова́ть, набива́ть.

tamper, *v.i*: ~ *with* тро́гать; по́ртить; вме́шиваться в; подде́лывать.

tan, *a*, рыжева́то-кори́чневый; ¶ *n*, зага́р; толчёная дубо́вая кора́; ~ *yard* кожёвенный заво́д; ¶ *v.t*, дуби́ть *(leather)*; обжига́ть; *(coll.)* дуба́сить; *v.i*, загора́ть.

tandem, *n*, велосипе́д-тэ́ндем; упря́жка цу́гом.

tang, *n*, ре́зкий при́вкус; арома́т.

tangent, *a*, каса́тельный; ¶ *n*, каса́тельная, та́нгенс.

tangerine, *n*, мандари́н.

tangible, *a*, осяза́емый, материа́льный.

tangle, *n*, спу́танный клубо́к; *(coll.)* неразбери́ха; ¶ *v.t. (& i.)*, запу́тывать(ся).

tango, *n*, та́нго.

tank, *n*, бак, цисте́рна; резервуа́р; *(mil.)* танк.

tankard, *n*, пивна́я кру́жка.

tanker, *n*, та́нкер; цисте́рна.

tanner, *n*, дуби́льщик; ~y, *n*, кожёвенный заво́д; tannic, *a*, дуби́льный; tannin, *n*, тани́н; дуби́льное вещество́; tanning, *n*, дубле́ние.

tantalize, *v.t*, му́чить; издева́ться над; tantalizing, *a*, мучи́тельный.

tantamount, *a*, равноси́льный, равноце́нный.

tantrum, *n*, вспы́шка гне́ва.

tap, *n*, лёгкий стук; кран; втулка, про́бка; отво́д; ¶ *v.t*, вставля́ть кран в; почина́ть *(barrel)*; де́лать надре́з на (де́реве); *(elec.)* отводи́ть; ~ *on* стуча́ть в/по; ~ *the wire* перехва́тывать телегра́фное сообще́ние; ~ *the line* подслу́шивать телефо́нный разгово́р.

tape, *n*, ле́нта; тесьма́; ~ *measure* руле́тка; ~ *recorder* магнитофо́н.

taper, *n*, то́нкая све́чка; ¶ *v.t. (& i.)*, су́живать(ся) к концу́; заостря́ть(ся).

tapestry, *n*, гобеле́н.

tapeworm, *n*, соли́тёр.

tapioca, *n*, тапио́ка.

tapir, *n*, тапи́р.

tapper, *n*, телегра́фный ключ.

tar, *n*, дёготь, гудро́н; смола́; *(coll.)* моря́к; ¶ *v.t*, ма́зать дёгтем; ~ *and feather* вы́мазав дёгтем, обваля́ть *(pf.)* в пе́рьях.

tarantella, *n*, таранте́лла.

tarantula, *n*, тара́нтул.

tardiness, *n*, медли́тельность; tardy, *a*, медли́тельный; запозда́лый.

tare, *n*, ви́ка; *pl*, пле́велы; *(com.)* та́ра.

target, *n*, мише́нь, цель; зада́ние; ~ *practice* стрельба́ по мише́ням.

tariff, *n*, тари́ф; расце́нка; ¶ *v.t*, включа́ть в тари́ф, оце́нивать.

tarmac[adam], *n*, гудрони́рованное шоссе́; бетони́рованная площа́дка; ¶ *v.t*, гудрони́ровать.

tarn, *n*, го́рное о́зеро.

tarnish, *n*, ту́склость; пятно́; ¶ *v.t*, де́лать ту́склым; *(fig.)* поро́чить; *v.i*, тускне́ть.

tarpaulin, *n*, брезе́нт, паруси́на.

tarragon, *n*, эстраго́н.

tarred, tarry, *a*, покры́тый дёгтем.

tarry, *v.i*, ме́длить, ме́шкать.

tart, *a*, ки́слый; е́дкий; те́рпкий; *(fig.)* ко́лкий; ¶ *n*, торт, сла́дкий пиро́г; *(coll.)* проститу́тка.

tartan, *n*, шотла́ндка.

Tartar, *n*, тата́р|ин, -ка; раздражи́тельный челове́к; tartaric, *a*, виннока́менный.

tartness, *n*, кислота́; ко́лкость.

task, *n*, зада́ча, зада́ние; *take to* ~ призыва́ть к отве́ту; отчи́тывать; *urgent* ~ неотло́жное де́ло.

tassel, *n*, кисточка; закладка.

taste, *n*, вкус; проба; глоток, кусочек; *have a ~ for* иметь склонность к; ¶ *v.t*, пробовать; вкушать, испытывать; *v.i*, иметь вкус/привкус; ~*ful*, *a*, сделанный со вкусом; ~*less*, *a*, безвкусный; ~*r*, *n*, дегустатор; **tasting**, *n*, дегустация; **tasty**, *a*, вкусный.

tatter, *n*, лоскут; *pl*, клочья, лохмотья; ~*ed*, *a*, оборванный; в лохмотьях.

tatting, *n*, плетёное кружево.

tattle, *n*, болтовня, сплетни; ¶ *v.i*, болтать; ~*r*, *n*, болтун, сплетник.

tattoo, *n*, татуировка; сигнал вечерней зари; ¶ *v.t*, татуировать; *v.i*, играть зорю.

taunt, *n*, насмешка; колкость, «шпилька»; ¶ *v.t*, насмехаться над; ~*ing*, *a*, насмешливый, язвительный.

taut, *a*, туго натянутый, упругий; ~*en*, *v.i*, туго натягивать; ~*ness*, *n*, натяжение; упругость.

tautological, *a*, тавтологический; **tautology**, *n*, тавтология.

tavern, *n*, таверна.

tawdriness, *n*, безвкусица; мишура; **tawdry**, *a*, безвкусный; мишурный.

tawny, *a*, рыжевато-коричневый.

tax, *n*, налог; ~ *collector* сборщик налогов; ~*free* освобождённый от налогов; ~*payer* налогоплательщик; ¶ *v.t*, облагать налогом; напрягать; утомлять; испытывать *(patience)*; ~*able*, *a*, подлежащий обложению налогом; ~*ation*, *n*, обложение налогом; налоги.

taxi, *n*, такси; ~ *rank* стоянка такси.

taxidermist, набивщик чучел; **taxidermy**, *n*, набивка чучел.

tea, *n*, чай; *high* ~ вечерний чай; *Russian* ~ чай с лимоном; ~*caddy* чайница; ~ *cosy* чехольчик (для чайника); ~*cup* чайная чашка; ~*pot* чайник; ~ *room* чайная, кафе-кондитерская; ~*set* чайный сервиз; ~*spoon* чайная ложка.

teach, *v.t*, учить, обучать; преподавать; *v.i*, быть преподавателем/учителем; *I'll* ~ *him* я проучу его; ~*er*, *n*, учитель, преподаватель, -ница; ~*ing*, *n*, учение; обучение; преподавание; педагогика.

teak, *n*, тик; ¶ *a*, тиковый.

team, *n*, команда; бригада, артель; упряжка *(horses)*, ~*work* бригадная работа; согласованная работа, слаженность; ¶ *v.t. (& i.)*: ~ *up* объединять(ся) в команду/бригаду.

tear, *n*, прорез, прореха; ¶ *v.t*, рвать, разрывать; *v.i*, рваться; ~ *along* мчаться; ~ *apart* разрывать на части; *(fig.)* раздирать; ~ *down* срывать; ~ *off* отрывать; ~ *one's hair out* вырывать волосы.

tear, *n*, слеза; ~*drop* слезинка; ~ *gas* слезоточивый газ; ~*ful* полный слёз, плачущий; печальный.

tease, *v.t*, дразнить; чесать *(wool)*; ворсить *(material)* ¶ *n*, задира; любитель подразнить; ~*r*, *n*, трудная задача/проблема; головоломка.

teat, *n*, соска.

technical, *a*, технический; специальный; ~ *offence* формальное нарушение закона; ~ *term* специальный термин. ~*ity*, *n*, техническая сторона; формальность; *pl*, технические детали; **technician**, *n*, техник; **technicolour**, *n*, цветная фотография; **technique**, *n*, техника; **technological**, *a*, технологический; **technologist**, *n*, технолог; **technology**, *n*, техника; технология.

teddy bear, *n*, медвежонок.

tedious, *a*, скучный, утомительный; **tedium**, *n*, скука; утомительность.

teem, *v.i*, кишеть, изобиловать; *v.t*, разливать; *it is* ~*ing with rain* дождь льёт; ~*ing*, *a*, переполненный; кишащий.

teenager, *n*, подросток.

teens, *n.pl*, возраст от 13 до 19 лет; *she is still in her* ~ ей ещё нет 20 лет.

teethe, *v.i : the child is teething* у ребёнка прорезываются зубы; **teething**, *n*, прорезывание зубов; ~ *ring* детское зубное кольцо; ~ *troubles (fig.)* начальные проблемы.

teetotal, *a*, непьющий, трезвый; ~*ism*, *n*, воздержание от алкоголя, трезвенность; ~*ler*, *n*, трезвенник.

teetotum, *n*, волчок.

tegument, *n,* оболо́чка, покро́в.

telegram, *n,* телегра́мма.

telegraph, *n,* телегра́ф; ¶ *v.t. & i,* телеграфи́ровать; **~ic,** *a,* телегра́фный; **~ist,** *n,* телеграфи́ст; **~y,** *n,* телеграфи́я.

telepathic, *a,* телепати́ческий; **telepathy,** *n,* телепа́тия.

telephone, *n,* телефо́н; **~** *box* телефо́нная бу́дка; **~** *exchange* телефо́нная ста́нция; **~** *switchboard* телефо́нный коммута́тор; ¶ *v.t. & v.i,* звони́ть по телефо́ну; **telephony,** *n,* телефони́я.

teleprinter, *n,* буквопеча́тающий телегра́ф.

telescope, *n,* телеско́п; ¶ *v.t. (& i.),* телескопи́чески скла́дывать(ся)/ выдвига́ть(ся); **telescopic,** *a,* телескопи́ческий; выдвижно́й, раздвижно́й.

televise, *v.t,* передава́ть по телеви́зору; **television,** *n,* телеви́дение; **~** *set* телеви́зор.

tell, *v.t,* расска́зывать; говори́ть; прика́зывать; отлича́ть; *v.i,* ска́зываться; **~** *off* отбира́ть; брани́ть; **~** *on* доноси́ть на; влия́ть на; **~** *in his favour* говори́ть в его́ по́льзу; **~er,** *n,* расска́зчик; счётчик голосо́в; касси́р; **~ing,** *a,* многозначи́тельный; вырази́тельный; **~tale,** *n,* преда́тельский; ¶ *n,* доно́счик, спле́тник.

temerity, *n,* безрассу́дство; отва́га; де́рзость.

temper, *n,* нрав, хара́ктер; настрое́ние; гнев; раство́р; смесь; *(metal)* сте́пень зака́лки; *fit of* **~** припа́док гне́ва; *loose one's* **~** выходи́ть из себя́; ¶ *v.t,* смягча́ть, умеря́ть; регули́ровать; *(metal)* отпуска́ть; зака́ливать, закаля́ть; **~ament,** *n,* темпера́мент; **~amental,** *a,* темпера́ментный; **~ance,** *n,* тре́звенность; уме́ренность; **~ate,** *a,* воздержанный, уме́ренный; **~ature,** *n,* температу́ра.

tempest, *n,* бу́ря; **~uous,** *a,* бу́рный, бу́йный.

temple, *n,* храм; *(anat.)* висо́к.

temporal, *a,* мирско́й, све́тский; вре́менный; *(anat.)* височный; **temporary,** *a,* вре́менный; **temporize,** *v.i,* приспособля́ться ко вре́мени и обстоя́тельствам; ме́длить.

tempt, *v.t,* искуша́ть, соблазня́ть; **~ation,** *n,* искуше́ние, собла́зн; **~er,** *n,* искуси́тель; **~ing,** *a,* зама́нчивый; соблазни́тельный; **~ress,** *n,* искуси́тельница.

ten, *num,* де́сять; ¶ *n,* деся́ток; *(cards)* деся́тка.

tenable, *a,* про́чный; приго́дный (для жилья́); защити́мый.

tenacious, *a,* це́пкий; упо́рный.

tenancy, *n,* аре́нда, наём; арендо́ванный дом; арендо́ванная земля́; **tenant,** *n,* аренда́тор, нанима́тель, съёмщик; жиле́ц.

tench, *n,* линь.

tend, *v.t,* забо́титься о; уха́живать за; обслу́живать; *v.i,* клони́ться, направля́ться; име́ть скло́нность; **~ency,** *n,* тенде́нция, скло́нность; **~entious,** *a,* тенденцио́зный.

tender, *n,* те́ндер; *(mar.)* посы́льное су́дно; *(com.)* предложе́ние; зая́вка на подря́дную рабо́ту; ¶ *v.t,* предлага́ть; вноси́ть; подава́ть (в отста́вку).

tender, *a,* не́жный, мя́гкий; боле́зненный; чувстви́тельный; **~foot** новичо́к; **~loin** филе́й; **~ness,** *n,* не́жность, мя́гкость.

tendon, *n,* сухожи́лие.

tendril, *n,* у́сик.

tenement, *n,* кварти́ра, аренду́емое помеще́ние; **~** *house* многокварти́рный дом.

tenet, *n,* до́гмат, при́нцип.

tennis, *n,* те́ннис; **~** *court* те́ннисный корт.

tenor, *n,* направле́ние; укла́д *(of life);* смысл; *(mus.)* те́нор.

tense, *a,* натя́нутый, напряжённый; ¶ *n,* вре́мя; **~ness,** *n,* натя́нутость, напряжённость; **tension,** *n,* напряже́ние, натяже́ние.

tent, *n,* пала́тка; **~** *pole* пала́точная сто́йка.

tentacle, *n,* щу́пальце.

tentative, *a,* про́бный, эксперимента́льный.

tenterhooks: *be on* **~** сиде́ть как на иго́лках, му́читься неизве́стностью.

tenth, *ord.num,* деся́тый; ¶ *n,* деся́тая часть; **~** *of June* деся́тое ию́ня.

tenuity, *n,* разрежённость; то́нкость; **tenuous,** *a,* разрежённый; то́нкий; непро́чный.

tenure, *n,* владе́ние; заня́тие *(of office);* срок владе́ния/слу́жбы.

tepid, *a,* теплова́тый.

term, *n,* те́рмин; срок, перио́д; семе́стр; *pl,* усло́вия; усло́вия опла́ты; ли́чные отноше́ния; выраже́ния; *be on good* ~s быть в хоро́ших отноше́ниях; *come to* ~s приходи́ть к соглаше́нию; ~s *of reference* компете́нция; ¶ *v.t,* называ́ть.

termagant, *n,* сварли́вая же́нщина.

terminal, *a,* заключи́тельный, коне́чный; семе́стровый; ¶ *n,* коне́чная ста́нция; коне́чный пункт; *(elec.)* зажи́м; **terminate,** *v.t,* конча́ть; *v.i,* конча́ться, истека́ть; **termination,** *n,* коне́ц, оконча́ние; истече́ние сро́ка; **terminus,** *n,* коне́чная ста́нция, вокза́л.

termite, *n,* терми́т.

tern, *n,* кра́чка.

terrace, *n,* терра́са; вера́нда; ¶ *v.t,* устра́ивать в ви́де терра́сы.

terracotta, *n,* террако́та.

terrain, *n,* ме́стность; по́чва; **terrestrial,** *a,* земно́й, сухопу́тный.

terrible, *a,* ужа́сный, стра́шный.

terrier, *n,* терье́р.

terrific, *a,* ужаса́ющий; *(coll.)* великоле́пный; **terrify,** *v.t,* ужаса́ть.

territorial, *a,* территориа́льный; **territory,** *n,* террито́рия; о́бласть, сфе́ра.

terror, *n,* страх; у́жас; терро́р; ~**ism,** *n,* террори́зм; ~**ist,** *n,* террори́ст; ~**ize,** *v.t,* терроризова́ть.

terse, *a,* вырази́тельный, сжа́тый; ~**ness,** *n,* вырази́тельность, сжа́тость.

tessellated, *a,* моза́ичный; вы́ложенный в ша́хматную кле́тку.

test, *n,* испыта́ние, о́пыт; ана́лиз, про́ба; экза́мен; крите́рий, мери́ло; *(chem.)* реакти́в; ~ *tube* пробирка; ¶ *v.t,* испы́тывать, проверя́ть; подверга́ть испыта́нию.

testament, *n,* завеща́ние; *(eccl.)* заве́т; ~**ary,** *a,* завеща́тельный, пе́реданный по завеща́нию; **testator,** *n,* завеща́тель.

testicle, *n,* яи́чко.

testify, *v.i,* свиде́тельствовать, дава́ть показа́ния; заявля́ть.

testimonial, *n,* аттеста́т; рекоменда́ция; **testimony,** *n,* показа́ние, свиде́тельство; заявле́ние.

testy, *a,* раздражи́тельный.

tetanus, *n,* столбня́к.

tether, *n,* при́вязь; *(fig.)* преде́л; *I am at the end of my* ~ я дошёл до преде́ла/то́чки; ¶ *v.t,* привя́зывать.

Teutonic, *a,* тевто́нский, древнегерма́нский.

text, *n,* текст, те́ма; ~*book* уче́бник, руково́дство.

textile, *n,* тексти́льное изде́лие, ткань; ¶ *a,* тексти́льный.

than, *c,* чем; *more* ~ *ten* бо́льше десяти́; *none other* ~ не кто ино́й, как.

thank, *v.t,* благодари́ть; ~ *God!* сла́ва бо́гу!; ~ *you!* благодарю́, спаси́бо!; ~*ful,* *a,* благода́рный; ~*fulness,* *n,* благода́рность; ~*less,* *a,* неблагода́рный; ~**s,** *n.pl,* благода́рность ~ *to* благодаря́; ~**sgiving,** *n,* благода́рственный моле́бен; благодаре́ние.

that, *pn,* тот, та, то; *(pn.relative)* кото́рый; кто; ¶ *c,* что, что́бы; *in order* ~ для того́, что́бы; ¶ *ad,* так, до тако́й сте́пени.

thatch, *n,* соло́менная кры́ша; тростни́к (для кро́вли); ¶ *v.t,* крыть соло́мой.

thaw, *n,* о́ттепель; ¶ *v.t,* распопля́ть; *v.i,* та́ять, отта́ивать; *(fig.)* смягча́ться.

the, *definite article* — *no equivalent in Russian;* ¶ *ad,* тем; *all* ~ *better* тем лу́чше; ~ *more* ~ *better* чем бо́льше, тем лу́чше.

theatre, *n,* теа́тр; **theatrical,** *a,* театра́льный.

thee, *pn,* тебя́, тебе́, *etc.*

theft, *n,* воровство́, кра́жа.

their, *a, & theirs, pn,* их; свой, *etc.*

theism, *n,* теи́зм; **theist,** *n,* теи́ст.

them, *pn,* их, им, *etc.*

thematic, *a,* темати́ческий; **theme,** *n,* те́ма, предме́т.

themselves, *pn,* себя́, *etc.* са́ми, *etc.*

then, *ad,* тогда́; пото́м, зате́м; *now and* ~ вре́мя от вре́мени; ¶ *c,* тогда́, в тако́м слу́чае; ~*ce,* *ad,* отту́да; ~*ceforth, ad,* с того́/э́того вре́мени, впредь.

theodolite, *n,* теодоли́т.

theologian, *n,* богосло́в; **theological,** *a,* богосло́вский; **theology,** *n,* богосло́вие.

theorem, *n,* теоре́ма; **theoretical,** *a,* теорети́ческий; **theorist,** *n,* теоре́тик; **theorize,** *v.i,* теоретизи́ровать; **theory,** *n,* тео́рия.

theosophy, *n*, теософия.
therapeutic, *a*, терапевтический; **~s**, *n*, терапия.
there, *ad*, там; туда; **~** *is*, **~** *are* есть; *here and* **~** там и сям; **~abouts**, *ad*, поблизости; приблизительно; **~after**, *ad*, с того/этого времени; **~at**, *ad*, при этом, по поводу этого; **~by**, *ad*, тем самым; посредством этого; **~fore**, *ad*, поэтому; **~in**, *ad*, в этом; в этом отношении; **~upon**, *ad*, затем, после чего.
thermal, *a*, термический, тепловой; горячий *(spring)*; **thermometer**, *n*, термометр, градусник; **thermos**, *n*, термос.
these, *pl.from* this.
thesis, *n*, тезис; диссертация.
they, *pn*, они.
thick, *a*, толстый; густой; плотный; глупый, тупой; **~-headed** тупоголовый; **~-lipped** губастый; **~-set** коренастый; **~-skinned** толстокожий *in the* **~** в самой гуще; *in разгаре*; *a bit* **~** немного чересчур; *lay it on* **~** преувеличивать; хватить *(pf.)* через край; *through* **~** *and thin* несмотря ни на какие препятствия; **~en**, *v.t. (& i.)*, сгущать(ся); усложнять(ся); уплотнять(ся); **~ening**, *n*, сгущение; уплотнение; **~et**, *n*, чаща, заросли; **~ness**, *n*, толщина; густота; плотность.
thief, *n*, вор; **thieve**, *v.i*, воровать, красть; **thievish**, *a*, воровской; вороватый.
thigh, *n*, бедро; **~-bone** берцовая кость.
thimble, *n*, наперсток; наконечник; **~ful**, *n*, глоточек.
thin, *a*, тонкий; худой; редкий *(hair)*; жидкий, слабый; **~-skinned** чувствительный; ¶ *v.t*, делать тонким/жидким; *v.i*, худеть; редеть; **~** *out (v.t.)* прореживать; *(v.i.)* редеть.
thine, *pn*, твой; свой.
thing, *n*, вещь, предмет; дело; факт; *pl*, вещи; багаж; принадлежности; *the only* **~** единственное; *it is a good* **~** *that* хорошо, что; *it is just the* **~** это как раз то, (что надо).
think, *v.t. & v.i*, думать, считать; мыслить; **~** *over* обдумывать; **~er**, *n*, мыслитель; **~ing**, *a*,

мыслящий, разумный; ¶ *n*, мнение; мышление; *to my way of* **~** по моему мнению.
thinly, *ad*, тонко; **thinness**, *n*, тонкость; худоба, худощавость.
third, *a*, *num.ord.*, третий; **~** *party* третья сторона; **~** *person* третье лицо; ¶ *n*, треть.
thirst, *n*, жажда; ¶ *v.i*, жаждать; **~y**, *a*, испытывающий жажду; иссохший *(soil)*; *be* **~** хотеть пить.
thirteen, *num*, тринадцать; **~th**, *ord.num*, тринадцатый.
thirtieth, *ord.num*, тридцатый; ¶ *n*, тридцатая часть; **thirty**, *num*, тридцать.
this, *a*, & *pn*, этот, эта, это; **~** *way* сюда; вот так.
thistle, *n*, чертополох.
thither, *ad*, туда, в ту сторону; *hither and* **~** туда и сюда.
thong, *n*, ремень.
thorax, *n*, грудная клетка.
thorn, *n*, колючка, шип; **~y**, *a*, колючий; *(fig.)* тернистый, тяжёлый.
thorough, *a*, тщательный, основательный; полный; **~bred** породистый, чистокровный; **~fare** проезд, проход; **~ly**, *ad*, вполне; основательно, тщательно.
those, *a.* & *pn*, те.
thou, *pn*, ты.
though, *c*, хотя, несмотря на; даже если (бы); хотя бы; *as* **~** как будто; ¶ *ad*, однако, тем не менее, всё-таки.
thought, *n*, мысль; размышление; намерение; внимательность, забота; **~ful**, *a*, задумчивый; глубокомысленный; заботливый; **~less**, *a*, необдуманный; невнимательный; беззаботный.
thousand, *num.* & *n*, тысяча; **~th**, *ord.num*, тысячный; ¶ *n*, тысячная часть.
thraldom, *n*, рабство.
thrash, *v.t*, бить; побеждать; *(agr.)* молотить; **~ing**, *n*, взбучка; *(agr.)* молотьба.
thread, *n*, нитка, нить *(& fig.)*; ход *(of screw)*; *(tech.)* резьба; ¶ *v.t*, продевать нитку (в иголку); нанизывать; **~** *one's way* осторожно пробираться; **~bare** потёртый; изношенный; *(fig.)* избитый; слабый.

threat, *n*, угрóза; ~en, *v.t*, грозúть/ угрожáть *(dat.);* ~ening, *a*, грозя́щий, угрожáющий; навúсший.

three, *num*, три; ¶ *n*, трóйка; ~cornered треугóльный; ~-ply трёхслóйный; ~fold, *a*, тройнóй, утрóенный; ¶ *ad*, втрóе, втройнé; ~score, *num*, шестьдеся́т; ~some, *n*, трóйка.

thresh, *v.t*, молотúть; *v.i*, метáться; ~ing, *n*, молотьбá; ~ *floor* ток; ~ *machine* молотúлка.

threshold, *n*, порóг; преддвéрие.

thrice, *ad*, трúжды.

thrift, *n*, бережлúвость, эконóмность; ~less, *a*, расточúтельный, неэконóмный; ~y, *a*, бережлúвый, эконóмный.

thrill, *n*, волнéние; трéпет; содрогáние; ¶ *v.t*, сúльно волновáть, захвáтывать; *v.i*, сúльно волновáться; дрожáть, трепетáть; ~er, *n*, боевúк, детектúвный ромáн/ фильм; ~ing, *a*, волнýющий, захвáтывающий.

thrive, *v.i*, преуспевáть, процветáть; разрастáться; thriving, *a*, процветáющий; бýйно растýщий.

throat, *n*, гóрло; ýзкий прохóд.

throb, *n*, биéние, пульсáция; ¶ *v.i*, бúться, пульсúровать; ~bing, *n*, биéние, пульсáция.

throe, *n*, сúльная боль; *death* ~ предсмéртные мýки, агóния.

throne, *n*, престóл, трон.

throng, *n*, толпá; ¶ *v.t*, заполня́ть; *v.i*, толпúться.

throstle, *n*, пéвчий дрозд.

throttle, *n*, глóтка, гортáнь; *(tech.)* дрóссель, регуля́тор; ¶ *v.t*, душúть; *(tech.)* дросселúровать.

through, *pr*, чéрез, сквозь, по; благодаря́, из-за; ¶ *ad*, насквóзь; от начáла до концá; *I am wet* ~ я насквóзь промóк; ~, *a*, прямóй, беспересáдочный *(train);* ~ *ticket* сквознóй билéт; ~out, *ad*, от начáла до концá; вездé; во всех отношéниях.

throw, *n*, бросóк; дáльность броскá; ~*in* ввод мячá в игрý; ¶ *v.t*, бросáть, кидáть, метáть; сбрáсывать *(rider);* ~ *aside* отбрáсывать; ~ *back* отбрáсывать назáд; отвергáть; ~ *down* сбрáсывать;

~ *in* добавля́ть; ~ *off* сбрáсывать; свергáть; ~ *open* распáхивать; ~ *out* выгоня́ть, выбрáсывать; отвергáть; ~ *up* извергáть; ~ing, *n*, бросáние.

thrush, *n*, дрозд.

thrust, *n*, вы́пад; толчóк, удáр; ¶ *v.t*, совáть, толкáть; ~ *aside* отбрáсывать, оттáлкивать; ~ *out* высóвывать; выгоня́ть.

thud, *n*, глухóй стук; ¶ *v.i*, пáдать с глухúм шýмом.

thug, *n*, головорéз, разбóйник.

thumb, *n*, большóй пáлец; ~screw тискú для большúх пáльцев; ~ *tack* чертёжная кнóпка; ¶ *v.t:* ~ *through* перелúстывать.

thump, *n*, тяжёлый удáр; глухóй звук; ¶ *v.t*, наносúть тяжёлый удáр *(dat.);* колотúть; *v.i*, пáдать тяжелó; бúться с глухúм шýмом.

thunder, *n*, гром; грóхот, шум; ~bolt удáр мóлнии; *(fig.)* гром средú я́сного нéба; ~cloud грозовáя тýча; ~storm грозá; ~struck как грóмом поражённый; ¶ *v.i*, гремéть; метáть грóмы и мóлнии; *it* ~s гром гремúт; ~ous, *a*, громовóй; ~y, *a*, грозовóй, предвещáющий грозý.

Thursday, *n*, четвéрг.

thus, *ad*, так, такúм óбразом; ~ *far* до сих пор.

thwack, *n*, удáр; ¶ *v.t*, бить, порóть.

thwart, *v.t*, мешáть *(dat.);* расстрáивать *(plans).*

thy, *a*, твой.

thyme, *n*, тимья́н.

thyroid, *a*, щитовúдный.

thyself, *pn*, себя́; сам, самá.

tiara, *n*, тиáра.

tibia, *n*, большáя берцóвая кость.

tic, *n*, нéрвный тик.

tick, *n*, тúканье *(clock);* отмéтка, «гáлочка»; тик *(cloth);* чехóл; кредúт; *(zool.)* клещ; ¶ *v.t*, отмечáть, стáвить «гáлочку» над; *v.i*, тúкать.

ticket, *n*, билéт; кáрточка; квитáнция; ярлы́к; спúсок кандидáтов; ~-collector билетёр, контролёр; ~-window кáсса; ¶ *v.t*, прикрепля́ть ярлы́к к.

tickle, *v.t*, щекотáть; веселúть; *my nose* ~s у меня́ щекóчет в носý; **ticklish**, *a*, щекотлúвый *(also fig.).*

tidal, *a,* прили́во-отли́вный; ~ *wave* прили́вная волна́; **tide,** *n,* прили́в и отли́в; пото́к, тече́ние; *high* ~ по́лная вода́, прили́в; ¶ *v.t:* ~ *over* помога́ть *(dat.);* ~ *way, n,* фарва́тер.

tidily, *ad,* аккура́тно, опря́тно; **tidiness,** *n,* аккура́тность, опря́тность.

tidings, *n.pl,* изве́стия, но́вости.

tidy, *a,* опря́тный, аккура́тный; значи́тельный; ~ *sum* кру́гленькая су́мма; ¶ *v.t,* убира́ть; приводи́ть в поря́док.

tie, *n,* га́лстук; *(sport)* ра́вный счёт; матч; *(mus.)* ли́га; *(tech.)* скре́па, соедине́ние; *(fig.)* обу́за; ~ *pin* була́вка для га́лстука; ¶ *v.t,* свя́зывать, завя́зывать; ограни́чивать; *v.i,* сыгра́ть *(pf.)* вничью́; сравня́ть *(pf.)* счёт; ~ *a knot in* завя́зывать узло́м; ~ *down* привя́зывать; ограни́чивать свобо́ду; ~ *up* привя́зывать; соединя́ть.

tier, *n,* ряд, я́рус.

tiff, *n,* размо́лвка, ссо́ра.

tiger, *n,* тигр.

tight, *a,* туго́й; пло́тный; сжа́тый; непроница́емый; те́сный, у́зкий; тру́дный; скупо́й; ску́дный; *(coll.)* пья́ный; *a* ~ *spot* тяжёлое положе́ние; ~**en,** *v.t. & i,* натя́гивать(ся), стя́гивать(ся); сжима́ть(ся); ~**ness,** *n,* теснота́; напряжённость; ~**s,** *n.pl,* трико́, колго́тки.

tigress, *n,* тигри́ца.

tile, *n,* черепи́ца; ка́фель; ~*d floor* ка́фельный пол; ~*d roof* черепи́чная кры́ша; ¶ *v.t,* крыть черепи́цей/пли́тками.

till, *n,* де́нежный я́щик; ¶ *v.t,* возде́лывать, паха́ть; ¶ *pr,* до; ¶ *c,* пока́ . . . не; ~ *then* до тех пор; ~*age, n,* обрабо́тка земли́; па́шня, возде́ланная земля́; ~**er,** *n,* земледе́лец; *(mar.)* ру́мпель.

tilt, *n,* накло́н; крен; *at full* ~ по́лным хо́дом; изо всех сил; ¶ *v.t. (& i.),* наклоня́ть(ся); крени́ть(ся); опроки́дывать(ся); повора́чивать(ся).

timber, *n,* лесоматериа́л; (строево́й) лес; ба́лка; *(mar.)* ти́мберс; ~*work* пло́тничная рабо́та; деревя́нное сооруже́ние; ~ *yard* лесно́й

склад; ¶ *v.t,* стро́ить из де́рева; ~**ed,** *a,* бревёнчатый; отде́ланный брёвнами; ~**ing,** *n,* лесоматериа́лы; пло́тничная рабо́та.

timbre, *n,* тембр.

time, *n,* вре́мя; срок; пери́од, пора́; раз; *(mus.)* темп, такт; *(sport)* тайм; ~ *and again* неоднокра́тно; *one at a* ~ по одному́; *at no* ~ никогда́, ни в ко́ем слу́чае; *at the same* ~ в то же вре́мя; тем не ме́нее; *at* ~*s* времена́ми; *for the* ~ *being* до поры́ до вре́мени; *from* ~ *to* ~ вре́мя от вре́мени; *in good* ~ то́чно, своевре́менно; *in* ~ во́-вре́мя; ~*-honoured* освящённый века́ми; ~*keeper* хроно́метр; *(pers.)* та́бельщик; ~*piece* хроно́метр, часы́; ~*-server* приспособле́нец; ~*-signal* прове́рка вре́мени; ~*table* расписа́ние; *have a good* ~ хорошо́ проводи́ть вре́мя; *beat* ~ отбива́ть такт; *three* ~*s* три ра́за; *what* ~ *is it?* кото́рый час?, ско́лько вре́мени?; ¶ *v.t,* выбира́ть вре́мя/назнача́ть вре́мя для; приуро́чивать ко вре́мени; рассчи́тывать по вре́мени; хронометри́ровать; ~*less, a,* ве́чный; ~*ly, a,* своевре́менный.

timid, *a,* ро́бкий, засте́нчивый; ~**ity,** *n,* ро́бость, засте́нчивость.

timing, *n,* расчёт вре́мени; хрономета́ж.

timorous, *a,* боязли́вый, ро́бкий.

tin, *n,* о́лово; жесть; консе́рвная ба́нка; ~*foil* оловя́нная фо́льга; ~*-opener* консе́рвный нож, откры́ва́лка; ~ *plate* бе́лая жесть; ~ *soldier* оловя́нный солда́тик; ~*smith* жестя́нщик; ¶ *v.t,* луди́ть; консерви́ровать; ~**ned,** *p.p. & a,* лужёный; консерви́рованный; ~ *food* консе́рвы; ~**ning,** *n,* луже́ние; консерви́рование; ~**ny,** *a,* то́нкий; звуча́щий как жесть; с при́вкусом же́сти.

tincture, *n,* отте́нок; при́вкус; налёт; ¶ *v.t,* окра́шивать; пропи́тывать.

tinder, *n,* трут; ~*-box* трутни́ца.

tinge, *n,* отте́нок; при́вкус; ¶ *v.t* слегка́ окра́шивать.

tingle, *n,* пока́лывание, пощи́пывание; ¶ *v.i,* коло́ть, пощи́пывать; зуде́ть; ~ *with* трепета́ть от.

tinker, *n*, луди́льщик, пая́льщик; ¶ *v.i*, починя́ть; ~ *with* возиться с.

tinkle, *n*, звон; звя́канье; ¶ *v.i*, звене́ть; позвя́кивать.

tinsel, *n*, мишура́; блёстки; ¶ *a*, мишу́рный.

tint, *n*, отте́нок, тон; ¶ *v.t*, слегка́ окра́шивать; подцве́чивать.

tiny, *a*, кро́шечный, малю́сенький.

tip, *n*, ко́нчик, наконе́чник; чаевы́е; намёк, сове́т; сва́лка; ¶ *v.t*, наклоня́ть; опроки́дывать, выва́ливать; надева́ть наконе́чник на; дава́ть на чай *(dat.)*; *v.i*, наклоня́ться; ~ *up*, *v.t.* *(& i.)*, опроки́дывать(ся); *(coll.)* сдава́ть; ~ *up a seat* отки́дывать сиде́нье; ~*up lorry* самосва́л.

tipple, *n*, алкого́льный напи́ток; ¶ *v.i*, пья́нствовать; ~**r**, *n*, пья́ница.

tipsiness, *n*, подвы́пившее состоя́ние; **tipsy**, *a*, подвы́пивший.

tiptoe: *on* ~ на цы́почках.

tip-top, *a*, первокла́ссный, превосхо́дный.

tirade, *n*, тира́да.

tire, *n*, ши́на; о́бод колеса́.

tire, *v.t*, утомля́ть; надоеда́ть *(dat.)*; *v.i*, устава́ть, утомля́ться; ~**d**, *p.p.* & *a*, уста́лый, утомлённый; ~**dness**, *n*, уста́лость; ~**less**, *a*, неутоми́мый; ~**some**, *a*, утоми́тельный; надое́дливый; **tiring**, *a*, утоми́тельный.

tiro, *n*, новичо́к.

tissue, *n*, ткань; *(fig.)* сплете́ние; ~ *paper* мя́гкая папиро́сная бума́га.

tit, *n*, сини́ца; ~ *for tat* зуб за́ зуб; услу́га за услу́гу.

titbit, *n*, ла́комый кусо́чек; пика́нтная но́вость.

tithe, *n*, десяти́на, деся́тая часть.

titillate, *v.t*, щекота́ть; прия́тно возбужда́ть.

titivate, *v.t.* *(& i.)*, прихора́шивать(ся), наряжа́ть(ся).

title, *n*, назва́ние, загла́вие; ти́тул, зва́ние; ~ *deed* докуме́нт, устана́вливающий пра́во на со́бственность; ~ *page* ти́тульный лист; ¶ *v.t*, называ́ть, озагла́вливать; ~**d**, *a*, титуло́ванный.

titter, *n*, хихи́канье; ¶ *v.i*, хихи́кать.

tittle, *n*, ка́пелька, чу́точка; ~*-tattle* болтовня́, та́ры-ба́ры.

titular, *a*, номина́льный; титуло́ванный.

to, *pr*, в, на; к; по сравне́нию с; по отноше́нию к; ~ *and fro* взад и вперёд; туда́ и сюда́; *a quarter* ~ *three* без че́тверти три; ~ *my mind* по моему́ мне́нию; *the road* ~ *London* доро́га в Ло́ндон; ~ *order* на зака́з; по ме́рке; *come* ~ приходи́ть в созна́ние.

toad, *n*, жа́ба; ~*stool* пога́нка; ~**y**, *n*, подхали́м; ¶ *v.i*, льсти́ть; подхали́мничать.

toast, *n*, подрумя́ненный ло́мтик хле́ба, грено́к; тост; *buttered* ~ грено́к с ма́слом; ¶ *v.t*, поджа́ривать (bread); пить за здоро́вье; ~**er**, *n*, прибо́р для поджа́ривания гренко́в, то́стер; провозглаша́ющий тост, тамада́; ~**ing**, *n*, поджа́ривание хле́ба; ~ *fork* ви́лка для поджа́ривания хле́ба.

tobacco, *n*, таба́к; ~ *pouch* кисе́т; ~**nist** *n*, торго́вец таба́чными изде́лиями; ~*'s shop* таба́чный магази́н.

toboggan, *n*, тобо́гган, сала́зки; ~ *run* доро́жка для ката́ния на сала́заках.

tocsin, *n*, наба́т; наба́тный ко́локол.

today, *ad*, сего́дня, в на́ши дни.

toddle, *v.i*, учи́ться ходи́ть, ковыля́ть; прогу́ливаться; ~**r**, *n*, ребёнок, начина́ющий ходи́ть, малы́ш.

to-do, *n*, суета́, сумато́ха.

toe, *n*, па́лец ноги́; носо́к *(of sock, etc.)*; ~*cap* носо́к; ¶ *v.t*, каса́ться носко́м *(gen.)*; ~ *the line* станови́ться в шере́нгу; подчиня́ться тре́бованиям; *(sport)* станови́ться на старт.

toffee, *n*, ири́с.

together, *ad*, вме́сте, сообща́; друг с дру́гом.

toil, *n*, тяжёлый труд; *pl*, се́ти, лову́шка; ¶ *v.i*, труди́ться; с трудо́м идти́, тащи́ться; ~**er**, *n*, тру́женик.

toilet, *n*, туале́т; убо́рная; ~ *paper* туале́тная бума́га.

toilsome, *n*, утоми́тельный, тру́дный.

token, *n*, тало́н; пода́рок на па́мять; знак, при́знак; *as a* ~ *of* в знак.

tolerable, *a*, сно́сный, терпи́мый; допусти́мый; **tolerably**, *ad*, удовлетвори́тельно; **tolerate**, *v.t*, терпе́ть; допуска́ть; **toleration**, **tolerance**, *n*, терпи́мость.

toll, *n*, пошлина; колокольный звон; ~ *bridge* платный мост; ¶ *v.t. & i*, звонить.

tomato, *n*, помидор; ~ *juice* томатный сок; ~ *sauce* томатный соус.

tomb, *n*, могила; гробница; ~*stone* надгробный памятник.

tomboy, *n*, девчонка-сорванец.

tomcat, *n*, кот.

tome, *n*, том.

tomfoolery, *n*, дурачество.

tommy-gun, *n*, автомат.

tommy-rot, *n*, вздор, чепуха.

tomorrow, *ad*, завтра; ¶ *n*, завтрашний день; ~ *morning* завтра утром; *the day after* ~ послезавтра.

tom-tit, *n*, синица.

tomtom, *n*, тамтам.

ton, *n*, тонна; *pl*, *(coll.)* масса; ~*s of money* куча денег.

tonal, *a*, тональный; **tone**, *n*, тон; атмосфера, настроение; ¶ *v.t*, настраивать; *v.i*, гармонировать; ~ *down* смягчать; ~ *up* усиливать.

tongs, *n.pl*, щипцы, клещи.

tongue, *n*, язык; язычок *(of shoe)*; ~*-tied* косноязычный; ~*-twister* скороговорка; *hold one's* ~ держать язык за зубами.

tonic, *a*, *(med.)* тонизирующий; *(mus.)* тонический; ¶ *n*, тонизирующее средство; *(mus.)* основной тон.

tonight, *ad*, сегодня вечером, ночью.

tonnage, *n*, тоннаж; грузовместимость; корабельный сбор.

tonsil, *n*, миндалевидная железа, гланда; ~*itis*, *n*, ангина.

tonsure, *n*, тонзура; ¶ *v.t*, выбривать тонзуру *(dat.)*, постригать в монахи.

too, *ad*, также, тоже; слишком; очень; ~ *long* слишком долго.

tool, *n*, инструмент; станок; орудие *(also fig.)*; ~*-box* ящик с инструментами.

tooth, *n*, зуб; зубец; ~*ache* зубная боль; ~*brush* зубная щётка; ~*paste* зубная паста; ~*-pick* зубочистка; *false teeth* вставные зубы; ~*less*, *a*, беззубый; ~*y*, *a*, зубастый.

top, *n*, верх, верхушка *(of tree)*; вершина *(of hill)*; макушка *(of head)*; гребень *(of wave, dam, hill)*; волчок ¶ *a*, верхний,

высший; *at the* ~ *of one's voice* во весь голос; ~*-coat* пальто; ~*-hat* цилиндр; ~*-heavy* неустойчивый, перевешивающий в верхней части; ~*-knot* чуб; пучок перьев/лент; ~*most* самый верхний; ~ *sail* марсель; ~ *secret* совершенно секретно; *from* ~ *to bottom* сверху донизу; *from* ~ *to toe* с ног до головы; *on* ~ *of* сверх *(gen.)*; наверху *(gen.)*; ¶ *v.t*, покрывать; подниматься на вершину (горы); обрезать верхушку (дерева); быть первым в/среди; превосходить.

topaz, *n*, топаз.

topic, *n*, предмет, тема; ~*al*, *a*, актуальный; ~ *event* злободневное событие.

topographical, *a*, топографический; **topography**, *n*, топография.

topple, *v.i*, валиться, падать, опрокидываться; *v.t*, опрокидывать; свергать.

topsy-turvy, *ad*, вверх дном; шиворот-навыворот.

torch, *n*, факел; фонарь; паяльная лампа; *(fig.)* светоч; *electric* ~ карманный электрический фонарик; ~*light* свет факела.

toreador, *n*, тореадор.

torment, *n*, мука, мучение; ¶ *v.t*, мучить, изводить; ~*or*, *n*, мучитель.

tornado, *n*, торнадо, ураган.

torpedo, *n*, торпеда; ~ *boat* миноносец; ~ *tube* торпедный аппарат; ¶ *v.t*, подрывать торпедой.

torpid, *a*, безразличный; вялый; тупой; онемелый, оцепеневший; **torpor**, *n*, апатия; тупость; онемелость, оцепенение.

torrent, *n*, поток; ~*ial*, *a*, проливной; обильный.

torrid, *a*, жаркий, знойный.

torsion, *n*, кручение; скрученность.

torso, *n*, туловище; торс.

tort, *n*, правонарушение, дающее основание предъявить иск.

tortoise, *n*, черепаха; ~*-shell* *(n.)* щит черепахи; *(a.)* черепаховый.

tortuous, *a*, извилистый; *(fig.)* уклончивый.

torture, *n*, пытка; ¶ *v.t*, пытать; мучить; искажать; ~*r*, *n*, палач; мучитель.

Tory, *n*, тори, консерватор; ¶ *a*, консерваторский.

toss, *n,* бросание; бросок; подбрасывание; сбрасывание; сотрясение; ¶ *v.t,* бросать, метать; подбрасывать; сбрасывать *(rider);* поднимать на рога; вскидывать *(head); v.i,* метаться *(in bed);* качаться *(of ship).*

tot, *n,* малыш; рюмка; ¶ *v.t:* ~ up складывать, суммировать.

total, *a,* весь, целый; полный, тотальный; ¶ *n,* итог, сумма; целое; ¶ *v.t,* подводить итог *(dat.);* подсчитывать; равняться *(dat.);* ~itarian, *a,* тоталитарный.

totter, *v.i,* ковылять, шататься; колебаться.

toucan, *n,* тукан.

touch, *n,* прикосновение; осязание; контакт; лёгкий приступ; *(art)* штрих; манера; *(mus.)* туше; примесь, чуточка; *a ~ of the sun* лёгкий солнечный удар; ~ line боковая линия; ~stone пробирный камень; *keep in ~ with* поддерживать контакт/связь с; ¶ *v.t,* трогать; касаться *(gen.),* прикасаться к; волновать; сравниться *(pf.)* с; *v.i,* соприкасаться; ~ up поправлять; ~ *upon* касаться *(gen.);* граничить с; ~ed, *a,* тронутый, ~ing, *a,* трогательный; касающийся; ¶ *pr,* относительно; ~y, *a,* обидчивый.

tough, *a,* жёсткий; крепкий; трудный; выносливый; ¶ *n,* бандит, хулиган; ~en, *v.t,* делать жёстким/крепким; ~ness, *n,* жёсткость; крепость, выносливость.

tour, *n,* поездка, путешествие, экскурсия; турне; объезд; ¶ *v.t,* совершать путешествие/ турне по; объезжать; ~ism, *n,* туризм; ~ist, *n,* турист, -ка; путешественник, -ица; ~ *agency* бюро путешествий; ~ *ticket* обратный билет без даты.

tournament, *n,* турнир.

tourniquet, *n,* турникет.

tousle, *v.t,* ерошить.

tout, *n,* навязчивый торговец, зазывала; ¶ *v.t.* & *i,* навязывать товар, назойливо предлагать.

tow, *n,* пакля; буксир; буксировка; *on ~* на буксире; ~ line бечева; буксирный канат; ~ *path* бечевник.

towards, *pr,* к, по направлению к; по отношению к; около; для.

towel, *n,* полотенце; ~ *rail* вешалка для полотенца.

tower, *n,* башня, вышка; ¶ *v.i,* выситься; вздыматься; ~ *above* возвышаться над; ~ing, *a,* вздымающийся; неистовый *(rage).*

town, *n,* город; ~ *clerk* секретарь городской корпорации; ~ *council* городской совет; ~ *crier* глашатай; ~ *hall* ратуша; ~ *planning* планировка городов; ~sman, *n,* горожанин.

toxic, *a,* токсический; ядовитый; **toxin,** *n,* токсин.

toy, *n,* игрушка; забава; ¶ *v.i,* играть, забавляться; ~ *with* вертеть в руках.

trace, *n,* след; незначительное количество; постромка; ¶ *v.t,* прослеживать; калькировать, копировать; чертить; **tracery,** *n,* узор; **tracing,** *n,* прослеживание; копировка, калькировка; чертёж на кальке; ~ *paper* калька.

track, *n,* дорожка *(also sport);* *(rly.)* колея, *(sport)* трек; гусеница *(of tractor);* путь; след; *off the ~* на ложном пути; *off the beaten ~* в глуши; уединённый; ¶ *v.t,* прослеживать; преследовать; намечать курс *(gen.).*

tract, *n,* трактат; брошюра; полоса *(of land).*

tractable, *a,* сговорчивый, послушный; легко поддающийся обработке.

traction, *n,* тяга; **tractor,** *n,* трактор.

trade, *n,* торговля; ремесло; профессия; занятие; ~*mark* фабричная марка; ~ *union* профсоюз, тред-юнион; ~ *wind* пассат; ¶ *v.i,* торговать *(in – inst.);* ~ *on* использовать в своих целях; ~r, *n,* торговец; **trading,** *a,* торговый; ¶ *n,* торговля, коммерция; ~ *station* фактория.

tradition, *n,* традиция; предание; ~al, *a,* традиционный.

traduce, *v.t,* клеветать на; ~r, *n,* клеветник.

traffic, *n,* (уличное) движение; транспорт; торговля; ~ *jam* затор в движении, «пробка»; ~ *lights* светофор; ¶ *v.i:* ~ *in* торговать *(inst.).*

tragedian, *n,* трагик; **tragedy,** *n,* трагедия; **tragic,** *a,* трагический;

трагичный; **tragicomedy**, *n*, трагикомéдия.

trail, *n*, след; тропинка; ¶ *v.t*, волочить, тащить; выслéживать; *v.i*, волочиться, тащиться; ~**er**, *n*, прицéп; *(film)* анóнс; реклáма.

train, *n*, пóезд; шлейф *(of dress)*; свита: *(mil.)* обóз; ~**-bearer** паж; *stopping* ~ пóезд с остановками; ¶ *v.t*, обучáть, готóвить; *(sport)* тренировáть; дрессировáть *(animals)*; объезжáть *(horse)*; направлять *(gun)*; *v.i*, тренировáться; готóвиться; ~**er**, *n*, инструктор; *(sport)* трéнер; дрессирóвщик; ~**ing**, *n*, обучéние; тренирóвка; дрессирóвка; ~ *college* педагогический институт.

trait, *n*, черта; штрих.

traitor, *n*, предáтель, изменник; ~**ous**, *a*, предáтельский.

trajectory, *n*, траектóрия.

tram[car], *n*, трамвáй.

trammel, *n*, нéвод; трал; *(fig.)* препятствие, путы; ¶ *v.t*, ловить нéводом; препятствовать *(dat.)*.

tramp, *n*, бродяга: (изнурительное) путешéствие пешкóм; тяжёлая пóступь; ¶ *v.i*, идти пешкóм, тащиться с трудóм; тóпать; бродяжничать.

trample, *v.t*, топтáть; *(fig.)* попирáть.

tramway, *n*, трамвáй.

trance, *n*, транс; экстáз.

tranquil, *a*, спокóйный; ~**lity**, *n*, спокóйствие; ~**lize**, *v.t*, успокáивать.

transact, *v.t*, вести *(business)*; заключáть *(deal)*; ~**ion**, *n*, дéло; сдéлка; *pl*, протокóлы; труды.

transatlantic, *a*, трансатлантический.

transcend, *v.t*, переступáть предéлы *(gen.)*; превосходить;~**ency**, *n*, превосхóдство; ~**ent**, *a*, превосхóдный.

transcribe, *v.t*, перепсывать, транскрибировать; расшифрóвывать; **transcript**, *n*, кóпия;расшифрóвка; ~**ion**, *n*, транскрипция; переписывание.

transept, *n*, трансéпт.

transfer, *n*, перевóд; перенóс; передáча: перемещéние; переводнáя картинка; ¶ *v.t*, переводить; переносить; передавáть; перемещáть; *v.i*, пересáживаться; ~

able, *a*, допускáющий передáчу, заменимый; ~**ence**, *n*, передáча; ~**or**, *n*, передáтчик, передающее лицó.

transfiguration, *n*, преобразовáние; *(eccl.)* преображéние; **transfigure**, *v.t*, преобразóвывать.

transfix, *v.t*, прокáлывать, пронзáть; *(coll.)* пригвождáть к мéсту.

transform, *v.t*,преобразóвывать; превращáть; ~**ation**, *n*, преобразовáние; превращéние; ~**er**, *n*, преобразовáтель; *(elec.)* трансформáтор.

transfuse, *v.t*, переливáть, дéлать переливáние (крóви); пропитывать; передавáть; **transfusion**, *n*, переливáние (крóви).

transgress, *v.t*, нарушáть, переступáть; ~**ion**, *n*, нарушéние (закóна); простýпок; ~**or**, *n*, правонарушитель.

transient, *a*, преходящий, мимолётный, скоротéчный; врéменный.

transistor, *n*, транзистор.

transit, *n*, транзит; проéзд; прохождéние; ~ *visa* транзитная виза; ~**ion**, *n*, перехóд; ~**ional**, *a*, перехóдный; промежýточный; ~**ive**, *a*, перехóдный; ~**ory**, *a*, врéменный, мимолётный.

translate, *v.t*, переводить;транслировáть *(radio)*; **translation**, *n*, перевóд; трансляция; **translator**, *n*, перевóдчик, -чица.

translucent, *a*, просвéчивающий, (полу)прозрáчный.

transmigration, *n*, переселéние.

transmission, *n*, передáча; **transmit**, *v.t*,передавáть;отправлять; **transmitter**, *n*, передáтчик.

transmutation, *n*, превращéние; **transmute**, *v.t*, превращáть.

transparency, *n*, прозрáчность; диапозитив; транспарáнт; **transparent**, *a*, прозрáчный; очевидный.

transpire, *v.i*, испаряться; окáзываться; обнарýживаться.

transplant, *v.t*, пересáживать; *(surg.)* дéлать пересáдку *(gen.)*; переселять; *heart* ~ пересáдка сéрдца.

transport, *n*, трáнспорт; перевóзка; ¶ *a*, трáнспортный; ¶ *v.t*, перевозить; перемещáть; ссылáть;~**ation**, *n*, трáнспорт, перевóзка; ссылка.

transpose, *v.t*, переставлять; перемещáть; *(mus.)* транспонировать

transposition. *n*, перестано́вка; перемеще́ние; *(mus.)* транспони́ровка.

transubstantiation, *n*, пресуществле́ние.

transverse, *a*, попере́чный.

trap, *n*, лову́шка, западня́, капка́н; *(tech.)* сифо́н, фильтр; дрена́жная труба́; экипа́ж; ~-door люк; ¶ *v.t*, лови́ть (в лову́шку/капка́ны); зама́нивать; обма́нывать.

trapeze, *n*, трапе́ция.

trapper, *n*, охо́тник, ста́вящий капка́ны.

trappings, *n pl*, попо́на, сбру́я; *(fig.)* украше́ния.

trash, *n*, дрянь, хлам; му́сор; ~y, *a*, дрянно́й.

travail, *n*, (родовы́е) му́ки; тяжёлый труд.

travel, *n*, путеше́ствие; ¶ *v.i*, путеше́ствовать; (пере)двига́ться; блужда́ть *(of glance)*; ~ler, *n*, путеше́ственник; ~'s cheque доро́жный чек; ~ling, *n*, путеше́ствие; ¶ *a*, доро́жный, похо́дный; путеше́ствующий; передвижно́й; ~ salesman комми-вояжёр.

traverse, *v.t*, пересека́ть.

travesty, *n*, паро́дия; искаже́ние; ¶ *v.t*, пароди́ровать; искажа́ть.

trawl, *n*, тра́ловая сеть, трал; ¶ *v.t*, тра́лить; тащи́ть по дну; ~er, *n*, тра́льщик, тра́лер; ~ing, *n*, тра́ление.

tray, *n*, подно́с.

treacherous, *a*, преда́тельский, вероло́мный; ненадёжный; **treachery**, *n*, преда́тельство, вероло́мство.

treacle, *n*, па́тока.

tread, *n*, по́ступь, похо́дка; ступе́нька; ¶ *v.i*, ступа́ть, шага́ть; *v.t*, топта́ть; дави́ть; ~le, *n*, педа́ль; подно́жка.

treason, *n*, изме́на; high ~ госуда́рственная изме́на; ~able, *a*, изме́ннический.

treasure, *n*, клад, сокро́вище; ¶ *v.t*, цени́ть; дорожи́ть *(inst.)*; ~r, *n*, казначе́й; **treasury**, *n*, казна́; сокро́вищница; the T~ госуда́рственное казначе́йство.

treat, *n*, угоще́ние; удово́льствие; ¶ *v.t*, угоща́ть; лечи́ть *(med.)*; обраба́тывать; тракто́вать; обраща́ться с, относи́ться к; ~ise, *n*, тракта́т; ~ment, *n*, лече́ние; об-

рабо́тка; обхожде́ние, обраще́ние; ~y, *n*, догово́р.

treble, *a*, тройно́й; *(mus.)* дисканто́вый; ¶ *n*, тройно́е коли́чество; ди́скант; ¶ *v.t. (& i.)*, утра́ивать(ся).

tree, *n*, де́рево; family ~ родосло́вное де́рево; ~less, *a*, безле́сный, го́лый.

trefoil, *n*, трили́стник.

trellis, *n*, шпале́ра; решётка.

tremble, *v.i*, дрожа́ть, трепета́ть, трясти́сь; **trembling**, *a*, дрожа́щий; ¶ *n*, дрожь, тре́пет.

tremendous, *a*, стра́шный, ужа́сный; грома́дный; потряса́ющий.

tremor, *n*, дрожь, тре́пет; сотрясе́ние; **tremulous**, *a*, дрожа́щий; ро́бкий, тре́петный.

trench, *n*, кана́ва, ров; *(mil.)* око́п; транше́я; ¶ *v.i*, рыть кана́вы/око́пы; выка́пывать.

trenchant, *a*, о́стрый, ре́зкий; ко́лкий.

trencherman, *n*, едо́к.

trend, *n*, направле́ние, тенде́нция.

trepan, *n*, западня́, лову́шка; ¶ *v.t*, зама́нивать; обма́нывать.

trepidation, *n*, тре́пет; смяте́ние; трево́га.

trespass, *n*, наруше́ние грани́ц; просту́пок; ¶ *v.i*, наруша́ть грани́цу; соверша́ть просту́пок; ~er, *n*, наруши́тель грани́ц; брако́нье́р.

tress, *n*, ло́кон, коса́.

trestle, *n*, ко́злы, подста́вка.

trial, *n*, испыта́ние, про́ба; проце́сс, суде́бное разбира́тельство; on ~ под судо́м; на испыта́тельном сро́ке; ~ run про́бный за́пуск/про́бег; про́бное пла́вание; испыта́тельный полёт.

triangle, *n*, треуго́льник; **triangular**, *a*, треуго́льный.

tribal, *a*, племенно́й, родово́й; **tribe**, *n*, пле́мя, род.

tribulation, *n*, го́ре, несча́стье.

tribunal, *n*, трибуна́л, суд; **tribune**, *n*, трибу́н; трибу́на.

tributary, *n*, прито́к; да́нник; ¶ *a*, явля́ющийся прито́ком; платя́щий дань, подчинённый; **tribute**, *n*, дань; pay ~ *(fig.)* отдава́ть дань.

trice: in a ~ мгнове́нно.

triceps, *n*, трёхгла́вая мы́шца.

trick, *n*, хи́трость; обма́н; трюк, фо́кус; вы́ходка, шу́тка; мане́ра, привы́чка; ¶ *v.t*, обма́нывать; ꜛнадува́ть; ~ *out* разнаря́живать, ~ery, *n*, надува́тельство.

trickle, *n*, стру́йка; ¶ *v.i*, струи́ться; ка́пать.

trickster, *n*, обма́нщик; tricky, *a*, ло́вкий, хи́трый; сло́жный; ненадёжный.

tricycle, *n*, трёхколёсный велосипе́д.

trident, *n*, трезу́бец.

triennial, *a*, трёхле́тний.

trifle, *n*, ме́лочь, пустя́к; *a* ~ *tired* немно́го уста́лый; ¶ *v.i*, шути́ть, забавля́ться; trifling, *n*, пустяко́вый.

trigger, *n*, куро́к; защёлка.

trigonometry, *n*, тригономе́трия.

trilby[hat], *n*, мя́гкая фе́тровая шля́па.

trill, *n*, трель; ¶ *v.i*, пуска́ть тре́ли; перелива́ться.

trilogy, *n*, трило́гия.

trim, *a*, аккура́тный; наря́дный; опря́тный; ¶ *n*, поря́док; состоя́ние гото́вности; ¶ *v.t*, подреза́ть, обтёсывать; отде́лывать *(dress)*; подра́внивать *(hair)*; уравнове́шивать; приспоса́бливаться к; ~ *one's sails to the wind* держа́ть нос по ве́тру; ~ming, *n*, отде́лка *(on dress)*; гарни́р, припра́ва *(to food)*; *pl*, обре́зки.

Trinity, *n*, тро́ица.

trinket, *n*, безделу́шка, брело́к.

trio, *n*, три́о.

trip, *n*, пое́здка, путеше́ствие, экску́рсия «подно́жка», спотыка́ние; ¶ *v.t*, опроки́дывать; подставля́ть но́жку *(dat.)*; *v.i*, бежа́ть вприпры́жку; спотыка́ться.

tripe, *n*, рубе́ц.

triple, *a*, тройно́й; утро́енный; ¶ *v.t*, утра́ивать; ~ts, *n.pl*, тро́йня; triplicate, *a*, тройно́й; *in* ~ в трёх экземпля́рах.

tripod, *n*, трено́жник.

tripper, *n*, тури́ст, экскурса́нт; tripping, *a*, быстроно́гий.

triptych, *n*, три́птих.

trite, *a*, бана́льный, изби́тый.

triumph, *n*, триу́мф, торжество́; побе́да; ¶ *v.i*, торжествова́ть; ~al, *a*, триумфа́льный; ~ant, *a*, торжеству́ющий, лику́ющий.

trivial, *a*, незначи́тельный.

troglodyte, *n*, троглоди́т.

Trojan, *a*, троя́нский.

trolley, *n*, вагоне́тка, теле́жка; сто́лик на колёсиках; ~ *bus* тролле́йбус.

trollop, *n*, неря́ха.

trombone, *n*, тромбо́н.

troop, *n*, гру́ппа, отря́д; (кавалери́йский) взвод; эскадро́н; *pl*, войска́, солда́ты; ~ *ship* тра́нспорт для перево́зки войск; ~er, *n*, кавалери́ст; солда́т.

trophy, *n*, трофе́й; добы́ча.

tropic, *n*, тро́пик; T~ *of Cancer* тро́пик Ра́ка; T~ *of Capricorn* тро́пик Козеро́га; ~al, *a*, тропи́ческий.

trot, *n*, рысь; бег; ¶ *v.i*, бежа́ть (ры́сью); *v.t*, пуска́ть ры́сью; ~ *out* выска́зывать.

troth, *n*, че́стное сло́во.

trotter, *n*, рыса́к; но́жка *(dish)*.

troubadour, *n*, трубаду́р.

trouble, *n*, забо́та, хло́поты; беспоко́йство, трево́га; беда́, го́ре; неприя́тность; беспоря́дки; боле́знь; *(tech.)* ава́рия, неиспра́вность; *take the* ~ брать на себя́ труд; потруди́ться *(pf.)*; *get into* ~ попада́ть в беду́; ~maker смутья́н, наруши́тель споко́йствия; ¶ *v.t*, беспоко́ить, трево́жить; надоеда́ть *(dat.)*; пристава́ть к; дава́ться *(dat.)* с трудо́м; ~ *oneself* беспоко́иться; ~d, *a*, беспоко́йный; ~some, *a*, хло́потный, тру́дный; капри́зный *(child)*.

trough, *n*, кормушка, коры́то; жёлоб; квашня́; котлови́на, подо́шва *(of wave)*.

trounce, *v.t*, бить; побежда́ть, разбива́ть.

troupe, *n*, тру́ппа.

trousers, *n.pl*, брю́ки.

trousseau, *n*, прида́ное.

trout, *n*, форе́ль.

trowel, *n*, лопа́тка, сово́к.

truant, *a*, пра́здный; прогу́ливающий; ¶ *n*, прогу́льщик; *play* ~ прогу́ливать.

truce, *n*, переми́рие; переды́шка.

truck, *n*, грузови́к; *(rly.)* ваго́н; обме́н; *have no* ~ *with* не име́ть отноше́ний с; ¶ *v.t*, перевози́ть.

truckle, *v.i*, раболе́пствовать.

truculence, *n*, свире́пость; агресси́вность; ¶ *a*, свире́пый, жесто́кий; агресси́вный.

trudge, *v.i,* плестись, тащиться, идти с трудом.

true, *a,* истинный, подлинный; правильный; верный; точный; ~ *copy* заверенная копия; ~*-born* чистокровный; ~ *to life* реалистический; как живой; *it is* ~ *that* . . . правда, что . . .

truffle, *n,* трюфель.

truism, *n,* трюизм; **truly,** *ad,* искренне; правдиво; поистине; точно; *yours* ~ преданный Вам.

trump, *n,* козырь, *(coll.)* славный малый; ¶ *v.t,* бить козырем; ~ *up* выдумывать, фабриковать.

trumpery, *n,* мишура; дрянь.

trumpet, *n,* труба; рупор; ¶ *v.t, (fig.)* возвещать; *v.i,* трубить; реветь *(elephant);* ~**er,** *n,* трубач.

truncate, *v.t,* срезать верхушку *(gen.);* сокращать.

truncheon, *n,* дубинка; жезл.

trundle, *n,* колёсико; ¶ *v.t,* катить.

trunk, *n,* ствол *(of tree); (anat.)* туловище; чемодан, сундук; хобот *(of elephant);* корпус; *pl,* трусы; *bathing* ~*s* плавки; ~ *call* вызов по междугородному телефону; ~ *line* магистральная линия.

truss, *n,* связка, охапка; гроздь, пучок; *(med.)* бандаж; *(arch.)* балка, ферма; ¶ *v.t,* связывать; стягивать.

trust, *n,* вера, доверие; *(com.)* трест; кредит; опёка; *on* ~ в кредит; на веру; *breach of* ~ злоупотребление доверием; ¶ *v.t,* доверять; доверяться *(dat.);* вверять, поручать; *v.i,* надеяться; ~**ee,** *n,* попечитель, опекун; ~**worthy,** *a,* надёжный, заслуживающий доверия; ~**y,** *a,* надёжный; ¶ *n, (coll.)* образцовый заключённый.

truth, *n,* истина, правда; ~**ful,** *a,* правдивый.

try, *n,* попытка; испытание, проба; ¶ *v.t,* испытывать, пробовать; судить; *v.i,* пытаться, стараться; ~ *for* искать, добиваться *(gen.);* ~ *on* примерять *(clothes);* ~**ing,** *a,* трудный; изнурительный; докучливый.

tub, *n,* кадка, ушат; ванна.

tuba, *n,* туба.

tubby, *a,* бочкообразный; толстый.

tube, *n,* труба, трубка; тюбик; метро; *cathode-ray* ~ электроннолучевая трубка; *inner* ~ камера.

tuber, *n,* клубень; **tubercle,** *n, (bot.)* бугорок; *(med.)* туберкулёзный бугорок; **tubercular,** *a,* туберкулёзный; **tuberculosis,** *n,* туберкулёз; **tuberculous,** *a,* туберкулёзный; **tuberose,** *n,* тубероза.

tubing, *n,* трубы; трубопровод; **tubular,** *a,* трубчатый, цилиндрический.

Tuesday, *n,* вторник.

tuft, *n,* пучок; хохолок; ~**ed,** *a,* с хохолком.

tug, *n,* рывок; буксир; ~*boat* буксирное судно; ¶ *v.t,* дёргать; тащить; буксировать.

tuition, *n,* обучение.

tulip, *n,* тюльпан.

tulle, *n,* тюль.

tumble, *n,* кувырканье; падение; ¶ *v.i,* кувыркаться; падать; бросаться; *v.t,* приводить в беспорядок, мять; бросать; ~*down, a,* полуразрушенный, развалившийся; ~**r,** *n,* акробат; стакан, бокал; ванька-встанька *(doll); (tech.)* опрокидыватель.

tumbrel, tumbril, *n,* телега; двуколка.

tumour, *n,* опухоль.

tumult, *n,* суматоха, шум; ~**uous,** *a,* шумный.

tumulus, *n,* курган, могильный холм.

tun, *n,* большая бочка.

tune, *n,* мелодия, мотив; тон; *in* ~ в тон; *be out of* ~ *with* идти в разрез с; быть не в ладу с; ¶ *v.t,* настраивать; приспосабливать; ~**ful,** *a,* гармоничный, мелодичный; ~**less,** *a,* немелодичный; ~**r,** *n,* настройщик.

tungsten, *n,* вольфрам.

tunic, *n,* туника; *(mil.)* китель.

tuning, *n,* настройка; ~ *fork* камертон.

tunnel, *n,* туннель; ¶ *v.i,* прокладывать туннель.

tunny, *n,* тунец.

turban, *n,* тюрбан, чалма.

turbid, *a,* мутный; туманный.

turbine, *n,* турбина; *turbo-jet* турбореактивный.

turbot, *n,* тюрбо́.
turbulence, *n,* бу́йность, бу́рность;
(tech.) турбуле́нтный пото́к; **tur-**
bulent, *a,* бу́йный, бу́рный.
tureen, *n,* су́пница.
turf, *n,* дёрн; бегова́я доро́жка; ска́ч-
ки; ¶ *v.t,* дернова́ть.
turgid, *a,* опу́хший; напы́щенный.
Turk, *n,* ту́рок, турча́нка.
turkey, *n,* индю́к, индю́шка; ин-
де́йка *(dish).*
Turkic, *a,* тю́ркский; **Turkish,** *a,*
туре́цкий; ¶ *n,* туре́цкий язы́к;
Turkmen, *a,* туркме́нский; ¶ *n,*
туркме́н, -ка
turmoil, *n,* беспоря́док, суматоха,
шум.
turn, *n,* поворо́т; оборо́т *(of wheel);*
о́чередь; переме́на; склад харак-
тера; услу́га; прогу́лка; вито́к
(of wire); (theat.) но́мер прог-
ра́ммы; ~ *of phrase* оборо́т ре́чи;
at every ~ на ка́ждом шагу́; *take*
a ~ *for the worse* принима́ть дур-
но́й оборо́т; *by* ~*s* по о́череди; ¶
v t. враща́ть, верте́ть; повора́чи-
вать; перевёртывать *(page);* зава-
ра́чивать (за у́гол); направля́ть
(attention); перелицо́вывать
(dress); точи́ть; *v.i,* враща́ться;
повора́чиваться, обора́чиваться;
станови́ться; ~ *away* отвора́чи-
вать(ся); увольня́ть; ~ *back* пово-
ра́чивать наза́д; ~ *down* откло-
ня́ть; убавля́ть *(light);* ~ *in (v.t.)*
загиба́ть; *(v.i.)* заходи́ть мимо-
хо́дом; ложи́ться спать; ~ *inside*
out вывора́чивать наизна́нку; ~
off (v.t.) закрыва́ть *(tap);* выклю-
ча́ть *(light); (v.i.)* свёртывать с
доро́ги; ~ *on* открыва́ть *(tap);*
включа́ть *(light); (fig.)* напада́ть
на; ~ *out (v.t.)* выгоня́ть; выве́р-
тывать *(pockets); (v.i.)* прибы-
ва́ть; ока́зываться; ~ *to* обра-
ща́ться к; принима́ться за; ~ *up*
(v.t.) поднима́ть вверх; загиба́ть;
засу́чивать *(sleeves); (v.i.)* появ-
ля́ться, приходи́ть; случа́ться;
~ *up one's nose* задира́ть
нос.
turncoat, *n,* ренега́т.
turncock, *n,* запо́рный кран.
turner, *n,* то́карь.
turning, *n,* поворо́т; перекрёсток;
враще́ние; тока́рное ремесло́; ~
point поворо́тный пункт.
turnip, *n,* ре́па.

turnkey, *n,* тюре́мщик, надзира́-
тель.
turnout, *n,* пу́блика; вы́пуск про-
ду́кции.
turnover, *n,* оборо́т; теку́честь ра-
бо́чей си́лы; *(cook.)* сла́дкий
пиро́г.
turnpike, *n,* заста́ва.
turnstile, *n,* турнике́т.
turntable, *n,* поворо́тный круг; диск
(of gramophone); прои́грыватель.
turpentine, *n,* скипида́р.
turpitude, *n,* ни́зость, позо́рное пове-
де́ние.
turquoise, *n,* бирюза́; бирюзо́вый
цвет.
turret, *n,* ба́шенка; *gun* ~ оруди́й-
ная ба́шня.
turtle, *n,* черепа́ха; ~ *dove* го́рлица;
turn ~ опроки́дываться.
tusk, *n,* би́вень, клык.
tussle, *n,* борьба́, дра́ка; ¶ *v.i,*
боро́ться, дра́ться.
tutelage, *n,* опе́ка, опеку́нство; **tute-**
lar, *a,* опеку́нский; **tutor,** *n,* на-
ста́вник *(at school);* руководи́тель,
тью́тор *(univ.); (law)* опеку́н; ¶
v.t, обуча́ть; дава́ть уро́ки *(dat.)*
руководи́ть *(inst.);* **tutorial,**
n, консульта́ция, встре́ча с руко-
води́телем; ~ *system* университе́т-
ская систе́ма обуче́ния под
руково́дством тью́тора.
twaddle, *n,* пустосло́вие.
twang, *n,* гнуса́вый вы́говор; звук
натя́нутой струны́; ¶ *v.i,* гнуса́-
вить; звуча́ть *(of string).*
tweak, *n,* щипо́к; ¶ *v.t,* ущипну́ть
(pf.).
tweed, *n,* твид.
tweezers, *n.pl,* пинце́т.
twelfth, *ord.num,* двена́дцатый; ¶ *n,*
двена́дцатая часть; *T~ Night*
кану́н креще́ния; **twelve,** *num,*
двена́дцать.
twentieth, *ord.num,* двадца́тый;
twenty, *num,* два́дцать.
twice, *ad,* два́жды.
twiddle, *v.t,* верте́ть; игра́ть *(inst.).*
twig, *n,* ве́точка, пру́тик; ¶ *v.t,*
(coll.) замеча́ть; поня́ть *(pf.).*
twilight, *n,* су́мерки.
twill, *n,* твил, са́ржа.
twin, *n,* близне́ц, дво́йник; ¶ *a,*
двойно́й; одина́ковый.
twine, *n,* бечёвка, шпага́т; ¶ *v.t,*
вить, плести́; ~ *round* обвива́ть-
(ся).

twinge, *n*, приступ (боли); угрызéние *(of conscience)*.

twinkle, *n*, мерцáние; огонёк *(in eye)*; ¶ *v.i*, мерцáть, сверкáть; twinkling, *a*, мерцáющий; ¶ *n*, мерцáние; *in the ~ of an eye* в мгновéние óка.

twirl, *n*, вращéние, кручéние; вихрь; рóсчерк; ¶ *v.t. (& i.)*, вертéть(ся), кружúть(ся).

twist, *n*, поворóт, изгúб; кручéние; искривлéние, искажéние; вûвих; закрýтка *(of tobacco)*; осóбенность (харáктера); ¶ *v.t*, крутúть, скрýчивать; изгибáть; вить; искривлять, искажáть; *v.i*, изгибáться; вúться; повóрачиваться; ~ed, *p.p. & a*, изóгнутый; искривлённый.

twit, *v.t*, попрекáть, упрекáть.

twitch, *n*, подёргивание, сýдорога; ¶ *v.t*, дёргать; *v.i*, дёргаться, подёргиваться; ~ing, *n*, подёргивание, сýдорога.

twitter, *n*, щебет, щебетáние; ¶ *v.i*, щебетáть; чирúкать.

two, *num*, два, две; ¶ *n*, двóйка, двóе; пáра; ~ *by ~* пó двое, попáрно; *in ~* нáдвое; *put ~ and ~ together* сообразúть *(pf.)* что к чему; ~fold, *a*, двойнóй; двухкрáтный; ¶ *ad*, вдвóе, вдвойнé.

tympanum, *n*, барабáнная пóлость; срéднее ýхо; *(arch.)* тимпáн.

type, *n*, тип; класс, род; образéц; *(print.)* шрифт; ¶ *v.t*, писáть/ печáтать на машúнке; ~writer пúшущая машúнка; ~writing перепúска на машúнке; ~written машинопúсный, напечáтанный на машúнке.

typhoid fever, *n*, брюшнóй тиф.

typhoon, *n*, тайфýн.

typhus, *n*, сыпнóй тиф.

typical, *a*, типúчный; typify, *v.t*, быть типúчным представúтелем/примéром *(gen.)*; олицетворять.

typist, *n*, машинúстка.

typographical, *a*, типогрáфский; книгопечáтный; typography, *n*, книгопечáтание; оформлéние.

tyrannical, *a*, тиранúческий, деспотúчный; tyrannize, *v.t*, тирáнствовать над; tyranny, *n*, тирáния, деспотúзм; tyrant, *n*, тирáн, дéспот.

tyre, *n*, шúна; óбод колесá; покрûшка.

U

U-tube, *n*, U-обрáзная трубá.

ubiquitous, *a*, вездесýщий, повсемéстный.

udder, *n*, вûмя.

ugh, *int*, тьфу!.

ugliness, *n*, урóдство; ugly, *a*, безобрáзный, протúвный, урóдливый; ~ *customer* неприятный/опáсный человéк; негодяй.

ulcer, *n*, язва; ~ate, *v.i*, покрывáться язвами; ~ated, *p.p. & a*, изъязвлённый.

ulterior, *a*, дальнéйший; потустарóнний; ~ *motive* скрûтый мотúв.

ultimate, *a*, послéдний, конéчный, окончáтельный; основнóй; ~ly, *ad*, в конéчном счёте; ultimatum, *n*, ультимáтум.

ultramarine, *n*, ультрамарúн.

ultra-violet, *a*, ультрафиолéтовый.

umber, *n*, ýмбра.

umbrage, *n*, обúда; сень, тень; *take ~* обúдеться *(pf.)*.

umbrella, *n*, зóнтик, зонт; ~ *stand* подстáвка для зóнтов.

umpire, *n*, судья; посрéдник, трéтейский судья; ¶ *v.i*, быть судьёй/ посрéдником.

unabashed, *a*, нерастерявшийся, несмутúвшийся.

unabated, *a*, неослáбленный.

unable, *a*, неспосóбный; *be ~* не быть в состоянии.

unabridged, *a*, пóлный, несокращённый.

unaccompanied, *a*, несопровождáемый; без аккомпанемéнта.

unaccountable, *a*, необъяснúмый; безотвéтственный.

unaccustomed, *a*, непривûкший; непривûчный.

unadorned, *a*, неукрáшенный.

unadulterated, *a*, настоящий, чистéйший.

unaffected, *a*, незатрóнутый; úскренний, непосрéдственный.

unaided, *a*, лишённый пóмощи; самостоятельный.

unalloyed, *a*, чúстый, без прúмеси.

unalterable, *a*, неизмéнный.

unanimity, *n*, единодýшие; unanimous, *a*, единодýшный, единоглáсный.

unanswerable, *a,* неопровержймый; трудный для ответа.

unappetizing, *a,* неаппетйтный.

unappreciated, *a,* недооценённый; непонятный.

unapproachable, *a,* недоступный, непристу́пный; беспод́обный.

unarmed, *a,* безору́жный, невооружённый.

unashamed, *a,* бессо́вестный, на́глый.

unasked, *a,* непро́шенный.

unassailable, *a,* непристу́пный; неопровержймый.

unassuming, *a,* скро́мный, непритяза́тельный.

unattainable, *a,* недосяга́емый.

unattended, *a,* несопровожда́емый; оста́вленный (без ухо́да).

unauthorized, *a,* неразрешённый; неправомо́чный.

unavailable, *a,* не имеющийся в наличии; **unavailing,** *a,* бесполе́зный, тще́тный.

unavoidable, *a,* неизбе́жный, неминуемый.

unawares, *a,* врасплох, неожиданно; неча́янно.

unbalanced, *a,* неуравнове́шенный.

unballast, *v.t,* выгружа́ть балла́ст с.

unbandage, *v.t,* разбинто́вывать.

unbearable, *a,* невыносймый.

unbeaten, *a,* не испыта́вший пораже́ния; непревзойдённый; непроторённый.

unbecoming, *a,* неподходя́щий; не к лицу́; неприли́чный.

unbelief, *n,* неве́рие; **unbeliever,** *n,* неве́рующий.

unbend, *v.t. (& i.),* выпрямля́ть(ся); разгиба́ть(ся); *v.i,* станови́ться приве́тливым/развя́зным; **~ing,** *a,* непреклонный, суро́вый.

unbiassed, *a,* беспристра́стный.

unbind, *v.t,* развя́зывать; распуска́ть; освобожда́ть.

unblemished, *a,* незапя́тнанный.

unblushing, *a,* беззасте́нчивый, на́глый.

unbolt, *v.t,* снима́ть засо́в с, отпира́ть.

unborn, *a,* ещё не рождённый.

unbosom oneself открыва́ть ду́шу.

unbound, *a,* свобо́дный; неперепле́тённый.

unbounded, *a,* безграни́чный; безме́рный.

unbreakable, *a,* небью́щийся.

unbridled, *a,* разну́зданный.

unbroken, *a,* неразбйтый, це́лый; непокорённый; непреры́вный.

unbuckle, *v.t,* расстёгивать.

unburden oneself отводи́ть/открыва́ть ду́шу.

unbutton, *v.t,* расстёгивать.

uncalled-for неуме́стный, ниче́м не вы́званный.

uncanny, *a,* жу́ткий, сверхъесте́ственный.

uncared for забро́шенный.

unceasing, *a,* безостано́вочный, непреры́вный; **~ly,** *ad,* непреры́вно.

unceremoniously, *ad,* бесцеремо́нно.

uncertain, *a,* неуве́ренный; неопределённый; изме́нчивый, ненадёжный; **~ty,** *n,* неуве́ренность; неопределённость.

unchain, *v.t,* спуска́ть с це́пи; освобожда́ть; раско́вывать.

unchangeable, *a,* неизме́нный, неизменя́емый; **unchanged,** *a,* неизмени́вшийся; **unchanging,** *a,* неизменя́ющийся.

uncharitable, *a,* немилосе́рдный, жесто́кий.

unchecked, *a,* необу́зданный, беспрепя́тственный; непрове́ренный.

uncivil, *a,* гру́бый, неве́жливый; **~ized,** *a,* ва́рварский, нецивилизо́ванный.

unclaimed, *a,* невостре́бованный.

uncle, *n,* дя́дя.

unclouded, *a,* безо́блачный.

uncoil, *v.t,* разма́тывать.

uncomfortable, *a,* неудо́бный.

uncommon, *a,* необыкнове́нный, замеча́тельный; ре́дкий.

uncommunicative, *a,* необщи́тельный, молчали́вый.

uncomplaining, *a,* безро́потный.

uncompleted, *a,* неоко́нченный.

uncomplimentary, *a,* неле́стный.

uncompromising, *a,* бескомпроми́сный; непрекло́нный.

unconcern, *n,* равноду́шие; беззабо́тность; **~ed,** *a,* равноду́шный; беззабо́тный; незаинтересо́ванный.

unconditional, *a,* безогово́рочный, безусло́вный.

unconfined, *a,* неограни́ченный, свобо́дный.

unconfirmed, *a,* неподтверждённый.

unconnected, *a,* несвя́занный, несвя́зный.

unconquerable, *a,* непобедймый.

unconscionable, *a,* чрезме́рный; бессо́вестный.
unconscious, *a,* бессозна́тельный; потеря́вший созна́ние; нево́льный; *be* ~ *of* не сознава́ть; ~**ness,** *n,* бессозна́тельное состоя́ние; бессозна́тельность.
unconstrained, *a,* непринуждённый; доброво́льный.
uncontrollable, *a,* неудержи́мый, не поддаю́щийся контро́лю.
unconventional, *a,* лишённый усло́вности, нешабло́нный.
uncooked, *a,* сыро́й.
uncork, *v.t,* отку́поривать.
uncorrected, *a,* неиспра́вленный.
uncouple, *v.t,* расцепля́ть; разъединя́ть.
uncouth, *a,* гру́бый, неуклю́жий; нескла́дный.
uncover, *v.t,* снима́ть кры́шку/ покры́тие с; открыва́ть; обнару́живать.
uncreated, *a,* существу́ющий изве́чно.
uncritical, *a,* некрити́чный.
uncrossed, *a,* неперечёркнутый; ~ *cheque* некросси́рованный чек.
unction, *n,* пома́зание; еле́йность.
unctuous, *a,* маслянистый; еле́йный.
uncultivated, *a,* невозде́ланный *(land);* нера́звитый *(talent);* некульту́рный.
uncurable, *a,* неизлечи́мый.
uncurl, *v.t,* развива́ть.
uncut, *a,* неразре́занный; несокращённый.
undamaged, *a,* неповреждённый, неиспо́рченный.
undated, *a,* недати́рованный.
undaunted, *a,* бесстра́шный.
undeceive, *v.t,* выводи́ть из заблужде́ния; открыва́ть глаза́ на.
undecided, *a,* нерешённый; нереши́тельный.
undecipherable, *a,* неразбо́рчивый; не поддаю́щийся расшифро́вке.
undefended, *a,* незащищённый.
undefiled, *a,* незапя́тнанный, непоро́чный.
undefinable, *a,* неопредели́мый.
undelivered, *a,* недоста́вленный; непроизнесённый.
undemonstrative, *a,* сде́ржанный.
undeniable, *a,* неоспори́мый, несомне́нный.
under, *pr,* под; ни́же; ме́ньше чем; при; согла́сно; ~ *age* несовер-

шенноле́тний; ~ *the circumstances* при да́нных обстоя́тельствах; ~ *cover* под прикры́тием; та́йный; ~ *penalty of* под стра́хом наказа́ния; ~ *way* на ходу́; в по́лном разга́ре; ¶ *ad,* вниз; внизу́, ни́же; ¶ *a,* ни́жний, ни́зший.
undercarriage, *n,* шасси́.
underclothing, *n,* ни́жнее бельё.
undercurrent, *n,* подво́дное тече́ние; *(fig.)* скры́тая тенде́нция.
undercut, *n,* вы́резка; ¶ *v.t,* подреза́ть; назнача́ть бо́лее ни́зкие це́ны, чем . . .
underdone, *a,* недожа́ренный.
underestimate, *v.t,* недооце́нивать.
underfed, *a,* недоко́рмленный.
undergarment, *n,* ни́жнее пла́тье; *pl,* ни́жнее бельё.
undergo, *v.t,* испы́тывать; подверга́ться *(dat.).*
undergraduate, *n,* студе́нт, -ка.
underground, *a,* подзе́мный; *(fig.)* подпо́льный; ¶ *ad* под землёй; *(fig.)* подпо́льно; ¶ *n,* метрополите́н; подпо́лье.
undergrowth, *n,* подле́сок: подро́ст.
underhand, *a,* закули́сный; ¶ *ad,* за спино́й.
underline, *v.t,* подчёркивать.
underling, *n,* подчинённый.
underlying, *a,* основно́й; скры́тый.
undermentioned, *a,* нижеупомяну́тый.
undermine, *v.t,* мини́ровать; подмыва́ть *(shore);* подка́пывать, подрыва́ть.
undermost, *a,* са́мый ни́жний, ни́зший.
underneath, *ad,* вниз, внизу́; ¶ *pr,* под.
undernourished, *a,* недоко́рмленный; *be* ~ недоеда́ть; **undernourishment,** *n,* недоеда́ние.
underpaid, *a,* ни́зко опла́чиваемый.
underpin, *v.t,* подпира́ть; подводи́ть фунда́мент под.
underrate, *v.t,* недооце́нивать.
under-secretary, *n,* замести́тель мини́стра.
undersell, *v.i,* продава́ть деше́вле други́х.
undersigned, *a. & n,* нижеподписа́вшийся.
underskirt, *n,* ни́жняя ю́бка.
understand, *v.t,* понима́ть; подразумева́ть; ~**ing,** *a,* понима́ющий; отзы́вчивый, чу́ткий; ¶ *n,* пони-

мáние; рáзум; взаимопонимáние; соглашéние, соглáсие.

understudy, *n,* дублёр.

undertake, *v.t,* предпринимáть; брать на себя; обязываться *(+ inf.);* **~r,** *n,* гробовщик; предпринимáтель; **undertaking,** *n,* предприятие; обязáтельство; обслуживание похорóн.

undertone, *n,* полутóн; *speak in ~s* говорить вполгóлоса.

undertow, *n,* отлив прибóя; подвóдное течéние.

underwear, *n,* нижнее бельё.

underwood, *n,* подлéсок.

underworld, *n,* преиспóдняя; дно óбщества, престýпный мир.

underwrite, *v.t,* подписывать; страховáть, гарантировать; **~r,** *n,* подписчик; страхóвщик; *pl,* страховáя компáния.

undeserved, *a,* незаслýженный; **undeserving,** *a,* незаслýживающий.

undesirable, *a,* нежелáтельный, неподходящий.

undetermined, *a,* неопределённый, нерешённый.

undeveloped, *a,* нерáзвитый; неразрабóтанный; незастрóенный.

undigested, *a,* неперевáренный; неусвóенный.

undiscernible, *a,* неразличимый; **undiscerning,** *a,* непроницáтельный, неразбóрчивый.

undisciplined, *a,* недисциплинирóванный.

undiscovered, *a,* неизвéстный, ненáйденный.

undiscriminating, *a,* непроницáтельный, неразбирáющийся.

undisguised, *a,* незамаскирóванный, открытый.

undismayed, *a,* необескурáженный, нерастерявшийся.

undisputed, *a,* бесспóрный; несомнéнный.

undistinguishable, *a,* неразличимый, неясный; **undistinguished,** *a,* невыдаюшийся.

undisturbed, *a,* нетрóнутый.

undivided, *a,* неразделённый, цéлый; дрýжный; объединённый.

undo, *v.t,* развязывать, расстёгивать; расстрáивать; уничтожáть, губить; **~ing,** *n,* гибель; уничтожéние; **~ne,** *p.p. & a,* несдéланный; погýбленный; *we are ~* мы погибли.

undoubted, *a,* несомнéнный, бесспóрный.

undress, *n,* домáшний костюм; *(mil.)* повседнéвная фóрма; ¶ *v.t. (& i.),* раздевáть(ся).

undrinkable, *a,* негóдный для питья.

undue, *a,* чрезмéрный; непрáвильный.

undulate, *v.i,* быть холмистым/волнистым; **undulating,** *a,* волнистый; **undulation,** *n,* волнистость; волнообрáзное движéние; нерóвность повéрхности.

unduly, *ad,* чрезмéрно.

undutiful, *a,* без чýвства дóлга.

undying, *a,* бессмéртный, вéчный.

unearned, *a,* незарабóтанный; *~ income* нетрудовóй дохóд.

unearth, *v.t,* выкáпывать из земли; *(fig.)* раскáпывать, отыскивать; **~ly,** *a,* неземнóй, сверхъестéственный.

uneasiness, *n,* беспокóйство, тревóга; нелóвкость; **uneasy,** *a,* беспокóйный, тревóжный; нелóвкий.

uneatable, *a,* несъедóбный.

unedifying, *a,* непоучительный.

uneducated, *a,* необразóванный, неучёный.

unemployed, *a,* безрабóтный; незáнятый; **unemployment,** *n,* безрабóтица; *~ benefit* посóбие по безрабóтице.

unending, *a,* бесконéчный, нескончáемый.

unenterprising, *a,* непредприимчивый, безинициативный.

unenviable, *a,* незавидный.

unequal, *a,* нерáвный; неравноцéнный; неадэквáтный; *~ to* непригóдный к; **~led,** *a,* непревзойдённый.

unequivocal, *a,* недвусмысленный.

unerring, *a,* безошибóчный.

uneven, *a,* нерóвный; нечётный.

unexampled, *a,* беспримéрный.

unexceptionable, *a,* безуслóвный; безукоризненный.

unexpected, *a,* неожиданный; внезáпный; **~ly,** *ad,* неожиданно; внезáпно.

unexpired, *a,* неистёкший.

unexplored, *a,* неисслéдованный.

unexpurgated, *a,* несокращённый, невырезанный.

unfailing, *a*, неизме́нный, надёжный; неисчерпа́емый; ~ly, *ad*, неизме́нно.

unfair, *a*, неве́рный, вероло́мный.

unfamiliar, *a*, незнако́мый, неве́домый.

unfasten, *v.t*, открепля́ть; отстёгивать, расстёгивать.

unfathomable, *a*, неизмери́мый, бездо́нный; непостижи́мый.

unfeeling, *a*, бесчу́вственный.

unfeigned, *a*, и́стинный, неподде́льный.

unfettered, *a*, освобождённый; свобо́дный.

unfinished, *a*, незако́нченный; необрабо́танный.

unfit, *a*, него́дный, непригодный, неподходя́щий; ненадлежа́щий; неподоба́ющий.

unfix, *v.t*, открепля́ть.

unflagging, *a*, неослабева́ющий.

unfledged, *a*, неоперившийся.

unflinching, *a*, бесстра́шный.

unfold, *v.t. (& i.)*, развёртывать(ся); раскрыва́ть(ся).

unforeseen, *a*, непредви́денный.

unforgettable, *a*, незабыва́емый.

unforgivable, *a*, непрости́тельный; **unforgiving**, *a*, стро́гий, непроща́ющий.

unfortified, *a*, неукреплённый; неподде́ржанный.

unfortunate, *a*, несча́стный; несчастли́вый; неуда́чный; ~ly, *ad*, к несча́стью.

unfounded, *a*, необосно́ванный.

unfrequented, *a*, ре́дко посеща́емый.

unfriendly, *a*, недружелю́бный, неприве́тливый.

unfruitful, *a*, беспло́дный.

unfulfilled, *a*, неосуществлённый, невы́полненный.

unfurl, *v.t*, развёртывать.

unfurnished, *a*, без ме́бели; необста́вленный.

ungainly, *a*, нескла́дный, неуклю́жий.

ungentlemanly, *a*, неве́жливый; неблагоро́дный, не подоба́ющий джентельме́ну.

ungodliness, *n*, безбо́жие; **ungodly**, *a*, неве́рующий.

ungovernable, *a*, необу́зданный, неукроти́мый.

ungracious, *a*, нелюбе́зный.

ungrammatical, *a*, граммати́чески непра́вильный.

ungrateful, *a*, неблагода́рный.

ungrounded, *a*, необосно́ванный, беспо́чвенный.

ungrudgingly, *ad*, ще́дро.

unguarded, *a*, незащищённый; неосторо́жный.

unhallowed, *a*, неосвящённый; гре́шный.

unhappiness, *n*, несча́стье; **unhappy**, *a*, несчастли́вый, несча́стный.

unharmed, *a*, невреди́мый; нетро́нутый.

unharness, *v.t*, распряга́ть.

unhealthy, *a*, нездоро́вый; боле́зненный; вре́дный.

unheard of несл́ыханный.

unheeded, *a*, незаме́ченный; **unheeding**, *a*, невнима́тельный.

unhelpful, *a*, бесполе́зный.

unhesitatingly, *ad*, реши́тельно, без колеба́ний.

unhindered, *a*, беспрепя́тственный.

unhinge, *v.t*, снима́ть с пе́тли; своди́ть с ума́.

unholy, *a*, нечести́вый; стра́шный.

unhonoured, *a*, нечти́мый.

unhook, *v.t*, снима́ть с крючка́; расцепля́ть; расстёгивать.

unhoped for неожи́данный.

unhorse, *v.t*, сбра́сывать с ло́шади.

unhurt, *a*, невреди́мый.

unicorn, *n*, единоро́г.

uniform, *a*, единообра́зный; однородный; фо́рменный *(clothing)*; ¶ *n*, фо́рма, фо́рменная оде́жда; ~ity, *n*, единообра́зие.

unify, *v.t*, объединя́ть, унифици́ровать.

unilateral, *a*, односторо́нний.

unimaginable, *a*, невообрази́мый.

unimpaired, *a*, неповреждённый, непострада́вший.

unimpeachable, *a*, безупре́чный.

unimportant, *a*, нева́жный.

uninformed, *a*, неосведомлённый.

uninhabitable, *a*, непригодный для жилья́; **uninhabited**, *a*, необита́емый.

uninitiated, *a*, непосвящённый.

uninjured, *a*, неповреждённый, непострада́вший.

uninstructed, *a*, необу́ченный, непроинструкти́рованный.

uninsured, *a*, незастрахо́ванный.

unintelligible, *a*, неразбо́рчивый.

unintentional, *a*, ненаме́ренный, неумы́шленный; ~ly, *ad*, ненаме́ренно, без у́мысла.

uninterested, *a*, незаинтересо́ванный; **uninteresting,** *a*, неинтере́сный.

uninterrupted, *a*, непреры́вный, непрерыва́емый.

uninvited, *a*, неприглашённый, без приглаше́ния; **uninviting,** *a*, непривлека́тельный.

union, *n*, сою́з; объедине́ние; соедине́ние; бра́чный сою́з; ~ist, *n*, член профсою́за; униони́ст *(hist, pol.)*.

unique, *a*, еди́нственный (в своём ро́де); уника́льный.

unison, *n, (mus.)* унисо́н; согла́сие.

unit, *n*, едини́ца; во́инская часть.

unite, *v.t. (& i.)*, соединя́ть(ся), объединя́ть(ся); ~d, *p.p. & a*, соединённый, объединённый; *U~ States* Соединённые Шта́ты Аме́рики; *U~ Nations* Организа́ция Объединённых На́ций; **unity,** *n*, еди́нство; сплочённость; *(maths.)* едини́ца.

universal, *a*, всео́бщий; всеми́рный; универса́льный; **universe,** *n*, вселе́нная, мир; **university,** *n*, университе́т; ¶ *a*, университе́тский.

unjust, *a*, несправедли́вый; ~ifiable, *a*, не име́ющий оправда́ния; ~ified, *a*, неопра́вданный, необосно́ванны.i.

unkempt, *a*, нечёсаный, неопря́тный.

unkind, *a*, недо́брый, злой.

unknowingly, *ad*, по незна́нию, без у́мысла; **unknown,** *a*, неизве́стный.

unlace, *v.t*, расшнуро́вывать.

unlawful, *a*, незако́нный, противозако́нный.

unlearn, *v.i*, разу́чиваться *(+ inf.)*.

unleash, *v.t*, спуска́ть с при́вязи; развя́зывать *(war)*; излива́ть *(anger)*.

unleavened, *a*, незаква́шенный, пре́сный.

unless, *c*, е́сли не; ~ *and until* до тех пор пока́.

unlettered, *a*, негра́мотный, необразо́ванный.

unlicensed, *a*, не име́ющий пра́ва/ разреше́ния.

unlike, *a*, непохо́жий на; не тако́й, как; ¶ *pr*, в отли́чие от; ~ly, *a*, маловероя́тный, неправдоподо́бный; ¶ *ad*, вряд ли, едва́ ли.

unlimited, *a*, безграни́чный, неограни́ченный.

unlined, *a*, без подкла́дки *(clothing)*.

unload, *v.t*, выгружа́ть, разгружа́ть; разряжа́ть *(gun.); (com.)* сбыва́ть.

unlock, *v.t*, отпира́ть, открыва́ть.

unlooked for неожи́данный, непредви́денный.

unloose, *v.t*, развя́зывать; отвя́зывать; открыва́ть.

unlucky, *a*, несчастли́вый, неуда́чный.

unmake, *v.t*, аннули́ровать; переде́лывать; уничтожа́ть.

unmanageable, *a*, тру́дно поддаю́щийся (контро́лю); тру́дный *(of child)*.

unmanly, *a*, сла́бый, изне́женный; недосто́йный мужчи́ны.

unmannerly, *a*, гру́бый, невоспи́танный.

unmarketable, *a*, не находя́щий себе́ сбы́та; него́дный для прода́жи, нехо́дкий.

unmarried, *a*, холосто́й, нежена́тый; незаму́жняя.

unmask, *v.t*, срыва́ть ма́ску с; *(fig.)* разоблача́ть.

unmentionable, *a*, сли́шком плохо́й, что́бы быть упомя́нутым; неприли́чный.

unmerciful, *a*, безжа́лостный.

unmerited, *a*, незаслу́женный.

unmindful, *a*, забы́вчивый, невнима́тельный; не обраща́ющий внима́ния.

unmistakable, *a*, несомне́нный, я́сный.

unmitigated, *a*, несмягчённый; абсолю́тный; отъя́вленный.

unmoved, *a*, нетро́нутый, непрекло́нный; неподви́жный.

unnamable, *a*, безымя́нный; неупомя́нутый; нена́званный.

unnatural, *a*, неесте́ственный; противоесте́ственный; бессерде́чный.

unnavigable, *a*, несудохо́дный; нелётный.

unnecessary, *a*, нену́жный; изли́шний.

unneighbourly, *a*, недобрососе́дский.

unnerve, *v.t*, лиша́ть реши́мости/ прису́тствия ду́ха.

unnoticed, *a*, незаме́ченный.

unobservant, *a*, невнима́тельный, ненаблюда́тельный; **unobserved,** *a*, незаме́ченный.

unobstructed, *a*, беспрепя́тственный; незасорённый; незава́ленный.

unobtainable, *a,* недоступный.

unobtrusive, *a,* ненавязчивый; незаметный.

unoccupied, *a,* незанятый; необитаемый; свободный.

unoffending, *a,* безобидный, невинный.

unopened, *a,* нераспечатанный; закрытый.

unopposed, *a,* не встретивший сопротивления.

unorthodox, *a,* неортодоксальный; непринятый, необычный.

unostentatious, *a,* ненавязчивый, скромный.

unpack, *v.t,* распаковывать.

unpaid, *a,* неоплаченный, неуплаченный; не получающий платы.

unpalatable, *a,* невкусный, неприятный.

unparalleled, *a,* беспримерный, не имеющий себе равного.

unpardonable, *a,* непростительный.

unpaved, *a,* немощёный.

unperturbed, *a,* невозмутимый. **~ness,** *n,* неприятность; непривлекательность; ссора.

unpleasant, *a,* неприятный; **~ness,** *n,* неприятность; непривлекательность; ссора.

unpopular, *a,* непопулярный.

unprecedented, *a,* беспримерный, беспрецедентный.

unprejudiced, *a,* беспристрастный.

unpremeditated, *a,* непреднамеренный, неумышленный.

unprepared, *a,* неподготовленный, неготовый.

unprepossessing, *a,* непривлекательный.

unpretentious, *a,* простой, без претензий.

unprincipled, *a,* беспринципный, безнравственный.

unprintable, *a,* непригодный для печати.

unproductive, *a,* непродуктивный, непроизводительный.

unprofessional, *a,* непрофессиональный; расходящийся с правилами/принципами профессии.

unprofitable, *a,* невыгодный, бесполезный; нерентабельный.

unpromising, *a,* не обещающий ничего хорошего.

unpronounceable, *a,* непроизносимый.

unpropitious, *a,* неблагоприятный.

unprotected, *a,* незащищённый, беззащитный; открытый.

unproved, *a,* недоказанный.

unprovoked, *a,* ничём не вызванный, неспровоцированный.

unpublished, *a,* неопубликованный, неизданный.

unpunished, *a,* безнаказанный.

unqualified, *a,* не имеющий (соответствующей) квалификации, неподходящий; абсолютный, безоговорочный.

unquenchable, *a,* неутолимый; неугасимый.

unquestionable, *a,* неоспоримый, несомненный; **unquestionably,** *ad,* несомненно; **unquestioned,** *a,* не вызывающий сомнения.

unquotable, *a,* нецензурный, неприличный.

unravel, *v.t,* распутывать; разгадывать.

unread, *a,* непрочитанный; *(pers.)* неначитанный, необразованный; **~able,** *a,* неразборчивый; слишком скучный.

unready, *a,* неготовый; несообразительный.

unreal, *a,* ненастоящий; нереальный, иллюзорный; **~ity,** *n,* нереальность, иллюзорность.

unreasonable, *a,* безрассудный; непомерно высокий, чрезмерный; **unreasoning,** *a,* немыслящий.

unrecognizable, *a,* неузнаваемый.

unrefined, *a,* неочищенный, нерафинированный.

unregenerate, *a,* невозрождённый, непреобразованный.

unregistered, *a,* незарегистрированный.

unrelenting, *a,* безжалостный, жестокий; неослабный, неуменьшающийся.

unreliable, *a,* ненадёжный.

unremitting, *a,* неослабный; беспрестанный.

unremunerative, *a,* невыгодный.

unrepeatable, *a,* неповторимый; нецензурный, неприличный.

unrepentant, *a,* нераскаявшийся.

unreserved, *a,* незабронированный; откровенный; **~ly,** *ad,* откровенно; безоговорочно.

unresisting, *a,* несопротивляющийся, нестойкий.

unrest, *n,* беспокойство; беспорядки, смута.

unrestrained, *a,* необузданный, несдержанный.

unrestricted, *a*, неограниченный.
unrewarding, *a*, невыгодный, нестоящий.
unrighteous, *a*, нечестивый.
unripe, *a*, незрелый, неспелый.
unrivalled, *a*, непревзойдённый, не имеющий себе равного.
unroll, *v.t*, развёртывать.
unruffled, *a*, спокойный; гладкий.
unruly, *a*, буйный, непослушный.
unsaddle, *v.t*, рассёдлывать.
unsafe, *a*, опасный, ненадёжный.
unsaid, *a*, невысказанный, непроизнесённый; *leave ~* не упоминать, не выражать.
unsalable, *a*, неходкий, не пользующийся спросом.
unsalaried, *a*, не получающий жалования.
unsalted, *a*, несолёный.
unsatisfactory, *a*, неудовлетворительный.
unsatisfied, *a*, неудовлетворённый.
unsavoury, *a*, невкусный; неприятный.
unscathed, *a*, невредимый.
unscientific, *a*, ненаучный.
unscrew, *v.t*, отвинчивать, развинчивать.
unscrupulous, *a*, неразборчивый в средствах, беспринципный; бессовестный.
unseal, *v.t*, распечатывать.
unseasonable, *a*, не по сезону; несвоевременный; unseasoned, *a*, без приправы; невыдержанный, несозревший.
unseat, *v.t*, сбрасывать с седла; ссаживать со стула; лишать парламентского мандата.
unseemly, *a*, неподобающий; непристойный.
unseen, *a*, невиданный, невидимый; *~ translation* перевод с листа.
unselfish, *a*, бескорыстный, неэгоистичный.
unserviceable, *a*, бесполезный, неуслужливый.
unsettle, *v.t*, нарушать порядок/ спокойствие *(gen.)*; выбивать из колей; расстраивать; *~d, p.p. & a*, неустройный; неустановившийся *(weather)*; нерешённый; неопла́канный.
unshakable, *a*, непоколебимый.
unshapely, *a*, бесформенный.
unshaven, *a*, небритый.

unsheathe, *v.t*, вынимать из ножен; *~ the sword* обнажать меч.
unship, *v.t*, выгружать; высаживать на берег.
unshod, *a*, необутый; неподкованный.
unshrinkable, *a*, не садящийся (при стирке); unshrinking, *a*, неустрашимый.
unsightly, *a*, непригля́дный; уродливый.
unsigned, *a*, неподписанный.
unskilled, *a*, неквалифицированный; неумелый.
unsmiling, *a*, неулыбающийся.
unsociable, *a*, необщительный.
unsold, *a*, непроданный, залежавшийся.
unsolicited, *a*, непрошенный; неожиданный.
unsolved, *a*, нерешённый.
unsophisticated, *a*, безыскусственный, простой; невинный.
unsorted, *a*, нерассортированный; неклассифицированный.
unsought, *a*, непрошенный.
unsound, *a*, нездоровый, хилый; гнилой, испорченный; ненадёжный; необоснованный; *of ~ mind* душевнобольной.
unsparing, *a*, щедрый; беспощадный.
unspeakable, *a*, невыразимый; отвратительный.
unspecified, *a*, неназванный, неупомянутый, неустановленный.
unspent, *a*, неистраченный, нерастраченный; неутомлённый; неупотреблённый.
unspoilt, *a*, неиспорченный.
unspoken, *a*, невыраженный, невысказанный.
unstable, *a*, неустойчивый.
unstamped, *a*, без штемпеля; не оплаченный маркой.
unsteady, *a*, неустойчивый; непостоянный.
unstinted, *a*, неограниченный.
unsuccessful, *a*, неудачный; неудачливый, несчастливый.
unsuitable, *a*, неподобающий, неподходящий.
unsullied, *a*, незапятнанный.
unsupported, *a*, неподдержанный.
unsurpassed, *a*, непревзойдённый.
unsuspected, *a*, не вызывающий подозрений; непредвиденный; unsuspecting, *a*, неподозревающий.

unsweetened, *a*, неподслащенный.
unswerving, *a*, непреклонный, твёрдый.
untainted, *a*, неиспорченный.
untamable, *a*, неукротимый; не поддающийся приручению; дикий.
untarnished, *a*, непотускневший; незапятнанный.
untaught, *a*, невежественный; необученный.
untenable, *a*, незащитимый; несостоятельный.
unthinkable, *a*, немыслимый; unthinking, *a*, легкомысленный.
untidy, *a*, неопрятный; в беспорядке.
untie, *v.t*, развязывать; освобождать.
until, *pr*, до, до сих (тех) пор; *not* ~ не раньше; ¶ *c*, (до тех пор) пока.
untimely, *a*, безвременный; преждевременный; несвоевременный.
untiring, *a*, неутомимый.
untold, *a*, нерассказанный; бессчётный, несметный.
untouched, *a*, нетронутый.
untoward, *a*, неблагоприятный, неудачный; несчастный.
untrained, *a*, необученный, неподготовленный.
untranslatable, *a*, непереводимый.
untravelled, *a*, нигде не бывавший; непроезжий *(road)*.
untried, *a*, неиспытанный, непроверенный.
untrodden, *a*, неисхоженный, непротоптанный.
untroubled, *a*, спокойный.
untrue, *a*, неверный; ложный; неправильный; *it is* ~ это неправда; untruly, *ad*, неискренне.
untrustworthy, *a*, ненадёжный.
untruth, *n*, неправда, ложь; ~ful, *a*, лживый.
untutored, *a*, необученный; неискушённый; без наставника.
untwine, *v.t*, расплестать, распутывать.
unused, *a*, неиспользованный; непривыкший; unusual, *a*, необыкновенный, необычный; ~ly, *a*, *ad*, необыкновенно.
unutterable, *a*, невыразимый; непроизносимый.
unvarnished, *a*, нелакированный; *(fig.)* неприкрашенный.
unvarying, *a*, неизменяющийся.

unveil, *v.t*, снимать покрывало с; торжественно открывать *(statue)*; открывать.
unversed, *a*, несведущий, неопытный.
unwarily, *ad*, неосторожно.
unwarranted, *a*, ничем не оправданный; недопустимый.
unwary, *a*, неосторожный.
unwashed, *a*, немытый, нестираный.
unwavering, *a*, твёрдый, устойчивый.
unwearied, *a*, неутомимый.
unwelcome, *a*, незваный, непрошенный; нежелательный, неприятный.
unwell, *a*, нездоровый.
unwholesome, *a*, нездоровый, вредный.
unwieldy, *a*, громоздкий, неуклюжий.
unwilling, *a*, несклонный; ~ly, *ad*, неохотно, против желания; ~ness, *a*, несклонность, нерасположение.
unwind, *v.t*, развёртывать, разматывать.
unwise, *a*, неблагоразумный.
unwittingly, *ad*, невольно, нечаянно.
unwonted, *a*, необычный, непривычный.
unworkable, *a*, неприменимый; негодный для работы.
unworn, *a*, неношеный; непоношенный.
unworthy, *a*, недостойный.
unwrap, *v.t*, развёртывать.
unwritten, *a*, неписаный; ненаписанный; ~ *law* неписаный закон.
unwrought, *a*, необработанный.
unyielding, *a*, упорный, неподатливый.
unyoke, *v.t*, снимать ярмо с; *(fig.)* освобождать от ига.
up, *a*, идущий вверх; ~ *train* поезд, идущий в центр/столицу; ~-*to*--*date* новейший, современный; ~--*and-down* холмистый; колеблющийся; ¶ *ad*, наверху, вверху; наверх, вверх; ~ *and down* вверх и вниз; взад и вперёд; повсюду; ~ *to* вплоть до; на уровне с; согласно/соответственно *(dat.)*; ~ *to now* до сих пор; *not* ~ *to much* неважный; *well* ~ *in* хорошо осведомлённый/сведущий в; *what's*

~? в чём де́ло?; ¶ *n*, подъём; ~s *and downs* уха́бы: *(fig.)* превра́тности судьбы́; ¶ *pr*, вверх по; вдоль по; ~ *the street* по у́лице; ~ *wind* про́тив ве́тра.

upbraid, *v.t*, брани́ть, укоря́ть.

upbringing, *n*, воспита́ние.

upcountry, *ad*, внутри́/внутрь страны́.

upgrade, *n*, подъём; ¶ *v.t*, повыша́ть (по рабо́те).

upheaval, *n*, сдвиг; переворо́т; *(geol.)* смеще́ние пласто́в.

uphill, *a*, иду́щий в го́ру; *(fig.)* тяжёлый, тру́дный; ¶ *ad*, в го́ру.

uphold, *v.t*, подде́рживать; приде́рживаться *(gen.)*; ~er, *n*, сторо́нник; боре́ц (за).

upholster, *v.t*, обива́ть; ~ed, *p.p.* & *a*, оби́тый; ~er, *n*, обо́йщик.

upkeep, *n*, содержа́ние; ремо́нт.

upland, *n*, гори́стая часть страны́, наго́рная страна́.

uplift, *v.t*, поднима́ть, возвыша́ть; ¶ *n*, подъём.

upon, *pr*, на; ~ *my soul!* че́стное сло́во!, кляну́сь!

upper, *a*, ве́рхний; вы́сший; ~ *deck* ве́рхняя па́луба; ве́рхний эта́ж *(bus)*; *get the* ~ *hand* брать верх; *the* ~ *ten* верху́шка о́бщества; ¶ *n*, передо́к (боти́нка); ~most, *a*, са́мый ве́рхний; наивы́сший.

upright, *a*, вертика́льный; прямо́й; че́стный; ¶ *ad*, вертика́льно; прямо́м; сто́йком; стоймя́.

uprising, *n*, бунт, восста́ние.

uproar, *n*, гам, шум; ~ious, *a*, бу́йный, шу́мный.

uproot, *v.t*, вырыва́ть с ко́рнем; искореня́ть.

upset, *n*, расстро́йство; беспоря́док; неожи́данное происше́ствие; ¶ *v.t*, опроки́дывать; расстра́ивать; наруша́ть; огорча́ть; *v.i*, опроки́дываться.

upshot, *n*, развя́зка, результа́т.

upside down, *ad*, вверх дном; в беспоря́дке.

upstairs, *ad*, наве́рх, вверх по ле́стнице; наверху́.

upstart, *n*, вы́скочка.

upstream, *ad*, вверх по тече́нию; про́тив тече́ния.

upward, *a*, дви́гающийся вверх, напра́вленный вверх; ~s, *ad*, вверх; ~ *of* свы́ше.

uranium, *n*, ура́н.

urban, *a*, городско́й.

urbane, *a*, ве́жливый, све́тский.

urchin, *n*, мальчи́шка.

urethra, *n*, мочеиспуска́тельный кана́л.

urge, *n*, побужде́ние, толчо́к; ¶ *v.t* побужда́ть, подгоня́ть; убежда́ть; ~ncy, *a*, настоя́тельность; кра́йняя необходи́мость; безотлага́тельность; ~nt, *a*, настоя́тельный, сро́чный; кра́йне необходи́мый; ~ntly *ad*, сро́чно.

uric, *a*, мочево́й; **urinal**, *n*, писсуа́р, ури́льник; **urinate**, *v.i*, мочи́ться; **urine**, *n*, моча́.

urn, *n*, у́рна; *tea* ~ ча́йник.

us, *pn*, нас, нам *etc.*

usage, *n*, употребле́ние; обы́чай; обхожде́ние.

use, *n*, по́льза; по́льзование, примене́ние, употребле́ние; *it's no* ~ бесполе́зно; *make* ~ *of* испо́льзовать; по́льзоваться *(inst.)*; ¶ *v.t*, употребля́ть, по́льзоваться *(inst.)*; применя́ть; обраща́ться/ обходи́ться с; *we often* ~d *to go there* мы ча́сто ходи́ли туда́; ~ *up* расхо́довать; ~d, *p.p.* & *a*, привы́кший; поде́ржанный, ста́рый; испо́льзованный; *get* ~ *to* привыка́ть к; ~ful, *a*, поле́зный; ~less, *a*, бесполе́зный; никуда́ не го́дный; ~ r, *n*, потреби́тель.

usher, *n*, швейца́р; билетёр, капельди́нер *(theat.)*; при́став *(in court)*; ¶ *v.t*: ~ *in* вводи́ть; возвеща́ть; ~ette, *n*, билетёрша, капельди́нерша.

usual, *a*, обыкнове́нный, обы́чный; *as* ~ как обы́чно; ~ly, *ad*, обыкнове́нно, обы́чно.

usufruct, *n*, узуфру́кт.

usurer, *n*, ростовщи́к; **usurious**, *a*, ростовщи́ческий.

usurp, *v.t*, узурпи́ровать, (незако́нно) захва́тывать; ~er, *n*, узурпа́тор, захва́тчик.

usury, *n*, ростовщи́чество.

utensil, *n*, посу́да, у́тварь; принадле́жность.

uterine, *a*, утро́бный; **uterus**, *n*, ма́тка; утро́ба.

utilitarian, *a*, утилита́рный; **utility**, *n*, вы́годность; поле́зность; *public utilities* предприя́тия обще́ственного по́льзования; ¶ *a*, утили-

тарный, практический; **utilize,** *v.t,* использовать, утилизировать.
utmost, *a,* крайний, предельный; самый отдалённый; величайший; *do one's* ~ делать всё возможное; *of the* ~ *importance* чрезвычайной важности.
utopia, *n,* утопия; ~n, *a,* утопический.
utter, *a,* полный, совершённый; абсолютный; отъявленный; ¶ *v.t,* произносить, издавать; ~ance, *n,* произнесение; высказывание, изречение; ~ly, *ad,* крайне; совершённо; ~most, *a,* самый отдалённый.
Uzbek, *a,* узбекский; ¶ *n,* узбе|к, -чка; узбекский язык.

V

vacancy, *n,* вакансия; пустота, пустое место; рассеянность; **vacant,** *a,* вакантный; свободный, пустой; отсутствующий *(look),* рассеянный; **vacate,** *v.t,* покидать; освобождать; **vacation,** *n,* каникулы, отпуск.
vaccinate, *v.t,* делать прививку *(dat.);* **vaccination,** *n,* прививка; **vaccine,** *n,* вакцина.
vacillate, *v.i,* колебаться; **vacillation,** *n,* колебание; непостоянство.
vacuity, *n,* пустота; **vacuous,** *a,* пустой; **vacuum,** *n,* вакуум; *(fig.)* пустота; ~ *cleaner* пылесос; ~ *flask* термос.
vade-mecum, *n,* путеводитель, карманный справочник.
vagabond, *a,* бродячий; ¶ *n,* бродяга.
vagary, *n,* каприз, причуда.
vagrancy, *n,* бродяжничество; **vagrant,** *a,* бродячий, странствующий; ¶ *n,* бродяга; празднношатающийся.
vague, *a,* неопределённый, неясный, смутный; ~ness, *n,* неопределённость, неясность.
vain, *a,* напрасный, тщётный; тщеславный, самодовольный; ~glorious, *a,* тщеславный, хвастливый; ~ly, *ad,* напрасно; тщеславно.
valance, *n,* подзор.
vale, *n,* долина, дол.

valediction, *n,* прощание; **valedictory,** *a,* прощальный.
valerian, *n,* валерьяна; *(med.)* валерьяновые капли.
valet, *n,* камердинер, слуга.
valetudinarian, *a,* болезненный, мнительный.
valiant, *a,* доблестный, храбрый.
valid, *a,* действительный, имеющий силу; веский; ~ate, *v.t,* ратифицировать, утверждать, объявлять действительным; ~ity, *n,* действительность; вескость.
valise, *n,* чемодан.
valley, *n,* долина.
valorous, *a,* доблестный; **valour,** *n,* доблесть.
valuable, *a,* ценный; дорогой; ~s, *n.pl,* ценные вещи, драгоценности; **valuation,** *n,* оценка; **value,** *n,* ценность; стоимость, цена; значение; *(maths.)* величина; ¶ *v.t,* оценивать; ценить; дорожить *(inst.);* **valueless,** *a,* бесполезный, ничего не стоящий; **valuer,** *n,* оценщик.
valve, *n,* клапан *(also anat.);* золотник; *(bot.)* створка; *(radio)* электронная лампа.
vamp, *n,* передок *(of shoe);* заплата; *(pers.)* авантюристка; ¶ *v.t,* латать, чинить; *(mus.)* импровизировать; соблазнять.
vampire, *n,* вампир.
van, *n,* фургон, машина; вагон; авангард.
vandal, *n,* вандал, варвар; ¶ *a,* варварский; ~ism, *n,* вандализм, варварство.
vane, *n,* флюгер; крыло *(of windmill);* лопасть *(of propeller);* лопатка *(of turbine).*
vanguard, *n,* авангард.
vanilla, *n,* ваниль.
vanish, *v.i,* исчезать, пропадать.
vanity, *n,* тщеславие; суетность; ~ *bag* сумочка.
vanquish, *v.t,* побеждать; подавлять. ~er, *n,* победитель, покоритель.
vantage point наблюдательный пункт, удобная позиция.
vapid, *a,* безвкусный, пресный; *(fig.)* плоский, скучный.
vaporize, *v.t. (& i.),* испарять(ся); ~r, *n,* испаритель; **vaporous,** *a,* парообразный; туманный; **vapour,** *n,* пар; туман.

variable, *a*, изме́нчивый, непостоя́нный; переме́нный *(also maths.)*; **variance,** *n*, разногла́сие, несоотве́тствие; измене́ние; *be at ~ with* расходи́ться с; противоре́чить *(dat.)*; быть в ссо́ре с; **variant,** *n*, вариа́нт; **variation,** *n*, измене́ние, переме́на; вариа́нт; разнови́дность; *(mus.)* вариа́ция.

varicose, *a*, расши́ренный; варико́зный.

variegate, *v.t*, де́лать пёстрым, раскра́шивать в ра́зные цвета́; разнообра́зить; **~d,** *a*, пёстрый, разноцве́тный; разнообра́зный; **variety,** *n*, разнообра́зие; мно́жество, ряд; *(biol.)* разнови́дность; *variety show* варьете́, эстра́дный конце́рт; **various,** *a*, разли́чный, ра́зный; разнообра́зный.

varnish, *n*, лак; *(fig.)* лоск; ¶ *v.t*, лакирова́ть; *(fig.)* прикра́шивать; **~ing,** *n*, лакиро́вка.

vary, *v.t*, меня́ть; разнообра́зить; *v.i*, меня́ться, изменя́ться; ра́зниться; расходи́ться.

vase, *n*, ва́за.

vaseline, *n*, вазели́н.

vassal, *n*, васса́л.

vast, *a*, грома́дный, обши́рный, безбре́жный; **~ly,** *ad*, о́чень, значи́тельно; **~ness,** *n*, грома́дность, обши́рность, безбре́жность.

vat, *n*, бак, чан; бо́чка, ка́дка.

Vatican, *n*, Ватика́н.

vaudeville, *n*, водеви́ль.

vault, *n*, свод; по́греб, подва́л; склеп; прыжо́к; ¶ *v.t*, возводи́ть свод над; перепры́гивать; *v.i*, пры́гать; **~ing** *horse* ко́злы, конь.

vaunt, *n*, хвастовство́; ¶ *v.t*, превозноси́ть; *v.i*, хва́статься; злора́дствовать.

veal, *n*, теля́тина; *~ cutlet* теля́чья отбивна́я.

vector, *n*, ве́ктор; носи́тель боле́зни.

veer, *v.i*, меня́ть направле́ние; лави́ровать.

vegetable, *n*, о́вощ; ¶ *a*, расти́тельный; овощно́й; **vegetarian,** *n*, вегетариа́нец; ¶ *a*, вегетариа́нский; **vegetarianism,** *n*, вегетариа́нство; **vegetate,** *v.i*, расти́; *(fig.)* прозяба́ть; **vegetative,** *a*, расти́тельный, вегетати́вный; *(fig.)* прозяба́ющий.

vehemence, *n*, стра́стность; **vehement,** *a*, стра́стный, нейсто́вый.

vehicle, *n*, экипа́ж, сре́дство передвиже́ния/перево́зки; сре́дство выраже́ния; носи́тель *(of infection, etc.)*; *(chem.)* раствори́тель; *vehicular traffic* движе́ние автогужево́го тра́нспорта.

veil, *n*, вуа́ль, покрыва́ло; *(fig.)* заве́са, покро́в; ¶ *v.t*, покрыва́ть вуа́лью/покрыва́лом; *(fig.)* завуали́ровать *(pf.)*, скрыва́ть.

vein, *n*, ве́на; жи́лка *(of leaf)*; **~ed,** *a*, испещрённый жи́лками.

vellum, *n*, то́нкий перга́мент.

velocipede, *n*, трёхколёсный велосипе́д; дрези́на; **velocity,** *n*, ско́рость.

velours, *n*, велю́р.

velvet, *n*, ба́рхат; вельве́т; ¶ *a*, ба́рхатный; **~ine,** *n*, вельвети́н; **~y,** *a*, бархати́стый.

venal, *a*, прода́жный, подку́пный; **~ity,** *n*, прода́жность.

vend, *v.t*, продава́ть; **~or,** *n*, продаве́ц, разно́счик.

veneer, *n*, облицо́вка; фане́ра; *(fig.)* лоск; ¶ *v.t*, облицо́вывать; обкле́ивать фане́рой; придава́ть лоск *(dat.)*.

venerable, *a*, почте́нный; **venerate,** *v.t*, благогове́ть пе́ред; **veneration,** *n*, благогове́ние, почита́ние.

venereal, *a*, венери́ческий.

Venetian, *a*, венециа́нский; *~ blind* жалюзи́.

vengeance, *n*, месть; мще́ние; **vengeful,** *a*, мсти́тельный.

venial, *a*, прости́тельный.

venison, *n*, оле́нина.

venom, *n*, яд; **~ous,** *a*, ядови́тый.

vent, *n*, вы́ход, отве́рстие; *~ hole* отду́шина; ¶ *v.t*, дава́ть вы́ход/во́лю *(dat.)*; выпуска́ть; излива́ть; **~ilate,** *v.t*, прове́тривать; *(fig.)* обсужда́ть; **~ilation,** *n*, вентиля́ция, прове́тривание; **~ilator,** *n*, вентиля́тор.

ventral, *a*, брюшно́й.

ventricle, *n*, желу́дочек.

ventriloquism, -quy, *n*, чревовеща́ние; **ventriloquist,** *n*, чревовеща́тель.

venture, *n*, предприя́тие; спекуля́ция; *at a ~* науда́чу; ¶ *v.t*, рискова́ть *(inst.)*, ста́вить на ка́рту; *v.i*, осме́ливаться, отва́живаться; ~some, *a*, смéлый; рискóванный.

veracious, *a*, правдúвый; veracity, *n*, правдúвость.

veranda[h], *n*, верáнда.

verb, *n*, глагóл; ~al, *a*, ýстный, словéсный; *(gram.)* отглагóльный; ~atim, *a*, дослóвный; ¶ *ad*, дослóвно; ~lage, *n*, многослóвие; ~ose, *a*, многослóвный.

verdant, *a*, зелёный.

verdict, *n*, приговóр; мнéние.

verdigris, *n*, ярь-медя́нка.

verdure, *n*, зéлень.

verge, *n*, край; обóчина *(of road); (fig.)* грань, край; *(eccl.)* жезл, пóсох; *(arch.)* стéржень колóнны; on the ~ *(of)* на грáни/ краю; ¶ *v.i*: ~ *on* гранúчить с; ~r, *n*, жезлонóсец, церкóвный служúтель.

verification, *n*, провéрка; подтверждéние; verify, *v.t*, проверя́ть; подтверждáть; verisimilitude, *n*, правдоподóбие; veritable, *a*, настоя́щий; verity, *n*, úстина; úстинность.

vermicelli, *n*, вермишéль.

vermilion, *n*, киновáрь.

vermin, *n*, вредúтели, парази́ты; ~ous, *a*, кишáщий паразúтами; отвратúтельный.

vermouth, *n*, вéрмут.

vernacular, *a*, нарóдный; мéстный; роднóй; ¶ *n*, роднóй язы́к; мéстный диалéкт.

vernal, *a*, весéнний.

veronica, *n*, верóника.

versatile, *a*, многостóронний; гúбкий *(mind);* versatility, *n*, многостóронность; гúбкость.

verse, *n*, стих; строфá: стихú, поэ́зия; ~d, *a*, óпытный, свéдущий; versicle, *n*, вóзглас; versifier, *n*, стихоплёт; versify, *v.i*, писáть стихú.

version, *n*, вéрсия, вариáнт; текст.

versus, *pr*, прóтив.

vertebra, *n*, позвонóк; *pl*, позвонóчник; ~l, *a*, позвонóчный; ~te, *n*, позвонóчное живóтное.

vertex, *n*, вершúна; vertical, *a*, вертикáльный; ¶ *n*, вертикáль; перпендикуля́р; ~ly, *ad*, вертикáльно.

vertiginous, *a*, головокружúтельный; крутя́щийся; vertigo, *n*, головокружéние.

verve, *n*, бóдрость, энéргия; сúла.

very, *a*, настоя́щий, сýщий; (тот) сáмый; ¶ *ad*, óчень; ~ *much* óчень; the ~ *same* тот же сáмый.

vesicle, *n*, пузырёк.

vespers, *n.pl*, вечéрня.

vessel, *n*, сосýд; корáбль, сýдно.

vest, *n*, мáйка; жилéт; ¶ *v.t*, облекáть; наделя́ть; ~ed, *p.p. & a*, облачённый; закóнный; ~ *interests* материáльная заинтересóванность; закóнные правá на имýщество; капиталовложéния.

vestal, *a*, дéвственный, целомýдренный; ~ *virgin* вестáлка.

vestibule, *n*, вестибю́ль, передня́я.

vestige, *n*, след; прúзнак.

vestment, *n*, одéжда, одея́ние, облачéние; vestry, *n*, рúзница; vesture, *n*, одея́ние.

vet, *n*, ветеринáр; ¶ *v.t*, проверя́ть.

vetch, *n*, вúка, горóшек.

veteran, *a*, óпытный, стáрый; ¶ *n*, ветерáн.

veterinary, *a*, ветеринáрный; ¶ *n*, ветеринáр.

veto, *n*, вéто, запрещéние; ¶ *v.t*, запрещáть, налагáть вéто на.

vex, *v.t*, досаждáть *(dat.)*, раздражáть; беспокóить; ~ation, *n*, досáда, раздражéние; ~ing, *a*, досáдный; ~ed, *a*, раздражóванный; *(fig.);* слóжный, спóрный.

via, *pr*, чéрез.

viable, *a*, жизнеспосóбный.

viaduct, *n*, виадýк.

vial, *n*, пузырёк, буты́лочка.

viands, *n.pl*, провúзия, я́ства.

vibrate, *v.i*, вибрúровать, дрожáть; звучáть; vibration, *n*, вибрáция, дрожáние.

vicar, *n*, прихóдский свящéнник; ~age, *n*, дом свящéнника; ~ious, *a*, замещáющий другóго; кóсвенный.

vice, *n*, порóк; зло; *(tech.)* тискú.

vice-, *prefix*, вице-, заместúтель; ~-admiral вице-адмирáл; ~-chairman заместúтель председáтеля; ~-president вице-президéнт; ~roy вице-корóль.

vice-versa, *ad*, наоборóт.

vicinity, *n*, окрéстность, блúзость; сосéдство; in the ~ поблúзости; óколо.

vicious, *a*, порóчный; злóбный; жестóкий; ~ness, *n*, порóчность; злóбность.

vicissitude, *n*, превратность.
victim, *n*, жёртва; ~ ize, *v.t*, мучить, преследовать.
victor, *n*, победитель; ~ious, *a*, победоносный· ~y, *n*, побéда.
victual, *v t*, снабжать провизией; ~s, *n pl*, пища, провизия, продовольствие; ~ler, *n*, поставщик продовольствия·
videotape, *n*, видеолента.
vie, *v.i*, соперничать.
view, *n*, вид: взгляд, мнение; кругозор; ~finder, видоискатель; ~point точка зрения; in ~ (of) ввиду; with a ~ (to) с намерением; ¶ *v t*, осматривать; рассматривать: смотреть на.
vigil, *n*, бодрствование; keep ~ бодрствовать; дежурить; ~ance, *n*, бдительность; ~ant, *a*, бдительный.
vignette, *n*, виньéтка.
vigorous, *a*, сильный, энергичный; vigour, *n*, сила, энергия.
vile, *a*, низкий, подлый: отвратительный; vilify, *v.t*, поносить, чернить.
villa, *n*, вилла; ~ge, *n*, деревня, село; ¶ *a*, деревенский: сельский; ~ger, *n*, деревенский/сельский житель.
villain, *n*, злодей; ~ous, *a*, злодейский; мерзкий; ~y, *n*, злодейство; мерзость.
villein, *n*, крепостной.
vindicate, *v.t*, оправдывать; реабилитировать; отстаивать; ~ oneself оправдываться; vindication, *n*, оправдание; защита.
vindicative, *a*, мстительный.
vine, *n*, виноградная лоза; ползучее растение; ~-grower виноградарь; ~-growing виноградарство; ~gar, *n*, уксус; ~yard, виноградник; vinous, *a*, винный.
vintage, *n*, сбор винограда, урожай винограда; вино урожая определённого года.
viola, *n*, альт; (bot.) фиалка.
violate, *v.t*, нарушать, попирать (rights); осквернять: насиловать; violation, *n*, нарушение; осквернéние: насилие; violator, *n*, нарушитель; violence, *n*, насилие; сила; violent, *a*, насильственный; нейстовый; сильный.
violet, *n*, фиалка; фиолéтовый цвет; ¶ *a*, фиолéтовый.

violin, *n*, скрипка; ~ist, *n*, скрипач; violoncellist, *n*, виолончелист; violoncello, *n*, виолончéль.
viper, *n*, гадюка; (fig.) змея; ~ish, *a*, ехидный, злобный.
virago, *n*, ворчунья, мегéра.
virgin, *n*, дéва, дéвственница; ¶ *a*, дéвственный; самородный (metal); (fig) нетронутый, чистый; ~ soil целина; ~al, *a*, дéвственный; невинный; ~als, *n pl*, спинéт без ножек; ~ity, *n*, дéвственность.
virile, *a*, возмужалый, сильный; virility, *n*, возмужалость; мужество; половая зрéлость.
virtual, *a*, фактический; ~ly, *ad*, фактически; virtue, *n*, добродéтель; достоинство; by ~ of благодаря; посредством; virtuosity, *n*, виртуозность; virtuoso, *n*, виртуоз: знаток, ценитель искусства; virtuous, *a*, добродéтельный, целомудренный.
virulence, *n*, ядовитость; опасность; (fig.) злоба: virulent, *a*, ядовитый; сильный. опасный; злобный; virus, *n*, вирус.
visa, *n*, виза; ¶ *v t*, визировать.
visage, *n*, лицо; вид.
viscera, *n.pl*, внутренности.
viscount, *n*, виконт.
viscous, *a*, вязкий, липкий; тягучий; ~ness, *n*, вязкость; тягучесть.
visibility, *n*, видимость; visible, *a*, видимый; очевидный; visibly, *ad*, видимо, явно.
vision, *n*, зрéние; видение; проницательность, предвидение; видéние; ~ary, *a*, мечтательный, дальновидный; призрачный, воображаемый; нереáльный; ¶ *n*, мечтатель; мистик.
visit, *n*, визит, посещéние; pay a ~ приезжать с визитом, навещать; отдавать визит; ¶ *v t*, навещать, посещать; ~ation, *n*, официáльное посещéние, инспéкция; (eccl.) божье наказáние, кара; ~ing, *a*, посещающий; ~card визитная карточка; ~or, *n*, гость, посетитель; инспéктор.
visor, *n*, козырёк (of cap); забрáло (of helmet).
vista, *n*, перспектива, вид·
visual, *a*, наглядный; зрительный; оптический; ~ize, *v.t*, представлять себé, мысленно видеть.

vital, *a*, жи́зненный; насу́щный, суще́ственный; живо́й; ~ity, *n*, жизнеспосо́бность, жи́зненность; жи́вость; ~ize, *v.t*, оживля́ть, обновля́ть; ~s, *n.pl*, жи́зненно ва́жные о́рганы.

vitamin, *n*, витами́н.

vitiate, *v.t*, по́ртить; де́лать недействи́тельным; лиша́ть си́лы; vitiation, *n*, по́рча; *(law)* лише́ние си́лы; призна́ние недействи́тельным.

viticultural, *a*, виногра́дарный; viticulturalist, *n*, виногра́дарь; viticulture, *n*, виногра́дарство.

vitreous, *a*, стекловидный, стекля́нный; vitrify, *v.t*, превраща́ть в стекло́/стекловидное вещество́.

vitriol, *n*, купоро́с; ~ic, *a*, купоро́сный; *(fig.)* язви́тельный.

vituperate, *v.t*, брани́ть, поноси́ть; vituperation, *n*, брань, поноше́ние.

vivacious, *a*, живо́й, оживлённый; vivacity, *n*, жи́вость, оживлённость.

viva voce, *a*, у́стный; ¶ *n*, у́стный экза́мен.

vivid, *a*, живо́й, я́ркий; ~ness, *n*, жи́вость, я́ркость.

vivify, *v.t*, оживля́ть; viviparous, *a*, живородя́щий; vivisection, *n*, виви́секция.

vixen, *n*, лиси́ца-са́мка; *(fig.)* меге́ра, сварли́вая же́нщина.

viz, *ad*, то есть, и́менно.

vizier, *n*, визи́рь.

vocabulary, *n*, слова́рь; запа́с слов; слова́рный соста́в; vocal, *a*, голосово́й; вока́льный; выска́зывающийся откры́то, шу́мный; *(phon.)* зво́нкий; vocalist, *n*, певе́ц, певи́ца; vocalize, *v.t*, произноси́ть зво́нко, вокализи́ровать *v.i*, петь вока́лизы.

vocation, *n*, призва́ние; профе́ссия; заня́тие; vocative, *n*, зва́тельный паде́ж.

vociferate, *v.t. & i*, крича́ть, ора́ть; vociferous, *a*, горла́стый, шу́мный, гро́мкий.

vogue, *n*, мо́да; популя́рность.

voice, *n*, го́лос; *(gram.)* зало́г; ¶ *v.t*, выража́ть (слова́ми); *(phon.)* произноси́ть зво́нко.

void, *n*, пустота́; ¶ *a*, пусто́й; недействи́тельный; ¶ *v.t*, опорожня́ть; *(law)* де́лать недействи́тельным, аннули́ровать.

volatile, *a*, лету́чий; *(fig.)* непостоя́нный; volatilize, *v.t. (& i.)*, улету́чивать(ся), испаря́ть(ся).

volcanic, *a*, вулкани́ческий; *(fig.)* бу́рный; volcano, *n*, вулка́н.

vole, *n*, полёвка.

volition, *n*, во́ля.

volley, *n*, залп; *(sport)* уда́р на лету́; ¶ *v.t*, отбива́ть/ударя́ть (мяч) на лету́; ~-ball волейбо́л.

volt, *n*, вольт; ~age, *n*, вольта́ж, напряже́ние; ~aic, *a*, гальвани́ческий; ~ meter, *n*, вольтме́тр.

volubility, *n*, говорли́вость, разгово́рчивость; voluble, *a*, говорли́вый, разгово́рчивый.

volume, *n*, том; объём; ~s of smoke клубы́ ды́ма; voluminous, *a*, объёмистый, обши́рный; плодови́тый *(of writer)*.

voluntary, *a*, доброво́льный; ¶ *n*, со́ло; volunteer, *n*, доброво́лец; ¶ *v.t*, предлага́ть; *v.i*, вызыва́ться доброво́льно; идти́ доброво́льцем.

voluptuary, *n*, сластолю́бец; voluptuous *a*, сладостра́стный, чу́вственный.

volute, *n*, волю́та; спира́ль.

vomit, *n*, рво́та; ¶ *v.t*, изверга́ть; *v i: I* ~ меня́ рвёт.

voracious, *a*, жа́дный, прожо́рливый.

vortex, *n*, водоворо́т; вихрь.

votary, *n*, почита́тель, сторо́нник.

vote, *n*, го́лос; голосова́ние; во́тум; ¶ *v.i*, голосова́ть; *v.t*, предлага́ть; одобря́ть; ~r, *n*, избира́тель; voting, *n*, голосова́ние; ~ paper избира́тельный бюллете́нь; votive, *a* исполненный по обе́ту.

vouch, *v.t*, подтвержда́ть; ~ for руча́ться за; ~er, *n*, распи́ска; тало́н, купо́н; ~safe, *v.t*, удоста́ивать.

vow, *n*, кля́тва, обе́т; ¶*v.i*, кля́сться, дава́ть обе́т.

vowel, *n*, гла́сный (звук), гла́сная бу́ква.

voyage, *n*, путеше́ствие; ¶ *v.i*, путеше́ствовать по мо́рю; ~r, *n*, путеше́ственник.

vulcanite, *n*, вулканизи́рованная рези́на; эбони́т; vulcanize, *v.t*, вулканизи́ровать.

vulgar, *a*, вульга́рный, гру́бый, по́шлый; простонаро́дный; просто́й; *the* ~ *herd* простонаро́дье чернь; ~ism, *n*, вульгари́зм, вульга́рное выраже́ние; ~ity, *n*, вульга́рность, по́шлость; ~ize, *v.t*, вульгаризи́ровать, опошля́ть; Vulgate, *n*, вульга́та.

vulnerable, *a*, уязви́мый.

vulture, *n*, гриф; (*fig.*) хи́щник.

W

wad, *n*, кусо́к ва́ты; па́чка; пыж; ¶ *v.t*, набива́ть/подбива́ть ва́той; wadding, *n*, ва́та; наби́вка; подкла́дка.

waddle, *v.i*, ходи́ть враззва́лку.

wade, *v.i*, перебира́ться по воде́, переходи́ть вброд; ~ *into* сме́ло вступа́ть в; реши́тельно принима́ться за; набра́сываться на, ре́зко критикова́ть; ~ *through* пробира́ться сквозь/че́рез; одолева́ть; ~r, *n*, боло́тная пти́ца; боло́тный сапо́г.

waffle, *n*, ва́фля.

waft, *n*, дунове́ние (*of wind*); струя́ (*of smell*); ¶ *v.t*, нести́; доноси́ть.

wag, *n*, взмах, кивóк; шутни́к; ¶ *v.t*, маха́ть (*inst.*); ~ *the tail* виля́ть хвосто́м; *v.i*, кача́ться.

wage, *n*, (*also pl.*), за́работная пла́та; ~-*earner* рабо́чий; получа́ющий за́работную пла́ту; корми́лец; ¶ *v.t*: ~ *war* вести́ войну́.

wager, *n*, пари́, ста́вка; ¶ *v.i*, держа́ть пари́; *v.t*, рискова́ть (*inst.*).

waggish, *a*, шаловли́вый, шутли́вый.

wag[g]on, *n*, пово́зка, фурго́н; ваго́н, вагоне́тка; подво́да; ~er, *n*, во́зчик; ~ette, *n*, экипа́ж.

wagtail, *n*, трясогу́зка.

waif, *n*, беспризо́рник.

wail, *n*, вопль, вой; ¶ *v.i*, вопи́ть, выть.

wainscot, *n*, пане́ль; ¶ *v.t*, обшива́ть пане́лью.

waist, *n*, та́лия; корса́ж, лиф; ~ *band* по́яс; ~*coat* жиле́т.

wait, *n*, ожида́ние; *lie in* ~ быть в заса́де; ¶ *v.t & i*, ждать; ~ *on* прислу́живать за столо́м; ~er, *n*, официа́нт; ~ing, *n*, ожида́ние; ~ *room* приёмная; зал ожида́ния; ~ress, *n*, официа́нтка.

waive, *v.t*, отка́зываться от; откла́дывать.

wake, *n*, поми́нки; (*mar.*) кильва́тер; *in the* ~ *of* по пята́м/следа́м; ¶ *v.t*, буди́ть; *v.i*, просыпа́ться; ~fulness, *n*, бди́тельность; бо́дрствование; ~n, *v.t*, буди́ть, пробужда́ть; *v.i*, просыпа́ться; пробужда́ться.

walk, *n*, ходьба́; похо́дка; прогу́лка пешко́м; алле́я, тропа́; *go for a* ~ идти́ гуля́ть; ~ *of life* профе́ссия, обще́ственное положе́ние; ~-*over* лёгкая побе́да; ¶ *v.i*, идти́, ходи́ть, гуля́ть; *v.t*, обходи́ть; води́ть; ~ *about* прогу́ливаться; ~ *in* входи́ть; ~ *off* уходи́ть; ~ *out* выходи́ть; объявля́ть заба́стовку; ~ing, *n*, ходьба́; ¶ *a*, гуля́ющий, иду́щий; ходя́чий; ~-*on part* роль без слов; ~ *stick* трость; ~ *tour* экску́рсия пешко́м.

wall, *n*, стена́; сте́нка; ~ *cupboard* стенно́й шкаф; ~ *eye* бельмо́; ~*flower* желтофио́ль; *be a* ~ *flower* остава́ться без кавале́ра; ~*paper* обо́и; стенгазе́та; ¶ *v.t*: ~ *up* заде́лывать (*door, etc.*); замуро́вывать.

wallet, *n*, бума́жник; су́мка.

wallop, *n*, си́льный уда́р; ¶ *v.t*, бить.

walnut, *n*, гре́цкий оре́х; оре́ховое де́рево.

walrus, *n*, морж.

waltz, *n*, вальс; ¶ *v.i*, вальси́ровать.

wan, *a*, бле́дный; изнурённый; поту́хший.

wand, *n*, жезл; па́лочка.

wander, *v.i*, броди́ть, стра́нствовать; блужда́ть; бре́дить; ~er, *n*, стра́нник; ~ing, *a*, бродя́чий; блужда́ющий; изви́листый; ¶ *n*, стра́нствие; бред.

wane, *n*, убыва́ние; ¶ *v.i*, убыва́ть, уменьша́ться, ослабева́ть.

want, *n*, нужда́; недоста́ток; отсу́тствие; *pl*, потре́бности; ¶ *v.t*, хоте́ть; нужда́ться в; недоста́вать; ~ed (*in advert.*) тре́буется...; ~ing, *a*, нужда́ющийся; отсу́тствующий; недоста́ющий.

wanton, *a*, бессмы́сленный, нену́жный; распу́щенный; своенра́вный; ~ *destruction* вандали́зм.

war, *n*, война́; ~ *horse* боево́й конь; ~ *loan* вое́нный заём; ~ *memorial* па́мятник па́вшим в войне́; ~*monger* поджига́тель войны́; ~

of attrition война́ на истоще́ние; W~ *Office* вое́нное министе́рство; ~*ship* вое́нный кора́бль; ¶ *v.i,* воева́ть.

warble, *v t. & i,* издава́ть тре́ли; петь; ~r, *n,* пе́вчая пти́ца; **warbling,** *n,* тре́ли, пе́ние.

ward, *n,* пала́та *(hospital);* подопе́чный; райо́н го́рода; ¶ *v.t:* ~ *off* отража́ть *(blow);* отвраща́ть *(danger);* ~en, *n,* нача́льник, дире́ктор; церко́вный ста́роста; ~er, *n,* тюре́мщик; сто́рож; ~robe, *n,* гардеро́б; ~ship, *n,* опе́ка.

warehouse, *n,* склад, пакга́уз.

wares, *n.pl,* изде́лия, това́ры.

warfare, *n,* война́, вое́нные де́йствия.

warily, *ad,* осторо́жно; **wariness,** *n,* осторо́жность.

warlike, *a,* вои́нственный.

warm, *a,* тёплый; *(fig.)* серде́чный; тёплый; горя́чий; ¶ *v.t. (& i.),* греть(ся), нагрева́ть(ся), согрева́ть(ся); ~ly, *ad,* тепло́, серде́чно; ~th, *n,* тепло́; серде́чность; горя́чность.

warn, *v.t,* предупрежда́ть; предостерега́ть; ~ing, *n,* предупрежде́ние, предостереже́ние.

warp, *n,* осно́ва (тка́ни); коробле́ние; ¶ *v.t. (& i.),* коро́бить(ся), искривля́ть(ся); извраща́ть, иска́жа́ть.

warrant, *n,* о́рдер; полномо́чие; оправда́ние, основа́ние; ~ *officer* уо́рент-офице́р; ¶ *v.t,* гаранти́ровать; руча́ться за; опра́вдывать; ~able, *a,* допусти́мый, зако́нный; ~y, *n,* гара́нтия; руча́тельство.

warren, *n,* (кро́личий) садо́к.

warrior, *n,* бое́ц, во́ин.

wart, *n,* борода́вка; ~y, *a,* борода́вчатый.

wary, *a,* осторо́жный.

wash, *v.t. (& i.),* мыть(ся), умыва́ть(ся); омыва́ть *(shore);* стира́ть *(clothes);* ~ *away* смыва́ть(ся) *(also fig.);* ~ *off* смыва́ть; I~ *my hands of it* я умыва́ю ру́ки; ~ *up* мыть посу́ду; ¶ *n,* мытьё; сти́рка; бельё; примо́чка; прибо́й; ~*basin* таз; умыва́льная ра́ковина; ~*house* пра́чечная; ~*leather* за́мша; ~*out* размы́в; *(fig.)* неуда́ча; ~*stand* умыва́ль-

ник; ~*tub* коры́то для сти́рки; ~er, *n,* мо́йщик; промыва́тель; промывна́я маши́на; *(tech.)* ша́йба, прокла́дка; ~ **erwoman,** *n,* пра́чка; **washing,** *n,* мытьё; сти́рка; бельё; ~*up* мытьё посу́ды.

wasp, *n,* оса́; ~'s *nest* оси́ное гнездо́; ~ish, *a,* злой; язви́тельный.

wastage, *n,* уте́чка; усу́шка; изна́шивание; неуспева́емость; **waste,** *v.t,* тра́тить; теря́ть *(time);* по́ртить; *v.i,* ча́хнуть; истоща́ться; ¶ *n,* изли́шняя тра́та; отбро́сы; отхо́ды; по́рча; поте́ри; пусты́ня; ¶ *a,* нену́жный; пусты́нный; невозде́ланный; *lay* ~ опустоша́ть; ~ *land* пусты́рь; ~ *paper* нену́жные бума́ги; ~ *paper basket* корзи́на для нену́жных бума́г; ~ *pipe* сто́чная труба́; ~ful, *a,* расточи́тельный.

watch, *n,* часы́; бди́тельность; наблюде́ние; *(pers.)* сто́рож; карау́л; *(mar.)* ва́хта; *be on* ~ быть наготове/насторо́же; ~*chain* цепо́чка для часо́в; ~*dog* сторожево́й пёс; ~*maker* часо́вщик; *(night)* ~*man* (ночно́й) сто́рож; ~ *lower* сторожева́я ба́шня, ~ *word* паро́ль; ло́зунг; ¶ *v.t,* наблюда́ть за; следи́ть за; смотре́ть; сторожи́ть; охраня́ть; ~ *out* остерега́ться; ~ *over* охраня́ть; ~ful, *a,* бди́тельный; осторо́жный.

water, *n,* вода́; прили́в, отли́в; *in deep* ~ в беде́; в затрудни́тельном положе́нии; ~*bottle* графи́н для воды́; гре́лка; ~*butt* бо́чка для дождево́й воды́; ~*carrier* водово́з, водоно́с; ~*closet* убо́рная; ~*colour* акваре́ль; ~*cooled* с водяны́м охлажде́нием; ~*course* ру́сло; река́, руче́й; ~*cress* кресс водяно́й; ~*fall* водопа́д; ~*lily* водяна́я ли́лия, кувши́нка; ~*line* ватерли́ния; ~*logged* заболо́ченный; напо́лненный водо́й; ~*man* ло́дочник; ~*mark* водяно́й знак; ~*melon* арбу́з; ~*mill* водяна́я ме́льница; ~*power* гидроэне́ргия; ~*proof (a.)* водонепроница́емый, непромока́емый; *(n.)* непромока́емый плащ; ~ *shed* водоразде́л; ~*spout* смерч; водосто́чная труба́; ~ *supply*

водоснабже́ние; ~tight водоне-
проница́емый; герметический; ~
tower водонапо́рная ба́шня; ¶ v.t,
полива́ть; ороша́ть; пойть (horses, etc.); v.i, слези́ться; his
mouth ~s у него́ слю́нки теку́т;
~ down разбавля́ть; ~ing, n,
поли́вка; ~ can ле́йка; ~ place
водопо́й; куро́рт, во́ды; ~less, a,
безво́дный; ~y, a, водяни́стый;
бле́дный.

watt, n, ватт.
wattle, n, плете́нь; ¶ a, плетёный;
¶ v.t, плести́.
wave, n, волна́; маха́ние, знак (ру-
ко́й); ¶ v.t, маха́ть (руко́й, плат-
ко́м, etc.); завива́ть (hair); v.i,
кача́ться; развева́ться; ви́ться
(hair).
waver, v.i, колеба́ться; колыха́ться;
~ing, a, коле́блющийся; колы́-
шащийся; ¶ n, колеба́ние; колы-
ха́ние.
wavy, a, волни́стый.
wax, n, воск; се́ра (in ear); ~works
восковы́е фигу́ры; ¶ v.t, вощи́ть;
v.i, расти́; прибыва́ть (moon);
станови́ться; ~en, a, восково́й;
мя́гкий как воск.
way, n, доро́га, путь; направле́ние;
мане́ра, спо́соб; о́браз де́йствия;
~s and means путй и возмо́ж-
ности; by the ~ (fig.) кста́ти; be
in the ~ стоя́ть поперёк доро́ги;
меша́ть (dat.); on the ~ по доро́ге,
по пути́; over the ~ напро́тив;
че́рез доро́гу; ~farer пу́тник; ~in
вход; ~lay подстерега́ть; ~-out
вы́ход; ~side (n.) край доро́ги,
обо́чина; (a.) придоро́жный; give
~ поддава́ться; обру́шиваться;
make ~ уступа́ть; отступа́ть;
make ~ for уступа́ть ме́сто (dat.);
дава́ть доро́гу (dat.).
wayward, a, капри́зный, своенра́в-
ный; ~ness, n, капри́зность, сво-
енра́вность.
we, pn, мы.
weak, a, сла́бый; нереши́тельный;
боле́зненный; ~ point сла́бое
ме́сто; ~en, v.t, ослабля́ть; v.i,
слабе́ть; ~ling, n, сла́бый чело-
ве́к; ~ly, ad, сла́бо; ~ness, n,
сла́бость; have a ~ for име́ть
скло́нность/сла́бость к.
weal, n, благосостоя́ние; рубе́ц.
wealth, n, бога́тство; изоби́лие, ~y,
a, бога́тый, состоя́тельный.

wean, v.t, отнима́ть от груди́; оту-
ча́ть.
weapon, n, ору́жие; ~less, a, безо-
ру́жный.
wear, n, но́ска; изно́с, изна́шива-
ние; оде́жда; ‘the worse for ~ истрёпанный, поно́шенный; ¶ v.t,
носи́ть; v.i, носи́ться; ~ out изна́-
шивать(ся); утомля́ть; истоща́ть-
(ся); ~ scent души́ться.
weariness, n, уста́лость; ску́ка.
wearing, n, но́ска; ¶ a, утоми́тель-
ный.
wearisome, a, утоми́тельный; ску́ч-
ный; ~ness, n, утоми́тельность;
ску́ка; weary, a, утомлённый,
уста́лый; ¶ v.t. (& i.), утом-
ля́ть(ся); ~ for тоскова́ть о.
weasel, n, ла́ска.
weather, n, пого́да; ~-beaten повреждённый бу́рями; обве́трен-
ный (face); закалённый; ~cock
флю́гер; (pers.) непостоя́нный
челове́к; ~ forecast прогно́з по-
го́ды; ~ glass баро́метр; ~ side
наве́тренная сторона́; ~ station
метеорологи́ческая ста́нция; ¶
v.t, выде́рживать (storm); v.i,
подверга́ться влия́нию атмосфе́ры.
weave, v.t, ткать; плести́ (also fig.);
¶ n, узо́р тка́ни; ~r, n, ткач,
-и́ха; weaving, n, тканьё; тка́-
чество.
web, n, паути́на; перепо́нка; ткань;
диск (колеса́); (fig.) сплете́ние;
~bed, a, перепо́нчатый; ~-footed
с перепо́нчатыми ла́пами; ~bing,
n, тка́ная ле́нта, тесьма́.
wed, v.t, выдава́ть за́муж; жени́ть;
венча́ть; выходи́ть за́муж за;
жени́ться на; v.i, жени́ться;
~ded, a, супру́жеский; (fig.)
пре́данный; ~ husband (wife) за-
ко́нный (-ая) муж, (жена́); ~
ding, n, сва́дьба, бракосочета́ние;
венча́ние; ~ cake сва́дебный торт;
~ day день сва́дьбы; ~ dress
подвене́чное пла́тье; ~ ring обру-
ча́льное кольцо́.
wedge, n, клин; ¶ v.t, вбива́ть клин в;
закрепля́ть кли́ном; ~ in вкли́-
нивать(ся) в.
wedlock, n, брак, супру́жество.
Wednesday, n, среда́.
wee, a, кро́шечный, ма́ленький.
weed, n, сорня́к; (coll.) таба́к; ¶ v.t,
поло́ть; ~ out вычища́ть; уда-
ля́ть; ~er, n, поло́льщик; поло́ль-

ная маши́на; ~у, *a*, заро́сший сорняка́ми; *(pers.)* сла́бый, то́щий.

week, *n*, неде́ля; ~*day* бу́дний день; ~-*end* уике́нд; ~'*s wage* неде́льный за́работок; ~ly, *a*, еженеде́льный; ¶ *ad*, раз в неде́лю; еженеде́льно; ¶ *n*, еженеде́льник.

weep, *v.i*, пла́кать; ~ *for* опла́кивать; ~er, *n*, пла́кса; пла́кальщик; ~ing, *a*, пла́чущий; плаку́чий *(willow, etc.)*; ¶ *n*, плач; опла́кивание.

weevil, *n*, долгоно́сик.

weft, *n*, уто́к.

weigh, *v.t*, взве́шивать *(also fig.)*; обду́мывать; поднима́ть *(anchor)*; *v.i*, ве́сить; име́ть значе́ние/вес; ~ *down* отягоща́ть, угнета́ть; *out* отве́шивать; ~ *bridge* мостовы́е весы́; ~ing, *n*, взве́шивание; ~ *machine* весы́; ~t, *n*, вес; тя́жесть; *(sport)* ги́ря, шта́нга; *(fig.)* бре́мя; ва́жность; влия́ние; ~*lifting* подня́тие тя́жестей; ¶ *v.t*, нагружа́ть; подве́шивать ги́рю к; отягоща́ть ~tless, *a*, невесо́мый; ~tlessness, *n*, невесо́мость; ~ty, *a*, ве́ский, тяжёлый; ва́жный.

weir, *n*, плоти́на, запру́да.

weird, *a*, стра́нный; сверхъесте́ственный.

welcome, *n*, приве́тствие, (раду́шный) приём; ¶ *a*, жела́нный; приéмлемый; ¶ *v.t*, приве́тствовать, (раду́шно) принима́ть; ¶ *int*, добро́ пожа́ловать!.

weld, *n*, сва́рка; ¶ *v.t*, сва́ривать; *(fig.)* спла́чивать; ~er, *n*, сва́рщик; ~ing, *n*, сва́рка.

welfare, *n*, благосостоя́ние, благополу́чие; социа́льное обеспе́чение; ~ *state* госуда́рство всео́бщего благосостоя́ния; ~ *work* рабо́та по социа́льному обеспе́чению.

well, *n*, коло́дец; ле́стничная кле́тка; *(fig.)* исто́чник; *oil* ~ (нефтяна́я) сква́жина; ¶ *v.i*, бить ключо́м; хлы́нуть *(pf.)*.

well, *a*, хоро́ший; здоро́вый; *all is* ~ всё в поря́дке; ¶ *ad*, хорошо́; вполне́; о́чень; ¶ *int*, ну!; *as* ~ то́же, та́кже; вдоба́вок; *as* ~ *as* так же как; ~*-advised* благоразу́мный; *you would be* ~*-advised* вам бы́ло бы лу́чше . . .;~*-attended*

хорошо́ посеща́емый; ~*-balanced* уравнове́шанный; ~*-behaved* благонра́вный; ~*-being* благополу́чие; ~*-bred* благовоспи́танный; ~*-disposed* благоскло́нный; ~ *done* хорошо́ сде́ланный; хорошо́ прожа́ренный; ~ *done!* молоде́ц!; ~*-informed* хорошо́ осведомлённый; ~*-meaning* име́ющий хоро́шие наме́рения; ~*-nigh* почти́; ~*-off* зажи́точный, состоя́тельный; ~*-read* начи́танный; ~*-spoken* уме́ющий я́сно выража́ться; уме́ющий поговори́ть; ~*-timed* своевре́менный; ~*-wisher* доброжела́тель; ~*-worn* поно́шенный; проторённый *(path)*; *(fig.)* иста́сканный.

wellington boot рези́новый сапо́г.

Welsh, *a*, уэ́льский, валли́йский; ¶ *n*, валли́йский язы́к; ~*man* валли́ец; ~*woman* валли́йка.

welt, *n*, рант *(of shoe)*; след от уда́ра.

welter, *n*, неразбери́ха, сумато́ха; *in a* ~ *of blood* в лу́же кро́ви; ¶ *v.i*, валя́ться.

wench, *n*, де́вушка; де́вка.

wend [one's way] направля́ться.

west, *n*, за́пад: *(mar.)* вест; ¶ *a*, за́падный; ¶ *ad*, на за́пад, к за́паду; ~ern, *a*, за́падный; ~ward, *ad*, на за́пад, к за́паду.

wet, *a*, мо́крый, вла́жный; дождли́вый; ~ *blanket (fig.)* челове́к, отравля́ющий удово́льствие; ~ *fish* све́жая ры́ба; ~ *nurse* корми́лица; ~ *paint!* осторо́жно!, покра́шено!; ~ *through* промо́кший до ни́тки; ¶ *n*, вла́жность, сы́рость; дождь; ¶ *v.t*, мочи́ть; увлажня́ть.

wether, *n*, кастри́рованный бара́н.

wetness, *n*, вла́жность, сы́рость.

whack, *n*, си́льный уда́р; *(coll.)* до́ля; ¶ *v.t*, колоти́ть, ударя́ть.

whale, *n*, кит; ~*bone* кито́вый ус; *have a* ~ *of a time* колосса́льно проводи́ть вре́мя; ~r, *n*, китобо́й; китобо́йное су́дно, вельбо́т.

wharf, *n*, при́стань, прича́л; ~age, *n*, портова́я по́шлина.

what, *pn*, что; ско́лько; како́й; ~ *for?* заче́м?; ~'*s up?* что происхо́дит?; ¶ *c*, что; *he knows* ~'*s* ~ он зна́ет, что к чему́; ~*ever*, ~*soever*, *a*, како́й бы ни, любо́й; ¶ *pn*, что бы ни; всё что; ~ *he says* что бы он ни говори́л; *nothing* ~ абсолю́тно ничего́.

wheat, *n*, пшени́ца; ~**en**, *a*, пшени́чный.

wheedle, *v.i*, подли́зываться; ~ *out* выма́нивать.

wheel, *n*, колесо́; руль, штурва́л; круг, оборо́т; *left* ~ l (*mil.*) пра́вое плечо́ впере́д!; ~*barrow* та́чка; ~*chair* кре́сло на колёсах; ~*wright* колёсный ма́стер; ¶ *v.t*, кати́ть; везти́; повора́чивать; *v.i*, повора́чиваться; е́хать (на велосипе́де); кружи́ться; (*mil.*) заезжа́ть/заходи́ть фла́нгом; *three-wheeled* трёхколёсный.

wheeze, *n*, сопе́ние; хрип; ¶ *v.i*, сопе́ть; хрипе́ть.

whelk, *n*, прыщ.

when, *ad*, когда́; ¶ *c*, когда́, в то вре́мя как; тогда́ как; ~*ce*, *ad*, отку́да; ~*ever*, *ad*, когда́ же; ¶ *c*, когда́ бы ни, вся́кий раз как; ~ *you like* когда́ хоти́те, в любо́е вре́мя.

where, *ad*, & *c*, где; куда́; ~**abouts**, *ad*, где, в каки́х края́х; ¶ *n*, местонахожде́ние; ~**as**, *ad*, тогда́ как: поско́льку; ~**at**, *ad*, по́сле чего́; на что; ~**by**, *ad*, посре́дством чего́; ~**fore**, *ad*, почему́; ~**in**, *ad*, в чём; ~**upon**, *ad*, по́сле чего́; ~**ever**, *ad*, где бы ни; куда́ бы ни; ~**withal**, *n*, сре́дства, де́ньги.

wherry, *n*, ло́дка; ~**man**, *n*, ло́дочник.

whet, *n*, пра́вка, то́чка; сре́дство, возбужда́ющее аппети́т; ¶ *v.t*, пра́вить, точи́ть; возбужда́ть (*appetite*); ~*stone* точи́льный ка́мень.

whether, *c*, ли; ~ *he comes or not* придёт ли он и́ли нет.

whey, *n*, сы́воротка.

which, *pn*, кото́рый; что; ¶ *a*, како́й; ~**ever**, *a*, како́й бы ни; како́й уго́дно.

whiff, *n*, дунове́ние; дымо́к.

while, *n*, вре́мя, промежу́ток вре́мени; *for a* ~ на вре́мя; *it is worth* ~ э́то име́ет смысл; сто́ит э́то сде́лать; ¶ *v.t*: ~ *away* (*time*) проводи́ть (вре́мя); ¶ *c*, & **whilst** пока́; в то вре́мя как; несмотря́ на то, что; тогда́ как.

whim, *n*, капри́з, при́хоть.

whimper, *n*, хны́канье; ¶ *v.i*, хны́кать.

whimsical, *a*. капри́зный, причу́дливый; **whimsy**, *n*, капри́з, при́хоть, причу́да.

whin, *n*, дрок.

whine, *n*, вой; хны́канье; ¶ *v.i*, выть; хны́кать; скули́ть.

whinny, *n*, ти́хое ржа́ние; ¶ *v.i*, ти́хо ржа́ть.

whip, *n*, кнут, хлыст; ~ *hand* контро́ль; *have the* ~ *hand over* держа́ть в рука́х; ¶ *v.t*, сечь, хлеста́ть; подгоня́ть; сбива́ть (*cream*); ~ *out* выхва́тывать; ~ *up* разжига́ть; (*coll.*) собира́ть; ~**per-snapper**, *n*, ничто́жный челове́к, молокосо́с; ~**ping**, *n*, побо́и; ~ *boy* козёл отпуще́ния; ~ *top* волчо́к.

whirr, *n*, жужжа́ние, шум; ¶ *v.i*, жужжа́ть.

whirl, *n*, враще́ние, круже́ние; вихрь; ¶ *v.t*. (& *i.*), верте́ть(ся), кружи́ть(ся); ~**igig**, *n*, карусе́ль; (*pers.*) юла́; ~**pool**, *n*, водоворо́т; ~**wind**, *n*, вихрь, смерч.

whisk, *n*, ве́ничек, метёлочка; муто́вка; пома́хивание; ¶ *v.t*, пома́хивать (*inst.*); сма́хивать; сбива́ть (*eggs*).

whisker, *n*, во́лос; *pl*, усы́ (*of cat*); бакенба́рды.

whisky, *n*, ви́ски.

whisper, *n*, шёпот; ше́лест, шо́рох; ¶ *v.t*, шепта́ть, говори́ть шёпотом; *v.i*, шепта́ть; (*fig.*) шелесте́ть, шурша́ть.

whist, *n*, вист.

whistle, *n*, свист; свисто́к; ¶ *v.t*, насви́стывать; *v.i*, свисте́ть; ~**r**, *n*, свисту́н.

whit, *n*, ка́пелька; *not a* ~ ниско́лько, ничу́ть.

white, *a*, бе́лый; седо́й (*hair*); ¶ *n*, бе́лый цвет; бело́к (*of egg*); *turn* ~ беле́ть, бледне́ть; ~ *ant* терми́т; ~*bait* малёк; ~ *elephant* обу́за; нену́жная вещь; ~*-haired* седо́й; ~ *horses* бара́шки (на мо́ре); ~*-hot* раскалённый добела́; ~ *lead* свинцо́вые бели́ла; ~ *lie* неви́нная ложь; ~**en**, *v.t*, бели́ть; отбе́ливать; ~**ness**, *n*, белизна́; ~**ning**, *n*, побе́лка; ~**wash**, *n*, раство́р для побе́лки; побе́лка; ¶ *v.t*, бели́ть;

(fig.) обелять; выигрывать «всухую».

whither, *ad. & c,* куда.

whiting, *n,* мерлан *(fish).*

whitish, *a,* беловатый.

whitlow, *n,* ногтоеда.

Whitsun, *n,* Троица.

whittle, *v.t,* строгать; ~ *away* стачивать; *(fig.)* сводить на нет.

whizz, *n,* жужжание, свист; ¶ *v.i,* жужжать, свистеть.

who, *pn,* кто; тот, кто; который.

whoa! *int,* тпру!.

whoever, *pn,* кто бы ни.

whole, *a,* весь, целый; невредимый; ~-hearted[ly] от всего сердца; ~-length во весь рост; во всю длину; ~meal непросеянная мука; ¶ *n,* всё, целое; итог; сумма; *on the* ~ в общем, в целом; ~sale, *a,* оптовый; *(fig.)* массовый; в больших размерах; ¶ *n,* оптовая торговля; ¶ *ad,* оптом; ~r, *n,* оптовый торговец; ~some, *a,* здоровый; благотворный; **wholly,** *ad,* полностью, целиком.

whom, *pn,* кого, *etc.,* которого, *etc.*

whoop, *n,* гиканье, крик; кашель; ¶ *v.i,* гикать, кричать; кашлять; ~ing cough коклюш.

whore, *n,* проститутка.

whorl, *n,* кольцо; завиток.

whortleberry, *n,* черника; *red* ~ брусника.

whose, *pn,* чей, чья, чьё, чьи; которого; **whosoever,** *pn,* чей бы ни.

why, *ad,* почему; ¶ *n,* причина; ¶ *int,* да ведь; ну!.

wick, *n,* фитиль.

wicked, *a,* злой; безнравственный; ~ness, *n,* злобность; нехороший поступок.

wicker, *n,* прутья для плетения; ¶ *a,* плетёный.

wicket, *n,* калитка; воротца *(cricket);* окошко.

wide, *a,* широкий; обширный, большой; *far and* ~ повсюду; ~awake бодрствующий; бдительный; *open* широко открытый; незащищённый; ~spread широко распространённый; ~ly, *ad,* широко, далеко; ~n, *v.t,* расширять.

widow, *n,* вдова; ~'s *weeds* траурное платье вдовы; ~ed, *p.p. & a,* овдовевший; ~er, *n,* вдовец; ~hood, *n,* вдовство.

width, *n,* ширина; *(fig.)* широта: полотнище; *10 ft. in* ~ шириной в 10 футов.

wield, *v.t,* владеть/править *(inst.).*

wife, *n,* жена.

wig, *n,* парик; ~ging, *n,* нагоняй.

wigwam, *n,* вигвам.

wild, *a,* дикий; невозделанный; буйный, нейстовый; распущенный; раздражённый; необдуманный; *be* ~ *about* быть без ума от; ~ *boar* кабан; ~ *cat (n.)* дикая кошка; *(a.)* рискованный; крайний; незаконный; ~ *strike* «дикая» забастовка; spread like ~fire распространяться молниеносно; ~ goose chase сумасбродная затея; ¶ & ~erness, *n,* дикая местность; пустыня; ~ly, *ad,* дико; буйно, бурно; безумно, необдуманно; ~ness, *n,* дикость.

wile, *n,* уловка, хитрость; обман.

wilful, *a,* своенравный, упрямый; умышленный; ~ly, *ad,* своенравно, упрямо; умышленно; ~ness, *n,* своеволие, упрямство; преднамеренность.

will, *n,* воля, сила воли; желание; завещание; *at* ~ по желанию; ¶ *v.t,* велеть *(dat. + inf.);* хотеть; завещать; *v. aux.* — expressed by future tense; ~ing, *a,* готовый, согласный; старательный; послушный; ~ingly, *ad,* охотно; ~ingness, *n,* готовность.

will-o'-the-wisp, *n,* блуждающий огонёк.

willow, *n,* ива.

willy-nilly, *ad,* волей-неволей.

wilt, *v.i,* вянуть, поникать; слабеть.

wily, *a,* коварный, хитрый.

wimple, *n,* апостольник, плат.

win, *n,* выигрыш; победа; ¶ *v.t,* выигрывать; добиваться/достигать *(gen.); v.i,* выигрывать, побеждать; ~ *over* склонять на свою сторону, убеждать.

wince, *v.i,* вздрагивать; ¶ *n,* вздрагивание, содрогание.

winch, *n,* лебёдка.

wind, *n,* ветер; дыхание; ~bag болтун; ~fall плод, сбитый ветром; бурелом; *(fig.)* неожиданное счастье; ~ gauge ветромер; ~ instrument духовой инструмент; ~mill встряная мельница; ~ pipe дыхательное горло; ~ screen вет-

ровбе/перéднее стеклó; ~screen
wiper стеклоочистúтель; get ~ of
пронюхивать; ¶ v.t, заставлять
задохнýться.

wind, v.t, мотáть, намáтывать; крутúть; обвивáть; v.i, вúться, извивáться; крутúться; ~ off размá-
тывать(ся); ~ up заводúть (clock,
etc.); взвúнчивать; (com.) ликвидúровать; ~ing, a, витóй, спи-
рáльный; извúлистый; ¶ n, на-
мáтывание; извúлина; ~ sheet
сáван; ~lass, n, лебёдка, вóрот.

window, n, окнó; витрúна (of shop);
~ sill подокóнник; ~ pane окóн-
ное стеклó.

windward, n, навéтренная сторонá;
¶ a, навéтренный; windy, a, вéт-
реный; труслúвый; многослóвный.

wine, n, винó; ~ cellar вúнный пóг-
реб; ~ glass рюмка, стóпка; ~
grower виногрáдарь; ~ growing
виногрáдарство; ~ merchant торгóвец винóм; ~ press давúль-
ный пресс; ~skin бурдюк.

wing, n, крылó; (mil.) фланг;
(arch.) флúгель; (avia.) авиабри-
гáда; pl, (theat.) кулúсы; ~ nut
крылáтая гáйка; ~spread раз-
мáх крýльев; ¶ v.t, окрылять;
ускорять; v.i, летéть; рассекáть
вóздух.

wink, n, моргáние; подмúгивание;
миг; in a ~ в миг; ¶ v.i, моргáть,
мигáть; ~ at подмúгивать (dat.);
(fig.) смотрéть сквозь пáльцы на.

winner, n, победúтель; winning, a,
выúгрывающий, побеждáющий;
обаятельный, привлекáтельный;
~ post фúнишный столб; win-
nings, n.pl, выúгрыш.

winnow, v.t, вéять; просéивать; ~
away (fig.) отсéивать; ~ing, n,
вéяние; ~ machine вéялка.

winsome, a, обаятельный, привлекáтельный.

winter, n, зимá; ¶ a, зúмний; ¶ v.i,
зимовáть, проводúть зúму; wintry,
a, зúмний.

wipe, n, вытирáние; ¶ v.t, вытирáть,
стирáть; ~ away, ~ off смывáть;
уничтожáть; ~ up подтирáть.

wire, n, прóволока, прóвод; телегрáмма; ~ dancer канатохóдец; ~
entanglement прóволочное заграждéние; ~ fence прóволочная решётка; прóволочная огрáда; ~

gauze прóволочная сéтка; ~
haired жесткошёрстный; ~ netting
арматýрная прóволочная сéтка;
~puller скрытый двúгатель; интригáн; ~pulling интрúги; ~ rope
прóволочный канáт; ¶ v.t, теле-
графúровать; связывать прóво-
локой; монтúровать проводá, дéлать проводку; окружáть прóво-
локой; ~less, a, беспрóволоч-
ный; рáдио-; ¶ n, рáдио; сооб-
щéние по рáдио; ~ receiver, set
радиоприёмник; ~ telegram радиог-
рáмма; ~ telegraphy радиотеле-
грáфия; ~ wiring, n, электропро-
вóдка, проводá; wiry, a, жúли-
стый; вынóсливый.

wisdom, n, мýдрость; ~ tooth зуб
мýдрости; wise, a, мýдрый; благо-
разýмный; ~acre всезнáйка; ¶ n,
óбраз, спóсоб.

wish, n, желáние; пожелáние; ~bone
дýжка; ¶ v.t, желáть (gen.); v.i,
желáть; хотéть; I ~ it were possible я хотéл бы, чтóбы это было
возмóжно; ~ a Happy New Year
поздравлять с Нóвым Гóдом;
~ful, a, желáющий; полный же-
лáния.

wish-wash, n, бурдá; wishy-washy,
a, жúдкий; (fig.) слáбый, бесцвéтный.

wisp, n, клочóк, пучóк.

wistaria, n, глицúния.

wistful, a, задýмчивый, тосклúвый.

wit, n, ум; острoýмие; (pers.) ост-
ряк; be at one's ~s' end не знать,
что дéлать.

witch, n, вéдьма, колдýнья; ~craft
колдовствó; ~ doctor знáхарь.

with, pr, с, вмéсте с; от; у, при.

withal, ad, вдобáвок; в то же
врéмя`

withdraw, v.t, брать назáд; отзывáть;
изымáть из обращéния; (mil.)
отводúть; v.i, удалять́ся, уходúть;
(mil.) отходúть; ~al, n, взятие
назáд; отозвáние; изъятие; уда-
лéние; (mil.) отхóд.

wither, v.t, иссушáть; v.i, высыхáть,
вянуть; ослабевáть.

withers, n.pl, хóлка.

withhold, v.t, удéрживать; скры-
вáть; v.i, воздéрживаться, удéр-
живаться.

within, pr, в, внутрú, в предéлах; в
течéние; ~ an inch of на расстоянии дюйма от; ~ a year в течéни‹

года; за один год; через год; ~ *call* поблизости; ¶ *ad*, внутри.

without, *pr*, без; вне, за; *do* ~ обходиться без; ~ *fail* непременно; *it goes* ~ *saying* само собой разумеется; ¶ *c*, без того, чтобы.

withstand, *v.t*, противостоять *(dat.)*; выдерживать.

witless, *a*, глупый.

witness, *n*, *(pers.)* свидетель; свидетельство; *bear* ~ *to* свидетельствовать; ~ *box* место для свидетелей; ¶ *v.t*, быть свидетелем *(gen.)*; заверять *(signature)*.

witticism, *n*, острота, шутка; **wittiness**, *n*, остроумие.

wittingly, *ad*, сознательно; умышленно.

witty, *a*, остроумный.

wizard, *n*, волшебник, колдун; фокусник; ~ry, *n*, колдовство.

wizened, *a*, сморщенный; высохший.

woad, *n*, вайда.

wobble, *v.i*, качаться, шататься; ковылять; дрожать *(voice)*; *(fig.)* колебаться; **wobbly**, *a*, шаткий.

woe, *n*, горе, скорбь; несчастье; ~ *is me!* горе мне! ~begone, *a*, удручённый, мрачный; ~ful, *a*, горестный, скорбный; жалкий.

wolf, *n*, волк; ~ *cub* волчонок; ¶ *v.t*, *(coll.)* пожирать; ~ish, *a*, волчий.

wolfram, *n*, вольфрам.

woman, *n*, женщина; ~hood, *n*, женская зрелость; женственность; ~ish, *a*, женский; женоподобный; ~kind, *n*, женщины; ~ly, *a*, женственный.

womb, *n*, матка; *(fig.)* чрево.

wonder, *n*, чудо; изумление, удивление; *it's no* ~ *that* неудивительно, что...; ¶ *v.i*, желать знать; интересоваться; ~ *at* удивляться *(dat.)*; любоваться *(inst.)*; ~ful, *a*, замечательный, прекрасный; **wondrous**, *a*, удивительный; чудесный.

wont, *n*, обыкновение, привычка; ~ed, *a*, обычный, привычный.

woo, *v.t*, ухаживать за.

wood, *n*, лес; дерево; дрова; ~bine *(Bot.)*, жимолость; ~ *carver* резчик по дереву; ~cock вальдшнеп; ~cut гравюра на дереве; ~cutter дровосек; ~land *(n.)* лесистая мест-

ность; *(a.)* лесной; ~louse мокрица; ~man лесник; лесоруб; ~pecker дятел; ~ *pigeon* лесной голубь; ~ *shed* сарай для дров; ~-wind деревянные духовые инструменты; ~work изделия из дерева; деревянные части строения; ~worker плотник; столяр; ~worm (жук-)древоточец; ~ed, *a*, лесистый; ~en, *a*, деревянный; *(fig.)* безжизненный, деревянный; ~y, *a*, деревянистый; лесистый.

wooer, *n*, поклонник.

woof, *n*, уток; ткань.

wool, *n*, шерсть; *go* ~-gathering витать в облаках; ~len, *a*, шерстяной; ~ly, *a*, покрытый шерстью; шерстистый; неясный; непродуманный; ¶ *n*, свитер.

word, *n*, слово; замечание; известие, новость; *by* ~ *of mouth* устно; на словах; *the W*~ Священное писание; ~iness, *n*, многословие; ~ing, *n*, формулировка; ~y, *a*, многословный.

work, *n*, работа, труд, занятие, дело; действие; произведение, сочинение; *pl*, завод; механизм; ~ *bag* рабочая сумка; ~house рабочий дом; ~man рабочий; работник; ~manship искусство, мастерство; ~room, ~shop мастерская, цех; ¶ *v.t*, управлять *(inst.)*; обрабатывать *(soil)*; разрабатывать *(mine)*; решать *(question)*; заставлять работать; *v.i*, работать; заниматься; трудиться; действовать; ~ *loose* освобождать(ся); разбалтывать(ся); ~ *out (v.t.)* решать; разрабатывать *(details)*; истощать *(mine, etc.)*; *(v.i.)* решаться; ~ *out at* составлять; *it will* ~ *out alright* образуется; ~ *over* перерабатывать; обрабатывать; ~ *up* разрабатывать; возбуждать; ~able, *a*, выполнимый, осуществимый; обрабатываемый; ~er, *n*, рабочий; работник; ~ *bee* рабочая пчела; ~ing *n*, работа, действие; обработка, разработка; эксплуатация; ¶ *a*, работающий; действующий; рабочий; ~ *capacity* трудоспособность; ~ *capital* оборотный капитал; ~ *class* рабочий класс; ~ *day* рабочий день; ~ *expenses* эксплуатацион-

ные расходы; ~less, *a*, без
работы, безработный.
world, *n*, мир, свет; ~ *War* мировая
война; ~*wide* распространённый
по всему миру; всемирно известный; ~ly, *a*, земной; искушённый, светский; опытный.
worm, *n*, червь, червяк; глист;
(tech.) червяк, бесконечный винт;
(fig.) ничтожество; ~*-eaten* исто-
ченный червями; ¶ *v.t:* ~ *oneself
into* вкрадываться в; ~ *out* выве-
дывать; ~*wood*, *n*, полынь; ~y,
a, червивый.
worry, *n*, беспокойство, забота, тревога; ¶ *v.t*, беспокоить, тревожить, мучить; терзать *(of dog);*
v.i, беспокоиться, мучиться.
worse, *a*, худший; ¶ *ad*, хуже; ~en,
v.t. (& *i.*), ухудшать(ся)
worship, *n*, поклонение, почитание;
богослужение; *your W*~ ваша
милость; ¶ *v.t*, поклоняться
(dat.), почитать; обожать; ~per,
n, поклонник, почитатель; присутствующий на богослужении.
worst, *a*, наихудший; ¶ *ad*, хуже
всего; ¶ *n*, самое худшее; ¶ *v.t*,
побеждать, одерживать верх над.
worsted, *a*, шерстяная/камвольная
пряжа.
worth, *n*, цена, стоимость; ценность; достоинство; ¶ *a*, стоящий; заслуживающий; *be* ~ стоить; *be* ~*while* иметь смысл,
стоить; ~*less*, *a*, ничего не стоящий, никчёмный; ~y, *a*, достойный; достопочтённый; заслуживающий; ¶ *n*, достойный человек; знаменитость.
would, *v. aux*, expressed by *Imperfective past*, *e.g.* '*he would sit for
hours*'; *or*, *in indirect statements, by
appropriate tense; or, in conditional
statements, by Conditional-Subjunc-
tive with* бы; ~*-be*, *a*, мнимый,
предполагаемый; с претензией
на.
wound, *n*, рана, ранение; обида,
оскорбление; ¶ *v.t*, ранить, обижать, задевать; ~ed, *a*. & *n*,
раненый.
wraith, *n*, призрак.
wrangle, *n*, пререкания, спор; ¶
v.i, пререкаться, спорить.
wrap, *n*, шаль, плед; обёртка; ¶ *v.t*,
завёртывать; закутывать; ~ *up*
кутать(ся); *wrapped up in* заку-

танный в; *(fig.)* погружённый в;
~per, *n*, обёртка; *(pers.)* упа-
ковщик, -ица.
wrath, *n*, гнев, ярость; ~ful, *a*,
гневный, рассерженный.
wreak, *v.t*, давать выход (гневу,
etc.); ~ *vengeance* мстить.
wreath, *n*, венок, гирлянда; кольцо
(smoke); ~e, *v.t*, сплетать;
обвивать; *v.i*, обвиваться; клу-
биться *(smoke)*.
wreck, *n*, авария, крушение; остов
разбитого судна; развалина; ¶
v.t, топить *(ship);* вызывать крушение *(gen.);* разрушать *(also
fig.);* *be* ~ed терпеть крушение;
рухнуть *(pf.)* *(plans);* ~age, *n*,
обломки крушения; ~er, *n*, грабитель; вредитель.
wren, *n*, крапивник.
wrench, *n*, дёрганье; *(med.)* вывих;
(tech.) гаечный ключ; ¶ *v.t*,
выбёртывать, вырывать; вывих-
нуть *(pf.);* ~ *open* взламывать.
wrest, *v.t*, вырывать; исторгать
(agreement, etc.).
wrestle, *v.i*, бороться; ~r, *n*, борец;
wrestling, *n*, борьба, реслинг.
wretch, *n*, несчастный; негодяй; ~ed,
a, жалкий, несчастный; никудыш-
ный.
wriggle, *v.i*, извиваться, изгибаться;
юлить; пробираться; *(fig.)* увиливать.
wring, *v.t*, выжимать; скручивать;
вымогать, исторгать; ~ *one's
hands* ломать руки; ~er, *n*, машина для выжимания белья.
wrinkle, *n*, морщина; *(coll.)* полезный совет; ¶ *v.t.* (& *i.*), мор-
щить(ся).
wrist, *n*, запястье; ~ *band* манжета;
~*watch* ручные часы-браслет.
writ, *n*, повестка, предписание; писание.
write, *v.t.* & *i*, писать; ~ *down* записывать; ~ *for* сотрудничать в;
(newspaper); выписывать, заказывать; ~ *off* аннулировать,
вычёркивать; ~ *out* выписывать
полностью; переписывать; ~r, *n*,
писатель, автор.
writhe, *v.i.* корчиться; мучиться.
writing, *n*, писание; произведе-
ние; *in* ~ в письменной форме;
~*-case* несессер для письмен-
ных принадлежностей; ~ *desk*
конторка, письменный стол; ~

materials письменные принадлежности; ~ *pad* блокнот почтовой бумаги; ~ *paper* почтовая бумага, писчая бумага.

wrong, *a,* неправильный, ошибочный; не тот; дурной; несправедливый; *be* ~ быть неправым; *something is* ~ что-то не в порядке; *go* ~ не выходить, не получаться; опускаться (морально); ~ *side* изнанка; ~ *side out* наизнанку; *on the* ~ *side of 40* за 40 лет; ~ *side up* вверх дном; ~ *way round* наоборот; *the* ~ *way* ошибочный путь; неправильный способ; ¶ *n,* неправда; обида, несправедливость; ¶ *v.t,* причинять зло *(dat.);* вредить *(dat.);* обижать; быть насправедливым к; ~**doer,** *n,* преступник; обидчик; ~**ful,** *a,* несправедливый, неправильный; ~**ly,** *ad,* неправильно; неверно.

wrought, *a,* обработанный; ковкий; сварочный; ~ *iron* сварочное железо; ~ *up (fig.)* взвинченный.

wry, *a,* кривой, перекошенный; ~ *face* гримаса; ~**neck** вертишейка.

X

X-ray, *n,* рентгеновый луч; ¶ *v.t,* просвечивать, делать рентген.

xylography, *n,* ксилография.

xylophone, *n,* ксилофон.

Y

yacht, *n,* яхта; ~**ing,** *n,* яхтенный спорт; плавание на яхте.

yak, *n,* як.

yam, *n,* батат.

Yankee, *n,* американ|ец, -ка, янки; ¶ *a,* американский.

yap, *v. i.* тявкать.

yard, *n,* двор; склад; *(rly.)* парк; верфь *(ship);* ярд *(measure);* ~-*arm* нок-рея.

yarn, *n,* пряжа; рассказ.

yarrow, *n,* тысячелистник.

yaw, *n,* отклонение от направления движения; ¶ *v.i,* отклоняться от направления движения.

yawl, *n,* ялик.

yawn, *n,* зевок; ¶ *v.i,* зевать; *(fig.)* зиять.

year, *n,* год; ~**ly,** *n,* ежегодник; ¶ *a,* ежегодный; ¶ *ad,* каждый год; раз в год.

yearn, *v.i,* томиться, тосковать; ~ *to* стремиться; очень хотеть; ~**ing,** *n,* тоска; сильное желание.

yeast, *n,* дрожжи.

yell, *n,* визг, пронзительный крик; ¶ *v.i,* визжать, кричать.

yellow, *n,* жёлтый; *(coll.)* труслйвый; ~ *fever* жёлтая лихорадка; ~ *hammer* овсянка; ¶ *n,* жёлтый цвет, желтизна; ~**ish,** *a,* желтоватый.

yelp, *v.i,* тявкать; визжать.

yeoman, *n,* йомен, мелкий землевладелец; ~ *of the guard* дворцовый страж.

yes, *particle,* да; ¶ *n,* согласие; утверждение.

yesterday, *ad,* вчера; ~ *morning* вчера утром; *the day before* ~ позавчера; **yesteryear,** *n,* прошлое.

yet, *ad,* ещё; всё ещё; уже; *as* ~ пока; до сих пор; *not* ~ ещё не(т); ¶ *c,* всё же, однако.

yew, *n,* тис.

yield, *n,* урожай, сбор плодов; размеры выработки; добываемый продукт; ¶ *v.t,* приносить, производить; уступать; сдавать; *v.i,* уступать; сдаваться; поддаваться; подаваться; ~**ing,** *a,* уступчивый; податливый; гибкий, мягкий.

yoghurt, *n,* югурт, простокваша.

yoke, *n,* ярмо; хомут; коромысло; кокетка *(on dress);* пара запряжённых волов; *(fig.)* иго; ¶ *v.t,* впрягать в ярмо; соединять, спаривать.

yokel, *n,* деревенщина.

yolk, *n,* желток.

yonder, *a,* вон тот; ¶ *ad,* вон там.

yore: *of* ~ давным-давно.

you, *pn,* ты, вы *etc.*

young, *a,* молодой, юный; ¶ *n.pl,* молодёжь; детёныши; ~**er,** *a,* младший; ~**ster,** *n,* мальчик, юноша.

your, *a,* твой, ваш; ~**s,** *pn,* твой, ваш; ~ *faithfully* с уважением; ~ *sincerely* искренне Ваш. ~**self,** *pn,* сам, сама, сами; себя; *you are not* ~ ты сам не свой.

youth, *n*, мо́лодость, ю́ность; ю́ноша; молодёжь; ~ *hostel* молодёжное общежи́тие, молодёжная турба́за; ~ful, *a*, ю́ношеский, ю́ный; живо́й.

yowl, *n*, вой, ¶ *v.i*, выть

Yugoslav (Jugoslav), *a*, югосла́вский ¶ *n*, югосла́в,-ка.

yuletide, *n*, свя́тки; ~ *log* поле́но, сжига́емое в сочельник.

Z

zany, *a*, ве́треный; ¶ *n*, вертопра́х.

zeal, *n*, рве́ние, усе́рдие; ~ot, *n*, фана́тик; ~ous, *a*, ре́вностный, рья́ный, усе́рдный; ~ly, *ad*, ре́вностно.

zebra, *n*, зе́бра.

zenith, *n*, зени́т.

zephyr, *n*, зефи́р.

zero, *n*, нуль; нулева́я то́чка; ничто́.

zest, *n*, жар, жи́вость; изю́минка.

zigzag, *n*, зигза́г; ¶ *v.i*, де́лать зигза́ги.

zinc, *n*, цинк; ¶ *a*, ци́нковый.

zip[-fastener], *n*, (застёжка) мо́лния.

zircon, *n* цирко́н.

zither, *n*, ци́тра.

zodiac, *n*, зодиа́к.

zone, *n*, зо́на, полоса́, райо́н.

zoo, *n*, зоопа́рк; зоологи́ческий сад; ~logical, *a*, зоологи́ческий; ~logist, *n*, зоо́лог; ~logy, *n*, зооло́гия.

Zulu, *a*, зулу́сский; ¶ *n*, зулу́с, -ка; зулу́сский язы́к.

GEOGRAPHICAL NAMES

Adriatic Sea Адриатическое мо́ре.
Africa А́фрика.
Alaska Аля́ска.
Algeria Алжи́р.
Alps А́льпы.
Alsace-Lorraine Эльза́с-Лотари́нгия.
America Аме́рика.
Andes А́нды.
Arabia Ара́вия.
Archangel Арха́нгельск.
Arctic Ocean Се́верный Ледови́тый
    океа́н.
Asia Minor Ма́лая А́зия
Athens Афи́ны.
Australia Австра́лия.
Azerbaidzhan SSR Азербайджа́н-
    ская ССР.

Balkans Балка́ны.
Baltic Sea Балти́йское мо́ре.
Berlin Берли́н.
Black Sea Чёрное мо́ре.
Bosporus Босфо́р.
Brazil Брази́лия.
Britain see Great Britain.
Byelorussian SSR Белору́сская ССР.

Cairo Каи́р.
Canada Кана́да.
Canberra Ка́нберра.
Cape Horn Мыс Горн.
Cape of Good Hope Мыс До́брой На-
    де́жды.
Carpathians Карпа́ты.
Caspian Sea Каспи́йское мо́ре.
Caucasus Кавка́з.
Ceylon Цейло́н.
Chile Чи́ли.
China Кита́й.
Cologne Кёльн.
Copenhagen Копенга́ген.
Cuba Ку́ба.
Cyprus Кипр.
Czechoslovakia Чехослова́кия.

Danube Дуна́й.
Delhi Де́ли.
Denmark Да́ния.
Dnieper Днепр.
Dniester Днестр.
Dover Ду́вр; Straits of ∼ Па-де-
    Кале́.

East Indies Ост-Йндия.
Egypt Еги́пет.

England А́нглия.
English Channel Ла-Ма́нш.
Estonia Эсто́ния.
Ethiopia Эфио́пия.
Euphrates Евфра́т.
Europe Евро́па.
Everest Эвере́ст.

Finland Финля́ндия.
France Фра́нция.

Geneva Жене́ва.
Georgia (USSR) Гру́зия; Джо́рд-
    жия (USA).
Great Britain Великобрита́ния.
Greece Гре́ция.

Hague, the Гаа́га.
Helsinki Хе́льсинки.
Himalayas Гимала́и.
Holland Голла́ндия.
Hungary Ве́нгрия.

Iceland Исла́ндия.
India И́ндия.
Indonesia Индоне́зия.
Iran Ира́н.
Iraq Ира́к.
Ireland Ирла́ндия.
Israel Изра́иль.
Istanbul Стамбу́л.
Italy Ита́лия.

Japan Япо́ния.
Jerusalem Иерусали́м.
Jordan Иорда́ния.

Kazakh SSR Каза́хская ССР.
Kenya Ке́ния.
Kiev Ки́ев.
Kirghiz SSR Кирги́зская ССР.
Korea Коре́я.

Latvia Ла́твия.
Lithuania Литва́.
London Ло́ндон.
Luxembourg Люксембу́рг.

Macedonia Македо́ния.
Madrid Мадри́д.
Malaya Мала́йя.
Manchuria Манчжу́рия.
Mediterranean Sea Средизе́мное
    мо́ре.
Melbourne Ме́льбурн.

567

Mexico Méксика; ~ City Méхико.
Moldavia Молдáвия.
Mongolia Монгóлия.
Montenegro Черногóрия.
Montreal Монреáль.
Morocco Марóкко.
Moscow Москвá.

Netherlands Нидерлáнды.
Neva Невá.
New York Нью-Йóрк.
Nigeria Нигéрия.
Nile Нил.
North Sea Céверное мóре.
Norway Норвéгия.

Oslo Óсло.
Ottawa Оттáва.

Pacific Ocean Тихий океáн.
Pakistan Пакистáн.
Palestine Палестúна.
Peking Пекúн.
Persia Пéрсия; **Persian Gulf** Персúдский залúв.
Poland Пóльша.
Portugal Португáлия.
Prague Прáга.
Prussia Прýссия.
Punjab Пенджáб.

Quebec Квебéк.

Red Sea Крáсное мóре.
Rocky Mts. Скалúстые гóры.
Rome Рим.
Roumania Румúния.
Russia Россúя.
Russian Soviet Federated Socialist Republic Россúйская Совéтская Федератúвная Социалистúческая Респýблика.

Sakhalin Сахалúн.
Scotland Шотлáндия.
Siberia Сибúрь.
Singapore Сингапýр.

Spain Испáния.
Stockholm Стокгóльм.
Sweden Швéция.
Switzerland Швейцáрия.

Tadzhik SSR Таджúкская ССР.
Tangier Танжéр.
Tanzania Танзáния.
Teheran Тегерáн.
Thames Тéмза.
Tierra del Fuego Óгненная Землú.
Troy Трóя.
Turkey Тýрция.
Turkmen SSR Туркмéнская ССР.
Tyrol Тирóль.

Uganda Угáнда.
Ukraine Украúна.
Ulster Óлстер.
Union of Soviet Socialist Republics Сою́з Совéтских Социалистúческих Респýблик.
United Kingdom Соединённое Королéвство.
United States of America Соединённые Штáты Амéрики.
Urals Урáл.
Uruguay Уругвáй.
Uzbek SSR Узбéкская ССР.

Venezuela Венесуэ́ла.
Venice Венéция.
Vienna Вéна.
Vietnam Вьетнáм.
Volga Вóлга.

Wales Уэ́льс.
Warsaw Варшáва.
Washington Вашингтóн.
Wellington Вéллингтон.
West Indies Вест-Индия.
White Sea Бéлое мóре.

Yellow Sea Жёлтое мóре.
Yugoslavia Югослáвия.

Zambia Зáмбия.